love
and
WAR

USA TODAY BESTSELLING AUTHOR

K WEBSTER

From USA Today Bestselling Author K Webster, comes a dark, suspenseful, and steamy romance box set of all seven interconnected books in the thrilling War and Peace series!

I was stolen from my boyfriend's arms by someone I loved and trusted.
A monster who betrayed me.
And now he's training me for something far more sinister.
I'm to be sold to the highest bidder.

There's no escape. No hope. I'm terrified of what's to come.
Because it takes an even worse monster to purchase a woman for millions of dollars.

My new captor is rich, handsome, and completely insane.
He's a twisted recluse who's set on keeping me locked in his self-imposed prison with him.

I have to escape.

Befriending him may be my only option.
Making him fall for me could be my weapon.

All's fair in love and war, right?
Not this time…

Includes the entire War and Peace series:
This is War, Baby (Book 1)
This is Love, Baby (Book 2)
This Isn't Over, Baby (Book 3)
This Isn't You, Baby (Book 4)
This is Me, Baby (Book 5)
This Isn't Fair, Baby (Book 6)
This is the End, Baby (Book 7)

Warning
The Love and War collection is a dark romance book series. Triggering themes including sexual violence, human trafficking, drug use, and self-harm are found in this series.
Please proceed with caution.

THIS IS WAR,
baby

My life had a plan. Until he invaded it and stole it all away.
My captor took me and I became a pawn.

His strategy changed and he sent me away to WAR,
because money is everything in this world.

In my WAR, though, I found peace.

I couldn't help but find love where I least expected it,
with a man who lived a battle every day of his life
…all inside his head.

But then my captor came back for me.
Yet, this time, battle lines had been drawn and I was protected.

So we thought.
Even though my WAR was raging,
my captor would fight to the death.

The good guys always win, right?
Not always.

All's fair in love and WAR, right?
Not this time.

PROLOGUE

Baylee
Three days before…

"Lower."

His slurp echoes in my bedroom and I tense up. Our eyes meet for a brief second before his tongue starts to lap at me again. My friend Audrey says when a guy eats you out, it's *the most amazing thing on the planet.* Yet as Brandon flicks his tongue everywhere except the part of me that seems on fire with need, I can't help but wonder if she was lying. She's always been one to embellish the truth. And right now, as my body tenses with the urge to explode, I never quite reach the climax I'm after. Audrey most certainly fibbed about this little detail.

Brandon grunts and his gentle thumbs stroke the insides of my thighs as he tastes me. The maneuver itself is sweet and one I have come to expect from my boyfriend of a year and a half. However, just once, I'd like for him to dig his fingers into my legs. To suck my clit that he seems to be dancing around. To force his way into me and break the barrier I'd gladly give to him if he'd take rather than ask.

I chew on my lip and ponder my bizarre thoughts rather than focus on the pleasure that seems to be slipping farther and farther away.

What would Dad do if he were to come in here and find Brandon between my legs? I stifle a giggle. He'd yank him away from me by his hair and drag him out of the house most likely—probably landing a punch or two on his handsome face before he sent him on his way. My amusement dies though when I think about him explaining what happened to *her.*

My mother.

Her pale lips would fall into the slightest of frowns and her blonde brows would pinch together. She'd become shaky and weaker than she already is with worry. That very thought sobers me up completely.

"Mmm," Brandon grunts from below, dragging me back to the task at hand.

I skim my gaze over his spiked brown hair and his bare shoulders. He didn't quite develop into the hot boy he is now until the summer before our senior year. Six months into the school year and I still catch myself grinning. I didn't expect to be in a serious relationship with the best-looking guy in school. But I'm certainly not complaining.

Well…

Maybe I am a little.

He's a great kisser and an attentive boyfriend.

But I crave for him to possess my body in a carnal way that matches the blazing of my heart— to bruise my flesh as his fingers dig into me while he takes me in such a way that suggests his body needs mine for life.

"I love you." His murmured breath against my clit jolts me and I wish he'd do it again. We're both learning here but I hope he learns a little bit faster.

"I love you too. Don't stop."

With newfound fury, he increases the speed at which he circles my sensitive flesh. So close and yet still so far away. I'd like to grab onto that spiky hair and hold him right where I want him. The thought sends a thrill quivering down my spine.

I hear a car door slam and my thoughts immediately go to my dad's best friend, Gabe. He's lived next door to us for nearly ten years now and they've been inseparable ever since. Images of his dark mop of hair that sometimes hides his brown eyes—eyes that seem to always twinkle with delight when he sees me—flood my mind. Lately, I think about him a lot.

Way too much.

When Dad's stressed about Mom's illness, he and Gabe spend hours drinking beer and whispering stuff I'm not privy to hearing. In a way, I'm glad Dad has someone to confide in. I just wish I could curl up between them like I used to before I grew boobs and started wearing makeup. Once I hit puberty, the way I used to climb all over him like he was my favorite tree ended as quickly as it'd started. Gabe now seems agitated every time I'm near him.

His dark eyes will flick over my body briefly, and with a flash of something that makes my belly ache, but he always moves them someplace else and affixes me with his annoyed glare instead. The disdain in his eyes only intensifies if Brandon is around. If looks could kill, I'd fear for Brandon's life.

It was as if he flipped a switch one day and didn't like me anymore.

I may be young but I'm not stupid.

I know, deep down, there's more than what is on the surface with Gabe.

That he wants me.

Brandon hits a spot that has me jolting upright. So close. So damn close. If he'd go back and spend a little more time there, I might find this elusive orgasm. I lean back and rest on my elbows so I can watch him. I'm beginning to lose faith in his abilities once again when something by the open window catches my eye.

A dark shadow.

Brandon swipes his hot tongue back over my clit and I buck as if I'm a live wire jolting with electricity. *More, Brandon. More…*

I close my eyes, hoping to leap over that blissful edge. My brain betrays the one before me though as thoughts of another man flood my mind—a man with messy hair and coffee-colored eyes.

A *man.*

Not a boy like Brandon.

"Oh God," I whimper and bite my lip, attempting to force images of my sexy boyfriend back to the forefront of my mind. "I feel close."

Brandon's tongue goes wild and I squirm against him. I want his tongue to own me. I want him to stick his fingers inside of me and probe where nobody but me has ever been before. I'm ready for so much more than what we've had—for the innocence of our relationship to die a quick death.

A creak of the floorboard in my bedroom has me jerking my eyes open. I expect to see Dad— to meet the furious glare of my father. But I don't.

Instead, it's something a thousand times more terrifying.

And I nearly come despite the alarm that renders me immobile.

I'm a sick girl.

A tall man, dressed completely in black, donning a ski mask holds a finger to his lips as he sneaks up behind Brandon. Terror seizes me and I'm unable to move a muscle. I want to scream. I want to scramble away. I want to know what the hell is going on. But I can't do anything but stare.

His dark eyes through the mask stay on mine as he prowls closer. Of course Brandon chooses that exact moment to hit the right spot. Spots darken my vision and I'm on the cusp of something euphoric.

But my dream is threading with a nightmare.

This darkness fits but it is also wrong and dirty. This can't be real—this can't be happening.

I'm confused, but the moment he grabs on to my boyfriend's hair and yanks him away from me, reality splashes me out of my lusty daze. I find my voice and I scream.

Everything seems to slow down and I'm rooted with my butt on the quilt Nana made for me when I was twelve. Brandon attempts to swing at the man but he's too slow—too young—too innocent.

Crack!

The man's fist connects with Brandon's nose and the sickening crunch has me dry heaving.

"Dad!"

Brandon crumples to the floor as blood gushes from his face. I need to help him. No, I need to get away. Fear releases its clutch on me and I scramble on the bed toward the door. I'm close when a powerful arm hooks around my middle and yanks me back.

His hand slaps over my mouth and my naked body heaves in his clutches. I attempt to wriggle from his unyielding grasp but he's too strong.

"Did you come?" he hisses against my head and frees my mouth.

The room blurs with my tears and I freeze. I know this voice.

"Gabe?"

"It was a yes or no answer, little girl. You have three seconds to answer the fucking question before I slit that pussy's throat."

His threat nauseates me and a sob catches in my throat. *Where's Dad?!*

"Three."

My voice. Why won't it work? Please, God. Help me!

"Two."

No! No! No!

"One. Times up." He reaches behind him and then brings around a huge knife out in front of me. A knife like that would kill Brandon.

"N-N-No!"

A throaty grunt vibrates through my back. If I had to guess, I'd say he is pleased by my answer. And by the way his erection presses into my back, I'd say excited too.

"Good answer," he mutters. "Now, say goodbye to your bedroom and your pussy-ass boyfriend. You'll never see them again."

His hand covers my mouth before I have a chance to belt out the scream that is now lodged in my throat. Surely this is some sort of joke. A plan for Dad to make sure I don't ever try to sneak around with Brandon under his roof.

Yes, that must be it.

All a game.

"Sorry, sweetheart, but this is going to hurt."

That's the only warning I receive before he cracks me over the head with a blunt object—probably the butt of his knife. Darkness steals over me, and the last thing I catch a glimpse of is Brandon's bloody, unmoving body. *You'll never see them again.* I can't handle the reality of that concept and the thought shoves me into oblivion.

chapter
ONE

Baylee

My head throbs.

Thump. Thump. Thump.

Where am I?

What day is it?

I'm aching and disoriented and cold. But that isn't what has me terrified. It isn't that I haven't eaten. Nor is it that I also haven't slept. No. What's terrifying is that I haven't seen anything but complete black in what must be days.

Anger bubbles in my chest at having been stolen by my neighbor. I can't prove it but I know his voice. He took me right from my bedroom. Dad never came. Brandon was badly hurt. And I haven't a clue as to where I am.

I think I hear a thud above me and I try to still my racing heart. Why would Gabe take me to lock me away in some dungeon and let me die? It makes absolutely no sense.

Another thud. Several of them. My heart flares to life and I hope maybe the cops have come for me. That my dad is leading a pack of angry policemen dead set on rescuing me. I'm too young to die. I had plans—plans that involved going to med school. Plans that I'd hoped involved marrying Brandon and having a bunch of babies. We're in love. God, I hope he's okay.

A sharp pain seizes my stomach and I whimper. I want to scream at him to feed me something—*anything*—but I've already tried that. The screams have fallen on deaf ears. Screaming doesn't get me food—screaming gets me a hoarse, dry throat. My cracked lips are the most apparent signs of my dehydration. The throat though, is awful. No matter how many times I attempt to conjure up spit to wet my throat, the most I can come up with is a small, thick ball of phlegm which only serves to nauseate me when I swallow it.

"Help." The croak belongs to me but it's nothing more than a whisper.

I've been all over this space, feeling my way through the dark, but have found nothing to be down here. Not one single damn thing. I've deemed one corner my bathroom. My bodily excretions are what decorate that corner now, not that there's much since I'm slowly dying from a lack of nutrients.

"Please." This time, my voice is louder but it will never penetrate these concrete walls. Reaching out, I once again finger the walls searching for a way out. How does a room not have windows or doors? How did he get me inside of this tomb?

Something skitters over my hand and I shriek. Must have been a spider. The normal girly-girl I was not long ago would have hidden in the pee corner to escape. This scared prisoner I've become though is hungry. I wonder if I could eat the spider. It would be disgusting but could provide protein.

Or poison.

Once again, I feel defeated. My luck, I'd gobble up that nasty spider only to die from the venom it carries. And then my dad would find my decomposed body hours too late or something.

He'd lose Mom and me both.

A scratchy sob pierces the air and I attempt to drum up tears. Nothing. I cry tearlessly for a minute and then swallow down the emotion. Mom was sick but she seemed hopeful. A liver could come at any time, she'd said. Dad, however, wasn't convinced. He researched. He reached out. He Facebooked the world. All in an effort to save the love of his life.

But time is running out.

For the both of us.

I should have told her how much I'd loved her before bed. Instead, I was too worried about hopefully taking that final leap with Brandon that would have sealed our relationship. Sex. I'd made him wait but I was ready. And now…

God, I am so stupid.

I'm not sure exactly how long I've been down here, but it's taking a toll on my sanity. Screamed until I was hoarse and voiceless. Cried until my stomach muscles were sore and aching. Spent unthinkable amounts of time fingering every crack and crevice in the darkness in an effort to find an escape route. Imagined every scenario about Brandon's fate, none of them good. At one point, I even tried to count as high as I possibly could—I was well over six thousand when I got bored and gave up.

I've been here forever.

Hours or days or months—my mind is on a black, endless terrifying reel.

I'm in an eternal, dark hell.

With nobody to talk to.

With no food or water or bathroom.

With nothing but the blackness and insanity slowly seeping through the cracks of my soul to keep me company.

A sliver of blinding light slices across the dusty floor in front of me and I stare at it with squinty eyes in shock.

"Gabe. Please." A tiny whispered plea.

I want to scream and cry and beg.

But I'm cold and tired. I'm disoriented and stressed. I just want to go home.

The slice of light becomes a distinct yellow square suspended about twelve feet above the ground. I blink several times in attempt to shield my sensitive eyes to the bright light. A silhouette—broad shoulders and wild hair—takes up most of the square, protecting me from the offensive light.

"How you doing down there, kiddo? Still alive and kickin'?" His deep voice is a gravelly rumble which used to excite me. Now, it scares the living crap out of me.

"I want to go home," I tell him in a firm tone, despite the wobble in my voice.

He chuckles though it is a humorless sound. Dark, evil, hellish…yes. Out of humor, absolutely not. Who is this man who I've known for the past decade? I've watched him with other women, flirtatious and desirable. I've heard him whisper dirty, sexual promises to girlfriends over the years and would even grow jealous of the attention he showered them with. I mean, I've fantasized about his strong, capable hands roaming all over me as he kissed me for crying out loud. And all this time, beneath the jokes and friendly façade was a demon from hell waiting in the shadows for the perfect opportunity to take what wasn't his.

"Baylee, baby, I told you already," he says in a menacing tone dry of any wit, "you're not going anywhere."

This time, the tears do come. Small, hot tears streak down my cheeks and drip from my jaw. "Why?"

If he doesn't plan on letting me escape, he at least owes me an explanation.

"Are you hungry?"

His blatant disregard for my question irritates me and I hobble over to the light that shines beneath him. My dirty, naked flesh is exposed but I want him to see me. I want him to see the little girl he was supposed to look after. The little girl he took for his own depraved reasons.

"Why are you doing this to me?"

I can't make out his features but I can tell he's annoyed with me. His tell—a frustrated hand running through his messy hair—rats him out. Hair that I know has a few streaks of grey at his temple. Hair that I used to dream about running my own fingers through.

"Sometimes, sweetheart, you have to make sacrifices. You, doll, are a sacrifice. Your part is small, but it is so significant."

His riddles confuse me.

"I want to go home, Gabe. Please, I won't tell anyone. I swear it," I vow. And it's the truth. If he were to let me go, I'd take the secret to my grave. If that meant regaining my freedom, I'd make that promise to him.

"Baylee, you're not going to tell anyone because there won't be anyone to tell. You've been initiated into a new world—a world you're not prepared to handle. Not even close."

I shiver and cross my arms over my chest. It should embarrass me that he sees me naked but I don't care about being modest. I care about getting the heck out of here.

"What do you want from me?" I demand with a nasty bite to my voice. I'm tired of being weak and begging. I want to go home.

"Ahhh, there's the feisty girl I know," he says, almost as if he's relieved. "If I let you out, promise not to run?"

No.

"Yes."

He laughs again and I decide I hate his laugh. "I don't believe you."

I shrug my shoulders and glare at him. "I've never given you any reason not to trust me." Unlike you, you bastard.

He nods finally. "Fine. I'm going to take your word. But what happens if you betray me?"

You've already betrayed me.

"I won't," I lie.

"You're right," he snaps. "You won't. Because if you do, I'll whip your ass with a stick from the yard for every step you manage to take away from me."

The hairs on my arms rise in alarm and my heart takes off like a hundred horses thundering away from me. "I won't run."

"Good. I want to clean you up and feed you. You're mine to take care of for now." He nods and then disappears.

I'm afraid he won't come back but a few moments later, he drops something into my prison. A rope.

"Climb," he instructs, voice cold and uncaring.

I shudder and wobble over to where it hangs before me. Sometimes in PE we climb ropes but not after having been starved for several days. The only reason I'm standing is because I'm running on pure adrenaline at this point. I reach for the thick rope and clutch it. It's rough in my hands and a sad realization comes over me. I'll never be able to climb this thing.

"Climb!"

I jump and reach higher on the rope. My attempt to hoist myself up ends up with me spinning wildly out of control, only managing to further nauseate my empty stomach. Dropping my feet to the dirt, I cry out. "I can't! It's too hard!"

"You have three minutes to get your ass up here or you'll die down there. You'll rot because you were too much of a fucking baby to climb up the damn rope. If you want to survive, Baylee, you're going to have to fight for it. Fucking fight for it!"

Tears blur the horrible world around me but rage blooms inside of me. I grab hold of the rope and try again.

Over and over again.

Sometimes I get a few feet up only to fall and land on my butt on the cold, hard ground. Other times, I slide down the rope and not only rub the skin from my palms but the inside of my thighs as well. It seems like forever but he finally barks out words that send me once again plummeting to my hell.

"Time's up. Nice knowing you, sweetheart. I thought you were stronger but clearly I overestimated your strength."

The door slams down and the light is gone.

My hope—my light in the darkness is vanished.

With a wail of defeat, I curl up on the chilled floor and close my eyes. I hope death is easy on me. I hope he's swift and steals me in my sleep. And I hope Mom finds me soon—wherever we end up on the other side.

Goodbye, world.

Goodbye, Baylee.

Aches. All over. Especially in my head and my belly. Groaning, I crack open my eyes.

Darkness.

Again.

How long was it since he closed me off this time?

Five minutes? Five hours? Five days?

I sit up and something touches my shoulder. A shriek escapes me before I realize it's only the rope. It still hangs from the ceiling. My heart thuds to life as I wonder if without the pressure of his stupid time limit, maybe I could make it.

But I can barely pull my weakened body to a sitting position. How would I ever be able to climb that thing?

I must, though.

I don't want to die down here.

Standing on shaky legs, I clutch onto the rope. It takes several tries, but I soon figure out that if I twist the rope around my leg as I climb, I can keep myself from sliding back down. My biceps scream in pain and I suck in gasps of air as I slowly inch myself up. When I'm finally near the top, I push the ceiling expecting resistance. But it moves. It moves!

I'm so excited that I nearly lose my grip and crash back onto the dirty cement floor below. At this height, I'd surely break a leg or an arm. Falling is not an option.

I slide an arm through the gap. The room is no longer lit and is dark, but moonlight shines from somewhere which means a window is nearby. Windows mean freedom. With newfound determination, I manage to lift the slat up and get my elbow onto the wood floors around the hole. Now that escape is within reach, I'm no longer weak and I find the strength to get my other elbow up. When I get my knee onto the surface, I nearly cry out in joy.

Almost there.

Now that my eyes have adjusted, I see that I'm in a kitchen. I slowly drag my body out of the hole and across the floor. And once I'm completely out and there are a few feet separating me from the opening, I cry. Silent, all-body wracking sobs.

So close.

A door is nearby and I can escape.

Climbing to my feet, I attempt to keep the shaking in my legs to a minimum. Each step is slow and painful but I'll be free soon. Just a few more. My fingers clutch the cold metal and I twist.

Free.

At last.

I smile for the first time in days.

Until the fire licks at my ass.

One. Two. Three. Four.

I've barely made sense of the pain when the strong arm is back around my waist pinning me against him. Searing hot pain brands my butt cheeks, and my moment of hope is replaced with fear. What is happening?

"I told you. For every step you tried to escape, I'd whip you. And you made it four steps before I caught you. Does it hurt, Baylee?" His masculine scent which used to warm and comfort me—even turned me on, later—infiltrates my pores. Now it only turns my stomach sour.

"Fuck you, Gabe," I snarl.

His hand slides up over my breast and pinches my nipple brutally. "I most certainly intend on fucking you, my brave, sweet girl," he says with a gravelly rumble. "But first, we're going to punish you for that naughty mouth."

I can't do this.

I should have died down there in that hole.

It seems preferable than to be in the steely clutches of this nightmare.

"Time to learn this new world of yours, sweetheart."

A shudder wracks through me as his thumb runs over my nipple, this time almost reverently. My flesh raises at his gentle touch and I nearly vomit.

"I like 'em dirty. And you're as dirty as they come. Soon, you'll be just as dirty on the inside," he murmurs against the shell of my ear, sending goosebumps over my flesh. "You'll like it too. In fact, you'll love it. One day you will thank me."

I will never thank him.

Ever.

chapter
TWO

Gabe

Sweet Baylee.

So innocent and pure.

It was almost too late. That fucker had nearly ruined her.

But she's mine to ruin. Every inch of her pale, dirty flesh. All mine. I've waited for so long. So fucking long. And now I have an excuse.

This past summer was the worst. Fucking agony.

Watching her bounce around in her tiny shorts and tight tank tops was painful. So goddamned torturous that I'd nearly yanked her out of that public pool one day and taken her long ago.

But the timing wasn't right.

Things weren't yet in place.

In my world, timing is everything. The early bird may catch the worm. But it's the patient bird who wins the dirt and all the worms in it.

Baylee is the most coveted worm of all.

So alive and free. Sexy yet unknowing of her allure to every man on this earth, aside from her father.

She was meant to be mine.

And she will be.

The girl isn't ready yet, but I will teach her.

Drag her through hell and then hold her on the other side. Nurse her soul back to health and heal all the broken parts of her. I'll be the sun and moon in her world. All thoughts will revert back to me. Always.

The training will be brutal. For her.

For me, it will be decadent perfection.

I will own every inch of her inside and out. I'll fuck her into oblivion. I will be the very thing she craves.

My plan will mean that I will lose her for a bit but when it all settles, I'll claim her again. She'll belong to me and nobody will say a fucking word. Her father will thank me. Her mother will hug me. Her boyfriend will hate me.

And she will love me.

chapter
THREE

Baylee

I kick my legs out in an attempt to make a connection with anything that will keep me from going back down into that hole. The house is so sparse though, definitely not the house he owns next door to my own. There's no furniture in the kitchen. Only wood planks stand between me and that black hell.

Gabe is a thousand times stronger than me, especially in my weakened state, and I'm nothing against his grip around me.

"Save your energy, sweetheart. You'll need it."

His warning chills my bones and I fall limp in his arms. At this point, the darkness is preferable to having him touch me and threaten me.

"Good girl."

This is the point where I give up. Whatever will be will be. I'm no match against a forty-one-year-old man. My father was someone I had always counted on to protect me because he was big and strong and fearless. Gabe kind of fell into the same category.

Until he stole me.

Then he became the villain in this story.

If Dad only knew his best friend betrayed him in the worst possible way, he'd kill him with his bare hands. I saw the way Dad pummeled a guy once. He'd gotten several licks in on him before the cops showed up. Some guy rear-ended us and my father exploded in fury. *"You could have killed my wife!"* She was already dying though. My mother and I screeched and cried while my dad punched that poor man relentlessly.

He defended us—*defended her*—with such a furious passion that the world trembled beneath his feet. My dad wasn't someone people messed with. At six foot five, he towered over most men, including Gabe. It wasn't the height that frightened people though. Something in my dad's eyes flickered with a barely contained rage. Even as a child, I sensed that he was brooding about something. That anger ebbed and flowed beneath the surface. Not at me or my mom. Not at Gabe. At the world. The world was always trying to cheat him and take from him. Life was unfair…and Dad hated that fact.

If he knew Gabe had taken me, he'd kill him. No doubt in my mind. Even though Dad loved Gabe like a brother, he didn't look at him like he looked at me.

I'm his only daughter.

His whole world.

The girl who looks like his wife but has his height, although not quite as tall, and his tenacity.

He would rip out Gabe's heart and serve it to me and Mom for supper.

A crazed giggle escapes me and Gabe freezes. "What's so funny?"

"Nothing," I say and then cackle. "I hope I come back and haunt you until Dad kills you."

His annoyed grunt satisfies me until he speaks. "You passed your first test. You're not going to die now. The worst part is over. It's time to train."

Train?

My mind fades to grey as I ponder what he means. In school, I train for track. I run miles and miles without getting winded. The high jump is my thing. Effortlessly, I flop over that bar as if it's the easiest thing to do in the world. I lift weights and eat right so Coach doesn't give me crap.

That's what training means to me.

But something tells me that Gabe isn't training me to run a marathon. Something tells me he's training me for something dark and sinister.

I'm so lost in my thoughts that I barely register being carried into a bedroom. The walls are made of wood and I realize we're in a log cabin. The floors, the ceiling, the walls, and even the bed are made of the wood that is now permeating my senses.

We're probably deep in the woods.

Nobody will ever hear me scream.

It's me against him.

"Are you sleepy, little one?"

For a moment his voice bears concern, and is familiar. Like the Gabe from before. The man I'd depended on to help me push my car when I'd run out of gas on the way to the mall when Dad was still caught up at work. The man who had playfully threatened my boyfriend not to harm a hair on my head or there'd be hell to pay. The man who had hugged me tight when my dog Molly got run over by a car and passed away.

Exhaustion overwhelms me and I sag in his arms. I'm so tired. So very, very tired.

"We'll talk in the morning," he whispers, almost sweetly, into my ear as he guides me over to the bed. "Over breakfast."

I burst into tears and he calms me with strokes on my grimy skin that should repulse me. But they don't. I want to close my eyes and pretend this didn't happen. I want to pretend he's here to save me.

"I'm scared," I choke out.

He yanks the covers back on the bed in the room and climbs in with me. It's only now that I realize he's wearing jeans but no shirt. My skin reacts and a cold sweat breaks out over me. I'm terrified, and yet, I want him to comfort me. I want him to promise me that this is all a bad dream and I'll wake in the morning in my own bed.

He drags the covers up over us and for the first time in days, I'm warm. Gabe is a monster and yet I'm twisting in his arms to get closer—to get warmer. My arm wraps around his middle and I bury my face into his bare chest.

"Shhh," he murmurs against my hair and then kisses me. "I have you now. You're mine, Baylee. All mine. Rest now and let me watch over you."

His words are enough to calm me and exhaustion steals me away.

After the hell I've endured over the past few days, this is heaven.

The devil is my savior.

Bacon.

My stomach grumbles and I come to. Blinking my eyes slowly, I take in the wooden walls that surround me in this sparse room. Where am I?

I'm in hell. I remember now.

The heavenly scent of breakfast wafting through the cabin, though, is enough to push away my worries and I focus on regaining my energy first. Every muscle in my body screams in agony. I'm not sure if I'll even be able to walk. The thought is alarming.

I must try though. Maybe we're near people. If I can get out the front door and run to the street, I could flag down a car. Someone could rescue me.

"I told you. For every step you tried to escape, I'd whip you. And you made it four steps before I caught you. Does it hurt, Baylee?"

What if it's a hundred steps to the road before he catches me? I shudder at the idea of him whipping me raw. My backside is still tender from last night. When I go to move my hand to finger the spot—to see if he broke the skin—panic threatens to drown me.

I'm tied up.

I'm tied up.

Holy crap, I'm tied up.

A tug of my legs indicates that my ankles are bound and strung to each post at the end of the bed. My wrists are secured together and rest on my belly under the blanket that's been pulled to my chin. I try to sit up but I have no strength left.

"Help!"

Something clatters in the kitchen. I hear normal sounds that one would expect to hear as someone cooked breakfast. And that is what terrifies me even more. Gabe is carrying on as if this is normal—as if this is okay.

It is absolutely not okay.

"Help!"

Heavy footsteps thunder down the hallway toward me and tears stream out of the corner of my eyes. I'm afraid. I want my dad. I want Brandon. I want someone who could help me.

"Good morning, sweetheart."

If I weren't tied up—if I were here under my own desires—I'd be in awe of the sight. The devil, disguised as an angel, stands in the doorway resembling a combination of both beauty and evil. His dark hair is still wet as if he's recently showered and he's once again shirtless. The man, despite being in his forties, still works out and has an impressive physique. His shoulders are broad and thick while his toned torso tapers down into a narrower waist. Dark jeans hang low on his hips and dark hair disappears into them. If things were different, I'd almost say he was hot.

But I'm his prisoner, not his lover.

So despite his body being hot, it's his eyes that are cold. Coffee-colored eyes are narrowed at me and his chiseled jaw is moving in a furious manner, reminding me of my dad when he gets angry.

"Time for breakfast," he grunts and storms toward me. He's carrying a plate and has a water bottle tucked under his arm. I'm upset and scared, but all I can think about is downing that water.

He sits beside me and I squirm away from him. My bindings don't allow for much wiggle room so the heat of his body envelops me.

"Why are you doing this? Is it sex? You want me for sex?" I demand with tears in my eyes.

He sets the plate down on the bedside table and opens the water bottle. I expect him to un-screw the cap, which he does, and give me a swallow, which he doesn't. Instead, he brings it to his full lips and takes a small sip.

"Mmm, cold."

I sniffle and choke back a sob. He probably wants me to cry and beg. Well, he doesn't deserve that.

"Want a drink, Baylee?"

With a frustrated sigh, I bite my chapped lip and nod. "Please."

He flashes me a pleased grin that roils my stomach. "Good girl."

I'm angry and want to swat the bottle out of his hands, but I'm not stupid. I need to be some-what compliant if I have any hope of leaving this place. He shoves some pillows behind me to prop me up which makes the blanket slip down to my stomach baring my breasts to him. The man who's always hidden his desire for me, blatantly eyes my breasts before sliding his eyes to mine.

Hunger.

I'm not the only one.

The flash of unbridled lust in his eyes tells me that he has plans for me—plans he's probably wanted to execute for quite some time.

"Drink."

I open my mouth and graciously accept the cold liquid. A tiny moan escapes me as I suck down the water with greed.

"That's enough, Baylee. You'll throw up if you drink too much. Why don't you have a try at eating something?" His saccharine tone sickens me and I glare at him.

"I'm thirsty."

"And you'll get more. You have to slow down though."

With an unconvinced nod, I jerk my gaze over to the plate on the table. A few scrambled eggs, a couple of sliced strawberries, and an unbuttered piece of toast.

"Where's the bacon?" I pout.

He chuckles and I cringe. I hate the sound. *Hate* his laugh. "Oh, baby, you're not getting bacon for a few days. One step at a time here."

"You act like you've done this before." My haughty tone wipes the smile off his face. Good.

"Several times, actually. But never have I enjoyed it so much." He winks and I frown.

Several times? What happened to the rest of the girls?

"Can you untie me?"

His lips draw up into a wolfish grin that frightens me down to the fabric of my being. "Baylee, I would love to untie you. And after training, if you're a good girl, not only will I untie you, but I'll let you shower as well. Would you like that?"

The deception in his words is thick.

"I don't believe you."

He shrugs and holds a piece of toast to my lips. "Not like you really have a choice though. If I were you, I'd take a chance and see what happens. Comply and you will be rewarded—that is my promise to you."

I take a bite and chew the dry toast. I'd prefer to suck down that entire bottle of water but I'm trying to behave.

"Good girl."

My belly aches from the food and I squirm in the bed. He's gone from the room and left me here. I wonder if he'll come back and make good on his promise. But with his return will be the training he's referring to. I'm not sure I'm ready for that.

Dishes clang together in the kitchen as he cleans up and I grow annoyed. The dishes can wait. I wish he'd come back, do what he plans on doing, and then let me shower.

What will he do?

The most obvious conclusion would be that he wants to have sex with me. Audrey told me that it hurts the first time but not too bad. Surely I can handle him inside of me. I was prepared to let Brandon make love to me. This is something I can do—something I must do.

"You ready?" His deep voice from the doorway jerks my attention to him. He stands there holding a large bowl of water with a rag hanging over the side.

I nod and attempt not to shrink away from him when he sits beside me. The bowl gets placed on the bedside table and I strain to watch his every move.

"Are you going to hurt me?" The wobble in my voice gives away my fear and I hate myself for it. "Please don't hurt me."

His smile is gentle, comforting even. "Sweetheart, I'm not going to hurt you today."

A lump of fear forms in my throat and I desperately try to swallow it down. *I'm not going to hurt you today.* But tomorrow? Or the next? My heart begins galloping at his words.

"Please tell me why you took me, Gabe."

He frowns. "I'll tell you what the plan is. How about that? Will that satisfy your curiosity?"

"Yes."

"I will. Right after training and your shower. I promise."

He soaks the rag in the water and then wrings it out before bringing it over to my dirty body. The rag is warm and I gasp when he begins to sponge bathe me. His movement is reverent, almost fatherly in nature, and bile rises in my throat.

I don't want him to touch me.

Or clean me.

Or even look at me.

He takes his time, washing my breasts first, and then cleans my face, neck, armpits, and stomach. As he gets lower, I attempt to drag my spread legs back together but they're immovable because of the rope.

"I have to wash that bastard from your sweet pussy. This wasn't his to take," he murmurs, an angry glint in his eye.

He pushes the blanket down to my knees and stares between my legs. Then, he draws the rag down and cleans me. All over the outer lips of my sex, he scrubs gently but in a determined fashion. It's not sexual and it doesn't turn me on. In fact, it repulses me. I want him gone from there. The rag is returned to the bowl and he squeezes the water from it once again. This time, when he goes back between my legs, I gasp in horror. He's cleaning my butt—the hole to be exact.

"Stop," I beg.

But he doesn't stop. He carefully cleanses my body one inch at a time. Thankfully, he returns the rag back to the water and disappears with the bowl. A chill from the air skitters over my flesh and goosebumps erupt all over my skin. When his footsteps thud back toward me, I tense up.

"Ready?" he questions from the doorway.

Tears well in my eyes and he blurs before me. I quickly blink them away so I can see him. I don't want him out of my sight.

"Please don't…"

He frowns. "Your pleas will fall on deaf ears. I can gag you, though, if you'd prefer. Up to you. But keep begging and I'll become annoyed. You don't want me annoyed, Baylee. You want to please me. Trust me."

I start to cry but I don't dare utter a word. He seems satisfied and drags the blanket the rest of the way from me, depositing it on the floor behind him.

"You're so perfect," he coos and runs a finger up my shin toward my thigh. "You have much to learn, so we're going to need to get started. Two weeks will come and go pretty quickly."

Two weeks?

And then what?

His finger trails lazily up my inner thigh and I cringe when he drags it along my sex. I can't do this.

"Most men don't like hair there. Soon, I'll reward you with a razor and you can clean this up." He tugs at the hair on my pubic bone and I cry out. "Shhh, remember what I said about the begging. I could gag you with the rag I cleaned your ass with. Would you like that?"

I shake my head in vehemence. "No." *Please don't* is on the tip of my tongue but he'd probably gag me for that.

"Okay then. I can see this will go well." His eyes become predatory as he drags his finger down my slit and pushes between my lips, connecting with my clit. He doesn't move, simply stares at me. "Did Brandon know how to touch you, Baylee? Did he ever bring you to orgasm?"

"N-No."

My chest feels as if it will rip apart and free my exploding heart at any moment.

"That's because he's a boy. You've never had a man with my experience draw pleasure from you."

A wobble from my bottom lip is my only sign of weakness. Of course he sees it and grins.

"See, I could get you off with just this finger," he tells me in a smug tone. "All I'd have to do is press and massage and circle right here." As he says *here*, I grow dizzy when stars dance around me. Despite my feeling afraid and betrayed, my body reacts. It embarrasses me and a shameful crimson heats my skin.

"Your skin is telling me you like this and I'm so glad. I want to prove to you my experience over his. That night, when I came for you, I could see the bored look in your eyes. I can assure you, when I'm between your legs, you'll only be thinking about me."

I swallow and close my eyes. Maybe I can pretend I'm someplace else. For a moment pretend it's Brandon instead, so I can endure the punishment he's about to unleash. The bed squeaks and I ignore it, clenching my eyes tighter.

I can do this.

Think of spiky brown hair.

Think of the sweet smile of my high school boyfriend.

Think about anything other than the—

"Oh!" I screech and yank my eyes open against my will.

Gabe raises a smug brow at me as his thick, wide tongue plows between my lips, dragging pleasure in its wake. His thumbs dig brutally into my thighs and I yelp. I don't want to watch him but I'm snared in his stare.

So hungry.

So primal.

So evil.

One hand leaves my thigh and he pushes a finger into my body. It's uncomfortable but not unpleasant. And with the way he's licking and sucking in all the spots Brandon couldn't find just days ago, I'm starting to lose my hold on sanity. It's hard to be upset and afraid when my body is being overwhelmed with such unimaginable sensations.

Concentrate, Baylee! He's a monster!

My breath stills in my throat as he curves his finger inside of me. He's probing parts of me that haven't been ever touched. It frightens me but my stupid body is rocking against him—betraying me. Again.

His teeth press down on my clit and I shriek in fear. But he doesn't hurt me. It's like he knows exactly what feels good and soon my fight begins to weaken. My thoughts are jumbled. All I can focus on is the way he tastes me. The slurping, ravenous noises that come from him. How his hot breath tickles me. And the way his fingers own the inside of me.

My thoughts dull as sensations take over. I'm no longer able to grasp on to the rational part of my head because all I can think about is the way my body has come alive.

A strange feeling takes hold inside me, an awareness that is as basic and simplistic as male and female, night and day, predator and prey. Yes, I am terrified. But there is also this undercurrent of something else. Something larger. *Lust?* Maybe. I have fantasized about this guy, dreamed about him touching me. I have hungered for his eyes on my naked skin. Imagined his mouth on my breasts. And now, here he is, *touching me*. And it is nothing like I had imagined.

It's too much.

Yet, it's not enough.

There's more, I can feel it.

Another nibble on my clit has me shrieking out in pleasure. This seems to excite him because he growls against my wet body and I shudder in response. My body stretches as he inserts another finger. So full with him. So overwhelmed by him. Even his manly scent has overpowered the earlier bacon aroma and taken root in my lungs.

I'm completely at his mercy.

Cast under his evil spell.

His spit and juices from my body are running down the clean crack of my butt and I want to be embarrassed. I want to squirm away from him. But, right now, I can't. My body is selfish for this moment after so many days of horror. The pleasure is as addicting as the water I greedily consumed.

I need this.

I need this to survive.

"Oh God," I mewl. "Oh God."

And then it happens.

One more hard suck of my clit seems to rip me open. An unearthly moan pours from me as my nerve endings come alive. I can feel them all at once, everywhere, and they seize me. Each and every one of them takes hold of me, clenching in ecstasy. My head throbs in unison with my wild heart and I nearly black out from desire.

It's overwhelming.

But for some sick reason, my body responds as if it needs this pleasure for nourishment, despite the horrified and disgusted thoughts running through my mind.

As my body shudders, it starts to leave as quickly as it arrived. His tongue still works me but he's slowed as if he knows this orgasm of mine is fleeting and it won't last forever. Tears stream down from eyes as I come to a nauseating realization.

He's going to give me more of these.

And I want them.

I want them so bad.

What the hell kind of person does that make me?

chapter
FOUR

Baylee

He sits up on his knees between my legs and smirks. "I knew you'd love that." With his fingers still inside of me, I feel as though I'm his accomplice in an act against myself. For a few brief moments, I joined his side and allowed him to carry out an agenda against me.

"I hated it," I lie. It's not truth either though. I'm conflicted and confused. A war rages inside of me between mind and body.

His face glistens from juices that came from my body and embarrassment once again washes over me.

"Don't lie, sweetheart. I've known you for a long time and can tell when you're doing it. I have plenty more to show you. Some of which you will love—other stuff you won't admit you love. But as long as you're with me, you'll feel only pleasure."

"You're a rapist pig!" I snap. I'm furious with myself for succumbing so easily to him.

He glares at me before launching himself on top of me. I scream and squirm but he crushes me with his weight. His mouth hovers over mine. My scent is all over him and I want to throw up.

"I haven't raped you," he snarls. "When I do take you, you'll beg for it. You'll *want* my thick cock inside of your tight cunt. Do you understand me, sweetheart?"

His erection presses through his jeans against my still wet sex.

"I'll never want you," I hiss and spit at him.

He grunts, makes a crude point of licking the spit from his face, and then begins brutally bucking against me. At first it hurts and I start sobbing again, but soon the build begins to burn in my pelvis. "You think you don't want this, but you do. Look at you. You can barely suppress your need for it."

Thrust. Thrust. Thrust.

I squirm and move but it only intensifies the sensation.

"I could pull out my dick and push it inside you. Is that what you want? To feel me deep inside of you, baby?"

I shake my head but close my eyes when he lowers his mouth onto mine. His kiss is possessive and I'm powerless against it. Poor Brandon kisses me sweetly and his skin is soft. Gabe kisses me with promise. Promise to take and possess. It only serves to madden and conflict me further. My body shouldn't respond so easily. It should recognize the wrongness of his actions and side with my mind.

But it doesn't.

His lips suck on mine. His thick tongue dances with mine. The shadow of dark hair that is growing on his face scratches my skin raw in a delightful way.

I'm going to orgasm again.

I can feel it.

His hardness rubs between the lips of my pussy and I gasp out in pleasure, acting out against the furious storm brewing in my head. My body wants this. The way he grinds against me is painful yet addicting, like the bliss of heroin surging through your veins after a hit. In your head, you know it's wrong. You know eventually it will kill you. And yet…your body craves it anyway. Against all rational reasoning.

I'm depraved.

"Stop," I breathe.

He deepens the kiss that tastes like me before pulling away. "I'm not going to fuck you right now, but I need to feel you."

His hand slides between us and he fumbles with his jeans. Soon, his erection slides up over my clit and I cry out.

"Oh God!"

A satisfied grunt escapes him before his mouth takes me again. I'm dizzy and lost in him. And the way his smooth, large cock slides against me is the most blissful sensation in the world. I'm wet and I wish—*I actually freaking wish*—he'd push it into me.

He's right.

Gabe won't have to rape me. I'll beg for it. I'm so stupid and—

"Shit!" I curse against his lips. This time, my orgasm seizes me for longer. I flutter my eyes closed and live in the moment. I try my hardest to draw it out for longer. And yet, like before, it's gone within seconds. As I come down from my high, wet heat spurts between us. I startle and my wild eyes meet his hooded ones that no longer seem frightening.

I've satisfied the devil, subdued him into a sleepy state.

"That was so fucking perfect, Baylee," he says, his fingers brushing my lips. "I knew you'd be the right girl for this. Soon, you'll hang on my every word. You'll beg for the orgasms that make you crazy. Your world will revolve only around me."

Terror, the elusive emotion, starts to make a reappearance. Not because I'm afraid of him, but because I think he's right. He knows my body better than I do and he's already proven how he can use it against me.

"I want my shower now." The nasty bite in my voice shocks him—and I don't miss the brief flash of hurt in his eyes—before he climbs off me.

"Very well. You deserve one after that."

And you deserve to go to hell.

The shower was heaven. I scrubbed his cum from my stomach until I was raw and sore. With the hot shower I was permitted to take alone, I was able to find clarity. To find my way back to reality.

He stole me.

He is a monster.

And I'll do well to remember that.

Once I turn off the water, I peek out of the shower to inspect the window. Maybe I could climb out and run. But then my eyes meet his bored, dark ones and I shudder.

"Thinking of running away?" His gaze travels over to the window. "It would be unwise of you."

I swallow and snatch the towel. Drying off behind the shower curtain, away from his leering eyes, I attempt to compose myself. I need to be smart about this. Once the towel is secured around my body, I tug the curtain away. He's smiling now and I'm once again afraid.

"No."

He frowns but doesn't probe me any further. "Come on, I want to show you something."

I climb out of the shower and follow him. He hasn't told me to drop the towel and I hold on to it as if it will shield my weak body from his expert touch. We make our way back into the bedroom. The bed has now been made with clean new sheets. A folded blanket sits at the end.

"Sit," he says and points to the bed.

I walk over and drop down to the soft bed. He strides over to a closet and yanks out a box. After he sets it on the floor, he rifles through what looks like photographs and pulls out a few. Once he's done, he makes his way over to me and sits close enough that our thighs touch.

"This is Sandy."

I gape in horror. A woman, probably in her early twenties, stares back at the camera devoid of emotion. She's naked and sprawled out on the bed like I was not even an hour ago. Panic ripples through me but I can't look away. Her hair is dark, a stark contrast to my long blonde locks, and her eyes are green unlike my blue ones. But she's dirty—as if she spent three days in a hole. Like me.

"This is sick, Gabe. You're sick."

He shrugs. "Yeah, I know." The next picture he shows me causes my breath to catch. Her mouth is on his erection. Empty eyes look up at him. It hurts to see this pic. She's gone. Whoever she was before is gone. Is this his plan for me?

"What happened to her?"

He wraps an arm around me and even though he's the monster, I lean into his comforting hug. "She belongs to another man now to do as he pleases. I sold her."

The world freezes at his words. *I sold her. I sold her. I sold her.*

"I-I-I don't understand."

He chuckles and I squirm away from him. His fingers bite into my bicep while he keeps me against him. "Of course not, sweetheart. Unlike these women, you're innocent."

"Are you going to sell me?"

He sighs and my heart crushes. "Yes, I am."

The reality hits me hard, knocking the air out of me. A wave of nausea clenches the pit of my stomach and pushes bile into my throat. The threat of vomiting is imminent. "B-B-But what about Mom and Dad? Gabe, you can't do this to me!"

The pictures flutter to the floor and he grabs my jaw in a brutal grip. He drags my face to meet his. "You don't have a choice in the matter. We only have two weeks. So if you want to be prepared for that world, I need you to pay attention to your training."

"No, I can't—"

"You'd sell for more being a virgin and all. And believe me, I have thought about it. But I'm greedy, and if anyone takes that from you, it will be me. Besides, I love you too much to send you to the wolves with no armor. I'm going to teach you, Baylee. I'll do fucking awful things to you so that when those monsters get their greedy hands on you, you'll be prepared. When they fuck you and hurt you, you can stare at them like Sandy did. With emotionless eyes. In all honesty here, I'm your savior. You should be thanking me."

Rage explodes from me. His matter of fact stare makes me want to claw his eyeballs out.

"Fuck you, Gabe!"

He shoves me back onto the bed and pins me before I can even think about moving. "Why thank you, sweetheart," he snarls, "I certainly will. I'll fuck every hole in your body until you bleed. And then I'll make you beg me for more. Is that what you want?"

Tears roll down the side of my face and I shake my head.

"Well, too bad. That part, I'm afraid, must occur because if I don't do it, they will. Can you imagine what it would feel like to get raped in the ass by some fat, bastard when you've never even been touched there? He would rip you apart. You would bleed out, baby. I'm going to teach you to enjoy sex—all the dark and dirty parts of it. So when they do take you, you'll like it. Your body will respond and you'll survive."

His words slide over me like oil and I gag. I can't do this. Images of terrifying men hurting me and touching me and fucking me is too much to bear. Gabe's wrong. I won't survive this. I don't belong here. I belong in my own bed worrying over simpler matters like school or my mother's health. Not in the clutches of monsters wondering if I'll live or die.

"I want to go home." My words are nothing but a whisper.

His lips draw up into a wolfish grin and his eyes darken. "You're never going back there, baby. Suck it up and accept your fate."

I will never accept this.

Ever.

"Do I need to tie you up this time?"

The deep voice drags me from my mental vacation. I'd slipped into some hopeless pit of despair—something reminiscent of the hole in his kitchen which now seems oddly safer than this bed.

I can't do this.

I'd rather die.

"Please."

"Please what? Tie you up? Give you more orgasms?"

I shudder at his words. "Let me go."

His harsh laugh startles me. "You're not going anywhere. You will stay with me for two weeks. Then we're going to San Diego where I'll sell you to the highest bidder. The better you behave—*the more you let me prepare you*—the higher the odds are that you'll get sold to someone wealthy. Perhaps someone who will care for you. You'll be… kept. Believe me when I say you don't want to get sold to some of those bottom feeders. They buy a lot which means, their slaves don't last long."

I stare blankly at him. *Slaves.* This is my life now.

"They die, sweetheart. Those bastards hurt and eventually kill them. I'd be fucking furious if they hurt what's mine." His tone is fierce and protective which confuses me.

"Why can't you keep me then?" My question is honest. If I have to be stuck in this world, I'd rather be here with him than some stranger, who could be far more evil than Gabe.

He raises his gaze to meet mine and shrugs. "I need the money," he says in a gruff, dismissive tone. "Ready for more?"

My mind is numb. This isn't reality. This is a nightmare. "Don't hurt me, Gabe."

He flashes me a crooked grin. "Baby, I'm going to hurt you, but you'll like it."

A shiver runs down my spine but I meet his stare with defiance. "Fine. Let's do this. Train me to be a fuck doll."

The scowl on his face is immediate and I realize my words struck a nerve. Good. A realization begins to course through me. He must not want to sell me. He's every bit the greedy bastard he confessed to being, and if he could, he'd keep me. I need to make sure that happens. Maybe if I meant something to him—something more than money—he would change his mind. He would lower his guard for me, and I could attempt escape.

He tugs the towel away from me and proceeds to undress. My eyes skim over his ridged frame and I freeze at seeing his erection. It's huge. His two fingers felt like an invasion—that thing will feel like it's impaling me.

"Did you ever suck Brandon's puny pecker?" he questions in a mocking tone.

I bristle and shake my head. "I relieved him with my hand. And he… he touched me some. We haven't really done much."

"And why do you think that is?"

I don't understand the meaning behind his question. "I don't know. Maybe because I'm high school," I sneer.

He laughs—the asshole laughs at me. "Cut the crap, sweetheart. I've been to every single one of your birthday parties since I moved in next door, including your eighteenth birthday. In the grand scheme of things, age doesn't matter. I want to know why you haven't let pussy boy fuck you yet."

"Because he hasn't tried." My honest words feel like a betrayal to both myself and my sweet boyfriend.

He crawls into the bed beside me and his fingers draw lazy circles on my stomach. "But you wanted him to?"

I let out a ragged, teary sigh. "Yes."

"Why?"

"What do you mean why?" I demand.

He smiles and the way his eyebrows quirk up, it reminds me of the look he gave me when he was between my legs. It causes my pelvis to ache and I hate myself for it.

"I mean, Baylee, why did you want him to? Was it 'love?'"

"Yes." I swallow but avoid his gaze by staring out the window where the midday sun pours in. "And because I wanted to know what it felt like."

His hand slides up over my breast, along my throat, to where he firmly clutches my jaw and drags my gaze back to him.

"Do you want to know how many times I thought about climbing into your window and fucking you on your bed?" His dark eyes narrow at me and his pupils dilate, as if he's getting off on the simple memory of his fantasy. With a flick of his tongue, he licks his lips and then growls. "Every single night since last summer. You taunted me in those tight clothes you always wore. I'm not fucking stupid, baby. I saw the way you watched me. How you'd bend over and give me a peek at that sweet ass. How you'd bounce around the house in a tight camisole with no bra on, with your tits on full display. You were playing games you had no business playing."

I gape at him. "I didn't ask for this!"

"No, but you wanted it."

"Not like this."

His grin stretches wide and reveals his perfectly white teeth which I'm sure will tear me to pieces one day. "But you admit you wanted me. Well, little girl, you have me. And I'm going to own every part of you until our time together is up."

So smug. So sure.

My instincts tell me to obey, but I want to rattle him and shake the very foundation his world is constructed upon.

"If you talk this much during sex, I'm guessing it will be a total snooze fest," I taunt with a snotty bite in my voice. He takes the bait and snaps at me.

"Playing games will get you hurt."

"So hurt me."

I smile in satisfaction at him. Screw you, asshole.

But my confidence dissipates the moment he slaps me. It was the fleshy part of his palm but it still stings.

"Ouch!"

He roars with laughter. "If that hurt, then we have a lot of work to do. Those men will devour you, baby. They'll tear apart your flesh and bruise every part of you. You have to toughen up if you want to survive."

His mouth lowers to my collarbone and he begins kissing me softly. It almost reminds me of how Brandon would kiss me. I wonder if he's okay. I'm sure half of California is looking for me by this point. Dad will have torn apart our entire neighborhood. And with Gabe missing too, he'll be an instant suspect. I've seen the crime shows Dad watches. It won't take long for the police to assume Gabe took me and then investigate his past. They'll search his phone records, discover property he owns or rents. And they will find me.

It's only a matter of time.

His tongue darts over my raised nipple and it hardens at his touch. Then he bites down. Searing pain rips through me, but before I can push him away, his tongue is back to massaging me. My heart rate is thumping along and can't decide if it's from fear or from yearning.

This can't be happening. Not to me.

He's once again doing all the things I seem to be powerless against. His mouth trails down my stomach and I gasp when he dips it into my belly button. My breathing becomes broken, heavy. My fingers crave to sink into his hair. Or rip it out.

"Get on your hands and knees."

I want to cry, I want to scream, I want to do anything but what he demands of me. He rolls away from me and heads back to his closet.

"Now, Baylee."

I scramble to do as I'm told and stare at the headboard. I've stumbled upon some shows on cable late at night. They never show anything but sometimes the man takes the woman from behind. In the movies, they seem to enjoy it. I try to convince myself that I can do this.

The bed sinks behind me and his warm hand grips my ass cheek. "This ass is fucking beautiful."

All too soon I realize, this is unlike anything I ever saw on late night television. Something cold and wet drags across my puckered hole. I instinctively buck, fighting the inevitable. Jerking my head over my shoulder, I'm horrified to see him teasing me with some metal thing. "What's that?"

He grins and winks. "It's a butt plug. Don't worry, it's small. We'll work up to something larger."

I'm already scrambling away when his fingers dig into my hips and he yanks me back to him. "Don't move, baby, or this *will* hurt." He begins pushing the ice-cold object into me.

"Please no."

"Relax and let me or I'll force it. Fucking understand?"

I whimper and nod. This is not a part of me that is meant to be seen. It's a part of me that *I* have never seen. I realize my fear stems in equal parts from deafening embarrassment at being touched in such a secret place, combined with the pain involved in being penetrated there. Closing my eyes, I attempt to conjure up images of Brandon. But all I can think about is *him.*

Gabe.

His dark, lust-filled eyes devouring me.

His unruly hair when it forms a veil over those evil eyes.

His full lips and hot mouth as it brings me pleasure, just as quickly as it spouts off words that bring me pain.

I jerk harshly and scream in pain at the intrusion, but he holds me steady. It's my inclination to clench in self-preservation but that only seems to make it worse. Eventually, I attempt to relax and it slides in.

It's foreign and unwanted and it doesn't belong there.

"It looks so pretty in your ass. From here on out, you wear this all of the time until you need to shit or when I'm ready to fuck you there."

I shudder and collapse onto the bed in defeat. It doesn't really hurt now but it's uncomfortable.

"Your mom told me you recently had the birth control shot. Is that right?"

I'm horrified at his words. "What? Why would she tell you that?"

"Let's just say I expressed my concern over the probability that Brandon was fucking you. I was making sure she knew the possibility of pregnancy was there. Turns out, she'd already taken care of it."

Technically Dad did. He'd carted me up to the female doctor and saw to it that I was examined. Of course he waited outside the examination room but afterwards, he informed the doctor of my decision to get the shot. Teens are irresponsible and forget to take pills, he'd told them. Such a personal matter and now Gabe has brought it up so callously. It's humiliating.

"I hate you."

He rolls me over onto my back and the plug jostles me from the inside. "And I love you, baby. Let me show you. Your first time should be perfect."

I start to cry again but his mouth finds my neck and soon he's sucking in that evil, erotic way that he seems to do so well. He kisses away my tears. Gently. His hands roam my body and I don't even try to fight him off. When his hand slips past my pubic bone and connects with my sensitive clit, I buck against him. I must have clenched my ass because an odd sensation throbs from inside of me. It isn't unpleasant either.

"Your first time will hurt but only a little. Then, you'll want me all the time, Baylee. As much as you want to eat and drink, you'll want me inside your pretty little cunt."

I whimper as he increases the pressure between my legs. He draws me closer and closer with each movement. I hate him. I absolutely hate him. Yet…

"Do you want me inside of you? Do you want to come all over my cock as I stretch you wide?"

His dirty words only seem to make me crazy for just that.

Yes.

"No."

"Don't lie, sweetheart."

The pleasure is so close. I want it, just like he said I would. Before I can stop myself, I beg. "Please."

"Please what?"

"I…" I trail off, unable to find the words.

"You want my thick cock inside of you?" he says. His words taunt me.

An embarrassed mewl croaks from me. "Yes."

The tip of his erection pokes at my opening and I squirm. I should want to push him away and take off running. But I don't. A sick part of me is curious and eager.

"I want your eyes on mine when I take you. Hear me, baby?"

I nod as tears leak out. "Okay."

His mouth seizes mine for a moment and his kiss is ravenous—for one split second, he kisses me like a man would kiss the love of his life. His tongue ventures gently into my mouth. He moans ever so slightly, a sound I've never heard from him before. It's all consuming and it helps me. It helps me cope with the reality of the situation.

I can do this.

"Look at me."

My eyes fly to his and they flicker with excitement. I also don't miss the adoring way he inspects me. That will be his weakness in the end. At least I hope it will be.

"I'm going to make love to you this first time, okay?"

A choked sob escapes me. "Thank you."

He grabs his cock and holds it steady. Our eyes stay glued together as he begins to press inside. At first, it's uncomfortable like when he put his fingers inside of me. But the farther he drives into me, the more painful it becomes. Without warning, he slams fully into me.

White hot pain explodes from within me and I scream. His mouth covers mine to quiet me but I'm losing my mind. He's too big. It feels like I'm being split open.

"Stop!"

He doesn't stop though and he plows into me over and over again. It feels like he's using that wicked knife of his instead of his cock. I'm cursing his very existence when his hand slides back between us. He continues his relentless pounding but now his fingers are on my clit again.

A few days ago, I was a normal virgin teenager who obsessed over her boyfriend and worried about getting into a good college. Now…

Now I'm some *thing* for this man to use and abuse.

Except now, instead of feeling sorry for myself, I'm gasping as he touches my clit that he's so easily mastered. The way he drove into me hurt at first but now it's dulling to a stinging sensation as another orgasm delightfully teases me.

He brings me to bliss and the only thing that exists is him.

Exactly like he promised.

I'm messed up—just as sick as he is.

"Oh God!"

His low, guttural grunt is the only precursor to his own orgasm. Shortly after, his cock seems to grow impossibly larger as he spurts heat inside of me. The warmth of it seeps out and stings my sore sex.

"I love you, Baylee. Say it back."

A sob catches in my throat as he dips to kiss me. With him still inside of me, it feels like we've somehow become one person. Like I am nothing more than an extension of him now. The thought terrifies me. I don't want to be a part of him.

But now…

Now he's a part of me.

"I love you too, Gabe." The lie on my tongue is just that, a lie. But dread washes over me as I wonder if it will one day become truth.

chapter
FIVE

Gabe

She's more than perfect. She's all mine. For now.

I didn't have to steal her virginity—she begged me to take it. And oh how fucking tight she was. I knew she'd be worth it…worth the wait. It was like we were meant to be. She would have been tight simply from being a virgin, but that coupled with the butt plug secured inside of her, it was like fucking bliss wrapped around my dick.

I can't stop thinking about that first time.

I say first time because I've fucked her over and over again for days now. Each time she gets braver. Says dirty things that still sound innocent coming from her lips. She claws at me and bites back. It's hot as fuck.

And she loves me.

This complicates things but it doesn't change the plan.

The plan is to sell her in less than a week.

I need the money.

But once I get it, I'll get her back. Baylee may be a pawn but eventually I will take back what belongs to me. And she does. Boy fucking does she. Never have I had a woman who complies so easily to my commands. Never have I ever had a woman who comes so easily from my touch.

She's no longer a girl. I stole that innocence away when I broke through her the first time. Now, she's completely woman.

A whimper from the other room startles me from my thoughts. The glow from my laptop is the only thing lighting up the living room. She has nightmares and I'm not delusional to think they aren't about me. Soon enough, she'll get past those. After this is all over, I'm bringing her back here and claiming her as my wife. She'll bear my children and life will go fucking on.

Another whimper.

I read through the e-mail again about the WCT or White Collar Trade location information. A wealthy San Diego real estate agent allows for the WCT to hold their monthly trades under the guise of a business convention. It's a black tie affair and the theme this month is "Innocent Flower." For Sandy and Brianna and Callie and the others, it would have been laughable. Those women were anything but fucking innocent. The dirty things they promised to do would scare the shit out of Baylee.

But my sweet girl, she'll steal the show. I might've stolen her virginity but innocence still radiates from her pores. I'll dress her up in a demure, white gown and affix gardenias to her silky hair.

Purity and sweetness.

Joy.

Secret love.

That flower is perfect and will draw the eyes of the richest men in the room. Most fucks will choose calla lilies or daisies but my Baylee is special and unique.

She whimpers again and I groan. Quickly, I place an order at the flower shop online so I can make sure they'll have what I need before closing my laptop to go to her. In her sleep, she's managed to kick off the covers and her perky tits point up toward the ceiling. I've been gentle with her until now. The occasional bite or bruising have adorned her pure flesh but I haven't hurt her like I promised.

I needed for her to get comfortable with sex first.

And boy is she comfortable. Earlier today, her wild blue eyes found mine and blazed with curiosity when I told her to ride my cock. Despite being unsure, she did. She was quite a vision with her head tossed back in pleasure.

I fell more in love with her in that moment.

But now, as the moon blankets her pale flesh through the window, I crave to prepare her. Those fuckers will hurt her. There's no stopping them. But I can ready her for the pain. And when it's all over, I'll bring her back to me so I can kiss away all of it.

"Baby, wake up," I whisper as I shed my clothes and walk over to her. "It's time to train."

Her eyes flutter open and she gazes at me as if I'm her whole fucking world. It causes an uncharacteristic ache in my chest but I push it away. I want the look gone because I'm about to destroy the pedestal she has built for me.

"Take your butt plug out."

Baylee

I squint at him in confusion. He never lets me take it out—when I need to go to the bathroom, he removes it for me. I've grown used to the way it feels inside and I'm almost worried to remove it on my own.

"I'm afraid to do it myself."

My admission seems to excite him. "Pretend you're taking a shit," he sneers.

I gape at him. "What? Why are you being mean?"

His eyes take on that bored stare that infuriates me. The past few days I've stupidly lulled myself into an irrational state of safety. I've allowed myself to slip into his trap and assumed he was really falling for me. Enough so, that he'd forget his whole idea of selling me.

"I'm not being mean. You have more training. Take it out now or I'll dump you back into the cellar."

I study his face for a moment longer and realize he's not kidding. Fear clutches at my heart but I sit up on my knees and spread them apart.

"Good girl. Push it out. Your body will know what to do."

Closing my eyes, I attempt to focus on relaxing and soon, I can sense that it is almost out. As soon as it drops to the bed, I gasp in relief.

He grunts his approval. "You have a three second head start, little girl."

I scrunch my brows together in confusion. "What? But you said—"

"I know what I said. Consider this permission. I'm going to count to three and then I'm coming for you."

We hold each other's stare for half a second longer.

"Run!"

His barked order jerks me to life and I scramble from the bed.

"One!"

I've been outside of the bedroom but never outside of the house. I'm not sure where he wants me to run but I make a beeline for the front door.

"Two!"

Crap! I fumble with the lock and jerk the door open. Tonight, the February air is beyond freezing and my body wants to shut down the moment a cool wind swallows me.

"Three!" he shouts from within the house. "Ready or not, here I come!"

My feet make purchase on the wood porch and I run. The steps, I easily hop down, and then tear off across the grass. Having been fed and hydrated over the past few days, my strength is up. I don't have much time to take in my surroundings but I do notice we're completely surrounded by woods like I'd determined.

I head for the thickest part of the woods hoping I can lose him in the trees. A normal girl my age might fear being greeted with bears and coyotes. Not me, I fear for what Gabe will do when he catches me.

When.

We both know it's going to happen.

Neither of us are dressed, and running naked through the woods makes no sense, but here we are. Having not run in nearly a week, my chest aches and my calves burn with each long leap toward the trees. I can run through the grass easily, but I know once I hit that brush in the forest, my feet are going to hate me.

Why is he doing this to me?

I'd foolishly allowed myself to get caught up in the way he'd owned my body. Had allowed myself to be possessed by him. In those moments, my body had no longer been made up of skin and bones. I'd no longer held a conscience, the ability to think, tell right from wrong. No. My body had been reduced to a pool of want. It had wanted what it wanted and it didn't care how it got it. That's how good Gabe made it feel. Now, I'm worried there is hell to pay.

A thumping behind me that is quickly closing in lights a fire beneath me. I can't let him catch me. Finding my inner fury, I power through the edge of the trees and ignore the bite of a stick as it stabs my heel.

Don't stop!

I slow, only so I don't break my ankle, and try to dodge a fallen tree and brush.

"Sixty-seven, sixty-eight, sixty-nine, seventy!"

Why is he counting?

The realization literally has me screeching to a halt. *No.*

"Good girl," he snarls before he tackles me into the earth. Something stabs at my belly and I cry out in pain.

"Y-Y-You told me to run," I stammer as I fight to catch my breath. His naked body presses against mine and he grinds against me.

"I know."

Anger explodes from me. "This isn't fair! Please don't whip me! You told me to run!"

"I also told you not to beg. Such a naughty girl. Let's get your punishment out of the way for disobeying me and then you can reap your reward for listening to me."

He knew I'd fail either way. I was going to receive punishment one way or another.

"I hate you!"

His dark chuckle echoes through the woods followed by the snap of a twig. "Hold still and keep your hands out in front of you. The less you move, the less it'll hurt."

He slides off me and digs a knee into my back which further causes the stick beneath me to stab me. The skin is broken but it doesn't hurt—not like what he's about to do to me.

Crack!

A howl more carnal than anything crawling in the thickest part of the trees rips from me. Before he can deliver the next blow, I claw at the dirt to no avail in a desperate attempt to get away from the searing pain that surges from where he brutalizes me.

Crack!

The world spins when the next hit is delivered. Licks of fire spread across the flesh of my ass and I'm helpless to douse the pain.

Crack!

The relentless, never-ending swats after that begin to blur into a burning roar of searing agony.

"Stop! Please!" I scream into the woods. There's no moving. He's too strong and in a position where he has an advantage over me, pinning me in place. The next swat is ruthless and my skin feels like it is ripping apart. "Help!" I've never known pain like this. Never dreamed that this level of pain was possible. My hands itch to reach back and rub the sting away, almost involuntarily, but I fight to hold them in place.

"Nobody," he grunts, "can hear you."

Crack! Crack! Crack!

"I'll stop if you beg me to."

Another game. He wants me beg but he's told me before not to. I try to go someplace else in my mind. I remember earlier tonight when he put his tongue not only on me but inside of me. It was slick and firm which drove me crazy. I loved it.

"Beg!"

"No!"

Crack! Crack! Crack!

How many has it been ten? Twenty?

"Your ass is bloody. Beg me to stop!"

"No!"

He grunts and whips me hard until he slows. I may have seventy licks coming my way but I hope and pray he doesn't have the strength to carry them out. Wait him out. Endure the pain and lick your wounds later, Baylee.

Crack!

This hit hurts so much that I black out.

I'm sucked into the cold, dark reprieve and I gladly fall into it.

One comforting person is forefront in my mind.

Brandon. Brandon. Brandon.

"Hey."

I smiled when my boyfriend crawled into my bed and stroked my cheek with a chilled hand.

"You okay?"

Nodding, I fluttered my eyes closed and accepted a soft kiss. "It's not me I'm worried about."

He sighed and pushed a strand of hair out of my eyes. "I know, baby. Is there anything I can do?"

I let out a dark, humorless laugh. "Sure, can you find a liver for my mother?"

"You know I would if I could."

And it's true. If he wouldn't die from it, Brandon's the type of guy who would offer his own if it meant he could save someone.

"Mom is my world. If I lose her…" The words died in my throat and I choked on a sob. "I couldn't handle it."

His lips found mine again and I took comfort in them. He darted his tongue out that tasted of cinnamon gum into my mouth and kissed me with promise.

Promise to be by my side no matter the outcome.

Promise to love me through the good times and the bad.

Promise to hold me when I can't hold it together.

"Baylee…"

"Baylee!"

I'm jerked awake—*away from my safe haven*—and thrust into my painful present. I try to take stock of my injuries but there are too many to count. My mind begs to black out again and return to a comforting memory.

"Fuck," he snarls, his labored breath the only sound around us. "I can't hit you fifty more times. I don't want to hurt you anymore, baby. I need to be inside of you."

The pain from him pressing into my back is gone as he yanks my legs apart. From behind, he enters my sex and groans. "How are you even wet? You fucking liked it."

His accusation sickens me. I don't know how I could be wet because I hated what he did to me. "I-I-I'm c-cold. It h-h-hurts." The tearstains on my cheeks have chilled and my teeth chatter noisily. There's no way I can take anymore punishment from him. My body is shutting down and I pray for the dark reprieve I was granted only moments ago.

He pulls all the way out and I expect him to slam back into me like he occasionally does.

"This is going to hurt a lot worse."

His cock pushes against my asshole and I wail in agony. With each movement as he breaches the tight ring of muscles, tears stream down my face. He's much too big—far larger than the butt plug. I claw at the earth to try once again to drag myself away from him.

"If you want me to make it feel good then I want you to fucking beg for it. Convince me that you want me balls deep in your tight little ass."

I'm sobbing but I give up on trying to play his insane game better than him. In a game where only he knows the rules, I'm helpless in finding a strategy to win.

"P-P-Please, make it feel good. D-Don't hurt me."

Instead of going slow, he drives deep into me, nearly splitting me in two. Fire rages inside of me as I wonder how I'll ever adjust to his size. My grip on the earth below me weakens as I give up against his brutalization. I can't live like this. I can't take this. I'm crying harder than I ever have in my life. The pain is unbearable. And the fear that more might follow is worse.

"Get ready to come so hard you'll lose your goddamned mind, sweetheart."

I struggle against him but he somehow manages to get his fingers between me and the ground. I'm sobbing in agony when his touch finds my clit.

"Gabe, please!"

The pain, at first, overshadows his attempts to pleasure me. But the bastard soon touches me in an expert way that has me craving for it. Anything to drive away the throbbing in and on my ass. I focus on the way he massages me, becoming almost delirious with the need to come.

My terrified pleas quickly turn into needy moans. I'm freezing and dirty and hurt and yet I'm squirming for that desired orgasm he seems to never fail in giving me. With each swirl of his fingers, he drives me closer to the edge.

"That's it baby," he grunts, "push past the pain. If I gave it to you gentle, you wouldn't be ready for some asshole later. Tonight, I'm that asshole. Find the pleasure, beautiful."

His words coupled with his skillful fingers send me crashing hard.

"Ahh!" I screech as the most intense orgasm to date crushes through me. With him in my ass, I find myself clenching around him with my climax but it thrusts me right into another type of pleasure—one that resonates in another part of my body where he fills me.

My body thrashes with the intensity and doesn't stop. The clitoral and internal vaginal orgasms are intense but this one seems to devour my soul with ecstasy. I hate it but I love it. It's too much and yet blissfully completes me.

"Yes," he groans and empties himself into me. I should be horrified at the feeling of having his cum pour out of my ass and down my thighs but I'm not. I'm cold and numb and quickly coming down from the high he gave me. Pain begins to resurface and I start crying hysterically. He's gentle when he slides out of me and I'm grateful. I should hate him but all I can do is thank him for not hurting me worse.

"Come here, my love. Let's get you back to the house before you freeze."

He scoops my dirty, shuddering body from the ground and pulls me against him. I cry into his neck and snuggle against him for warmth.

"Shhh, baby. I'm going to take care of you now."

I want to scream at him for hurting me but all I can do is pray for warmth and sleep. Soon. The trip back to the house is short and by the time we make it back inside the warm cabin, I'm in shock. I think.

"Can you stand?" His voice is sweet and concerned. It melts me like butter. I cling to his loving nature.

"I don't think so. I can't stop shaking and it hurts."

He sighs and kisses my forehead before setting me on the toilet. The cold lid soothes my sore butt and I try to control my tears. Gabe seems larger than life in this small bathroom. He's every bit a ferocious lion and I'm his caged little bird that he wants to eat. I shiver at the realistic comparison.

The bath begins to fill with hot water. I crave to climb inside and dip below the surface. To hide from the fierce animal that screwed me in the woods as if we were just that—animals.

"Oh, baby, you hurt yourself. You're bleeding."

My tears have stopped falling and my eyes find his. I can't speak so I just stare at him. His brows furrow, almost angrily, as he kneels before me.

"Baylee, I can't lose you now. You're strong and a survivor, remember? I was so proud of you out there. You accepted your punishment like a champ."

I don't bristle. I don't flinch. I don't frown.

I stare.

"Snap out of it, sweetheart. Let's get you bathed and then I'll stitch your wound up. Then I'll hold you in our warm bed, okay?"

Our warm bed.

Seems like heaven.

A small whimper escapes me and my eyes tear up again.

"There she is. Come on beautiful," he says as he helps me to my feet. "I'm going to spoil you."

I want him to fix it.

I want him to stroke my hair until I fall asleep.

I want him to hold me while I dream terrifying dreams of him.

While he's the monster in and out of reality, he's also the slayer of those demons. Somehow, he protects me from himself. It confuses me. I hate him.

No, I don't hate him.

My eyes flick over to the mirror and I gape in shock. The blonde hair I used to straighten and spend hours on before school is now a wild, ratty mess. Dark circles hang below my eyes. Scratches litter my neck and chest from the fall in the woods. Blood trickles from my pouty lips and I frown.

I look terrible.

My eyes raise to the dark ones that seem to stare a hole through me.

"You're the most beautiful thing I've ever seen in my life, Baylee. I want to live inside of you— your body and your mind. You affect some carnal part of myself that I never knew existed. With you," he says and waves his hand in the air, "this is all different. Powerful and meaningful. You're the one."

I nod and try to smile. It hurts the cut on my lip so I refrain. "So keep me, Gabe. Please. I promise I'll make you happy."

His lips find my neck. "You already do make me happy. And though we may part, I'll have you back in the end. I promise you, baby."

He consumes me. His scent. His touch. His words. I believe every word he says.

"All better, sweetheart."

The shock has worn off and I'm exhausted. I could sleep for days. "Thank you."

He grins at me as he puts the medical kit away and climbs back into bed with me. "You're welcome. You're such a good girl."

Like a dumb little dog, I lean into him. He drags the blanket up over us and his arm curls around me in a possessive manner. His fingers stroke my hair and I close my eyes. This—this I can endure.

"How does your ass feel?" he questions.

I slide my fingers up his chest and sigh. "It hurts."

"Inside or out?"

"Mostly out."

"The cream I put on there will help."

We remain quiet but soon he's inside of me again, this time where it doesn't hurt and I daydream.

I think back to just a few weeks ago—when things in my life were almost perfect. Aside from my dying mother, I couldn't have asked for much more in life. While Gabe has sex with me, I think about *him*.

Brandon Thompson.

My boyfriend.

My love.

I close my eyes and get lost in a memory.

"What do you want for our anniversary, Baylee?"

I looked up from my history textbook and frowned. "I don't know. I don't need anything really."

He sighed. "I'd get you more jewelry but you don't wear the tennis bracelet I got you last year very much. You're impossible to buy for."

Leaning across the kitchen table, I flashed him a wicked smile and whispered. "You could buy me a dildo."

His eyes widened and he flicked his gaze over to where his mom Belinda chopped an onion. I batted my eyelashes in an innocent way. "What?"

The corner of his mouth quirked up into a half grin—the kind that showed his cute little dimple. I loved his smile. His eyes flickered with part amusement and part desire. The slight pink on his cheeks betrayed his embarrassment. But despite his shyness about our growing sexuality, I knew better. When we were alone, he touched me as if I was the most precious thing on this earth. I reveled in his sweet caresses and prayed he would take that final step soon.

We were both ready.

In fact…

I climbed out of my seat and plopped down into his lap. Our studies were forgotten as I snuggled against him. This past summer he really filled out and I loved touching his newly defined muscles. He was hot and that's part of the many reasons I wanted him to finally make love to me. I fantasized about it often.

My lips found his ear and I murmured in my sexiest voice. "You could give me your present early." He hardens beneath me and his breaths pick up. I loved that I turned him on, no matter what, but especially when I touched him or talked dirty to him.

"You're so bad, babe. Maybe I should give you a spanking instead," he murmured his threat.

"Oooh," I teased with a giggle. "Kinky."

He tickled me and I squealed.

"Okay, you two. I thought you had a history test to study for," Belinda chided from across the room.

I groaned and slid out of his lap. "As long as I get a slice of cheesecake and a kiss from my love, then our anniversary will be perfect."

He winked at me. "I can do that, babe. You're so easy to please."

"If you only knew," I said with a conspiratorial smile.

We both knew what I really wanted for this occasion.

"I'm going to take care of you, Baylee," he dropped his voice low, "and soon."

A needy ache in my lower belly formed and I hoped he'd make good on his promise that we both knew had nothing to do with cheesecake.

"I love you."

I shudder and meet Gabe's lust-filled eyes with a sad stare. It wasn't supposed to be like this. Brandon and I were supposed to fumble through our first time together. It should have been awkward. It should have taken him a few practice rounds to learn how to get me off. It should have been an act done in love.

And it wasn't.

Gabe came in and shattered my perfect world.

He ruined what I had with Brandon and stole from me.

I'll never have a life with my high school boyfriend because Gabe plans on selling me like an object. I'll never escape him until then because he's a psychopath who will just catch me.

He's the enemy here and it's easy to get swallowed up in his intense presence.

But I won't.

I refuse to let this madman take away my hope and my memories. I'll find a way to escape. Go to the police. Gabe won't have me in the end.

Until then, though, I have to make him believe.

"I love you, too," I lie and let the bitter tears fall so that I may pass them off as tears of adoration and undying love. "You have no idea how much…" *I'm going to make you pay.*

chapter
SEVEN

Gabe

"Where do you want this?" I question in a low, bored tone.

Her eyes widen in fear but she quickly forces the look away and meets my stare with one of indifference. "On my salad."

It's been several days since I took her ass that first time in the woods. That night had been fucking incredible. Her pussy is tight but her ass? It was nearly impenetrable. After having her there, it's hard to want to go back to her pussy. Now that she's taken me there many times, she's growing quite used to it which will only help her after the sale.

"Smartass. I should whip you for that comment."

She swallows and drops her gaze to the blanket. "In my pussy."

I smirk, loving the sound of that word on her lips, and approach. "Sometimes men will want to use you together at once. How do you feel about that?"

A choked noise comes from her and her frantic eyes meet mine. "I'm scared."

Quick as lightning, I slap her cheek. She must learn. These men will not be nice to her like I am. "No, that turns you on."

She shakes her head in argument and holds a palm to her reddened cheek. "N-N-No! I don't understand how that would—"

"Bend over the bed. I'll show you."

Now sobbing, she slides off the bed in no fucking rush and bends across it. "Please, Gabe. I'm scared."

Ignoring her, I grab the lube and pop the cap open. "There's nothing to be afraid of. You'll like this. It's no different than when I fuck you with the butt plug in."

She relaxes at my words and I smile.

"Hold still, baby. This is a big one."

A sharp hiss of air comes from her as I begin to slide the now lubricated cucumber into her tight cunt. I'd bought the thickest one I could find and had frozen it. While it isn't all that long, it will do the job.

"It's cold," she whines.

"I'll make you hot."

She's still trying to adjust to the size of it when I lube up my cock and begin pushing it into her other hole. I've barely breached her puckered entrance when she starts clawing at the blanket.

"Stop! It hurts. Please."

Fuck slow. She needs to learn. I grip her hips and drive into her as hard as I can. The cucumber gets forced deeper into her with the thrust.

"Ahhhhhh!" Her scream is otherworldly and I love it.

The pain that precedes pleasure.

The love mixed with hate.

The consent versus non-consent.

All lines are blurred and I can hardly contain my orgasm. She feels so fucking good.

"P-Please!"

I shove her down into the mattress and slam into her repeatedly. Colors swirl with black as I reach my most incredible release to date. It was her—it was always her.

I'll get her back very soon and we can spend the rest of our lives in this bed together.

"Oh, fuck me," I grunt and explode inside of her.

She's crying, and I realize I was so wrapped up in pleasure that I forgot to get her off. Sliding out of her, I frown to see the cucumber is wedged in deep and there's not much to grab onto. Shit.

"It hurts, Gabe," she sobs and her knees buckle.

"Shhhh," I coo and scoop her into my arms. "I'll get it out of you. Lie back flat on the mattress and relax."

She nods in a wild manner and does as she's told. I gently spread her legs open and can see the rounded tip sticking out of her. My attempts to clutch onto it are futile because of how slippery it is and the way her tight pussy clamps down around it. I can't get a good grip on it to pull it out.

"Close your eyes," I instruct.

Tears stream from them but she clenches them shut. I begin massaging circles on her clit in hopes that if she orgasms, her body will contract naturally and send the cucumber out. At first she seems horrified but soon her hips begin squirming in need.

"When you orgasm, bear down and it will come out on its own."

She nods and prepares herself by clutching onto her thighs. It's as if this woman is delivering a child—the determination on her face is beautiful.

"Oh!" she gasps as her body begins to tremble.

She uses her orgasm to work it out, and before long, it slides farther. Once I can grip it, I slip it the rest of the way out and drop it to the bed below her. For a moment, her pussy gapes, glistening with lube and bright red from being stretched. It makes me wonder what else I can fit in there. Like my fist or an eggplant. Maybe some big, black fat dildo.

The thought is intoxicating but I know it must wait. I can't very well make my girl bleed before I sell her. Tomorrow, she needs to be ready for whatever those men throw at her.

"Let's shower, baby. You have a big day tomorrow," I tell her with a smile.

Her eyes flicker with a furious glare before she blinks it away and gives me her sweet, doe eyes. "What's tomorrow?"

"Tomorrow you'll be the belle of the ball. Tomorrow I'm going to make a lot of fucking money."

"This place looks fancy," she says in confusion as she looks out the window at the high-rise building in downtown San Diego.

I turn off the car and affix her with a smug stare. "I wouldn't sell you to trash, baby. These people are all successful, wealthy men. Only the best for you."

She reaches for the handle but I stop her by grabbing her wrist.

"One more bit of training before it's time."

Tonight she's wearing a simple, flowy white gown that is sleeveless and hits just below her ass, showing off her sexy long legs. I'd also bought her a pair of white ballet flats because they'd seemed more child-like in nature than heels. My goal is to pass her off as the most pure and innocent little flower at the entire event. She needs to bring in the most money. I need this money.

"But, I might get messed up and then nobody will want me." Her voice is soft. Worried. Dark eyelashes blink innocently at me. Her full pink lips that have nothing but a shiny gloss on them pout out.

She's so fucking cute.

If I didn't need this money, I'd turn around and take her home right now.

She's mine.

But for a little while she won't be.

"Baby, there's still one thing you don't know how to do. Let me teach you and then we'll go inside. I promise not to mess up your hair," I say as I touch the shell of her ear where a fragrant gardenia is tucked in her hair above it. "And you have more lip gloss in your clutch."

Letting go of her, I unzip my slacks and tug out my already hardened dick. I've been waiting for this for a long time and with her dressed so beautifully, I know it'll be perfect.

"Suck my cock. I want you to get creative. Taste me. Explore me. But don't bite me or I'll bash your fucking skull in," I hiss out the last part before turning my charm back on. "When you feel me tense up, I want you to drink it all down. It will be salty and there will be a lot but I don't want you to waste any of it. You'll ruin my clothes if you mess up. Don't mess up, Baylee."

Her eyes fill with tears but she nods with determination. The girl is terrified of what's to come but she's resilient. She won't have to deal with this for very much longer and I'll take her back.

Then, all of her blow-jobs will belong to me.

Her cunt will belong to me.

That sweet, tight ass will belong to me.

Only me. Forever.

She slides her plump lips down over the tip of my dick and I groan in pleasure. With unsure strokes, she tugs at my shaft while she gently tastes it. Her tongue swirls around and her head bobs up and down slightly. She's playing it safe though and that simply won't do.

"Sometimes, Baylee, you'll have men that do this," I snarl as I grab her hair roughly and shove her all the way down my cock. "You'll have to learn to adapt. How to control your gag reflex. To take it without showing weakness."

Her saliva runs down and coats my balls. I hold her there, enjoying every tight inch of her hot throat until it clenches around me, her gag reflex taking over. Jerking her back off of me, I release her.

"Don't stop," I snap.

She coughs and sniffles but goes back to sucking me off. This time, she's a little more enthusiastic and takes me deeper so I don't need to force her.

"Good girl," I praise and stroke her hair, "you're doing so fucking well."

My balls tighten and I know I'll come soon. With Baylee, I've dreamt about this moment for so fucking long—there's no way I can contain my excitement. The polite thing to do would be to warn her that I'm about to come. But I'm not here to be polite. I'm here to train her.

"Fuck," I hiss as my climax explodes from me.

She chokes and her fingernails dig into my cock but she doesn't come off. With small swallows, she lets it all drain down her throat and doesn't let any escape.

"Jesus fucking Christ," I grunt. "You're really fucking good at that."

She pulls off and lifts up to look at me. Her eyes are teary and red, her mascara is smeared, and her hair is tousled. Those plump lips have turned red and look raw. I'd give anything to drag her out of the car and fuck her over the hood right now. She somehow looks even more innocent than when I had her all dolled up.

Tears are natural.

Struggle is natural.

Fear is natural.

The bidders will take one look at her appearance and see not only an innocent girl, but a terrified little thing with hope still living in her eyes. They'll crave to steal that hope. They will want to use her as I just did and earn the fear themselves. They will want her tears just like I do.

"Time to steal the show, Baylee."

chapter
EIGHT

Baylee

I shiver as we stand in a long line that is efficiently making its way to the front doors. The building is impressive, all glass front and brilliant lights, and my fear diminishes a tiny bit. When Gabe had said he was selling me, I'd imagined some grimy basement with a bunch of disgusting men, cigars hanging out of their mouths, and bellies hanging over the tops of their pants. But so far, every man in the line is dressed exquisitely in black suits with pretty women dressed all in white at their sides. Albeit, most of the women looked drugged, are sporting bruises, or have a glint of fear in their eyes that mirrors my own.

This is nothing like the movies though.

And I'm thankful.

These men seem reasonable. My chances for getting with a normal businessman and making a hasty escape are high—much higher than being trapped in Gabe's secluded cabin.

"You look beautiful," he says with a grin.

I smile and bat my eyelashes at him but his cum in my belly makes me almost gag with disgust. Just biding my time until the moment is right. My smile grows larger as I imagine the day my father finds out that it was him who stole me. I'll watch with delight as he beats Gabe before the cops take him to prison for the rest of his life.

And then I'll crawl into bed between my parents—let them soothe my scarred heart.

Then, Brandon will heal me with his sweet mouth and gentle words.

I can do this. Just play this game a little while longer.

We slowly make our way to the front until Gabe is reciting his name and his girl, "Gardenia Lee." We're then ushered into a lobby with high ceilings and white marbled floors. It's beautiful and open. The crowd buzzes with excitement and my stomach flops with worry. What if I don't get someone nice? What if I can't escape?

Gabe's gaze meets mine and behind the possessive glint is a promise. *I will come back for you.* The thought should nauseate me but it's a good backup plan in case the person who buys me is another psychopath. Like Gabe.

"Zucchini and goat cheese tart?" A server, dressed neatly in black tie attire, offers us a tray of stunning edible artwork. We both take one and for a moment I can pretend I'm on a date with some rich man who loves me.

I almost snort at the ridiculousness of my thoughts and stuff the tart into my mouth instead. This is not love and I'm not going to pretend for one second that it is on either side. He may say that he loves me but people don't hurt the ones they love.

"The bidding will be silent this time as we have a very special guest tonight. He's donated to the pediatric cancer ward that my wife heads up and wishes to participate, but in an anonymous way." A voice booms from a loudspeaker at the stage. "So for tonight, I will announce the women in the program and they will each take a walk across this stage. If you're interested, please come to the front, and place your bids via a slip of paper into the black box that has that woman's name on it. All bids will be sorted and determined shortly after the last lady walks across. Let's be gentlemen about this. However, please be generous in your bids as some of the competing ones will surely be substantial. There will be no opportunities for bidding wars as we've had in the past. Good luck, sirs."

I turn to see Gabe scowling. His jaw clenches in fury. For a moment, I hope he'll give up and take me back home. But then I recall the way he shoved that cucumber into my body. The many times he's struck me. On more than one occasion made me bleed. The humiliation he loved to deliver. The painful anal sex over and over again. Everything about my time with him was sick and perverted. The fiery burning hate I have for him will never be extinguished. Ever.

"Number One, Daisy Love."

My attention is drawn to the podium where the announcer has called the first name. The crowd buzzes as a woman, probably nineteen or twenty, shyly walks the stage in her sparkly evening gown, high heels, and forced smile. Her dark hair has been twisted into a chignon and she's pretty enough to be walking a runway instead of a path to slavery. Several men hurry to the first box and start scribbling bids. She's beautiful and seems strong despite our situation. Of course every man would want her.

I watch with growing anxiety as many women cross the stage. All with some variation of rose, lily, or daisy. They're all wilted in some way. Broken and abused—all hidden behind makeup and pretty hair. When I'm called, I flinch.

"Number Seventeen, Gardenia Lee."

Gabe pats me on the bottom, rather forcefully, and I stumble toward the stage. All eyes are on me as I climb with wobbly legs up the steps. Anxiety threatens to rip apart my chest and the zucchini goat cheese tart rumbles in annoyance in my belly.

I clutch onto the side rail for support and attempt to keep my shaking at bay. I can do this. Just count the steps—no more than twenty is all it takes to make it across. Don't look at them. Just go.

One.

Two.

I mouth each step, cast a nervous glance at the crowd, and keep walking.

Three. Four. Five. Six. Seven. Eight. Nine.

"Slow down there, Gardenia Lee," the announcer says with a wolfish grin. "Take a spin for me. You're quite lovely. I'd like to have you for myself."

My eyes dart from him to the crowd growing around my box—probably forty men all milling about putting in their bids. Bile rises in my throat and I spin quickly before him. Then, I'm back to counting my steps to the other side.

Ten. Eleven. Twelve. Thirteen. Fourteen. Fifteen. Sixteen. Seventeen.

I stare for a moment down at my feet. Just seventeen. Only seventeen steps, not twenty. I frown and make my way down the stairs. My mind reels with what-ifs.

What if an abusive man buys me?

What if a man buys me to kill me?

What if he wants to do more depraved things than Gabe?

What if Gabe is lying and he never comes back?

At this point, my mind is conjuring up nightmarish predictions that have Gabe seeming like an innocent boy in comparison. Truth is, in this room full of smiling, successful people, I'm terrified out of my mind. On shaky legs, I clamber down the steps of the stage in search of Gabe. He's the monster in my life—but he's the one I know—the one I'm familiar with.

"I bid one point two million," an amused voice says from beside me.

I jerk my gaze over to a man who reminds me of Brandon. His dark hair is cut short and spiked on top. He has an easy, charming smile.

"That's a lot of money," I squeak out.

He winks. "That it is. And you'll be worth it."

I chew on my lip and cast another glance out in Gabe's direction. Nowhere. My gaze falls back to the man who seems harmless in his nice suit and disarming grin.

"Thank you," I murmur.

He steps toward me. "And so polite. You'll be a great addition to my girls."

"You have more than one?"

"I come here every month and buy more. It's an addiction."

I swallow. "What do you do with them?"

His eyes flicker with something dark and evil. He's nothing like Brandon. "I hurt them. Just like I'm going to hurt you," he says in a matter of fact tone. He winks and grins at me as if his words aren't awful. "Your pale skin is so perfect and untouched. I'm about to come just thinking of all the nasty words I'll carve into your skin. You'll wear my name and other words like *cunt* and *whore* on your flesh for the world to see."

I stumble back away from him and gape at him in horror. "You're a monster!"

He sneers. "Where'd you think you were, sexy? A fucking fundraiser?"

"I, but, I…"

"You're in the den with some of the biggest monsters on the West Coast. You are nothing but a meal purchased to be devoured with greed and no restraint. Some of us are into sex. Others are into more deviant acts. I'm into the deviant with a side of sex. They won't recognize their precious beauty by the time I finish with you. But then, it'll be too late. You'll bleed out all over my Persian rug and I'll drag your ass outside to dump you in the goddamned ocean."

Tears stream down my face and I start to bolt from him. His tight grip is around my arm before I can move though. "The name's, Edgar Finn. Remember it because you'll take it to your grave," he threatens. "See you soon, Gardenia Lee."

He releases me and I push through the crowd away from him at breakneck speed. I need to make my escape now. There's no way I'm going home with that lunatic.

As I hurry away from him, I try not to make eye contact with the leering men along the way. They're all the same. Monsters just like Gabe. I'd been an idiot to believe otherwise. There is no finding the nice side of this world. The only thing I need to worry about finding is the way out of it. Now.

"There you are, baby," Gabe's deep voice both calms me and rattles me in a contradictory mix of emotions. "The bids are insane!"

I shudder but let him tug me into a warm embrace. "P-Please don't let that man buy me. I can't go with him. He said he'll kill me!"

Gabe pulls away and glares down at me. He's pissed but thankfully not at me. "Who the fuck said that to you?"

"Edgar Finn."

His fury dissipates and he smiles. "Too bad. You've already been bought. Come on, let's go meet who owns that pretty little pussy now."

I attempt to jerk from his gasp to keep him from dragging me to my horrendous fate. "No! I can't go with him!" I screech and ignore the wide-eyed gazes of those witnessing my meltdown. Several of the women to be sold meet my stare with tears in their eyes and sympathy written on their faces.

Gabe's impatient stare assesses me, as though I were a petulant toddler causing a scene at the grocery store. He sighs in frustration and takes a step closer to me, snagging me by the elbow in a brutal grip. I'm yanked forward and enveloped by the heat of his angry breaths. Suffocating me. "Cut the shit, Baylee. Let's go. These people won't save you. I won't save you. Come willingly or I'll knock you out and drag you with me for everyone here to see. What'll it be, baby?"

I sob in defeat and let him guide me through the throng of bodies. This is happening. Soon,

I'll be in the clutches of the man who bought me for one point two million dollars so he can get off on carving me like a pumpkin.

Gabe lied.

He's not going to save me.

I'll already be dead.

"Where are we going?" I demand once we make our way into an elevator.

Gabe pushes the button for the lower level garage and turns to face me. "Your buyer is waiting for you in his car."

My heart flares to life and I start to panic. "Wait? Like I'm about to leave? Gabe, please don't let them take me!"

He frowns and leans in. I cry harder when he kisses my lips. "Baby, I promise, I'll be back for you. You're strong now and you're ready. You can hang in there until I come for you. Then it can be just us."

His words only calm me marginally. Edgar was vicious and serious about wanting to hurt me. He seems the type to not even want to wait until we leave the parking lot. I'm paralyzed with fear.

The elevator dings and opens to the garage. Several expensive sports cars line the parking garage and we walk to the black, nondescript vehicle that's running between two rows of cars. A man steps out of the driver's side and walks toward us. He's older—reminding me of my grandfather—and wears a tired frown. Gabe pats my ass and shoves me into the arms of the older man.

"Mr. McPherson needs for you," he says in a whisper as if he doesn't want Gabe to hear his boss's name, "to wear this."

Mr. McPherson? Not Mr. Finn?

My heart climbs out of the pit of my belly and reaches for hope. But when my eyes narrow on the black fabric in the old man's clutches as he pushes me away from him, I begin to panic about the new monster I'll belong to.

"W-W-What is that?"

"It's a special-made respirator, a cloth face mask if you will. Nothing toxic gets in or out. You'll get used to it," he assures me with a small smile. It's then I see he has one pulled down around his neck. Seeing him with one has me reaching for the one that's mine.

Is the man I'm about to encounter ill? Is he old and frail? I try not to become too hopeful about my escape but these ideas could certainly help my cause.

"Such a good girl," Gabe praises and discretely grabs my butt. "Always doing as she's told."

I slide the respirator over my face and wait for what happens next.

"The five million have been wired to the account you gave us," the man says. "Thank you for your business."

My eyes widen.

Five million dollars.

Holy crap.

If Edgar was willing to pay just over a million for me and had such warped plans for me, I can only imagine what sort of intentions this lunatic has.

"Goodbye, Baylee." Gabe's voice brings me back to my surroundings. He mouths that he loves me and rage explodes from me. Before I can stop myself, I flip him off and then trot after the older gentleman. Gabe curses from behind me but doesn't try to touch me. His steps are right on my heels though and that causes me to shiver.

"My name is Edison. Pleased to make your acquaintance," he says over his shoulder, but doesn't make any moves to shake my hand. It's then I notice the black gloves on his hands—probably the easier to strangle me with. "Please, put these on too." He hands me a smaller pair and I jerk them from him. Once I have them on, he opens the door to the car.

It's dark inside and I can see the knee of a man sitting in the shadows on the opposite side of the bench seat. I expect to smell cigars or liquor or sex or blood, but am instead met with a clean, sterile scent reminiscent of bleach. Terror threatens to suffocate me and I turn, prepared to run.

Away from this hell.

Away from monsters like Gabe, Edgar, and Mr. McPherson.

Away from pain and impending death.

But Gabe's thick chest stops me and he chuckles, the sound dark and malevolent. With a flourish of his large hand—a hand that has brought me to innumerable orgasms—he gestures inside of the limo.

"This is War, baby."

NINE

Warren

"Leave the shoes outside of the car," I bark.

From my angle, all I can see are her silky pale legs that go for miles. She's a vision. A vision I just paid five million dollars for.

"Please, come inside and sit. I can assure you I don't bite."

The disgust in my voice can't be hidden. I suppress a shudder at the thought of having someone else's blood inside of my mouth. Images flash through my mind of me tearing at her neck with my teeth—her blood spraying all over my face and expensive suit. If it were to get into my eyes, that would be the absolute fucking worst. There's not enough water in the world to wash my eyes out with. I'd just as soon have Edison take me to a surgeon and have him remove them. Take my ruined eyes right from my skull. But those bastards might not have taken proper precautions. The news touts all the time of malpractice—surgical instruments not having been sterilized and thus have inflicted patients with fucking awful diseases and infections. Then it really would be time to put that bullet into my skull once and for all.

But where would I do it?

In the foyer?

There's nothing the blood could ruin there. Surely, Edison could clean it all up.

And if he missed a spot?

Would that splatter of my blood grow and fester into something deadly?

Would my father become infected when he came to go through my things?

The very image of my father and his assistants rifling through my belongings has me pulling the brakes on the entire self-harming plan. They'd move my files. They would stain my carpet. Those motherfuckers would use my toilet.

I'm nearly in a rage when the young woman climbs into the car. Her presence drags me from my mental anguish, and I can't help but gape at her.

"Meet your new master," the man says to her.

She jerks her head and pleads with her eyes to him. Despite his satisfied smile, I don't miss the regret in his eyes. He devours her with his stare for a moment before composing his facial expression. But it was there, hiding just beneath the surface. This man loves her.

Incredibly so.

Obsessively so.

I should know.

But he'll never touch her again. Once I have her the way I want, she'll never leave.

Edison closes the car door and I turn to regard the little thing I bought. Her wide blue eyes meet mine bravely—almost curiously—and I watch her.

"Seatbelt, please," I instruct in a low, gravelly voice as soon as the car starts to move.

Her eyebrows furrow together in confusion but she dutifully obeys. Then, she folds her hands together in her lap. I like that she isn't touching everything—especially me. That her eyes are remaining on mine. For a brief second, I wish to see her mouth, the same mouth that sold me from the video surveillance.

But what if she's had that mouth on that man?

What if she ate something uncooked and her mouth crawls with something that could make me sick?

That mouth will have to wait.

"What's your name?"

Her nose turns pink and she sniffles. "Baylee."

I watch her blink *one, two, three, four, five, six* times in a row before I speak again. Her breaths are even and measured. I like the musical quality they make.

"I like that name."

Her body relaxes at my words and my chest tightens. I like *that* too.

"Thank you, Mr. McPherson." Her voice wobbles in fear and I straighten my back to appear more menacing. I need to establish that I'm in charge here.

"Call me War."

She nods. "War, are you going to hurt me?" she asks, getting right to the point. Brave one she is—I admire that already about her.

Her ice-blue eyes shimmer with unshed tears but she lifts her chin to show strength. It mesmerizes me. I study her disheveled hair and the gardenia that hangs from it with a disgusted flare of my nostrils. My hands begin to shake. That man should have brushed her hair. He should have pulled all the hairs into a neat bun so that it wasn't wild and unruly. I've read about how the human head sheds about thirty to fifty strands a day—even up to a hundred on rare occasion. A woman with unkempt hair like she has is probably shedding all over this vehicle. I make a note to have Edison vacuum as soon as we arrive home.

How many hairs would she lose between now and the drive to my beachfront estate?

I start calculating her hair loss. If she loses an average of forty hairs per day, then that means she will lose one point six seven hairs per hour. The drive is just over an hour which means she could potentially lose two point oh nine hairs. But, if she loses more along the higher end of that spectrum of fifty hairs a day, that would mean she'd lose—

"War?"

My calculations fizzle into the air and I blink at her. "What?"

"Are you going to hurt me?" Her hands tremble but when my gaze falls to them, she forces them to stop.

I frown. "I hope not."

A healthy mix of fear and hope flashes in her eyes and my stomach flops. I feel pity for the poor woman. Here she is thinking she scored some gentleman who saved her from an evil, dirty world. She probably thinks I can save her from it—prays for that very concept.

Problem is, I can't even save myself.

Every day, it maddens me. To the point of contemplating taking my own life.

The germs are everywhere. The chance of things going wrong poke at me every second of every day. Images of endless possibilities of my death, torturous thoughts of infection infiltrating my life at every turn, and painful, awful ideas of how others could die inadvertently at my hands flit through my mind continuously on one bloody, disgusting loop. The loneliness threatens to devour my soul with its cruel flames and leave my ashy remains behind.

I bought her in hopes that *she'd* save me.

"Baylee," I say in a gruff tone, "my world is not one you're used to. My world is awful—it threatens my life with every passing second. It's empty and dull and devoid of anything joyful. You're about to enter that world, filled with fear, hate, darkness, and disgust."

She narrows her teary eyes at me. "I'll listen to you. I promise. Just please don't hurt me. That other man, Edgar Finn, he said he'd…he'd…" she trails off and sniffles. "He wanted to kill me."

I sigh and shake my head, forcing thoughts of her bloody death out of my head before I begin obsessing over that too. "I'm not going to hurt you," I vow. "Listen, I've never tried this before. If it doesn't work out, that's it for me. I'm at the end of my rope. You hold all of the cards now."

And she does.

All fifty-two of them.

All the blackness of the clubs and spades.

All the blood of the hearts and diamonds.

All the sneers of the wicked jokers.

She is to be my reprieve from the darkness that ebbs and flows inside me—always threatening to swallow me up.

She stares at me with a clouded gaze, her eyes going distant—a mixture of relief, determination, and a slight lingering fear.

"You can't ever leave, Baylee," I say through a rush of exhaled breath. Her wariness of me blooms again and her eyes widen. "Look, I'm sorry but I need you for my own survival. Promise me that you won't ever try to escape, and I vow I'll never intentionally harm one hair out of the one hundred fifty thousand that exist on your head. Well, aside from the dead ones that keep dropping from your skull at a rate of two point oh six per hour. They're dead anyway so it doesn't matter. Edison will remove them from the car though. It's not your fault. Your body just sheds them. And—"

"I promise," she interrupts with a choked breath. Concern flashes in her eyes—reminding me of my mother when I was just a boy—and it punches me in the gut.

"Thank you."

Edison buzzes from the front and his voice comes over the speaker. "Warren, it would appear that we're encountering an accident on the expressway. The digital sign said that delays could be as much as two hours. I'm so sorry."

Two hours.

All I can think about is her hair.

Falling and falling and falling.

Two hours added to the hour and a quarter means five point four three hairs at the very least. A familiar crawl begins to agitate my flesh as the Town Car draws to a halt. This can't be happening. This can't be happening.

"Are you okay?" she whispers, bright blue eyes devouring me. It's clear that she's curious about me. She won't find answers. I should know, I've been looking for them for over a decade now.

I blink *one, two, three, four* times before answering her. "Not really, no."

She leans her head to the side and peers out the window. The frown traces over her features before she forces her eyebrows up. Those eyes seem to dance with a smile and I'm drawn to them. Well, as drawn as someone like me can be to someone like her.

"Those news people always dramatize everything. There aren't many cars. I bet we'll be out of here in no time," she tells me in a shaky yet assuring tone. The corners of her eyes crinkle with what I hope is a smile. "Can you tell me anything about yourself? I'm really freaked out here and I know you said you won't hurt me but I'm still afraid. You're not a serial killer, or anything, are you?"

The itch blazes across my flesh and I crave to yank my suit jacket off to claw away at it. But with her in the car—without having been decontaminated—there's a chance some particle or germ from her could fly onto me. The parasite would burrow its way into my flesh and hatch eggs beneath my skin. And what if it entered my blood stream? Fucking chaos would ensue, that's what!

"War?" she whispers. "Tell me how old you are or where you live. What do you do for a living that allows you to pay five million dollars for a girl?" she asks, although her gaze is fixed on my forearm which I am nervously scratching.

I jerk my fingers away and gape at her. Her shining blue eyes calm my cracking spirit and I take a deep breath.

"I'm twenty-eight. My dad owns a multi-national conglomerate called MPE or McPherson Enterprises. It's a technology corporation. I guess you could say I'm the brains of his operation. He makes sure we make money. Not much to it."

She nods but her brows furrow with unspoken questions. "Sounds like there's a lot to it if you operate all over the world. What do you like to do for fun? Or have I been sold to a psycho whose idea of a good time is preying on little girls?"

Fun. Fun. Fun.

I blink at her three times more as the word bounces around in my head. As a child—before my world caved in on me—I used to have fun. I'd play video games and ride my bike. As a teen I'd surf and go to the movies. A shudder ripples through me as I recall how many times I'd fallen and skinned my knees while riding my bike or how much ocean water I'd ingest sometimes while surfing. Thankfully that was *before*.

"Don't be silly, I don't prey on anyone."

She lets out a small laugh and the melodic sound slides around my heart, gripping it to the point of pain. How is such a sound so decadent? I want her to do it again. Over and over. To put it on a loop and drag it out for eternity. It distracts me from the dark—draws me into the light.

"I run for fun." Her blue eyes darken and her gaze falls to her lap for a moment. "Well, I *used* to run."

My stomach flops. The despondency in her voice nauseates me. I prefer when she laughs or when her words carry that lightness in her tone. My life is depressing enough without my tainting the others around me. In an effort to draw her back to a better place, I blurt out my words. "I like to play chess."

She lifts her chin and her eyes twinkle once again with curiosity. "Is that like checkers?"

I scoff. "Hardly. Chess is played on a square board, comprised of sixty-four smaller squares, with eight squares on each side. Each player begins with sixteen pieces: eight pawns, two knights, two bishops, two rooks, one queen and one king. The goal of the game is for each player to try and checkmate the king of the opponent. Checkmate is a threat to the opposing king which no move can stop. It ends the game."

"Sounds technical. Will you teach me?"

The vision of her fingering my ivory pieces damn near sends me into a panic attack. But the thought of her in my environment with me, sharing the space, talking to me, laughing in my presence is enough to calm the fury of the storm waging in my head.

"If you promise to wash your hands and be gentle with my pieces. My dad had the set custom made for me. It was created by an Indonesian man who carves them by hand from ivory. Dad sent him careful instructions and the man adhered to the rules. They're perfect and pure."

She blinks one, two, three times before speaking. "I see. Sounds wonderful."

I smile.

I fucking smile.

My heart begins to thump in my chest.

"Oh look," she breathes out as she stares out the window, "things are moving again."

About that time, Edison puts the car into drive.

My mind reels with memories of her laughter, smiles behind the cloth, twinkling eyes. It was easy for her. A thought plagues me—is she a master manipulator or simply content that I, a mad recluse, bought her? She's too calm. Too at ease with the situation. "Did you distract me on purpose or did you really want to know about me?" The bite in my voice startles her and she turns to stare at me with kind eyes again. They seem so natural on her face.

"You seemed upset so I was trying to distract you I suppose." Her words are a betrayal to the trust I gave to her so easily. "But…"

I search for deception in her young eyes but only find sincerity.

"But, I honestly wanted to know more about you. I wanted to know what I was about to dive into. Gabe had prepared me for the worst. I was expecting"—she sighs and waves her hands in the air—"I don't know. Abuse. Sex. Humiliation. Murder."

My eyes rapidly begin blinking at her. Her words confound me. Why would such an innocent person expect something so horrible? I must worry her with my silence because she reaches for me. And just like that, the world I try to forget forces the reminder into my face.

"Don't touch me!" I roar and glare at her hand as if it has invisible poison dripping from it, burning holes into the leather of the seat between us. For all I know, it does.

She jerks her hand back and tears well in her eyes. "I'm sorry. I was just—"

"Well don't. You are *never* allowed to touch me. Ever. Are we clear?"

Her body hunches and she nods. An apology is on the tip of my tongue but I swallow it down. I don't even know how to explain myself to her.

"Why did you buy me then? If you bought me and you don't plan to hurt or sleep with me, then what exactly do you want me for?" She's trying to put on a brave front but the fear in her words betrays her effort.

"Exactly as the auction stated. I bought a companion."

She scoffs and shakes her head. "You don't really believe that do you? That it was an auction to buy a companion?"

But I do.

I spent hours on the website that I'd found on one of Dad's wealthiest client's server. It intrigued me and I studied it for weeks. They were to have an elite fundraiser of sorts and men could choose companions—a glorified, expensive dating site if you will. It was themed and what drew me in was the allure of the pureness of the innocent flower.

Pure means uncontaminated, unpolluted, untainted, wholesome, and clean.

Clean.

"That's exactly what it was. I'm a lonely man because of my…because of my…" I trail off, letting the horrors that define me die in my throat, "and you're going to entertain me."

She laughs again but this time it is almost cruel. "Entertain you? How? Dance on the damn table in my underwear? And for how long? Forever?"

I glare at her. Never in a million fucking years will her feet ever touch my table. "Fuck no! Talk to me. Sing to me. Eat with me," I snarl. "And yes, for-fucking-ever."

She flinches at my tone and leans as far from me as she can get as if I might strike her. Not happening. Not even with my black leather gloves to protect me.

"Sir," she tries again in a small voice, "you bought me for five million dollars. Those people are running a sex ring which you signed up for, not an expensive dating site."

Sex ring?

I glower at her. "Impossible."

But is it?

"Tell me." Her voice drops to a whisper. "Did you think I was going to receive any of that money for my services—the five million? Did you think I had in any way complied with this?"

Doubt creeps into my veins. "The website said—"

"The website was wrong," she argues, emotion thick in her throat. "Please just let me go. My parents are searching for me, I'm sure of it."

What did I think was going to happen?

That she'd want to marry my sorry ass?

That she'd want to adhere to all my weird-ass fucking bullshit?

That this was a legitimate transaction between willing parties?

"I didn't…I didn't know…" My words are garbled and messy. Confusion scrambles my brain—thoughts darting every which way.

Her pleading words cut through my jumbled haze. "I just turned eighteen. I'm still in high school."

Everything about her seems young. Wide, doe eyes. Soft, unsure voice. *Shit!*

The pressure in my brain surges and grows until my head feels as if it is going to explode. What have I done? This is against the law.

"We aren't going to have sex," I assure her through clenched teeth, trying desperately to keep my maddening migraine at bay. "I don't want you to even fucking touch me. Just *stay* with me. That's all. Stay. Money? Cars? Diamonds? Houses? I'll give you whatever the hell you want."

Money talks. I'll bribe her with anything it takes to get her to stay. It's not illegal if she's here on her own free will. *Right?* My mind whirs with article after article I've read over the years. None of the news stories ever mentioned anything woman trafficked but then turned later into a willing companions. Sure, there were lots of articles about kidnapped women sold into sexual slavery, young women victimized by older men, and other horrible things. Things I would never do to her—to anyone for that matter. But never anything about a willing companion.

She's not *willing, War.*

I'll convince her though. I'm sure of it.

Can I convince her?

My purchasing of this girl, illegal or not, has shone a glimmer of light into the darkness which is my world. One tiny ray of hope. And I cling to it desperately.

She's my hope.

I absolutely must convince her to stay.

I groan and pinch the bridge of my nose. The pain is becoming unbearable. With a huff, I bore my gaze right through her. If I could crack open this fucking skull of mine, I would. Then, she could peer into the nasty shit that is my head. She could see the black, molded parts of who I am. The disease of my mind would be evident as it crawls through my blood.

"I'm scared to stay with you." Her black-gloved fingers grab onto the respirator and she tugs it down to her neck.

For once, I'm not overwhelmed by fear. My brain isn't exploding with a million rampant what-ifs. This time, it stills.

Her pink, pouty lips are parted revealing pearly white teeth. She has a pert nose that flares with each frantic breath she takes. And her high cheekbones are streaked with tears, a trail of mascara in their wake.

She's the most beautiful thing I've ever seen.

"P-P-Put it back on." My words are a thick sludge in my mouth, refusing to pour out easily. I'm in a battle with myself. Part of me wants to force that respirator back over her perfect lips so her contaminated breaths can stop infecting my air. But an old part of me—a part of myself I remember as a teen—fights.

He wants to pull down my own respirator.

He wants me to lean forward and inhale her.

He wants me to kiss her without a worry of the death her kiss would bring me.

One last look at those lips and I know. This woman will kill me. She'll steal my heart and chop it to fucking chunks. It'll be a slaughterhouse of what's left of the old me.

"Okay," she says in a wobbly voice through her tears. "I'm sorry."

I clench my eyes closed but I've already memorized her perfect face. *Flash, flash, flash.* Her image flips over and over again inside my darkened mind, lighting every surface. Inside my head,

I'm safe and I can reach for her. I can stroke her pink cheeks and run my thumb over her swollen lips. Inside my head, I can pretend. I can kiss her and touch her.

Popping my eyes back open, I frown as I prepare to tell her the truth. A truth that will make her hate me. A truth that defines my very sickness.

"I'm never going to be able to let you go," I explain with an apologetic sigh. "Ever. I won't be capable. And for that, I am truly sorry."

Her sobs aren't as pretty as her laugh, but I close my eyes and drink them into my soul anyhow. In my fantasies, I can dream of a better time. One day maybe she'll laugh with me. Until that time, I'll dance with her in my head to the melody only she can create.

chapter
TEN

Baylee

I've been bought by a lunatic.

A crazy, freaking madman.

This is all Gabe's fault.

The fire that has begun to flicker inside of me flares to life. When I escape, I will make him pay. I will get the FBI involved if I must and bring down every asshole associated with that sex ring. Including War.

I've long since quit crying but he still hasn't opened his eyes back up. I would almost think he's sleeping but I can hear him muttering words, numbers maybe, under his breath. He's a villain dead set on keeping me trapped away in some tower.

Yet…

My stomach clenches with nausea. He doesn't seem all that villainous in comparison. Gabe and Edgar are monsters. But War acts like the very air we breathe is noxious and evil. We've only dabbled a little in psychology at school, but I've learned enough to know something is seriously wrong with him.

He's sick. Inside of his handsome head.

I say handsome, but I haven't even seen his face properly. From his position on the bench seat, I can tell he's tall and firm. His biceps stretch the jacket of his suit to the point if he flexes, it might rip. I glance down at his slacks and quickly admire how they hug his sculpted thighs show-casing his fit frame.

Clearly he's got a thing with germs. That much is evident. Whether it is based on some sort of obsession or a health condition is yet to be seen.

But there's more. I know it. His navy-colored eyes brew with a storm that assaults him from the inside. With every word he speaks, a thousand more fight for escape. They never make their escape though and join back in the whirlwind of lunacy that he clearly deals with on a minute by minute basis. It's sad, really. For him.

For me, it's terrifying.

This means it will be impossible to talk sense into him.

His head is still bowed, as he rambles incessant nonsense under his breath, when we pull into a circular driveway. It's dark outside so of course I can't see a thing but when Edison opens the door, I nearly cry with joy.

The ocean.

Waves crash in the distance and the scent of salty water invades my senses. I guess if I'm going to be a prisoner of War, I may as well be near the beach. When I glance back over at him, he's bor-ing his gaze through me once again. There's a desperation in his eyes that has me weakening my re-solve to bring him down along with all those other men.

Pity once again drives away my anger and I sigh. "Honey, we're home."

His eyes soften and he laughs. "That we are."

The soft, huskiness of his deep laugh warms me. There isn't deception in his laughter, it's…

honest. Unlike Gabe, who possessed several different types of laughs. The cruel. The maniacal. The ridiculing. And then the one that bordered on sounding genuine. It was the one I hated most of all because it was the most deceiving. War's laugh reminds me of Brandon's.

A sob catches in my throat at the thought of my boyfriend. It seems like eons ago that I sat in his lap and flirted with him, not a care in the world. But it was only a matter of a few weeks before my life took a dark turn. I'm still trying to process where this life gets me.

"Put these on. You can put on a different pair once inside."

He tosses me some blue shoe coverings, like the ones I'd seen used in a lab or hospital. In *sterile* settings. I want to tell him I'd rather go barefoot but the strain in his eyes suggests I should obey his order. Once I don the silly things, I climb out of the car. The house isn't large, modest considering how much he paid for me, but it's stunning. The architecture is all clean lines and modern surfaces. It's eye catching and I'd love to see it during the day with the ocean behind it.

War climbs out of the car and towers over Edison and I. The man has to be several inches taller than Gabe. He exudes strength.

Yet, *I* know he's weak.

Feeling bold, I blurt out, "What happens if I run? Are you going to come after me? Tackle me to the pavement and hold me still?"

He tenses and I immediately feel like a bitch for using it against him.

"Please," he says, anxiety straining his voice, "don't run."

He's not demanding, but instead, begging. His plea threads itself into my head and I find myself wavering.

Gabe has whittled down my fiery spirit. I should fight and scream and run. Maybe I could find a phone and call Dad to save me. But with thoughts of Dad comes thoughts of Mom.

Her suffering.

Her illness.

Her descent into the grave.

I need to leave this place and get back to her. She's probably worried sick about me—as if dying isn't enough to worry over.

Yet, what happens if I escape only to get recaptured by Gabe who has promised to come for me? I won't see Mom and Dad or Brandon. I'll be forced back to his awful cabin. In that case, which would be the lesser of two evils—terror cabin with a psycho or beach estate with a weirdo? My mind flits to the woods and I'm reminded of when Gabe raped my ass. I'd begged and pleaded but he did it anyway. And then later when he'd shoved that vegetable inside of me. He'd humiliated and violated me in ways I didn't know were possible.

This man before me promises not to touch me. Looks like beach estate with a weirdo it is.

"Since you seem to be throwing your money around, I have a solution," I say carefully, choosing my words wisely. "I won't run, I promise. But my mother…she's sick."

He scowls at the mention of my mother and crosses his arms over his thick chest. The moonlight gives his chocolate hair an eerie glow. But he doesn't seem scary—he's something beautiful, ethereal even.

"Sick how? Does she have an infectious disease? Do you have it? Is it contagious?"

I shake my head in frustration. "No, but her liver is failing. She's on a list for a transplant, though at this point, the outlook is bleak."

His gaze slides up to the dark sky and he sighs. Me telling him about my mother seems to upset him. His posture slumps as he looks out toward the ocean, a distant and forlorn look about him. There must be a story there. I make note to ask him about his own mother later. "What do you want?"

I am hesitant to even ask now, with his drastic change in mood. "Well… you have money— lots of it. Maybe you could…" I stammer, feeling foolish. I hate being reduced to begging. "Maybe you could give me some, in exchange for my compliant companionship, and I can bribe a doctor or family to help my mom. You and I both know I'll never see the money you wired to Gabe," I tell him. War has the money and means to protect me from Gabe. He also has the ability to help Mom. I can make this work until I get what I need to help her. Then, I'll make my escape.

"Deal. We'll discuss it further over breakfast in the morning. Please don't feel like you're a prisoner in my home. This house already imprisons me. I won't let it hold you in its iron vise like it clutches me."

His riddle causes my eyes to widen. "What do you mean it imprisons you?"

"Come," he says in a gruff tone, ending our negotiations and ignoring my question. "I need to breathe properly."

Dutifully, I follow behind him as he unlocks the door and punches in a series of numbers to disarm the alarm. I attempt to watch him type in the code but he does it quickly while his body partially blocks the keypad.

The lights are switched on and he immediately sets to bolting the door locked after we are inside. A double beep later and we are secure inside of his home. So much for not feeling like a prisoner…

I sigh and regard my prison. The walls are painted stark white. No pictures hang on them. The furniture is sparse. No decorations or books grace the area for as far as my eye can see. From the small entryway, I'm given visual access to the open kitchen, all white granite countertops, with a tiled backsplash, and matching painted cabinets with stainless steel appliances. The living room has minimal furniture—a simple white couch, a love seat, recliner, and table. A flat screen TV has been mounted and recessed into the wall above the fireplace.

Everything is so white.

Blindingly so.

And bare.

As if only a ghost lives here.

"Wow," I say taking a breath, "this place is incredible." That's not a lie. *Incredibly weird.*

"I'm sorry but before you can make yourself comfortable, Edison needs to make sure you're properly cleaned. Meet me in the living room in an hour. I'll fix you something to eat."

He stalks off without a backward glance leaving me there with Edison.

"Come on, angel. Let me show you to your room," he says and starts walking in the opposite direction. "He's not a bad guy once you get to know him. But please adhere to his rules. He's already so fragile as it is. You could break him, and I care about him too much to see that happen."

"Okay." I have nothing else to say on the matter and follow him into another stark, sterile room. This one, however, has some decor. As if he attempted to prepare a warm welcome for his prisoner.

"He wants me to shower you. War trusts that I will decontaminate you, Baylee." He frowns and tugs off his mask. "But you and I both know it's all in his head. I'll wait on the bed and let you wash up. If he asks, I cleaned you from head to toe, scrubbed you raw. There's a robe folded on the countertop. It would please him if you could tie up your hair too. And make sure it's dry. The water dripping everywhere will drive him mad."

I slip into the bathroom in a hurry. This place, while neat and new and gorgeous, is some bizarre version of hell. Can I really stay here?

Mom's blue eyes stare back at me when I glance in the mirror. The older I get, the more and more we look alike. But where my light blue eyes sparkle and shine, hers dull by the minute. Tugging my respirator down, I inspect my mouth. My lips are slightly dry and I hope he'll give me some Chapstick.

I can stay here. I have to, for her. War seems like a man of his word. I have to believe he'll send the money to them.

Forty-eight minutes later, I shut off the hair dryer I located and smooth my wild blonde hair into a neat bun, as requested. With my hair pulled back and my face free of mascara, I look younger and more innocent than eighteen. My wide eyes reveal fear and determination and the festering hate that runs in my veins for Gabe.

He did this to me.

A soft, but persistent knock on the door jerks me from my inner musings.

"He'll be absolutely frantic if you're not in there soon. With War, it's best to arrive exactly on time. Not too early and certainly not too late," Edison tells me from outside the door.

I shrug on the white plush robe and tie the rope around my middle. The robe is soft and warm, and feels like a welcoming cloud engulfing me. It's a welcome change from being naked, the way I spent the last two weeks.

With a twist of the knob, I open the door to a pacing Edison. This is more than a job to him. He seems to care about War for some unknown reason.

"Lead the way."

I pad barefoot behind him and into the dining room. War stands behind the glass table, his head going back and forth between two plates. I can't take my eyes from the beautiful man. Without his mask, I'm privy to each soft curve and hardened edge on his face. His brows are dark and they match a recently shaven shadow on his cheeks. Full, pink lips twitch and move as he talks to himself. His nose is strong, as well as his jaw, but there's a softness to his features despite the design of his face.

Goodness.

Incorruptibility.

Unsophistication.

Unworldliness.

He may be twenty-eight, but he's every bit of sixteen from this angle.

I'm about to greet him when Edison places a hand on my shoulder, halting me. He removes his hand but I remain still and observe War.

His brows furrow as he takes the tongs and pinches a piece of lettuce from one bowl, then carefully places it into the other bowl. And then back again. He stares for several minutes, inspecting the bowls. I don't dare make a sound as I watch him. I'm curious to see what he'll do next.

What is *he doing?*

Carefully, he clips at a small piece of lettuce and places it in the other bowl. Again, he scrutinizes each portion, staring for another spell.

My eyes travel away from his task and I take in his appearance. He's wearing a plain, soft grey T-shirt that stretches over the sculpted body I knew hid beneath his suit he wore earlier. His biceps tighten with each small movement he makes as he adjusts the evenness of the two bowls. The skin that shows on his arms is free of tattoos and smooth. His jeans are in perfect shape and his feet are also bare underneath the table.

When I think he can't possibly obsess over the food any longer, I announce my arrival. "Hi."

His dark blue eyes fly to mine and for a moment they flicker with happiness. "Bay."

The gruff, almost reverent way he says my name sends a tingling down my spine and I smile. "War."

Behind me, Edison clears his throat. "If there's nothing further, I'll be heading back home," Edison says as he shuffles away. "You know Dorothy worries if I'm out too late."

War watches the old man walk away and with the turn of his head, he reveals a nasty scar from his temple all the way along his jaw to his chin. It's thick and wide. Whatever happened had to be painful. As soon as Edison is gone, War reactivates the alarm using the keypad near the French doors which overlook the ocean near the kitchen table.

Then, his eyes are back on mine in a flash as he makes his way back to the food. "Sit. I made us some salad."

I take a step toward the table and bile rises in my throat upon seeing sliced cucumber all over it. I'm assaulted with memories of Gabe.

My breath is stolen as I recall the terror that immobilized me when the icy vegetable became lodged inside of me. The way I had to push it out. The horror and humiliation at having Gabe between my legs coaxing the stupid thing out. I shudder and attempt to drive away the sickening memory.

"No," I say with a gasp. "I can't eat that." My eyes clench shut and I steady myself with my hands on the back of the chair.

"You don't like salad?"

Lifting my teary eyes to his, I bite my bottom lip and shake my head no. "I did…I mean, no. It's not that. Gabe. He did despicable things to me with a cucumber."

His face blanches and his hands begin shaking wildly. "But that's food. You can't…how could…I don't understand." Then his eyes widen in horror. "He didn't."

I swallow and nod. "He did."

With an angry huff, he snatches both bowls up and storms past me. Instead of scraping the bowls, he dumps them, bowls, forks, and all into the trashcan with a loud clatter. He then heads for the sink where three soap bottles line the back. I watch with brazen fascination as he spends a good five minutes scrubbing his hands with all three soaps. Once he's dried them, he turns to look at me. His hands blaze red. His eyes devour me for a moment before he clenches his eyes shut.

"I'll never be able to eat cucumber again."

I laugh bitterly. "You and me both."

His eyes reopen. "Um, are there any other foods…did he…"

I interrupt him with a shake of my head. "No. Maybe we could order a pizza or something instead."

He cringes at my words. "Do you know how disgusting restaurants are? The people who work there, they don't wash their hands. You can't trust them to cook the food to the proper temperatures. They use meat!"

I gape at him. "Okay…what do *you* want to eat?"

He starts to pace. Up toward the sink five paces, equal and measured, and then back toward me at the table. Five more paces. Equal and measured. I itch to reach out and stop him with my hand. However, although I've only known him for a few hours, I strongly suspect doing so will send him into a meltdown.

He mumbles rapidly and tugs at his hair. The muscles in his back ripple and tighten with each movement.

"I could make some spaghetti squash with red sauce and—" he stammers but then curses. "Fuck! No, squash is too much like cucumber. No eggplant. No carrots. No pumpkin. No zucchini. Goddammit!"

I chuckle to diffuse his breakdown. "I'll eat anything you want to offer me. We can eat salad if you want, just no cucumber. The rest are fine. I swear. Please, I haven't eaten since this morning."

His face lights up with determination. "Right, sit. I'll make you something delicious and inoffensive." His worry seems to dissipate. *Who the hell is this guy?*

I lean against the counter, ignoring his order for me to sit, and watch this complicated man obsess over our meal. His cuts into the tomatoes are precise and exactly the same width. He makes sure of it before he presses the knife down. The entire time, he mutters under his breath. In the quiet of his home, I can understand what he's doing. He's counting. Everything.

Pieces of lettuce.

Slices of tomato.

Slivers of onion.

Handfuls of croutons.

Seconds that pass.

Breaths we take.

I want to chime in and tell him he should have more since he's practically a giant but I don't. It's clear to me that he *needs* for it to be even. He needs to go through these rituals to feel right in his head.

After he finishes with the salad—cucumber free—he uses a measuring cup to give us both the exact same amount of homemade dressing. He then sets to scrubbing the dishes he used. He spends another ten minutes washing and drying the knife. I'm starving but I don't dare interrupt a process that he's seemed to have perfected.

I wonder how long he's been like this.

And better yet, what made him this way?

I can't help but ponder over what he would think about the cellar I was dumped into when Gabe stole me. And the way Gabe used me in the woods.

Would he even care?

Would he want to protect me?

I know I can't stay here with him forever but I can certainly stay long enough to do what needs to be done for Mom. Despite War's weird habits, it does seem a little safer here than when I was with Gabe. At least he's not forcing me to partake in depraved activities like I just came from.

"I'm sorry that took so long," War huffs, interrupting my thoughts. "I have issues."

I smile at him as we take our seats. The salads are perfect…and even. "This looks amazing. Thank you."

He nods and sets to cutting his food into bite-sized pieces. I, on the other hand, am ravenous and don't have time for manners, so I all but inhale my food. The urge to lick the bowl afterwards is intense but a choking sound drags me away from the lingering morsels.

The handsome man's features are twisted into one of absolute disgust. "You eat like a starved dog," he hisses and then follows it with a gag. "This was a bad idea."

I roll my eyes and smirk. "I guess licking the bowl is out of the question."

I've never seen a man run so fast in my life.

chapter
ELEVEN

War

Exactly three minutes every day.

That's how long it takes me to shower.

Not twelve seconds less, not forty-five seconds longer.

Always three minutes.

I know this because I count. Every second. Every minute. Every breath. The average adult breathes twelve to eighteen breaths per minute. I breathe twenty-two breaths per minute. Always. No variation. So in one shower, I take sixty-six breaths.

As I tug on a pair of slacks, I contemplate how many breaths she takes when she showers. Her breaths are unmeasurable—sometimes rapid when she's afraid or upset and similar to mine when she's behaving in a calm manner. Calculating her breaths in one shower is an endless, unsolvable problem. What if she takes ten-minute showers? Or forty-minute showers?

I'm about to consider several different variations when I pause to simply consider her in the shower. The very image of droplets sliding down her smooth, pale forehead and wetting her dark eyelashes is captivating. Her blonde hair would grow darker from being wet and it would hang smoothly down her back. And her smile—it would reveal her perfect, pearly white teeth and the kindness that lies within.

If she's smiling, she's breathing slower. Perhaps thirteen or fourteen breaths per minute. But the variable I'm still unsure of is the length of her showers. I'll have to ask her to time them.

I glance up at my long mirror on the wall and frown. For over ten years, I've been this man I don't know. Ever since…well, anyway, I'm him now.

And I hate the very fucking air he breathes.

All twenty-two breaths per minute.

Today, I'm wearing a pair of charcoal-colored fitted slacks, black dress shoes, and a crisp pale blue dress shirt that matches her eyes almost perfectly. I'd seen to ordering three online in similar colors in an attempt to find a perfect match. If none of those work, I'll have to call the manufacturer and have a special order made.

Normally, even at home, I slip a tie around my neck and dutifully knot it just as Dad showed me when I was ten years old. Sometimes, I wish the knot would turn into a noose and hang me. I've contemplated how many breaths I would take before my air supply would become completely cut off. Three? Four? Twenty? The answer defies me and I can't seem to ever push it from my mind.

Along with the million other rampant thoughts that run my fucking life.

"To hell with it," I snap in defiance. It's me who struggles to survive in a battle against myself. Every now and again, my true self wins—even if only momentarily.

I toss the black tie onto the bed and start to stride from the room. I've barely made it to the door before I'm stalking back over to it. Carefully, I roll it up neatly—it takes two tries to get it exactly the way I like it—and I place it back in the drawer where it belongs. My breaths seem more rapid, so I unbutton the top few buttons to breathe more easily.

Every day for years, I've had my morning ritual. Shower. Dress. Eat. And then work. But today, along with the discarded tie, I have the urge to break from the mundane and peek in on where she sleeps. Last night, I'd left in a childish huff at seeing her eat like a pig. The human part of me wanted to feel sorry for her—sorry that she was so hungry that it forced her to eat that way. But the monster who controls my every thought was disgusted. If I weren't afraid of what the stomach acid would do to my teeth, I'd have stuck my finger down my throat and thrown up after I'd sought refuge in my bathroom.

I have no idea what she did after I left her.

Did she finger every surface of my house? I make a note to have my maid, Greta, do a massive sterilization. She hates when I go on my benders but when I triple her pay those days, she quickly quiets down. My mind craves to consider every single thing Baylee touched but I force it away and burst from the room. I'm shocked to find her curled up on the couch sipping on some coffee.

"The couch is white!" I hiss out in greeting, instantly hating the words that came out.

She blows on the mug and arches a perfect eyebrow at me. "I know I'm a *teen* and all," she mutters sarcastically, "but I'm *not* a toddler. I won't spill it. Good morning, by the way."

Once again she throws her age at me, causing me to feel like more of a bastard than I already am. "Morning," I tell her gruffly, this time less angry. "Did you sleep well?"

Her brows furrow together and she sighs. "Best sleep I've had in two weeks to be honest. With Gabe, I didn't really get to sleep."

I run a hand through my hair. Last night, I tossed and turned wondering about what that man did to her. When she mentioned the cucumber, I was disgusted. And not because it was food—but because he hurt her. I may be fucked in the head but I'm not a virgin to the female anatomy. Before my world closed in on me, I quite enjoyed sex.

If I'm being truly honest and not dwelling on the dirtiness of the act, I fucking miss it.

But then images of exchanging bodily fluids—fluids which another person has shared with another and so on and so on starts to fester in my mind. I can't even watch porn without wanting to scream.

"What did he do?" I don't want to know the explicit details, and yet, this is why I bought her. To entertain me. To accompany me. To talk to me.

She sets the mug down on the end table and stands with her back to me while she faces the wall of windows overlooking the ocean. My mind momentarily frets over whether or not she'll leave a coffee ring on the wood. But when she stretches, arms high over her head, my mind blanks.

The white robe she's been given lifts and rewards me with a view of her lean upper thighs just below her ass. Her arms fall back down and with it, the robe covers more of her flesh. My fingers crave to lift the edges of the fabric and reveal her perfect skin to me again.

I want to touch her.

The thought alarms me.

I don't want to touch anyone. Ever again.

"What *didn't* he do?" she mutters and steps close to the windows. I'm afraid she'll put her fingertips on the glass and smudge the crystal clear view. It sets my jaw on edge but I bite my tongue. The despair in her voice distracts me and I find myself eager to know more about her. "After he kidnapped me, he took me to some remote cabin. For days, he trapped me in his cellar. I was forced to climb out on my own only for him to beat me and tie me to his bed."

A sob catches in her throat and her shoulders hunch. I take one, two, three, four steps toward her. When I notice my hand is stretched out, reaching to comfort her, I jerk it back.

"Then what?"

"It's kind of confusing. I mean, I have a boyfriend and I love him dearly," she murmurs and crosses her arms across her chest. Her back remains to me and I wonder if it is difficult for her to say these things directly to me. "But Gabe was my neighbor. I'd trusted him for so long. In fact, I'd always had a bit of a girly crush on him."

"He hurt you?"

She turns to look at me, as if I just asked the most ignorant question, especially after last night's admission about the cucumber. My neck tightens with stress as I wait for her to mar the untouched glass. Instead, she drops her hand, leaving the glass in crystal clear perfection.

"He gave me orgasms. Plenty of them. I didn't want them, War, but they felt good. I had no control over my body and I hate myself for that."

I take another step. Her sweet scent doesn't poison me. It intoxicates me in a way that has my head spinning. I like her scent. I like the way it fills my lungs and cleanses me.

"That's not your fault."

She sniffles. "Then, he took my virginity. It hurt so much but then…"

"You liked it?"

A sob pierces the air. "I-I-I did. I betrayed my boyfriend because I liked when Gabe had his way with me. He was always clear about selling me. After he fucked me over and over again, I had in some way hoped he'd just keep me. That we could stay in that cabin and I'd make do." She lets out a deep breath that fogs the window in front of her. I watch with a mix of horror and fascination as she draws a "B" with a heart around it on the foggy glass.

My mind begs to flip the fuck out but something stronger within me wants her to continue. And as the fog fades, the smudge of her letter remains barely noticeable. It adds warmth to my ridiculously cold space. I'm alarmed to learn I like it there. Trying not to obsess over her artwork, I urge her on. "Then what?"

"One day… he told me to run and when I did, he caught me. That night, in the cold forest, he violated me. Robbed me of another first."

The growl in the room startles us both and she turns to look at me. I understand quickly, the protective growl belongs to me. Shit. I'd normally be flipping the fuck out talking about anal sex, despite how much I'd wondered about it as a teen, but right now, all I can think about is beating the fuck out of Gabe.

Her sad eyes meet mine and she takes a small step forward but doesn't touch me. We're a mere twenty-four inches apart. I haven't been this close to someone out of my own volition since my high school girlfriend. For a few brief moments, in her broken presence, I feel like the strong one. I feel as though I'm normal.

"And the cucumber," she hisses out bitterly and I cringe, "he used to penetrate my sex with while he drove into me from behind. 'Oftentimes two men will want to take you at once. You must be prepared,' he said."

My chest threatens to explode with fury. A single strand of her blonde hair has escaped her bun and my fingers twitch to stroke it away from her forehead. Not because it's out of place but because I want to see her face better. I want to comfort her.

And I fucking can't.

Fisting my hand, I snarl out my promise. "I would never hurt you like that. He sounds deranged, Bay."

Tears well in her eyes and I lean in toward her. I want her presence invading me. Despite not touching, my flesh reacts to her proximity. Goosebumps prickle my flesh. The hairs on my arms seem to lift and point toward her as if she carries some magnetic current that my body is attracted to.

So young.

I swallow and look over her head toward the ocean. It's beautiful, and one of the few things I won't allow my mind to become obsessed with—pondering the many creatures and organisms that infest it.

Instead, I think about her.

My mother.

The way her dark hair would whip around her in the wind while I would chase the waves. She'd force me out of the water every so often to ruffle my hair and press a kiss to my forehead. Sometimes, she'd hand me a sandy cracker to munch on to keep my energy up so I could keep playing.

I won't allow my mental disease to ruin those memories. They remain virgin against the dark cloak of hatred and despair that rages continuously in my head. Always threatening to do harm. But no matter how fucked up my head may be at a particular moment, I can always return to her and our days at the beach.

One of the few calms in this life.

And now…

Now I've found another one.

Gorgeous blue eyes are staring at me, glistening with tears, when I return my gaze back to her. She's so beautiful, and for a moment, I could almost forget everything and kiss her.

Forget the germs.

The numbers.

The what-ifs.

The blood.

And bury myself in the pure distraction.

This time, reality, not my affliction, deters me and I force words from my mouth I wish I didn't have the balls to say. "You're only a child. I won't hurt you like he did. I swear on my mother's grave."

A tear rolls out but she lifts her chin in defiance. "I'm *not* a child, War. I'm eighteen. Besides, after what happened to me, I'm no longer innocent. I'm every bit woman."

"I don't care if you're eighty, Bay. I will never touch you without your permission."

Her eyes widen and her mouth parts. "But you'll touch me if I ask you to?"

After my flagrant display of my afflictions last night, I'm sure she's confounded by my words. Hell, I'm fucking confounded by my words.

"Another day, perhaps."

A small smile tugs at her lips which only further frustrates me. How can she be so pleased with my answer? I'm no fucking better than that bastard who stole her. I mean, I *bought* her for crying out loud.

"Let's talk about your family," I say in a gruff tone before stepping away from her. My eyes slide over to the glass and a tightness clamps over me at seeing her "B" on the surface again. The tightness is unlike anything I've ever known. It almost feels possessive.

A ragged breath escapes her. "I thought if maybe we wired them some money and sent a letter stating I'd run off with you, they'd buy the story long enough to help Mom. I know my Dad though. He won't stop until he finds me."

Anxiety explodes inside of me. The thought of people crawling all around my house in an attempt to steal her away makes me livid with rage. She's the first shard of happiness in this goddamned world I've seen in over a decade. I can't let them take her.

"But he's not the problem. It's Gabe. He's already promised to come for me soon. In fact, I wouldn't put it past him to already be stalking us now." Her body shivers and I ache to hold her. "He's kind of obsessed with me."

I'm kind of obsessed with you.

I fist both hands and huff. "Gabe will never touch you again. I'll kill that motherfucker if he steps one foot onto my property." The words are technically a lie—the images of that man's blood everywhere threaten to make me sick. But, if it came down to protecting her from him, a little blood might be necessary. Greta would really fucking hate me then. "I'm going to call my attorney to set up an arrangement of transferring funds to them without it getting traced back to me. You need to write down your address and your parent's names. I'll see to it they receive the money."

She nods but frowns. "And how will I let them know I'm okay?"

That part's easy.

I'm a computer genius.

I'll run the source e-mail through so many encrypted servers, nobody will ever find out where it came from.

"I'll give you a computer with an e-mail as long as you promise to never divulge your whereabouts."

"I promise. But War, Gabe knows your name. He's not stupid."

I run my fingers through my hair in frustration. "Not my last name. Only the auctioneer had that information. I won't let him take you."

She chews on her lip and nods, but still seems unconvinced. I want to reach over and pluck her plump lip from between her teeth. To run my tongue over it to soothe the damage she's caused with her nervous habit.

My cock thickens in my pants and I nearly jump for fucking joy.

"Come on," I say with a grunt, not revealing the happiness that's running through my veins. In these few moments with her, I've felt freer than I ever have. "Let's eat some breakfast and then we'll get started."

chapter
TWELVE

Baylee

Today has been a long one. I'm exhausted. The food sucks. And I'm still donning a stupid robe. Yet, it's also been productive. After I'd given War my information, he e-mailed his attorney and instructed him on how to funnel the money so that it appeared to have come from an anonymous donor. He'd also managed to order me a selection of clothes online. The man becomes one with the computer when he sits down at it. All his anxieties seem to dissipate as he throws himself into whatever task it is he's trying to accomplish.

All afternoon, I'd sat in a cozy chair in his office while he worked. His fingers had tapped away as codes danced upon the computer screen. I'd been fascinated but after the last weeks of turmoil, my body was clearly exhausted because before long I had fallen asleep. When I'd awoken, he was no longer in the office but he'd covered me with a blanket. The kindness on his part wasn't missed.

His office, like the rest of the house, is bare. No décor. No rugs. No curtains. Just the necessary furniture and technology. He has a simple filing cabinet that I'm sure is meticulously in order and one framed picture sits on the desk, seeming out of place in the stark room.

While he'd worked, I hadn't pried but now that I'm awake and alone, I'm itching to look at it. The frame is simple and black—not a fleck of dust or a fingerprint on the glass.

A small boy with a mop of brown hair and bright blue eyes beams at the camera. His parents, wearing matching grins, stand behind him. The ocean is the background and it's a picture of happiness.

So how did this little boy, who's clearly War, turn out to be the troubled man who's terrified of life?

The picture reminds me of my own family and tears begin to well in my eyes at the thought. Setting the picture down, I swipe the hot tears from my cheeks with the back of my hands. Mom and Dad are probably sick to death with worry over me. I'm probably all over the news by now. God, I miss them both so much.

"Everything okay?" A gruff, yet anxious voice, questions from behind me.

Not at all.

Everything sucks.

I shrug my shoulders and sniffle. "I miss my family."

A rush of breath escapes him and I turn to peek at the man. Today, he's especially handsome and almost relaxed. After last night, I'd assumed I'd have to deal with the uptight germaphobe twenty-four-seven. But then, this morning, he'd come out and seemed more human. As if he was attempting to climb out of his bubble—even if it were only one finger at a time.

"Edison delivered some freshly laundered new clothes for you," he says softly. "They've been put away in your room. You must be eager to get out of that robe."

I nod and force a smile. "Thank you. When can I contact my parents?"

His jaw clenches and the strain in his eyes matches mine. We're both fumbling through this crappy situation in our own distinct ways. "I've created an e-mail account. For your own safety, I'm going to read them before you send them. I'll also read their replies."

He said *them* and *replies* as in more than one.

Initially, I had assumed I'd send one e-mail to let them know I was okay. But now…now, hope blooms in my chest.

"Can I e-mail them now?" The excitement in my voice is evident with each rising octave as I speak.

"Why don't you dress first and then we'll work on that? My attorney also assured me the first transfer has been made."

"First transfer?" I question.

"I didn't want to send it all. Insurance if you will. I sent a little to help them out this first transfer. If I give them everything they need right away, you'll have no incentive to stay with me." His voice is tight and his brows are furrowed.

The man has millions of dollars and he's going to send them "a little" at a time. Maybe he's no better than Gabe after all. Rage explodes from within me and I fist my hands at my sides.

"*I* promised you I'd stay and *you* promised me lots of money in return. My mother needs it, War. She's dying," I remind him with a fierce glare.

He winces at my tone and hangs his head. His mouth moves ever so slightly as he mouths words, numbers, nonsense—who the heck knows. Both of his hands slide into his hair and he grips at it, as if he can yank answers from his head. I almost feel sorry for him and his internal battle he's waging. But that changes nothing because he's still making things hard on me.

"Whatever," I huff and damn near shove past him. He's lucky I have self-control and compassion for others—even if they are sick individuals. I know he'd probably pass out if I touched him. And no matter how angry I am at the moment, I'm not cruel.

When I step close enough that our chests nearly touch, I expect him to jerk out of the way or hiss at me to stay away from him. Instead, he snaps his wild gaze to mine. My fury quickly dissipates as I get swept up in his stormy eyes. His eyelids droop closed and he leans in to inhale me, mere inches from my cheek. From this proximity, I can smell his soapy scent.

"Knowing you're naked under here drives my already crazy head onto a new plane of madness— one I don't understand and can't navigate," he whispers against my hair, his breath tickling me. "So it's in your best interest to find clothes first and then we'll continue this conversation afterward."

His words twist inside of me and my knees wobble. "Why does it make you crazy?" I can't help but goad him. I'm curious to know what it is about me that disrupts his normally structured life.

"Because," he groans and a shudder ripples through his massive frame. "I want to touch it."

"My naked body?"

A hiss of his breath sends a wake of goosebumps creeping down my neck. "Yes."

"Send my parents the money they need to make this happen and you can touch me all you want," I murmur. Did I just try to bargain for more money with my body? I'm sick.

He growls, that same possessive growl from earlier today, and jerks away from me much to my dismay. "Go get dressed, Baylee."

I huff at his clear rejection and storm away. It isn't until I'm safe inside my room that I burst into tears again. Gabe prepared me for sexual abuse and pain. Not…whatever it is War is. It's confusing and difficult for me to navigate.

Thankfully, the clothes in the bureaus are all simple and comfortable. For some reason, I'd expected business suits. Something demure and conservative. Items that matched War's crisp, professional style. Instead, I find several pairs of jeans folded neatly in the drawers beside some yoga pants. Many T-shirts are tucked away in another drawer. I also find socks, bras, and underwear. The undergarments are all simple.

Nothing ostentatious.

Nothing sexy.

Just normal.

And I couldn't be happier.

In the closet, I find a few nicer things including a couple of dresses but still no shoes. Why didn't he give me any shoes? I slam the closet door with a huff and storm back over to the dresser. I'm sure he'd prefer the dresses, but after his blatant display of control, I want to dress as unappealingly as I can for him. With that in mind, I choose a pair of fitted jeans and a soft pink V-neck shirt. I tug my hair out of the bun and weave it into a long loose braid in front of my shoulder.

When I emerge, a delicious aroma fills the kitchen. I find that something is baking in the oven. I didn't know War even knew what delicious was.

"Greek-style vegetarian lasagna," a deep voice rumbles from down the hallway.

I snap my gaze from the kitchen to see him standing several feet away from me. His dark hair is now slightly disheveled as if he's been running his fingers through it. The dress shirt is completely unbuttoned baring his fitted white tank underneath. He's rolled up his blue sleeves, showcasing beautiful forearms, and his hands are shoved into the pockets of his slacks. The expression on his face is still the almost feral one from earlier, and I'm surprised when a quiver of excitement runs down my spine.

Yesterday, he was such a mess.

Today, he's messing with *my* head.

Today his normal obsessive patterns and displays are there but a different side of him pulsates from behind those composed behaviors. I want to scratch at him and free that side.

"I'm ready for the e-mail you promised," I clip out and attempt to keep my cheeks from reddening. I'm supposed to be angry at him, not drooling.

"Come into the living room," he says in a low, seductive voice. A voice you could nearly make love to. "I want to give you something."

On shaky legs, I follow him out of the kitchen. The sun is setting and it will be dark soon. He leads me to the couch and motions for me to sit. Once I'm seated and attempting to regain my composure, I stare up at him. For a moment, hunger flashes in his eyes before he stalks off.

Okay…

Moments later he returns and sets a laptop down on the coffee table. "This is yours. You'll have access to the Internet and the e-mail account I set up for you. Social media accounts are blocked for your own safety. I have safeguards in place to make sure you don't accidentally divulge your location."

Our eyes meet and I hold his stare. "Thank you."

He frowns but offers a curt nod. "Dinner will be ready in thirty minutes. We'll dine together, so send your letter now while I take a quick shower."

I force a smile as he starts to walk away.

"Oh," he says with a shy voice and turns to flick his gaze down over my body, "I want you to know that you look really nice. Pink is a great color against your flawless skin. With your blonde hair spilling out over the top of it, you remind me of an autumn sunset behind the ocean. Simply beautiful."

And on that note, he strides away.

I blink after him for several moments. Something he said on a whim was quite possibly the nicest compliment anyone has ever given me. And here I'd thought he'd be repulsed by my simple clothes and messy hairstyle.

Instead, he thinks I'm as pretty as the sunset above the ocean he so clearly loves.

With an annoyed, but secretly satisfied grunt, I flip open the sleek MacBook and open my e-mail. I have one unread message.

From War.

Peace,

I'm sorry it has to be this way. Give me time, and I promise I'll make it up to you. Your light is already seeping into the dark parts of my soul and I'm not about to let that slip away for a second.

Call me greedy. Call me smart. Whatever it is, I know I can't live without that light. I've been existing for so long in the darkness. Alone. Twenty-two breaths per minute.

Today, I forget to count them though.

War

I stare at his words and a flurried mixture of guilt and satisfaction settles over me. I'm a distraction from his mind. The fact that he's called me Peace only further proves what he thinks of me.

War,

I'll hold you to that promise.

Peace

After I hit send, I open a new e-mail. Dad doesn't have e-mail but Mom does to help her keep up with our extended family in Indiana. I wonder how exactly War plans on keeping me from writing her the truth about where I am.

But then she'll tell Gabe.

What will Gabe do to them if they realize he was behind everything?

He'd probably kill them. After all that he did in the cabin, I can't imagine him doing anything less. The man is psychotic.

Mom,

I pray to God you're feeling okay. I hope that somehow they've moved you up on the transplant list. I'm sorry I left without as much as a goodbye. I met someone and we're in love. I'll try and contact you when I can. Hopefully, this will all be over soon and I can come back home. I'll bring you a seashell souvenir. You always loved taking us to the beaches in southern California. I love and miss you and Dad so much.

Love,

Baylee.

P.S. Please don't mention this e-mail to Gabe. This is a private family matter and I'd appreciate it if we kept it inside of our family.

Pleased with my e-mail littered with hints to my parents that Gabe probably wouldn't pick up on, I hit send. I frown though when it sits in the outbox. Many attempts later, it still goes nowhere. With a huff, I sit the computer down on the table and pace the floor in front of it. Safeguards. That really meant he was going to monitor each e-mail before I hit send?

I glance back down at the screen when I see a flash of movement. I'm dumfounded when the cursor moves, opens the e-mail, and my words change before my very eyes.

Mom,

I pray to God you're feeling okay. I hope that somehow they've moved you up the transplant list. I'm sorry I left without as much as a goodbye. I met someone and we're in love. I'll try and contact you when I can. One day we'll come for a visit. I'll bring you a souvenir. I love and miss you and Dad so much.

Love,

Baylee.

PS…please don't mention this e-mail to Gabe. This is a private family matter and I'd appreciate it if we kept it inside of our family.

What the hell?

I abandon the computer and storm toward his bedroom. When I burst into the room, I take a moment to admire the sight and almost forget why I'm there.

War sits on the edge of his bed, one leg hanging off and the other bent with a laptop resting on it. The towel around his hips gapes open revealing a hairy thigh dangerously close to his cock. He's affected by me just as I am by him. It's kind of hard to hide an erection when all you're wearing is a towel.

Water rivulets are running down his sculpted chest from his recent shower. His dark hair is wet and messy on his head.

He's a picture of perfection.

A chiseled god of a man.

Beautiful.

My cheeks burn because I can't even formulate words to say to him. I'm no longer angry but instead snared in his intense gaze.

"I changed a few things," he says in a gruff tone as he drags his laptop over his lap covering what I'd already seen.

"That was invasive, War." I'm glad to have finally remembered the reason I barged in here in the first place. It was to chew him out, not ogle him. "I didn't give anything away."

He sighs and swipes some hair from his eyes. "Invasive is having a fleet of fucking FBI agents terrorizing my home. I may have problems, Bay, but I'm not at all stupid. Your little hints will be used to find you."

Tears well in my eyes. "I just wanted to let them know I was okay."

He flicks his gaze over my body before closing his laptop. "And you did. But I told you, we'll have to play this by ear. I need you, Baylee. We have to do this my way."

"Fine. Whatever *Master*," I utter sarcastically. "Once again, I'm reminded I'm your prisoner. When can we eat? I'm starving and ready to go to bed."

He rises to his feet and I can't help but skim over his chest once more before meeting his glare. The white towel hangs low revealing dark hair which leads right to the bulge beneath the towel. I avert my eyes to the floor because if I keep staring at him, I'll lose my hold on sanity. The thoughts whirring around in my head are unnatural and wrong.

"You're not my prisoner," he says softly. His steps are slow and unsure but soon he's towering over me just inches away, the heat of his body nearly melting me to the floor. "But you *are* like a miracle drug, Bay. For some reason, I don't obsess over numbers and germs and patterns. Each time you open your mouth, I'm fixated on your words. I'm drawn to the way you say them. When I'm around you, I don't obsess over my problems because I obsess over you."

The man is certifiably crazy. His words and actions are no better than those of Gabe, yet I find my lips turning up on one corner into a half-smile. I like that I control his happiness. It opens a dark door inside of my head—one that Gabe never let me see. Gabe controlled every aspect of me.

War's not the one in control here despite his monitored e-mails, vegetarian meals, and clothing choices he's picked for me. No, he knows I hold the power.

I just wish I knew what to do with that power.

"Why do you like me so much?" I question, lifting my eyes to meet his smoldering stare. "Why do I have the ability to make you not think about those things?"

He leans forward and takes a deep breath. "I have no idea. But I want to explore it. You have no clue how relieving it is to not be assaulted by the demons in your head—even if only for a few moments. I'm exhausted. So fucking exhausted. And for the first time in what seems like forever, I'm living a little outside my head and it's refreshing as hell."

My eyes find his tender ones and I shiver. His stare penetrates inside of me and carefully unravels every secret thing about me. I feel exposed at his visual dissection.

I raise a palm to his cheek but don't touch him. His entire body shudders at the nearness of me. Moments earlier, I was angry with him but when he flays open his heart and exposes raw parts of him, I can't help but be intrigued.

He clenches his eyes closed and grinds his teeth. His muscular chest heaves with each breath he takes. I watch as his eyebrows pinch and relax over and over again as if he's battling with his mind once again.

"I wasn't trying to hint to my parents in hopes that you'd take the fall for something Gabe started, you know," I say and drop my hand.

His eyes open and he frowns. "I know. And it's not your father I'm worried about. You said so yourself—Gabe will find you if you're not careful. I'm just being careful, Baylee, not crazy."

A shudder ripples through me at the thought of being in Gabe's rough clutches again. I'll do anything not to let that happen again. Even if that means letting War have his control over my e-mails. "Okay then. I'll be more careful," I concede.

He smiles at me, as if my words have the power to make him happy, and I can't help but return the gesture.

"How'd you do that anyway—getting on my computer like you were some ghost? If I'm being honest here, that was creepy," I tell him with a feigned disgusted curl of my lip.

His warm laughter fills the room—deep and throaty—and it smooths away any lasting annoyance about his taking over my message to my parents. "If I told you, then I'd have to kill you." He waggles his eyebrows and attempts to plaster on a fierce gaze to which I laugh.

"I'll take my chances."

He saunters over to his closet and disappears. I can hear hangers moving as he hunts for something to wear. "Actually, it's called remote access," he calls out from inside. "The computers in the house are all joined to the domain. From the server, as admin, I can manage any computer in this house easily. I was logged in remotely from my laptop to the server, and then to your computer. Then, I—"

"Oh my God," I groan and head back to the doorway to leave his room. "You'll kill me with boredom. Forget I asked."

More of his boyish laughter, muffled by the closet, causes me to smile but I hurry and leave his space where I wonder about what he looks like under his towel. Being this close to him—smelling him, hearing him, almost feeling him—is too much for comfort. My body is hyperaware when I'm near him and I'm not sure I like that about myself.

I'm supposed to be afraid or angry, but there in War's room listening to him chuckle, I'm not. I'm far from how I'm supposed to be feeling. In fact, for the first time in a few weeks, I feel safe and dare I say happy.

And that is what scares me.

chapter

THIRTEEN

War

One week with Baylee and my life has drastically changed.

Everything seems softer. Quieter.

The hammering in my head—the constant banging of numbers and calculations, of bloody possibilities, of sickening disasters—is all quieted whenever she's around. I lose track of all of that, and focus on her.

Her voice.

Her movements.

Her scent.

We're both trying to figure out this situation. She, at times seems to tiptoe around me, careful of her words, when I'm particularly moody and the monsters in my head creep up on me. And I try not to obsess over her. Obsessing over her is easy. I've timed every single thing she does. I know that she chews every bite of food almost nearly the same amount each time. Twenty-six. Twenty-six chews. I also know that she blinks twenty-four thousand four hundred eighty times a day. Seventeen blinks per minute. Twelve hundred blinks per hour. This is the average—but the variance is so nil, I can almost count on her blinking seventeen times each minute.

I know this because I stare at her. A lot. Not just her pretty blue eyes but most often her mouth. Pouty and pink and perfect. It's hard to look away when she turns her gaze my way—to not stare at her lips.

And the girl can talk. I never imagined, although I'd been plenty hopeful, that the sound of someone's voice could lull most of my demons to sleep. Demons that roar and slash the inside of my head to fragmented bits are now being silenced. As if she wields a sword, her tongue, which they solemnly fear.

Her reverent and soft, almost whispered, stories of her mother.

Her fond, proud tales of her father and how much she felt protected by him.

Her happy memories of school and track. And even her boyfriend Brandon.

I could listen to her speak for eternity. To put her voice on an endless loop that would get me through my maddening existence.

With Baylee, my life has become positively endurable.

And Jesus Christ do I wish it were mirrored by her.

To have her revel at *my* words, even though they're much less in quantity than hers. To have her stare at *my* mouth as if it had the power to perform miracles like hers seem to do. To have her listen to *my* stories and memories with intense interest.

But that's far from the case.

With every frown she tries to hide. Every tear she swipes away. Each unanswered email from her parents, I know.

She's nothing but a well-paid prisoner.

I've spent the better part of the week obsessing over how to change this. Over what to say and how to interact with her in hopes that she will begin to look at me with different eyes. To not regard me as the warden of her sentence but rather the sun in the sky. Bright and brilliant and beautiful. Because that's how I see her. She blinds me with her innocence. Her humor. Her wit and charm. I'm a blind man seeing for the first time when around her.

She's my savior.

"Still no response," she utters from the kitchen doorway, her bottom lip quivering.

I frown at her. "Give it some time."

"I know they've been worried sick. You'd think they'd be happy to know I was safe and not kidnapped, even though I was. Why aren't they responding?"

A single tear rolls down her cheek and I crave to comfort her. Despite the demons being silenced, I still can't imagine myself ever willingly touching her. That's the part that sucks. I want to gather her in my arms and kiss away her heartache.

But I'd be stupid to believe I'd ever be able to do such a thing.

"Anything could have happened. Maybe her phone has been shut off or something."

She frowns. "Maybe. I wish I knew what was going on. I feel so cut off from the world here."

This time, I'm the one feeling guilty. I've locked her down on her computer from anything that could give her access to the outside world. She has a weather app—as if I'd even let her outside—and open links to many stores to which my credit card is attached to so she can shop as much as she wants.

But news. Social media. Forums. Nothing. All blocked. For her safety, of course.

"They'll reply soon," I assure her. "I'm sure they're worried about you and miss you. There could be many reasons as to no response. We'll get through to them eventually."

I turn away from her so she can't see my features and stare down into the dishwater. Lying isn't one of my strong suits. Even as a kid, I didn't lie often without giving myself away. Truth is, her parents aren't worried. And that worries me.

Not one single news article has mentioned anything about a missing girl named Baylee Winston. No missing person reports filed. Not one single mention on any of their social media accounts.

I know this because I've fixated on learning about where she came from, who she is, what her parents were like, what sort of home she grew up in. All things to confirm her stories and to paint a more detailed picture of the woman in my home.

Her mom wasn't one to post often and the last post was over a month ago—her and Baylee curled up in bed. It was cute and it endeared me to her even more.

Problem is, if your child went missing, wouldn't you blast that information all over the place?

I researched her father's page and he's posted a couple of pictures of a carburetor he'd been working on. Last post was this week. That shit had me in mental fits all night. There's no way I can tell her that nobody is looking for her.

Just that goddamn lunatic, Gabe.

She walks past me and leans her hip on the edge of the counter, deep in thought, and stares out the window just past the kitchen table that overlooks the sparkling Pacific. Today, her long blond hair hangs damp to the middle of her back. It's unkempt and loose—a notion that would normally terrorize me. Yet, here I am wishing I had the mental strength to pull her into a comforting embrace and stroke her silky hair. To slide my fingers into her blonde tresses and kiss her like there's no tomorrow.

A somewhat normal gesture between a man and a woman.

With Baylee, I can almost imagine what normal gestures in a normal life would look like. A life where she's my confidant and lover. A life where I'm happy and we have a future. At one time, I felt that way about my high school girlfriend, Lilah. That was *before*.

Before the monsters.

Before the blood.

Before the misery that attached itself to my soul.

I let my mind wander away from the vision in front of me and back to the past—a place I don't let it go often.

"I'm not pregnant."

I'd been pacing her bedroom outside of her small bathroom for three whole minutes waiting on the outcome. When Lilah had said she missed her period, I flipped the fuck out. If I got her pregnant, Dad would kill me. I didn't even want to imagine what her dad would do to me.

"Come out here," I thundered from the other side of the door.

She cracked the door open and her tearstained cheeks showed proof that she was crying. I pushed into the small space and enveloped her in a bear hug. While I squeezed her, I glanced over at the test and breathed a sigh of relief to see that she was telling me the truth. I wasn't even eighteen yet and she'd just turned sixteen. Our lives would be over if we had to take care of a baby.

"Why are you crying?" I questioned while I stroked her brown hair.

She sniffled. "I don't know. I kind of hoped that we would have a baby. That we could get married and be a family."

I tensed at her words. As much as I loved Lilah, I wasn't ready to be a dad. Her dad was a fucking asshole so I knew why she would have loved to leave home and create a new family. But, I actually liked my parents. I was in no hurry to grow up fast.

"In time," I promised, "I'll get you away from here."

She gripped my black T-shirt and started tugging it off me. I hadn't been in the mood but the moment she rubbed my cock through my jeans, I hardened immediately. We just got through a pregnancy scare and I was ready to be inside of her again. This time, though, I wouldn't forget the condom.

"Make love to me, Warren," she begged.

We made quick work of shedding our clothes and once my dick was safe inside the rubber, I lifted her onto the countertop, shoving the test away, and entered her forcefully.

"Yes," she shrieked and leaned her head up against the mirror while I drove into her. My mouth found her neck and I suckled her flesh there, loving the taste that was her.

"War," a sweet moan, yet an unfamiliar one, drags me from my distant memory and I freeze.

I'm pressed up against Baylee, my dick grinding into her belly with my teeth nipping at her bottom lip. Her fingers are threaded into my hair and are gripping me desperately. For one brief second, I am able to enjoy the moment of having her—if only for a short time—before the monsters who'd been semi dormant start raging in.

What if I lost control and sunk my teeth into her lip?

Would the blood spray all over my white kitchen?

Would she bleed out all over the tile, saturating everything in its wake?

Shit!

I slam my eyes closed and jerk away from her ignoring the burn on my scalp where she'd been gripping my hair. My dick throbs painfully but it isn't that head that's winning this war.

I touched her.

I kissed her.

I tasted her.

I nearly dry fucked her against the countertop in my kitchen.

Are her panties wet?

"Fuck," I hiss out and scrub my palms with my cheeks. "Fuck!"

Her concerned voice attempts to wade through the darkness in my head but as it nears I swat at the air in front of me.

"S-S-Stay away!"

I stumble back until I crash into the edge of the stove behind me. My mind screams to get to my bathroom—to wash my mouth and my hands and my cock. If I could wash my soul, I'd do that too.

What the fuck have I done?

War. War. War.

My name is a worried chant over and over again in the kitchen but I scream at it. I swat at it. I threaten it. With each breath I take, I will it away. *Just go the fuck away.*

The sobs only feed the darkness inside me. I don't understand why she's crying but it makes me fucking crazy. It's too much. I have to get away from her.

Away.

Away.

Away I go until I'm in the hot shower in my bathroom scrubbing her from me. All the places I touched her. The places she touched me. I want it gone.

It isn't until I'm redressing that the black storm dissipates. I blink my eyes in confusion as I wonder why I flipped my shit. I was lip locked with the woman whom I've been obsessing over in the past week and I'm too much of a lunatic to accept it. To be normal. To kiss away her pain. Instead, I only inflicted more pain. Emotional lashings that she doesn't deserve and can't possibly understand. Hell, I can barely understand them.

Shit.

With a huff and growing determination, I stalk toward her bedroom. On the other side of her door, I hear the occasional sniffle. With a grunt, I push through the door, ready to face her and apologize. When my gaze fully takes in the scene, I nearly forget all and shove her onto the bed.

Baylee stands beside the bed completely nude, her clothes discarded into a pile beside her on the floor. She's working at braiding her wild blonde hair. Our eyes meet and time freezes.

I expect her to retreat or call me names.

I expect her to cover herself or to tell me to leave.

Instead, she runs her fingers through her hair to divide it into three equal sections and speaks softly. "What was that about?" Tears well in her eyes and the rejection painted there stabs at me.

"Jesus," I groan and run my fingers through my hair. "I don't fucking know."

And that's the truth. I have no idea what came over me. What possessed me to block out the constant misery swimming inside of me and throw myself into a perfect kiss. Sure, the memory of Lilah sparked my bravery—reminding me of a time when I was capable of doing such things—but it was all Baylee's lips I was kissing.

Perfect.

Pink.

Pouty.

"You want me."

I drag my gaze from her mouth and scrunch my brows together as I meet her teary stare. God, I would kill to kiss her again. To feel the soft way her lips caressed mine. The way her tongue, hot and slippery, felt inside of my mouth dancing with my own.

Turning before I do something stupid, again, I lean my forehead against the doorframe and grunt out my reply. "You have no fucking idea how much."

"I'm confused, War." She swallows loudly. "Why'd you run away from me then? Was my kiss that awful? Do I repulse you?"

Yes.

"No," I lie, "I just…"

"Your mind can't stand the idea of touching me, but your body is an entirely different story."

I pull back and meet her glare. Her body is a vision, and I *do* want to be inside of her. I want to fuck like a man who's been imprisoned for a decade. The release that she holds is alluring as hell. Too bad my head fucking hates me.

"This isn't easy," I mutter, "being at odds with myself."

She picks up one of the nightgowns I'd bought her and tugs it over her naked body. It's pale pink and made of silk. Despite it being sleepwear, it's sexy as fuck. The slinky material hugs her gorgeous tits and showcases her alert nipples. It may nearly go to her knees but it's the hottest damn thing I've ever seen on a woman.

"It isn't easy for me either," she whispers.

Her eyes are tired and I can tell she'd rather go to sleep than hang out with my crazy ass. Frustrated, I run my fingers through my hair and huff. "I'm trying, Bay."

She frowns and the hard look from before dissipates, giving way to a more compassionate one. "What do you want then? I feel like I'm walking on eggshells here, and unsure of where to go."

The image of her pale feet stepping on sharp shards of shells constricts my chest. Would the hard points puncture her skin? Would she bleed all over the fucking floor? Worse yet, is there a possibility that the shell could become lodged under her skin? Could she somehow be at risk for salmonella if the bacteria enters her blood stream?

Would she die?

"War," she says in a calm, soothing tone and approaches me hesitantly, "what do you want to do? Watch a movie? Talk?"

Her words snap me out of the horror show in my mind. Her pretty lashes bat against her cheeks one, two, three, four, five, six times before I find my words. "Actually, I was going to teach you chess," I murmur. "That is, if you wanted to learn still. I know you've been bored and this could entertain you."

A tiny smile tugs at the corners of her lips. "I do want to learn. Should I wash my hands first?"

Baylee may be barely eighteen, but she is one of the most mature women I have ever met. Her soul is first and foremost compassionate, like my mother's was. She cares about the well-being of others. Of me. Even if I did just act like a complete asshole after our kiss.

Most people think I'm a freak, hence the hiding away on my beachside estate. My father protects me the best that he can but occasionally my issues are exploited by others. Because of the success of my father's company, I'm sometimes dragged into the public eye for scrutinizing. They usually give up after enough refusals to comment and my hiding away for sometimes months.

But even with my escapes from the limelight, I often will come across someone who is horrified by my behaviors. Whether it be a postal worker delivering a package or a friendly neighbor popping over to say hi. They all learn quickly that I'm a fucking mess. Each and every one of them glares at me with disgust written all over their faces. Snarled lips. Wide eyes. Slack jaws.

Get over it. It's all in your head.

I get so fucking tired of that line. Of course it's in my goddamned head. If I knew how to get it out, I'd have already found a way to crack open my skull and scoop the shit out. Smear it all over the fucking walls and light it on fire. Watch it burn to the shitty-ass ground I have to walk on every single day.

"War?"

Her brows are pinched together in concern. Once again she amazes me with her selflessness when it comes to me.

"Yes, please. Use the soap in the kitchen. Wash them twice just in case. Sometimes bacteria can get left on your hands even after three minutes of solid washing with soap and water. That's why I wash for four minutes the first time and then four minutes more the second time before playing chess. By then, everything should be removed." I rattle off my words. "Should being the key word. My chess pieces are precious to me and need to be handled properly. So just in case, wash your hands twice. Four minutes each."

Her eyes widen and she sets to chewing on her lip. All horrifying thoughts of germs crawling all over her fingertips and infecting my rooks, bishops, pawns, queens, and kings scamper from my mind as I focus on her mouth. The bottom lip is plump and swollen. Ripe for sucking.

Thirty-seven minutes and sixteen seconds ago, I had my mouth on hers. The monster inside of me screams at me—reminding me of the insane amount of microorganisms that are most likely inhabiting her tongue and gums. Those microbes are how diseases are transferred.

Fucking stop already.

I blink one, two, three times and lick my own lips. I'd been in such a hurry to scrub her from me but now I'm wishing I could still taste her. My body thrums to kiss her again but the demons in my head laugh in my fucking face.

You. Can't. Do. It.

"How will I know how long four minutes is?" she questions, grabbing my attention again.

I frown. "You count. That's what I do. Two hundred and forty seconds each. Total of four hundred and eighty seconds."

She bursts into a girlish laughter that distracts me. It's innocent and light and I want to bathe in the sound of it. Her voice is one I could listen to all day long and never grow weary.

"Maybe you should buy me a watch so I don't mess up," she finally says once her humor has died down. "Until then, can you do it with me?"

I'm already shopping online in my head. Sizes and brands and thicknesses of watches I've seen in passing filter through my head like a personalized catalogue. Her wrist is so delicate and dainty but her spirit is strong. I will have to find something that harnesses both.

"Warren. Focus."

I blink at her and try to shake off the thoughts that are maddening me. Rose gold? That would be stunning against her pale flesh and—

"War," she snaps, walking past me and nearly brushing against my shoulder. "Think about all that's running through your head later. After our chess game. I'm ready to learn."

With a deep sigh, I nod and stalk after her toward the kitchen. The globe of her ass jiggles with each step she takes and my cock responds almost magnetically to her. Explosive thoughts dull and fade as I focus on her gorgeous figure.

She dutifully washes her hands.

The suds lathering up nicely on her perfect skin and I become mesmerized.

I find it difficult to focus on anything around her, anything near her, anything but her.

And once again, I lose count.

chapter
FOURTEEN

Baylee

"Your turn," I tell him as I slide my white, ivory bishop diagonally and sit back in the chair.

His brows pinch together and I watch with fascination as his eyes dart all over the board, no doubt configuring many different outcomes with every possible move he can think of. The man is obsessed—*no surprise there*—with this game but I've never seen him so in his element. It took him a good ten minutes to set up the board. I could tell after the first two pieces that he wanted to cleanse them all with his soft cloth, but all it took was one shameful glance my way before he pushed the cloth away and set up the board.

It took a while for him to explain the rules to me, but once I had a decent understanding, we began. With each move, he'd ask me if I were sure. I know he was trying to help but it made me second-guess each placement of the chess pieces. It was as if he played himself for so long that he couldn't bear to win so easily. Clearly I'm no match for him.

"Are you sure you didn't want to move your rook there instead?" he points to a black square.

I scrunch my nose and lean forward. The rook seems like he protects my king so I don't want to move him. No other moves seem possible aside from the bishop. Tapping my bottom lip with my fingertip, I consider what he might have planned against me.

"I think so…"

He grunts and hovers his hand over the board. "Checkmate." With finesse, he lifts the knight and leaps it over a pawn to attack my king.

Our eyes meet and he smirks at me, satisfaction written all over his face. It's a handsome look on him. I've always been competitive when it comes to board games but with one look, I want to lose all the games with him—just to see that cocked eyebrow and smile lifted on one side.

"You cheated," I say with a laugh.

His gaze falls to my mouth and I watch his Adam's apple bob in his throat as he swallows. Now that the game is over and he isn't fixated on the board, I've become his new obsession. He skims over the silky material of my nightgown, slowing at my breasts, and then drops his eyes to my bare thighs.

I could have changed into something more decent but I kind of liked feeling sexy for him. The thought of him losing control again and kissing me more dizzies me. His mouth on mine had been decadent. War is lost inside of his own head most of the time, but for that moment, he'd lost himself in me.

And I liked it.

I chew on my lip, savoring the lingering taste of him there, and slightly drag my gown up my legs, revealing more skin on my thighs. With my eyes on him, I watch for any signs indicating that what he sees excites him. He clears his throat but his stare is on my legs. I'm not wearing anything under the gown. The idea of spreading apart my legs to show him has me dampening for him.

Gabe may have been a psychotic prick but I sort of miss his expert touch when he wasn't hurting me. If War, the gentle soul he is, touched me, I think I'd enjoy it a whole hell of a lot more.

Feeling brave, I lean back against the cushions of the couch stretching so that my gown inches up even more. Across from me in the armchair, he sucks in a rush of air.

"Bay." His voice is a low growl—almost a warning.

It excites me and a shiver of desire tickles across my flesh. "Yes?"

"Please stop."

Tears of rejection sting my eyes at his uttered words and I hastily drag my gown back to my knees. Heat creeps up my neck from being caught and I can no longer look at him. "I'm sorry," I choke out, embarrassment garbling my words. I flick a glance back up at him. He's staring up at the ceiling and his mouth is moving. Counting and counting. Finally, he drags his eyes from the ceiling.

He groans and his pained eyes meet mine. The muscles in his neck tighten and he seems as if he's physically restraining himself from pouncing on me. The idea is confusing considering seconds ago he shot me down after my poor attempts to get him to touch me. I want him to touch me though. Badly. I want to feel his sweaty skin pressed against mine.

"You're torturing me."

I scrunch my brows and frown at him. "Because I'm annoying you? You don't want me?"

War is an ocean I'll never be able to navigate. His head a sea of unchartered, choppy waves. I feel as though I'm an inexperienced swimmer in a sinking boat and he's the treacherous, stormy waters threatening to pull me under into the darkness with him.

Something tells me I'll drown.

That I'll never understand what goes on inside his head.

I'll lose my mind trying to figure him out.

"Jesus," he curses and runs his fingers through his hair, "of course I want you. I'd be a fool not to."

I chew on my lip and tears well in my eyes again. "I guess I don't understand then."

My words seem to anger him and I don't know why. Further proving my thoughts, he scowls at me. "She replied."

As if cold water has been splashed over me, I jerk upright. "Wait? What?" I demand. "Who replied? Mom? Why didn't you tell me sooner?"

He shrugs his shoulders and leaves the room. I don't miss the bulge in his pants. He'd been turned on despite the way he'd acted—as if I was an annoyance for displaying how I felt. I'll break into his head one day.

Hastily, I drag the laptop onto my knees and open my email.

Baylee,

Where in the hell are you? Give me your location so I can come get you. I've been worried sick.

Dad

Tears blur the screen in front of me and I choke back a sob. Dad is pissed at me because he assumes I put them through all this heartache for selfish reasons. If only he knew it was that bastard. His best friend who stole me and put me into this position.

Dad,

Why did it take you so long to respond? I'm somewhere safe. Don't worry about me. Did you happen to get any money? To help with Mom? I love you, Daddy.

Baylee

I swipe a tear from my cheek and lose myself to a memory of my dad.

"You're too young to date, Baylee," Dad snapped as he washed the grease from his hands after a long day at the machine shop he worked for.

I chewed on my lip and glanced at the door. Brandon would be here any minute to "study." What Dad didn't know was that we were boyfriend and girlfriend at school. We held hands and he walked me to all my classes. Technically we are dating even though we didn't go anywhere to do it. He'd even kissed me many times after school when no teachers were around. I'd felt his erection through his pants and he'd, on more than one occasion, touched my breasts through my shirt. I would not be telling Dad that though.

"But Dad, all the other girls my age—"

He slammed his fist on the counter and affixed me with a firm glare. "I don't give a damn about those other girls. They'll end up pregnant before graduation. Not my daughter."

Tears welled in my eyes and my shoulders slouched in defeat.

"Oh, Tony," Mom chirped as she entered the kitchen, "let her date. Don't you remember when we were her age? We'd been together since the eighth grade."

My dad's scowl melted away at hearing her soothing voice. She stepped into his hug and he kissed the top of her blonde head. "That's exactly why I don't want her dating. I know what we did and at what age we did it."

I cringed at thinking of what my parents did. I wasn't clueless though and pushed away thoughts that would make me puke.

"But Brandon's a nice guy and—"

Ding dong!

My eyes widened as Dad went back to glaring. "Your study partner is the guy you want to date? Hell no."

My skin heated and I flashed my mom a horrified look as Dad stormed away to answer the door. I chased after him and peeked around my dad's broad shoulders to see a frightened Brandon staring up at him. Brandon was cute today still in his baseball shirt. His dark hair was spiked up perfectly. Someone might poke their eye out if they got too close.

"Tony," Mom warned.

Somehow, even though Dad was the gruff, tough one, Mom always seemed to win when it came to him. She'd always been my ally and best friend.

"You want to date my daughter?" Dad snarled.

Brandon's Adam's apple bobbed in his throat and he managed to get out a husky reply. "Yes, sir. I like Baylee a lot."

Dad grunted and waved for him to enter. "What is it exactly that you 'like' about my daughter?"

Brandon stepped in, his body slightly quivering and his eyes darted over to mine. He was so good looking. One day he'd grow into a handsome man. His height towered over mine but Dad was still taller. Brandon was muscular but not as big as my dad who did physical labor all day at the shop. Dad's beard was thick and his dark hair hung in his eyes making him look like a feral animal in comparison to Brandon's clean-cut appearance. I knew women found Dad attractive because I'd heard on more than one occasion my mom get jealous of a few of our overly neighborly neighbors.

"I like her smile. She's one of the nicest people I know," Brandon said softly and his gaze found mine. "I like that she cares about people at school and makes it a point to talk to everyone no matter if they're cool or not. And I like that she runs the track not as if she's running from the world but as if she's running toward it, embracing all that life has to offer her."

Mom let out a sigh and I couldn't help but grin at my secret boyfriend.

"So poetic," Gabe mocked with a chuckle as he entered through our open front door. My eyes tore from Brandon to regard our neighbor and my dad's best friend. His eyes always seemed to follow me from room to room. It was as if he looked through me into my head and could understand my most secret thoughts. He unnerved me—even if he was really hot for an older guy.

"Whatcha think, Gabe?" Dad asked. "This boy good enough to date my Baylee?"

Brandon swallowed down his apparent nerves but straightened his back to meet the glare of Gabe.

"As long as they're not having sex, I don't see the harm in her dating a boy." Gabe's eyes flitted down my body and a chill ran through me. My boobs have grown and Brandon's not the only one who noticed them. I'd caught Gabe staring on more than one occasion. I kind of liked that he liked my body. It made me feel more grown up than I was.

"They're not having sex. Ever," Dad said firmly.

Brandon nodded in a clipped manner as if to agree with my dad. My heart did a nosedive because I'd already been having many dirty fantasies involving Brandon and I. Chewing on my lip, I darted my gaze back to Gabe. He did that thing where he gave me a look that seemed to implant itself inside my head. A look that said, I'd have sex with you because I'm a man. My lower belly started to ache and I had the urge to run to my room away from the awkward situation.

"Gabe, Tony," Mom blurted out suddenly, "get out here and start the grill. The kids have some studying to do. Leave them alone, and Brandon, I hope you'll join us for dinner."

Brandon let out a rush of relieved breath. "I'd love to, ma'am."

Gabe seemed unimpressed but I was very impressed. Brandon was a sweet, sexy boy but he sure did hold his own with two fierce men. I thought I fell for my boyfriend a little more.

"Fine," Dad groaned but grabbed Brandon's bicep. "But if I so much as hear you think about hurting my daughter, we'll be having you for dinner, all right."

With that threat, he released his arm and stormed out the door with a smirking Gabe on his heels.

A chime from the computer alerting me of a new e-mail startles me from my memory. I blink away the tears and open the e-mail.

Baylee

Yes, I got the money. Money that isn't needed. What's needed is my daughter. Come home. You're a teenager and if I find out who has you, I'll ruin them for kidnapping my daughter.

Dad

I gape at his reply. I'd expected him to be angry, but he's acting out of character. For a moment, I wonder if Gabe is the one replying. That idea sends a shiver down my spine and I shake away the terrifying thought.

Dad,

Why isn't Mom replying to me? Is she in the hospital? Did they find a donor? And I'm not sleeping with him. There's someone else that should be ruined—a monster that is too close to home.

I pause and delete the last sentence for fear if Gabe really is the one behind the e-mail. Even if he didn't write it, I know it'll only be a matter of time before he reads it. He and Dad are close, and if Dad thinks I've been kidnapped, he'll no doubt use Gabe's help and share with him this information. This whole thing is complicated and exhausting. I continue my e-mail.

Please just accept the money we send and use it for Mom. I promise when things are better, I'll come see you both. Things have been hard, Dad. Trust that I'm still your daughter and would only be doing seemingly hurtful things if there were a reason. You know me better than to assume the worst. I love you and look for more money. Can you let Mom reply?

Baylee

Tears well in my eyes and then spill down over my cheeks. Less than a month ago, I was spending my days flirting with my boyfriend between classes, training for a track meet after school, and having long talks with my mother about my childhood, my relationship with Brandon, and my future.

Fast forward a few weeks and I'm craving physical attention from a man who purchased me for companionship, worrying over whether Gabe will come back for me, and attempting to get my father to understand my situation without telling him.

My, how things have changed.

A ding on the computer has me jerking my attention back to my inbox. I let out a tiny sigh of disappointment to see that it's from War, who's undoubtedly hiding from me in the other room. Away from my childish advances.

Peace,

You're more than I could have ever imagined. I know you're not happy but I think with time you could be. Please forgive me for selfishly wanting you all to myself for a couple of hours. I knew the email would upset you and all I wanted was to make you happy.

It's the least I can do for all that you have done for me.

War

I swipe away my tears and tap away a response.

War,

It's hard to be happy when your life is a big, confusing, frightening mess. Granted, I'm not fearful around you, but I am fearful for the simple fact that Gabe is still out there. Most assuredly, he's there with my parents or at least in contact with my dad. I feel disconnected with the outside world. I could be contacting the police, explaining to my parents about Gabe, anything. I'm not though. I'm pretending to be your doting companion with you. And while playing chess with you, eating your super healthy vegan meals, and chatting to you about every single thing I can think about to keep the boredom at bay passes the time, I'm still stuck in this box. Your house. Locked in. Away from everyone.

I know you say I'm not a prisoner. Well show me.

I know you say you'd be a fool not to want me. Prove it.

I know you hate Gabe for what he's done to me. Then help me.

Right now, I'm like your annoying little puppy that you got stuck with. You're afraid I'll get dog hair all over your pretty couch or pee on the floor. That I'll bark too loudly and the neighbors will find out you have a yappy dog. You don't want me to chew on your stuff, yet you give me nothing to play with.

I'm not happy, War.

I'm sorry.

Your puppy you've been saddled with,

Peace

Feeling satisfied with my e-mail, I fire it off to him and glare at the screen. My fingers tap impatiently on the device as I wait for a response from him or my parents. Minutes later, my computer pings again.

Peace,

I could have done without the puppy peeing reference. Jesus. That shit is fucking with my head just thinking about it. Look, I'm sorry too. I'm not a monster, Bay. I made a mistake—buying you like I did. I was too delusional to even think through the consequences or outcomes of such a fantastical plan. Now, I get it. And that's at the expense of you. For that, I apologize. I'll make it up to you, I promise.

Until then, know this. You're not a puppy to me.

In fact, you're as far from annoying as one could get.

You're a light in my dark world. I'm not ashamed to admit that. And you're right, I'm holding you prisoner just as I promised not to. Your Internet access is no longer restricted. Find out what you can about your parents and Gabe. Do whatever makes you happy. But please don't create a trail that leads back to us. That means no posts on Facebook or anything of the sort. Please.

War

PS—the code to the alarm is 1200, the same number of times you blink per hour.

My heart thunders to life. The code, although weird, is no longer a secret. Internet access is no longer restricted. Finally, I can start to make a plan.

War,

Thank you.

Peace

Flipping over to the Internet, I immediately type in: ***Missing Person, Baylee Winston.*** Another chime on my computer alerts me to an e-mail. Toggling back over to my inbox, I pray it's my parents. Unfortunately, it's only another e-mail from War.

Peace,

There's something you should know.

Nobody's looking for you.

I didn't know how to tell you sooner and don't know what to make of it.

I'm so sorry, Bay.

War

I shake my head in argument and flip back to my Internet browser. Several long minutes of researching prove he was right. There isn't one single article of me missing. This makes no sense. I've been gone for over three weeks. Only in the past week have my parents been notified that it wasn't against my will, even though it actually was. So why is nobody looking for me?

Looking over my shoulder, I make sure he isn't coming and attempt to sign into Facebook. Repeatedly, I try my password and it's wrong. It was Winston20. Both of my parents and Brandon knew the password. Did one of them change it?

Quickly, I whip up a fake account under the name Winnie Stone. Mom and Brandon have their pages locked down from people who aren't their friends, mine doesn't seem to exist, and Dad's is open.

Recent pictures.

Of stupid car parts.

I don't understand.

With hot, angry tears in my eyes, I fire off another message to War.

War,

Why aren't they looking for me?

Peace

I want to scream at him to get his coward self in here and stop hiding away from me so we can discuss this but I'm too overwhelmed. Fear roils my belly and bile creeps up my throat. Something is wrong.

I exist, dammit!

So why in the hell does it seem like I disappeared from the face of the earth and nobody even noticed.

Peace,
I don't know why. But I'll figure it out. I promise.
War

I'm tired of his broken promises. And I've certainly never been great at patience. It's time to find out what's going on. Even if that means breaking my promise to War.

Tonight, I'm leaving.

War

She didn't respond back to my e-mail. Why the hell would she? I mean, I've acted like a complete ass toward her. Not given in to her innocent advances. Withheld useful information from her. Lied to her. She probably hates me.

As she should.

I *paid* for her.

Fucking *paid* money for her.

I'm no better than Gabe.

My logical side attempts to reason with me. *Let her go. Drive her back to Oakland and deliver her to her parents. Stop obsessing over her. Move the fuck on.*

Yet, the irrational part of me fights. *But I don't want to let her go. If I take her back, Gabe will hurt her. Again. If I don't take care of her, who else will? Her parents certainly don't give a damn. What parent doesn't report when their child goes missing? Something doesn't add up.*

Ignoring both sides of the argument for now, I check my email for the twenty-eighth time since my last message. Nothing. Stretching out on my bed, I pour through documents filed at the court house in her county, her parent's bank records I hacked into, police reports, news articles, and anything tied to the Winston name.

Not one single shred of evidence that indicates she's missing.

With reluctance, I type in the Oakland police department in my browser and peruse through the names of the detectives. Since Baylee was involved in a sex ring, maybe she does have a case but it's under wraps. It would make sense especially if the Feds were involved.

There are several names of detectives that handle missing persons. Rita Stark is one of them. Her name makes me think of my clean house and stark white walls. Her name calls to me. I quickly copy her email address and open one of my many encrypted e-mail accounts. Maybe she can shed some light on Baylee's situation.

Detective Stark,

I apologize in advance for coming to you under such anonymous conditions but I have my reasons.

Would there be any circumstances why a missing person would not go be broadcast publicly and no reports be made? Perhaps if they were involved in a bigger case?

Sincerely,

Mr. Pacific

Panic skitters through me as I hover the cursor over the send button. I know for a fact the dinky Oakland Police Department won't be able to trace this message back to me. Fear of them finding out by some tiny miniscule detail like the made up last name though has me editing my email. Once I've changed my signature to *Mr. Atlantic* instead, I hit send before I change my mind.

I climb off the bed and start pacing the room. Ten steps one way and ten steps back. Over and over again until I'm sure I've worn a hole in the carpet. When I check my email again, there's one sitting in the inbox.

Mr. Atlantic,
What an unusual question. Perhaps we could discuss it further over the phone?
555.672.4359
Stark

I frown and type a response.

Detective,
While I understand where you're coming from, it won't work. I am simply trying to find an answer to my problem. If a person, let's say still in high school, goes missing, what are the reasons as to why someone wouldn't report them? This is an important matter and I'd appreciate your honest feedback, not attempts to discover my identity. That, you'll never know.
Mr. Atlantic

I don't have to wait long for her reply.

Mr. Atlantic,
I'll bite on the anonymous name, for now.
This isn't a certain young man that slung my files off my desk in a fit of rage is it?
Listen, son. I will tell you what I told you before. If she went missing, her parents would have reported her missing. And I did look into your suggestion of truancy at her school. Her father decided to homeschool her and withdrew her from school the afternoon before you said she went missing. Your fantastical story of someone taking her while you two were in the middle of an explicit sexual act is quite creative and detailed, but I'm afraid it isn't enough.
You must understand something. Her mother is very sick. I know you're her boyfriend but sometimes families do things like homeschool their children when a parent is dying. The need to travel to doctor appointments out of state, especially if they find a donor like in her mother's case, and spending time with the loved one before their passing is important. I understand your frustration, I really do. But until someone, besides you, reports her as missing, I'm afraid our hands are tied.
Come talk to me again. This time, leave the anger at home. I want to help you.
Stark

I blink several times at the computer. She's referring to Brandon. Brandon knows she was stolen and the police don't fucking believe him. Swallowing down my unease, I respond.

Detective,
This isn't who you think it is but you've certainly answered my questions for now. I'll be in touch.
Mr. Atlantic

This time she doesn't reply. I probably shouldn't have said anything but I hate the idea of Baylee's parents blowing her off for whatever reason. It doesn't add up and Stark needs to open her eyes to that fact.

I've wound myself up researching Baylee's life to the point that I'm in a full blown episode. Since I can't make sense or bring order to her situation, I've resulted in tackling things I do have control over.

Like my closet.

For the past two hours, I've tried everything on to make sure it still fits, rearranged the shirts in order of newness, inspected each garment for imperfections like split seams or tears, and bundled up clothing to donate. I've also made a list of everything I need to buy to replace the donated items.

Once I'm done with the closet, I organize each dresser drawer.

Then the bathroom cabinets.

And then all the files on my computer.

I can't get my mind to sit still and millions of different reasons as to why her parents haven't reported her missing flit through my head.

Maybe they really did think she ran off with someone. Gabe even. But wouldn't they be worried about their daughter disappearing with an older man?

Maybe her mother got called with a donor. But would they run off for surgery and not report their child as missing?

Maybe they know she's missing and they don't care. But who could not care about Baylee?

That last option is impossible.

Maybe Gabe killed them. But why is there still normal activity on their bank records and why the hell is her father posting mundane shit on his Facebook?

I'm no closer to finding answers and it's scrambling my brain.

I need to call Dad.

"Warren," Dad's gruff voice crackles on the other line. "Is something wrong? Are you okay?"

I rub my palm up my cheek and into my hair. "Yeah, Dad. Just wanted to hear your voice."

The line is silent for a moment before he speaks again. "I'm glad you called. What do you want to talk about? Want me to bore you about the New York client I'm finalizing a contract with?"

I smile and crawl into bed. "Please."

For the next half hour, through plenty of yawns, Dad regales me with slightly embellished stories of his new client meant to make me laugh. I chuckle and find my eyelids drooping as the evening wanes on.

"Dad," I murmur, "I'm going to go now. Thanks for boring me to sleep."

His deep laugh soothes me, reminding me of when I was a small boy and would crawl into his lap before bed. "Always. I'll be back in San Diego in three weeks or so. We'll catch up then."

"Thanks, Dad."

We hang up and I lie in bed wondering how I'll explain Baylee to him. He won't be happy, that much is for sure.

I drift off with Dad on my brain.

"Lilah's here."

I flinched at hearing her name and dragged the pillow from my face to peek up at my father. His dark hair was streaked with greys that weren't there two months ago. Two months of hell and my father was quickly becoming an old man.

"Tell her I can't right now," I murmured and started to cover my face again with the pillow.

Dad growled from the doorway. The moment I heard it creak all the way open, my heart started to race. I'd told him time and time again to stay out of my fucking room. The pillow was yanked from me and I looked into his glowering eyes as he hovered beside my bed.

"*Get up and go talk to that girl. You have to at some point. Now, Warren!*"

I flinched at his tone but I was already scrambling from the bed away from his nearness onto the other side. My flesh seemed to flare up because of him being in my room and I started to scratch at my forearms that were on fire.

"Get out!" I hissed.

His glare softened and he clenched his jaw. "Break up with her then. She's been here every day like a lost little puppy. I can do almost everything for you but this is something I can't do. End it and then she'll go away forever."

The thought of losing my girlfriend—the one I loved so fucking much gutted me. But how did I keep her? I couldn't even leave my room without having a damn panic attack. Dreams from that night haunted me.

So.

Much.

Blood.

And it poisoned my brain. I couldn't think straight. All I could understand was the dirtiness and disease and toxins that surrounded me. Disgusting problems which I could control by holing myself in my room and taking several showers a day.

It helped me.

It calmed a raging storm within me.

I felt a sliver of peace when I was scrubbing my hands raw under the scalding water.

But it was times like now, when the outside world came crashing in on me, that I lost my mind.

"Dad," I begged, my voice choked up with emotion and threatening tears, "please go away. Tell her to go away too."

His eyes dropped and his bottom lip drew down, a slight quiver to it. I hated seeing my father so upset but I didn't know what else to do. I couldn't comfort him. Not emotionally. And certainly not physically.

"I'm so sorry." A garbled sob escaped him before he stumbled out of my door in an incredible rush.

Hot tears burned my eyes and I clamped them closed. Balling my fists up at my side, I let out a roar of frustration. The anger inside of me was explosive and if it weren't for me having a meltdown over the aftermath, I'd destroy my room with my two bare hands.

Punch holes in every wall.

Shove everything from every surface onto the floor.

Rip my clothes from their hangers.

Tear my comforter and sheets into shreds.

Yank at the edges of the carpet and pull it right from the concrete.

Crush the mirror above my dresser.

Anything to match the way I felt inside. Punched to death. Shoved and shoved. Ripped to shreds. Torn in two. Yanked around. And crushed to bloody, gory bits. My heart was the worst—I didn't even think it beat anymore. I would have liked to have taken my pocket knife and gouged a deep hole just under my ribs, shoved my hand through the bloody flesh, and gripped the black organ in my fist. Then, I wanted to rip it from me, detach it from my soul and inspect what was left. My guess was, nothing. Black, rotten pieces but nothing as it was before.

Dr. Weinstein said these gruesome thoughts were normal for my condition. That, through therapy, we could talk through these grim imageries.

But I didn't want to talk about any of it.

Not what happened to them.

Not what I was always thinking.

Not how I was too much of a fucking lunatic to hug my girlfriend or sit on the bed next to my father without my head crushing in.

Dr. Weinstein was wrong. I was not fixable. You couldn't fix what was wrong with me. It wasn't *mental—it was fucking tangible. I could feel the dark, twisty parts of me infecting every cell, membrane, and bone in my body.*

I was tainted.

With her blood.

Their blood.

And the disease of my despair.

There was no cleansing something so tainted.

This was who I was now.

This was War.

chapter
SIXTEEN

Baylee

I stare at the clock on the nightstand and when it reaches exactly three in the morning, I make my move. Soundlessly, I creep out of the bed. Along the way to the dresser, I shed my gown and open the drawers hunting for clothes in the dark. I'm sure I could turn on a light but I don't want to clue him into what I'm doing. A sliver of light could wake him. I need a head start, not for him to catch me in the act.

Once I've located jeans and a sweater, I dress with haste. I'm annoyed, once again, that I don't have shoes. Running away is going to be hard without them. Frustration threatens to let a sigh out but I choke it back. Instead, I snatch out two pairs of socks and double up for the protection.

Slipping out of my bedroom is easy and quiet. I've managed to make it to the front door undetected. My fingers hover over the keypad of the alarm. Panic causes my chest to constrict and my heart to nearly pound out of it. Pushing those numbers will make a sound. How far will I get before he realizes I'm out the door?

I've peeked through my bedroom window enough times to know the driveway is about a hundred feet to the street. Across the street are bars, restaurants, and shops. If I can just make it across, I can blend in and hide.

But everything will be closed.

I swallow down the fear of running alone along the storefronts. Right into the arms of Gabe. Clenching my eyes closed, I shake my head.

If Gabe were here, he wouldn't wait. I know him. He's arrogant enough to come right through the front door. I'm not going to run into him.

Someone will find me.

A passing car.

Someone taking a late night stroll.

Drunks trying to make their way home from the bars.

Anyone.

I snap my eyes back open and grind my teeth together. I can do this. I'm a fast runner—shoes or not. War isn't going to count my steps—I mean, he probably will—but not in an effort to punish me should he catch me.

He's not going to catch me.

He's too afraid.

My germs will eat him alive.

The thought urges me on and I have to stifle a maniacal laugh.

1-2-0-0.

The beeps as I mash the buttons are like blasts on an air horn in the silent house. A dull roar resounds in my ears as adrenaline kicks in. *Run, Baylee!*

I'm out the door and charging down the driveway before I even realize what I've done. I just ran away. From War. My heart sinks and I push away the unusual feeling of loss as I distance myself from the house.

Seventy-seven steps.

I have been counting them—a lingering memory of Gabe reminding me of every step I take. My knees buckle and I nearly stop. But then a voice jerks me back to life.

"Baylee!"

War's booming voice thunders from behind me. Despite the loudness of it, I sense the pure anxiety in the way he said my name.

"Please!"

One simple word, and my legs slow to a near stop on their own accord. Ninety-two steps. I'm nearly to the desolate street. Risking a glance over my shoulder as I retreat from him, my mouth opens in surprise to see him charging for me. If things were different, I'd ask him how he's managed to come outside without his respirator or shoes for that matter. His bare, muscular chest is ethereal and spooky under the moonlight. And yet…I like what I see. Even if that means what I'm seeing is a wild-eyed man chasing me.

A car horn blares at me as the vehicle swooshes past me, jerking me from my stare down of War and I snap back to attention. I drag my gaze up and down along the row of buildings across the street.

Nothing but darkness aside from a hotel about a mile down the road.

I can do this.

I can make it.

My legs finally wake up and I start jogging across the street. There aren't any cars at the moment so I easily make it across. I've still got my eye on the big hotel when something stabs the bottom of my foot.

Pain cripples me and I stumble forward. Something grabs at the back of my sweater and I'm jerked back to my feet. I snap my head over my shoulder to meet the feral eyes of War. His nostrils are flaring in anger and I almost don't recognize his foreign glare.

He's zoned out.

An animal.

And I'm in his unpredictable grasp.

"Jesus," he snarls and snatches my wrist.

He doesn't flinch. He doesn't fret about germs. He just drags my limping ass back to his home.

And like an injured fool, I hobble after him while he mutters out numbers and words that make no sense. My heart is racing but my focus is on where he touches me. His touch, despite the need to get me to his house, is firm and gentle. I almost wonder if I could jerk out of his grasp. Yet, I don't want to. I'm defeated and hurt and all I want to do is lie down under a blanket. Tears roll down my cold cheeks and I let out a sob.

How will he punish me?

When we get inside, he slams the door shut and releases me. I cry harder as his shaky hand flies over the numbers of the key pad. He's changing the code, I know it. My eyes are blurry and out of focus from crying so I don't make out the new one.

"I have to shower," he snaps at me and storms away leaving me a quivering, sobbing mess in the entryway.

A shudder wracks through me the moment I see the blood all over the marble floor. It's soaking through the socks and leaving a trail with every step I take. I should be worrying over how angry War is about my running away.

But all I can think about is how horrified he'll be to see the blood.

Hoping on one foot, I make my way into my bedroom to shower. Once I'm clean and have my bleeding foot under control, I can clean up the entryway.

The shower is hot and the blood does slow. When I feel brave enough to look at the damage, I sit down and draw my foot up to my knee under the warm water. A long, but not necessarily deep gash runs along the fleshy part of my heel. I use my finger and thumb to open the cut in search for any remaining fragments of glass or metal, whatever it is I stepped on. Nothing remains but it continues to bleed. When I'm clean and it finally slows, I climb out of the shower and wrap up in a towel.

I hobble out of the bathroom in search of clothes and am shocked to find a first aid kit sitting on my bed. Once I've bandaged up my cut and dressed, I limp back to the entryway to clean up my mess.

War, like a man possessed, is on his knees scrubbing with bleach at the floors. The blood no longer remains but he scours at the floor as if he's ridding it of invisible toxins. He's donned his black respirator and is wearing yellow gloves that hit midway up his muscular forearms. I can tell he's freshly showered as his wet, messy hair is sticking out in every direction, bouncing as he scrubs. He's wearing nothing but jeans and he looks good. Really good.

Tears well in my eyes again as realization washes over me.

I ran from someone who needs me. He needs me in his world for it to make sense. I may not understand why my parents haven't gone public with my missing whereabouts. I may not understand how I am to outsmart Gabe. And I certainly don't understand why I feel guilty for running from War.

But I do.

My chest aches and I long for his possessive touch around my wrist.

"I'm sorry," I tell him, a quiver in my voice as I blink my eyes to drive away the tears. "I shouldn't have run."

He mumbles. He's counting. Each scrub back and forth along the smooth marble. Numbers in the hundreds.

"War," I say louder. "It's clean."

He jerks his head over his shoulder and for a moment, his gaze scares me. His normally beautiful eyes have turned dark with mania. With a quick tug, he draws the respirator down and his jaw clenches in an angry fashion. But the look is fleeting. The scrub brush clatters to the floor as he stares up at me.

"I was fucking terrified, Baylee."

Guilt trickles through me and I bite my bottom lip to keep from crying again. His gaze softens as he glances down at my mouth and then back at me again.

"You promised me," he chokes out as he stands. "You promised me you wouldn't leave me."

I let the tears fall again and glance down at my feet. "I'm sorry. I didn't think it through. All I wanted to do was find my parents and figure out why they aren't looking for me."

He lets out a sigh and I look over at him. Dark shadows under his eyes tell me he's exhausted. Because of me.

"What did you step on?" he questions, changing the subject.

I shrug. "I don't know. Glass or metal. Nothing is left and I cleaned it thoroughly."

He groans and his hands begin to tremble. "The metal—" he curses, "—it could infect you. Poison you."

"I had a tetanus shot last year and I poured half the bottle of alcohol on it before bandaging it up. I'll keep it clean."

My words seem to calm him and he relaxes a bit. "We'll talk about this tomorrow. Get some rest, Baylee. I'm going to shower *again* and then go to sleep."

Without another word, he turns and strides down the hallway away from me.

"War," I call out. I hate myself for asking this question but I need to know the answer. "Are you going to punish me for leaving?"

He jerks his head over his shoulder to stare at me, an incredulous look on his face. "No, Bay. I could never hurt you. I'm not like him. When are you going to understand that?"

And with that, he disappears into his bedroom.

I flip off the lights and crawl back into my bed where I cry myself to sleep. And for some reason, I'm crying for him.

For making him do things he can't handle.

Chase me.

Touch me.

Brave the outside world.

Clean my blood.

I cry because despite everything, I'm already starting to care for him and that scares the hell out of me.

I could never hurt you.

Then why do I ache for you, War?

chapter
SEVENTEEN

War

Four days is a long time not to speak to someone living in your home. I mean, we've spoken, but we haven't talked—really talked. Every time I think about the way she left that night, hell bent on going home, I get angry all over again.

I trusted her. I gave her the fucking code to the house for crying out loud. I gave her the chance to spread her wings a little and boy did she fly. She flew right out the goddamned door, nearly into oncoming traffic, and directly into harm's way.

A shudder ripples through me as I recall how truly terrified I was that night. Not only for her safety but for my own as well. I'm not the kind of man who leaves his house. Only in emergencies. And even then, I take every precaution to protect myself. But that night? I couldn't think straight. All that mattered was getting her back home safely.

My mind had zeroed in on her and nothing else mattered.

Nothing.

It wasn't until she was locked back up in my home that anger began to set in. This is the main reason we haven't spoken much in several days. Each time I start to bring it up, I can feel my blood practically boiling. I'll give myself a heart attack if I'm not careful.

The horrifying thought of having surgery—the cracking open of my chest, the tools working beneath the flesh—damn near sends me over the edge.

Luckily, Dad sent some program requirements for his new client from New York and wanted to know if I could come up with some customized programs for them. Of course I could. It's taken all my energy and focus, but I've finally come up with something I'm sure the client will love.

And for the tune of four million dollars, they should love it.

I'm tapping away on my laptop in my office when a soft rapt on the door distracts me.

Dragging my gaze to the doorway, I frown to see Baylee standing there. Not because I don't want to see her but because when she's around, all I can do is stare at her. Angry or not. She's a vision. A piece of art. Something too pretty and too pure for this world.

Today, she's wearing a pair of yoga pants that hug her toned legs and a bright yellow fitted sweater. My gaze travels over her perky breasts all the way down to her bare feet, the right one still bandaged.

I snap my gaze back up to hers. "How's the foot? Did you clean it today?"

Same questions every day.

"Yep," she says with a frown.

"Did your dad reply?"

More of the same daily questions.

Her eyes well with tears and she plops down in the chair in my office. "Yeah. He's being really weird, War."

I clench my jaw together to keep from blabbing the fact I've been in contact with the local police department of where she lived. Stark has reached out a few times after our initial contact, baiting me to come see her. Each message has been left unanswered.

With my palm, I scrub my cheek and sigh. "What'd he say?"

She swipes a tear away and my eyes zone in on the wet part of the back of her hand. It glistens in the light and I become fixated on it, ignoring everything she's saying.

"…and basically that's it."

I blink one, two, three times before lifting my stare to her face. "So he still simply demands you come home or to tell you where you're at? Never divulges anything as to why he hasn't reported your missing whereabouts?"

I'm hoping it was the same reply as it has been for the past few days since I wasn't paying attention to anything other than the soft, wet flesh of her hand.

"Nope. He's leaving me in the dark. His harsh tones though remind me of Gabe. Have you found out anything?" she questions and then looks past me to the screen that's filled with complicated code. "Never mind. I can see you've been busy with something else."

She stands quickly and storms from the room.

With a groan I follow her. Her blonde hair is the only trail she leaves in her haste to make it to the small room I long ago converted to a gym. I stand, filling the doorway, as she picks up two weights and begins rotating, curling them toward her breasts. Once again, I'm drawn to staring at her body. The way the black pants hug her nice ass. So much for being pissed at her.

"When you're done pouting, I have something for you."

She stiffens and throws me a confused look. Her eyebrows are pinched together and though she's mad at me, I can tell she's curious about what I have for her.

Leaving her, I head for my bedroom and retrieve the box from the delivery that came in earlier this morning. I'd gone a little crazy, and for a moment, I hope she won't think I'm a fucking lunatic.

"I'm done pouting." Her amused voice from the doorway warms me and seeing her bright smile has me forgetting all about why I've been upset with her. I've missed her smile.

"Good," I say with a grin, "now close your eyes and don't open them until I say you can."

She arches a questioning brow but I don't budge until both eyes are closed. I saunter over to her and get a closer look at her. Her soft pink lips are slightly parted and I crave to run my finger over her bottom one.

"What do you think it is?" My hot breath, inches from her face startles her and her eyes flutter. "Don't open them."

Her nose scrunches and her brows furrow together as she thinks. "I don't know, makeup? Perfume?"

Maybe I should have bought her something girly instead. I didn't ever consider she'd want something like that. Does she really feel like some abused prisoner? My heart is pounding as I quickly rethink my gift to her.

"No." My tone is gruff, aggravated even.

She frowns, most likely from my mood change, and not the fact I didn't buy her those things but now it's all I can think about. I'm going shopping just as soon as I can for both.

Dragging myself from her alluring presence, I make my way over to the bed and pull open the flaps of the box. Then, I carry it over to her and set it at her feet. Panic washes over me. I hope she likes what I got her.

"Open them."

Her eyes find mine first and they twinkle with excitement. It's in this moment I decide I want to buy her gifts all the time. Every single day.

When her eyes fall to the box, she frowns but reaches inside. She retrieves a pink pair of flip-flops and when her eyes meet mine there are tears in them. "You bought me shoes. Lots of them."

Uncomfortable with her lack of enthusiasm, I shift from one foot to the other. "I thought that maybe…I assumed that after, you know…that you—"

"I love them."

We hold each other's gaze for eighty-six seconds and then she breaks away to try them on. Every single pair. The enthusiasm I assumed wasn't there is in full force as she babbles on with glee. I've never been so captivated by her. So utterly engrossed in everything that is her.

The lingering scent of her body wash.

The animated way she waves her hands in the air when she talks.

The cute way she walks down her imaginary runway and pivots just as a model would.

"Why did you buy me shoes? I mean," she says softly as she approaches, "I can't go anywhere anyway."

I cross my arms over my chest and glance out the window. The window which points to the road she once ran from me on. Suppressing a shudder, I turn my attention back to her.

"The code is still 1200. I never changed it."

She gapes at me, her pouty lips parting and then closing again as if she's trying desperately to formulate words. "B-B-But you were so mad. I betrayed your trust."

I shrug my shoulders. "And I bought you. Let's call it even."

Biting down on her bottom lip, she contemplates my words. The woman can think all day if that means I can stare at her unabashedly. I love watching the way her eyes sparkle with excitement or the way her cheeks turn pink when she is embarrassed. Simply put, she's beautiful.

"Listen," I say, my voice gruff, "I was serious when I said you weren't my prisoner. I want to keep you safe from that asshole and to enjoy your company. Even though we had an agreement that you'd stay if I sent money for your mother, that doesn't mean under duress. If you want to leave, you can go. I'd fucking hate it but would understand."

She shakes her head adamantly. "No, the money is important to Mom. It could get her the lifesaving surgery she needs. My dad may be acting strangely and Gabe may have a hand in that, but I won't jeopardize what you're doing for her in order to get back home to them. Quite frankly, I'm struggling to understand how they haven't ever reported me as missing. I don't think running home will give me that answer. In fact, I worry it could be detrimental to me in the end," she says softly and smiles. "Besides, I kind of like it here. Now that I have shoes of course."

My heart soars when I realize she really isn't going to leave me. At the moment anyway. She's staying by choice which means, even with all my bizarre afflictions, she isn't completely disgusted by me.

"In that case," I tell her with a smirk, "I better buy you more shoes."

"Aren't you going to move your queen?"

She stares down at the board and chews on her lip. The wheels are turning as many different moves flip through her mind. "I don't want to," she says finally and lifts her gaze to mine. Her cheeks tinge pink and she gives me the look—the embarrassed one. I'm beginning to recognize each and every expression on her pretty face. The defiant ones when she's not in the mood for tofu but instead insists on anything with peanut butter in it. The happy ones when she's recalling stories about her past or tales of how she's unbeaten at her school in the high jump. Even the fearful ones when she's deep in thought, haunted by Gabe and all he did to her. My favorite expression, though, is her embarrassed one. Her full bottom lip gets toyed with by her top front teeth. Those gorgeous blue eyes become hooded, almost as if she's trying to hide the expressiveness in them from me. And her nose and cheeks change colors just enough to reveal her shyness. All in all, it's fucking cute.

For two weeks now, our days have been predictable. We spend a good amount of time working together trying to make sense of what's going on back in Oakland. Her dad still demands for her to come home, although less often and there is never any mention of her mom. He's confirmed he's receiving the payments but that's all he'll elaborate on. When we're not focused on that, we hang out. Just as I originally bought her to do. But now, it's becoming less about our negotiation and more about each other. Bottom line is, we have chemistry.

Too bad I can't do anything about it.

So many times I've longed to reach across the chess board and stroke the back of her hand as she makes her move. I've caught my gaze lingering on her smooth, bare legs in the mornings when she's still wearing her gown. And I can't keep my eyes off her ass when she struts around the house in a pair of fitted jeans.

It's her mouth, though, that I dream about day in and day out. The one kiss we shared was an accident and it damn near sent me over the edge but lately, it's all I can think about. I'm too much of a pussy to broach the subject—to see if she'd let me try again. I know she would. I see the mutual glint of need in her eyes matching my own. Problem is, I don't trust myself. I can't guarantee that I won't flip out on her again. This time, I believe it would hurt her feelings more so than the first time. And I don't ever want to hurt her. Ever.

"Let me think," she says softly and moves her pawn back. "War?"

I sit back in my chair and take in her new expression. Worried. Unsure. Something on the tip of her tongue.

"Yeah?"

"This is probably terribly rude but I need to ask."

I swallow down the unease forming in my throat. Honestly, I'm surprised she hasn't asked sooner.

"What did they diagnose you with?"

When I don't answer, she moves her pawn instead of the queen and I'm once again baffled at her strategy. But I don't stick around to question it. With a huff of frustration, I stand and stalk back toward my bedroom. We were having fun. I was focused on her. There wasn't a need to start yanking out my skeletons for dissection.

"War!"

Ignoring her, I stomp into my room and slam the door. I'm not sure what I was expecting but it wasn't for her to sling the door open and charge over to me. When she grabs the back of my T-shirt and yanks it toward her, I freeze.

What the fuck is she doing?

"You can't just run away in the middle of a conversation when you don't like where it's going," she seethes.

My skin erupts into invisible hives that begin to burn and itch but I refrain from clawing at them. For the moment.

"Let me go."

"Not going to happen until you tell me."

I jerk away from her grasp and spin around to face her. I'm sure she's taken aback by my furious glare because she stumbles back a step. Prowling toward her, I take satisfaction in the way she retreats until her back hits the wall. The craving to kiss her again is intense. Slamming both palms to the wall on either side of her head, I dip close to her and inhale her sweet scent.

She licks her lips and my cock thickens with need. My reactions to her are becoming more and more unpredictable. I'm not myself around her and that's a good thing.

"Tell me," she murmurs, her hot breath upon my own lips.

Each breath is ragged and uneven. Nearly impossible to count or predict how many she'll take in a minute.

"I'm dark inside. Ugly. And broken. Ruined. I don't need labels to tell me that," I hiss and lean into her another inch. So badly I want to scoop her into my arms and kiss her like she deserves to be kissed.

"I don't think you're any of those things," she whispers. "In fact, I happen to think you're a good man. Beautiful on the inside and out."

I close my eyes and let her words wash over me. Jesus, I want to taste her again.

"Baylee." Her name is a grunted prayer on my lips. "Will you kiss me again?" My cock twitches and I let my mind go blank. The vortex that is her sucks me in easily and I let it.

"Yes."

At her whispered response, I take my hand from the wall and tentatively run my fingertips along her jaw. Her bright blue eyes blaze with a need that matches my own. She lets out a gasp when I run my thumb along the other side and grip her face in my hand. Those perfect pink lips part open and her eyes flutter closed.

God, she's alluring as hell.

Dipping down, I barely brush my lips against hers. The action sends wild excitement buzzing through me. My brain struggles to grab statistics about mouth-to-mouth germ transferring but I snuff out those thoughts.

She is my focus.

My only thought.

When she lets out a tiny moan, I dart my tongue out and taste her. She's sweeter than the orange juice we had this morning and I want to devour her. To stick my tongue deep into her mouth and run it along every surface just to know her from the inside out. I want to tangle my fingers in her golden locks and hold on to her indefinitely.

But what if I pull to hard?

Would her hair be torn from her scalp?

Would it bleed all over my white carpet?

Stay in the moment, War.

Kiss her. Kiss her. Kiss her.

I try to drive away the maddening thoughts that are now popping around me like gunshots on a battlefield but it's too much. The moment one of her palms touches my cheek, I jerk away from her. My heart is thundering in my chest, my cock is proud and at attention behind my jeans, but my brain is on overdrive.

Twenty billion oral microbes.

Seven hundred or more possible strains of bacteria.

Thirty-four to seventy-two different varieties in each person.

Hers mixing with mine.

The combinations are endless.

Streptococcus mutans. Porphyromonas gingivalis.

Staphylococcus epidermidis, Streptococcus salivarius, and Lactobacillus sp.

Crawling and crawling and crawling all over the inside of her mouth—the same mouth I'd fantasized about tonguing every crevice.

"War," she says in a firm tone that snaps me from my thoughts. "Calm down. Brush your teeth. Shower. Do whatever it is you do and then let's finish our chess game."

My eyes find her concerned ones and I relax, even if only marginally. Focus on something else. Not her mouth. Anything.

"Uh," I grunt and run my fingers through my hair. I tug at it but don't let go. "Why won't you move your queen, Bay? It's the only move." Chess has always been a good focal point when my brain threatens to explode. I can focus on the strategies and become obsessed with moves, not germs and gore.

She starts toward the door but gives me a tender smile. "Because the queen always protects the king." And then she whispers the last part. "Even from himself."

Her strategy makes no sense to me…

And yet, a sense of calm washes over me as she leaves the room.

Turns out, I don't need the shower after all.

Just a little mouthwash and a lot of chess will bring balance back to my world.

I think I just semi-averted a meltdown—a first in my book.

And that was solely because of her.

Baylee.

chapter

EIGHTEEN

Baylee

"This," he grinned and handed me a dainty tennis bracelet, "is for you."

A couple of girls nearby giggled—the excited type of giggle—at Brandon's romantic notion. We'd been going out since last year, when we were juniors, and were very much in love.

"It's so pretty. I love pink," I gushed and batted my lashes at him as he latched it around my wrist. "Thank you, Brandon."

"Our one year anniversary is important."

My cheeks reddened and I glanced around. No teachers were around so I slid my fingers around his neck and drew him forward. Our mouths met and he kissed me sweetly.

"God, Baylee," he groaned after our kiss. "You make it really hard to function at school."

He dragged his backpack into his lap and flashed me a shy smile. Today, he was especially cute because his normally perfectly spiked hair had become messy from the rain we ran through this morning to get from the bus to the school. I liked when he wasn't all perfect and put together.

"I wish we could spend more time together outside of school. You know how crazy my dad is though. He'd be happier if I didn't date until I was thirty!"

We both laughed and he leaned in again for another kiss. Rain drops began pelting us and the giggling girls from earlier were now screeching. We were left all alone in the courtyard.

Brandon seemed to sense this and our kiss became deeper. His backpack fell to the grass and he pulled me into his lap so I was straddling him. It was cold and we were getting soaked but I couldn't get enough of him. I grinded against his erection and he moaned into my mouth.

I had been thinking about sex a lot lately. If Brandon and I could ever get together alone, I'd probably let him have sex with me. I loved him and he loved me. It seemed right.

"Touch me," I murmured against his mouth.

Both of his palms found my breasts through my hoodie and he squeezed. It sent a thrill through my body and I continued grinding against him in order to find relief.

"I want to have sex with you," I blurted out and stared into his blazing, hungry eyes.

"We will one day, babe. I promise," he assured me and then laughed. "But not here on school grounds. I'm working on a baseball scholarship…not expulsion."

I giggled and kissed him again.

"If I got expelled for having sex at school, my dad would kill me. We better save it for another time."

His eyes danced with humor as he swiped a soaked tendril of hair out of my eyes. "I'd never let him kill you. I would steal you away and keep you safe. You're my girl, Baylee Marie. I'm going to make you my wife one day."

Gah, if only those girls could hear my boyfriend now.

I beamed at him. "I love you."

"I love you too, babe."

We kissed until a teacher snapped at us.

Getting detention with my boyfriend was worth kissing him in the rain.

After all, it gave us more time together. Even if we couldn't talk or touch, we were there. Together.

A loud ringing jolts me awake from my dream. The sun has long since risen and I'm curled up on the sofa, a blanket covering me. I'd fallen asleep on the couch last night after too many hours on my laptop. War, of course, couldn't put me to bed but he at least tried to make me more comfortable. I wonder why he didn't just wake me up. A smile plays at my lips when I think about how we'd shamelessly flirted over dinner.

"I'm not that terrible of a kisser, you know," I teased as I took a bite of my spaghetti. "You didn't have to pretend you were having a mental breakdown."

He smirked and raised an eyebrow. "Maybe it wasn't your technique. Maybe it was your breath. I can practically smell your garlic breath from here."

"Hey!" I scoffed and tossed my napkin his way. "I'm a great kisser and I taste like heaven."

His eyes dropped to my mouth and he grew serious. "That you do, Bay. That you do."

My cheeks burned at his comment and I looked past him toward the setting sun.

"You look beautiful tonight. More so than usual," he told me softly.

A smile played at my lips as our eyes met. "I'm wearing a boring white sweater and jeans. Hardly beautiful."

"Women who taste like heaven are usually angels," he told me thoughtfully. "And you, dressed in white, are every bit heaven sent."

His words caused me to melt.

"I can be naughty," I assured him with a wicked grin.

He rolled his eyes. "If your naughty skills are anything like your chess skills, you're still ninety-nine point nine percent angel. A sucky chess playing angel."

"You're an asshole," I groaned but couldn't help but smile.

I liked that he thought I was beautiful.

He watched me like I was the sun in his sky.

I seemed to put him under a spell and to be honest, I loved it.

A sound from War's phone stopped our flirting and he dragged it from his pocket. His smile fell and he started typing away, almost angrily.

"What is it?" I questioned, my brows furrowed in concern.

He lifted his gaze to mine and by the way he clenched his jaw, I knew he was holding something back from me.

"Tell me," I muttered.

With a frown, he leaned back and looked at his screen. "Detective Stark."

I blinked several times at him in confusion. "Who?"

"Rita Stark. Oakland PD. I've been," he said and scrubbed his face with his palm, "in contact with her about your case. Or lack thereof more accurately."

My heart rate quickened. "What do you mean? Why aren't you telling me everything, War?"

"I wanted to have more information before I told you. And now I do."

I gaped at him like he was a moron for stopping. He quickly continued.

"A couple of weeks back, I contacted her and asked her why someone wouldn't report their child missing."

"And?"

"She thought I was Brandon."

I froze at his mention of my boyfriend. With War it was easy to suspend reality and play house in his castle on the ocean. But times like these, when my past collided with the present, I had a hard time merging the two worlds.

"He's okay?"

War nodded and revealed what he knew. About how Brandon had come to see her. Nobody believed *him. My parents had withdrawn me from school. How Stark thought it was all some elaborate story from a sad boy who hated the fact his girlfriend was being homeschooled.*

"So why didn't you tell me all of that, War? What the hell is going on?" My voice had risen several octaves and I stood from the table.

He shrugged and let out a huff. "Because it wouldn't do anything, Baylee. We knew something was fishy. Now, though, things have gone from fishy to unbelievable."

"What happened?"

"Stark replied. Said Brandon's parents filed a missing person report on their son. He just vanished. Stark is certain he's gone off the grid to look for you. She doesn't think he was taken or anything. But she's asked about my identity. And blatantly asked if I had you in my possession."

My flesh grew cold on my cheeks and my jaw hung slightly open. "What did you say?"

"I told her Gabe's name. I said she needed to open an investigation in regards to him and some illegal activities he'd been involved in," he said and turned his phone to me. "I told her to open her eyes and look into sex trafficking rings in California. Now she seems to be concerned about your whereabouts."

I took the phone from him and read all their emails.

"Do you think she'll talk to Dad and Mom? I just can't believe they'd go on with life as if I never existed." Hot tears formed in my eyes and spilled over.

His gaze fell to my wet cheeks and he frowned. "I don't know. Obviously she was being vague to me in her messages and is probably doing everything in her power to find out who's sending those messages to her. Of course it'll never lead back here. You're safe with me."

"How can we find out what she does? She's not going to just come out and tell you her plan, who she's going to question, or anything. I feel so helpless, War!"

He reached for me, briefly, but jerked his hand back as if he remembered he wasn't capable of comforting me. "You're not helpless. You have me and I am quite resourceful. Your parents are spending the money I'm sending. Every dime is being withdrawn. I've been researching every lead to find out what's going on. We'll figure it out, beautiful. Just like I promised."

My anxiety lessened at his words. "And then what? After we figure it all out? After we discover my parents don't give a shit about me. Huh?"

His eyes meet mine and he pins me with a serious stare. "I'll take care of you no matter what because I do give a shit about you. You're mine, Bay."

I'd spent the rest of the night on the computer next to War on the couch. Both of us tapping and clicking our way through the web in search of answers and only coming up with more questions.

My thoughts return to our kiss from earlier in the day yesterday. It started out so carnal and needy. For a moment, he'd shoved away his demons to kiss me. While it only lasted seconds, it was beautiful and perfect.

But it's my dream last night about Brandon that still hangs thick in the air. After I discovered he was missing and had been searching for me, I'd thought a lot about him. What happens if this detective finds Gabe and hauls him off to jail? Will Brandon come back home? Will I go back home? Do my parents even want me? Will things go back to normal?

Images of War sitting alone in this house with nobody to talk to. Nobody to eat with. Nobody to play chess with. It's all too much. He's grown on me too much to abandon him and run back home. Even if Gabe went to prison and all went back to normal, I don't think I could ever leave War on his own again.

It would crush him.

The doorbell rings again and I leap from the couch ignoring my stiff muscles. The memory of our kiss and my lingering dream of Brandon are momentarily put on hold as I make my way to the door. Hobbling over to the door, I question who could be here at this ungodly hour. Maybe another delivery of shoes. The notion has me reaching for the doorknob with a smile on my face.

But as I reach for it, a deep voice startles me.

"Don't answer it."

I turn and regard a sleepy War with furrowed brows. "Why not? It's probably just a delivery."

He growls and storms over to me. "Because," he hisses, "what if it's him? Did you even look? I have the alarm on for a reason, Bay. To protect you. The deliverymen always leave the packages on my doorstep per my instructions. Whoever is here is not delivering anything to me."

Fear of Gabe assaults me and my knees buckle.

I could have just opened the door to him. I'd allowed myself to grow comfortable in War's home and forgotten what was truly at stake had that man found me again. He could have snatched me up and taken me to his stupid cabin before I even knew what hit me.

I'm frozen as memories assault me.

Frozen cucumbers.

Butt plugs.

His large fingers probing and stretching every hole in my body.

A shudder wracks through me. Mom would be screwed and I'd live the rest of my life getting tortured by that sadistic monster.

No thank you.

"I'm sorry," I tell him with tears in my eyes. "I didn't think."

He relaxes and I can see that he itches to comfort me in some way. Problem is, with War, there is no way. Only words, no embraces. "It's okay. Go get dressed. I'll figure out who it is."

Hurrying away from the door, I make my way into my room. I locate a pair of jeans and T-shirt and dress in record speed. By the time I finish, I can hear raised voices in the other room.

Oh, God.

He's here.

Snatching up a tall, metal candleholder from the bedside, I raise it and creep out of the room prepared to crack it over his head. War comes into view first, his features contorted into an angry scowl. I hold a finger to my lips to warn him. His face pales and he raises a hand.

"Bay, no!"

Charging from around the corner, I ready myself to kill Gabe. I'm furious for the horrors he put me through and am eager to break his skull. Then, this can all be over. I'm about to swing the candlestick when War snatches it from my grip and rips it away from me.

The man in the foyer is *not* Gabe.

He turns to regard me with a frown and I can see that this man is older and has greying hair mixed in with his dark hair. The man is almost an exact image of War.

"Baylee, this is my dad, Loveland McPherson." War's jaw is clenched in frustration as he sets the candlestick down on the entryway table.

I blink at the older man several times before responding. "I'm Baylee Winston, Mr. McPherson."

My words seem to drag the man out of his stupor and he reaches a hand out for me. "Call me Land. And I must say, I've never known War to have anyone over before. Ever. Are you two…" he trails off as if searching for the right words, "together?"

Glancing at War, I plead with my eyes for him to handle the explanation.

He nods and clears his throat. "Dad, Baylee is my, uh, girlfriend."

Land frowns at me before he flicks his gaze over to War. "And, son, how *old* is your girlfriend?"

chapter
NINETEEN

War

Fuck.

I didn't expect Dad to show up for one of his random visits. I mean, I know it had been awhile since he'd last visited, so I knew I was due for another. But the timing is horrible. He won't understand about Baylee.

Her bottom lip trembles and I can almost feel her heartbeat in my ears. Thump, thump, thumping. I crave to hold her body that still quivers from the fear of thinking Gabe was here. The man is a fucking monster. I'm not sure I even want to know what all he's done to her. It might make me crazier than I already am. Or homicidal.

"She's still in high school."

I wince and then count the seconds until he explodes. With Dad, it's coming.

One, two, three, four…

"ARE YOU KIDDING ME RIGHT NOW, WARREN THOMAS MCPHERSON?"

In a natural move, I stand between her and him. My dad wouldn't hurt her. Ever. But I still don't like him being near her while he's pissed. She's had enough bullshit lately to have to deal with my dad's tantrum too.

"Dad, listen—"

"No! You listen to me, son! This is un—"

"I'm here on my own free will!" Baylee shouts over us. "Land, I'm okay. I promise. And we haven't had sex if that's what you're worrying about. I'm here to keep War company."

Dad's furious body that ripples with rage relaxes. "What about your parents? Do they know you're here?"

She lifts her chin bravely. "I'm eighteen and I have been in contact with my dad. He knows I'm with your son. I promise, I'm not War's prisoner. He's helping me, too."

Dad flits his gaze from her to me. "How much did you pay her?"

"Can we talk about this later?" I question through gritted teeth.

He nods and I heave out a breath of relieved air. Turning around to face Baylee, I give her a smile. "Why don't you go and shower. I'll make you some breakfast."

She seems hesitant to leave but finally turns and bounces off toward her room. I stare at her perfect ass until she disappears around the corner.

"Tell me all of it. Now, Warren," Dad hisses out.

I sigh and motion for him to follow me. "I'm going to cook breakfast. We'll talk in the kitchen."

While I start pulling things out of the refrigerator, Dad respects my needs by spending a good ten minutes at the sink washing up past his elbows. It was a battle in the beginning but after passing out on several different occasions as he tested my will on the matter, he'd finally bent to my needs. And I don't even have to look at him to know he's left his shoes by the door as well and is donning blue surgical booties.

"Start talking, Son."

I begin chopping vegetables to make vegan omelets and sigh. "I'm lonely, Dad."

"I know this," he says softly and begins pulling glasses out to fill with orange juice. "But you've been lonely since Lilah. You haven't had one single female companion since her in fact. I'm not necessarily shocked that you've clearly paid a woman to entertain you but what I'm fuming about is her age. So I will ask you once again to tell me all of it."

My dad and I have always been close but when Mom died, we knew we only had each other after that. He expects the truth from me and I've never had a reason to lie. Now included.

"I stumbled across a site online. It seemed professional and legit. And it was fucking expensive," I say with a grumble. "I'd called ahead and spoke with the coordinator. They changed their event to a silent auction to accommodate my needs and even agreed to keep my participation anonymous. From the car, I watched them all prance across stage. But one stood out."

I've stopped chopping and I fixate on a small square tile on the backsplash. There are seven hundred and forty-six tiles on the backsplash. I've counted them. Five hundred and twelve are pure white and two hundred and thirty-two are slightly marred. And two have cracks near the sink. My gaze travels over to the two cracked ones. Perfect aside from the fissure that runs right down the middle. Most days, I crave to get a Dremel tool and grind them out of the backsplash. But other days, I focus on the imperfect ones as a reminder. Maybe I can find another person, like me, and we can exist in a sea of perfection—broken but still beautiful and necessary.

"Son…"

I blink and continue. "She counted her steps across the stage. Seventeen steps, Dad. Her mouth moved as she counted and I became fixated on her. For a moment, I'd hoped she'd been like me. Different. When the man delivered her to my car and she spoke, I knew I wasn't going to let her go."

"Warren, I don't think this sounds legal. There's more to this isn't there? What did you pay for her?"

I groan and avoid his eye contact. "Five million."

"Jesus fucking Christ, son!" he hisses. "What were you thinking?"

"I wasn't. I was just tired of being alone."

"So, you paid a teenager five million dollars to be your companion? Why is she still here?"

"Well, it's more complicated than that, Dad. I didn't understand what I was doing when I bought her. It was some sort of sex ring. I swear I didn't know," I tell him, shame causing my voice to go husky.

"Look at me."

I drag my gaze to his and frown. "I bought her from some asshole who did sadistic shit to her. Stuff that has twisted her head up. Evil bastard. And the shit he did to her against her will…" I trail off and shudder. "So incredibly sick."

"So you know all of this and you still kept her?"

"I'm fucking lonely!" I roar and slam the knife down on the countertop. "I wanted to die. Again. Those thoughts were swarming me, like they often do. I was drowning in them. But then Baylee came along. She makes me forget, Dad. I actually *want* to touch her."

My dad, after having had dealt with my issues for over a decade now, softens and his brows furrow together. "You want to touch her?"

I nod and smile sheepishly. "I kissed her. Twice."

His eyes widen and his brows fly to his hairline. "You kissed her? So you actually touched someone on your own free will? You didn't force her did you?"

"No, I didn't. In fact, she seemed upset the first time when I pulled away and had a fucking meltdown. I had to take a long ass shower to wash her off me. But…"

Dad is no longer angry. He seems hopeful.

"But then, as soon as I came back to her, I wanted her again. She's addicting. I want to hear her voice, see her smiles, and bask in her warmth. For the past few weeks, I've wondered if I have a chance at healing my fucked up head. That maybe she is my answer."

He nods thoughtfully. "If you have faith that she can, then it's most certainly possible. Promise me one thing though, War. Promise me you'll respect her boundaries and wishes. You're a good man and I don't want this thing weighing on your conscience or sending my only son to jail. You're not like the man who hurt her. You're my son and we've got morals."

I go back to chopping when he speaks again.

"So she's a millionaire at eighteen," he says, astonished.

"Well, not exactly."

He grunts. "But you just said—"

"Gabe has the money. The man I bought her from."

Risking a glance at my dad, my shoulders slump at his furious stare. "After all those things he did and…"

I huff. "I know. But what am I supposed to do about it?"

"I don't know, call the goddamned cops on him!"

"Dad, it's not that easy!" I snap and immediately feel guilty for yelling at him. "Besides," I soften my tone, "I'm in contact with a detective in Oakland. I've been giving her information that won't lead back to me in hopes they'll catch Gabe. Her parents never filed a missing person's report. Something is going on and I'm not about to send her back to the lion's den where that asshole will come back for her. She's safe here. Besides, we worked out another deal."

He waits expectantly.

"I've been sending money to help her mom. She's sick."

A groan rumbles from his chest and he turns away from me. His gaze falls to the windows that overlook the Pacific Ocean. I know he's thinking about Mom. Our thoughts always drag back to her. She's the reason I am who I am today.

"So you're dumping more money just to keep this girl? You do understand you'll be broke and heartbroken before it's all said and done." His voice cracks and I wish I could hug him. I've not been able to do that since I was a teenager.

"What else can I do? I was desperate. With Baylee, life is different. Less lonely. I know you may not understand all my reasoning but trust that I'll be smart. I'm not going to hurt her but I'm also not going to let her go. I can't. Not now."

I hear someone clear their throat from behind me. "Am I interrupting?"

Whipping around, I smile at her. She's freshly showered, her blonde hair pulled into a messy wet bun on top of her head. The dark jeans she's wearing hug her figure and the baby blue sweater does nothing to hide her gorgeous tits. My cock reacts to seeing her, and I quickly turn back to my task of cooking to hide my erection. "No, we were just talking about how I came to acquire you."

"You told him?" she questions as if she's shocked.

My heart speeds up to see her from the corner of my eye beginning her hand washing ritual. She doesn't have to count. I'll count for her. But after today, neither of us will have to. Another gift for her should arrive at some point this afternoon. I ordered it not long after she arrived but it was being custom made to my specifications.

"Why wouldn't I tell him?" I say with a chuckle. "He's my father. I tell him everything. Didn't you tell your dad everything?"

Dad leans against the counter and watches our exchange with interest.

"Well," she says slowly and starts to turn off the water, "not everything."

Her cheeks blaze red with embarrassment and I laugh. But when she turns off the sink, my laughter dies in my throat.

"Not done. Forty-eight more seconds," I bark out a little more harshly than I intended. Dad grumbles behind me but doesn't say any more on the subject.

The water turns back on and she continues to scrub her hands. "Now?"

I start frying the vegan omelets and sigh. "Not yet."

The seconds pass by but I don't tell her when the time is up. A few more moments of washing never hurt anyone.

"Baylee," Dad says in a soft voice. "I'm sorry for what happened to you. You're a victim. And if you decide you want to leave, you call me. I'll drive you home myself."

She shuts off the water this time and I don't stop her. "I'm okay right now. Thank you, Mr. McPherson."

"Please, call me Land. You're strong and you're brave. Thank you for attempting to help my son, no matter what your motives are for doing it. That means the entire world to me and I'll do whatever I can to return that favor."

In a surprising move, she hurries over to him and throws herself into his arms. He hugs her tight—*like I wish I could*—and strokes her back in a way that always comforted me as a child. I'm jealous of both of them. That they can hold each other and I can't hold either of them.

He murmurs whispered assurances and I finish the food up, careful to make each omelet the same size with equal portions of vegetables and tofu in them. Once I've added some sliced bananas to the side, I carry the plates to the table. She finally breaks away from his embrace and flashes me a shy smile.

"So tell me about yourself, Baylee. If you're someone special to my son, then you're someone special to me," Dad says after we settle at the table and begin eating.

She sighs and her eyes focus past him at the ocean as if she's recalling happy memories. "I run track and am pretty good at it. My parents Tony and Lynn are good to me, and we live in a modest home in Oakland. I plan on going to Berkley next fall. Well, I *did* plan to go there."

My father and I both frown. Guilt slices through me and I stuff another bite into my mouth as she continues.

"I love to read. Swimming is something I enjoy, especially in the ocean. Um, that's all I guess."

"Did you know War used to surf?"

Her eyes widen in surprise and she darts her gaze over to me. I grunt my confirmation and she smiles.

"I didn't know that. I don't know much about your son, I'm afraid. I mean," she says with hesitation, "besides the obvious. He doesn't tell me anything."

Dad glances at me, sadness and fatigue marring his features. "There's a lot to my boy. His sickness plagues him but he's still in there. I see him fighting to the surface sometimes. I'm glad that you're able to break through to him some."

"I'm right here," I complain and stab at a banana. "She's not my shrink."

He frowns and I wince. I shouldn't have said that. My father has only tried to help me ever since I lost my shit. It's not his fault I'm the way I am. He's only done everything he can to provide for me, accommodate my issues, and love me enough for two parents.

"What do you want to do when you, um," Dad says with a grunt, "grow up?"

I groan at his word choice but she doesn't seem to be affected.

"If you mean after high school," she says with a grin, "then I'd hoped to go to school on a track scholarship. I was always intrigued with medicine because of my mom. But now…"

I lift my gaze and meet her compassionate one.

"Now I'd like to get into psychology."

Her words are genuine and not meant to cut me. She's curious about my condition and it has sparked a desire to learn more. I should feel irritated that yet another person wants inside of my black brain.

But with Baylee?

I want her there.

"Have you been down to the ocean yet?" Dad asks as he stands and carries his plate to the sink.

She shakes her head. "It's the middle of winter. The water's probably cold…" she trails off, her sadness not letting her finish the argument.

He turns to me but speaks to her. "Nonsense. It's almost seventy degrees today. Sure, the water will be a little chilly but you'd do well to get some sunshine. If it's okay with you," he says and his eyes meet mine, "I'd like to take her for a walk along the beach."

"Dad, I don't know if—"

"Really? I would love that. May I, War?" Her pretty blue eyes glitter with an excitement I've yet to witness. She's beautiful. And so deserving. How could I ever tell her no?

But the sand.

The salt from the water.

The wind blowing debris all around her, into her mouth and hair.

"Uh," I start and pinch the bridge of my nose.

She could bathe after.

Imagine how cute her nose would be with a little pink on the tip from the sun.

And she'd smell like memories that aren't tainted.

"Of course, Bay. I'll clean up while you two enjoy yourselves. But I can't promise I won't go fucking nuts if you track sand into my house. In fact, I'll have a broom waiting for you on the front porch. Make sure you hose off, too."

Her delighted squeal as she rises from her chair makes it all worth it and I find myself grinning.

chapter
TWENTY

Baylee

I can't believe he let me out of the house, especially after my running away attempt. I'm nervous, fearing that Gabe could be lurking anywhere, but with Land within reach, I'm comforted. He makes me feel safe, like my dad always did.

"My son's a good man, you know."

Our feet squeak in the white sand as we trudge toward the crashing waves. I'd changed into a summer dress that billows in the wind and I realize this is the freest I've felt in weeks. I owe Land for that.

"Yeah," I say, probably not as convincing as he likes.

"There's a reason for the way he is, Baylee. And he's been," he chokes out, "so lonely for so long."

Tears well in my eyes. Despite having been stolen by Gabe and then sold to War, things feel different here. War doesn't hurt me. The only times my feelings get hurt are when I want him to touch me and he won't.

Well, he can't.

His mind won't allow him to.

But I don't miss the unmasked desire. Desire that ignites a flame inside of me. Shame courses over me as I consider what Mom and Dad would think about my sexual infatuation with a man I was sold to. What they would think of how I crave to make normal love with him.

And Brandon?

The boy I loved with my whole heart?

He's becoming more of a distant memory rather than a reality of someone I'll ever be with.

"It's pretty here," I say with a sigh, hoping to change the subject. Trotting off ahead of him, I grab the hem of my dress and run into the sudsy surf. The water is like ice but I welcome the way it envelops my ankles. Feeling braver, I wade out to my knees.

"Shit," Land curses, "that's cold!"

I laugh and turn to see him tip toeing toward me. "Big baby," I tease.

His chuckle warms me and he wraps an arm around me. Land is affectionate and it slices my heart thinking about how he'll never have that with his son again. I lean into his hug and let him hold me for a while.

"He had a girlfriend once," he says slowly, almost wistfully. "Of course, I didn't care too much for her. Lilah was rough around the edges. I suppose it wasn't her fault. Her dad was a damn idiot, but still. It grated on my nerves that they were together. Warren had potential. He was extremely smart and technical. But around her, he sort of walked around with hearts in his eyes."

I try to imagine a younger War. A War who was in love with a girl from the wrong side of the tracks.

"At the time, I'd been selfish. Tried to subtly push him in other directions—directions that she could be no part of. My Paula was not impressed with my actions. She'd reminded me of a time we'd been young, dumb, and in love."

"She sounds like a lovely lady. You speak fondly of her."

His grip around my waist tightens and his voice becomes hoarse as if he might cry. "She got pregnant, my Paula. At forty-four years of age. It was a miracle and a blessing."

I smile at his words.

But then he goes on to tell a horrifying story that roils my breakfast in my belly. A story that paints a vivid image of how War became the man he is today. The story of the loss of his pregnant wife causes Land to choke on his emotion.

A huge wave crashes toward us and if Land hadn't have gripped on to me at the right time, it would have knocked me over. My dress, now wet, clings to my thighs and I shiver.

"Come on," Land says gruffly and guides me out of the water and onto the warm sand. Together we sit and stretch our legs in the sun.

"What did you have?" I shouldn't ask but I'm curious.

He swallows and doesn't speak for a few moments. "A little girl. Constance was her name."

Was.

Tears brim in my eyes and I drop my gaze to my toes that are dusted with white sand and still dripping with ocean water.

A tear rolls out and I sniffle. He seems to sense my sadness for him and his wife because he pulls me against him again in a side hug. I like Land and am grateful for his presence.

"Poor War. My boy, my sweet boy."

His words are hollow and sad as he replays scenes so horrific involving War that I'm not sure I'll ever get them out of my brain. I try to quiet my sobs after hearing the details but they won't quit.

"After…after we lost them," he chokes out finally, the worst part of his words over, and I reach for his hand to grip it. "I lost War too. Not like I'd lost them but he'd become a shell of himself. And then, he turned into this person I was unsure how to help."

Something tells me he doesn't tell this story often—if at all. We both grow silent aside from our sniffling.

"Why couldn't the doctors help him?" My question is almost a whisper getting lost in the wind. I shiver and he hugs me tighter, rubbing his arm up and down my bicep that's covered in goosebumps.

"They tried. Believe me, they tried. But my son," he says with a teary chuckle, "is a stubborn one."

A smile plays at my lips. That he is. "I'm familiar," I tease.

"He spent five weeks in the psych ward after the accident, his obsessions grew and grew despite the constant psychiatric evaluations and therapies. The psychiatrist explained to me that he had PTSD, anxiety, depression, and OCD issues among other new problems including a delusional disorder. He seemed miserable there, so finally, I took him home where we struggled for months trying to learn how to cope. Together. Eventually, when his obsessiveness over blood and germs became too much, I'd asked if he'd feel more comfortable in his own place. A place where he could control the environment. I'd bought him this house in an effort to make him feel close to his mother and to give himself space. As time went on, I became angry at him for his behavior—as if he had some way to change it. We fought but eventually I decided having my son was more important than trying to make him heal when he wasn't ready."

I turn my head over my shoulder and look back up at the house. A dark shadow stands at the window.

War.

That poor, beautiful, tortured soul.

"What about his girlfriend?"

He groans. "Lilah? She only made things worse. Out of desperation for him to return to his normal self and either reconnect or break up with her, I'd invited her over while he was staying with me. I'd already learned to respect his no touching rules, but she'd barged in and had thrown herself at him. What she didn't know or understand was that War was no longer the boy she knew. When he pushed her away and roared at her to not touch him, she burst into tears and spewed nasty words at him that don't need repeating. I ended up dragging her out of my home and that was the last we'd seen of her. War tells me she's married now with three kids."

Turning back to look at the ocean, I sigh. "I feel so bad for him. For you. I'm so sorry. You both must have been so devastated."

He climbs to his feet and then tugs me up too. We embrace and I bury my face into the warmth of his chest. I wish I could do more to help them.

"Come on," he says finally, "let's get you back inside before you freeze. Besides, War looks like he's about three seconds from breaking from his cage to come fetch you himself. That boy likes you."

The fondness that he speaks of his son with warms me. It's easy to forget my problems after hearing Land's story.

"What am I going to do?" I ask as we walk to the house. "I can't stay here forever. Once my mom gets the help she needs, I'll need to leave to be with her. Or worse yet, if Gabe figures out where War lives, he'll come for me. Either way, War will be hurt."

Land remains calm for a short while. "Just give him a chance to love you. Even if it is only for a short while. Then, when it comes time for you to leave on your own free will, I will be here for him to pick up the pieces once again. He deserves a sliver of, albeit brief, happiness in his dark world. And you're just the right person to give him that."

"What happens if my choice is taken from me? If Gabe finds me?" I shiver as I remember the terror of being chased in his woods and the things he did to me after.

"War and I will protect you. I swear it on every penny I own in this world."

A beeping wakes me up and I stretch. It's been over a week and a half since Land came to visit and my feelings for War have intensified. I can no longer hardly keep my hands to myself. On more than one occasion, I've had to physically refrain from touching him. After learning about what happened to his mother and sister, I crave to comfort him. To understand him. Land had given me insight into the issues that plagued War.

PTSD.

Depression.

Anxiety.

OCD.

A delusional disorder.

I've been a witness to his issues for over a month now. When I'm not trying to contact my dad, I'm researching all of his conditions until the late hours of the night. I want to understand him. I need to fix him.

Now that I'm getting to know him well, I watch for his non-verbal cues to better understand what he won't tell me. Sometimes I ask him to tell me stories of his childhood or the beach—times I knew he'd been happier. We've played chess every night, and every day we laugh until it hurts. He's funny, flirty, and incredibly good looking. I'm completely crushing over this flawed man.

And I know the feeling is mutual.

The intense desire he feels for me is evident every time our eyes meet and it thrills me to no end knowing he wants me. I just wish there was a way we could break through his mental barrier so it could happen.

Dad went silent which has upset me. No more replies. No more scathing demands for me to come home. Nothing. Despite my attempts to reach out to him or Mom, I'm met with silence. Thankfully, as promised, War has continued to wire money to them each day. Dad may have his reasons for cutting off contact with me but Mom deserves all the help she can get. And I know my parents, my father would die if anything ever happened to her. He will do everything in his power to save her.

I push the button on my watch to silence the beeping and can't help the smile that plays at my lips. After that day Land took me to the beach, War surprised me with a watch. He'd told me he wanted rose gold because it reminded him of me—a sweet notion in itself—but then decided it should be bold, pink, and waterproof. He revealed that it fit me better because I was brave and indestructible. A shiver runs through me again at the memory of his sweet words.

"Bay," he says softly and enters my bedroom, interrupting my thoughts that are all over the place this morning. "I have something I want to give you."

I sit up in bed and push the hair out of my eyes. His gaze falls to the T-shirt I'd slept in for a moment before he smiles at me.

"I have fresh coffee waiting for you at your spot," he assures in a playful tone that has me crawling out of bed after him. His eyes flicker with a hunger that can frequently be seen in his stare. I walk past him, inhaling his fresh, manly scent on the way to the sofa that has a great view of the ocean.

"What's this?" I ask, seeing a black hatbox sitting on the table. It's tied with a pretty, hot pink ribbon. I sit down on the sofa and give him a confused look.

He smiles, almost as if he's embarrassed, and sits surprisingly close to me. "I got you a gift."

"You don't have to buy me anything," I chide but can't help the excitement bubbling to the surface.

"Well, in that case, I suppose I'll return it—"

"Not so fast, mister!" I say with a laugh and playfully swat at him.

He beams at me and I adore the twinkle in his eyes.

Turning, unwillingly, from his handsome face, I grab hold of the ribbon and tug. After I lift the lid, I gasp.

"You hate it."

Ignoring his words, I lift the pair of pink Nike's from the box and stare at them. Underneath the shoes are some running shorts and a sports bra.

"What is all this?" My voice is breathless and I don't let go of the tennis shoes.

"I thought perhaps you'd enjoy running along the beach for exercise. You know, since it means so much to you. From my perspective, I can watch you all the way to the restaurant, a mile to the left, and the big dock about a mile to the right. It'd be a great length to—"

Without thinking, I launch myself at him. I'm thrilled and wrap my arms around him in a gracious hug. It isn't until a few heartbeats later that I realize what I've done. Tearing from him, I stand and look down at him.

"I'm so sorry! Oh my God!" I let out a ragged breath of air upon the realization that I touched him in ways he'd flip out over.

His jaw clenches and his hands fist at his sides. The internal battle that wages in his head is in full force. I have to do something.

"Warren, look at me."

Eyes remain fixed on the coffee table and he doesn't respond.

Doing the only thing I can think of, I grab the hem of my shirt and tug it from my body. My tiny scrap of black panties are the only thing keeping me from being completely nude.

"Warren, look at me."

It takes everything in him to drag his gaze to my body but when he does, the relaxing of his muscles is almost instant. His hands are no longer in fists and he rakes them through his chocolate-colored hair in a way that makes me think he's controlling himself from touching me.

"Follow me," I instruct.

He blinks a couple of times but stands on shaky legs.

"I won't touch you but you need to shower so you'll feel better. Come on."

I walk off toward his bedroom and am thankful to hear him padding behind me. Once I make it to his bathroom, I push my panties down and start the shower. His shower is a nice walk-in, tiled shower with plenty of space for the two of us. When steam starts to fill the bathroom, I turn to see his hulking frame taking up the doorway.

"Take off your clothes, Warren. I'm not going to hurt you."

He swallows but heeds my direction. With a quick grip of the bottom of his shirt, he tugs it off his body and up over his head in one swift movement. I chew on my lip when his muscular chest is bared to me. What I wouldn't do to touch that chest.

"I'll be waiting," I say, a hint of sauciness in my voice, and step into the warm spray.

My hope is that he won't leave me hanging. I want him in more ways than I should. And helping him is my priority.

"I used to be able to run a mile in six minutes. Do you think I can beat that with those shoes? They look awfully fast." My hope is to distract him with numbers. It must work because he steps into the shower and my mouth hangs open. The man's body is a beautiful sight to behold. His height combined with his lean physique is a turn on, and my pelvis begins to ache with need.

"I think you could beat that time. Easily." His response is more than I could have expected and I sigh in relief.

I grab the bar of soap and lather up my body in a slow, teasing way. His eyes never leave where my hand travels. It's as if he's fixated on what it'll do next.

"Your turn." I hold out the bar by one end and he carefully takes it from me.

With the same level of excitement, I watch him cleanse himself. His cock, thick and long, points at me as if to accuse me for being some seductress.

"Why are we showering together?" he questions as he sets the bar down on the ledge.

I pout at his words, wondering if maybe he doesn't feel the same desire for me as I do for him. "I thought that maybe…"

His dark brow raises in an amused way that has heat creeping over my flesh.

"Since this is a safe place for you," I try again, "that maybe I could touch you or you could touch me. We're clean."

Dark blue eyes find mine and hope flickers in them. My body craves to climb up his firm chest and sink myself on his hardened cock but I know better. Instead, I wait for his next move.

War

She watches me with narrowed eyes, the same competitive look she gives me when we play chess. In her eyes, she's calculated all of the moves and she's certain she will win. But for me, I've counted thousands of other variations. Move upon move upon move of how things could and should go.

This time, she might win.

Chess may be my game that I dominate.

But this?

This is clearly her territory.

My heart thumps in my chest as I contemplate whether I have the strength to do what she wants. Is it really that simple?

Suds run down her pert tits and my cock feels like it may explode with a long overdue release. I want to do so many things to her but I don't know that I can.

"Can I touch you? All you have to do is tell me to stop and I'll let go, War. Trust me."

Her smile is kind but her eyes are hungry. I do trust her. Problem is, I don't trust myself. What if I push her away from me in a moment of mental breakdown? Would she crack her head on the tile? Would blood run down and mix with the water at our feet?

I clamp my eyes closed.

I can't do this.

What if—

"Warren, look at me."

It's almost painful having to open my eyes, but I do. Staring back at me is the most decadent woman on this earth.

"Let me feel you," she says firmly and my dick twitches at her words.

Her arm stretches for me and I flinch when her fingertips tickle the flesh over my heart. Our eyes meet and I nod. She's right, I do want her to touch me. It feels safe in here. When they start to move down, I groan. My dick bobs up and down as if it begs to be caressed next. But she ignores my eager cock and pokes a finger into my belly button. Her smile is wicked and I chuckle.

"Okay so far?" she purrs.

That voice, low and seductive kills me.

"More than okay."

Her eyes shine with pride and her other hand begins to explore me. I should be obsessing over all sorts of chaos that normally plagues me but all I can think about is each cell in my body coming alive at her tender touch.

She revives dead parts of me.

She's the sun, water, and earth. And I'm a seed that has hope to grow into something strong and beautiful. Because of her.

One of her hands slides up my shoulder and cups the side of my neck. Her eyes darken and her other hand moves purposefully downwards.

"Jesus, Baylee," I say with a growl.

A choked gasp is the only sound I make as she softly grips my erection. Bliss explodes from where her small fingers touch me there. I'd expected the crawling, itchy sensation to overtake me at any second. The burning and the flood of awful thoughts.

But they never come. All of my focus is on the millions of nerve endings in my shaft all eager for her to stroke me to heaven.

"My God," I hiss out when she begins moving up and down along my length. My eyes start to close but I force them back open. Right now, I'm safe. With her. If I close my eyes, the demons will suck me under and it will all be ruined.

"Does that feel good? Am I doing it okay?"

I grit my teeth and nod at her. Every other stroke, her fingernails graze my testicles and I nearly lose it.

"I won't last long. It's been so long and—"

"Shhh," she murmurs and pulls her hand from my neck so she can knead her breast with it. "Come for me, Warren. I want you to let go and feel how much I want you."

Her thumb and finger pinch her pebbled pink nipple and I groan. So close. The sight arouses me even further, like nothing I've ever seen before, and I can't control myself any longer. A burn deep in my lower abdomen seizes me and I come without warning.

"Baylee!" I snarl out, but never take my gaze from hers.

She intensifies her actions as I throb out my release. It splatters her soapy belly before running down toward the drain. When I'm no longer twitching, she slides her hand off and sets to cleaning herself off. As if she knew I'd lose my shit about having my cum all over her.

What she doesn't know is that a fire has begun to burn inside of me.

Seeing my cum spurting all over her body awoke some carnal part of me.

A part that needs to possess and take what's mine.

Baylee *is* mine.

But can I do it? Can I actually make love to her?

"I want to touch you," I mutter. I wonder if the words were even spoken aloud. My gaze falls to her breasts, not because they're beautiful because they are, but I can't look at her. What if I fail? What if I pussy out and can't offer her the same pleasure in return?

Her even, melodic breathing calms me and I count five of her breaths before I have the courage to look back up at her.

"Is that okay?"

Pink, perfect lips turn up in a sweet smile and it spurs me on. I'll push through whatever mental barriers I can in order to have her. I will do whatever it takes. I can do this.

"More than okay."

I push a palm against the tile beside her and lean in. She gasps at my proximity but doesn't move.

"Spread your legs," I instruct with false bravado. I want to behave like a normal man, not some scared as hell boy. "I don't know if I can do this but I really want to fucking try."

She flashes me a naughty grin and does as she's told. Then, she gathers her half wet hair up in her fingers and piles it on top of her head. My girl is smart. She's keeping her fingers occupied so she doesn't accidentally touch me and ruin the moment.

Leaning in close to her, hovering just above her mouth, I make my move. With a shaking, unsteady hand, I lower it to cup her pussy. She flinches from my touch and lets out a tiny, pleased sigh.

"Want me to touch you?"

She nods and chews on her bottom pink lip. It drives me wild and my cock is already thickening again, ready to play once more. Slipping my finger between the lips of her sex, I locate her throbbing clit and massage her. It's been ages since I touched a girl—Lilah had been the last—so it takes a minute to figure out the right pattern.

"Oh, God," she whimpers and her eyes flutter closed. "Yes, that feels good, War."

My name on her lips makes me want to beat my fists on my chest. I love how it sounds. I don't want her to murmur it, but to scream it. Intensifying my movements, I draw her closer to the edge of ecstasy. I've never seen her look more beautiful than she does now with her mouth parted open and her eyes closed. A pinkness tinges her nose and cheeks as she grows closer to climaxing.

"Can you touch me inside, too?" she murmurs and jolts against my touch.

I grunt, unsure on whether or not I'll lose my mind and decide to at least try. Slipping my thumb to her clit, I then plunge my middle finger into her hot, tight center.

Jesus fucking Christ.

I can't think about anything aside from the way her body clenches around my finger, almost brutally. Images of how my cock would feel buried inside of her are the only ones in my diseased head at the moment.

"Yes," she moans, "deeper!"

Without thinking, I slip my free hand from the wall to grip under her thigh. I lift it up and it allows me better access inside of her. My finger grazes the pea-sized nub inside of her and she shudders wildly at my touch.

"Ahhhh!"

I massage that spot inside of her harder and force her into another orgasm before she even comes down from the first. When she lets out a pained sob, I slip my hand out of her and catch her before she collapses in the shower. Ignoring awful images, I delay those thoughts and stay in the moment with her. Gathering her soapy, languid body in my arms, I pull her to me—against my firm chest and hard cock.

Our heartbeats are now in competition on which can make it to the finish line first. The moment isn't ruined by talking or acknowledging that this hasn't happened to me in over a decade. Instead, we bask in the frozen moment of time.

"Are you okay?" she questions after some time. "I'm afraid to move. I can't tell you how good it feels for you to hold me."

I close my eyes but images of me holding her until I crush her ribs and puncture her lungs terrorize me. Quickly, I jerk them back open.

"I'm better than fine. I'm afraid to let you go."

But the water starts to cool and I'm forced to break from her so we can rinse off before the water turns to ice.

After we're both wrapped in our own towels and are standing in the bathroom, she speaks again. "What are those for? Do you take all of them?"

"Fluoxetine, fluvoxamine, sertraline, clomipramine. All antidepressants prescribed to help with OCD," I say softly. Then, I point to another group on the countertop. "Zoloft, Prozac, Paxil, Klonopin, Valium. I've tried them all at least once. They never work."

She frowns and picks up the clomipramine. "I read good things about this one. A lot of studies had said it helped."

"That's the one that I tried to pick non-existent scabs from my belly. Apparently in some people, the anxiety worsens. Besides, I feel better when I don't take anything at all."

"Oh," she says, a hint of disappointment in her voice, and sets it on the countertop. "I see."

Needing to change the mood, I stalk out of the bathroom and into the bedroom. "Why don't you put on your new outfit? I'll make us some breakfast before your run."

I turn just in time to see her reaction. Her breathtaking smile lights up not only her soul but mine as well. It's a sight to behold. A sight I'll never tire of seeing.

My hot breath against the glass revives her smudges from when she first got here. The B encircling the heart warms me. I'll never grow tired of seeing it here. My housekeeper was informed to leave it be when washing the windows.

She's been running for two hours now back and forth up the beach. I miss her voice and her smell but I love how happy she seems. A couple of times she stops to suck down one of the three water bottles she took down with her in her bag. Other times she stops to stretch. And every so often, she turns toward the house and waves. I know she can't see me from where she's at but I always wave back.

The things she does to my heart are wicked.

Ever since she gave me the world's best hand-job known to man, I've been unable to force her from my mind. Not that I'd want to anyway. For the first time in a long time, I'm able to get lost in something that doesn't bring pain or heartache my way. She gives me something to look forward to. Baylee gives me hope.

Which is why…

I took the fucking Klonopin.

If it helps, even a little, I could touch her more. Kiss her maybe. Taste her. The thought isn't as abhorrent as it would have been a week ago. In fact, it's all I can think about. My mouth waters and I practically drool for a taste of her.

Perhaps tonight, I can dull my senses enough to get lost inside of her. What I wouldn't give to be able to thrust into her tight pussy and rain worshipful kisses all over her neck and face. To let my fingers dance all over her flesh in an effort to bring her multiple orgasms.

I can do this.

At least I fucking hope so.

The timer dings and I rush to turn the heat off of the mushroom bourguignons I'd been cooking for the past two hours. Only another ten minutes left on the mashed cauliflower with garlic and chive. I hurry back to the window and look up and down the beach for her.

No blonde ponytail swishing back and forth as she runs.

No perfect ass in black spandex shorts.

No long legs striding down the beach effortlessly.

"Shit!" I hiss and my panic rises, threatening to suffocate me.

What if he took her?

Did that motherfucker come onto *my* beach and take *my* beautiful Baylee?

With a growl, I storm toward the front door. I sling it open, ignoring my fears and prepare myself to run after them. Instead of running for her, she nearly runs into me.

"Jesus, I turned my head for one second and thought he'd taken you. You scared me," I tell her with a relieved growl.

Sweat trickles down her bright red cheeks and she grins at me. "I was tired and hungry."

I swallow down my unease and let the joy of having her back in my presence overtake me. A week ago I'd be having a shit fit about all the toxins she's bringing into my home. But today, I just want her home.

"Why don't you run and shower. Dinner is almost done."

She flashes me another cute smile and bounces off. After I reactivate the alarm, I try to still my racing heart. Will it always be this way? Me worrying over her to the point of unhealthy obsession. I already can't work or sleep. And the only reason I eat is because she spends her meals with me. It's like if I have to have a moment without her, I'm fucking depressed about it.

Another timer sounds and I stalk back into the kitchen. While she showers, I set the table, careful to present each plate in a perfect, even way. Our wine glasses are both filled three quarters of the way full. Exactly the same amount.

I'm not one to drink but I keep it on hand for the rare times when I can't cope and want to drink away my insanity. I don't let it happen often but it does happen. Tonight, if I can manage to drink a little wine on top of the Klonopin, maybe I can calm the fuck down enough to make love to her.

I wait, watching the doorway, for what seems like ages before she finally appears. She's freshly clean but her cheeks are still a little red from her run. Her hair has been pulled into one of those neat buns she knows I love and she's put on a sleeveless black wrap dress which ties on one side. It's kind of short and distracts me momentarily. Her feet are bare—just the way I like them.

"You look incredible," I rush out, craving to pull her into my arms.

She blushes at my words and takes her seat at the table. "This looks amazing, War."

I turn on some music that calms me before sitting down with her. If we tried hard enough, we could almost imagine we were on a real date at a nice restaurant like normal people.

The evening goes off without a hitch and as we drink more wine, I feel a calm like never before settle over me. I'm not sure if it's the Klonopin, the wine, or just Baylee that's got me so relaxed but whichever it is, I am thrilled.

After dishes are done and put away, we retire into the living room. This time, she wins at chess and I don't care. I'm buzzed and happy.

"Checkmate!"

Her scream is loud and I start laughing so hard I cry.

"It's not funny!" she complains. "I win!"

"I let you win," I try to tell her through my tears.

She snatches a pillow cushion and heaves it at me. "Asshole."

I flash her a flirty grin that has her blushing. "You should take off that dress."

Her mouth pops open in shock and then she narrows her eyes at me. "Are you drunk, Warren McPherson?"

Smirking, I shrug my shoulders. "Maybe I just want to see your amazing tits again."

My cock has been at half-mast all during our chess game but now as she stands, her heated gaze never leaving mine, it practically rips through my slacks in an effort to be set free.

"You want me to strip for you?" she purrs, batting her eyelashes as she sashays over to the stereo. She bends over and my eyes fall to her perfect ass then along the backs of her creamy thighs and muscular calves.

"Depends."

She scoffs and puts her hands on her hips tossing me an annoyed glare. "Wrong answer. The answer is always yes when a woman asks if you want her to strip for you."

I chuckle and boldly rub my cock through my pants. Her eyes follow my action and she bites her lip. "Baylee, if you're going to be one of those strippers who teases me and leaves her underwear on, then I'm not interested. I want to see that pretty pussy and that fine ass."

She gasps, clearly embarrassed by my words, and turns away to find a song. Soon, the thump of a bass has her swaying to the beat. Her body begins moving along with Justin Timberlake as she "brings sexy back."

The music seems to be able to filter in through my ears and flow along my veins with my blood. Within seconds, I feel alive like never before. My cock aches to be inside her. My tongue waters to taste hers. My heart thumps with the beat in an effort to gallop right out of my chest and into her waiting arms.

She finds my gaze and holds my stare as she tugs at the ties on her dress. It falls open revealing nothing but skin from her collarbone to her now smooth pussy. I blink several times before attempting to speak.

"Oops, I forgot to wear them. You still interested? If not, I can tie this back up and—"

"Drop the dress and come here so I can look at you properly," I order in a low, seductive tone. My skin buzzes and I think my cock might rip through my pants at any moment.

She lets the dress fall to the floor as she slowly moves toward me. Her body is all smooth curves. I have never wanted something so much in my entire life. For so long I've been shut off from the world and now it's as if the very best thing out there is presented to me on the shiniest fucking platter.

I'd be a fool not to at least try and take it.

I will have my Baylee tonight.

Even if it kills me.

chapter
TWENTY-TWO

Baylee

A hunger like never before burns behind his eyes and all I want to do is add fuel to that flame. With War, he's always holding back, always living inside of that head of his, always afraid. But now, maybe the wine has gotten into him because he's hungry.

For me.

His tongue darts out and he licks his lips as if he wants to wet them before he puts them on my body. I'm slick between my legs with desire for him to lose control and take me. With Gabe, he'd been in control and I was a victim. Sure, I enjoyed a lot of what he did to me. But with War, I want whatever he has to offer. This morning, in the shower, it'd been heaven. Touching him and him touching me was erotic and addicting.

I want more.

"Do you like what you see?" I taunt and feign shyness as I approach.

His eyes darken and his gaze is smoldering. "You're the most beautiful thing I've ever seen."

My first instinct is to be embarrassed by his words but his breathtaking smile is convincing enough to make me believe him. Tugging at my hair tie, I let my damp hair fall around me in loose waves in front of my shoulder. His eyes watch my every move.

"What now?"

He rises and takes slow steps toward me as if either he's afraid of me or he's stalking me, it's hard to tell. But by the ravenous glint in his eyes, I'd say the latter. When he makes it close enough for our chests to barely touch, he lifts a hand and brushes some hair from my eyes.

"You make me feel again, Bay." His eyes are narrowed as he inspects my features closely. I love looking at him closely because I can see flecks of green in his blue eyes. I can see the long silver scar along the side of his face more clearly and now understand he came to get it from the accident after what happened to his mother. I also like that I can see his full lips twitching at the corners as if he might break into another smile at any moment.

"You make me feel like we're the only two people in the world," I murmur back.

He lifts his hand and I close my eyes as he runs his thumb along my bottom lip. "So perfect," he says in a breathy whisper that tickles my face. "I want to kiss you."

I flutter my eyes back open and lean toward him. His scent is always so clean yet distinctly man. If I knew it wouldn't freak him out, I'd lick his neck to see if he tastes like a man too.

"So kiss me, Warren McPherson. And mean it this time."

His eyes darken, no doubt remembering our first kiss not long after I'd arrived and the second one much later. He'd zoned out that first time, as if he were recalling his past, and kissed me like he wanted to fuck me against the kitchen counter. The second time, he'd seemed disgusted as the demons took over his mind. But tonight, I want him to kiss me like he wants to make love to me in his bed.

"So bossy," he says with a wicked smirk. He tangles both hands into my wild hair and draws me to his lips. The moment he grazes his across mine, a fire ignites between us. His tongue darts out, tentatively tasting my lips before pushing through and gaining access to me. I let out a pleased moan and happily meet his tongue with mine.

While he kisses me as if he'd love to devour my soul, I start undoing the buttons on his dress shirt as quickly as I can. I want him naked like me. I want him inside of me.

"Is this okay?" I murmur as I start pushing his shirt off his broad shoulders.

He groans and nips at my lip. "Better than okay."

I smile against his lips before pulling away to focus on his pants. He sheds the shirt and tank underneath as I attempt to free his thick cock from its prison. When he's finally standing naked in all his glory before me, I grin.

"Does the wine really help?" I question, my eyes landing on his proud cock.

He growls and scoops me into his arms. Never breaking stride toward his room, he flashes me a naughty smile. "It seems to be helping just fine. Let's make love before it wears off." His voice is tight when he says the words, no doubt fearing when the monster in his head will take back over.

Tomorrow, I'll pressure him to drink more wine. Clearly, he loosens up enough to lose his af-flictions, even if only temporarily. I'll take what I can get.

When we arrive at his bed, he gently sets me down and a flash of apprehension crosses his features. I recognize the look.

What if?

What if?

What if?

"Shhh, quiet that head of yours, War. Grab a couple of towels, I'll lie on them so we don't mess up your blankets," I tell him.

Relief washes over him and he nods. I get a lovely view of his butt as he strides off to get tow-els. Moving out of his way, I let him obsessively cover his bed in not two but six towels. I suppose he's expecting a big mess.

I crawl back onto the bed and lie down on my back. With my best come hither stare, I non-ver-bally beg him to come make love to me.

"Bay," he says with a groan and runs his fingers through his hair. "There are certain things I don't think I can do—certain things I don't think I can let you do."

I frown and sit up on my elbows. "Are you going to make love to me?"

He nods but once again the demons fight for him. "I just…I just can't put my mouth there knowing…knowing…" His horrified expression knifes at my heart. In his mind, he won't be the lover I need him to be.

What he doesn't understand is…I just need him.

"Warren, come here and put your cock inside of my tight pussy," I taunt in a low, seductive voice. "I'm practically quivering with the need to have you inside of me. I don't care about that other stuff. I just want you."

He lets out a rush of air and nearly pounces on me. "Thank you, Bay. Thank you so much for being you."

His mouth covers mine as he settles his massive, warm body over mine. I hook my ankles around his waist and urge him closer. Each time his thick erection slides between the lips of my sex, I cry out with desire.

"Please," I beg against his wet mouth.

He reaches a hand between us and positions it at my entrance. "Our juices will mix," he says with a shudder and withdraws slightly, "the probability of—"

"We'll clean ourselves right after," I interrupt in a firm tone. "I promise. Don't make me beg for your big cock because I will. All night long."

His brows furrow in determination, hunger flashing in his eyes, and he nods. Slowly, almost painfully so, he pushes into me. I want to scream and beg and cry for him to slam into me, but I know this has to be on his terms.

"Jesus!" he hisses when he is seated completely inside of me. I can feel his cock throbbing and my pussy contracts with each pulse. We almost don't even have to move, our bodies knowing what to do without us.

"You've been missing out, huh?" I mutter and wriggle my hips.

He groans and begins a slow thrust into me. "Maybe I've just been waiting for the perfect woman."

"Go faster," I say with a grin.

It's just the encouragement he needs. His hips buck against me, each thrust getting harder and harder. I try to kiss at him but he lifts up so he can watch me as he makes love to me.

"You're so tight and fucking perfect," he says with a grunt. "It's never felt this good."

I smile and then moan when he hits me deep. Curls of pleasure in my lower abdomen start their dance and I know it won't be long before I climax with him deep inside me.

"I like it too, War."

War satisfies a part of me that I never knew existed. He seems to own parts of my soul that I never knew were available for others to take. But he doesn't just take from me. In its place, he gives me parts of him that I will treasure forever.

"I won't last long, Bay. It's been so long."

"Shhh, just come. I want it."

I'm close but I don't care about my release. I want him to let go of ten years' worth of stress and sadness and despair. I want him to pour it all from him and never let it back inside.

"Bay!" he grunts out my name seconds before his heat explodes inside me. He doesn't quit his thrusting and I'm soon following.

Stars dance before me. Millions of them. I want to count them for him. Tell him exactly how happy he makes me in a numerical form he can understand.

"Oh God," he murmurs and buries his face into my neck. "You're so fucking beautiful when you come. I want to make you orgasm over and over again just to see the look on your face."

I run my fingertips along the bare, contoured flesh on his back. I'm not sure how long he'll let me inside of his heart and head, but I'll be selfish and enjoy it while I can. After some time, he begins to tense up.

"Baylee, can we…"

"Shower?"

A huff of hair tickles my neck. "Please."

I nod and smile. "That's normal you know. So don't start thinking you're some weirdo because you want to clean up. Can I sleep in your bed after?"

He lifts up and gives me a look of sadness that overwhelms me nearly to the point of tears. "I want you in my bed every night. I want you in my arms every second of every day. And tonight, I will take you as long as I can have you."

I let the tears well in my eyes. When one races down my cheek, he swipes it away.

"But forgive me if my mind takes over and makes me its fucking hostage again. Promise me, beautiful."

As if I'd do anything else.

"I promise. I'm still yours even when you don't want me."

His face darkens. "You're always mine and I'll never stop wanting you."

As he sleeps, I stare at his handsome face. The bathroom light is on so his features are shadowed. Even in the dark. In the shadows. He's still innocent and pure. Warren has led a sheltered life from his own volition. His mother made a choice that ruined her son for life.

My thoughts drift to my own mother. I miss her so much. There have been times I thought about calling Land to ask him to take me home. Not that I plan on staying there but so that I could check on Mom.

But once I was home?

I'd be right in the clutches of Gabe.

What would he do this time?

I shiver at the thoughts of him finding more objects to use on me. More chases through the woods. More pain. More mental head games.

No, I can never go back to that again.

I belong here with War.

A smile plays at my lips and I stroke his hair. His dark lashes jut out over his cheeks and his lids twitch every so often as he dreams. I could get used to staring at him every night while he sleeps.

My heart feels intertwined with his in a way Brandon's never had a chance to be. War and I've made love. Our connection is on a cellular level that I'm afraid can never be severed. Not that I want it to be. I'm afraid I'll feel lost and alone without him. The idea of leaving him is no longer an option I want to consider. I want to see my parents, sure. I miss Mom and Dad, incredibly so. But with Gabe in the picture, I know I'll live with that fear always hanging over me.

With War, I'm not afraid.

I feel powerful and cherished.

I feel cared for.

I even feel loved.

Leaning forward, I press a kiss on his cheek. His breath quickens and he frowns in his sleep. I hold in a chuckle and snuggle closer to him. My thoughts drift to earlier in the shower when he'd shown the first signs of coming down from the wine.

His eyes darted back and forth as if he were trying to listen to all the voices in his head at once. He raked his fingers through his wet hair and shuddered before meeting my gaze with an intense one.

"Let me clean you. I need to rid you of that bacteria. If you got a urinary tract infection or vaginal infection, I'd feel horrible."

My eyes widened as he dropped to his knees and I palmed the cold tile behind me to brace myself. He lathered up a rag with soap and then began an extremely thorough cleansing of my inner thighs, lips of my pussy, and even my ass. It was nothing like the time Gabe cleaned me. This was done out of pure obsession for my health and wellbeing. Instead of taking offense to his actions, I ran my fingers through his hair and massaged his scalp.

Once my skin was rubbed raw but squeaky clean, he rose to his feet.

"My turn," I told him with a smile.

I could tell he wanted to do it—to get every microbe off his body but he clenched his jaw and conceded by handing me the rag. With vigor, I soaped down the rag and then knelt down like he'd done moments before.

Taking my time, I scrubbed his cock and balls like he'd done for me. His hand stroked along the side of my wet hair and he groaned. The soft cock in my hands was growing harder by the second.

"Maybe you cleaning me was a bad idea."

I looked up at him and grinned. "Or a good idea. Depends on who you ask."

He tugged me to my feet and then pushed me against the tiled wall. "I'm all clean but I want to make love to you again," he murmurs against my lips, "before all this slips away from me. I can feel it slipping, Bay."

I linked my fingers around the back of his neck and let him lift me. A moment later, he was deep inside of me. The burn from his obsessive cleansing was overshadowed by the intense bliss at having him stretch me with his thickness.

Our leap into oblivion was quick and after another careful cleansing, we turned off the shower and got out. I wasn't in any hurry to let his demons come rushing back in to steal him away from me which is why I took the eighteen-minute shower with him. I knew this because he timed us.

When we'd finished, I was worried he would push me away and want to sleep alone. Instead, he made no moves to send me away. I stood beside the bed and watched as his muscled frame flexed and tightened with each towel he picked up. Then, he discarded them in a hamper and climbed into his bed.

"I need to feel you," he murmured as he pulled back the covers and motioned to the bed beside him.

With a huge grin on my face, I scrambled into the bed and molded my body against his hot one. His fingers found my hair as he gazed at me with an emotion that nearly brought me to tears. War has eyes that sometimes let you glimpse into his soul. And right now, I had full access.

"Did you know you have between 120,000 and 150,000 hairs on your head?" he questioned and twisted a wet lock around his finger.

I smiled at him. "You told me a time or two."

He continued to regale me, despite having told me before, on how many hairs an average human loses all the while playing with mine. Even though I'd heard it before, it was still fascinating and necessary for him to share that information with me.

"Up to a hundred strands a day in rare cases," I said, remembering a conversation before. "That's a lot."

He groaned but flashed me a sweet smile. "Tell me about it. If I let myself think about it, I'd go mad wondering how many you've shed since you've been here."

His eyes began their darting and I knew he was calculating. He thrives on details. The forces that normally possess him seemed to be in control when he could explain them to me. I also got a run down on my average breaths, heartbeats, and blinks per minute. But what got me was my smiles.

"Sometimes, your smiles run together," he said thoughtfully and ran his thumb along my bottom lip. "For someone who likes to count, this is difficult to calculate. When we play chess, you smile once. And it lasts the entire game. I live for that long precious smile."

I smile again recalling his words as I stare at the handsome sleeping man. His obsessions and compulsions may horrify others, including him. But I like learning about them because they're a part of who he is. As much as running is a part of my life, his quirks are a part of his.

"Momma," he mutters in his sleep. "Momma, no."

Frowning, I inspect his features. He's upset about something he's dreaming about. A part of me wants to wake him. But the selfish part worries he'll be back to his old self when he does wake. I'm worried he'll have a fit and kick me out of his room where I won't be able to touch and smell him. Where I won't be able to pepper kisses all over his face when the mood strikes.

I reach between us and grip his flaccid cock in an attempt to draw him from bad dreams to a pleasant reality. With each stroke, he hardens and soon his hips are bucking against my hand.

"Shhhh," I whisper as I roll him onto his back. "I'll take care of you."

He cracks his eyes open and they widen. I recognize the fear in them—the fear of germs and catastrophes and touch and me. But I don't let him recoil. Instead, I straddle him and sink my body on his thick cock.

A pleased groan rips through him and his hands find my hips. His eyes have slammed shut and I smile, realizing I've won over his mind, even if for a short while. I've never been on top before with him so I'm unsure what to do at first. He seems pretty content to simply have me there. But soon, his fingers dig into my hips and he urges me to move. It takes a minute to get the hang of it, adjusting to his thickness, but I eventually start bouncing on him with vigor.

From this position, he's deep inside of me and reaching me in places that make me crazy. My breasts bounce and the slapping sound of my skin against his only serves to make me wetter for him. His hands slide up and begin kneading my breasts. When he pinches my nipples, my vision goes black with pleasure and I lose myself to an orgasm.

"Oh God!" I shriek and spasm around him.

It must send him over the edge because he hisses and throbs out his release inside of me.

"My Baylee. My sweet, sweet Baylee."

I don't climb off of him but instead rest on his chest and bury my face in his neck. His palms stroke my back. He doesn't urge me to get off of him. I'm relaxed and sated.

Warren is my whole world.

And I think I'm his too.

For now.

War

"When we get married, I want to move to New York," Lilah mused as she took a hit of her joint. She attempted to pass it to me but I waved her off. It's something we didn't agree on, but I didn't press her to quit despite her many attempts to talk me into trying it.

"Our family is here in San Diego," I said with a frown. "Mom is pregnant. I can't leave my little sister or brother to move to New York on a whim, Li."

She pouted and I instantly felt guilty. "Warren, I can't stand my family. You know that. If we marry and move there, it won't matter about my age anymore. We can be free to make love all day and do whatever the fuck we want."

What I wanted was to get a degree in computer engineering and go into business with Dad like we'd talked about on numerous occasions. He had a business plan and everything. All he needed was my techy brain to learn more and we'd be in business. His plan was solid for where he wanted to take his company. And I was supposed to be a part of that. Running off to New York with Lilah was not a part of that plan.

"We can make love all day here," I said, my voice faltering.

She narrowed her eyes at me, understanding my hesitation, and slid off the bed to sit on the floor in front of me. Her glare stayed on me as she began unzipping my jeans and pulled my dick out. This was her thing. The girl would give me blow-jobs all day long as long as it meant she got her way.

As soon as her mouth wrapped around my dick, I snapped my eyes closed in pleasure. I hated that she could control me so easily with her mouth. While she bobbed her head up and down, taking me deep in her throat, I wondered if Dad would be okay with us leaving. I'd need his support for a move like that and—

My phone started beeping over and over again with texts, to the point I couldn't ignore it, despite needing to come so desperately. Lilah didn't quit as I read Dad's text.

Dad: GET HOME NOW! MOM LOST THE BABY! I'M ON THE PHONE WITH HER NOW—CAN'T TALK!

I shoved Lilah off my cock and was already yanking my pants up as I ran for the door, texting him back that I was on my way.

"What the fuck, War?!"

Ignoring her, I zipped my jeans up and snatched my keys. "I have to go. Love you," I blurted out as I ran for the door.

She cussed me out and called me a pussy. Her words stung but I didn't have time for explanations. I needed to get to Mom. The drive was a blur and all I could feel was the sticky saliva that had now dried on my dick. If I had the time, I'd have washed her off of me. Lilah was fucking insane. There was no way I could ever leave Mom and Dad. Especially now. Lilah would get over it and we'd stay in San Diego.

Slamming my car into park, I jumped out and bolted into the house. I could hear wails upstairs in her bedroom so I took the steps two at a time in an effort to get to her quicker.

"Mom!"

Her back was to me, but all I could focus on was the blood. So much fucking blood. And she was sitting right in the middle of a darkening, growing pool of it.

"I love you, Warren," she sobbed. "Please forgive me."

I peered over her shoulder and my jaw dropped to see the tiniest baby in her grasp. So bloody. So innocent. Not breathing. My heart lurched into my throat and I swayed with dizziness when I saw Mom bring the handgun up to her mouth. I didn't have time to stop her when a blast roared through the bathroom.

Time stopped. My eyes clamp closed. The bang echoed over and over and over again as I tried to find the nerve to reopen my eyes. It wasn't until I felt something trickle down past my nose and over my lips that my senses forced me to face my fears.

Popping my eyes back open, I stared in horror at the scene. Blood was everywhere. It coated the entire front of my body. Chunks of flesh were stuck to my throat and cheek. I scraped them off quickly. Dark hair hung from part of the fleshy pieces and I gagged at the sight.

This was my mother.

This was my mother.

Holy fucking shit I had to get her to a hospital!

Without hesitation, I began gathering all of the larger pieces of her skull and brain and collected them in a towel. I could have sworn I heard my dad calling for me but it had to be a hallucination. He was in LA. I was the man of the house while he was gone and it was my job to fix this. To save my mother. When I went to take the baby from her lap, I realized I had a sister. Her umbilical cord was still attached inside Mom. I'd seen on TV how they could save the baby sometimes as long as it was still connected.

With newfound determination, I scooped Mom, my sister, and the towel full of pieces the doctors would need into my arms. I slipped in her blood but managed not to drop her. The trip down the stairs and out of the house would later become complete black memories. I didn't recall how I got to the car, yet there I was, buckling my mother in, so she would be safe.

I climbed into the driver's seat and tore out of the driveway. Miles and miles, I drove at full speed trying to get to the hospital in time. I could save her. I could save my mother and sister. She'd become one of those famous stories the whole world found out about. A medical miracle. And I would be her hero. There was no reason for her to ask for forgiveness for anything. Everything was going to be fine.

"Momma," I choked out, "hang in there. Please. I need you. The baby needs you."

She was quiet and wouldn't respond. I risked a glance at her and my world ripped apart.

This was a fucking nightmare.

A replay of some horror story I watched as a kid.

The gore isn't real.

The blood is fake.

I would wake up soon.

My stomach heaved as I realize the half blown out skull belonged to my mother. It wasn't a small wound. Half her head was gone. There was no way anyone could survive such a blast. She was dead. My sister was dead too.

What the fuck!

My skin began burning and itching where her blood and brain matter clung to me. I started to panic trying to wipe it away.

"Get it off of me!" I screeched and released the steering wheel to scratch at my flesh.

But in a matter of seconds, we hit a bump. The car jerked. I tried to grasp the steering wheel. But for the second time that evening, I was too late. We were airborne. A half-second later, we crashed head first off the side of the road.

The car was flipping one, two, three, four, five, six times.

Or twenty.

Or once.

Everything was a dizzy, painful blur.

When we finally came to a stop, all that could be heard was the hissing of the engine and my ragged breaths. And as I began to black out, I counted them.

One.

Two.

Three…

"War!"

I blink my eyes open and find that I am staring into the prettiest blue ones I've ever seen. I plead with my mind to allow me to stay there. With her. With an angel.

But I have to get this shit off of me.

"Get away from me!" I bellow. "I have to get it off me!"

Shoving her away from me, I stumble out of the bed and toward my shower. With shaking hands, I turn on the shower as hot as it will go. I need the soap and the water and the rag. I need to get this fucking shit off my skin.

Oh God.

Is it in my mouth?

I start scraping my fingernails on my tongue until I'm gagging. From behind me, I hear crying and I can't tell if it belongs to me or my sister or an angel.

"T-T-The water is too hot, War!"

A slender arm reaches past me to change the temperature. I reflexively slap the hand away. "Don't touch it!"

A shriek followed by sobs is all I hear as I start to step into the scalding rain. I need it gone. I need the blood down the drain and away from my orifices.

"Warren, please!"

Hands clutch on to my bicep and I go black with crazed rage. Spinning to face my attacker, I shove as hard as I can until they are out of the bathroom. My trembling hands slam and lock the door.

The heat is my salvation.

I will burn away the blood.

Stepping into the shower, I wince as the water scorches my flesh. I cry out and slam my fists into the tile. Pain explodes all over my knuckles and I gape in horror to see blood streaming from them.

Her blood.

Her blood.

Her motherfucking blood!

Snatching up a rag, I start scrubbing at my knuckles. I must wash every trace of her from my flesh. It stings and the blood only seems to run heavier.

I scrub and scrub and scrub.

Until…

A crash startles me.

"Warren." A deep voice.

I blink and shiver. The scalding water has somehow turned to ice. I'm confused and disoriented. I could swear it was just hot.

"Time to get out, son."

My dad.

I turn to the voice and shudder. My body aches and my heart feels empty. I'm missing a part of it. I start to claw at my chest in an effort to piece it back together when Dad grabs hold of my jaw. I've barely had time to process that he's touching me and to fight him off when he shoves something down my throat.

"D-D-Dad," I choke out, gagging on the acrid taste of the pill. "What's happening to me?"

"You're just having a panic attack. I gave you something to calm down. Get back into bed and sleep." His voice is calm and soothes my pounding heart as he wraps a towel around my shoulders.

But the ache in my chest…

It's unbearable.

"Dad, it hurts," I tell him, a sob hanging in my throat. "Something's gone."

His eyes search mine and he nods. "Baylee's safe. Go to sleep and I'll have her visit you when you're feeling better."

Baylee. Blue eyes. Blonde hair. Breathtaking smile. An angel.

Nodding, I stumble over to my bed and climb in under the covers. It's warm and smells good. Like her. Like the missing piece of my heart.

She's safe, he'd said.

I let out a sigh of relief and with it hope to push the confusion out, too. Three long breaths later and I'm losing my hold on consciousness.

The pounding in my head is intense. And the sun shining in on me is practically blinding me. I squint and try to recall the night before.

Why the fuck do I feel like death warmed over?

Why do my muscles ache as if I ran a fucking marathon?

And why in the hell do I feel like I could sleep for a week?

I sit up and take in my surroundings. The bathroom door is wide open with the light on. A towel is on the floor halfway between here and the bed. And voices.

A rich, deep, loving one.

A sweet, soft, beautiful one.

I love these voices and want to hear more of them. As if on cue, I hear heavy footsteps thundering my way. When they stop, Dad stands in the doorway. He's dressed casual today in a pair of jeans and T-shirt. His hair is messy and he has dark circles under his eyes.

"Hey, Dad. What're you doing here?"

He frowns and casts a glance over his shoulder before stepping over to the bed. "You had another delusional episode. I'm here to make sure you don't hurt yourself and…"

I squint at him, not understanding his words.

"Baylee. I don't want you to hurt Baylee either."

My heart flutters to life and begins galloping out the door past him. "I need to see her." I'm already stumbling out of bed and heading my naked ass to my closet. He starts making my bed knowing I won't leave this room until it's done.

"Warren, do you remember much from last night?"

I remember dinner. I remember the dress. Baylee's amazing fucking body. I remember making love to her and holding her tight. It was heaven.

"We made love," I admit as I dress.

He remains silent until I come out. I button my shirt and regard him with a raised brow.

"What, Dad? It was consensual. And," I say almost shyly, "I think I love her."

His gaze falls to the floor and he clenches his jaw. "Do you remember hurting her?"

I gape at him. "What?"

"Last night," he reveals, "you became severely paranoid and delusional. You struck her, Warren. And then you shoved her."

The blood drains from my head and dizziness washes over me. "N-No. You're mistaken. I would never hurt her."

He walks over to me and frowns. "Son, she's bruised on her arm and winces when she walks. She's trying to play it off but she's hurt. Whatever you did to her, hurt her."

I struck my Baylee.

The woman I made love to not once but three times.

This can't be.

"I need to see her," I snap and storm barefoot down the hallway. When I reach the living room, she's curled up on the couch sipping coffee. Her eyes are red and she looks like she's been crying. The devastated look she regards me with crushes my soul.

"Baylee." I stalk over to her but stop just before I reach her. I want to touch her and hold her and kiss her. But as I reach my hand toward her, I know I won't be able to. "I'm so sorry. What have I done?"

Tears well in her eyes and she looks past me to my dad. "Are you hungry?"

Her weak attempt to change the subject unnerves me. Of course I'm not fucking hungry. I'm worried sick that I abused the only woman who heals me.

"No. Jesus, Bay. What happened? Whatever it is, I am so sorry."

A tear trickles down her cheek and she nods. "I know. I'm not upset with you, War. You weren't really yourself."

Running my fingers through my hair, I suppress a rage-filled scream. "Are you afraid of me?" If she is, I'll pack her bag now and send her back home to the safety of her parents.

She shakes her head and the tears continue to spill. "I'm afraid *for* you. Things were perfect and then…" she trails off and lets out a ragged sigh, "you were gone."

I clamp my eyes closed and try to remember what happened.

Flashbacks of my dream of Mom and Constance.

Flashbacks of the scalding shower.

Of Baylee trying to help me. I did hit her. I did push her away from me. I'm worse than Gabe. I'm the rotten filth of the earth. I am sick and undeserving of someone as perfect as her.

All it would take was one bullet.

That's all it took for Mom.

No pain of having miscarried. No depression and grief at having lost a child. Nothing.

Click and boom.

Her life ended and she was nothing but sticky blood painted on my shirt.

I shudder. Could I do that to my father again? Spray my brain all over the walls and leave him to clean it up. What would that do to Baylee? Somehow, I don't think it would make her happy. In fact, I think, perhaps she'd be crushed and ruined. The thought of ruining her steals my breath.

She's a perfect, pure, sweet smelling gardenia.

And all I do is crush her in my fist.

"Warren, I'm hungry."

Her voice snaps me from my dark thoughts and I stare at her. She's standing now and the sun surrounds her from the windows giving her an angelic aura. Such a vision.

"I'm hungry for pizza," she says in a firm tone. "And either you can make me some of your vegan crap or I'll call Pizza Palace. I think you owe me." Her lips curve up into a sweet smile and I can't help but reciprocate.

Of course I'll cook her something.

I'll give her anything she wants.

Baylee

I lift my hand from the warm water and sigh. Today started off terribly but it ended well. When War woke up in the wee hours of the morning flipping out, I hadn't known what to do. His eyes were crazed and he spoke like a madman. All I wanted was to calm him.

But he was far from calm.

He'd hit me when I tried to turn the water cooler but it didn't deter me, despite the strength with which he'd struck. Now I'm sporting a big purple bruise. When he shoved me though, I was frightened. I'd landed hard on my butt and my breath was knocked from me. All I could think was to call Land and get his help. Turns out, he lives less than five minutes away, and was here before I could formulate what to do next. I was thankful when he'd gone in there, forced War to take a Xanax, and then put him to bed.

Land makes me feel safe. Not that I'm afraid of War. I'm afraid of that monster that lives inside of War's head. A monster that I don't really know or understand but would be glad to murder any day of the week. War is a victim of that beast which only managed to stay away for a little while before he came raging back with claws bared and a thirst for blood.

This is normal.

This is who he is.

This is War.

Land's words keep replaying over and over in my head. I selfishly wish I could fix my War. Help him heal and become human again.

This afternoon, he'd returned mostly to his normal self. He obsessed over the homemade pizza and even threw a conniption when Edison showed up with store-bought cookies. But, to make me happy, he suffered through and watched with a frown as I ate them up. It wasn't until I licked my lips and flashed him a seductive grin that he seemed to relax about the cookies.

I'd actually enjoyed spending the day with War, Land, and Edison. It made me miss Mom and Dad more but Dad still won't respond to my e-mails. To say I'm hurt is an understatement.

The alarm sounds as it activates and I sigh. Land and Edison must have gone for the evening. That leaves me alone with War and I'm not sure how things are with us. I'd like to think that we could forget about his episode last night but I can't be certain. All I know is that I miss him.

I hear a timid knock followed by the sound of his voice. "Baylee? Can I come in?"

I shiver and turn to see his powerful presence standing in the doorway. His gaze falls to the water where my naked body is hidden beneath a sea of foamy bubbles and I can't help but smile. I like that he's distracted by thoughts of my body.

"Yeah."

He awkwardly makes his way into the small bathroom and sits on the edge of the tub. His jaw clenches as his eyes drag along my wet flesh. "I'm so sorry."

I lift my hand from the water and draw hearts in the suds. "What happened?"

A loud sigh escapes him and he pinches the bridge of his nose. "I have a delusional disorder. When my OCD gets severely out of control on occasion, I'm more prone to episodes sparked by paranoia and fear and my haunting past. The crash from the pill and the wine coupled with memories of my mom were too much. I spiraled out of control," he huffs out and meets me with a serious stare. "If I'd done something to you…"

I shake my head. "Don't even think about it. Yes, you hurt me. Will I heal? Quickly. But for me to be with you, I need to understand you. I want to help you, War. You have to open up to me."

His lips press into a firm line. "I know and I'm working on it. I hate not being in control of myself. It's embarrassing for you to know all the broken, wrong parts of me. I fucking hate the way this shit rules my life."

I scrunch my brows together and recall some of the things I'd learned while researching his conditions. "You know there are psychotherapies you could try. A therapist could help."

He grumbles but nods. "I think with time—with you—I could try them again. I want to get better for you, Baylee."

Sitting up in the water, I watch him as his gaze falls to my breasts. "We'll get through this. You know that right? I know we'll find a way to be together."

A breathtaking smile spreads across his face. The man is handsome and when he smiles, the world tilts on its axis.

"You're beautiful. And I'm lucky you haven't run for the hills."

I laugh and splash at him, loving the now boyish grin I'm met with. "Who says I'm not planning to run tomorrow?" I tease but then regard him seriously. "I'm not going anywhere. I was actually hoping you could make love to me again." I'm not sure if he'll take my bait but am thankful when his eyes darken.

"You still want me? Even after…" he trails off, shame morphing his features into a frown.

"I can't help but want you. I mean look at you," I tell him playfully, "you're hot."

He flashes me a wicked smile that makes its way straight to my core. "You're an amazing woman, Baylee. Don't ever think for one second that you're anything less," he says softly. "When you get out, I have something for you."

As soon as he's gone, I'm already standing in the tub, eager to find out what he wants to give me. His gifts always make me happy. I dress in my robe sans underwear and smile to see him stretched out on my bed.

"That was quick," he says with a smirk. "You and your love for presents."

I laugh and bounce on the bed beside him, careful not to touch him. Once I'm settled, he opens his palm up to me. Inside are two rose gold earrings in the shape of a heart with a *B* inside.

"These are pretty," I say softly and open my palm to him so he can drop them into my hand.

He flashes me a shy smile as he gives them to me. "That first day when you longingly stared out at the ocean and wrote your initial with a heart around it on the foggy glass, I'd been a little fucked in the head about you marring my clean glass. But then…"

"I don't even remember doing that. It used to drive Dad crazy when I'd write on the windows of his car but Mom always said they were little Baylee notes left all over, and that he should appreciate them." My voice wobbles and I choke down the emotion of thinking about her.

"Well, I did appreciate it. For once, I didn't strive for perfection," he says, "I wanted something better than perfection. I wanted you."

"This is so thoughtful. Thank you, War."

He shrugs. "I took a picture of it so the jeweler would get it exact. It may seem obsessive but I really wanted it—"

"They're beautiful, War."

I take my time putting them in each ear and then beam at him.

"Listen, Baylee," he says slowly and brings his gaze from my ears to my eyes. "I'm not going to take that medicine anymore. The side effects always seem to be worse than the actual problem."

He'd confessed earlier today to taking Klonopin before the wine, hence the unusual reactions. My heart sinks and I wonder if that night would be the only night we'd ever spend together.

"But, that being said, I can't stop thinking about you. I can't stop thinking about the way it felt to be inside of you. To kiss you. To make love to you. Medicine or not. Wine or not. I want to try to be with you again." He sighs and scrubs his face with his palm. "I can't promise I'll never have another episode again, but as long as my mind is clear from the drugs, I vow to never hurt you again. I may not be able to touch you, but I won't ever put my hands on you in anger for as long as you live."

"You know, those pills are meant to be taken each day and not sporadically. Most have a two week or more loading dose before noticeable changes. I've been reading up on ways to help you. You're not giving your body enough time to adjust to them I'm afraid," I tell him firmly.

His jaw clenches but he nods. "Maybe we can research it together. I'm willing to try if that's what you want."

I nod and will the tears away. I miss the man from last night but I also want the man in this bed with me. "So what now?"

He leans forward and tugs at the rope on my robe. It falls open and reveals my breasts. "We see what happens."

"See what happens," I murmur as I slip out of the robe and toss it away.

He climbs off the bed and undresses. I'm in awe of his sheer, masculine beauty. All contours and curves. Beautiful. He strides off and returns with a towel. "I'd feel more comfortable with this underneath us."

I smile and nod. My eyes never leaving his, I climb onto the bed and lie on his newly situated towel. His entire body trembles as he watches me with both fear and anticipation. The eagerness squashes his apprehension because he slowly slides between my spread legs.

"Focus on me, War. Focus on how good I make you feel. Kiss me. Don't think, just do."

He launches himself on me and our lips smash together. I let out a moan that has his erect cock pressing against my belly. Running my fingers up his ribs, I then rake them through his hair.

I need this man. Desperately so.

"Make love to me."

"God, Bay," he groans as he positions his cock against my entrance. "I can't think when I'm with you."

I cry out when he pushes into me. "Good. Don't think. Just be with me."

Our mouths tangle again and he bucks into me over and over again. The slapping of our flesh echoes in my room and with each pound into me, I grow closer to orgasm. My body thrums with desire for him to touch me all over, but right now, I'll take what I can get. His mouth on mine, his body connected inside of me—it's enough.

"So perfect," he chants over and over again.

My body writhes beneath his, growing closer with each breath to an incredible orgasm only he can give me. "I'm close."

He grunts and his finger finds my throat. His strong hand cradles my neck and he holds me as he loses himself to a body shuddering climax. My name is on his lips—a violent whisper as he releases more of his inner hell by means of pleasure.

The heat that pours into me stings but it signals my own climax. I cry out and give in to the bliss he saturates me with.

This has to be love.

Thirty minutes later, we're sufficiently cleansed—after an almost too hot shower—and are curled up in his bed this time.

"You're the sun on the horizon. I ache for you," he says in a soft, pained voice, his eyes falling to my lips. "I don't get it, Bay. If I think hard enough about it, I start obsessing over something crazy;

tainted meat or airborne bacteria. It consumes me. But all it takes is looking at you and the storms that rage inside of me suddenly dissipate."

He runs a tender thumb along my cheek and I shiver with delight.

"All I care about is you, woman. You're my peace."

"Then make love to me again, Warren. Take me over and over again until we become one."

And he does.

Three times in fact.

Three more towels and three more showers later, I'm exhausted but happy. He holds me in his strong arms and I melt at his touch. Nothing else exists with War. Just us.

"Still no response?" War calls out from the kitchen.

I stretch my long legs out and wince in pain. Every muscle aches this morning. Yawning, I set my laptop on the table and turn to watch him. His back is turned as he cuts vegetables for breakfast. "Nothing. It's so weird. Dad can be a jerk sometimes but it's strange for Mom to not ever respond. She isn't one to get mad or hold grudges. It makes no sense. Do you think something happened to her? Do you think Gabe did something to them?" A shudder wracks through me at the possibility.

He walks from the kitchen into the living room and regards me with a frown. "The money keeps getting withdrawn according to my research. I don't understand why they aren't speaking to you." I wonder about his methods of research but seeing how he flies through screens on the computer, I can bet they're illegal means of obtaining information.

"How much have you been sending them? I'm not going to leave you no matter what, so you may as well tell me."

He lets out a rush of air and darts his gaze to the ocean. "Only fifty thousand a day."

I blink at him and wait for him to laugh. To tell me he's joking. But he doesn't.

"Wait," I say carefully, "you said you were sending them a little at a time."

He nods and heads back for the kitchen. "That is a little."

Considering Dad only made forty-seven thousand in a year, I'd say his wire transfers are more than a little. Jumping up from my seat, I hurry into the kitchen after him. "War, that is not a little. That is ridiculous. You let me scream and yell at you—bribe you with my body. All along you were sending outrageous sums. Mom should have been more than able to afford a liver transplant. Why aren't they responding to me?"

He stalks over to me and draws me to him. I'll never tire of his comforting presence. I inhale him and lean my forehead on his chest.

"I don't know. I didn't want to tell you but I've been all over the Internet searching for a trail on them. What they're doing. Everything seems normal. Debit card is being used. Bills are getting paid. And my transfers are being withdrawn. I'm not sure what's going on but everything appears to be business as usual there. I'll keep checking into it though."

I nod as he pulls away and continues making our food but my mind is still flitting through a million what-ifs. The worst what-if is…what if they're dead?

That thought is unbearable and I won't give voice to it. Instead, I'll focus on my time with War and together we'll figure out a way to expose Gabe. Then, I'll sort out making amends with my parents.

This will work.

War is my happily ever after.

chapter
TWENTY-FIVE

War

Two months later…

That motherfucker is smart. It's as if he knows I'm tracking his ass. Dad and I have been working to find evidence against the White Collar Trade I'd bought Baylee from and have even passed along the information to Detective Stark who asked me a billion more questions I didn't know the answers to. I still cringe thinking about my reasoning and stupidity for acquiring Baylee in the first place. But, I will never be sorry for rescuing her. Because, in the end, she's out of that bastard or any bastard's clutches. She's safe and I will never let her go.

I sigh as I sift through more land records in search for this cabin Baylee spoke of. Gabe no longer lives next door to her house. Records indicate a new family moved in not long after he abducted her. I just need to locate where he went.

"Do we have any crackers?"

I click off the land records and swivel in my desk chair to look at my woman. It amazes me that she was able to drag me from the hellish depths of my mind back to reality. I still have difficult days from time to time. I still won't touch meat even if it is the only thing left on the planet to survive on. And of course I don't go to the beach with her, or anywhere else for that matter.

But I *can* touch her.

I even managed to give Dad the world's most awkward hug the other day.

Baylee spends all day long researching OCD psychotherapies and makes me try some of them since I refuse to be seen by a therapist just yet. I'm not ready but I keep assuring her I will be. Mostly the therapies she's found involve retraining my brain and talking through the pain of what happened to Mom. I might not be close to being completely healed, but I'm happier than I've been in my entire life. Dad practically lives over here because not only does he adore my girl, but he loves being able to spend time with his son free of afflictions for the most part.

"Did you look on the bottom shelf in the pantry? I think there still may be a sleeve," I tell her. Anxiety infects my chest and my heart begins to race once I really take in her appearance. "Are you okay? You look pale, Bay."

She makes a face and groans, crossing her arms over the T-shirt she's wearing. "I don't feel so hot. I'm going to call Land to see if he'll bring me some ginger ale."

I stand from my chair and walk over to her. "Do I need to call a doctor? Dad is friends with one who could come over."

"No," she mutters and accepts my hug. "I'll be fine. Just feeling a bit blah today. Maybe I've been running too hard lately."

I frown but slide my hands down to her ass. She's not wearing panties under the oversized shirt she stole from me and if she weren't feeling so sick, I'd already have dragged her back to our room to make love to her.

Now that I can more easily touch her, I find it hard keeping my hands off her. There are certain things I haven't yet been able to bridge—the idea of oral sex, for example, still seems abhorrent to me, giving or receiving—but we have sex more than most humans do, I'm sure. Recently we've done it doggie-style a few times too. I feel like, in time, I'll jump all the hurdles between us and nothing will stand in our way ever again.

"Go call Dad and put some pants on before I try to make you better with my cock," I tell her with a growl. "I'll finish up in here and then I'll make you something to eat."

She giggles. "Such a tease, Warren McPherson."

I grin crookedly at her. "I love you, Baylee. I just want you to know that. Through sickness and in health," I promise and my smile falls. "I know you don't believe that—that I'll run at the first sign of illness. But I won't. I'm here, beautiful. Always."

She sniffles and presses a kiss against my chest. "I love you too."

With a smile, I kiss her hair and release her. "Good, now go grab some crackers."

Once she's gone and I'm settled at the computer, I start perusing the records again. I toggle back and forth between screens looking at remote cabins outside or near the San Francisco area and cross-reference them to the land records.

Nothing.

With a sigh, I open a new search and go back to hunting for the sex ring site. You can't just type in White Collar Trade and find it. Last time, it had been pure luck when I'd found it. Apparently these people create a new website each time and kill the previous after the event. I have to back track back to when I found the one Baylee was at from one of Dad's client's servers. There are no other sites on his computer and I want to scream.

Until…

I keep thinking back to the man who ran the event. Surely there is a lead there. He'd only referred to himself as "Buck" and we'd never met in the flesh, but he'd mentioned that proceeds from the event would go to his wife's pediatric association at the hospital. I do remember the hospital name he'd spoken of when we'd talked over the phone. A few searches later and I've found her hospital, name, and husband.

Forrester "Buck" Whitehead.

And the very first thing that shows up on his Facebook page is a link to his obituary.

My stomach flops as I follow the link dated last week.

Murdered.

In his office.

Items stolen from his files.

"Fuck!"

I'm out of my seat and stalking out of the office without a backward glance.

"Baylee!" I call as I stride down the hallway. "Baylee, we have a serious fucking problem!"

When I round the corner, I freeze.

My Baylee, my sweet fucking Baylee, is crying silent tears. Her eyes, which were happy ones just moments ago, are pleading for help now, as the monster I hoped to only meet again in hell stands there, in my foyer. He holds his hand over her mouth with one hand, his other bulky arm tight around her waist, a gun in its grip. Her back is against his chest and she breathes heavily.

"Let go of her," I snarl, fisting my hands at my sides. I briefly contemplate what I could use for a weapon. My quick assessment of my surroundings yields nothing and my heart sinks. "How did you get in here?"

He laughs, the sound dark and evil, and digs the gun into her ribs. "I knocked on the fucking door. My baby opened it right up for me."

She must've thought he was Dad.

Jesus.

Tears roll down her bright red cheeks and she apologizes with her eyes. My Baylee.

"Let go of her."

He shakes his head. "Actually, Warren *McPherson*, I will *not* let go of her. She's mine. Always was and always will be."

I start for him but he halts me with his words.

"Take another step and I'll put a bullet in her skull. Just like Mom. Isn't that right? Your mom blew her fucking brains out all over you. That's what made you into such a goddamned nut job?"

Bile rises in my throat and I can almost feel the sticky residue on my flesh. "Gabe, please. If you want money, I can give you fucking money. You can have it all. Just please don't hurt her. Leave us and we won't tell a soul."

He drags the barrel of his gun along her rib cage and then between her breasts toward her throat. She whimpers but he doesn't take his hand from her mouth. "I don't want your fucking money. I already have millions from you, asshole. That shit doesn't compare to the tightness of this little one's ass. Some things, money can't buy. Time's up. Baylee's coming home with me."

I charge for him but he shoves the barrel inside of her mouth. Jesus Fucking Christ. If that gun goes off. My Baylee will be… She'll be…

Images of what damage the bullet could do to her horrify me. I claw at my head in an attempt to run them away from my mind. There'd be no way she'd survive. Her blood would splatter the wall behind them—like Mom's coated the front of me that day she delivered Constance too soon.

So.

Much.

Fucking.

Blood.

"D-Don't…" I clench my eyes closed. *I don't know what the fuck to do!*

"Open your eyes, asshole. You need to see this."

I open my eyes and glare at him. Her eyes stay on mine as she sobs. I've never seen her so terrified—so upset. It scares the shit out of me. I want her smiles back, goddammit!

"Suck on the barrel, Baylee. Let's show your boyfriend how you always obey me," he murmurs against her hair. "How you're *my* good girl."

She shakes her head, but he rams the gun deeper inside making her gag. The morning sun pours in through the windows and blankets them, causing her blonde hair to shimmer in the light. Every bit an angel in the devil's grip. I want to save her. Save my angel that saved me. I want to grab him by the throat and throw him off the balcony. To take his gun from him and paint the sand the color of his blood from his head.

The sound of Gabe's sinister growl fills the room, interrupting my desire to murder him. "You're going to suck on the goddamned gun or I'll fuck your ass with it instead. I know how you like your ass played with, baby."

She opens her mouth, fully accepting the gun, and once again shoots me an apologetic look. What the fuck does she have to apologize for? This bastard is shaming her by using her body for his own twisted enjoyment.

"Good girl. Keep sucking. But one false move, Baylee and I'll pull the trigger."

When he shoves the barrel deeper into her mouth, causing snot to drip down her lip and over her chin, I gag. I fucking gag like a pussy. The demons are revolting in my head, threatening to take over, and I'm trying desperately to keep them under control. He starts to slide the barrel in and out of her mouth to which she squirms.

Don't fucking squirm, Bay. Don't do it.

"Shhhh," Gabe says with a grunt and nips at her shoulder. "You're doing so well. I missed you, baby."

And I watch, unable to protect her, as he fucks her mouth with that gun. Each time he withdraws the gun, it glistens with her saliva mixed with snot and I fight to keep from gagging. Memories of my mother—of Constance—assault me and the room spins around me. Her sobs echo around me only making me feel like less of a man for not being able to help her. I wish I could fucking help her.

I could charge at him.

But he seems the type to pull the trigger because he's a psycho bastard.

He chuckles, the sound dark and revolting to my ears. "Listen to her breathing picking up," he tells me with a smirk. "I know her better than you. She's enjoying every second of this. My girl is depraved."

I glare at him. "Fuck you."

He laughs but when she starts to wiggle, he snarls against her ear. "Don't fucking try it, baby." She lets out a sob—almost rage-filled as he nibbles at her ear. Her tears don't stop but she sags in his arms. My Baylee is so weak.

"Good girl, sweetheart," he says and drops a kiss to her temple. "And for the next act of our show," he says to me, ignoring her cries. "You get to watch *my* girl deep throat."

My skin grows cold and I start to grow dizzy.

Focus, War.

Don't let this asshole win.

When he's preoccupied, make your move. Charge for him.

"Go to hell," I snap at him before speaking to her. "Bay, hang in there. I love you."

Gabe grabs a handful of her hair and forces her to her knees in front of him. "Your lover boy wants you to hang in there. Can you hang, baby?" he taunts. "Suck on this gun like it's your last goddamned meal. Who knows, maybe it is. Or maybe you'd rather suck on my cock instead. Do you want your boyfriend to watch?"

I snarl and attempt to stay still. She shakes her head in vehemence and heeds his instruction. The moment she starts bobbing her head on the gun, my world tilts again.

Sucking and slurping.

Dark chuckles and whimpers.

My stomach churns at the thought of him accidentally pulling the trigger. Parts of her brain blowing all over my home, covering every white inch of it. I gag again.

Stop fucking thinking about it!

"How's your deep throat these days anyway, baby?"

He shoves his gun as far as it will go and this time, she's the one that gags. Loud, sloppy, wet. A croak echoes off the entryway walls before she sprays vomit all over it and the front of his jeans. Falling to my knees, I claw at my throat. Don't throw up, too. Don't fucking throw up. This shit will be everywhere.

The walls.

The floors.

Her clothes and mine.

FUCKING FOCUS!

He laughs and releases her. "Without further ado, the grand finale…"

I tear my gaze to his. "You're fucking sick."

His gun raises and he points it at me. "And you're fucking dead."

Pop!

Pain explodes in my chest.

Nooooo!

I clutch my chest and hiss when blood blooms out over my fingers. Just like Mom. Just like the day she died. So much blood. It won't stop.

My eyes blink.

One.

Four.

Or was it three.

Black and black and black.

"WAR!!!"

That voice. *Her* voice. It's my heavenly oasis although it sounds distant. I don't want to close my eyes but they're already shut and I'm spiraling into the darkness.

"War is over." The sick twisted voice knifes its way into my darkness.

War is over.

Gone, gone, gone.

Goodbye, my Baylee. You kept me happy from the very first time I laid eyes on you.

I blink them open and get a brief glimpse of her reaching for me as he drags her away.

Closed.

And you kept me happy the last time I laid eyes on you.

Wherever I go, I'll only think of you.

My Baylee.

My Peace.

This is Love, Baby is up next…

THIS IS LOVE, *baby*

My War was over and I had lost. My captor reminded me I was nothing more than his pawn.

His strategy never changed…it was always me.

But what he didn't know was that LOVE always wins.

In my War, I'd found not only peace but LOVE as well.

I'd been through a battlefield with my War and LOVE was
what brought us to the other side.

Our LOVE was beautiful and pure. Undying.

My captor thinks he has won this war. That I will LOVE him.

What he doesn't know is this time, I'm the one with a strategy.
I'm always thinking several moves ahead of him, my War taught me that.

I will outsmart him and find peace again.

This is a war I will win.

My LOVE will conquer all.

PROLOGUE

Brandon

I pace the living room and let out a rush of relieved breath when I watch the green flashing light on my phone app start making its way back toward Oakland.

He has her. He fucking has her.

But not for long.

Stalking over to the mantle, I tug a framed picture down. The prick smiles back at me and my anger explodes. That motherfucker…

I stop that train of thought and remind myself I need to save my energy. Having a meltdown and destroying the house because of what he did won't do any good. I need to preserve my anger. For Gabe. Because when I get my hands on that asshole, I'm going to fucking gut him.

Run along to your stupid cabin, old man. When you least expect it, I'm coming for you.

My phone chimes and I close the GPS app that shows the movement of his car to check my texts.

Mom.

I swallow down my rage. Where was she months ago when I needed her most?

Mom: Could you at least come home to have dinner with us, Brandon? We miss you.

Fuck her. Growling, I type back my response.

Me: You know I won't rest until I find her. I'll take a raincheck.

She fires back a nasty retort. Always the same with us.

Mom: Son, you're going to have to accept that she ran away. If she'd been stolen, like you said, it would have been all over the news. A broken nose doesn't mean she was taken. You know my stance on this.

The rage bubbles up inside of me again—I'm angry all the time these days. I don't think I've smiled aside from when I look at pictures of her. Baylee Winston. My girlfriend.

Me: Fuck you, Mom.

This time, I smile. After months of searching for her and following Gabe's every move, I will finally have her back with me.

I press a kiss to her picture on the frame and set it back on the mantle. Then, I stalk over to my duffle bag. I throw some of her clothes, a few bottles of water and some snacks inside, and the 9mm pistol I'd stolen from Tony.

For over four months, I have worried about her.

For over four months, I have wondered if she was suffering.

For over four goddamned months, I cried myself to sleep over her.

Gabe stole that time from me—time I'll never get back with her. He stole my girl right out from under my damn nose and with it, he broke a part of me I'm not sure can ever be fixed.

Now, it's time to show him how much he underestimated me. That I'm not some kid who can be pushed around. He'll live to regret he ever stepped foot in her bedroom that night. Regret he ever took my love from me.

It's time to make him pay.

And, it's time to get my girl back, once and for all.

chapter
ONE

Baylee

My chest aches.

The living, beating organ that seemed to pump only for War has begun to shrivel up and die along with him. No more pattering from simple touches, stolen glances, or murmured words. The strong cadence has dwindled to a sad, irregular beat that will never again be counted.

My heart is dead.

Crushed.

Flat lined.

He didn't deserve this!

Tears burn my already irritated and swollen eyes as memories from our time together flash by me. My heart has shut down and my brain has taken over. Memory after perfect memory of the man I loved flit by like a horrible slide show meant to mentally torture its victim.

I'm that victim—a victim of my own memories.

They slay and cut me with each passing thought.

His lips which were always moving. Always counting.

Those wise, navy-colored eyes—eyes that held so much pain but were kind and pure.

The soft, tender touch of his fingertips along my breasts and ribcage as he explored my flesh with a mix of hesitation and wonder.

Pain threatens to rip me in two. This useless heart of mine is pounding. Thunderous. And excruciating. Now I understand how one could die of a broken heart. It's happening to me. I'm drowning in despair.

The devil slayed my heart when he killed my War.

And now I'm back. With *him*. Gabe, the monster who haunts my nightmares.

We hit a bump and I attempt to focus on the present. To focus on a way to get away from the man who has stolen me for his own selfish perversions—again—and to push down the pain I feel over losing the man I loved.

It's dark in the trunk he forced me into. When he shot War and then dragged me out of the house, I'd been hysterical and tried to bolt from his grasp. Since I was behaving like a rabid animal, he treated me like one by trapping me in here for the drive to who the fuck knows where. A stale, stagnant odor lingers in the stuffy air, choking me. And, though I've never had a thing with small spaces, I swear if he doesn't let me out of here soon, I'm going to wig out.

Nausea overwhelms me again and my stomach grumbles. I fan my face in an effort to cool down and not throw up but it only makes matters worse. For several minutes, I retch and retch until there's nothing left but despair in the pit of my belly. Slobber runs down my chin, mixed with the countless tears I've shed, making my face wet and sticky. The acrid taste of vomit lingers on my tongue, and my now soaked hair sticks to my face. The stench overtakes the trunk and I shakily roll to my other side in an effort to escape it.

When Gabe dragged me away from War, I was hysterical. I'd clawed his face and ripped my way through the flesh on his cheek with vicious delight, nearly catching his eye in the process. It earned me a dizzying backhand to the face that still has my head pounding but it had been worth it. I'm no longer the docile child he once knew. The frightened animal he thinks he so easily trained and subdued.

I'll make his life a living hell.

It's only fair since that's what he's done to mine.

I'll hurt him in every way I can.

I'm jolted when the car picks up speed and I roll forward inside the trunk, knocking my head against something hard and metal, from what I can tell. It only serves to dizzy me further, which doesn't help my roiling belly.

I pick at the carpet lining some more in hopes of accessing the taillights. I'm craving air—anything other than the sour smell of my vomit that hangs there instead. Mom and I watched a movie on Lifetime once where a girl had been stuffed in a trunk. She'd managed to tear away the lining, break the taillight, and wave to motorists behind her, which in turn saved her.

Problem is, in the movie, the girl made it look easy.

In real life, the carpet is really wedged under the metal and in my weakened state, I'm finding it difficult to—

Riiiip!

I let out a crazed laugh when the material finally gives and I gain access to the bright, red light of the taillight. With all my might, I push, beat, scratch, punch, kick, and pick at the stupid plastic. It doesn't budge. It doesn't give in the slightest little bit. So, it definitely doesn't break off and fall into the road as we drive.

No, that would be too easy.

This isn't a Lifetime movie.

This is a horror flick starring the devil himself.

Defeated tears stream down my cheeks and I lie back, trying to catch my breath. In all of my efforts, I'd become drenched with sweat and now my muscles ache from the exertion. A horrifying thought claws at me.

Will I suffocate in here?

The air suddenly seems too thick. Too hot. Too limited.

How many breaths do I have left?

If War were here, he'd calculate exactly how much time I have left. He'd tell me the precise number of breaths to take so I'd have plenty to spare. He'd hold me and comfort me, telling me I was safe with him.

A loud, all-body quaking sob rips from me.

The loss of my lover, my friend, my safety—it's too much to bear. A piece of me is gone. Forever. Not just my heart, but my soul. It's been fractured and stolen from me. I'm no longer a whole person—just a broken, leftover mess.

Gabe finally ruined me once and for all.

I've been abused and tortured by this man—and it's far from merely physical. Whereas before, he'd wrecked my body and my mind, he's now obliterated the very parts of me that make up who I am. I'd actually managed to right myself after how much he wronged me. War's love was crucial in that healing process.

But now?

Now, he's fucked with my head to the point that I don't even exist anymore. Gabe has managed to flay my heart and rip away every good part of me.

I'm a cold, lifeless shell.

And my War is gone.

A wave of sickness washes over me and I close my eyes. I pray for God to just take me, too. To take me to a place where War and I can live free of afflictions and psychopaths.

Exhaustion plagues me and I let it steal me away. I want to get lost in the blackness of unconsciousness and block out the misery. But every time I relax and give into it, blue eyes are at the forefront of my mind.

Darting back and forth.

Concerned.

Loving.

Hungry.

Beautiful.

He'd been shocked as he clasped a hand over his chest, blood blooming over his pale fingers, staining not only his skin and clothes, but his mind too. I cringe to think of what his last thoughts must've been like. The horrifying demons in his head. Laughing at him. Mocking him. His final memory of me was to stand there idle, having to watch Gabe brutalize me in front of him. The realization of his own impending death growing imminent, and the uncertainty of what would happen once he was gone.

It's all my fault. In a moment of carelessness, I opened the front door and let that bastard right in. And he killed the love of my life.

I'd finally been able to help War live again.

Only to watch him die.

I'm not sure how long we drive for or how long I remain frozen, War's blood gushing on replay in my mind. It feels like eternity—a sentence I'm being tortured with. Nobody should have to watch someone they love die before their eyes. It isn't something I'll ever be able to erase from my mind.

Madness will kill me in the end.

Another wave of queasiness has me gagging.

Just breathe, Baylee. Calm down.

One, two, three, four.

I slow my breathing and focus on what I can control.

My fingers slide under my T-shirt and I rub my abdomen. I hadn't confirmed it, but I recently missed my period. Since then, I've battled the occasional upset stomach and my breasts are always sore. Deep down, I know I'm carrying War's baby. I just know it. When Land came over, I was going to ask him to set up an appointment for me with his doctor friend, so I could confirm.

A child with War. It was a blessing. Something created from the purest love. Age is no matter when two hearts connect and become one. It was soon, but it was right. Conceiving his child in love was something natural and beautiful. I'd been eager to confirm and share the news with him.

I know War. He'd have been over the moon with excitement. He would have taken care of me and been a perfect father. I would have married him and everything would have eventually fallen into place.

But now he's gone.

I cling on to hope, though, that there is a baby growing inside of me. His baby. A baby that looks and acts like him. Something to remember him by.

And with a baby comes great responsibility.

I'm responsible for protecting an innocent being from that monster.

I will do what needs to be done.

Nagging thoughts invade my mind. What if I'm not pregnant? What if it's all for nothing? What if I make it through to the end—this idealistic baby being the prize—only to find out there is no baby? *Then what, Baylee?*

Bile creeps up my throat again and I swallow it down, running my fingers over my sore breasts.

I'll hold on to the hope anyway. War would want me to fight that beast, not roll over and die. He'd want me to smile again.

But I can't take this!

The exhaustion weakens me, once again, and I'm no longer able to even think anymore. The darkness invades and I let it steal me away—hopefully for forever.

God, I miss War.

"Come on," Gabe says with a growl when he opens the truck. "You need a shower before you get in my bed. You smell like shit."

I squint at the late afternoon sun pouring down on me and sit up. I'm not sure how long I was passed out for—must have been hours. Fighting to keep my eyes open in the bright sunshine, I attempt to take in my surroundings. Trees, trees, and more stupid trees. We're back at his cabin—no surprise there. He clutches onto my elbow and helps me out of the car. My knees buckle—stiff from being stuffed in a trunk for hours—and he holds me up by my arm.

"I missed you, baby." His voice is saccharine sweet and it makes me want to claw at the other side of his face. "Did you miss me?"

He must be even crazier than I thought. "No."

He jerks me around to face him, his strong hands now gripping my shoulders, and shakes me. His fingers dig into my sore muscles and I yelp out in pain. Gone is War's gentle touch. Gabe's harshness momentarily stuns me.

"What, did you grow some backbone while you were with that freak? He's in a body bag now, Baylee. Accept it. You have no one but me. We can either do this the hard way or the easy way. Personally, I sort of get off on your struggles, so you'd only be making me happy. Having a hot blonde tied to your bed is what most men dream of." He barks out a derisive chuckle.

I glare at him, tears welling in my eyes. *Fuck you* is on the tip of my tongue, but the words would probably give him a hard-on. And he'd probably hit me again. Instead, I bite my tongue and grit my teeth as a single, hot tear rolls down my cheek and drips from my chin. Gabe is too powerful for me. I would never be able to overtake him, which is exactly why I have to be smart about this. "Can you at least make me some toast while I shower?" My voice is low and scratchy. I guess screaming for hours in a trunk will do that to you. My question is an attempt to drive the conversation elsewhere—into more amicable territory. "I'm not feeling so well after that ride in the trunk. You know how I get motion sickness." Another tear streams down my face. "Please."

His gaze becomes soft and he strokes my hair. "Of course, angel."

I swallow down the bile in my throat and let him drag me into the small cabin. A faint scent of bacon lingers in the air and the mere whiff of it makes me queasy again. But I have to get it together. The thought of Gabe suspecting even for one moment that I'm pregnant with War's baby is a horrifying one. I shudder to imagine what terrible things he'd be capable of doing with that information.

He guides me through the bedroom that still gives me nightmares and into the tiny bathroom. Once there, he finally releases the death grip he had my arm locked in. "Make it quick and don't try anything stupid. I don't think I have to remind you of the rules, do I? Every step, baby. Every step."

I shudder and nod, rubbing some circulation back into by arm. He smiles and leaves me alone in the bathroom. The shower is quick, even though I want to stay there for hours, and soon I'm dried off. My toothbrush is still here so I brush my teeth quickly and redress, pulling the same T-shirt I had on over my head. War's T-shirt.

Sounds from the kitchen alert me to the fact that Gabe must be preparing food. I creep over to the doorway and cast a glance down the hall to the front door. If I could manage to steal his keys, I could make a run for it. I've been training every day for two months on the beach. Some days, I would even run barefoot. I never want to be helpless again like I was in those woods not long ago. It is possible for me to make it. Especially if he were incapacitated.

But if I don't?

There are easily over seventy-five steps between where I'm standing and the car.

Seventy-five lashings would be brutal.

I shiver and turn toward the kitchen, resolving to devise a better plan later when I have some time to think. A plan that includes making a run for it while he's asleep or in the shower. Anytime other than now when I can barely stand on two legs. Right now I need my strength.

"Smells good," I tell him and slide into a kitchen chair that wasn't here the last time I'd been here. My eyes graze over the familiar open cellar door in the floor, in the middle of the kitchen. A shudder passes through me remembering the time I spent tossed down there and I force myself to stop looking at it. Why is it open? Had he planned on putting me in there had I not been compliant?

"You smell clean now," he says with a smile and puts a plate down in front of me. "But the shirt has to go. You know better, baby."

I nod and attempt to hide my reluctance at having to take off the only piece of War I have. He must sense my moment of hesitation, though, and grabs the front of my shirt, hauling me out of the chair. I cry out when he passes the cellar. Thankfully, he drags me over to the counter. When he picks up a sharp knife, I start to cry.

"No! Please!"

He doesn't cut me, but instead saws down the front of the shirt until he slices it right off. Once he rips it from my shivering body, he tosses it into the dark cellar hole.

His fingers curl around my hair and he yanks me until I'm staring into his almost black eyes that seem to pulsate with rage. "That was your only warning," he hisses, spittle raining down on my face. "Next time, it'll be you that goes down there."

I swallow back a sob. "Yes, I'm sorry."

His hand releases my hair and both palms find my now bare ass. With incredible strength, he easily hauls my weakened body against him, nearly stabbing me with his erection, which I couldn't help but feel digging in my stomach through his jeans. "Hurry up and eat. We have plans."

"I'm so cold."

He's tied my arms to the bed and I can't stop shivering. My legs are free and I wonder if I can somehow choke him with them.

"I know, Baylee. I'm about to warm you up." His smile is predatory as he sets to removing all of his clothes. I cringe when he starts my way but he hesitates, a scowl immediately taking over his face. "Where's my willing girl? Where'd she go? Don't tell me that fucker polluted your mind. You're mine, baby. You're home."

Images of War flood my mind and my lip quivers with unshed emotion. "I'll never be yours." My voice comes out in a hoarse whisper.

He sits down on the bed beside me and grips my jaw in his brutal grasp, turning my gaze to meet his. "This was all part of the plan, Baylee. Remember? I promised you I'd be back for you and I delivered. I'm going to take care of you now. I love you."

This delusional bastard thinks he loves me.

Love doesn't make you kidnap someone.

Love doesn't make you violate someone.

Love doesn't make you murder someone.

No, psychopathy does. And Gabe is a complete psychopath.

Screw him!

I spit in his face. "I fucking hate you."

He assesses me silently, his only movement coming from his free hand, which reaches up to wipe the saliva from his face. A slow smile lifts one side of his mouth. *Oh God.* In an instant, his hand slips from my jaw and seizes my throat, squeezing me until I'm choking.

His nostrils flare as he leans forward and practically spits his words at me. "Do that again and things will go very bad for you, Baylee. I'm not against punishing you into submission. This *will* work between us. And if it doesn't, I will cut your broken heart out because if I don't get to have you, nobody else can. Do you understand, baby?"

Stars glitter before me, but I manage a small nod that immediately rewards me relief. His grasp is gone and his large palm slides down my throat and between my breasts. He fondles my nipple between his thumb and finger while I suck in air with greedy gulps.

A violent shiver courses through me—the chill of the air, the frightening man before me, and the painful loss of my lover, all taking their toll on my body.

"Look at me," he says in a deceivingly soft tone, and sits up on his haunches. His dark hair is wild and unruly on his head. A pair of demented eyes snare me and my gaze locks with his. "Good girl." His praise doesn't comfort me, only haunts me, causing me to shudder again. "You've been through so much. I'm sorry about that. But I promise I'll make it better."

He slides his hands to my knees and parts them. My resistance is futile as he easily settles himself on top of me, his hardened cock pressed into my belly. I expect him to enter me, but instead, he pulls the covers up over us, and then buries his face against my neck. His scent envelops me and I feel as though I might choke on it. Thick. Heady. Wicked.

Silent tears roll down my cheeks as he presses soft kisses against my neck just under my ear. It would be preferable for him to just fuck me to death rather than whatever the hell he's doing. I don't want his comfort or solace.

I want War.

A sob pierces the air and he coos in response, his hot breath tickling my ear. "Shhh, baby. Let me fix you."

The world around me tilts and I'm nauseated. I don't want him touching me—invading me—in all the places I'd given to War. I'd willingly given every part of myself to War and belong only to him.

Gabe cradles my cheek with his palm and regards me with tender eyes. "I don't know what all went on with that asshole, but you have to know we belong together. I promise, it won't always be so hard, Baylee. One day you'll be the mother of my children and my wife. It's all I've ever wanted. Ever since the moment I moved in next-door to you, and laid eyes on my wise, sweet little neighbor. I knew you belonged to me in that moment."

I'm too stunned to speak and his mouth covers mine, further silencing me. He sucks on my quivering bottom lip before biting it gently. When his tongue shoves its way into my mouth, I close my eyes and mentally retreat.

I can't do this.

I can't be his prisoner for life.

I refuse to be his kept woman.

When he starts sliding his cock against my clit, I jolt my eyes open. He breaks from our one-sided kiss and looks between us as he thrusts.

"Gabe," I manage to choke out, "I don't want to do this."

He flashes me a warm smile. "Not yet, but you will. Just like last time, sweetheart."

I shake my head as he continues to slide back and forth between the lips of my pussy. He doesn't enter me, just continues to rub against me. Unwanted sensations—my body being manipulated into responding to his touch—begin to ripple through me. I clamp my eyes closed and focus on anything other than what he's doing to me.

I won't let him win this time.

I've grown up a lot since the first time he took me.

I have control over my body, not him.

A jolt slices through me and I cry out. It's a quiver of pleasure, of want, and I hate it. Absolutely hate the way his familiar touch once again steals the rein of control from me.

"You love it when I do this," he tells me smugly as he continues his gentle bucking against me. "I bet your pussy is getting wet."

I shake my head at him and the tears continue to roll out. "I hate you."

He groans when the tip of his cock slides against my opening. I attempt to clench my thighs together, but with him between them, there's no stopping him. I'm granted a momentary reprieve when he pulls away just a bit.

"Let's see, baby."

His finger pushes into me and I cry out. He doesn't do anything except for sticking it inside me, only to pull it right back out. I refuse to look at him and the disgusting look of triumph that I know I'll find. I keep my eyes snapped shut.

"Ahhh," he says with a pleased laugh, "I was right. Your body does still belong to me."

He drags his wet finger around one of my nipples and teases the hardened peak. I wiggle to no avail.

"I won't let you rest until you come for me. We can do this all day, Baylee. I've waited for you while you were gone. I didn't share myself with anyone knowing I'd have you back where you belong eventually."

I sob when he goes back to sliding his cock against my throbbing, betraying bundle of nerves.

Think of War.

Think of War.

I'm trying to block him out when I feel his hot mouth on my sex. Jerking my eyes back open, I glare down at him. His tongue takes over and my squirming only serves to make him more ravenous.

Licking and slurping.

Biting and sucking.

There's no possible escape for me from his pleasure assault and it's making me crazy. If my body gives in, I'll not only betray myself, I'll betray War.

"Mmm," he moans against me, his hot breath only making my struggle to remain strong harder on me.

His finger is back inside of me in an instant as he continues to taste me. I roll my eyes back into my head and attempt to ignore the curling of the impending release twisting its way through my lower body like a sharp knife.

The craving to climax is strong.

Sickening.

Torturous.

I hate the way my body begs for it. How it quakes and quivers in need.

My mind pleads for another way but I know it's hopeless. I'm once again prisoner to the villain who plays my body as if it were an instrument only he knows how to play. Each muscle in my body aches and burns as I do everything in my power not to let him win.

But he does win.

His fingers know parts of me inside that surrender to his demands. Parts that aren't connected to my heart or mind.

A shudder, hard enough to rattle the earth beneath us, overtakes me. It's pain and hate and fury all rolled into one exhausting release. My pussy clenches around his fingers and my own duplicitous juices run from my body along the crack of my ass, wetting the bed beneath me.

What have I done?

With reluctance, I reopen my eyes and take responsibility for what I allowed to happen.

I loathe him.

But who I loathe more is myself.

I'm no longer the Baylee I once knew. He's found a way to sever the last thread of connection to who I was. The last thread to my life with War. I am nothing, floating and black. My soul wails in hopeless defeat.

"There, there." He kisses the inside of my thigh once I've come down from my unwanted orgasm. "That was perfect. You're perfect, Baylee."

I lie there, unmoving like a child's doll long forgotten in the yard. Discarded and used. Broken and useless. My thoughts are blank and my heart doesn't beat. I just stare and stare and stare into nothingness. His next words don't frighten me or upset me. I don't recoil in disgust or beg for him not to.

"I'm going to make love to you now."

I simply stare.

I am no longer War's peace. I am nothing. I am Gabe's vacant little doll.

Nothing.

Nothing.

Abso-fucking-lutely nothing.

chapter
TWO

Brandon

I shoulder my duffle bag and start toward the door when a thought occurs to me.

She doesn't have any clue. Not one single clue.

My girl has been stolen, most likely raped and beaten, been someone's prisoner for nearly four months now. Her spirit is probably broken. She'll miss her parents. I'm sure she'll be scared out of her damn wits.

I run my fingers through my overgrown dark hair. The boyish spikes are a thing of the past and I've embraced the wildness of what it's come to be. Much like myself. No longer stiff and in place, behaving for everyone to see. No, it's unruly. Unmanageable. Rogue. Like me. I've spent months searching for her. Months dealing with more questions than answers. Months missing her so badly, my heart physically aches in my chest.

And while I don't understand, and quite frankly, am furious about the correspondence she had made, I'd been smart enough to know it was probably under duress.

My Baylee loves me. She always has.

I can't wait to take her from that motherfucker and hold all of the broken pieces of her. I'll mend her and heal her. Take the pain away from her. Provide the shoulder she needs to lean on. It's what we do. Baylee and I are made to weather any storm. If we can get past all of this bullshit, we can do anything.

I stride through her home and make my way into her parents' room to find what I'm looking for. On her father's bedside table sits a picture. A picture of her family. The frame long since replaced after having been broken not so long ago.

Baylee—recently turned seventeen in the picture—sits between her parents on the bleachers. It had been baseball season, and she'd forced them to come to one of my games. Tony, for once, was actually smiling. Almost as if he'd grown used to seeing me around and could perhaps stomach the idea of her and I being a couple. Lynn wore a smile of beauty and grace as she side hugged her daughter. It was one of the last times Baylee's mother had been well enough to leave the house.

I swallow down a thick ball of emotion and grit my teeth. Lynn had always been good to me. When Tony and Gabe would mess with me, like they often liked to do, she'd always shoo them off and mollify me with motherly smiles my own mother could never give. It was like she, too, knew Baylee and I weren't just some passing fling, but instead true love. That we were meant to be.

I loved Lynn as if she were my own mother.

Baylee is going to be devastated.

Giving her the news via email seemed impersonal and wrong. I always knew I'd be the one to hold her through what would inevitably be the worst time of her life. I just didn't realize that it would be so in more ways than one.

With a sigh, I set down the duffle bag and unzip it. I stuff the picture into it and on a whim decide to grab Lynn's white sweater which she always kept on the chair near her bed. I look around the room, pondering whether or not I should take anything else. She'll need memories. I don't want her to be denied of any of them.

I snatch a few more things and toss them in the bag. After zipping it back up, I stride back through the house to leave. A loud, sudden bang on the front door nearly stops my heart.

My blood runs cold in my veins, nearly turning to ice, as I freeze in my tracks. I've been staying in this house for a while now and nobody has come over. Hoping it's just a neighbor I can easily get rid of, I prowl over to the front door and peek through the small window. I lock eyes with the shrewd brown ones of Detective Stark.

Fuck.

Another pound startles me. "We can see you in there," her partner's deep voice booms through the door. "Open up. We'd like to ask a few questions."

I grit my teeth and reluctantly pull open the door. Stark widens her eyes in surprise before she schools her expression.

"Brandon Thompson? Funny seeing you here," she says carefully, her eyes darting behind me into the house. "Do your parents know where you've been?"

I shrug my shoulders and drag my gaze to her badge on her belt to avoid her scrutinizing stare. "I'm eighteen. I wasn't missing, just needed my space. She knows I'm alive and well."

She makes a cluck with her tongue and our eyes meet again. "I see. We actually came to pay a visit to Mr. and Mrs. Winston. May Detective Shilling and I come inside and ask a few questions?"

Glancing at Shilling, who chews on a toothpick like it's a piece of gum beside her, and then back at Stark, I shake my head no. "Uh, didn't you hear about Mrs. Winston? She's dead."

Stark's partner slides his hand over his gun, the movement almost unnoticeable. But I see and cringe.

"Her liver finally shut down and she passed on," I add quickly before they start getting the wrong idea.

Stark waves her hand at her partner, trying to calm him, I guess. "Yes, we knew she was very ill," she says solemnly.

Shilling nods and relaxes. Slightly.

"Where's Mr. Winston?" Stark questions, her eyes flitting behind me again as if she's cataloguing everything in the house.

"He's not here—went into San Francisco to see a friend," I say and wave behind me. "But you're welcome to come inside and have a look around. I can tell you want to. But if you'll excuse me, I was on my way out."

When I start to walk over the threshold, Stark stops me. "What's with the bag, Mr. Thompson? Heading somewhere?"

I nod. "Talked to my mom. I was headed back home to stay with them. At least until I find a job and can get on my feet."

Stark narrows her eyes at me. "I see. So, Mr. Thompson, you're telling me you've been staying with Mr. Winston this whole time?"

My palms begin to sweat so I make a fist with them. "Yeah."

"Check it out, Shilling. I'm going to chat with Mr. Thompson for a minute."

Shilling shoulders past me and begins nosing around the house.

"I gotta tell you, son," Stark says with a sigh, "I'm awfully curious how, just a few months ago, you acted like Anthony Winston was your enemy—that he was a part of some elaborate scheme to get rid of his daughter—and now you two are roomies? Can you explain that to me?"

I clench my teeth and glare at her. "My opinion of him hasn't changed. We'd formed a sort of alliance to search for Baylee. Remember her? The missing girl you blew me off about? Plus, he's been having a hard time since his wife died, and he is my girlfriend's father. So, I've been here because obviously Baylee can't be. Is that a crime, Detective?"

Her gaze softens and her lips press into a line. "Of course not, Brandon. Actually, that's what we came here to talk about. Baylee and where she's been—what she's been up to. Have you had any contact with her?"

An ache forms in my chest. "No, I haven't spoken to her." It's true. I haven't heard her sweet voice. Her throaty giggle. The soft way she moans when I kiss her.

Stark lets out a sigh, almost seeming relieved at my words.

"The house appears to be lived in. No signs of a struggle or altercation. There's nothing here," Shilling says from behind me.

Stark nods and motions for me to follow her. "Mr. Thompson, we'd like you to come down to the station so we can ask you a few more questions."

"So ask them now," I bark out, trying not to seem so eager to get away from them.

Glancing down at my watch, I nearly cringe knowing these people are wasting my time.

"I'd rather do it up at the station. In my office. We can do this the hard way or the easy way. Just a few questions."

"Questions about what?"

She frowns. "Gabriel Sharpe for one."

I wince at hearing that asshole's name. "I don't know anything about that stupid fuck." But my menacing growl does nothing to conceal my hatred for him.

"Well, that's not all. I promise, we won't keep you long. Like I said, the easy way."

Our eyes meet and I challenge her. "And if I just leave?"

A soft chuckle leaves Shilling as Stark bristles at my question. "Then we do it the hard way. I have my partner here search your bag and if we find anything missing from this home, we'll haul you in for trespassing and larceny. You could also be charged with aiding and abetting."

"What?" I bellow out in disbelief. "Aiding and abetting with what?"

She crosses her arms over her chest and stares at me. "With aiding and abetting Baylee Winston in the attempted murder of Warren McPherson."

I blink at her several times in shock. Surely this woman has lost her goddamned mind. "What the hell are you even talking about? Who the fuck is Warren McPherson? Baylee was kidnapped. Stolen. She's not a murderer!"

Stark cocks a dark eyebrow and nods toward the squad car and my truck. "I know the story you've told me, and I'd like to believe you, Brandon. That's why I want to get your statement at the station. We'll need your help in bringing Baylee in. She's a person of interest. Any information you might be able to provide will help us in our cause."

Unfuckingbelievable.

"This is ridiculous." I run my fingers through my hair again and curse.

"You can meet us there. How about that? We'll talk, clear some things up, and then you can be on your way," she tells me in a placating tone that reminds me of Lynn. Motherly and concerned. "I know you want her back. If she's innocent, like you claim, we'll get to the bottom of it."

Rage bubbles inside of me.

Now that they think she tried to murder someone, they're suddenly interested in where the fuck she went. Not for the near four months that I've been going crazy searching for her.

I want to strangle this woman and say, *I fucking told you so.*

I want to tell them everything I know about Tony Winston and his psycho best friend, Gabe Sharpe.

I want to tell them how Baylee wouldn't hurt a soul. She's an innocent. A motherfucking victim.

My phone buzzes in my pocket alerting me to a notification from the GPS app that's tracking

Gabe's movement. I've already wasted too much time with these dumbass detectives when I should be stalking where Gabe's taking her.

But I know they won't get off my ass until I talk to them. Stark's firm stare tells me so. I need to shake these guys off me so I can get to her. For a brief moment I consider telling her that I'm going after Gabe, but then I remember how much help she was before.

I don't have time for their bureaucratic bullshit and red tape.

I need to get to her. And soon.

"Fine," I concede with a huff. "I can't stay more than an hour though. I promised my mother I'd be home for dinner." My stomach grumbles as if to punish me for teasing it with a mention of my mother's home cooking when I know I won't be getting that shit anytime soon.

Stark nods and flashes me a warm smile. "You're doing the right thing, kid. Thank you."

Four hours.

For four goddamned hours I've sat here answering their questions.

When was the last time you saw Baylee Winston?

Do you know the current whereabouts of Gabriel Sharpe?

How would you describe Baylee? Was she ever violent?

Were Gabriel Sharpe and Baylee Winston collaborating to con the reclusive billionaire out of his life and money?

Where is Anthony Winston and why would he hide the fact that his daughter had gone missing?

On and fucking on.

I evaded. Anything to get them off my back and hurry the hell up.

"Are we done here?" I demand for the millionth time, my patience wearing incredibly thin.

Stark, ever the calm one, raises a dark eyebrow at me. "Shilling just called your parents to let them know you've been located and are safe," she says with a hint of smugness. "He also told them you'd be late for dinner. Although, they sounded a bit surprised to hear that you'd be joining them at all."

Fuck.

"There's also no reason for you to lie about going to your parents unless you really don't want anyone to know where you were actually headed. Where were you really going in such a hurry, Mr. Thompson?" she questions, suspicion evident in her voice.

"This is stupid. I was going to see a friend." A growl rumbles in my chest. "Besides, I'm eighteen, Stark. There's no reason for you to have called them. It's none of their business."

I flick my gaze to the clock above her head, wanting to slam my fist into the table. Another three hours or so and he'll be back at the cabin. I think about the gun in my bag in the truck. How it will feel to shove the barrel into that asshole's mouth and pull the trig—

"Detective," a mousy woman with a greying mop of hair interrupts, peeking into the interrogation room. "Mr. Thompson is here to see his son."

Rubbing a palm over my face, I groan at the feeling of dread spreading through my body. The last thing I want to do is be forced to face my father now, after all this time.

"He can wait until we finish up here," Stark snaps.

"No," the woman squeaks, "actually it can't wait. He's here with an attorney and is demanding to see him right away."

Jesus fucking Christ. My father just has to go to the extreme. I could have handled this. I was almost done and on my way to find Baylee.

But now?

Now I'm going to look even guiltier. Spend even more time here. And possibly lose track of them.

Shit!

"Fine," Stark grumbles, "send them in."

Seconds later the door swings open and my father storms in with a scowl painted on his face. I stand abruptly and glower at him.

"I had this handled," I grit through my teeth. "They were just asking questions about Baylee. I was about to leave. I didn't need a lawyer or my dad to come save me."

My father approaches and looks down his nose at me. "You look like hell, Brandon. Are you on drugs?"

I can't help but roll my eyes. *Fucking typical.* "Leave," I seethe at him, fisting my hands at my sides.

He laughs at me before grabbing a fistful of my T-shirt. I know he's pissed at my disappearing but he no longer has any influence or control over me.

"Okay, Mr. Thompson, that's enough," Stark snaps as she stands.

"Son," he says, shaking his head, "you clearly can't be left to deal with matters on your own. You only ever end up doing something stupid. You went and got yourself mixed up with that girl. You're throwing your entire life away for her. Her hot-headed asshole father doesn't even like you. She's not worth—"

"SHE'S WORTH EVERYFUCKINGTHING!"

I snap. Blame it on the day of being poked at and forced into shit that I didn't want to do after months of being ignored by the very people in this room. Rage overwhelms me and I nearly go blind with it. I can't stop the rush of anger. Can't stop where it takes my fist. I can't evaluate the repercussions of my action until it's too late.

Crack!

The rest is a blur of chaos.

A blur of shouts.

A blur of force as I'm wrangled into cuffs by a fucking woman.

A blur of threats by my father. Warnings by his attorney. And my Miranda rights being read to me by Stark.

A blur that doesn't fade until I'm sitting on a cold bench behind bars, beside a bunch of other criminals.

I'm so sorry, Baylee.

I'm so fucking sorry.

chapter
THREE

Baylee

I sit on the shower floor with my chin on my kneecap as I hold my legs to my chest. The heat of the water does nothing to warm my frigid soul. I'm dying from the inside out. The past few hours have been permanently blocked from my mind. I won't allow myself to dwell on what happened.

Because it will kill me…

My thoughts focus on War and hot, angry tears fill my eyes. I was his—all his—and Gabe took that away from me. A shudder ripples through me and I let out a sob. My wrists still burn from the rope and I lift them up to inspect them.

When I do, the dark veil lifts in my mind and the memories of only moments ago assault me worse than the act itself.

I'd fought against those ropes.

Squirmed and wriggled.

Thrashed and spit and snarled.

But in the end, he took me anyway.

And once it was done, I broke. Gabe snatched onto my already bruised and bleeding spirit—and snapped it in half. He stole the last thing I had for War. Greedily robbed it all for himself.

The motherfucker even had the audacity to tell me he loved me.

I stand on shaky legs and scrub that vile man from my body. I can't help but think of War and our time together, as I fervently scour away every particle from my flesh, to the point of pain. Every smear of his saliva. Every drop of his cum. Any lingering scent of the devil himself. All of it burned from my body by my vicious scrubbing and drained away into the depths of hell, where it belongs.

"Baylee…"

I flinch at hearing his voice, low and menacing, and I drop the rag onto the floor. Gritting my teeth, I prepare to shred his face if he so much as thinks about entering this shower with me.

"What?" I snap.

He chuckles, the darkness in it a threat itself. "There's my girl. Thought I'd lost you there for a spell when you went all catatonic."

His shadow behind the curtain moves over to the mirror and I hear him turn on the sink. He sets to brushing his teeth as if we're some stupid married couple getting ready for bed.

I hate how comfortable he is with what he's done.

Absolutely hate him.

"You developed feelings for him." His words aren't a question but instead an accusation. Silent tears roll down my cheeks as I think about War. "Baby, they have a name for that. It's called Stockholm syndrome. It's a psychological disorder. You only *think* you have feelings for him because he was your captor. It's not uncommon."

My blood boils and I want to charge through the curtain and beat his face against the mirror. To smash his flesh against the glass and revel in the way his blood smears the reflection.

If only I knew for sure that I could take him. In my angered state, I imagine I almost could.

"I'll never feel anything for you but hate. I'll *never* fall in love with you," I hiss back at him.

The shower curtain is suddenly yanked open and I shriek in surprise. His gaze drags over my naked flesh before those evil eyes bore into mine. "You won't have to fall in love, sweetheart, because I'll drag your ass into it with me."

We glare at one another for several long seconds. When he reaches for me, I go wild. I claw at him and scream. He manages to grab onto one of my arms and jerks me out of the shower into his firm grasp.

His bare skin against mine nauseates me and I wiggle to free myself.

"Let go of me, you asshole!"

I've lost it. I can't remain calm for the sake of my maybe baby. I can't even get myself under control and use my head long enough to determine an escape plan. All I can do is think about murdering this man with my bare hands.

"Baylee," he snarls, squeezing me hard enough to nearly break my ribs, "calm your shit or I'll knock your ass out."

Ignoring him, I lean back before slamming my forehead against his chin—hoping to hurt him more than myself.

"Fuck!"

We continue to scuffle—me like a live wire in his arms—back into the bedroom. My body is slippery and wet, but he still manages to hold on to me. When I get a glimpse of blood dripping from his lip, I'm overcome with joy. So much so that I cackle with glee.

"Calm the fuck down, woman!"

Only when he wrenches my arm behind me and twists it painfully do I stop my movement, giving in to loud, defeated sobs. The adrenaline seeps out of my body with every passing breath and all strength leaves with it.

"Take this," he orders, prying open my mouth. "It'll calm your ass down."

I gag as his fingers force the acrid pill past my tongue and into my throat. My teeth clamp down but he manages to free his hand before I can do any real harm. His strong palm presses my chin up to keep me from trying to spit it out. I can feel the mysterious pill slowly make its way down my dry throat.

"Baylee, I'm sorry."

I stiffen in his arms as his palm rubs innocently over my belly. Recoiling away from it would only give him suspicion to what I'm protecting, so instead, I bite my lip and breathe as normally as I can. My stomach roils as the pill settles and begins to do its job. I pray to God that if I am pregnant, it won't harm the fetus. "You're not sorry. You killed him. I *loved* him."

He stays silent for a long time and I wonder if he was even listening. Or if he's planning his retaliation for what I'm sure he interpreted as defiance. His grip on me finally loosens, but I'm too exhausted to fight and I'm already feeling numb from whatever it is he gave me. "Shhh, let's talk about it tomorrow. I've been too rough with you, I think. Expected too much, too soon. You're a good little girl, and I don't want to treat you like a prisoner."

He manages to climb into bed with me in his arms. When he drags the warm blanket up over us, I nearly moan in relief. His heavy arm holds my body against his—my back to his front. Even though my hair is soaked, he buries his nose in it and kisses my skull.

Every muscle in my body is on fire. My brain is fried. And my heart is gone.

I'm helpless to his forced cuddling.

So instead, I close my eyes and pretend his body belongs to another. That I'm receiving warmth from a man who is as pure as freshly fallen snow.

"I love you," he murmurs.

The voice is wrong but the sentiment comforts me.

I love you too, War.

I'm not sure if the words are spoken aloud or in my head, but soon I'm drifting off to a place where I'm free. Free to love and kiss and adore a complicated man.

At peace with War.

"What are you doing?" I ask, sucking in a gasp of air as his finger dances along my shoulder blade, pushing my hair away in a gentle move.

War smiles. I don't have to see it because I feel it. And I smile too.

"Counting your freckles. There are so many," he says in a quiet, almost shy tone.

I laugh and turn to look at him over my shoulder. He's propped up on one elbow and inspecting me as if he's trying to memorize every single square inch of my flesh. Everything about him is beautiful. The way his dark blue eyes twinkle when he's counting. How his full lips move in just the slightest way. And the way his brown hair hangs over his right eyebrow in a messy yet sexy way.

"How many are there?"

"Four hundred and thirteen," he tells me. His voice is resolute. Convinced. Completely sure. "So far."

Closing my eyes, I bask in his gentle touch. He calms me just as much as I seem to calm him. The world is no longer a threatening place when we're together like this. We're in our own world—one which is safe and filled with love.

As I drift off to sleep, he counts my freckles while I count every happy beat of my own heart.

Birds chirping.

They don't sound like the seagulls I'm used to waking up to.

Maybe they're sick.

My body is heavy and sore to the point that I almost feel drugged. I can't even manage to get my eyelids to lift.

Still too exhausted to face the day, I bury my face against the warm, firm chest in front of me and hug him closer to me. War always warms me. All the way down to the innermost parts of me. For some reason, I'm incredibly achy today and don't want to move.

Perhaps it's me that's sick, not the birds.

I think about how odd my body has been. The nausea. The sore breasts. The missed period. I'm nervous to bring it up to him, yet excitement threads through me. We've created something from our love. I'm certain there's a little love bud growing inside of me.

A smile graces my lips and I press a soft kiss to his chest. I slide my palm down along his lower abdomen until I'm gripping his hardened cock between us. His soft breaths tell me he's still asleep and I almost giggle aloud, knowing I'm about to wake him up.

I crack open an eye and tilt my head to look up at him.

My world spins and darkness swarms in like a horde of angry bees.

Not soft, peaceful features and a familiar scar.

Instead, dark, hard lines and edges. No scar.

His hot dick in my hand feels like an abomination and I jerk my hand from it as if it were a snake filled with poisonous venom. Short, choppy breaths rush from me as I inch myself away from the evil that lies before me.

The memories come crashing down around me. War. The gunshot. The blood. Bile rises in my throat and a scream remains lodged there. Sunshine from the window blankets us but it's a farce.

I'm not in a cozy cabin, happily whisked away with my lover.

I'm in hell with the devil. I'm his prisoner.

But I'm not bound.

A thrill kick starts my dead heart to life. I slip out from under Gabe's heavy arm. His soft snores an indication that he's still deep in sleep.

This is my moment.

This is my opportunity.

Probably one of the few I'll get.

I slip off the bed and nearly collapse. My legs are aching and shaky but I don't let them deter me in my pursuit for escape. Quickly, I snatch up his discarded shirt and yank it over me. Since Gabe is much taller than me, the shirt hits me mid-thigh, providing enough coverage for me to get the hell out of here.

The floorboard creaks beneath my feet and I jerk my gaze over to Gabe. No change in his movement. I have to go. *Now!*

On tiptoes, I hurry out of the bedroom and down the hallway toward the front door. It isn't locked—why would it be? Nobody would burst through the devil's front door on their own accord. I wrench it open as quietly as I can.

Squeeeeeak!

The door protests when I open it and it's loud. There's no turning back now. I have to go.

I push through it and stride down the steps. The memory of a few months before—him chasing me through the woods—is at the forefront in my mind. If anything, it only spurs me to go faster. With long strides, I ignore the bite of the gravel driveway on my bare feet as I put as much distance as I can between me and that godforsaken cabin.

"Goddammit, Baylee!"

His furious words from behind me make my heart freeze and I almost stumble. Ignoring the hateful way his words echo in my head, I run faster than I ever have toward the road. Heavy footsteps and frustrated grunts can be heard behind me. My panic overwhelms me with fear and tears well in my eyes, blurring the world around me. When my bare feet make purchase with the smooth, chilly concrete of the road, I almost cry out with joy. Running becomes a thousand times easier and I soar with long strides.

I focus on the road ahead of me and the prize is my ultimate escape.

I don't count my steps. I don't worry about his punishments.

Gabe will *not* catch me this time.

The grumble of an engine just around the bend is just the spark I need. My long legs carry me farther and faster than ever before. I risk a glance behind me and nearly cry out.

A monster chases me.

Bare feet and bare chested, only jeans covering his long, powerful legs.

Dark hair flapping in the wind.

Eyes black with rage.

Muscled chest flexing with the promise of recapture and retribution for my actions.

His mouth is contorted into a horrifying snarl, and I wonder if he'll tear through my flesh upon catching me.

He will not catch me this time.

Jerking my head forward, I pound along the freezing pavement toward the vehicle that now comes into view.

Thank you, God!

The black truck is barreling down the road. Too fast. Too out of control. It'll hit me, I think.

Then I can be with War…

I beam and look up into the early morning sky.

Take me with you, War.

The threat of tears burn in my throat as the sound of screeching tires echo around me. The truck never makes impact, though, and instead slams to a complete stop. A door flings open and I charge toward it.

"H-Help!" I croak, my voice dry and hoarse from exertion.

A man steps out and looks past me. "Get in the truck!"

The voice is comforting and familiar. I don't think twice about running past him and crawling into the cab of the truck. When I lift my gaze out of the windshield, I see just how close Gabe is. But instead of running right for us, he veers off to the tree line and reemerges with a large, thick branch.

"Let her go and I won't crack your skull open," Gabe barks out at the man whose face is hidden from me.

I could slam the door shut and drive off. Leave the man to deal with the monster on his own. The thought is fleeting and I don't let it win. If I left the man, Gabe would slaughter him. It would be that man's death sentence.

"She's coming with me, Gabe."

The voice. Familiar. Warm. Easy. And how does he know his name?

Before I can contemplate much more, a gunshot goes off, shattering the early morning tranquility. Gabe's shoulder jerks back and he gapes at the man in shock. He doesn't take another second before turning and hauling ass back to the cabin. Another gunshot goes off but it misses Gabe's retreating form.

"Baylee," the voice whispers. "Jesus, my Baylee."

The man steps into the open doorway of the truck and dips his head down to look at me. Pained, green eyes assess me. I'm so shocked, I simply stare at him with my mouth agape as he shoves the gun into the back of his pants.

"B-B-Brandon?"

He drops into the seat and reaches for me. I flinch slightly, still overwhelmed by the events of the last few minutes. Brandon frowns at my reaction.

"Babe, it's me."

His expression is sad. Tentative. His green eyes are all over me mixed with pity and relief. Brandon's once perfect hair is a wild mess that hangs in his eyes. His nose is slightly crooked from when Gabe broke it. Dark shadows mar the flesh under his eyes and his eyebrows are pinched together.

He looks older. Harder. Stronger. Almost frightening.

But then he smiles. His entire face lights up and my heart patters to life in my chest. He would never hurt one single hair on my head.

"It's really you," I sob.

His eyes flicker with happiness—something they always did when we were together—and he nods.

I scramble from my seat and into his arms. His warm, strong arms envelop me and I let him hold me as I wail against his neck. The embrace is familiar and comforting.

"Shhh, I have you now. This ends today, babe." He strokes my tangled hair and drops a kiss to the top of my head. After the hell I've been through, it feels almost heavenly to be back in Brandon's arms. I'm safe. This can all be over soon. But it won't be over until we put some distance between us and Gabe.

"We have to leave. He'll be back!" I shriek and jerk my gaze back to the road. I find no sign of Gabe. No sign of bloodshed. Not even the branch he had in his clutches. But I'm not naïve enough to be lulled into any kind of false sense of victory. Not yet. There's no doubt in my mind that he's run off to get his own gun or his car or God only knows what. Gabe doesn't give up. Not without a fight.

Brandon slams the truck door closed while I fall back into the seat right next to him. His body heat warms me and I remember a time when I sat snuggled up to him in this very truck. Back when life was simpler. The tires screech as he puts it into drive and gasses it. But instead of hauling ass up the road like I expect him to, he heads in the wrong direction. In the direction of the cabin. When he pulls into the driveway, I panic.

"Stop! What are you doing?" My voice is near hysterical.

"Wait here," he growls.

I'm clawing at his arm as he climbs out of the truck and storms off toward the cabin. My heart races in my chest and I'm at a loss as to what to do.

Gabe will kill him. Just like he killed War.

I can't lose Brandon, too.

chapter
FOUR

Brandon

My heart is on overdrive.

I have her.

I fucking have her.

And the need to protect what's mine is overwhelming. I won't let this asshole hurt her anymore. That's why this has to end now. *He* has to end now. I'm going to put a bullet between his eyes. Gabe Sharpe will never have the chance to put his hands on me again. And he'll never have the power to hurt my girl. Not ever again.

He is dead.

I let anger—*a newfound aspect of my personality*—wash over me in a red, vicious wave. Images of what he did to her. Thoughts of what she went through at his sadistic hand. Nightmarish visions of the horrors she faced. All ripping and clawing at the inside of me, fueling me on. Feeding the rage to pounce on the monster. To fucking destroy him.

The 9mm is still hot from when I fired it at him moments before. I'd felt invigorated the moment he jerked back when the bullet clipped his shoulder. I may not be the best marksman and I may not have landed my target, but I'd at least hit him. Weakened him. No longer was he the impenetrable force who was impossible to take down. This time, I wouldn't miss my target. I *will* kill this motherfucker.

Baylee grows eerily quiet behind me in the truck as I ascend the front steps of the cabin with the gun drawn and pointing toward the door. I wish I'd ordered her to lock the doors but there's no time. He's inside, no doubt, planning his own attack against us.

An attack he'll never carry out.

When I reach the front door, I waste no time and twist the knob. Once inside, I listen for movement. A scuffling in the back draws my attention. As much as I'd love to taunt him, demand answers, and make him suffer at the hand of my endless torture, there's no time.

With slow, measured steps, I make my way through the small living room and peek my head into what appears to be a kitchen.

"Stop right there, pussy boy."

My 9mm is trained on him but unfortunately, he has one pointed at me as well.

"This ends today, Gabe," I snap. A quiver in my arm makes the gun shake and his calculating eyes zero in on the trembling of my weapon. Surely mistaking it for fear. I'm not afraid, though. What he's seeing is the uncontrollable rage that quakes through me.

His laugh is deep and echoes in the small kitchen. "We both know how this ends, kid," he snarls, the short-lived humor in his voice gone. "I kill you and then I fuck my girl."

"She's not your girl, you fucking idiot."

A dark, amused eyebrow lifts and he smiles. "You don't honestly think she's yours, do you?" he taunts. "You're not enough for her. You weren't then, and you sure as fuck aren't now. She needs a man. A man who can protect her." He looks me up and down, and curls his lip in disgust, as if his findings leave much to be desired. "A man who can at least eat her pussy and hold her attention while he does it. I'm sure even that freak has that on you since she seems to think she's actually in love with him." His mouth lifts into a sinister smirk. "She tell you about him, *kid?*" He emphasizes the word kid. Another taunt. Another jab at my expense about how I'll never be good enough for Baylee. Same shit I've gotten from Tony for nearly two fucking years.

His words cast a shadow of doubt over my heart. There's no way Baylee could love the sick fuck who bought her. She's strong and smart. If anything, she may have played the role for her own survival, but she'd never fall for someone who could be a part of something so heinous.

"Fuck you, you rapist, pedophile piece of shit!" I fire off a shot but he's already charging for me.

He lands a splintering punch across my jaw that momentarily dazes me. My gun is still in my grip so I attempt to shove it against his rib cage, but he rolls the moment I squeeze the trigger. A window shatters as the shot hits it instead.

Gabe underestimates me and I twist in his grip to where I'm on top. I free my fist and blast him in the nose. *Payback's a bitch, asshole.* The satisfying crunch fuels me and I slam my fist forward again. This time, he hits me in the ribs, knocking the breath out of me.

It's just enough.

One stalled second to catch my breath and he's back on top of me.

Pop after pop with his fist across my jaw, he overtakes me and I start to weaken.

Shit!

"She wants him, pussy boy," he spits out as his hand finds my throat.

He's a goddamned liar and I won't let him rile me. I twist and scream in rage. The grip on my throat tightens and his laugh is maniacal.

"She fucked that freak and loved—" he starts, but a crack of something impacting his skull shuts him up. His dark eyes drop closed as he collapses on top of me.

A baseball bat wielding, crazed angel stands before us.

I'm dizzied and confused but I know it's Baylee—in all her furious glory—standing before me.

"D-Did he hurt you?" she stammers out as she drops the bat to push Gabe off of me.

I help her shove him away and blink away the daze. "I'm fine. Where's my gun? I'm going to kill him."

When I start for it, she launches for me. I'm shocked at her strength as she tackles me. Her pretty blue eyes are wild with fury as she pushes me back down to the floor. The gun is forgotten as I focus on how it feels to have her long legs straddled around me.

God, I fucking missed her.

"What are you doing?"

Tears well in her eyes and I slide a hand into her messy hair, drawing her to me. Those lips. Those perfect lips need kissing and tasting. She needs me to make it all better. Her mouth parts open and I can almost taste her sweet tongue on mine. But when I'm inches away, she slaps her palm over my mouth and widens her eyes.

"You can't kill him," she hisses. "At least not until I have answers from him."

A growl rumbles through my chest but one shake of her head silences me.

"Help me tie him up. I know where he keeps all the fucking rope." Her words drip with hate and venom. She doesn't need to tell me what he's done to her—her demeanor tells me enough.

Rape.

Torture.

Mind games.

Her crazed eyes tell me so.

"Yeah," I agree with a huff once she releases my mouth and sits up. "But when you're done, he's dead. Fucking dead."

Tears well in her eyes and she gives me a clipped nod. "The rope is in the bedroom closet."

She slides off me, and despite the day's chaos, I immediately miss her heat. Hopefully, soon

I'll have her in my arms where she belongs. When I stand, I nudge the gun to her. "If he moves, shoot him."

Her blue eyes find mine and she gives me a small smile. "With pleasure."

Gabe hasn't woken up yet, but he's not going anywhere. I've made sure of that. He's tied to a chair in the kitchen with a dishrag, Baylee's idea, gagging his mouth shut. Once he was secure, I watched her as she slipped into some sort of trance.

Her once lithe, toned body now appears wilted and fragile. Skin that used to glow from a year-round California tan, is lackluster and washed out. Blonde hair that used to hang in silken waves in front of her shoulders is now tangled and dull.

But the part of her that's the most different are her eyes.

Her sparkling, innocent blues have been replaced.

They're darker now. They hold secrets—secrets that will probably haunt her for the rest of her life, and I wonder if she'll ever find the strength to divulge them. Her eyes bear the pain she's endured and I'd give anything to make it go away. To see the soft look she used to gaze at me with once again.

"I brought you some things. You should shower and dress," I say softly, letting my eyes drag over her scantily clad body. When I'd rescued her, she'd been wearing nothing but a T-shirt despite the frigid morning air.

I cringe to think what would have happened had I not been released on bail sooner. If my mom hadn't have thrown a hissy fit to get me out of there, despite the fact I hit my father. The moment I was released, I was back in my truck, hauling ass out to this cabin, without so much as a muttered word of thanks.

I was almost too late.

But I wasn't.

I'd been there at exactly the right time.

It was fate.

"You think he'll bleed to death?" Her whispered words draw me from my mind and I follow her stare to Gabe. His head is leaning forward and his eyes are closed. After I shot him, he'd thrown on a T-shirt and the blood from his wound has soaked the sleeve. But it's not gushing. I had only clipped him—barely grazed the bastard.

"I wish," I huff and run a hand through my unruly hair, my newest habit, "but I think it's just a flesh wound. He'll probably be just fine."

She nods and leaves the room without another word. With a sigh, I trot out to the truck and retrieve my bag. Once back inside, I hear the shower running so I make my way into the bedroom and set to pulling out some things for her.

The room reeks of sex.

Of him and her.

Together. In this fucking bed.

It nauseates me.

She hasn't told me what he's done to her, but I know. He was inside of her, tarnishing not only her virginity, but her sanity. Baylee's different. How could she not be? And I hate what he's done to her.

I'm lost in my thoughts when she emerges, wearing only a towel. The circumstances are shit, but I can't help the way my cock thickens at the sight of her. We can finally be together. I'll finally be able to make love to her, make her feel safe again.

"Do you feel better?" I question with a hoarse voice.

Her eyes meet mine for a brief second before she drops them to the floor. Taking her cue, I walk over to the window to stare out while she dresses.

"You brought my favorite hoodie," she murmurs softly, ignoring my question. "Thank you."

She shuffles around behind me dressing, and it takes everything in me not to turn around and watch her. But she's been through too much. I won't victimize her too.

"If I remember correctly, it's my hoodie," I tease, a smile hinting at my lips. "You stole it."

A small chuckle escapes her and it's bliss—fucking bliss to hear it again. Her perfect, throaty laugh. "It looks better on me anyway."

I can't help but peek over my shoulder at her. She's already slid on her yoga pants over her panties and is tugging the hoodie over her head. Her small breasts—bare because I didn't think to grab any bras—jiggle as she pulls it on. Before her head pokes through, I turn away and adjust my erection. "That it does, babe."

The bed squeaks behind me as she sits. I turn to see her slipping on her socks and tennis shoes. It bothers me that she's sitting on that bed—a bed they shared last night—but I refrain from saying so. Instead, I stride over to her and sit beside her. My arm snakes around her waist and I hug her to me. She winces and freezes in my arms which only serves to anger me. It makes me want to jerk away from her and go back to the kitchen so I can beat the fuck out of Gabe.

"I'm going to take care of you," I vow. "I swear to it."

She lifts her chin and turns to look at me. "How's Mom? And where's Dad? Why weren't they looking for me?"

I can't help but sigh at her words. I knew this conversation was inevitable. I'd hoped for more time to hold her. To kiss her. To hug her. To love her. More time before having to crush her. To break what's left of her spirit.

"Babe, maybe now's not the time—"

"Don't."

I frown and scrub my palm over my face. My tongue is thick and sticky in my mouth, unable to find the right words.

"Tell me," she urges, the plea in her voice desperate. "Please, Brandon."

"Baylee…"

Our eyes meet, my lips just inches from her quivering bottom one. A single tear rolls down her cheek and drips from her jaw. "N-N-No."

"She passed away," I choke out, emotion threatening to suffocate me. "I'm so sorry."

"God, no." Another tear chases the last one and her nose darkens to a deep shade of red. "My poor dad." She stifles a sob but the tears run down her cheeks as she silently cries.

Rage bubbles in my chest, eradicating the sadness I felt for her and her mother, at the mention of Tony.

"When?"

I slide a hand along her cheek and swipe away some of the wetness with my thumb. "A few days after you were taken."

Her eyes dilate and her sadness quickly morphs into anger. "A few *days?* You mean, t—this was all for nothing!" Her statement is shrill and she stands abruptly. Matching her stance, I rise to my feet and grab onto her shoulders.

"That bastard didn't even tell me!" she shrieks and attempts to jerk out of my grasp but my grip is too strong. "And my dad! He never mentioned it once while I emailed with him, Brandon! Not once! Where the hell is he? Why wasn't he looking for me?"

A wash of dread trickles through me and I make a decision. She's had enough for one day. I won't be the bearer of any more bad news.

"I don't know where he is. But when I went by your house to get your clothes, a neighbor said he'd gone to San Francisco." The words easily roll off my tongue. "Maybe he was sparing your feelings. Maybe he wanted to tell you in person. And maybe he really is looking for you there."

Her entire body wracks with sobs and I hug her to me. Me, comforting her, it feels like where

I belong. I've held her crying body on numerous occasions as she struggled with coming to terms with her mother's illness.

"San Francisco? What the hell's in San Francisco? Something's not right, Brandon. Do you think Gabe hurt him?"

I freeze. "I wouldn't put it past him. He hurt you."

She nods and tilts her tearstained face to regard me. "I've lost everyone."

I press a kiss to her forehead. "You haven't lost me. I'm still here."

As if my words enrage her, she jerks away from me. Guilt flashes over her features, leaving me puzzled for a moment. Then, she storms from the room on a mission. I chase after her to find her standing in front of Gabe with her hands on her hips, staring at him.

"Wake up!" she snaps and grabs a handful of his hair, pulling his head back.

Gabe doesn't even flinch. He's breathing but he's out cold.

"We can interrogate him later. You should eat something and rest a little."

She jerks her gaze to mine, disgust written all over her face. "We're not staying here long. As soon as he wakes up, I'll get him to tell me where my dad's at, and then we'll go find him."

I cringe, knowing this conversation with Gabe won't end well. "Fine," I say, placating her, "but you will eat. You're pale as hell."

She relaxes a bit as I walk over to the refrigerator. I open the freezer, hoping to find something easy to make her. Instead, I only find foil-wrapped vegetables.

"What a fucking weirdo," I murmur in disgust as I widen the freezer to show her.

Her face blazes crimson as she charges for me. I gape at her as she starts grabbing them from inside and begins chunking them at Gabe. They may as well be rocks because each one that manages to hit him makes a thud. I stand there in stunned silence as she throws every last one of them at him.

My Baylee. My sweet, sweet girl. She's lost.

All that's left is this angry, distraught little animal. I'm afraid she'll never be the girl I once knew and loved.

Doesn't mean I could ever stop loving her. If anything, I love her even more. We've both changed. Not just her. She and I are different. We've seen things—done things that have altered who we are and forced us to grow wise beyond our years.

When she has nothing left to throw at him, she slaps his unconscious face over and over again. I let her release some of her inner rage and emotion before scooping her into my arms. Her hand clutches onto my neck as I stride with her into the living room. I sit down and bring her with me into my lap.

She smells clean and her skin is soft. My arms grip her tight against me as she curses God, sobs, and screams. We stay like that until she's nothing but a quivering, sniffling, hiccupping shell of herself.

"Rest now, Baylee," I murmur against her damp hair. "You're safe now."

chapter
FIVE

Baylee

"When we make love, I forget to count your breaths," War murmurs in the dark, his fingertip tickling over my ribcage as he drags it up and down along my skin. "But they're quicker and more frequent. I like the way they sound, sharp intakes followed by whimpering exhales. And the ragged, uneven way about them is perfection."

I smile and snuggle against his warm body. "Maybe we should do it again. You know," I tease as I kiss his neck, "so you can count them."

A deep, rumbling chuckle reverberates from him, and I fall deeper for him. His laughter has the ability to work itself under my skin and imbed warmth there for eternity. With each laugh or smile, he fills me. I'm whole with this complicated, beautiful man.

"Bay, I'll make love to you any day," he says with a growl, "but I can assure you I'll always forget to count."

He rolls on top of me and nudges my thighs apart with his knee. When he rests his hardened cock against my belly, I let out a gasp.

"When we fuck," he murmurs, making sure to enunciate the word as he thrusts against my body, "I only think about you. The black abyss inside my head is obliterated by your light. I'm too absorbed in your tight body and swollen lips. You chase away my demons. I'm nothing more than your servant—put on this earth to worship you until the end of time."

His words cause a heat to burn through me, all the way from my heart to my core. I squirm against him and thread my fingers into his dark hair. "Fuck me then, servant," I taunt, pulling his head down to mine.

He must be turned on by my dirty talking because he lets out an animalistic grunt and forcefully enters me. My body is wet and ready, as it always is with him, and I moan against his lips.

"One," he mutters aloud as he bucks against me. The delicious tightening in my lower body intensifies with each powerful thrust into me. He's counting my breaths and I'm counting stars.

"Two."

All of them.

"Three."

Glittering behind my closed eyelids as I greedily grab for the orgasm his body will no doubt give me. His lips steal over mine and he kisses me hard enough to steal the breath right from my lungs.

I love all the parts of War.

But when he makes love to me, he owns not only my body but my mind as well. We become one and I relish in the way we connect in blissful harmony. His hand slides to my breast and he squeezes reverently. Our lips don't disconnect as he fucks me right over the edge.

"Oh, God!"

My words seem to have a ripple effect because his cock feels as if it grows inside me before he bursts his release into me, marking me as his.

And it's true.

I'll never belong to another.

War owns me and I own him.

Together we are peace.

"My sweet Baylee," he croons, his lips now peppering kisses all over my face. "You're so goddamned perfect."

I smile and tenderly stroke his cheek with my thumb. "And so are you."

His body crushes me and I revel in the way he consumes me. Despite his afflictions, he's strong and powerful in his own unique way. Warren McPherson is a force to be reckoned with. He's a dark storm, raging from his inner demons. I have an appetite for his destruction. My soul craves to be completely overtaken by him.

Lucky for me, though, War would never hurt me. He may be chaos, brewing and festering on the inside, but with me, he handles me with surety and gentleness. My War protects what belongs to him as if it is precious.

I am precious to him.

"How many breaths?" I question as he pulls out of my body, his hot cum running from me and warming a trail between my butt cheeks as it leaves.

He grunts as he climbs off the bed in search of a towel. "I was at three breaths before time stopped."

The bathroom light flicks on and soon I can hear the water running in the shower. He returns with the towel, the light silhouetting his muscular frame. His hands make quick efficient work with the towel as he cleans me before guiding me out of the bed.

"Time stopped for you too?"

He stops before opening the shower curtain and regards me with a crooked smile. Dear God, this man has the most handsome face. The silver scar along one side from his accident only serves to intensify his rugged appearance.

"Time stopped for me the moment you sat down inside my car that night. With you, I could finally take a break from the maddening chaos ticking by, second by second. With you, I could breathe. With you, I could be happy."

I stand on my toes and press a kiss to his cheek. "Our own little world."

"Don't ever leave our world, Bay. Stay with me forever."

Tears well in my eyes, but for once, they aren't from worrying over my parents or Gabe or anything else for that matter. They're happy tears. "I wouldn't ever dream of leaving."

He drags me into the shower and I let out a moan as the scalding spray washes away the evidence of our lovemaking.

"Baylee…"

The voice is wrong.

It doesn't belong to my War.

I look around but he's no longer in the shower with me, the steam from the water growing thicker and thicker, obstructing my view.

Our world has dissipated and darkness cloaks around me, blinding me.

"War…" I call out with a sob. "War!"

"Baylee!"

I blink open my eyes and stare into two dark green orbs. They're not my War's icy navy blue ones. The warmth that had only moments ago surrounded me is replaced by a chill I can feel all the way to my bones.

The voice again. Raspy and ragged. Choked and angry. And still not belonging to the man from my dreams or the person I'm wrapped around.

"Brandon?"

I close my eyes to rid myself of the confusing dream and reopen them, hoping it will be War instead. But, my gaze fixates on Brandon's intense glare.

"Who is War?"

The blood turns to ice in my veins and I shiver. Brandon hugs me tighter to him. We're sprawled out on the couch with my back to the cushions and him facing me as we lay on our sides. One of his big hands is resting on my ribcage, his thumb running back and forth along the underside of my swollen breast. His knee is between my thighs, resting against my pussy. The hardness of his erection presses against me alerting me to the fact he's enjoying our contact.

It all feels like a betrayal to War.

"Brandon," I murmur, dragging my gaze away from his, "he was…"

His knee moves and I let out a whimper. My dream was so vivid and my nerve endings are still alive. The simple touch of his nudge sends my heart racing.

"He must've been something to you, babe," he says in a hushed tone, a hint of revulsion in his voice. "Otherwise you wouldn't have been riding my leg and moaning his name."

To reiterate his point, he drags his thumb over my nipple and I gasp, my hips involuntarily bucking against him.

"Brandon, stop," I whimper.

He groans but his hand leaves my breast and underneath my shirt to rest on my hip. "I thought you were dreaming about me." His voice is husky and I can sense the feeling of betrayal in it.

"I…" I trail off, not sure of how to explain this to him. "He…"

"Did you fuck him?"

I flinch at the harsh way he spits out the crude words.

"It wasn't like that. I loved him," I choke out with a sob.

"Like you loved me?"

A tear rolls down my temple and our eyes meet again. "I loved him differently."

He swallows and breaks our stare. His face is a storm of emotions. Eyebrows pinching together in anger, followed by sorrow as if he might cry. Nose flaring with each upset breath. Lips pressed into a line to keep from spewing words of hate at me.

"I searched for you." His voice is a mere whisper. "This whole time, I searched for you when nobody else would." When his watery green eyes meet mine, I ache to soothe the boy I once loved. Our love was simple and easy. Our love was nothing like the otherworldly, all-consuming love I had with War.

Had.

Because he's dead now.

"And *you* found me," I tell him, the emotion in my throat making it ache.

His palm finds my cheek and he strokes it with the pad of his thumb. "Will you love me like you loved him?"

Before I can answer him, the voice—the one that stole me from my sweet dream and turned it to a nightmare—beckons me.

"B-Baylee."

My heart thumps in my chest. Brandon scrambles off the couch and is already stalking into the kitchen before I even roll myself off.

"This is all your fault, you bastard!"

I round the corner in time to see Brandon backhand Gabe across the cheek. Gabe makes a grunting sound from the force of Brandon's hit. When he rears back to hit him again, I push him away.

"Stop it! I need answers and if you knock him out, I won't get those answers," I shout and give him another shove.

He grumbles under his breath but doesn't go at Gabe again. Gabe, who doesn't look much like himself because of his swollen face, bloody nose, and bright red cheek, lifts his head to look at me. His dark eyes lock with mine.

I expect to see anger or fury.

What I don't expect is to see a flicker of regret.

"Why didn't you tell me she died?!" My voice is shrill and I hug my arms to my chest to keep from hitting him myself. "I was here, getting violated by you, all the while unknowing of the fact that my mother had died."

Brandon growls behind me, but I ignore him and keep Gabe in the sights of my rage.

"I didn't know she died, sweet girl. It wasn't until after I sold you that I learned the truth," he says, voice dropping low as his gaze flits over to Brandon briefly. "When I came back, I'd learned she'd passed. I was planning on telling you today but you ran away…"

I search his eyes for deception but find none. If anything, I sense what appears to be despondency. An emotion I didn't think Gabe was capable of. He's sad she's gone. Before he'd gone psycho by abducting me, he'd been close to my parents.

"Why wasn't my dad looking for me?" I blurt out, the thought of my father causing my heart to ache. "War and I searched for anything related to my kidnapping and there was nothing. Is my daddy hurt? Did you hurt him?" Tears well in my eyes and I shudder. I'm not sure if I'm strong enough to hear the answer.

Gabe turns his head to glare at Brandon and spits out his words. "Why don't you ask Brandon that question?"

I jerk my head to see Brandon's chest heaving with rage. Before I can stop him, he darts forwards and slams his knuckles across Gabe's temple, rendering him unconscious.

"What the hell did you do that for?" I screech and throw my hands up in the air.

He lets out a fierce growl that chills me. "He was getting loose," he says, motioning to the rope holding Gabe to the chair. "He'd managed to loosen the rope around his wrist. I'll string him up tighter. Why don't you go lie down and rest? You're awfully pale, babe."

Ignoring the wooziness from not having eating today, I hold my palm out to him. "Fine. But I want to try and reach my dad. Give me your phone."

"It died," he murmurs while working to tighten the rope in quick, sharp movements. "I don't have the charger with me."

I want to challenge him on his words, but I don't. Brandon always carries a portable phone charger in his truck. Why wouldn't he have it with him? My mind whirls with reasons as to why he'd lie to me, coming up empty. Brandon has never lied to me. Not once. He's always been the one person I could count on.

"What did he mean?" I question, my thoughts lingering on Gabe's earlier words.

Brandon flits his gaze over to me and frowns. "About what?"

"About my dad. What did he mean about asking you? Is there something you know and aren't telling me?"

He throws his hands in the air and immediately he becomes defensive. "W—What? You think I have something to do with all this? Come on, Baylee," he says with a hiss of disbelief, his eyes darting back between me and Gabe's unconscious form in a way that has me on edge. "I checked in on your dad while you were gone. He'd lost Lynn and I knew you would want me to make sure he was okay. Jesus Christ! And then one day he upped and vanished. Why do I feel like I'm the goddamned villain now?"

Guilt floods through me and I shake my head in argument. "I just…"

"Believed that monster over me." He clenches his jaw and I can tell he's trying not to cry.

My emotions take over and I reach a shaky hand over to touch his shoulder. I want to comfort him. Because of my own exhaustion and grief, I'm taking it out on Brandon. I'm believing that monster over him, just as he says. "I'm sorry, Brandon."

With a big sigh, he reaches up and clutches my hand that covers his shoulder. "It's okay, babe. We'll get through this together. I promise."

chapter
SIX

Brandon

I lied to her.

Again.

How many times will I have to lie to her?

Leaning against the counter, I cross my arms over my chest and watch her leave the kitchen. As soon as she's gone, I pull my phone from my pocket and turn it off so it won't buzz or ring while she's around. The last thing I need is for her to discover that I have it and that it is working just fine.

A dull throb begins to form behind my eyes and I sigh out in frustration, stuffing my phone back into my pocket. Stark had said Baylee was wanted for questioning in the attempted murder. When Baylee whimpered and moaned his name while she slept, I knew.

Gabe was right. She is, for some God-awful fucking reason, in love with him.

The thought enrages me.

It makes me want to lift the slat of the hole to the cellar and push Gabe to his death for being the cause of all of this.

But mostly, it hurts.

My mind can't comprehend how she could feel anything for her captor. Except for intense hatred. Fuck, this guy is no different than Gabe. How could she not see that? I'd honestly assumed she was lying—possibly playing him in order to survive.

Once I saw her running down the street and then later had her in my arms, I almost laughed at myself for having entertained such a stupid notion even for a second. Of course my girl couldn't love some monster who paid money to fuck her. Of course she still loved me with all of her heart, like I love her.

But now?

Now I know it wasn't a fucking act.

She does love him. I see it in the way she won't hold my gaze—the guilt pouring from her eyes giving her away. I feel it in the way she avoids my touch, instead pushing me away.

I have to fix this.

And if that means lying to her to keep her safe, so be it. It isn't normal for her to have fallen for someone who paid money for her. Clearly, he fucked with her head. Soon, she'll come to this realization and come back to me. I'll get my girl back.

A few tiny lies mean nothing in the grand scheme of things. Those lies will protect her mind and her heart. As her boyfriend, the love of her life, I will make sure I do whatever it takes to protect my girl.

"I'm hungry."

The voice from the kitchen is weak and shaky. Baylee, who sits curled up on one end of the couch, eating a sandwich meets my gaze with wide eyes.

"You don't deserve to eat, asshole," I call out, and then stuff a chip in my mouth.

Baylee's lips press together in a firm line. Her eyes are darting back and forth from me to the food on her plate. Finally, she sets the plate on the coffee table and snatches up the uneaten other half of the sandwich.

"I'm going to talk to him," she says as she stands.

Anxiety floods through me as she stalks off to see Gabe who had *unfortunately* regained consciousness. If he doesn't keep his mouth shut, he could ruin everything. Dropping my plate to the table, I jump up and stride after her.

"Where's Dad?" she demands and dangles the sandwich in front of him.

He eyes it hungrily and meets her gaze. "I don't know."

"Liar," she hisses.

His glare snaps to me and he smirks. I fist my hands at my sides. If I hit him again, she'll definitely be suspicious.

"I'm not lying, sweet girl. I was with you the whole time. After your auction, I came back to check in with Tony, and he was gone. He hasn't returned any of my calls. It's like he's disappeared."

Baylee approaches him and holds the sandwich to his mouth. He takes a bite and flashes her a grateful smile as he chews. I hate the way he looks at her—as if they share something I'm not privy too. He's probably thinking of how he popped her fucking cherry. Fucking bastard!

"Why did you need to check in with him?" she questions.

His dark eyebrows furrow together and I know he's warring with whether or not he should tell her the truth. If he explains the fact that her father had something to do with it, it'll only infuriate her, and the chance of him eating a bullet is likely. "I wanted to check on Lynn for you, baby," he lies, his eyes finding mine.

Truth is, he never showed up to check on Tony. This, I know for a fact. I could out him on his lie, but then she'll be back to demanding to know where her father is.

She can't know.

Ever.

Her hand becomes shaky as she feeds him another bite of the sandwich. I'm not sure why she's showing him kindness. He doesn't deserve one second of her time unless it's spent making him pay.

"Don't cry," he says softly after he swallows, his gaze turning soft. "She loved you. I'm sorry she was taken so soon."

She shoves the rest of the sandwich in his mouth and then turns to face me. Tears stream down her red cheeks and she runs into my waiting arms where she belongs. As she sobs and I embrace her, Gabe and I maintain eye contact. He seems satisfied at toying with me. Almost as if the asshole thinks he holds the fate of my relationship with Baylee in his hands.

For some reason, he didn't mention Tony's involvement in her abduction. I'd like to think it's because he's a pussy and doesn't want her to be angry with him. But deep down, I feel like he doesn't want to break her already fractured heart further. Tony and Lynn were his friends.

He clearly has something up his sleeve. I'll make sure he never gets the chance to pull out any of his tricks though.

This game is nearly over and I'm already calling victory.

"Can you take me to Walmart?" Her voice is a muffled whisper against my chest. "I need a few things and then we can get back to dragging answers from that prick before we go to the police."

Her soft voice pulls me from pondering what Gabe's motives are and I stare down at her. Despite her flushed wet cheeks, she lifts her chin and bravely gazes up at me.

The idea of her face plastered all over the Walmart security cameras while she's wanted in connection of an attempted murder, sends panic skittering through me. Stark would have her team all over us before we even managed to fill the shopping cart. Fuck that. We're not going anywhere. But just when I think I have the balls to tell her as much, she speaks again.

"Plus," she says with a shaky voice, "I'd like to see my mother's grave."

The very idea that Baylee didn't get to say goodbye to Lynn is heartbreaking. If I could bring her mother back to her, I'd do it in a second without a moment's hesitation. I would do anything for her. *Anything.*

Which is why I pull slightly away from her and run my fingers through my hair while I battle with indecision. All the reasons as to why this is a bad idea fly at me like baseballs barreling at me in a batting cage. I wish I could knock them all away from me and give her everything she asks for.

But I can't.

I won't make stupid mistakes like going into public knowing they're looking for her. She's already been through too much. I'll protect her from this too.

I slip my palm to her neck and run my thumb along her jaw. "Sure, baby. We'll go see your mom's grave." The Walmart trip will have to wait for another day. "Go get in the truck and I'll finish him up."

A grumble echoes in the kitchen and my shoulders tense at the sound.

"What the fuck does that mean?" Gabe demands from behind her.

I flip him off. "Exactly what you think. You're dead, asshole. Time's up. You've ruined shit enough and I'm done with you fucking with my girl."

He laughs at me. "Your girl?" he says with a tsk. "Brandon, Brandon, Brandon. We've been through this and—"

"SHUT UP!" she screeches. "Brandon, you're not killing him." She snaps her gaze to Gabe. "Yet."

Gabe, seeming unaffected by her threat, smirks at me. "By all means, take your 'girl' to dinner. Go *woo* her. I'll just hang out here. Bring me a doggie bag."

She grabs my hand and drags me from the kitchen. "Why do you even challenge him?" she huffs as we make our way into the living room. "You can't win with him." Her tone is annoyed and impatient. It stings that she'd chastise me for wanting to protect her from his predator ass.

"Apparently I can't win with you either," I mutter under my breath. "I'll wait outside."

"Did you get what you needed?" I ask as she climbs into the truck with a bagful of shit. Earlier when we'd pulled into the parking lot of the aging drugstore in town, she'd seemed suspicious as to why I didn't take her to Walmart. But I just shrugged my shoulders, feigning indifference, and told her this place was closer.

She nods and rummages in the sack until she pulls out a small plastic box. Tossing it into my lap, she narrows her eyes at me and says coolly, "A phone charger. You can charge it when we get back to the cabin."

I give her a clipped nod as I try and figure out a way to avoid her using my phone. Once she sees her face on the news as a person of interest, she's going to really lose her shit. I don't need her completely breaking apart. Not when I'm finally here and attempting to put her back together again.

Putting the car into reverse, I reach over and push play on my Big Wreck CD. This was an album that we always listened to together. I'm hoping to help her remember better times—times when our relationship wasn't strained. Times when we were free to love without worry.

From the corner of my eye, I see that she bought a small purse and is quickly shoving shit into it. It all appears to be girly makeup, a hair brush, and other stuff. I didn't really think to grab those things in my haste to get to her. All I cared about was finding her and then never letting her go.

The cemetery is about forty-five minutes from the cabin and I dread having to drive in silence. She now stares out the window as if she longs to be anywhere but inside this truck with me.

"I'm sorry, babe. I shouldn't have been an asshole earlier. I'm just totally at my max with stress about this whole situation. All I want is to help you. That's all I've ever wanted."

Her head turns to me and she offers me a small smile. It's not much but I'll take it.

"Do you remember that time Dax Stevens poured hand sanitizer into Mr. Duncan's coffee while he stepped out of the classroom?"

She nods and looks out the window.

"God, the whole class was laughing so hard when he came back in. He was so eager to tell us about the Civil War that he downed practically half his cup before he realized it didn't taste right. When he puked in the trash can, you almost threw up." I flash her a grin. "Dax got in so much fucking trouble. His dad probably beat his ass for getting expelled over that shit."

"Poor Mr. Duncan." A small chuckle escapes her and it's fucking musical. It breathes hope into a brittle part of my heart that had been recently darkened.

She leans forward and switches the song she always skips over to the next one we both love. My chest swells with happiness. We can fix this. I just need to breathe life back into my girl. Make her remember the good times.

Reaching over, I hold my hand out to her. And like a million other times we rode around in my truck together, she grasps my hand and our fingers thread together.

Everything is going to be okay.

chapter
SEVEN

War

White and then black.

White and then black.

White and then voices.

"Warren."

A blur stands in my vision and I attempt to blink away the haze. When my eyes find their focus, my father comes into view. His dark hair is disheveled and his eyebrows are drawn together in concern. Lines that weren't there before crinkle along his forehead. My dad looks older. And stressed as hell.

"Warren, do you remember what happened?" His voice shakes as he asks his question.

I try to speak but it's then that I realize something is in my throat. A tube maybe. Shaking my head, I attempt to conjure up my memories.

Something niggles at me.

Something heavy.

As if my heart is aching.

"Son, you were shot. Do you remember that?"

Again, I shake my head no.

His frown is immediate. "Do you remember Baylee?"

Baylee. Baylee. Baylee.

My heartrate speeds up and I can hear it on the monitor. The sound is comforting and I find myself needing to count the beats. How many of those rapid beats would resound on the monitor in a minute's time? My eyes dart all around the room in search of a clock. Finding nothing, I decide to count them. One, two, three, four, five, six—nearly two beats per second. Two beats per second means one hundred twenty in one minute. Is that normal? Is it abnormal? Is it the reason I'm in the hospital instead of being shot like Dad claims?

I forget to count when I'm with you.

The voice, *my voice*, echoes in my head over and over again. That phrase seems to be a mantra I've created for myself. Because of her.

I close my eyes and I see her bright blue eyes. Kind and compassionate. Hungry and loving.

She loves me.

And I love her.

Reopening my eyes, I plead with them to my father. To ask him where she is. Everything is confusing and hazy but when it comes to thinking about her, I can recall every tiny detail of her beautiful face.

"I'm sorry but…" Dad trails off and reaches my hand. I jerk it away before he can touch me.

My heartrate thunders in my achy chest and the beats are out of control. The machine is dinging noisily at my side. Why is he sorry? What happened to her?

"We'd like to ask you a few questions, Mr. McPherson," a woman says from somewhere else in the room. "Or should I call you Mr. Atlantic?"

The panic in my chest doesn't subside and I'm at the point where I feel as if it might rip right down the middle at any second. My skin would tear while the bones would crack as my heart makes its escape. Blood would spurt and spray the dingy, yellow ceiling tiles, making them a brilliant red instead.

An attractive older woman steps into view, her brown eyes narrowing at me. I don't know her yet she appears to know me. Before she gets too close, Dad stops her with his arm.

"That's close enough, Detective Stark."

Stark?

Why does that name ring all sorts of bells in my head?

She nods her acquiescence. "We'd like to talk to you about Baylee Winston and Gabriel Sharpe. She's wanted for questioning right now for her involvement in your attempted murder. We have reason to believe she was Mr. Sharpe's accomplice. Is it correct that you were sending funds to help her mother?"

The room spins and I snap my eyes closed to keep from throwing up. With this tube down my throat, who knows what would happen. I could drown on my own vomit. It would spew and spew but would have nowhere to go. Gobs of stomach acid would find their way into my lungs, burn through the tissue, and eventually suffocate me. Then who would help Baylee?

I reopen my eyes and affix my gaze to my father. With furrowed brows I plead for him to explain to her that Baylee is my love, not some criminal. He frowns and nods, a knowing look on his face.

"Parking is a nightmare around here," another voice complains, interrupting our exchange when he enters the room.

A middle-aged man with a receding hairline strolls in with his hands on his hips. I become fixated on his unusually long fingernails—too long for a man—on each hand. Black. Dirty and filthy underneath. And crawling with bacteria. Who the fuck doesn't clean under their fingernails?

My dad is saying something to Stark about Baylee but I can't take my horrified stare from the man who takes those same disgusting fingers and retrieves a discolored toothpick from his front pocket. He pops it into his mouth between his teeth and starts gnawing on the thing like he's a goddamned beaver.

Smack. Smack. Smack.

The sound grates on me but the sight is much worse.

Moisture forms on his lips and I shudder to think of how many millions of disgusting microbes are infesting that mouth of his.

He pinches the end of the toothpick to whittle between two of his teeth. I want to look away from this sick show but I'm completely glued to his revolting behavior.

When he slips the toothpick from his mouth, inspecting the end of it, I gag.

A small chunk of something mushy sits on the tip. His tongue darts out and he slurps it off causing my stomach to clench in protest.

What kind of fucking pig did they let into my room?!

The room spins and my world goes dark as I attempt to force the images out of my mind. But the vision is already permanently etched there. I can almost sense the toxic microbes from inside his mouth tainting the air around me and my lungs ache from the very idea of that shit finding its way in there. I can practically feel it crawling inside of me, contaminating every inch of my insides.

I gag again and again.

A commotion resounds in the room. Shouts and voices. I ignore it all as I try to calm my heart, which is clawing painfully in my chest to get away from the contaminated air I've breathed in. Just when I think I'm about to pass out, a cold blast enters my vein. At first I assume it's something horrible and toxic, but then it travels quickly and blissfully up my arm, leaving a numbing wake in its path. It can't get to my brain fast enough.

I beg for it.

Crave it.

Need for it to numb the madness.

And it does. Soon, I'm attempting to blink my eyes open to tell them Baylee is my savior, not some monster.

But I can't open my eyes. I can't tell them about her.

"I'm cold."

Her brilliant blue eyes are staring at me. The tube is gone. All that exists is her. "I'll keep you warm."

She rewards me with a breathtaking smile. The urge to kiss her is overwhelming. My arm snakes around her and I haul her to my chest. Our lips meet in an unrushed kiss. She tastes divine and I don't ever want to disconnect from her.

I thread my fingers through her hair and hold her in place while I taste every inch of her mouth. So perfect. So goddamned perfect.

"I love you," I murmur and then suck on her bottom lip. My cock lurches with excitement against her thigh.

"I love you too, War," she whispers and lets out a tiny moan that's my undoing. "Now make love to me."

Pushing her to her back, I spread her thighs apart and push into her hot center.

The pleasure is overwhelming and the world goes black.

I fuck her into the nothingness of my mind, where she belongs. Where she can save me in a way only she knows how.

"Stay with me here," I beg as the blackness blinds me.

"I wouldn't dream of leaving you."

Black and black and black.

And Baylee.

chapter
EIGHT

Baylee

I'm numb.

I've stared at her tombstone for a solid hour, trying to understand how this all happened. How I lost my mother when I thought I was helping her this whole time. If she died that first week, why was my father taking the money War was sending? What was Dad doing with it when he should have been looking for me and why the hell is he in San Francisco?

Brandon clears his throat from beside me, jerking me from the thoughts that are on a continuous reel in my head. "You want to grab a bite to eat? It'll be dark soon."

My stomach grumbles but I ignore it. Instead, I stare at the grey granite.

Lynn Marie Winston.

Beloved Wife and Mother

The angel wings engraved into the rock are gorgeous. I wonder if Dad paid for it with War's money. Money I negotiated my body and my companionship for. Of course, once I got to know War and fell in love with him, it hardly seemed like a negotiation or prison sentence.

It was my home.

He was my home.

But still. How could Dad accept War's money so easily but not tell me my mother had died? The realization that he never once mentioned what happened to her kills me. I want to find him so I can demand answers to all the questions inside my head.

The wind picks up and chills my flesh. My hoodie does nothing to warm the cold, emptiness in my bones. In my aching heart. In my fractured soul.

I hug my purse to my side and think about the pregnancy test inside. I've been dying to learn the truth about whether or not I'm carrying War's baby. I need to know one way or another for closure. I'd also like to get ahold of Land. I want my child to have a relationship with their father's father.

Brandon snakes an arm around me and hugs me to his side. I hadn't realized I was shivering but his body warms me. Well, on the surface at least. He'd relaxed on the way here and was back to being the friendly, all-around good guy I was used to. It's going to break his heart when this all blows over and I explain to him that I don't love him—not like I love War. That we're better as friends.

The thought of telling him this—after all he's done for me—nauseates me. But I won't live a lie. My heart belongs to War, whether dead or alive. I can't get past him. I will never get past him. And if this baby exists, I'll pour all of my love for War into it. I'll spend the rest of my life giving that baby everything it deserves.

"Babe," Brandon says and kisses my temple. I shudder at his affection, but hopefully he attributes it to me being cold. "We can come back tomorrow. And the day after. And every day after that if it makes you feel better. But I need to get some food in you before you blow away with the wind."

He tries to make light of the situation and it irritates me. I stiffen in his arms and clench my jaw so I don't say anything hurtful. Truth is, I'm angry and upset and devastated. My mother is dead, War is dead, and my father is apparently missing. Meanwhile, Brandon is acting like he wants to slip back into old roles and play house.

His hand slips to my throat and he uses his fingers to turn my jaw to face him. The gesture is firm but still gentle. Our eyes meet and I wonder if he can sense the fury emanating from mine. "Hey," he says softly, and I relax a little. "I didn't mean to upset you. This is a big clusterfuck and I'm trying to navigate it without a rule book. I'm sorry."

He lowers his lips to mine, and when I attempt to jerk away from him, his fingers bite just a little into my flesh, holding me still. The desperation in his eyes chases away the light, and for a moment, I gape at his sudden change. His lips are on mine a second later. Needy and overly eager. I wait just a fraction of a moment to see if the old spark returns.

It doesn't.

It's just lips and tongue.

Wetness and cinnamon gum.

Nothing about his kiss consumes me—not like War's did. The only reason he's been awarded this kiss in the first place is because his grip is strong and I can't easily break away. When he moans into my mouth, I freeze. I don't want to kiss him. I want him to give me some space. Sliding my fingers into his hair, I tug until his lips break from mine.

"Brandon," I murmur, my voice laced with annoyance.

He ignores the sting of me pulling his hair and instead, steals another kiss. His weight topples me over into the cold earth and soon he's grinding his erection against me. The man kisses me as if he's starved for me—as if I'm the one person who can fill some of his emptiness.

The entire action reminds me of Gabe and my heart speeds up. My palms find his chest, and I try to push him away but he's so strong. When he grinds painfully against me again, I lose it and manage to jerk my mouth from his, turning my head sharply to the right. His mouth moves on to my neck and earlobe, hot breath tickling my flesh.

"God, how I've missed you, babe. Missed us. This." He emphasizes his point by nibbling on the skin.

I see red about the same time I see a stick. It isn't thick but it'll do. With quick, forceful whaps I whip him on the back of the head until he rolls off and away from me. Scrambling to my knees, I point the stick at him accusingly.

"What is wrong with you, Brandon?" I demand and toss the stick into the grass. "My mind is a mess and this certainly isn't helping."

He has the sense to look ashamed. His darkened eyes return to the sparkly green I know and trust. Crimson heats the top of his cheeks as he runs his fingers through his messy hair. "Jesus, Baylee. I'm so sorry. I just missed you and—"

"Thought you could make out with me on my mother's grave?" I finish for him, my voice venom-filled as I stand up. My words wound him and I'm glad. I know he's been through a lot, but so have I.

He looks up toward the sky with a groan and then pins me with an icy glare before stalking off toward the truck. "And you don't have to worry," he calls out over his shoulder, "that'll be the last time I try and comfort you again. But my feelings for you—my craving to touch you—can't just be flipped off with the push of a button, unlike you."

Guilt washes over me as he leaves me. Maybe I was too harsh. This has to be difficult for him too. When I left, we were hot and heavy for one another. We had plans. A future all mapped out.

But then I was sent to War.

And everything changed.

Nothing will ever go back to the way things used to be.

By the time I reach the truck, he's squatting down beside it. When I round the vehicle to inspect what he's looking at, my heart sinks.

"I dropped it. It's dead now."

The phone is shattered and the screen is black. My brows furrow as suspicion trickles through me. I used to drop my phone all of the time and never once shattered it. Sure, I cracked it a time or two, but it never shattered. He had to have thrown it when he had his angry tantrum. I want to shout at him for being a hot-headed asshole or to demand why he'd destroy our only connection to the outside world. Instead, I lift my chin and wordlessly go back to the passenger side to climb in. Casting one more glance at my mother's final resting place, I silently make a vow to her.

I will find a way to be happy, Mom.

A way to be safe.

I will protect myself and nurture the love in my heart for War.

You don't have to worry about your little girl anymore. I'm all grown up.

I won't let anyone control my life but me.

The drive back to the cabin is silent and it's driving me crazy. My mind buzzes with all sorts of questions. Everything out of his mouth seems like a lie and I want to shake the truth from him.

"Do your parents know you came to save me?" I ask and flick my gaze over to him.

He shrugs and continues to stare ahead of him. "Nope. They don't give a shit about anything except for school and baseball. Neither of them cared about what happened to you. That's why I left. I've been looking for you ever since."

I frown and look out the window lost in my thoughts for a while. It surprises me that Brandon would move out. Where would he even go? Has he been working this entire time? I'm shocked that he would give up so much for me. When my stomach lets out a grumble, I turn back to regard him. His shoulders are rigid and tense while his hands grip the steering wheel. The muscle on his neck flexes every other second as he clenches his jaw. He's clearly still angry about what happened at the cemetery.

"I'm hungry," I tell him. "We passed a diner earlier on the way to see Mom's gravesite. Can we stop there and get some dinner on the way back?"

He snaps his head over to me and his eyes are wild with anxiety sending my heart galloping right out the window. "No. We'll hit a drive-thru on the way back."

His head jerks back to the road and I glare at him. Whatever is going on inside his head is really starting to piss me off. "I don't want to go to a drive-thru. I'm not necessarily eager to get back to the cabin. I need some more time away. Why are you in such a hurry to get back anyway?"

He shrugs his shoulders, feigning indifference, but he's too stiff to pull it off. His lies are so easy to read. "I'm tired. We're not going to the diner. McDonald's or Taco Bell?"

"Brandon," I snap, "what is wrong with you? I just told you I don't want to go back right now. Why can't you respect that? Don't you even understand what kind of shit I've been through? That cabin is the last place I want to be right now. I want to go to the diner!" My voice is shrill and I'm seconds away from clobbering him for being an asshole.

His hand swings my way, causing me to flinch, and he points his finger at me. "We're not going to the goddamned diner, Baylee!" he hisses, his eyes wild with fury. "Now get over it."

I gape at him in shock.

There's no way in hell I'm getting over it.

"Stop the truck," I seethe and gather my purse in my lap.

He cuts his eyes back over to me and panic flashes over his features. "What? Why?"

"Stop the stupid truck!" I shriek. "I'm over it! I'm over how weird you're acting and your constant lies. I can't take it anymore! STOP THE TRUCK!"

The tires screech as he slams on the brake and pulls the vehicle over to the shoulder. As soon as it stops, I climb out and begin storming toward town. I can hear his heavy footsteps crunching on the gravel behind me as he follows me.

"Baylee, stop. Please," he begs. The crack in his voice makes my heart ache but I ignore it and continue stomping away.

"Baylee!" His voice is sharp and his fingers bite into my bicep as he physically stops me. "What the fuck is wrong with you?"

Whirling around in his grip, I stand on my toes and glare at him. "What the fuck is wrong with *me*?" I demand in a high-pitched voice. "What the fuck is wrong with *you*? Tell me what's going on, Brandon. I know you're lying to me too, just like everyone else. So just stop it. Fucking stop it. You were the one person I had left to count on to give me the truth and you're evading me at every turn. I can't lose you as that person. I'm out of here. If you're going to lie to my face, I'm fucking out of here."

The anger melts from his face as his chin quivers and pain seems to rip apart his features. He lets out a garbled sound and gathers me into his arms. "Baby," he says in a hoarse whisper against my hair as he strokes my back. "I'm so sorry. I just wanted to protect you from the authorities. They think you're involved in his murder and I couldn't let them take you away from me. Not again. I can't lose you now after everything. You're my girl and I love you. Things may not be the way they were before but I promise you we can fix this. I'm here until the very end for you, Baylee. Please tell me you can see this."

He's still babbling and only one word sticks out.

Murder.

Murder.

Murder.

I mean, I knew he was dead, *my War*. But for some reason, I still held onto a shred of hope he'd somehow survived. Deep down in the dark depths of my heart, I wanted to believe he'd lived. Yet he hadn't. My War was completely over.

"Oh, God," I sob and collapse in his arms.

He kisses my hair over and over again as he tries to soothe me. I inhale his familiarity and let it bring comfort to me. I'm a shuddering mess and all I can do is clutch onto his T-shirt to keep from hitting the gravel.

"Baylee," he says in a thick voice, his own tears wetting my hair, "I swear to God I will love you and take care of you. Let me help you remember what we had. Remember our love."

Love.

Love.

Love.

Another sob rips through me and he holds me tighter. The grief and stress from the past few days overwhelms me, rendering me weak. He seems to sense my breakdown because he slips an arm beneath me and picks me up. I curl up against his chest while he carries me back to the truck. Once he opens the door and sets me on the seat, his red, tearstained eyes are washing over me. His fingers find my chin and he lifts it so our eyes meet.

"I'm sorry for keeping that from you," he tells me, his brows bunching together. "I'll take you to the diner. We'll just be careful." He reaches under the seat and pulls out his baseball cap. I watch his determined, handsome face as he places it on my head and tucks my hair inside of it. "There, now you're a boy."

I try to force a smile but my lip ends up quivering it away.

"Hey," he says, his green eyes glittering with the playfulness I know, "let's go get you a strawberry milkshake before beat my ass with my baseball bat. You get mean when you're hangry. Hunger is not a pretty look on you."

This time I do smile and it's genuine because his own grin is so infectious. Just like old times.

"I'm sorry for flipping out," I murmur, my voice squeaking a bit as I swipe at my wet cheeks with the back of my hands. "I don't mean to keep taking it out on you. Thank you for all you're doing to help me through this."

He leans in and kisses me softly on the corner of my mouth. "We're in this together, babe. Until the very end."

"Will that be all?" the waitress questions, her eyes lingering on Brandon. A familiar, yet ridiculous pang of jealousy, grates at my nerves at her blatant ogling of him.

"No," I clip out, making sure to keep my face hidden beneath the baseball cap, "I need to order a chicken finger special to-go."

She scribbles on her note pad and then scurries away. When I lift my eyes to Brandon, he's frowning.

We'd had a fairly quiet dinner until this point. He'd been looking over his shoulder every five seconds while I tried not to think about my mom death or my dad's disappearance. And especially not what happened to War. Every time I did, my heart would ache and tears would well in my eyes. It was easier just to focus on my greasy fries and milk shake. To distance myself from the all-consuming pain.

"What?"

"Did you order that for," he spits out the next part as if he's disgusted, "*him?*"

I lift my chin and nod. "I'm trying to draw information out of him. I know there's more he's not telling me about my dad. Maybe if I'm nice he'll give it to me and then we can go find him."

He rolls his eyes and curses under his breath as if I'm just a stupid girl who knows nothing. I'm once again irritated by his moody behavior.

"What?" I demand.

Shrugging his shoulders, he stares off into the crowded restaurant. "It's not going to work, babe. Gabe's a liar. He'll manipulate you into letting him go. Then, he'll hurt you again," his voice drops to a whisper. "We need to get rid of him."

I study his features. The clenching jaw. The way his nostrils flare with anger. How his narrowed eyes scrutinize me. I don't know this man. The boy who hugged me earlier and cried into my hair when he thought I was leaving him, I know him. This guy though, the asshole, I can't even begin to understand who he is and I certainly don't like him a bit.

"I don't want it to be easy on him, believe me. But he needs to pay for what happened to me and what he did to those I love. I want him to think about what he's done every day in a tiny prison cell for the rest of his life. Once we get what we need from him, we'll call the police." My voice is firm and unwavering. I've thought a lot about this. Brandon and I are just two young adults. We're not killers. I won't let him kill for me and I certainly want to be a good parent to my future child. Murdering someone, even the devil, is a bad start to motherhood.

He scoffs at my words. "The police? We can't get them involved. We've been through this, babe. They think you're involved in War's *murder.*" He bares his teeth slightly as the last word rolls off his tongue. It cuts me deep and affects me more than being accused of the one who did it. "Remember?"

Murder.

Murder.

Murder.

The world spins around me and my belly rumbles as my dinner threatens to make a reappearance. I swallow to keep from throwing up and hiss at him. "How could I forget? I was there. *Remember?*" Tossing his word back at him, I meet his glare before I start scooting out of the booth. "I need to go to the ladies room." Snatching up my purse, I hightail it past the flirtatious waitress and into the bathroom.

Once inside with the door locked, I slip into the stall and open my purse. Tears roll down my cheeks and drip from my face as I hunt for the pregnancy test I'd purchased. On autopilot, I open the test, and follow the instructions in taking it. Once I do, I sit on the restroom floor as I wait for the result. My eyes close and I think about War.

He really is dead.

No denying that now.

It's been completely confirmed.

As if that weren't excruciating enough, the police think I was involved, too. I would never hurt him. Ever. Surely I can speak to them—find Land and have him vouch for me. I didn't kill War and they'll soon be able to prove that. Gabe will go to prison for his sins. Everything will work out.

I glance down at the test on the floor beside me. I'd splurged on the easiest to read, most expensive test. Brandon sent me in with a wad of cash and I bought the best.

One glimpse at the one grey word on the display screen tells me what I already knew in my heart. Tears blur the bathroom around me and I let loose a flood. My body aches and I cry until I'm hyperventilating.

Pregnant.

This baby has no father.

This baby only has me.

I'm not completely alone in this world.

What if this baby is Gabe's?

The terrifying thought has me clutching my stomach in absolute disgust. There's no way. This baby is in no way his. For one, the shot lasts for three months. I'd been given the depo shot about a month before Gabe took me which meant it would have worn off while I was with War. I know for a fact I had a normal period not long after coming to stay with him at his beach house.

This is mine and War's baby. Not Gabe's. No damn way.

I sob for a good twenty minutes before I find the strength to pull myself back together. This baby needs me now. I'm going to figure it all out for my little one.

On shaky legs, I stand, deposit the test and packaging into the trash, and then wash my hands and face in the sink. Carefully, I take my time smudging on some of the new concealer and base I'd purchased to hide my red, puffy face. Once I look halfway composed, I leave the bathroom.

I crash into a solid, warm chest. Arms wrap around me and I shiver.

"Everything okay?"

No. Everything is not okay.

"Everything's fine. I'm just tired."

Satisfied by my answer, he releases me and saunters over to the waitress who's carrying a take-out bag. Wordlessly, we head back to the truck and make our way back to the cabin.

As soon as Brandon heads for the shower, I carry the food into the kitchen to attempt once again to coax answers from Gabe.

"Who killed your puppy?" he greets as I set the bag on the counter and set to opening his food.

"Enough with the games, Gabe. Tell me where Dad is."

He watches me with furrowed brows as I bring a chicken strip over to him. His nostrils flare, inhaling the greasy meat, and he groans. I wave it near his mouth but don't get close enough for him to bite.

"Never took you for a torturer, sweetheart," he says with a hint of grumpiness in his voice.

"And I never took you for a rapist murderer but here we are." I break the chicken piece in half and raise a brow at him. "You want food, you talk."

He frowns. "I don't know where Tony is."

I toss one half of the chicken into the hole and revel in the horrified way he stares after it. "Wrong answer."

"Fucking hell, woman. Just give me the goddamned chicken. I'm starving over here."

I laugh, not girly and carefree but freakish and maniacal. "You're starving? Try three days, asshole. Then tell me how much you're starving. It's been one day," I hiss out. "You can handle it."

His dark eyes meet mine and then they peruse my body. "I need to take a piss," he says suddenly. "I've been holding it all damn day, Baylee. I'm the monster, not you. Have some pity on an old man."

I know he plans on trying to overtake me. Gabe sees himself as brilliant and as the master when it comes to the two of us. I'm not as innocent as he thinks, though.

"Should I untie you? Let you piss out the back door?" I ask sweetly and bat my eyelashes at him as I break apart the second half of the chicken strip.

He groans when I toss another piece into the hole. "I promise, I won't run," he says and then his voice turns low, "and if I do, you can spank me, little girl."

"Fine."

His eyes widen in shock for a moment before he masks it with a pitiful stare. I push the small piece of chicken into his mouth and he chomps hungrily on it. We don't speak anymore as I feed him more of his food which he devours. Once I think he's had enough, I untie both feet that are secured to the chair. Brandon tied his hands behind his back and wrapped rope around his chest and the chair. I leave his hands bound but untie him from the chair.

"My hands?" he asks and curses as I help him stand. He's clearly woozy because his knees buckle and he would have fallen if it weren't for me holding onto his elbow.

"You're going to piss out the door but your hands aren't getting untied," I tell him simply.

"How am I going to get my dick out?" he snaps and his body seems to grow stronger by the second.

I lift my chin and meet the devil's glare head on. Unafraid. "I guess I'll have to pull your dick out and help you." Quirking up an eyebrow, I smirk. "Unless you're shy. Not like I haven't seen it before."

He rolls his eyes but I still see them working out a plan. Slinging open a drawer, I locate a steak knife and point it at his cock. "If you try and run away, I'll stab you. If you try and hurt me, I'll cut your dick off," I tell him in an even voice.

His eyes widen and he smiles. "My sweet girl is something of a badass. Sure you don't want a quick fuck before Captain America gets out of the shower? You know I'm the only one that makes you purr like a goddamned kitten. The way my tongue knows just how to taste you so you're coming all over my face. God, I miss your sweet honey dripping down my chin. Would go great with those chicken strips."

I grab a fistful of his shirt and guide him to the backdoor, ignoring his vulgarity. I'm sickened to discover he's hard through his jeans. Rat bastard. With a huff, I unbutton his pants and unzip them. His giant dick practically attacks me as it falls out.

"Oh, sweetheart, just like that," he faux moans as I tug him free.

I roll my eyes. "Just piss already."

He wasn't lying about needing to pee because he wastes no time. Once he's done, I push him back into his pants and redress him. As soon as I shut the door, he throws his body at me. The knife drops from my grip and clatters to the floor. My heart thrums in my chest as he pushes his shoulder into my back and shoves me into the wall. Even hungry and tied up, he's still stronger than me.

"Listen to me," he hisses and brings his hot breath to my ear as he grinds his hard cock into my back. "That boy is fucked up in the head. More fucked than me. *Trust me.* You think I'm crazy? He hides his crazy, which makes him much more dangerous."

I still my body, surprised at his words, and stop trying to fight him. "W-What?"

He grumbles and kisses me just below my ear. "I love you, sweet girl," he murmurs. "I know you think I'm a monster but I love you so fucking much. And that pussy boy in there, he's gone mental. He'll hurt you."

I gasp when he sucks my earlobe into his mouth. "*You* hurt me!"

His hips rock against me before he speaks. "And I'm sorry, okay? But don't you see he's different? Fucking *hear* what I'm saying, baby."

My mind flits back to the way he's been acting today. The awkward way in which he practically mauled me in the cemetery. All of his lies. Gabe's previous words about asking Brandon where my father was.

"What did you mean anyway when you told me to ask Brandon where Dad is? He said he went to San Francisco. Is that the truth? Do you think he knows something he's not telling me?"

His body relaxes behind me and his voice becomes a low growl. "I'm sure he knows *a lot* more than something, baby. That boy isn't right."

"Brandon is a good person," I argue in his defense.

"He'll lie and hurt people," he replies gruffly, as if I should see this as clearly as he apparently does. "*Anything* to keep you as his girl."

I shiver at his words. "He wouldn't hurt anyone."

His laugh is dark and humorless. "Little girl, he already has."

"What? You're lying," I snap.

He kisses me again and another shudder wracks through me. "Just get the hell out of here. Leave his crazy ass here. I can deal with him. But you, my love," he says in an admonishing whisper, "need to get the fuck away from him."

Heavy footsteps thunder into the kitchen and I hear the cocking of a gun. "Get the ever-loving fuck away from my girl or I'll pump your head with every goddamn bullet in this gun."

Gabe presses another kiss to my neck before pulling away. Brandon charges forward, gun raised like he might hit him again, but I intervene.

"Enough, Brandon!" I huff and gesture to Gabe, "Just tie him back to the chair."

Brandon curses but slams the gun onto the counter so he can wrangle Gabe back to the chair. Once he finishes, I regard my longtime friend who looks so different from the boy I once knew. He's still every bit as ripped as the last time I saw him. But now, as he dons only a pair of jeans and no shirt on his chest, I can see some things have changed. His once pure flesh has been inked up in a gigantic dragon tattoo that covers his shoulder and part of one pec. Fire pours from its mouth surrounding where his heart is. Inside the fire is a name.

My name.

Baylee.

His dark green eyes almost glow with the rage that ripples from him. With each angry breath he takes, his muscles tighten and twitch making his dragon seem alive. The fire looks as though it's licking and twisting on his flesh, charring the boy from my past and revealing the demon from within.

Gabe's lying.

I think.

Brandon stalks toward me and I flinch. I don't miss the scowl on Gabe's face as he watches Brandon's every move. Nor do I miss the furious glare of disgust as Brandon notices my small retreat away from him.

But then, as if suddenly someone doused the demon with holy water, he returns. Green eyes glitter to life and a smile quirks up on his lips as he flashes me a flirtatious grin.

"Like what you see, babe?"

It alarms me how quickly he was able to change moods. As if he could sense my unease and wanted to calm me.

Forcing a laugh, I wave at the chicken. "Feed him that, will you? I'm going to take a quick shower."

Without waiting for an answer, I leave his confusing presence and hurry to the bathroom. Once inside, I lock the door and sit down on the lid of the toilet.

Gabe's words won't stop replaying in my head, despite my desire to discount them as his own lunatic evaluations.

There's something going on with Brandon, though. And I don't like it one bit.

I've got to figure out a way to get away from him. From both of them.

And soon.

chapter

NINE

War

They keep me drowning and lost in a sea of prescribed darkness. Each time I find clarity, the icy chill of calming bliss wraps its tentacles around my mind and drags me back under. Oftentimes I fight. I fight for her. My sun and moon. The only light inside my goddamned head.

But each time, she's gone.

I promise myself as I begin to wake up that I won't let them steal her from me. As each and every memory of my girl comes back to me, I greedily horde all of her smiles, frowns, and peaceful stares into my memory bank. My goal is to put them into a place in my mind so that if I'm pushed back into the darkness, I can find her burning bright somewhere in the fucking abyss.

"War."

Dad's voice has spoken to me intermittently, a constant lifeline in my dark hell. Sometimes I'm able to grasp onto it and pull myself out. Other times, no matter how hard I try, I can't seem to latch on and free myself.

The nurses and doctors think they're helping me by sedating me but the medications don't help. They thrust me right back into the nightmares I've grown so accustomed to. But this time, it's harder to break free of them. This time, I feel more lost than ever before.

The few moments of clarity I've had were spent obsessing. Being stuck in a hospital, it has nearly driven me to the brink of ultimate madness, knowing the entire building is crawling with toxins and germs.

"War."

I hear my father again. This time, I reach for him. His warm hand envelops my own and it pulls me from the darkness. Not long ago, I'd have been horrified to touch him but now I crave his comfort. With several slow blinks, I see my worried father keeping vigil at my bedside.

Baylee.

I try to say her name but I'm still unable to speak. I'm not sure what this means but I'm completely unaware of what's going on with my body. I feel as though I'm a hurricane of thoughts trapped in an unmoving corpse.

"You have to get better, son," Dad tells me with tears in his eyes. "You're living in your head. I need you out here with me, boy."

My throat aches with emotion but no tears come. I know I'm not paralyzed because I can feel his grief all the way down to my toes. But, I can't move or speak.

Just blink.

"Baylee needs you." His words cause my eyes to burn. I wish I could cry for my girl. To show any signs of improvement so I can get her back.

But the moment I blink, the threat of tears disappears.

"Do you have any idea where he could have taken her? The police have gone to her house but she's not there."

I close my eyes and her pretty blue orbs blink back at me. Perfect, small nose tinged in pink from the sun. Pouty, peachy lips ripe for tasting. God, I want to touch her.

Reopening my eyes, I try to scan my body to find exactly what's wrong with me. What it is that seems to be sitting on my chest holding me pressed against the bed. But when my eyes peruse over the blanket, I don't see any weights. Just a thin hospital gown.

"You were shot," Dad says softly and points to my chest. "Do you remember?"

My eyes meet his and I nod. It's difficult with the drugs in my system but he sees.

"The bullet went through your shoulder. It hit one of your ribs on the way and cracked it but didn't break it. The bullet punctured your left lung, which collapsed during surgery. You're intubated until your lungs heal a bit more. Eventually you'll be able to start some pulmonary therapies to regain usage of that lung."

I close my eyes again and wonder if the bullet had been infected with anything. Had Gabe touched it or not handled it properly before loading it into that chamber? What if he'd been in contact with something toxic? Does that mean it could potentially poison my bloodstream?

The heart monitor begins racing which only causes me to panic more. Each time I awake and my mind gets out of control with my obsessions, the nurses come back in to "calm" me down.

But it doesn't calm me down. It sends me hurtling right back into the dangerous depths of my mind.

Warren, chill the fuck out.

Dad squeezes my hand and I pop my eyes back open. He's frowning and keeps glancing at the heart monitor.

"Relax. I need you here with me. We need you to get better so we can find where he took her," he says firmly, his voice the stern one he'd use whenever I was in trouble as a boy.

I nod again and this time the tears do well in my eyes. He's right. I need to pull my shit together so I can get well and help the police find my girl. She's out there in his clutches as we speak. The motherfucker is most likely doing unspeakable things as I sit here fading in and out of black.

"Is everything okay in here?" a nurse questions as she comes into my room.

I nod at her and she flashes me a sweet smile. "Good to see you alert and awake today, Mr. McPherson. Dr. Watson is hoping to be able to extubate you today. Get you off that ventilator. He's also sending in Dr. Daniels for a psych evaluation later. But first, I'm going to grab some supplies and I'll come drain the blood from your chest tube."

She scurries off and I dart my widened eyes to my dad.

"Listen, War. You have got to be strong. Stay strong for her and get yourself well. Dr. Watson was able to repair your lung but you're not in the clear. You're going to have to fight harder against these episodes or they'll keep pumping you with that mind-numbing shit. I need you to do whatever it takes to get yourself through this."

I nod and furrow my eyebrows in concentration as the nurse comes back in the room. My eyes remain locked on Dad, tuning out her mindless chatter, as she sets to sucking out blood and fluids from my chest.

Don't think about it.

Don't think about it.

"Son, do you remember that time we saw that stingray over at Coronado's beach? He had to have been four feet long. Just swam right up to you."

His twinkling eyes meet mine and he grins. I nod and try to smile around the tube in my mouth.

"Your mother started screaming like a wild banshee. You'd have thought you were being attacked by a great white, not a stingray. How old do you think you were? Ten? Eleven?"

Nodding, I smile again. I remember at first being terrified by the sea animal but then I couldn't take my eyes from it. I'd reached out my shaky hand and stroked the smooth side of the creature, careful to stay away from its tail, before it floated back out into the water. By the next big wave, it had disappeared. Dad told me animals know a kind spirit—that they're drawn to them. He said that magnificent creature was fascinated by me as much as I was about him. A mutual respect and curiosity between species. To this day I still wonder about that stingray.

"Wasn't so bad," the nurse chuckles and starts cleaning up. "Last time we had to sedate you. You'll be walking out of here before you know it." She winks and leaves me here with my dad.

"Good job, son. I knew you could do this. Focus on the good—focus on Baylee. We're going to get her back. Just as soon as we get you out of here, we're going to find her and keep her safe so that bastard never messes with her again."

My nod this time is curt and I stare at him with an intensity that I hope conveys my serious determination to get better so I can help her.

"Now rest," he urges and squeezes my hand. "You're going to need your strength because when we leave here, you're going to slay that dragon and save your princess."

I close my eyes and immediately bring forth those innocent, kind blue eyes. She's been through so much and I can only imagine what she's going through now. But she's unflappable and resilient. Her strength is more than a thousand men. My girl will survive that asshole's clutches. I just need her to keep staying strong until I get there.

Dad was wrong.

I won't be saving a princess.

No, I'm going to save my queen.

chapter
TEN

Brandon

Once I hear the shower running, I toss the piece of chicken back into the styrofoam box and sling the entire thing into the cellar.

"What did you say to her?" I snarl through clenched teeth.

Gabe's eyes remain narrowed as he watches my every move and takes his time chewing what little of the food I gave him. Once he swallows, he smirks at me. "I told her she'll never be satisfied with your limp dick."

A deep growl rumbles in my chest and I seize his throat with my hand. "Fuck off and tell me what you really said. Do you think you have enough air to last through her shower? Little Baylee isn't going to come rescue you, dumbass."

He refuses to speak, so I squeeze hard enough to cause him to struggle in the chair. I enjoy the way his face turns purple. So fucking purple. Death will never be a good enough punishment for the bastard who stole my girlfriend. But I'll sure enjoy seeing him die, that's for damn sure.

"W-What…d-d-did…"

I release his throat and he gulps in air.

"What did you do to Tony?" he rasps out.

My eyebrows fly to my hairline but I quickly mask away my look of shock. "I didn't do anything to him." Dragging my gaze from his penetrating glare, I stare at the doorway and listen for signs of Baylee. The shower is still running.

"You're lying and she'll find out, you little shit," he seethes and struggles with his bindings as if he'd actually be able to tear through them to get to me.

"No, Gabe," I tell him calmly and lean forward until my face is inches from his scowling one. "She won't find out. I'm going to make sure of it. Because before we leave this shithole, I'm going to cut your throat."

He scoffs. "Oh, yeah? And then what? You two gonna ride off into the sunset together? You're fucking delusional, kid. Have you seen the way she looks at you?"

Rage surges through me, painting my insides red with hate. I ball my hands into fists. One more stupid word out of his mouth and I'll break my promise to Baylee about not hurting him. "She loves me."

My entire body quakes with barely contained fury. He keeps pushing and fucking pushing. I don't know how much longer I can take his shit before I snap.

"No, she *likes* you. You were a teenage crush. Nothing more than a pussy-ass boy. You're friend-zoned now. She just doesn't know how to break it to you and your fragile little wussy feel—"

Hate overwhelms me and my restraint is no longer something I have control over. Before I can think better of it, I backhand him across the side of the head, hard enough to reopen a cut on his eyebrow which immediately starts bleeding. He spits out a wad of blood and glares at me.

"Mark my words, boy."

With a huff, I storm out of the kitchen ignoring his psychotic laughter that echoes behind me. It takes everything in me not to beat him to a bloody pulp.

Stalking back into the bedroom, I dig around the duffle bag until I find one of Baylee's favorite nightgowns. It's my favorite too—an old, oversized pink thing with Tweety Bird on the front. She loves it because it was handed down to her from her mother. I love it because it's short and shows off her pretty long legs. Also, I locate her a sexy black thong and toss it onto the bed as well.

The shower shuts off and I pace around the room waiting for her. Between her distant behavior toward me and Gabe's taunting and threats, my nerves are shot. I need to fix this.

"I laid out your clothes," I tell her with a proud grin.

She's wrapped up in a white towel that stretches over her gorgeous tits and hangs just low enough to cover her pussy. I crave to finally lose my virginity to her. *Soon.* Her eyes fall to the bed and tears well in her eyes.

"I love that nightgown," she murmurs, emotion making her voice hoarse. "It used to be Mom's." Her long legs glide over to the bed and she fingers the thin, worn fabric as the memories assault her. When her shoulders quiver with silent tears, I stride over to her and hug her from behind.

"That's why I brought it, babe. I want you to be happy. To remember Lynn. I grabbed a few pictures for you too."

Her sobs are quiet, but I'm overcome with joy when she lets me hold her. My arms are locked around her stomach and I keep her back pressed to my front. As she cries, I press kisses to her bare shoulder. I want to tear the towel from her body and make love to her. To pump into her and kiss away her sorrow.

Soon.

After some time, she sniffles away the last of her tears. "A thong. Really Brandon?"

I chuckle and tickle her sides, making her squirm away from me. I shrug. "I just grabbed the stuff I like seeing you in. Was I supposed to grab the granny panties that were shoved to the back of your drawer?" I question and smirk at her.

She rolls her eyes and throws the black scrap at me. "I'm not wearing those."

I feel myself grow hard as I shove her panties into my pocket. "You won't see me complaining," I tease and drag my eyes down her body, eying her suggestively.

"Go away and let me get dressed," she huffs but the playful tone is still in her voice.

"I'll just be brushing my teeth."

Once inside the bathroom, I quickly brush my teeth in hopes that we can at least kiss while we cuddle before bed. I drop my jeans and leave on my black boxers. When I finally emerge from the bathroom, she's bent over the bed tugging the sheets into place and baring the backs of her smooth thighs to me.

The idea of sleeping in this bed still fucks with my head, but having her curled up next to me will outweigh the fact that Gabe fucked her on it. "Tomorrow, we're leaving. With or without his compliance. I'm ready to take care of you and staying here is a constant reminder of what that asshole did to you. A reminder of what he did to us."

She whirls around and glares at me. Her bare tits are visible through the thin pink gown and her hardened small nipples poke through. What I wouldn't give to put my teeth on one of them and—

"Us?" she snaps. "He did nothing to you here in this cabin, Brandon. But me? He did everything to me. Don't say shit like that."

I growl and storm over to her. She flinches again and it pisses me right the fuck off. "Stop acting like you're afraid of me, goddammit!" I say with a low rumble in my voice. "I'm not going to hurt you. You're my everything. And just because you're upset doesn't mean I should be the recipient of every outburst you have. He's the one who raped you, not me. Gabe fucked what was mine, not me. So he did do something to me in this cabin. He robbed me of what was supposed to be mine. *Ours.* Next time you want to have a bitch fit, remember that I was the one to rescue you from that, because it seems like you are easily forgetting. I'm the one who fucking loves you. I'm the only one who wants to keep you safe. So cut the shit, Baylee."

Tears well in her eyes and her body quakes with sobs. She throws her arms around my waist and buries her face against my chest, heating the flesh where her name is surrounded in tattooed flames. It seems fitting and right.

"I'm sorry, Brandon. I'm just so upset. Everything hurts. Losing my mom and War," she sobs. I try not to flinch at the mention of that asshole. "And not knowing where Dad is. Being around Gabe, knowing he's the blame for all of this. But being around you is the hardest. You want things from me that I simply can't give to you right now."

Right now.

But she didn't say not ever.

My heart soars and I stroke my fingertips up and down her spine causing her to shiver. "It's okay. Let me hold you while you sleep."

She tenses in my arms but I don't let it affect me. I peel myself from her and motion toward the bed. Then, I walk over to the bag and retrieve a picture for her, as well as her mother's sweater. When she sees them, her cries turn louder as she releases the grief she's been holding on to. I help her into the sweater before she crawls under the covers, clutching the picture. It only takes me a few minutes to turn off the lights and then join her beneath the sheets. She lets me pull her back against my front.

I want to roll her onto her back and push into her tight body. But I don't. I refrain and settle with simply holding her. My fingers stroke her skin everywhere in an attempt to calm her. When her hiccups eventually turn into soft breathing, I know she's fallen asleep.

We lay there for hours, her sleeping and me awake holding her. When she rolls onto her back, I stare down at her pretty face, the moonlight from the window casting an ethereal glow on her pale flesh. Her lips are parted open as she takes even breaths. Dark lashes flutter as she dreams. Leaning forward, I press a kiss to her pouty lips. So soft and perfect like I remember.

My dick thickens against the side of her thigh and I am fucking desperate to make love to her. She may no longer be a virgin but I am, and she's the one I want to lose mine to. The way it was always supposed to be. For the both of us. I'm about to come simply from the idea of it. I drag my fingers over her stomach gently and then up to her breasts. With one finger, I tease the hardened peaks of her nipples through her gown. Then, I slide my finger up her throat, over her chin, and stop at her lips.

Pushing my finger into her mouth, I revel in the heat that she breathes over my flesh. I run the pad of my fingertip over her pink tongue and over the grooves of her teeth. Once my finger is damp, I pull it from her mouth. Rolling to my back as well, I push down my boxers enough to allow my stiff and eager cock to spring free. With my wet finger, I circle the tip of my cock. Knowing her juices are on me is enough to almost have me come right there.

I groan when a bead of pre-cum rolls down the head of my soft tip.

I want her to taste it.

Heat warms my body as I jerk my hand from my dick and bring it back to her lips. I push my finger back into her mouth and drag my smear of semen along her tongue. A soft moan escapes her and it makes me ravenous for her.

Removing my finger once again, I then drag the bottom of her gown up to her belly button, revealing her pussy to me.

God, what I wouldn't give to devour her right now.

But she's not ready for me.

I should roll back over and go to sleep.

Yet, I know I can't. I need to touch her and make her feel better again. Even if I am only able to reach her subconscious.

Grabbing onto the back of her thigh, I pull her knee toward me until it touches the bottom of my thick shaft. I slightly buck my hips against her thigh and groan at how perfect her smooth leg feels against it.

My fingers slide over her cunt and I probe at her opening with my longest finger. She's slightly wet. I drag my finger over it several times. The craving to taste her is intense. I pull my finger to my mouth and suck on it.

God, she tastes fucking amazing.

And now she's all mine.

I need to fuck up Gabe once and for all. Get her away from all of this.

Just her and me.

Once my finger is good and wet, I slide it back over her slit. I find her opening and slowly push into her. She whimpers and my cock lurches with desire.

"Mmm," she purrs in her sleep.

It spurs me on and I fuck her with my finger lazily. I revel in the way her body grips it. She may have fucked those two men, but she's still tight. To further prove that fact, I push another finger into her. And then another. Her body accepts me and grows increasingly wet. My cock will stretch her further. Her cunt will take it—every thick inch of me.

With my free hand, I jerk at my dick in unison with each plunge of my fingers into her heat. One day soon, we'll fuck. Once I'm finally able to break down her walls, I can make love to her sweet body at all hours of the day. She'll remember our love and find her way back to me.

Another small whimper fills the night air and it's all it takes before I'm overtaken by my climax. Hot semen spurts all over my belly and I hiss out in pleasure. I'm beginning to relax from my high when she speaks. It's murmured and in her sleep but I still catch it.

"War."

A whispered plea. A reverent evocation. A fucking slap in the face spoken in a way in which I have never once heard my name come from her lips.

The name splashes over me, arctic and icy. I jerk my hand out from inside her. Fury surges through me to the point I'm physically shaking. Tiny threads of what was left of my control and sanity pluck one by one as the anger sweeps through me like a rampant tornado decimating everything in its path. I can actually feel the snap inside me—the shredding of the gentle boy I was before as the reborn man rips from within and bursts out. The man I've become flexes and snarls because he knows this means war. I can't lose her to Gabe, only to lose her to his other guy too. She belongs to me. It's always been that way and now I have to fight for her. The old me couldn't handle it but the new me is flexed and ready to demolish anything in my path. Fuck that asshole for stealing her body from me and fuck that other prick for stealing her heart. I'm going to do everything in my power to keep her away from that motherfucker in the other room. And soon.

With a grumble, I climb out of bed and clean my cum from my stomach. Lifting my fingers to my nose, I inhale her scent. I certainly won't be washing her from me anytime soon. Tomorrow, every time I eat or scrub my face in frustration, I will catch a whiff of her. It will get me through the times when she isn't acting like herself.

I make my way back over to her and slide into the bed. Once the covers are pulled back over us, I wrap my body around hers to keep her warm. Sliding my hand back under her nightgown, I palm her breast and my mind flits to the past as I drift off to sleep.

Tony's cell phone rings from where it's plugged in on the bedside table and I jolt to an upright position on their bed. Every time his phone rings, I'm flooded with a mixture of anxiety and hope. Anxious that it could be someone looking for him, hopeful that it could be Baylee.

But it isn't her.

It never is.

The only contact I get with her is through a questionable email address that shows up in Lynn's inbox on her cell. Where I play the role of her angry father. Baylee must be playing a role too, because her emails are bullshit and don't even sound like her.

A growl rumbles in my throat to see the call is from an unknown number. I swipe the button to answer the call but don't say anything.

"Tony?" a familiar voice questions.

Gabe.

This is the first time he's tried to make contact with Tony.

"Where is she?" I spit out.

The line is silent for a moment before he chuckles. It pisses me right the fuck off.

"She's been sold. But something tells me you already knew that."

Blinding rage causes my fingers to grip the phone in my crushing grip. I'd throw the damn thing at the wall if it didn't mean I'd lose my main line of contact to her. Instead, I sling the framed picture on the nightstand careening with the back of my hand and relish in the sound of the glass shattering as it hits the floor.

"Her sorry excuse for a father told me all about your scheme," I snarl, hoping to bait him.

"Scheme? What scheme?" he questions, his tone sarcastic but I don't miss the underlying hint of concern. "Where is 'ol Tony anyway, pussy boy?"

"Well, he isn't fucking here, dumbass." I pace the floor along the bed and fist my free hand. His voice seems to pour accelerant on the fire blazing within me.

The line goes silent and I pull it away to make sure it's still connected. Finally, he lets out a breath of frustration and I smile in satisfaction knowing I'm getting to him.

He laughs but it's dark and humorless. "Someone grew some balls since turning eighteen."

"Where is she?" My tone is low and deadly.

"She's gone," he says, "for now. But soon I'll have her back. Not that it matters to you anyway."

"YOU WON'T HAVE ANYTHING!" I roar.

His heavy breathing has become louder on the other end of the line and he practically spits out his next words. "I will have everything—I've had everything. She belongs to me you little shit. Tony knew what he was doing when he agreed to all of this. He knew what could happen."

"That you'd rape his daughter?!"

"You can't rape the willing, pussy boy. And boy was she willing—such a needy, greedy little girl. So ripe. So fucking juicy. It may not have been part of the original…scheme, but when the opportunity presented itself, I took it. Jesus, I'm getting hard just thinking about slurping up that wet pussy of hers. Fucking delicious. And, goddamn, that ass of hers was so tight—"

Before I can control myself, I heave the phone across the room with more force than any baseball I've ever thrown. It hits the dresser and shatters. My lifeline to the man who stole her is gone. The rage is out of control and I storm out of the house so I don't ruin my sweet girl's home. Instead, I take my anger outside and beat the fuck out of the trunk of a thick oak in the backyard. Once my knuckles are busted open and bloody, and I am depleted of energy, I walk to the corner of the yard and sink to my ass on the dirt. Hot tears threaten but I don't let them fall.

This fucker won't win. He'll show up and I'll force him to tell me who he sold her to. If I have to kick his ass into next week, I will. If I have to break both his arms, I will. If I have to kill him, I fucking will. I will do whatever is necessary to pull the information from him. And when he finally gives me what I want…I'll save her. I will find my girl and bring her back home.

I need to be smart. Vigilant. Her hero.

He'll turn up soon. Either here, his job, his bank. Somewhere. And when he does, I'll be waiting.

chapter
ELEVEN

Baylee

"Shhhh."

His lips are all over mine. Sweet and needy. But they feel all wrong. I don't want his lips on me. And now his tongue is pushing its way into my mouth. Rubbing against my own tongue. Taking and owning.

"Stop," I whimper into his mouth.

He ignores me and dives deeper. His palm covers my breast through my nightgown and he squeezes almost painfully. I cry out and try to push him away.

"Stop!"

His mouth tears from mine and he's no longer desperate. He's fierce. Green eyes glower down at me as he covers my mouth with his palm. I struggle against his heavy frame but I'm not strong enough. This boy who I once loved is turning into a monster. He's hurting me.

A whimper escapes me and his eyes darken. He stares at me as if he's contemplating how to devour my entire being. How to extract it from my body and run his tongue along it.

I shudder in his arms. He seems to enjoy my discomfort, though, because he grins baring his perfect teeth to me.

"I've been waiting for you, babe. To lose my virginity to the woman I love. You came back to me. The time is now."

A scream remains lodged in my throat as I struggle against his hold. He laughs and then attacks my neck. His teeth bruise the flesh as he bites down hard. He works to silence my cry with his hand, tears rolling down my cheeks. It feels as though blood is gushing from me and when he pulls away to look at me again, my horrors are confirmed.

His white teeth are stained red and my blood drips from his chin. The green eyes morph into the color of coffee, before turning almost black. And he's no longer a boy, but the devil who owns this cabin. He slams his thickness into me and I scream. My blood drips from his chin and splashes onto my face. With each drip into my eyes, I become blind. The world around me turns red with my blood. The devil fucks me straight to hell.

"That's my baby inside of you," he taunts.

I shake my head in vehemence. I'm waiting for my white horse to show up, carrying my hero. But then I remember he's dead.

He can't save me.

Can't save me from their evil.

The demonic eyes find mine and he tears his hand from my mouth, instantly replacing it with his tongue. It plunges inside so deeply that I retch in response. The taste of the metallic blood—my blood— and the way he tries to fuck my throat with his thick tongue is too much.

I gag and gag and gag.

"Baylee."

The voice is soft and sweet. I miss it so much.

"Mom?"

I'm now in the cemetery and I'm staring at her tombstone. The air is cold and the monsters are momentarily gone.

"Baylee," she whispers again, her voice wrapping around me in a comforting hug. "Help me…"

The earth moves in front of her grave and I scramble over to it. Her long slender finger pokes through the dirt and wiggles at me.

"Mom!" I screech and begin clawing at the ground.

"You left me," she tells me sadly.

With a shake of my head in disagreement, I dig and dig until her arm is free to her elbow. Grabbing onto it, I pull with all my might. Soon, her dirty face emerges and her blue eyes stare at me almost in an accusing way.

"You left me."

I'm sobbing as I completely free her from the dirt. Her frail body collapses on mine and I get a whiff of decomposing flesh.

"Mom, I'm here. I'm here," I tell her and rake my fingers through her filthy blonde hair, hugging her to me. "I wanted to save you. I thought War's money could save you. Mommy, I tried."

She lets out a groan, her breath a deadly stench. "You were too late, honey. Too late."

When my body begins to shudder with hysterical sobs, I close my eyes and try not to throw up. But when I reopen them, I'm back in the forest behind Gabe's cabin. The monster with the coffee-colored eyes is standing above me unbuckling his jeans. He pulls out his cock and I try to run. One step, two step, three step.

His weight is suddenly on top of me. Crushing. Deadly. Soul consuming. He smashes my face into the brush and I'm choking on leaves. Sticks poke at my face. Ants crawl into my ears. The jingle of his belt jolts me into action and I squirm to avoid his harsh punishment.

"Three steps, three licks," he taunts before the fire tears across my flesh.

"Ahhhh!"

My scream could wake the dead. Maybe Mom will come save me even though I couldn't save her.

"Baylee! Wake up!"

My eyes fly open and a dark shadow is on top of me, holding my arms down against the bed.

"Help me!" I screech and squirm against my attacker. "Get off me!"

"Jesus, it's me," he says softly. "You were having a nightmare and were flipping out. I was afraid you were going to hurt yourself."

My body somewhat relaxes once I realize it's Brandon—not the monster from my dream. Memories of my mother fade away. The forest dissipates in the air around me. Smells, sounds, pain—they all flee and leave me in peace.

"There she is," he coos and presses a kiss to my forehead.

Only then do I realize our position. He's on top of me, his cock pressed against my bare pussy with only the fabric of his boxers preventing him from pushing into me. My legs around his hips. His strong grip on my wrists pressing into the bed on either side of my head.

"Brandon…" I start but he shushes me with a soft kiss on my lips.

Anxiety washes over me and my heart thunders inside my chest as if it might explode at any moment.

"I'm going to take care of you, babe," he murmurs against my mouth. "Always."

A shudder ripples through me when he grows hard. It's enough to throw me out of my daze. "Get off me!"

He jerks away and stares down at me, shock morphing his features. You'd think I'd just slapped him. If he'll free my hands, I'll do just that. But he rolls off and away from me, pain contorting his features.

"I'm not him," he chokes out. "I'm not that fucking monster. I love you."

I scramble out of the bed and back away toward the bathroom. But it's when I hear him crying—soft, masculine sobs—that I begin to ache inside. He's right. He's not a monster like Gabe. But he's not the playful, innocent boy I left behind either. The Brandon I knew before would never pin me down. Never take anything from me unless I was ready to give it. I should be grateful for Brandon. And I am. He's here when nobody else would or could be. The man—and yes, he's all man now—only wants to look after me. To love me. But why can't he understand that right now, I just need my friend?

"I'm sorry," I whisper and continue my retreat toward the bathroom in the dark. "I have nightmares about him and the stuff he's done to me. I was scared."

He climbs off the bed and strides over to me. His strong arms wrap around me and pull me to his sculpted chest. "It's okay. You're drenched in sweat. Take a shower and you'll feel better. I'll grab you a bottle of water for when you get out."

I want to be thankful for his gentleness. Want to be able to accept it for what it is. I let out a sigh when he kisses the top of my head. He leaves me to head for the kitchen. Making my way inside, I turn on the light in the bathroom and kick a discarded towel out of the way. I lock the bathroom door behind me and head over to the mirror.

My hair has dried from my last shower and is a mess on top of my head. Dark circles paint the flesh under my eyes. A quiver has set in on my bottom lip and tears stain my cheeks. I'm crushing under the weight of all that's happened to me.

I twist my hair into a quick bun and then turn on the shower. Seconds later, I'm standing under the hot spray, hoping to wash away my nightmares forever. I quickly rinse my body but when I bring a washcloth between my thighs, I wince. My pussy feels slightly sore as if I've recently had sex. But the last time was last night with Gabe. A shudder ripples through me and I push away another nightmare, as a dark sense of foreboding comes over me.

With everything that's happened, my body has been thrown out of whack.

Pregnancy hormones and all that.

I remember falling asleep with Brandon protectively curled up behind me. Waking up, entwined in him, as if we'd been—

No. He wouldn't. As much as I know he wants to, he'd never violate me like that. I need to stop painting him as a villain and lean on him as a friend. Perhaps he had a wet dream, while I was having another nightmare. I have to chuckle at the irony. Because if I don't I'll start to cry.

I'm going to take care of you, babe.

I remember his words to me once he ripped me from sleep. I have to trust that he is doing just that. Even though I don't trust anyone right now. But I need a friend. Incredibly so.

When the water grows cold, I step out and begin to dry off.

Then I hear it.

Shouting.

What if Gabe got loose and is hurting Brandon?

Panic sets in. *I can't lose Brandon too.* My desperate resolve from just outside this godforsaken cabin two days ago comes rushing back over me. I might not entirely trust Brandon anymore. He might be deceiving me in some way that I *will* sniff out. But he's all I've got. I didn't let Gabe steal him away from me then. And I will not fucking lose him now either.

Not wasting any time, I bolt from the bathroom naked and down the hallway. I'm just pushing through into the kitchen but then slam to a halt.

Brandon's green eyes are glowing with manic rage. His hair is drenched with sweat and his shoulders quake with heavy breaths as he drags Gabe in his chair over to the hole of the cellar. I open my mouth to plead for him to stop—that if Gabe doesn't tell me what happened to Dad, I'll never have any answers. But instead, I stand there stunned silent and reaching out to him.

Gabe's dark eyes find mine and they're sad. He mouths that he's sorry before he drops heavily down the hole. The sickening crunch resounds over and over again in my head. Chair splintering.

Bones breaking. Over and over again. No other sounds. No movement or moans or noise of any kind follow the sound of his descent.

I hate Gabe.

Detest his existence.

But I wanted him to suffer.

Humanely.

In prison.

To always think about his crimes and pay for them over his lifetime.

"W-W-What did you do?" I stammer out and meet the enraged glare of Brandon. Pushing past him, I make my way over to the hole that Gabe was pushed into. I fall to my knees and peer inside. My stomach clenches into a fist as I clutch onto the sides of the floor to keep from hurtling down into the abyss with him. Gabe's lying on his side facing the darkness of the cellar. A pool of blood forms around the middle of his body and he's unmoving. The chair is smashed into a several pieces around him. His neck seems to be turned in an awkward way and I wonder if he broke it upon impact. Tears are streaming down my face and I angrily swipe them away with the back of my hand. Finding the cellar door, I pull it closed and then latch it shut. I can't look at his broken body any longer.

With a scream of frustration, I scramble to my feet and charge for Brandon. "Why? Why did you do that?" I demand, fresh, hot tears chasing the ones before them race their way to my jaw and drip onto my breasts. "You killed him!"

His eyes hungrily lick up and down my naked form before they're back on my teary ones. They soften at the sight and he slowly approaches. "The nightmares wouldn't stop until he was dead, Baylee. I'm healing you. I'm fixing you, babe."

Fury explodes within me and I attack. My fists become tiny weapons of destruction as I try to beat some sense into him. When my hands don't seem to be doing the job, I set to shoving him. He lets me push him against the counter. I slap at his face and am about to claw his stupid eyeballs out when he snatches both wrists and yanks me to him. His face is bright red, anger twisting up his handsome features into something ugly and hateful. I want to rip the look right from his face.

I shake my head at him and jerk my wrists from his grasp. "Don't touch me. You can sleep on the couch tonight for all I care," I hiss at him. "I don't want to talk to you right now."

The unmasked rage begins to melt from his features. His face falls into a frown—clearly heartbroken—as I storm from the room. Once inside the bedroom, I lock the door and then crawl into the bed.

This time, when I dream, Brandon takes the place of the monster. And this new monster is equally terrifying.

The birds chirping outside the window wake me up at dawn. My entire body aches from crying and exertion. With Gabe gone, I'm ready to leave this hell hole once and for all. Maybe Brandon did me a favor. Although I will never let him know that. But by him getting rid of our villain, maybe now I can move on. Problem is, I don't want to move on. I want to go to the police. Tell them about the cabin and all about Gabe. Expose the WCT sex ring but leave War's name out of it. And most importantly, I want to find Land. If I can't count on Brandon, I know I can count on Land to help me find my dad. He'll want me in his life once he learns I'm carrying a part of his son.

And life will get better. I can control that much.

I couldn't control what Gabe took from me.

I couldn't control my mother's death.

I couldn't control War's fate.

I couldn't even control gaining the answers I wanted and the closure I needed from this whole mess.

But I am going to take care of myself from here on out. And I will control that.

A soft knock on the door makes me jump. I quickly throw on my clothes from yesterday before opening it.

Brandon's face is contorted into one of guilt and regret. He rests his forearms on the door frame and leans into the room, eyes on mine.

"Baylee," he murmurs. "I'm sorry."

I gather up Mom's sweater, my nightgown, and the picture frame. Ignoring him, I stuff them all into my small purse, making it bulge. "Take me to the police station. Now."

He leaves his position in the doorway and stalks over to me. I refuse to show weakness anymore and I square my shoulders, looking him in the eye. When his hand reaches for me, I swat it away.

"We can't do that," he says with a sigh of frustration. "They'll take you to jail."

I roll my eyes. "I'll take my chances."

He growls and runs his fingers through his hair. "Listen, babe. Let's talk this through first."

"No. There's nothing to say. You killed a man. I told you not to hurt him. I told you I we needed answers out of him. But you did whatever the hell you wanted to anyway. I need some space from you."

I start past him but he grabs my wrist. His almost glowing green orbs find mine and his brows furrow. "That is exactly why we can't go to the police."

With a huff, I jerk my arm from his grip. "I thought you were worried about *me* being taken to jail. It's your own ass you're looking to save? Well tough shit. Besides, it was self-defense, Brandon. Wasn't it?"

"He was hogtied, babe, and he was covered in cuts and bruises *we* gave him. They'll see it as premeditated murder or some shit. You can't let them take me away from you now. Not after everything we've been through."

Guilt tries to wash over my anger, but I don't let it. Not this time. "Either you take me to the police, or I find my own way. Your choice."

A streak of anger flashes in Brandon's eyes before he masks it and releases a sigh of defeat, his hands scrubbing over his face. "Fuck, Baylee! Aren't you listening to me?" I jolt backwards because in the next second, he's in my face, hands gripping my arms, shaking me. "We cannot go to the fucking police. The whole time you were gone, I tried to get their help. The whole fucking time. They wouldn't believe a word I said. They were only interested in talking to me once that freak who *bought* you was killed. We have no proof. We have no witnesses. My parents sure as hell aren't going to help us, and—" He catches himself and lowers his tone. "And yours can't help us either, babe. You want answers? You want to find your dad? Fine. Let's go to San Francisco and start asking around. I'm with you. But we have to take matters into our own hands."

I move my gaze from Brandon's stormy one, and look over to one of my arms which he is still squeezing. His movements are jerky when he releases me and takes a step back, almost as if he hadn't even realized he was holding me so tight.

"Fine. I just want out of this cabin. We can figure out the rest once we're on the road."

A smile lights up his face and he nods. I leave the room so he can pack up and spend the next few minutes standing near the hole in the kitchen. The cellar door is still closed and latched. A part of me wants to pull it open—to peer into the dark abyss. I would almost expect him to be standing there with his arms crossed over his bulky chest waiting for me to toss him the rope so he can climb out. But the little girl inside of me refuses to open that door. I know he won't be standing there. He'll be curled up and stiff in the same position as last night. And I can't see him like that. I'm not strong enough to deal with the finality of it.

I shouldn't feel remorse or sadness. I shouldn't feel guilt. I shouldn't feel as though I'll burst into tears at any moment from having lost another person in my life.

A hot tear streaks down my cheek, though, and I let out a sob. Gabe had become a monster, but for ten years, he wasn't. I know, deep down, he did love me. Even if that love was born of something sick. It doesn't make sense to me but my heart still hurts.

I consider some of his last words to me. How he tried to warn me about Brandon being dangerous. It was almost laughable, considering the source—a source who stole an underage girl, forced her to have sex with him, sold her, only to later shoot and kill the person he sold her to. Gabe took and took and took. But in that moment, he gave. And in his final moments, he gave too. When he told me he was sorry. What it all means, I may never know.

Swiping away my tear, I shake my head. *These are the pregnancy hormones talking.* It probably meant nothing. It was probably just another one of his twisted head games. There's no way I'm going to mourn the loss of Gabriel Sharpe. He took my innocence, took my love, and who knows what else?

All he gave me in exchange was heartache and pain.

And the monster he created.

He gave me the dragon.

He gave me Brandon.

"Where are we going?" I question as we hit the expressway that will take us to San Francisco.

"I thought I could take you shopping and that we could stay in one of those boutique hotels that overlook the Golden Gate Bridge. I'd always planned on taking you there for your eighteenth birthday. But then…" His voice cracks and I risk a glance at him. His features are more innocent and reminiscent of the boy I knew. Maybe he needed out of that cabin too because now, in his truck with the sun filtering in through the windshield, he looks like the Brandon I remember.

"Then Gabe ruined it all. I know," I say with a frustrated sigh. "We're going to look for my dad there too, right?"

He lets out deep breath. "Of course we are. Is that okay?"

Nodding, I reach into my purse and pull out the picture of my parents and I that Brandon had given to me. Mom is stunning as usual and my dad is fierce and handsome. My eyes glitter with innocence in the photo, and I miss the girl I once was. An ache forms in my chest as I realize I have nothing to remember War by. No pictures. No trinkets. Nothing.

"That was quick," he says with a smirk. "You and your love for presents."

I laugh and bounce on the bed beside him, careful not to touch him. Once I'm settled, he opens his palm up to me. Inside are two rose gold earrings in the shape of a heart with a letter B inside.

"These are pretty," I say softly and open my palm to him so he can drop them into my hand.

He flashes me a shy smile as he gives them to me. "That first day, when you longingly stared out at the ocean and wrote your initial with a heart around it on the foggy glass, I'd been a little fucked in the head about you marring my clean glass. But then…"

"I don't even remember doing that. It used to drive Dad crazy when I'd write on the windows of his car but Mom always said they were little Baylee notes left all over, and that he should appreciate them." My voice wobbles and I choke down the swell of emotion thinking about her causes.

"Well, I did appreciate it. For once, I didn't want the perfection," he says, "I wanted something better than perfection. I wanted you."

My fingers trail up my neck and I gently touch the earrings he gave me. Tears blur the world around me, but a smile forms on my lips. His sweet gift and his child. What more could I ask for besides his warm, strong presence? It would have to do. I would have to do this. For him. For us.

"You never told me which neighbor said my dad went to San Francisco," I mutter and cut my eyes over to him. "It wasn't Gabe, we know that much. Was it Mrs. Stephens?"

His body stiffens and he shoots me a nervous glance. "Yeah," he says with a grunt, "but then I also found a note inside saying the same thing when I went to get your things. I guess he left it for you in case you ever came home."

A note. Funny how he's just now telling me about said note. I frown as I try to imagine my father leaving me this note. It's not his style. I also have a hard time believing he'd leave our home after recently having lost Mom to go someplace to look for me that I wasn't even at. He had no idea where I was, so why would he search in San Francisco. Why not just go to the police?

"Hmmm."

He shrugs his shoulders as if he doesn't know much more on the subject so I let it drop. I'll definitely be involving the police to help find my father. Something isn't adding up and I need answers.

The rest of the drive is quiet and when the piers start coming into view as we travel along the Embarcadero, he turns and flashes me a grin.

"Clam chowder for lunch?"

My stomach growls and I remember I'm eating for two. I nod and offer him an appeasing smile. "Sure."

chapter
TWELVE

War

"How are you feeling?" my nurse named Cathy asks. "Do you need some more water?"

I cringe, wondering where their water comes from. Has it been properly purified? Has it been poisoned by the germs of someone coughing too close to the open water source? My mind starts to go *there*—to the black places that rip apart my sanity. But, before I let it eat me alive, I focus on her. Not nurse Cathy, but *her*. My Baylee.

Reaching for my cup, I pull it to my lips and sip. "I have plenty. Thanks." My voice is hoarse after having the tube in my throat but I feel much freer. Dad had to leave to meet with a client but should be back any time.

"Good," she says and smiles at me. "This morning we're going to do some pulmonary therapies. Doc wants you out of that bed and doing some light activity. We'll start by taking that catheter out and going to the restroom. You're a big, strong boy. You can do this."

I wince when she reaches for me but am thankful she's donning a pair of latex gloves. The obsessions running rampant in my head are maddening but something bigger, more important is at stake. My Baylee. So, with thoughts of her in mind, I accept Cathy's assistance. Another nurse enters the room and closes the door behind her. *Fucking hospitals.* Anytime they do anything invasive, there has to be a witness. To make sure nurses like Nurse Cathy aren't molesting me or anything. It just prolongs the process and, therefore, my unease. Cathy works to remove the catheter while I grimace and groan. The heaviness in my chest still feels like a grown man is sitting on top of me. Every breath I take is short and labored. She assures me this is normal and that my body will heal as long as I continue to work to help it along. And I am. I will do whatever it takes.

"Good boy," she sings like a mother praising a toddler after I piss into the plastic container attached to the toilet seat. It burns like hell. "You did more than I hoped for." Her hand pats me on the shoulder and I shudder reflexively at her touch.

Baylee.

Baylee.

Baylee.

I exhale the stress of her touch and focus on the therapies. We've spent a good twenty minutes doing simple exercises beside the bed when Dad shows back up. Stark follows in behind with her disgusting partner. Thank fuck there's no toothpick in his mouth.

"Mr. McPherson. So glad to see you up and around this fine morning," she chirps, a little too fucking peppy for this early in the day.

Dad shakes his head and rolls his eyes.

"Looks like we're done with therapy for a couple of hours, big guy," Cathy says and helps me back into the bed. She scurries off and I turn toward Stark expectantly.

Her long, brown hair hangs in front of her breasts. She's wearing a neat, fitted grey suit and black heels. The woman is actually pretty for her age. I guess her to be close to Dad's age. Her dark eyes probe me, narrowing as if she can peel off the top of my skull and look inside. I'd gladly show her the darkness if she promises to take some with her when she exits.

"Mr. McPherson, this is my partner Steve Shilling. I'm not sure if you remember him or not." *How could I fucking forget his disgusting ass?* "You were still sort of groggy from your surgery," she says and then frowns. "I'd like to ask you a few questions about Baylee Winston."

"I told you that—" Dad starts, but she cuts him off.

"I took your statement, Mr. McPherson, and now I'd like to hear his."

Dad sighs but nods toward me. I meet her eyes and furrow my brows together. "Baylee didn't shoot me," I grumble. "That psychopath Gabe did."

"Gabriel Sharpe?" Her question is more of a statement. The woman may be questioning me but it seems as if she knows more than she's letting on.

"Yes, and he took her. He took my girl."

She raises both eyebrows at me and glances at Shilling. "You do realize she's just that, right? A girl."

Anger bubbles in my chest. "She's eighteen. Have I done something wrong? Why are you here—again—instead of searching for her?"

Dad strides over to my bedside and touches my shoulder. His touch causes me to stiffen, but unlike before, it soothes rather than madden me. And that is all because of Baylee. Her ability to slay the demons in my head so that I can be somewhat human. Normal even. Well, almost. "Calm down, son."

"Anyway, her age is beside the point right now," Stark clips out in annoyance. "What I'm trying to make sense of is her disappearance, Brandon Thompson's involvement, her neighbor's involvement, and the sudden disappearance of her father. Additionally, I'd like to inquire more about the sex ring you alluded to in your emails. How did you come to acquire Miss Winston, Mr. McPherson?"

Her barrage of questioning has my head spinning and Dad glowering at her and shaking his head.

"Perhaps we should contact our lawyer," he says with a growl. "You've got no right to barge in here and accuse my son of anything. He's innocent of whatever it is you're cooking up. Warren loved that girl and she loved him back. He protected her from that bastard and took care of her when her own father turned his back on her. You're barking up the wrong tree, detective."

A smile plays at her lips. "Just tell me what you know so we can do our job to find the missing girl and to put this madman behind bars."

Dragging my gaze from hers, I inspect the tray on my bedside table with disgust. I can handle the applesauce but that chicken broth shit looks deadly. They'll have to knock my ass out and pour it down my throat because I won't willingly allow it anywhere near my mouth.

"Mr. McPherson…" she trails off, jerking my attention from the abomination they want me to ingest.

"I, er…saved her from that place. I'd thought I was donating to a hospital, some pediatric foundation. My sister died when my mom delivered her prematurely. It was my way of contributing to other families in need." The lie stumbles off my tongue but I'm not about to go to prison. I'll die before that happens. Not with Baylee out there in danger. "Anyway, I took Baylee to my house. She told me all about how Gabe took her straight from her bedroom, to some cabin out in the middle of nowhere, raped her repeatedly, and then sold her to a sex ring called White Collar Trade that was hiding under the ruse of a pediatric fundraiser benefit."

Shilling jots down my notes as Stark nods and approaches me. I don't flinch and work to remain resolutely composed. The last thing I need is for her to sense my weakness and pick apart my mental illnesses. My gaze meets Dad's irritated one but he nods for me to continue.

"Forrester 'Buck' Whitehead was his name," I tell her. "It was his wife I donated to. You should be able to find record of the funds transfer. I'm not sure if you know this or not, but he was murdered. Gabe killed him to find out where Baylee was hiding. He knew they'd have my last name at the very least."

Her partner continues to take notes, but at a more hurried pace.

"We'll look into that," she says and frowns. "What do you know about Brandon Thompson?"

I shrug my shoulders and it pulls at the incisions on my chest. Grimacing, I shoot her a pained look. "Not much. Besides that he was Baylee's boyfriend…before." I look up to find both detectives looking at me expectantly. Detective Shilling has stopped the note taking, his pen suspended in the air as if waiting for me to continue. "We grew close while she stayed with me. Long after she turned eighteen, we fell in love. I'm going to marry her and protect her as soon as we find her."

Stark's gaze softens. "Do you think Brandon could have anything to do with Baylee's disappearance?"

I shake my head. "No, I don't think so…he's just a kid. Gabe came for her alone."

"Can you tell us anything concerning the whereabouts of Anthony Winston?"

My mind is whirring. "No. Where is her mother? Maybe they had to leave town because they found a donor?"

She sighs and shakes her head. "Mrs. Winston passed away a few of months ago. Liver failure. No foul play."

I attempt to sit up but grow dizzy. My mind is on overdrive as I attempt to piece together what she's telling me. "What made you ask me if I thought Brandon had anything to do with any of this?"

Her partner and her exchange a look.

Stark clears her throat before continuing. "We found Brandon at the Winston residence a couple of days ago. He was acting erratically and was in a hurry to leave." She shrugs.

"Do you think he was there the whole time? This entire time while Baylee was gone?"

Stark stiffens and her dark eyes meet mine. "We have our suspicions that he may have been. We're also concerned about Anthony Winston. He's a missing person of interest."

I run my fingers through my messy hair. "I've been sending money to them for her mother. They were withdrawing it too. This makes no sense. Baylee didn't know she died. Jesus," I groan and slam my eyes shut. "She's going to be so fucking gutted."

"Shilling, we need to check into the money. Follow the trail," she barks out at him over her shoulder.

Shaking my head, I reopen my eyes. "Something is off here. I'd set Baylee up with a secure email to let them know she was okay while I kept her safe from Gabe. Her dad would reply but she'd said he sounded different in his responses. Angry and demanding. I'd assumed it was Gabe attempting to lure her back into his clutches. But now, I don't know."

"How do you know the money was being withdrawn, Mr. McPherson? If you wired it, you wouldn't know if it was being spent or not." Her eyes are darting back and forth as she attempts to figure out what the fuck is going on.

I sigh and glance at Dad who is frowning. "I'm," I say, pausing to choose the least incriminating word, "*resourceful* on the computer. I followed the trail and noticed the money was being withdrawn. Baylee and I assumed it was for her mother's benefit."

Stark places a hand on her hip and sends me a knowing nod. "So you were *resourceful*," she repeats carefully, "in the same way you were *resourceful* in finding a way to contact me in an untraceable way?"

I nod and take a bite of the applesauce still sitting on the tray from my forgotten breakfast, hoping to push the bile down my throat. This shit is complicated and every second we waste, Baylee is in more danger.

"Mr. McPherson," she bites out sharply. "I'm no fool. I have reason to believe you may have been connected in some illegal activities. However, I'm not one to pass up an opportunity to bring a child molester and sexual predator to justice. Additionally, I'm not one to ignore a lead to bringing down an entire sex ring. So, I'm going to take your word that Miss Winston was indeed your girlfriend and that she was staying with you as your guest, consensually. Until she tells me otherwise herself, I'm going to use your help on this investigation."

Dad and I exchange a confused glance before she continues.

"That is why I'm going to have you use your *resources* to help us. Are you up to following any leads you have on Mr. and Mrs. Whitehead, the White Collar Trade, Anthony and Lynn Winston's financial information, details about Brandon Thompson and his whereabouts, and everything you can glean from Gabriel Sharpe?"

Furrowing my brows, I nod. "Of course I am. I want to bring my girl home."

"Good. My captain would have our asses if I brought the Feds in on this one. I don't want their help—they'll trample through this entire investigation with their bureaucratic bullshit and we'll be removed. Our chances of finding Baylee will be less because they'll focus on the WCT, not her. Besides, this story will bring national media attention to our precinct. We could finally get the funding we need to put a technical forensic analyst on payroll, which in this digital age, is necessary. At the moment, we don't have one, which is why I could never track you down after you sent those messages. But now, we have one working for free. You. Pro bono, right?"

Shilling and Stark both stare at me with expectation in their eyes. Dad is frowning and now pacing with his arms crossed over his chest. But when he glances over at me with his lips pressed together in a firm line and nods, I turn my gaze back to Stark.

"Yes," I assure her, "I'll do whatever needs to be done as long as we get Baylee back."

She smiles at me but when my dad stops pacing to glare at her, her smile fades.

"My son won't go to jail for this," he clips out in a cold tone and gestures to me. "You need to give us your word he won't be implicated in any way for his involvement."

Stark glances at Shilling and nods. Her smile is gone but she seems fine with his request and approaches my bedside. Her proximity unnerves me but I grit my teeth and hold still. "Mr. McPherson, with your help on this case, we would be willing to provide you with immunity in exchange for your assistance. After all, we're after the bigger fish here. Gabriel Sharpe and the WCT are the biggest whales in the Pacific. We get Sharpe, we get your girl. We bring down WCT, and we get a whole bunch of girls."

"The doctor says he'll be here in the hospital for another week, maybe two," Dad interrupts. "He's in no shape to be helping right now and—"

I meet her gaze with a serious one of my own. "I'll do it. Dad, I can access everything I need from my laptop and can get to work here in the hospital. Get me that, my phone, and my wireless access point. I'm going to get them whatever they need to help find Baylee."

He groans but nods in resignation. "Of course, War."

Stark pats my knee and smiles. I'm shocked that I don't recoil from her touch. But my mind isn't focused on her anymore. It's flying through code and possibilities. My mind is counting numbers, recalling articles about sexual crimes in California, and contemplating thousands of different avenues I can travel via the Internet to exploit the parties involved. It was Baylee's wish to bring down this sex ring. She mentioned it to me on numerous occasions. If I can help give her that and bring her home at the same time, I will. All for her.

"Thank you," she says and pulls her card from her breast pocket. She tosses it onto the table and extends her hand for me to shake it. "We'll be in touch. Get me anything and everything you can find."

My eyes fall to her slender hand. The nails are clean and polished. She doesn't seem to be crawling with diseases, unlike her partner. With a swallow, I shove my fear down and clasp her warm hand. The handshake is brief, thank God, and then she releases me. They leave without another word and my eyes travel to find the worried ones of my father. My hand quakes from residual fear from touching her but I force myself not to obsess over it. Instead, I take another spoonful of my applesauce as I think about her—my Baylee.

Pretty blue eyes.

Sweet smile.

Compassion that radiates from her like a million rays more brilliant than the fucking sun.

Swallowing the food, I look over at my dad and clench my jaw. "We're going to get her back."

His lips press into a firm line and he nods. "Of course we are, son."

The police may want the bigger fish to fry, but not me.

I want my Baylee.

My heart.

My peace.

Brandon

"Don't touch my girlfriend," I snarl, spittle spraying his face.

The salesman at the department store has the sense to look ashamed and jerks his hand from her arm and holds both palms up in defense. I'd been watching both of them laugh for the past five minutes as he held up different styles of jeans for her to look at and it was pissing me the fuck off.

"D-Dude," he stutters, "I was being friendly."

"She's not yours to be friendly with," I snap.

Thin arms wrap around my middle and try to pull me away. "Stop it, Brandon."

I relax in her embrace. "Think twice before hitting on a girl who's taken."

"I wasn't hitting on your girl, man," he says and shoots Baylee an apologetic glance. "I'm gay."

He gives her an awkward wave and turns to leave us.

"Thanks for all your help," she clips out as she releases me and the storms away.

Fucking great. I trot after her and watch as she angrily snatches up all her bags full of clothes and necessities from the bench I'd abandoned.

"Can we go to the hotel now?" she grits out and shoots me a glare. "I'm tired."

Frowning, I nod and follow after her toward the parking lot. Once we've loaded the bags into the truck and get in, she's composed herself.

"I want my own room."

I'm already shaking my head. *Fuck that.* "No."

She snaps her head over to glare at me. "Why the hell not, Brandon? I don't even know who you are anymore. You're violent and unhinged. I need space."

Violent?

Unhinged?

Of fucking course I am!

She was stolen right out from under my goddamned nose. They raped and fucking tortured *my* girl. Fuck them and fuck her attitude right now. I saved her yet she has no gratitude whatsoever.

"I don't have enough money for you to get your own room. Sorry." My lie and the firm tone I deliver it with silences her and I put the truck in drive. Eventually she finds her voice again.

"Unbelievable," she mutters and crosses her arms across her chest, glaring out the window.

The trip to the hotel is quiet. Things will be rocky until we find our way again. I'll always be wary and fucking suspicious of anyone who even breathes her way after all that's happened. It's my duty to protect my girlfriend. I failed once and I sure as hell am not ever letting that happen again.

We pull up to the front of the hotel. It's swanky enough that a valet clerk greets us. "Good afternoon. Would you like us to park your vehicle while you check in?"

The clerk brings over a cart and we load our things up. Baylee remains all but mute with her eyes downcast. I shouldn't have flipped the fuck out at the department store—I know this—but I was pissed. That fucker, gay or not, was touching her. I'm responsible for her now and that means protecting her from everyone.

"Come on," I tell her and pat her bottom as we walk into the hotel. The lobby is all brick on the inside but with an elegant, modern décor to give it a rustic yet restored feel. There aren't hotels like this back in Oakland and I'm eager to spend some alone time here with my girl.

Baylee walks off to stare at a painting on the wall. It's of the ocean. I'll have to take her to the beach soon. Her shoulders have relaxed and she seems much calmer than she was in the truck where she looked like she wanted to rip my head off.

"Do you have a reservation, sir?" the slender woman at the counter asks.

She's pretty, her blonde hair pulled back in some up-do thing. Red paints her lips making her look like a whore. An expensive one but still a whore. She doesn't compare one iota to Baylee's natural beauty. Upon making eye contact, she frowns. Her eyes skitter over my young, boyish face and she predetermines I can't afford her pricey hotel. It's written all over her face and it annoys me. I flash her an easy grin, despite my irritation, which causes her to smile back. Truth is, I'd love to throw wads of hundred dollar bills in her face but I can't be an arrogant asshole. I need her help.

"Actually, no," I say sadly, "but I really want to surprise my girlfriend with something fancy. This is her birthday present."

The girl's lips press into a firm line when she glances over to see Baylee, looking stunning as hell in her simple yoga pants and my hoodie. I'm sure she's working out a way to nicely tell me no.

"I see," she says softly and taps at the computer. "Unfortunately, sir, it appears we're booked." *And there it is.*

I raise an annoyed eyebrow at her in question but then quickly pull my lips into a frown, doing my best to give her the puppy dog look. It must work because she has the sense to look embarrassed and her cheeks turn pink. Do whores even blush?

"You don't have anything available?"

She chews on her red lip. "Well," she lowers her voice. "We have one of the VIP suites we keep open for emergencies. But it's pricey, sir."

I smirk at her. "I can handle it, miss."

"Umm," she says and then sighs, "it's two thousand dollars a night."

"Two thousand a night!" Baylee hisses as she approaches. "I thought you didn't have any money! No, Brandon, we're going to the Holiday Inn."

A growl escapes me, startling both the women. I yank out my wallet and slap my credit card down on the granite countertop. "Book us for the week. The suite."

The suite is huge and overlooks Fisherman's Wharf, which is bustling with evening activity. There's a crab restaurant that I want to take her to and maybe take her to one of the shops after to buy her an engagement ring.

The thought of sliding a pretty diamond on her slender finger sends a ripple of excitement through me. This is it. I always knew I'd marry her—I just assumed it would be after college. But, with us both high school dropouts now, there's no reason to wait. Who needs college when you're fucking loaded anyway?

I smirk down at the crowd below before turning to regard Baylee. She's sitting on the small sofa in the suite with her purse in her lap. Her eyes aren't roaming the beautiful space or gushing about how fucking cool it is. Instead, she's wringing her hands together.

"What's wrong? Do you not like it here?" I question and saunter over to her.

She flinches when I sit down beside her on the couch and just like every time before—which there have now been several—it irritates me. Everything I do is *for* her. All of it. If only she knew the things I've gone through. Endured. The things I've done. The dark paths I've taken.

Her left foot is tapping rapidly. I am about to repeat my question when she says, "We need to call the police and tell them about Gabe's body at the cabin. I'm ready to tell them what I know about the sex ring as well. There were some bad people, Brandon," she says, her sparkling blue eyes finding mine. "If anything, maybe they can go after the other assholes who are still selling women into human trafficking and sex slavery out there. These are innocent women, Brandon. Women like me, who were taken and sold as if they were commodities rather than people. Not all of the buyers are good, honest people like War."

I run my fingers through my hair and groan. She's defending that freak again. Her speaking to the police doesn't sit well with me but I feel like she's slipping through my fingers. The last thing I want her to feel like is that I'm imprisoning her or controlling her. Gabe did enough of that to her to last a lifetime. Baylee is a free spirit. Independent and strong. I need to give that to her so she'll trust me. We're slightly broken and I need to do whatever I can to fix it.

"Fine, we'll call them together. You can talk and I'll sit here. We'll have dinner afterwards."

She shakes her head and grabs hold of my hand. Her touch ignites a fire within me and my heart thumps to life.

"I'd like to do it on my own," she whispers, tears filling her eyes, making them look like tiny Caribbean oceans. "I'm embarrassed about the things that happened to me. Please. Let me do this on my own. You can order us some take-out and bring it back. It shouldn't take long."

I clench my teeth hard enough to make my jaw ache as I search her eyes for deception. But I find none. They only reflect the Baylee I know. Sweet, innocent, untarnished by the cruel fucking world. God, I love her.

Sliding a hand into her hair, I then rub the pad of my finger over her temple. She's so beautiful. Gabe tried to stomp on my gorgeous girl's nature and body, but she survived. Baylee not only made it through, but it somehow made her even more alluring. She's no longer that delicate flower the world was threatening to crush. No, now she's sporting some sexy-as-hell thorns.

"Please," she utters and then leans forward, parting her lips.

I'm so stunned that she's initiating a kiss, I don't realize that's exactly what it is until her soft lips are pressed to mine and a small whimper pours from her. It slides down my throat and strokes the pelt of my inner beast. The dark parts inside of me shimmer briefly to life.

I crave to deepen the kiss. To push her down onto the sofa and kiss her like there's no tomorrow. My cock begs for me to tug her yoga pants from her body and sink inside her tight heat.

But I can't.

She's barely warming back up to me.

I won't ruin it out of desperation to mark and claim her for the first time.

It takes everything in me but I pull away from her kiss and grin. "Sure, babe. I'll get us some food."

She beams at me, but for a brief moment something flashes in her eyes. I don't recognize the glimmer. It's dark and foreign. Before I can pinpoint what it is, she reaches forward and pushes some of my hair from my eyes.

"You need a haircut," she says and then laughs. I search her face for sadness or anger. Or anything. Something was there but now it's gone. Now she's happy. Almost too happy.

"Babe," I start slowly, "is something wrong? You looked upset for a minute."

Her eyes widen and she bites on her lower lip. I drop my gaze to her mouth and crave to nibble on it too. Later. Definitely later.

"I was just wondering…"

I arch an eyebrow at her in question.

"Where'd you get all this money, Brandon?"

My eyes tear from hers and I flick them to the painting on the wall behind her. Black brush strokes up and down. Left and right. Smudging together, attempting to hide the red blob beneath. It kind of feels like my heart. Like I have a black paintbrush of deceit trying desperately to cover up the hate. What the hate made me do.

"Brandon." I feel her hand squeeze mine. "Tell me."

With a sigh, I meet her eyes. "I took his money. That freak you were with. He took what was mine, so I took his money." The bite in my voice is sharp and not meant to sting her, but it does.

Her eyes widen and her plump lips part open. "The money War sent for Mom? You took his money?"

The way she says his name, as if he's precious to her, sends ice through my veins. "Your dad had clearly bailed. Fucking asshole," I snap. "After I found the note, I'd seen in the emails that he was receiving money for your mother and she had already died. I figured we could use it, babe. It's our money to start over. We can buy a house and—"

"Wait." She shoves of the sofa and retreats a few steps. "You read those emails between Dad and me? And you didn't try and reply back to me?"

Shit!

I blink my eyes several times to try and figure out a way to dig myself out of this hole. "Babe…"

"No! Don't 'babe' me. You could have reached out to me then. You could have told me Dad had left and that Mom had died. Why didn't you reply to me? I thought you loved me!"

Tears well in her eyes but she doesn't look sad anymore. Her face is red. Her fists are clenched. Her breaths are labored. She's pissed the hell off. *Fuck. Fuck. Fuck.* I'm growing more nervous by the second. She's slipping through my fingers faster now, and I don't know how to make it stop. I need her to understand.

Without thinking, I grab onto her hips and haul her to the wall next to the painting. "Love. I *do* love you. And you loved me too but then the moment someone else stuck their dick inside you, you forgot about that love. Reduced it to nothing but a fucking memory. Did you ever even think about me?"

"This isn't about you and me!" she cries out and shoves at my chest, but I don't move. "This is about your lies—about you deceiving me! This is *not* about us or our love." My girl is tiny and weak. Snatching both of her wrists, I push them against the exposed brick above her head. She squirms her body but when I smash my hips against hers, pinning her to the wall, she freezes. Terror swims in the pools of her eyes. Fucking terror. She's afraid. Of me.

"Of course this is about us," I hiss, dropping my voice to a whisper. "Or course it's about our love. Tell me. How could you forget about me so easily? Not one second of one day went by where I didn't think about you, babe. I obsessed over finding you."

She presses her lips together when I lean forward, but I kiss her anyway.

"Baylee, I didn't respond to those emails because I assumed it was someone pretending to be you. I was confused." It's mostly the truth. She didn't seem like herself at all. Not my sweet Baylee. My girl would never willingly run off with someone else when she had me.

The terror melts away as her expression changes to one of determination. It doesn't fit, considering our proximity and the anger emanating from me. She should still be quivering and frightened, but she's not.

"I'm sorry, Brandon." Her words weave themselves through my heart and slip under the black smudges. I hold them there closely. Guard and protect them. Nurture and love them. You're right. "It probably must have been very confusing for you. I'm so sorry."

Relief floods through me and I let out a rush of air. Crisis fucking averted.

"I love you, Baylee Marie," I murmur as I release her wrists and then slide my palms down her arms and to her hips.

She's still stiff but she lets me kiss her this time, her mouth opening to give my tongue access. God, she tastes so fucking good. I can't wait to taste all of her. My mind flits back to the brief taste I snuck from her last night, and although I know I was a bastard for doing it, my cock hardens at the mere thought. I need more. To consume her as I make love to her. I need her like I need goddamned air.

"I'm hungry," she murmurs when I finally break away. "I'll make the call while you grab the food."

I want to tell her I'm not hungry for anything but her. That I would rather spend the night licking and nibbling every part of her flesh. How I'd love to bury my tongue deep between her thighs and bring her pleasure. But then her stomach growls and I pussy out. I do need to feed her. The pleasure can wait. We have the rest of our lives.

"I'll be back as fast as I can. Make the call and don't leave this suite," I instruct as I pull away.

She smiles and it quickens my heart. "I'll be right here when you get back."

Her words unnerve me but I'm not sure why. She's grinning and her eyes are shining but it's almost too much. Like the time she told me she loved the necklace I'd bought her for Valentine's Day, and then later admitted she didn't wear much silver because it irritates her skin. I'd been shocked and saddened that she could lie so easily to spare my feelings. At the time, I thought it was sweet. But now, now I wonder if she's lying to me again. To keep me calm. Why would she lie to me?

I narrow my eyes at her and frown. "Don't leave while I'm gone."

She blinks and her smile falls. "I promise I'll be here when you get back with our food."

This time I do believe her.

chapter
FOURTEEN

Baylee

The moment the door slams closed behind him, I rush to the window. Several minutes later, I see his messy dark hair blowing in the wind as he emerges from the building below and trots across the street to a busy restaurant. When he turns to look up at the hotel, I duck away from the window and locate the phone.

He said to not leave.

And I won't.

Not yet.

Not until I call the police. I'd been biding my time alongside Brandon since the cabin. I don't know what's happened to him, but I'm not sticking around to find out. He's an angry, unstable, and volatile man whom I don't even recognize.

Like the possessive way he behaved at the store earlier. I'd been horrified by the way he confronted that poor man for simply being nice to me. I know he's keeping things from me. And I *know* he's lying—I can feel it—and it scares the hell out of me. The way he took War's money—it might not have been a blatant lie, but it was deceitful. Gabe may have been the psychopath in my story who dragged me into his deranged world, but Brandon's erratic and controlling behavior fill me with the same sense of dread. And I refuse to lead a life of misery in anyone else's steely clutches for as long as I live. I decide not to think about it too deeply, because if I do, I'll fall apart. So, for now, I push it to the back of my mind. I need to find Land. He'll keep me safe and help me get on my feet. We will search for my dad. Then, together, we can raise my child—his grandchild—in a non-toxic environment.

It's time for me to stand on my own two feet.

I can do this.

It doesn't take long for me to locate the number for the Oakland PD. Quickly, I dial and try to keep my fluttering heart calm.

"Detective Stark, please," I mutter to the receptionist who answers. She tells me to hold and I'm soon listening to elevator music.

"Stark speaking."

Her voice radiates authority and my nerves seem to hum with anxiety.

"Umm, hi, this is Baylee Winston."

I hear her rushed breath come through the phone. "Miss Winston! Are you okay? Are you safe?"

I look toward the front door of the suite, expecting to see Brandon's angry form materializing there.

"Um, for the moment. But I, uh, need to talk to you."

She shuffles some papers and her voice is serious. "You have my undivided attention. Where are you, Miss Winston?"

I sigh and will the tears away. "San Francisco."

"San Francisco? Are you still with Gabriel Sharpe?"

A tear rolls down my cheek and I sniffle. "No. I escaped, but then Brandon showed up and found me. Then, um…"

"And then…what, Miss Winston?"

"He—" I pause because whatever I say will implicate Brandon. The thought of him getting in trouble makes my chest ache. He may no longer be the boy I once knew, but that doesn't mean he deserves to be put away as a result of Gabe's actions.

"I'm listening."

"He died. There was a struggle…and he fell into the cellar at the cabin. The cellar where he was first holding me captive."

The line goes silent for a moment. "Where can we find his body, Miss Winston?"

I rattle off directions to the cabin, as best as I can, since I don't know the address. When I finish, she speaks again. "Can you come down to the station so we can get your statement? Or can we come to you? Where in San Francisco are you, Miss Winston?"

"It doesn't matter. I'm not coming in. Well, not yet at least." Picking up the phone receiver, I walk back over to the window to watch for Brandon.

"Okay." Her heavy sigh comes through the line. "Well, can you at least tell me more about the White Collar Trade group?"

I swallow down my emotion and nod even though she can't see me. "They were all rich men in suits. A fancy real estate company in San Diego. I don't know any of their names except for one. Edgar Finn. He told me he would carve me up after he had his way with me and then dump me in the ocean. I'm afraid he's hurt or done…worse to other women like me, and I don't think he planned on stopping any time soon."

She's taking notes. I can hear the scribbling of her pen on paper.

"Miss Winston, do you know where your father is? Are you staying with him?"

A sob catches in my throat at the mention of my dad. "No, I don't know where he is," I choke out. "I'm…" The last remaining shred of my loyalty to Brandon holds me back. I squeeze my eyes shut and hope to God I'm doing the right thing. "We came to San Francisco to look for him. Brandon said Dad left a note stating he'd come here. But we haven't done anything to look for him yet. He wanted to come to this fancy hotel, and—" I realize the words are rushing out of my mouth and stop to take a deep, calming breath. "He's acting really weird. I'm scared, Ms. Stark."

"Rita," she says softly, "call me Rita."

"I didn't kill War, you know. Brandon told me you guys think I did, but I didn't," I tell her firmly as hot tears roll down my cheeks. "I loved him. So much. Gabe came back for me and shot him, Rita. There was so much blood…he didn't deserve it. He was sick and that kind of death was the worst possible way for him to go."

"Honey," Rita says, her voice growing firm, despite the pet name, "Mr. McPherson's not dead. He's alive. I spoke to him today at the hospital."

My heart stops. My world spins and I grab on to the frame around the window to keep from collapsing. "W—What?" I whisper, not trusting my voice. *Alive. Alive. Alive.* My War is alive. "I don't understand. Brandon told me he died."

"Really? He was touch and go there for the first day, from what I understand. He was in critical condition. Suffered a bullet wound to the chest, but no, Baylee. They expect him to make a full recovery. He's very worried about you, in fact."

My choked gasp is the last thing that comes over the line as quiet sobs wrack my entire body. With my back to the wall, I lower myself to the floor, no longer able to support the weight of my own body.

"Thank you, thank you, thank you…" I don't know if I am saying it to Detective Stark or God or whoever, but in the midst of hell, this news is heaven.

"I'm so sorry you didn't know, honey. We've been trying to reach you." She's quiet for a moment, and then, "I personally questioned Mr. Thompson about the *attempted* murder of Mr. McPherson, though, so he was aware that Warren didn't die. I'm concerned that he may know more about the disappearance of your father than he's letting on. Tell me where you are so I can come get you, Baylee. I have reason to believe you're in danger."

My hands begin to tremble and my heart thunders in my chest as if it may burst out at any moment. "He killed Gabe," I blurt out. "He pushed him into the cellar."

"Get out, now," she orders. "Find a public place and call me. I'll call the San Francisco PD and have them pick you up until I can get there."

My mind races with thoughts of War. I need to get to him. To touch him and kiss him. To see if her claims are true.

My breathing is completely out of control. I'm heaving breaths as if I just finished running a marathon. "He's at Fisherman's Wharf at one of the restaurants, picking up dinner. I can leave now before he gets back but I have to go now."

"Call me as soon as you—"

I hang up the phone and rush over to the shopping bags. I'd purchased a backpack to carry my clothes. Quickly, I unzip it and rip the stuffing from it. I shove my purse and a few of the new clothes into it. Finding his duffel bag, I search for the pictures of my family, which he'd put in there. I snag those too and then zip my backpack up.

Pulling my hoodie over my head, I tuck my hair inside and shoulder the bag. War's alive. The love of my life and father of my child survived being shot. I need to get to him. With Brandon on his way back any time, I have to make every second count. I avoid the elevators and head for the stairwell. I sprint down four flights of stairs, ignoring the ache in my calves and the wooziness in my head. When I reach the bottom, I peek my head out the doorway.

Brandon is striding into the lobby with a bag full of to-go containers in one arm and a bundle of red roses in the other. He's smiling, like he doesn't have a worry in the world, and it causes a slight pang in my chest for my friend. The old Brandon. But he's no longer here.

Once he disappears into the elevator, I bolt from the stairwell and past the receptionist. The moment I make it outside, I veer to the right and trot down the sidewalk in search of a cab.

Cabs are everywhere so I quickly hail one and hop inside as soon as it stops.

"San Diego," I blurt out, "hurry!"

The dark-skinned man turns and glares at me. "Too far. I don't leave San Francisco."

I jerk my head over my shoulder and look back at the entrance of the hotel. There's no sign of Brandon, but I know it won't be long.

"Fine," I huff out, "take me to the bus station. Please hurry!"

He grumbles but peels out and into the traffic. I keep my eyes affixed on the hotel until it becomes a blur. Brandon hadn't emerged yet. I breathe a sigh of relief and sag into the backseat of the cab, but I know it's not over. He's going to be furious once he realizes I ran.

It took everything in me to kiss him and smile at him when I wanted to shake him. For trying to control me. For lying to me. For hiding things from me.

He hid the biggest thing of all.

War.

Had I known War was still alive, I certainly wouldn't have been sitting at that cabin with him and Gabe. I would've been in War's arms. Kissing away his pain.

The tears start and they don't stop, despite the annoyed looks the cab driver sends my way. I cry the entire way to the bus station.

The bus ride was several hours long but I managed to get in a nap. My sleep was disturbed, though, with interchanging images of both Brandon and Gabe. Each were taking their turns violating me. In the dream, War was dead and bloody. I couldn't speak or move or cry. All I could do was stare into their eyes—a demented set of coffee-colored ones alternating with an evil set of greens—as they relentlessly fucked me.

When an old lady woke me up to tell me we were near the bus station, I'd screamed. Actually screamed in terror. She'd scurried off, surely in a hurry to get away from the crazy, screaming teenager on the bus.

Now, I'm sitting in the back of another cab with the side of my head on the cold glass. It's after midnight and I'm still on a mission to get to the hospital.

"We're here," the cab driver grunts out.

I dive my hands into my purse, inside my backpack, and pull out the last of the cash I had left over from the shopping trip with Brandon earlier in the day. After I shove a few bills into his hands and tell him to keep the change, I climb out of the cab and practically limp into the hospital. My entire body aches from the exertion. I'm sure it doesn't help that all I've had to eat today since lunch was a Snickers bar I'd procured from the bus station vending machine. I can barely keep my eyes open but the adrenaline fuels me in my effort to find War.

"I'm looking for Warren McPherson," I say to an older woman manning the front desk. Her long grey hair is pulled into a ponytail and she looks up at me with kind eyes.

"Sure honey," she chirps, way too friendly for as late as it is. "Looks like he's in room 1200." *The same number as his alarm code back home.*

1-2-0-0

He's alive. A feeling of warmth that I hadn't felt since Gabe ripped me away from War coats my insides at hearing that room number.

My heart flutters in my chest and I beam at her. "Thank you!"

"Wait," she says, and then frowns. "Visiting hours were over three and a half hours ago. I'm afraid I can't let you go back there."

The emotions from the past four months overwhelm me and I burst into tears. Loud, ugly sobs. She quickly stands and comes out from behind the desk to pull me into a hug.

"Oh, honey."

"He—he—he doesn't know he's going to be a father…please," I tell her through my tears. "I thought he was dead. I need to see him. Please."

She pats my head and pulls away, gracing me with a kind smile. "Come on," she says in a whisper. "It's my break. I'll take you there. You've been through a lot, honey. That much I can see."

I hug her back to me. "Thank you. Thank you so much."

With her arm over my shoulder, she guides me down the complicated web of hallways and to his room. The hallway is dim. His door is pushed forward, but not shut. "Go on, honey. Go see your man," she says and winks, "but if they catch you in there, you tell them you snuck in there yourself."

Nodding profusely, I thank her one more time before slipping into the dark room. The sound of a heart monitor is music to my ears because it confirms he's alive, just like Rita had said. But panic sets in. What if he doesn't want to see me? What if he's regressed and the thought of my touch horrifies him? I swallow down my fears and take a few steps into the room. Peeking my head around the corner, I nearly cry out with joy.

My War.

His large frame fills the entire bed and a simple white blanket covers him. He's wearing a standard hospital gown and his hair's a mess. I crave to smooth it out of his eyes and rain kisses all over his beautiful face.

Approaching slowly, I shed my backpack along the way. I drop it to the floor and take his warm hand in mine.

"Oh, God," I barely choke out before sobs wrack through my entire body.

He jerks slightly, waking up. His full lashes fluttering to reveal the navy-colored eyes that complete my existence. The entire world fades away except for the both of us, two halves of a perfect whole. Two magnets drawn together by unmeasurable forces. "Bay?" his sleepy voice rasps out. "Is this a dream?"

My eyes find his half-lidded ones and my tears blur the man before me for a moment. "Not a dream. I'm here and you're alive."

His hand squeezes around mine and he tugs me to him. Bliss. All I know is this is bliss. My heart, so broken and bloody, is rapidly healing with every second in his presence. I blink a few times to let the tears escape and he comes back into view.

"Thank God," he murmurs and pulls me until our faces are inches apart. "I've been going out of my fucking mind worrying about you. God I've missed you."

I drop my lips to his and kiss him tenderly. His lips aren't soft like usual, they're cracked and dry but they're perfection to me. I've missed them so much. We remain barely touching—simply inhaling one other. He's hurt and I'm afraid I'll make it worse I even move. But then his fingers thread into my hair and he palms the back of my skull, pulling me closer. The hunger—the all-consuming urgency—explodes through him and I fall into him. Just like each and every time. I can't help but get swept up in the incredible hurricane that is him. He pulls me into the eye of his storm where it's safe and calm. War loves me with the gentleness no other can give to me while the chaos ensues around us.

When I let out a happy sigh, his tongue dives into my mouth and he tastes me as if I'm the most delectable thing he's ever had the pleasure of tasting. I slide my fingers over his cheek that's sporting a few days' worth of scruff and kiss him deeper. His mouth has a way of wiping away all the hurt and pain, and instead filling me with hope and love.

When we part, my face is cupped in his hands and he holds it a few inches from his, his eyes flitting all over me. "I need you closer," he murmurs against my lips. "Get into the bed with me."

I kick off my tennis shoes and delicately climb in next to him. His arm wraps around my back as he hugs me to him.

"I'm afraid to touch you," I murmur, my fingertips delicately dancing along his flesh as if he might disappear at any moment. "War, I thought you were dead and that…that…" I shudder in his arms.

He strokes my hair and presses a kiss to my forehead. "Shhh. I'm here, Bay, and I'm not going anywhere. As long as you're here, I'll make it through this. How did you get away from him? What did he do to you?"

More tears spill out and I shudder in his arms. "He hurt me…again, but he's gone. Don't worry about me. We're together now."

I tilt my head up to look at him. His stormy blue eyes are devouring my appearance. I hope he can't see the horrible memories of what Gabe did inside my head. If he knew that Gabe raped me, he'd probably be disgusted. I'd become tainted in his eyes. Filthy. Like the infectious bacteria he so ferociously avoids. I want to enjoy this moment. I know it's a conversation we need to have. But I can't put those images in his mind. I can't bear the thought of rehashing the events of the last two days right now. Not when I just managed to escape.

When I find his eyes in the darkness, they are looking at me studiously. He sighs and nods slowly. "Okay," he whispers as if he recognizes the fact that any questions he dares to ask should be asked with caution. Because he isn't going to like the answers. "You're safe now, beautiful. When I get out of here, we can go back home where I'm never letting you go."

Home.

War is my home.

"My mom died," I tell him, my chin quivering. "This whole time she's been dead, and I never knew. I went to her gravesite. God, I miss her."

He hugs me to him. "I'm so sorry. Detective Stark told me. I fucking hate that for you."

Our lips meet for a moment and he kisses me while his thumb swipes away my tears.

"Brandon told me you'd died," I choke out. "I was dead inside. My heart died right along with you."

My sobs overwhelm me and he holds me tight against his side.

"Shhh," he coos. "I never went anywhere, Bay."

"He's not the same person," I hiss out, my lip wobbling wildly. "I was happy when he saved me but then I wasn't. I don't love him. Not anymore. But it's more than that, War, he's unhinged. He has these elaborate ideas about us being together. I watched him shove Gabe to his death in that cellar. His eyes were hate-filled… I'm afraid he'll never cope with you and I being together, which is why he lied. And I think he has something to with my dad being missing."

His brows furrow together and he frowns. "Yeah, I started getting a feeling when talking to Stark and it wasn't a good one. Jesus, Baylee," he says and drops a kiss to the top of my head, his hands around my face trembling. "We'll call her in the morning. She can deal with Brandon. You're safe with me now."

I want to believe him but fear still niggles inside of me.

"Go look in my bag," he says with a smile. "I brought something of yours to have up here with me, but now you can have it back." His fingers tenderly stroke along the outer shell of my ear and he touches my earring.

Nodding, I climb out of bed away from his warmth and dig in his bag. I find a Gala apple and jerk my gaze over to him. "Can I have this? I'm starving."

"Yes, Jesus, please eat. I hate that you've been out there in survival mode. You can rest now. You're free," he tells me gruffly.

I take a bite of the apple and finally find what he wanted me to have. Chewing, I pull out my pretty pink watch and slide it on over my wrist. "I wish I had this on when I left," I tell him sadly after I swallow. "The trunk was so dark…I didn't know how many hours had passed. I had nothing but your shirt on my back to remember you by."

He sits up in bed, eyes wide and furious. "Trunk?" I hear the beeps on the machines next to his bed speed up, an indicator of his anger. "I wish you had it too, *believe me*," he says with a growl that I've missed so much. "Now get over here because I'm already missing you and you're only five feet away."

With my apple in hand, I bounce back over to him and then crawl back in beside him. His lips press a kiss to my forehead and then my nose. I let out a sigh when he trails kisses along my cheek and to my ear.

"I love you, Baylee."

I shiver in his arms and let his touch soothe away all of the pain—the physical and emotional—that both Brandon and Gabe made me endure.

"Bay," he murmurs, his hot breath against my ear, "I didn't obsess or count while you were gone. If I had, it would have swallowed me up. It was you—always you. Every breath, every thought, every blink. You were in each and every one. When they had me drugged after my surgery, it was your light that shone in the darkness of my head. Had you not been there, I'd have lost you forever. The demons would have ruined me once and for all. They were there—always there, threatening me, but you saved me. Every time."

I find his mouth with mine and kiss him hard. His mouth overtakes mine, his tongue lapping up the juicy remnants of the apple as we kiss. When I break away, I smile at him.

"You saved me too, War. When I was stuck in a nightmare, I dreamed about you. It was my heaven."

He kisses me again and the apple slides from my grip. It hits the floor with a thud and rolls away until it thumps against the wall.

"Don't eat that," he chuckles against my lips. "I very much like kissing you, but so help me, if you pick that thing up…"

I giggle and look into his gorgeous, expressive eyes. "But I'm really hungry," I say and then grow serious, "because I'm eating for two."

chapter
FIFTEEN

War

Two.

Two.

Two.

That number is quickly becoming my favorite and I count over and over again. One, two, one, two, one, two, one, two.

Black monsters run from my head as something beautiful fills the space. A woman and child. Beautiful. And mine. I'm blinded by the sweet, perfect light of it.

I blink at the sun, my Baylee, so radiant and blinding I almost have to look away. But I don't. The brightness that shines from her is nourishment to my starved, black soul. I want to bask in all that's her for eternity.

"Did you hear me?" A slow grin plays at her lips and her blue orbs shimmer with emotion, her eyes blinking. One, two. "War, I'm pregnant. We're going to have a baby. It'll be the three of us"— *one, two, three*—"Are you happy?"

Happy?

I'm fucking ecstatic.

Three's my new favorite number because it includes me. Baylee, our baby, and me. One, two, three. Love doesn't come in the shape of a heart, it clearly comes in triangles.

"I'm more than happy, Bay," I murmur against her pouty lips. "I'm complete."

One point two seconds later and I'm ravishing her. My teeth bite and nip at her lips as my hands roam over her perfect body. A baby. My woman is pregnant with *our* child. The ache in my chest is because the love inside of me is trying to claw its way out and envelop her in an everlasting embrace. The throbbing from my surgery is ever present, but it is nothing in comparison to the pain I felt when she wasn't with me. With Baylee in my arms, the entire world fades to black while she shines brilliantly in the middle.

She's my center.

My nucleus.

My only reason.

I can only exist fully with her.

And I am nothing without her.

"God, I love you," I murmur as we kiss, "and this." My fingers slide under her hoodie and I stroke her soft skin on her belly. "I love this too."

She lets out a whimper when my fingers trail up her flesh and then I flutter them over one of her breasts. Her nipple hardens at my touch and I grin at her. "I even love this," I assure her and pinch it between my thumb and finger.

"War," she murmurs and straddles my waist. "I need you to make it all go away. Touch me all over. Please."

She tugs her hoodie from her body and bares her full tits at me. Her nipples point right at me as if to accuse me for not saving her from Gabe. I tug her closer and put one in my mouth. My tongue teases the hardened peak and then I gently bite down on the tender flesh. A pleased gasp releases from her and my cock thickens between us. She seems to realize this at the same time and grinds herself against me. The groan that leaves my chest is one of pure bliss and it dizzies me.

"Shit," I say as wave of darkness passes over my vision. "I need to lie back for a second."

"Oh my God," she hisses in horror. "I keep forgetting you're hurt. I'm so sorry. I should—"

She starts to climb off of me but I grip on to her hips to keep her in place. "No, don't leave me. I just need to catch my breath."

Her lips pout into a small frown that does nothing to help my aching cock. "I just missed you so much."

"Come here," I say with a smile and tug her toward the crook of my arm. To my dismay, she shrugs the hoodie back on first before sliding back up against me. Her legs remain stretched across my thighs as if she's attempting to latch onto me indefinitely. "Dad is going to be so fucking happy you're back. I should text him and let him know you're safe."

She snuggles against me. "Text him in the morning. I'm so exhausted I can barely move."

"Okay." I stroke her hair. "And Bay, in the morning? After we call my dad and Stark, I want you to go down to the emergency department and get yourself checked out." She stills against me. I don't know the details, but I don't need to. I know that monster violated her. Again. It's written all over her face. And when she lifts her head to look at me, her watery eyes and the shame in her expression is all the confirmation I need. She offers me the same silent, tentative nod that I offered her just moments ago when this topic came up, before putting her head back down on my chest. She doesn't want to talk about it. Whether it's that she doesn't want to talk about it at all or that she doesn't want to talk about it with me, I don't know. But it will need to be dealt with. She may be safe now, physically. But emotionally, my Baylee is anything but okay.

I continue stroking her hair while my mind begins playing out a future for us. A future where Baylee wears more than the earrings and watch I gave to her, but also a ring.

"Quiet your mind, Warren McPherson," she says thickly as sleep begins to steal her.

I smile, letting my thumb slide along her jaw and then rest it on her pulse point. "Shhh, quiet your mouth. I'm counting the beats of your heart against me."

She lets out a small sigh and soon breathes in a soft, rhythmic way that lulls the monsters inside me right to sleep. But there, in the darkness of that hospital room, I resolve to help Baylee fight her demons, just like she helped me fight mine.

I won't let her exist in the darkness. I'll bring her into the light.

With a yawn, I hug her to me and follow quickly behind.

I've finally found Peace again.

I wake with a start.

Cold, bitter, emptiness threatens to swallow me whole.

My warmth—my radiant, brilliant sun—has vanished and thrown me back into the darkness.

"Breakfast, Mr. McPherson?" Cathy chirps as she waltzes into the room, carrying a tray of food she and I both know I won't eat.

I'm already climbing out of bed. "Where is she? Where the fuck is Baylee?"

Her eyes widen and she sets the tray on the table beside the bed. "Who? Are you feeling okay, Warren?

"She was here. Baylee came into my room last night. She got away from him—both of them actually—and I held her in my arms. So where the fuck is she? Call hospital security! Have them look over the security footage! We need to call Detective Stark!"

She frowns at me and then looks down at the floor. Her features quickly morph into one of shock as she bends over to pick something up. "This her shoe?"

I nod and once again the world spins.

"Sit down before you faint, Warren. I'll call security." She rushes out the door and I pick up my phone as I sit on the edge of the bed. I call and leave a message for Dad, telling him to hurry up with a change of clothes. Then, I phone Stark next.

"Stark," she barks out.

I launch into a crazy man's babble. "He took her. I think Brandon took her. She was here last night—said she got away from him. But her shoes are still here. Stark, she wouldn't leave without her shoes. Not to mention, she wouldn't leave me. Goddammit she's pregnant with my baby! You have to fucking find her!"

She lets out a string of expletives that would make a sailor blush. "We're on it. I already issued an APB on Brandon's truck after I spoke with Miss Winston last night. We'd pinpointed the location of the hotel she called from and his credit card activity matched, but when we arrived, they were both gone. I have no doubts Brandon is looking for her. Unfortunately, Baylee isn't my only concern right now."

I brutally grip the phone and clench my teeth. "What the fuck is your concern besides finding my goddamned fiancée?"

She huffs, clearly frustrated with my tone. "The cabin was empty. There was no body. No sign of Mr. Sharpe."

The room spins again and I lie back against the pillows for a minute. "What do you mean there was no body? You mean to tell me that bastard could be the one who took her?"

Jesus Christ.

This can't be fucking happening.

Again.

There's only so much that girl can bear. And why the fuck did I not hear her leave last night? We'd both fallen asleep and I didn't wake to her struggling or screaming. No way would she have left willingly.

Not my girl.

"His car was gone too. We've put out an APB on his vehicle as well. Stay put, Mr. McPherson," she commands. "We're on it. Find out what you can on Edgar Finn, will you? That'll keep your mind occupied while we locate Miss Winston."

She hangs up on me and I scrub my face in frustration.

Like fuck I will.

I am stuck here until Dad shows up with clothes. I can't exactly take to the streets barefoot. I feel like a prisoner in this fucking room. Crawling back out of the bed, I pull up the app on my phone that I'd installed awhile back. The green flashing ping gives me a false sense of security—I know it doesn't tell me if she's hurt—but it at least tells me where she is. I keep it open and under my watchful eye while I take a quick piss. By the time I've splashed water on my face, Cathy shows up with my dad and a security officer.

Everyone has somber looks on their faces and I think I might snap. "Someone please talk to me."

"This is really against hospital protocol, but since MPE is such a generous benefactor—" the security guard stammers but is interrupted by my father.

"And we appreciate that. Can you please just tell us what was on the footage?"

"Of course," he says, clearing his throat. "About an hour ago, a man in scrubs was seen entering this room pushing a wheelchair," the security officer tells me, his breath heaving. "Several minutes later, he came back out with a young woman in the chair. She appeared to be awake. Didn't look to be injured on the footage. The man's face was covered. They're still sorting through the parking lot footage."

"Shit," I hiss out and then run my fingers through my messy hair. "I'm leaving. I have to find her."

She shakes her head. "Sir! You've just had surgery to repair a pneumothorax. You can barely walk without getting winded. I strongly advise against that."

I toss my phone onto the bed so Dad can see and nods, passing me a bag of clothes. "Cathy, will he be okay if he stays put in the car? Once we get Baylee, we'll come back. Just tell me he'll be okay to leave for a short while."

She frowns and waves her head in a disproving way. "Sir, he has a chest tube in place and a wound vac. Even if he wants to leave against medical advice, I need a doctor here to D/C the tube, get prescriptions for antibiotics—because he will probably get an infection if the chest tube is discontinued early—and provide me with discharge orders. These things will take me some time."

The mention of antibiotics makes the hairs on the back of my neck stand. I try to fight the black that threatens to consume me at the mention of the risks involved with leaving the hospital early. The fact that my lung, according to Cathy, will likely fill with infectious pathogens.

My breathing grows shallow. It's an involuntary response.

But I remember the look in Baylee's eyes last night—the one that she was trying so desperately to keep from me that spoke of pain, and humiliation, and sadness.

I remember that she needs me.

And I remember that it's my turn to fight for her, like she fought for me. To bring my queen into the light.

"Just do what you can, please," I beg. "My fiancée is in grave danger."

Nurse Cathy looks between my father and I and nods. "I'll see what I can do," she says, making her way out of the room.

I work to take a few more calming deep breaths, but I sense my dad approaching and open my eyes to find him in front of me. One side of his mouth lifts into a small smile.

"I'm proud of you, son."

chapter
SIXTEEN

Brandon

"Are we almost there?" she asks, a cold bite to her voice. Her arms are crossed over her chest as she glares straight ahead of her.

I grit my teeth and give her a one word answer. "Almost."

Her mouth sets into a thin line and I let my anger fill me up and fuel me on. She acts like she's the one who was put out for having to leave the hospital. Not once did she consider how I'd feel. How I'd feel when I came back ready to spoil her with flowers and dinner only to find out she'd bailed on me. It didn't take rocket science to figure out she'd gone to see him. And sure as fuck, I found her wrapped around him. Like she belonged to *him*.

I *deserve her love.*

It gutted me.

Fucking gutted me.

She's lucky I didn't end him right there once and for all. I craved to yank out the knife I'd bought, after returning to an empty hotel suite, and slash his throat. To watch it spray the ceiling and shower down around her. He deserved to drown in his own goddamned blood. The rage fights to consume me as I grip the steering wheel tighter, so I don't do anything stupid like turn around. If I turned around and went back, I'd surely kill him. And if I killed him, she'd never forgive me. Her attention would be on him, not me.

I *deserve her attention.*

We're walking a fine fucking line here.

Between right and wrong.

Love and hate.

Black and white.

The lines are becoming blurred and I'm tired of playing Mr. Nice Guy.

"Here we are," I say as I pull down a long driveway that leads to a little house by the beach. "Home sweet home."

She huffs at me and is already wrenching the door open before I have the damned truck turned off. I watch her run toward the house. It was easy getting her here. All it took was telling her the one thing she so desperately needed to hear. *Come with me if you want to see your dad.*

She'll be so disappointed.

I'd hated the look of regret she'd shot over at that freak when she crawled out from under his heavy arm. I'd nearly gone mad with blinding rage when she pressed a soft kiss to his forehead. And I'd wanted to punish her—punish my sweet, sweet Baylee—for willingly cheating on me with that motherfucker.

I *deserve her apologies.*

But instead, I'd put on a brave face and wheeled her right out of that hospital. Helped her into my truck and drove her straight here. My girl had gone without a fight because she wanted to see her precious daddy. The same daddy who didn't give two shits whether or not she got raped by men more than twice her age. It was just one more deep cut she wounded me with.

I was the bad guy.

Even after all this. After I'd stood by *for years* as the perfect, patient boyfriend.

I deserve to be the good guy.

As I climb out of the truck, my mind flits back to the beginning. Back when nobody believed me that she'd been taken. A satisfied smile stretches over my face.

"Where the fuck is she, Tony?"

He has the sense to look fucking ashamed. Leaning back in his armchair, he tilts the bottle of Jim Beam back and swallows a healthy gulp before speaking. "I don't know."

Fury overwhelms me and I fist my hands at my sides. I want to bash his goddamned skull in.

"She's dead, Brandon," he says.

The room spins as I consider his words. "No-No-No!"

"Not Baylee," he snaps and his violent bloodshot eyes meet mine. "My wife. Lynn passed away. It was all for nothing. Now I've lost my baby, too."

With a snarl, I stomp over to him and grab onto his shirt. Yanking him to his unsteady feet, I spit in his face. "What was all for nothing?"

He shrugs his shoulders—fucking shrugs them—and has the audacity to look down at me as if I'm still that pesky kid he always thought me to be. I'm no longer that shy kid who wants to date his daughter. I'm his worst fucking nightmare and I won't stop until I have the love of my life back in my arms.

"Baylee. The sale. Gabe tried but it wasn't enough. The money will come too late… Lynn couldn't cope with losing Baylee. I never anticipated she'd deteriorate so quickly. That losing Baylee would cause her to give up." A choked sob rips from him.

I curl my lip in disgust at his words and shove him away from me. "I fucking knew you were involved. You had a hand in selling your own daughter on the black goddamned market!"

He roars at me and charges. The man is bigger than me, but I'm furious. My rage is that of a hundred men. When he reaches me, I greet him with a fist to his gut. Then, I crack my elbow across his face and send him hurtling to the floor. He lands on his ass with a grunt. I waste no time and launch myself at him. Over and over again, I smash my fists against his face. His teeth cut open my knuckles on one hand and they are now dripping with blood all over the pristine living room rug.

"You're a disgusting piece of shit," I snarl in between labored breaths. "She's your child." My entire body is quaking with rage.

"G-G-Gabe," he stutters out and spits out blood along with a tooth, "said she'll only be gone for two weeks. He p-promised he'll get her back before anyone hurts her. He vowed to keep her safe and get me the money to save my wife."

Tears fall out of his eyes but I have no pity for the sorry-ass motherfucker. The man who used to intimidate me now sickens me. He's nothing but a piece of fucking trash. A piece of trash who'd negotiate his teenage daughter's body for money.

"Where did he take her?"

Heat reddens his face. "He said it was best if I didn't know the details. That if he went to prison for her kidnapping, I'd still be here with Lynn."

I gape at him. "And you believed that bullshit?"

He doesn't have to nod or speak for me to know he did.

"Did you ever think about Baylee, Tony?" I demand. "Did it ever occur to you how fucking scared she would be? Did you even once consider that Gabe was lying to you—that he would fuck your daughter? The man looks at her like she's a piece of meat he wants to sink his teeth into and you sent her away with him."

His eyes widen and realization seems to wash over him. "No…"

"Yes. He probably fucked her the moment he got her to wherever the hell it is he took her. There probably never was any money. I bet he concocted the entire thing so he could fuck your daughter like the goddamned pervert he is!"

"Get the fuck off me," he roars. "Don't talk about my daughter like that. Gabe is family. He loved her—"

"He loved her, all right," I sneer. "I watched him love her from afar all the fucking time. While you were too busy trying to intimidate me away from your daughter, he was fantasizing about getting into her teenage panties. And if for some wild reason he does sell her without harming her, do you think for even one second she'll be safe? Baylee is sweet and innocent. Those monsters will destroy her."

He tries to shake his head, but my hands are around his neck before I can stop myself in my attempt to hold him still. My vision begins to cloud, blackness taking over the edges.

"She won't be the same, Tony. You may as well have killed her yourself because if she comes back, she won't be the same Baylee!"

His face turns an ugly shade of purple and his eyes bug out of his head as he desperately claws at my wrists. This motherfucker deserves punishment for what he did.

"I will find her," I grunt out as I squeeze his neck harder and enjoy the hissing sounds coming from him. "And all she'll have left is me. I'm going to marry her and give her a bunch of fucking babies. You'll be a sad, distant memory. The man who sold her. The man who betrayed his own daughter because he was too stupid to realize he was being played by his own best friend. How does it feel, Tony? How does it feel knowing I'm going to ruin you like you ruined your own daughter?"

His eyes flutter closed and his hands slip away from my wrists. I could stop right now. The pulse in his throat is faint but still there. I think. Dragging my gaze away from him, my eyes find the picture of Baylee on the mantle. Her senior picture. She's wearing a pretty denim jacket over a white lacey dress with cowboy boots. The smile she wears is bright. That girl deserves so much more than the piece of shit parent she was left with.

She deserves me.

With a sigh of frustration, I release my grip. "I'm doing this for you, babe," I mutter aloud, my gaze still on her picture.

"Where the hell is he?" she screeches from the porch and stomps for me, jerking me from my memory. "Where the hell is my dad, Brandon?"

I *deserve to slay her monsters.*

Her hand is already raised, poised and ready to slap my face. As soon as she nears, I snatch her dainty wrist and twist it painfully behind her.

"Ow!" she cries out. "Let me go!"

A crazed laugh rumbles around us and I shiver. For a moment I wonder if it's Gabe coming back to haunt us but then I realize the laugh is mine.

I *deserve her loyalty.*

"Did that freak give you this?" I snap and jerk the same wrist up so I can take a closer look at what's on her arm.

"Stop, Brandon," she says in a wobbly voice, all her fire snuffed out.

I yank the watch from her arm and heave it as far as I can throw it, which is pretty damn far considering I was a pitcher for the varsity baseball team. If we weren't standing on sand, I'd have stomped it into a million pieces.

I *deserve to spoil her.*

"Get in the house, babe," I grunt. My hand squeezes her forearm as I guide her inside. "We need to talk."

I'm surprised to find the house unlocked. It makes me wonder if the owners are nearby. Out for an early morning walk or some shit. They'll regret coming home, that's for sure.

I *deserve to have her all to myself.*

She puts up a resistance when I start pushing her toward the stairs. "You promised me you'd take me to my dad. That's the only reason I left with you. Where is he?"

Ignoring her, I all but drag her up the stairs and down the hallway. When I find the master bedroom, I toss her onto the bed and glare down at her.

I *deserve her body.*

"Take off your clothes," I snap.

At first, her eyes widen in shock but then her nostrils flare and she scowls at me. Her cheeks and neck redden but I've known her long enough to know it isn't from embarrassment. She's pissed. How is it she's scared shitless of Gabe but I don't frighten her one bit?

I *deserve her fear.*

"Baylee Marie Winston," I bite out, "if you don't take your goddamned clothes off right now I will cut them off you." For effect, I yank the knife out of my pocket and wave it at her.

I *deserve her terror.*

Tears well in her eyes but the fury remains. She's still not fucking afraid of me. With her angry eyes locked on mine, she whips off my hoodie. The same hoodie I'd seen her in hundreds of times at school. The hoodie with "Thompson" emblazoned on the back that let every guy at school know she was mine.

Was.

I *deserve to give her my last name.*

I run my fingers through my hair and let out a rage-filled scream. "Why, Baylee? Why did you do this to us? You used to love *ME!*"

She crosses her arms over her breasts and glares at me. "Where. Is. My. Dad?"

I *deserve her undivided attention.*

Storming over to her, I surprise her when I grab onto her jaw, my fingers digging brutally into the flesh. "Naked, babe. You're still half dressed." When I drag the knife along her breast and down over her belly, she winces in fear. Fucking finally.

I *deserve her hot cunt.*

"Okay, Brandon, okay."

I release her and watch as she shimmies out of her pants. As soon as her perfect pussy is on display, I ache to taste it. To put my mouth on her hot cunt and remind her of why she loves me— not that bastard in the hospital.

I *deserve her entire body.*

"What are you going to do?" she demands, her teeth gritting together. I'll give it to my girl for her bravery—she's one tough bitch after what Gabe put her through.

I kick my shoes off and start unbuckling my belt. "What I should have done a long time ago."

I *deserve to fuck her into tomorrow.*

She starts to squirm away from me but I seize her ankle and yank her back over to the edge of the bed. "Brandon, don't do this," she begs, fear finally threading her words. "This isn't you."

I *deserve her pleas and screams.*

I smirk, not feeling at all like that timid little pussy boy she once loved. "You're right, babe. I'm different and I'm tired of being a fucking virgin while you fuck every goddamned prick on the West Coast. Keep your eyes open, Baylee. I want you to know who's fucking you this time."

I *deserve all of this.*

I waited for her.

I rescued her.

I killed for her.

I deserve her.

My Baylee.

chapter
SEVENTEEN

Baylee

Brandon's normal twinkling green eyes are dulled into something dark and deviant. I don't recognize his voice, his hateful smile, or the menacing expression and crazed look in his eyes. He's not the boy from high school—the boy who was shy about giving me my first kiss or meeting my parents for the first time. This isn't the boy who I cried for when Gabe took me.

Gone is the boy from my past.

This man is a product of Gabe's actions.

Gabe created the monster before me.

"Please," I beg again as his grip becomes tighter around my ankle. "I'm pregnant," I blurt out.

His green eyes spark to life as he takes pause. I watch in wonder as his gaze darts back and forth between me and my belly as if trying to make sense of my words. I hear a creak on the wood floors in the bedroom. A pair of eyes peer back at me just beyond Brandon. A familiar pair of eyes. A pair of eyes that belong to the devil.

I'm seeing things.

Brandon seems to snap out of his daze and works at his jeans to free his cock. While he's preoccupied, I rear back with my free foot and kick him with every bit of force I can dredge up in his chest. It doesn't faze him, though, because he laughs and twists my ankle in his grip to the point of pain, causing me to yelp out.

"You must be deaf because I clearly heard her demand for you *not* to touch her." As if the devil has any room to talk. Brandon freezes as Gabe steps closer, pointing a gun at him.

So I'm not seeing things.

A bruised and bandaged up Gabe enters the bedroom. He walks with a slight limp and winces.

"I killed you," Brandon murmurs in disbelief as if he's seeing a ghost. "You were dead."

Gabe laughs but then coughs. "No, you beat me, when I couldn't defend myself, and then you dumped me into my cellar. You broke bones, but you didn't break *me*," he mutters through gritted teeth. "Drop the knife on the bed and step away from her."

Brandon lets the knife fall on the edge of the bed and takes three slow steps away from it. Gabe winks at me and I shiver.

"How did you get out?" I ask softly. There was no way out. I should know, I was in that cellar for days and felt every surface looking for an alternate escape route.

He remains perfectly still, only his eyes sliding over to meet mine when he says, "There was a window. You just never found it, baby." He shrugs dismissively like I just lost a simple coin toss over who has to do the dishes that night.

I sit up and glare at him, reaching for my hoodie and sliding it on over my head. "There was no window!"

"There was. It was painted black near the ceiling. It was hard as hell finding all the brick grooves to stick my toes in so I could scale the wall but, I managed," he says in a triumphant tone. "Too bad you two were long gone before I got out. Otherwise, we could have had fun together."

Brandon starts toward Gabe but he aims the gun fitted with a silencer at his head.

"Don't even try it, pussy boy. Why don't we start by you telling Baylee what you did to Tony?"

My eyes find the enraged ones of Brandon. His jaw clenches as if the boy I knew from before is clinging on desperately. Begging him not to make things worse. I can't help but be thankful for the truth that Gabe will no doubt force from him.

"You know nothing," Brandon snaps. "I did nothing."

The muscle in Gabe's forearm flexes as his finger hovers over the trigger. "I'm not stupid. You and I both know what you did."

Brandon grunts and runs his fingers through his hair. His eyes dart back and forth between Gabe and I as he searches for the right words. When his furious glare lands back on Gabe, he fists his hands and spats out words that has my already fragile psyche cracking. "Tony deserved it after what he did."

My heart thunders in my chest and I shake my head in denial. What did my dad deserve? What did he do? "No." The word is a whisper and I'm not sure either of them even heard it.

Gabe frowns and shakes his head in disproval. "Did you tell Baylee that *you* killed him? Surely she has ascertained as much by now."

"No, you're lying." I swallow down my emotion and blink away the tears blurring my vision. "Tell me where my dad is, Brandon."

Brandon grits his teeth and jerks his gaze to me. The fire in his eyes is burning bright and hate-filled. He's lost. So lost. "That night," he snarls, "that night when *he* fucking took you, I woke up with a broken nose and a broken heart."

"Awwww," Gabe taunts.

"Shut the fuck up," Brandon snaps. "I went into their bedroom and woke up your dad. I told him what happened. Do you want to know what he did?"

My brows scrunch in confusion. I can imagine a million different scenarios. Dad hitting him. Dad freaking out with worry. Dad accusing him of doing something to me.

"He dragged me out of that room, so your mother wouldn't wake, and he punched me in the stomach. Then he threatened me. He told me to shut the fuck up or he'd do it for me. To not tell a soul anything because as far as I was concerned, you ran away. It wasn't until a few days later when I came back, after your mom had passed away, that I learned the truth. He told me that he did what he had to do for the money. To save your mother. End of story."

"I don't understand," I murmur. None of this makes any sense.

Brandon huffs and lets out a cruel laugh. A laugh so similar to Gabe's it sends goosebumps popping up all over my flesh. "Your dad was in on your abduction and sale, Baylee. It was all planned."

Time stops as I consider his twisted words. There's no way my father would sell his daughter for money. Absolutely not.

Sitting up on my knees, the hoodie hitting me mid-thigh, I point my finger at him angrily. "No, I don't believe this." Anger surges in my chest at his insinuations. "You're a fucking liar, Brandon. Dad wouldn't let Gabe *abduct* me, *rape* me, and then *sell* me. No!"

Gabe chooses that moment to pipe up. "It's truth," he says and has the audacity to look regretful. "It was the only way to make sure Lynn got moved up on the transplant list or considered for a private donor that could be paid off. It was business and you were a pawn, sweet girl." Then, his eyes slide over my bare legs and he flashes me one of his wicked, psycho grins. "Besides, Tony didn't give me his approval to sleep with his daughter. How was I supposed to know we were going to fall in love? That was just a bonus, beautiful."

We are *not* in love.

He is fucking delusional.

"This was all for nothing…" I trail off, choking on my words. "What about those other girls? Did you love them too or were they just practice?"

Gabe runs his fingertips over the top of my foot and I shudder. "Sweetheart, believe me when

I say it was *not* all for nothing. It was worth *every* second. And, yes, my little hobby of mine with the WCT opened the door for something bigger. It revealed to me a way to help your father save your mother and to give me you. Everyone wins. You were worth so much more than those broken girls though. You were meant to be mine, sweet girl. Forever."

Tears roll down my cheeks as the betrayal sinks in at being used in their game. The black knight and the black rook taking out all the pieces in my world, including their attempt at taking my king. My father's ultimate betrayal spins in my head, threatening to finish me off. Lifting my chin, I remember War's words.

The rules state the pawn is the weakest piece.
But if the pawn makes it to the other side, it gets promoted.
The pawn can become queen.
And then it's not weak at all.

"Mom knew?" My voice wobbles.

Gabe smiles, almost tenderly and shakes his head. "She didn't. Your mother would have never agreed to that."

Another tear streaks down my cheek and I cling to the fact that not everyone has betrayed me in this life. I almost believe that had they just asked me, I'd have gone willingly. I would have gone off to War to save my mom. Gabe didn't have to terrorize me in the process. We could have found a way. I would have done that for her. I would have done *anything* for her.

But nobody asked me.

They just used me.

I was exactly like he said. A fucking pawn.

"Go on, Brandon," Gabe urges. "Tell her how you killed him while she was with that freak. You probably beat him just like you beat me, you angry little shit. Tell her how you buried him in their own backyard."

"How do you know this?" Brandon says with a growl. "Did you dig up his fucking body?"

I'm shaking my head in denial and send a pleading glance to Gabe who frowns at me. His brows are pinched together and I see the flash of sadness in his eyes. He may be a monster now but he was Dad's best friend. Surely knowing that my father is dead wounds him too.

Jesus, my dad is dead. I can't even fathom the word.

Dead.

The same dad who protected me and loved me.

A man who wasn't all brute and gruffness, but also had a sweet, teddy bear side.

A man who somehow was desperate enough to sell his own daughter to save his wife.

If only he'd have asked me. I would have gone willingly. I am certain of this. If it meant saving, Mom, I'd have done it in a heartbeat.

Gabe lets out a huff of frustrated breath and glares at Brandon. "Me," he waves to his battered body, "dig up his body like this? Hell no. I kind of figured you lost it and finally let him have it. Hell, I don't even know if you shot him or stabbed him or what the fuck you did. But you have already proved yourself to be a damn lunatic. When I went into their backyard and saw the picnic table had been moved to the corner of the yard, I knew. You covered your tracks well but you were hiding something. That something was his body. How *did* he die anyway? You beat her old man into a bloody fucking pulp? Did you slit his throat?"

"He had it coming to him!" Brandon screams. "He deserved to pay for what he allowed to happen to her!"

Understanding begins to crush in on me.

Brandon killed my dad.

He really did it.

Gabe flashes me a regretful look before plastering on an angry scowl for Brandon. "This would have all worked out just fine if you would have just backed off, pussy boy. Now you went and fucked it all up for Baylee and I. You broke her heart when you killed her dad. And now I'm going to break you."

I hold my hands up in the air a moment to stall him. My mind is fracturing quickly and I need all the answers I can get before I lose myself altogether. This breakdown has been a long time coming. I'm teetering on the very edge, about to plummet into my own mental hell. "How did you find us?"

Gabe takes my hand and squeezes it in an affectionate way. Hurt, fucking hurt, flashes in his eyes when I jerk it away. I'm disgusted with him—with both of them. With a small sigh, he continues. "All it took was me doing a quick internet search to learn freak boy, who'd pickled your brain into thinking you loved him, was surprisingly alive. And I know you sweet girl, once you figured out he wasn't dead, you were still hypnotized enough to go right back to him. But when I got there to retrieve you, lo and behold, *he* was kidnapping you. Doing all my dirty work for me." He shakes his head and smirks at Brandon. "I have to say, pussy boy, you have some balls on you. Guess they finally dropped when you turned eighteen."

I'm no longer listening to them. I slam my eyes closed and try to drown them out. But I can't. The darkness swarms in and suffocates me with the truth. Truth that he's really dead. This is too much. Brandon is not a murderer. He wouldn't murder my father.

Please be a lie.

Please.

But it's not a lie. It's truth and he's a murderer. The boy I loved as a teenage girl grew into something sick and fucking twisted. He sought revenge when it wasn't his to seek. Brandon Thompson stomped all over his own innocence when he stamped out my father's life.

"Fuck you," Brandon snaps, jerking me from my overwhelming grief. I pop my eyes open and swipe away the tears I hadn't noticed were falling down my face.

Gabe's glare becomes furious as he steps toward Brandon. "Shut up! I'll put a bullet through your skull before you can take your next breath," he roars. "I'm not done with story time. Tell Baylee how you lived in her house for months jacking off to pictures of her while you waited for me to find her, you sick fuck. Tell her. When I called Tony after I sold Baylee to give him the money and to update him, you were there playing fucking house in *her* house. And did Tony ever emerge from that house? *No.* Because you *killed* him. You were just waiting there so when the time came, you could swoop in and save the fucking day. Ride off into the sunset with *my girl* knowing you murdered her goddamned father."

I shudder and reach for my panties. There's no way I can sit here and listen to another second of this. I have to get the hell out of here and back to War. If I can manage to slip off the bed and make a run for the doo—

"Leave them off," Gabe barks, waving his gun at me and motioning to my panties in my fist. "I'm not done looking at you, sweetheart." He winks at me and flashes me a heated grin.

Bile rises in my throat. I'm trapped in a sick parallel universe where there's not one devil, but two. A nightmare of insanity. Not only a battle between two evils but an epic war. Two twisted murdering men. Two men who have used my body for their benefit, manipulated me, murdered one of the men I loved in this world, and nearly destroying the other. And as collateral damage, they had a hand in killing my mother too.

Anger surges through me, chasing away the betrayal and grief threatening to swallow me whole. These two men think they have a right to me and my body. But only one person truly owns me, and it's my heart he owns. That man is honest and pure and wholesome. Deserving. He's an angel—the father of my child who has earned his peace. Peace I vow to give him.

It's time to end this war, for my War.

My mind stops considering ways to escape but instead how to outsmart them both.

I need a plan to get rid of them. And quick.

Time to show them I'm not a pawn. I'm the motherfucking queen.

This is war, baby. And I will win.

With a deep breath, I inhale the strength of what needs to be done. Yesterday I was worried that murdering Gabe would somehow taint me as a mother. That it would make me unfit. But now, as I feel the hate and jealousy throbbing between these two men, I know it's the only way. They'll never stop.

Prison doesn't stop people like Gabe or Brandon—not when they're this far gone.

Death is the only probable sentence.

The battle lines are drawn, my strategy in this war is in place.

"Gabe." I let out a sob. Brandon's brows knit together in suspicion, as if he's already figured out my plan. Gabe is clueless though as his dark eyes dart along my body, probing and assessing, before they land on my quivering bottom lip. "He killed *my* daddy. He killed *your* best friend. What if he kills *me* too? He was about to rape me if you hadn't intervened when you did. I don't think it would have ended there either." My words are honest and I know he senses that—I *need* for him to sense that for this to work. Brandon *is* unstable. There's no telling what he would have done once he'd had his way. Would the guilt have consumed him? Would he have ended both our lives?

Gabe's smug stare is wiped off his face as he snaps his angry gaze to Brandon. My heart rate speeds up as I realize this could work.

"What the fuck, Baylee?" Brandon bites out. "Like the motherfucker would even care what the hell I did with you. He was chasing your half-naked ass down the street when I showed up! The man's a goddamned monster! I'm the fucking hero here, babe!"

I stare at him for what feels like eternity as I search for the boy I once knew. My heart pleads for one sliver of the kind soul who I loved. I wish his green eyes would light up with the familiar happy spark I remember. But instead, I'm met with an empty, soulless glare. With fury and hate.

That boy is gone.

He's been long gone for a while now.

Not only did I lose both parents, but I lost him.

I lost Brandon too. Lost him to the darkness. Lost him to the evil. Lost the boy who grew up being my only real friend, my first love. His physical form may remain, but the Brandon I once knew is gone.

I inhale a deep breath and prepare myself to finish this. I'm not battling with Brandon, I'm fighting this *thing* he's become. It should make what I have to do a little less painful, but it doesn't. My heart is ripping in half with each passing second but my mind is already making its lethal move.

"But he wouldn't ever truly hurt me. Not like you were going to do," I argue and send Gabe a terrified look. One that says Brandon is scarier than he is. "Gabe loves me. He always brings me pleasure after the pain. You will only bring me pain!"

Gabe growls and his chest heaves. He's always been jealous of Brandon. Now, it works to my advantage.

"I did everything for you!" Brandon roars. His face reddening. His forehead creasing. His neck bursting with thick pulsing veins. "I gave up my life, school, baseball, my fucking parents for you!" He launches at me, his giant frame tackling me to the mattress.

I attempt to shove him away but he's too strong. "I didn't ask you to and I certainly didn't ask for you to kill my dad!"

Brandon's hand wraps around my throat and he squeezes. "This is how I killed him," he spits out, his hand crushing my windpipe. "Just like this." His gorgeous features have contorted into something vengeful and wrong. He doesn't want us to be together. He wants me as his prize. His possession. His reward for having given up so much for me. I'm nothing more than a trophy to add to his bookshelf back home. And now he wants me dead.

"Take your goddamned hands off her," Gabe hisses from behind him, "or I'll paint the headboard with your blood."

Tears stream down my face and I reach for Gabe, as if he is my savior. The devil has been my savior on more than one occasion. And I'm counting on him now.

"Baylee," Brandon says, his voice a desperate plea, ignoring Gabe's threat. He smashes his lips to mine, causing me to cry out when his teeth split open my bottom lip. His grip is gone and he cradles my throat reverently. "Jesus, I'm so sorry. I love you."

And in that moment, I believe him. His bright green eyes shimmer with emotion revealing the tenderhearted boy I once knew. I hate that it all came to this. Absolutely hate it.

Pop!

Time freezes as Brandon's wide eyes regard me before something blinds me. My eyes close and I try to drive away what I just saw. The horror is overwhelming and I feel myself losing hold on the present as I hurtle to the past. A past where green eyes used to make me shiver with delight and my heart would patter right out of my chest when a certain smiling, spikey-haired boy would walk me to my locker.

"Why is the marching band playing in the hallway?" Audrey questions, a dark eyebrow arched in question. "It's so noisy!"

I laugh as I hurry and yank my history book from my locker. Shoving it into my backpack, I stand on my tiptoes to try and see around the crowd in the hallway. Something's going on. It's not a pep rally day, so I'm confused about the chaos. Even though Audrey seems agitated, she's sporting a goofy grin that matches my own.

Kids all around us are giggling and so are we until I recognize the song. As soon as the tune of 'Keep on Loving You' by REO Speedwagon becomes recognizable, I can feel the familiar burn on my cheeks. This same song was playing at the skating rink where he first told me he loved me. My smile grows larger when my boyfriend rounds the corner and beams at me. He's carrying a single red rose but it may as well be a thousand. The boy makes me feel like I'm the only girl on the planet.

When his gorgeous gaze meets mine, I hear the collective gasps of all the girls in my grade. Brandon is the good-looking boy who doesn't even realize how beautiful he is. He's sweet and caring. A tenderhearted guy who loves his girl hard.

God, I'm so freaking lucky.

"Hey, babe," he says with a wink as he approaches and the band grows silent. When he falls on his knee, several girls squeal, including Audrey. "Will you go to the homecoming dance with me, Baylee Marie Winston?"

My knees buckle and my jaw hurts from the smile that stretches across my face revealing my teeth which are now finally free of braces. With a shaky hand, I accept his rose and nod.

"Yes, of course I will go with you!"

He launches from the floor at me and tackle hugs me against the locker, his strong arms enveloping me in a heated embrace. Warm lips meet mine and he kisses me as if I'm the only girl he could ever want.

"Thank you," he murmurs against my lips.

I lean my head back against the locker to better look into his expressive jade-colored orbs. "For what?"

"For letting me love you," he says, his brows furrowing together in a serious manner. "I'll never stop. No matter what. Always know that, babe."

They are earnest words and weave themselves into my heart. Is this the all-encompassing love Mom always gushes about when she talks about Dad? Because I feel it. From the ends of my hair, all the way down to the tips of my toes.

Brandon is my best friend and I love him.

"Promise me you'll always be mine," he says sternly, his eyes darkening slightly. "Promise me, Baylee."

My heart stops for a moment in my chest.

His declaration terrifies and thrills me at the same time.

"Always, Brandon."

A choked sound jerks me from my memory and my eyes fly open. I shriek when I realize Brandon's heavy body has collapsed on me. He's still—too still. Something warm trickles down my cheek toward my ear and I start gagging upon the realization that it's his blood. All over me.

I start screaming and squirming to get him off me. Gabe hobbles over to the bedside and pushes Brandon onto the floor, the heavy thud echoing in my heart. My eyes remain fixated on his unmoving form. The only thing moving is the blood as it continues to pour from his forehead.

He's dead.

Gabe killed him.

The devil slayed the dragon but he took my sweet boy away in the process.

Despite my horror over having seen it actually play out, this went as planned. In our war, my strategy was to use one opponent to take out the other. And it worked. I need to move on to my next move. If I lose my focus now, I'll completely break down and I can't. I have to be strong.

For the baby.

For War.

For me.

"Gabe," I sob, my entire body shuddering, "you're the only person I have left."

He leans down over me and strokes my hair in a loving way. "I told you that you were all mine, baby. I love you."

I nod in vehemence, as if I wholeheartedly agree with him. The bile in my throat is sour and stings. I'm seconds from throwing up everywhere.

Breathe.

Observe every move.

Take out your opponent.

There's only one pawn standing between you and your king.

Taking several calming breaths, I wave toward the bathroom door. "Could you grab me a towel?" I ask in the most level tone I can muster, hoping I can distract him long enough to implement part two of my plan. All I need is a few seconds' distraction.

His eyes narrow and he runs his finger along my bare calf. "But you look so pretty with this blood all over you. His fucking blood," he snarls as if the very thought of Brandon disgusts him. "You should wear it proudly, baby. It makes me want to suck on your clit until you wake the neighbors with your screams."

I tremble and hold back my tears. I should have known I couldn't outsmart Gabe. He's like the black knight, anticipating all of my moves before I even make them.

I am not a weak pawn.

I am the queen.

Quickly devising a new plan, I peel the blood soaked hoodie from my body and toss it away. Brandon's blood is beginning to dry on my throat so I quickly smear it down over my bare breasts.

Gabe's eyes darken and he growls. "Jesus, you look so fucking hot right now, sweet girl."

I flash him a shy smile. "I should be trying to run," I whisper. "But all I can think about is having you inside me."

He groans and crawls onto the bed beside me, taking Brandon's spot. "Straddle me. My body hurts too fucking bad to do this any other way. I want to play with your pussy while I watch that blood run down your tits."

I sit up, sliding my palm across the bed, I make contact with my saving grace, and do as I'm told. My hand fists the wondrous piece and I twist my arm behind my back, pushing my tits forward to dazzle him with. All done in a graceful, fluid motion. The bandage on his nose has me halting my movement. "I don't want to hurt you," I lie. Truth is, I want to sit on his face and smother him with the pussy he seems to adore.

"Oh, baby. Such a sweet girl. You just sit there and look pretty—I'll do all the work."

Nodding, I ease myself down to straddle his waist just above the top of his jeans, my naked body vulnerable and shaking. I close my eyes and think of War. His gorgeous smile. His moving lips as he counts my breaths. His gentle and loving touch.

Breathe.

I can do this.

For War and our baby.

Gabe grips my thighs almost brutally, which has me jerking my eyes back open. This monster has always thought he owned my body. Making me come against my will. I want to make him pay for hurting War, causing Brandon to get lost in the darkness, for the role he played in the deaths of my parents.

I could almost get off on the idea of Gabe's death.

Over and over again, I think about his neck being spilt open from ear to ear. His blood, responsible for the deaths of everyone I love, will pour from him until his heart stops beating.

I'll leave this nightmare he dragged me into. I'll go to college. I'll raise this baby in a loving home with War in peace. I'll go on and live when it was Gabe's plan to take it all away.

I'll spit on his grave and laugh all the way into the sunset of my own twisted happily ever after.

chapter
EIGHTEEN

Baylee

The thought of Gabe's death is responsible for an all-consuming nearly orgasmic shudder that ripples through me like never before. It's not sexual though, it's a buzzing, electric adrenaline I've never experienced. My body responds with anticipation to eradicate him once and for all from my life, not the feeling of his filthy tongue on my clit as he'd like for it to be.

The rage festers inside me, fueling me. Egging me on. My grip tightens around my sanctity in my fist as I wait for the perfect moment.

"You're something else, baby. So sweet and innocent at times, and fucking naughty as hell at others." He sits up on one elbow and drags his gun along my bare belly. I try not to recoil in disgust and flash him a seductive smile instead.

"Thank you."

His dark eyes widen in surprise. "For what?"

"For getting rid of him," I say with a shiver. "He was different. Scary different."

He drags the still warm barrel of the gun to my sex and teases my clit with it before letting it trail back up. "I'm kind of pissed off you find him scarier than me. That boy was always a pussy. Maybe," he murmurs as he pokes the gun almost painfully into my lower belly just above my pelvic bone, "*I* should scare you a little more."

My widened eyes meet his and he grins. If this were six months ago in my living room and he were poking me with his finger, that grin would have been charming. But not now, now it chills me to the bone.

"I'm not scared of you," I tell him, my voice level. "Because I love you." Those words fall out easily too, but they're a big fucking lie.

"I love you too, sweet girl," he tells me, his dark eyes warm like melted chocolate. His thumb slides over my belly just below my navel and he winks.

I make my move and lean forward to kiss him.

I'm coming for you, black knight.

As soon as our lips touch, he groans. Before he can deepen the kiss, I jerk away from him and swing my arm around. I'm clumsy with the weapon that feels too big in my slender hand, but it's my only shot. I let my anger strengthen me as I stab downwards into his chest.

"What the fuck?" he roars. "What did you do to me?"

Despite his weakened state, he slings me away from him and I bang my head on the headboard. The devil rises from the bed, his malevolent presence scorching me with his eyes. He drops his gaze to Brandon's knife which now sits firmly wedged to the hilt in his chest.

Blood.

So much.

Seeping and seeping at a rapid rate from his wound. A wound I gave him.

His shaky hand attempts to pull it out, but it won't move. He darts his eyes all around as if to pull answers from the air on what to do next. But it's too late. Too late for the devil. This avenging angel already took his choice away from him.

"Baylee," he rasps and uses what little bit of energy he has to lunge at me.

Screaming, I try to push him away from me but he grabs onto my hips and presses his warm mouth to my belly kissing me reverently, almost sweetly. Possessively even. My stomach roils in disgust and I choke down the bile threatening to spew out at any moment. His warm blood pours from him and runs down between my legs, soaking the bed below my bare ass.

But just when I think I can't take anymore, it's over.

Quick.

Painless.

Finished.

His body stills and remains unmoving as I slide out from beneath him.

"Checkmate," I whisper and shove his lifeless body away.

My teeth are chattering from the adrenaline rush and all I can think about is getting out of this house.

But I stop for a moment to admire my handiwork.

Gabe. The damn devil. *Dead.*

With shaking hands, I drag my yoga pants on without panties. I grab Brandon's bloody hoodie from the bed and tug it over my head.

I'm done with this life.

It's finally over.

Those bastards aren't coming for me anymore. I can take my time. But I'm ready to put my past behind me and start over with War.

I need order.

I need simplicity.

I need to feel safe again.

My heart races in my chest and I can't seem to get it to slow. If War were here with me right now, he'd press a thumb to the pulse at my throat and count each rapid beat.

God, I need him.

With a deep breath, I open the front door and inhale the fresh scent of freedom.

"Bay."

I jerk my gaze to the heavenly voice that somehow thunders through the madness in my head and blink in confusion to see the man approaching me slowly.

Beautiful but flawed.

Weak yet so strong.

Mine.

"War."

I'm afraid to move. Afraid to chase off the vision of him. He seems so real. So close. So present. I want to thump myself in the head to remind myself that War is in the hospital.

"Are…are you okay?" His voice cracks and his hands tremble at his sides.

Land materializes from the behind him with wide eyes and I put a palm to my chest as if to still my pounding heart. "You're really here."

War winces but takes several more steps toward me, not deterred by my shuddering body.

"Bay, beautiful, please tell me you're okay."

Tears stream down my face and my knees buckle. Blackness eats away at my vision, causing me to sway. "I am *not* okay."

And darkness envelopes me.

But with it comes a warm, all-consuming strength. It embraces me and keeps me safe. I unravel inside of my own head and let the warmth overtake me.

"For the love of God, Bay," he chokes out, "*Tell me* you're okay."

The deep, husky voice parts through the gloom in my mind and I reach for it. I blink my eyes open and inhale a scent that belongs to my lover. My friend. My equal. My War.

"You're really here right now with me," I sob, "and we're *going* to be okay."

His hand strokes my blood-soaked hair as I cling to him. He flinches when I touch the left part of his chest where he was shot, so I settle for the right.

"I was so scared." My tears drench his shirt and he continues to hold me.

"I was fucking terrified when I realized you were gone," he says, his words muffled somewhere in my hair. "As soon as I realized what happened, I left the hospital to come for you. Your watch was fitted with a tracking device—in case Gabe ever came back for you. But when he did come for you, you weren't wearing it. This time, though, I was going to find you and save you."

"You did save me," I whisper as I pull slightly away, searching his stormy eyes.

He smiles and his gaze skitters down my throat. "Bay, you saved yourself."

His eyes become fixated on my flesh and realization washes over me like slick oil. Suddenly, a thought overwhelms me to the point I nearly vomit.

Blood.

So much blood.

I'm dripping in War's worst nightmare.

Shit!

I try to peel myself from him but he grips me tighter. "Warren, I'm covered in…I'm covered in…"

He grips my hair and tugs my head back. "I see, beautiful. Believe me, I see." Our eyes meet and his perfect mouth quirks into a half-smile. "But love will make you do crazy things. Like do absolutely anything—slay any dragon, even the imaginary ones in your head—for a chance to have the one you love in your arms once more. You own me, Bay, and you always win when it comes to battling my heart against my delusional mind. I love you." He gives me a small smile. "I'm going to kiss that dirty mouth of yours now."

I half sob and half laugh as his mouth descends upon mine. Our lips connect and he devours me as if he needs my love for nourishment. So I feed it to him. Every part of me, I give to him in our kiss. The promise of my love. Children. Loyalty and friendship. My heart.

"Kiss me again," I order.

He smiles and dives back in. "Anything for the queen."

The sound of the sirens grows louder as the police get closer. War, Land, and I have been sitting on the front porch waiting for them to arrive and deal with the situation. Land has been on the phone, answering questions from Detective Stark. She asked him to keep us out of the house until they arrived. Something about contaminating the crime scene and disrupting evidence. I didn't care, though. I was perfectly content sitting next to War on the porch swing with his heavy arm draped around me.

I haven't said much, and have let War's whispers soothe me. He's been counting and muttering since we sat down. I know he's still with me because every so often he presses a kiss to the top of my head. But he doesn't stop. It's as if he's found a way to cope with the blood and the insanity. I don't dare disrupt that. I don't need to ask him if he's okay, I know he's weak and exhausted. Aside from his muttering, he's not moved much.

When a black Crown Vic comes bouncing down the drive, red and blue lights flashing, I let out a sigh. *It's almost over.*

A pretty brunette climbs out of the car and stalks over to us. Her scowl hardens her features but when she sees me, her face softens. The clomp of her boots on the wood porch indicate her arrival and she squats down in front of me.

"Miss Winston?"

I lift my head and regard her. Dark brows furrow together as her eyes quickly asses the blood all over me.

"Are you hurt?"

Shaking my head, I glance over as two uniformed cops and another detective in a suit walk inside the house. "I'm okay. It's not my blood. War needs to get back to the hospital, though." He stiffens beside me at the mention of his name but then quickly relaxes.

"Of course, hon. We're going to secure the crime scene and then I need to ask you a few questions before you leave to get medical attention. Wait here and I'll be back in five," she instructs as she stands.

When she doesn't move, I lift my gaze to hers and she frowns.

"Miss Winston," she says softly, almost motherly in nature, "I'm sorry this happened to you. We're going to continue to bring down every other perp who had any dealing with the White Collar Trade group. Together, with you and Mr. McPherson's help, we're going to catch these guys. Every last one of them."

My mind flits back to that day I met War. Before I climbed into his car. When the monsters lurked around in their five thousand dollar suits, expensive haircuts, and dashing grins. A time when they bought and sold women as if they were nothing more than a simple business transaction. Trading in a used vehicle for a sexy, sleeker model. Their wolfish smiles were terrorizing to all the lost sheep in the flock. If I could help save even the sixteen other girls I saw walk across that stage, it would be more than I could have ever expected. Men like Edgar Finn will go to prison and rot for their crimes against those women. Women like me. Detective Stark can prevent that man from carving up women for sport.

I'll do whatever the hell she needs as long as she makes that happen.

"Thank you," I tell her, meeting her gaze with a firm stare of my own.

"Stark, we have a problem," the other detective says through the doorway. "I think you need to come see this."

She stalks off and my veins freeze. What sort of problem do they have? Will I somehow be in trouble for defending myself?

Not even thirty seconds later, Stark bursts through the door with her radio in hand. "I want a chopper in the air casing a five-mile radius of the crime scene. We need the coast guard on alert. We're looking for a Caucasian male, forty-one years of age, and severely injured. Suspect is on foot and his blood loss trail indicates he went into the ocean. The prick is most likely dead, but I won't sleep until I zip him up in the body bag myself."

I stiffen.

This was supposed to be over.

"Bay," War murmurs into my ear, "it's going to be okay. Calm down."

But I can't calm down. Jerking from his grasp, I run the length of the porch and make it to the railing just in time to puke over the side. I try to ignore Stark's voice, which only seems to make things worse, but her words still find their way inside my head.

"Contact the local news and have them make an emergency police bulletin. We're looking for a man named Gabriel Sharpe. Suspect is considered to be armed and extremely dangerous despite his life-threatening injuries."

Hearing his name—confirmation that it isn't over—sends me over the edge. Black crushes in around me and I go down, submerging into the darkness.

chapter
NINETEEN

War

Focus. Focus. Focus.

Baylee. Baylee. Baylee.

Shit!

I'm naturally predetermined to freak the fuck out about the things I can't control—blood, microbes, disease, toxins, her pain. My mind threatens to crack down the middle and split in half so the terrors can wreak their havoc on me. It seems imminent.

But I can control it.

I have to.

I will.

My fingers thread through her blood-caked hair as Dad drives us to the hospital and I find my calm. Baylee needs me and I won't let her down now. I've been getting better, because of her, and I will be the one to help her through this. My precious Bay has been to hell and back. She's had to be strong for so fucking long and now it's time to reverse the roles. I will be the one to carry her to the end. The road won't be an easy one and she'll need a lot of counseling, but I'll be there for her every step of the way. The demons in my own head are dead to me. They can go fuck with someone else because I'm over it. Fucking over it. I'm done fighting those bastards because I am fighting for her.

She is the most important part of me.

She's the *only* part of me that truly matters.

"You okay back there, son?" Dad's voice questions, the shakiness in it telling me he's not as strong as he lets on.

"Yep," I clip out and meet his eyes in the mirror with a firm gaze of my own. "I just want to get Baylee taken care of. That's all that matters to me, Dad."

He presses the accelerator and we glide around a slower car as he makes his way back to the hospital. We'd left Stark and the fucking chaos of emergency vehicles to get medical attention for both myself and Baylee with the promise they'd be by later to question us.

"Ten minutes, War. Hang in there kiddo."

Her hot breaths as she sleeps burn through my jeans on the top of my thigh, almost scalding me. I stroke away her hair and admire her pretty, blood-stained face.

So beautiful.

So perfect.

So worth the fight.

I *can* look at her blood smeared face without losing my fucking mind because it's *her*. It's not blood and disease and disgust. *It's her.* Bay. Deserving of love and so much more. She's mine to love and care for. And I won't fucking let her down.

Jerking my head back up when we hit a speed bump, I let out a relieved breath to see we're turning down the side road that'll lead us right to the hospital. When we pull up to the front, Dad jumps out of the car and hurries to open my car door. Baylee sits up, groggy from her short nap, and her frantic eyes dart around.

She's looking for him.

Expecting him to step out from a shadow.

To take her again to do only God knows what.

But he's not here.

As she realizes this, she climbs out with Dad's assistance and I all but jump out after her, eager to keep her close to me. My eyes fixate on the crusty smears on her cheek and I reach for her, the urge to touch her as necessary as my next breath. The blood doesn't scare me anymore. The pale skin and disoriented look on her face does though. When her knees buckle, I'm there to gather her light frame into my arms. People are shouting around us but I hold my girl to me.

I won't let you fall, Bay.

Not now, not ever.

"Son, you need to readmit yourself. You don't look well." Dad's concerns roll off me and I blow them off.

Nothing matters except her.

When she fainted earlier, they rushed to admit her. I stayed by her side, clutching her small hand, while they assessed her. She was severely dehydrated and in dire need of fluids. Now that she's being taken care of properly, the color is beginning to return to her face. Her soft, rhythmic breaths as she sleeps are music to my ears.

And yes, I count every fucking one of them.

"I'll be fine," I assure him as I run my thumb across the top of her hand, ignoring the searing ache in my chest. I could really use some pain meds, but it'll have to wait. The last time I closed my eyes, Brandon took her right out from under my nose. I'm not eager to leave her vulnerable again.

"Warren, she's going to be okay. But if you don't get back into a bed soon, you won't be okay. She needs you to be strong for her. Besides, there's a uniformed cop just outside her door. Nothing will happen to her."

I process his words. If she were awake and coherent, she'd be pressuring me to get medical attention. He's right. I do need to get better for her. She would want it that way.

"Fine, but you stay with her. Just to be safe. She only has us, Dad. Take care of her for me," I tell him gruffly as I stand on shaky legs. "Promise me."

"Of course," he vows, his voice serious and it comforts me.

Leaning forward, I run my thumb along her now clean cheek and then press my lips to hers. "I love you, beautiful. Take care of yourself and our baby. We'll go home soon and put this behind us. I swear to you I'll make it all better."

Her eyes flutter open and she smiles, albeit a small, quick one, before she slips back into a much-needed sleep. I kiss her one more time and then stand. The room spins, my dizziness overwhelming me, and I stumble. Dad, thankfully, is there to prevent me from careening to the floor where I know for a fact is crawling with disgusting microorganisms. He ushers me over to the door and calls over a nurse.

"My son needs a room. And preferably one nearby. I need to look after both my kids."

The nurse finds me a wheelchair and not long after, she's wheeling me into a room three doors down from Baylee. Three is my lucky number. When she begins turning down the blankets, I shudder. All of the horrors from the day wash over me like the black fucking plague.

"Are you okay?" she questions from the bedside, alarm marring her features. "You look like you've seen a ghost."

I shake my head and gesture for the bathroom with a quivering hand. "I'll be fine,"—*and I will*—"but I will need a shower ASAP."

The monsters in my head taunt me—images of Bay's bloody face multiply in my head, one on top of the other, until it's one messy blur of bloody love.

Gore.

Dripping and oozing from my Baylee.

It's in her mouth, her eyes, her nose, and her ears.

She's choking on it. And vomiting over and over.

I need to help her!

In the darkness of my mind, I reach for her—I reach for my light. I wade through the sea of bones and blood, the stench making me gag, and I go to her.

I'll protect you, Bay.

"War?"

I blink my eyes open from my nightmare and slowly take in the scene around me. A new hospital room. The clock on the wall tells me it has been two hours, eighteen minutes, and six seconds since I last saw her. She was sleeping and safe.

With a sigh of relief, I scan the room and am thankful not to see Dad sitting in one of the chairs. He's making good on his promise to look after her. My eyes do find the dark, kind ones of Dr. Daniels. The psychiatrist.

"Warren," his deep, calm voice thunders through the foggy remnants of my bad dream. "How are you doing?"

I clench my eyes closed for a moment to drive away the bad images of Baylee and recall better ones. Her pretty blonde hair bouncing in her ponytail as she runs along the beach. The excited way she would clap her hands together when she'd beat me at chess. How musical her voice sounded when she'd giggle at something I'd said.

When I reopen my eyes, I'm smiling.

She saves me every time.

"Talk to me, man," he says, his own grin turning his lips up on one side. He's a light-skinned black man with eyes the color of the way Baylee likes her coffee. I don't think he can be any older than me from my quick assessment. "Where'd you go just then?"

Shrugging, I take note that the searing ache in my chest has lessened thanks to a healthy dose of pain meds upon my being admitted again. "It was nothing."

And that is a lie. Bayle is everything.

"War. Be frank with me. Give me the gory details."

Jerking my gaze back to Dr. Daniels, I sigh. "I had a nightmare earlier. There was blood. Everywhere."

He smiles which immediately causes me to frown. "On your girlfriend?"

"Fiancée and mother of my child," I correct, scrubbing my jawline with my fingertips and level my gaze at him. "But then, when I felt those old demons closing in on me, I focused on *her*. Baylee's always been my savior—my light in the maddening darkness. I'm going to be a father now. Getting well isn't just about me anymore. It's about my family."

He nods and sits on the foot of my bed. I don't jerk away from him. I don't wonder about what he had to eat today or whether or not he washed his hands after he used the restroom. Instead, I want to know how he'll *help* me. How he'll *fix* me.

"Do you love her?"

I glare at him as if he's the one losing his mind, not me. "Of course I fucking love her. She's everything to me."

"Good. Then you're going to need to get yourself better for her. I just visited with your fiancée before I came to see you. She's going to need your light, Warren."

My heart rate quickens and I furrow my brows together in question. "But how can I be her light if I can't stop these thoughts every time I close my eyes?"

He breaks eye contact and pats my shin. "You were getting better, weren't you? I've read your history and talked with your father," he says and lifts his gaze to regard me. "Miss Winston was helping you, right?"

I nod without hesitation. "She cures me, Doc."

He smiles. "She's definitely been instrumental. With my help, I think we can continue get you on a path to a healthier life. You've already come leaps and bounds. With some talk therapy on a weekly basis and the proper dosage of anti-anxiety medication, you can live a normal life, War. I know you want that for yourself."

"I want this for *her*," I tell him with conviction.

I cringe at the idea of spilling all my problems to this guy. But then again, he doesn't seem judgmental. He actually seems like he wants to help me.

"The medications I've taken in the past seem to mess my head up even more though," I admit and pinch the bridge of my nose to ward off a headache that's forming. "I want my head clear for her."

He knits his brows together in a thoughtful manner and nods. "I agree. In the past you weren't getting the proper help you needed. But that's why we'll work through this together. This has to be a team effort, War. I don't need you seeing me as the bad guy. I was just in there with Miss Winston, and she needs you. She needs for you to be the strong one. That poor girl has been through so much. I believe you can do what it takes to get better for you and your family. We can talk about whatever bothers you and we can get you on a medicated regime that actually works. What do you say?"

I close my eyes and try to imagine a life where I walk through a store, hand in hand with Baylee, as we shop for baby furniture and then eat at a restaurant overlooking the ocean. One where I'm not continually assaulted with what ifs, gory imageries, and microbes by the millions. The idea is so fantastical, so out there, that I actually laugh. When I open my eyes, Dr. Daniels isn't amused. But he's not annoyed either. He's calm and simply waiting for my answer. With a sigh, I tell him the only answer that matters now that Baylee is a part of my dark, twisted world.

"Yeah, of course. Help me get this sick shit out of my head."

A week of psychotherapies and medicinal cocktails for my mental health, and pulmonary therapies for my physical health, and I'm finally ready to go home. And boy am I ready to get back to reality. A few days ago, Dad took Baylee back to Oakland for her father's proper burial beside her mother. Stark, as promised, has had uniforms following them around just in case Gabe tries to show back up.

Fortunately for us, he hasn't. The medical examiner claims that Gabe's blood loss would have been too much to survive without receiving immediate medical attention. And since the blood trailed all the way to the ocean, they're convinced that he likely drowned.

I'm glad the fucker's survival rate wasn't viable after what Baylee did to him. It was a small price to pay for all the heartache and pain he put her through. She still won't speak of what he did to her after I was shot. Nor do I press her. My Baylee's different. Vacant and quiet. She forces smiles for Dad and me, but as soon as no one's watching, she's back to picking lint off her pants or gnawing on her fingernails.

She's stressed the fuck out.

I can see the worry in her eyes. That he'll show back up and take her again. I wish I could find a way to make her relax and trust that he got what he deserved.

Once we're back home, together, I'll find a way to bring her back to me.

I'm not giving up on her now. Not after everything.

"You all ready?" Nurse Cathy questions when she comes into the room pushing a wheelchair.

Baylee trails in behind her with her arms folded across her chest. I wish she would come over to me and crawl into my bed. I crave to press my lips to hers and kiss away all her worries. Unfortunately, she doesn't show me her familiar spark and I don't push to see it. Not yet. So instead, I press gently whenever and wherever I can. Eventually, I'll push through the wall she's forming around herself. I'll get to her like she got to me.

We'll fix this.

"I'm ready for things to go back to normal," I tell the nurse but my gaze drifts to Baylee. She fidgets uncomfortably in her chair but doesn't make eye contact. My heart squeezes in my chest. Each day, the distance between us grows wider and wider. I'm afraid any farther and she'll disconnect from me altogether. I'll die before I let that happen. When we get back to the house, things *will* fall back into place like they once were.

My head is clearer with the newest concoction of antidepressants and anxiety meds. The blood and germs and toxins are dulled in my mind and my skin no longer crawls when people come too close. I can't help the way my mind obsesses over exactness, though. Perfection. Details. It's as if my OCD has worsened in some ways. I knew it was getting bad when I tried to count each tiny square between the woven threads that the hospital blanket was made up of. Dr. Daniels told me he was seeing progress on my end though, and I wasn't going to ask for another medication to thrust me into oblivion.

Once I'm settled in the wheelchair and Baylee stands to follow, she reaches a hand out to me. The movement is subtle, her hand barely coming forward. But it's something. It's everything. A spark.

Without hesitation, I snatch her hand and bring it to my lips. Hope twinkles briefly in her eyes before she breaks our gaze.

One tiny spark at a time is all I'm asking for. Soon, our love will be back to blazing and consuming everything in our path. I'll feed the flames. I will torch the past. All for her.

Hang in there, Bay.

I'm going to make you all better.

chapter
TWENTY

Baylee

It's been over a month since we've been home.

At night, after War's breaths even out, I cry myself to sleep.

Even with Land and War around me all the time, I'm alone.

Even with our love child growing inside of me, I'm drifting.

Dad's gone.

Mom's gone.

Brandon's gone.

And Gabe is somewhere.

It's not that I'm really even afraid of him. If he were alive, he'd have come back for me already. Stark promises they've cased every hospital in the state and not a word on his arrival or anyone matching the description of his injures. *He's dead*, she swears.

I want to believe her.

Maybe rationally I do.

But sometimes, late at night as I cry in bed, I can almost feel his presence. The devil warms me and I drift off to sleep, weak and exhausted.

I hate the things he did to me.

Yet, my heart aches from missing him in the same way I miss Brandon, Mom, and Dad.

It's stupid and bordering on crazy, but it's the way I feel. How I could miss both a monster and a dragon? How I could miss a father who would sell his daughter to save his wife?

Since we've been home, War spends an ungodly amount of time holed away in his office. He's obsessing. He's scouring the Internet for clues and leads. Anything to point them in the direction of the WCT and people who were involved. Stark had gotten a judge to approve a warrant for Forrester Whitehead's office and home. They turned both places upside down looking for evidence but he was good. 'Ol Buck and his wife knew how to leave absolutely no trails back to their affluent clientele. And as for Edgar Finn, turns out it isn't so easy to get into the finance mogul's home without reasonable cause. Apparently my testimony isn't enough, without some sort of substantial evidence.

So for a month now, War has done what Stark has asked him to. He's been trying to hack into both Mrs. Whitehead's and Edgar Finn's financial information. War is good at what he does but they're just better at hiding their trails.

"How's my grandbaby?"

Land's voice sends a jolt of warmth through my heart, thawing out the frozen, black parts of it. I roll over in bed and see him smiling in the doorway of War's room. He, like me though, wears a false smile. And me, like him, pretends as well. I plaster on a fake grin. "Your grandbaby makes me sleepy."

It's the truth. Sort of.

I'm pretty sure losing all of your loved ones will make you depressed and that will make you sleepy, but I let him think happier thoughts.

Unborn babies make their pregnant mothers tired.

Of course.

"You've been in bed all day," he says softly, his smile falling. "Maybe we should take you in to the doctor. See about switching out your prenatal vitamins or something. Have you made an appointment with the therapist Dr. Daniels suggested?"

The concern written all over his face reminds me of when I'd be sick and my dad would take care of me. Mom was great about making me homemade chicken noodle soup or buying me new books to read to keep my mind off being ill. Always trying to find a way to make me better. But Dad? Dad would hold me and just let me be his baby for however long it took to get well.

Tears streak down the side of my face and soak the pillow I'm laying on. The ache in my chest hurts more than normal and I try to swallow down the emotion that seems to have seized my throat.

"I miss my mom and dad," I choke out with a sob. I'm embarrassed that I sound like I'm twelve years old again, needing my daddy to make it all better. But that's exactly how I feel. Young. Alone. And scared of the outside world.

Wordlessly, Land rounds the bed and climbs in next to me. He wraps a warm arm around my middle and hugs me to him.

"I'm so sorry, Baylee," he says, his own voice thick with emotion. "I wish I could take it all away."

When I start to cry, he follows in behind me, his deep sobs in melody with my higher pitched ones. Together we cry for those life took from us. I know he hurts for his wife and daughter. I'm bleeding over my parents. And together our hearts sometimes ache over War. The sweet, broken man whose afflictions occasionally steal him away from us.

In our own way, we lean on each other.

We lie like that for some time. Land's fatherly presence reminds me of my own and it comforts me.

"I'll never replace your dad," he says softly, "but I'll protect and love you like you are my daughter. When that boy gets stuck inside his head from time to time, I'll be there for you."

I swallow down the tears. War has been great. Determined to bring down the WCT during the day but still attentive to my emotional needs at night. He makes sure I eat, hovers when I'm not wearing my fake smile, and crushes me with his warm embraces. We've yet to make love again and I have my reasons. War wants in desperately. But it's me who's stuck inside *her* head. It's me who can't let go of the past several months. It's me who pushes him out when I crave him more than anything.

"War and I will always take care of you," Land assures me. "You're our family now, Baylee. Got it, kid?"

His last words are playful but I know he's serious. I can feel it deep inside my heart. Knowing I have at least two people in this world willing to love me and look out for me lessens the burden that has been weighing my mind down.

"Thank you, Land. You have no idea how much that means to me." And with a smile, I add, "So will you take me to get my belly button pierced?"

He chuckles loudly and then feigns a deep, fatherly voice. "I don't think so young lady. Not while you're living under this roof."

We both laugh and my heart feels lighter.

One day at a time.

We can do this.

Together.

War runs his fingers through his hair and huffs in frustration. "Nothing. Fucking nothing."

I'm curled up in the chair in his office, needing to be close to him. "No money trail?"

"Nothing that will hold up in court. They're all meticulous as fuck," he grumbles and slams his fist on his desk, startling me.

He continues clicking on webpages but doesn't turn around to regard me. My mind drifts to that night. The night I encountered that horrible man.

"I bid one point two million," an amused voice says from beside me.

I jerk my gaze over to a man who reminds me of Brandon. His dark hair is cut short and spiked on top. He has an easy, charming smile.

"That's a lot of money," I squeak out.

He winks. "That it is. And you'll be worth it."

I chew on my lip and cast another glance out in Gabe's direction. Nowhere. My gaze falls back to the man who seems harmless in his nice suit and disarming grin.

"Thank you," I murmur.

He steps toward me. "And so polite. You'll be a great addition to my girls."

"You have more than one?"

"I come here every month and buy more. It's an addiction."

I swallow. "What do you do with them?"

His eyes flicker with something dark and evil. He's nothing like Brandon. "I hurt them. Just like I'm going to hurt you," he says in a matter of fact tone. He winks and grins at me as if his words aren't awful. "Your pale skin is so perfect and untouched. I'm about to come just thinking of all the nasty words I'll carve into your skin. You'll wear my name and other words like cunt and whore on your flesh for the world to see."

I stumble back away from him and gape at him in horror. "You're a monster!"

He sneers. "Where'd you think you were, sexy? A fucking fundraiser?"

"I, but, I…"

"You're in the den with some of the biggest monsters on the West Coast. You are nothing but a meal purchased to be devoured with greed and no restraint. Some of us are into sex. Others are into more deviant acts. I'm into the deviant with a side of sex. They won't recognize their precious beauty by the time I finish with you. But then, it'll be too late. You'll bleed out all over my Persian rug and I'll drag your ass outside to dump you in the goddamned ocean."

Tears stream down my face and I start to bolt from him. His tight grip is around my arm before I can move though. "The name's, Edgar Finn. Remember it because you'll take it to your grave," he threatens. "See you soon, Gardenia Lee."

He releases me and I push through the crowd away from him at breakneck speed. I need to make my escape now. There's no way I'm going home with that lunatic.

As I hurry away from him, I try not to make eye contact with the leering men along the way. They're all the same. Monsters just like Gabe. I'd been an idiot to believe otherwise. There is no finding the nice side of this world. The only thing I need to worry about finding is the way out of it. Now.

I shudder at the memory. "Do you think he really kills them? Edgar Finn I mean."

War swivels in his chair and stares at me, the worry over me written all over his face. When I'm being closed off, which is a lot of the time, he pours himself into his work. His weary gaze skims over my face and he frowns. "I wouldn't be surprised. All of them are monsters."

Licking my dry lips, I sit up in the chair, suddenly eager for his undivided attention. "He bragged to me about killing those girls and dumping them in the ocean. Do you really think he does that? Wouldn't people find their bodies? Do you think it was all an act to terrorize me or was he for real?"

His eyes zero in on my mouth as I speak and a shiver, the first sign of life in nearly a month courses through me.

"You're so beautiful, Baylee," he murmurs, completely ignoring my questions. But I don't care. I'm too enthralled in the way my body that seemed to be slowly dying has shown some real signs of life. My heart is beating erratically inside my chest and my breathing picks up. His mouth barely moves and I can tell he's counting. Counting my beats, my breaths…he's counting me. The smile on my lips is immediate.

And it makes me so damn happy.

"How many?" I question after what feels like a minute.

His cheeks turn pink and he smiles sheepishly at me. "Nineteen blinks, fourteen breaths, and one big smile I haven't seen in a long time."

Tears well in my eyes before one spills out and streaks down my cheek. His eyes follow its path and he stares at it as it hangs from my jaw. With a shaky hand, he reaches out and touches it, wetting his fingertip. The breath I seemed to have been holding rushes out quickly and I jerk my eyes to his.

I can see it in his eyes. He craves to kiss me. To hold me and caress away my pain. But I don't know if I can handle it. Each time he attempts to touch me in a way that is more than just friendly, I shy away.

I'm too fucked up for him now.

When I lean back his face falls, and with it, my heart plummets to the floor. I want to push through this thick wall in my head. To climb over it and into his warm, waiting arms. Why can't I just get the fuck over it?

I rub my hand over my belly and vow that tomorrow I'll call the therapist Dr. Daniels suggested. I need to get better for the three of us. This baby *will* enter this world in a happy, loving environment.

"Edgar Finn seems like a braggart. He seems the type to want to show others his handiwork. People like him are narcissistic," I spit out in equal parts disgust of the monsters in this world and the lingering thought that War and I are still worlds apart. The latter my entire doing.

His eyes glaze over as he gets lost in thought. I watch with sick satisfaction as he rolls the pad of his finger and thumb together, smearing my tear over his flesh. My heart pumps with overwhelming joy that he seems obsessed over touching a part of me.

Just give yourself to him.

But then he snaps out of it, used to my constant denial, and swivels back around. His fingers fly over his keyboard like a man possessed. I chew on my lip and try not to burst into full on tears at not being able to be the woman he deserves.

"You're a genius," he mutters over his shoulder to me. "I was so fixated on his financials, I didn't think about his house. Stark may not be able to get inside without a warrant, but we can get inside. He pays a monthly fee to Pacific Security each month. All I need to do is access their database and locate his account. A rich bastard like him is sure to have cameras on his property. Maybe we can find something."

Disappointment fades away as I hurry to my feet and watch in awe over his shoulder as War flies through the programs with ease. He's a natural born hacker and there's not a firewall that's impenetrable when it comes to him. I just wish he knew how to hack inside my mind and tear down the wall that divides us.

"Bingo," he says with a satisfied growl.

Without thinking, I slide into his lap to get a closer look. His strong arms wrap around my waist and his lips find my neck. Hot, quick breaths tickle my flesh and my heartrate thumps to life for the first time in weeks. The feeling is exhilarating and I missed it so damn much.

"God, I've missed you," he murmurs against my skin and then presses a kiss there. I want his kisses everywhere. All over me. Inside me. Owning and taking every inch of my broken being.

I'm about to completely give in to his eager touches when I freeze in his arms. I had momentarily zoned out but he'd just found something. Something important. Tugging away from his love that burns so bright it scalds me, I look up at the monitor. "Oh. My. God."

Eight squares fill the screen. There's no movement on six of them. Just empty rooms. But one reveals a room with several women huddled together on the floor, they seem to be comforting one another. It's not that room that's so terrifying though.

As if reading my mind, he releases my waist to reach for his mouse and then opens the eighth square to make the visual on that room full screen. There's no audio but the visual is crystal clear.

Edgar Finn.

He stands next to a bed wearing nothing but a pair of pants. His chest heaves as he takes deep breaths. Other than the small movement he makes breathing, he's otherwise unmoving and fixated on the girl on the bed. Her stomach and thighs have been crisscrossed with bleeding cuts. Something, a rag maybe, gags her mouth and she's bound with an appendage tied to each post of the bed.

A bloody star fish.

Just waiting to be released back into the sea.

"You'll bleed out all over my Persian rug and I'll drag your ass outside to dump you in the god-damned ocean."

But she's not bleeding out all over his rug. The blood slowly seeps from her wounds and runs down, soaking the comforter beneath her. Her eyes look past him and straight into the camera.

I recognize the look in her eyes. A look of despair and resignation. One that has come to the realization she'll never see her family again.

"We have to save her," I mutter, my voice barely audible as I jump to my feet. The room spins and his strong hands find my hips to steady me. He tries to pull me back into his lap but I start pacing the room. "Warren, you have to save her."

When Edgar Finn starts moving closer to her and the glint of his blade shimmers in the light, I feel bile rising in my throat. Bolting from the office, I run as fast as I can to the guest bathroom and barely make it to the toilet before throwing up.

That girl. Nothing more than a commodity. Something for him to consume and then discard.

"You are nothing but a meal purchased to be devoured with greed and no restraint."

I'm haunted by his words and it does nothing to help my nausea. I wish Land were here this evening instead of catching up on some work at the office. He could bring me a cold rag and some ginger ale. Land would take care of me like Dad would have. Instead, I'm left to deal with the sickness, the rage of what Edgar is doing, and the demons of my past all alone.

But you're not alone.

War wants in. You have to let him in.

He will save you from yourself, Baylee.

War's voice comforts me as he shouts at Stark over the phone, no doubt telling her to save that girl. His heavy footsteps can be heard as he paces around his house. He may not be able to physically comfort me right now, but I steal any comfort I can get. And just hearing him sound so powerful and strong has my nausea settling.

Let him in.

On shaky legs, I stand and quickly brush my teeth. After I wash my face, I make my way over to the guest bed and crawl onto it. Curling into a fetal position, I let my emotions take over. I cry myself to sleep hoping and praying they can save that girl.

Someone needs to save her from the monster.

And one day she can move on and be free again.

I just hope she doesn't turn out like me.

Drifting.

Lost.

Alone.

She *deserves* to be free.

chapter
TWENTY-ONE

War

I stare at my phone.

With each second that ticks by, the next slower than the last, I grow more and more impatient. It pisses me off but I can't speed things up. So, instead, I just stare at my phone willing Stark to call me back. But the call never comes. Finally, at just after midnight, I receive a text.

Stark: We got the bastard. An "anonymous" tip of a woman being harmed was enough to get the warrant we needed. Finn is in custody. The other eight women are being treated for minor injuries. Girl number nine is in the hospital but expected to fully recover. You did well, War. Thank you.

I let her words wash over me and I can't fight the grin that spreads over my face. My initial reaction is to scream it through the house. To tell Baylee we've taken down one more monster in this godforsaken world.

But then I remember she's already gone to sleep. After those horrifying images showed up on the video feed, she disappeared. I could hear her retching in the bathroom but I was too hopped up on adrenaline to let it get to my head. I'd wanted to go to her—to comfort her in her time of distress—but Stark needed to get to those women. I had to make sure I sent them right into the lion's den before it was too late.

My feet carry me to the doorway where she sleeps and my heart sinks. She's still curled up into a little ball, making her seem so much smaller. Day by day, the medicine makes me feel stronger. Levelheaded and calm. But I've been too focused on Finn. I haven't stopped obsessing long enough to focus on my poor, sweet girl breaking apart before my very eyes.

Jesus, I'm a fucking idiot.

She whimpers, and I'm striding into the dark bedroom before I even stop to consider what I'm doing. This past month she has pushed me away every chance she gets. I've allowed her to—tried to give her the space I thought she needed. But not anymore. I'm going to get through to her. I'll break through to her. Maybe she doesn't need space at all. Maybe she needs *me*. My fisted hands clench at my sides as the urge to touch her becomes overwhelming. I want to fix her like she's fixed me. I need to hold her and kiss away her pain.

So fucking do it!

With a growl of part determination and part desperation, I drop a knee onto the bed. Leaning forward, with shaky hands, I push them beneath her and drag her light frame into my arms.

I expect a shiver of horror to course through her as the nightmares of Gabe plague her.

I expect her mind to take over and play tricks on her—for her to shout and screech and claw at me like she's done so many nights recently.

What I don't expect is the way her body reacts to mine. She's warm and curls up against me. Her fingers thread into my hair and she holds on as if I might vanish at any second. My heart thrums with love at having her in my arms. I hug my beautiful girl against my chest and kiss her cool forehead.

"War?" she questions, the grogginess in her voice revealing disbelief. Almost as if she thinks she's dreaming me.

"I'm so sorry, Baylee. I'm sorry I've never been enough of a man for you," I apologize and kiss her sweet, pink nose as I carry her down the hallway to our bedroom. "But I swear to God I'll always try for more. I won't ever stop trying to be better, healthier, and the man you deserve. And I'll never stop fighting for you. You once told me the queen always protects the king, even from himself. Well, beautiful, I'm returning the favor. I'm not going to give up on you. Not now, not fucking ever. I love you, Bay."

She starts to cry but I calm her with soothing hums of songs that always seem to still the raging beast inside my head. I swipe at the light switch, darkening the room, before peeling back the blankets. When I set her down, she lets out a sigh of relief and slides under the covers. I don't even bother getting undressed and crawl in after her. Our bodies mold together and her cool skin begins to warm from the heat of mine. With every ragged breath she takes, my touch seems to breathe life back into her.

My lips are pressed against her messy hair near her ear. Moments ago, I was worried to touch her for fear of her rejection. But it's clear to see she needs me now. Desperately. And I can't seem to get enough of her. I want to fuse my soul to hers. To tether us in a way we'll never be separated again.

She twists in my arms to face me, and even in the darkness, I can feel her pretty blue eyes on mine. Her hot breath tickles my lips but it doesn't make me recoil from her like it would have several months ago. Instead, I lick my lips wetting them because I'm hungry for her. Fucking ravenous. My Baylee has changed me for the better.

"Thank you," she rasps out, emotion thick in her voice.

I hug her closer to me until our lips brush against each other. "Shhh, I'm never letting you go."

Her fingers lightly feather up my neck and then brush against my cheek. "Kiss me and don't ever stop for the rest of our lives."

Capturing her face in my hands, I tilt her head before diving in to kiss her. Her hot mouth is ready and grants my tongue easy access. The touch of hers against mine is enough to send a thousand volts of desire coursing through my body. Suddenly, the kiss becomes inadequate. Unfulfilling. I need more of her. All of her. Our kiss is nothing more than a tease. A small taste. A tiny sample of our love.

I need every single part of her.

Every last drop.

My tongue waters to lick every inch of her flesh. I want to memorize the taste of her and have it fill my mind. The desire to learn every part of her flesh with my mouth is overwhelming.

Breaking from our kiss, I grin at her needy yelp, and yank off her T-shirt. She's not wearing a bra so in my very next breath, my lips are on her right breast as I push her onto her back. I'm starved for my sweet Baylee. The hunger for her is growing into a formidable force that can't ever be sated.

"Oh, God, I've missed you," I murmur before sucking her sensitive nipple into my mouth. She lets out a gasp and then her fingers are in my hair. Tugging and clawing, she shoves my face against her tit, needing me every bit as much as I need her.

As I nibble on her flesh, my fingers find the waistband of her yoga pants and panties. She wiggles her ass as I slip them from her body. I pull away from her and sit up on my knees. In the darkness, all I can make out is her shadowy form. Using my fingertips, I touch her swollen lips and then drag them down her throat, between her breasts, and along her still flat belly. When I run them over her pubic bone, she lets out a whimper.

"Baylee," I plead as I push her knees apart, "can I taste you? I need to taste you."

She lets out a sexy kitten-like mewl that has my cock straining to get free of my jeans. "Can you? Will you freak out? I don't want to gross you out." The shaky way she says her words lights a fire to the madness inside my head. It rages within me, eager to burn away the demons and burn bright with her light.

"You could never in a million years gross me out," I vow. And I mean it. Never fucking ever.

Her legs relax at my words and she lets them fall to the sides. I lean forward and inhale her feminine scent that's only unique to her. As I lower myself to her pussy, I become dizzied with the desire to devour her.

I've never been so sure of anything in my life.

"You smell so…" I trail off, trying to find the right words, "clean."

She giggles, a sound so pure it should be banned from this ugly world and only reserved for a place like heaven. "Way to make a girl feel special, War."

Her laughter dies in her throat the moment my lips hesitantly brush against her pubic bone. I lightly press a kiss there that has her breaths coming out in quick succession. The desire to count them is overshadowed by the craving to learn every inch of her pretty pussy.

At first, I kiss her slowly until I reach her clit that seems to be throbbing with need. Using my thumbs, I open her like a special gift I don't believe I've earned, and taste her almost tentatively.

Sweet.

Sexy yet pure.

A taste like nothing else on this earth.

"War," she moans as I drag my tongue along her slit.

The way she says my name drives me crazy—crazy in a good way and I want her to do it over and over again. I want to count how many times she chants it. And I hope it will be an uncountable number.

My tongue seems to know exactly what she wants because soon I'm sucking and lapping at her, and she is squirming like a woman possessed on the bed. Her fingers have long since threaded into my hair and she pushes and pulls me to where she wants me. I let her be the guide and use my tongue for her own sexual gratification.

"Don't stop," she pleads and holds my head in place.

Of course I won't stop. I don't think I'll ever stop. A part of me wonders if she's my cure. Some magical remedy to my afflictions. Because when I'm between her legs, consuming all that is her, I can't think of anything else.

Just Baylee.

My Baylee.

Forever.

"Oh God!" she shrieks one, two, three seconds before she thrashes against the bed with an orgasm I've never had the joy to experience with her. An orgasm that takes hold of her soul and rattles it ruthlessly. Her moans and yelps are a chant I don't understand but somehow feel deep down in my bones. Pure bliss and soul satisfying pleasure.

I gave that to her.

And I'll keep giving until I take my very last breath on earth.

"That was…" she trails off.

I press one last soft kiss to her clit before I sit back up on my knees. Her heavenly body is invading my senses—taste, smell, touch. For a man who obsesses over cleanliness, I find myself wanting her scent on me at all times. A constant reminder of the love of my life—a way to get me through my day.

It's addicting.

Distracting.

And oh so fucking delicious.

"Do you need to, um," she questions softly, almost embarrassed, "brush your teeth?"

A warm chuckle erupts from me and I crawl between her spread legs, hovering above her. My lips brush against hers and she lets out a soft gasp.

"I quite like your taste, Bay," I tell her truthfully. "I'd like to keep you there for a little while longer if that's okay with you."

She laughs, so soft and sweet, but I silence the sweet sound with my mouth. I want her to taste what I taste. To understand just how perfect she is to me. Her fingers dance along my rib cage as I kiss her and she hugs me to her. My cock is straining against my jeans and I want to yank it out so I can make love to her. But I want to tend to her needs first.

"Baylee, my strong, sweet, beautiful girl," I praise as I pull away from her and sit up on my knees. "I'll never get enough of you. Marry me, please."

I can feel her smile. I don't have to see it to feel it. With Baylee, she smiles with her soul. You can feel that shit. It isn't something you have to see because her smile is a living, breathing entity.

"I thought you were supposed to get on one knee," she teases.

I run my palms over her belly and stroke her reverently. "Technically I'm on two. Does that mean I'm doubly serious about my request?"

Instead of waiting for an answer, I'm eager to bring her pleasure again. My lips find her belly and I kiss with soft, gentle kisses. Then, I kiss her more firmly—I suck her sweet flesh into my mouth and taste her. After forty-nine seconds of this, she's turned into a live wire beneath me.

"War, I need more."

With a half-grin, I slip my finger between her legs. Pushing into her now dripping pussy with my finger, I go back to licking and sucking the skin on her abdomen. Her breaths come out short and uneven, the urge to count them gone, and my mouth soon finds her supple tits. Our bodies connect and thrive when they're together. I don't have to think about what I'm doing with her, it just happens exactly the way it should be.

"Yes! God, yes!" she cries out as another orgasm seizes her.

When her body stops shuddering, I chuckle and slip my finger out of her. "Is that a yes to marrying me?"

The air in front of me swishes as she swats at me. "The answer to your question, Warren, is yes multiplied by infinity. And don't you dare start trying to calculate what that number is. Just know it's infinite and a number that can never be counted because it's too great. It's never-ending."

Crawling back over her, I find her lips again and kiss her in a gentle manner. "Thank you."

"For what? You haven't even gotten off yet," she says with a laugh. "I'm the one having all the fun here."

With my thumb, I stroke her smooth cheek which I know is slightly red, even in the dark, from her orgasm. "Thank you for loving me. I'm hard to love, Baylee. It takes a special person to love someone like me."

Her fingers push through my hair on the sides of my head and her thumb slides along the uneven scar on my face. "It was never hard for me," she whispers. "It was always too easy. Like breathing or talking. Loving you came second nature. You were meant for me."

I bury my face against her neck and press kisses into the flesh below her ear. "The medicine is helping me, beautiful. I can do this—for us. Thanks for never giving up on me."

She lets out a gasp when I suck a little too hard on her skin. "War was never over for me. I will always fight for you. Thank you for fighting for me too."

Smiling, I trail kisses back up along her cheek until I find her mouth again. "We don't ever have to fight again," I assure her. "We've won. Love always wins, Bay."

When she starts to cry, tears of relief, I kiss away each one. I revel in the salty release of her pent up worries, sorrows, and fears tasting each and every one as they leak out of her eyes. Soon, she won't have to cry ever again. I'll make sure of it.

Until the last of her tears are released, I'll lick them all away. My Baylee tastes of sunshine, the salty Pacific, and hope.

But most importantly, she tastes like peace.

chapter

TWENTY-TWO

Baylee

I'm here.

With War.

At last.

The steaming hot water washes away the pain and horrors I've been harboring. Although the water remains clear, I can't help but feel as though I'm washing away the blood from the casualties in my war. With a tearful, bitter, dark laugh, I confess what weighs on my heart—the main reason I haven't been able to connect physically with War. "He fucked me, War," I murmur, unable to meet his eyes as he stands outside of the shower dutifully taking his medication. "And Brandon would have if he'd been given the chance."

Silence stretches out between us as he unbuttons his jeans and pushes them down his muscular thighs. He kicks out of them on his way over to me so that he's completely naked. The man is built like an immortal god.

"They didn't love you though. Not like I do. Fucking means nothing without love. Remember that." His voice is calm and it blankets me in a warmth the water will never match.

He steps into the shower and helps me wash. I keep waiting for him to obsess over how Gabe tainted me or poisoned our baby with his bodily fluids. I expect him to recoil from this dirty woman I've become. Instead, he washes me while he hums a song by the Pixies.

Where Is My Mind?

The song that he's played on occasion while we play chess soothes my quivering heart. It infects the dark thoughts inside of my head and weaves with it images and memories of War. His touch, his scent, his overwhelming desire to care for me. His love. Soon, the shower is off, my mind and body are renewed, and my War is guiding me to his bed.

Towels are dropped.

And that's okay.

Afflictions are lost.

And we don't notice.

Love leads the way.

And we gladly follow.

"I'm going to hold you, Bay, and never let you go." His words are a vow meant to protect me, not imprison me. And I believe them.

I lift my finger and draw a heart over his own. Then, I trace a 'B' inside of it. With my invisible mark, I stamp my presence on his soul and permanently etch a part of me onto him. Breaking away from him, I climb on top of the bed and let his searing gaze burn off any last remnants from the blood of the monsters of my past. "Make love to me Warren McPherson."

His eyes meet mine as he crawls on top of me without hesitation. Our mouths connect in a needy flurry and his hard cock pushes into me without warning. I moan out in relief at having him inside me, stretching my body to limits in a way only he can. The connection becomes one and I jolt back to life. Dragging my nails over his shoulders, I kiss him deeper than ever before. I need him to taste the love I have for him.

My War is hungry for it too.

My love satisfies him and he grunts as he bucks into me.

Bliss and passion and desire and perfection are all rolled into one as we chase the release we both need. Not a selfish release, but one we only find together. A mutual orgasm of the souls.

The black king and white queen are the only ones left on the board that's no longer devoid of color. It drips with the crimson blood of the defeated and we stand in victory. Together.

"My Baylee, my sweet, sweet Baylee," he murmurs against my lips as his body tightens with his climax. The throbbing of his cock inside of me sends my body into a flurry of shudders as I orgasm with him. When he empties himself into me, he relaxes and his gaze meets mine. A smile plays at his lips.

"War is worth the peace." My words are honest and true. War is worth everything.

"Focus, on your move, Bay," he says from across the board.

He doesn't think I'm focused but I am. I'm hyper focused. But not on our chess game. Instead, I'm obsessing over having him in my mouth. It's been a couple of days since our lovemaking reunion when he went down on me, and I've been squirming with need to return the favor ever since. Each time, I attempt to, I see the shame and horror flicker in his eyes.

He's afraid of his own reaction.

That he won't be able to handle it.

But I'm determined to win. I will find a way to suck on his cock and when I finally get to, he'll wonder what he's been missing all along. My confidence is unwavering. Some things you just know.

"There. I'll move there," I tell him absently and move a pawn that undoubtedly opens me up for an attack on his part.

His frown is immediate. "Are you sure?"

I nod, a sly smile forming at my lips. I'm planning an attack of my own. He draws his attention from me and back onto the board. I see it in his eyes as they dart all over the place. He's calculating each and every move. His brain is on overdrive, trying to figure out a way to take out the queen.

Little does he understand, he's always had her.

Tearing my nightgown from my body, leaving me naked, I stand and make my way over to him. He's still staring at the board and hardly notices my movement. When I step in front of his view of the board between his spread legs, his eyes travel up my bare flesh until his heated gaze meets mine.

"You're cheating," he says, a low growl rumbling in his throat.

I shiver when his hands find my hips. "Close your eyes."

His jaw clenches but he does as he's told. With a satisfied smile, I drop to my knees in front of him. He lets out a grunt when I grab onto the waistband of his pajama pants and tug them down his thighs. War's cock, thick and proud, bobs out and points up at the ceiling.

"Baylee, I don't know if this is—"

But I don't give him a chance to argue and run my tongue along the tip of his dick.

"Jesus Christ, woman," he hisses out.

My hand curls around his shaft, and I stroke it while I tease him with my tongue. It isn't until I fully wrap my lips around him and slide down his cock where it hits the back of my throat that he finally seems to let go of any insecurities about this act.

His hands dive into my messy hair and he groans out in pleasure. It turns me on to see him enjoying it and I pull out every trick I can think of. I suck him hard, I run my tongue around in uneven patterns, I even let my teeth graze along his sensitive flesh a few times. I'm not a pro at dick sucking but judging by his sharp intakes of air, I think I'm doing okay.

"Bay," he growls in warning, "I'm going to—"

I know what he wants but I don't let him off easy. Instead, I take him as deep as I can go knowing it'll send him over the edge. A roar of pleasure rips from his chest and soon after his cock throbs as it spurts out his hot release. His salty taste isn't offensive and I swallow him down until he's got nothing more to feed me.

Slowly, I ease my mouth off of him and search his eyes to make sure he enjoyed it. His head is tilted back against the cushion of the chair and his lips are parted. He's gorgeous as hell, and I can't wait to do it again just so I can see this look of pure ecstasy on his face.

"Checkmate," I tell him with a laugh.

His head snaps back down and his searing gaze is on mine. I've never seen such an unmasked look of desire on him. His furrowed brows, darkened eyes, and clenching jaw indicate he's hungry for me.

"We're not done playing, beautiful," he murmurs and melts me with his scorching stare. "Come here and let me show you how the game is played."

I grin at him and climb into his lap. Once I'm straddling him, he guides his cock into me and then clutches onto my hips, pushing me all the way down. He stretches and fills me perfectly. Like we were designed to fit each other exactly.

"Kiss me," he orders in a low, seductive tone.

My lips descend on his and I moan into his mouth when he begins bucking into me. The sensation is too much and not enough all at once. Even though I'm on top, he's the one doing the fucking. All I can do is close my eyes and enjoy the ride. His strong fingers grip into my ass as he pounds his love into me.

Chess pieces clink and clatter behind me, his legs no doubt hitting the table as he makes love to me. I nearly come from the simple fact that he doesn't stop to obsess over his precious game. He doesn't care about anything else but me. Just like he promised.

"Oh God," I yelp out when a blissful orgasm slices through me, temporarily blinding me with a mix of love and lust in one perfect concoction.

His heat pumps into me and I shudder with the last of my climax. I'll never get enough of this man. When we both come down from our high, I collapse against his chest and stare off into the ocean behind him, a smile gracing my lips.

I shiver when his fingertips run up and down along my back. My palm slides over his red scar on his chest and I thank God again that he survived that day.

"You're such a cheater," he says, a smile in his voice. "And I should punish you for what you made me do to my white furniture."

Leaning back, I gaze into his beautiful, loving eyes and arch an eyebrow at him. "Punish me how?"

My taunting question has his softening cock twitching back to life. He smacks my ass with both hands and I squeal with laughter.

"That's a start," he says with a smirk. His hooded eyes meet mine and my body thrums to life. "For the second part of your punishment," he muses as he stands with me in his arms. His pajama pants fall to the floor and he steps out of them on the way back to our room. "I think I'll carry you into the bedroom," he says, just as he does that. "Push your back against the wall." I let out a gasp when the cold wall hits my skin. "Hold your hands to where you can't move." My pussy contracts with excitement when he firmly pushes them to the wall. "And…"

"Fuck me into tomorrow?" I quip with a saucy grin.

He narrows his eyes but his cock is fully hard again inside me, at my words. "Actually, this is punishment, remember?" he reminds me with a raised brow. "So, I thought I'd explain to you how a firewall on a server works. You see, it's a system that's meant to keep viruses and—"

"No!" I squeal in mock horror. "Put me out of my misery already. Fuck me to death, War, because there's no way I can sit and listen to your boring computer mumbo jumbo for another second."

He chuckles but thrusts forcefully into me. "As you wish, my love."

The world around us once again fades away.

Horrors of our past slowly smolder to ash and swirl from us bit by bit, no longer having a place in our hearts.

Heat of our present ignites into a raging, uncontrollable beast of a blaze that ravages the two of us, never promising to cool.

And the beauty of our future is blinding with a fire so powerful, it will decimate anything in its path, aside from our love.

His mouth over takes mine and we climax hard together. When I flutter down from my high, my eyes meet his and he smiles.

I drag my gaze over his bottom lip that looks good enough to bite and grin back at him. "My War."

"My peace."

EPILOGUE

War

Two years, one month, fourteen days, sixteen hours, eight minutes, and forty-seven seconds later…

My hot breath on the glass materializes another heart.

My Baylee, always leaving secret notes for me.

I smile and stare out toward the ocean. Her long blonde hair whips to her left as the wind barrels along the coast. It tries its damnedest to knock her over but she remains steadfast and strong. The queen in my world.

With her back to me, I can't see her swollen belly but I know it's there. Just this morning, I rained kisses all over that belly and was met with little nudges against my mouth. Our son will be a playful one like his mother. I can't wait.

I watch Dad as he opens the ice chest between them on the blanket and hands her a bottle of water. I'm envious of that bottle—her tongue and mouth doing things my cock is now certainly familiar with. With Baylee, each day drives me further and further away from my afflictions. All it took was one blow-job from my girl and I didn't care if I died an awful death from the worst diseases known to man. It was all worth a few beautiful minutes of her lips on my dick.

And the first time I tasted her, sucked and nibbled on her sweet clit, I was a goner. When it came to her body, I was free. She was a healer, not an infection. I'll never get enough of what she so gladly offers me.

I'd be a fool though if I said we were perfect. We're far from it, in fact. Twice a month, Baylee and I attend our counseling sessions. Most times, we go together but on occasion we go alone. There are some memories my girl still has trouble dealing with—the loss of her parents, the fact she was a victim of sexual violence, and the betrayal of three men she cared deeply for. And I tend to flip the fuck out from time to time—the fear of losing the ones I love to disease, accidents, or some freak murderer hangs heavy in my heart continuously and no matter how hard I try to shake it away, I simply can't. But together, we emerge from the darkness that shadows our minds and we find a way to survive. Happily.

Together we find the light.

Baylee stands and she shields her eyes as she looks up at the house. She doesn't have to see me to know I'm always watching her. My heart flops when she waves and blows a kiss in my direction. I wish I could run down the stairs now and trudge through the gritty sand toward her. To take her in my arms and kiss her pretty mouth.

Of course I can't.

Well, at least not yet.

When she turns her back to me again, I drop my gaze down to the glass near the floor. It's smudged all to hell and gives Greta hives when she comes over. I beg her not to clean them away but she pulls the know-it-all motherly card and says it needs to be sterilized. That I can't capture every memory in the way of snot and slobber. The memories stay in the heart and mind, she says, not on glass. My how the roles have changed.

I flick my gaze over to the clock on the wall and my heart begins to thump wildly in my chest.

It's almost time. Thirty-eight more seconds before Baylee says it's okay. If it were up to me, I wouldn't count the hours and minutes and seconds. I'd lose them all in the scent of blonde curls, bright blue eyes, and slobbery grins.

But I've learned my lesson.

When I break Baylee's rules, we spend the rest of the day battling tears and meltdowns.

So, I count the hours and minutes and seconds.

Twelve seconds left.

Flickering my gaze back to my dad, I smile to see him hugging her. Those two cling to one another and it fills my heart with joy. She's the daughter he lost. And he's the father she lost. A perfect pair, those two.

Click.

I'm already stalking away from the window toward my bedroom as soon as the last second passes. The time is now. For kisses and soul-melting babbles.

"Dadadadada."

I stop in the doorway, frozen by the sight of perfection. My little cherub stands in the play-pen, grinning at me with the world's cutest toothy smile. Her blue eyes glitter with excitement when she sees me and she reaches for me. Stepping over Baylee's discarded nightgown and one of my shoes, I make my way over to my baby.

"Hey there, angel. Did you wake up?" I scoop her into my arms and kiss the soft hair on her head.

She babbles about her dreams, speaking a language only she knows, while I carry her over to the bed to change her. The sheets and blankets are a mess with Baylee's psychology books still open to the last chapter she was reading for her college classes. A couple of years ago, I'd have flipped out over the mess. Now, I can't stop smiling because it means Baylee has left her mark on my life.

"Did you poo-poo? You know Mommy changes all the poo-poos," I chide playfully as I grab the wipes and a diaper from the end table.

"Mamamama," she explains and scrunches her nose.

She's so fucking cute, I laugh out loud. "Fine, you get out of it this time."

Like the practiced dad I am, I change her with only a few gags that I'm pretty sure are nor-mal for something that smells that rancid. Once she's in the pink bathing suit Bay left out for her, I carry her on my hip toward the door.

"You ready to go play with Gramps and Mommy at the beach?"

She buries her sweet face against my chest and I melt. My girl has me wrapped around her tiny finger and I don't care to ever be released.

"Papapapa."

"Yeah, Gramps will be excited to see you."

I step outside of my home and inhale the warm, salty air. Once upon a time, I shuddered at such a concept—breathing sea air. Now, I practically need it to survive. Barefoot, I trot down the steps and through the hot sand toward my family. When Baylee sees us, she stands and waddles my way. I'll never tire of seeing her big and pregnant with our children. Before it's all said and done with, we'll have our own little army.

"Hey, honey," she calls out to me. "Hey, cutie."

Hannah reaches for her mommy and Baylee takes her. I come around behind her and wrap my arms to touch the sides of her belly. My mouth finds the shell of her ear and I kiss it tenderly.

"Papapapa!" Hannah shrieks upon seeing him and wriggles to be set down.

We both laugh the moment Hannah is free and clumsily makes her way to Gramps who is waiting with an undoubtedly sandy cracker my mother would approve of.

"Mmm," Baylee murmurs, turning in my arms, "I thought you'd never get here."

I flash her a grin before threading my fingers in her hair and kissing her deeply. "Believe me, I was counting the seconds."

She sighs in happiness and together we watch as my dad plays with our daughter. Finally, after a few moments, my wife looks up at me with tears in her eyes and runs her fingertips over the scar on my chest. "War, the battles were worth it. The pain, the blood, the casualties, the paths our lives took. It was all worth it because it led to this. Whatever 'this' is"—she motions between me and our family—"I don't ever want it to end."

I plant a kiss on her forehead. Making the same gesture of my hand, I explain exactly what "this" is.

"This is love, baby."

Baylee

I press a kiss to War's soft lips and smile at him. Today he's beautiful in the bright sunshine. A few tiny freckles dot his nose and his navy-colored eyes twinkle with delight. His grin stretches across his entire handsome face lighting up all of his features. The wind tousles his brown hair in every which direction making him a sexy, disheveled mess. Just the way I like him. Simply perfect.

He's right. This *is* love.

My heart nearly bursts with joy any time my husband bounces our adorable daughter on his knee or rubs my belly reverently. His smiles are frequent and they are a salve to parts of my heart that are still hissing from being burned. Not a day goes by where I don't think about what led me to War.

Fate had a plan.

The psycho bitch knew we were meant to be together.

What she didn't tell me was it would cost everything I loved to be with him.

Mom. Dad. Brandon.

And even Gabe.

My therapist tells me it's okay to miss them. Three men who supposedly loved me but ended up cutting my heart out, each one in their own way, still managed to make my heart ache from time to time. She tells me it's normal. *I find it far from normal.* The ache for them feels like a betrayal to War. And that sense of betrayal breeds anger.

After all this time, I'm *still* angry.

Apparently that's normal too.

She assures me eventually I can move past all the anger. That I should forgive them for what they did. Even Gabe. *Especially Gabe.* So I can move on, according to her. By letting go of the pain of my past, I can make room for all the good things my future has in store.

And most days, I am able to find the strength to agree with her. I search deep inside my splintered heart and I seek out the goodness each one had to offer. Before disease and money and stress drove them to carry out terrible atrocities on the one they loved most. Those days, I feel strong. I'm a warrior—a hero in my own story.

It's the other days that are hard. The days where I feel like I'm the last one on the board protecting her king with the bloodiest damn sword around. Guilt drips from me like blood from all of the casualties in my war. Those days, it's crushing. Those days, I don't feel strong at all.

But the war is how I found my peace.

The war was worth it.

War was worth it.

When I feel our son rolling around in my belly or when Hannah falls asleep against my chest, I know. I know that every single second of this was all necessary in some fucked-up way. The battle was truly ugly but my peace is more beautiful than words could ever describe.

"Oooh," Hannah babbles and points at the choppy ocean. She toddles closer toward the water's edge and I trail behind her as War and Land dive into discussion about a new client behind us. My daughter is brave and doesn't fear the crashing waves. Instead, she squeals and runs toward them. No hesitation. No reservations. No strategy.

She doesn't worry about the evils of the world because she has two parents who do enough worrying about that for her entire lifetime.

My daughter is free.

War and I will be the parents who protect her.

She'll never know the terrors we faced. Life, for her, will be perfect. We'll make sure of that.

"Mamamama!" she tells me with a sweet giggle and splashes into the warm water. A wave rushes toward us causing her to lose her balance and she plops onto her butt in the sand. I smile and reach for her small hands to help her stand back up. Once she's stable again, I clasp my fingers around her tiny wrist and let her guide me along the shore.

I'm lost in thought, a smile playing at my lips when the familiar sick dread washes over me. A shiver skitters down my spine and I jerk my head over my shoulder. My therapist assures me that because I never had closure with Gabe, I'll always be paranoid to a certain extent. She tries to get me to relax and not worry about what I can't control. He's dead and I need to move on.

Yeah, I get it.

But each time, I look over my shoulder. I expect to lock eyes with his heated coffee-colored ones. To be paralyzed in fear as he descends upon me like the beast from hell devouring his next dark soul—to make me pay for those in my destructive wake. Brandon's blood on my hands plagues me worst of all. I helped shape him into the dragon that annihilated the sweet boy from my past. And when I had a hand in slaying him, I became the biggest player in Gabe's twisted mindfuck game.

A game where there were no winners.

Just death and blood and loss.

I'm simply surviving one day at a time with my broken king at my side. Together we fight the dark demons of our past by focusing on the blonde angels in our future.

A rumble of thunder in the distance makes me jump and I squint to see where the storm is coming from. Dark clouds are forming further on down the coast which means it won't be long before the bad weather makes it here.

War's laugh cuts right through my sullen haze and wraps itself around my heart. Whenever I let these guilty thoughts infect me, he always finds a way to push them back out and instead fills me with his love.

It's enough.

It's more than enough.

And it works.

I can let down my guard and enjoy the moment. As the wind picks up and blows my hair into my face, I close my eyes and let out a small breath. Life is good. This *is* love, like he said. Fate may be the evil bitch but it's Love who's the stubborn one. Love doesn't care if you think you're underserving or unworthy. Love doesn't give a rat's ass about your past or who you've hurt along the way. Love doesn't care if you have blood on your hands.

Love is selfish and she always gets what she wants.

And Love is the one who's teamed up with Fate. They, for some crazy-ass reason, think I deserve this beautiful life.

The war in my heart still wages on.

But this?

My gaze flits from my daughter's blonde curls to War's joyous grin as he watches us from beside his father. I rub my belly and smile back at them. *This is peace, baby.*

Johan

If you love someone, set them free.

Whoever made up that crock of shit line should be shot in the head. If you love someone, you should protect them. Watch over them. Make sure they're happy. You should do whatever it takes to see their breathtaking smile over and over again.

You most certainly don't set them free.

That would be stupid and unsatisfying.

I know love and it grows each day with every grin on her pretty face—smiles I can't seem to get enough of.

"A storm's rolling in," a sexy, husky voice says behind me, distracting me from my thoughts.

I groan in pleasure when she wraps her arms around my waist and lays her cheek on my bare back. Alejandra is my angel. My miracle. And I owe her my life.

"The beach is still busy," I muse as my eyes zero in on the little girl playing in the sand farther up the beach. "What do you think? Another thirty minutes and it'll be pouring down rain?"

She pulls away and then finds my hand. I squeeze her soft palm before bringing it to my lips and pressing a kiss to the back of it. Alejandra has the hands of an angel. My wife is a surgeon and a damn good one at that. She's always babbling after a few days' worth of rounds about the many lives she's either improved or saved. I listen with rapt attention because I owe it to her. Because at one time, she saved me.

Her long, almost black hair whips around her in the wind. I remember the first time I saw her. The day I stumbled onto the deck of her old house farther up the coast, soaking wet, pushed through her back door, and collapsed on her kitchen floor. She'd been shocked at first but when she crouched next to me to take my pulse, I'd stared straight into her honey-colored eyes and said, "I'm not ready to die."

Her shocked features turned sad for a moment before a look of sheer determination took over. Alejandra saved me that day on her kitchen floor. She performed what I call a miracle and nursed me back to health in her home.

My wife never asked questions.

She never probed into my past.

Alejandra protected me when I was unable to protect myself.

"God sent you to me," she'd said with utmost certainty.

And I never argued.

Maybe it was divine intervention. God must have been playing in our lives because when I'd seen the wedding photos on her mantle later after I'd healed, I saw her kissing a man with dark, wavy hair and deep brown eyes. I learned it was her late husband. Alejandra was a widow. And her previous husband resembled me. Little did she know, she'd traded in her good guy with one of the bad. But maybe, just maybe, God didn't care. He knew deep down I deserved a second chance at happiness. I'd always be a bad guy, but bad guys deserve love too, right?

Long before she moved from Venezuela to California, she'd been married to Johan Cruz-Diez. He'd been the love of her life before a sudden and massive heart attack stole him from the stunning doctor.

And man, is she stunning.

Alejandra has curves in all the right places. I love clutching her thick thighs when she rides my cock, her big tits bouncing heavily in front of me. My dick twitches and I smile. She's also quite a needy freak in bed. I guess losing your husband and then finding him again will make a woman insatiable. I'm all too happy to satisfy her needs.

"We better close up the patio umbrella so it doesn't blow away, Johan," she tells me as she bends to pick up a shell. I admire her big, round ass in her turquoise bathing suit that makes her skin seem more tan than usual. Her ass is fucking divine.

"I'll take care of it," I promise and squeeze a handful of her ass as she stands. "I want you naked and on your knees when I get back inside. I'm ready to fuck my beautiful wife."

Her eyes close and she lifts her chin toward the heavens, her thick, red lips parted. I know she's thanking God for sending me to her. After that day she healed me, she always called me Johan, her dead husband's name. And I never corrected her. It simply made it easier to obtain an identification as him and fall into the perfect life he left. Into his wife's tight, gorgeous ass.

Definitely divine intervention.

And here I thought God didn't like the devil. That he was an outcast shunned from heaven. Clearly, I was mistaken.

"I love you, Johan," she tells me, a fierce love burning bright in her eyes.

Tugging her to me, I spear my fingers into her wild hair and kiss her hard enough to steal her breath. When she's gasping for air, I pull away and flash her a grin. "I love you too, sweet girl."

She beams at me before bouncing away back toward our home. I know in another fifteen minutes, she'll be screaming Johan's name as I shove my cock into her tight ass. I'll come all over her back and tell her how much I love her too.

Of course we both know her love will never measure up. It'll never be the true love that owns the rest of my heart—a love that's actually a genetic piece of me. But like we've done from day one, Alejandra and I play our parts to indulge the needs of each other. It's what makes us happy.

It's how a perfect marriage works.

My gaze drags back over to *her*. The one with the brilliant, bright smile, pretty blue eyes, and silky blonde hair. I ignore the men behind her as they gather up blankets, toys, and lawn chairs. I even ignore the pregnant one—the one with long, pale locks that whip in the wind. The one who used to consume my every thought.

Not anymore.

She now shares that place with someone equally important.

Someone just as perfect.

And *that* is true love.

The last day I was with her, I overheard her telling her stupid, pussy boy ex-boyfriend that she was pregnant. Pregnant with *my* child. She didn't need to say those words—that I was the father—I knew.

I frown thinking about 'ol pussy boy. A better man would mourn his death, feel things like guilt, remorse, pity, but I am not a better man. Quite frankly, I feel nothing for him. I do have to hand it to him though for fighting for what he wanted. And he did put up a good fight. But in the end, we were at war. He was in my way and there could only be one man left standing—no room for boys.

My thoughts leave the past as I stare at my future. Pride blossoms in my chest and I grin at the little girl playing on the beach. Of course, she can't see me from this distance, but I know it's her. I'll watch over my beautiful daughter each day and then one day, when she's old enough to understand, I will explain to her who her real father is. Maybe when she's seven. Her mother certainly seemed well aware of me by that age—the age I pulled my car into the driveway next to her house that first time. Those blue orbs of hers shimmered from her front porch with curiosity and instant adoration. I expect it will be the same way for my daughter when that time comes.

I will pull her into my arms and never let go.

I'll give Alejandra the child Johan was never able to.

I'm a patient man and will make this happen, in time. Until then, I'll enjoy my new life. The life Johan wasn't man enough to hang onto.

With one last longing gaze at my child who is now saddled on her mother's hip, I turn and leave her. As raindrops begin to pelt me, I trudge through the sand back to the house and up the steps of the back deck. Efficiently, I work the handle of the umbrella and secure it as I promised my wife I would.

Once inside, I shove my swim trunks down to the floor and follow the trail of sand that leads to where she'll be waiting on her hands and knees. With my dick in hand, I smile at how sweet life really is, and fist my cock several times to prime myself for Alejandra's tight hole.

They say the good guys always win, right?

I chuckle darkly to myself.

Not this time.

This Isn't Over, Baby is up next…

THIS ISN'T OVER,
baby

They'd won the battle and I held up the white flag of defeat…

But the war wasn't OVER.

I suffered the aching loss of what they had stolen from me.

OVER and OVER again, my heart broke.

The white Queen and the black King had taken OVER the game

and ruled for what seemed like eternity.

Until one day, eternity was finally OVER.

I was the dark knight who would rise again and conquer.

I was the man who would win OVER the most important piece on the board.

A slayer. A protector. A father.

A new king with the blackest of hearts.

And head OVER heels in love with…

The little princess who owned my twisted soul.

Sometimes the villains don't just want their happy ending…

They demand it.

This isn't OVER, baby.

This will never be OVER.

chapter
ONE

Gabe
The Past

"Next."

My father's bored, gruff tone grates on my nerves and I itch to tug at the knot of my tie. But his shrewd nearly black eyes are on me—always on me—waiting for me to show one tiny sliver of weakness. Weakness is what he feeds on. What he has for breakfast, lunch, and fucking dinner. And he's been feeding on me since I was ten years old. So instead, I fist my hands and I keep my features relaxed as I wait for his stupid little show to fucking end. He may be hungry, but I won't be the one feeding his crazy-ass monster tonight. No, one of the shivering, bound, and crying girls standing in front of our fireplace will. As the next girl stumbles into the room, I close my eyes and let my mind flit to the past. Almost eight years ago, my life changed with the whap of a belt against my flesh.

"Your whore mother left us." That was his only explanation of why Donna Sharpe wasn't in the living room slurping down one of her signature dirty martinis after school one day. I'd been confused because, quite frankly, at ten, I had no idea what a whore was. When I cried for the loss of the calmer parent in my home, my father changed. His annoyed expression turned into one of rage, and that day he took out every ounce of his fury of her leaving on me. His expensive leather belt on my bare ass tore the skin to shreds.

But that's not what broke me.

He crushed me later that night. When the house grew silent, and I'd cried myself dry, he stepped into my room and promised to make it all better. That night, he kissed away the pain on my backside, and in the process, twisted my head into a tangled mess of strings that he would go on to pull whenever he wanted.

My father devoured my innocence, and now that he can no longer feed on me, he's transforming into a starved animal. His need to prey on the weak disgusts me. It only shows he isn't as strong as he thinks he is. He may traipse around in five thousand dollar suits and drive an expensive sports car, but my dad is a pussy.

It took this past summer for me to come to this conclusion. When he'd come into my room after I'd spent a week at summer camp, something in me snapped. I'd watched other guys my age sneak off with girls at night. Kids all around me were happy. Naïve. Untouched. And I realized that I owed him nothing.

But he owed me everything.

The moment he slurred out my name and dragged the covers off my half-naked body, the fear and revulsion that always made me immobile was no longer present. Instead, rage—a glorious fucking feeling—lit a fire inside of me and I exploded. The fucker put up a good fight for a drunk asshole, but I bashed my fists against my father's face until he was unmoving. My knuckles were bruised and achy, but my pride was restored.

My father never touched me again.

Instead, he treated me like an annoyance. A burden. A fucking bother. Like nothing ever happened.

But *everything* happened.

That night, I transformed.

I became someone better.

I became my own monster. A monster dead set on not letting him feed off me ever again. I became invincible as far as he was concerned.

Next month I'll be graduating from high school, and I'll go on to college. Away from my father. Away from my hellish past. I'll make a life and become someone. For once, I'm not the scrawny, lanky kid with the messy hair and quiet disposition. After that night, I began working out—fueled on by the desire to always be stronger than that beast. Eight months later and I had filled out everywhere. My shoulders were broad, I had abs, and I was no longer someone he could intimidate. Girls started to notice me and guys wanted to be my friend.

I was no longer weak.

"They're all so terrified," Grant Sharpe's gravelly voice growls, interrupting my thoughts when the last girl comes to stand beside the three others.

Four girls.

All of them young.

Some my age, some considerably younger.

But one stands out among the others.

A girl with bright blue eyes and messy blonde hair eyes the group in the living room with disgust. Where the other girls are crying and huddling together, this one looks as though she wants to slaughter every one of us.

My father, his best friend, Lance, his accountant, Gordon, his attorney, Jack, and me. Four girls, four men, and me. These "pussy parties" as good 'ol Dad called them, were nothing more than a sick form of human trafficking of under-aged girls. Lance, Gordon, and Jack are all married, and their wives think they participate in monthly poker night with my father. Something innocent and legal. None of them know.

I've always known.

At fifteen, I walked in on one of their parties by mistake when I was supposed to be sleeping. It was then that I became the official mascot. The kid they poked fun at while they smoked their cigars and bid on girls. I hated every second of it. You see, father, in his spare time, recruited girls for a human trafficking ring. And their monthly "poker night" was where they test drove the merchandise before they sold them to the distributors.

Despite hating what happened during them, I began to look forward to those nights. Those were the nights when I would watch girls who were weak and breakable. I was stronger than them. Not the weakest in the bunch. For one night a month, I was a man.

Of course, he never let me do anything but sit and watch from afar, a hard-on straining in my slacks and heat burning my cheeks. I'd craved to lose my virginity to one of them. I even fantasized about falling in love with one of them—had thoughts of rescuing them from the biggest villain I know and running far, far away. But each time, my hopes and dreams were snuffed out as every one of my father's friends took their pick and disappeared to the other rooms of the house. By the next morning, they were always gone.

Tonight wouldn't be any different except when girl number four's eyes meet mine, I see a flash of something that stirs my heart. She's caged and wild. Everything in her screams to be set free. The girl is different. Not weak at all.

My gaze skims over her naked flesh and lingers over her perfect tits. Small and perky. I can almost feel my mouth watering with the need to suck on her nipple. A small groan escapes me the moment my dick thickens. I continue skimming over her flesh. Unlike the other girls, she's dirtier. Bony. Hardened. She has a small tattoo of a black heart on her hipbone. I become fixated on the ink that mars her flesh and wonder how old she really is. The other three girls are sixteen or seventeen, but number four looks like she might be eighteen or nineteen. Our eyes meet again, and something passes between us.

Not a plea.

Not fear or terror.

A threat.

I will kill all of you. Just untie me and watch.

The smile on my lips is immediate, and I wink at her, flashing her a message of my own in one simple glance. *I'd cut you loose and help, if I could.*

"What's the matter, boy?" Gordon says with a sneer from beside me. "You got a thing for one of the pieces? Which one? Let me guess…" He trails off and saunters over to them. They shriek— all of them but number four, of course. She bares her teeth at him, and I wish he'd get close enough for her to take a bite. "Not this one. Her tits are too big for a little boy like you, and this one looks like a fucking boy with her stupid haircut. This other girl has some fucked-up acne and you're way too pretty for that, Gabey," he mocks. Then he continues down the line until he stands in front of the last girl. "But this one. She's something special, isn't she? Is this the one you like?"

A growl rumbles in my chest, but I swallow it down, knowing *he's* watching me. When I don't answer, Dad tosses a piece of ice from his glass at me. "Answer him, Gabriel."

I swallow down the fury and swat the ice out of my lap onto the floor. "Four. I like four."

"My name is Krista. I am *not* a number," she hisses, spittle spraying him.

He wipes at his cheek with the back of his hand. "Krista," he says with a dark chuckle. "You'd eat that boy for lunch. He's kind of a wimp. You need a man like me or his daddy over there. A man who'll fuck you until you bleed. Gabriel wouldn't even know where to stick it in."

All the men laugh at my expense, and my cheeks blaze with embarrassment.

"I know where to put it," I snap and cross my arms over my chest. I may be a virgin, but I'm not stupid.

Gordon laughs again and grabs a handful of her tit. She yelps out in pain, and I'm already at my feet before I even realize I've blown my cool facade.

"Let go of her," I bark out. My jaw clenches and one of my newly defined muscles ticks in my neck. "I want to buy her." The words are spoken before I even register what they mean. But as soon as I say them, I stand behind them.

She'll be the girl.

I'll save Krista and show them I'm not weak.

Her determined eyes meet mine and they flash with appreciation. She sees me as an accomplice. A stepping stone to get her the hell out of here.

"Absolutely not." Father's voice causes prickles of rage to wash over my flesh.

"Ten thousand," I blurt out.

I know how these things work. These guys pay a certain amount for the girl they want, and Dad collects the money. Once a year they go to Vegas with the money in the pot, somewhere I'm not invited—mascot or not—and they have a boys' weekend where God only knows what takes place. The most any of them have ever paid was six thousand and that was for a pretty Hispanic girl who shockingly had her clit pierced. She certainly wasn't a virgin, but they all wanted her.

"You don't have ten thousand." Dad laughs and slaps the leather of the arm on his recliner. "You don't have shit, Gabriel. It's all mine, remember?"

I swallow down my hate for the man and jerk my gaze to meet his glare. "I have a trust fund," I seethe. "Mom started it for me, remember?"

He doesn't like his words thrown back at him and the reminder of my mother has him quaking with unmasked rage.

"Oh, come on," Lance says, poking fun at me, "let the wimp get his dick wet. The kid's not as scrawny as he used to be. Maybe it's about time he fucks for the first time."

I let Lance's comment roll off me as I keep my hardened stare on my father. Dad's lips pull into a sneer. "You're not eighteen yet, mama's boy. So don't go getting all high and mighty."

"I'll lend it to him, Grant," Jack says, and I jerk my gaze over to where he sits with his fingers steepled in front of him, hiding his wolfish grin. "Plus sixty-nine percent interest."

His friends all laugh, each one bolder than usual as they fly high on their high dollar cocaine, but I snap my glare back to my father who regards me coldly, a humorless expression marring the face so similar to the one I see in the mirror each morning. Several seconds pass while he remains motionless. I know he's contemplating ways to hurt me, but I don't care. In a couple of months, I'll be out of here anyway so it doesn't matter.

"Five thousand. Lend him five grand. I'll pay the other half because we're going to share her." His words dig a knife deep into my gut, but I don't argue. Instead, I give him a clipped nod.

"Fine."

The men holler with obnoxious cheers, but I tune them out as my eyes find Krista's. She now seems shaken, and I momentarily wonder if it's by the idea of two men having her instead of one. I implore her with my gaze to be strong. Her lip trembles, but a certain understanding passes between us.

I will save you, beautiful. Just give me a chance.

The rest of the evening is a blur as the men negotiate what—scratch that, *who*—they want. Apparently, the one with the boy's haircut was their choice piece of meat because they engage in a bidding war over her. Once the money passes hands and the men drag away their prizes, I turn to Dad.

"Take her to your room. I'm giving you an hour with her before I come up. Don't try anything stupid," he barks out as he stands and strides over to the bar to refill his tumbler.

I nod, adrenaline surging through me, and make my way over to Krista. As soon as I reach for her, she shies away and turns her back. I grab on to her bicep and pull her to me. My lips find the shell of her ear and I whisper into it. "Trust me, sweet girl."

Then, I guide her out of the living room and toward the stairs without sending a glance my father's way. She stumbles up the steps, but I'm there to keep her from falling. Soon, we're in my room and I'm shutting the door. Once I've locked it, I smile at her.

"You're so beautiful," I praise. I know I sound like a fucking fool. I'm not exactly Casanova with the girls, but it's the truth. Underneath all the dirt and bravery, she's really pretty. Her lips are full and pink. I love how slender and pale her neck is—I crave to mark it up with my teeth. My dick reacts to the mental image, causing the heat of embarrassment to singe my skin.

"Untie me," she orders.

I frown, disappointed in her not acknowledging my compliment, and motion for her to turn around. "Don't try and run away. Dad'll end this as quickly as it started if you do. Play along with me and when the time is right, I'll get you out of here. But you have to trust me, Krista."

"If that's your way of asking me to go steady, I'm going to have to pass. Your *family* is a touch too dysfunctional for my taste," she snaps and wiggles her purple fingers at me.

I sigh because there isn't any response to what I already know. With a grunt, I drop to my knees behind her and start to work at the knots at her wrists. Her ass is perfect, and I'm overcome with the strong urge to kiss it.

"How old are you?"

She huffs. "Almost nineteen."

My eyebrows knit together as I wonder what made them pick up a girl who wasn't young like the others. "Don't tell my dad that. You're seventeen like me if he asks."

She doesn't respond. The moment I've loosened her wrists, she slips out of my grasp and runs to the other side of my bed. Her hand is free from the bindings in an instant and she snatches my bedside lamp up.

"Stay away from me!" she hisses and casts a wary glance at my bedroom window.

I shake my head at her as I stand. "Put the lamp down. And you'll eat pavement if you jump from that window. Let me handle this, beautiful."

"Stop calling me that!"

Another pang of disappointment washes through me. "Please just put it down. If he comes in here and sees you like this, he won't be as nice as me. Let me figure out a way to get you out of here."

Ignoring me, she throws the lamp in my direction but it doesn't go very far, since it's still plugged in, and lands on the bed. She's fiddling with the window by the time I reach her. My arms wrap around her and I pin her naked back to my chest.

"Stop," I order. Having her bare flesh pressed against my suit has my dick hardening. She's dirty, but a faint scent of lotion—something unfamiliar to me—floods my senses. It smells fresh and clean. It's a direct contrast of the girl wiggling in my arms.

"Let go of me!" she shrieks. "Are you hard right now?!"

Her words have me clenching my eyes closed. *Fuck. Fuck. Fuck.* "No," I lie and wrangle her over to the bed. "I told you to stop moving."

She cries out when I tackle her onto the bed. Her body is beneath mine, and I have to look away from her wild eyes, so I don't go crazy with the need to thrust into her. Her thrashing is only serving to make me more excited.

"If he thinks I can be a man, he'll leave me be. So just go along with this and he'll leave us alone. I'll get you out of here. Trust me, you want me fucking you and not him. He's a cruel bastard."

Her body trembles, but resignation courses through her. "Don't hurt me."

Grinning, I slowly pull one hand from beneath her and stroke a blonde strand from her eyes. "I would never hurt you."

I lean forward and press a soft kiss to her lips. I'd kissed a girl named Julia at summer camp because the other kids dared us. After what was the most dizzying and exhilarating moment in my life, she laughed at me and told everyone I tasted like cucumbers. Something tells me this kiss will be better. Krista won't belittle me because she needs me to be her hero.

I'll be her fucking hero.

"He's probably listening on the other side," I whisper to her. "Get it together for me, sweet girl."

Her eyes well with tears and she nods. "Okay."

I reluctantly release her and right the lamp back on the table while keeping my eyes on hers. Her perky tits bounce with each nervous breath she takes. When I shed my jacket, her eyes widen with fear.

"I. Won't. Hurt. You."

She nods again and tears her gaze from me as I undress. My dick is nothing to be ashamed of and I want her to see it. I want her to see I'm all man—not a wimp like my dad and his friends say. Her curiosity wins out because she once again flits her eyes over to me. I watch with pleasure as she skims over my body with a look of interest.

Once I'm fully naked, I crawl onto the bed beside her. I'm not sure what to do with her, but I know what my dad expects. He is going to want me to take her. Hard. The way he and his repulsive friends do. And once he takes his turn, I'll make him sorry. I'll save her from this hellhole, and we'll go somewhere. Together.

"I have a confession," I say with a smile as I tenderly stroke her flat stomach.

She shudders at my touch but regards me with pinched brows.

I can't look at her when I say it. "I'm…a, um," I struggle, my father's taunts echoing in my head. "I'm a virgin. I know how sex works, though, so you don't have to worry about me putting it in your ass by accident…like they said," I rush out and then snap my mouth shut. *So much for not making a stupid ass out of myself.*

Her eyes flicker to mine. "We don't have to do this," she murmurs. "We can pretend."

Groaning in frustration, I run a shaky hand through my hair. I hadn't thought of that and now

I feel foolish that I'm three seconds from losing my load against her naked thigh. I need to fix this. "What I mean is, I have had sex." My eyes clamp closed and I hate the way my cheeks burn with shame. "It's just been—"

Her eyes widen. "It's just been what?"

A heavy sigh rushes out of me. *God, why do I have to be such a fuck up?* I push myself up and turn my back on her, sitting on the side of the bed, my head hanging between my legs.

I hear the bed shift, and after a second, she's sitting next to me.

"Hey, are you okay?"

I shake my head and let out a bitter laugh—a laugh that's far from funny. "My dad…he used to force me," I mutter. Our eyes meet and her concerned, furrowed eyebrows motivate me to continue. "He used to force me to do things a dad shouldn't do with his kid." There. I said it. I drop my gaze to the floor and fixate on the carpet to avoid her gaze. I've confessed, and now it's hanging in the air between us—dirty and dark but no longer hidden. And, although I can't stand the thought of looking over at her, at seeing the pity probably in her eyes, it feels good to get it out. To share it with someone. I've held it in for all these years. His filthy secret.

"I'm so—"

I jolt and glare at her. "I don't need your pity."

"Did I say I felt fucking sorry *for* you?" she snaps, but then flashes me a small smile. "What I was going to say was that I'm sorry your dad's an asshole. People like us deserve better than the lot that's given to us."

People like us.

Abused. Beaten. Molested. Hated.

My chest aches from her words and I lie back down on the bed. "Uh…"

A pound on the door saves me from the mortifying moment.

"Yeah?" I bellow.

Krista scrambles to sprawl out next to me on the bed and flashes a quick smile at me as she tenderly runs her fingers along my chest. "We don't deserve this," she whispers. "We'll get out of here. There's a whole wide world out there for people like us—a world where *we* get to decide our fate."

Such a concept is mind-blowing. A world without a greedy, sick, manipulative father sounds pretty good to me.

"Did you fuck her yet?" he demands, interrupting my thoughts.

I grit my teeth and say the words I hate myself for saying. "Yes, Dad."

His laugh is demented on the other side of the door. I can hear the key turning in the lock and soon his giant frame fills the doorway. My entire body quakes at seeing him in my room after so long. His eyes lazily skim over us and he shakes his head.

"Nice try, Gabriel. Fuck her. I'm going to watch."

She whines, but I run my fingers over her stomach in a way I hope soothes her.

"I can't do it with you in here," I growl and my jaw clenches.

He smirks as he sits in my desk chair. "Wouldn't be the first time I've watched you come."

The room spins as flames of embarrassment engulf me. I force out the things he's done to me—the things my body did that were out of my control—and I quiver with hate.

"Fuck you," I snap.

He laughs but thankfully doesn't respond. "Just fuck the girl and we're all good, son."

I roll myself on top of her and my lips graze along her ear. "I'll be so gentle. I swear. Please let me so I can get you out of here." My words are soft and nearly inaudible.

Her slight nod is enough, and I waste no time. Our lips meet again and this time, she lets me kiss her like I kissed Julia from summer camp. Krista tastes sweet, like gummy bears, and I want to suck on her tongue all night. My kiss must turn her on because she untucks her legs from beneath me and wraps them around my hips. The heat of her pussy pressed against my aching dick is too much. I want inside of her so bad, but I don't want to rush this.

"Just hurry," she begs.

I groan with disappointment and sit up slightly. Using my hand, I stroke myself for a second. Blindly, I poke at her opening and am met with tight resistance.

"Wrong hole," she bites out.

Dad laughs from behind me, and I nearly lose my hard-on. "I'm sorry," I grit out, overcome with shame. I move the tip of my cock up a couple of inches.

She squirms and spreads her legs further as if to help me find the right place. Her pussy feels dry, not at all like what I'd imagined it would feel like, and I'm still having trouble pushing it into her. My dick is practically weeping with need and it causes it once again to slide between her ass cheeks.

"Jesus," she whimpers and grips me. I nearly go blind with bliss. Letting go of the embarrassment of her having to put me inside her, I allow her to guide me to the right place. As soon as the thick head of my dick makes it past the dry opening, I easily slide the rest of the way in. My dick throbs with the need to come. I hold still for a moment, so I don't lose my load right away.

I fall back against her and try to kiss her, but she keeps her lips pressed together. I'm humiliated that she's treating me like I'm the villain. With gritted teeth, I thrust into her as hard as I can. She yelps, and it dizzies me. I do it again and again, her small moans driving my need. I'm about to explode at any second.

"Stop."

Dad's harsh command has me halting and jerking my angry gaze over my shoulder. "The fuck, why?"

He rises from his seat and stalks over to the side of the bed. "Hurt her."

My cock begins to soften as I shake my head. "No."

Fuck my life. His salacious glare confirms that he knows he's got me. "Fucking hurt her or I will."

She whimpers again, and I gape at him in horror. "No."

He pulls his 9 mm from his slacks and points it at her. "Now."

The need to rescue her from his bullet wins over and I do the only thing that feels right. I slide my hand to her throat and grip it. She immediately clutches my wrist and claws at me, her eyes wide with an unspoken plea. Instead of releasing her, I hold her tighter. I'm saving her. If I don't do this, he'll kill her. I won't suffocate her—just hurt her a little, like he says.

"Perfect," he says with a growl.

Ignoring him, I thrust deep into her. My cock is hard again and I like the way her body grows limp beneath mine. I like the way her pretty pink lips are slightly purple.

"Will you kiss me now?"

She tries to nod, and I release her neck slightly so I can press my lips to hers. God, she tastes so fucking good. I'm pounding into her like a madman when my dad once again stops me.

"Did you even give her an orgasm?"

I jerk my head to him and once again my cheeks burn. "I, uh…"

"Let her ride you. You can access her clit better that way."

She gasps for air the second I release her throat to roll onto my back, our bodies still connected. Tears roll down her cheeks, but she doesn't try to evade me. Her sad eyes meet mine and she places her palms on my chest.

I don't even know where her clit is. Clumsily, I fumble between her legs until I touch something that makes her clench around my dick. The little nub stands out between her pussy lips and I massage it slowly. She continues to work her hips in a way that sends tingles down my spine while I rub her back in return. It's fucking sensational.

"Oh, God," she whimpers, and I realize I'm actually about to make her come. I intensify my efforts and seconds later, she's shuddering above me and shrieking. Her pussy clamps down around my cock and I explode inside of her.

My eyes slam shut as her body milks me for all I've got. It's the best feeling I've ever experienced. I'm still basking in the orgasmic glow when she's unceremoniously ripped from me.

"My turn."

I gape, too stunned to move, when he pushes her over the end of the bed. His dick is out, and he spreads her cheeks apart before slamming into her. She screams in pain, her eyes finding mine in panic.

"Stop!" I roar and rise to my knees ready to attack him.

He grunts and waves his gun at me before shoving it against the back of her skull. "I'm not finished fucking her tight ass yet."

She once again begs me with her eyes and I see red. Krista is mine to make love to. Not fucking his! I've made a promise to myself I'll save her. I won't let him ruin one more person. When I launch myself at him with a hate-filled scream, a bang echoes around the room. Something warm splatters my thigh and I nearly pass out.

No!

In a moment of uncontrolled fury, I tackle him off of her and wrestle him to the ground. The gun is still in his hand, but when I stomp on his throat with the heel of my foot, he groans and releases it. Once I snatch it from his uncoordinated drunk grip, I stand and tower over him.

My gaze travels over to the unmoving body of Krista, and I swallow down the bile in my throat. Leaving him choking on the floor, I rush over to her to check her pulse. I quickly ascertain that she won't be coming back from the deathly gunshot to her head. There is no pulse. She's dead. Fucking dead. I promised her I'd saved her and I didn't deliver. I *am* a goddamned pussy.

"Awww," he rasps out from behind me. "What're you going to do, boy?"

I growl and aim the gun at his cock. This man has done nothing but take and take from me. Well, now I'm the one taking whatever the hell I want. And right now, I want his pain. Another bang and he's howling for a God he's never worshipped to save him. *Yeah fucking right.*

"Fuck you."

I don't know if his life flashes before his eyes, but mine certainly flashes before mine.

Bitter images of a shattered childhood. A mother who once loved me—who used to take me to the zoo or the children's museum while Dad was away on business trips to offer a tiny bit of normalcy for her son. But my father's fists eventually ruined all that was good in her life, so she drank away the pain. Until the day she gathered the courage to save herself. She left me behind though. With a monster. A father who never hugged me. Never took me to Little League practice. Never loved me.

Never gave a flying fuck.

With a roar of over ten years' worth of pain ripping from my chest, I unload the rest of the bullets into his chest and skull. I keep pulling the trigger, even once the magazine is empty, unable to stop the outpouring of emotions that are flooding through me. He deserves more than death— he deserves hell. When the red haze of hate finally lifts, I watch with morbid satisfaction as the blood—crimson and thick—around his ruined body seeps into the expensive carpet. My chest is heaving, I'm dripping in sweat, and the room reeks of a pungent coppery odor of both a monster and his last victim.

"Who's the pussy now, old man?" I mutter to his corpse.

I take one last look at poor, bloody Krista before turning back to him. With all the disgust and hate from a decade of his punishments rushing through me, I spit on him and then kick his body.

It's finally over.

And one thing is for fucking sure.

I'm *not* weak.

Not anymore.

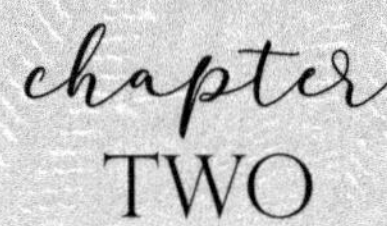

chapter
TWO

Gabe
The Present

"Johan," Alejandra pleads, her olive-colored hands clawing at my chest. "Don't leave me."

I'm an animal locked in a goddamned cage.

Pacing and angry.

Unfuckingcontrollable.

I push her away from me and stalk toward the window over the kitchen sink. It's my stalker post. Most days, I spend hours and hours praying they'll go down to the beach. And don't even get me started on when it rains. When I don't see them. Those days, I can barely hold it together.

"Our time is through, Alejandra," I say as I grip the countertop and peer out the window. "I have unfinished business. Business that doesn't involve you."

Her continued sobs grate on my nerves. I clench my jaw and squint my eyes. From this distance, I wouldn't be able to see her face. Not that she's out there this afternoon anyway. Sometimes, I climb up on their back porch after dark and watch them through the glass because I need to see her. Tonight will be one of those nights.

I close my eyes and envision her bouncy blonde curls. She gets bigger and smarter every day. Her laughter, which I can hear through the glass, is adorable as hell. Sometimes I feel like crashing through the glass, slaughtering the entire goddamn family, and taking her back home with me where she belongs.

I may be a psychopath, but I'm also her father.

To destroy her entire life would fuck her up. Just like my father fucked me up. And I will not be that asshole. Even I have some morals.

But lately, it's becoming harder and harder to stay put knowing she's growing up without my presence in her life. I know Baylee will love the child with all she's got. That's who she is, despite knowing I'm the girl's father. If the father was Satan, Baylee would still love her all the same.

"Johan…"

I tense at Alejandra's teary pleading. "You know that's not my fucking name," I say with a growl, refusing to look at her. It's been a little over two years since I stepped foot in her old kitchen where she brought me back to life. Where she slipped me right into the role of her late husband. We never discussed my real name. The crazy bitch just went right along living in her pretend bubble.

Well, I'm tired of fucking pretending.

"My name is Gabriel Sharpe."

She wraps me in a hug from behind and it relaxes me a bit. Whenever her big tits are smashed against me, I tend to get distracted. "I'll call you Gabriel if that makes you happy. But please don't leave me. I love you."

I turn to regard her. Her palms slide up my chest to my cheeks, which now sport a thick beard. She practically digs her nails into my flesh to make me look down at her. Brown, bloodshot eyes behind wet lashes look up at me.

"Don't leave me."

Inhaling a deep breath, I attempt to calm myself. I'm comfortable here. If I took the girl, I'd be on the run. Baylee wouldn't stop until she found her. I would have to kill the child's mother and that just isn't fucking happening.

I close my eyes. But perhaps, I could take them both…

"Gabriel," Alejandra whispers in desperation. "Stay."

Blinking my eyes open, I regard the beautiful woman. I'd miss her. I don't know what to do but this peeping Tom bullshit isn't cutting it. My daughter turned two a few months ago, and she doesn't even know me.

"Why? I'm not your real husband, love. You know this. My heart is there," I grumble and point at the window. "With her."

Tears stream down her face and she stands on her toes to reach me. "Your heart can be in both places. Besides," she murmurs and threads her fingers into my hair. "I have a reason for you to stay."

She tugs me lower and her hot breath tickles my ear as she whispers her reason. Her words have their intended effect on me because another moment later I'm on my knees worshipping her.

Kissing.

Adoring.

Thanking.

Alejandra's right. I can have the best of both worlds. And I will.

chapter
THREE

Hannah
Nearly sixteen years later…

Nature versus nurture. The debate that my eleventh grade Psychology teacher Mr. Collins couldn't seem to stop talking about last year. Over and over again. Were our behaviors as humans learned? Did the people who raised us teach us and mold us into the adults we were all becoming? Or, was it ingrained in us since birth. A simple genetic code woven together the moment our fathers spurt their seed into our mothers. A delicate pattern of traits and characteristics meshed together to create a unique human.

Mr. Collins believes in nurture. He was a child born to a crack whore and spent his entire life in the system, bounced from one abusive foster home to the next. It wasn't until he landed in a little old lady's home that he finally learned how to behave. He learned kindness and love. She taught him to be a man of integrity. To be accountable for his actions. To own up to his shortcomings and conquer this life.

I can remember the way his brown skin would glisten with a sheen of sweat as he lectured us with the passion of a thousand men charging into battle. It was mesmerizing and beautiful. His dark brown eyes would narrow as he snared each one of us in his gaze. He would preach about how it doesn't matter who you were born to—or the blood running through you—that you could become whoever you wanted.

To say he inspired me with his lectures was an understatement. I loved Mr. Collins. Loved the way he would place a hand on another student's shoulders as he worked out a problem with him on his assignment. Or the way he'd high-five the basketball players in the hall when they'd win a game. I even loved how he'd attend every softball game I played in with his wife and two kids. How his smiles never waned.

But as much as I loved Mr. Collins, he was wrong.

My parents have brought me up in this world with fierce love and protection. They've doted on my brothers and I. Provided us with everything we should ever need. Been there through good times and bad.

I believe human nature runs in our blood. That no matter what we do to change who we are, we'll always be a fragment of who are parents were. At least. Mr. Collins will always be the boy who came kicking and screaming into this world addicted to crack. That despite not knowing his real parents, he carries on their traits and behaviors. Maybe even unknowingly.

My father, Warren McPherson, has psychological problems. I know this because, despite my parents' desire to hide every single bad thing from my siblings and I, some things just won't stay swept under the rug. They can't hide the way my father counts seconds. His mouth always moving. His eyes darting back and forth as various scenarios torment him from the inside. He can flash me a grin and tickle my middle, but I see the struggle within him.

It's in his blood.

It's in *my* blood.

My mother has dozens of bookshelves at home filled with the works of Freud and Jung and

Horney. Books I've taken into my room and studied. Books that have both torn apart Mr. Collins's beliefs or supported them. Many of her books are highlighted, the pages frayed and torn from overuse. They talk of such things like obsessive compulsive disorders. Delusional disorders. Trauma related disorders. Personality disorders. And so on and so on.

Panic attacks used to seize me. Started when I was twelve years old, not long after the accident. I'd sit up in bed at night gasping for air that didn't seem to exist. Clawing at my throat until my dad would burst in, turn on my lamp, and speak calm words to soothe my mind. Mom always tried, but it was Dad who could reach me. Dad who always pulled me from my own inner darkness. Dad who, in the end, physically saved me.

Mom keeps a constant lock on her emotions. She hides them away with her smiles and her love. Never reveals what makes her who she is—what hides the true person within. She shelters my brothers and I from the world. Keeps us in our happy little bubble. Nurtures us.

But my nature always wins out…

I see a glimmering in my father's eyes—a certain recognition. Often, he tells me I remind him of his mother. His jaw clenches and his lips stay sealed, but I can tell he wants to grab me by the shoulders and explain the history that runs through me in greater detail. Explain how it taints my mind and heart.

My brothers don't understand. They're too much like Mom. Fierce and strong.

It's Dad, though, who recognizes I'm different.

"Mom would kill you if she saw you wearing that, Han."

My thoughts are ripped from the forefront of my mind and dragged away, back into the dark corners, as I affix my brother Ren with a devious grin. "Good thing she's in Italy then, huh?"

My overprotective younger, but taller, brother waves his phone at me with a smirk on his face. "I could show them. What do you think, Calder? Should I send Mom and Dad a picture of our underdressed sister?"

Calder, our fourteen-year-old brother, doesn't even look up from his phone as he inhales a slice of pizza and shrugs. When our parents aren't around, which isn't often, we tend to do crap they wouldn't approve of. Like eat foods we're not normally allowed to eat, go to parties we shouldn't go to, and dress like we've been threatened not to. Typical teenagers.

But it's Ren who keeps us all in line, despite me being the oldest. Ren is like Mom's secret spy. Lets us get away with just enough but pulls rank when we do something our parents would flip out about. It's irritating. And what's even more irritating is that after the heat of the moment is over, I can admit he was right to do so.

I'm the rash one—although Dad prefers brave.

I'm the quickest one to get angry—although Dad calls me passionate.

I'm the one always questioning why there are certain rules—Dad calls me intelligent.

"I'm almost eighteen," I bite at him in defense. "God, ever since you got your driver's license, you act like you're some big man. You're not Dad, little brother."

Nobody could ever be my dad. If anyone is like him, it's me. Not Ren. Ren is just like Mom. Definitely nature with him too.

"You look like a slut." His harsh words sting, and I flip him off.

The last person to call me a slut was Mrs. Collins after Mr. Collins was fired from our high school. I'm not a slut, though. She'd been sadly mistaken. I'm still a virgin. I don't mess around with boys, or girls for that matter. I'm just me. It wasn't my fault he fell in love with me.

You're delusional, he'd said that day.

You need help, he'd hissed that afternoon.

But the heart wants what the heart wants.

My heart wanted Mr. Collins. And he wanted me too, no matter how much he tried to deny it. I saw the way his eyes would turn molten when I'd bend over his desk to ask him a question. The way they'd darken when my cleavage was hanging in his face. The way his cock would harden between us when I'd throw my arms around him and hug his neck before class each day. The way his breath would come out in a sharp gasp when I'd whisper something inappropriate.

He'd been nurtured to be a good, faithful man to his wife. To follow the norms of our society and obey the rules. Because that's what the old lady had taught him to do.

But he couldn't deny his true nature.

His eyes refused to say no when I unbuttoned my shirt and revealed my breasts to him one day after class. His fisted hands and barely controlled restraint were proof his blood was running hot. That it wasn't a matter of nurture—it was his true nature surging wildly through his veins. He wanted me. Badly. Had we had more time, I could have been the one to give him a real lesson on the subject of nature versus nurture. To prove his trivial theories wrong.

All it took was one moment, though. One irritating moment, for someone to be in the wrong place at the wrong time and become a "witness" in the way he "leered" at my breasts. The way he'd "used his power of position over me." That he was staring at the tits of a "victimized, under-aged girl."

Mrs. Simms cried for me that day. Held my shirt together and ushered me out of that classroom and straight to the principal's office, despite the begging and cursing of Mr. Collins behind us. Stood on her soapbox and defended my honor against "that predator." I still miss Mr. Collins. Later that spring, it was Mrs. Collins who marched out onto the softball field at one of my games and told me I was a slut. That was after she slapped me. Took both coaches and my mother to drag her off that field.

I'm *not* a slut.

"Screw you," I snap and flip Ren off. "And you're an asshole."

Storming out of the kitchen, I stomp back toward my bedroom. Ren thinks he can judge me, but I don't see anything wrong with my black skirt and pink halter-top. I'm going to a college party so I should look at least college age. It's not like I'm trying to seduce my teacher or anything. My best friend, Kiera, will be wearing something no doubt way sluttier.

I am *not* a slut.

Once I'm in my room, I stand in front of my long mirror to look over my appearance. The short skirt shows off my long, toned legs—legs I work my ass off for in the gym and on the softball field. And the halter-top, thanks to a great push-up bra, makes my boobs look bigger. I look sexy. Ren can fuck right off.

With a huff, I switch on my hair straightener and set to smoothing out my long blonde hair. Once I'm satisfied that it's sleek and frizz free, I apply some makeup. Ren can get his panties all up in a wad after he sees me when I'm all made up. Tattle to Mom later if he wants.

You're rebellious and impulsive, she'll say.

But Dad will say I'm strong-willed and determined.

I smile at the mirror, and my blue eyes flicker with excitement. I've given myself smoky eyes, darkened my thick lashes with mascara, and applied some dark lipstick on my full lips. I look older. Definitely college aged. Tonight, I'm going to get laid.

That is, if I don't wuss out again.

My mind drifts to my last boyfriend, Brody. We'd dated for a while, and I was ready to lose my virginity to him last fall. But then, at the last minute, I freaked. God, he was furious. He'd said that for a rumored slut, I was a cocktease. When I gripped his bare balls in fury and gave them a tight squeeze, I forced him to take back his words. I am *not* a slut. With tears in his eyes, he retracted his words. Brody Stephens vowed to never say another word on the subject. And Brody's been true to his promise. Kid doesn't even make eye contact when we pass in the halls.

Sometimes I wish I would have just slept with him. I wish I would have just gotten over the worry of the painful loss of my virginity, and we could be dating as we speak. Who knows, maybe he'd have even wanted to marry me after we graduate. Most women these days want to go off to college and have successful careers before they get married or start their families. Not me. I want love…and I want it now.

My mind is lost to visions of me in a white dress with a handful of sweet-smelling daisies in my grip when my phone alerts me. When I pick it up, I see that it was Ren.

Ren: I'm sorry I was a dick.

Letting out a sigh, I type out a response.

Me: I'm not going to get pregnant. I'll be fine.

Ren: Call me if you need a ride home. I don't care how late it is.

I smile. He's so much like Dad, even named after him—Warren or Ren because it's much cooler. And while I appreciate my brother's protectiveness, sometimes he's overbearing. I wish he'd find a girlfriend, so he'd stop harassing me. Actually, scratch that. Thoughts of his last girlfriend have me shuddering.

Me: Thanks, Dad, but you'll have your hands full keeping an eye on Calder.

At this I laugh. Our younger brother is a zombie. While I'm athletic with softball and Ren's always on his board in the ocean, Calder doesn't get up off the couch. Mom says he's a techie like Dad. I just think he's a lazy ass.

Ren: Fuck off…but be safe while you fuck off.

Grinning, I start tucking everything into my purse, including my phone.

Before I leave my room, I take one last look in the mirror. Dad would say I was beautiful. I just hope some guy at this party thinks so, too. Starting college as a virgin is not on my list of things to do.

I'm going to do everything in my power to pop the proverbial cherry.

I may even have to act like a slut.

But I am *not* a slut.

"Oh my God," Kiera yells into my ear over the loud thumping music. "The guys here are all hot. And big. I bet they all have big cocks too unlike those losers we go to school with."

I laugh and peruse my friend's appearance. Her black hair is cut into a chin-length blunt bob. She's half Korean and has elegant features. Creamy skin. Almond-shaped eyes. High cheek bones. Super petite frame. But her eyes are the palest blue you've ever seen. That comes directly from her father's Scandinavian decent. She's gorgeous and pretty much lands any guy she smiles at.

"I feel out of place," I groan, and self-consciously run my palms down the front of my skirt. Earlier, I'd thought I looked hot. Now, I worry that I've made a damn fool of myself by trying too hard.

Kiera swats me on the butt, causing me to giggle.

"We're both hot so shush. Let's go find Corey," she says, grabbing my hand and guiding me through the throng of dancing bodies.

Corey is a guy she met at work who goes to college at the University of San Diego. He'd boasted that his fraternity was holding this end of year blow-out party and he invited her. Told her to bring her hot friends.

"Kiera!" A tall, lanky guy calls out. His brown hair is kind of long and hangs in his eyes, like in a young Justin Bieber kind of way. "My Asian angel!"

She laughs and swats at him, her flirt game in full effect. I flash him a fake smile. He's not that cute, but she seems into him. She always had Bieber Fever…

"And who are you? Malibu Barbie?" he questions with a half-grin. His brown eyes are rimmed bloodshot red. The guy's higher than a kite right now.

"Han McPherson," I say politely and hold my hand out to him.

His gaze lingers at my chest for a brief moment before he takes my hand. "Like Han Solo?" He laughs as he kisses the top of my hand. God, what a nerd. Kiera is in trouble for this crap. I thought we were coming to meet cool college guys, not Star Wars geeks. Older, more refined men. Someone who was going to take my virginity with style and finesse.

Refraining from rolling my eyes, I give him another tight smile. "Something like that."

"Come on," he says, never letting go of my hand. "Let me introduce you two ladies to some friends of mine."

Kiera laughs from beside me as Corey drags me through the frat house. We end up in a dark living room of sorts. People are lounging all over the place. It reeks of weed, and I think a couple over in the corner may even be having sex against the wall. I'm already over this party. Ren would be pissed, but he'd come get me if I called.

"Cheer up. We'll get a beer or something and then you can relax. You're wound up way too tight," Kiera says into my ear. "God, Corey is so hot. I'm going to get him drunk and then make crazy love to him."

I snarl my lip up in disgust. "With him? Are you sure?"

With a big grin, she nods. Then, she bounces off after him, leaving her best friend standing in the middle of a roomful of strangers.

"Pretty lame, huh?" A deep voice rumbles from behind me.

I turn to see a good-looking guy towering over me. He has hair as black as Kiera's, but it's long in front and styled to stick out in every which way. His grey T-shirt hugs his broad shoulders and massive chest. And his biceps, all the way to his wrists, are covered in tattoos. I drag my gaze from his body to look into his eyes. Bright green. Curious. Mischievous. And older…by several years. I bet he could pop a cherry without calling a girl a cocktease when she showed apprehension. I bet he would make a girl beg for it. I'm completely enthralled by him.

"I'm Julian," he tells me with a wide, crooked grin that makes my knees wobble a bit.

"And I'm Hunter."

Another guy, around the same age, comes to stand beside Julian. Hunter, as he calls himself, is even more beautiful than Julian. He's wearing a red polo shirt that barely fits him. The guy is ripped but he's missing all the tattoos Julian has. And Hunter has bright blue eyes and blond hair. Typical All-American guy. Abercrombie & Fitch models in the making. They're both hot as hell and Kiera's missing out.

"Uh, I'm Hannah."

They're both smiling at me, and I feel like melting right here on the floor in front of them. I'm so out of my league, but I won't deny I don't love the way they both devour me with their gazes. Their attention is on me. Consuming me. Drinking me up. I hope they get drunk on it.

"You look like you could use a beer or something. Loosen up, babe," Hunter says with a grin before walking away.

"We were just about to leave this lame party but then…"

I lift my gaze to meet Julian's twinkling jade orbs. His eyes are kind. Despite his outward, rugged appearance, he looks like the kind of guy you definitely would one day bring home to Mom. "Then what?"

"I saw you. Just standing there looking beautiful and bored. I figured misery loves company," he says in a low tone. He dips his head closer to mine and brushes his lips against my ear. "Plus, I knew I couldn't leave this party without hearing your voice or seeing your smile."

My cheeks heat and a shiver ripples through me. *God, Kiera is totally missing out!*

"You're a real life Romeo, huh?" I tease, my attempt to keep my voice light and playful fails. A tiny tremor of excitement makes my voice wobble. Would he be a gentle lover or like one of those guys who tied up a woman and spanked her until she came?

He reaches up and brushes a strand of hair that's stuck to my lipstick away from my face. His fingertip sends jolts of desire coursing through me.

"Babe, you have no idea."

I'm saved from any more stupid remarks on my end when Hunter returns. He hands us each a red solo cup. In an effort to hide my embarrassment, I take several chugs.

"Wow!" I choke out. "That's so strong. What did they put in it? Gasoline?"

Both men—*and God how they are men*—laugh at me. My mind briefly imagines a scenario with both of them. I'm sandwiched in between while each one of them fights to pleasure me. Their fingers and teeth scraping along my flesh as they both vie for their own piece. Heat burns from my cheeks, along my neck, and to my chest. I'm probably way out of my league, but I've melted into a puddle of want and desire. The only way I'm leaving these two is if someone drags me out of here.

I take another sip of the gasoline to hide my reactions to the sex on sticks standing before me. Neither of them seem to mind and continue their blatant staring. The heated level of interest in both of their eyes excites me and gives me hope about how the rest of the evening will go.

"You go to school here?" Hunter questions, standing too close for comfort. I can smell his delicious cologne, and I try not to inhale him.

"No. A different college," I lie.

They exchange a look. Julian grins and leans in to whisper in my ear again. "Don't lie, babe. Your eyes darken when you do it. A dead giveaway. You're in high school aren't you?"

Defeated, I nod.

Maybe I won't be losing my virginity after all.

The downfall with older men…they're too afraid to pursue the carrot dangling in their face for fear of society's rules and labels.

His palm finds my lower back, and he chuckles. The deep reverberation ignites every nerve ending in my body. "That's okay. You seem pretty mature to me. I won't tell anyone. Our little secret."

Maybe this one likes the carrot…

I flash him a thankful smile before chugging down the rest of the disgusting contents of my cup.

"Damn, girl," Hunter says with a smirk. "Slow down or some stupid frat boy's going to come steal you away from us. You'll wake up in the morning with an STD and pregnant or some shit."

When I gape at his crudeness, Julian growls from beside me. "Fuck off, Hunter. We'll look after her. I dare any of these asshole punks to take advantage of her. Fucking dare them."

Hunter shrugs his shoulders in defense. "I got your back, bro."

He takes my cup before sauntering off somewhere. When I turn to thank Julian for sticking up for me, I'm ensnared by his heated gaze. My eyes drop to his full lips. His lips are much more delicious looking than Brody's or Mr. Collins's ever were. I want to kiss him. He's so beautiful. I'm not sure I'll ever get the opportunity to kiss someone this good looking ever again. Standing on my toes, I swallow down my nerves and make my move. Closing my eyes, I brush a soft kiss against his perfect lips.

When I reopen my eyes, he's almost glaring at me. But the good kind of glaring. The kind of glaring that makes me think he wants every single part of me. Another shiver courses through me.

He gently grips my chin and stares at my lips. "That will never be enough." Then, his mouth descends upon mine. His kiss is urgent, but expert. It's as if he's kissed me a thousand times and knows exactly what I like. I let out a small, satisfied moan, running my fingers through his hair.

"Maybe she should be afraid of *you*," Hunter jokes, causing Julian and me to reluctantly pull from our kiss.

With a wink, Hunter hands me another cup. We spend the next few minutes discussing which classes they take here at the college. Julian's going to school for business, and Hunter's studying pre-law. They seem older—as if they are closer to Mr. Collins's age than mine—but I don't question them. Nobody lies about going to college. Well, unless they're younger and wish they were in college.

I don't miss the fact that while we talk, Julian stands close to me, almost possessively. Hunter seems to see it as a challenge because he touches me as often as he can. By the time I've finished my second glass, I'm dizzy and having a hard time keeping up with the conversation.

But one thing's for sure, they're both pretty to look at.

"You don't look so well, babe," Julian says, taking my cup. "I'm cutting you off."

I nod and relinquish the remnants of my gasoline.

"Come on, let's get you some fresh air. Do you have someone you want to call?" he questions.

He all but drags me out to the front porch where people are everywhere making out. It makes me want to make out with him, too, but I am afraid I'll puke. And that would be too ridiculously embarrassing.

A gust of cool air whips around me and I inhale the refreshing air.

"I really wanted to get to know you but you're about to pass out, babe," Julian says, nervousness in his voice. "There's no way in hell I'm leaving you at this party in this state. Some fucker will mess with you."

His words are like molasses. Sticky. Messy. Sweet. God, I'm so confused.

"Let me see your phone. Want me to call your mom? Dad?" he questions.

I have the sense to shake my head. "P-Please, no," I slur. "C-Call Ren. That's my bro—"

The last thing I see is Julian's worried gaze before the world turns black.

chapter

FOUR

Hannah

"Hannah," a deep voice rumbles. "Can you hear me?"

I blink my eyes open slowly. Dark green eyes are focused on mine. "Mmm."

He frowns and glances somewhere else before looking back at me. "I think you have alcohol poisoning or something. I've been calling your brother over and over, but he's not picking up. Even tried a Calder on your phone. Should I call your parents?"

I'm shaking my head, but it only makes me dizzier. "No—Italy—Ugh."

I fade out once again. When I reopen my eyes, Julian is carrying me.

"Shhh," he whispers. "I'm taking you someplace safe. Hunter's dad is a doctor. He'll make sure you're not going to die on us, babe. Just try to rest."

His words are like a lullaby, and I fall back asleep.

"Hannah."

I crack open my eyes. I'm trying to take stock of my surroundings, but I don't recognize anything around me. The room seems expensive. And I'm lying on top of a bed. My heart rate spikes, but Julian's tender touch on my forehead calms me.

"Relax, babe. You're safe. Hunter's talking to his dad now, downstairs. We're going to get you well."

I nod but can barely keep my eyes open. He leans forward and presses a kiss to my lips. Stupid me had to get too drunk to kiss back the hottest guy I've ever seen. Kiera's probably worried sick about me. I try to ask for my phone, but it's too much of an effort.

"He said to give her this," Hunter says from the doorway. He stalks over to my side and looks down at me. His eyes don't have the same kindness Julian's have, and a tremor of fear paralyzes me.

"N-No," I tell him, eying the syringe warily.

Julian clutches my hand. "Babe, you're sick. We're going to help you."

My eyes close the moment the bite of the needle stings my thigh. I'd expected a rush of awareness. Not more grogginess. I try to sit up, but my body fails me. I'm panicking, but Julian's comforting voice is once again at my ear.

"Shhh, rest now."

My entire body feels numb. I can't even wiggle my toes. When I go to open my eyes, it's a struggle. Words are garbled in my mouth. Nothing makes sense.

"So damn sexy."

This deep voice warms me, but I'm also confused. When I finally manage to open my eyes, I see Julian sitting beside me, without his shirt on. My gaze flickers over his hard chest for a moment before looking back up at him.

"You're such a good little girl," he tells me calmly. His fingertip tickles my inner thigh. I'd shiver, but my entire body feels useless. "You went along with everything so well. I think you should be rewarded."

My eyes widen, and he chuckles. His laugh now freaks me out. I don't like it. "L-Let—"

"I like it when you're quiet," he tells me. Then, his fingers slide up under my skirt. My heart thunders in my chest as he slides my panties down my thighs. He's gentle as he removes them completely. "This should work."

I'm horrified when he pushes my panties into my mouth. I start to gag, and he laughs.

Shit!

What have I done?

Everything goes black again. I'm not sure how long I'm out for. But I wake with a start.

Two green eyes look up at me from between my legs. I'm naked. *Shit, I'm naked!* I can't really feel what he's doing to me. His tongue is on me, that much I can see. Tears streak down my cheeks as I attempt to scream through my panties. All I hear are muffled moans and the disgusting way he slurps at me.

"So sweet," he growls. "Are you a virgin?"

Terror immobilizes me, and our eyes meet. Gone is the handsome guy I met earlier. His true colors come out, and I'm staring into the eyes of a monster.

I watch helplessly as he rips the foil off a condom and slides it on his thick cock. He grabs my thighs and pushes them apart. And then, he's inside me.

"Fuck!" he hisses as he thrusts into me. "You're so goddamned tight."

I'm crying hysterically, but I'm unable to move. *I don't know what they gave to me!*

"You're such a pussy," Hunter laughs as he saunters in without a shirt. "You always make love to them. Maybe she just wants to be fucked rough and hard."

Julian ignores him as he pounds himself into my body. I thank my lucky stars that at least I can't feel him. Beads of sweat form on his wrinkled brow and his once styled hair is now disheveled. His mouth parts open to let out a groan.

"I want her again after you're done," he says to Hunter as he slides out of me.

My eyes fall to the condom on his dick. It's blood tinged, which makes me gag.

"Pull the panties out of her mouth," Hunter instructs with a growl. "I like to hear them scream."

Julian yanks them from my mouth, and I do find my voice. Words don't form, but a garbled scream does roar from me.

"Scream all you want, bitch. Nobody's coming for you."

Hunter sheds his clothes and puts on a condom. I start screaming some more when he flips me onto my stomach. He yanks my thighs apart and laughs. "Ever been fucked in the ass before?"

I finally find words. "Y-You can't d-d-do this!"

He grabs a handful of my hair and jerks my head back. His mouth finds my ear. "Why? Because you'll tell them we raped you? Just try it, bitch. After we've had our fill of fucking you, we're going to put your cum dumpster ass in the tub. We'll wash you clean. Then, we'll drop your unconscious body on the bed of some shithole motel. When you wake up, you'll remember shit. And if you try and tell the police, they'll have no physical evidence. Jesus, you teenage whores are all the same. Fucking stupid and easy. Newsflash, Hannah. You've been had. You fell for our shit and now you must deal with the consequences of your stupidity."

My tears are just a continuous stream down my hot cheeks. This can't be real. He releases my hair and drops me back to the bed. I'm crying so hard I think I might suffocate, which is preferable to letting two monsters rape me.

"Don't fuck her ass, Hunter," Julian warns. His warning infuriates me. As if what he did to me was any better.

"Why? Because I don't have any lube? That's what her pussy is for. You already lubed it up for me, man," he says with a dark chuckle.

It's then that I feel him push into me. Hours ago I was a virgin and now, I'm not. Hell, earlier tonight I'd wanted to lose my innocence, but certainly not like this. Not for two men to have had me. This is so screwed up. I wish it were a dream!

"Still so tight even though fuckwad over there popped your cherry. But that ass is mine," he growls. "You just—"

A sickening crunch has Hunter stalling.

"What the fuck? Who the fuck are you?" he starts, but then I hear another sickening crunch.

Wetness splatters on my back where I've regained some feeling. Hunter, who was filling me just a moment before, is suddenly ripped from inside me. I wonder if Julian decided to be a man and put a stop to this. The crunching sound won't stop, though. Over and over again it replays inside my mind. I want to make it stop.

"Jesus," a gravelly, deep voice hisses. "What did those motherfuckers do to my sweet girl?"

I'm gently urged onto my back. My eyes meet the fierce chocolate brown ones of an older man. His dark eyebrows are furled together, and he looks pained. Is he a cop? He scowls, but for some reason, I'm not afraid of him. I know. He's my savior, not like the villains who were taking advantage of me only moments before.

With a huff, he wraps me in a sheet and pulls me into his arms. My eyes flit around the room. Two bodies. Two rapists with their heads smashed to gory bits by a baseball bat that lies in the middle of the floor. Blood is everywhere. So mesmerizing. Beautiful. I should be horrified by the sight, but all I can think about is how they got what they deserved. Someway, somehow, I had an angel looking out for me. One look in his protective eyes, and I don't feel an ounce of fear.

He would kill for me.

That's what his eyes say.

And he did.

Twice.

I'm completely in and out during the drive. I don't know where he's taking me. A part of me momentarily shudders imagining he's a monster too. But he saved me. He killed those assholes to get me out of there. Monsters don't rescue raped girls. Do they?

Mom and Dad are going to kill me. Right after Ren gives me the longest *I-told-you-so* speech known to man. God, I'm the dumbest person on the planet. I fell for such a stupid scheme. And now I'm a statistic.

"We're almost to my house," the deep voice assures me. "I'd take you home, but your parents aren't even there, are they?"

I stiffen at his words and cut my gaze over to him. "How do you know that?"

He offers me a comforting smile. "I live about a half mile up the beach—can even see your house from mine. Your parents and I go way back. My wife Alejandra is a surgeon. You should let her take a look at you when she gets home. Then, in the morning, we'll get you back to your house. Unless you want to go home in the state your in…"

I close my eyes and can imagine the horrified stares of my brothers. Hell no.

"You could be lying to me," I say with a tremble of my voice. "Those guys who took me—"

"They're dead. You don't have to worry about those maniacs anymore. I promise you're safe here. Do you want to call your parents and tell them what happened?"

I don't have my purse so I can't text them. I'd have to call them from this guy's house, and I definitely don't want them leaving Dad's business trip in Italy because I was the big dumbass who got herself raped twice in one night.

"Did you say you know my parents?" I question.

His eyes meet mine and with absolute honesty he says, "I know them very well. In fact, I've known your mother since she was seven years old."

A weight is lifted from my shoulders and I nod. "I'd like to get myself together then before I tell them what happened if that's okay with you. I want your wife to make sure I'm okay. Those assholes gave me something. I couldn't fight them off or even move."

He clenches the steering wheel as if he's furious on my behalf. Once again, I'm warmed by my savior's presence.

"Sir," I say in a whisper. "What's your name?"

"My name is Gabriel Sharpe. Call me Gabe." He smiles at me. "Pleased to officially meet you, sweet girl."

Maybe I will let this man and his wife help me.

"We're here," he says as he pulls into a driveway to a beautiful home on the beach. A home that is not far from mine. So he was telling the truth. "See," he points through the window. "Your house is that way."

I nod as he climbs out of the car. When he opens my car door, I attempt to move my legs. They're still useless, and I look up at him with tears in my eyes. "They paralyzed me," I hiss out in frustration.

He kneels down in front of me and furrows his eyebrows together. I can tell he was handsome in his younger years. Hell, he's handsome now. Much more handsome than Mr. Collins.

"It's probably only temporary. Alejandra will know what they did. My wife is good at what she does. Let her help you."

He slides his arms beneath me, and I shiver. Now that my mind is clearing, parts of my body are prickling back to life, too. I can smell Gabe's scent—something spicy maybe—and I like it. He holds me like my dad does. As if he wants to protect me from the entire world. If it weren't for him showing up when he did…

"How did you know to find me there?"

His eyes flicker down to me, and he frowns. It mars his beautiful face, and I wonder what it'd look like if he smiled. My fingers twitch out of need to touch his beard. God, what is wrong with me? I don't even know this man. "I was driving by and saw two men carrying you into that house. I kept driving, but something niggled at me. Told me it wasn't right. I'd made it all the way home when I decided I needed to ease my conscience. Turns out, the feeling in my gut was accurate. I'm sorry I didn't get there sooner." Sorrow whispers over his features, causing my belly to ache for him. Out of a need to comfort him, I give in to my curiosity and touch his beard. It's coarse and wiry with a few grey strands sprinkled in. I like it.

I wonder what it would feel like against the soft, fleshy parts of me. Would it feel scratchy or would it tickle? A wicked shiver ripples through me.

He doesn't remark to my touching him and silently lets us into the home. Once inside, he turns on the entryway light. The home is well-decorated and smells nice. Like cinnamon and nutmeg. Family pictures on the wall once again put me at ease.

"I'm going to have to wake her up and explain what happened so she doesn't panic. Would you like to bathe until then?" he questions.

My heart patters in my chest as he climbs a flight of stairs. But once again, I'm met with more family pictures. He's here to look after me. Gabe knows my parents. I'm safe.

"Um, what're their names?" I blurt out as he enters a large bathroom. "My parents, I mean." A girl can never be too safe.

He smiles, and it's as brilliant as I imagined. "Baylee Marie Winston was your mother's name before she married Warren McPherson. Your grandfather is Loveland McPherson. And you, my dear, are Hannah. Let me guess," he says with a chuckle. "Your mom hates cucumbers." His laughter is even more beautiful than his smiles. It warms me to my core.

I return his smile. "Well, she's allergic. Dad is too, I think." Both of my parents shudder at any mention of cucumbers. One time, when I was younger, while she was shopping for produce, I pulled one from the bin and chased my little brothers with my "wiener" as I called it. She yanked me up so quick and spanked me right there in the store. I'd never seen her so mad before.

He winks at me. "Trust me now?"

Nodding, I relax in his arms as he carries me into the bathroom. He sets me on the toilet seat while he starts a bath. I check him out from behind while he fills the tub and pours bath salts into the steamy water. His dark jeans hug his muscled frame well but are stained with blood. The white T-shirt he's wearing is fitted and splattered with more blood. Gabe is all man—hard and chiseled and hairy in all the right places. Made Mr. Collins look like a pussy wannabe. Gabe should probably look scary, but to me he screams comfort and safety. And something else I can't quite put my finger on… Another shiver.

"Can you get in or do you need my help? If you need my help, I can assist. Don't worry," he says with a growl. "You could be a daughter to me. I'm not interested in what's under that sheet if that's worrying you."

His words both disappoint me and relieve me. Disappointment because I don't want to be thought of as a daughter to this man. But at the same time, I know I wouldn't even know what to do with a man like him. I'd be way in over my head. So definite relief that he doesn't want me because I'm not sure I could deal with any more stress in one night. I'm going to need some serious therapy after this night…

"I need your help," I tell him bravely. He may not want me, but it doesn't change the fact that I want him…to help me.

He nods and strolls over to me. For his age, he's incredibly fit. His chest is defined and ripples with every movement. I should be embarrassed that after such a horrifying night, I'm lusting over my savior. Has to be some sort of PTSD or something. Whatever it is, my mind likes the way his eyes assess me and wash over me, as if I'm precious to him. It makes me want to see more of it. He kneels in front of me. His eyes meet mine as he slowly peels the sheet from my shoulders. Our eyes meet, and he silently asks my permission. A slight nod is all I give, and he doesn't waste any time removing it from my body. I shiver as the cold air meets my naked flesh. I continue to study his features with interest. Even though he was my savior, I'm not blind to the fact that his dark eyes hold villainous secrets. Secrets I want to unlock and discover.

He stands back up and then slides his arms beneath me. The hairs from his forearm tickle the underside of my thighs, a signal that my feeling is coming back.

"Don't drown," he says with a chuckle as he lowers me into the water.

It's hot, and the parts of my flesh that are coming back to life sting. Whereas the dead parts still feel nothing. What a bizarre feeling.

His gaze flickers over my body as he assesses me. "Did they hit you?"

I shake my head as tears well in my eyes. "Nope. Just…raped me." I let out a harsh laugh. Of course, my first time would be against my will and unenjoyable. Fit for a slut. If only Mrs. Collins could see me now…

A murderous glare paints his features, and I like it. I like that he hates those men just as much as I do.

"They'll never hurt anyone again," he says with conviction, his eyes meeting mine.

Blinking back my tears, I nod. "Thank you, Gabe. You saved me, and I can't thank you enough."

Our eyes meet for a long moment. A million different emotions flicker in his eyes. I want to reach inside his head and pull each one out. Ask him about each and every one of them. Find the part of him that wants me too and dissect it. Make him look at it with me. Explore it alongside me where I feel safe and cared for.

His jaw clenches and he tugs off his shirt, revealing his exquisite chest. My eyes inspect a mottled scar on his chest, and I wonder how he came to get such a nasty wound. "Bathe. I'm going to take a quick shower and talk with Alejandra. She can be a little over the top when she's upset. And this is really going to upset her. Just warning you," he tells me as he wads up the bloody shirt in his strong hands. I want to look in his eyes, but I can't help but stare at his rigid chest and broad shoulders. Dark hair between his pecks and another patch just below his navel. I'm completely mesmerized. I bet Mr. Collins had a soft, protruding belly. Maybe even man boobs. He'd never look like the god of a man before me. All Gabe would need is a staff and a toga, and he'd be right out of the Greek mythology we studied freshman year. He doesn't look like he'd be Zeus or Poseidon. No, Gabe looks like he could be Hades. Splattered with the blood of his enemies. Evil and sinister, yet powerful and protective. Knows what he wants and destroys all those in his path. And I could be Persephone. He could steal me away and take me to the underworld where I belong. With him. My black thoughts would be welcome and normal there. Gabe certainly doesn't look like he belongs here. Neither do I.

When our eyes meet, his dark ones are like molten lava. Heat straight from the depths of hell. I'm spellbound by that look and want to see more of it.

"Relax, sweet girl," he instructs before stalking out of the bathroom, leaving me alone to my bizarre thoughts and inner ramblings of a madwoman.

With a sigh, I do just as he says. Now that I'm alone and rational thought begins to seep in, I finally come to terms with what happened to me. They raped me. Those assholes raped me. Neither asked, they just took. And as each moment passes and feeling begins to return to my body, I am more and more aware of their violation. Tomorrow, bruises will mottle my thighs and belly. My sex will be sore and hurting. But it'll be my mind that suffers the most—as if I could afford the extra affliction there. The drugs will clear my system, and I'll be fully aware of the gravity of what happened.

This is going to severely fuck with my head.

chapter
FIVE

Gabe

"YOU DID WHAT?" Alejandra screeches as she slings on her robe.

I lean against the doorjamb, running a towel through my wet hair, and glare at her. "They fucking raped her, woman. What the fuck was I supposed to do?"

She yanks the ties on her robe and knots it at her waist. "You took her. You took your daughter. They'll come for you, Johan."

Our eyes meet and her chin quivers.

"Gabe," I seethe.

Nodding, she swallows down her emotion. "*Gabe*, they will come after you. Your past is—"

"Is in the past," I hiss. "Now's the time I can have a relationship with her. All these years, I've dealt with the pain of not having a relationship with my daughter. She's almost eighteen. If she likes me, it won't be up to Baylee anymore. Hannah and I can finally be together. She's my daughter, Alejandra. You know this. And by default, that makes her your family too. So cut the shit and help me."

My wife storms past me in a huff. But before she can pass, I snatch her bicep and squeeze. "Accept this. It is a part of me. If you can't deal with this, then I can't deal with *you*." Her eyes widen at my threat. We both know what I mean. I won't leave my life here. However, if she thinks she can ruin this, I'll fucking ruin her.

"Fine."

Leaning forward, I press a kiss to her forehead. "Thank you, beautiful."

She relaxes marginally and pulls away. I follow her as she gathers her medical bag. Together, we enter the bathroom.

There, an angel sleeps.

My angel.

Perfect and gorgeous.

An exact replica of her mother.

My heart aches inside of my chest.

"Hannah," I whisper as I sit on the ledge of the gigantic tub that seems to swallow my daughter. "This is my wife, Alejandra."

Her eyes flutter open and her panicked blue eyes fly to mine. Upon seeing me, she calms. It only makes me more protective over her. Our connection is natural.

"Sweetheart," Alejandra says in the tone she reserves for her patients, "tell me what happened."

I start to leave, to give them their privacy, but Hannah yelps and reaches a shaking hand for my arm. "Please don't leave me."

Her gesture fills me with a warmth I didn't think my cold, hollow insides were capable of anymore. With a nod, I sit down on the floor beside the tub and hold her hand. Her voice wobbles as she retells the entire painful story of those bastards who hurt her, but she doesn't cry. She's angry and embarrassed. I'd expected tears and horror, not the vengeful look on her face. Alejandra, being the professional she is, is efficient in diagnosing her problems and assessing her for injuries.

"You shouldn't have bathed her, Gabe," Alejandra chides. "The hospital won't be able to process her for DNA."

Hannah splashes in the water as she tries to sit up. "No! If you take me to a hospital, then he'll go to jail. He saved me!" Her terrified blue eyes meet mine, and I see a flash of adoration in them.

My heart swells in my chest, and I squeeze her hand. "I'm not going anywhere."

Alejandra sighs. "You're right. After your bath, though, I want to check you for vaginal and rectal tears."

Hannah's face grows bright red and her plump lip wobbles in horror.

"Go grab her some hot tea and something to eat. You're overwhelming her," I snap at Alejandra, flashing her a warning glare. "I'll get her out of the bath."

Alejandra flickers her gaze to Hannah for a moment and I sense jealousy radiating from her. She better back the fuck off and remember her place around here.

"Alejandra," I say with a low growl.

She has the sense to jump and nod. Understanding once again softening her face. As soon as she rushes from the bathroom, I stand to hunt for a towel. I locate a large white one and bring it over to the tub.

"How are you feeling?"

Her teary eyes meet mine. "I'm starting to hurt. I guess that's a good thing. Means my feeling is coming back."

The washcloth is fisted in her hand. Her body quakes as she desperately attempts to hold her tears in. This girl is brave. Tough as shit.

"Were you able to clean yourself?" I question, my voice hoarse with emotion. If those assholes weren't already dead, I'd fucking gut them this time and let her watch them as they bled out. I would pull their beating hearts from their bodies and lay them at Hannah's feet so she could crush them until they stopped twitching.

"Not like I wanted to." Her eyes flicker with something I don't fully recognize or understand. Not sadness or frustration. Something else.

She hands me the cloth, and I nod my understanding. With clinical efficiency, I clean her in the places they violated her. Once I'm satisfied those motherfuckers are no longer on her, I meet her gaze. Her full lips are pressed together but she stares at me as if I'm her entire world.

I want to be her entire world.

Always.

Our connection is thick. You could cut it with a knife, but now that I've had her in my home, I won't ever let anyone sever the way we seem to be tethered to one another.

"Let's get you out of there, sweet girl," I coo as I help her stand on shaky legs. Quickly, I wrap the towel around her. She may be able to walk, but I don't take any chances, scooping her light frame into my arms.

I carry her downstairs to the guest bedroom. Once inside, I lie her on the bed and then find the switch to the lamp. As soon as the light floods the bedroom, I see that her wide blue eyes are once again on me.

"How old are you?" she questions, her slender fingers reaching out to touch my bare chest. Her touch, so innocent but curious, warms me.

I clutch her hand and pull it to my heart so she can feel how it beats for her. "Old enough to be your father."

Releasing her, I start toward the door.

"Don't leave me," she begs, her entire body shivering.

"I'm going to find you something to wear, sweet girl. I'll be right back."

When I come back, Alejandra is sitting at her bedside, stroking her hair and trying to get her to sip some tea. My wife will be rewarded later for helping me. I'll make her cunt weep all over my lips when we finally get back to bed. After murdering those fuckers and rescuing my Hannah, I'm desperate for some sort of physical release.

"Hey," I say gruffly as I stride over to the bed.

Hannah reaches for me and frowns. I take her hand and turn my gaze to my wife. "Now what?"

Alejandra's eyes become sad. "I really need to check you, sweetheart. To make sure you aren't bleeding inside. Since your body is numb, you may not be able to feel how hurt you could be. Were you a virgin? Did they use condoms?"

Hannah nods at her.

"Just close your eyes," Alejandra says calmly, "and it'll all be over soon."

Hannah's eyes fly to mine. "I'm scared."

A fierce growl rumbles in my chest. "I'll be right here, baby."

At this, she smiles at me, as if I've given her the moon right from the sky. If it were possible, I'd reach right up there and pull it down for her.

Sitting beside her, I half pull her onto my lap. I stroke her soft hair as Alejandra sets to work. She positions Hannah's feet flat against the bed so her knees are up. Then, she slides on some latex gloves.

"Will it hurt?" The shivering girl in my arms claws at my forearm, as if I might try and leave her during such a time.

"No," Alejandra assures her. "You'll feel some discomfort, but I need to check you out." My wife lubricates her fingers and begins to examine her.

I close my eyes because I can't watch. I'd much rather think of the surprise in that sick fuck's eyes when I swung that baseball bat at his face. How his skull cracked the moment the bat made its impact. The minutes pass by quickly.

"You're inflamed, which isn't uncommon for someone with no prior sexual history. However, there aren't any tears that could become infected or need stitching. Your rectum seems untouched. We can thank God both men used condoms. Considering the circumstances, you were very lucky."

I shoot Alejandra a relieved look. "Thank you."

"Of course. Gabe, can I talk to you for a minute in the hallway?"

Hannah twists in my arms, her eyes wide with fear and her fingers gouging holes in my chest. "What's happening? What's wrong?"

I stroke her cheek with my finger, hoping to calm her. "Nothing's wrong. I'll be right back. Promise."

She relaxes, and I slip out from beneath her to follow Alejandra out. Once the door is closed behind us, she flips out.

"This is deep shit, Gabe. We have a victimized girl, your daughter whom you stole, in our house. And, you murdered the two men who raped her. This is bad, Gabe. Very bad."

I glare at her and seize her throat. She gags when I haul her down the hallway and into the kitchen. Pushing her against the cabinets, I get in her face.

"It was bad when you rescued me all those years ago. You knew what you were getting yourself into. Now, get the fuck over yourself, woman. I'm going to help her. I'll spend every waking minute with her until she asks to go home. I need this. You know I need this. For my goddamned sanity. Either get on board or get the fuck out of my way. I won't bring the law to our house if that's what you're worried about. Do you understand me?"

She nods. "But what if you leave me for her? What if you run away to live your life with your daughter? I can't lose you."

Same song and dance with us.

"Keep pissing me off, and I'll do just that," I threaten.

She lets out a pained sob. "What do you want? I'll do whatever you want."

"Go to sleep. This will look better in the morning," I assure her.

Her lips find mine and she kisses me. I don't kiss her back. She's already left a sour taste in my mouth. "I left two pills on her bedside table. One is a muscle relaxer and one is a Xanax. She'll need to sleep. Other than that, she's going to be okay. By tomorrow, she should be able to walk around like normal. Her mind will be ruined, though, Gabe. She's been through a traumatizing event. I'll do what I can to help her."

Sliding my hands to my wife's generous ass, I give it a squeeze. "Thank you. I owe you so much for this."

She leaves without another word, and I make my way back to the guest bedroom. When I peek inside, Hannah's still wrapped in the towel. Her wide eyes soften once she sees it's me. Relief floods her pretty features.

"You should dress," I tell her as I come into the room and close the door behind me. "You're shivering. Do you need help?"

Her eyes fall to the scar on my chest and linger there.

"Yes."

I stride over to the silky gown I stole from Alejandra's drawer and slide it over her head. She pokes her arms through the holes as I tug it down over her bare breasts and stomach. Once she's covered, I drag the blanket over her quivering body.

"Do you want me to leave so you can sleep?"

She shakes her head wildly. "N-No. Can you sit with me? Tell me stories of how you knew my mom. She's never mentioned you."

My chest squeezes and a flash of anger surges through me. It pisses me off Baylee never told her about me. Not one single thing.

"Sweet girl," I say as I sit down on the other side of the bed. "Not all the parts of my story are good. In fact, most of it is awful. I guess to understand my relationship with your mom, you'll need to understand me."

She lifts the blanket urging me to get under the covers. I'll probably suffocate with these sweat pants on, but that's the kind of shit you do for the one who belongs to you. With a sigh, I slide underneath and pull the covers up over us. As if it's her instinct to do so, she snuggles up against my side. I hug her to me. It's as if a missing part of me has finally been reconnected. I feel whole and invincible. One tiny moment of her in my arms will never be enough. I'll need her here over and over again.

"To understand me, we're going to need to start from the beginning. Back when I was about your age," I tell her.

Her fingers flutter over my chest hair and she nods. "I want to hear it. All of it."

"I once fell in love with a girl named Krista. She was beautiful and feisty," I murmur, "just like you."

My mind escapes to the past and I tell her all of it. What my father did to me, the sex ring him and his friends were a part of, and finally every gruesome detail of how I murdered my sick father. She doesn't flinch. She doesn't recoil. She doesn't cry.

She just keeps drawing hearts on my chest, over and over again, until I wonder if her fingernail will eventually cut right through my flesh. Now that's a scar I'd wear proudly.

This girl is brave and unflappable.

This girl is mine.

chapter
SIX

Hannah

When he stops telling his story and regards me with the saddest eyes I've ever seen, it breaks something inside of me. As a child, he was molested. It's sickening.

"I'm so sorry," I tell him, my voice a shaky whisper. "He deserved everything he got. Everything."

And I believe that wholeheartedly. I should be worried that this man killed two men to rescue me and admitted to killing once before, but I'm not afraid. In fact, I'm dying to know more.

"Did you love my mom once?" I ask bluntly.

He strokes the back of my arm with his fingertips, causing me to shiver. "My love for Baylee has morphed and transformed over the years. At first, it was a fierce need to protect. Kind of like with Krista. And like you. But then, she grew right before my eyes and became this beautiful piece of art. My love for her changed. It became distorted, but it was real nonetheless. I can even admit that there was a time I thought I hated her. Now I know it was just a fleeting emotion. I was simply angry with her."

"Why?"

"She fell in love with someone else."

"My dad?"

He stiffens in my arms and changes the subject. "Are you hungry?"

I shake my head and sit up. "Do I look like her?"

His eyes skim over my face, causing him to frown. "Exactly, baby. Almost exactly."

A smile plays at my lips. I'm not sure why, but I like the fact that this old friend, maybe even boyfriend, of Mom's who was so in love with her says I look like her. It makes me wonder if they slept together. Was he a good lover? Did she scream his name in pleasure?

"Do you think I'm pretty?" I ask, batting my lashes at the handsome older man.

His lips pull into a half-grin. He pushes the hair out of my eyes. "Beautiful, actually. So fucking beautiful."

My heart thunders in my chest. "She never talks about her father. I've asked a lot but she always changes the subject. Did you know my grandfather?"

His dark eyebrows pinch together, a painful expression painting his face. I want to reach into the air and pull the words back. To apologize for making him sad. To go back to him telling stories that make him growl and tense, not ones that make him upset.

"I'm sorry. I didn't know—"

He surprises me by hugging me tightly. "Shhh. I'm going to tell you everything. I just miss Tony. He was my best friend."

My throat aches with emotion. He's the one gutted, and yet here I am the fool trying not to cry against his warm, firm chest as he holds me. "Tell me about him."

He chuckles, the sound thick and rich. It blankets and soothes me. "He was big. Had one of those Viking beards and a perpetual scowl. Everyone was afraid of him. Well, aside from Baylee and her angelic mother. Did she ever tell you about Lynn?"

I nod. "She talks about her often. That's why I don't understand why she doesn't mention my grandfather, Tony. I don't know much about him."

The room goes silent, and I wonder if I'm bothering him by asking too many questions. If he sees me as a curious child rather than an inquisitive woman who looks like an old love of his. Eventually, he lets out a sigh before launching back to the past.

chapter
SEVEN

Gabe

My past follows me wherever I go. Not a day goes by when I don't think about the night that ended it all. The night I dispatched my father who killed Krista in cold blood after brutally raping her. Her blue eyes haunt my nightmares. For thirteen years, I've thought about her non-stop. Every time some asshole tries to pull a fast one over me, I think of her.

That night, after I sought my revenge, I found my father's friends still in our house. I showed them what Grant Sharpe had turned me into. Naturally, they were scared. Not just from me but afraid of what would happen if I were caught. Their shitty deviant ways would be dragged out into the open for all to see. It was in their best interest to help me.

And so from that point on, my father's best friend, Lance, became my mentor. He gave me money until my twenty-first birthday, where I was given access to my trust fund my mother set up and my inheritance that went to me after my father's death. Anytime I got into too much trouble, Lance was there to guide my way back out of it.

I'm not going to lie. I went through a dark phase. Did things I certainly regret. But now I'm attempting to turn over a new leaf. Which is exactly why I'm headed to a boring house in a boring suburb on a boring day.

Lance says I can't keep blowing through my money or I won't have any left. He also says my bullshit is leaving a trail that leads back to them. So, in an effort to chill the fuck out, I'm trying to start a new life. Who knows, maybe I can meet someone and settle down.

I'm squinting to read the addresses on the street when I lock eyes with her.

A woman.

Her shoulder-length golden hair blowing in the wind as she makes her way to her mailbox. When she sees me, she grins and waves.

Krista?

I slam on my brakes, but I can't peel my eyes from her. Not to be a dick, I wave back. She turns and bounces back up toward her house. It's then I realize her address is right next to the one I'm moving into.

Talk about fate.

With a smile on my face, I pull into my driveway. I'm climbing out of my car and about to call out to the woman making her way up the porch when someone steps out of her home. The Viking motherfucker zeroes in on me and glares. He's massive and borderline psychotic looking. Our eyes stay on one another as he pulls the woman into his arms and hugs her.

Well, fuck.

My first instinct is to climb back into my car and haul ass out of here. The last thing I need is a territorial war with some fuck face over his woman. I've spent a lifetime being fucking bullied by kids from school, my father's friends, and my father himself. I don't need this shit.

"Are you the new neighbor?" Her voice is like a musical breeze—soft and tantalizing. It instantly threads its way inside my head and takes root there. "I'm Lynn Winston. This is my husband, Tony."

I'm snapped from my daze to see them walking toward me. Shutting my car door, I saunter over to them with false bravado. In actuality, I wish there were a hole to crawl into instead.

"Gabriel Sharpe," I say in a deep voice and extend my hand to the Viking.

He grunts but takes my hand. "Good to meet you."

Next, the angel takes my hand. "Welcome to the neighborhood. I was marinating some steaks if you want to come by for dinner tonight. Tony and I'd love to give you a proper welcome."

Tony's gaze lingers on where she grasps me, and I quickly jerk my hand from her grip. "Uh, sure. I'll bring over a case of beer. I mean, if that's okay. Do you drink beer?"

Tony growls and Lynn chuckles. I like her laugh. "I don't, but this brute here does. Could you pick up a two-liter of orange soda too?"

I'm nodding. I find that she could ask me to donate my skin and I'd cut it right from my body. Something inside of me wants to give her what she wants.

"It's settled then. See you at, seven, Mr. Sharpe."

I laugh. "Gabe. Please call me Gabe."

I'm still wound up thinking about her as I drive back to my new home from the store. This Lynn lady looks so much like Krista it's scary. But she's happy. Unlike poor Krista, Lynn has a life worth living. She doesn't have to run or to fear men like my crazy dad.

She's safe.

And that makes me happy.

Happy is an unfamiliar emotion. Sometimes, I'm satisfied. And hell, with the right woman, I can feel pretty damn good. But never do I feel a thumping in my chest like this. The way my blood rushes to my ears and I can't fucking think straight.

I wonder if she would leave the Viking for me.

Pulling into the driveway, I let out a huff of frustration. The woman is happily married. I'm not going to fuck with that. No way. I turn off the vehicle and head to the trunk. Once I pull out the case of beer and two-liter of orange soda, I shut the trunk and flicker my gaze to their porch. Staring back at me is the mini version of Lynn. A small girl. Beautiful and innocent.

Mine.

The thought, so sudden and fierce, startles me. Fuck that! I'm not some sicko. But it's nothing like that, I assure myself. It's much different.

"Did you get my orange soda?" she asks, her voice sweet like cotton candy.

I'm grinning like a goddamned fool. Walking up to her, I hand her the big bottle. "Is this for you?"

She beams, her blue eyes twinkling, and reveals a couple of missing teeth. "It's my favorite. What's your name? How old are you? What's your favorite television show? Do you like to swim?"

My heart squeezes. Maybe fate sent me here because I need normalcy. If I can get past the Viking, having Lynn and this little girl in my life could be good for me.

"Gabe. I'm thirty-one. I don't really watch much television but I do love to swim. What's your name little girl? How old are you? Do you interrogate strangers often?"

She giggles, and I swear it's a salve to my burned soul.

"Baylee Marie Winston. I'm seven. What does interrogate mean?"

I kneel down in front of her. "It means to ask questions. You ask a lot of them."

She scrunches her nose up. "Daddy says I'm nosy. Mommy says I'm curious. What do you think?"

Does it make me a fucking creep that I want to hug her to me and never let go? Deciding that it does, I push the thought from my head.

"I think you're inquisitive. And that's a nice trait to have," I tell her with a grin.

Her blue eyes sparkle. "I like you, Gabe. Will you take me swimming?"

Ruffling her hair, because she's too fucking cute not to, I shrug. "I don't know, sweet girl. Maybe one day you, me, and your parents can all go. We have to convince your dad to like me first. I don't think he cares too much for me."

She leans in to tell me a secret. "Daddy doesn't like anybody, but Mommy will make him."

At that, she bounces off with her orange soda in hand. Her pigtails, almost white in color, flop back and forth as she runs up the steps.

My life is finally starting to look up.

Thanks to a couple of intervening angels.

chapter
EIGHT

Hannah

"So my grandpa was grumpy? That's why my mom doesn't speak of him?" I question. The two pills I took earlier have relaxed me and sleep keeps dragging my lids down. "I don't understand."

He strokes my hair in such a way it makes me even sleepier. "There's more. I'm not sure you want to hear about it, though. Your mother and I sort of went to war. It was your grandpa who did some unforgivable things to her. She hated him for what he did."

My palm splays on his toned belly, and he covers my hand with his. "You were just my grandpa's friend? What was my mother to you?"

"She was my everything." His tone is low and gravelly. The way he says it, in such a possessive way, has a sliver of unwarranted jealously trickling through me.

"Oh."

"But then…" He trails off.

I look up at him and his chocolate-colored eyes are liquid love. "Then what?"

"Then you came along."

"Me? I'm nobody to you."

His chuckle warms me down to my toes. "Sweet girl, you became my everything."

Furrowing my brows together in confusion, I let out a sigh. "I don't understand. You don't know me."

His fingers slide through my hair near my cheek as he murmurs his words. "I've watched you grow and blossom into such a brilliant, beautiful young woman. I've been to most of your softball games. Watched you from afar. The team is nothing without you, by the way."

His words of praise wash over me like a cold spring rain and cleanse me. But then, my blood turns to ice when I wonder if he saw *her*. Mrs. Collins. When she went psychotic in front of my entire team and family.

"I'm not that good."

"Better than Jameson, Cartwright, and Brown," he argues.

If he knows the three best players on my team, then he *does* come to our games. So why is it he's never revealed himself until now?

"So the Viking eventually became your friend because you get sad when you talk about him. Am I right?"

He laughs. "That he did. They became the family I never had. Lynn was so…" He trails off as if to think of the perfect word. "She may have looked like Krista, but she was gentle and kind. Krista would have ripped your throat out with her teeth had she had the chance. And then little Baylee grew up right before my eyes."

"You fell in love with my mom?"

His body grows tense. "It was way more complicated than that. You see, Lynn was dying. They didn't have a lot of money. I'd exhausted most of mine from acting like a jackass all those years, so I was no help. My sexual tastes were outside of the norm and that forced me to satiate that need in ways my father would have been proud of."

This time, it's me who is the one hardening at his words. I sit up on one elbow and frown at him. "What sort of sexual tastes?"

His fingertips drum at his stomach and his eyes darken. With every breath he takes, his nostrils flare and his jaw clenches. "Depraved. Devious. Sick sexual tastes," he breathes. "Nothing a little girl should know about."

"I want to know."

He's quiet for a moment. "I bought and sold girls. When I needed cash, I took them, trained them, and made a quick buck."

"Just like your father," I say in astonishment.

Nature versus nurture.

It's in Gabe's nature to be like his father.

My theory remains hole-proof.

"Yes," he growls, "just like my goddamned father."

Instead of shuddering at his angry tone, I snuggle back up against his warm, hard body. I wasn't judging him. Simply stating a fact. I'm like *my* father, Warren McPherson, and his mother. Certain parts are just broken inside our heads. The good parts of me intricately twisted with the bad. Struggling every day to keep my head above the water so the black abyss doesn't suck me down forever. I've had a few dips into darkness over the years. I have no right to judge anyone.

"Then what?"

"Well, after going to these trades over the years, I took notice of the ones who sold for the highest. Once I had a game plan, I was able to bring in higher profits. Every day, Lynn grew more and more sick. Tony became depressed. And my sweet Baylee was so sad. I wanted to fix them all. They were my family."

I smile and begin drawing hearts on his chest again.

"One day, your mother was bouncing through the house, in nothing but a red swimsuit, hunting for sunscreen. I wanted her so fucking bad in that moment. She was no longer the daughter of my friend. She was a woman. Curvaceous. Beautiful. Her body was ripe. An untouched virgin. I wanted her for my own selfish reasons."

"She looked just like me?" I can't help but remind him.

His fingers stroke my hair. "Exactly."

"Did you sell her?"

He flinches at my words. "How could you possibly come to that conclusion?"

"Grandma Lynn needed money. You wanted my mother. If you were smart, you could have had the best of both worlds. You could have slept with her, trained her, and then sold her. Then you'd have the money to save Lynn. But since you loved my mom, you could then rescue her afterward." I expect him to laugh at my hypothesis, but he doesn't.

His eyes narrow and I can see him attempting to peel back the layers inside my head. *Good luck.* "You're a smart girl, Hannah."

"I understand true love."

"Do you now?"

I nod and wait for him to continue.

"Well, your mother wasn't the happiest camper. Once Tony reluctantly agreed to the plan, I was to take her right from her bedroom window. I took her and…"

"Did you make love to her?"

He rolls over onto his side and glares down at me. "Among other things, Hannah. When I say little girls don't need to hear these things, I mean it. Eventually, after I broke her in, I sold her. The plan was to swoop right in and take her back. But everything went to shit after that. Her ex-boyfriend killed Tony for his involvement. Lynn passed away, the grief was too much to bear. And Baylee was nowhere to be found. The man who bought her went to expensive lengths to keep his name out of it. My girl was lost, in the hands of some monster, and I didn't rest until I got her back."

"So you *did* rescue her," I say with a smile. My fingers once again rise to touch his beard. "You were her hero."

His eyes clench closed. "I tried, but fuck if her ex-boyfriend wasn't a pain in my ass. Not to mention, your mother fell in love with her captor. Stockholm Syndrome bullshit."

"But you loved her, and she loved you. Ever since she was a little girl," I argue, my voice rising several octaves.

He opens his eyes back up and skims them over my features. "She didn't love me anymore. I was angry and lonely and heartbroken. My friends were dead and my sweet Baylee no longer belonged to me. Not truly. When her psycho ex tried to kill her, I put a bullet in his skull. She seemed so relieved to see me—for what I'd done. I knew we could put all the heartache behind us and move on together. That she would be my wife one day. But…"

His hand grabs mine and he drags my fingertips over the scar on his chest. Our eyes meet and what I see in his breaks my heart. Tears well in my eyes but don't spill out.

"But what?"

"She stabbed me. She stabbed me because she loved him instead."

"Her ex?"

"No, Warren McPherson," he bites out with a sneer, "your father."

I'm stunned silent. "My father *bought* my mother?"

"For millions."

A tear streaks down my cheek as I attempt to put together what he's saying. It explains my parents' secret love story they never divulge. It explains a lot actually.

"I'm so sorry," I blurt out. I love my mother and father, but right now my heart aches for the man whose heart thunders in his chest beneath my fingertips.

"Don't be sorry," he says with a smile and leans forward, kissing my nose. My stomach feels as if it does a flop inside of me. What would he do if I parted my lips and kissed him on his handsome mouth?

"But, my family hurt you," I murmur.

"Shhh," he whispers. "I'm fine. Look at me now."

"Gabe, why am I everything to you then? Why do you follow me and watch my games? Is it because I look like her? Do you want me, too?" I question, hope filling my voice.

His gaze softens. "Of course I want you. I've always wanted you since day one. But I also wanted you to be happy. I never wanted to hurt you or ruin your life."

I bask in his warm gaze. "But you have a wife. Won't she be upset?"

"She'll have to deal with it, sweet girl."

Mrs. Collins didn't have to deal with it. *I* had to deal with it. This time, the roles are reversed. It thrills me.

He rolls onto his back, and I can't help but slide my knee over his hip. My fingertips skim over his hard torso as I attempt to find the courage to make my move. I lean forward and kiss his cheek near his ear. "I want you too," I whisper. Then, I kiss along his jawline until my lips hover over his. They barely brush over his soft mouth when I'm flipped over on my back and am staring into his furious brown glare.

"What the fuck are you doing?" he barks.

I frown and try to run my fingers through his hair. My efforts are thwarted when he grabs both wrists and pins them to the bed. His body is heavy on mine. I should be afraid. Terrified, like I was when Julian and Hunter were having their way with me. Instead, I'm hot and needy and desperate. If he weren't so heavy, I'd wrap my legs around his hips just to feel his erection against my clit. Just the vision of such a perfect scenario sends a quiver of excitement pulsating through me.

"We want each other," I tell him.

We have a silent stare off for a moment before he speaks again. "Not like this, sweet girl. Jesus!"

I squirm against his grip, but he only tightens his hold. The way he devours me as if I'm his entire world has me desperate to come at his touch. He's strong and powerful and wicked. His wickedness attracts me. Gabe truly is Hades. I want to be his Persephone. I want us to explore the depths of the darkness together.

"You said I look just like her," I argue. "You said I was pretty."

His glare becomes murderous. "Beautiful. You're fucking beautiful."

The anger in his voice, so fierce and sure, makes me smile. "So why won't you make love to *me*? Why won't you kiss *me*?"

The fury is wiped right from his face as shock settles in. "What?"

Wiggling my legs free, I hook them around his waist and drive him against me with the heels of my feet. His body is warm against my tingling, needy sex. "I can be her. Krista or Lynn or Mom. But this time, nobody stands in your way. Don't you feel this connection? I want you inside of me, erasing what those bastards did. You, Gabe."

His cock between us comes alive at my words. The sweatpants between us feel like a punishment, and I wish they were gone.

"Baby," he murmurs and buries his face against my neck. "Fuck, I should have said something sooner." His grip on my wrists is gone so he can slide his arms around my body to hug me. I'm completely trapped in his heavy hug. "We can't do that."

Tears of rejection sting my eyes. "Why not?"

His hot breath is once again on my ear. It sends desire zapping through me. I wiggle my hips in hopes of feeling his cock rub against my clit—anything to relieve this fiery need.

"We can't do this because…" His words are hoarse and ragged. He bucks against me, just once. Stars blind me as pleasure surges through me.

"Do it again," I mutter.

He's panting into my ear. The uneven breaths make me crazy. I want to hear them as he splits me in two with his massive cock that's simply teasing me now.

"Please," I beg.

His groan is a painful one—as if touching me is the hardest thing he'll ever have to do in his life. But he heeds my wishes. He grinds against me so hard, I think his cock may tear through the material and find its way inside of me.

"Oh God," I gasp. I've never felt so alive and wanted by a man. My mind is going crazy with images of him fucking me forever.

"Fuckfuckfuckfuck," he chants into my ear. "Fuckfuckfuckfuck."

His entire body shakes as if he's trying desperately not to give in to what we both want. He surprises me when he thrusts against me slowly, but not as hard. With each movement, his cock presses against my clit in just the right way.

"Please don't hate me after this," he murmurs against my ear.

"I swear it."

With my vow still hanging in the air, he suckles gently on my earlobe as he uses his cock to drive me closer to orgasm. I've come many a times with my own fingers but never at the hand of another. My entire body tenses as my climax nears. I'm desperate for it. So needy for the release.

"Come, sweet girl. Soak my pants with your juices," he growls.

His words are enough to send me over the edge. The darkness I tried to avoid swallows me whole. I'm no longer Hannah McPherson—the weird little girl who does inappropriate things. I'm no longer the girl who falls in love with teachers and doctors and coaches. I'm no longer the girl who runs a razor along her wrist simply to watch the blood spill all over the perfect white bathroom tiles. I'm no longer the girl who tries to drown on purpose so the lifeguard will save her. I'm no longer the girl who spent three weeks two summers ago in a mental health facility for delusions and obsessions and a multitude of other things.

My orgasm consumes me, and I cry out his name.

I'm no longer that girl.

Because now I am his.

I belong to Hades.

I am Persephone.

chapter
NINE

Gabe

Love is a wicked little creature. It slithers into your life and sinks its teeth into you whether you like it or not. Love doesn't care about morals or social norms or familial boundaries. Love takes whatever the fuck it wants.

And right now, love has me crazy with the need to rip my sweatpants off so I can sink my throbbing cock inside of her. I'm so desperate to do so, I think my chest might explode at any minute. Fucking insane with need.

Somehow, though, I manage to enjoy her sweet orgasm until it subsides and then pull myself up off of her. When I sit up on my knees, I can't help but admire how fucking beautiful she is. Her blonde hair is a halo around her soft features. With each ragged breath she takes, her chest heaves. Tiny nipples poke through the sheer fabric, and it makes me want to bite them. Her legs remain spread apart. My eyes fall to her sweet pussy, which glistens with her arousal.

This is so wrong…

But it feels so right.

Tearing my gaze from her cunt, I meet her blazing blue eyes with a stern look. "We can't ever do that again." My words cause her to frown. Rejection mars her pretty features and her lip wobbles.

"Was I not good? Do you not want me?"

The way she whispers those questions, so unsure and sad, has me wanting to give her whatever the fuck she wants—morals be damned.

"You were perfect," I tell her with a smile. I can't help but reach out and stroke a blonde strand of hair away from her pretty face. "I'm just a sick bastard who takes what he wants even when it's the wrong thing to take. I'll go to hell one day for all of this."

Her brows furl together. "I'll go with you."

My heart beats to life in my chest, and I can't help but smile at her. "You don't belong in hell, sweet girl. You're an angel."

She sits up on her elbows and gives me the evilest grin I've ever seen on a woman. My goddamned traitorous cock strains in my pants.

"I'm no angel."

Running my fingers through my hair, I attempt to spill the words that need to be said. "Baby," I say with a sigh. "There's a reason I followed you all these years."

She blinks at me innocently. Not an angel, my ass.

"I'm your father."

I expect tears and screams and fists. What I don't expect is for perfect, angelic laughter to fill the room. She laughs until tears of amusement stream down her cheeks. I watch as her tits jiggle through the silky material.

"You are not," she argues, a huge smile on her face.

I grab at the hem of her nightgown to cover her still wet cunt. It's fucking distracting me. "I am too. When your mother stabbed me, she'd said she was pregnant. It had to be mine."

Hannah reaches for the waistband of my sweatpants. Once she has it in her grip, she tugs it down and my cock bounces out enthusiastically. My dick weeps at the way she licks her lips hungrily. It takes every ounce of humanity left inside me to push away from her and tuck the eager thing back into my pants.

"Hannah, no."

I climb off the bed and take several steps away. "I'm your biological father. What we just did was wrong. It certainly can't happen again."

She sits up and draws her knees to her chest. Her pretty features fall as sadness takes over. "I have a father."

Her words sting, but I shake them off. "I know, but I'm the one who gave you life. It's my DNA inside you. I'd like to have a relationship with you, though. To take you places and buy you things. To spend time with you."

At this, her face lights up with a breathtaking smile. "Really? You want to see me again?"

"I want to see you every goddamned day for the rest of my life. And not from afar. I want you close to me. I need to make up for lost time."

She relaxes in the bed and stretches out. "I'd like that too. But my parents can't know. They'll forbid it. I just know it."

I reach for her and pat her thigh. "Our secret."

"I'd plug your name into my phone but I think it's still at that house."

Squeezing her thigh, I wink at her. "Get some sleep. I'll get your phone back."

She nods, and I go to leave the room. When I get the door open, she calls out for me.

"I love you," she mutters, her eyes flickering with a thousand emotions.

The words infect my heart and disease me with her—all of her. "I've been waiting eighteen years to hear those words. I love you too, sweet girl."

Going back to that house was probably smart. I'd left clues and shit everywhere. After several hours of cleaning, collecting her things, and disposing of the bodies, I felt much better about not getting caught. The last thing I needed was the police to take her away from me again. Now those fuckers are swimming in the Pacific. My hope is the fish and saltwater will take care of any lingering evidence.

By the time I got home and cleaned up, the sun was rising. Not one to miss a workout, I've been lifting weights ever since. My mind is focused on her. My sweet girl. I finally have her. Sweat pours from me as I power through an exhausting workout after no sleep. I can't sleep knowing she's in the other room. I'm not sure I'll ever sleep again.

I curl the barbell to my chest and let out a grunt. My dark eyes find their reflection in the mirror. Every muscle is flexed and hardened. Sweat drips from each strand of my hair as it hangs in my face. I'm wired and high on adrenaline. I'd go up and fuck Alejandra to relieve some of this energy, except I don't want to. My focus is elsewhere. And, just as Alejandra feared, it might never be back on her again.

"Gabe?"

The sweet voice is music to my ears. With a groan, I set the barbell down and turn to find the voice. Hannah stands in the doorway to my home gym, wearing that thin little gown with no panties and a mischievous smile on her face. She plays with the hem of it, revealing her creamy thighs, and I force myself to look back up at her face.

"Good morning, beautiful."

She beams and then runs to me. Apparently, my sweat doesn't bother her because she throws her arms around my neck and kisses my cheek. "Good morning, beefcake."

Chuckling, I look down at her. She's all smiles and bright eyes this morning, despite what a fucked-up night she had. "Beefcake?"

She smirks. "If my brother saw how ripped you were…he'd be so jealous. He's sixteen and spends all of his free time working out. The poor kid has a few muscles but he's got a long way to go."

I stroke her soft hair and inspect her features. "Did you sleep well? How does your body feel?"

Her eyes drop to my mouth and she sighs. "A little sore but I'll be okay. I'm going to have to go home, though."

She lifts her gaze to mine, and it's sad. I can tell she doesn't want to leave, which makes my heart fucking soar. "Yeah, sweet girl, you're going to have to go home. But," I say, breaking from her warm grasp, "I got you a present."

Sauntering over to the countertop along the far wall, I retrieve her purse and phone. She takes them from me and lets out a sigh of relief. "You went back."

I nod. "There's no evidence left of you being there. Or me for that matter."

Her fingers tap away on her phone. Then, she looks up at me. "What's your number?"

I snatch a towel from the bench and dry my face and hair. Once I locate my phone, we exchange numbers.

"Put me in your phone as Persephone," she instructs, mischief painting her features. "You'll be Hades in mine."

Lifting up an amused brow, I do as I'm told. I'd rather have aliases in the event her mother ever got ahold of her phone.

"Are you ready for me to take you home, Persephone?" I question, one corner of my lips quirking up.

Her cheeks turn red, but she shakes her head. "Not really. I want to stay wrapped up in your arms with you telling me stories forever." She bites on her bottom lip and sends me a look no daughter should ever send her father.

Clearing my throat and hiding my reaction with the towel, I start toward the door. "We'll find ways to hang out, sweet girl. Trust me. And one day, if you want, you can come live with me. We have to be careful, though. Your mom will get me sent me to prison if she ever finds out."

Twenty minutes later, after I've had her dress in a pair of Alejandra's yoga pants and a tank top, I walk her out to my car. She's quiet as we get in. The sun is finally above the horizon in the east.

"This isn't over, baby," I tell her and reach over to squeeze her hand. "This is the start of something we had stolen from us. Nobody can take that away from us now."

She smiles at me. "I'll probably drive you crazy."

"Never."

"I'm kind of a stalker."

"So am I."

At this, she grins. "I guess we have that in common."

"I guess we do," I agree and wink at her. "Don't ever feel afraid to call me or text me. Any time is the perfect time. All of the time is the perfect time. I'm yours now, sweet girl, and you're mine."

She shivers but nods. "Always."

When I drop her off in front of her house, she turns to look back at me, shielding her eyes from the sun. I can see her nipples through the tank, and I hope she finds something decent to wear before she traipses around in front of her brothers. She blows me a kiss that melts my fucking heart before bouncing back into her house.

My sweet girl.

All mine.

It's been five days since I saved her from those monsters. Since I brought her into my home and nursed her physical and emotional wounds. Five days since I fell in love with the most beautiful girl in the world.

Alejandra isn't pleased with my leaving every day to take Hannah to dinner or to a movie or for a walk along the beach. She wears a wary expression but doesn't speak out against me. Wise woman. I do as I please. I make up for lost time. I hug my girl. I spoil her rotten.

"What do you want to do today?" I question as we weave down the road, the warm air whipping around us through the open windows.

She has her toned legs stretched out and her bare feet propped up on the dash. "Let's go find a secluded beach and swim. I haven't been swimming in ages, and it's hot today."

"Did you bring your swimsuit?"

"Nope." She flashes me a wide grin, but I can't see her eyes behind her shades. This girl grows naughtier by the day. Like finding her biological father suddenly gave her a license to behave badly. I don't mind if she's bad, though, as long as she's bad with me. Where I can protect her and look after her.

"When do your parents get back?"

"Tomorrow," she says with a groan. "They're not going to let me leave all of the time like I've done this week. I don't know what we'll do then."

Anxiety makes my chest ache. I've grown used to seeing her every day as soon as she gets out of school. Today, she skipped school altogether, so we could spend the entire day together. "We'll find a way, sweet girl. Even if I have to steal you away."

Words like that should make her fearful, but she only giggles. "It's not stealing when your victim willingly goes with you."

Arching an eyebrow at her, I look at her in question. "So you're my victim now?"

"I can be your victim if you want me to be." Her lips pout out, and she runs her fingers through her wild blonde hair.

"What do you want for your birthday?" I question to change the subject from the dangerous territory it had gone to as I turn onto a gravel road I know leads to a quiet part of the ocean.

"Hmm," she ponders as we park. When I turn off the car, she turns to look at me. "I want you."

"You have me."

"That's all I want," she murmurs. I want her to elaborate, but she climbs out of the car. Before her door even closes, I'm already out of the car and trudging through the sand after her. The wind picks up and whips her hair off to the left. She'd worn a loose summer dress, which flaps in the wind. With every gust, it gives me a glimpse of her round ass barely contained in a pair of pink panties.

Swimming is a bad idea.

When she reaches the water's edge, she grabs the hem of her dress and peels it away. I freeze in my tracks. My jaw clenches as I watch her shed her bra and then finally those tiny panties. Her body is perfect—exactly like Baylee's. My traitorous cock agrees.

Swimming is a very fucking bad idea.

"The water's warm," she calls out, flashing me a grin and a view of her perky tits before she sinks into the ocean. "Come swim with me, Gabe."

I tear my shirt from my body and lose my shorts. The wise thing to do would be to leave my boxers on so I don't get carried away with Baylee's twin in the water.

I've never been a wise man.

I'm a man who thinks with his cock.

And my cock thanks me the moment I shove down my boxers and charge after her. The water is warm like she said.

"I'm a bad influence on you, sweet girl," I tell her and grab her wrist to pull her closer moments before a wave nearly drowns us both. When we reemerge, sputtering water, I pull her all the way to me.

"How do you know I wasn't bad before?" she questions, her arms snaking around my neck.

"Because I've been watching you this entire time. You're a good girl."

She leans her forehead against mine. "Did your stalking reveal the time my parents put me in a mental hospital?"

I tense at her words. "They fucking did what?"

She leans back and holds her wrist up for me to see. "Do good girls cut their own wrists just to see the blood?"

I press a kiss to the scarred flesh there. "Why would you do that?"

"Because I don't think like normal people. My brain is wired differently."

"Different is good. Hell, I'm as fucking different as they come."

"Good girls don't steal and tell lies to their friends, so they'll hate each other. Good girls don't watch their younger brother stroke his cock at night. Good girls don't take their shirt off for their forty-year-old teacher and try to break up his marriage. Good girls don't want to fuck their..." she looks down at my lips but doesn't finish her statement.

I close my eyes because she's driving me fucking crazy. "We can't fuck, sweet girl. I know I seem like a fun friend who showed up when you needed him most. But I'm more than that. Your creator. Your father. A piece of you."

Her eyes cloud over and she looks past me down the beach. "If I could prove you weren't my real father, would you make love to me?"

A growl rumbles from my chest and I squeeze her to me. "You're mine."

She brushes her lips across mine. "I know. Whether you're my father or not. I'm yours. I became yours the moment I heard the sickening crunch of that baseball bat."

Another wave hits us, and my palms find her ass to keep her from going under. She wraps her legs around my waist. My cock presses against her sweet center, desperate to push inside of her.

"Why are you doing this?" I grumble.

"Why are you fighting this?"

"I'm a bad man who does very bad things," I snarl, my restraint holding on by a precariously thin thread. "I'm better when I'm with you. Let me be a better man."

Her eyes mist over and her lip wobbles. The rejection she wears on her face cripples me. "I don't want you to be a better man. I want you to be you."

Slipping my thumb into her mouth, I grip her jaw with my other fingers and hold her so I can look at her. "Don't make me cross that line, sweet girl. There's no coming back once it's been crossed. I'll never let you go. Ever."

Her teeth sink into my flesh as anger flashes in her eyes. I yank my grip from her and glower at her.

"You let *her* go," she snaps.

I grab a handful of her hair. "Because of *you.*"

When her hand clutches onto my cock, black bleeds into my vision. The sunlight is snuffed out as darkness creeps in. Out here in the water, we're two halves of a whole. Society's rules mean fucking nothing. I'm about to cross that line when someone hollers at the shoreline.

I jerk my head over to see some asshole. "You can't swim here. Private property. You've got five minutes to get out of here, or I'm calling the police."

He stomps away. I wonder if I could choke the life out of him in those five minutes. If I had my knife, I'd slice open his gut and drag his entrails into the water for the fish to feed on. This fucker just ruined our moment.

I take a deep breath.

A moment that would have changed everything between us.

A moment that would have killed something before it even began.

"Come on," I tell her and forcefully rip her from my body. "We need to leave." I all but drag her out of the water.

She pouts as she pulls her clothes back over her wet flesh. I brood while I dress. Neither of us says a word. We're both pissed and frustrated and confused.

"Now what?" she questions once we're settled back in the car.

"I take you back home."

She scoffs. "I don't want to go home."

Slamming my fist into the steering wheel, I turn to glare at her. "And I don't want to fucking lose you because I fucked you during a moment where I let my dick do the thinking. You're mine, Hannah."

"Not yet," she murmurs.

I clench my jaw but don't argue. She's right, though. This girl won't be mine until we're far, far away from this hell hole where our families, and the negativity they bring, are in the way.

"Not yet," I agree and squeeze her hand. "But soon."

chapter
TEN

Hannah

Soon.

Soon.

Soon.

That was several months ago. Ever since the day I almost got him to fuck me, he's been strangely resilient to my advances. Mom and Dad have long since come home. And as predicted, my time with Gabe has diminished to mostly on weekends. Our phone calls last until the wee hours of the morning and our texts never stop. I just wish we could have more.

But at least he watched me graduate. When I'd walked across the stage, I found him in the crowd and blew him a kiss. My parents would never see him in the sea of people. It was my public promise to him. A proclamation of my love. And I didn't miss the way his dark eyes lit up with love.

"Your move," Dad reminds me.

I blink away my daze and skim my eyes over the chess pieces. No matter my play, he'll win. Dad always wins. "I'm thinking," I stall, twisting my peace sign necklace in my fingers my dad gave me when I turned sixteen.

He smiles and leans back. "What's there to think about, Han? I'm going to win. May as well get it over with."

Ignoring his taunting, I lean forward with my elbows on my knees. After a moment, I look into his navy blue eyes. My dad is handsome and sweet. And my *real* father. One hundred percent. I'd wanted to explain that to Gabe, but then I feared he might not want to see me after that. That, I couldn't bear.

"Do you remember that time I cut myself?" I question, my voice even and unaffected.

His eyes close and his face blanches. "All too clearly."

"We have a rare blood type."

He swallows and nods. "Rarest of them all. O negative. Only six point five percent of the population has that blood type. But you and I both have it."

"Is it weird your blood flows through me?" I question. His face is pale and his shaking hands draw into fists. "That it mixes with mine and somehow works?"

"I'm thankful. It saved you."

"Dad?"

His eyes open, and I see the darkness flickering there. He's thinking about it. He's calculating the probability of how I should have died. That a girl with a rare blood type's chance of living after such a traumatic "accident" should be dead. Not alive and well and happy playing chess with him. The numbers practically dance out of his head into the air. It's painful for him, that much I can see. Not just thinking about what happened to me. The close call. What's painful is his need to keep a lid on his darkness.

For years I tried to keep my lid on too.

But now I don't like the lid.

I prefer the darkness to the light.

I want to free it.

"You know I love you, Dad. No matter what."

"I know, Han."

Scanning the board, I find the most satisfying move. The most satisfying win for my dear father. Once I move the rook, opening up my queen, I stand and give him a kiss on his cheek. "You win, Daddy."

His smile is wide and the love in his eyes chases away the darkness that lingered there only moments ago. "I always win." He winks. "Why don't you get off to bed? Tomorrow the five us can take a beach day. Soon you'll go off to college, and we'll miss you. Get some rest and tomorrow will be just us. Ren can surf. Your mom can run. Calder and I can take turns dunking you like old times."

Laughing, I give him a quick squeeze around his neck. "Sounds perfect."

"Night, honey," Mom says from the doorway.

I look up from my phone where I was texting Gabe and smile. "Night."

Her brows furrow together and she stares at me for a long time. "Where'd you get that ring?"

A pink diamond on a platinum band sits on my ring finger. Gabe gave it to me for my eighteenth birthday a couple of months ago. He'd put it on my right hand, but when I'm alone, I wear it on my left and pretend he's my husband. I never wear it at home, though, for this very reason.

"Um," I start, slightly shocked at her taking notice. Lately, she's too wrapped up in everyone else to notice something like my jewelry. "It's from my boyfriend."

Not totally a lie.

Gabe just doesn't know he's my boyfriend.

Details.

"What's his name?"

Crap.

"Julian Hunter," I blurt out. As soon as I say the names of my rapists, I wish I hadn't.

Her eyes narrow and she purses her lips together. "Is he good to you? Why haven't we met him?"

I sit up and twist the band around my finger. "You've met him plenty of times. Not my fault you can't remember him." I can't help but fuck with her.

She frowns. "When did you meet him?"

"While you were in Italy."

"I see. How old is he?"

"Older," I challenge.

Her arms cross over her chest and she gives me the sternest look she can muster. "I want to meet him. Invite him over tomorrow for our family beach day. I'm sure he's lovely, but I don't feel comfortable with you seeing him without us having met him. You know how we feel about these things."

"Why? Did something happen to you to make you worry about me so much?"

She swallows and her hands ball into fists. "No."

I challenge her with my gaze. She's lying straight to my face.

"Why don't you talk about Grandpa?"

"Hannah, you're not—"

"Were you raped when you were younger?"

"No, I—" Her eyes widen in shock, and I can see the wheels turning in her head.

Another lie. "What, it's not rape when you have feelings for your attacker?"

She storms over to me and slaps me. "Don't you dare talk to me that way ever again. You know nothing, Hannah. Nothing."

A cruel laugh escapes me. "No, *Mother*, you know nothing."

We glare at each other for a long moment. My phone buzzes. Before I can yank it away, she has it in her grip reading our texts. Invading my privacy.

"I miss you, sweet girl," she whispers aloud. "Is his name really Hades?"

I snatch my phone from her. "Privacy, Mom!"

"Get some sleep," she seethes. "Tomorrow we're discussing what's gotten into you. I'm going to call Dr. Gibson. The medication isn't working like it used to. Your moods are all over the place."

In a fit of rage, I throw my phone as hard as I can at her. It misses her face because I *made it* miss her face. If I wanted it to hit her, she'd have a broken nose as we speak. Instead, my phone now sits cracked and dead on the floor.

She doesn't say another word, just slips out and closes the door behind her. Tears stream down my cheeks. I'm not going to see Dr. Gibson again. Last time, he asked me questions about my sexuality. Had I ever had anal sex? Did I watch porn when I was alone? How many times did I masturbate a week? All questions to help him diagnose me, he'd said. His words danced the line between helpful doctor and perverted old man. I didn't miss the way he eyed my thighs every couple of minutes. I refuse to let that man give me more medications that'll have me as a vegetable on his black couch ready and waiting for his wrinkly fingers on me and in me.

Hopping off the bed, I find my duffle bag I use when we travel for softball. I stuff as many clothes that will fit inside. Once I've thrown in my makeup and medications—just in case—I zip it up and plan my escape. Before I leave, though, I pull open my laptop and send Dad an email.

Daddy,

I can't stay here anymore. Mom wants to medicate me, and I don't feel like myself on all of those medications. Summer's here now, and college is around the corner. I'm going to stay with a friend until I get myself sorted out. I love you.

Han

I know Dad won't read the email until morning. Once I send it, I snatch up my bag and push open my bedroom window before they set the alarm for the night. I'm outside and halfway to Gabe's before I give in to tears. The walk takes about thirty minutes. Soon I'm standing at his front door with my fist poised to knock.

Ever since that first night, we've never come back to his house. I've only ever seen his wife once. I'm nervous about seeing her again.

With a sigh, I knock softly on the door. A few moments later and it opens. I stare into the eyes of a girl no older than Calder. Her brown hair is pulled back into a ponytail, and she eyes me curiously.

"Can I help you?"

I vaguely remember her from the family pictures on the wall from that first night. "I'm here to see Gabe," I tell her.

Just then, Gabe's massive frame fills the doorway behind her. He takes one look at my tearstained face and crushes me with a comforting hug. I let out a sob as I grip his T-shirt.

"What happened?"

"I left. I thought maybe we could…"

He pulls away and looks at the girl. "Brie, go on up to bed."

"Who is she?" she questions.

"Someone very special to us. Go to bed now."

When she disappears, he hauls me into the entryway. I set my bag down and swallow down my emotion. "What's your blood type?"

His brows furrow together. "AB positive. Why?"

My smile is so big it hurts my face. "Can I stay here tonight?"

"Of course, sweet girl."

He hefts my bag from the floor and guides me to the bedroom I stayed in the first and only time I was here.

"Will you stay *with* me? Like last time?"

He nods. "I'll be right back."

While he's gone, I undress and then find an oversized T-shirt in my bag. Once I've pulled it over my head, I climb into the warm bed that somehow smells like Gabe. Rubbing my thighs together, I wonder what it'll be like to have him.

I *will* have him.

Closing my eyes, I part my legs and touch my bare pussy. I lean back against the pillows to relax. My fingers massage my sensitive flesh while I dream of the dangerous man I've become so close to. With each swirl of my touch, I get closer and closer. But it's not close enough. It's not good enough. It's not *him*.

"Mmm," I whine.

A soft click of the door has me reopening my eyes. He leans against the closed door, his dark eyes shadowed by his hair that curtains around them. Somewhere along the way, he took off his shirt and dons only a pair of low-slung holey blue jeans. He's fucking hot, and I want him inside of me.

"What are you doing?" he grumbles.

I meet his gaze and then push a finger inside of myself. "Trying and failing to orgasm."

His jaw clenches.

"You could help me," I murmur and can't help but taunt him, "Daddy."

He closes his eyes and gives his head a shake, as if to drive the depraved thoughts from his head. I don't want them to go away, though. I want to see them and dance with them and live with them and make love to them.

"Sweet girl," he growls. His voice is low and angry. I want to unleash his fury. I want to be his victim.

"Why won't you fuck me?"

He storms toward me, furious and violent, and I nearly come at the sight because he's so beautiful. I part my lips to gasp with pleasure. "You're poking a bear that's been in hibernation for a long time."

Arching a brow at him, I give him a challenging stare. "Maybe I need the bear to maul me."

His eyes caress my flesh. "The bear would fucking hurt you. The bear is unstoppable. The bear is cruel."

"It's a good thing I'm not Goldilocks then. I'm not running from you, Hades. I'm running *to* you. We were meant to find each other. I can be her…Krista, Lynn, Mom. Just do it already. I'm dying for you."

He launches himself at me, causing me to cry out in surprise. His fingers grip my wrist and jerk me away from touching myself. "Stop it," he orders. His chest is heaving as he pins it to the bed. The way his fingers dig into me makes me fight him more. I like the bite of the pain.

"No."

"Fucking stop," he snarls. "I'm going to hurt you."

His mouth is close to mine so, I lift forward and bite his lip. My mouth is forced from his when he brutally grabs my jaw. I punch his side with my free hand, which causes him to lose his grip on my face. We struggle until I have him right where I want him.

Between my legs.

"There," I purr, my eyes meeting his enraged ones. "Much better."

His tongue flicks out, and he licks away the blood I drew from his bottom lip. I want to lick that lip too, but he won't release me. Both of us breathing heavily as we stare each other down.

"You're fucking with my head, sweet girl."

Smirking, I dig my heels into his ass. "I'd rather fuck *you* instead."

His growl melts my insides.

"That night, when those motherfuckers raped you," he murmurs, "they fucked your head up too. You think you want this, but you don't."

His words infuriate me and I explode. "Fuck you, Gabe!"

I squirm enough to free my hand and I claw at his face. As soon as my fingernails meet his flesh, he slams my hand back onto the bed. His breath is minty and sweet and just a hair from my lips. This time, I lean up and kiss him. I don't bite him, but instead run my tongue over his wound. When I let out a whimper of need, his little thread he clings so desperately to snaps.

Pop.

"So wrong," he hisses before spearing his tongue deep into my mouth. He kisses me expertly, as if he's been practicing his entire life just for me. We're no longer fighting against one another. Now we're fighting to climb into each other. My fingers rip at his hair as he kisses me like I might disappear.

"I won't disappear," I voice my thoughts against his lips.

"Fucking damn straight you won't."

His mouth swallows mine again. I lose all sense of reality as the beast consumes me. I need him inside of me. I'm trying to voice this need, but his kiss is too powerful. He doesn't stop nipping and sucking and tasting me until he lifts up briefly to undo his jeans. I don't get any sort of warning to the fact he's made his decision until I feel the tip of his cock against my wet pussy.

Gabe isn't slow or sweet or gentle.

He just drives into me with one powerful thrust that has me screaming—a scream he swallows with a kiss. His cock is thick, so thick, and I feel like he's going to split me in two. Thrust after thundering thrust, he fucks me like it's his right to do so. I've never felt so wanted or loved in my entire life. It's as if he wants to live inside me.

I want him to live there too.

"Don't stop," I manage to murmur when he lets me gasp for air.

"I'll never fucking stop," he snarls.

His fingers slip between us, and he massages my swollen clit. The sensations are too much. I try to clench my legs together, but this beast between my thighs makes it impossible.

"I want you soaking my cock, sweet girl. Make that pretty pussy juice all over me. I want it all. Fucking give it to me," he orders with a growl.

The sensations mixed with his words drive me wild. But I need more...

"I want you to look at me when I come," I tell him bluntly. "Look. At. Me."

His eyes turn nearly black, but he heeds my request. I stare into his dark, vicious eyes and I see me. I see my own monster staring back at me. Oh, what a beautiful monster she is too.

"You're so fucking perfect," he huffs, "and mine."

I let out a choked sound of pleasure as an orgasm takes hold of me with force. My body jolts and quivers as I climax hard. His grunting only lasts another moment before scorching heat fills me. Every inch of my insides are coated by the beast on top of me. He slows his bucking into me until the twitching of his cock subsides. Then, he buries his nose into my hair at the base of my neck.

"I have no moral compass, Hannah."

I laugh. I'm sure his words were meant in warning, but they only comfort me. "Neither do I."

"What the fuck?" he grumbles. "That was so fucked up, but I loved every second of it. I'm waiting for my dick to wake back up so I can fuck you again. I want inside every single one of your holes. Those motherfuckers may have taken your virginity, but I'm going to take your ass one day. Every tight inch."

Shivering, I scratch my fingernails down his spine. "Run away with me. Let's leave this town."

He lifts up and indecision paints his features. "I have Brie to think about too, sweet girl."

His words irritate me. He has *me* to think about. I try to push him away from me, but he's like a brick house. After several unsuccessful attempts, he chuckles.

"Are you pouting?"

Not meeting his eyes, I shake my head. "No."

"Liar."

"I'm not pouting."

"Look me in the eye."

My gaze snaps to his, and I hope he sees the jealousy and anger in them. "I didn't think about my family when I ran to you."

Guilt morphs his features and he peppers kisses all over my face. "No, you didn't. You're reckless and irresponsible and uncaring of others."

I glare at him. "Okay, Mom."

His gaze darkens. "I'm your fath—"

"Yeah, about that," I interrupt. "You're not."

He doesn't blink. Just stares at me. I watch with amusement as his jaw clenches several times. "Impossible."

"Possible."

"But I know—"

"Well, you're wrong. I have the rarest blood type. So does my father," I whisper, "Warren."

He flinches at the name. Instead of arguing, he pulls out of me and climbs off the bed. He pulls up his jeans over his hips and points at me. "Get dressed. Now."

Frowning, I shake my head. "No."

"Don't test me, sweet girl."

With tears springing in my eyes, I climb off after him. When I'm near him, I throw my arms around his neck. "I'm sorry. I didn't mean to taunt you. Please don't make me leave. I love you." A choked sob escapes me. "We can pretend. I can be her. Please let me be her."

His fingers tangle in my hair and he jerks my head back to the point of pain. I let out a whine when his mouth sucks on the flesh just to the left of my throat. "When I said you were mine, I wasn't fucking joking. You think I'm going to let you go? Now? Fuck that. *We're* leaving. Tonight."

I sag in his arms, relief washing over me. His mouth is all over my neck marking me as his. With each nip and suck, I grow hungrier for him. I need him inside of me again.

"Will she try and stop you?" I question.

His chuckle is downright evil and sinister. Straight from the depths of hell. I love how it warms me from the inside out. "She can fucking try."

Smiling, I slide my fingers into his hair and grip him.

"Grab a quick shower, sweet girl," he says and slaps my ass. "I need to go deal with Alejandra."

"How was your shower?" he asks as he hauls a suitcase to the front door.

"Would have been better *with* you."

He smirks at me. "Tomorrow I'll bathe you."

With that promise, he walks out the front door to load the vehicle. While he's preoccupied, I tiptoe up the stairs to see how he "dealt" with Alejandra. I wonder if he dealt with her by using a baseball bat to her beautiful face. Would her blood color the walls? Grinning wickedly, I peek my head into the bedroom doors until I find the master bedroom.

Inside, I'm sickened by what I see.

Fucking sickened.

Alejandra's wild eyes meet mine, and she whimpers through the gag in her mouth. She's been tied to each poster of the bed. But she's *alive*. Unharmed.

Eyeing the knife he used to cut the rope, sitting on the nightstand, I walk over to it. She implores me with her eyes to use it to free her. To cut her loose so she can stop Hades from dragging Persephone into his hell.

I don't think so.

Persephone *wants* to be dragged into the dark underworld where she belongs. With her love, her life, her Hades.

Alejandra is a complication. A complication we don't need.

"He's mine now," I tell her as I sit beside her on the bed. "I hope you enjoyed him while you had him."

She glares at me but can't speak through her gag.

I hold up the knife. Sharp. Serrated. Long. Wide. A knife like this could really hurt someone. It would make such a mess.

Dragging the tip between her breasts, I watch with glee as the knife tears through the fabric easily. I wonder if it tears through flesh, muscle, and bone all the same. Her muffled screams are beautiful. A symphony of sadness, anger, and jealousy. I love her screams because they're a means to an end.

I want Gabe to tie me up and make me scream too.

But my screams will only be the beginning.

"Did he tell you he was my Daddy?" I taunt.

Her eyes widen and she nods.

Leaning in toward her, I grin. "Did he tell you he fucked me earlier? Made me come all over his cock? That we're going to run away together so we can fuck all of the time?"

Tears well in her eyes and she shakes her head in denial.

"True story," I tell her. "He's been waiting for me all this time. And now I'm here. Ready for him. He's all mine now."

Our eyes are glued to each other when I drag the tip of the knife up her chest to her throat. She starts to cry when I find the giant artery that pulsates in her neck.

"What happens if I poke a hole here?" I question. "Does the good doctor bleed out?"

Not waiting for her response, I push the tip of the knife into her flesh above the pulsating vein. She garbles words through her gag. The small hole I poked gushes for such a small hole. Crimson leaks out around the tip of the knife soaking her pillow behind her.

I'd always heard when you slice the carotid artery, it sprays everywhere.

They never educated us on what happens when you poke it.

But what about when you twist your knife into the thick vein? Do I get a bloody spray then? Will it be as climactic as I'd hoped?

The knife twists slowly in my grip. Her flesh tears against the blade. A bigger gush seeps out, but still no spray. The movies were all wrong. I'm severely underwhelmed.

Releasing the knife, I slide off the bed and stand.

"I'll take good care of him," I promise. And I'll never break that promise.

With that, I hurry down the stairs toward my future.

My love.

My life.

Mine.

chapter
ELEVEN

Gabe

After six hours in the car, we finally pull off the old highway down a dirt road situated between two mountains just outside of Tucson. Hannah is asleep, and the sun is just barely coming up over the desert horizon. A few years ago, I took some of the money I had stockpiled away from when War bought Baylee and purchased this private land. It was always my hope to whisk Hannah away one day. To convince her to stay with me.

What I didn't anticipate was her revealing that I'm *not* her father.

At first it made my heart fucking bleed, but the animalistic craving for her just wouldn't go away. I'd needed her in some primitive way since the moment I scooped her bloody body from that rapist's bed. It grew and morphed into something I refused to unleash. I love her and crossing a line like that could have been detrimental. Turns out, I worried for nothing.

I can now have her any fucking way I want her.

The drive down the narrow road takes another thirty minutes until I arrive at the stucco home I'd had built for this moment. It's not a large house. Just a couple of bedrooms. But it's new and has all of the amenities we could ever need. I'd even had the builders put in a pool. This will be our paradise. Our home. Our forever.

And now I don't just get to take care of her, I get to fuck her too.

Talk about happily fucking ever after.

My mind drifts to Alejandra. I'd meant to end her life. It's what I should have done. But then I thought of Brie. My sweet little Brie. She'll need her mother. One day I'll come back for her, but not until the aftermath our departure will bring dies down. Brie doesn't need to leave her school or friends. Alejandra will be a good mother to her until I come back.

I park inside of the garage and look over at Hannah. She stirs, rubbing her palms in her eyes. Her blonde hair is messy, but she's still perfect.

"We're here," I tell her.

We climb out, and I take her hand before we enter. A cleaning lady comes once a week to keep the place free of vermin and dust. On the way here, I'd given her a call to ask her to bring a few things to the house. I'm pleased to see a bowl of fruit on the island as we enter the kitchen. I know the refrigerator and cabinets will be stocked with food, too.

"Cute place," Hannah praises as she prances through the house touching everything in sight. I follow after her, watching her tight ass jiggle every time she moves.

"The best part is outside."

She pulls open the sliding glass door and squeals when she sees the sparkling pool. "Let's swim!"

I chuckle and hook my arm around her waist before she dives in fully clothed. "It's six in the morning. Let's rest and we'll swim when the sun's out."

She pouts but relaxes against my chest. "What will we do until then?"

"Sleep," I propose.

Not giving her a chance to argue, I clutch her hand and guide her through the house toward the bedroom we'll be sharing. I'd had the other room set up for her, but now I don't want her anywhere but in my bed.

"Take off your clothes and get in the bed," I order, pulling off my own shirt.

Her eyes darken and a smile plays at her lips. "Do you like tying girls up?"

My cock twitches at her words. Visions of my sweet girl bound and at my mercy twist my mind up. Dirty, dark thoughts have my body dying to do so many things to her.

"Yes." My voice is husky and dry.

"Are they bad girls?"

"Sometimes."

"What do you do to them?"

I smirk. "Whatever the fuck I want."

"Would you do that to me?" A golden eyebrow arches up in challenge.

I'm not sure what she wants from me. "Only if you ran from me. There's no getting away now, sweet girl."

Fear doesn't flicker in her eyes. Desire does.

She edges over, taking a few steps in my direction. "So if I ran from you, you'd drag me back and tie me up? What would you do then?"

A low growl rumbles in my throat. "I'd whip your ass for leaving me." I unbutton the top of my jeans and kick my shoes off.

She looks down at her tennis shoes and sends me another challenging stare. "Then what?"

"I'd fuck you until you begged me to stop."

"What if I didn't want you to stop?"

"Trust me, you can't handle what I would do."

She closes the distance between us and licks her lips in a seductive way that has me fisting my hands at my sides to keep from mauling her. "I bet I could. I bet I'd want it."

"I don't think so."

Both of her palms run along my pectoral muscles. "I'm not Krista or Lynn or Mom. I'm better," she snips out. "You'll see."

I'm about to argue back when she shoves me as hard as she can. I lose my footing and fall on my ass. It's then that I see a flash of blonde as she bolts from the room. That bad, bad girl.

Clambering to my feet, I don't hesitate as I chase after her. The backdoor slams as she runs from me—fucking runs—fully knowing the consequences of such an act. Her blonde hair flies out behind her like she's some kind of flying fairy.

I'm going to catch her.

I'm going to hurt her.

The Arizona dirt under my feet stings as I tear after her, but I ignore the bite of the tiny pebbles against my soft flesh. All that matters is catching that girl so I can fuck her.

"Getting slow in your old age?" she taunts over her shoulder.

Letting out a growl, I power after her. She may have played softball, but I work my ass off at the gym. Her legs are no match for mine. Soon, I'm close to her. I reach out, but she zigs hard to the left and then zags quickly to the right. I'm momentarily stunned but catch back up. This time, when she's close, I tackle her. She cries out when her knees hit the dirt.

"Don't fight me," I hiss.

But, boy, does she fight me. Her fist swings up and clocks me in the jaw. Amazingly, she rolls out from beneath me and starts to take off again. I grab her ankle to yank her back to me. I fucking maul her like the bear I am and press her chest into the dirt. She lets out a moan, but still fights me as I tear her shorts from her body. Once I have them to her knees, along with her panties, I don't waste any time pulling my cock out. I'd expected her cunt to be dry, but she's wet, and it greedily sucks me into her body.

"Oh yes," she moans and clenches around me.

I grab her hair and yank her head back. "Why'd you fucking run from me?"

"To see if you'd catch me," she pants.

Grunting, I drive into her hard and fast. I'm going to come inside of her. As soon as I get off, I'm going to give her the ass whipping of a lifetime.

"Of course, I'd fucking catch you. I'll always catch you."

She moans as if my words please her. "This feels good, Gabe."

"Are you going to come with my dick inside you? I can't reach your needy clit from here, sweet girl."

Her body writhes beneath me. "Yes!"

And, boy, fucking does she. Her pussy clamps down around my cock, which makes me explode inside her. I come so hard, I think I might pass out. An old guy like me does not need to be running through deserts chasing little fuck dolls. I'm too old for this shit.

"Jesus!" I hiss as I spurt out the last of my seed. "You trying to fucking kill me?"

Her fingers clutch the dirt, and it's then I notice she's wearing the ring I gave her on her wedding finger. It makes my chest swell with manly pride. She's mine.

"You promised to bathe me," she murmurs, her back heaving with exertion. "And I'm really dirty."

Groaning, I slide out of her and stand on shaky legs. My dick still drips with my release, splashing her white ass—an ass I'm going to royally fuck up later. I tuck my cock back into my jeans and fasten them before helping her to her feet. She drags her clothes back up over her dirty body. When our eyes meet, I love the way hers shine with pleasure. Her little monster has been sated.

"You're bleeding," I point out and gesture to her knees.

She shrugs. "I'm guessing it won't be the last time you make me bleed."

I turn away from her, so she can't see just how fucking crazy she makes me. "Come on."

Hand in hand, we walk back to the house. When we reach the back door, we strip out of our clothes so we don't drag dirt into the new house. I guide my dirty girl to the massive bathroom and start the walk-in shower. Once it warms, I pull her under the hot spray with me.

"That was stupid," I tell her. "After everything I've told you about me. About what I've done, who I've killed, people I've taken and tortured. You still poke the bear. What happens when I hurt you? Will you wake up one day and realize you've had enough?"

She wraps her arms around my waist. "I'll never have enough. That was the single most exciting moment of my entire boring life. I don't want to quit you."

I smile and hug her to me. "It's a good thing. Because there's no getting away. Ever."

After our shower, I can tell she's dragging. Her eyes droop and she practically stumbles into the bed. I sit on the edge of the bed watching her until she passes out. Then, I make my move. With quiet efficiency, I bind each of her wrists and tie them to the headboard above her head. She doesn't stir, and I bite back a laugh.

Once I'm sure she's secured, I jerk her knees apart and stare at her pink pussy.

"Wake up, sweet girl," I coo.

She mumbles and then lets out a needy whine once she realizes her predicament. "What are you doing?"

"Punishing you."

She laughs—fucking laughs at me. "Like you punished your wife? I peeked in and saw her all trussed up. Did you give her pussy a little fuck before you left?" Her eyes darken with jealousy.

Now it's my turn to laugh. "She was always a placeholder until you came back to me. And no, I didn't fuck her. I just wanted her to stay."

"Like a good dog."

Her pupils are dilated and she looks wild with fury.

"Are you on drugs?" I demand, my fingers biting into her thighs so I can part her for me.

She smiles wide and her tits jiggle as she laughs. "Not anymore."

My fingers slide down to her cunt and sure enough, when I push a finger into her, she's wet for me. "What do you mean, not anymore? Were you using?"

Her body bucks as I finger fuck her. I almost stop to force her to talk to me, but she speaks before I have to. "Unless you call antipsychotics and antidepressants a drug addiction, then no, I wasn't using. Just doing as Mom and those doctors asked. But now that I have you, I don't have to take them anymore."

I clench my teeth together and push another finger into her. She moans as I stroke her G-spot. "You *only* need me," I agree.

Her eyes brighten with adoration. "Only you."

Now that I have her full attention, I feast upon her sweet pussy for the first time. The scream of pure bliss fills the room and she bucks against my face, greedy for the pleasure I intend on giving. I suck on her throbbing clit as I fuck her tight pussy with my fingers. Her cunt tastes of sin, and I gladly enter the dark side with her juices running down my chin.

"I need…I need more…"

I insert another finger inside of her, but not to fuck her with it. I want to get it wet. Once it's sufficiently drenched, I slide back out. When my finger probes the tight hole of her ass, she cries out in surprised shock.

But I don't give her a moment to argue. I push into her virgin hole slowly. My tongue continues to assault her clit while my fingers do their magic on her pleasure holes. Soon, she's screaming like a demon as she comes all over me. Her body tightens around my fingers, to the point that I wonder if I'll ever get them back out of there.

"Oh, God, that was…"

"I'm not finished, sweet girl. There is no 'was.' This is all happening *now*. I'm going to own every part of you until all you think about is me one hundred percent of the time."

She shakes her head. "I already think of you all of the time."

"When you're hungry and you think of my cock, when you're thirsty and you think of my cum, when you're tired and you think of my chest as your pillow, when you're needy for a fuck but I'm already pushing inside you," I bite out. "Then you'll be where you think of me all of the time."

"Right now, I could mention your mother or father or brothers and you'd think of them. I want your thoughts, sweet girl. Every single fucking one of them."

"Untie me," she begs, her breaths shallow. "I need to touch you."

Growling, I twist her until she's on her stomach. Then, I drag her legs off the bed so her ass juts out at me. "I'm not done touching you first."

"What are you going to do?"

I lean over her and growl in her ear, "Don't you remember? I owe you a whipping."

She starts to argue but I hit her ass hard with my palm. It stings my flesh. Her yelp gets my cock hard as fuck.

"Did that hurt?"

"Yes!"

"Want me to do it again?"

"No…"

Lying little girl. I can tell by the way her body shudders with need that she doesn't want me to stop. Her monster inside is begging for it. Begging to be beat into submission.

"Beg me to hurt you."

"Only if you call me Persephone," she bites back.

I laugh and hit her ass harder this time. The bright red mark of my hand will no doubt turn into a bruise later.

"Do you like that, Persephone?"

"Yes, hit me again, Hades."

Smirking, I step away to find my belt still looped around my jeans. Once I slip it from my pants, I make my way back over to her red ass.

"Beg."

"Hit me again! Please!"

Thwap!

She screams and wriggles away, but I dig my fingers into her thigh to pull her back to me.

Thwap! Thwap! Thwap!

At one point, she kicks backward and narrowly misses my balls. Despite her begging, she doesn't like it.

"You wanted me to hurt you," I snarl and whip her several more times. "But now you want to kick me away?"

"Stop!"

"No!"

She twists back around onto her back and kicks me right in the jaw. I stumble backward until I fall on my ass. Her wild eyes are dilated to the point they almost look black. That caged monster is running free.

"What do you want me to do then?" I demand, my chest huffing.

"Release me so I can claw your fucking throat out," she screams.

With a full-bellied laugh, I throw my head back. "Not yet, sweet girl. Not yet."

This time when I stand and head for her, I'm prepared for her attack. When she kicks, I grab her ankle and twist her back onto her belly. Her ass cheeks clench together as she prepares for the next blow. But it doesn't come. I crush her with my weight and suckle on her neck. My palms slide underneath her and pinch at her nipples. I thrust my cock against her sore ass until she's whimpering.

"Please…"

"Please what, my beautiful girl?"

"Please fuck me."

I chuckle. "I want to take your virginity."

"My ass?" she whimpers.

"If you're good and you relax for me, I'll reward you like you would not believe."

Her entire body goes limp. "Okay."

With a grin, I lift up and push my rock-hard cock into her cunt to wet it first. Despite this girl wanting to kill me moments before, her pussy is fucking drenched. Bad girl.

I pull out of her wet hole and then press against her much tighter hole. Her screams are otherworldly as I inch into her slowly. Everything in me begs to slam into her, but I love her and hurting her more than she can handle right now just isn't on my list of things to do. I want her to enjoy this. She cries against the mattress but remains deathly still as if moving one single bit will make it worse on her.

"Such a sweet, sweet girl," I praise. "Take my cock in your tight ass. Tell me how much you love it."

"I love it," she moans.

I wrap a hand around her waist until I locate her clit. With soft circles I bring her to the edge of bliss while I slowly pump into her. "Does that feel good?"

"Yes."

"Want me to stop?"

"God, no," she hisses. "Don't stop. Oh my goooood!"

As soon as her climax overtakes her, her quaking body clenches around my cock like a vise. I'm helpless to make it last any longer because the moment she loses control, my release gushes deep inside her, filling her up.

"Fuck!" I snarl as my cock drains inside of her. "Fuck!"

My cock softens after a moment, and I slip it carefully out of her. She's limp as I untie her hands. Her body remains unmoving when I scoop her into my arms to carry her back into the shower. Those pretty blue eyes refuse to meet mine as I set her to her feet inside the shower and start cleaning her.

Finally, I've had enough of her games.

"Open your eyes and look at me."

When she finally opens them, I expect to see fear with a little bit of hate. What I don't expect is hunger and possession and love.

Clenching her jaw in my grip, I make her look up at me. "I love you, sweet girl. Don't you ever forget it. Even when you feel like you can't take it anymore. When you think you hate me. When you consider running away for real. Remember, I love you. I have since before you were born."

Her fingers claw at my shoulders as she draws me closer. "Every second with you only binds my heart more intricately with yours. You're the one who will want to run away in the end. I'm difficult and hard to handle. Just ask my parents."

At this I laugh. "I'm difficult and hard to handle too. Seems we were meant to find each other."

chapter
TWELVE

Hannah

The heat of the afternoon sun warms me. I've been out here for hours and should probably go inside, but I don't want to. I'm relaxed and happy. In heaven. With my king of the underworld. My Hades.

I peek an eye open and watch him over the top of my sunglasses as he drags a net along the pool surface gathering bugs and debris from the water. Every muscle in his body flexes with each movement. Large biceps and forearms are bite-worthy, complete with bulging veins and just enough arm hair to make a girl go crazy. He dons a pair of swim trunks that hang low on his waist, revealing a sexy little V with a trail of dark hair right in the middle that leads straight to his hidden massive cock. I'm hungry and want to rip those shorts right from his body.

He kneels by the edge and scoops a handful of water into his palm. His hair had fallen into his eyes but now he splashes it with the water so he can slick it back. The water droplets run down his face dripping onto his solid chest. I lick my lips. I'm thirsty too. Men who look this good should be rich and ridiculously famous with big breasted women hanging all over them. Not secluded in the middle of the desert with a girl who barely knows her way around the bedroom.

Yet, here we are…

I've been rewarded by some higher power, that's for sure.

When I go to sit up, I let out a whine that has him jerking his head toward me. His black aviators on his nose hide his dark eyes, but I know they flicker with desire. Despite the pain he doled out last night, I'd come so hard. I'm still in a post-anal-sex stupor. After he whipped me and then fucked me until I lost my sanity, he'd cuddled with me. So much so that we'd slept through the morning, and most of the day away. I'd made us a quick meal before we came outside to enjoy the sunshine before it disappeared.

"Your ass hurt, sweet girl?" he calls out as he returns the net to its hook on the wall, his full lips quirking up into a half grin.

I stand and amble over to him. "Maybe."

"Want me to kiss your bruises?"

Our mouths meet for a quick kiss. "Do I really have bruises?"

His chuckle heats me from the inside out. "There's no doubt, baby. I didn't go easy on you."

Pulling away from him, I walk over to the water's edge. Then, I look over my shoulder at him giving him a wicked smile as I drag my toe in the warm water. With my eyes on his, I inch the bottoms of my black swimsuit down my thighs, baring my ass to him. The reaction is instantaneous, and his cock strains through his swim trunks. I love the effect I have on him. So immediate. So greedy and needy and downright possessive.

"Is it bad?" I question, a slight pout in my voice.

He charges for me and palms my breasts as he hugs me to him, letting me feel his throbbing erection against my sore ass. "So bad," he growls. "But fucking beautiful too. Purple and blue. Like a goddamned masterpiece."

I twist in his arms and palm his pectoral muscles, making sure to turn him right where I want him. "Will this earn me more?" With a hard shove, I push him backward into the pool. The splash is loud. His dark form lurks in the deep end and his aviators flutter to the bottom. I pull my bottoms back up and wait for him to resurface with my hands on my hips.

But he doesn't resurface.

He just sinks to the bottom.

He's fucking with me.

We play chicken. Each of us waiting out the other.

My heart races in my chest while I wait for him to gasp for air and chase after me. For him to spank me and call me his bad girl.

But he doesn't resurface.

He just remains still at the bottom.

He's fucking with me.

Right?

"Gabe," I yell. "Not funny!"

Nothing.

Did he hit his head on the bottom?

Panic seizes me. Do I still remember CPR from tenth grade?

He's fucking with me.

"Gabe!"

Time ticks by quickly and he doesn't move. At all. Not one tiny bit.

He's not fucking with me.

"No!"

Without another moment of hesitation, I dive into the water. I swim quickly to him and wrap my arms around his waist. He doesn't move or jerk or anything. His body is heavy, but in the water, I'm able to drag him toward the shallow end. When I can touch, I roll him over to his back. Dark hair clings to his eyes and his mouth hangs open.

"No!" I screech and slap his face. "No!"

I drag him over to the steps so I can attempt to feel for his pulse. When I can't seem to find the thumping that should be there, I start to panic. I need to do CPR but I don't know how I'll get him out of the pool. A sob rips from my chest and interrupts the quiet desert air. My mouth hovers of his. I press my lips to his and blow air into his mouth. This isn't how they taught me to do it in gym class, but it's the best I can do.

"Breathe, goddammit!" I beg.

I'm so busy trying to force air into his lungs, I barely register his palm cupping my breast. As soon as I realize this, his tongue spears into my mouth while his other hand grips my hair.

"You're not dead!" I scream at him.

But he will be for freaking me out.

Fisting my hands, I rain punches down against his hard chest until he grabs both wrists and immobilizes me.

"I don't die, sweet girl." He winks. Smug motherfucker.

"I hate you!"

He releases my hand to grip me by the throat. With his fierce, smoldering eyes on mine, he walks me out to the deep end by my neck. I'm not choking because the water makes me practically weightless and I can still touch. But when we get out to where I can't touch, it becomes a struggle to stay afloat and the grip on my throat does start to choke me.

"Take it back," he seethes, his lips inches from mine.

I kick at his balls but the water thwarts my efforts.

"So help me, Hannah. Take it back or I'll drown you right now."

"Fuck you!"

His eyes flicker with rage, his fist squeezing around my throat. "Say it."

When I don't, he begins pushing me under the water. My hand grips his wrist that's clasping my throat. He dips me to my chin.

"Fucking take it back," he orders.

"No!"

Dunk.

I'd barely gotten a breath of air before he submerged me. I kick and struggle, landing a knee to his stomach. His grip loosens, and I rise to the surface. I've barely sucked in a deep breath when I'm pushed back under.

"Take it back!" he roars above the water.

Reaching forward, I grab his nipple and twist until he lets me go. I swim away from him, deeper into the water. When I think I might get away, a firm grip around my ankle yanks me back. My lungs burn with the need to breathe air. His handle on me is loose enough that I could get away, but I'm assaulted by memories of the accident.

Jace Friedman is twenty-three and beautiful. He's thirteen years older than me but surely a man like him could want a girl like me. I haven't developed breasts yet but I'd be a great kisser, I just know it. If only I could convince him to even look at me. I'm sure once I got his attention, I'd have it forever.

The waves are super choppy today. Mom told me to stay in the shallow part but she's got her hands full with Calder. He's crying because there's sand in his juice box.

Would Mom even notice if I drowned?

She only notices when I do something bad.

Drowning is bad…

"Mommy! Watch this!" I call out moments before I do an impressive cartwheel in the shallow water.

She doesn't look up. She babies my brother instead.

Pouting, I wade out into the water. The waves are crazy and try to swallow me whole. Some days I wonder what would happen if they swallowed me. Would I become a mermaid and live at the bottom of the sea?

Maybe Jace is a merman…

I'm lost in a daydream where Jace and I swim along the ocean floor, collecting pretty shells for my daddy, when a gigantic wave crashes over me. It yanks me back with it, and when I go to reach my toes out to touch, I can't find sand. Only water.

Panic seizes me, and I thrash in the water.

Jace will save me.

Don't swim.

If you drown, he'll have to come out here and rescue you. He'll have to wrap his big, muscled arms around you and put his lips on you.

Thrashing to the surface, I splash and scream. I'm proud of my act, but then another wave hits me sucking me under. This time, I don't care about the slow lifeguard. This time, I try to swim to the surface. But I'm confused and I can't tell which way is up.

My lungs hurt and I want to breathe!

I'm fading out when something grabs my arm.

Jace?

The grip is tight, and I'm dragged to the surface. As soon as I gasp for air and choke out seawater, my eyes meet the terrified blue ones of my mother.

"My baby girl," she coos and hugs me to her chest. "You scared me half to death, baby."

I start to cry and hug her tightly as she swims us back to shore.

Maybe she pays more attention than I realized.

"Sweet girl," a deep voice rumbles through my daze. "Where'd you go, baby?"

I look into a pair of dark brown eyes in confusion. "Jace?"

Those dark eyes swirl with rage. "Who the fuck is Jace?"

Reality swoops in and settles around me.

Gabe. My Hades.

"A lifeguard when I was ten," I tell him, my voice hoarse. "I was confused."

It's then I realize that I'm in his arms, and we're sitting on the steps in the pool. My thoughts are murky and the past still lingers.

"Look at me," he orders, his chocolate-colored eyes swirling with emotion. Anger and rage and fear and sadness and love. And me. "Take back what you said. We're not leaving this pool until you do."

Tears well in my eyes and I wrap my arms around his neck. I straddle him and press my lips to his. He squeezes me against him as if he never wants to let me go. I'll die if he ever does let me go…

"I don't hate you. I couldn't ever hate you," I murmur against his mouth. It's the truth. He scared the shit out of me. All I could think about was being alone. Without him. A world without him simply doesn't exist anymore. Nothing else matters but him.

"I'm sorry I held you under. I'd never let you drown," he says. "You know that."

Our teeth clash together as we kiss with the need to devour the other. His fingers rip at my swimsuit, both top and bottom, until I'm naked in his arms. He somehow manages to squirm out of his trunks and one breath later he spears me with his cock.

"Oh God!" I shriek.

"He can't hear you now that you're with me," he growls and nips at my bottom lip.

I tilt my head back as he bucks into me. His mouth finds my neck. Teeth and more teeth. Biting and tearing and scraping. He hurts me. He may even make me bleed. The bruising, the cuts. I love it. I need it.

All it takes is his fingers on my clit while he fucks me, and I'm lost. Gabe is this dark thunderstorm that came up over my horizon, decimated everything in his path, and swept me away with his torrential presence.

Who needs light when the dark nourishes your entire being?

Not this girl.

"Yesss…" My words trail off as I climax hard enough to see glittering stars in the middle of the day. His heat fills me as he roars like a bear tearing apart his prey.

Gabe tears me apart.

Rips and shreds me.

And then he somehow puts me back together better than I was before.

It's magic.

"I love you, sweet girl," he murmurs against my throat. "Too much. A love like this will eventually kill one of us."

Gripping his hair, I tilt my head down to look into the sated monster's eyes. My eyes zero in on his perfect lips, and I lick mine. "I hope it's me then. What a way to go…"

His features harden and he grips my jaw, his thumb biting into the soft flesh below my cheek. "A life without you is no life at all. I can assure you, I will die before you. Not because of my age, but because I can't mentally fathom something happening to you or being here without you. My mind would crush in on itself. If you needed to breathe, I'd give you my last breath. All for you, sweet girl."

We remain conjoined, his cock soft inside of me. I bury my face into his neck and cry. His words scare me. I don't like thinking of a life where one of us exists without the other. I only want to know a life where the two of us live together. Alone. In the desert. Secluded from society and reality. A piece of heaven.

He climbs out of the pool with me in his arms, kicking out of his shorts the rest of the way. I shiver when we make it inside and the air conditioning chases away the warmth from outside. He doesn't set me down until we're standing in the shower and the water turns hot. Then, he slides me off his cock and onto my feet. I'm shuddering from the cold, but also from fretting about his words. They haunt me.

I'm obsessed with them.

I'd give you my last breath.

Tears choke me up, and I hug my middle.

Well, Gabe, I would suffocate before I accepted it.

Powerful arms wrap around me. I'm safe and warm in his embrace. No threats or stress or heartache. Only happiness and love.

Gabe

We've been locked away in our secluded paradise for days. The time passes slowly and quickly, and sometimes I think it simply stops. I've given up caring about what day of the week it is, or anything else for that matter, because she's all that matters.

But sometimes, late at night, after I've fucked her pretty much until she passes out, I think about other stuff. I think about my Gabriella. Little Brie. So sweet and smart like her mother. Beautiful. Too innocent for this world. Soon, she'll be old enough for boys and shit. That makes me crazy fucking furious. She'll need me to look after her and protect her.

I could bring her here…

But what about Alejandra? She doesn't fit into this equation. Hannah is my love, my fucking angel. Alejandra doesn't fit.

Fuck.

My conscience, some bastardy intangible thing that seemed to vine its way through my mind from the moment Alejandra told me she was pregnant. No matter how hard I try to cut it away—to leave it in the past—I can't. It's still there sprouting beautiful little flowers named Brie.

She's probably upset and confused at how her daddy could abandon her. And I *did* abandon her. I left her without a goodbye because I'd had Hannah on the brain. I'd let my obsession fuel and guide me.

I'd left my own flesh and blood because my dick told me to do so.

Hannah stirs beside me in the dark. My thoughts are interrupted when the blanket slides down my stomach past my cock and down my thighs. Warm lips wrap around my soft dick, but it wakes right the fuck up. She's been practicing late at night, so I can't see her face. I think it gives her confidence to try weird shit. Like, just yesterday, she tried to stick her finger up my ass. That ended when I flipped her over and drove my dick inside hers instead. Tonight, she's not trying to get in my ass, but instead tongues the tip of my cock like it's a lollipop. She's fucking teasing me on purpose.

She distracts me.

My moral compass is obliterated in her presence.

As long as she's touching me. Laughing. Chatting my ear off. Just looking at me. I'm completely focused on her. Nothing else exists. I'm blissed the fuck out on her. Only when the world goes silent does my conscience slowly wake.

I'm not this man.

I don't have complications.

Life is simple. I take what I want. I get what I want.

But what happens when what I want threatens to tear me apart and drag me in opposite directions.

Hannah's teeth sink into my cock causing me to hiss. She doesn't bite hard enough to make me bleed, but she bites hard enough to force my attention back on her. My sweet girl hates to be ignored. She hates it when she's not sitting pretty on her pedestal.

In fact, she goes a little crazy.

We discovered that yesterday when I made her stay at home while I ran to the store. I didn't need anything, but I needed to check in on Brie. At the house, there's no signal whatsoever so I had to find out. Brie didn't respond to my text. I'd even dragged my ass around town for an hour. Nothing. Crickets. Alejandra, even though I left her tied up, would have gotten loose eventually, or Brie would have released her. So when I bit the bullet and called my wife, I had expected her to answer. Nothing.

It's been bothering me ever since.

What really bothered me was when I came home. Hannah's face was red from crying. She'd thrown all of the lawn furniture into the pool. I'd found her sitting with her legs dangling in the water. Naked. Crying. Furious.

It took a lot of soothing words and finally an ass whipping followed by an angry fuck to calm her ass down. Then she just cried until she fell asleep. While she slept, I found her empty duffel bag under the bed. The medications sat there untouched. I'm fucking worried as hell that she truly does need that shit. She doesn't act like the girl I met. The girl I met was subdued. An animal, yes. She was caged, though. Then, I set her free.

Now, I don't know how to cage her back up when she acts like a madwoman.

I'll simply have to force her to take the meds again. She'll get over it. It'll piss her off, but she'll calm the fuck down eventually.

"Fuck!" I snap when she bites me again. Yanking at her hair, I pull her away from my dick. "Bite me again and I'll tie your ass to the bed for a week. Don't test me, sweet girl."

She laughs like a fucking lunatic and goes back to sucking my dick like a motherfucking pro. When I'm about to come, she grips my balls to the point of pain before taking me deep in her throat. The girl's a wicked vixen, and I come without abandon. All down her warm little throat. And when she gags, I push on her head so she'll take it deeper.

I release her when the last of my cum spurts out. She slips away and straddles me. Not because she wants to fuck but, because she wants to be the center of my world. Grabbing her elbows, I pull her to my chest to hug her and press a kiss against her hair.

"I want you back on your meds in the morning." My words hold no room for negotiation.

She stiffens in my arms. "Why?"

I let out a sigh. "Because you need them."

"Says who," she bites out.

"Says me."

"You're not my dad."

I growl and flip her over onto her back. "No, you're my fuck doll, sweet girl. You're my woman, my soul, my motherfucking other half. But you need them and you'll do as I say, or I'll force them down your throat just like I forced my cock down it."

She rages beneath me, further proof that she needs the shit. Thankfully, I'm stronger than her little bad ass. Eventually, she gives up and relaxes.

"You think I'm crazy too. Just like Mom. Just like those doctors."

Pressing my lips to hers, I kiss her softly and breathe my words against her. "I don't think you're crazy...I just don't want to lose you to your impulses."

She wiggles. "Fine."

"That's it. Just fine?"

"You want to control me? Control me. I'll take the pills. I'll be your little zombie girl until the end of time if that makes you happy."

I let her curse and rage and hate for the rest of the night.

And the next morning, she takes the fucking pills.

Things have gone back to normal once she got back on her medication. No more wild child moments. No more tantrums. No tearful breakdowns.

Just her.

And me.

In motherfucking bliss.

But I have to know how my daughter is doing. I need to check on her. To give her some sort of explanation and a promise that I will come back for her. She's probably beside herself with stress and worry. Brie's an innocent. Such a sweet, brilliant girl. As much as I belong out here with my Hannah, I can't help but feel torn. Her little heart will be broken.

"We almost there?" Hannah questions from the passenger seat, twisting her peace sign necklace between her fingers. "I'm hungry."

I learned my lesson last time and no longer leave her at home alone when I go places. She rides shotgun and tells me a million different stories about her childhood—the ones I wasn't privy to being behind the glass and in the shadows of her life.

"Another fifteen minutes and we'll be on the outskirts of Tucson. We'll find a diner or something once we get there."

She nods and sticks one of her feet out the open window, wiggling her bare toes in the wind. Her dress lifts up and shows her pale pink panties which makes driving fucking impossible when I want to pull over and fuck her with my fingers instead. The girl likes to fuck. A lot. She's giving this old man a run for his money.

Dragging my gaze from between her thighs, I wonder if I'll be able to buy some gym equipment for this house. I'd not considered it when I had it furnished but after a week of not working out, it's driving me crazy. Running through the desert and swimming laps in the pool simply aren't cutting it. My body is used to a more rigorous regime.

"Do you think they're worried about me?" she questions, her head rocking to the beat of the music.

I think about how Baylee has hovered over her children over the years as if they may vanish at any moment. How War is always glancing at exits and people as if everyone is a potential child kidnapper. They're obsessed with their children's safety. And even though their oldest daughter is eighteen, I can imagine they're stressing the fuck out.

"Do you want to call them?" I blurt the words out before I can stop myself.

She bites on her lips and shrugs her shoulders. "Maybe. Can I think about it?"

Smiling, I reach over and grab her hand. "You can do whatever you want, sweet girl. I'm going to check on Brie so I don't care if you check in, as long as you don't tell them where you're at or that you're with me."

She jerks her hand away and glares at me. "Why are you going to call her?"

Passing a slow car, I gun it before answering her. "She's my daughter. I need to let her know I'm okay and I love her."

Her mood darkens, and she crosses her arms over her chest. She's silent for the rest of the drive, and I wonder what's cooking inside of her head. I wonder what the fuck we're going to do when the meds need refilling and we don't have them.

Then, what the fuck?

"Pedro's Mexican Restaurant?" I ask when we pass a billboard boasting of the best enchiladas this side of the border.

"Sure," she says with a cold bite to her voice. "Oh, and I do want to call them. Thank you." I don't like her tone but I brush it off. I'll be sitting in on that conversation.

When we pull into a decrepit parking lot of the questionable looking restaurant, I pull out my phone and am thankful to see bars of service.

"You first," she says and clasps her fingers together.

With a sigh, I dial my daughter's number. No answer. Alejandra still doesn't answer either. I know she's pissed I left her tied up to the bed, but I could have done much worse. She of all people knows this. If she's keeping me from talking to Brie because of this shit, I'll make her pay dearly for it.

"No answer?" she questions.

"Nope. I'm going to try the hospital. Alejandra should be there."

She nods and gives me a beautiful smile. "Okay."

I dial the nurse's station where they can page her to talk to me.

"Surgery," a bland voice barks, "Nurse Brenda speaking."

"Hey, Brenda," I greet. "It's Johan. Is Alejandra available? I need to speak to her. It's urgent."

The line goes quiet for a moment. "Um, I, uh…" The phone is muffled as she speaks to someone else, but I can still hear her.

"What did they say to do if Johan calls?" she hisses to someone.

The response is muffled, but I understand. "Patch him through to Detective Larson."

"Um, yes, Johan," Brenda says with a shaky voice, "let me transfer you."

"Brenda, she doesn't have a phone there. You page her and she comes to the phone. Why are you trying to send me to a detective?" I demand with a growl.

"Do you really not know? I told them it wasn't you. You're good to her, and she loves you. But they didn't want to listen to me," she murmurs.

"Know what?"

"Alejandra was murdered a week ago."

Blood boils inside of me, and I shoot Hannah a scathing glare. She smirks. She motherfucking smirks at me. Swallowing, I let out a hiss. "I didn't fucking know this. Where's my daughter?"

"Well, since you weren't there and Alejandra has no other family in the US, she's been taken by child services. I'm so sorry. I thought you knew—"

She's cut off, and I hear a scuffle of voices. Then, I'm put on hold. What the actual fuck? Seconds later, the phone rings as it's forwarded. I hang up before it connects to this Detective Larson.

"What the fuck did you do, Hannah?" I demand.

Her eyes narrow and darken. "She was a complication. You said so yourself many times this week."

Running my fingers through my hair, I suppress the urge to throttle her. "What. The. Fuck. Did. You. Do?"

"I did what I had to do for us," she snaps and crawls over the console onto my lap to straddle me. Her wild eyes meet mine and she smiles like the devil. "I pushed that blade into her pretty little neck. Watched her bleed out all over the bed while you packed the car. She died before we even left the house."

I grab her by her throat and choke the shit out of her. She yanks at my wrist, but I don't let go. "You left my fifteen-year-old daughter home alone with her dead mother's body? You left her to find that shit by herself? What the fuck's wrong with you, Hannah?"

When she grows limp in my grip, I release her. She gasps for air but wastes no time attacking me. Her claws are bared, ready to rip my eyeballs out, but I snatch both of her wrists before she exacts any damage.

"She would have taken you away from me," she tells me, her voice defeated and her lip wobbly. "I didn't want her to come between us."

Closing my eyes, I lean my head back against the seat rest. "She and I were never truly in love, sweet girl. I would never have left you for her. Fucking ever. But letting Brie find her that way? You really fucked up, baby."

Her lips smash against mine and she threads her fingers into my overgrown hair. "Please forgive me," she breathes out her plea. "Please. I didn't think about what would happen. I just did it."

I slide my palms to her ass and squeeze. Her tongue finds its way into my mouth. She kisses me hungrily. When I've had enough of her apologetic kisses, I tug at her hair to pull her away from me.

"They're looking for me now. I'm obviously the main suspect. Of course, they're looking for Johan, not Gabe, but it won't take long to connect me, I'm sure."

A tear streaks down her cheek. She's not sad about the fact my daughter had to find her dead mother tied up to the bed. She's sad because she thinks the fucking police might take me away from her.

"No more bullshit, Hannah. You have to get your act together and do exactly as I say. If they're looking for me, then we're not safe here. You can make the call to your parents, but then we're getting rid of this phone."

She nods in agreement. I swipe the tear away with my thumb and kiss her nose.

"Be a good girl."

I hand over the phone and she dials a number.

"Put it on speaker," I instruct.

With another push of the button, the ringing can now be heard by both of us.

"Hello?" a kid answers.

"Ren?"

"Holy shit! Hannah? Where are you? Mom and Dad are freaking the fuck out!" he shouts.

She frowns. "I'm fine. I swear. How's everyone? How's Dad?"

"You know Dad. He's obsessed with locating where you're at. You left your smashed phone here, but he's been on the hunt. They're super panicked because the day after you left, there was a murder up the road a little ways. I didn't think we had to worry about you since you emailed Dad but they still have been stressed about the whole thing. You should come home, Han. They won't eat or sleep or smile. They're sad."

I bring my lips to her neck and suckle the flesh there. My mind whirs with shit I now need to be aware of. Every trip to town is going to be a problem. Fingerprints are a problem. If they connect the two, it's a huge fucking problem.

"I'm not coming home, Ren. I'm in love."

He groans on the other line. "You're always in love, sis. At least talk to them."

When I nip at her flesh, she lets out a gasp. "Okay. Mom, though. I don't want to talk to Dad." I jerk away to read her features. Her eyes are teary. She's a daddy's girl and doesn't want to hear his disappointment.

"Mom?" Ren calls out. "Han's on the phone."

Not a second later, Baylee's breathy voice fills the line. My cock hardens from the sound of it I've missed for so long.

"Baby girl? Where are you? I'm so sorry we had a fight. Just come home and we'll work it out. God, I'm so glad you're okay."

Hannah grabs my wrist and guides my hand between her legs. Once she's shown me how wet her panties are, she gives me a wicked grin. *Finger me*, she mouths. I push a finger into her hot, tight center and revel in the way she gasps loudly.

"I'm better than okay, Mom. I'm in love."

Baylee sighs into the phone. My finger drives in and out of my sweet girl's cunt as she speaks with her mother. "You're not in love. With whom? That Julian Hunter?"

She smirks. "No, I lied. That's not his name."

Don't, I mouth to her in warning. I don't like the wicked gleam in her eyes.

"Is it your teacher?" Baylee questions, horror lacing her voice.

Hannah laughs, a little on the maniacal side. "Nope."

"Coach Phil?" Baylee's sigh is one of exasperation.

"Not this time."

"Stop playing these games and tell me." Baylee's voice is tight and fierce. It's a façade, though. I know when she hides her fear. She's fucking terrified for her daughter right now.

"You play games all the time, *Mother*," she snaps. "You lie and keep the truth from me. Truths I should have been told ages ago. But no, you hid it all in your obsessive stupid effort to protect me. A lot of good it did. I was raped by two men, *Mother*. Are you hearing me?" Hannah starts to cry, and I hug her. "Two men!"

"Hang up," I murmur against her hair.

"No."

I growl, but she pulls away from me and swipes at her tears.

"What are you talking about, Han?" Baylee asks, her voice a mere whisper.

"When you were in Italy, I was drugged, dragged away to some stranger's house, and they fucked me, *Mother*. They forced me and I couldn't do a damn thing about it because I was paralyzed against their attack. Maybe if you'd told me how *you'd* been kidnapped and raped, *I'd* have known what to do!" she screams, fat tears rolling down her cheeks. "You did this to me!"

Baylee starts to sob on the other end. "Where are you? Who are these men who hurt you?"

"Julian and Hunter," she laughs, the sound sinister and harsh.

"Why didn't you go to the police?" Baylee demands. "Why didn't you tell us?"

"Because *he* saved me."

"Who?"

"Hades."

The line goes dead silent for a beat. And then, "Who is Hades?"

"He slaughtered those bastards and carried me out of that hell. He nursed me and loved me. He told me stories, *Mother*. Stories about my grandparents. Stories about *you*."

"No," I hiss and grab for the phone, but she wriggles away.

"No," Baylee's voice echoes mine.

"And then he made love to me, *Mother*. He showed me what true love is—love you threw away because you chose your captor over him! He's mine now, and I love him!"

"Hannah!" Both Baylee and I shout at the same time.

We wrestle for the phone, and I finally wrench it from her hand. I snag both of Hannah's wrists in my grip while she hisses and curses at me. Yanking her onto the console beside me, I hold her against me while I greet her mom. She squirms but isn't going anywhere.

"Miss me, sweetheart?" I growl into the phone. "And don't you worry your pretty little heart out. She's safe with me."

"YOU MOTHERFUCKING UNDYING MONSTER! I SWEAR IF YOU TOUCH MY DAUGHTER I WILL CASTRATE YOU AND—"

I hang up before she can finish the sentence. "Get your ass over there." Hannah tenses and lets out a gasp when I release her. "Don't speak. Don't move. Don't goddamned do a thing but sit there and think about the fucking mess you've made."

As soon as she scrambles into the seat, I climb out of the car and slam my phone into the concrete. I stomp on it several times until it's crushed and dead. I don't get to look at any pictures of Brie or *any-fucking-thing* because I don't need them tracking us here. I'll have to find a way to see Brie once I figure out what the fuck I'm going to do.

I climb back into the car and peel out of the parking lot. We're silent as I drive through and get some burgers from a fast food joint on our way home.

My heart is full with this girl. Fuller than it ever has been before. I love her.

But she's making me fucking crazy.

It's time to domesticate my wild animal.

I'm going to have to tie her ass up and teach her how to behave.

We're too far into this for either of us to back out now…

chapter
FOURTEEN

Hannah

He refused to utter a word the whole way home. And the moment we pulled into the garage, he put on some running clothes and ran far, far away from me. I cried the whole time. I'd cut open Alejandra's throat *for us*. So she wouldn't try and steal him from me. So she wouldn't call me a slut like Mrs. Collins did. I did it *for us*.

But I suppose it ruined things.

Now he's wanted for a murder *I* committed.

And now, because I just couldn't help but taunt my mother, my parents know I'm with Gabe. I don't even want to begin to think what sort of means Dad will go through to get me back. As far as I know, he's probably already hacked into every surveillance camera in the US looking for footage of me to see where I'd gone off to.

Dad *will* find me.

Shit!

I chew off my fingernails as I wait for Gabe to return. It's growing dark, and I miss him. I want to throw myself at his feet and beg for forgiveness. I want to formulate a plan for us to become new people so we can hide away from those who hunt us.

He needs to come back home.

I need him.

Need. Him.

I fucking need him!

I find some Windex and set to cleaning every window and mirror in the house to distract myself from the terrors plaguing my mind. Once I've done that, I clean the toilets. Vacuum. Sweep. Scrub the shower. Then I count my pills. I obsess over how many I have left and what happens when I run out.

Will Gabe grow tired of me?

Am I too crazy for him?

Was I a fun fuck and now I'm simply a psycho, murdering thorn in his side?

I'm pacing the living room ripping at my hair when the back door opens up. When I drag my gaze over to him, he ensnares me with an evil glare.

A look that says, *I'm going to devour you.*

I flash him a wide, relieved grin. I *need* him to devour me—to promise me it'll all be okay. To comfort me. To erase this anxiety that's turning the inside of my head blacker than black.

My smile seems to infuriate him further, though. When I reach for him, he hisses at me.

"No."

His one word sends ice through me, chilling every vein in my body.

"What do you mean, *no*?"

He stalks over to me and snatches my wrist. It's painful and possessive. The way his thumb digs into my flesh sends relief fluttering through me. "I mean," he growls, "play time is over. Enough with this bullshit. It's time for your punishment."

Punishment last time was intense pleasure. He whipped my ass but made me come harder than ever before. His punishments don't seem like punishment at all. They seem like rewards. I'm confused because he doesn't look happy. He looks pissed.

"Okay," I tell him and then bite on my bottom lip.

He drags me into the bedroom. As soon as we're inside, he grabs up the rope he'd used before and binds my wrists together. Then, he once again uses a longer rope to tie it to the headboard. There's enough slack that I can easily stand beside the bed.

"What now?"

He tugs off his soaked T-shirt and tosses it to the floor. "You can wait there until I decide what I'm going to do with you."

"Are you mad at me?"

His jaw clenches and his eyes cloud over with darkness. "No, sweet girl, I'm not mad at you." He stalks toward me. His fingers dig into my hip as he draws me to him. I part my lips open when he lowers his face to mine. *Kiss me, Hades.* "I'm fucking furious."

Instead of kissing me like I'd wanted, he releases me and storms off into the bathroom. Anger surges through me. He can't just tie me up like some wild animal. I yank and pull at my bound wrists in an effort to loosen them. He's a pro, though. I'm not going anywhere. After several minutes of cussing and screaming, all of which he can't hear while in the shower anyway, I give up and sit on the edge of the bed.

My mind flits to Calder and Ren. I wonder if they miss me. Do they even notice I'm gone? Is it a relief not having their crazy sister there, fucking shit up as usual? Ren's probably free to have an actual girlfriend now. Without me there to terrorize her and sabotage their relationship. He's probably happy. Probably having sex with her as I sit here bound and helpless. She's probably a teenage whore. Just like that last girl he dated, Sidney. Sidney was perfect with her soft brown hair and bright green eyes. He doted on her. Treated her like she was the damn queen of the world. Ren stopped hanging out with me, his sister and best friend, so he could make out with the bitch. It pissed me off.

But I got rid of Sidney.

One day when she and Ren were out swimming, I snooped in her phone. Found all of these naked pictures she'd sent to Ren. So, I forwarded them to all of the male-sounding names in her contacts on her phone, along with some special messages to each of them, even making sure to add the stupid little tag she always puts when she texts.

Want to hang out later? xoxo Sid

My boyfriend doesn't kiss like you do. xoxo Sid

I'm horny. xoxo Sid

You're hot. xoxo Sid

I wish it were you instead of him. xoxo Sid

Including Calder. Calder, being the noble brother he is, later showed Ren the text Sidney had sent. *I wish it were you instead of him.*

I'd planned on drugging her and making a really racy video I could put on YouTube, but it never came to that. My brother broke up with her. She denied the claims and said her phone was hacked, but many of their mutual friends at school also confirmed receiving the text from Little Miss Innocent. Her reputation was ruined. And I had my brother back.

But now that I'm gone, is Ren glad?

Did he find another "good" girl?

Does he fuck her on my bed?

My fists ball up and my entire body trembles with fury. I've always been jealous of girls talking to my brothers, especially Ren. I don't know what I'll do if they ever get a wife.

Maybe she'll meet the same fate as Big Tits Alejandra…

"Have you had enough time to think about what you did wrong?" Gabe's deep voice drags me from my angry thoughts and into the present.

Jerking my head over to his voice, I find him standing in the doorway completely naked and drying his hair with a towel. He's no longer pulsating with rage. Instead, he seems amused now. One of his dark eyebrows is quirked up in question. A small smile tugs at one corner of his lips.

I want him to lie down on this bed so I can sit on his face.

I want to feel the way his recently thinned out beard feels against my inner thighs.

To have his tongue taste a part of me no other man but him has tasted.

I'm his and he is mine.

"Untie me. Let me touch you," I plead.

He chuckles, but it's not humorous. It's sinister. Dark. Deadly. It turns me right the fuck on. "Nope. We're only getting started, sweet girl."

Defeated, I hunch my shoulders and tear my gaze from his body that I'm positive was sculpted by gods with super powers. "I didn't mean to make a mess of things."

He finds a pair of sweatpants in a drawer and drags them up his muscular thighs, denying me the view of his nice cock. Then, he pulls on a shirt and some shoes. I guess we're not going to have makeup sex.

"You didn't mean to. But you did. Now, we can't enjoy our time here as a couple. Now, I have to make plans. I have to be vigilant. I have to keep a motherfucking eye over my shoulder twenty-four-seven," he seethes. "Not to mention, you murdered the mother of my only child and left her to find her by herself. No child should ever have to see their parent's bloody corpse. I have no idea where they've taken Brie because of you. You. Did. This."

Huffing, I snap my head up to glare at him. "For us!"

He stalks toward me, and I jump to my feet to meet him head on. His fingers thread in my hair, yanking my head back to look up at him. "You're out of control, Hannah. It's time you calm your ass down."

Sneering, I bare my teeth at him. "Good luck trying to control me. My parents and doctors couldn't. What makes you think you can?"

With a hard shove, he pushes me onto the bed. Before I can kick him, he anticipates my go-to move and grabs both shins immediately. "I can and I will. I'm going to run into town to buy a few supplies to break you in."

At this, I burst into tears. My blurry gaze finds his as my lip trembles. "Please don't leave me again."

He scowls and rests a knee on the bed between my spread thighs. The heat makes me rub my leg against his to seek relief and comfort. Then, he lowers himself over me to get close to my face. "You don't care anything about me breaking you in, do you? I could beat your ass until it killed you and you still wouldn't give a shit. No, you're afraid of something else entirely. You're afraid of being left alone. Afraid I won't talk to you. You're afraid of losing me." His eyes grow distant as he mulls this over. "Very interesting. Looks like we'll have to try something different."

"Don't leave me," I beg.

He grazes his lips across mine but doesn't kiss me. "That's exactly what I'll do."

Before I can plead my case any more, he jerks away from me and exits the room. I scream and cry for him. He's still in the house. I know because I can hear him rooting around in the kitchen. Finally, he comes back.

Holding a roll of duct tape.

"No," I sob. "I'll die. What if I hyperventilate and die?" My tears are coming out as steady streams now. With every ragged breath I take, my entire body quivers. "I'm scared."

Riiiip!

The tear of a strip of duct tape makes the same sound of my heart ripping from my chest. He's found a way to hurt me and it works. It hurts. So fucking bad.

"I won't forgive you for this," I murmur.

Our eyes meet and uncertainty flickers in his. But in the end, he wrestles me down and slaps the tape over my mouth. "Yes you will, baby. I need to do this."

If my eyes would do as I command them to, I'd scorch him with my fiery rage. Burn his body to the ground where he stands.

But then you'd be alone. Without him.

Tears spill over. Snot runs down the strip of tape. My heart ceases to beat.

"You're going to be okay. I'll be back. When you're fucking losing your shit, remember I'm doing this for you. For us. Just like you did what you did to Alejandra. For us. Sometimes we have to hurt the one we love in order to keep them," he says softly. His hand reaches out and he strokes my cheek. I lean in to his touch. "Sometimes we have to hurt them so they don't hurt themselves much worse. I'm doing this for us, sweet girl."

My entire world goes black with loneliness when he steps away. His footsteps thunder through the house until the door slams shut.

I'm alone.

All alone.

This is going to kill me.

"Wake up, beautiful. I brought you a present."

I stir from my fetal position on the bed to find Gabe stroking the hair out of my eyes. It's dark in the bedroom and the light from the bathroom illuminates his face in an eerie way. He leans forward and kisses my forehead. I need his mouth on mine. I need him to free me so he can make love to me. I need to touch him back.

His fingers grab the edge of the tape. With one quick yank, he rips it away along with probably a layer of my skin. I cry out, but he soothes me with his mouth on mine. He kisses me tentatively, but I try to maul him despite my bound position. My body seeks his desperately. I attempt to wrap my legs around his hips, but he stops me with his words.

"Don't you want to see your present first?"

I let out a whine. "No, I need you inside of me."

His growl makes my entire body quiver with need. "Later. First, I want to show you something."

He leaves me alone on the bed. Soon, I'm blinded by the overhead light. Squinting, I sit up on the bed to look for him. What I see at the end of the bed infuriates me.

"Her name is Maria."

Maria, an olive-skinned woman, stares at me with wide, bloodshot eyes. Her mouth is covered in duct tape and she's bound to one of the kitchen chairs. She looks terrified. Her brown eyes plead with me? Sympathize with me? Worry for me or with me, I'm not sure. All I'm sure about is the fact she's naked. Her big tits jiggle with each movement and her bushy cunt sits wide open by the way she's bound to the chair.

With a growl of my own, I snap my gaze to Gabe and spit out my words. "Why is there a naked woman in our bedroom?"

He arches a brow and shrugs. "She's your punishment."

"Did you fuck her?" I seethe.

His lips press together in a firm line. He shakes his head. "Not yet."

Animal. He thinks I'm a wild animal? He'll learn this when I escape and tear his eyeballs right from his skull!

"You cheating asshole! I will kill you for this!" I scream at him, sliding off the bed so I can stand. "I'll cut your cock off and feed it to the vultures!"

He smirks. Stupid man.

"So jealous," he tsks. "Are you jealous of every woman or just the ones in my life?"

I think about Ren and all the girls who talk to him. How I hate them all. I think about when other girls would talk to Mr. Collins, and I wanted to choke them. I think about how Dad fawns all over my mother like she's the queen of England. But mostly, I think of Gabe touching Maria's hairy cunt with his perfect fingers—fingers that were meant for me and me only.

"I'm not jealous," I lie, my eyes cutting over to the woman, who now seems even more terrified. "Especially not of her. Is she a whore?"

Gabe laughs. "Not a whore. Just a lady who worked at the grocery store. A lady who couldn't say no to the proposition of sex with a man like me."

Hissing at her, I struggle at my bindings. "He's mine! How dare you?!"

Tears stream down her face and she shakes her head as if to argue his words. Gabe doesn't lie to me. The bitch wanted him. Wanted to sink her hairy pussy on his thick cock.

I want to hurt her.

To cut her throat like I did to Alejandra.

"I need to pee," I lie. Technically, I do have to pee, but I want him to cut me loose so I can get to her.

"I bet you do."

He saunters over to me, no longer wearing shoes or a shirt, and unties the part that's hooked onto the headboard. His grip is tight on the rope as he guides me into the bathroom. Since I'm bound, he has to slide my panties down my legs.

After I pee, he wipes my pussy for me but doesn't put my panties back on. I hope he compares our pussies and realizes mine is a thousand times better.

"Why are you so mad, sweet girl?" he taunts. "You're going to have to control your jealous impulses. You can't kill every woman I pass on the street because you don't like the way she looks at me. We'd both end up in prison before the end of the week."

"You're mine," I snap. "She thinks she can come in here after minutes of knowing you and take you away from me. I hate her."

He pushes me against the bathroom wall with his hands on my hips. His lips descend upon mine in a soft kiss. I groan against his mouth and hike my leg around his hip.

"Make love to me, please."

"Not yet," he murmurs, his fingers fluttering over my rib cage toward my breasts. "Soon, baby."

I relax in his arms. "I don't want her here."

"I know. But you need to learn to deal with her presence without wanting to kill her. Prove to me you can go three days without cutting her throat, and things can go back to the way they were. I can trust you again."

The very idea of keeping her for three days makes me want to rip my hair out strand by strand. Instead, I nod. "Fine."

His hand slips around to my front and finds its way under my dress. He massages my clit in an almost reverent way that has me shuddering with excitement.

"See what good girls get?" he coos, his teeth nipping at my bottom lip. "Treats. Good girls get treats and rewards."

I moan and nod. "I'll be so good. I swear it."

His fingers make quick work, bringing me to orgasm in record speed. My pussy drips with the need to have him inside of me. Just when I think he's about to fuck me against the wall, he pulls away. "If you're good tonight, I'll untie you in the morning."

Ignoring his statement, I pout. "Why won't you fuck me, Gabe?"

His eyes darken as his gaze slides over my lips to my throat. "You have to work up to that reward."

With tears in my eyes, I nod. "I'm sorry."

"I'm sorry too, sweet girl. Just be good and we'll work through this. Then we can both have what we so desperately want. Each other."

chapter
FIFTEEN

Gabe

We somehow made it through the night. I slept with my sweet girl in my arms and managed not to fuck her, despite every cell in both of our bodies begging me to. The bitch from the grocery store kept whimpering. It wasn't until I knocked her ass out I was able to sleep.

Hannah's still asleep but I promised her if she were good, I'd reward her. Carefully, I untie her wrists and set her free. I hope she doesn't disappoint me. She'd slept in her dress from yesterday since she was tied up, but now I want it gone. It'll be tempting not to fuck her once she's naked, but I'll have to refrain.

"Sweet girl," I murmur against her ear. "Wake up."

She moans, a sound so sweet and pure it wakes my dick up. I push her dress up her hips so I can see her pussy in the morning light. I'm desperate to taste her this morning. As I crawl between her legs, spreading her apart for me, I make the mistake of glancing at my captive. Her eyes are wide and repulsed by what I'm doing. But five bucks says when I finish, she'll be greedy for my tongue too.

Bringing my lips down between Hannah's thighs, I inhale her unique scent. I love the way she smells and tastes. So fucking delicious. Without further hesitation, I dive into my sexy breakfast. I nip and suck and taste every part of her that I know comes alive only for me. Hannah no longer sleeps, but instead bucks and moans on the bed. Her fingers, now very free fingers, rip at my hair to both beg me to stop and beg me not to all in one motion. I devour her until her sweet pussy soaks my chin with her orgasm. I don't stop my assault until she's relaxed and shivering on the bed.

When I lift up, our eyes meet and love shines in hers so brightly I wonder if it'll blind me. I love the adoration and dedication to me. It's addicting. Fucking perfect. She just needs to learn to control herself.

As she comes down from her high, her smile is wiped off her face when she sees Maria. I watch as her soft blue eyes blaze with rage, her entire body tensing with fury. Her little monster is jealous as fuck, and we need to deal with it.

"Sweet girl," I warn and slap her wet cunt with my hand. "Calm the fuck down."

Her wild eyes meet mine. "She watched us. That whore watched us."

Smirking, I push my finger inside of my woman. "Do you think it turned her on? Do you think our prisoner likes watching us?"

Hannah drags her gaze back over to the woman. "She better not have enjoyed it."

"But what if she did?"

She clenches her fists, and I swear she's seconds away from attacking the woman. But with incredible self-control, she relaxes. "I would want to punish her."

Good girl.

No psychotic rages or tantrums.

No fucking meltdowns.

She's using her words.

"I would want to punish her too," I agree with a smile. "Prisoners aren't supposed to enjoy what we did. They're supposed to hate us."

Hannah sits up on her elbows. "How would you punish her?"

"How would you punish her?" I counter.

Her eyes flit over to the bedside where I left my knife. For a brief moment, I worry I'll have to tackle her on the bed to keep her from cutting the hostage. Then, she gives me a sweet smile. "I'd whip her with your belt."

Grinning, I push deeper into her pussy with my finger before pulling all the way out. "Good answer, sweet girl." I suck on my finger and meet her eyes. "And how would we know if she got turned on or not?"

The woman whimpers from behind me.

Hannah's eyes widen, a wicked grin forming on her lips. "We see if she's wet."

"I guess I'll have to see—"

"No," she snaps, grabbing my wrist. "Don't touch her dirty pussy. I'll check."

I lift my brows in surprise as she crawls off the bed, bypassing the knife to make her way over to Maria.

"Do you want my man?" she demands.

Maria shakes her head no as tears streak down her cheeks.

"We'll see."

Smirking, I watch as Hannah bends over in front of the woman. The woman's screams are muffled behind the duct tape as my girl shoves her finger inside of her. She doesn't remove her finger right away. Instead, she slides it in and out of the woman. Hannah's a sly one. She's not merely checking to see if the woman is wet. No, she's trying to make her wet on purpose. With the heel of her hand, she rubs against Maria's clit as she finger fucks her. The woman gasps and squirms. Pure horror lingers in her eyes. But the longer Hannah works her magic, the more the woman relaxes. It isn't until the woman shudders that I know Hannah brought her to orgasm literally single-handedly.

She slips her hand out of the woman and holds the proof in front of me. "She enjoyed it. Now let me whip her ass."

"I want to hear her scream," Hannah says as she drags the leather of my belt over Maria's big ass. "I need to hear her."

Sighing, I grab a handful of the woman's dark hair and yank her head up. "She'll beg us to free her. Say all sorts of shit to fuck with your head. Can you handle that?"

She nods that she understands. The second I rip the tape away, the woman begins her begging. "P-P-Please l-let me g-g-go!"

Hannah cackles, the sound wicked and not from this world. "You're going to pay for lusting over Hades. He's not yours to look at."

The woman starts to plead again, but Hannah begins whipping her with the belt. Over and over and over again, I stare in wonder as my girl becomes the beast who lives within. Her eyes cloud over with rage. She doesn't stop or slow or hesitate.

She just whips and whips.

The woman screams but eventually passes out from the pain. Hannah just keeps doling out the punishment. The leather has torn the woman's ass up and it bleeds from several lash marks. I figure it'll slow Hannah, but she doesn't stop. Not when I order her to. Not when I shout at her. She only stops when I wrestle the belt from her hands. Even then, she struggles to get at the woman.

"You're done. Good girl," I praise, my mouth against her ear as I hold her tight.

Her body relaxes in my arms. A sob releases from her throat. She cries and cries. Not for the woman on the bed. She cries for us. Me and her. Hades and Persephone.

"Shhh," I murmur. "You were perfect, baby."

She lifts her head and kisses me hard. Our teeth bump together before we find our needy rhythm. Soon, her fingers are clawing at my sweatpants trying to free my cock.

"No," I snap, grabbing her wrist. "You're still being punished."

Apparently, my cock is being punished too. I'm dying to push inside of her slippery cunt and make love to her. But I need to calm her ass down first.

"Please," she begs.

"Soon." It's a motherfucking promise.

"Okay." She concedes easily, which shocks me. "Will you at least shower with me?"

"Not only will I shower with you but I'll also eat your pussy for breakfast, lunch, and dinner. Cheer up, sweet girl."

At this, she beams.

"Did you like the pancakes?" she questions.

She'd gone all out for breakfast. The girl is a great cook. I'll get fat if I'm not careful around her. "It was so good I think I need a nap now."

I must not have slept well because my eyes keep drooping. In fact, I'm really fucking tired.

"Come on," she purrs and helps me to my feet. "Let's get that whore out of our bed so we can lie back down."

The room spins when I stand. I stumble behind her, trying to understand what's going on. Confusion and disorientation cripple me. When we reach the bedroom, she yanks at the woman to push her to the side. Then, she undresses me and helps me lie down on the bed. I'm in and out of consciousness as she unties the woman's hands. Maria is rolled onto the floor with a loud thump. Hannah kneels out of view while she does something to Maria. I go to open my mouth and ask her what, but I pass right the fuck out instead.

"Wakey, wakey sleepyhead."

I crack open an eye to see the most devastatingly beautiful woman straddling my bare chest, naked. Her hair is wild and messy. She's spent some time doing up her makeup because I almost don't recognize her. Her eyes are rimmed in smudgy black liner, she's caked on black mascara, and shadows rim her lids, all of which make her blue eyes pop like two sparkly gems. She's painted her lips a dark shade of pink that makes them look fuller and more suckable.

I need to touch her.

But the moment I reach for her, I realize I'm in a bind. Literally. My sweet girl has bound each of my wrists to the top two corners of the bed and each of my ankles to the opposite end. I'm naked and completely at her mercy. My cock twitches with excitement, but unease trickles through me.

She's unpredictable as fuck.

"God, you look hot," I praise, my eyes once again falling to her pouty lips.

She beams at me, her eyes sparkling with delight. "So do you."

A growl rumbles in my chest. "Untie me, so I can fuck your pretty little cunt, sweet girl."

I can feel how wet her pussy is as she grinds it against my belly. A little lower and I'll make good on my promise.

"I thought I was still being punished," she says thoughtfully, her finger dragging along my chest. When she reaches my nipple, she twists it until I hiss in pain. She lets go and then leans forward to suckle on it.

"I don't give a shit about punishments right now," I mutter. "I just want inside of your hot, tight body."

She squirms above me. Her eyes dance with indecision. I can tell it excites her that I'm at her mercy, but the girl likes getting fucked. She likes it when I hold her down and force my dick into her ass while biting down on her shoulder.

"You left me," she pouts, her teary eyes finding mine. "You left me to find her."

My body stiffens, but I keep her gaze on mine. "Just to bring you closer to me. Just to try and show you you're stronger than your impulses." She tears her eyes from mine to look up at the ceiling. "Baby, look at me."

Her lip wobbles, but she meets my stare with a firm one. "You broke my heart leaving me like that. I'd have rather you'd hurt me physically. But leaving me tied up, that was cruel and torturous, Gabe. Now, I want to punish *you*."

My heart rate skitters to life at her words. "Sweet girl," I warn, my voice low and menacing. "Don't do something you're going to regret afterward."

Blonde eyebrows furrow together as she scowls. "I just want you to know what it feels like." Her voice is a fucking scary hiss. "I want you to feel the way you sliced my heart."

"I'm sorry," I whisper. "I didn't realize how fragile you were."

Her face falls for a moment. I think she might give in and untie me. Instead, she lifts her chin and meets my stare with a brave one of her own.

"I'm not just fragile. I was broken since the day I was born. You can't destroy what's already smashed and fragmented. All I've been searching for, my entire life, was someone to hold all the pieces together. Even if they had to bleed a little in the process. I thought you were that person, Gabe."

"I. Am. That. Person."

Unconvinced, she slides off of me, leaving a wet trail from her pussy in her wake. I want to hold her down on this bed so I can worship every inch of her flesh with my lips.

"I drugged you," she says as she reaches for the knife on the table. "Smashed those sleeping pills you keep in the cabinet to bits. I put them in your orange juice. Don't worry. I only put enough in there to knock you out, not kill you."

"I'm awake now, Hannah. Let me go so I can apologize properly."

She sits beside me and drags the tip of the knife down the middle of my chest. A scraping sound can be heard, along with my ragged breathing, as she trails it along the lines of my defined stomach toward my cock.

I need to distract her.

"Baby…"

"What did you do to my mother?"

Both of my brows fly to my hairline in shock. Now is definitely not the time to talk about this. "I don't know what you mean."

She pokes the flesh of my stomach, just hard enough for a bead of blood to surround the tip of the knife. "I mean, you gave me the general gist. You raped her. The girl you loved so much. But I want details."

"Untie me and I'll tell you," I vow.

Her brows scrunch together as she contemplates my words. "Tell me and I'll untie you."

A motherfucking impasse.

"Hannah…"

"Did you hurt her?"

"Yes."

"Did you fuck her in the ass?"

"Yes."

"Did you tie her up?"

"Yes."

"Did you do that thing to her with your tongue?"

"Hannah—"

"JUST ANSWER THE FUCKING QUESTION!" she shrieks and slices my flesh along my stomach. Our eyes meet, and hers flicker with a mixture of curiosity and horror. She didn't cut me deep, but it's bleeding.

"I did. But I didn't love her like I love you. I didn't realize it back then. Not until I had you in my arms, did I realize what real love is." My words are honest and true, and I hope they fucking work.

She drops the knife back onto the end table and runs her fingertips along the cut on my stomach. Then, she brings her bloody fingers up to her face to inspect them. Her giggle is not cute or adorable—it's fucking wicked.

"Hannah," I growl in warning.

Her eyes flit to mine and she runs her tongue along her finger, tasting my blood. "Not as good as I thought it would taste," she muses aloud. Blood is smeared on her chin. She's wild and untamed. If she'd just fucking cut me loose, I'd bend her back into submission with the tongue she so loves.

"Where's the whore?" I question, distracting her.

She points to the corner. The woman is wriggling in the chair, but a blanket has been placed over her head.

"You got her in there all by yourself, baby?" I smile at her. "You're really good at being bad."

My praise washes over her like a cleansing rain. She flutters her lashes at me before climbing off the bed. Then, she pulls the blanket from the woman. Maria's mouth is still covered with the duct tape, but now tiny cuts paint her face. Blood trickles from each one. The woman's hair has also been cut crudely from her head. Her once long, almost black hair is gone. Just patches remain.

"She tried to escape," Hannah tells me, a slight waver in her voice.

"Good thing you stopped her, Persephone."

The name causes her to pause and jerk her head toward me. Hunger flashes in her eyes. Her body lunges onto mine, her lips attacking mine as she tries to swallow me whole. I groan into her mouth and meet her tongue thrust for thrust.

"Get on my cock, good girl. Ride it like you own it because it's yours. Not that whore's or your mother's or Alejandra's. Only yours. Fuck me, baby," I order between our kisses.

She moans in agreement. My eyes roll closed when she sinks her tight heat on my aching dick.

"Such a good girl. God, you're so fucking beautiful. I've never seen someone so goddamned pretty in my entire life. Eyes as blue as the ocean, baby. Tits so perfect I have dreams of coming all over them. I love you, angel."

Her body quivers at my words. My little beast fucks me like the madwoman she is. With every bounce on my eager cock, I get closer and closer to coming inside my girl.

"I love your crazy, fucked up head," I tell her with a grunt. "Even when you do twisted shit like drug me, tie me to the bed, cut me open, and then fuck me. After I spurt every last drop of my orgasm into you, you're going to untie me so I can worship you. Do you understand, sweet girl?"

She whimpers at my words and quickens her pace. Her fingers dig into the flesh on my chest as she fucks me harder. When her pussy clamps down around my throbbing cock, I lose it before I can warn her. Thankfully, she's coming too, and we both cry out in pleasure.

My heat fills her.

Every inch of her.

I mark her as mine because she is. All mine.

Even when she's a crazy bitch.

When we both stop shaking with our explosive orgasms, she climbs off of me all too quickly. I don't like the sudden loss of her.

"I don't want her here," she tells me as she scrambles over to Maria. "I want her gone."

I sigh and shake my head. "Untie me and I'll get rid of her."

"She wants your cock."

"Baby…"

She rips away the duct tape from Maria's bloody face and begins untying her. The woman is shaky. Her terrified eyes meet mine in question.

"Clean his cock off with your mouth, and we'll let you live," Hannah barks at her. "Now!"

The woman nods frantically and scrambles onto the bed. "P-Please don't hurt me. I'll do as you say. L-Let me go, and I won't say a word. I promise."

Hannah smiles sweetly at her. An angel's smile with devilish intent. "I promise."

Gritting my teeth, I bite back words that will interrupt Hannah's plan. She wants to do this, so I'll fucking let her. It won't end well, but it's not like I expected otherwise when I lured Maria into my car.

"Suck it off of him."

My eyes lock with Hannah's as Maria grabs on to my cock. The touch makes it twitch back to life. I harden in her hands but don't lose eye contact with my girl.

"She makes you hard," Hannah seethes.

"No, you make me hard, baby," I counter. "*Your* dick sucking lips are what's making me hard. I want *your* lips on my dick, not hers."

She seems satisfied with my answer and climbs onto the bed. I groan when she reaches for the knife and then straddles my face, so she can face Maria. I'm blinded the moment she rubs the lips of her still dripping cunt on my mouth. Knowing what she wants, I lap at her pussy lips and tease her clit while I bury my nose between her ass cheeks.

Maria continues to suck our juices from my cock. I'm fully erect now and wonder how pissed Hannah will be if I shoot cum all over Maria's bloody face.

"Oh, yessss," Hannah purrs and rocks against my tongue. "More, Hades."

"Please, he's clean. Let me go," Maria begs. Stupid fucking woman.

"You're not done yet, whore!" Hannah's voice is a snarl as she leans forward toward Maria. "Take him down your throat!"

My eyes close when the tip of my cock slides down Maria's throat. I bite at Hannah's clit, which seems to drive her wild. She's grinding on my face while Maria deep throats my dick. This is hot as fuck. I'm going to come again.

"Fuck!" I hiss. "Fuck!"

Maria gags and Hannah screeches. "Stay!"

My dick is all the way down Maria's throat. Hannah keeps Maria's face pressed down against me, forcing her to stay there. Our hostage struggles and gags and a gush of hot liquid tells me she vomits too.

And my sick fuck ass comes so fiercely that I nearly black out.

"FUCK!" I roar against Hannah's cunt. I suck on her clit so hard, she screams loud enough to wake the dead.

More heat gushes around my dick as I drain the last of my seed into the mutilated woman's throat with the girl of my dreams quivering with pleasure on my face.

When the room grows silent, Hannah climbs off of me.

Maria's fucking dead as a doorknob.

Her vomit and blood soak my thighs and dick. The knife Hannah had sticks out from the side of Maria's neck, just below where my cock was only moments before. I snap my gaze to see Hannah smiling serenely. She yanks the knife from the dead woman's neck and turns her attention to me.

"Now, let's get you taken care of."

Hannah

"Am I too much for you?" I question, worry tainting my words.

He reaches for me and pulls me into his arms, my back to his front, disrupting the calm water around us. Hot breath tickles my neck as he whispers his reply. "Not enough. Never enough. I'll always want every single part of you."

My eyes close and I lean my head back. His palms circle to my front so he can pinch my nipples. After a late evening of digging a grave and cleaning the big mess I made in the bedroom, we'd settled for a midnight skinny dip in the pool. Gabe didn't freak out or try to subdue me the moment I cut him free. Instead, he'd hugged me to him and whispered how perfect I was. How much he loved and adored me. How much he wanted to apologize.

I've been glued to him ever since.

Most of what happened with Maria is a fog. I don't want to think about it. I just want to forget it happened. To move on with my lover.

"Get on my cock, sweet girl," he murmurs against my earlobe, his dick nudging me between the cheeks of my ass.

I lift on my toes in the water. The tip of his cock pokes at my entrance making it easy to slide down over him. From this angle and behind me, he pushes against my g-spot in a way that makes me see stars without him even having to move.

"Mmm," I gasp.

He pinches my nipple with one hand and teases my clit with the other. "Mmm is right, baby. Fucking delicious with you on my cock."

I cry out when he begins to thrust against me. Each time, a pleasure-filled zing courses through me. It only takes a few pounds into me before I come with a shriek. Moments later, his heat fills me. He kisses the side of my neck but doesn't release me.

"What were you going to go to college for? Before…me." His words sound sad.

"I don't know. I figured maybe business so I could help Dad with his company. I'd not really considered it much," I tell him. Much to my mother's horror, I couldn't make a decision. Nothing interested or excited me. Until now…

He grabs my hips and pulls me off his cock. Then, he twists me so we're facing each other. "Why do I feel like saving you that night ruined your life?"

I frown and run my fingers through his wet hair. "You saved me for forever. I was drifting until I met you."

His eyes search mine for truth. That is the total truth. For once in my life, I feel complete.

"Everything is so fucked up right now," he murmurs, grazing his lips against mine. "But there's no other place I'd rather be."

He devours me with a kiss that steals pieces of my soul. His darkness, altogether different than my Dad's, complements mine. Together, we make twisted sense.

"Do you love me?" he asks.

"You know I do."

His lips trail away from mine, kissing my cheek and jaw until his teeth are nibbling at my ear. "Then do something for me."

"Anything."

"Spend the summer here with me. Together. We'll kiss and fuck and watch movies and swim. Just us." His lips move down to my neck, just below my ear, and he sucks on the skin there. "But then, let's go get my daughter."

I freeze at his words. My palms find his chest, and I push him away. Pain twists his handsome features. Even though he suggested it, he's not demanding it. With his molten chocolate-colored eyes, he's begging. My dark, delicious man is pleading with me.

Could I do that?

Share him with his fifteen-year-old daughter?

Would she hate me for what I'd done to Alejandra?

"I don't know…"

His jaw clenches and he gives me a clipped nod before tugging from my grasp. I watch, with my heart in my throat, as his naked form climbs out of the pool. He dries off quickly and then ties the towel around his waist.

"When people are in a relationship, they give and take. It has to be a team effort to make it work. If I learned anything from living with Alejandra, it was that a marriage could work as long as one of the partners wasn't being selfish. But," he growls, "if one of the partners has no regard to the other's wishes and feelings, resentment begins to form. And with resentment, dislike. Eventually hate." He looks me over with a cold glare. "I really don't want to fucking hate you, baby."

With those words hanging bitterly in the air, he leaves me.

I'm alone under the stars.

Sore from our latest fuck.

Heart aching from our latest mindfuck.

Fragmented and holding the bloody shards of myself in my own hands.

Loneliness is the worst demon lurking in my head. Eventually, that demon will be the one to kill me in the end.

I wade over to the steps and sit on the middle one. Burying my face in my palms, I think about what my life has become. What I've lost and what I've gained. What I could lose. Sobs overtake me, and I let my mind drift to other times I've been selfish. Times it didn't do anything but cause me heartache and pain.

"Your dad's so cool," Missy tells Brandi. "I can't believe he got us a hotel room for your birthday."

Brandi laughs as she turns off the lamp. "Not that cool. He's in the other room and won't let us lock the door."

A shiver quivers through me. "He's just keeping us safe."

My bed partner, Lana, has already passed out. She's the only girl on our softball team who can fall asleep anywhere. Coach has even yelled at her for napping in the dugout a time or two.

I stare up at the ceiling in the darkness. Brandi's dad, Coach Phil, may be cool but his new girlfriend, Stephanie, is not. She's much younger than him and walks around with her nose in the air as if she's too good for him. Truth is, he's too good for her.

After an hour or so of listening to the sound of my three favorite teammate's snores, I slip out of bed. I want to go watch Phil while he sleeps. At our games, he's always mad and his face is bright red as he barks out orders. When he's not at the games, he's more relaxed and even playful. I love him when he's playful. Sometimes I think he's even flirting with me.

Not that a man like him would be interested in a fifteen-year-old girl…but I still like to dream about it.

I've spent the night at Brandi's plenty of times and know Phil is cute when he sleeps. His full lips part as he sleeps with an arm slung over his eyes. Phil isn't one of those big muscle dudes, nor is he really hot. He's handsome in his own way. Fun smile, bright green eyes, messy hair. I love how tall he is. How he towers over me.

Sneaking into his bedroom is easy. The girls never wake. I pad over to his bedside and ignore dumb Stephanie, sleeping with her back turned to him. If I slept in his bed, I'd always cuddle with him.

The pale moonlight shines in through the window casting a glow on his sleeping face. My fingers beg to touch him. He hugs us all the time and pats us on the back when we make a good play, but we never really get to touch him.

I trace my fingertips over his lips and let out a slight sigh before dropping my hand. I'm about to go back to bed when his eyes flutter open. Confusion furrows his brows together before he expresses concern and sits up.

"Everything okay, Han?" he whispers.

Seeing his gaze on me, I want more. I shake my head. He slides out of bed, wearing nothing but a loose pair of boxers. When he goes to search for some clothes, I whimper. The sound has him glancing at the bed before gently grabbing my shoulders. He guides me into the bathroom. The light blinds us both.

"What's wrong?" he questions as he closes the door.

My eyes greedily devour his hairy chest. I never knew he had a tattoo. He's not trim or fit, but I don't care. I like his body. My gaze falls to his boxers. I've watched enough porn late at night on my computer to know he doesn't have a boner. But his penis seems big anyway because he bulges from his boxers. I wonder what happens when he gets hard.

"I think I pulled a muscle," I tell him with a whine, loving the way his concerned eyes wash over me.

"Your bicep from throwing? Do I need to rub some cream on it?"

"Actually," I tell him, biting my bottom lip. "It's on my thigh." I hoist my leg on the countertop and then lift my gown to show him. My eyes remain on his as I brush my fingers along my inner thigh. When the tip of my finger grazes my panties, I jolt with excitement. His worried expression darkens.

"Hannah, perhaps you should go to bed. We can see if it's better in the morning."

I massage the area in question and summon tears. "B-but it hurts now." My chin quivers and a tear snakes out.

He rakes a hand through his hair in frustration but his eyes remain glued to my thigh as if he's attempting to figure out what to do about it. A shiver of delight ripples through me when he takes a step forward.

"Let's see," he murmurs and kneels before me so he's eye level with the area in question.

A gasp escapes me when his strong fingers touch the flesh there. If only he'd move them a little in the opposite direction. Would he make me cry out like those women in the porn movies?

"Right there," I tell him.

His fingers deftly work the muscle and his brows remain furrowed in concentration. I sneak a peek and can't help but be excited to see his erection tenting his boxer shorts. He's turned on by rubbing my thigh. I'm turned on too.

"Does that feel any better?" His voice is tight and strained.

I grab hold of his shoulders to steady myself. "A little."

He lets out a sigh of relief when I drop my foot back to the floor. When he goes to stand, I grip his shoulders. Our eyes meet for a brief moment. With my toes, I touch his hardness through his boxers. A hiss rushes from him, and his eyes snap shut. He lets me rub on him with my foot for a few long seconds before he stands abruptly.

"No, Hannah." His green eyes blaze with fury. "You shouldn't have done that."

With his entire height above me, I cower away from him. On the softball field, he can be quite intimidating. But like this? He's terrifying.

"I'm sorry," I whisper.

His eyes skim over my body before he clenches his teeth and points a long finger at me. "This never happened."

My lip wobbles and I nod.

"You speak one word of this to anyone and you'll be off the team so fast you won't even know what happened. People won't believe you, Hannah."

Our moment was there, we both felt it. He was hard beneath my touch. His groans and breathing told me he enjoyed it. I want it again.

"Phil," I murmur and selfishly reach out to touch him. "I want you."

He huffs and takes a step toward me, snatching my wrist. Then, he leans forward, so close I think he might kiss me, but utters his hateful words. "You're a child. I don't want you. Now go to bed and remember my warning."

The bathroom door creaks open and my eyes meet the surprised ones of Stephanie. Her nose isn't in the air. No, her nostrils flare with anger. Tears well in my eyes as I fear a lashing from her too. But she shocks me when she pushes inside and digs her claws into Phil's bicep.

"What are you doing?" she demands. "Why are you half naked in here with a little girl?"

I'm not a little girl.

"You don't know what you're talking about," he replies with a grumble. "She had a bad dream and I was comforting her."

Stephanie shoots him a scathing glare. "Out. I'll comfort her."

His shoulders hunch as he goes to leave, but not before sending me another look of warning. Once he's gone, she wraps me up in a hug. I need a hug after the rejection I just suffered.

"Did he…oh my God…" She trails off. "Did your coach, um, touch you?"

He touched my thigh. I touched his penis.

"No."

"Oh sweetie, thank goodness. It looked much worse, I suppose, from my end," she says, her voice coming out in a relieved rush.

"I still feel terrible," I admit. "My, uh, dream was a nightmare. In my dream, someone hurt me." But my dream was reality. Phil hurt me in reality.

"Listen, honey," she whispers and hugs me again. "You're awake now. And if you ever need anything, you come to me. Not Phil. The way he was in here with you in nothing but his underwear and touching you, that was inappropriate. I hate to think of what it could have escalated to had I not come inside."

I could tell her the truth. Bask in her comfort. Revel in the way she soothes my heart that still stings. But I don't.

Because I'm selfish.

If I tell what happened, not only will Phil try and kick me off the team, but he may also get in serious trouble. Then, they'll take him to jail or make him stop coaching. I wouldn't be able to see him again. I wouldn't know if we could have ever had another chance like tonight in the bathroom.

Because I'm selfish, I lie.

"Coach is a good man," I tell her firmly. "He would never take advantage of a little girl." The words taste like venom on my tongue, but I say them anyway. "Plus he's an old man. Ew."

She laughs, and I let out a crazed giggle of my own.

"I like you, Hannah."

"I like you too, Stephanie."

My thoughts vanish into the air the moment I hear a slam from inside the house. Gabe's form paces around the kitchen as he searches for something. Gabe would have liked Stephanie I think. She was a bad girl too. I still remember the scandal of her ending up pregnant by Phil's younger brother. It put our coach in such a pissy mood for an entire season. Wasn't until he held his "nephew" for the first time that he began to thaw. He never made eye contact with me again, though. And the only time he remotely smiled at me was when Mrs. Collins came onto the field and slapped me.

It was a smug grin.

A smile that said, *I fucking knew you were trouble.*

If only he knew how much trouble I was now…

I climb out of the pool and dry off. Once I make it inside the chilly house, I find Gabe leaned against the counter with a bottle of Jack in his grip.

"You should go to bed," he says, his voice low and gravelly.

I shiver at his words. "I'm not tired."

He tilts his head back and parts open his lips to swallow back a swig of the amber liquid. His Adam's apple bobs with the motion. My mouth waters to lick him there. Once he swallows, he turns his hard gaze on me, snuffing out the heat that was kindling inside me. "Fine. But I'm not in the mood to babysit. Go find something to do. Without me." His words flay me. Cut me right open and make me bleed.

"You're an asshole."

He smirks. It reminds me of the smirk Phil gave me that day. "And?"

With a huff, I storm over to him and steal his bottle. I take a swallow of the nasty stuff. His eyes flicker with irritation when I take another swig. He yanks the bottle from my hands so he can drink.

And so begins the next half hour of our evening.

Angry glares.

One bottle of Jack, quickly emptying.

Two hurt people.

A fire that seems to be building again with every second that passes.

"You look so much like your mother, it's fucking disturbing," he blurts out, his eyes narrowing and falling to my breasts still hidden in my towel. "Your tits are nicer, though. You…not so much."

I flip him off. "I bet you wish she was here, so you could make love to her. Is that why she's so special? You made love to her and told her she was perfect and shit?"

His laugh is more like a loud bark. "She was special because I fucked her just like I fuck you. Hard and without apology. Your mother, unlike you, denied how much she loved it, though. Unfortunately for Baylee, her weepy cunt couldn't lie."

Snarling my lip at him, I shake my head in disgust. "You're a pig."

"And you're a psycho."

When I haul off and kick him, he pounces on me, tearing my towel from my body in one fluid movement before backing me up against the counter.

"Apple doesn't fall far from the tree. I bet your pussy's dripping for me right now, even as I talk to you like you're a piece of shit."

"Maybe my pussy is wet because I'm thinking about stabbing you and burying you with your whore girlfriend, Maria," I seethe.

He chuckles and his eyes light up with amusement. "You're feisty as fuck."

His palm cups my breast. When he dips down to suck my nipple into his mouth, I let my head fall back, enjoying the sensation of his tongue on the sensitive flesh. I latch my fingers into his hair while his kisses my breasts.

"What did you do to my mother that made her hate you so much?" The question always lingers in my mind.

Hot breath tickles my flesh. "It was either the time I fucked her ass with a cucumber shoved up her tight cunt or the time I shot your precious daddy in the chest. I'm really not sure."

His words should disturb me. But you can't disturb the disturbed. A giggle starts in my throat and soon I'm full-bellied laughing with tears rolling down my cheeks. He pulls away with an arched eyebrow and a half-smile on his lips.

"Do I entertain you?" he muses.

I nod and guide his hand between my legs. "You're crazy like me."

"You just now figured this out?"

He slightly sways and I giggle again.

"It explains why she's *'allergic'* to cucumbers," I tell him, a wicked grin on my face.

"I could make *you* develop that *'allergy'* too," he threatens, but it falls flat since he's smiling.

Running my fingertip over his lips, I murmur my naughty words. "You could try."

I officially know what it would feel like to have two men at once. Gabe wasn't gentle or kind or loving as he fucked my ass with a frozen vegetable up my twat. He didn't assure me everything would be okay. He didn't make any sort of empty promise.

He just fucked me until I came so hard I collapsed.

The entire time, I imagined it was Phil's frozen prick inside of me while Gabe drove into my ass. It made for a fantasy that would only ever happen in my dreams. And, oh what beautiful dreams they were.

After we finished and cleaned up, he wouldn't stop laughing at me. I was annoyed, but I couldn't help but be tickled by his boyish amusement.

He said I was too good to be true.

Nothing but his own fantasy come to life.

It was then, in our perfect post sexual haze, that I gave him what he wanted.

"I want you to be happy. When the summer is over, let's go get your girl and bring her home to us."

Once I uttered those words, Gabe flipped me over and made love to me so sweet, it made me cry. With our fingers intertwined while he thrust into me and our eyes connected, he whispered promises I hope he can keep.

About forever.

About family.

Love.

Us.

"This isn't over, baby," he assured me. "It's only just begun."

chapter
SEVENTEEN

Gabe

Three and a half weeks later…

We're out.

Been out for five days.

I'm going to kill her.

Stroking her blonde hair while she lies with her head in my lap, I contemplate my next move. There's always online Mexican drug companies. Or, I could get her a fake ID so we could see a doctor. But the testing could take more time than we can afford. I don't need them to waste precious fucking time trying to diagnose my girl. I already know what she needs. She needs the goddamned Clozapine and Celexa or I'm going to choke her to death.

When she's high and happy and in love, the girl fucks like a goddess and we can't get enough of each other. But when she hits her lows, I worry she'll cut my throat in my sleep. She's unpredictable. She's unstable. She's motherfucking insane.

I'm going to have to do something that could really be dangerous to us both.

I'm going to have to go to War.

Sure, the fucker probably wants to put a bullet through my skull—even though I doubt the pansy could stomach it. Hannah's worth whatever shit I have to go through because I need her well and whole again. I was an idiot to ever think she could exist free of medication. I'd had no idea the depth of her mental illness.

"I love this movie," she says softly, her finger drawing hearts on my kneecap. "It's so romantic."

I chuckle and raise an eyebrow. "Dracula is romantic? Or is Luke Evans just sexy? You're kind of hot for villains."

"Villains need love too," she retorts.

That they do.

And in our story, we're both the motherfucking villains.

"Sweet girl?"

"Mmm?"

"I want to take you on a trip. We can go swim at that secluded beach. This time I'll let you fuck me," I say with a smile.

She sits up and flashes me a worried look. Her brows are furled together as she bites on her bottom lip for a hair before speaking. "Why? That's awfully close to home. What if someone recognizes us?"

I run my thumb along her bottom lip. "We'll be fine. San Diego's a big city. Plus, I need to get something for you while we're there."

Her pupils dilate for a moment, anger flickering in her eyes. "What?"

"Your fucking meds."

She scrunches her nose and snarls her lip. "I don't need them. I'm fine, see?" Her slender fingers motion at her face. And today, she is fine. So fucking fine. I wish I had her like this all of the time. It's when she's not fine that's the problem. Her ups and downs are too high and too low. We need to coast in the motherfucking middle.

"I love you," I assure her. "You know this. And that is why I am doing this for you. Trust me, baby."

She straddles my hips and wraps her arms over my shoulders. Her lips are pouting, but her eyes tell me she'll concede. "How do you plan on getting my medication?"

I close my eyes and let out a sigh. "I'm going to have to contact your dad."

"No."

Popping my eyes open, I glare at her. "What do you mean no?"

"You're not going to hurt him."

I cup her cheek and drag my thumb along her full bottom lip. "I swear to you, beautiful, I'm not going to fucking hurt him. He might try and hurt me, but I'm not going to touch a hair on his goddamned head. He can refill your prescription, though, and get it to me until I can secure your new identification and doctor. We have to do this."

She frowns. "Dad might involve the police. What happens if he sets you up? They'll tear us apart. I can't live without you. I'm happy for the first time ever."

"I'll be careful."

"You don't know my dad. He's smart and can hack into any computer network out there. If we weren't out in the middle of nowhere, I have no doubt he would've found me already."

Once upon a time, he evaded me and holed away my Baylee. But I found them. I always do. And they never found me again. I've got this.

"We'll make it work. I promise you."

"Hello?" the deep voice answers.

I lean against the shitty pay phone with my eyes on Hannah. She'd wanted a cherry Icee at the convenience store. Instead of blending in, she's drawing motherfucking attention from every male who walks past her. Her blonde hair blows in the wind while she sucks on the red straw as if it's the most delicious fucking thing she's ever wrapped her lips around. The short dress she's wearing keeps flapping up, and I swear to God, if some asshole approaches my girl, I'll beat the shit out of him in the parking lot.

"War?"

A growl in response. "Gabe?"

"We need to talk," I tell him bluntly. "About Hannah."

"Jesus Christ," he hisses into the phone. "She better be all right."

I can hear tapping on his computer. The motherfucker is probably trying to triangulate my location or some shit. "Stop trying to find us," I tell him. "We're coming to you."

"You're bringing her home?" The surprise is evident in his voice.

"Fuck that. She doesn't want to come home. But we do need something that belongs to her."

He remains silent.

"I need you to refill her prescriptions. Today."

"She's been off them for a few days now," he clips out. "Is she okay? Has she tried to hurt herself?"

I think about Maria's bloody bloated corpse. And that was when she actually was on meds. I don't even want to think about Hannah at her worst.

"She hasn't tried to hurt herself. She's safe and happy. But I'm afraid I can't keep her that way all of the time without them."

He lets out a breath of frustration. "What am I supposed to do? Just hand over my daughter's meds and pray you don't shoot me in the chest again?"

I smirk. "Don't be a pussy. That was nearly two decades ago. You lived. And yes, that's exactly what I want."

"We want to see her. To talk to her."

"Not going to happen."

"Why the hell not?" he demands.

"Because I'm not fucking stupid. You'll try and convince her to come home."

The line goes silent again. "She can't come home."

At this I laugh. "Wow, man, she really was too much for you to handle like she said. Poor girl. I can fucking handle her."

He growls again. "I can handle her just fine. I love my daughter. Problem is," he says lowly. "She's wanted in connection of the murder of Alejandra Cruz-Diaz. Alejandra's husband is wanted as well. Her fingerprints were all over the house and the murder weapon. This is really bad for her."

My eyes flit over to Hannah. She's sitting on the hood of the car, looking like the finest damn hood ornament a man has ever seen. The girl sticks out like a sore thumb. If she's wanted, I need to hide her.

"Okay, so we meet in private. How do I know you're not going to set us up?"

"Because I'll come alone. I can't tell Baylee. She'll flip out and want to bring an army against you. They'll take Hannah away from us," he spits. "Put her in a prison cell where she cannot survive. Or, she'll want to commit her to an institution. We've gone 'round and 'round about it. Hannah needs love. That's what my daughter needs. And I'm supposed to believe you of all people have found a way to reach her? That you have some sort of fucked-up love for her?"

I smile. I do have a fucked-up love for her. "Sounds like you don't have much of a choice in the matter," I tell him, my tone smug. "What about Coronado Beach?"

He curses, and I half expect him to hang up on me.

"Fine," he snaps. "I can get the medications filled this morning and meet this afternoon. I'm going to see her, though. You only get the meds if I can hug my daughter."

Annoyance flits through me, but I concede. He's her father after all. I'd do anything right about now to hug my own daughter. "Deal."

"How do I know you won't grow tired of her? Just like everyone else? Swear to me you'll bring her home before you do anything stupid." His plea is meant to be threatening, but it's filled with devastation.

"I'm not bringing her home and I'm not going to hurt her. But I can give you something in return. For insurance."

"I'm listening."

"Find my daughter. Gabriella Cruz-Diaz. They took her somewhere, and I need to find her. She belongs home with me and Hannah."

He huffs. "And how is this insurance for me?"

"Because if you find her, then I'll let you see your daughter again. And if we need more medication, I'll let you see her again. And if you're a real good boy, War, I may let you see her from time to time. Don't fuck this up."

"I can work with that. See you in a few hours."

The fucker said he'd be alone.

I should have known better.

"Is that Ren with Dad?" Hannah asks, shielding her eyes from the sun.

When we'd gotten to the beach earlier, we'd decided to make a day of it while we waited. I fucked her in the ocean with people swimming around. It was hot and wicked. And my sweet girl didn't care that we had spectators. She just moaned and begged for an orgasm until I silenced her with kisses.

So much for not drawing attention to ourselves.

"I told him to come alone," I mutter with a growl as I stalk over to our bags where my 9 mm hides inside. I towel off and pull my T-shirt back on, never keeping my eyes off the pair.

War is cautious, his eyes searching the crowded beach, and he wanders along hesitantly. His boy Ren wears an angry but determined scowl on his face, clearly the more badass of the two as he follows behind. It isn't until War's gaze finds Hannah, toweling off beside me, that he visibly relaxes.

As soon as he sees her, his eyes dart over to mine. The unease is wiped right from his face as his brows furl together angrily. He looks like an overprotective bear ready to maul me for even breathing the same air as his daughter. His little cub behind him already has his claws out.

Too bad for the little bears…

Their Goldilocks is the motherfucking dragon.

A fire-breathing, full on psycho, unpredictable beast.

And she just happens to look like a fucking swimsuit model in the process.

"Hannah," War calls out, his eyes back on his daughter.

She lets out a gasp, and much to my dismay, runs for her daddy. Her cute ass jiggles in her tiny swimsuit. My cock jerks in my trunks at the sight.

Her arms sling around her father's neck the moment she nears him, and he pulls her to him in a tight embrace. The boy stands behind them, his menacing glare gone, and I swear the little pussy looks like he might cry.

Trudging through the sand up to them, I lift my chin to acknowledge them. War's gaze flies to mine and his nostrils flare with fury.

"You just don't die, do you?" he snarls, his entire body stiffening. "A damn cockroach."

Hannah jerks away from him. "Dad, be nice."

War's jaw clenches and the boy fists his hands beside him.

"Where are the meds?" I demand, crossing my arms over my still-wet chest. "You aren't reneging are you?"

He snaps his gaze over to his son and shakes his head. "No," he huffs. "They're in the car."

"Han, come home with us," Ren urges, almost inaudibly to her. "It's not too late."

War's features crumple in devastation. "Ren, we talked about this. She can't come home."

Smirking at them, I grab hold of Hannah's wrist and haul her to me so her back is flush with my chest. Both War and Ren glare at me as I wrap my arms around her bare middle.

"Did you hear that, sweet girl?" I whisper on a hot breath into her ear. "You can't go home. Did you want to go home?"

She shakes her head and turns to look up at me. I plant a wet kiss on her fat lips, just to piss them off.

"Can you please not rub this in our face?" War snaps.

"I love him," Hannah proclaims. "We're not trying to make you mad."

War runs his fingers through his hair and casts a wary glance farther down the beach. "Was it you? Did you kill that woman?"

She freezes in my arms. "What woman?"

"Alejandra Cruz-Diaz."

I watch War as he studies her. His eyes dart all over her face, assessing her well being. He pulls his lips into a disappointed frown. I can see that he doesn't need for her to answer to know the truth. He knows, beyond the shadow of a doubt, his daughter killed my wife. As much as that thought crushes him, he is still protective over her. I hate to admit it, but he's a good father. She deserves a good father.

And now she deserves a man who can carry the torch in his stead.

I'm a good father too.

But I'm a very bad man.

Good thing she's a bad girl too.

"It just…" She trails off, her slight body tensing in my arms. "I don't know what happened, Dad. She would have tried to stop us."

War closes his eyes, and Ren stalks off back to the car. I keep my eyes on the boy, in case he tries to do anything funny.

"Listen to me," War says, his voice deep and broken, as he reaches for her hand. "What you did was horrible. And they want to arrest you as soon as they can find you. But I can't stand to think what would happen to you if you went to prison. They'd hurt you."

He pulls her from my grip, back into his arms.

"I'm sorry, Daddy," she says with a sob, her slender arms tight around his waist. "I didn't mean to."

We all know she meant to. Little lying girl.

"I know," he coos as he strokes her wet hair. "I'm going to do everything to keep you safe. Is he good to you? Now is the time to tell me the truth. People are everywhere. If he hurts you, I'll find a safe place to keep you. I'm dying to send him away to prison where he belongs."

She lifts her head to look up at him. "He understands me. Like you do sometimes. But he understands me all of the time. Plus, he protects me. When you and Mom were in Italy…"

Her body quakes with sadness. I'm tempted to rip her right out of his arms so I can hold her. Instead, I let him have his fucking moment with his daughter.

"Did Mom tell you what those men did to me?"

War lets out a garbled choke and he grips her shoulders to look at her. "She said they assaulted you."

"Sexually," she hisses. "And Gabe saved me. He killed them for hurting me. He's been protecting me ever since. Sometimes even from myself."

At the last bit, War's shoulder's hunch. "I'm so sorry, baby."

With the backs of her hands, she swipes away her tears and slips under my arm, pressing her hot cheek to my chest. "I'm happy now, Dad."

War's gaze meets mine, and he shoves his hand into his pocket. When he pulls out a phone and offers it to me, I shake my head.

"I'm not stupid. You're not going to track us." I laugh at him.

He scowls and thrusts it at me again. "This is so I can warn you if the authorities are onto where she's at. I've hacked into the San Diego PD's network and am following the progress on her case. It's also to inform you of when I locate *your* daughter. And, yes, it's also so I know where the fuck my daughter is in case I need to see her. So take the phone and don't destroy it. You'll get the meds, and we'll both have our insurance."

I snatch the phone from his grip and glare at him. "Find Brie. And so help me, if you screw me over, you'll pay dearly." Baring my teeth at him, I let the threat of my thinly veiled words sink in. For effect, I slip my hand around Hannah's throat and stroke her flesh gently. His eyes flit down for a brief moment before they're back on me.

"I'll find her. And I'm not going to screw you over."

Grinning wolfishly at him, I nod. "You just made yourself a deal with the devil."

chapter
EIGHTEEN

Hannah

One week later…

"Tell me a story," I murmur as I wipe the slobber and leftover cum from my bottom lip. His eyes hold a certain twinkle for the rest of the day when I wake him up with a blow job.

"What kind of story?" he questions.

I crawl my nearly naked body back up the bed and curl against his chest. His fingers thread through my hair, working out the tangles from sleeping.

"A story about my grandparents."

He chuckles. "More about the Viking and his angel?"

"Yeah."

"Tony and I didn't get along too well at first. It was your mother and grandma who took to me in the beginning. I tried with the fucker. Man, how I tried. But every time I thought we were cool, he'd bark out some warning or snide comment. I'd damn near given up on a friendship with the asshole when…"

I lift up to look at his face. The smile falls, and his eyes darken. His features become hard as he remembers.

"What happened?"

"My dad's friends showed up." He sighs and scrubs his face with his palm. "Lance, Gordon, and Jack. They wanted to include me in on a new business venture they were working on."

"That's nice, though, right? You said you'd nearly run out of your money."

A growl rumbles in his chest. "There was still a matter of some assets—a fuckton to be quite frank—that I'd inherited from my father. Accounts that were set up in such a way that I'd only become a trustee upon my producing a child. Bullshit money that I knew I'd never see a dime of. It was money that they knew of nonetheless."

"You have Brie now," I offer.

He laughs. "I also have millions from your father. I don't need that money."

"But you did, Gabe. You needed it back then."

His body tenses beneath me. "That I did."

"So what happened?"

"We were sitting in my living room and I told them I'd have to pass on their offer. They wanted to take their sex trafficking shit to a whole new level. Online forums hidden in the dark web. Places where men could shop for pretty much any type of sex they were into. Old bitches. Fat ladies. Pregnant mothers. Little girls."

I curl up my lip in disgust. "Gross."

"At one time, I might have gone along with their 'gross' business venture. But I was too damn enthralled by Lynn and her daughter to even care about that shit at the time. I told them as much. They'd probably have left if it weren't for Baylee letting herself in, per usual, and prancing right over to me like she owned the place in her little purple swimsuit begging for me to take her to the pool.

I'd seen their hungry gazes all over her. She was a fucking kid, and they licked their old lips like she was on the goddamned menu."

His hand fists my hair but he doesn't pull on it. My panties, the only thing I'm wearing, become wet at his possessive grip on me.

"I told them to leave. I'd made plans with my neighbors and that it was time to go. Gordon just wouldn't stop looking at her with his beady eyes. Asked her if she wanted to come sit on his lap. I wanted to bash his fucking face in."

"Did she?"

"Fuck no!" he roars, a possessive growl rumbling through him. "I kept her in my lap where she belonged. Jack went on and on about how little blondes were a favorite. Could bring in a hefty sum. To reconsider their offer. When I refused and threatened to haul each of their old asses out to their car by the damn throat, the situation escalated."

"Did they hurt her?"

"They fucking tried. Gordon pulled a gun out of his briefcase and pointed it at me. Baylee was too wrapped up in trying to braid my hair with her back to them. She had no fucking clue. Those pricks told me to put her in their car. Like they were going to fucking take her from me."

"Were you scared?"

"I was fucking petrified!"

"Did they get her? Did they take my mom from you?"

He laughs, and the dark, sinful tone cloaks me. "I gave her a little kiss on the head and told her to go play Mario in my bedroom. That I'd be in there shortly—after I dealt with some business with the men. As soon as the bedroom door slammed shut, I rose to my feet. If I had to, I was going to take all three of them out."

The room goes silent. His body visibly shakes with rage.

"The dumbass still had his gun trained on me when the Viking bursts through the front door, a murderous glare on his face. He didn't like his little girl playing alone with me. All it took was one meaningful look at Tony and then flicking my gaze back at Gordon for him to understand the situation. Your grandpa was perceptive. As if on cue, he lunged for Jack while I charged for Gordon. The old fuck never squeezed off a shot. My fist broke his nose upon impact and I wrestled that gun out of his hands. I was beating the fuck out of him when someone got me in a chokehold from behind. Fucking Lance. I'd always sort of looked up to him as a fill-in father figure. Hell, his boy and I even used to be friends for a while there. These friends of my father's were the only fucked-up family I had, and they turned on me. For money. Lance was the trustee on all of those accounts. If something were to happen to me, he'd handle the appropriation of funds at that point. And since I wouldn't let them use my money, they planned to take matters into their own hands."

"Did they overtake you and Grandpa?"

His laugh, this time, is humorous. "A Viking and a monster? Three old men never had a chance. Your father pulled Lance off me and proceeded to beat the fuck out of him. When they were all three moaning and groaning but incapacitated, he helped me load them into their trunk. Stuffed all three fuckers inside."

"My grandpa helped you? Why did he do that? What happened to the men?" I question.

"We retrieved your mother from the bedroom and sent her back next door with her mother. Then, he followed me in his car. I drove and drove upstate until I found a piece of my dad's old property Lance had 'bought' from me. I'm still not sure if I sold it to him for a fair price or not— my guess is the latter. The assholes were screaming and begging from the trunk."

"What did Grandpa say?"

"When we got out, he asked what those men wanted. I told him about the sex trafficking business venture they wanted to start. I also told him how they looked at little Baylee. How they wanted to take and hurt her. His face was bright red with fury, and he nodded. That nod was the beginning of our friendship. He climbed into his car and waited for me. I set a rock on the gas pedal of their car and sent them careening into the secluded lake to drown. We never spoke of it again, but Tony had my back from that day forward. I watched over his daughter and wife, and he looked out for me. He became my best friend. My motherfucking brother."

I slide a leg across his waist and cage in his head with my arms. My long, messy hair hangs down, tickling his face. "I'm glad you killed them."

"Why? Because they were bad men? I'm a bad man too, sweet girl."

I laugh and peck him on his nose. "No, because it made you and my grandpa grow closer. Because it gave you a best friend. My grandpa knew you would take care of his girls."

He becomes quiet and his eyes close. "I still miss that fucking Viking. And the angel." He lets out a sigh. "And your mother."

I stiffen at his words. "I thought you loved *me*."

"I *do* love you."

"What would you do if you ever saw her again? Would you want her?" I probe, tendrils of jealousy threading their way through me.

"I have you. I don't need Baylee anymore."

"But what if she wanted you. What if she showed up naked right now? Would you fuck her?" My voice quakes and tears well in my eyes.

"Hannah," he growls in warning.

A tear slips out and lands on his forehead. Our eyes meet. His dark gaze penetrates me.

"Would you tie her up and take her ass, like old times?" My voice is cold. "Would you want to hear her scream and beg?"

His cock twitches beneath me.

"No."

Rage surges through me.

"LIAR!" I fist my hands and start hitting his face. "Your cock still wants her!"

Before I can land another punch, his strong fingers are around my throat squeezing. I hiss out, clawing at his fingers for him to release me. He flips me over onto my stomach, pressing my face down into the mattress. I squirm and scream and claw at the bedding.

"My cock wants you, you fucking psycho," he seethes. His other hand rips my panties down my thighs and yanks them away. He shoves his knee between my legs to part me open for him. I let out a furious scream when he slams his hard cock—hard for my mother—into my still wet pussy.

"Stop it! I hate you!"

He grunts and fists my hair, yanking me back. "You love me, you lying bitch!"

A traitorous moan rips from my throat as he pounds into me. "Fuck you!"

His full-bellied laugh sends ripples of pleasure coursing through me. He pounds into me roughly, like the savage he is, until I come around his cock with a wail. No sooner do I drench him with my juices, does he pull out and then slam into my ass.

"Ahhh!" I screech. The sudden intrusion there leaves me breathless, tears pouring down my cheeks. "You're hurting me!"

He groans as he fucks me without slowing. "Good!" he snarls. "You deserve it for being a jealous cunt. You know it's you. It's always fucking you. So get the fuck over it already."

You know it's you.

It's always fucking you.

His words have their intended effect, and I relax. With every thrust that his huge cock fills my ass, I grow closer and closer to another orgasm. This one is an orgasm of the soul. My entire body spasms with pleasure. My only thought on him.

You know it's you.

It's always fucking you.

I moan in relief when his hot seed bursts inside of me. His cock seems to double in size, threatening to rip me in two. "Gabe!"

He hisses out my name as he comes. When his cock stops throbbing, he slips it out of me and crushes me with his body. I let out a whimper when his mouth finds my neck.

"I love you, sweet girl. Don't you ever fucking forget it. But keep this jealous shit up, and I'll punish you until you can't walk. Is that what you want?"

Shaking my head, I give him the answer he desires. "No."

"Good girl."

You know it's you.

It's always fucking you.

"I just worry someone will take you away from me. I worry I'm not as good as my mother. That you miss her." My honest words cause him to take pause.

"Nobody is ever taking my girl away from me, understand?"

"Okay."

"And I do miss your mother. But that doesn't change how I feel about you. You're my world," he murmurs.

You know it's you.

It's always fucking you.

You're my world.

"Gabe!" I shriek.

He storms into the kitchen, worry painted over his features. "What?"

"The phone is buzzing. It's Dad."

A groan escapes him as he answers. "War."

All irritation leaves his face as he listens. He gives me a quick glance before stalking out the back door. I watch from the window as he paces along the pool. His hand waves in the air as he seems to yell at my dad through the phone.

Are the police coming?

Will they take me away from him?

I'm still frozen in fear of what's to come when Gabe bursts back through the door with the phone outstretched to me. "Here."

Confused, I take the phone and put it to my ear. "Are they coming for me, Daddy?"

A rush of breath comes out on the other end. "No, baby. They're not coming for you."

"I was scared."

"Don't be scared. I was giving Gabe information about his daughter. But I want to see you. I'm coming to Arizona."

A flutter of butterflies takes flight in my belly. "Are you bringing Ren or Calder?" The hope in my voice is evident. Then, my voice drops. "You're not bringing Mom are you?"

He sighs, clearly frustrated. "Your mother still doesn't know I've made contact with you. Neither does Calder. I'll bring Ren again, though."

I smile at knowing my dad is keeping our contact a secret from her. She would only try to ruin it all by making Gabe go to prison. Mom would destroy me by attempting to destroy him.

"I love you, Daddy."

"I love you too," he assures me, adoration flooding his voice. "I'll see you tomorrow."

When I hang up, I turn to see Gabe leaned against the counter. His palms scrub his face in frustration.

"What's wrong?"

His dark gaze lifts to mine and his brows furrow. "Everything."

Bouncing over to him, I throw myself into his arms. "Tell me. Dad seemed fine on the phone. Was he lying?"

His body is tense and his heart is pounding in his chest. "It's not about us. It's about Brie."

Irritation courses through me. "What *about* her?" I attempt to keep the scathing tone down, but I know he senses the harshness in my voice.

"War's found a lead. And," he hisses against my hair, "it's fucked up. So fucked up, sweet girl."

Lifting my head, I search his warm brown eyes. With his brows pinched together in frustration, he seems every bit his age. Lines crinkle the corners of his eyes, and larger lines mar his forehead. Giving him an encouraging smile, I run my fingertips through his hair on the side of his head. Strands of grey streak at his temples.

He's a silver fox.

My sexy old man.

Delicious.

"Hannah."

Blinking away my daze, I frown. "What?"

"Did you take your medicine today?"

Rolling my eyes, I push away from him, but he grabs my elbows hard enough to bruise me. "Yes, *Daddy*," I smart off.

Annoyance flickers in his eyes, and I immediately hate that I choose all of the wrong moments to let my crazy shine through.

"I'm sorry. What's happening with Brie?" I smile sweetly at him and bat my eyelashes.

He hauls me to him for a bear hug. "Some rich fucking family is taking necessary steps to adopt her. This is wrong." The despair in his voice makes my chest ache. "She's fifteen. Who the fuck wants to adopt a fifteen-year-old girl?"

"But you're her father. They can't just do that anyway."

"Johan Cruz-Diaz is listed as her father on her birth certificate. Johan Cruz-Diaz was wanted in connection with the murder of his wife. That is," he lets out a huff, "until they found his death certificate from before Brie was ever conceived. The State of California has no legal documentation of her *real* father."

A small current of excitement courses through me. "What does that mean?"

"It means the only way I can claim her is to submit to a paternity test. But as soon as I do that, since the police are heavily involved, they'll nail my ass and haul me off to prison. They found those fuck face's bodies who raped you. It won't be long before they tie that shit to me too. Thankfully, your parents have kept silent on how they know 'Johan' and have feigned innocence because they know the moment they say anything about what happened with Baylee and I all those years ago, this shit will go national. If it goes national, we're fucking screwed. They're trying to protect you, but that means protecting me too."

Just me and Gabe…

"I'm sorry," I tell him, my bottom lip trembling. But I'm not sorry. I'm happy. "What are you going to do?"

"I don't fucking know. War's getting me names and shit. He's coming to see you tomorrow. I don't think this is a setup or anything. His concern for Brie was surprising. I'm curious why he was so fucking concerned come to think of it."

While he broods and his mind races with worry over Brie, I silently thank the heavens for letting her find a family who wants her. She can be their daughter and have a normal life. Her teen years can be spent doing traditional things. If she came with us, she'd be locked away. He'd have to homeschool her.

He would spend all of his time doting over her.

Apologizing about her dead mother.

Choosing her over me.

And I would become angry.

I know how I am.

I would be jealous just as he always accuses me of being.

Then, I would hurt her too.

A single tear rolls down my cheek. Gabe's attention returns to me—where it should be—and he swipes away the wetness with his thumb.

"We'll get her back," he promises, as if that's the reason why I'm upset.

I nod and another tear rolls out. If we get her back, she'll be cooking under the Arizona sun in another homemade grave with that whore, Maria, who Gabe brought home. Brie, although I only saw her once, was pretty and looked sweet. She looked like a daddy's girl…like me.

She would have easily stolen him from me.

My body begins to shake as the gravity of reality sets in. If he finds her and brings her home, it will be the end of us. A choked sob escapes me. The man I love blurs in front of me. He shuffles and soon I'm scooped into his arms. I clutch desperately to him as he carries me into our bedroom.

"Shhh," he coos as he sets me to my feet. His deft fingers tear at my clothes until I'm naked and shivering. Once he's naked too, he slips an arm around me and guides us onto the bed. In the next breath, he's inside me. "You're perfect, sweet girl. So perfect."

I cry as he makes love to me. His full lips suckle on my neck and his teeth nip at the flesh. My fingers thread into his hair as I guide him to my mouth.

"Kiss me," I beg.

"Always."

And this is why it needs to be just us.

Gabe, my furious and raging storm, brings me calm. He pulls the real Hannah from the darkness to wrap his arms around her so she won't be lonely. Together, we fulfill a need nobody else ever can.

His fingers skim over my flesh, worshipping me with his touch as he thrusts into me. He rubs against me in such a way that has my body jolting with pleasure. It's him. It's not his touch or his expertise or his taste or his words.

It's.

Just.

Him.

"Oh, Gabe," I cry out, ripping at his hair as I climax.

He kisses me deeply as I feel him release inside of me. His heat warms me. I wish we could stay joined like this forever. No worries of Brie or my mom or anybody.

Just us.

When he pulls out of me and lies beside me, I let out a disappointed sigh at the loss of him. His seed trickles out of me, soaking the bed below. Watching me with a peaceful look, he circles his fingertip around my nipple.

He gives me the most breathtaking smile I've ever seen.

My heart thumps to life in my chest.

"Sweet girl…"

"Mmm?"

"I swear," he says and presses a kiss to my nose. "I'll get her back. Then we'll be a family. I promise."

The blood in my veins turns to ice.

"A family." My voice is a whisper.

"*My* family." His voice is a growled proclamation.

I nod in agreement because he looks so happy. I even try to smile back. It doesn't reach my eyes, though. The moment he has her in his clutches, all of this will be destroyed. *She'll* be his favorite. I bet she doesn't have to take medications. I bet she behaves and follows rules. I bet she's never hurt a soul. The pretty teenage girl with the wide brown eyes will obliterate my whole world.

I'm going to have to ask my dad tomorrow for a favor.

A huge favor.

And he'll say yes because I'm *his* little girl.

Gabe

As the sun rises, I sip my coffee and watch the long driveway, my 9 mm tucked safely in the front of my jeans. War may not have anything planned, but I'd be a dumbass not to prepare anyway.

Nobody is taking her away from me.

Over my dead fucking body.

If I were a smart man, I'd pack my sweet girl up and drive her ass halfway across the country to a new location. Someplace safe. Someplace hidden. Texas, maybe.

But, apparently, I'm stupid.

I'm stupid because love makes you that way.

Crazy fucking stupid.

I let out a sigh as I think of my baby—the baby War is going to help me get back whether he wants to or not. A smile tugs at my lips as I lose myself to a memory of her.

Gabriella Alejandra Cruz-Diaz.

Not legally a Sharpe, but still mine.

So fucking perfect.

We've been home for over six weeks, and Alejandra is finally back at work. Her tight body bounced back only leaving a little more meat on her ass than usual. No complaints here. She let me fuck her long before she was cleared to have sex. But she said she was a doctor and she was fine. Again, no complaints.

"My Brie," I murmur, running my thumb along my baby girl's soft cheek. So fucking soft. "Such a good baby."

Her dark lashes blink open revealing her pretty brown eyes. Alejandra claims she looks just like me. I don't see it. To me, she looks like herself. A tiny, perfect baby. Mine. I hope one day she'll look like Alejandra though. The woman's a knockout. If Brie even looks half as good as Alejandra, I'll be cutting some throats, no doubt, by the time my daughter hits puberty. Boys wouldn't fucking dare touch my girl.

She starts to whimper so I stand with her swaddled in my arms and step out onto the back patio. After one colicky night where she screamed nonstop for fucking hours, I took her outside. I was so frustrated, and Alejandra was beat. I'd contemplated tossing her in the ocean. Not really, but I was over the screaming. Over it.

Thankfully, though, her screaming stopped the moment the warm, salty wind touched her skin. The crashing of the waves seemed to soothe my upset baby. And now, every time she cries, I take her outside. It calms her. Always.

"There we go," I murmur as I sit in the lounge chair on the patio. "You like this, Brie baby?"

Her chunky legs kick inside the blanket like she's trying to go somewhere. I chuckle and press a kiss to her forehead.

"Not yet, pretty girl. When you get older, I'll take you swimming."

I tear my gaze from my child and let my eyes wander down the beach toward the familiar house I'm always stalking.

My other daughter.

She's three now.

I know this because I saw the big hot pink balloon tied to the mailbox the other day. It was in the shape of a three.

It took some stalking on my part, but I also learned her name was Hannah. Such a pretty name for a pretty blonde little girl. Mine.

"You have a sister," I tell Brie. Her eyes are heavy but she fights to remain awake. "One day, you two will be friends. We'll do everything together. As a family."

Brie's mouth quirks up on one side with a smile. Alejandra says she isn't really smiling—that it's gas—but to me, she's fucking smiling. Who the fuck smiles when they have gas?

"I knew that you'd like that," I say with a laugh. "Don't worry. You'll always be my little baby."

Her tiny hand swats at me. When I hold my finger up, she clutches onto it. Those wide brown eyes find mine and they fucking twinkle. This little girl has a grip on my heart so tight, I fear one day she'll suffocate me with her love.

What a way to go…

My mind is brought back to the present, and I think about Alejandra. We mostly had good times. When she became pregnant with Brie, we grew closer. I miss her and hate that she's gone. But it was always going to be this way for us. The moment I had my Hannah in my clutches, Alejandra would be gone. I hadn't planned on killing her, but it's probably easier that she died. She'd have done everything in her power to keep the three of us together as a family.

But she didn't fit in the equation.

Hannah fits.

And Brie.

I try to imagine a world where they are friends. Would Hannah take my daughter under her wing and be kind to her? Would she fill the void Alejandra left?

Blinking away my stupid fantasy, I let out a low grumble.

Of course, she wouldn't be fucking kind.

I'd have to watch her every second of every day.

Brie could become a target.

Fuck.

With a hiss of frustration, I rake my fingers through my hair. I'll figure out a way to have them both. There has to be a way. Brie will have to toughen up. There's no changing Hannah.

But can my little girl be who she needs to be around my wild woman?

I think of Brie's innocent giggles when she gets tickled about a show she's watching.

I think of the way her wide brown eyes become watery when someone hurts her feelings.

I think about how she, even at fifteen, is a daddy's girl—always wanting to curl up on the couch with me to watch movies.

Hannah, her mother's killer, would smash her sweet world.

Hannah, the unstable wild woman, would smash her.

My chest aches as I ponder how to fix this. I love Hannah with all my heart. She's beautiful and sexy as fuck. I've never had a lover be able to keep up with my insatiable need and extreme fetishes. But hell, Hannah helps me pick out the fattest fucking vegetables at the store and provokes me to do the most depraved shit to her. She's perfect.

A click of the door behind me jerks me from my thoughts. Hannah saunters out wearing nothing but my white T-shirt. I can see her dark nipples through the material, and five bucks says she's not wearing panties. Dirty girl. Her hair is messy and tangled. Those bright blue eyes are tired and bloodshot. She chews thoughtfully on her fat bottom lip. I want to fucking chew on it too.

"Good morning, beautiful."

She flashes me a brilliant smile before climbing onto my lap to straddle me. Her palms run up my bare chest and I'm instantly hard beneath my jeans.

"Morning, handsome." She leans in and presses a sweet kiss to my lips. I watch her every movement as she slips the gun from my jeans, hesitates for a brief moment, and then sets it down on the table beside me. "You look sad today."

I palm her ass and am satisfied to know I was right. No panties. "Just thinking."

Her brows scrunch together. "About what? Are you tired of me yet?"

And this is why my head is a fucking mess. Brie has a chance. Brie's sweet and smart and compliant. Maybe this rich family could give her the love and guidance and safe environment she needs. My daughter could thrive like she always has.

Yet, out here in the Arizona desert?

Brie would be a captive.

She'd be trapped with two monsters: the one she loves but doesn't fully know and the one she doesn't know at all, who also killed her mother.

Gabriella would be miserable.

She may grow to resent me. Hate me even.

Unfuckingacceptable.

Hannah wins this war. Nobody but me understands her. Nobody but me can control her. Nobody but me can keep her safe from everyone in the godforsaken world…but especially from herself.

The choice has been made.

"I could never grow tired of you," I vow, earning a grin from her. "Just you and me, baby, until the end."

I've barely spoken the words before she's tearing at the button of my jeans. She tugs the zipper down to free my eager cock. Without any hesitation, she sinks her wet pussy down along my length, gasping in pleasure once she's completely seated on me.

I grab the hem of the T-shirt she's wearing and yank it over her head so she'll be bare for me. Her hips buck in a slow, teasing manner. Leaning forward, I suck her pink nipple into my mouth and bite down hard enough to make her whimper. She spears her fingers into my hair to latch on. When her hips rock against me harder, I suck and nibble at her tits until she's making obscene noises that I've never heard before.

"So fucking perfect," I praise as she bounces on my cock like I'm her favorite riding toy.

Her mouth parts open in pleasure, so I shove my finger into it, coating it with her saliva. She makes a sexy show of sucking on my finger like she does my cock and I nearly come right then. Jerking my finger back out, I then use my other palm to pull on her butt cheek. A small whimper, fear laced with excitement, escapes her as I tease the tight hole of her ass with the tip of my wet finger.

"I'm going to shove my finger up your ass," I say with a growl as I nip at her tit, "and you're going to love it."

She nods and leans closer to me, giving me what I want. I push my finger deep inside her and relish the way my cock squeezes with the extra pressure.

"You like that, sweet girl?"

"Mmm."

"Tell me."

"I like when you fill me up with…you. All you."

I fuck her ass slowly with my finger while she bounces in a quick rhythm on my dick. Her pussy keeps clenching and her ass as well, so I know my girl will be coming like a hurricane soon. Wild, uncaring, intense.

"You like it when I control and punish you. You're not a sweet girl at all, are you?"

She shakes her head, but then abruptly tilts her head back. "Oh God!"

Using my free hand, I pinch at her clit. She screeches and clenches down around me harder than before. So I do it again and again and again, each time more brutally. This not-so-sweet girl rakes her claws down the front of my chest, no doubt drawing blood, making me hiss in pain.

"Fucking bad girl," I chide as I bite on her breast. My thumb and finger twist her clit, just enough to have her raising off of me to escape the pain. But just when I think she's trying to get away, she drops back down on my cock and shudders so hard I think she'll collapse. Her pussy clamps down around my throbbing dick as she goes wild with her orgasm.

"Gabe," she moans, her body still quaking.

I yank my finger from her so I can grab onto her hips. She's tiny and fucking perfect and doesn't argue when I lift her up off my cock only to impale her ass in the very next movement. Once again, those wicked claws rip at my flesh as she cries out. Her body falls forward against me, shivering and trembling. When her teeth scrape against my neck, and she bites me like a rabid goddamned dog, I explode inside of her hot, tight ass. My dick pumps until the girl bleeds me fucking dry.

"You're going to kill me."

She giggles—a sound too pure for the act we just committed—and sits up to look at me. Her eyes are no longer bloodshot and tired. They twinkle with love and happiness. I make this girl happy. Me. She's the right decision. The only decision.

Brie will be okay.

Brie is strong and capable.

I'll make sure the fuckers who want her are good people.

And then I'll let my baby girl go, so she can be safe.

So I can take care of this girl.

The girl who I have loved, in some capacity or another, for her entire eighteen years of life.

"Come on," I say and slap Hannah's ass with both hands. "Let's get you cleaned up so your daddy doesn't see how dirty you really are."

Her lips quirk up on one side wickedly. "Only you know how truly dirty I am. Only you."

She climbs off of me and jiggles her sexy ass back into the house.

I look down at my softening cock and smile.

Hannah is the right decision.

"That's Dad's car," she breathes and bounces on her toes.

My eyes are drawn to the back of her tanned thighs. After we had showered, she made us a gigantic breakfast and ended up putting on a cute little yellow dress. She braided her blonde hair down her back making her look a thousand times more innocent than she really is. I'm aching to take her in that dress, but know I won't get the chance until they leave.

A cloud of red dust billows behind War's car as he travels up the road. Another five minutes and I'll have to share my girl with him. Storming over to her, I lift the back of her dress and palm her ass.

"Bend over. Right now," I order.

She laughs but bends to touch her toes. Hastily, I yank my cock out and stroke it while I push her panties to the side. A second later, I'm inside her. Fucking her in that innocent little dress.

"Touch your clit. You don't have much time to come, sweet girl."

With my grip on her hips, I pound into her ruthlessly. She moans and groans, but her finger feverishly rubs at her clit. As the car nears, I wonder if they can see what I'm doing to her. Just the thought of War or her little brother watching me fuck her has me coming deep inside her hot cunt.

"Are you close?" I demand, my dick still throbbing and leaking my seed into her.

"Yes!"

I yank at her braid and she screams in pleasure. I know she's climaxing the moment her pussy squeezes the fucking life out of my cock. She's mid-orgasm when I yank back out of her, letting her panties slide back into place. Her dress falls over her ass. Nobody would ever be able to tell.

As I tuck my dick back into my jeans and shove my gun into the front of them under my shirt, I watch as she straightens back up. She glances at me over her shoulder and grins at me. Her cheeks are rosy after having just come.

With satisfaction, I watch a trail of my cum race down the inside of her thigh toward her knee. If the goddamned car weren't pulling into park right as we speak, I'd clean her sexy legs up with my tongue.

"Dad!" she chirps and takes off running to the car.

Her dress bounces up, revealing her panties with each long stride she takes. My dick starts to harden again until War climbs out. All serious and Debbie Fucking Downer.

"Han," he chokes out in relief, wrapping his arms around her for a tight embrace.

The boy climbs out of the passenger seat and glares at me. Still a little prick, I see.

"What's up, kid?" I greet, just to fuck with him, and acknowledge him with a lift of my chin.

He waves a middle finger up toward the sky. Smartass. Dragging my gaze back over to my girl, I wait for them to approach.

"Well, come in," I say. "It's hot as hell out here. Might as well talk about this shit where there's air conditioning."

I usher them into the house, careful to take up the rear. I'm not turning my back on either one of those motherfuckers.

War's gaze darts all around as he inspects the space. Hannah's a messy girl, but I make her clean up her shit. Germ boy should be fine.

"Looks like you're being treated nice," he says tersely. His eyes cut over to mine. I expect disgust or hate, not fucking gratitude.

"Good girls get nice things," I say with a smirk.

His face reddens and his jaw clenches. The boy beside him fists his hands.

"You're an angry little shit, aren't you?" I ask Ren.

He laughs sardonically. It comes out as a cruel bark. "You don't even know."

Rolling my eyes, I slap Hannah on the ass. "Why don't you get them some of that lemonade you made this morning? Your brother certainly needs cooling off."

When she runs off to pour them a drink, I gesture for the couches. War and Ren take a seat, side by side, on the couch. I plop down in the middle of the love seat and arch a questioning brow at War.

"Tell me what you know about this family."

He lets out a rush of breath, releasing some of the hostility he brought in with him. "They look great on paper. Wealthy. Philanthropic. Always volunteering. It appears they have one child already. A girl about Gabriella's age. I'm wondering if they maybe couldn't have any more children? Maybe they wanted her to have a friend? The girl, despite their wealth, remains homeschooled. Again, it could be due to social issues or perhaps a health problem. Their finances are clean. No criminal record. And they live about an hour north of San Diego. From all outside perspective, they seem legit."

My heart clenches at having her live with another family, but this family doesn't sound like the foster fucks I've heard about on the news who hurt children. They seem normal.

"Anything bad?"

"Not bad, per se," he says with hesitation.

I level a *don't-fuck-with-me* look his way. "Out with it."

He scrubs his face with his palm. "They hold a lot of social events at their house. Looks like parties for political people, a few celebrities, and even local authorities."

"Are these like ragers or some shit?"

Ren snorts, and I give him a glare.

"What?"

"Ragers? You really are old," he bites out.

Ignoring him, I frown at War. "Are these wild parties? Is Brie in danger being around them?"

He shakes his head. "Not from what I can tell. It just seems like the wrong people could slip in…" His eyes narrow at me and his brow crinkles with worry. It actually fucking moves me once I realize what he's so goddamned concerned about.

He's concerned for her.

My Gabriella.

"You mean, people like *me* could get in and see her?" A smile tugs at my lips.

He nods. "Yeah."

"Why do you seem to care about her, man? You fucking hate me."

War glances over his shoulder into the kitchen. Hannah is flitting around making the drinks, a serene smile on her pretty face. She enjoys this shit—being the center of attention.

"I do. But she's just"—he turns to look at me—"an innocent. I hope she gets the life she deserves."

I clench my teeth knowing Hannah stole what little normal and deserving life my Brie did have when she murdered Alejandra.

"I'm glad for your concern. If these people are good to her, then I'm cool with them. But I like that I can slip in and check on her whenever I want."

His eyes are blue steel as he fixes me with his hardened gaze. "Don't hurt them, Gabe. I gave you this information so you could see your daughter, not do something stupid like slaughter their entire family one day on a whim."

"It's not me you have to worry about," I assure him, flicking my gaze to Hannah, who waltzes into the living room carrying the tray of lemonade. She even cut lemon wedges to put on the rim of the glass. Suzy fucking homemaker.

Understanding washes over War, and his features fall. He knows what his daughter is capable of. He knows that, unlike me, she can't be reasoned with. Her moods and emotions dictate her actions. Warren McPherson knows the safest place for his daughter is with me. And only I can prevent her from hurting people like the ones who want to adopt my daughter.

"Here, Dad," Hannah says sweetly as she hands him a lemonade. "Made with bottled water and fresh lemons. I made sure to wash well beforehand too." She winks at him and then hands one to her brother. When she makes her way over to me, she boldly sits in my lap. We share her lemonade, much to the horror of War and Ren judging by their disgusted gazes.

"What's the name and the address?"

War lets out a sigh and pulls out an envelope from his pocket. Hannah snatches it and hands it to me.

"What now? We all best friends?" I taunt, pulling Hannah back against my chest.

Both the man and the boy glare at me, their gazes turning murderous when I let my palm slide up her bare thigh. I stop just before where her dress hits her upper thigh.

"Oooh, Ren," Hannah says with excitement, "we could go swimming."

My girl would prefer her world this way: the three men she seems to care about most under one roof doting over her. If that makes her fucking happy, and her family doesn't try any shit, I'll indulge her. Anything to see that beautiful smile on her face.

"Go swim, sweet girl. Your dad and I still have business to discuss."

chapter

TWENTY

Hannah

"What's wrong, Ren?" I ask, shielding my eyes from the sun.

He's sitting at the edge of the pool in nothing but his plaid shorts with his legs dangling in the water. I already tried to get him to swim with me, but he refused. His eyes never leave our dad, who now sits at the patio table with Gabe talking in hushed voices.

"He's not going to hurt Dad," I tell him firmly.

Ren drags his gaze to me and frowns. "You really fucked up, didn't you, Han?"

"I didn't fuck up."

"You killed that woman. Gabe's wife."

I stiffen at his words. Legally, they were never married. She was not his wife. But I will be one day. "It was an accident."

He scoffs and begins emptying his pockets. Ren looks bigger—broader. Like maybe he grew since I saw him last.

"It was on purpose, and you know it," he snaps, calling me out like usual. "Own what you've done."

He slips into the water and dunks under the surface. When he reemerges, he gives a shake of his head to knock off the water and then runs his fingers through his unruly hair, slicking it back. His dark eyelashes are thicker looking now that they're wet.

"Own it," he hisses, splashing me with the water.

"She was going to try and break us apart," I tell him with a huff. "He's the only person who gets me."

Ren's jaw clenches and he regards me with a dejected look. "I got you, Han. I always got you."

My bottom lip wobbles. He and Dad were the only ones who I truly could connect with.

"I'm sorry," I whisper, hot tears welling in my eyes.

He lets out a sigh and opens his arms to me. I throw my arms around my brother's neck to hug him tight. We're not ones to be openly affectionate, but I've missed him and apparently he's missed me.

"Come home with us," he begs against my ear, in a voice low enough for only me to hear.

"I can't."

"Please."

Sniffling, I look over at Gabe who's watching me like a hawk. The aviators in front of his eyes can't hide his scowl. It thrills me to know he's jealous of my little brother.

I've seen Ren's cock before.

Many times as he's fisted himself to orgasm through the crack of his door late at night.

Ren, while well endowed, has nothing on Gabe.

Hell, the cucumbers have nothing on Gabe.

With a smile, I turn back to regard Ren, who's still holding onto me like I might vanish from his life forever. I can feel Gabe's possessive gaze on me which has me wanting to taunt him.

"Do you have a girlfriend?" I question.

Ren's hard gaze softens and his lips quirk up on one side. "No, but I like this girl."

Curling up my lip in disgust, I scoff. "Who is she? Is she prettier than me?"

Ren rolls his eyes and tries to push me away, but I lock on tighter. "You're such a fucking weirdo, Hannah. You're my sister, you perv. I'm guessing you're pretty by the way that motherfucker stares at you, like he wants to eat you, but to me you're just my sister."

"But this girl?"

He sighs but smiles. "She's just cute. I want to get to know her."

"Is she nice?"

"Seems that way."

I glance over my shoulder and Gabe has repositioned himself to where he's leaning forward with his elbows on his knees. His hands are fisted and his lips are pressed firmly together as Dad talks. Ren was right, Gabe does look like he wants to eat me. And he eats so well…

"Earth to Han."

Blinking away thoughts of Gabe's scruff scratching the inside of my thighs as he tongues my clit, I shiver and look back at Ren.

"As long as she's good to you, I'm happy," I relent with a huff.

Ren is all smiles at that. I know that wicked smile. Before I have a chance to jerk away, he clutches onto me and drags me under the surface with him. I squeal and squirm under the surface. Bubbles of laughter leave my brother as he terrorizes me like usual.

Finally, I kick him in the balls, leaving him sputtering and surging to the surface. I swim away from him and when I resurface, I yell at him. "Brat!"

The next hour becomes a war between my brother and I. Who can kill who first. Who will beg for mercy by the end. Eventually, Dad stands and whistles for us.

"You two kids get out. Your mother still doesn't know about this…" He sighs, shooting Gabe a frustrated glance. "Situation. Ren and I need to head back, so I can call her. She's not answering my texts."

Ren dunks me one more time before he swims over to the side. I watch my brother's back muscles flex as he climbs out. His shorts mold to his ass. The girl he likes will be lucky to get a boy like Ren. He's a catch. She better be good to him…or else.

Gabe's eyes are on my body as I get out of the pool. I wore his favorite bathing suit on me—a skimpy black thing that my mother would hate—and he's been licking his lips in appreciation ever since.

He wraps a towel around my shoulders and pulls me to him. "You know how difficult it is to listen to him talk when I've got an hour long hard-on for his daughter? Fucking impossible," he whispers against the shell of my ear.

I shiver and let out a giggle as I rub my ass against his impressive need behind me. "Thank you," I say, my voice growing serious. "Thank you for putting everything else from the past behind you to let me see them."

He kisses my neck before pulling away, flashing me a wide smile. "Anything for you, sweet girl."

I can hear the crunch of gravel out front and I wonder who could be visiting. Gabe tenses, unease in his gaze.

"You brought the cops here?" he snaps at my father.

Dad growls. "Hell no. I wouldn't jeopardize seeing my daughter."

"Stay here," Gabe orders and stalks off into the house.

I take my opportunity and pounce. "Dad," I hiss, "you can't let him take her. Do whatever you have to do but don't let him take Brie."

Dad frowns and glances over at Ren. "Why? Are you afraid for her safety? Will he hurt her?"

No, I will.

"This is just no life for her. She belongs with those people. I'm afraid Gabe will take her and then she'll be unhappy. Plus," I say lowly, "I don't want her here."

Dad's jaw clenches. "Hannah…"

"We won't let him take her. That's a promise," Ren barks. "You're right. She belongs to those people. I'll make sure he doesn't do anything stupid."

I beam at my brother. "Thank you."

Dad's gaze is worried as he skims it over me. "If things get weird or you become unhappy, call me. I will come for you."

Leaning forward, I kiss Dad on the forehead. "This is the happiest I've ever been. Tell me you see that."

He sighs and Ren grumbles, but they both nod in agreement.

"Like you said," I remind Dad, "I don't belong in prison or some institution. I belong with him. He can protect me and keep me safe."

Dad goes to say something when we hear a screech.

A familiar screech.

"WAR!"

Mom.

chapter
TWENTY-ONE

Gabe

Baylee.

My angel.

Bright blue eyes. Pretty blonde hair.

Exactly the fucking same as the day she stabbed me in the fucking chest and left me to die.

And furious.

I've never seen her so mad in my entire life.

"You psycho motherfucker! What have you done to my family?!" she screeches. Her body trembles as she looks past me into the house. "Where is she? What have you done to my daughter?"

I grin at her. "Hey there, sweetheart. Miss me?" When I take a step forward, she pulls a gun from her purse and points it at me.

"Don't move!"

I do as the woman—and God is she all woman with her soft curves and long legs—says and stay still. Footsteps thunder from behind me. She lowers the gun slightly just as War shoves past me.

"Babe, put the gun down," he urges, his tone calm and comforting.

Baylee doesn't drop the gun, though. Her face crumples as she starts to cry upon seeing Hannah and Ren walk past me out of the house. "You let my babies into the same house as him? You came to see him and didn't tell me?"

Smirking, I shoot War a look that says *Pussywhipped fucker is in trouble.*

He groans and slips the gun from her grip. "She didn't want you to come. She thought you would institutionalize her. The only reason Ren and I are here is because he let us see her in exchange for her medications. And I'm helping him find his daught—"

"DOES IT LOOK LIKE I GIVE A FUCK ABOUT HIM?" Baylee's entire chest heaves as she sobs so hard she nearly fucking chokes.

Hannah glares at her mother with more hate than a daughter should ever have. "You should leave, *Mother*. You aren't welcome, *Mother*." My sweet girl storms over to me and throws herself into my arms. She makes a great show of kissing me on the mouth.

"Oh my God," Baylee hisses. "I'm going to throw up."

And she does. The poor woman wretches and wretches. Despite being the doting husband, War takes a few steps away. His throat works up and down as he gags. The boy—maybe he does have balls—pulls Baylee's hair back while she vomits and he attempts to soothe her.

"I'm going to call the police. You're going to prison, you sick fuck!" Baylee threatens. "You'll never see my daughter again. You'll pay for touching her!"

"I LOVE HIM!"

Baylee's bloodshot eyes find Hannah, and her bottom lip trembles. "No, you don't. Believe me, baby girl. He's gotten into your head, but you don't love him." Baylee reaches into her purse and pulls out her cell phone. "Get your sister, Ren. We're going home. War, shoot him if he moves."

"Mom, please don't call them," Hannah begs. "I'm happy. You're ruining everything!"

Baylee snaps her gaze to mine as she speaks. "Detective Price," she says coldly into the phone,

"I'm at his property, and he *does* have my missing daughter. Yes, the sick bastard I told you about." An angry pause and her nostrils flare. "No, I will not leave until you all arrive. I'm staying here until that man is in cuffs and doesn't have his dirty hands on my daughter!"

Hannah sobs. "Why is she doing this?"

"Because she loves you. Because she doesn't understand us."

"I can't live without you," she cries and presses her mouth to mine for a sloppy, wet kiss. "Don't let her take me."

"Shh," I say, hugging her to me. "We'll figure something out."

She jerks from me and screams at Baylee. "I killed Alejandra! I cut her throat with a knife. And then I killed Maria while Gabe was tied up. I cut her throat, too!"

Baylee's flesh pales and she drops the phone into the dirt. "No…no, baby. No…"

Hannah's entire body shudders with rage. "I killed them, and it made me happy! I killed them because they tried to come between Gabe and me. I'll kill you too if you do the same!"

"Hannah!" Ren shouts.

War pulls Baylee to him a moment before she collapses. His face is crumpled in devastation. His boy is seething mad.

The cops will be here soon.

And that detective is still on the line. The phone is still lit up in the dirt.

Pulling my gun from the front of my jeans, I aim it right at the back of Hannah's head. "Well, it's been real fucking exciting, but I'm over this shit. Hannah didn't kill anyone. You all hear that? Nobody. I, Gabriel Motherfucking Sharpe, killed Alejandra Cruz-Diaz, two rapist motherfuckers, some dumb bitch from a Tucson grocery store, and a shitload more."

Three sets of eyes are wide and worried as they stare at us. Hannah remains completely still. I grab on to the back of her swimsuit bottoms and pull her to me. Sliding the end of the barrel against her temple, I hiss at them. "Get in your goddamned cars and leave before I splatter her brains all over the stucco of this house."

Baylee shakes her head. "No. Not without my daughter."

"She's not yours anymore, sweetheart. I've staked my fucking claim on her. Now leave already, dammit!" I roar, shoving the gun hard enough into Hannah's temple to make her cry out in pain.

But I know better.

My girl is fearless and tough.

Her ass rubs against my cock like she'd love nothing more than for me to fuck her right here in front of her family.

"Gabe," War snaps, his body trembling with anger. "You promised not to hurt her."

"And you fucking promised not to bring your wife!"

"I didn't bring her," he growls. "She must have found out on her own. Just don't hurt my daughter." His head snaps over to his son. "Take your mother to the car. Drive far away from here. I'll take care of this."

"But Dad—"

"DO IT!"

Baylee screams as her son drags her away. I'm fixated on how her ass jiggles as she fights him that I don't see War take a few steps forward. The gun he'd taken from her is now pointed at me.

"Just let her go, man. You're too far gone now. The police are on the way. I can still look out for Gabriella, even when you're in prison. But you have to let Hannah go. Please." He must have grown some balls in the last two decades because his hand doesn't shake or waiver. His steely blue eyes are fixated on me with the promise of death if I don't comply.

"Gabe, don't listen to him. He won't hurt you if I'm with you. Just get the keys and we'll go. Just the two of us," Hannah begs tearfully.

I inhale her wet chlorine-smelling hair and murmur against her ear. "No matter what, you know

I love you. We'll be together forever in some shape or another. Souls as powerful as ours don't let prison or death or *any-fucking-thing* tear them apart. You hear me?"

She sobs and shakes her head. "No! Stop it!"

"Say it back, sweet girl. Tell me you love me back."

Baylee climbs out of the passenger side of the car and runs for War.

"Say it," I hiss and nip at Hannah's ear.

"I love you so much." She cries so hard she doubles over, as if I've caused her great pain.

Everything that happens next is a blur of commotion. Baylee rips the gun from War's grip, like the crazy protective mama bear she is, and raises it at me. With a grunt, I shove Hannah as hard as I can away from me to protect her from the inevitable.

A second later.

Pop! Pop! Pop!

Turning on my heel, I charge back into the house and—*pop!* A motherfucking burst of pain hits me in the back, and I nearly stumble on my way to the back door. I can hear screaming and crying and fucking feet pounding behind me.

But as soon as I reach the back door, I fly through it and charge away from the house. Away from the woman hell-bent on killing me. Away from her family. Away from my Hannah.

Pop!

Another fiery blast of heat explodes on my ass cheek. She shot me in the fucking ass!

Pop!

I run like the damn devil and don't look back, despite the excruciating pain rippling through me. I run until I can't hear Baylee's screeches of hate. I run until I can't hear Hannah's sobs as her heart breaks. I run until the pain from my gunshot wound radiates through my chest and constricts my lungs.

A mile.

Maybe ten.

I don't know how far I run, but that's all I do until my vision grows black and cloudy.

It's daylight out but everything is black.

Black.

Blink.

Black.

Blink.

I suck in a breath, only to find I can't get it to enter my lungs.

That bitch shot me, and I'm going to actually fucking die this time.

Unbelievable.

Despite being blind and suffocating, I keep charging forward until my legs cease to work. I tumble into some thick brush. Cactuses or bushes—I don't know fucking what—scratch and pierce me as I crash.

I try to stand again.

I try to breathe.

I can't.

Baylee finally fucking did it.

But it isn't Baylee's perfect face I see in the darkness.

No, it's my sweet girl, Hannah.

My perfect, psycho, unstable girl.

I love you, Persephone.

See you in hell.

chapter
TWENTY-TWO

Hannah

Six months later…

The wallpaper is dancing again. Flowers that move and talk. One flower named Fred tries to council me often.

You'll have to forgive her one day.

I snarl. *Never.*

But she's your mother, Fred argues.

My mother killed the man I love. She killed him and then committed me to a fucking institution.

Fred the flower laughs. *Your mom is a bitch it would seem.*

At his words, I laugh too.

I go to claw at my head to try and rip the confusing drugs from my head, but then I remember. I'm wearing these stupid little mitts since I kept trying to claw at my chest earlier. When your heart is dead, you don't want it in your chest anymore. They make sure I'm in a constant state of euphoria to keep me from talking about him.

Obsessing.

Obsessing.

Obsessing.

And also, so I don't hurt myself.

Or anyone else.

Dr. Feelgood is coming, Fred warns.

I cackle as I remember not long after I first was institutionalized. I'd attempted to seduce the doctor. Surely an old, fat fuck like him would want some young pussy. I would do anything to get the hell out of here—even sleep with that loser. Gabe's soul would probably haunt him until the end of time, but he'd forgive me. He'd want me to do whatever it took to get out of here. But Dr. Feelgood rejected my advances. And he didn't like it when I tried to stab him in the throat with his pen either.

He's gay, I tell Fred.

We both laugh.

You should get some sleep, Fred says seriously. *The nurse said you'd require more sleep nowadays and—*

Fred's words are cut off as the heavy thud of the bolt lock to my room disengages. I try to focus my blurry gaze on the nurse. A man. It's never a man. But they say I'm strong. Perhaps they need someone strong to hold me down these days.

"Hey, baby," I slur, attempting to focus on the man wearing blue scrubs. "Let me loose and you can do whatever you want."

He stalks forward, and I writhe in my bed, unable to make my body function like I want it to because of the mind-altering drugs surging through my veins. "Shhh."

His palm finds my breast, and I jolt with shock. So warm. So powerful. Possessive. Maybe I can seduce him. He definitely doesn't seem gay, unlike Dr. Feelgood.

I whimper when the nurse's hand slides up over my belly. He lets out a hiss of pleasure. Then, he slides back down my belly toward my pussy. His fingers lift my gown and push past my panties. Even through my confusing haze, I buck against his touch as he pushes inside me.

I haven't been touched like this since…

Tears well in my eyes, only further blurring the world around me.

"Come for me, sweet girl."

I'm hallucinating again.

Always the fucking same.

Always him.

Always Gabe.

"Yes," I moan.

"Shhh…"

His fingers expertly touch me until I'm exploding with pleasure. Fred the flower winks at me.

"Time to go home," the nurse says.

Home?

"Not with her. I'm not going anywhere with her," I seethe and rage. My mother is responsible for all this. My fate is all her fault. That I'll die in this wretched place. Alone. Sure, Dad comes to visit on occasion, but it upsets him too much. In his eyes, I'm gone. Unreachable. Lost. Vacant.

The nurse's finger—a finger that smells like me—shushes me against my lips. "Not with your mother. With me. Where you belong."

He pulls a shiny, big knife from the back of his scrubs and saws through my ID bracelet with ease. When he frees me of it, he slips a white doctor's jacket over my gown. I blink through my haze to read the tag.

Dr. Stephchinski.

Dr. Feelgood's *other* name.

I'm then scooped up like I'm a sack of potatoes.

"I can see they're feeding you well, sweet girl."

I squint and try to focus on his face.

Brown eyes.

Handsome smile.

"Gabe?"

"Shhh."

He carries me out the door, swiping his security access card through the reader. I don't even get to say goodbye to Fred. That flower was my only friend. I squint, looking for Dr. Feelgood or his other nurses, but nobody comes. The hallway floor is painted in a radiant shade of red. One of the crazy patients must have gotten into the art closet. Had a heyday spattering red paint all over the place.

So pretty.

Like blood.

Brilliant.

Door after door, he swipes his magical card and I become entranced by the musical sound it makes each time as we make it through the maze of the facility. It's heavenly and freeing.

"Are you an angel?" I ask.

His lips press a kiss to mine and soon a frigid gust of air chills my exposed skin. It's black outside and cold. "Your dark, avenging angel."

I smile.

Just like the angel who saved me once before…

"Am I dying?"

"You're not dying," he says with a chuckle as he loads me into his car.

The car door slams. Then, he climbs into the driver's seat beside me. A moment of clarity hits, and I focus on him.

Gabe.

Mine.

He's alive and he came for me.

His palm finds my belly and he strokes the very swollen flesh. "Sweet girl…"

"She's yours," I assure him.

It's certainly not Dr. Feelgood's or Fred the flower's.

"I know."

"How?"

"Because everything about you is mine. Even that clearly very big baby girl kicking inside you. Mine. Every single part of you belongs to me."

I sigh when he kisses me quickly on the lips before peeling out of the parking lot.

"I love you, Hades."

He stretches his arm out and strokes my cheek in a reverent way. "I love you too, Persephone."

"Are we going to hell?" I question, yawning big.

He laughs. "Not today, baby. Not today."

"Where then?"

"A place almost as hot…"

I reach for him and he takes my hand. "Where?"

"Texas."

"Texas…" I echo. "Should we name her Dallas? Is that where we're going?"

We sail along the dark highway, and he leans in to steal a kiss.

"We're going to Corpus Christi."

"The beach," I say with a happy sigh. "Christi. Let's name her Christi."

I fight to keep my eyes open, but fatigue drags me under.

"Get some sleep, sweet girl."

Jolting upright, I shake my head in vehemence. "No! If I fall asleep, this will all be a dream. I don't want this to be a dream."

He squeezes my hand and gazes at me in the darkness. The red glow from the dash lights makes him look like some sort of evil villain. A monster. *Beautiful.* Villains need love too, though. "This isn't a dream," he assures me. "Besides…" His lips quirk up into a wolfish grin. "Even a dream couldn't keep me away from you. Some nightmares simply won't die. Some nightmares will haunt you until your last breath."

Leaning back against the seat, I relax and run my fingers over my belly. "I trust you. Don't ever leave me. Please."

"I'll follow you anywhere," he says with a low, possessive growl. "Even into the darkness. Especially, into the darkness."

I'll follow you anywhere.

Even into the darkness.

Especially, into the darkness.

EPILOGUE

Gabriella

One year later…

I stare into the vanity mirror in my room.

My room.

What a joke.

Nothing belongs to me here…not even me.

I belong to *him*.

To be paraded around and groomed.

I'm to join two powerful families by marriage.

All in due time. It's what *he* tells me every chance *he* gets. Due time really means the moment I turn eighteen. In eighteen months, that is, I'll be wed to one of the Rojas brothers. Esteban, second in command to his father, who has a terrible scar running down his cheek. Duvan, the hot but scary college kid, who likes to taunt Esteban for fun. And finally, Oscar, the youngest brother who is still in high school, like me. He seems the better choice of them all and is sweet to me… but it's not like I'll have a say in the matter.

He will choose for me.

He always chooses for me.

I look down at the black dress *he* bought for me to wear tonight. It had been hanging on my closet door when I awoke this morning. He'd purchased it and brought it to me. His decision. My *real* father always let me make my own choices. My real father loved me…

Until he didn't.

Until he chose that girl over me. The murderer.

Tears well in my eyes as I think about finding my mother that day. Tied to my parents' bed. Eyes wide and glazed over. Blood soaking her throat and the bed below.

She was stolen from me.

By that crazy bitch.

And then he was stolen from me too.

I was left for others to decide my fate.

And Heath Berkley was more than happy to take the rein over my life.

Heath is the man who makes all of my choices now.

A shudder ripples through me as I try to block out his scent, which always lingers in my room. I block out the way he touches me when his wife Izzie isn't looking. The quick hugs. The stolen kisses. The way his hand caresses my thigh when he's had too much to drink…

I swallow down the bile rising in my throat and stand quickly. Rushing over to the window, I pull it open to suck in some fresh air.

Vienna says *father* would get angry if he saw me open the window.

Vienna worries too much.

I feel sorry for my *sister*, Vee. She's my age. Pretty with bright red hair and a smattering of freckles on her cheeks. Her green eyes are the color of grass…

Heat floods me, and I shake away the feeling.

My *sister* was the reason *he* adopted me.

The Rojas brothers didn't want a redhead. Those Colombian boys weren't interested in a ginger. Their words, not mine. They wanted someone like them. My exotic Venezuelan features I inherited from my mother make them salivate every time they see me.

Like tonight.

They'll be drooling like a bunch of starved dogs.

Sometimes I wonder if I can run away from it all… Would *he* find me? Of course, *he* would. Heath is successful in everything he does. I know this because he tells me so.

The sound of bass thumping from a vehicle starting has me jolting out of my thoughts and practically hanging out the window. This is the real reason I open the window. The real reason Vee worries.

The boy comes twice a week like clockwork to mow.

It's the highlight of my crappy life—watching him pull his T-shirt off and toss it into his suped-up black truck. Watching the way his shoulder muscles flex when he weed eats. The way his shorts hang low on his narrowed hips, showing a delicious V that leads straight down.

But mostly, the way his eyes always lift to find me staring down at him and twinkle to see me.

Always.

Each and every time, he flashes me a handsome grin that makes me weak in the knees and gives me a wink.

I live for that moment.

I'm boldly staring at his sculpted chest when he lets out a whistle. My eyes dart to his and my cheeks flame at having been so blatantly caught.

"What's your name, Princess?"

I laugh. "Princess?"

He puts his hands on his hips and gives me a crooked grin. "You look like a sad little princess locked away in a tower."

At this, my laughter dies. His words are spot on. "Gabriella. You can call me Brie."

"Pretty name for a pretty girl."

The heat from my cheeks spreads to my neck, revealing my embarrassment. "What's your name?" I question, avoiding his compliment.

Before he can answer, Heath's black SUV turns into the driveway. The boy pretends to fool with the mower until the garage door closes behind Heath. I know I only have a matter of minutes to get the window closed and wait dutifully for Heath to fetch me.

"The name's Ren," the boy calls out. His features harden and his chest flexes. A muscle in his neck ticks and a sheen of sweat forming on his throat glistens in the sun. It has me wondering if he tastes salty. I've always preferred savory over sweet. "One day I'm going to save you from that tower, Princess Brie."

Our eyes stay locked for a long moment until I hear footsteps thundering for me down the hallway. I wave quickly and slam the window down. I've just turned around and smoothed out my black dress when the door nearly flies off the hinges.

I force a pleasant smile on my face and greet the wicked dragon in my story. With fluttering lashes, I sashay over to him and give him his expected kiss on the cheek.

When I pull away, his icy blue eyes skim over my dress and he frowns. "This isn't you, baby," he motions at me. "Too long. Put on the green fitted one you wore a few months ago. We want you to be pretty tonight. Business is business, sugar."

I hate the green dress. Low-cut. Short as can be. Molds to my every curve. The last time I wore it, I thought Esteban and Duval would shed blood in our living room over me in the dang thing. Those two dogs hate each other enough as it is without dangling a teenage steak with a nice rack wrapped up in a tiny green bow in front of them. They literally growled at each other.

Looks like tonight, I'll be teasing the dogs again…

"Sure," I tell him with a wobbly smile as I head for my closet.

His strong hand snags my bicep and he pulls me to him. I suck in a sharp breath, suppressing an all-body-consuming shudder, when his arms wrap around my middle and he hugs me to his large frame. "I missed you, Gabriella," he tells me, his nose nuzzling my hair. "I always miss you."

This time, though, instead of noticing how he inhales me or how his palms drift to my hips, his fingertips sprawled out over my lower stomach, or how he grows hard behind me, I think of *him*.

Ren.

The lawn boy.

My dragon-slaying prince.

Time's a tickin,' Ren. There are more dragons waiting to swoop in—three in fact. Eighteen more months and I'll belong to one of them.

But quite frankly, the one with the sharpest teeth behind me may not be able to wait that long. It takes everything in him not to devour me as it is. Time is of the essence.

I'll be the princess in the green dress surrounded by salivating dogs.

Tick tock.

This Isn't You, Baby is up next…

THIS ISN'T YOU, *baby*

I was a pawn.
Weak and someone easily manipulated.
To be played with as he saw fit.
Until YOU.

YOU shone light in my now dark world.
It was YOU who made me smile.
For the first time in this game, I had hope.
All because of YOU.

The more powerful pieces on the board, however, were a threat to YOU and me.
They would win at any cost.

Two kings ruling with an iron fist.
Allies or opponents, it was hard to tell.

YOU promised to save me.
Told me we would win.
But then I was on the wrong side of the board.

This isn't YOU, baby.
And I don't know what to do.

The game is almost over and I'm counting on YOU.
Tick, tock…

PROLOGUE

Ren
Age Sixteen

"This is stupid, Dad," I say with a grunt. "We should have called the cops and had them follow us to Coronado Beach. That prick belongs in prison."

Dad leans back in his office chair and swivels to regard me. Frown lines mar his otherwise smooth forehead, and I swear he's sporting a few greys that weren't there last month. The meeting with Gabe and Hannah at the beach several days ago has taken a toll on my father. It's driving him crazy not being able to tell my mother. The guilt is written all over his face. "We can't and you know that. They'll take her away from us."

I wince at his rough tone and pinch the bridge of my nose in frustration. "I know," I concede. "I just hate him. Hate that the old fucker is with Han."

"Language, son," he grunts before turning back to his computer where he's been looking up Gabe's daughter's whereabouts. "I hate him too. He's evil and unpredictable but…" he trails off.

So is Hannah.

We're both thinking it but neither of us voice it.

She killed Gabe's wife, for crying out loud. If we called the police, they'd take away my sister right along with him. And while that would upset our family, it would devastate my father. He loves her with damn blinders on. Sees past her moments of crazy that the rest of us in this family can't always overlook.

"Heath Berkley looks good on paper," he says as he toggles between screens. My dad is smart as shit with computer stuff. I'm not stupid enough to not know that what he's doing is illegal. But when it comes to his family, I think Dad would do whatever needed to be done. "I just wish there was a way we could keep an eye on her. She's our only insurance. The Berkleys live about an hour from here. It'll be hard to stay on top of her."

While Dad flips through his financials, I scroll through my pictures to some selfies Hannah took with my phone. In the pictures, my sister looks calm and casual. The storm that brews sometimes in her eyes isn't present in the photos. It saddens me. I fucking miss her crazy ass.

"Jesus Jacopo."

"What?"

"That's the name of the kid who mows their lawn. They don't use a fancy lawn service. Just some kid," Dad states as if this means anything to me.

"Okaaaaaay," I draw out, furrowing my brows together in confusion.

"I'm going to call Jesus and double what he makes in an entire season working for them. You're going to take his place."

At this I laugh. "No, Dad."

"Ren," he grumbles. "You're sixteen with no job. Just because we aren't hurting for money doesn't mean you'll get away with not having a job. Most males have a job at sixteen. It's like a rite of passage."

I huff. "Hannah didn't have a job."

"Hannah's different. We've discussed this."

I curl up my lip in disgust. "So, I'm supposed to mow lawns for some family just so I can spy on psycho Gabe's daughter."

He frowns and turns to regard me. "The girl lost her mother and her father without any explanation. It isn't fair for her. Just do this for our family. Please."

Guilt surges through me. Not because of the girl but because Dad has never really asked me to do anything of such importance. I don't want to let him down.

"Fine. But if she's insane like her dad, I'm out."

I pull up to the sprawling gated Berkley Estate. They're clearly loaded as hell. The house is gigantic and so is the damn yard. I could be surfing this summer but instead, twice a week, it looks like I'll be the Berkeley's indentured servant.

Thanks a lot, Han.

With a huff, I climb out of the black truck my parents bought me eight months ago. My irritation shows as I stomp to the back of my truck and wrangle my brand-new lawnmower out. Dad purchased the lawn equipment for me last night. We spun a story for Mom and she believes I'm mowing to earn some extra cash to start paying for my own car insurance. Dad droned on and on about how teens need to earn things, so they don't turn out to be spoiled brats. After all that's happened with Hannah lately, I don't even think Mom was really listening.

At first, as I begin mowing the big ass lawn, I'm pissed. I crank up some Nine Inch Nails on my headphones and ignore the world around me. I'm supposed to be keeping an eye out for this Gabriella girl, but she's nowhere to be found. Just me and the damn never-ending yard. When I become completely drenched in sweat, I yank off my wet T-shirt and stuff it into the back of my shorts. It's then when I feel it.

Someone staring at me.

Stopping the mower, I swipe at the sweat on my forehead as *Closer* starts thumping its bass in my headphones. I drag my gaze along the windows of the house. The shades are all drawn and I wonder why I feel like someone is watching me. When I glance up at the second floor, I lock eyes with a brown-eyed girl. The same brown eyes as that motherfucker who is banging my sister. *Gabriella.* But this girl's eyes don't look evil. They look sad. She peeks at me from behind the glass with her plump lips in a pout. A red-headed girl pops in beside her to see what she's staring at. Then, the other girl tries tugging Gabriella from the window.

Gabriella reaches for the glass—almost as if she's reaching for me—and my heart rate quickens in response. She disappears and I feel disappointed almost immediately. A protectiveness—much like I always felt with Hannah—settles over me. The girl can't help she's the spawn of Satan. Right? She needs people like Dad and I looking after her. Right?

I restart the mower, and this time, I don't rush my work. For the next several hours, I meticulously trim and weed-eat the massive yard. After I load my equipment back into the truck, I can't help but look back at her window.

Gabriella sits perched on the ledge. She's wearing a pair of jean shorts and her short legs are stretched out along the window as she paints her toenails. Long, wavy dark brown hair hangs in front of her shoulders.

I wonder if her hair is soft.

The thought jars me, and I shake it out of my head. When she notices me frowning, she frowns too.

I want to see her smile.

Lifting my chin, I give her a small wave and a huge grin. She sits up and in return gives me the most breathtaking smile.

She's beautiful.

I'm disappointed when she leaves the window once again. But as I climb into my truck, I have a whole new outlook. This job just got a whole lot more interesting.

Don't worry, Gabriella, I'll look after you now.

chapter ONE

Brie

Three years later

"Hair up or down?" Vienna questions, her back to me as she fusses with her dark red locks. "Dad will want it up." At this she sends me a pouty look in the mirror.

Just the mention of her father—my adopted dad—Heath Berkley has my skin crawling. I've been under his roof since I was fifteen. And now that I'm nearing my eighteenth birthday, the vibe around him has gone from creepy to menacing. I feel like time is ticking by way too quickly and when it finally hits its mark, I'll be in for a rude awakening.

"Wear it down. You look like Ariel from *The Little Mermaid*," I tell her as I scroll through my phone. When Vee and I turned sixteen, Heath got us phones.

There aren't many people in my contact list. Heath, his wife Izzie, Vee, Oscar Rojas, and…Ren.

"Ugh, that's what your boy toy always says too." She sticks her tongue out at me.

As if on cue, he texts me.

Romeo: Can I crash the party tonight?

A smile tugs at my lips. We've been out a few times on dates when Heath is away on business, although those dates have dwindled since Ren went to college. He's taking a crap ton of courses and no longer mows our lawn. However, since he's out of school for the summer, we can go back to seeing each other again. Besides Vee, he's my closest friend.

A friend who I've kissed more times than I can count.

A friend who I want to do much more with.

A friend who never fails to text or call me each day.

I just wish we could be more than friends.

Me: Heath wouldn't like it. You better not.

"Green dress or red dress?" Vee questions. Her red eyebrow is raised in question. I'd kill to have her silky hair and cute, freckly face. Everything about her is adorable.

"Red clashes with your hair," I say with a laugh.

She huffs at me but tosses the red dress.

Romeo: I miss you.

My heart flutters at his words. I haven't seen him since spring break when we snuck off for a beach day with his brother Calder and Vee. Heath just thought us girls were going shopping. Had he known we went off with boys, he'd have forbidden it. That day, under the warm March sun, Ren and I made out like…well, teenagers. He nearly grinded me into the sand where, might I add, I had my first orgasm. Luckily, Calder and Vee were on the Jet Ski, so they didn't notice my embarrassing moans. If we hadn't been low on time and out in public, I'd have begged Ren to take my virginity right there on the beach.

"You should get dressed," Vee says with a huff as she zips up her fitted jade-colored dress. "Dad doesn't like it when we're not ready to go."

I roll my eyes at her. "Why? He'll just make me change anyway."

At this, her pale cheeks burn bright red. I know she's embarrassed about how her father acts around me. Like I'm a piece of property. Neither she nor I will discuss why he's this way. It's awkward for us both. The only thing that makes sense about my life is the fact that she and I became best friends. She was a lonely, homeschooled child while I'd lost everyone closest to me. We were naturally drawn to one another. I hurry and fire off another text to Ren before Heath gets here.

Me: I miss you too.

Vee spritzes some perfume on and fusses with her eyeliner. She's looking especially stunning today. I know she's attempting to please her dumb dad. And probably hoping to lure one of the Rojas brothers into liking her.

It won't work.

None of the Rojas brothers—not even Oscar—are interested in her. It's why I'm here in the first place. To be married off to one of them. And while I get along with Oscar the best, I don't want to be married off to anyone. I had plans. College. A career in filmmaking. And then later on down the road, marriage and a family. But ever since Dad lost his mind and ran off with the psycho who killed my mother, my plans got slaughtered too.

"Earth to Brie," Vee snaps, looking feisty with her hands on her hips.

God, I wish they would like her instead so I would be off the hook. Life would be a lot simpler that way.

"What?"

"I asked if you were texting with Ren. Has Calder asked about me?" She bats her eyelashes sweetly. I don't know why she's asking about Calder. Last time he tried to kiss her, she avoided him. Since I've known her, she's been obsessed with Oscar. And even though Calder is a hot, nice guy, she just doesn't seem too into him for some reason.

"Ren wanted to crash the party," I say with a laugh. "And no, he didn't mention Calder."

She pouts, and I swear it makes her look sultry, as she tosses her red hair over her shoulder. "Dad would have a fit if Ren showed up. In fact, if he knew you two sort of dated, he'd go nuts."

I let out a huff. "And that's why he'll never know. As far as your dad's concerned, I'm his dumb little puppet."

Vee's eyes well up with tears and I worry she'll mess up her newly applied makeup. "I'm sorry," she tells me for the millionth time since I came here. "But I'm not sorry you're my best friend. If Dad hadn't adopted you…" Her words trail off and her lip trembles. "I was lonely until you came to live with us."

I toss my phone on the bed and pull her in for a hug. She's taller than me, especially now that she's wearing heels, so I basically get a face full of boobs.

"You're my family now, Vee. I'm happy I have you."

We're still in a sisterly embrace when tension crackles through the air. I can always sense his presence before I ever see or hear him.

Heath Berkley.

The man who owns me.

"Vienna, baby doll, your mother was looking for you. The wait staff is arriving for the party, and she needs you to help direct them where to go," he says in a smooth tone that makes me shiver.

"I'm sorry," she whispers against my hair before releasing me.

As soon as she exits the bedroom, Heath pounces.

Like a black panther stalking its prey, he strides over to me. His knuckles lift my chin so our eyes meet. "Why aren't you dressed?"

Irritation trickles through me and I narrow my gaze at him. "You always make me change anyway."

He steps away from me and regards my outfit with a disgusted look. "You know I hate when you wear this shit." He waves at my black yoga pants and oversized T-shirt. "Take it off."

I'm stunned by his words as he storms into my massive closet. Hangers clang together as he searches for something for me to wear. When he reemerges, a scowl paints his features.

"Off."

"W-What?" I hiss. "Not while you're watching me."

His face reddens and a vein in his forehead pulsates with rage. Normally I do as he says, but he's never asked me to undress in front of him before. I have to draw the line somewhere.

"Gabriella, take off your goddamned clothes before I take them off for you," he growls.

Tears pinch the backs of my eyes, but I refuse to let him see me cry. For three years, I've lived in this house and hidden my emotions from him. Not once have I let him see how broken I am inside at having seen my mother's bloody, dead body or how devastated I was that my dad chose her killer over me.

When he takes a menacing step toward me, I let out a yelp. "Gabriella." His low, warning growl has me peeling off the big T-shirt. Had I known he was going to force me to undress in front of him, I'd have worn a bra. As soon as the shirt hits the floor, his eyes flicker with desire. I don't miss the way his slacks bulge with his erection. A shiver of fear ripples through me.

"Pants."

Swallowing, I slowly push the material down over my hips toward my knees. Thankfully I have on a pair of black lacey boy short panties. He stalks over to me and brushes some hair away from my face. His scent chokes me, and I nearly gag.

"So perfect," he praises, his fingertips tangling in my hair. He presses a soft kiss to my mouth. My entire body freezes. Heath has kissed me but never on the mouth. Usually on the cheek, forehead, or the top of my head. "Please wear a bra with this dress." His voice is husky. The heat from his body nearly scorches me although we are barely touching.

"Okay."

"Now, Gabriella."

I jolt away from him and scramble to find a bra. Once I've put it on in record speed, I start for the dress he's laid out on the bed. When I bend over to grab it, he steps behind me. His large hands find my hips and he pulls my ass against his hard-on.

"Do you feel what you do to me?"

I swallow and try not to cringe. Embarrassment causes my flesh to heat. "I'm sorry?"

He chuckles and his thumbs rub circles on my hipbones. "I'm not."

A shriek escapes me when he pops my ass softly with his hand before striding away from me. Before he exits, he turns to regard me with a sly grin. "What do you want for your birthday?"

My freedom.

I yank the dress quickly up my body to hide from him. "I don't want anything." *From you.*

Our eyes lock and he pins me with his heated glare. "Three more days, Gabriella. And then I'm going to give you something we both will enjoy."

At that, he slips out of my room and disappears.

I have to get out of here.

Heath's parties are something out of a fairy tale. He spares no expense when it comes to hosting such events. Everyone who is anyone is invited, the food is incredible, and the décor is impressive. I've met more celebrities than I can shake a stick at. Under normal circumstances, this might be cool.

But nothing about this situation is cool.

What people from the outside don't see is the cesspool of the vilest criminals all dressed up and fancy as hell in one room making subtle and refined negotiations. Heath Berkley is not an honest self-made man. He's heavily involved in the drug circuit. I know for a fact that his biggest alliance is with the Rojas family. Camilo Rojas is one of the richest men in Colombia. His cocaine empire is virtually untouchable by the American feds. He doesn't come to the US much—he instead has his two eldest sons, Esteban and Duvan, do most of the overseeing for his drug trafficking. His alliance with Heath is what keeps the feds off his ass. Heath lines the pockets of politicians, influential police personnel, and our local government so they'll overlook what comes through his shipyard via shipping containers.

So far, the business marriage between these two families has worked out well. But about five years ago, the Colombian government began harassing Camilo. They're as corrupt as he is and have been extorting a crap load of money in exchange for not blasting Heath's name to the feds—the ones who actually do their jobs and aren't dirty—the ones he can't pay off no matter how much money he waves in their faces. Their mere "business" relationship makes their criminal activity that much more obvious. Why else would a wealthy Colombian family be so well connected with a rich American one? Especially since the American family owns a gigantic shipyard that primarily sends barges to Buenaventura from the Port of San Diego.

For the past several years, Heath and Camilo have slowed on both production of the coke and the distribution here in America to keep the Colombian government off their backs. However, when they finally have me married into the Rojas family, they can make a great show of the actual marriage of the two powerful families. Their relationship will no longer be a red flag.

Of course, I'm not supposed to know any of this.

But, like I said, Oscar, the youngest Rojas son, is actually my friend and has a really big mouth.

"Oh my God, Brie," Vee whines and sips on the champagne we're only allowed to have about eight times a year at these lavish parties Heath hosts. "Oscar looks so hot tonight. His hair is getting longer. He looks more like Esteban every day but a whole lot less scary."

I laugh and scan the growing crowd for our friend. He lives and goes to school in Bogotá, just a day's drive from where his father's shipyard is located and apparently around the corner from where one of the warehouses is located. We don't see Ozzy every time Heath has his parties so I'm glad to know we'll see him tonight.

"Are Duvan and Esteban here too?" I don't want either of them to be here. Where Oscar treats me as a friend and makes me laugh, his two older brothers treat me as a prize one of them will eventually sink their teeth into.

"Yep, and old man Camilo. Must be a big deal for the whole family to be here," Vee says and chugs her champagne. "I'm going to make out with Oscar. I'll shove him into a dark room and do dirty things to that firm body." When she starts fanning herself, I laugh.

"Do you even know how to do dirty things? Last I checked, you were a virgin too, nerd," I tell her with a smile.

A big body comes between us and slinks an arm around each of us. As soon as I inhale the familiar cologne, I know it's Oscar. "What's that? You both want to lose your virginity to me at the same time?" he says playfully. "I can arrange that. It'll be our little secret."

I chuckle but Vee bristles. Her idea of flirting with Oscar lately is to give him the cold shoulder. On many occasions, I suggested she switch up her approach. Maybe just dress slutty and attack. She always turns her nose up at that idea and prefers to play hard to get. Possibly a little too hard to get.

"I'm going to go talk to Dad for a bit," she says coolly. "See you around?"

He shrugs as she pulls from his grip. As she walks away from us, her hips sway and I know deep down she's hoping he'll follow her. Sometimes I want to push him in her direction. But we all know it's our parents who have the final say on who dates who.

And right now, it's still up for debate.

At least until three days from now…

"Come on," Oscar says and grabs my hand. So much for sending him her way.

He drags me through the throng of people and down the hallway. When we reach one of the many guest bedrooms, he pushes through it. After he shuts the door, he gives me a crooked grin that I know must melt some hearts back in his hometown.

"Miss me?" he asks, waggling his dark eyebrows.

Laughing, I give him a playful shove. "I missed hearing about all of your female conquests. Have you had sex with the entire female population there, Ozzy?"

He unbuttons his jacket and tosses it over a chair before sprawling out on the bed. "Maybe even a small percentage of the male population too. You know I can't turn down a killer body."

Rolling my eyes, I kick off my heels and crawl onto the bed beside him. This is our thing. Usually, Vee is right in the middle. Find Oscar, hide from the parents and his brothers, and laugh all night. It feels weird without my best friend. But she knows where to find us.

"You're a douchebag," I tell him with an exasperated huff but hug his middle.

"A douchebag you're going to marry." He turns and regards me with a grin.

I scrunch up my nose in irritation. "I wish it were you and not one of your asshole brothers."

"Duvan's not that much of an asshole. Just acts like a dick most of the time because of Esteban. Always has to prove something. He's better than he used to be though. Rehab really cleaned him up." I never even knew Duvan had done drugs. I mean, they're all sons of a drug trafficker, but I never thought they actually did them. He turns on his side and stares at me, a frown tugging at his full lips. His fingers push some hair from my face. "But it's me. I'm going to marry you."

I love Oscar. I truly do.

But I don't want to marry him.

We're friends.

Besides, things are beginning to get serious with Ren.

"Ozzy…" I trail off.

His eyes are molten with love and it breaks my heart I don't feel the same about him. I wish he'd look at Vee this way instead.

"Brie," he murmurs and slides a palm to my hip. "It's what Papá has decided."

Hope blossoms in my chest. At least with Oscar, the idea of an arranged marriage doesn't seem so frightening. He's the type of boy who'd never settle down, so I'm sure he wouldn't care if I dated Ren on the side.

"Really?"

He slides his fingers into my hair and grips me gently. His eyes darken as he drops his mouth near mine. "Really."

And before I can register what's happening, his mouth is on mine. Demanding and eager. He deepens his kiss the moment I open my mouth to ask him to stop. His heavy body slides over mine and his erection pokes at me through our clothes.

"So hot and mine now," he murmurs against my mouth.

His kiss has left me breathless, but I start to protest. "Ozzy—"

He lets out a groan as his hands roam my body. "We can finally have what we've always wanted."

When his fingers pinch my nipple through my dress, I cry, "What has gotten into you?" He never acts like this. "Oscar, we can't do this. I'm seeing someo—"

He silences me with another kiss. My heart races in my chest as I try to wriggle free of his expert touch that starts to roam south. Turning my head to the side, I let out a groan. "Please stop." I push at his massive shoulders, but he's immovable. He suckles at my neck as he manages to shove my dress high up my thighs. This is going too far. "Oscar, no. I don't…" I trail off. "…want this."

His hot breath causes me to shiver. Balling my fist, I prepare to punch him in his ribs until he gets off of me. But it's too late. I lock onto a pair of familiar green eyes that glimmer with betrayal in the doorway.

Vee.

No!

"Vienna!" I call out over Oscar's shoulder. "You idiot! Look what you did!" I slap at his head, but he just gives me a wicked grin.

"What?" he says in a smug tone. "You liked it."

I shudder in disgust. "Get out! You're an asshole!"

I go to kick him, but he jumps off the bed out of the way.

His brows furrow in frustration. "You love me and when we get married, I'll—"

"You'll do what, little brother?" a deep voice says from behind him. "Last I checked, you weren't in the running for this little contest."

Normally, I hate Duvan but today I'm thankful for his presence. Oscar just crossed a major line.

"Fuck off, D. You know she and I are better suited for each other," Oscar grumbles and adjusts his erection in his slacks. "She doesn't even like you or Esteban."

Duvan steps from behind Oscar. My eyes meet his almost black, rage-filled glare and I suppress a shudder. His gaze falls to between my legs where my dress is still lifted. I squeeze my thighs shut to hide from him. When his darkened gaze meets mine, he stalks over to me. The hunger in his eyes scares me.

"Out, brother," Duvan bites out, his tone a no-nonsense growl.

Remorse washes over my friend's face. His eyebrows are pinched together and his eyes flicker with regret. For him to maul me like he did is way out of character. We've always been friends and nothing more. "I'm sorry, Brie. I just wanted us to—"

"NOW!" Duvan roars.

I flinch at his barked order. "Please check on Vee," I beg. Oscar gives me a single nod before turning and slamming the door behind him.

Now that we're alone, Duvan's hardened stare softens. He quirks up one side of his mouth in a knowing smirk. "You look hot as fuck when you're aroused, tigress."

"I wasn't aroused," I argue with a glare of my own.

He chuckles, and I have the urge to slap him upside the head too. "Little Ozzy turns you on. And just think, I'm bigger and better than him in every way. When we're married, I'll show you just how much bigger of a man I truly am."

I narrow my eyes at him as I climb off the bed. He doesn't stop staring at me as I quickly smooth my dress down over my thighs and cross my arms over my still hard nipples. *Thanks a lot for that, Ozzy.* As if he can read my mind, he smirks.

"You can't hide from me. I'll be seeing what's under that dress and be inside of you by the end of the week, tigress. And that's a motherfucking promise."

chapter
TWO

Ren

"Have you heard from him?" I ask as I pace my room at home. I can hear Mom banging pans around. She's been in a pissy mood ever since Dad left for a meeting in Chicago. But apparently, women shouldn't fly this late in their pregnancy, according to Dad. Mom's about to pop with a baby boy any day now. My parents call the kid an "oops" baby. Calder and I call him a "pull out method gone bad" baby…but never to their faces.

Dad grunts on the other line. "Not in weeks. Last I knew, they were in Destin, Florida. They've travelled all along the Gulf Coast ever since he took her from the mental health facility. She called to tell me she loved me. I don't know if she's just happy or what, but she sounded really good, Ren."

Rolling my eyes, I sit down on my bed and run my fingers through my hair. I just came back home yesterday for summer break from college and I'm already dying to see Brie. If Mom wasn't being so emotional, I'd have left her already to go see my girlfriend.

Is she really your girlfriend?

Annoyance flits through me. We haven't made it official, but I'm not fucking anyone else or even talking to anyone for that matter. The only girl I ever talk to is Brie. She's hot and has a body that drives men wild but it's her sweet soul that has me wrapped around her little finger.

Our relationship is based on lies…

"He asked about Gabriella," Dad says, jerking me from my inner thoughts. Guilt infects me. Standing up, I start to pace again.

"And?"

"Just mentioned he's been by to see her from afar a few times over the past three years. He says she looks happy and that she deserves a safe, loving home. He says that every time." He sighs in frustration. "I didn't dare tell him what you told me."

"That her adopted dad looks at her like he wants to eat her?"

"Fuck no," Dad hisses. "That psychopath would slaughter everyone in this damn city if he thought for one second that Heath Berkley was shady around his daughter."

"But he *is* shady, Dad." She never mentions it, but I've witnessed firsthand how Heath devours her with his gaze. On more than one occasion, I've seen him hug her in a lingering way that goes beyond how a guardian should hug a girl.

"Until we have more information, I'm not going to bring it up to him. He's unstable and he still has your sister. And…" he trails off. "My grandchild."

Gabe has kept his lips sealed about their child, but we know the baby has to be just over two years old now. When he broke her out of the facility, Hannah was six months pregnant.

"I'm dropping by tomorrow to ask if they need summer lawn help. I'll find out what I can," I assure him. My gaze stops at the mirror and I almost laugh. I'm as big as Dad now but more filled out, thanks to my obsessive workout schedule. We still have the same deep blue eyes, chiseled jaw, and messy brown hair. Dad says I have Mom's smile, though.

"You haven't told them your real name, have you?" he asks.

Guilt once again surges through me. Mom doesn't know I mowed lawns for three years where Gabe's daughter lives. Dad doesn't know that Brie and I have been friends for the past year and a half. And he certainly doesn't know that we're quickly progressing to more than friends, especially after I nearly blew my wad in my swim trunks making out with her on the beach during spring break.

What sucks the most, though, is that Brie thinks my last name is Loveland.

But if she ever knew my sister was the one who killed her mother…

"How's your mom?" he asks, dragging me from my dark thoughts.

"Banging shit around in the other room," I say with a chuckle. "Calder's spending the week with some friends on their yacht. So, it's just me left to deal with her wrath. Thanks a lot, Dad."

He huffs. "Go cheer her up. God knows you're the only one who can. She hung up on me earlier because the client I'm working with asked me to stay three more days to go over some different concepts for their firm. Your mother didn't take that news lightly."

"I swear to God if I have to be in that delivery room, you're dead to me, Dad," I groan.

He lets out a loud chuckle. "That's pretty much the same thing she said to me earlier, but with a lot more curse words."

We chat a little about how final exams went before I let him go. I change out of my jeans and pull on some gym shorts before leaving to go find my mother. When I make my way into the kitchen, she's cleaning out the fridge and chucking old bottles of salad dressing into the trash.

"Hey, Mom," I chirp and lean in to kiss her on the cheek.

The tension leaves her body and she flashes me a wide smile. "Hey, baby. What do you want for supper? It's just the two of us. We can order pizza if you want, or I could make you one of your favorites."

Shrugging, I lean against the counter and regard her. My mom is young looking for her age. And now that she's pregnant, she looks about twenty years younger. "Pizza is fine."

She continues throwing stuff into the trash, but she's lost her furious edge. "You look bigger. You've been working out too much."

I smirk and snag an apple from the bowl on the counter. "I don't think there is ever such a thing in a guy's mind."

"Do you have a girlfriend?" she queries, her head still hidden in the fridge.

"Meh, nobody serious." Lies.

"That's good," she says with a grumble. "You're too young to settle down with just one girl. Wait until you get your degree and then you can date more seriously."

"Yeah, yeah," I agree just to get her off my back. While she cleans, I pull up the pizza delivery app on my phone and order two large pizzas. Since she's been pregnant with Mason, she's been craving bacon much to my vegan father's horror. Her pizza is bacon with extra bacon plus bacon.

Her shoulders loosen as we chat about school and Calder and the baby. Whenever the topic strays toward Hannah and she gets teary-eyed, I change the subject. The doorbell saves us from our latest near conversation about my sister.

"I'll pay the pizza man if you'll bag up that trash and take it out," she says before waddling out of the kitchen. I'm knotting the plastic ties when I hear her screech.

Fuck, if her water broke, Dad is dead.

"Please don't tell me you're having the baby—" My words die in my throat upon seeing Gabe in our doorway holding a bundle of blankets. It's been years since I've seen him in the flesh. "What the fuck are you doing here?" I fist my hands, preparing to beat the old man's ass. I'm about to drive my fist into his nose when something squirms in his arms.

"Baylee, hear me out…" His plea falls on deaf ears.

"Ren! Call 911!" she hisses. Her hands automatically fall to her belly as if she's protecting Mason from the psycho prick.

Gabe takes two long strides toward her and snatches her by the shoulder. "I said fucking listen to me," he seethes.

Mom's eyes widen in fear.

"Let her go!" I roar and storm toward him.

It's then the blanket falls away and a curly blonde-haired toddler with big brown eyes wearing a royal blue dress grins sleepily at me. Gabe releases my mother's shoulder and thrusts the baby toward her. "Baylee, meet your granddaughter."

Mom is frozen as she simply stares at the child. When the baby sees me again, she grins so wide and lets out a squeal. "Teev! Teev!" She's reaching for me, but I don't know what to do. Fuck! Of all days for my father to be out of town.

"She thinks you look like Steve from Blue's Clues. The kid's obsessed with those DVDs," Gabe says softly, his tone wistful. He presses a kiss against the baby's head. "She turned two a few months ago. That's your Uncle Ren," he tells her.

"Teev! Teev!"

My heart thumps in my chest. The little thing is starting to get fussy because she's reaching for me and I haven't taken her. With a grunt, I storm over and pull her into my arms.

"Why are you here?" I demand, my eyes never leaving the little girl who looks like Hannah, but with Gabe's eyes.

He runs his hands through his hair and gives Mom a pointed look. "Baylee, you have to take her." His gaze falls to her belly and his jaw clenches. Mom remains deathly still, her glare fixed on him. "She isn't safe."

The baby tries to stick her pudgy finger in my nose, and I laugh. "What's your name, little girl?"

She giggles and buries her face against my neck. "Teev." Her sigh only further melts my heart.

Gabe tears his gaze from Mom and frowns at me. "Toni Lynn Sharpe."

Mom sucks in a hiss of air. "You motherfucker…"

"Hannah named her after her grandparents. And now…" He lets out a groan of frustration. "You have to take her."

"This is madness. I'm calling the cops," Mom seethes.

But even though she's making threats, her eyes keep sneaking over to little Toni. The child must be tired because her squirming stops and her breathing evens out.

"No, madness, Baylee, is having to keep a constant fucking watch on your kid so your jealous wife doesn't hurt her in the middle of the night. Madness is having to tie your wife to the goddamned hotel room bed so you can give yet another perfect little girl in your life to another family…*again*…so your wife doesn't kill her. Madness is staying with an unhinged and unpredictable woman that should be locked away because you know she's better off with you than anywhere else." His chest heaves with labored breaths. Dark circles rim his eyes and his hair is messy, probably from the way he keeps running his fingers through it. He's exhausted. "Madness is not begging her to abort the child she's now growing in her belly that you know she'll grow to hate. I've never claimed to be a sane man." His head hangs in shame. "But, goddammit, I love this kid and I love my wife and I love the one on the way. I'll do whatever it takes to keep them all safe."

Mom remains stock-still but a solitary tear runs down her cheek. I walk over to her so I can wrap an arm around her. "Hannah wants to hurt the baby?"

This doesn't surprise me. It pisses me the fuck off, but it doesn't surprise me.

"I fell asleep on the couch the other day and awoke to find Toni shivering in front of the bathtub. The bathroom door had been closed so she couldn't get out, her eyes were red from crying, and she kept telling me, 'Momma, no.' Toni was angry with her mother for leaving her for fuck knows how long. She could have fucking drowned or gotten hypothermia or some shit.

Hannah was out back tanning by the pool at our new house reading a fucking magazine like it was no big deal." His body ripples with rage. "But it was a big deal. And worse yet, she keeps doing shit like that. Little stuff. Accidents keep happening. Hannah gets bolder and bolder as her pregnancy progresses and I'm afraid one day I won't be there in time. When she's pregnant, she doesn't take her meds. Claims they're bad for the baby. We don't exactly have a primary care physician to support her claims."

Mom's sobs come out sounding like she's choking for air. "My Hannah…"

"Teev. Nanna," Toni says, lifting her head so she can look at me.

Gabe gives me a tired smile. "She wants a banana, Steve."

"Here, Mom," I say firmly. "Hold her while I go grab her a piece of fruit." I don't give my mom a chance to argue and deposit the chunky thing into her arms. Even though I don't like Gabe's crazy ass, he's definitely the lesser threat right now. My sister has really fucked up our family. It's even wearing Gabe down.

When I come back with the banana, Mom is twisting her body holding the little girl to her chest. Toni's playing with Mom's hair.

"Momma?"

"No, your momma is sleeping, remember?" Gabe says, his voice soft and gentle. "That's your grandma."

"Mom-mom?"

My mother runs her fingers through Toni's blonde curls. "Yes, I'm your mom-mom."

Toni grins at her and then reaches for me once she eyes the banana. "Teev!"

When she calls me Teev, my heart pounds hard in my chest. I've barely met this kid and she feels like family. I knew I was an uncle, but I never got to *be* an uncle. Now I'm Uncle Teev.

"Baylee, please," Gabe pleads.

I open the banana and break off a piece for my niece while Mom struggles internally. She sways gently with her granddaughter glued to her hip.

"I hate you," she reminds him, although her voice has lost its bite. "I wouldn't be doing this for you."

Gabe lets out a rush of relieved breath. "I don't care who you fucking do it for as long as you just do it."

Mom shoots me a determined look before regarding the man that tortured and terrorized her at one point in her life. "For how long?"

He scrubs his jaw with the palm of his hand. "I've been researching some drugs that are safe during pregnancy that might help. If I have to drive her to Mexico to obtain the shit, I will. Once she has the baby, I'm hoping she'll calm the fuck down again. I've already made plans to get a vasectomy once we've settled somewhere."

"Fine," she murmurs and kisses Toni on her fuzzy head. "Do you have things for her? Is she allergic to anything? How can I get ahold of you if there's a problem?"

"No allergies and everything's out in the car. I'll call and check in," he vows. His jaw is set and his eyes are narrowed. I believe that he will. It's clearly killing this monster to have to leave his baby.

"Take care of my daughter, and I'll take care of yours," Mom tells him.

He pulls the baby from her arms and squeezes her. "Daddy has to go bye-bye to get things for the baby in Mommy's belly. Then we'll come back for you. Uncle Steve will take you to the beach, I bet, if you're a good girl. Are you going to be a good girl, Toto?"

She nods and gives him a slobbery kiss. "Dadda go bye-bye."

"Thank you," he murmurs and seizes my mother in a quick hug with his free arm. "I owe you big for this."

Mom wriggles free from his grip and takes Toni from him. "You owe me big for a lot more than just this, Gabe."

Me: I miss you.

Me: Can I see you tomorrow?

Me: Maybe you're having too much fun at this party without me.

She hasn't responded in hours and I wonder if I should crash the party like I playfully warned. I climb out of my bed where Toni is curled up snoring and begin arranging pillows, so she doesn't fall off when my phone chimes with a text from "Juliet." The whole Romeo and Juliet thing started when I picked her up one day, while Heath was away on business, to take her to a movie. I brought her a single white rose and she said I was a natural Romeo. And since she took to calling me Romeo on occasion, even going as far as programming it in her phone, I thought it was only fair she was Juliet. The parallelism isn't lost on me. Two feuding families. Two people who aren't supposed to date and still do so in secret. Of course, she doesn't know my reasons.

Juliet: I don't know if I'll get to see you tomorrow. I'm in trouble.

Me: Can you talk right now?

I'm waiting for her to respond when my phone starts ringing. I answer it quietly and slip out of my bedroom, so I don't wake the baby. Hannah's room is still decorated all girly, but Mom packed up a lot of her stuff last year. She told me earlier she was going to fix it up for Toni while she stays with us.

"Hello?"

A familiar female voice exhales into the phone. "Ren."

Simply hearing Brie's voice settles me.

"Why are you in trouble?" I question. "What happened? Are you okay?"

She half chuckles half sobs. "It's a long story."

"It's a good thing I like long stories then, huh?"

"I'm not sure I can talk long enough to get the entire story out," she says with an exasperated huff.

"So, give me the *Cliff Notes* version."

I can hear her sniffling but don't prod her. Eventually, she lets it all out in a rush. "You know Heath adopted me, right?" I remember back when we went to see Gabe and Hannah years ago before shit hit the fan. Dad explained to us that this good, respectable family had stepped in to adopt her since she had no one to take her in. At the time, it seemed odd, but I never really questioned it.

"Yeah."

"I told you it was because my parents both died," she says with a tiny squeak. "I lied, Ren."

I lied too.

"It's okay, B. Tell me what really happened."

Her voice grows wobbly as she speaks. "My mother was murdered by this girl and…"

Fuck. Fuck. Fuck.

"And what?"

"And my dad somehow…" She pauses and an exasperated huff of air comes over the line. "Fell under her spell, I guess. He ran off and left me for her. Allowed me to get adopted by a criminal family."

I pinch the bridge of my nose and attempt to keep calm. "People make mistakes. He still loves you." My attempt to assure her is met with a hiss.

"If you love someone, you don't set them free. You hold on to them. He let me go," she chokes out. "He broke my heart." A sob escapes her.

"Brie…"

"I was basically bought as a bargaining tool."

Wait, what?

"Heath adopted you—" I start but she cuts me off.

"Legally, yes. But he wants to marry me off to one of the biggest cocaine suppliers in Colombia. I'm nothing but a business transaction and—"

My skin grows cold and I fist my hand. "He wants to fucking marry you off? You're seventeen, Brie!"

Her laughter is cruel. "It's a part of their plan. It *will* happen."

"But what about us?" I can't believe I'm even hearing this nonsense. "This is stupid. This is the twenty-first century and we're in America. That kind of shit doesn't happen around here."

She grumbles. "It *does* happen, Ren. It *is* happening."

"When?"

"I'm not sure exactly. I turn eighteen on Saturday, but all three Rojas brothers are in town this week for this party. Heath and Camilo are meeting in Heath's office downstairs right now. Then they're going to call us in to let us know the verdict."

I let out a grunt. "I'm coming to get you. My parents can keep you at their house. We'll keep you safe from those men." They already have one of Gabe's kids. What's one more?

"Ren, I—shit!" she hisses.

"What?"

"I have to go. I've been summoned."

"I'm coming for you."

chapter
THREE

Brie

"I'm sorry." Oscar hangs his head in shame as we walk down the long hallway that leads to Heath's massive office. "I just missed you and knew you were turning eighteen soon and that there was a good chance since we were so close that I would be married off to you. I didn't anticipate that it would blow up in my face. I just want…us."

I let out a sigh and grab his hand. "We're too young to be put in this situation anyway. In all honesty, I want it to be you. If I have to marry someone, I'd rather it be my friend. At least then, I'd be free to see Ren on the side since this whole thing is just for show anyway."

Oscar stops right outside the office door and turns to regard me. His brown eyes are narrowed and a small frown tugs at his lips. He lifts his hand and rubs his thumb across my bottom lip. "If we're to be married, it would never be for show to me. I'd want you—all of you. You would be enough for me. And I'd hope that I could be enough for you."

I blink stupidly at him and shift nervously on my heels. "Oh." Oscar is Mr. Playboy. Mr. Non-commitment. I never would have guessed he'd take this whole arranged marriage thing seriously. I sure as hell don't. How can you love someone you're forced to marry? I take in Oscar's handsome features and wonder if I could ever love him in a husband capacity.

I'm not sure that I can.

Gripping his wrist, I pull it away from my mouth. "Vee likes you. What we did was wrong on so many levels. She saw and now she's heartbroken. We betrayed our best friend, Ozzy."

Anger flashes in his eyes and he jerks his hand from my grip. "She'll have to get over it once we're married."

I swallow and give him a weak smile. "You could see her on the side like I plan to see Ren."

He lets out an angry growl and seizes my jaw with his strong fingers for just a moment before he crashes his lips to mine again. This time, I put up more of a fight and tear my mouth from his. His erection grinds into me against the wall. I'm about to punch him in his gut when the office door swings open.

Immediately, I feel *his* presence.

Terrifying and menacing.

Possessive.

"Gabriella." The way my name is spoken, so harsh and feral, has Oscar jerking away from me.

"Mr. Berkley," Oscar says, his head bowed in respect before he stalks into the office.

My gaze meets Heath's and he glares at me. He's furious and about to blow a gasket. As far as Heath knows, I don't date. If he knew that I was dating our lawn boy on the side while having impromptu make-out sessions with one of the Rojas brothers at every turn, he'd probably chain me up in my bedroom and forbid me to ever leave.

I shudder at that thought.

He closes the office door so that we're alone in the hallway. Then, he advances on me. His body is heated and I can feel the warmth rippling from him even though he isn't touching me. When he speaks, I can smell the expensive liquor on his breath.

"This is unacceptable behavior," he hisses.

I swallow and meet his fiery gaze. "I'm sorry. It just happened."

"Oscar's tongue in your mouth just happened?" His scathing tone makes me shiver. "I'm not stupid."

"Heath," I plead. "We're friends and we were just messing around—"

His palm pops me across the cheek, echoing loudly in the hallway. My eyes brim with tears and one manages to escape. It streaks down my cheek, hot and angry, before dripping from my jaw.

"You hit me," I choke out, surprise in my voice.

His jaw clenches and he leans so close I think he might lick my tear right from my cheek. "You're getting out of line and need to remember your place—your duty. You're lucky I didn't whip your ass in front of the entire goddamned Rojas family to remind them that you're still a little girl for a few more days. *My* little girl."

I'm not his. I will never be his.

He grabs my elbow and drags me into the office behind him. Four pairs of eyes burn into me. I try not to make eye contact with any of them, but I end up sneaking a glance at Oscar. His elbows are on his knees and his face is in his palms. He looks upset. When I flit my gaze over to the older brothers, Esteban remains stoic and impassive while Duvan flashes me a smug grin.

Heath rounds his desk and sits in the leather chair bringing me into his lap with him like I'm some little girl. *You're still a little girl for a few more days. My little girl.*

"We've made our decision," Camilo says, his voice gruff from decades and decades of smoking. He's a heavy cigar smoker and the thick scent permeates the air around us. I lift my gaze to the old, white-haired man. To most, he looks like a grumpy grandpa. But Oscar has told me stories. Of how he's broken each bone in a man's hand one by one for attempting to steal some coke from him. Or how he strangled a man to death with his bare hands for talking badly about his sons. Or how he has more bodies buried on his property than most cemeteries.

Oscar tends to embellish the truth at times, but I somehow sense when it comes to Camilo, it's all true.

Heath wraps a possessive arm around my waist and pulls my back against him as he leans forward to address the men. His palm rests on my lower belly, his pinky nearly touching me where I know he'd love to have a go at. "On Saturday morning we've arranged for Judge Griffiths to come by and do a small ceremony. You'll be a Rojas by lunchtime and then you'll catch a flight with your new husband back to Bogotá where you'll spend your honeymoon."

I freeze in his arms and jerk my gaze over to Oscar. He won't look at me and his shoulders are hunched. It's not him. It's one of his brothers. "We're not staying in California? What about Vee?" My voice comes out as a whine. What about Ren? "I don't know anyone there."

"You'll know your husband." Heath chuckles and it reverberates through me. "And darling, surely you're not stupid enough to think that she is going to miss your absence. Vienna is devastated right now. What you and Oscar did was atrocious. Not only was my daughter interested in him, but you're not his to put his hands on. You never were."

I swallow and flick my gaze to Esteban. His eyes glitter with desire. It makes me shiver. He's so gigantic. I can't ever read his thoughts. For the most part, he's calm and collected. But when Duvan pokes at him, he rages like a homicidal bear. Oscar told me there's always been a rivalry between his two older brothers. That they both want to take over once Camilo retires or dies. Plus, I get the feeling that maybe Esteban has hurt people who they care about. Whenever I probe, Oscar always shuts the conversation down.

Over the years, I've studied Esteban and Duvan when they've visited, knowing one of them could be my future. I'm terrified of the unknown with either of them. Esteban always seems to be hiding his intentions for me. As if he locks away some hideous monster that wants to devour me.

A shudder ripples through me and I quickly divert my eyes to Duvan who watches me with narrowed eyes. He leans back in his seat, seemingly aloof, but I sense a blaze that all but burns from within him. In his nearly black eyes, a furious flame flickers in the dark. I'm afraid if I stand too close, I'll get burned.

Duvan is no better than Esteban. He's always been crude—he blatantly fucks me with his eyes. His words border on menacing and flirtatious. I'm afraid he's a barely caged animal. Women are naturally drawn to Duvan because of his ridiculously good looks, but it's me he always watches from every corner of the room while Vee and I laugh with Oscar. Not those other women. Me. And the intensity with which he does it scares the hell out of me.

Why couldn't it have just been Oscar?

Easy. Playful. Nice.

My friend.

His brothers are far from friendly.

Camilo leans forward and pins me with a fierce glare that sends a shiver rippling through me. "My two eldest sons have each presented their arguments to me as to why they shall be the one to bind our two families. While both presented valid points, in the end, the victor is Duvan."

I stop listening after the mention of his name.

Duvan Rojas.

My future husband.

"What…what was the deciding factor?" My bottom lip wobbles and another stupid tear sneaks out.

Camilo beams at me, reminding me a little of Oscar when he does. "He thinks he can love you. And as these boys know well, I loved their mother completely and without fail until cancer took her away from us in '04. Our marriage was arranged long ago and, at that time, I loathed the idea of marrying her. But I grew to love her, and Duvan has the ability to love you too. Esteban will always love his career—our family business—more. While that is an admirable quality, love will only make this family union more valid."

Love?

I'll never love Duvan.

"Why couldn't I have just married Oscar?"

Oscar lifts his head and his eyes are red rimmed. My heart breaks in two for my friend.

Camilo reaches over and squeezes Oscar's knee. "My boy is too young to settle down. He has his whole life ahead of him. Duvan has completed his college studies and Esteban is pushing thirty. It is time for them."

I bite back the retort that *I* am too young to settle down. That *I* have my whole life ahead of me. That *I* am still a virgin and have no idea how to be a wife.

I clear my throat instead. "May I be excused?" My voice is but a whisper for fear of letting my anger bleed through.

Heath grabs my hips and lifts me to my feet, his hands lingering for a moment. When I flit my gaze over to my future husband, his jaw clenches. His narrowed eyes remain fixed on where Heath is touching me. I can almost feel the flames about to burst from him.

Great, my soon-to-be husband is possessive too.

"Get some sleep, Gabriella. Tomorrow, Izzie is going to take you to the spa and shopping. You'll need some new clothes for your move."

My eyes once again trail over to Duvan. He stands and eyes me like I'm a steak he's about to cut into. Knowing him, he's probably sharpened his blade for the occasion. Duvan is solid muscle and stands well over six feet tall. His shoulders are broad and always seem to stretch the fabric of his dress shirts. The tie around his neck is loosened and the top button undone, revealing a hint of a colorful tattoo. His black hair is always disheveled in a just-fucked kind of way. He's hot, no doubt. But he scares me.

"Tell Izzie just a trim. Your hair is the perfect length right now," Heath blurts out. I jolt in surprise. Usually, he keeps his demanding and controlling ways to himself.

"Come on," Duvan grits out. "I'll walk you to your room."

I accept his elbow and let him guide me from the office. I'm still too stunned to speak, and quite frankly, I'm terrified of this man. He doesn't say a word as he guides me to my room. People are still milling about the house, the party in full swing, yet he doesn't acknowledge any of them along the way. We pass through the living room and I feel someone staring. It makes my heart beat and I miss my dad—my real one. If he were here, he'd put a stop to all of this. Or, the father who raised me would have. The one I knew before that lunatic came along.

Hysteria builds in my chest.

This is really happening.

My eyes lock on Vienna's green ones that are red rimmed. A look of satisfaction and relief flashes over her features to see Duvan at my side. I give her a small smile, but she looks down at her feet instead of returning one.

"Will I still be able to talk to my friends?" I murmur as we head down another hallway.

Duvan chuckles. "I'm not your master. You can do whatever you want, tigress."

Hope blossoms in my chest. "Thank you."

"Come here," he says, his muscled arms open and inviting me for a hug.

A quiver of fear races through me but I step toward him. I'm pulled against the big, hard man and it isn't as terrifying as I expected. I remain stiff and uncomfortable in his grip, though.

He pats my back but holds me to him when I start to pull away. I lift my gaze to his. His nearly black eyes glint with promise. "I'll give you a lot more to be thankful for."

I swallow and force a smile. "Okay."

His arms fall to his side, and I scurry away from him toward my room. Before I slip inside, I turn to peek at him once more. He's leaned against the wall, watching me with his bulky arms folded across his chest.

"Brie…"

An angry scowl paints his face, and for a moment, I'm afraid he'll say something mean.

"Yeah?"

He seems to deliberate his words for a second, making the moment almost become awkward. "Promise me you'll do whatever the fuck you want with your hair. He doesn't own you," he growls, his nostrils slightly flaring.

The smile that graces my lips this time is honest. "I promise."

At that, he winks and then turns on his heel.

"You're too young to date," Dad says simply and kicks his feet up onto the coffee table. Saturday nights we watch eighties movies. Dad chuckles the whole time while I tease him about their clothes and hair. It's our thing while Mom's at work.

I stick out my bottom lip and pout. "Fifteen is not young, Daddy."

His brown eyes swirl with barely contained rage. "It's too young for my daughter to date. You can date when you're sixteen. Maybe." He scratches his beard with his fingertip. "Actually, eighteen. You can date when you're eighteen."

I huff and cross arms over my chest. "This is unfair."

He wraps an arm around me and pulls me into his side despite my pouting. "Life's unfair, Brie baby. Get it through your thick skull." He taps the top of my head with his fingertip and then kisses my hair.

"But all the other girls at my school date."

"And all the other girls will get pregnant or get their hearts broken or get an STD. My girl will be safe." He hands me a piece of red rope licorice, and I snatch it from him despite my irritation.

Letting out a sigh, I text my friend Lennon back.

Me: I can't go out with Jacob.

Len: WHAT?! WHY? HE'S THE HOTTEST GUY AT OUR SCHOOL!

Lennon is a drama queen.

Me: I know. Lame.

Dad can read my text, but I don't care. He's pretending to watch the movie, though.

Len: Maybe I should date him…

Rolling my eyes, I tap out my response.

Me: You can date him for three years and then he's mine. ;)

Dad lets out a chuckle and a smile tugs at my lips.

"If you were allowed to date, there would never be any contest. Lennon's lucky I'm doing the poor girl a favor and making the playing field more even," he says, a smile in his voice. "Plus, I'm getting too old to have to kill little boys for getting handsy with my little girl."

I laugh. "You wouldn't kill them."

"Oh, but I would."

Snuggling against my dad, I realize I'm happy. Jacob is kind of lanky and kind of hairy and kind of has an annoying laugh. And he probably hates eighties movies.

Maybe Dad does know best.

I wake from a heavy sleep when I hear something hit my window. Another tap has me slipping out of my bed and stumbling through my dark room toward the cause. When I lift the window and look out, I find a hot, shirtless boy looking up at me, his black baseball cap flipped backward on his handsome head.

"Ren!" I hiss. "What are you doing here?"

The party guests have long gone home but someone could see him out there.

"I came for you, like I promised." He flashes me one of his signature crooked grins that make me weak in the knees. I haven't seen him in so long. He looks bigger and somehow hotter.

"I'll sneak out."

I leave the window and slip into the bathroom to brush my teeth quickly. My hair is a wild mess, so I gather it all up and twist it into a bun. I'm wearing a thin nightgown that hits me mid-thigh. Rather than changing, I decide to leave it on. I snatch a pair of flip-flops and tiptoe over to my door. Slipping through, I start past Vee's door when she whispers my name. I freeze before poking my head into her room.

"You okay?" I ask.

"Where are you going?" Her voice is cool but not hateful.

"To see Ren."

She sniffles as she sits up in her bed. "Are you seeing him or are you running away?"

"I'm just going to go talk to him," I promise. My voice chokes up as I whisper my apology. "I'm sorry about tonight. It wasn't what it looked like."

Her thin arms cross over her chest and she purses out her lips. "Don't be gone long or I'll tell Dad you're with Ren Loveland." I hate that she ignores my apology.

Heath doesn't know anything about Ren, other than the fact that he mowed our lawn, and I'd like to keep it that way.

"I promise."

When she doesn't reply, I take my leave and exit her room. Every step through the house seems like I'm a big elephant thundering through the halls. I'm sure Heath will wake and be furious with me. Luckily, though, I manage to escape unscathed.

When I reach the gardens, Ren is nowhere to be found. I start down the driveway toward the road when two strong arms wrap around me from behind. I've been in his arms enough times to know it's Ren.

"I missed you, beautiful," he says and hugs me to him.

Relaxing in his arms, I let out a sigh. "I missed you too."

He releases me and snatches my hand. "Come on. Let's go across the street to the beach."

We sneak off of Heath's property as Ren guides me onto the beach behind a sandy dune. He's already prepped the area with some blankets and an ice chest. I smile because he looks so handsome in the moonlight as he sets to smoothing out the blanket before sitting. Then, he pulls me into his lap so that I'm straddling him.

"God, you smell so good," he groans and buries his face in my hair. "I'll never get enough of how you smell."

Knocking his hat off, I let out a giggle and thread my fingers into his hair that seems longer than the last time I saw him. "I taste even better," I tease.

His palms find my ass and he pulls me closer to him. He's hard beneath me and the urge to grind against him is overwhelming.

"I'll be the judge of that," he growls before crashing his mouth to mine.

Ren's kisses are always fervent and needy. I like how he seems to devour me each time. His hands roam my body as if he's worshipping me with his touch. I've never felt like someone not only wanted me, but that they needed me too. Ren makes me feel needed.

I let out a soft moan when his tongue pushes into my mouth to taste my own. My fingertips are greedy. I run them along his bare neck and shoulders and to his chest as we kiss. When I run them between us toward his belly button, he lets out a hiss. His erection jolts with excitement.

"This nightgown is such a damn tease," he murmurs against my mouth, his palms slipping underneath it to stroke my back.

"So, take it off," I urge him and actually do grind against him this time.

"Fuck!"

His able fingers tear my gown from my body in one quick movement before coming around to my front. He kneads my swollen breasts with his large palms. I look down at his hands on my flesh. His large hands easily cover both of my barely C cups.

"Look how fucking perfect you are," he praises, his thumbs running across my hardened nipples.

Our eyes meet and his are like looking into a mirror.

Lust and excitement.

Need.

Desire.

"Just say the words, beautiful."

"I need you. All of you."

He lets out a pained groan before flipping me onto the blanket on my back. His eyes dance over my flesh as an appreciative smile graces his lips. I chew on my bottom lip as he tugs my panties from my otherwise naked body.

"Are you a virgin?" he asks, his voice deep and husky as if the thought excites him.

"Not for long," I taunt.

He gives me a crooked grin that makes me blush and begins undoing his shorts. When his large cock springs free, I shiver. Ren must take this to mean that I'm cold because he grabs the extra blanket and wraps it around his back. He then covers me with his chilled bare flesh. His cock presses against my pubic bone making me squirm with need.

"Are you on the pill?"

Nerves light up my flesh and I nod. "Are you, um, safe?"

He nods. "I've only been with one girl and it was a few years ago. We used condoms every time."

"Okay," I manage. "Will this hurt?"

His brows furl together. "I hope not."

I spread my legs as he prods at my entrance with the tip of his cock. He doesn't push into me like I expect and wish he would. Instead, he teases my sensitive clit with the head of his penis until I'm clawing at his shoulders.

"Ren, please…" I murmur.

He chuckles and the sound nearly makes me lose it. "Once you come, I'll give you what you need, beautiful."

His words dance on my flesh and tickle me right toward the edge. With sure movements, he rubs against me until my body seizes up with pleasure. It's then he chooses to push into me with one powerful thrust. The sharp pain is overshadowed by the climax still rippling through me. And when I come down from my high, he slowly starts to move inside of me.

"You're perfect," he murmurs against my lips.

I'm completely caught up in his gaze that alights my entire soul. I've been looked at as if I'm something to be ravished and devoured, never revered and worshipped. Ren elicits that feeling of belonging that I no longer have now that my parents are both gone. He lets out a groan and murmurs an apology as he comes quickly inside me. My insides feel raw and torn and burning, so I'm glad he wasn't inside of me long.

But where he's slipping out of my body, he'll never slip out of my heart.

"Ren," I say with a sigh and cup his cheek.

He kisses me on the lips and lies on his side to stare down at me. "Brie."

"I've been waiting for far too long to do that."

His laugh is sexy and deep. "I've been waiting to do that since I saw you up in your tower, princess."

"Juliet to you, Romeo," I tease.

His eyes darken and he forces a smile. "I'm running away with you."

If only it were that easy.

If only I could just run away with Ren Loveland and become Mrs. Loveland instead of Mrs. Rojas.

"Where would we go?" I question, indulging him. Heath wouldn't let me get far.

"Far away from here," he assures me. "I could keep you safe."

I frown and play with a strand of his hair. "What about college and your parents? They won't like you running away."

He doesn't answer and I know it's because his wheels are turning. Ren's a good guy. Not someone to up and abandon his life for a girl.

"I'm going to talk to my dad about this. I can help you before Saturday. Maybe you could even come to my college," he says softly. "We'll figure it out."

I give him a single nod. "Maybe."

We both grow quiet. I've been out here too long already and should get back in case Vienna decides to rat me out.

"Call me tomorrow and let me know what your dad says."

He grins at me. "Have I ever told you you're beautiful?"

My heart swells in my chest. "A time or two."

His sexy smile is my undoing. "You're beautiful."

"That's three," I tell him with a smile. "And you're sweet."

After a lingering kiss on the front porch, Ren reluctantly pulled away from me. Our eyes were glued to one another until I shut the door quietly behind me. My body is sore and I feel raw inside where he made love to me. But I feel different. Grown and whole. Stronger. I'm smiling as I creep down the hallway.

"Gabriella."

Heath's voice sends a quiver of fear racing down my spine. I don't see him in the darkness but I'm pretty sure the voice came from one of the guest bedrooms. When I peek my head inside, I can see his silhouette sitting on the massive mahogany framed bed. The moonlight shines in and illuminates part of the overly ornate room.

"I was just getting a drink of water," I tell him quickly as I approach him inside the room.

His chuckle is dark. "Last I checked, the water in the Pacific Ocean isn't drinkable, darling."

I freeze when he stands. His shadow stumbles forward. He's completely wasted. Crap!

"What were you doing down there? Who were you with?"

I'm still trying to form words when I hear the door close behind me and the lock turn. My heartbeat is thumping so hard in my chest, it nearly hurts.

"I was just taking a walk," I lie.

His heat envelops me and his hands grip my hips from behind. "So, you weren't whoring yourself out with the lawn boy?"

I jolt at his words. "I, uh, Heath—"

He pushes me forward, and I fall to my elbows on the bed. A tremor of fear paralyzes me for a moment before I jerk into action. His belt jingles and I scramble to jump off the bed. A strong hand grabs my ankle, yanking me back. My stomach is dragged across the duvet and my nightgown is pushed up, baring my back to him. He yanks my panties down my thighs.

Surely he's not about to do what I think he wants to do.

If he tries to touch me, I'll tell Duvan.

The very idea that I see Duvan as someone who could protect me from Heath alarms me.

"Your panties are drenched with his cum," Heath seethes.

I'm about to plead for him to let me go when I hear the swoosh of something cutting through the air a second before pain sears across my ass.

He whipped me with his belt!

I scream out in both horror and pain. But Heath is stronger than me. He keeps me pinned to the bed with one hand while he begins whipping me relentlessly with the expensive leather. My flesh stings and burns and I know it will be marred with bruises. The tears I've always kept at bay now run freely down my cheeks as if the dam of three years' worth of pain is being released.

He beats me until I go limp.

He whips me until I begin to black out.

He abuses me until I completely check out.

chapter
FOUR

Brie

"Just a half inch off the ends," my adopted mother, Izzie, instructs the overpriced hairdresser. "She's getting married on Saturday and needs to look beautiful."

At this point, a marriage to Duvan seems preferable to the monster Heath has become. After he whipped me last night, he carried me upstairs and put me to bed. I woke up as he was dragging the covers over me. When I started crying again, he proceeded to press kisses to the tender flesh he had destroyed. I quickly dried my tears so he would go away.

And he did.

Thank God.

I haven't seen him since.

I'm trying to come up with a plan to get away from him, so I don't have to see him ever again.

"Aren't you a little young to be getting married?" Mario asks. His perfectly sculpted black eyebrow shoots up his brown face to his hairline.

I give him a false smile. "I'm seventeen. That's not even legal, is it?"

He scoffs, but Izzie swats at me. "Mario, she's being dramatic. Her birthday is Saturday."

Mario narrows his eyes at me in the mirror. "A marriage for your birthday. I mean, I always knew I was a queen, and that was my dream since I came out of the closet at age eight, so I totally get fantasizing over a white wedding, but damn girl, is that what you really want?"

Izzie pins me with an icy glare.

I shrug my shoulders and swallow down the emotion choking me. "It will get me out of their house and that'll be the best birthday present ever," I murmur. A shudder ripples through me remembering the way Heath hurt me last night. "It's definitely better than my current situation."

Izzie huffs and storms off. "Ungrateful child," she hisses under her breath before calling out over her shoulder. "Half an inch. I'll be next door at the restaurant getting a cocktail. Come find me when you're through."

My phone chimes with a text and I don't recognize the number.

Unknown: Remember, do whatever the fuck you want with your hair. You don't belong to him anymore.

A genuine smile lifts the corners of my lips up. I program his number into the phone and am thankful I have a way to contact him now, in case I run into any more trouble with Heath.

Me: Do you like Mohawks?

His response is immediate.

Duvan: I can assure you that once we're married, the last thing I'll be concerned about is your hair.

I chew on my lip and find Mario reading over my shoulder.

"Is that the lucky groom to be?" he asks.

I nod even though it sounds silly. "The one and only."

"So, the evil bitch wants you keep your hair long and the future husband wants you to do whatever makes you happy?"

"Pretty much."

"What makes you happy, Gabriella?"

I run my thumb over the glass of my phone. Ren makes me happy. My friends Oscar and Vee make me happy. And…

Tears well in my eyes. "I don't know, other than a handful of my friends."

Mario lets out a sigh and hands me a magazine. Selena Gomez is on the cover sporting a sexy, messy new hairstyle. It's shoulder length with lots of layers and side bangs. "It's never too late to become someone new."

I stare at the smiling woman on the page. At one time, I wanted to go to college and do big things with my life. Once I realized I was being groomed for marriage, I stopped caring about anything aside from the few personal relationships I had. I had no hobbies or interests. I just coasted.

It's time to stop coasting and take control.

"This will make me happy," I tell him and point at the celeb's stylish cut.

He winks at me in the mirror. "And it's going to make me happy to see the look on that witch's faces when she comes back."

Cutting off eight inches of hair truly is freeing.

Watching a rich, manicured woman have a meltdown that would give most toddlers a run for their money is satisfying.

And watching the man who thinks he controls your world sling shit off his desk because you disobeyed a direct order is gratifying.

Ren and I texted back and forth all day. I didn't mention to him what happened with Heath. I was embarrassed and worried he'd think I was too much trouble. He told me how wonderful it was finally getting to make love to me. I told him about how sore I was but also that I don't regret a thing. He was supposed to sneak over again to see me tonight, but I made up an excuse saying I was really tired. I promised that he could take me out for my birthday tomorrow night. Come hell or high water, I'll have one last Friday night as a free woman.

Heath screams and rages and accuses Izzie of being a terrible wife while I ignore him. Duvan has texted me a couple of times today asking about clothing size and food preferences. He hasn't been awful and I'm thankful. He even told me that my new hairstyle suits me better than the old one when I texted him a picture earlier. It left me with a lingering smile all day.

Duvan: What do you want for your birthday?

I want you to kill Heath. The thought has me stifling a giggle.

Me: I don't need anything.

Duvan: I didn't ask what you needed. I'll give you what you need…I asked what you wanted.

While Heath spazzes out on Izzie, I try to think about what I actually want. Nothing. I don't want anything.

Me: I don't want anything.

Duvan: Are you always this difficult?

I snort.

Me: I'm just learning how to be difficult. You're in for a real surprise. With age comes wisdom.

"Izzie, leave," Heath snaps.

She hastily exits his office and slams the door shut. My phone buzzes, but I'm afraid to look down at it.

"Are you conversing with that goddamned lawn boy? Did he put you up to not only being a whore, but also into whacking off all your hair against my wishes?" he seethes.

Rage surges through me. "For your information, I was texting with my future husband."

His nostrils flare with fury. "Duvan is more preferable than me? You think you're going to be so damn happy as his little Colombian princess? Wake up, Gabriella. You're being sent to the lion's den. I won't be able to protect you anymore."

My heart stops in my chest. Not because of his threat. No, fuck that. I'm stunned because he actually believes he's been protecting me all this time. He was the one I needed protection from!

Me: Can you come over here? Heath is out of control.

I hit send and level a glare at Heath. "I'm leaving tonight and I won't be coming back."

He barks out a cold laugh. "Camilo Rojas will have you killed if you walk away from what we've been cultivating for three years."

His threats don't bother me. I know how terrifying Camilo can be. But right now, I don't care. The Rojas family is preferable over this guy.

"I'll be back for this sham of a wedding Saturday," I snap and jerk to my feet. "And then I never want to see you again. You won't ever be able to hurt me again."

Fury twists his features into an angry scowl. He stalks over to me and grabs a fistful of the front of my dress, yanking me to him. "You'll always belong to me, Gabriella. There's a bigger plan than you can see. When everything falls back into place, you'll be right back where you belong."

I blink at him in confusion. He releases me with a huff and runs his trembling fingers through his hair.

"If you ever repeat that, I'll slit your throat in your sleep."

With my phone in my grip, I bolt from his office and down the hallway. I run through the house without slowing. Once I'm outside, I take off down the driveway. The blare of an engine barreling down the road has me slowing. Duvan's black Challenger whips into the driveway and he's out of the car the moment he throws it in park.

I've seen Duvan angry with Esteban before, but I've never seen him like this—wearing a white tank top, his hair tousled, a baseball bat in hand, and a look that would frighten even the devil.

"What the fuck did he do?" he snarls and charges for me.

Most normal people would probably run at the sight of such a menacing man racing toward them with a baseball bat in his white-knuckled grip.

Good thing I haven't been a normal person for a long time.

I'm scared of the evil that lives inside the home behind me.

When he nears, I throw myself into his arms and let him hug me. His raging fury seems to simmer because his tense muscles relax.

"What do you want, tigress?" His breath is still coming out in angry huffs.

"I want to leave. There's nothing here for me. Just…" I trail off. "Can you keep me safe?"

He lets out a possessive growl that warms me.

"Don't let her fool you, boy!" Heath yells from the porch. "Your fiancée was off prancing around with the lawn boy last night. She's no longer as pure as you think she is."

Duvan stiffens, and I fear what his reaction will be. He pulls away and tucks me into his side under his arm. In his other hand, he swings around his baseball bat. "We've agreed this was a marriage of necessity and not one of exclusivity. She can fool around with whoever she wants as long as when I call for her, she's there for me."

I'm not sure why Duvan is lying for me, but I'll take it.

"Does your father know you're okay with your wife being a whore?" Heath fists his hands at his side. As if he'd have an actual chance against the baseball-bat-wielding Colombian god.

"Does my father know you want to fuck little girls?" Duvan bites back.

Heath blanches. "Learn your place, boy." His voice quivers slightly.

"And understand who truly is in power here," Duvan snaps, his voice low, his tone deadly.

They have a silent standoff before Heath storms back into the house. Duvan releases me and points at me with the bat.

"Get in the car, tigress. If that bastard ever speaks to you like that again, I'm going bash his motherfucking head in with this bat. Got it, babe?"

I nod and smile at him. "Thank you."

His smirk, which used to seem smug and asshole-ish, now seems to be one of his more endearing mannerisms. I find I'm beginning to like it.

That smirk means he knows he'll win.

And when it comes to protecting me from Heath, I need him to win.

I run the hairbrush through my now short, wet hair and stare at my reflection. Duvan's staying in a suite at some five-star hotel his dad owns just outside of San Diego. There's an extra room in the sprawling suite that he's offered me. The gesture came as a surprise to me. I'd expected Duvan to be villainous and cruel. Abusive maybe. Or that he'd try and force himself on me.

I never expected him to care.

"Dinner's getting cold, tigress," he calls out from the other side of the bathroom door.

"Uh, I'm coming!"

I shrug on the soft, plush white robe over my naked flesh and exit the bathroom. Duvan lies on his side wearing nothing but a pair of jeans. He's laid our food out on trays on the bed. My eyes flit to his bare skin that's marked up in beautiful ink. I never knew he had full sleeves on both arms and that his entire chest was covered with them. I'm still staring when he laughs at me.

"Dinner is over here," he says pointing. "That's all that's on the menu. At least for tonight," he says with another smirk, his eyes glittering.

Heat floods my cheeks and I roll my eyes. "I was just looking at your tattoos. I always wanted one."

He sits up and lifts a brow. "Of what? Where?"

I shrug and sit on the bed careful not to flash him under my robe. His eyes skim over my bare thighs before he looks up at me.

"You don't know much of anything, do you?" he questions.

Frowning, I flip him off and steal the roll from my plate. "I know I love bread. And mashed potatoes. And Earl Grey tea. I love gyros and cupcakes and steak. I love that red rope licorice you can only buy from real candy stores." I love that last thing because it was something my dad and I shared when I was a kid. Something that Mom used to get grossed out over. We'd make a great show of smacking loudly as we ate an entire bag of it on the way home back from the mall.

"So, you like food. Your hips don't lie, tigress. Do you know what makes you sad? Because you got all kinds of sad just now and I know it wasn't because you're craving red licorice."

My heart skips a beat in my chest. "My dad—my real dad—and I would always get it to tease my mom. She hated that stuff."

He takes the roll from my hand and butters it for me. When he hands it back, his brows are pinched together. "I miss my mother too. I get it, Brie."

I take a big bite of my bread to keep from crying. We eat the rest of our meal in silence. Once he's cleared away all the dishes and put them outside the door, he turns to regard me with his hands on his hips.

"Ready for your present?"

A small smile tugs at my lips. "Why are you being so nice to me? I didn't imagine this was how it would all go down."

He shrugs and saunters away to the closet. "I'm not always a bad guy, you know." I can hear something rustling in the closet. When he reemerges, he's carrying a bright pink birthday bag stuffed way too full of lighter pink tissue paper. It's totally a man's wrap job. I let out a giggle.

"Hey, I never claimed to be good at *everything*," he says with a grumble and sets the bag down on the bed.

The smile on my face is genuine. For someone who doesn't offer them a lot, you notice when you do. I sit down on the bed and he sits across from me, his eyes on mine as I pull out the million sheets of tissue. When they disappear, I dive my hand into the bag and pull out a slim white box.

"You bought me a MacBook Pro?" I say in astonishment. "Why?"

He laughs. "Most people would just say thank you."

I lift an eyebrow. "Thank you, but why? It's too expensive."

"Nothing is too expensive for *my* family," he scoffs. "Besides, I thought you might want a way to Skype with your friends. Might be easier with the computer."

Sitting up on my knees, I lean forward and hug his neck. "Thank you. That means a lot to me."

He pats my back. "And I also thought if you wanted to look up college courses and whatnot, it'd be much easier on that thing."

I pull away from him, my face just inches from his, and frown. "You'll let me go to college?"

His brows pinch together. "I told you I wasn't your master, Brie. I want to help my father with his business. And I want to help you. Getting away from Heath will be the best thing that ever happened to you."

Without thinking, I kiss his cheek. He smells clean and spicy and safe. "Thank you so much. But how did you know I wanted to go to college?"

He smirks and it warms me. "Oscar is good for some things, you know. Apparently, he's full of useful information, even if I have to beat it out of him."

I laugh. "You didn't hurt him."

His black irises twinkle with shards of purple in the brilliant hotel room lights. "Nah, he's just a kid."

When I bristle at his words—because Oscar is actually older than me—Duvan winces.

"You know what I mean. He's my little brother. Anyway, since you two are friends, I thought maybe you could go to his college since we'll be living in the same town."

"I don't know what to say," I tell him in a shaky voice. In just one night, I've gone from feeling doomed to feeling hopeful.

"Just say you won't fuck my brother." His growl is possessive, and a shiver quakes through me. "He's been into you from day one, tigress."

"I'm not interested in your brother that way, but..." I knit my brows together in confusion. "I thought you said we could still see other people."

The hope that had been blooming in my chest comes crashing to the ground when he scowls.

"Other people. Not my brother." His tone is no nonsense.

"But Ren?"

"The lawn boy?"

Heat burns my cheeks and I start to pull away. He palms my cheeks, looking me straight in the eye. "Is he your friend?"

Technically, yes. And more. "Yeah."

"Does he make you happy?"

"Absolutely."

"Then, tigress, see him all you want. Just come home to me at the end of the day. We have an image to uphold." He winks at me.

Guilt floods through me that I've just asked my future husband if I can still have a boyfriend. But Duvan and I were both groomed for this marriage. Both pushed into something that wasn't our plan.

"Are you going to open your other present?" he questions with a grin that now makes me happy.

I reach into the bag and pull out a terribly wrapped package. When I open it and notice it's a DVD, I flit my gaze to him in question. "A movie?"

But when I flip it over, I notice it's not just any movie. It's THE movie. THE movie I used to always watch with my dad. THE link to my childhood and my past.

"How did you know?" I wobble out.

The cover is a blur, but I know it's *The Breakfast Club*. I've watched this movie a thousand times with Daddy. He's defended Judd Nelson's character John Bender countless times stating bad boys are cool, but would go on to affirm that I would never be allowed to date one.

I look up at one of the *baddest* boys I know.

Amusement is no longer coloring his features, though. He looks worried and nervous and unsure. On Saturday I would be old enough to date, and I'm not only dating a bad boy, but I'm also marrying one.

What would Daddy think of that?

"It was a guess," he says softly. "Did I guess right?"

I can't find the words and simply nod. "H-How?"

The smirk is back. "Let's just say on the many times you tried to avoid us when we came to visit, you'd blare that godawful song by Simple Minds."

"Don't You (Forget About Me)," I say with a laugh. "And it's the best song ever."

"It didn't take rocket science to think maybe just maybe you'd be into it." He shrugs. "Plus, by the way you would always tease Vienna about being a modern-day Molly Ringwald, I put two and two together. I'm older than you, you know. I'm familiar with that era. Most chicks your age don't know shit about the eighties."

I laugh. "I'm an old soul then. It really is the best, you know."

He holds his hand out to me. "Want to watch it together and then I can make a better deduction afterward?"

With a burst of happiness surging through me, I climb off the bed and hurry over to the television. Ten minutes later, we're settled on the couch, and I'm reciting the movie word for word. Just like old times. Just like when I had a home and when I was happy. When I risk a glance at Duvan, he's simply staring at me.

I give him a thankful smile and curl up into his side, basking in the momentary peace that he's provided us.

And I wonder, is happiness finally a possibility for me?

Ren

"I cannot believe we have Hannah's kid, a kid she had with Mom's psycho rapist, living in our house," Calder says in astonishment as he pushes the grocery cart down the diaper aisle.

"She has a name, asswipe."

He shrugs as he looks at the list Mom gave us. "Toni. Yep, got it. Named after he-who-shall-not-be-named," he deadpans.

I whap him upside the head and snag some Pull-Ups off the shelf. Mom said Toni should be potty-trained by now and was on a mission to be the one to teach her. Her grandchild hasn't even been here for two days, and she's already in possessive grandma mode. Hell, Dad hasn't even been home yet to meet my niece and she's already a part of our household. He wasn't pleased that Gabe showed up but he's looking forward to seeing Toni.

"How's it going with your girlfriend anyway? You made her your girlfriend, right? Or are you still pussyfooting around?" he asks over his shoulder as he pushes the cart.

"She's my girlfriend," I tell him with a growl.

"So, you fucked her."

I kick him in his ass and he laughs.

"What? You wouldn't be getting all shitty unless you fucked her. Does she know she's fucking the brother of the crazy ass woman who killed her mom?" This time, he takes off running with the cart, so I don't hurt him again.

When I catch him, I snap, "She doesn't know. Nor will she ever find out."

He turns and raises his hands up in defense. "Dude, I'm not going to tell her."

"Have you told Vee?"

A flash of anger morphs his otherwise chill face into a scowl. "I'm not talking to Vee."

"Why not?"

"She's not fucking interested. I'm not going to chase her around when she's wet for another guy."

An old lady passing by gasps at my brother's crude language.

"Whatever, man," I grunt.

"Do Mom and Dad know you're fucking Gabe's daughter? Wait, does that like make her your niece since he's fucking our sister?" He stops to scratch his head as if he's trying to figure it out.

"Calder, shut the fuck up," I grumble. "Of course they don't know and don't be disgusting."

He shrugs. "Me? I'm not the one mixing bodily fluids within the family tree, bro," he chuckles, clearly amusing himself.

I stop the cart and glare at him.

"Maybe you ought to come clean, man."

"I can't."

"Why the hell not? I like Brie. She's cool as shit. Not at all the type to not forgive you over something lame."

But it's not lame.

Our entire relationship was forged from lies.

"I just can't, okay? She's dealing with some heavy shit right now. I have to find a way to help her."

He turns down the cereal aisle and starts tossing in random boxes of cereal. Mom and Dad gave up on trying to make my brother eat healthy long ago. If he weren't a runner, he'd be a chunky fuck. Luckily, he has good genes and he isn't opposed to exercise.

"Where are you taking her tonight?" he asks.

"Dinner and a movie. I even booked a hotel room."

He snorts. "A way to a woman's heart is not through her pussy, dumbass."

The same old lady is coming down the aisle and utters that we need Jesus.

"I just want to spend some time with her alone and then I'll figure out a way to keep her," I tell him in exasperation.

He levels a hard glare at me. "You can't keep her. She's not a stray dog, Ren."

I pinch the bridge of my nose and exhale in frustration. "You know what I mean."

"You should probably just back out before it's too late."

"But they're going to marry her off into a criminal family!"

Calder stops to check out some chocolate covered granola bars. "And you want to get in the middle of that?" He doesn't even look at me. "Is she in danger?"

I think back to the texts we exchanged earlier. Her future fiancé was cool with our arrangement to see each other and had taken her in. Something had gone down between her and Heath, but she wouldn't say what—just that it was ugly. She said the guy, Duvan, was being nice and keeping her safe. I was jealous, but her safety and happiness overshadowed the twinge of green in my mind.

"Nah, she's with Duvan."

"Who the hell is Duvan?" he asks and stands back up. My brother isn't as solid as I am, but he's slightly taller than me.

"Her fiancé."

Calder starts laughing so hard, people pass by the cereal aisle just so they can glare at us.

"What?" I snap.

He doubles over and holds his belly while I fume. "You know this whole ordeal is super fucked up, right?"

"Whatever. Let's get out of here. Can't fucking take you anywhere. I'm taking my girl out while you get to help babysit an equally fucked-up situation."

His grumbled response lets me know I got him.

"Oh," I say as I toss some animal crackers from an end cap into the cart, "Speaking of bodily fluids, I hope Mom goes into labor while I'm out with Brie and that you have to witness every horrifying second all by yourself."

When he gags behind me, I let out a snort of laughter, thankful that I didn't get Dad's sensitive gag reflex.

She's been way too quiet.

Contemplative.

Somber.

"Are you having regrets? About having sex with me?" I blurt out as we pull out of the restaurant.

"What? No," she says and grabs hold of my hand. "I'm sorry if I'm all over the place. Just been a long couple of days. Where are we going?"

I glance over to her and give her a wicked smile. "I'm taking you to a hotel so I can give you your real birthday present." When I waggle my eyebrows at her, she giggles. The sound is sweet music to my ears.

"And here I thought my necklace was my real present." She fingers the silver chain. It's simple but pretty. A silver crown and the letter *B*. I'd debated between a *G* and a *B*. When she opened it and thanked me, I was overjoyed to know I chose well. Apparently, Heath calls her Gabriella and she's grown to loathe her own name.

The drive to the hotel isn't long and when we pull into the parking lot, she climbs over the center console to straddle me. My dick immediately responds to having her so close. When I took her virginity, it was fucking bliss. I'm dying to be inside her again.

"I'm almost free," she murmurs as her mouth crashes against mine. Her fingertips skitter over my shirt and up my chest sending ripples of anticipation pulsating through me. When she starts grinding against me, I lose it and grab her ass hard.

What I don't expect is for her to cry out in excruciating pain.

"What the hell, Brie? Are you hurt?"

She whimpers and shakes her head. "It's nothing."

"The hell it ain't!"

With a huff, she yanks at the door handle and climbs out. I scramble out after her.

She rounds the front of the car and lets out a weary sigh. "Ren, it's nothing."

My jaw clenches and I shake my head as I approach. "Don't lie to me."

But you're lying to her…

Guilt softens her features, and she tugs at her bottom lip with her teeth. "It was Heath. The night we had sex, afterward…he was waiting up for me. He knew I'd been with you—knew your name and everything. Vee has been upset with me. I think she must have told him."

I tangle my fingers in her sexy-as-fuck short hair and crash my lips to hers. My kiss spills all the secrets I can't verbally say. God, I hope she understands. When we both pull away and are winded from our needy kiss, I lean my forehead against hers.

"What did that motherfucker do to you?"

She swallows and lifts her chin, meeting my gaze firmly. "He whipped my ass with a belt."

I don't think I have ever been spanked in my entire life. Hannah got Mom's hand a few times when she'd do something really bad in public but never Calder or me. Dad never once spanked us. My mind has trouble comprehending how a grown ass man would spank an almost eighteen-year-old woman. "He hit you?"

Her brows furrow with anger. She turns around and lifts her dress. Out here in the parking lot, anyone can see but neither of us seem to care. I kneel behind her and tug her panties down slightly over the bottom of her cheeks. What I see causes me to explode with rage.

"THAT MOTHERFUCKER!"

Dark purple marks paint her flesh like some fucked-up piece of artwork. In some places, the bruises are actually scabbed over. He hurt her. He fucking hurt her.

"Why didn't you tell me sooner?" I seethe. I'm not angry at her. I just wish I could have fucked him up for doing this to her.

"There's nothing you could have done. The damage was already there. It doesn't matter," she assures me. "After Saturday, Duvan will look after me. I can have his protection and still see you. It won't be as easy with me leaving the country, but we can Skype, and I'll be back to visit."

I freeze at her words. "Wait? You're leaving?"

She nods slightly, her eyes not meeting mine. "Camilo says that we have to—"

"What about what you want, Brie?" I clutch her short hair and pull her to my chest. She lets out a sob, squeezing me tight.

"It's going to work out," she assures me. "I promise."

"They're smuggling you out of the country, away from me!"

She frowns. "I'll get to go to college." A twinkle in her eyes tells me she's excited about that notion.

"You can go to college here with me," I plead.

"I have to do this, Ren. You can't protect me like Duvan can. It's still you whom I want though. I've made this crystal clear to him. He's fine with it. Things will just be weird for a bit."

I'm still scowling when she reaches between us and grabs my dick. It springs to life at her simple touch.

"I thought I was getting my real birthday present," she says coyly. She's changing the subject and it's working. "Please."

❧

The hotel is nice. I'd used the express kiosk to check us in before whisking my feisty princess up to our room. Once inside, she wasted no time pulling her slinky black dress from her body and showing off her sexy black bra and panties. My dick, which remained painfully hard, nearly ripped through my jeans to get to her.

"I wanted to go slow and make this special," I growl as I tear through the buttons on my shirt. "But you're just too fucking fine. I need inside of you now."

She laughs and pulls the rest of her clothing away. In the bright hotel light, I can see every perfect inch of her svelte body. Brie has curves in all the right places and yet still maintains a toned physique. Her tits are on the small side, but they'll fit perfectly in my mouth.

"Come here," I demand in a low tone as I get completely naked.

She bounces into my arms, her legs wrapping around my hips immediately. I walk her over to the door and lean her back against it.

"I want to fuck you against this door. Any objections?" I raise a challenging brow at her.

Her fingers thread into my hair and she wriggles in my arms. "My only objection is that you're taking too long."

I position my cock against her and drive into her in one quick thrust. She cries out my name, ripping at my hair. "More, beautiful?"

"I want it all," she murmurs, her head tilted back in pleasure.

My mouth finds her neck, and I suck on her olive-colored flesh as I pound into her. I massage her clit while I fuck her knowing that if I want us to come together, it's going to have to be soon on her part. The last time I was inside of her, I came way too fast. She feels that damn good.

"Ren!"

I pinch the sensitive bundle of nerves, and she comes hard around my cock. Her body quivers in my arms like she's a live wire. With a groan of pleasure, I release my hot seed inside of her. When we both stop spasming and jolting, I press a kiss to her swollen lips.

"I'm going to do this to you all night," I vow and tug at her bottom lip with my teeth.

"I suppose this is a pretty good birthday present after all," she teases.

I thrust into her again, even though I'm softening, and she lets out a moan. "Don't act like it isn't the best one you got."

Her eyes darken but then she blinks away the look.

A pounding on the door makes her shriek. I slip out of her and lower her to her feet.

"Who is it?"

"Hotel manager."

"Go hide under the blankets," I say with a laugh as I jerk my pants on up over my still wet dick. Once she's hidden in the bed and I'm dressed, I open the door.

The older woman's eyes go wide when she flits her gaze to my chest for several long seconds. "Uh…" She shakes her head away and lifts up a clipboard. "Mr. McPherson? I'm sorry, but our computers went down on the kiosks and we're having to manually retype everything in the old-fashioned way. I've already input the information I could pull from my laptop, but payment information reserved online isn't saved anywhere. I'll just need you to verify your address and I need to get the card number from you again. Then I'll be out of your hair. My apologies for the interruption."

She rattles off my address and phone number while I locate my card from my wallet. Once she has me sign the form, she leaves. I return my card to its place and toss the wallet onto the dresser.

"Now, where were we," I say with a growl, my dick already hard for her again. I've barely got my pants unbuttoned when my gaze meets hers.

Her eyebrows are pinched together and her mouth is parted.

"Are you okay? What's wrong?" I demand and reach for her.

She pins me with a serious stare. "What did she call you?"

Fuck.

I clench my jaw and shake my head at her. "Brie…"

"What did she call you?" Her tone is calm. Too calm.

Pinching the bridge of my nose, I let out a breath. "Warren McPherson."

"Do you have a sister?" she demands, her voice raising a couple of octaves. "More importantly, what is her name?"

I close my eyes. The name is on my lips, but I can't say it. I can't cut her anymore. When I re-open my eyes, I implore her to listen.

Understanding washes over her like a bucket of icy water. She hisses at me—fucking hisses like a cat—and scrambles away from me as if I might be diseased.

"Her name is Hannah," she utters, horror evident in her voice. "Your sister's name is Hannah."

As soon as the name rolls past her perfect, plump lips, I know I've majorly fucked up.

"Brie, listen—"

"No," she says, her voice wobbly, as she dresses in record speed. "You lied to me."

Fuck!

Running my fingers through my hair, I shake my head. "My name is Warren 'Ren' Loveland McPherson. That wasn't a lie."

"IT WASN'T THE FULL TRUTH EITHER!" she screeches and digs through her purse.

I start for her, but she fucking hisses again.

"STAY AWAY FROM ME!"

"Brie, just listen to me—"

"You knew. You knew it was me all along. Why, Ren? Why?" Fat tears roll down her cheeks and the betrayal in her eyes makes me sick to my stomach.

"Let me explain."

She fires off a text and glares at me through her tears. "You have exactly fifteen minutes to say your piece. My ride will be here for me and I will be gone. Tick tock."

I scrub at my cheek with my palm. "My dad asked me to look after you."

"Why? Keep an eye on the girl who was now an orphan because your sister killed her mother? Was this some kind of guilt thing?" Her words are a vicious snarl.

"Jesus, Brie, no." I start for her and she takes a step back. "Just hear me out."

She remains eerily quiet as I recant the past three years. How her father asked us to look after her. How Dad paid off the old lawn boy so I could take his place. How I eventually fell for her on my own.

"How I felt about you was never a lie, beautiful."

Her throat bobs as she swallows. "Your sister killed my mother. Your sister stole my dad."

I don't even touch on the fact that she has a half-sister she doesn't know about who lives across the hall from my bedroom. "I'm nothing like my sister. You know that."

"Blood was everywhere," she whispers so softly I almost don't even hear. "Everywhere. I climbed on top of my mother and tried to hold her cold neck together. Ren, I tried to give a corpse CPR." Her body quakes but the sob never escapes.

"I'm so sorry, Brie."

"Me too. I'm so sorry but I can't do this with you. This wasn't just a lie. This was a massive cover-up of the most horrific time of my life." She starts for the door and swings it open. "I can't get over this. I'll never get over this."

A massive scary-ass motherfucker comes up behind her and I freeze.

"Everything okay, tigress?"

His glare is menacing and penetrating. He's the type of guy who is feral—the type of guy who looks just crazy enough that he'd bite your jugular with his teeth for looking at him wrong.

I must be asking to be made into a meal because I'm looking all kinds of wrong at him.

"Just take me home, Duvan." She turns and buries her head in his chest.

Duvan. Fucking Duvan.

Her motherfucking fiancé.

Home?

He pins me with a warning glare before ushering her out of the room.

"Brie!" I call out to her in the hallway.

I don't get a response as the only girl I've ever really cared about walks into the elevator and out of my life for good.

The elevator doors begin to draw to a close, and as I stand there paralyzed with Brie's *fiancé's* death glare burning into me, a trembling Brie in his arms, one thought circles around in my head.

Thanks a fucking lot, Han.

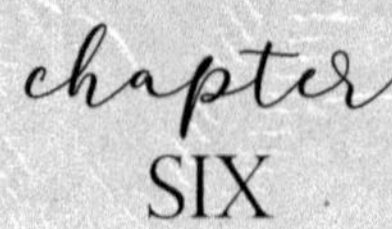

chapter
SIX

Brie

I'm hollow and empty inside.

Dead.

He lied.

Duvan wisely remained silent while I stewed over Ren's dishonesty. This wasn't a lie about how much money one makes at their job or embellishing the size of a fish they caught. This isn't even like one of Oscar's lies where he tells us about how he slept with Taylor Swift and that her recent album is about him.

No, this was lying about who Ren was.

Everything he told me, he did so while he hid the truth of who his family is. It was his family who entered my life and tore it to pieces. His sister stole and stole from me. And he lied and did so in a way that assured I wouldn't know who he was—who she was to him. The fact that he's been in touch with my father was the icing on the cake. My own father who *I* have not spoken to in over three years. My own father who chose my mother's killer over me.

I'm disgusted.

The ride back to Duvan's hotel is a blur.

I vaguely remember him walking me upstairs. I hardly recall him running me a bath. I don't even remember getting into the bath at all.

I'm simply in total, mind-blowing shock.

Duvan's deep voice rumbles in the other room as he talks on the phone, but I can't make out his words. Eventually, he returns to me, concern painting his features.

"Time for bed, tigress."

I stand in the water and he wraps a towel around me. Earlier today he'd taken me shopping. He didn't choose for me like Heath always would. No, Duvan sat in a chair scrolling through his phone while I picked out the items I liked. When I step into the bedroom I'm staying in, I find some yoga pants and a hoodie lying on the bed. A pair of pink panties sits on top.

His kindness makes me break down in tears.

And I don't stop.

Three years of pent-up hurt and betrayal all pours out in one evening. He doesn't ogle me or try to touch me as he helps me dress. He doesn't tell me what a bastard Ren is. He doesn't do anything but help me.

"Look at me," he says, lifting my chin. "You cry this shit out tonight. I'll give you something to relax. And then tomorrow, you begin living your fucking life. All this heartache stays here. We won't bring it with us."

I nod, desperately trying to swipe the tears away. "Okay."

"Okay," he agrees with a gentle smile and brushes a stray tear from my jaw.

He leaves the room and returns with a bottle of water. I take the pills from him and swallow them down. When I crawl into the bed, he sidles in beside me. His comfort is the only thing fueling me on right now.

"Sleep, tigress."

And I do.

My marriage to Duvan is official.

I am Gabriella Rojas.

Married at eighteen and flying to another country with her husband.

We've barely spoken, aside from our murmured vows in front of the judge and our families. I've floated along in a fog. The medicine that Duvan gave me last night helped. I'm trying to get the courage to ask him for some more.

The ache in my heart hurts.

"Duvan?" I ask, my voice husky.

He's been staring out the plane window. Quiet. Too quiet. It unnerves me.

"Hmm?"

When he turns to look at me, he's frowning. His jaw ticks, and I wonder what he's thinking.

"What's wrong?"

He reaches over and takes my hand. "Just happy to get home. Ready to leave all this behind."

"Can I..." I chew on my lip as nerves eat away at my stomach. "What you gave me last night really helped me."

He lifts a dark eyebrow. "All you have to do is ask for it, tigress."

"Can you give me those pills again?"

His hand dives in his pocket and he produces two pills—as if he knew I'd need them. I choke them down and chase them with my water.

"Thank you."

He gives me a small nod. "It's my duty as your husband to take care of you now."

The degree of seriousness as he says this makes me shiver.

My husband.

He's my last thought before I drift off.

"This is our bedroom," he says after he flicks on the light. The sprawling mansion situated on the outskirts of town is an architectural masterpiece. Whereas the rest of the city is a myriad of buildings and homes from crumbling to pristine, his house—our house—is the fanciest of them all.

"We're sleeping in the same bed?" I blurt out.

His eyes darken and he plucks at the buttons on his shirt. "Isn't that what husbands and wives do? That's what we did out of wedlock last night, did we not?"

I swallow and nod, my eyes fixated on his motions.

"This house is beautiful," I praise, hoping to change the subject. "I think it's the nicest one around here."

He chuckles. "It is the nicest house," he affirms with barely disguised pride. "And here, in Bogotá we are royalty. Do you understand?"

I nod but freeze when he wraps his arms around me from behind.

"Relax, tigress."

The meds from our flight have worn off, and I'm feeling edgy. "What sort of things are there to do around here?"

He twists me in his arms and pins me with a scary glare that has me cowering. "You are never to leave this house without me. Are we clear?"

I blink at him in confusion and nod.

His fingers lift my chin so that I can't avoid his menacing gaze. "Not because I'm a controlling asshole, Brie. But because it's dangerous out there. Not everyone likes our family. We have enemies. Enemies dead set on destroying our empire."

Relief courses through me. "Okay, I promise I won't go anywhere without you."

This seems to please him and he grins at me. And then he kisses me. Not a quick peck like at our wedding, but deep. Consuming. Claiming.

My palms find his hardened pecks to steady myself, so I don't get kissed right out the window. His big hand wraps around the back of my neck as he pulls me deeper into his kiss. I let out a surprised moan. The way his tongue dances with mine is delicate yet dominating. Like a tiger who goes easy on his tigress because he doesn't want to scare her off. But he still ripples with strength and power. I know he could maul me to death if he truly wanted.

He eventually pulls from our kiss and flashes me what is becoming one of his signature smirks. "I wanted to kiss you like that at the ceremony."

I laugh. "Why didn't you? That would have made this trip a lot less nerve-wracking."

His eyes darken and his jaw clenches. "They don't need to know how I really feel," he mumbles. "Love and family are a weakness in my life. You show your enemies what's valuable to you and they will try and take it from you."

"But it was your family and my adopted one."

"Heath is an enemy. Esteban is an enemy."

I'm shocked at his revealing words about how he truly feels about his brother, and it sparks my curiosity. "Why is your brother an enemy?"

His brows furl together. "Once I graduated from college, our father wanted us both to work alongside him. Esteban had grown used to calling a lot of the shots. Then he had me to contend with. We've been at each other's throats for a couple of years now. Since the moment we'd been told one of us was going to marry you, and that you weren't to be simply given to the eldest, Esteban has had a major fucking chip on his shoulder. He's always wanted it all. Our father makes us earn what we want. And Esteban has hated that our entire lives."

"I'm glad I got you then. He seems awful." That's the truth. I love Oscar dearly as a friend. But he's not frightening. Oscar could never protect me like Duvan can.

"It wasn't an easy fight, tigress."

"But you fought for me anyway."

He lifts his hand and strokes away my bangs that hang in my eyes. "I'll fight for you from here on out. You're mine now." The way he says the last part isn't threatening. It's in an affectionate way. Mom would have liked Duvan, I'm sure of it. Dad would have hated him. Bad boys and all that.

"Can I have more of those pills?"

He stares at me for a long second. "Not those. Now that we're home, I have something better."

When he comes back with a glass tray, I furrow my brows.

"Cocaine? I don't do drugs."

"This is your empire now. Your legacy. Know your product, tigress," he says in a matter-of-fact tone as he messes with the white powder, arranging it into neat lines. "Besides, the shit I gave you before was to calm you down. Now it's time to perk you up. It's time to be happy."

He snorts a line and I shudder. I can't do that. No way.

"Come here."

My feet stumble toward him and I eye the tray like it's diseased.

"Duvan…"

"You don't need that whole line. Look," he says and takes my finger. He uses my fingernail to scoop up a tiny bit. "Just this amount." Our eyes meet as he brings the substance to my nose. "Sniff and done."

Sniff.

And.

Done.

His eyes are intense and on mine as he swipes away the dust under my nostril.

"I don't get what the big deal is…" Blood seems to rush loudly in my ears and my body thrums with electricity. The sadness I was just dwelling on is chased away by a feeling unlike anything I've ever felt before.

I'm flying…

"I'm going to feed you. Put on something comfy," he instructs with a wide grin and a wild glint in his eye.

I'm flying…

"Tell me something funny," he orders, his lazy grin never leaving his face all through dinner.

I pick up my wine glass and frown when I notice it's empty. "I don't have anything funny to tell you."

He chuckles and motions to get the waiter's attention. Everyone in the restaurant seems to sneak stares at us. Duvan wasn't lying when he said we were royalty. The people won't look him in the eye. They hold doors open for us and pull chairs out for us. They never make us wait.

"Oh, tigress," he chides. "You're going to have to start figuring out what you like. Because when you find it, I'm going to give it to you."

I beam at him. The bump we did back at the house has long since dissipated and I'm glad the alcohol has taken over. I'm feeling loose and relaxed.

"What'll we do next?"

"Here," he says.

I open my palm and he drops a yellow pill with a smiley face into my hand. "What's this?"

He smirks and it makes my heart flutter. "Something funny. Now you know."

Laughing, I toss the pill into my mouth and go to chase it with his wine. He pushes my water glass toward me.

"Chase it with that, mi amor."

Mi amor.

My skin heats and I gladly guzzle the cold water. "Now what?"

He stands and whistles for the waiter. They exchange a look and the waiter nods. We leave without paying. This is all so weird.

"All hail King Duvan," I snort as we leave the restaurant to his waiting car.

He tickles me, and I squeal as I climb into the vehicle. "So now you know something funny and I know you can laugh. We're both learning new things at every turn."

I lean against his shoulder in the backseat as the driver takes off like a bat out of hell. Duvan rests his palm on my bare knee. The dress I wore has ridden up, giving him a view of my silky thighs. His fingers begin running up and down against my flesh causing me to tingle. The tingling seems to zip right to my core with each caress. By the time we reach the house, I'm squirming with need.

"Duvan…" I trail off as we climb out of the car and he drags me into the house.

"What, mi amor?"

Mi amor.

I giggle, and his laughter echoes around me. "I like your laugh."

He reaches forward and grazes his thumb across my nipple through my dress. "I like your tits in this dress."

My entire body quakes with need from his one simple touch. "Why do I feel so happy?"

His fingers tangle into my hair and he pulls me into a kiss. I moan loud and desperately against his mouth. "Besides being here with me," he says with a wicked grin. "You're flying high on Ex."

"Ecstasy?"

He grabs my hand and pulls me through the house. When we reach his massive bedroom—our massive bedroom—he wastes no time in tearing off his shirt. I gape at his colorful chest the moment he bares it to me. The muscles flex and harden as he smiles at me.

Why does he have to be so hot?

"Tell me what you really think," he says smugly.

I slap my hand over my mouth and giggle. "I said that out loud."

He flashes me a smoldering look. "Take your dress off," he says low, a streak of moonlight illuminating his face in the otherwise darkened room.

I'm stunned stupid when he shoves his pants down. He isn't wearing any underwear, and his giant cock bounces heavily out in front of him. I'm staring boldly at it and lick my lips in an effort to wet them.

It's so big.

"Biggest you've ever seen," he confirms, and struts toward me.

The giggles overtake me again at having blurted out my thoughts. But when he begins dragging the dress up my body, I let out an embarrassing moan. I break out in goose bumps everywhere that the fabric touches on my skin.

"I'm going to make you happy, mi amor."

Mi amor.

"You like it when I call you mi amor?" he asks.

Shit, I said that out loud.

He smirks as he tugs my bra from me. When I look down, I'm staring in awe that my panties are missing.

"Where did my panties go?"

His laugh warms my soul. "You gave them to me in the car."

"I did?"

He nods and kisses me again. Deep in the recesses of my mind, I scold myself for jumping right into bed with this man. My husband. But right now, the argument is not making a strong enough case against it.

"Mi amor…"

"That's not my name," I protest.

He chuckles. "Brie…"

I swat at him. "I like when you call me tigress. Maul me, Mr. Tiger."

His hand seizes my throat, and I stare at him. No fear. No worry. Nothing. He walks me backward with his hand gently gripping my throat. I let out another giggle when he pushes me onto the bed. I'm still laughing at him as he grips my thighs and drags me to the edge of the bed.

"Are we consummating our marriage?"

He smirks.

Jesus.

I clench my thighs together and he takes great satisfaction in prying them apart. When he lowers himself to his knees, I sit up on my elbows to see what he's up to. He drags his nose along the slit of my pussy, and I shiver. My nerve endings are alive and sensitive.

"I'm going to eat this pussy. You're going to come so hard, you will see motherfucking stars, mi amor."

Mi amor.

Biting my lip, I nod. I want him to make me feel good.

A low, guttural groan escapes me when his thumbs pull apart the lips and he runs his thick, flat tongue along the most sensitive part of my body.

"Oh my God!"

I squirm and try to get away. One lick and it's too much. It's intense and I don't want it, yet I need it.

"Stay still so I don't have to tie you up," he breathes against my pussy.

Stars.

He promised them.

And they're everywhere.

"Good girl," he praises, his words doing their part to turn me on as well.

My orgasm takes hold of me, and when it subsides, his tongue works me into another one. I've ripped at his hair, tugged at my tits, and screamed in a mix of bliss and frustration.

"I. Need. You—"

His tongue pushes into me and the sensation is unlike anything I've ever encountered. I'm on the edge of another earth-shattering climax when he bites down on the top of my pussy with his tongue buried deep inside me.

This time, I see white.

Just white.

The all-body-consuming, intense pleasure has stolen me from this reality and dumped me into another plane of existence. I ride out the glorious waves, one ripple after the other.

And then I'm full.

So full.

A musky tongue is dancing with mine.

The tiger is tearing me up.

Marking me and owning me.

Obliterating the sad girl and pulling the tigress from her ashes.

"My Brie…"

His musical words sear themselves into my soul.

"Duvan."

chapter
SEVEN

Brie

I wake with a thundering in my skull and a brown-eyed woman about my age staring at me. She gives me a shy smile over getting caught.

"Um, hi," I croak and absently pat the bed beside me. Duvan is gone.

When she notices me looking for him, she frowns and shakes her head.

"Did he leave?"

She nods and smiles again. Then, she motions for me to follow her. With a groan, I slink out of bed. The air hits my bare flesh causing me to yelp out in surprise. Last night is a blur, but I'm naked and sore and hungover. Bits and pieces remain in my memory bank.

I remember Duvan taking me to dinner.

I remember him kissing me like he wanted to crawl inside of me.

I remember his tongue.

And then he took me.

Closing my eyes, I recall the way his black eyes drank me in while he did things with his tongue I didn't know were possible. Then, he crawled on top of me and drove into me with such strength, I thought he'd rip me in half.

He was huge and he mauled me.

And I liked it.

I reopen my eyes to find the woman staring at my chest, her eyebrows furrowed in concern.

"I'm going to shower. I'll be right out," I blurt out and dart past her to the bathroom. Once inside, I get a look at myself in the mirror. I look like hell. My hair is sticking up in every direction, my eye makeup is smeared everywhere like I'm some rabid raccoon, and purple hickeys mark up my neck and breasts.

Oh, Duvan, what have you done to me?

My head is clear, but it hurts like hell. Two days ago, I'd slept with someone whom I thought I loved. And he betrayed me in the worst possible way.

Now?

I'm going at it with my new husband like Ren didn't matter.

But he did matter.

God, my heart hurts.

I swallow down the emotion bubbling in my throat. Ren was a mistake. Duvan is my life now. He's been nothing but good to me since I discovered we were to be married. I've been treated with respect and he's pleasured me beyond my wildest dreams.

Leave it all behind and focus on being happy. That's what Duvan wants me to do. So, I'm sure as hell going to try.

After a long, invigorating hot shower, I'm thankful that the girl isn't in my room when I come out. I dress in some light grey lounge pants and a loose black tank top sans bra. Duvan said I could dress however I wanted. It feels weird not to be putting on fancy dresses for Heath's personal enjoyment.

It also feels unusual being in the house without Duvan. I wonder why he left without waking me. Did he go to work? What exactly does a Colombian drug lord do? Does he go to a factory and watch them make cocaine? Does he drive to fields and oversee crops? I know nothing about drugs and their origin.

But you liked them last night…

Shame heats my cheeks and I slip my feet into a pair of flip flops before hurrying out of the room. If I dwell on certain things for too long, I feel guilty. And right now, I'm too exhausted for guilt.

It's time to be happy.

Duvan's house is gigantic and modern while still maintaining a country feel. Giant windows line the front and back of the house. The front overlooks a flat field and the back is nothing but thick trees, like you'd see in the rainforest. I know he has a barn and a workshop. He promised he'd take me to tour the entire property this week.

A woman is humming a sad song as I enter the kitchen. It's the same woman who woke me up. She's pretty. A little taller than me. Most definitely from these parts. Her black hair has been braided neatly down her back and she wears a crisp uniform. As she fries up some bacon, I realize she must be our cook.

We have a cook?

"You didn't have to cook anything. I could have had cereal," I tell her.

She turns to me and gives me a sweet smile. Then she wags her finger at me and *tsks* before going back to her cooking. I frown wondering why she doesn't speak. Does she understand English?

"I don't know Spanish," I tell her and then bite my lip.

She turns off the stove and deposits the meat onto an already prepped plate of eggs and fruit. A smile graces her lips as she motions for the small bistro table in the kitchen. The woman seems so proud of her meal, so I sit and accept her generosity.

"Thank you. What's your name?" I question, taking a bite of the savory bacon.

Her hand covers her mouth and her eyes drop to her feet. "O."

"O?"

She nods and her eyes find mine again, twinkling with delight.

"I'm Brie."

Her hand goes to her mouth again and she peeps out, "Beh."

"Brie."

"Beh."

I frown because I wonder why she doesn't talk well. Finally, I just accept it and smile. "Yep, Brie."

She points at me and then pats her chest where her heart is and points upstairs. Then, her eyebrows pull together as if it's a question.

"Do I love Duvan?"

Her smile is adorable and she nods. The excitement glittering in her eyes has me instantly warming to her.

Thrusting my hand at her, I show her the sparkling diamond on my ring finger. "He's my husband. We're still getting to know each other."

She lifts her eyebrows as if she understands. Then she taps at the watch on her dainty wrist before tapping her chest and pointing upstairs.

"With time I will love him?"

This time when she smiles, she reveals perfect white teeth and nods. She seems positively pleased I understand what she's saying.

"Do you know when he will be back, O?"

She simply shrugs her shoulders before scurrying over to clean up. I gobble up the delicious breakfast. It helps for the massive hangover I'm nursing. The shower and the food helped but my body still aches—every muscle, my head, and inside as well. Not just where Duvan took me but my heart.

My heart hurts.

Sad memories of Dad and Mom have been brought to the surface. Knowing Ren's sister was the person to kill my mom and seduce my dad is a wound on my poor heart that won't stop bleeding.

O leaves the room once she finishes up. After I eat, I clean my dishes and roam the house looking for her. I find her in a small room with a tiny desk. The room is painted sunshine yellow and has a window that overlooks the barn. I can see some chickens pecking at the dirt. She fiddles with a laptop and I realize it's my laptop.

When she stands back up, she motions around the room and then points at me, grinning.

"This is my office?" I question.

She nods and then surprises me by pulling me in for a hug.

"Thank you," I murmur, patting her back.

Once she leaves, I sit down at the chair. The room is free from decoration and a little trickle of excitement begins to build at the prospect of making it mine. I want Duvan to come home, so I can thank him for making me feel welcome.

I open my computer and find an email from Duvan.

Tigress,

I see Luciana has shown you to your office. My American Express Black Card is under the laptop. Feel free to shop online for anything you need. Also, you can use it to enroll and pay for tuition if you decide you want to go to Oscar's university in the fall. I'm away dealing with business this morning, but I'll be back soon. Last night was fun, mi amor. Dress comfortably, and I'll show you something when I get back.

- D

I'm smiling as I finish his email. It's surreal being here. I'm not sure what I expected marrying a drug lord, but it wasn't this. It is romance and a feeling of belonging and happiness. I'd imagined cartel criminals and torture and filth.

Not this.

Not chickens outside my window.

Not being treated like royalty.

Not a pattering of hope in my chest.

I start browsing for the courses at Oscar's college when my Skype app chimes. Toggling over, I open it and accept the incoming call. As soon as it connects, Oscar's handsome face fills the screen.

"How are you, Mrs. Rojas?" he questions with a sad smile.

My cheeks heat and I fight a grin. "I'm good. Beautiful country. Just looking up courses at your school. How's everyone? Vee?"

He leans back in the chair and swivels. Familiar pastel purple fills the screen. Oscar is in Vee's room which means she's probably listening. I wish we could patch things up.

"Heath is still a dick as always. Vee and I have been hanging out the last couple of days. Feels weird without our third wheel."

I let out a sigh. "I miss you guys. You too, Vee," I call out, hoping she'll hear me. "When do you come back home?"

Oscar shrugs his shoulders. "I'm trying to talk Vee into taking a trip there for the summer with me. But…"

I frown. "She doesn't want to see me."

Guilt draws his features into a pinch. "I told her we were just playing around. It's not a big deal."

I wince at his words. "Actually, Oscar, it was a big deal. You and I both know it should have never happened. We were both confused and the moment got away from us. I'm with Duvan now and I'm happy."

Oscar forces a smile but it doesn't reach his eyes. "What about Ren?"

The breath in my lungs expels out in a huff as if I've been sucker punched. "W-What about Ren?"

His eyes dart over to Vienna somewhere in the room before he looks back at the screen. "I thought you were going to see him on the side."

I shake my head. "I broke up with him. I'm going to try and focus on my marriage."

I hear whispering and then he rolls his eyes. "You tell her," he grunts before swiveling the screen around.

Vee's bright red hair fills the screen. Her pouty lips are parted in shock and her green eyes are wide. "Uh…"

God, I miss my best friend.

"Vee, I'm sorry."

She frowns but nods. "Okay."

We stare silently for a moment and Oscar sniggers. "You two are terrible at being mad at each other. I never seen two women more depressed in all my life. Make the fuck up already."

Vee and I both giggle and just like that the three of us are comfortable again.

"Well," Vee says with an exasperate sigh, "now that we're over that, I was going to say that just because you're trying to make it work with Duvan, doesn't mean you can't be friends with Ren. You two were friends before anything transpired between you. Brie, you don't have family any-more, it's just your friends in this life."

The ever-present ache in my chest cracks open and I feel as though I might start to cry at any moment. "You don't understand. It isn't that simple. He…"

"He lied," she says bluntly.

"How do you know?"

Oscar pops in next to her. "He came over. I don't even like the guy and I felt sorry for him. He was devastated when he found out you were already gone."

My brows scrunch in confusion. "He told you?"

They both nod and anger blooms in my chest.

"So now you see why I had to end it. His sister killed my mother!" A sob rips from me and I shudder.

"Oh, Brie," Vee says sadly. "You need a hug."

"Luciana!" Oscar hollers.

Footsteps patter into the office and then Luciana is hugging me from behind.

"Why doesn't she talk?" I question through my tears.

Oscar's face darkens into something murderous. "Why don't you ask Duvan?"

A flash of anger surges through me. Did Duvan do something to her?

"Just talk to him," Vee pleads. "Ren is just as heartbroken as you."

"He lied to me which means Calder lied to you too. It was all lies. That is not friendship. That is not love. It's wrong," I snap.

Oscar shrugs and Vee shakes her head in disappointment.

"Nobody is asking you to be buddy-buddy with him. Just let him apologize. He's your friend.

Let him be one. You're all the way off in butt fucking Egypt," she grumbles. "You need all the friends you can get."

I drag my gaze from theirs and stare off at the chickens. "I need to go."

As soon as I hang up on my friends, O, now known as Luciana, escorts me back to bed. I'm thankful when she hands me the same two pills Duvan gave me the night Ren broke my heart. They're not the happy pills, and I'm thankful. I don't want to be happy right now.

I just want to forget.

"I'm scared," I tell him, my legs straddling the surfboard. Ren and I are both floating in the choppy waves as he tries to explain how surfing works.

"There's nothing to be scared of. It's fun," he assures me with a panty melting grin.

God, he's so hot.

Vee and I've been off with him and his brother Calder a few times. They're funny guys, and I know his brother likes Vee. It's been nice to get out some after being under Heath's thumb for so long. I don't constantly see my mother's dead body in my mind or remember how Dad hugged me goodnight the night of her death and how it had felt like goodbye. Looking back, I should have seen the signs. Begged him to wake up and realize a psychopath was in our home. Pled for him to not leave me.

But that girl, Hannah McPherson, stole everything from me.

I was too late.

Too naïve.

And now I'm all alone.

"Do you ever wish you could go back in time?" I question. "Say something that you should have said from day one?"

His eyes flash with understanding and he nods. "Every day." He bores his steel blue eyes into mine, trying to convey unspoken words. It makes me wonder what he regrets in this life.

"I miss my parents," I say sadly.

A wave crashes into us and we're both knocked off our boards. When we resurface and swim back to shallower waters, Ren grabs my wrist. He pulls me to him and my heart rate skitters in my chest.

Oscar always tries to kiss me, but I never let him. I wanted my first kiss to be special.

Ren's wet hand slides into my hair and he narrows his smoldering gaze at me. His nostrils flare slightly. I can see desire dancing in his eyes.

Ren Loveland wants me.

This time, my heart stops beating completely.

I've been crushing on this boy since I first saw him mow our grass. He's starred in countless dreams where he kisses me dizzy and steals me away. We've been out a few times as friends, but right now, nothing feels friendly at all.

This feels like way more than friends.

His mouth descends upon mine and his soft lips that taste salty like the Pacific crush against mine. He kisses me with a soft possessiveness that makes my heart kick start back to life. I moan when his tongue slides against mine. A simple swipe where he tastes me for the first time. Ren tastes minty with a hint of salt—like kissing the ocean on Christmas day.

I'm gasping for air by the time he releases me. His lips press one more soft kiss to my mouth before he pulls away. A satisfied half-smile plays on his lips.

"I like kissing you," he says and runs his thumb over my swollen bottom lip.

I slide my palms up the front of his chest to his neck and give him a naughty grin. "So do it again."

"Wake up, mi amor."

I groan and attempt to roll away from the sound. But then, soft lips start kissing my neck. At first it is sweet. A peck here, a peck there. Until it becomes hungry. Duvan suckles on my flesh and bites hard enough to make an embarrassing sound come from my throat. He somehow speaks to a primal part of me. I squirm from his kisses and turn to face him in the bed.

His dark hair is gelled and in one of his just-fucked hairstyles. Black irises, with a hint of purple, shimmer in delight. A slight dusting on his cheeks lets me know he skipped shaving this morning. With the afternoon sun pouring in, he's absolutely gorgeous.

If I were braver, I'd ask him to make love to me.

After the day I've had, I just want to be held.

"Stop giving me *fuck me* eyes," he says with a pained groan. "I promised I'd show you something, and it wasn't my dick I had in mind."

I laugh and it feels weird after all the sadness that had nearly consumed me earlier. "I wasn't making faces at you."

His smirk is immediate. "You made the same face when I was between your legs last night. Before I pushed into you and made you mine." He uses his thumb to swipe my bangs out of my eyes.

I'm glad he's back home. Earlier today, despite talking to my friends, I'd felt hollow and alone. Now I feel…

Complete.

"Nobody has ever done that to me before. It was…" I trail off, heat warming my cheeks.

"Something you want to do again?" he quips with a black, arched eyebrow.

I swat at him and he laughs.

"What, mi amor? Just like those hips tell me you love to eat, those eyes tell me you loved having my tongue between your legs."

When I go to protest, he grabs my hips and hauls me to him. His mouth crashes to mine in a fervent, needy kiss. Duvan is quickly filling a void I didn't realize existed. He takes his time kissing me while his hand roams up and down my body. I let out a whimper when his palm slips under my shirt. He groans when his hand cups my bare breast.

"No bra," he murmurs and pinches my nipple. "I like you this way."

I laugh and lean into his touch. My entire body is thrumming with the need to be consumed by him. He must read my body language because he begins kissing down my chin, along my jaw, and down my throat.

"Take your shirt off, tigress. I want to see your pretty tits," he instructs as his fingers dig into my lounge pants. He drags them off my body, along with my panties, while I tug off my shirt. Once I'm completely naked, I feel too exposed. My thighs rub together in an effort to hide and I place my palms over my breasts.

He sits up and works through the buttons of his dress shirt. I can't help but stare as he sheds both it and his white undershirt. His sculpted chest ripples like some fancy moving artwork as he undoes his slacks. The jingle of his belt reminds me of how Heath whipped me and has me shuddering. Thankfully, he pushes them down and I'm soon distracted by his massive cock.

I start to throb with pain just looking at it. I'm still sore from last night and I worry it'll hurt today.

"Look at me, mi amor."

Mi amor.

My heart does a flop.

His black eyes are nearly purple as they shine with adoration. He takes my right hand with his left and threads our fingers together. Then, he does the same for the other. My heart thunders in my chest when he leans forward, pressing our conjoined hands against the mattress on either side of my head.

"Spread your legs," he urges, his mouth teasing mine.

I swallow down the fear of pain before opening myself up to him. He doesn't enter me at first but instead rubs his veiny cock against my clit.

"Are you happy?" His murmured words cause my skin to erupt into a thousand goose bumps. "I am right now."

He hisses with pleasure with each stroke against me. I squirm with need. I'm no longer worried about the pain. I just want him inside me. Filling me. Completing me.

"Duvan, please," I beg.

The tip of his cock stops at my opening and he pokes me there. "You want this?"

I try to free my hands so I can grip his hair to pull him in for a kiss, but his hands tighten around mine. "I want this," I say with a whine of frustration.

His chuckle warms me to my soul. I'm dripping with desire for him. If he keeps rubbing against me, I'll come simply from that. But I want to come with him deep inside.

"Get ready, tigress."

That's his only warning before he slams his hips forward, shoving his thick cock all the way into me. The burn from last night is awoken, and I cry out in pain.

"Too much!"

But then his mouth is on mine, and he's kissing me like I'm the only person he'll ever do this with again. Like I belong to him and he belongs to me. The sensation throbbing from my heart is foreign, but I like the high that surges through me.

"Not enough," he argues, his hot breath tickling my lips.

He kisses me deeply as he thrusts into me over and over again. Each time he rubs against my clit as he slides into me, I get closer to the edge of bliss. I'm at his mercy and can't move my hands, but I feel safe. He's giving me what I want.

"Come for me, baby. Come all over this fat cock that was made just for you."

His words ignite flames that race through my veins. I'm high. I'm high off the feelings my husband evokes within me.

"Oh, God!" I shudder with pleasure and my thighs squeeze against his powerful hips.

He lets out an animalistic groan before his heat gushes into me. My sore pussy stings when his cock seems to throb even larger than before with his release. But soon it softens and I'm given relief. His fingers release mine and he cups my face.

"My Brie."

I give him a lazy smile. "Duvan."

Ren

Toni slaps me in the face, and I jerk awake. Her wide brown eyes twinkle with mischief.

"Teev. Nanna," she coos.

I hug her to me and kiss her soft curls. "You want a banana, Toto?"

Calder, Mom, and I have all taken to calling her Toto. She's so fucking cute but she's most attached to me. Mom is efficient with caring for her but she doesn't just hold her to hold her. I think she's afraid of getting attached. Thankfully, Dad came home yesterday. Toni was nervous around him but when he took her down to the beach before it got dark, she came back glued to him and remained that way for the rest of the night.

I was happy to get a break.

After the hell I went through with Brie, I haven't been in the mood for anything. I've dragged through the last couple of days as if I'm a damn zombie. I'd even resorted to trying to get Vee to talk to her. I met another one of the infamous Rojas brothers and much to my dismay I actually liked the guy. I'd wanted to hate their family because they took my girl from me.

But she's not my girl.

She made it very clear after we made love for the second time that she saw me as a lying monster. The pure look of devastation in her eyes was one I wish I could erase indefinitely from my mind.

"Teev, nose." Toni pokes at my nose and giggles. Her sweet laughter helps soften the ache in my chest.

"Toto, nose," I say back and tap hers.

My bedroom door opens and Mom waddles in. "Hey, kiddo. Did Toni sleep in here again?"

I nod, yawning. "She was crying in her bed, and I felt sorry for her."

Toni scrunches her face and her lip starts to quiver. "Dadda bye-bye."

Hugging her to me, I stroke her silky hair. "He'll be back," I lie. I have no idea if he will or not. He's not called since he dropped her off on our doorstep. Last night, Dad came clean to Mom about how he'd still been in contact with Gabe. About how he'd still been keeping tabs on Gabriella. Everything. She'd reacted better than I expected. Only a few tears.

"I made omelets, guys," Dad says, poking his head in the door. His eyes peruse Mom's pregnant belly and he grins before walking over to her.

She flashes him a smile back before stepping into his hug. "I'm so glad you're back home."

My parents are affectionate. A little too affectionate, if you ask me, considering Mom's pregnant again.

"Did somebody say food?" Calder questions as he saunters in past our parents and steals Toni from my lap. This kid is spoiled at our house.

"Yeah and it's going to get cold," Dad states. He kisses Mom on the head before leaving to finish up breakfast.

"Did you tell Mom about your broken heart?" Calder asks and then nuzzles his nose against Toni's cheek. She squeals and grabs his hair. He spends the next minute trying to pry her tiny fists from his head. Eventually, he peels her from him and holds her out like she's a bomb about to detonate.

"Who broke your heart?" Mom questions.

I flip Calder off, and he chuckles as he leaves the room carrying his little baby bomb with him.

I run my fingers through my messy bedhead and groan. "It's too complicated."

She sits down on the bed beside me and grabs my hand. "Apparently, I know complicated. I'm babysitting my death-evading rapist's baby who also happens to be my granddaughter. If that's not complicated, I don't know what is."

Mom has always comforted me. It's like she knows I've always been on my best behavior to take the load off of her since Hannah was such a handful. She's always had a special place in her heart for me because of it. Unspoken words and knowing smiles always told me she'd appreciated that I was a good kid.

Unfortunately, I'm not her good kid anymore.

"I fell in love with Gabe's daughter."

She pats my hand. "I think we all have. Toni is a sweet little thing. She reminds me of Hannah at this age."

I let out a sigh and turn to regard my mom. She's always been pretty. One of my good friends Kyler used to crush so bad on her. I told him he was sick because she's my mother. "Not her. Gabriella."

She stiffens and frowns at me. "The one your dad was keeping an eye on?"

"Yeah, I mowed the lawn where she lived. It was me keeping an actual eye on her."

Mason rolls in her stomach, and she pulls her hand away from mine to rub her belly. "Oh, Ren," she murmurs, tears welling in her eyes. "Why?"

I swallow down the emotion and shrug. "I didn't want to. I hated who she was at first. I hated that Dad asked me to do it. But then…"

"She's beautiful?"

"Yes." I remember how captivated I was when I first saw her. How all the irritation and resentment melted off of me like ice cream from a cone on a hot day. "I wanted to know the sad girl. Mom, she was so sad."

Guilt flickers in her eyes and she nods. "Your sister has ruined a lot of lives. She needs help. Hannah was getting the help she needed until he broke her out of there." She makes a sour face. I remember clearly when the detectives showed up at our door telling us about how an unknown man slipped in, slaughtered most of the night staff, and stole away my sister. Our entire family was sickened at the news.

"I spoke to her one day and from that moment on, I needed to know her. One day when she was swimming with her adopted sister in the backyard, I found the courage to ask her if she wanted to come hang out with Calder and I. It started out friendly. The four of us would go see movies or go to the beach. She was sweet and funny and brave."

Mom smiles. "I'm glad she's found some happiness. I'm sure it couldn't be easy for her to lose both parents. And then she had you."

A spike of guilt shoots through me. "I lied to her. If she knew I was Hannah's brother, I knew she wouldn't want to have anything to do with me. I told her my name was Ren Loveland. We never spoke about our families. Brie is guarded when it comes to her past. But even though she held back her emotions, I could see how she hurt from it. I hated Hannah for doing that to her, and that I had to lie to Brie."

"Oh, Ren," Mom says sadly. "I'm sorry you've been dealing with this. Did your dad know?"

I shake my head. "I told him what he needed to know but never that I was falling in love with her."

She leans her head against my shoulder. "Love is strange."

Letting out a sigh, I nod in agreement. "As I fell deeper for her, I hated the secret that hung in the air between us. I'd threatened Calder not to say anything. One day I was going to find a way to tell her." I pinch the bridge of my nose and squint my eyes. The pain in my chest is a dull throb. "Her adopted dad is someone vile. A criminal. He had arranged for her to marry into some Colombian drug family when she turned eighteen."

"What?" she snaps and looks up at me, concern washing over her features.

"He'd found out she and I had sex for the first time and he whipped her, Mom. He whipped her like she was some child, not practically a legal woman. I wanted to save her from it all. She's too innocent to get wrapped up in all that. Brie just wanted to go to college and have a normal life." I choke down the emotion threatening to make me cry. I've only cried once and it was when grandpa Land died about ten years ago.

"Does Gabe know all this?" she asks, astonishment in her voice. "He's not the type to let someone hurt what belongs to him."

I shake my head. "He doesn't know. Hell, I didn't know what was happening until a few days ago. I mean, I knew Heath was an asshole, but I never realized what was going on. She agreed to let me help her and wanted to be with me. I took her out for her birthday. Everything was perfect until…"

"Until it wasn't. She found out your secret," Mom whispers.

"She was fucking devastated. I broke her heart into a million pieces. And then she left. She ran off and married some punk named Duvan, flew off to Colombia, and hates me with every ounce of her being."

Mom sniffles and I'm shocked to see tears rolling down her cheeks. "Come here, baby." She hugs me to her and strokes my hair. "If you two had something, she'll come around. She's angry and upset. She feels betrayed by one of the closest people to her. I understand how it feels when you are victimized by someone else's lies and actions. It hurts deep. A cut that takes forever to stop bleeding. But even the deepest cuts do heal."

Toni comes running into the room with banana smeared all over her face. She has a mischievous grin that reminds me of my sister. Mom stands and scoops the messy toddler into her arms.

"Are you mad I betrayed you too?" I question, my voice hoarse.

Mom's blonde brows furrow together. "How could I ever be mad at you, son?"

"I fell in love with Gabe's daughter."

She sighs and kisses Toni on the head. "So did I, Ren. So did I."

"Are we going to get our asses kicked?" Calder questions as he eyes Heath's gigantic mansion from the passenger seat.

"Vee said he's with Camilo at the shipyard and will be for most of the day. Come on," I order as I climb out of the truck.

We both saunter up to the front door. When I go to knock, Vee answers the door. Her bright red hair has been curled into tight, spiral curls and her makeup is a little on the heavy side. The dress she is wearing looks like she bought it from a hooker.

"Ummm…." I can't help but gawk at her unusual appearance. "Are you okay?"

She frowns and her bottom lip juts out in a pout. Calder stiffens beside me. "I'm fine. Come in."

I turn to see Calder glaring after her. The lime green skintight dress she's wearing barely covers her small ass. He growls at me. "What the fuck is she wearing?"

Shrugging, I follow after her. She guides us up to her bedroom. When we enter, the kid Oscar from yesterday mumbles a "what's up" before turning his attention back to his phone. Calder folds his arms across his chest and gives Oscar the stink eye. I guess he's still bitter about Vee choosing the Colombian kid over him.

"You think you can get her to talk to me?"

Vee fingers one of her curls and scrunches her nose up. "Ozzy and I talked to her earlier. She was really broken up about what happened. I think we might be able to trick her into talking to you."

I groan and shake my head. "No. She's still too angry. Let her cool off and then maybe I can accidentally be here one day when you call her. I don't want to make things worse than they are."

Oscar sits up and grins. "Smart. You know our girl better than I thought. Brie can't stay mad forever. Trust me, I know. I've pissed her off thousands of times and she still loves me." He waggles his eyebrows at me. I should be irritated that he's close to her and his brother married her but I'm not. It only gives me relief that she's capable of forgiveness.

When I glance at Vee, her lips are in a pout as she stares at Oscar. Calder is tense as fuck and I'm afraid if we don't get out of here, he's going to beat this kid's ass over Vee.

"Calder and I were going to hit a sub shop and then hit the waves. You surf?" I ask Oscar.

"He sucks," Vee offers with a giggle but then starts digging through a drawer that holds bathing suits.

"I don't suck," Oscar groans.

"Well Ren's pretty awesome at it," she tells him, holding up two different bathing suits. "Turquoise or black?"

"Black," both Oscar and Calder say at once.

Her eyes light up and she beams. "I'll be right back. Try not to miss me too much." She gives a pointed look at Oscar and then shoots the same one to Calder before bouncing out of the room. Both guys stare after her. When Oscar looks over at Calder, I see it. A look of awareness. Two minutes ago, he couldn't give two shits about the girl that was practically begging him to look at her, yet now he's got a competitive gleam in his eye.

Calder fists his hands and stalks out of the room. "I'm waiting in the car."

"You're pretty badass at this shit," Oscar says after spitting out a mouthful of saltwater.

Calder and Vee are sitting side by side on the beach in deep conversation. His hand is in the sand behind her and she's leaning slightly toward him.

"My dad taught me how to surf," I tell him. What I don't tell him is that Dad would only do it super early in the morning before any beachgoers were present. The uninterrupted sound of the crashing waves seemed to soothe some of his OCD ways. It was definitely a coping mechanism for all the shit he'd been through. I'd eventually learned the basics from him. It was a time we could spend together alone without Mom or my siblings. Those quiet moments were ours. "Been doing it since I was a kid."

"The only thing Papá ever taught me was how to get a woman into my bed. He said," he tells me and lowers his voice to sound like his father. "You have to romance them, Ozzy. Wine and dine them. Tell them what they want to hear. Your mother always liked to be told she was a great cook. Most days, the food tasted like salted cardboard but I praised her cooking until the day she died. Women just want to be complimented and adored."

I laugh. "Your dad sounds funny."

His hand skims through the water beside him. "Papá is cool sometimes. Most times he's an arrogant prick. I'm used to him, though."

"Is he nice to Brie?"

He lets out a sigh. "He sees her as a tool. Both him and my oldest brother Esteban. I thought Duvan was that way too. But then..."

I wince at the idea of her being married to that criminal. "Then what?"

"He proved me wrong. Duvan sees her like I do. As a person. Funny and gorgeous and full of secrets that you can't help but want to uncover. She was my friend. I liked her too, you know." His eyebrows pinch together in pain. I hadn't realized it before, but he's apparently disappointed she's married to his brother. "I thought it would be me that my father chose. I hoped it would've been me anyway."

A flare of jealousy flickers inside me. "I loved her."

His eyes narrow and he challenges me with his stare. "I loved her too."

Vee's laughter can be heard over the waves and it breaks the tense moment.

"Is she safe with him?" I ask, my voice low.

His lips quirk into a half smile. "Duvan won't let a soul touch her. He'll do anything to protect her. I know my brother. It's what he does."

"What do you mean?"

"He took care of my friend Luciana when my brother Esteban hurt her. Claimed her as his own property, which meant she was untouchable. That's just how our family is. When you stake claim on something, our family respects that claim. Brie was Papá's decision but once my brother made his claim, she became safe from anyone, including Papá."

"What happened to Luciana?"

A flash of anger washes over him and he grunts. "Esteban was fucking her mother. Luciana's father works for Papá. He's very trusted and high up in command. When Luciana and I walked in on them, he turned into a monster. He strutted over to us completely naked after swiping his knife from his pants. Luciana's scream was horrifying. We weren't anymore than maybe eleven years old. She thought he was hurting her mother. Esteban kept telling her to shut the fuck up. When she didn't…"

He grips his board and growls.

"What?"

"He cut out her tongue, man."

I choke down the bile rising in my throat at that image. "Are you fucking kidding me?"

"He told both her mother and I that if we said anything to Carlos or Papá that he'd cut our tongues out too. The story he told them later was that he'd rescued her and I from some gang in the heart of the city but he was too late to keep them from hurting her. Carlos and Papá slaughtered six men who they thought were responsible. Esteban got away with it."

"But you just told me," I mutter.

"I also told Duvan. He watched over Luciana and when she turned sixteen, he hired her as his help. She lives in the apartment over his garage. She washes his laundry, cleans the house, and cooks for him. I still remember the murderous look on Esteban's face when Duvan smugly told him Luciana was his and under his protection."

A wave crashes behind me nearly knocking me off my board. "He'll protect Brie from him?" I may hate the dude but I met him. He was a scary motherfucker. If anyone can protect her from tongue stealing psychos, it would be him.

"He'd die before he let anything happen to either one of them. She's safe, Ren."

chapter
NINE

Brie

"Put these on."

Duvan hands me a pair of big rubber boots that are three times the size of my feet. He's still wearing the smug smirk that has kept my insides in constant turmoil since our exertions in the bedroom earlier. Afterward, he took me into the shower and washed me. It was intimate and I felt cherished.

"These are big," I tell him as I kick off my flip-flops.

"I ordered some in your size. They'll be here in a few days," he assures me with a wink.

My core throbs and I clench my thighs together. He's driving me crazy with how he can work me up with just a look. When we step outside, he grabs hold of my hand and we walk down to the barn. The chickens all strut around pecking and clucking.

"They're cute," I tell him.

He laughs and it scares a couple of them away. "They're dinner."

I gape at him in horror. "What? Why?"

"I'm kidding. Luciana uses the eggs but we don't slaughter them. They're like pets," he tells me with a grin and kisses me.

Relief floods through me. "Thank God."

He drags me through the barn showing me incubators for the eggs, a couple of horses, and where they keep the extra feed for the chickens. Duvan goes into great detail about what's involved in caring for the animals. I find myself focused on his smiling mouth as he gushes about the animals. He loves them. He's at peace here in his home.

"Why do those hens not have any feathers on their back?" I ask as I point to one.

He pulls me in front of him so that my back is against his chest. My heart rate quickens when he fists my hair and jerks my head back. I let out a needy moan that has his cock twitching against me.

"Because that's why."

"Huh?"

"The rooster pecks at the hen as he fucks her."

"Chickens fuck?!"

He laughs and the hot breath in my ear makes me crazy with need. "The rooster pulls at her feathers like I pull on your hair. Kinky bastards."

His palm slides to my pussy and he rubs me through my lounge pants.

"I can't get enough of your cunt, tigress. How am I supposed to work and help run a business when all I want to do is bury my dick in you at every turn?"

I let out a whimper. His fingers massage me expertly, and my panties grow wet from his touch.

"I threw out your pills."

Panic darts through me. "The white ones or the yellow ones?"

His laugh rumbles from behind me. "Not those, mi amor. Your birth control pills. I want to put a child in you. We're a family now. I want us to have children."

My mind races with his statement, but I let go of it for a moment to feel my orgasm consume me. Afterward, when I've practically turned into jelly in his arms, I twist to look at him.

"That seems fast, Duvan."

I haven't been around many babies in my lifetime. I wouldn't know what to do with one, much less having one rely on me. Not to mention, I barely know Duvan. The idea of carrying his child worries me.

"I'll convince you." His smile is dashing and boyish. It sends warm ripples of joy like arrows straight to my heart.

A smile tugs at my lips, despite my hesitancy. "You think so, huh?"

All I get in response is a knowing smirk and a wink. "Come on, I have something I want to show you."

I'd imagined he'd wanted to show me his tongue or something. Instead, he dragged me back into the house and took me to a locked basement.

"Are you going to lock me in your dungeon until I say yes to having your little tiger cubs?" I question.

He chuckles as he guides me down the dim stairway. "I'm going to show you my man cave." His fingers thread with mine, and I take comfort in his touch. A week ago, I'd have been terrified to willingly go into a dark basement with Duvan Rojas. Now, I'm wondering if there'll be a bed for him to fuck me on. "Besides," he says in a smug tone. "You won't have to say yes. It'll just happen."

I roll my eyes at his sure tone but don't hate the idea of having a child with him. It's progress I suppose. I just didn't expect it so soon.

Once we reach the bottom, he turns on another light. The smell of chlorine stings the inside of my nose and curiosity has me looking past him to find where it's coming from. On the far wall are three large, solid metal safes. They are surrounded by glass and a door fitted with a keypad.

"King Duvan is 007?" I say with a laugh and skim my fingers along the steaming water of the hot tub that bubbles in the center of the room. The left wall is a gigantic sectional sofa and on the right wall are cabinets, a refrigerator, and a sink. "This isn't a man cave, it's a bat cave!"

He shakes his head. "Have a seat."

I plop down on the comfortable sofa. He enters in a code that he doesn't try to hide from me and I watch as he opens the safe on the left. Inside is filled with blocks of powder. His product. And many prescription pill bottles. He gathers armfuls of stuff and then comes back into the room.

"What's all that? Are you trying to kill me?"

His eyes turn black and he shakes his head. "I would never hurt you. Nobody will ever touch you."

The earnest tone with which he says these words has me swallowing down my unease. "Okay."

He relaxes and holds a baggie to me. "This is our premium coke. Our cash cow, if you will. We make a fuck ton of money off the production and sale of this shit." His finger dips into the bag and then he tastes it. "You can tell the quality of cocaine just by tasting it."

His finger is once again coated with the dust but this time, he holds it to me. I narrow my eyes at him in question, but he simply nods for me to mimic him. Flicking my tongue out, I taste the bitter powder.

"Yuck."

He laughs. "You weren't complaining about it last night."

"That was different."

"Want a bump?"

The rush from last night is still fresh in my mind. I give him a small nod, and he hands me the little baggie. Like yesterday, I use my fingernail to scoop a bit of the powder up. Our eyes meet, and he watches me with intensity as I snort the powder. His smirk sets my nerves on fire and he takes the bag from me.

"These are roofies. They sell for a fuck ton on the street. Don't take those," he says with a stern look. "These are your pills that help you relax. Vicodin and Xanax. They're addictive so only take them when you need them. There are other pills similar to these in the safe."

I eye the pills and my heart feels like it's dancing inside of me. "Can I count them?"

He pins me with a smoldering know-it-all stare. "That bump of coke is working its magic, I see."

As soon as he hands me the two bottles, I dump them out into two piles. I count them three times to be sure. Forty-seven Vicodin and twenty-three Xanax. "What happens when you run out?"

He points to his safes. "I have plenty, and I can get more. Don't you worry about that."

"What are those?"

"Oxy," he holds up a bottle. "Probably too much on your little body so stay away from those." Then he shows me a bag of some crystals. "Crystal meth. I have a few friends I keep this around for. It'll fuck you up and make you claw your skin off. Don't ever fucking take it."

I nod in agreement.

He lifts another bottle. "This is the Ex. They're easy to find. Little yellow pills with smiley faces on them. You can have as many of those as you want, mi amor."

My heart flutters at his words.

"Can I have one now?"

His face breaks out into a smile. "They're yours. All of this is yours. If you make friends, you can sell it to them. If you want to use it, you can. It's your empire too. This is all for recreational use and has nothing to do with the business side. We have entire warehouses for that shit."

"Is that where you went this morning?"

He nods. "I'll take you there one day maybe."

His answer satisfies me. I continue my education of his drugs. "What's that?"

"That's heroin. It'll bliss you the fuck out. Pretty addictive. Years ago, I had a habit that got me sent to rehab." His eyebrows knit together as if he remembers the rough time. Oscar had mentioned it in passing and I can see it wasn't a pleasant part of Duvan's past. "You better stick to the small stuff, tigress."

I eyeball the heroin with a curled lip of disgust. "I don't do drugs."

"Sure, you don't." He snorts with laughter and plucks a yellow pill from the bottle. My lips part and I accept his offering without hesitation. *Okay, so maybe I do do drugs.* The pill is acrid on my tongue, and I'm thankful when he gets up to grab me a water bottle from the fridge. I swallow the pill and look at him in question.

"I'm showing you all this now because I want you to have fun while you can. Once I put a baby inside you, you have to stay clean. We'll lock this shit up for nine months and live a boring life," he says with a wicked gleam in his eyes.

My skin starts to tingle and I have the urge to take off my clothes. "I want to get in the hot tub."

While he gathers his drugs up to put back in the safe, I strip out of my clothes until I'm naked. I clumsily climb up the ladder and fall into the hot water. The bubbles seem to assault me in a way that's almost dizzying when accompanied with the Ex. I become fixated on one of the jets. The hot, powerful spray hits my thighs and I know exactly where I want it. I lift up so I can feel it on my clit. The moment it hits my super sensitive nerves, I cry out in pleasure. Soon, strong arms are wrapped around me from behind, pulling me against a hard chest away from the blissful bubbles.

"No," I complain.

But then his mouth is suckling on my neck and his fingers are applying more pressure between my legs than the water ever could. My eyes roll back in my head. I shudder with the need to come again.

"This feels good. I need more…"

"More what, baby?"

I'm frustrated until he sinks his teeth into my neck. A million explosions of pleasure detonate inside me.

"T-That. I need more of that."

He bites me again while pinching my clit roughly. It makes me squirm in his arms. I want it but I don't. Oh, God but I do.

"More…"

He twists me around in his arms. The moment my legs hook at his waist, he impales me with his sizeable cock. I moan when his hand goes to my throat. "I want to squeeze you here." His thumb and finger bite into my flesh, which sends more pleasure shocks through me.

"Do it, please," I beg.

His grip is powerful and strong. I'm completely at his mercy but don't fear anything. He makes me soar. He makes me feel safe and cared for.

"So fucking perfect," he snarls, his hands squeezing me to the point I can't breathe.

I fall limp in his arms and he thrusts his hips into me over and over again. My hands find his hair so I can grip onto him. His touch completes me. I want him to squeeze me until I break.

"More," I hiss out, blackness eating at my vision.

He reaches between us and pinches my clit so hard I sob. But as soon as the pain hits me, my orgasm obliterates my entire existence. I black out completely and ride off on this dark wave.

Something stings my cheek and I drag my eyes open.

"Jesus, fuck!" he rasps out. "I thought I killed you." His dick is still inside me and still hard.

"Did you come?"

He shakes his head and we become feral again. Our mouths attack each other as he climbs out of the hot tub with me in his arms. He lowers me down onto the sofa, our wet bodies soaking the fabric below.

"I want to own every piece of you," he mutters, his cock driving into me powerfully. "Every hole. Your entire soul."

"You're a romantic," I tell him with a giggle.

He growls as he hooks my legs over his shoulders. When he thrusts this time, I can feel him deep in my stomach. "How can I make you happy?"

I stare into his dilated eyes and bite my lip. "Duvan, I think I am happy."

His mouth crushes mine, and we kiss until the darkness steals me away.

Each day gets easier than the last. Duvan spoils me with presents and food and pleasure. I've spoken to Oscar and Vee regularly. And the hole in my heart lessens with each passing moment. I am happy right now.

Luciana and I have figured out how to communicate. She has a phone so we text. The girl is actually quite funny. I was shocked when she confessed she always had a crush on Duvan. She'd been prepared to hate me but then said I was too nice to hate.

I'm definitely happy.

What Duvan doesn't know is I dug my birth control pills out of the trash. He's been super eager to get me pregnant while I, however, am not so keen on the idea. I keep the pills hidden underneath all of my bras in my drawer. It's not him, it's me. The idea of getting pregnant so fast scares me. What if Duvan grows bored of me after a few months? I'd hate to think how messy that would be if I were pregnant with his child.

He's been at the warehouse all day. Even though I asked to see it, I think he's avoiding taking me there. I'm beginning to go stir-crazy being cooped up in the house. If I didn't think Duvan would have an aneurism, I'd take a walk through the city. But he warned me of the dangers. Of enemies lurking about. So, instead, I pine for him all day while he's gone and try not to drive Luciana crazy with my questions about the family. The only things she won't tell me are anything about Esteban or why she's mute.

When my phone rings, I nearly fall out of my chair scrambling to answer it.

"Hello?"

"Tigress," Duvan growls, and I'm instantly overcome with desire for him.

"When will you be home?"

He lets out a sigh. "I have some business to take care of tonight. Some associates are coming over. Esteban too."

I cringe at the mention of his brother. "You didn't say he was coming back."

"Esteban cut his American trip short. He flew in this morning. We had some theft issues that we had to deal with," he explains. "I need you to listen to me."

His tone grows icy, and it makes me freeze. "Sure."

"Remember what I said about enemies?"

I swallow. "They can't know your feelings?"

"You're my wife on paper. Nothing more than a business transaction," he bites out harshly. "Someone to sink my cock into at night when I'm tired of the whores."

Tears well in my eyes and I blink them back. "W-What?"

"That is how I will have to talk to you," he says softly, a twinge of regret in his voice.

Understanding washes over me. I've been living in my happy bubble for enough time now that I completely forgot the fact that I'm married to a dangerous man. Another reason to keep taking my birth control.

"So you'll treat me differently in front of them."

"Remember how you used to hate me?"

My heart aches at the Duvan I once knew making a reappearance. "I didn't like *him*."

"Tonight you will hate *him*."

A shiver washes through me. "Are you going to hurt me?"

"What? Jesus, fuck, no," he grumbles. "I just can't let them see what you mean to me. They'll expect you there for dinner, but then I want you to feign a headache or something. Go upstairs to bed and keep the door locked. Do you understand, tigress? This is so fucking important."

The hairs on my arms prickle in apprehension. "I understand, D."

"Good," he says in a relieved tone. "Will you wear a sexy dress for me?" His tone is soft and sweet, completely unlike the tone in which Heath used to order me what to wear. I actually want to please this man.

"I'd rather wear nothing," I tease.

He growls again and it sounds deeper through the phone line. "I'll strip you down soon enough."

chapter
TEN

Brie

After hanging up with Duvan, I spent a lot of time dressing up for him. I'd actually put on makeup whereas the rest of this week as his wife I went clean faced. I even styled my hair almost as nicely as Mario did it at the salon. The dress I selected is black and short. It is tight at my breasts with a low scoop neck and poofs out like a little girl's dress on the bottom half. A bright pink sash tied just under my breasts completes the look. I'm not ready to wear the matching pink pumps so I opt for flip flops until our company arrives.

While waiting, I log into my computer to see if Oscar or Vee are on. I'm shocked when I see an email in my inbox from Ren. My heart throbs in my chest and I swallow down the bitterness. What could he possibly want from me? We have nothing more to say to one another.

Curiosity gets the best of me, and I open the email.

Brie,

I'm sorry. So sorry. I know you'll never forgive me, and quite frankly, I don't deserve your forgiveness. But what I would like is your friendship. A fresh start. I'm not like her. What my sister did to your family has disgusted me from day one. She ruined what we could have had. I'll never forgive her for that. Mostly, I wanted to let you know I've been hanging out with Vee and Oscar. Oscar's pretty cool. He surfs better than Calder. Calder has the hots for Vee but she's obviously not into him. It feels weird, all of us hanging out without you. Empty. Different. Everyone feels your absence and nobody likes it. Wherever you are, I hope you're safe and cared for. I know you've moved forward with Duvan and I can respect that. But I can't let you out of my life. This isn't even about me. It's about you. You deserve friends who care deeply for you. You and I had something beyond attraction. Beyond friendship. I know you felt how both of us would come alive in the presence of each other. As hard as it is, I've come to accept it will only ever be one-sided. I'll always be your Romeo, even though you'll never be my Juliet. But please at least be my friend.

Ren

Just one letter, hearing his voice through his words, and I'm aching with sadness. It wasn't fair that our budding romance was stolen from us because of his lies. But would I have ever given him the time of day had I known the truth from day one? Most certainly not.

God, why is my life so complicated?

Ren,
I'm safe.
I'm happy.
Duvan is good to me.
Tell Calder I said hi.
Brie

I was probably nicer than I should have been, but he's right. When I was at one of my darkest moments at Heath's house, it was Ren who showed up looking every bit the part of Prince Charming and shone light back into my life. Without him, I'm back in the darkness.

At least Duvan holds me in his warm arms in the darkness.

Ren responds almost immediately.

Brie,

Thank you. Thank you for responding. I'm always here if you want to talk. We can even Skype if you need to. Any time. I'll make time for you, Brie.

Ren

I let out a relieved sigh. I don't know why a weight feels as though it's been lifted, but I suddenly feel lighter. So light I could float away. Snapping the computer shut, I stand quickly and scan my office. My posters I'd ordered arrived yesterday. Now, *The Breakfast Club* and *Dirty Dancing* posters adorn the walls. It feels a little bit homier.

I'm staring at Patrick Swayze when I hear commotion downstairs. It sounds chaotic and boisterous. Sounds like the party has arrived. Luciana spent all afternoon cooking for tonight. Her anxiety levels were palpable and it's times like these that I wish she could speak. I check my makeup before slipping my heels on. With an excitement to see Duvan, I clomp down the stairs in record speed. The moment I enter the living room which is filled with cigar smoke and full of scary men I don't recognize, I freeze.

Every single pair of wolfish eyes devour me. Neither Esteban or Duvan are in here. My excitement is extinguished as fear overwhelms me.

"*¿Quieres chupar mi pinga, puta?*" one of the men hisses and he grabs his crotch in a vulgar manner.

I take a step backward and put my palms up. "Um, *yo no hablo a español muy bien.*"

That's the only phrase I can actively recall from my Spanish homeschool studies.

"I said," the man says in a thick accent. "Want to suck on my dick, whore?"

"She's not a whore, Santiago," Esteban's familiar deep voice growls. "That is Duvan's wife."

Santiago eyes me up and licks his lips in a salacious way. "Duvan shares his pussy. Where is Luciana anyway?"

I perk up at the mention of her and frown. "Duvan and Luciana slept together?" A twinge of jealousy ripples through me. As soon as the words leave my mouth, I want to wrangle them back in.

Esteban closes in on me, and I flinch at his proximity. His black eyes are cold, slithering over me. The long scar along the side of his face shimmers like a silver snake from the overhead light. He always wears his hair clipped close to his head and a neatly trimmed beard does nothing to hide the sharply chiseled jaw he shares with his two brothers. He leans down, inhaling my hair much like a panther would the moment before he eats his smaller, weaker prey. "No, but he lets these guys fuck her from time to time."

"Oh," I squeak out.

He leans in and whispers in my ear, his hot breath not warming me at all. In fact, it sends chills racing down my spine. "I don't fuck her because she's useless to me without a tongue."

A shudder ripples through me. "W-What?"

"Bitch got what she deserved."

The blood in my veins turns to ice. I'm frozen in my spot when Duvan rounds the corner. He notices my dress first, his black eyes flickering with appreciation. But then he eyeballs his brother who looks like he's about to maul me. All it takes is one fiery gaze from Duvan, and I know he's shown all of his cards in the blink of an eye. One of the men sniggers. Another mutters something about tearing up that pussy. And Esteban pats me on my ass. "Good girl," he murmurs.

I try not to run into Duvan's arms. Instead, I approach him with hesitation, my eyes lowered to the floor. When I reach him, he takes my hand.

"This is my new wife. We're now connected to the Berkleys in San Diego. Coke production is about to increase tenfold as we expand our trafficking in the US," he tells them blandly, as if they all should know. "Getting hitched to a tight teenage cunt isn't half as bad as I thought it would be."

The men laugh at my expense. I remain silent with my head bowed.

"Looks like love to me," Esteban says with a cruel laugh.

Duvan shrugs his shoulder. "I love when my cock is buried in her tight ass."

I clench my butt cheeks and a shudder passes through me. The men laugh at me again.

"Um, I'm going to see if Luciana needs any help," I peep out and turn to leave.

Duvan's grip bites into my bicep and he glares coldly at me. "You're not the help, Gabriella." His menacing stare has my anxiety spiking. He promised me it would be this way. All part of the act.

"Please don't hurt me again. I'm still sore from the last time," I whisper.

I can pretend. I pretended all the time with Heath. Putting up a mask and hiding is what I'm good at.

Santiago hears and whistles like he's proud of Duvan. "If you ever need help keeping the bitch in line, me and Pablo love a little tag-teaming." Pablo, another scary-ass-looking man, licks his lips and winks at me.

They're all men here.

I'm nothing but a little girl way out of her league.

Duvan grabs my wrist and jerks me over to a chair. He sits, then tugs me into his lap. His hand grips my hair and he yanks me back so he can reach my ear. "Mrs. Rojas, run your sexy ass along and bring us some blow. The good stuff we like."

He lets go of me, pushing me back out of his lap. The men's hungry glares are on me as I hurry away from them. On my way to the basement, I nearly run right into Luciana. Her brown eyes are wide. She's frantic. Terrified.

"Did Esteban cut your tongue out?" I demand with a hiss.

Tears well in her wide brown eyes and she nods. When she opens her mouth and shows me a small nub, all that's left of her tongue, I feel bile rising in my throat.

"Oh, my God," I whisper, taking her cheeks in my palms. "I'm so sorry. I had no idea."

She sniffles and touches my nose before pointing to the basement, worry flickering in her eyes. "Beh."

"I know," I assure her. "I'll get them what they want. We're not done discussing this."

The men laugh loudly in the other room causing the both of us to jump. She grabs my shoulders and pushes me toward the basement. "Beh," she says, pointing.

With a nod, I hurry down the steps careful not to trip in my heels. The chorine-scented air immediately calms me. It reminds me of all the times Duvan and I've had sex in the hot tub. Mostly it's been after taking the ecstasy because it just amplifies the effect. But, we did make gentle love in it a time or two which was nice too.

I quickly push the buttons on his keypad and am granted access into his safe room. Like I've seen him do many times, I open the safe that houses what he's asked for. My hands shake so much I end up knocking several bottles onto the floor. Thankfully they don't pop open and spill. I grab a Xanax for myself to calm my nerves. Once I swallow it dry, I grab what Duvan's asked for and hurry out of the safe room.

When I exit, my eyes lock with Esteban's. He's leaned against one of the posts in his expensive suit wearing a stupid, knowing smile. I hate that he thinks he has something on Duvan. Lifting my chin, I try not to let him see my fear of him. He's like a dog chasing a scared kid—once he knows you're afraid, he'll give you something to be afraid of.

"Little Brie," he says in a low grumble. "All grown up and playing wife. Queen of the Colombian Cocaine Cartel. Aren't you just so fucking sweet?"

I swallow and pin him with a fierce glare. "I'm not sweet, Esteban. I'm so goddamned sour you'll want to cut your *own* tongue out."

At this, he bellows with cold laughter. "Speaking of," he snarls and grips my jaw in his brutal grip. "Let me see that sour tongue of yours."

The tray of cocaine and paraphernalia rattles in my hands.

He leans forward and nuzzles his nose against mine. "Shhh," he murmurs. "I'm not trying to scare you. Just show me, and I'll let you run along upstairs, so you can continue your charade."

I stick my tongue out at him and lightening quick, he latches onto it with his finger and thumb.

"Ahh!" I cry out, nearly dropping the tray.

He steadies it with his free hand, narrowing his eyes at me. "Don't drop that or Duvan will be furious, sourpuss." My grip tightens. "You see this?" He lets go of the tray and I hear the switch of a blade. The shiny silver glints in the light as he waves it in front of me. "This was the blade I used to saw that piece of shit tongue of hers from her mouth. The little bitch cried. She struggled. And she bled so much I was sure she would die from blood loss." The tip barely scrapes along my raised taste buds, scratching them just slightly. A coppery taste fills my mouth in its wake. "Luciana crossed me, and I showed her what happens when someone pisses me off. Do you want me to show you what happens when *you* piss me off?"

I shake my head and the blade pokes me. It stings and a trickle of blood slides down my throat. The reflex to gag is strong, but I hold it in my throat for fear of swallowing with the sharp object pressed against my tongue.

"Then don't act like I'm stupid and don't see what I see. There's more to the picture that you aren't aware of, sourpuss." He slips the knife out of my mouth and licks my blood from it. "Mmm, you do taste sweet."

He releases my sore tongue and I swallow the blood in my mouth. The tray remains in my death grip. I'm sure Duvan would forgive me but I don't give Esteban the satisfaction of seeing my terror.

"Funny," I tell him as I storm away from him. When I get to the bottom of the steps, I give him a bored look. "Heath told me the same thing when he threatened to slit my throat. A bunch of big 'ol lions intimidated by a little tigress." I blow him a kiss and stomp up the stairs.

By the time I deliver the drugs to Duvan and sneak back into the kitchen with Luciana, I'm feeling woozy. I hadn't eaten much for lunch so the Xanax is hitting me hard. My limbs feel heavy. Everything is beginning to tingle its way to numb. And the room keeps tilting.

"Luciana," I mutter. "I need to eat something."

Her black brows knit together in concern. She abandons the stove to look me over. Then, she looks up at me in question. She makes a motion of putting something into her mouth and swallowing before questioning me with her eyes.

"Xanax," I tell her, sliding to the floor onto my butt and leaning against a cabinet. "They don't usually make me feel so out of it."

Panic washes over her and she darts her gaze to where the voices are being loud in the living room.

I hold up my hand stopping her. "Don't go get him. He'll be worried, and they'll see that. Please don't mess this up for us."

Understanding dawns in her eyes and she nods with a frown. She busies herself making me something. When she sits down beside me, she spoon-feeds me some hot rice that goes with the meal she's preparing. At least the rice should soak up some of the medicine.

She's still fussing over me when the basement door opens and Esteban steps into the kitchen. His eyes zero in on me on the floor, a predatory look in them. Luciana scrambles away, clearly terrified beyond reason, and gets back to her cooking. My eyelids feel heavy.

I close them once.

When I reopen them, I'm in Esteban's arms.

I close them again.

And then were descending the stairs.

I close them again.

This time, I'm on the sofa.

"What did you take, sourpuss? Did you accidentally roofie yourself?" he questions, his tone cold and cruel.

My mind flits back to the pills. I thought I grabbed the Xanax. Could I have grabbed something else? I remember what the roofies looked like so that wasn't it.

"I kind of like you down here at my mercy. You can't mouth off when you can't talk. I bet I could fuck that tight ass that we both know Duvan hasn't touched and you'd hardly utter a peep. I bet I could shove my cock down your throat until you suffocate and you wouldn't even fight me off."

My heart rate quickens at his words but I feel numb and useless.

His hand palms my thigh. I can't even feel it, but just the thought of him touching me scares me to death.

"If you can't feel that, then we're going to have some fun while your dear husband entertains his guests. What do you think? We probably have a good twenty minutes until Luciana finishes dinner. What sort of trouble can we get ourselves into in the meantime?"

I watch through half-lidded eyes as he pushes my dress up. His hand disappears underneath and I'm thankful I can't really feel what he's doing. But I do feel pressure. He's pushed his finger or fingers into my pussy.

Every bone feels heavy and worthless. A tear leaks out of my eye but I can't stop whatever terrible things he has planned. The pressure is suddenly gone. He then tugs my panties down my thighs. Once they're off, he inhales them before pocketing them.

"Let's see what has my brother so fucking obsessed with you," he says through clenched teeth.

I'm afraid to close my eyes so I glare at him as he pulls my legs apart.

"So pink and tight. I can see the allure," he states. Esteban wiggles three fingers at me before pushing them inside me. A small, terrified whimper escapes me. It seems to light up the deviant fire in his eyes. When he pulls them out, he sucks on them. "I'm going to give you something you will love."

I nearly pass out when I hear the jingle of his belt. He doesn't undo his pants but instead slips the leather from the hoops of his slacks and lays it on the couch beside me. And then he disappears.

Shit!

I'm praying that Luciana ignores my wishes and tells Duvan. If he knew I was alone with Esteban, I doubt he'd be up there partying.

My adrenaline has spiked, which has me much more alert than moments before. Even though I feel numb, a buzz of electricity seems to course through me. If I could just make my legs work. I find some strength and roll onto my side. He's still out of sight. With a groan, I work to slide my lifeless hand under me. It obeys, so I start to push up on it. I'm still attempting to right myself when a pair of dark slacks appear in my vision. He reaches down and strokes my hair out of my eyes before pulling my arm back out from under me, causing me to hit the cushions with a thud. Esteban sits beside me next to my head, but I don't make out what he's doing. Just sounds. Crackling of a bag. Flick of a lighter. I'm once again trying to sit up when he yanks my arm up above my head.

The jingle of the belt confuses me. Pressure wraps around my bicep. I twist my head up slightly but can't make out what he's doing.

"Get ready to feel so good, sourpuss," Esteban tells me, his voice gritty.

I feel a slight pinch followed by warmth. The warmth travels up my arm as if he's let loose a snake under my skin. It wiggles its way through me, creating a blissful wake behind it. I start to black out as Esteban stands. I know I'm supposed to be worrying what he plans to do to me but all I can think about is this glorious sensation powering through me. I want it to reach my toes. I want to bathe in it.

"Mmmm." It's all I can manage as the warmth devours my entire being.

I want to fuck the warmth.

To have its babies.

To roll around in it and taste it.

"Sourpuss," Esteban snaps, causing my eyes to jerk open. He lifts my legs and sits on the sofa. Then he drapes them over his lap. I'm wondering what he'll do but I'm too dazed to worry. I blink lazily at him as he picks up the remote and turns on the television across the room. It's still paused from where Duvan and I started watching *Dirty Dancing* the night before last. Esteban hits play, and I'm consumed by happy memories of my father.

"I can dance like that," Daddy says, peeling a strip of rope from his red licorice. He turns to waggle his eyebrows at me.

I curl up my lip and don't believe it for a second. Not even my sixth-grade music teacher can dance like that and he knows how to do the Moonwalk. "Liar."

Daddy laughs and swats the candy at me. I steal it and stick out my tongue. When "Love is Strange" starts playing, Daddy stands up and holds his hand out to me. I stick my tongue out so he starts dancing into the middle of the living room by himself.

"Sylvia," he says.

I laugh. "You're dumb, Daddy."

"Oh, Sylvia!"

I'm giggling so hard that Momma comes from the kitchen to laugh at us. When Daddy sees her, he motions for her like Patrick Swayze does in the movie. Momma shakes her head at him and tosses the dish rag onto the couch before sashaying over to him.

"Yes, Mickey?" Momma says.

They proceed to mimic my favorite part of the movie word for word. Daddy wasn't lying. He's got the moves and so does Momma. I'm so giddy to watch them dance together that when he hauls me to him, I don't fight him despite not knowing how to dance. He grabs both my hands and gives me a smug grin. "Told ya, Silvia. Hop on and see how it's done."

With a smile that hurts my face, I stand on Daddy's bare feet. He moves us effortlessly around the living room spinning and dipping me until I'm dizzy with happiness. When the scene finally ends, he kisses my forehead. "Never doubt your dad."

I hug him. "I love you, Daddy."

"I love you too, Sylvia."

"You like this," Esteban tells me and motions at the television I'm smiling at.

I nod and it makes me sleepy. My mind craves to chase my dad back into the shadows of my memories.

Esteban laughs, and it doesn't sound so evil right now. When I drag my gaze back to him, he's stroking my thigh while he watches the movie with me like we're a couple. Where he touches me feels like fire, which makes me squirm.

"Shh," he says, his hand sliding up between my legs and brushing my clit, "this is the best part."

My eyes roll back in my head and I lose myself to the movie. I'm in it. I'm no longer in Colombia. I'm no longer in the basement. Instead, I'm Sylvia and Daddy is Mickey and we're dancing like we were born to do it. The bliss courses through me, but a familiar, beautiful sensation builds at my core. When I find the strength to open my eyes, Esteban is watching me like a hawk. His fingers work me between my legs. I want to stop him, I think. I'm so confused.

The memory has left me high on happiness.

And with the way Esteban is touching me, I stay in a blissful cloud.

I wish it were Duvan, though. My husband. A giggle escapes me. I miss him. My laughter dies and tears roll down my cheeks. Esteban chases my sadness with more pleasure. When I close my eyes, I imagine how Duvan touches me. So reverent. But when I try to see his face in my vision, he morphs into Ren.

Ren's steel blue eyes are imploring me to forgive him.

He takes my virginity over and over again.

I come hard each time.

A groan jerks me from my white cloud and Esteban is glaring at me. He shows me his glistening hand before forcing his wet fingers into my mouth. My sore tongue stings from his touch.

"Take a little nap, sourpuss."

He pulls away from me and stalks out of the basement without another backwards glance. Dragging my eyes to the television, I lose myself in another one of my favorite movies.

I can't nap though. It's my favorite part...

"Baby," I sing. "Oh, baby..."

Brie

"Shhh," the voice whispers in the black shadows. I'm in my bed, but it's so dark. Something tightens around my arm.

"Duvan?" I croak.

A hand cups my breast over my dress and squeezes painfully. I'm sore between my legs which causes panic to skitter through me.

"Relax," Esteban says, his familiar voice making itself known. "I can feel your heart racing. You'll go into cardiac arrest if you don't calm down."

My entire body aches and I'm on edge. I feel as though I'm needy. But for what, I'm not sure. "Duvan!" But the sound coming out isn't loud at all. It's a hoarse whisper.

"You two must have had quite the story planned out before we got here because as soon as I told Duvan you weren't feeling well in the basement, he seemed relieved to fetch you and put you to bed. Now he's having a grand fucking time getting wasted downstairs. My brother forgets I have keys to every room in his home."

"D-Did you rape me?"

Esteban laughs, the chill sobering up my body quickly. "Not yet, sourpuss."

"No," I hiss.

He strokes my hair. "You'll beg for it soon enough. I won't have to force you."

"Duvan!" My croak is louder.

"You want more, don't you? It's been a few hours since your hit. I can tell you're craving it already. Funny how the shit just takes you by the throat and doesn't want to let go," he says softly.

The lamp flicks on and the bright yellow light has me squinting. I groan and try to sit up. He fiddles with something on the nightstand. Then, I hear the familiar sounds from earlier. They unlock something inside of me. A hungry animal that wants more. When he turns to give me an evil grin, I don't shy away from him.

"What is it?" I manage to ask.

He brings his face close to mine and breathes hot breath that smells like whiskey in my face. "Heroin."

I shake my head. "I don't do drugs."

He growls as he tightens something around my arm. "You do now."

His eyes find mine as he jerks my arm to him. I watch in a brief moment of horror as he presses a needle into my flesh. When he depresses the warmth into my vein, I frown at him.

"Why?"

He smiles. "Because you were supposed to be mine. This empire was supposed to belong to me. But all of that was ruined. Now it's time to fix things."

Heat surges through me, and I let out a breath of relieved air. "You and Heath are working together?"

He stiffens and grabs my jaw. "What the fuck are you talking about?"

"Bad men…"

The heated bliss has me fading fast.

Searching for Daddy.

And Duvan.

And Ren.

I'm looking for the good men. Where are they?

Esteban grunts and soon I hear the door slam behind him. I chase my dancing daddy into the darkness…

"How you feeling, tigress?"

Duvan.

It's daylight and I'm confused. "Hmmm."

"You really did have a migraine," he says, regret in his tone. "I thought you were pretending like we talked about. I'm so sorry I didn't get you something for the pain."

My body thrums with need. I had something for the pain last night. Esteban gave it to me.

"Did you convince them?" I question.

"I did." His lips find my neck and he kisses me softly, suckling my flesh between his teeth. I yelp out when he touches me between my legs. He stiffens and murmurs into my ear, "Did I hurt you?"

I could tell him what Esteban did but everything is so confusing and hazy. Would he kill Esteban? Worse yet, would he kill me?

My mind replays to the way Esteban touched me. I remember coming all over his fingers. Oh, my God, I enjoyed his assault. Guilt has me swallowing down my confession.

"I need you," I beg Duvan. If he will just fuck the memory away, I can better assess how to tell him what happened. I'm not sure I can even tell him though.

Duvan undresses me—he's already naked—and then he's inside my sore pussy. He grunts as he drives into me. I can't look into his perfect purple-black eyes. Instead, I stare out the window.

He makes love to me, and after a long shower together, he's gone. The guilt running through my veins is enough to want to make me throw up. Luciana is nowhere to be found. I find myself downstairs and staring into the safe on a hunt for what Esteban gave me last night. It takes a bit but eventually I find a baggie of brown crystals. I know from the movies you somehow cook it before you send it into your veins. But I have no idea how to do any of it. Just seeing it there in a form I can't utilize has me angry and on edge. I shove everything back into the safe, ignoring the shakes. Once I'm upstairs and in my office, I call Oscar.

"Brie!" he answers with an excited chuckle. "I missed—what the hell happened to you?" His dark brows are furled together in concern on the screen.

"I'm not feeling well."

He lifts a skeptical eyebrow. "Did my brother do something to you?"

If you only knew…

"Duvan didn't hurt me," I tell him in a firm tone.

His gaze softens before turning murderous. "Esteban?"

Tears well in my eyes and I divert my gaze. "I'm fine."

"What the fuck did he do?"

Our eyes meet, and I shake my head. "Nothing, Ozzy."

The front door slams downstairs, and I slam my laptop closed without saying goodbye. Rushing down the stairs, I hurry to meet Duvan. Thank God I couldn't figure out the heroin because he would have walked right in on me.

"Did you forget something?" I ask in a cheery tone, hoping to mask my unease.

But it isn't Duvan standing in the entryway. It's Esteban.

"I came to give you what you need."

My heart skips at his words. "I don't need anything from you."

He shrugs and saunters past me toward the kitchen. The basement door slams shut, and he's gone. I wait for ten whole minutes for him to return. Standing idle makes me think too much. I think about finding my mother. The blood. Her blue flesh. Her dead eyes. I think about a psycho stealing my daddy's love from me. I think about how Ren broke me with his lies. I think about how I betrayed Duvan—my husband—when Esteban shoved his fingers inside of me.

A deep ache forms in my chest.

I'm almost in a daze as I open the basement door, willingly about to step foot into hell with the devil. Fear consumes me, but it isn't until I hear familiar eighties music playing downstairs from the television that I start clambering down the steps. When I get to the bottom, I see Esteban sitting on the couch with the drugs next to him.

The need inside me starts to fester and crawl.

I want to claw right through my chest to rip it from me. I hate the way he gives me a familiar, knowing smirk that disarms me like Duvan's does. This man touched me against my will. Made me cheat on my husband. Forced drugs into my system. Cut the tongue from my friend's mouth.

And yet here I am sitting on my knees beside him on the sofa.

Here I am dragging my gaze from his to stare at the television.

Here I am offering my arm to this monster.

"I'm not so bad, sourpuss," he says.

But he's worse than bad.

"Wait," I blurt out, drawing my arm back to me. "I can't do this."

"Nobody's telling," he says, his hand patting my thigh.

I close my eyes. He takes my arm gently which only angers me. Why would he be nice right now?

"I hate you," I seethe under my breath.

The needle bites into me, and I let out a moan as soon as the heat enters my system. He pulls me into his lap and hugs me to him, the needle still dangling from my flesh. His breath tickles the side of my neck. "You need me. And I need you. This was supposed to be ours."

A tear rolls out as the bliss fully overtakes my body. I relax against him. He doesn't touch me sexually thankfully but he's affectionate, which feels even worse.

"Now tell me about Heath's plan, sourpuss."

I swallow and remember the way Heath threatened my life. "He seems to believe I won't be here for long. That I'll be back with him." Frustration chases away my high and I let out a sob. "It's not working."

His palms roam my breasts through my clothes, and I can feel his erection beneath me. "I'll give you more after you tell me what his plans are."

I turn my head to frown at him. "I don't know, but he scared me."

He softens his gaze before running his fingers through my hair. "I believe you." His lips press to the side of my mouth. "Such a good girl. I'm going to take your pants off."

The panicked look I give him makes him chuckle. "The vein in your thigh is better, sourpuss. Get your head out of the gutter."

Shame washes over me as he lays me onto the couch. I keep my head turned toward the television so I don't have to focus on what he's doing. My pants—and panties, for that matter—get yanked down my legs. I'm disgusted with myself, that I've stooped to befriending Esteban so he'll get me high. When a jolt of pleasure shoots through me, I glare at him.

"No."

His smile is devilish as he pinches my clit again. "Do you want me to leave?"

I close my eyes and have the urge to kick him. "No."

"I didn't think so."

Tears stream from my eyes as he massages me. I hate that my body responds to his touch—that the need to orgasm is almost as intense as the need for him to shove that damn needle into my leg.

I refuse to beg him but I have to bite down on my bottom lip to keep that promise to myself. When he ceases his ministrations just as I get close to coming, I curse at him. But he stops to drop more crystals onto the spoon. I swear my entire body jolts with the need to shake him so he'll hurry the fuck up. My mind fades in and out of this reality as he cooks the drugs. And after what feels like an eternity later, I distantly feel him dragging the needle along my thigh. He pinches my clit with his free hand and gives me a conspiratorial grin.

"Ready to lose your motherfucking mind, sourpuss?"

With a twist of my clit and a poke to my thigh, he makes good on his promise. I lose control as an out of this world orgasm compliments the best high I've ever known. I'm lost in my own blissful haze as he cleans up the mess and walks away.

And now, my only thought isn't about Ren or Daddy or Duvan.

It's about Esteban.

And when the fuck will he come back?

When I wake up, I'm groggy and sore. Shame and regret nearly cripple me. I'm both extremely thankful and sickly sad that Esteban isn't down here with me. I find myself climbing the stairs on shaky legs on a hunt for him. As soon as I burst through the kitchen door, I find Luciana crying. Her entire body shakes.

"What's wrong?" I demand, my voice hoarse.

She stares at me in horror. I realize I must look a sight with only a shirt on. Jesus, I didn't even put any pants back on! He's fucked me up so hard with this shit, I can't even think straight. When I look at the clock, I realize I've slept most of the day away downstairs. Luciana is sporting a bright red bruise on her cheek that's fading into purple.

"Did he hurt you?"

Her shaky fingers go to her mouth and she makes a motion of zipping her lips. Anger bubbles inside of me.

"Where is he?"

She once again does the stupid zipping motion and I want to throttle her. Instead, I hobble back downstairs to search for my pants. I'm just picking them up off the floor when I hear his voice behind me.

"Looking for me?"

"What are you doing to me?! What did you do to her?" I scream, throwing my pants at him.

He ducks and his gaze peruses my body as he stares at my naked bottom half. "I *fucked* her because you don't want me *fucking* you. At least not yet."

"I-I need to call Duvan," I mutter, my hands shaking violently. "This is messed up. This is out of control."

He stalks forward. "He's being detained."

"What?"

"A fire at the warehouse. He's quite busy."

I run my fingers through my hair. "You need to leave, Esteban. JUST FUCKING LEAVE!"

Three long steps and then he's in my face. "Are you sure about that, sourpuss? Would you know what to do?"

A longing begins to burn deep within me, but I fight it. "No more. I don't want to do it anymore."

He snags my throat in his grip. "*It* wants to do *you*."

"Please," I hiss out.

"Please, Esteban, will you pump my veins full of that shit while you make me come again?" he asks, his voice light despite the hostile glare he's giving me. My body reacts to his words much to my horror. I rub my thighs together to drive away the need.

"Stop!"

"Stop making you feel so damn good?"

Tears roll from my eyes and I hate how weak I am in his presence. "Yes."

"Yes, you want it?"

"N-No."

I can barely breathe as he squeezes my throat. My eyes roll back into my head. When I feel him touching me between my legs, I squirm and jerk my eyes back open.

"Want me to leave and fuck with Luciana instead?" he questions, his eyes liquid fury.

The idea of him raping her again has me gagging. "N-No."

"You want me to stay and make you feel good?"

My face scrunches in a painful frown. The ache in my heart hurts but the growing need for the stupid drug is vining its way around both my mind and my heart. It's claiming both and crushing them.

"It's either her," he murmurs and licks a tear from my face, "or you. I'm not as nice to her. What'll it be, sourpuss?"

I reach my hand up and grab his wrist. "Not her."

He beams in a way I've never seen before and he almost looks as handsome as Oscar. Playful and carefree. Happy. Esteban is a monster who takes joy in terrorizing his victims. "I was hoping that would be your answer. Want it in your thigh again?"

I close my eyes remembering the way the drug chased away reality. How I coasted into oblivion with a smile on my face.

"Yes."

He releases me and I fall onto the couch. I'm in a haze of self-hatred and lust over the heroin while he messes about in the basement. When he returns, he helps me sit up.

"Take off your shirt," he demands.

"No."

His eyebrows furl together in fury. "I'm really hating that word coming out of your mouth," he snaps. "Maybe I should cut out your fucking tongue so you'll quit using it."

I take off my shirt.

I'm completely naked and twitching for what he's about to give me. My mind and my body are at odds—an epic battle my body is winning. They've already slaughtered my heart somewhere along the way.

"What did you take last night anyway?" he questions, his fingertip running down between my breasts toward my navel.

I close my eyes and pretend it's Duvan. "Xanax."

His hand leaves me as he prepares the heroin. "Not Xanax. You got too fucked up way too quickly. Sure it wasn't Dilaudid?"

"I'm not sure. What's that?"

"A strong pain reliever. The Xanax were pushed to the back. The Dilaudid cap was screwed on crooked," he tells me. I try to drown him out but the sounds of what he's doing sends a ripple of need coursing through me.

"What is it?"

He rubs my thigh and I open my eyes to look at him. "It's similar to heroin. An opiate. Gives you a high almost as good as this," he says and waves the syringe at me. "Just so you know." His wink is conspiratorial.

Dilaudid.

I won't forget that name.

"Esteban," I murmur, my voice raw and shaky. "I need Duvan. Please call him."

His face darkens. "I've taken care of him for a bit. All you need is me. You'll see soon enough. You'll crave me just like you crave this hit. Then, once he's gone for good, we'll rule like we were born to. It was never supposed to be him."

"Please…"

His hand rubs over my stomach in a gentle, reverent way. "Shhh," he says in a gravelly voice. "Let me do this."

He takes my wrist and pushes the needle into the vein there. I stare in fascination as he squeezes the pure heaven into me. The familiar warmth surges through me like fire on dry brush. It ignites every nerve ending and sets my soul aflame. My eyes roll back and I let out a moan of pleasure.

I'm lost in my own little world when I hear something tear. Then a manly, guttural groan. And then I'm crushed and filled. I'm suffocating on the scent of a monster. He's consuming me and I'm running from him, chasing my high into oblivion.

I wake up shaking and confused. Every muscle in my body is on fire with pain. My brain is muddied with fragments of Esteban. I groan when I try and sit up. It's then that I notice the raw pain between my legs. Hot tears streak down my cheeks. Four used condoms are tied and discarded on the floor beside the sofa. Bile rises in my throat.

I'm going to be sick.

On weak legs, I wobble across the basement to the steps. I'm just climbing the bottom one when the door swings open. A dark figure stands in the doorway and I realize it must be night since light isn't pouring in from the kitchen.

"Where are you going, sourpuss?"

"How long have I been down here?" I croak. I'm not sure when was the last time I ate or drank anything.

"It's after midnight," he says with a *tsk* and clomps down the steps toward me. "All you wanted to do was fuck and get high all day long."

No.

I swipe at the tears on my cheeks and shake my head. "I n-need to get away from you. I need to call Duvan. Where is Duvan?!"

He continues his descent, a wolfish smile tugging at his lips. "I told you, he's being detained. It's just us, Gabriella."

I wince at hearing my name. Hearing it pulls my mind back to reality a bit. "I'm going to find him."

His eyes darken as he skims his gaze over my quivering naked body. "It's a long way to the warehouse. What happens when you get there and you need your fix?"

Hissing at him, I stumble away from him when he approaches. "I don't need a fix!"

My body trembles in protest. Lies. I need it and I need him.

"Shhh," he says softly and walks past me to the safe room. "Let me help you. I can help get rid of those shakes and then I'll drive you to him."

Another quake ripples through me and I double over in pain as a severe throb twists my stomach into a knot. A loud grumble comes from my belly. "I-I don't need that," I tell him, my bottom lip wobbling wildly. "I need food. I need clothes. I n-need you to go away."

But my eyes are watching him with intensity as he pulls out his supplies from the safe. I want to focus and notice every detail so I don't need his help anymore. Another pang rips through me.

"I'll feed you after this, sourpuss," he assures me in a calm tone. He sets his tray full of stuff down and begins pulling off his suit jacket. Each movement is slow and calculating. I hate how he's taking his time. Darting my gaze to the drugs, I try to ignore the hunger pain in my stomach.

"Esteban…" I murmur. "Please help me."

His nearly black eyes lift to mine and he flashes me a sincere smile. "Come here and sit beside me. Let's talk. I'll give you what you need and then I'll feed you. Together we can go find Duvan."

My shoulders hunch. I want to believe him. God, how I do. It would be much easier than fighting my conscience that is clawing for attention. I keep pushing it away because it hurts less that way.

"You promise?" I croak.

He nods and pats the sofa beside him. I have to step past the used condoms, which make me shudder harder.

"D-Did you rape me?"

His body tenses at my words. Our eyes meet and irritation is present in his. "It's not rape if she comes screaming your name."

I close my eyes and am met with fragments of memories. Esteban inside of me. Pushing himself and the liquid bliss into my veins. I did come. He made it all feel so good.

"I can't do this anymore," I choke out, tears blurring him in front of me. "I don't even know who I am anymore."

He grips my bony hips and hauls me into his lap so I'm straddling him. When his fingers whisper over my sore arms, I shudder with need. I cry out when he bites my breast. "You're mine now. That's who you are, sourpuss. Mine. Just like it was supposed to be."

A full-bodied sob wracks through me. He's hard between my legs and I'm disgusted. Yet I can't bring myself to move away from him. Self-loathing swarms around me like a furious storm cloud, whipping at me from every direction.

"Help me," I murmur. "Somebody help me."

I feel the tightening on my bicep. And then I feel a pinch. As soon as the heat rushes into me, I roll my head back and stare up at the ceiling. The pain and worry and sadness and despair are chased away into the darkness. I'm once again stolen by the pleasure that's dancing through me and the fingers that are now probing me.

I'm trapped in a nightmare.

Esteban is the monster.

And I can't fucking escape.

Stars dance and glitter around me. Nothing makes sense anymore. He takes away my pain despite being the one to dole it out to me. I'm on a seesaw of confusion. Up and down, trying to decide between right and wrong.

"There, there, angel," he coos, dragging me up, up, up into my high. "I promised I'd take care of you." And then he's bringing me down, down, down onto him and him deep inside of me. "Come and then sleep."

I come.

And then I fall against his chest and sleep.

Somebody help me…

chapter
TWELVE

Ren

"Something's wrong."

I lift my gaze to stare at Oscar. He's been trying to get ahold of his brother Duvan for several days now. Nothing. Vee sits cross-legged on her bed beside him and frowns at me.

"Brie isn't answering our Skype calls either. Has she responded to your emails?" she asks me.

Pinching the bridge of my nose in frustration, I shake my head. "I thought she was still trying to warm up to being friends with me. When's the last time either of you spoke to her?"

Oscar stands and starts pacing the bedroom. "She was behaving strangely last time I talked to her. Seemed nervous and frantic. Then she just hung up on me." He scrubs his face with his palm. "I can't get in touch with either of my brothers. Something's most definitely wrong."

"I'm calling my dad. He's been spending a lot of time at the shipyard with Camilo so he hasn't been home this week but I think he ought to be able to help us," Vee says as she dials her dad and puts him on speakerphone.

I bristle at the mention of him. The dickhead put his hands on Brie and I'll be damned if I ever trust a word he says. But if she's in trouble and he can help, I'll listen. While the phone rings, I text Dad.

Me: Have you spoken to Gabe lately?

Dad: He called and checked in last night while you were out.

I hold up my finger to Vee and Oscar excusing myself before stepping out into the hallway to call him.

"What did he say?" I demand the moment he answers.

"Toto, go see mom-mom," he says gently. I can hear Blue's Clues playing in the background and him saying something to Mom before the sound of a door clicking shut muffles the music. "He gave me a number to reach him at. Was checking on Toni and wondered if I'd heard anything about Gabriella. Why?"

"Did you tell him about her marrying Duvan Rojas?"

He lets out a swoosh of air. "I didn't think it was necessary to give him the details and send him on a damn killing spree. Besides, you told me she was happy."

Pain makes my chest ache, and I shake my head in frustration. "She may very well be happy. But we can't reach her. Duvan's brother Oscar and I are worried about the both of them."

The line grows quiet. "I have to tell him." A growl resounds on the other line. "Jesus, I have to fucking tell him."

I flip my ball cap around so that it's backward and lean my shoulder against the door jamb. "Don't send him into a psychotic rage just yet, Dad. Let me find out what I can and I'll let you know."

He sighs and I can hear his chair squeak. "Be careful, son. I don't like you wrapped up with these people."

I bristle. These people are my friends. And one of these people, I'm heartbroken over. "Then maybe you should have thought about that before you involved me."

Dad curses, and I instantly feel like an ass for blaming him.

"Look," I say in exasperation. "I'm sorry. Just…" I trail off when Oscar pops his head through the door and shakes his head at me. "Just see if you can tap into her phone records. See what she's been up to. Emails. Social media. Anything. We need to make sure she's okay. And if she's not…"

"We'll send her father after her."

I bite my tongue but agree. "Yep. Gotta go, Dad."

If she's not okay, there's no way I'll trust waiting on Gabe to go in and help her. He already abandoned her once, I can't help but wonder if he'd do it again. Hell, my parents are already dealing with one of his kids as we speak.

"You got a passport, my man?" Oscar asks.

I scrub my face with my palm. "Yep. Give me time to pack a bag."

"I'm coming with you," Calder says, his mouth set into a determined frown. "You won't let Dad come, but I'm going."

I cringe thinking about the argument Dad and I had when I came home to break the news to him. Gabe's not answering the number he gave him. Like I said, I can't trust him to do a goddamned thing. When Mom heard us arguing, I told her I was going on a summer trip to South America with some friends. It wasn't a lie. And Dad didn't want to get into it with her so he stormed off.

He'll get over it.

"It's fucking dangerous, bro," I grunt as I shove clothes into a suitcase. "We don't know what we're walking into down there."

He shrugs and saunters over to me. "More the reason for me to be there and have your back."

"Mom will never let you go," I retort.

"I'm not a kid anymore."

I glance over at my brother who recently turned eighteen and sigh. "Fine but when we get there, you're staying at the hotel with Vee."

His blue eyes brighten at the mention of Vienna. "Why is she going?"

I rummage through my drawers yanking out socks and underwear. "Brie's her best friend. She's worried."

He groans. "She just likes that asshole. I don't know why she's so obsessed with him."

And, God, she is. Every time I look at the girl, she's gazing at Oscar like she wants to be the mother of all his babies. The guy doesn't even see her. I mean, literally, he sees her. But he doesn't look at her the way she looks at him.

Unfortunately, she doesn't look at Calder the way he looks at her.

What a clusterfuck.

"Whatever. If you're going and Mom's not going to beat your ass, pack a bag. I don't have time to wait."

He's gone in a flash to pack. I can't help but wonder if this is a shitty idea. For all I know, she's happy playing wife—*God, how I fucking hate that word now*—to Duvan. We may just show up and piss her off.

While I wait for Calder to pack, I open my laptop. I have a picture saved on my desktop. It's one Vee took of us. Brie's hair was longer then and blows in the wind. My arm is wrapped possessively around her waist. Her smile is breathtaking. The brown in her eyes seems to sparkle with mischief—a look that's hot as hell on her. My eyes are different too. Happy and proud to have her by my side.

I waited too long.

My secret always kept me from plunging too deep with her. So many times over the past couple of years I'd wanted to profess my love to her. To make love to her and promise her my heart. It teased the tip of my tongue but never rolled out. The secret of my betrayal always hung like a thick curtain of disgust between us. No matter how much I wanted to move forward with her, I simply couldn't. Not with such a divide between us.

Now, I wish I'd have told her the first time I'd kissed her. Perhaps then, we could have talked it through. Worked on shit. Maybe if I'd not been a goddamned pussy, she'd be here with me now. In my arms instead of his.

Perhaps then she'd be wearing a promise ring from me instead of a damned wedding ring from Duvan Rojas.

I fucked up.

Royally.

Opening up my email, I check to make sure she hasn't messaged me. Nothing since the last time we corresponded. Swallowing down my unease, I tap out an email to her.

Brie,

I hope you're happy. You're quiet and not responding. We're all worried about you. If you're happy, though, I'm happy for you.

Do you remember that time we ate at Fish Paddy's on the pier? Calder and Vee went to throw french fries at the seagulls, but we stayed behind and shared a piece of key lime pie. Remember how you told me you'd wanted to go to film school? How you'd wanted to write a screenplay one day that would top Sixteen Candles? I laughed at you and asked you why you watched old ass movies all the time. You got this pretty glimmer in your eyes and said, "Old movies have the best music."

I teased you and we went on our way. What I didn't tell you was that I found Sixteen Candles on Netflix. And a whole bunch of other cheesy eighties movies. I watched them because I had to know what made you love them. I needed to know what made you so intrigued with them that you wanted to go to film school.

I have to say…I'm still trying to figure it out, Brie.

I'm kidding.

You were right, beautiful. The music is pretty badass. Still won't replace my Nine Inch Nails or Pearl Jam, but I may or may not have made a playlist that reminds me of you…

"Don't you…forget about me…"

Ren

PS – I hope you have that song stuck in your head now because I do. Thanks for that, woman.

"Ready?" Calder asks from the doorway, a bag thrown over his shoulder and a ball cap pulled over his head.

I hit send and snap my laptop shut. "I don't think I'll ever be ready to see her with that Rojas fuck."

Calder lets out a sigh. "Believe me, brother, I know exactly how you feel."

Turns out, we aren't able to get a flight out until tomorrow evening. The four of us have decided to crash in Oscar's hotel room until then. None of us have heard from Brie, and I'm about to go fucking crazy with worry.

"What are you studying, Oscar?" I ask as I flip through pictures on my phone of Brie and me.

He blabs on about family business and shit. I'm only half listening as I obsess over Brie—my girl before it all went to hell. Oscar is still talking when we hear a bang on the hotel room door.

"Probably my father," he groans.

But when he opens the door, Heath Berkley storms in past him. "Where is she?"

Anger surges through my veins at seeing him. I'd give anything to knock him in his perfect, white goddamned teeth. When I lean forward in my chair, Calder taps me on the knee and shakes his head at me.

"Daddy," Vee whines. "I'm going to see Brie."

Possessiveness flashes in his eyes at the mention of Brie, his jaw ticking furiously. "She's with Duvan for now. She's fine. You're not going out there."

For now?

My ears perk up and I listen attentively.

"Why not? It's not like I haven't been before," she argues, her pale cheeks turning pink with anger. "We vacationed there many times when I was a kid."

He growls and storms over to her pink suitcase sitting in the corner. "When you were a kid, Vienna. Not since you've become a woman. Things are different over there than they are here. All it takes is one person to recognize that you're my daughter and to see how beautiful you are, and they'll try to get to me through you. I won't have you traipsing across the world into a hornet's nest."

"I'm eighteen now, Dad!" she snaps. "I can do whatever I want."

When he lets out a furious hiss and stomps toward her, Calder rises from his seat with both fists clenched. He's poised and ready to attack.

"It's not safe," he snarls, fury contorting his features.

"But you let Brie marry Duvan and willingly sent her over there?!" Her voice is shrill and her bottom lip trembles.

His eyes flicker over to Calder and then me. As if forgetting his daughter, he sneers. "Jesus, the goddamned lawn boy is here too? You all fast fucking friends now, Oscar? Does your brother know you're hanging out with the asshole who fucked his wife?"

Storming over to him, I grab the front of his button up shirt and pull him toward me. Spit showers over him as I hiss my words. "Does Duvan know you put your hands on his wife? Whipped her ass like she was some small child? You're a sick fucking pervert, old man."

He jerks from my grip. Oscar steps between us while Calder grabs me by the shoulders.

"Heath," Oscar says in a clipped tone. "We're going to see my brother and Brie. They're family and our friends. This is nothing more than a trip to check and see how they're enjoying married life. I'll keep Vee safe."

A look of disgust washes over Heath's face. "If one hair is harmed on her pretty red head, I'll gut you in front of your entire family."

Oscar, always the easygoing dude, tenses. His shoulders square and he glares at the old man with a menacing stare. "I'm sure Papá would love to hear how his business partner just threatened his son."

Heath has the sense to look fearful. "Whatever. Keep her safe."

I relax when the asshole hugs Vee before slamming the door behind him.

"What a dick," Calder mutters under his breath.

Oscar turns toward us and scowls. Worry paints his features. "Stick with me and you'll be fine. But as a precaution, I want you both to have eyes on Vee at all times."

Calder folds his arms across his muscular—despite eating a shit-ton of sweets at every turn—chest and smirks at Oscar before winking at Vee. "Not a fucking problem."

chapter
THIRTEEN

Brie

"Beh."

Thundering in my head.

"Beh."

I groan and attempt to swat away the person attempting to wake me from my glorious slumber. A sleep where I find peace. My parents. Our old beach house. Memories of a time when I was happy.

"Beh!"

"What?" I snap and drag an eye open.

Luciana's brown eyes are darting all over me as she seems to check me over. A single tear streaks down her cheek and her bottom lip quivers. "Beh."

My entire body aches and I'm shivering. Shivering so much it hurts. When I crack open the other eye, I glance down to see I'm naked and bruised. Sticky and dirty. I'm burning between my legs which causes horrible fragments to slice through my mind, cutting my soul into bits. I touch between my legs and let out a gasp when they come back into view bloodied.

I'm panicked for a moment until I realize I must have started my period.

"What time is it?" I murmur as I try to sit up. "How many hours have passed?"

She frowns and holds up five fingers. A crack of thunder makes us both jump. "Five hours?"

My eyes close again in an attempt to escape the neediness raking its way along the inside of every vein in my body. A craving—unlike any hunger pain I've ever experienced—grips my entire being. I'm a prisoner to this starvation for the drug that's had me in its hold for what…twenty-four hours? I realize I have no clue as to what day or time it is. Nothing makes sense.

"I need to get out of here," I croak as I reopen my eyes. But even then, I'm letting my gaze flit over to the safe. Esteban is nowhere around. And while it's relieving to know he won't be using me anytime soon, I can't help but panic.

What if he doesn't come back?

How will I get the heroin into my body?

"I need your help," I manage to say as I sit up. As much as I'm starving for food and a shower, my other obsession strangles me and won't let go. "I need you to help me."

She assists me in standing. But when we tug in opposite directions, she frowns. "Beh," she whispers and shakes her head no at me.

Fury surges through me and I tug from her grip. "You don't understand," I snap. I'm stumbling into the room and trying desperately to open the safe while she whines from behind me. I get the door open after several failed attempts and hunt for the heroin.

"Where the fuck is it?!" I screech.

Pill bottles crash to the floor as I search the depths of the safe. My hands shake violently and I attempt to remember the name of the pills Esteban told me about. Blood from my period runs down the inside of my thigh, but I don't care. A loud grumble causes my stomach to seize up in pain, but I ignore it. The thundering in my head nearly matches the storm waging outside, but I push past it.

Luciana tugs at me. "Beh!"

"No! Just leave me alone!" I scream at her so loudly, I nearly throw up from exertion.

She's still attempting to pull me from the room when my eyes land on the dark, almost black, eyes of Esteban. He's sitting on the couch with a knowing grin on his lips. I have no idea when he showed up but my heart skips several beats when I see him. Not from fear or disgust, but from excitement.

Luciana freezes, her gaze trained on him, a horrified expression on her features. "Beh," she says, a sob clogging her throat before she shakes her head no.

But I'm long gone on a stumbling mission for the drugs. Esteban's face lights up when he sees me. He wiggles a syringe at me. "Miss me, sourpuss?"

I fall to my knees in front of him and offer my arm to him. "Yes."

His thumb caresses my sore flesh and he frowns. "We've blown all these out." He points to my other arm. "And those." Then, his hand waves at my thighs. "Those too."

Panic seizes me. "W-What do we do then?" My voice is a shriek and bile rises in my throat.

"Luciana," he barks at the woman I'd long forgotten. "Make Brie something to eat."

She sobs but scurries away to heed his instruction. Once she's gone, he regards me with a soft smile. "I could put it here." His thumb drags along the side of my throat. My pulse leaps at his touch. Fear should be playing with my emotions, but it's long gone.

Only need.

Only desire for the heated bliss.

Only a craving like I've never experienced.

"Please," I croak, my throat parched.

He leans forward and suckles on my throat. His tongue is where I want the needle. I grip his thighs and let out a frustrated mewl. He roughly pinches my nipple as he kisses my neck. I'm not turned on, just desperate.

"Esteban…"

He sucks hard enough to leave a bruise before popping from my flesh. His dark eyes meet mine, twinkling with mad delight. "Just getting that vein nice and fat for you."

I try to focus on how he's cooking the heroin. How he gets it into the syringe. How much. But my mind isn't taking notes. It's just counting down the seconds until it goes black again.

"Come here," he urges, tugging me into his lap. The blood from my period soaks him through his slacks, and I don't even care. I just need him to do what he does best. Take me away.

His fingers fist my hair and he jerks my head to the side. The bite of the needle hurts worse in my neck, but as soon as the heat surges into me, I roll my eyes into my head. I hear the jingle of his belt and vaguely comprehend him lying me down on the sofa on my belly. His cock is soon inside me.

I don't care anymore.

I'm going, going, gone.

"Tigress!"

I blink open my eyes in confusion. Duvan doesn't come to me in my dreams anymore. Is he here now? My words come out as a whimper and nothing more. The pumping into me has stopped.

Screaming and screaming.

Warm hands are on me, turning me over onto my side. My eyes wash over Luciana once before falling behind her.

Duvan.

Is he really here?

Bruises along his cheekbone. Blood crusted around his nose. He's soaking wet and wearing a hate-filled scowl as he rears his fist back. I hear a crunch and then another. It takes me a moment to realize he's hitting Esteban.

This is real.

"N-No!" I hiss out, my voice unrecognizable to me.

When Duvan's eyes meet mine, I see a look that tears my soul right from my body. A heartbreaking expression that matched my own when I'd looked in the mirror after I found my mother's dead body.

Despair.

Revulsion.

Disgust.

Hate.

"I'm s-sorry," I slur out. My body relaxes, the bliss taking full control of me finally.

Luciana slides out of the way and Duvan falls to his knees beside the couch. His fingers spear through my tangled hair. I expect him to yell at me. To tell me what a whore I am. I'm shocked to tears when his full lips whisper over mine, gently kissing me.

"My poor, tigress. I'm so fucking sorry," he murmurs. The pain in his voice is like tiny knives cutting through me. It hurts me to hear them.

"You came back for me." I'm not sure if I thought the words or said them aloud. Either way, he understands because he nods. His lips press hard this time to mine. A choked sound escapes him before he pulls away. The strong, fearless Duvan has tears spilling down his tanned cheeks.

"I'm going to kill him. For you," he vows, his voice a cold rain washing over me. "I'm going to cut him, limb by limb, until he pays for what he's done to you."

"Wha!" Luciana cries out.

Duvan jerks away and utters a, "FUUUUUCK!"

The rest is a blur.

I don't remember him coming back.

Or him scooping me into his arms.

Or the entire walk back to our bedroom.

The warmth of the shower seemed to soothe my soul some but even it was a fading moment.

Finally, I felt safe.

chapter
FOURTEEN

Duvan

I'm going to find the motherfucker and slit his goddamned throat. After I slice his cock off and feed it to him. Fucking Esteban. My damn brother.

Not anymore.

Rage quakes so violently through me, I fear I'll wake Brie. It's been at least ten hours since I cleaned her up and wrapped my body around hers in our bed. Ten hours where I couldn't sleep but instead replayed the betrayal of my brother over and over again in my head.

I did this.

I brought her here knowing this could happen.

But I'd been selfish. Thought I could protect her here. Thought I'd have her all to myself.

How did this happen?

One minute we're playing pretend for my brother's benefit.

The next I'm tied to the chair in my office at the warehouse while his goons beat the shit out of me.

For five fucking days, I worried myself to the point of exhaustion.

I knew whatever Esteban was doing to my tigress was sick. It's his way. He's a twisted bastard like our father. Brutal and a goddamned lunatic.

Despite it being after noon, the tropical storm named Inez has come ashore. The winds are howling loud enough to wake the dead. I should check on my chickens but I refuse to leave her side.

He starved her.

He drugged her.

He fucking raped her.

Fury, more violent than the storm outside, ripples through me. While I was tending to her, he'd fled the house despite my breaking his nose and beating the hell out of him. I've put a call out to one of my most trusted men, Ravi, and told him to find my brother. I'm going to enjoy slicing him into tiny fucking pieces. Enjoy making him pay for everything he did to her.

Her skin has grown hot and she starts to shiver in my arms. She'll soon wake, craving her beloved drug. I've already instructed Luciana to flush it all. To rid my safes of anything that could harm Brie any more. Aside from the meds I'll need to help wean her off, the rest has got to go.

"Mmm," she croaks, her eyes still clenched closed.

I stroke her wavy hair out of her face. It's long since been washed and air-dried. When I helped her shower last night, I almost lost my fucking head. Her body was littered with so many bruises. So many track marks. And once I finally determined she was bleeding from her period and not from sexual abuse, I had Luciana assist me with finding her a pad to line her panties with.

My sweet, brave tigress is safe.

She's clean and I'm going to heal her.

"Ow," she murmurs, her entire body shaking. Not from the chill of the air but from need. Her road to recovery is just beginning. She'll hate me before it's all over with.

I tug her into my arms and hold her quaking, emaciated self. I fucking hate how bony she feels in my grip. How hollow and breakable she is. My own body hurts from the blows I'd suffered to my ribs, but it won't keep me from holding her.

"I missed you, mi amor," I murmur against her hair, which now smells like lemon and honey. A smell I never want to leave my presence again.

Her fingers splay out over one of my bruised pecks and she whimpers. "Duvan. You're really here." A sob wracks through her.

"I'm here, baby," I assure her through clenched teeth. "You're safe now."

She relaxes against me, her lips pressing against my throat. "Where's…"

I stroke her hair and kiss the top of her head. "He's gone now."

At my words, she tenses. When her head tilts up and her dulled eyes spark to life, my heart throbs in my chest. God, how I fucking missed her.

"I n-need…" she trails off, horror painting her gorgeous features.

"I know," I murmur. Our eyes meet. An entire conversation passes between us with just one look.

"No," she says, sitting up. Her eyes glance down at the hoodie I'd put on her. She tugs at it in confusion before turning her now wild gaze to mine. "No, Duvan!" She rips at the hair on her head before letting out a crazed scream. "You can't do this to me! You don't understand!"

I grab her wrist and yank her to me. She's weak so she falls onto my chest without much effort on my part. Once I have her squirming body tight in my grip, I growl out my words. "Oh, but I do understand, tigress. I've been there, baby. I'm going to fix you. Hate me all you want, but I'm going to find my sweet girl again."

A wail escapes her. Her fidgeting body becomes jelly in my arms as she gives up. "I'm not your sweet girl," she cries, her tears soaking my bare chest. "I did things."

I close my eyes and take a ragged breath. I'm going to cut off his balls and fucking choke him with them. "I know, tigress. I know."

Her sobs become hysterical cries with uncontrollable hiccups and desperate gasps for air. I simply hold her through her meltdown.

"Y-You don't know," she chokes out. "I…I did those things willingly…"

Kissing her head, I let out a sigh. "I know, but it wasn't your fault. Esteban knows how that addiction fucks with a person. He lived it with me. Back when I couldn't take care of myself, it was my brother who dragged me to rehab."

"Oh, God," she moans. "This hurts. I can't do this!"

I grit my teeth. "You can and you will. I'm going to help you."

She squirms and rages in my grip but she's still too weak. Esteban didn't feed her enough. And we have a long road ahead of us. She'll undoubtedly lose more weight before I can put any back on her.

Rolling her over onto her back, I grab her wrists and pin them to the bed. Tears leak from her eyes. She's so fucking broken. It rips through me like the raging storm making all the windows in my house rattle.

"Woman, listen to me," I growl. Her body relaxes but her lip continues to tremble. "I love you, tigress. I'm going to fix you." While I was beaten and tortured, I imagined over and over speaking those words to her. *I love you, tigress.* Each time, I could almost envision her brown eyes widening with surprise and her sexy lips tugging into a smile before she said them back. *I love you too, Duvan.* Of course, the perfect things only happen in dreams… This is our nightmare.

A sob escapes her. "Then just give me a little bit. You know how to do it. Please, Duvan. Help me. It fucking hurts!"

I hate to see her in pain, but it's fleeting. Just a phase. "I *am* helping you."

"No," she argues, her voice hoarse. "You're hurting me. If you love me like you say, then give me just one little hit."

I close my eyes to avoid her angry glare. She makes me weak, but I'm doing this for her. "I'm sorry."

She spits on me and hisses. "I fucking hate you!"

I swallow before kissing her forehead. "I know and I'm sorry."

"You have to eat something. You can't stay holed up in this bedroom forever, Brie. Do you want to go with me to feed the chickens? It's finally stopped raining."

She doesn't answer me. For two days, as she's slowly detoxed, I've attempted to bring her out of the shell she's seemed to disappear into. When she's not yelling at me or sleeping, she's throwing up and begging for death. I'm worried to fucking hell over her.

"Tigress…"

"Just go."

"Baby…"

"Leave me alone."

"Brie…"

"No!"

"*Debemos de estar juntos…*"

The Methadone has been critical with her heroine withdrawals, but it's not perfect. God, how she suffers. My poor girl has claw marks all over her stomach and thighs from the never-ending itch that consumers her. In some places, she's even drawn blood a couple of times. Depression also seems to be taking its toll on her. Not being able to shoot up with what she'd grown accustomed to, she's dealing with some all-time lows. It's damn heartbreaking to watch her sob all hours of the day, begging for the drugs. But it's the nausea that's by far the worst on her. Nothing is appetizing to her and she throws up a lot of what I do get her to eat. Having been exactly where she's at myself, I know precisely what a soul-shredding experience she's going through.

But we *will* get her through it.

"When I get better, I want to leave. With or without you, I want to get the hell away from this place," she spits out, her back still turned to me.

I stride over to her bedside and kneel before her. She tries to hide her hand but I find it anyway, squeezing it in my grip. "Without me is never an option." My tone is fierce and leaves no room for objection. I repeat my earlier words. "*Tenemos que estar juntos.*" *We need to be together.*

"Don't you have work to do or—" she starts but we both jolt when we hear a car door slam outside.

"Stay here," I order as I rise to my feet. If that bastard came back, I'm putting a bullet through his skull. The springs on the mattress squeak behind me, but I'm already on a mission of yanking my gun from my bedside table. It's chambered and ready to fire by the time I creep out of the bedroom. When I glance back, Brie is out of the bed and on my tail. As much as it's good to see her out of the damn bed, she's much too pale to be up, and I don't want her anywhere near Esteban. "Get back in the room," I order with a hiss.

She glares at me. "No."

Gritting my teeth, I continue my trek down the hallway and down the stairs. Keys jingle at the front door a moment before it swings open. I raise my gun, ready to blow my brother's head off his shoulders.

But it's the wrong brother.

A mixture of annoyance and relief filter through me.

"What the fuck, man? Why the hell aren't either of you answering our calls?" Oscar demands, his voice deep with emotion.

I lower my gun but the moment more people start piling through the door, I jerk it back up.

Oscar holds his palms in the air and approaches me. "Dude, calm the fuck down. These are my and Brie's friends. And Vee. We're here to check on you guys."

My eyes lock with the blue eyes of the guy Brie was seeing before me. A surge of jealousy spikes through me. "Why are you here?"

He starts to shoulder past Oscar toward Brie, but my brother holds out his arm to stop him. Smart man. I'm too amped up with the need to destroy our older brother. This kid might accidentally take a bullet in his place. After all, he broke my wife once before. I won't put it past him to do it again.

"Brie," the fuck murmurs to her. "What the hell happened to you, beautiful?"

I'm about to punch him in his throat when she pushes past me and runs straight into his arms. Esteban fucked her God knows how many times but seeing her willingly—completely sober—run toward her ex-boyfriend, I find myself raging with betrayal.

"Duvan," Oscar growls, swatting my arm with the gun down toward the floor. "Let's fucking talk about what's going on here." He shoves me into the kitchen until my eyes no longer can glare at the man holding my wife. Once we're in the kitchen, he takes the gun from my grip before setting it onto the countertop. "Talk."

An ache forms in my chest, and I glare at my brother. "Esteban."

His jaw clenches. A storm brews in his brown eyes. "Did he hurt her?"

I scrub at my overgrown scruffy jaw before spearing my fingers into my messy hair. "He had Santiago and his men beat the shit out of me while I was tied to my office chair. And while they were doing that to me…" I close my eyes. Thoughts of how I found her grip my thoughts—with my brother's dick inside of her bloody cunt—and I boil over with rage. My fist slams into the cabinet door, splintering it into several pieces. "He raped my wife." I snap my glare to Oscar. His mouth gapes open, and sadness crumples his features. At one time I'd been jealous of his puppy love for Brie. Now, I'm thankful he cares for her and not in some sick, perverted way like Esteban. "He got her so fucked up on heroin, man. She hates me because I've forced her into detox."

A flash of understanding glimmers in his eyes. "You were a bitch too if I remember correctly. That stuff will steal your soul."

I nod and my jaw clenches again with anger. "She hates me right now, and you bring in that motherfucker. How am I supposed to bring her back to me with him here?"

Oscar relaxes and shakes his head. "He's cool, man. Ren isn't the type to go after your girl. He cares about her. We all do. If anything, we're your saving grace. She can talk to Vee, maybe get a break from you."

I shake my sore hand, now starting to throb from punching the cabinet. "She doesn't need a break from me," I hiss. "I was away from her for five goddamned days!"

He winces at my tone. "Where's Esteban now?"

"Fuck if I know. When I find him, I'm going to slit his fucking throat, though. I'm going to let her watch as he bleeds out all over the damn floor," I seethe. "*La venganza es mía.*" *Vengeance is mine.*

The sound of both girls sobbing in the living room has my body firing back to life and me reaching for the gun. Oscar groans and shoves me away. "Chill the fuck out, *hermano*. She's fine. Clearly, she's dealing with some shit. Back away from her a bit."

I stomp past him to peek around the corner. Vee rocks Brie in her arms on the sofa. Ren and some other fuckface who looks like him tower over the two girls, poised and ready to comfort them. It pisses me off. "That asshole his brother?"

Oscar tenses and gives me a clipped nod. "Yeah."

"Why the fuck's he here?"

He gives me a sour look. "Who the hell knows, but he is. Have you spoken to Ravi?"

"Last we talked, he'd not seen any trace of Esteban or Santiago or the gang. My men know he's a dead man walking."

Oscar nods. "Does Papá know?"

"No," I spit out. "He won't know until our brother's heart fucking stops. You know Papá would try and protect him. Tell us boys to work it out like we're still goddamned kids. There's no working out the fact he had my ass beat while he drugged and fucked my wife!"

My brother stalks over to me and places his hands on my shoulders. "Look at me, Duvan."

I snap my fiery gaze to his determined one. "What?"

"I have your back. He doesn't deserve to fucking live for touching her," he snarls, the jealousy in his tone making my blood pressure spike. "Together, we keep her safe."

His eyes are clear and not deceptive. I trust his words. His puppy love for my wife will keep him true to his promise.

"Don't let him take her from me," I growl, an ache forming in my chest.

He scowls. "Never. Esteban won't touch her again."

Tugging at my hair, I give him a tired gaze. "I'm talking about the lawn boy."

chapter
FIFTEEN

Ren

What the fuck happened to my girl?

Weeks ago she was a feisty, vibrant woman with curves all over her beautiful body. Her brown eyes shone with intelligence and hope. The smile she used to reward me with is long gone.

Brie is a shell.

Empty and used.

The light in her eyes is gone.

Desperation exists there.

Fuck!

"Tell me what happened," Vee urges as she strokes Brie's messy hair.

I clench my teeth in frustration. Brie's so bony. Her cheeks are sunken in. Dark circles ring her dead eyes. The hoodie she's wearing hangs off her shoulder, baring the emaciated flesh there. Rage bubbles up inside of me. My fists tighten and the urge to pummel her husband's already bruised and swollen face is overwhelming.

What the fuck happened here?

"Brie…" Vee's urges only cause her to cry more. I'm dying to push Vee over and plop down beside my girl so I can hold her.

My girl.

I nearly bark out a bitter laugh. She's not mine anymore.

"I don't want to talk about it, okay?" Brie snaps and claws at her thighs through her pants. Her lip is curled up in anger as she swats Vee away.

Vee's gaze meets mine and her eyes well with unshed tears.

"What the fuck happened?" I bark out to anyone who will listen.

Brie looks up at me, and for a brief moment, she resembles the young, innocent girl I once dated. Before I took her virginity, and Duvan gave her his name. When she was just a girl with no worries. Just a sad girl with a sad past.

Now she's much more than that.

A broken girl.

Dead inside.

"Come on," I tell her and hold my hand out to her. She seems desperate to escape Vee's mothering. With a flicker of relief in her eyes, she lets me pull her from the sofa. "Take me somewhere we can be alone."

She guides us up some stairs on unsteady legs and to a small room at the end of a hallway. It's painted bright yellow. As soon as we enter the girly space, I can see this room is hers. An office fit with an antique desk and an oversized comfy chair. Posters line the walls that remind me of her. *Dirty Dancing. The Breakfast Club. Sixteen Candles.* Her favorites.

"Sit with me," I instruct.

The woman who was pissed and brokenhearted over my lies of who I really was is distant. This new woman is different. Harder. Sharper. Feral. She scratches at herself all over as if she's crawling with bugs. It makes my heart physically ache for her.

"I'm withdrawing from heroin," she sneers when she catches me staring.

When she doesn't offer up any other explanation, I sit in the large chair and tug her down to sit beside me. She's shivering so I pull her against me to warm her up. It feels right having her at my side again. Her skin is hot to the touch, and she's far too pale for my liking. Neither of us speaks while she all but convulses as the long minutes of her recovery drag on in what feels like slow motion.

On several occasions throughout the day, I wonder if she should go to a hospital. Duvan comes in occasionally, with tender looks for her and glares for me, to bring her medicine or to attempt to force food into her. At one point, when she started gagging when he'd popped in, he carried her off to the bathroom so she could throw up.

I've never felt so helpless in my entire life.

Seeing someone so sick with need but no way to help them.

As much as I hate her husband, I'm glad he seems to know what she needs. When she shivers, he brings her a blanket. When she complains of body aches, he offers to massage the parts that hurt or hands her ibuprofen. When she starts to sweat, he brings her ice packs and popsicles.

All I'm good for is emotional support.

No words are needed as she suffers.

She just suffers.

In suffocating silence.

"You need to tell me what happened, Brie," I mutter, my words soft and imploring. Oscar gave me the quick horrifying version after she'd gone to bed last night. I'll stay in denial until I hear it from her.

Yesterday had been awful. When she'd grown tired of hiding away in the office, Duvan took her to bed. I'd hated seeing her leave with him but she clung to his shirt as if he had the power to heal her. If he can heal her, I sure to hell hope he does and fast. My brother and my friends all wore the same matching expressions. Last night, I told them to book flights for tomorrow. With every passing moment, Brie seemed weaker and more physically exhausted. Having us here only seemed to make her recovery harder. And that's the last thing I wanted to do. Much to my surprise, Duvan truly does have this handled.

She swallows but doesn't speak right away. I'm afraid she'll ignore me altogether. But then she clears her throat and shaky words spill from her mouth. Words so vile and fucked up, I want to scoop them all up so I can crush them with my fist. She robotically recounts her life during those hazy, awful five days while I viciously attempt to keep my rage to a dull roar.

With each horrifying thing she says, I stroke at her hair and promise her it will be okay.

I hope to fuck that it will.

"And now," she says in a whisper, "the need physically hurts. I want to claw out this festering inside of me. It's like a billion microorganisms are squirming around inside of me all begging to be fed. I want to feed them."

Last year, a buddy of mine from college kicked a bad heroin addiction. That shit is no joke. I'd never seen a man cry like that before. And here, my girl is suffering just like he did. But worse. Not only is she attempting to get clean, she's also dealing with the guilt of trading sex for a hit.

Now I completely understand the hate-filled rage in Duvan's eyes when we came through the door. He'd thought we were Esteban. With one glance, I know that if it had been his brother, the motherfucker would have been dead on the spot.

At least the prick is good for something.

Even if he couldn't protect her before, he seems dead set on trying now.

"Do you want to come home? I could take you to my house and—"

She sits up and regards me with teary eyes. "I am home. *This* is my home."

"Okay," I say slowly, swiping a rogue tear from her pasty cheek. "Would you like to come visit me?"

Her laughter is not like cheerful bells as it once was. It's cruel and mocking. "And hang out with the mother of the girl who killed *my* mother? No fucking thank you."

Once again, I want to throttle my sister for ruining every goddamned thing in her path.

"Think about it," I say with an edge to my voice. "Besides, I think there's someone you might want to meet."

She frowns. With her this close to me, the urge to grab her face and kiss her is strong. But after the shit storm she's been through, and our rocky "friendship" coupled with the fact that she's fucking married now, I refrain.

"Who?"

I tread lightly, carefully choosing my words. "Brie, you have a sister."

Her face remains impassive.

"And I think you should meet her when you feel better. She's so cute—"

"No." The word comes out like a violent hiss.

We stare at each other for a long moment before I tug her against my chest. Words are only riling her up so I simply hold her instead. She settles for this thankfully. Together we sit for hours in silence as her body shakes and shivers. Shouts and conversation, while muffled, can be heard beyond the office walls. Occasionally, the door creaks open, and Duvan checks in on her as he did yesterday bringing her food and medications once more. She lets him nurse her back to health. All I can offer is to just hold her. God, how I wish I could do more.

And I hate that, come tomorrow, I'm going to have to let her go so he can bring the smiling girl she once was back to us.

chapter
SIXTEEN

Duvan

It's been two long weeks of watching my wife howl and suffer from withdrawals. Fourteen torturous days of exhausting all of my resources to hunt for Esteban. Fourteen goddamned days of only getting to touch her when she falls asleep and I am able to tug her into my arms so I can sleep with her protected in my bed with me. Thankfully, my brother and his friends left after two days of visiting. It was hard on them. Seeing her lows. As much as I was eager to get that Ren fuck out of my house, I hated the way she seemed so empty afterward. Those couple of days he was here, she clung to him. Not like she wanted to fuck him or anything…but like she needed him. I want to be the only man she needs. She cried so hard when they left. Broke my fucking heart for her.

Slowly but surely though, Brie returns to her hollow body.

She eats a little more each day. Throws up less and less.

Her body begins to fill out slightly and the color returns to her skin.

I even heard her laugh a time or two with Oscar or Vee via Skype.

I've kept my distance. I've let her chat with her friends. Email back and forth with Ren. I've done what my wife needs.

And now I need to win her back.

Sure, she's pissed I made her detox off the heroin. I was enemy number one. Even Esteban—her fucking rapist—was more preferable to me. At least he would give her what she wanted, she'd spit at me.

Each vicious lashing of her tongue, though, only strengthened my love for her. It grew the need to protect her. She was mine and I vowed, just like when we wed, to protect her until the day I died.

I failed her once.

I won't fail her again.

Footsteps pad down the hallway outside of our bedroom door, and I hope Luciana keeps quiet while she cleans. I want Brie to stay asleep in my arms all day. Each morning, she's all too eager to escape me to sulk.

I've yet to do more than hug her but now I need to let her know how I still feel about her. I need her to remember how she feels about me…before she forgets.

I press a soft kiss to her soft, parted lips and then one to her cheek. Then along to her jaw. Along her slender throat. And on to her collar bone. When I slip a hand under her T-shirt, she lets out a sweet noise that urges me on.

"Tigress," I murmur against her throat as my fingers gently pinch her nipple. "Let me love you back together again."

She tenses upon hearing my words, but I don't give up. I find her mouth again. This time, I kiss her urgently. I kiss her as if she's the drug *I* need. The addiction I am suffering from. At first, she resists. Her anger is still palpable. But when my palm slides down her taut stomach heading south, she lets out a gasp that has me deepening our kiss.

When her fingers thread into my hair, I groan a sound of relief into her mouth. We can fix this.

She and I can find each other again. I break away long enough to tug her T-shirt from her body. Her swollen breasts beg for attention, her small erect nipples teasing me.

"You're a vision unlike any other on this earth," I tell her, my voice serious.

Her eyes lock on mine and she lifts her hips so I can pull down her yoga pants along with her panties. Once she's naked, I spread her open and visually feast upon my wife's sexy cunt.

"So perfect," I praise, my fingertips delicately tracing a trail between her tits toward her recently shaved pussy. "Tell me this was for me…" Her cheeks turn slightly pink, and she nods. "Good," I growl before giving her clit a tiny pinch that makes her whine with need. "I'm hungry for you, mi amor."

"I need to feel something good again," she murmurs, her voice an unsure whisper.

I'll make her feel so damn good.

I bury my face between her thighs and run my tongue along her slit. She lets out a cry of pleasure. I've barely touched her, yet she's already writhing in need.

"You need this, don't you? You need to come all over my tongue to feel better. Am I right, Brie?"

She hisses out a *yes* before tangling her fingers in my hair. I ravish her wet cunt until she's quivering so hard I think she's having a seizure. The moment she starts to come down from her new high—a natural high I gave her—I slip a finger inside of my wife's hot body. It's been nearly a month since I've been inside of her. I'm dying to be with her again.

"Are you ready, mi amor?" I question as I pull my finger from her body. It glistens in the morning light pouring in through the window. "Tell me you need this."

Her eyes are hooded and she chews on her bottom lip in a way that nearly has me coming in my boxers. God, she's fucking gorgeous.

"Tell me," I growl.

"I need you to put me back together again."

Sweet goddamn music to my ears.

I suck her juices from my finger before pushing down my boxers. Once I'm fully naked, I climb on top of my wife so I can watch her.

I need to see the way her eyes widen when I push into her.

"Oh, Duvan…"

I need to feel the way her body stretches just barely wide enough to allow my cock entry.

"Yes…"

I need to kiss away her loud moan as I drive into her as deep as her body will allow.

"Mmmm…"

Our teeth clash in a needy way as I kiss the fuck out of her. My hips seem like they're spring loaded. Thrust after powerful thrust without any sign of slowing. Her body grips my cock in such a way, it takes every part of me not to shoot my load into her well before she's ready to orgasm again.

"I love you, tigress," I murmur against her mouth.

She nods but doesn't repeat the sentiment. I'm not stung by it. This girl has been to hell and back. I'll wait her out. Eventually, I will hear those words from her…even if it's the last thing I hear on this earth.

"Duvan," she cries out. "This feels…"

All it takes is sliding my hand between us and grazing a finger across her sensitive clit to have her bucking wildly beneath me. A climax so soul gripping it makes her gasp for air ripples through her body—from her cunt all the way to her curled toes. Her body clenches beautifully around my cock until I'm unable to hold off any longer. With a gush of heat, I release my seed into her. I mark her and erase every place where my bastard brother was inside her.

She is mine.

When the quakes of pleasure seem to subside from her and my dick softens, I lift up so I can see her beautiful face. Her cheeks are still pink. Those haunted brown eyes now shimmer with a hint of peace. And the full lips I've missed so desperately are swollen and curve slightly up on one side into a half-smile.

"What were you going to say?" I question, an eyebrow quirking up.

Her smile widens and it's fucking beautiful. "This feels…" Once again, she trails off.

"This feels like love?" I quip.

"This feels right," she says with a nod. "Thank you."

It's not exactly what I wanted to hear, but I'll take it. It feels perfect to me. She's all I'll ever need. Fuck this family business. Fuck this country. Fuck everyone and everything but her.

"I want to take you on a honeymoon," I tell her. "Let's leave. We'll vacation somewhere fucking epic and then we'll talk about a better future. A future where you're always safe."

Our eyes meet and I see the desperation in hers. The need to feel secure and protected. I'll fucking do whatever it takes to keep her free of harm.

"What sort of future?"

I run my thumb over her bottom lip and grip her chin. "One where you can see your friends more frequently. One where you aren't a sitting duck. One where we could have a family."

Tears well in her chocolate orbs and she kisses the pad of my thumb. "You'd do that? Leave this place for me?"

Leaning forward, I rest my forehead against hers. "Tigress, I would do anything for you. Just let me. Let me be that man."

Her fingers link behind my neck and she nods. My dick that had begun to slip out of her slippery opening hardens back to life. Slowly, I thrust into her.

"What do you say?"

She locks her legs around my waist and keeps me still for a moment. "Let's do it. Let's go find our happily ever after."

I kiss her hard as I drive into her. When we're both gasping for air and on the brink of another orgasm, I nuzzle my nose against hers. "I'm going to love you until your heart stops bleeding from all the deep lacerations you've endured, that life has so cruelly inflicted."

"And what if it never stops?"

Lifting up, I smirk at her. "Then I'll simply keep loving you until mine stops beating in my chest." I suck on her bottom lip when she lets out a wail, her orgasm stealing her momentarily away from me. When I come this time, I nearly black out from the pleasure. Sex was always one of my favorite activities. But sex with love, well, that's quickly becoming an obsession.

I've always had an addictive personality.

And I'll gladly inject her into my soul for the rest of my life.

"I miss them," Brie says as she sits down on the sofa beside me in the living room. We've yet to go downstairs since Esteban ruled over her like a mad king in my basement.

"I know you do, tigress," I tell her and slide her down on the cushions in front of me. She lets me pull her to my chest. I push the button on the remote and *Stand By Me* starts playing again. I'm not sure if she's actually paying attention to the movie or lost in her thoughts. Either way, I hug her close and keep my lips pressed against her neck.

"Are we safe?" she questions, a twinge of fear in her voice.

I stroke her hair away from her face and tug at her earlobe with my teeth. "Ravi and my men have eyes on the house. They're also hunting for my brother. You're safe."

She turns in my arms, ignoring one of her favorite eighties movies and frowns. "I asked if *we* were safe."

Her worried frown has me smiling. God, she's so fucking cute. "You worried about me?"

I love the way her cheeks blush when she gets embarrassed. Like now. Sexy as fuck.

"I just want to leave this place. I want to pack a bag and start over. This," she waves around the living room but indicating more than this space, "isn't you. You're better than this. You've got a college degree in business and a good head on your shoulders. We can have a better life. I don't need much." Her gaze drops to my lips before darting back up to my eyes. "Just my friends and my family. You're my only family, Duvan."

Gripping onto her hair, I kiss her hard. I want her to feel how much I love her. To understand that she's my family too. When she pulls away from our kiss, I grin at her.

"We leave in the morning. I'll have Luciana pack up your posters and stuff. We'll have them sent wherever we land," I promise.

"What about Luciana?"

It warms me that her and my housemaid have grown so close. Luciana was always a scared little mouse. After what Esteban did to her, she was afraid of her own shadow. But when he victimized Brie too, they connected in a way no two other people could. They became best friends. It's cute how they text all goddamned day about the weirdest shit—never ever touching on what happened—but instead blabbing on about Justin Bieber, Dirty Dancing, and cat videos of all things. I've never seen Luciana laugh as much as when she's around my wife.

"While we honeymoon, I'm sure she'd love to visit her mother. But know this. Luciana goes where I go. She's my responsibility to look after. Now that we're married, she's *our* responsibility," I tell her. "When we find someplace permanent, she'll come too."

"What if she doesn't want to come?" she pouts.

I laugh and peck at her nose. "She'll come. We'll bribe her with Justin Bieber shit."

Brie snorts. "You're right. She'll come."

We both relax, lost in our thoughts. Her finger traces the tattoos on my bare chest. After some time, she looks up at me. "I'm ready for that tattoo."

Smirking, I raise a brow. "Is that so?"

"Will you get one with me?"

"Baby, I'll do whatever you want. Where do want it?"

She scrunches her nose as she thinks. "Somewhere I can look at it every day. Maybe my wrist."

I pull her bare left wrist to my mouth and kiss the flesh. "There?"

A smile graces her lips. "Yeah. Definitely there."

"What do you want?"

Without hesitation, she murmurs, "A heart. With tiger stripes inside."

"Tiger stripes for my brave little tigress. I like it."

She beams at me. "What will you get?"

"I'll get the same."

Her lip curls up. "You'll get a girly heart on your wrist?"

Tugging her wrist back to my mouth, I suckle her. "I'll have you there with me. Who the fuck cares if it's girly? You're girly, and I want you on me."

She giggles and snuggles against me. "Let's do it as soon as we land wherever it is we're going."

"That's a promise, mi amor."

"Where are we going anyway?" she questions, her hand slipping between us. When she grabs my cock, I groan in pleasure.

"Wherever the fuck you want to go," I promise.

She laughs, the sound soft and sweet. "That's because I have your cock in my hand." My eyes close as I relax in her grip. I'm most definitely fucking addicted to her.

"Fine, we're going to Venezuela. I thought you might want to see where you're from. Plus," I tell her through gritted teeth as she strokes me just inside my sweatpants. "They have beaches. And

I'm dying to fuck you in the ocean, mi amor." I peek open my eyes to gauge her reaction. Instead of laughing, she's quiet.

Her eyes are watery when she looks up at me. "Thank you."

I smirk. "Don't thank me yet. You haven't had my cock while we snorkel."

A snort of laughter on her end has me chuckling. "You better keep your peter in your pants when we swim in the ocean. Just yesterday Luciana sent me a video of a guy swimming naked. A fish swam right up to him and took a bite of his dick. He came out of the water with a fish hanging from his cock!"

I cringe at what that must have felt like. "Luciana has to stop sending you crazy shit and—" The words die in my throat as she eases herself down my body. Her lips wrap around the weeping head of my cock and all thoughts of anything but her perfect fucking mouth dissipate around me.

"I love you, tigress," I hiss through clenched teeth as she takes me deep in her throat.

Our eyes meet, and hers twinkle with happiness.

I fucking make her happy.

Her molten browns tell me she loves me too.

I don't need to hear the words.

I see them.

I know it with every goddamned fiber of my being.

Gabriella Rojas loves me.

chapter

SEVENTEEN

Ren

She's happy.

As much as it rips my heart straight from my chest, I can't help but smile back at her via our Skype session. Now that we've been back in San Diego for a few weeks, and we know Brie's safe with Duvan, I feel empty and lost. We'd finally reconnected after our fight where she said she hated me. Selfishly, I'd wanted her to fall for me again. For us to pick back up where we left off.

But she's in love.

With another man.

A man I drove her to with my lies.

Those two days I'd seen her, she suffered immensely. I'd even overheard Duvan talking to Oscar about the long road of recovery she had ahead of her. With everyone there hovering, she'd seemed more anxious. So brittle. I knew in order for her to get better, we needed to leave. So we did. I trusted that fucker to bring her back to her old self and surprisingly he did.

That was what was so hard.

Despite her anger and sickness from the heroin withdrawal overwhelming her, I'd seen the slivers of her love for him shining through. It was something solid and unbreakable. And it was something that I knew gave her hope. I'd have been an ass to fuck with that. In the end, I was the friend she needed and let him be her husband.

"Margarita Island looks like the best honeymoon destination. I still can't believe Duvan rented a house there," Vee gushes. "How long will you stay?"

Brie's lying on her side chewing on some red licorice. "I don't know. I like it here. Duvan and I have seen all the sights. Next week he's going to take me to my mom's birthplace to see if we can locate some of her extended family." Her voice grows soft, and she avoids looking at me. Vee squeezes my knee in support while I swallow down the disgust. There will always be a wedge between Brie and I—friends or not—since my own flesh and blood murdered her mother. "Anyway, enough about us. What are you two up to?"

Vee flashes me a smile. "Ren's going to take me into the city to look at apartments near the college. We'll be going to school together in the fall. I doubt we'll have any classes together, though."

Brie's eyes narrow and she sits up on her elbow. "Where are Oscar and Calder?"

"Calder's on babysitting duty. My mom had Mason while we were in Bogotá, so now that we're back, she and Dad have needed the extra help," I tell her. What I don't tell her is that he's babysitting her half-sister Toni. Ever since she shut down when I mentioned her sister, I've kept my lips sealed until a better moment presents itself. If she ever comes to visit, I'll encourage her to meet my little Toto.

"And Oscar is helping his dad. Esteban hasn't resurfaced yet," Vee chimes in. But as soon as she says Esteban's name, she flinches.

We both watch Brie for a reaction. Her eyes dart to the screen. A flash of hunger flickers in them. A need for what he forced upon her. While we were visiting a few weeks back, she painstakingly rehashed every morbid detail of how Esteban quickly got her hooked on heroin and every sick moment of how he made sex a part of the packaged deal. Brie was devastated she'd stooped to such a low level.

Nobody blames her.

Not me.

Not Calder.

Not Vee.

Not Oscar.

And certainly not her husband, Duvan.

Brie looks over her shoulder and then back at us. A haunted look passes over her features. "Sometimes I miss it…I miss him…" Her words are low and hollow. She swipes at a tear and sniffles. "It's stupid and disgusting, but sometimes I think if he walked through the door right now, I'd be excited to see him. A feeling of warmth would pass over me as I anticipate the heat of the heroin. Oh, God, I feel like a sick, sick girl…"

"You're not sick," Vee assures her. "You went through something so terrible. I'm sorry you had to go through it alone."

Brie, looking unconvinced, flickers her gaze to mine. "Do I disgust you?"

I gape at her like she's lost her mind. "You could never disgust me, Brie. Never."

When a door shuts behind her, she sits up and plasters on a smile. Soon, Duvan saunters into the room in nothing but a pair of swim trunks. His body is tatted up, and it makes me feel stupid for the one tattoo I have. Like I'm just a poser with my tribal wave on my left pectoral. This motherfucker is colored on every visible part of his flesh. It looks cool as hell on him, and I'm jealous.

I'm also jealous that he gets her.

My Juliet.

The girl I had in my grasp but lost because of the lies that stood between us.

His arm wraps around her and he hauls her to him. As soon as they touch, she relaxes against him. I see it. I see the comfort and love so obvious it may as well be a blinking sign over them. As much as I hate the guy and how he swooped in behind me, picking up the broken pieces of her, I'm glad he was there to put her back together again. I'm thankful as fuck he's found a way to make her smile.

She deserves to be happy.

After all she's been through, Brie needs peace.

If that Colombian fucker can give it to her, I can accept that.

But moving on is going to be such a bitch. The very idea of dating again has my stomach roiling in disgust.

I'm so zoned out, watching the way he strokes her arm just above her elbow that I don't realize they're talking to me. "What?"

"Pay attention, dork," Vee says with a laugh and bumps me with her shoulder.

I blink away my daze and drag my eyes from his fingers to Brie's face. "What's that?"

"I asked," Duvan mutters, slight contempt in his voice, "if you liked our new tattoos."

Brie's cheeks redden and she looks down at her lap.

"I didn't know you wanted a tattoo, Brie," I say leaning forward so I can see better.

Brie shrugs and lets Duvan drag her wrist to the screen. It's a heart with black and yellow stripes like a tiger. Inside on one of the yellow stripes, written in black, is his name. Duvan. He then holds his wrist out. While the artwork looked cool on her arm, aside from donning that fuck's name, his looks gay. Duvan has the same girly heart with matching stripes, but Brie's name is on his.

They got matching goddamned tattoos.

This really is serious.

All tiny rays of hope I'd had for them to realize their marriage was not one out of love, but instead one of arranged necessity, fly out the window. People who are merely together out of arranged necessity don't get each other's names tatted on themselves.

From here on out, Brie really will really only ever be a friend.

Fuck.

"I, uh," I say and yank my hat off. Running my fingers through my thick hair before shoving my cap back on, I then flit my gaze to Brie and give her a weary smile. "I need to check on Calder and make sure he hasn't lost the kid or some shit. Vee, I'll be in my truck on the phone. Brie," I murmur, "it was good seeing you. I'll speak to you soon."

Vee reaches for me, but I'm already off her bed and stalking toward her bedroom door. I hear Brie asking about me, but I don't have time to listen. When I sling the door open, I nearly run right over Heath.

"What the fuck are you doing here?" he hisses. But even though he hates me, his attention is in Vee's room.

"She's happy. Leave her the hell alone," I growl as I shove past him.

He mutters something to me, but I stalk far away from him. And far away from Duvan's possessive hold over the girl I thought I belonged with.

This shit is fucking ridiculous.

I'm sitting in my truck, blaring Nine Inch Nails, when Vee slips out through the front door ten minutes later. Since she doesn't have Oscar to impress, she isn't dressed like a ho. Today she's wearing a simple lime green dress that fits her slim figure and a pair of matching flip-flops. Her dark red hair has been braided into some fancy design down the front of her shoulder. Toto would call it an Elsa braid if she were here. Vee's definitely a knockout. It makes me wonder why Oscar just strings her along. And she strings Calder along. It's all so fucking pathetic.

"Loud much?" she grumbles when she climbs in.

I roll my eyes when she pushes the button to silence my vehicle. "We going to eat first?"

She arches a sculpted eyebrow up at me. "You're being a grouch," she pouts but then her gaze softens. "Look, it sucks loving someone who doesn't love you back. Trust me, I know. But you have to move on. I've known Brie for three years. The only time she's ever looked that happy was on the few occasions with you. They're married now. Just let them be."

"I'm not doing a damn thing, Vee," I snap as I put my truck into reverse. "It's too late for me. She's moved on."

She's quiet at that. I flip the radio back on in an attempt to drown out the awkward silence. "Aren't you happy for her?" she asks finally after we've been driving for several moments.

I cast a weary gaze her way. "I'm so fucking happy."

She frowns and starts to pick at her nude-colored nail polish. "Why is it that people like us never get what we want?"

I chuckle, but it's humorless. "I don't know. I'm not sure I'll ever get what I want…" My jaw clenches as I replay how he touched her over and over again in my mind. Sure, Brie and I have forged forward some semblance of a friendship, but it will never be enough for me.

"You're a guy…" she says softly. "Why doesn't Oscar see me? Like how you and Duvan see Brie?"

I glance over at her. Her full pouty lip trembles. I can't see her eyes now that she's donned a pair of sunglasses, but she's visibly upset. From my vantage point, she's actually a sexy woman. All long legs, narrow hips, and big-for-her-size tits. She practically throws herself at Oscar, and he teases her with subtle touches or glances. But not once has he gazed hungrily at her. Not once have I see that look in his eyes. A look that shows a craving for her. Calder's eyes, on the other hand, never leave Vee. Ever.

"He sees you. Just doesn't appreciate how hot you are," I tease with a half-grin, hoping to lighten the mood in the vehicle. We're both fucking depressed as hell.

"I'm not hot," she says in a way that tells me she wants me to argue.

So I do to indulge my friend. "Keep telling yourself that, mermaid girl."

A smile tugs at her lips. "Calder calls me Ariel too."

"Calder says a lot of nice things about you," I confide. "Unfortunately he sees *you* like *you* see Oscar. It's unrequited."

Her plump lips form a tiny '*O*' and she jerks her gaze out the window. She fiddles with the hem of her dress while her mind works with unsaid thoughts. Finally, she speaks again. "It would be easier if I could just let Oscar go and date Calder."

I shrug as I pull into the apartment complex we're supposed to be visiting. When I park the car, I turn to look at her. "Don't toy with my brother, Vee."

She gapes at me, a slight flare of anger flickering in her green eyes. "I only said it would be easier. I didn't say I was going to. Sheesh, I'm not a bitch, Ren." With a huff, she climbs out of the truck and stalks toward the management building.

I grumble and climb out after her. Once I reach her, I grab her by her elbow. "Just stop. I'm sorry, okay? I'm just being a dick because the girl I love is fucking married, has her husband's name tattooed on her wrist, and is on a dream honeymoon on some Caribbean Island."

Vee's hardened gaze falls. "I'm sorry too."

Pulling her to me, I hug my friend. She rests her cheek on my chest, her arms wrapped tightly around me.

"Maybe," she says, lifting her head to look up at me. Her jade-colored orbs almost glow with mischief. "Maybe, we should hook up. We're both desperate for people we can't have."

The very thought of betraying my brother has me sick to my stomach. "Ha…ha. Calder would string me up by my nuts." I tap her on her forehead. "Get that dumb thought out of your head right now."

She scoffs and rolls her eyes. "Fine. But you know you'd have a good time with this body. Am I right?"

This girl is trouble. "Don't start, mermaid girl. Wrong brother. If you're going to try and get over Oscar, don't use me for it. I'm sure Calder would love to have a good time with 'this body.'" I mock her with her own words.

Her eyes lose their luster. "This would be a whole lot easier if Oscar would just see me, dammit."

I take her face in my hands so I can look into her glistening eyes. "Be yourself, Vee. Every time you're around Oscar, you dress like a skank."

She growls and tries to move from my grip, but I hold her still.

"You're too willing. Too available for him. Make him work for it. If he thinks he can't have you, he'll want you. I saw several times when you were chatting with Calder the way Oscar would look pissed about it. He may not want you, but he doesn't want anyone else to have you either. Us guys, sometimes we need big hints," I tell her and press a kiss to her forehead before releasing her.

She steps away and folds her arms over her ample chest while she thoughtfully chews at her bottom lip. "He looked jealous, you think?" The hope in her eyes saddens me. Oscar is a dick. He's got this hot chick practically humping his leg and he blows her off until my brother is in the room. Then, and only then, does he show any interest besides platonic friendship.

"You've been around him since you were a baby. To him, he sees you as something stable. That when he finally finishes being a manwhore, you'll still be there for him if he ever decides to settle. Are you willing to wait until then?" I ask, rubbing the back of my neck where tension from the past few weeks seems to have permanently settled.

"I want him to shit or get off the pot," she huffs.

A couple of guys exit the management building and leer at Vee. The bigger guy murmurs something to another one before he whistles appreciatively.

"Fuck off," I holler and reach for her wrist. "Come on. You're not staying here."

"But we haven't even looked at the apartment yet!"

Ignoring her arguing, I drag her back to the truck and push her inside. Once I'm in and the air conditioning is blasting us, I regard my pouting friend with a frown. "You'll get your ass taken advantage of around here."

"Maybe that would make Oscar jealous," she snaps.

I reach out and pat her hand that rests on her thigh. "Don't do anything stupid, woman."

She groans. "It's a good idea in theory."

"Except then you'll have some dumbass guy wanting to get in your pants while you try and bait Oscar. He's not just going to go away after. You'll have more problems than you bargained for."

"Like Calder…" she trails off.

I nod, feeling bad for my brother. "You just need to make Oscar see what he's missing."

"Will you help me?"

Seems like a fucking joyous task but it's not like I have anything better to do. "I'll do my best."

She squeezes my hand and widens her expressive green eyes at me. "Thank you, Ren. You're a good friend."

"I'm not making any promises," I tell her.

Her smile is bright. "That's okay. All we can do is try, boy."

Boy, my ass.

I could bench press her scrawny butt.

"Can you do something for me too? Can you get Brie to move back here? I know she'll be with that fucker but at least I'll know she's safe. Can you do that?"

"I'll try," she says.

"Then I'll try too."

She holds her hand out to mine and I give it a shake.

I sure hope Vee has the ability to get her friend to come back.

I fucking miss her.

It's been several weeks since Vee and I went apartment hunting. Unfortunately for her, Oscar has been flying back and forth with his father. He'd given his dad the scoop on what had gone on with Esteban, and they were trying to find him. It was my hope they'd find him and we could all take turns beating that motherfucker's ass but in actuality Camilo needs him to make sure shit is running smoothly in their country. Oscar has taken over much of the crap Duvan did before he bailed with my girl so we hardly see him anymore.

I've seen Vee plenty of times while we chatted with Brie via Skype but we've not hung out much more than that. But tonight Oscar's in town, and she's dying to make her move. I'm less than thrilled because she expects my help. However, Vee's been making good on her end of the deal. Each time we Skype, she's mentioned to Brie that they could move back. Small and subtle. Talks about college and stuff they'd always planned to do together. Brie's eyes seem to dance with what-ifs. I hope to hell Vee can convince her.

"Grab me another beer," I holler at Vee.

She's moved in to her new apartment now, one close to the school but with less leering neighbors. I don't feel like she'll get abducted on the way to her car at least. One less thing I have to fucking worry about.

"Do you think this is better?" she asks as she rounds the corner carrying two Coronas.

My gaze flits over her tiny black shorts and green Aztec print halter top that reveals far too much cleavage. It's better than the spandex tight red dress she had on earlier, though. We're not going clubbing. We've planned to watch a movie for crying out loud. But still…it screams *look at me*.

"Your tits are barely contained. It's not a whole lot better than the dress. Don't you have a T-shirt or something you could wear?" I ask with a groan.

She curls up her lip in disgust as if I've just asked her to show me her old man porn collection or some shit. "I still want him to remember I'm a woman, dumbass. A T-shirt is not going to remind him I have tits."

I roll my eyes as she hands me a beer and plops down beside me. "When's he supposed to get here?"

Her lips wrap around the end of the bottle and she sips. If she does subtle crap like that, she'll have no problem getting Oscar to notice her. I don't think any guy is blind to a woman wrapping her plump lips around a bottle. Every guy's thoughts immediately go...*there.*

She's about to answer when the door swings open. Oscar strolls in with his keys in one hand and a six-pack of beer in the other. Despite the unusual circumstances in which I've come to know the guy, I actually really like him. Unlike his brother Duvan, he's cool and funny as hell. And he's a pretty good surfer. I wish he'd snap the fuck out of it though and claim this girl before the wrong asshole does.

Conversation, like usual, is easy for the three of us. Oscar regales us with tales of the asshole men who work for his father and how he riled them up at every chance he got while visiting. Vee updates him on Brie and Duvan. I remind them about the concert tickets in September I purchased tickets for the three of us to go to. After we finished off the beer and our second movie, we moved on to some strong-ass cocktails which Vee made. We're all relaxed to the point that I don't mind her head in my lap while she blabs on about the classes she's enrolled for. The tension in my neck has loosened somewhat.

Oscar's gaze seems to roam her bare legs on his own accord. I don't even think he's noticed yet that I'm stroking her hair. Through half-lidded tipsy eyes, she gives me an appreciative smile. I wink at her and enjoy relaxing with my friends.

At home, I can't fucking relax. I'm eager for class to start back up so I can get back to the dorms. Mom and Dad have their hands full with a toddler and a newborn. We've yet to hear from Gabe as far as I know, which only serves to piss me off. Home is most definitely not relaxing.

"Have your legs always been this smooth?" Oscar questions, his brow lifting with one corner of his lips.

Vee laughs and kicks at him where he sits on the other end of the couch we're sharing. He's seemed to loosen up. I don't miss the hunger in his eyes that he's trying to mask. "You're drunk, Ozzy."

He smirks. "You're the one who can't handle her liquor. Why the hell did you make this shit so strong anyway?" His fingers tickle her thigh and she squeals. "Make me another drink, bartender."

She sticks her tongue out at him, but I can see happiness glittering in her green orbs. The fucker is finally paying her some attention. But by the time she returns with another round of drinks, Oscar is frowning as he texts. He doesn't even utter a *thank you* when she hands him his drink.

Her sad gaze finds mine and my heart aches for her. "Come here."

She sets the drinks down and sits down beside me. I can tell she's seconds away from crying. The liquor is depressing her and it's making a quick job of it.

"What's wrong?" She and I both know what's wrong.

"Nothing," she says in a wobbly voice.

Her tears begin to fall, thanks to the alcohol, and I hug her to me.

"Shh," I murmur, stroking the side of her arm. "Don't cry."

I'm attempting to comfort her when a glass slams against the coffee table, startling us.

"What the fuck did I miss?!" Oscar bellows as he rises to his feet.

"Maybe pay some attention and you'd know," I growl out.

Without warning, she's physically pulled from my hug by Oscar. His scowl is murderous when it meets mine as if I were the one who made her cry. Then, he drags her squirmy ass into her bedroom. The door slams shut, and I'm left wondering what the hell just happened.

God, I wish he'd just fucking wake up.

My thoughts drift to Brie. Sexy, stunning Brie. Such a sad girl with a brilliant smile. I'd do anything to see her smile right now. To have her in my arms. Jesus Christ, I miss her.

Simply thinking of her has my dick aroused and eager to come. The last time I came—not by my own hand—was at the hotel before Brie walked out on me. And before that was when I'd taken her virginity. I close my eyes to remember how perfect that night had been. How beautiful and ethereal she'd been under the moonlight. The way her body squeezed my dick so hard, I thought I'd pass out from pleasure.

She moans and—

I pop my eyes open with realization that it's Vee's moans I'm hearing. Good for her. She finally got him to fuck her, it would seem. As proud as I am for her, I'm still hard as hell and have Brie on my mind. Shamelessly, I unfasten my shorts and pull my proud cock from my boxers. With my eyes closed, I let Brie take center stage in my fantasy while Vee's moans in the background give it the realistic edge my normal whack off sessions don't have. I fist my length with a death grip and run my thumb over the topside of my shaft. When it slides over the tip, I hiss out. My dick jolts in my hand.

"Brie," I murmur, my voice but a whisper.

Her brown eyes—eyes I miss seeing in the flesh—are focused on me as I stroke myself. I can almost imagine it's her. Her mouth. Her lips. Her wet tongue. All tasting me and bringing me closer to climax. With every thrust into my fist, I get closer to blowing my wad down her imaginary throat.

"Fuck," I hiss out as my balls draw up in pleasure.

Heat spurts up the front of my shirt as my release escapes me. My mind lingers on Brie and I drag out the fantasy as long as possible. When I've finished and tucked my cock back into my pants, I open my eyes and acknowledge that I'll never have her again.

That one day soon I'm going to have to move the fuck on.

Easier said than done.

I rip my soiled shirt from me and toss it away. The moans from the other room have stopped. It almost sounds like she's crying again. If I didn't think I'd get my ass kicked, I would go in there and check on her. Oscar shouts something muffled. It has me rising to my feet in alarm. But then she's back to moaning. With a huff of frustration, I plop back on the sofa and start to pass out.

Where do I even go from here?

Rolling to my side, I push thoughts of my bleak future away and gladly welcome ones of when Brie was beneath me in the sand. She'll always be nothing but a memory to me. For at least one night under the stars and another against the hotel door, she was mine. It may have been fleeting but they were our moments.

I may not ever have *her* again.

But *that* memory I'll hold on to until the day I die.

"Are we going to talk about what happened last night?" I question as I pour syrup all over my pancakes.

Vee winces, as if my words physically pain her, and stabs at her eggs. "Which part?"

"You and Oscar. Did he finally wake the hell up?"

She chews on her eggs and regards me with sad eyes. "Yeah."

I lift an eyebrow at her. Even though she got what she wanted, she seems unhappy. "Why were you crying last night? I thought you got laid. Isn't that what you wanted?"

Her nose turns pink and her bottom lip wobbles. "We didn't have sex. Oscar was jealous and he finger fucked me into several orgasms. And just when I thought we were going to finally do it…"

She sniffles and lets out a huff.

"What?"

"He said he's too busy for a relationship. That if he fucked me that's all it would be. A fuck." A tear races down her cheek. "I told him I would take whatever I could get."

I cringe at how desperate that must have sounded. "What did he say?"

"He told me no. When I started to cry, he kissed me. God, he kisses so good. And then he got me off again. Afterward, we fell asleep wrapped up in each other's arms."

Her fingers are trembling as she attempts to open a packet of sugar to add to her coffee. I reach over and take it from her hands. Once I've torn the packet open and dumped it into the steaming liquid, I regard her once more.

"It seems like progress, Vee."

She gives me a sour look. "He friend zoned me. Fucked me with his perfect fingers and then friend zoned me."

I make a mental note to call Oscar and have a man to man talk with him. Vee's too sweet for him to string along. If he doesn't like her, then he needs to move on. Fingering her in her bedroom not once but twice is confusing the poor girl and leading her on.

"Duvan did just up and leave with Brie. And Esteban is missing. Do you think he actually is busy helping his father?"

She shrugs and swallows. "Maybe."

"Maybe you just need to take a step back. If he's busy, you'll never have his full attention," I tell her gently.

Her green eyes burn with fury and her nostrils flare. "Our fathers are business partners. He and I could be partners too. I could help him."

I'm already shaking my head. "You do not need to be fucking involved in that cartel shit, Vee."

Her gaze loses its fiery edge. "I was born into it. I'm already involved. He just needs to wake up and realize how great we could be together."

I pull my baseball cap off and run my fingers through my hair before giving her a tired look. "Have you ever thought that maybe you two *aren't* good together?"

She frowns. "Nope."

I ignore the roiling of my stomach. The syrupy scent that hangs heavy in the air isn't helping my hangover at all. "Promise me something," I say finally and then regard her with a serious stare. "If he doesn't make a move by the end of the summer, promise me you'll get out there and date again."

Her brows furl together as she ponders my words. Finally, she lets out a huff. "Fine, I promise."

I roll my eyes because I don't believe her one single bit. "You're not just lying to me, Vee. You're lying to yourself."

Her nose turns pink as she wobbles out her words. "Lying to myself is the only way I've managed to keep my heart intact."

Brie

Two months on Margarita Island

"Tell me a story, tigress."

We're lying on a blanket under an umbrella being lazy today. After a week of visiting with my mother's cousin, I'm exhausted. It was nice meeting Louisa, and she was so great to me, but the constant reminiscing only depressed me. I found most stories funny about their childhood. However, every single one of them reminded me of the fact that she's gone. It doesn't hurt any less after three years.

"What kind of story?" I question as I curl against his bare chest. The artwork on his sculpted torso is fascinating. I've spent hours just tracing my finger along the different curves of each design. Moments like those, we can go forever without speaking but so much is spoken silently.

Duvan gets me.

Deep down, he knows me better than I know myself.

"One that makes you happy, mi amor," he murmurs, his fingers brushing over mine on his chest.

I settle in the crook of his warm arm and let out a sigh. Closing my eyes, I think back to a time I truly was happy and carefree.

"Daddy," I say as I dig my small shovel into the sand. "I want a sister. Constance from school has three sisters. I just want one. Nobody wants to play with me."

He chuckles and looks off into the distance of the beach. Daddy always looks in the same direction. Like he's waiting for someone to come see him. "Your momma is busy fixing hurt people all the time at the hospital. She doesn't have time for another baby."

"I'm not a baby," I pout.

Daddy pulls the shovel from my hand and helps me square away the sides of the castle we're making. "You're my baby. Always will be."

"I'm seven, Daddy," I tell him with a huff. "I want to be your big girl."

He brings a sandy finger to my chin and lifts it so we're staring at one another. My daddy is strong and fearless like the dragon in my storybook. I'm the princess and Mommy is the queen. "You're my Brie baby. Still a big kid but still my little girl."

I crack a smile at him. "I still want a sister."

His eyes shine and once again he flits his gaze down the beach. "Maybe one day you'll have one, kiddo."

He says his words with such sureness, I can't help but believe him. Maybe I will one day.

"Ally says her daddy isn't nice," I tell him, my voice soft—so soft it almost gets lost in the sound of the waves crashing close by. "He must not love her if he isn't nice."

"Is that so?"

I look up at him and see that his frown matches mine. "Will you always love me?"

He takes my hand and narrows his eyes at me. "Brie," he assures me. "I'll always be your daddy. I'll always love you no matter what. And if…" He scrubs at his face, rubbing sand across his skin. "If anything should ever happen and I'm taken away from you, don't forget that. I will always try to be the best man I can for you, baby girl. Don't let anyone ever tell you I don't love you. No matter what they say I've done or what I'm capable of. My love for you never wanes. I'll always do what needs to be done to protect you."

His words are sad, and they make me sad too. I start to cry. He coos and pulls me into his lap. My daddy hugs me until I stop sobbing about stuff I don't understand.

"Love is strange, baby. It comes in all different forms and sizes. Sometimes it makes sense like the love I have for you and your mom. Other times, it's confusing. Sometimes you have love for a person that doesn't even know you. One day, you'll find yourself all twisted up over love. It'll make your heart hurt and your mind messy. But, sweet girl," he says in a fierce tone, "don't ever let it get away. You deserve love. And in this family…" He chuckles and lets out a tired sigh. "In this family, we do some crazy things for love. In this family, we don't let love go."

I'm still lost in lingering thoughts of my dad when Duvan clutches my hand.

"I'm sorry, mi amor."

Shrugging, I swallow back the tears that are threatening to spill. "I just wish he'd have held true to his promise. He let me go, Duvan."

He sits us up and takes my cheeks in his hands. The almost black usual irises have turned purple in the sunlight. I could stare into his eyes all day long.

"Brie…"

I frown. He hardly calls me by my name. "What?"

"One day you need to forgive him. He fucked up, tigress. But maybe…" he trails off and brushes a kiss on my lips. "Maybe love started to get confusing. I mean, love is a complicated little fuck. Back when we first met you, I'd have never imagined falling so hard for someone my father wanted me to marry. Yet I did. And did you ever envision yourself with the likes of me?"

My lips curve into a smile. "No. Not at all."

He takes my wrist and kisses my now healed tattoo. Each time he does it, it sends ripples of electricity straight to my heart. "Come on," he says with a chuckle. "Let's get showered and dressed. I'll take you out to dinner. We've still yet to fatten your skinny ass up."

I laugh for his benefit, but my belly does a flop. I am gaining weight even though he doesn't seem to notice. My stomach is pudgier than normal, and my boobs even seem to have grown. I don't want to get his hopes up unless I know for sure, but I missed my period. A huge part of me is scared shitless about the possibility I could be pregnant. After the heroine addiction and the hell I endured with Esteban, I slept with Duvan without protection. It had been days since I'd taken my birth control and I wasn't in the right frame of mind to remember to take it.

What if I am pregnant?

The smaller, slightly braver part of me, is secretly excited. And in about fifteen minutes, I'll have my answer. Earlier today while Duvan napped, I walked down to the drugstore to buy a test. He'd woken up when I came back so I hid the test in my purse until another time.

Now's the time.

We make it inside our beachside house rental and he makes a beeline for the shower, peeling clothes off along the way. I can't help but grin as his muscled ass tightens with each step away from me. Duvan is nothing but sheer tattooed muscle. I've licked every inch of him and my mouth waters for more.

There's no way I'm not pregnant.

I've never been so horny in all my life.

The shower turning on springs me into action. I find the test and slip into the bathroom behind him. He's already stepped into the shower so I do my business while he rambles on about a seafood restaurant he found online that he wants to try. I mutter the appropriate answers while I undress and wait for the test.

Three minutes.

"You getting in or what, tigress?"

I let out a squeak and set the test down with a clatter. "Yep!"

He launches into a story about his dad, but I'm too zoned out to listen.

One word.

One word.

One word.

Pregnant.

Tears well in my eyes and elation floods through me. I'm not sure what I expected, but overwhelming excitement wasn't it. We're pregnant. Holy shit. Vee is going to freak out when she finds out.

"Duvan…"

He pops open the shower door and furrows his brows in concern. The god of a man is all perfectly chiseled lines and grooves. A distinct 'v' on his lower abdomen paves the way straight down to his thick cock. Even flaccid, the man's dick is beautiful. When my gaze rises back to his handsome face, he's smirking at me.

My God, that smirk.

It kills me.

"Someone's hungry for more than that seafood restaurant I found us," he says in a smug tone.

I laugh and join him in the warm spray. He hauls me into his arms kissing me sweetly on the top of the head.

"Duvan," I start but then chicken out.

He grips my chin and tilts my head up to look at him. "Out with it, mi amor."

His black hair is slicked back and his eyelashes seem darker and longer now that they're wet. Water races down his temple. My mouth waters to lick it right from his cheek.

"I'm pregnant."

I'm beaming at him, but his smile falls the moment I say the words. Dark brows furl together in what seems like an angry manner. Panic wells inside of me because this was not the reaction I was expecting.

"S-say something," I choke out. He becomes a blur as my emotions get the better of me.

His hands slide into my partially wet hair. I'm dragged toward him so that his mouth can consume mine. He kisses me hard enough to make my heart nearly stop beating. The kiss is so passionate and filled with love, I feel it with every fiber of my being.

"Are you happy?"

His nose nuzzles against mine. "Tigress, I'm fucking thrilled. Thank you for giving me a baby. You two will never want for anything."

I'm hoisted into his arms, and he's sliding me over his erect cock. He pushes me up against the shower wall while he fucks me. All the while whispering promises of a perfect life together.

"You're safe now," he coos into my ear.

And I am safe.

I'll never be able to express the gratitude I have for him saving me from Esteban. The addiction I was forced to endure was something I could have so easily succumbed to. Had it not been for Duvan's fierce need to protect, I could still be in that dark vortex Esteban sucked me into. That overwhelming urge to keep me safe is what ultimately birthed this love between us. When everyone else abandoned me, was stolen from me, or betrayed me, Duvan was there to defend me. It was his arms that held me together when I felt like I'd break.

He's my rock.

Strong. Powerful. Unwavering.

"I love you, tigress," he murmurs as I climax fiercely in his arms. "Don't you ever forget that."

I'm too drunk on him and his words to respond. He spills his seed into me. When it runs back out, he steals my heart forever.

I love you too, Duvan.

"You sure you're ready to tell them?" he questions. "Even *him*?" The slight twinge of disgust makes me smile. Duvan is jealous of Ren. While Ren and I have remained friends, my heart belongs to my husband.

"Aside from you, they're my only family. I want them to know we're expecting."

He nods as he sets up the computer so we can await their call. I greedily take the package of red licorice he had shipped here from his hands. While I smack on the candy, he fiddles with the DVD player. Soon, we're curled up watching Dirty Dancing. It reminds me of my daddy. Of times we spent together watching this very movie.

But it also brings back memories of Esteban.

Of the basement.

The heated bliss and the strange pleasure he forced on me.

Each and every time I think of Duvan's older brother, a sense of hot excitement surges through me. My heart does an actual leap in my chest. That is…

Until my disgust catches up to me.

The horror of what I'd become…

Of what I let him do…of what I begged him to do…

It all crashes down around me, squashing any sense of peace in my world.

Instead of explaining to Duvan why I don't want to watch one of my favorite movies, I let him tug me up beside him on the couch. We cuddle in each other's arms while we wait. It's only been a few days since I took the test, but he talks to my belly all the time. My world is completely calm and serene and so damn happy when that man's lips are pressing kisses to my stomach. When he's whispering to his baby in my stomach. When he's loving the both of us so hard it makes my heart ache.

A sudden chiming alerts us to the fact they're calling through. We sit up and as soon as I hit the button, three familiar faces grin back at me. Oscar is broodier than usual on the left. Vee sits in the middle. And Ren sits on the right with a slight uneasiness marring his features and his arm casually slung around Vee. I shoot Duvan a quick questioning look, and he shrugs it off.

"Hey, guys!" I greet with a smile.

Vee leans forward and touches the screen. "God, I miss you. When are you moving back?" Her pouting is cute. I miss that girl so much.

"Soon," I lie. In fact, I'm trying to convince Duvan to purchase the rental we're staying in. It may only have one bedroom, but surely we could make it work. Babies don't need their own rooms, do they?

"Have you seen or heard from our brother?" Duvan asks, straight to the point.

Oscar groans and pinches the bridge of his nose. He's clearly stressed having to pick up Duvan's slack. "Some of the guys say he headed east. Probably just rumors but stay safe anyway, man."

Duvan gives me a peck on my cheek and whispers to me. "Nobody will hurt you ever again, mi amor."

I believe him.

His words wash over me like the rain we've had all day today.

Cool and refreshing. Cleansing.

Vee starts babbling about her new apartment. I don't miss the haunted look in Ren's eyes. Oscar looks so tense he may snap. I've never seen my easygoing friend seem so frustrated.

"Anyway," Vee chirps. "Tell us the big news. What's going on?"

Duvan kisses my cheek before splaying his hand on my stomach. "We're having a baby."

Vee screams so loud I start laughing until tears are running down my cheeks. There's all kinds of commotion happening on the computer screen and with the storm crackling outside, but all I'm focused on is the way Duvan murmurs dirty stuff into my ear.

"Bye," I yell at the screen and swat at it.

Vee's still screeching, but the tone has changed. In fact, they're all yelling at us. As if we did something wrong. Duvan's hand slips up to caress my cheek. Time slows for a long moment.

His black eyes, shimmering with purple staring deeply into mine.

A perfect man for me who gave me a perfect gift.

Chaos from my friends that doesn't feel right.

Something is wrong.

And then I see *him*.

The evil glint in his eyes telling me all I need to know.

My mouth pops open to scream—a scream that matches that of my friends—and Duvan silences it with his kiss.

And then it's over.

So quick, I can't believe it's happened.

Hot liquid gushes down around me, and Duvan lets out a gurgle. His confused stare meeting mine as he clutches at his neck.

Blood.

So much blood.

Oh, God.

This can't be happening.

Wake up, Brie!

This is a nightmare.

No! No! No!

"I'm s-so s-s-sorry," Duvan stammers out, the crimson flood around his fingers becoming uncontrollable. "I-I l-love you, t-tigress."

Tears are streaming down my cheeks and I'm trying to help him hold his neck together.

And it's too much.

Oh my God, it's too much.

Blooming and blooming around our fingers like the most hideous scarlet flowers to ever grow. The most hated flowers in the universe.

"No!" I choke out. "No!"

His eyes dull and he blinks slowly. He collapses on me and his breathing slows. I can't move my dying heavy husband. He's too big!

A sob wracks through me so hard I think I'll throw up. My fingers grip at Duvan's hair as I try to get him to look at me.

"P-Please, don't you dare die," I sob. Nothing else around me matters but him. Not his killer. Not my friends.

Just me and my love.

"I love you, Duvan."

His breath comes out in a ragged rush before he murmurs a final word. "Tigress."

Beat.

Beat.

Beat.

The sound of my own heart is thundering in my head, but no other sound comes through. My body grows cold. Shivers begin to ripple through me. A blankness settles over my mind.

Beat.

Beat.

Beat.

Nothing makes sense. I'm scrambling far, far away from reality inside my head. I want as far from the truth as I can get. I want to crawl into the black hole of despair in my brain only to never escape.

Beat.

"Gabriella."

Heath's cold voice drags me from my safe haven into my hell. My senses assault me all at once. A brutal beat down of my psyche. The people on the computer are still screaming. The man on my chest is dead. And the monster standing behind the couch is soulless.

Eyes that once looked upon me as if I were a treat his mommy wouldn't let him have now glare at me like he wants to tear through my flesh with his teeth and then suck on the bones after. The giant knife he used to slit the throat of my husband drips with blood. A knife similar to the one that fatally cut through my mother's neck too.

He's going to kill me too.

I'm going to die.

Duvan, our baby, and me. We'll be together at least.

"Not today, Gabriella," Heath hisses. "I've come a long way for you. A promise is a promise. And I promised I'd be back for you."

My eyes roll back as I succumb to shock. The heavy weight is gone and I'm floating. It isn't until I'm laid on something soft that I reopen my eyes. I'm on the bed—a bed I've made love to Duvan countless times on—and Heath is cutting my clothes right from my body.

I can't move.

I can't think.

I can't feel.

I just stare at the monster. He isn't careful as he tears the shorts off me. I'm nicked by the sharp blade on my hip bone when he cuts my panties from me. The tank I'm wearing is easily sawed through.

Blood.

So much blood.

All over my hands and upper body.

His hands.

The knife.

Bile creeps up my throat, and I turn my head to the side so I don't drown in my own vomit. Heath's belt jangles as he prepares to fuck me. Just beyond my dead husband's body.

And I can't do anything about it.

I pray for him to push the tip of his blade into my chest so I'll bleed out too. I want him to dump my dying body on Duvan's so we can race into the afterlife together.

"I've been waiting so long for this," Heath hisses.

Blink.

Blink.

Blink.

And then *him*.

Elation surges through me like the heroin used to cause. Hot and exciting as it rushed through my veins. Heath will pay for this. I can see it in my hero's eyes.

Dark and murderous.

Hate-filled.

My heart flops.

Hope soars inside me like a thousand eagles taking flight.

A knife, much bigger than Heath's glints in the bedroom light. Thunder booms outside like a prologue to the massacre that shall be.

Stabbing and stabbing and stabbing.

Death crashing around us like the storm waging outside.

I can't help but get high off the vengeance. More satisfying than any hit of bliss that ever swam through my veins. I want to thank the man with every ounce of my being who singlehandedly crushed a demon that had somehow escaped from hell.

A devastated scream I recognize as Vee's from the computer, makes my skin crawl.

Heath croaks and crumbles to the floor. His dick is hanging out but he never got to do what he came for. I stare at his unmoving body on the floor. If I had the energy, I would spit on him.

"Brie baby."

I drag my gaze from the psycho on the floor to the hero standing beside my bed. He sits down next to me and pushes my sticky hair from my face. A tender expression crosses over his features, and I'm instantly comforted.

"Is he alive?" I choke out.

He turns and regards Heath on the floor. "That motherfucker is dead."

"And my husband?"

This time, he frowns. Sadness washes over me. All this time, I had him painted as a monster. He's no monster.

He.

Came.

For.

Me.

"No."

A tear streaks down my cheek. "But I loved him."

"I know, baby."

"I will never love anyone like I loved him…"

He narrows his eyes at me and gives me a smile I remember fondly. "You will. It'll be different, but you will. Love is strange, Sylvia." Warm memories surge through me at the silly name.

I close my eyes and let my last happy moments with Duvan wash over me on repeat. His laughter. His touch. His decadent scent. His doting nature. His jokes. His strength. His ability to find my broken heart and mend it.

His love…

My body physically aches from this loss. I'm not sure the pain will ever subside. With a shaking hand, I reach out to *him*. "I want to go home, Daddy."

This is Me, Baby is up next…

THIS IS ME, baby

The game was over and they stole the victory away from ME.
Cheating. Lies. Corruption. Death.
This pawn never stood a chance.

But then he came for ME.

He plucked ME from my nightmare and kept me safe.
My heart was in tatters and my soul was lost.

Until the beast in ME woke up.
She was hungry and furious and didn't play by the rules of their game.
We were a vicious team. And we changed the game altogether. I took
what was theirs because they took what was mine.
ME against them.

That is…until I had someone else with ME.
Someone who vowed to fight alongside ME until the very end.

I don't want the love he has for ME.
But the beast in ME still craves to take everything she deserves.

He should run far away from ME.
Instead, he runs straight for ME.

This is ME, baby and I am going to ruin them all.

PROLOGUE

Brie
The day before…

"I feel like for once, I have a future. Something I can actually look forward to," I murmur and absently rub my still flat tummy. One day it will swell with our baby. The idea both elates and terrifies me.

Duvan chuckles and sits up on his elbow on the bed beside me. In the morning light, his eyes are a brilliant purple, not a trace of black in them. I could stare into them for hours. "I want you to wake up every single day and look forward to the next. You've had too much heartache in your life, mi amor. It's time to live. It's time to love. It's time to be happy. You deserve it."

His fingertip brushes against my bottom lip before he drags it along my throat toward my collarbone. When he skates it over to my nipple, I let out a gasp.

"I'm most definitely happy right now," I tell him with a grin. My nipple stands at attention as if to affirm my statement.

"Good," he growls as he climbs over my naked body. "I won't ask you for much, but your happiness is something I need, tigress. I want it. I desire it. I fucking crave it. Seeing your genuine smile or hearing your sweet laugh is better than any drug I've ever experienced. You're the real deal." His lips dance across mine. "You're mine."

I hook my legs around his hips and slightly lift up from the bed in a needy way. When he's inside of me, owning me and pleasing me, I feel whole. Perfect. A part of something much bigger than I ever dreamed of.

"I need you," I tell him, my voice almost a whine.

He nuzzles his nose against mine before pulling slightly away to look down at me. A strand of black hair falls down over his right eye, and he rewards me with a crooked grin. It sets my skin on fire with the need to have him before I go crazy. "You don't need me," he murmurs. But as he slides his thick cock against my clit, I know it's a lie. I need him with my entire being.

"I can't seem to function without you," I admit. With each slide against me, he makes me wetter and wetter. One wrong move and his teasing charade will be over. He'll be seated deep within me where he belongs.

His thumb strokes my cheek. "You are your own person, Brie. You may need my cock inside of you right now but you don't need *me* to exist. You're like some beautiful planet that hasn't been discovered by anyone but me yet. I come visit because I love being there with you. But you don't need me there to thrive. You exist in the vast black nothingness because you were meant to. You were always the plan…everyone around you, including me, is simply a part of the plan."

Tears well in my eyes and I blame my stupid emotions. He hardly ever calls me by my name. It startles me to the point that I begin to examine his vague words. I don't like the ominous nature of them. Like he's unknowingly warning me of a life without him.

I can't exist in a life like that.

"Tigress…" His growl has me locking eyes with him. "I'm not trying to make you sad. In fact, in about thirty seconds, I'm going to make you really fucking happy." He closes his eyes for a brief moment before blinking them back open. "I just want you to know that you're stronger than you give yourself credit for. I learned this about you the very first time I saw you. Your face was so impassive yet a storm brewed in your eyes. I could feel the heat of your fury at being a pawn between my father and Heath. That eventually you'd tire of their bullying. That one day you'd incinerate them both with your fiery wrath. I've seen your strength on many occasions. It hasn't been fully unleashed, but baby, it's there."

He swipes away a tear on my cheek and kisses my nose. My chest aches with a dull pain that begins to form there. I hate the tone with which he says his words. As if he and the rest of the universe know something I don't. Something that will completely blindside me one day. Something that will force me to call upon those alleged strengths he's so confident I own.

"Don't ever leave me," I choke out. I'm not sure where the insecurity is coming from but I can't bear the thought of him growing bored with me one day.

His mouth smashes against mine in a deep kiss. A kiss that makes promises he's yet to voice. That he'll be with me forever. I moan into his mouth as he slowly pushes his cock into me. With Duvan, I want him to split me in two. For him to burrow his way so deep into my soul, I'll never get him out.

"I'll always be with you, mi amor," he vows between our wet, breathy kisses. His hips buck in a slow and torturous way against me.

"Here." He taps my temple.

"Here." He runs his fingers between my breasts, lingering long enough to feel my thundering heartbeat.

"And here." His hand splays across my stomach.

I nod in agreement and dig my heels into his ass to spur him on. I need my tiger to maul me. To destroy my being and mark me as his. "Always with me," I echo, my voice quivering with the anticipation of a very close orgasm.

His kiss deepens as he thrusts harder into me. Duvan touches me in all the right places. Says all the right things. Smells exactly the right way.

"Oh, God," I whimper a second before my body convulses with an orgasm.

He grunts against my mouth, his hot breath tickling me, as he finds his own release. His hot semen fills me, but it's actually *him* who fills my heart.

"Tigress," he says, a smug tone in his voice. He pulls away and lifts a black eyebrow at me. The shadow from not shaving in a couple of days is a sexy look on him. My pussy throbs just looking at my handsome husband. "I'm going to make you love me one day."

All I can do is beam at him.

He won't have to make me.

Because I already do.

I love you, Duvan Rojas.

ONE

Gabe

The day of…

Love is strange. At least that's what I always told my baby girl. That it's messy and confusing. That half the time it doesn't make sense. That sometimes, it morphs and changes into something new.

What I didn't tell her is that love is ugly too.

As a father, I wanted to shelter her from heartache and pain. There was no way I was going to crush her and tell her that sometimes love really fucking hurts.

And yet…

I should have warned her. I should have explained to her that sometimes love is like a dull knife that takes pride in gouging out little pieces of your heart, one painful dig at a time.

Love has fucking destroyed my daughter.

Glancing over at the passenger side of the rental car, I let out a sigh of frustration. She looks so tiny curled up in her seat. Her hair is messy and caked in blood. Those high cheekbones, which are exactly the same design as her mother's, are tearstained and almost as red as the blood that covers her.

I tear my gaze from her sleeping form and focus on the dark road ahead of me. The rain is coming down in buckets due to the tropical storm, which makes trying to drive in it a bitch. I'm dying to get on my phone and call War. To flip the fuck out on him for not warning me sooner about what was going on.

"We can't be sure," he'd said. *"Everything looks okay from afar."*

But it wasn't fucking okay. Some motherfucker had a hard-on for my daughter. The prick was supposed to take care of her so she'd be safe and loved. A stand-in father if you will. This life was supposed to be preferable over the one I could have given her with Hannah. She was supposed to thrive and live life to the fullest.

Not this.

She wasn't meant to be forced to marry some pussy at eighteen, carted off to South America, and then have to witness the brutal murder of her *husband*.

Just thinking the goddamned word has me on edge. My knuckles turn white on the steering wheel as I clutch it with fury.

If only I'd not been wrapped up in Hannah, I could have noticed the signs sooner. I should have known better than to leave Ren and War in charge of looking after my daughter. Those two idiots can't identify evil from a mile away, not like I can. Hell, I'm married to it. I recognize the unhinged parts of people. Hone in on them like a fly on shit. If I'd taken one minute out of my goddamned life with my wife and Toto to look beyond the surface of Brie's new life, I'd have seen the signs. Something would have alerted me.

I could have saved her from all of this.

Clenching my jaw, I attempt to calm the fuck down. My daughter needs me to be her strength. I've got a lot of apologizing to do. I need to fix my broken baby girl.

My phone rings in my pocket, jerking me from my inner hatred. I yank it from my pocket and bark out a harsh, "Hello?"

"How is she?" War demands. "Ren told me what he saw during the Skype session—"

"I could have saved her sooner," I snap, interrupting him. "You and your son were supposed to be watching her. How could you not see any of this earlier? The clues were there, were they not?"

The line is quiet for a moment. "Gabe, is Brie safe?"

"Yes. Now answer the fucking question."

He huffs into the line. "Perhaps if you wouldn't have gone all Bonnie and Clyde with my daughter, you would have noticed the signs your own damn self." Even though his words are meant to bite, they don't.

"*Your* daughter needed me," I hiss back.

"*Your* daughter needed you." His retort isn't pissy…it's matter of fact.

"Jesus," I complain. "This is all my fault."

A commotion in the background on his end grows quiet. "Your other daughter needs you too."

I scrub at my cheek in frustration. I'm fucking tired as hell, having been on a non-stop journey all over the goddamned globe ever since I was first made aware of that sick asshole Heath Berkley. I'd made it my mission to slaughter his ass once Ren told me all about the depraved things he'd done to her. Things he'd witnessed, but also the stories that came from her adopted sister too. I'd called with the intent to check on Toto and ended up slamming my phone down after a long, detailed account of exactly what my daughter had been dealing with.

"How's Hannah? Is she being…"

War sighs and it makes my anxiety spike. "She's being nice. For the most part. We haven't had to restrain her or anything. Toto seems happy to see her."

I let out a breath of relief. "She's still not allowed to be alone with her," I remind him.

"Don't worry," he assures me. "Bay hasn't let Toto out of her sight since Han showed up."

Thank fucking God.

"Are you bringing her back to San Diego?" he questions. "Gabriella can always stay with us in case…" he trails off.

"Hannah loses her shit?"

He huffs. "Bay researched medicines that were okay for Han to take while pregnant. I'm going to order them and have them shipped here as quickly as possible. So maybe—"

War.

Always trusts Hannah can get better.

Hannah will *never* get better.

That, I know for a fact.

"Get the shit ordered," I grunt.

"Do you want to talk to her?"

I roll my head on my shoulders in an attempt to loosen my tight muscles. "No."

Silence.

"She's been asking for you," he murmurs.

"Speaking to me will just rile her up. We need her calm. Tell her you couldn't get ahold of me," I instruct.

I've been driving in the dark for hours. Long after the ferry ride that was choppy as fuck due to the storm. I don't know where I'm going but I'm just getting her far the hell away from that blood bath.

My poor Brie baby has seen too much blood in her lifetime. Her mother and now her husband. If I could rewrite history for her, I would.

"When are you coming back for the rest of your family?" he questions.

I glance over at my broken daughter and sigh. "I don't know. I need to assess how she's doing first. As soon as we've landed somewhere, I'll update you."

Before he can get any more words in, I hang up.

Brie sniffles from beside me. Her tired eyes blink open, and then she tells me exactly where she wants to go.

And of course I'll take her there.

Thirty-one hours is a long goddamned drive. We stopped off at some roach-infested hostel before we entered Colombia. I was able to get Brie to take a shower, but she's been in a state of shock. Thankfully, she's slept most of the time.

The GPS signals we're at our location. Fucking finally. I'm not at all comfortable staying here, but we have no choice. We need to rest for a few days before we travel any further. I feel like it's all I've been doing for the past week as I hunted for that prick Heath. Now that he's no longer a threat, I can focus on my daughter.

She sits up in her seat and squints in the darkness. The house is one of the fancier ones we've seen. I like that it sits on the outskirts of town, far away from any hoodlums. I can keep her safe here for now.

As soon as we park, she clambers out of the vehicle and sprints toward the house. But before she makes it very far, she doubles over and vomits into a bush. I grab the bag I'd stuffed my clothes into, as well as another one I'd filled with some stuff she had at the home on the island. I'm not sure if I grabbed everything she needs, but I didn't want any evidence of her left at the murder scene. I hope I took everything and that she won't get tied back to what happened there.

"Brie baby," I say softly. "Don't just charge in there. Let me make sure it's safe."

She pauses as she starts up the porch steps. Her teary eyes find mine and she nods. "He could be here."

The chilly way in which she says those words causes unease to crawl up my spine. I killed the monster in her world. Fucking stabbed every vital organ I could push my knife into. Heath Berkley can't hurt my daughter ever again. She must still be in shock if she doesn't remember that.

I clutch her shoulder before passing her on the porch. Thunder grumbles nearby and I know we've only been given a brief reprieve from the hammering winds and rain. I unsheathe my knife. Soundlessly, I drop our bags to the floor beside the door and twist the knob. It turns without resistance, which makes alarm bells ring inside my head. The door makes a squeak of protest when I push inside.

Darkness.

I can hear the hum of the refrigerator but not much else.

"Stay there," I instruct in a whisper.

On silent feet, I make my way through the darkened living room. Every few minutes, the lightning illuminates the space, showing me my path. I clear the front room and kitchen first. I'm just walking down the nearly pitch black hallway when I hear the familiar click of a gun being chambered.

Fuck.

I slash my knife in the direction of the sound—at least where I think I heard it—but it's wrong. In the next instant, I'm tackled. It catches me by surprise and I crash into a wall, knocking a picture to the floor, causing it to shatter. My attacker attempts to choke me from behind.

But I'm bigger.

With a roar, I flip the little fucker off my back. He hits the wood floors with a loud thump. In the dark, I wave my knife out in front of me in an attempt to slash him wide open. When I hear the ragged breathing nearby, I lunge forward. But he's too quick and he kicks my knife out of my hand. I manage to find the asshole's throat, gripping it in a punishing vise.

Cold metal meets my temple and I freeze.

And then light.

Blinding fucking light.

"Daddy!" Brie cries out from behind me. "Don't hurt her!"

Her?

I glare down at a girl not much older than Brie. Her eyes are wild and her nearly black hair is messy. Her hand—which she is holding a gun with, pressed to me—trembles severely.

"Luciana," Brie says with a sob.

The girl beneath me lets out a cry of relief at seeing my daughter. They must be friends. I snatch the gun from her grip and rise to my feet. She quickly jumps to hers. Her brown eyes are narrowed as she scrutinizes me.

"This is my dad." Brie runs over to the girl and they hug. When they pull apart, Luciana frowns at her.

"Beh?" she seems to say in question and then taps her heart.

Brie lets out a ragged sob and shakes her head. "H-He's g-g-gone."

Luciana starts to cry too, and the two girls lock together in an embrace. Meanwhile, I stand there looking stupid. I don't know what's going on or how to fucking fix it.

"Are you alone?" I demand with a growl.

The girl looks over at me and nods.

"Esteban…" Brie murmurs. "He's not been by?"

Terror flickers in Luciana's eyes. She shakes her head. Why the fuck won't she talk?

"Daddy," my daughter says. "We're safe. He's not here."

Hot anger surges through me. The fact that my daughter has more than one man to fear has my teeth grinding together to the point that I wonder if I'll break them. I want to grab Brie by the shoulders and shake the answers out of her. Problem is, she's so fragile, I'm afraid it would crush her.

We need to get some sleep and gain our bearings.

Then she can explain this entire fucked-up world she's been living in.

"I'll grab our bags and lock up," I say with a huff. "Luciana, can you make sure she eats something?"

Luciana nods and breaks from their hug. When she starts past me, I snag her wrist. "What's the matter? Cat got your tongue? Why won't you talk?"

She lifts her chin bravely and glares at me. Then, she opens her mouth. I gape at the little stump in her mouth. What the fuck?

"Esteban." The name is whispered from Brie behind me.

This motherfucker is right at the top of my shit list. Jerking my head to Brie, I lift a brow in question. "Who's this Esteban character?"

Her eyes well with tears—I'm surprised she still has any left—and she drops her gaze to the floor. "He's nobody." She pushes past me and I hear her footsteps as she runs up the stairs.

Luciana makes a sound of disagreement. I turn to look at her. Her lips are pressed into a firm line.

"Esteban hurt you?" I demand.

She narrows her eyes and nods.

I grit my teeth and look up at the celling for a moment before meeting her gaze again. "And did he hurt my little girl?"

Tears pool in her brown eyes, making them look like melted chocolate. Her bottom lip wobbles as she makes a motion of giving herself a shot into her forearm.

"HE FUCKING DRUGGED HER?" I roar, my chest heaving with fury.

The young woman flinches at my tone and nods wildly.

"Is that all?" I'm seething mad.

She swallows and shakes her head. My fears come to life when she mouths the word: *rape.*

The wall beside me never saw it coming.

I blast my fist through it. One. Two. Three times until the young woman grabs at my elbow.

When I finally turn to look back at her, she's blurry. So fucking blurry. I stiffen when she hugs my middle.

A choked sound escapes me.

Luciana pulls away and reaches a small hand up to my face. She swipes away wetness from my cheek before making a motion of holding a phone to her ear. I pull mine from my pocket and hand it to her.

Her dark hair curtains around her face as she taps away with lightning speed. The heat keeps streaming down my cheeks. I can feel it dripping from my jaw.

My Brie.

My poor baby girl.

She hands me back my phone, and I see she's written a message on my notes app.

Esteban is an evil man. He cut my tongue from my mouth when I was a little girl. He's done terrible things to Brie. He forced heroin on her and raped her. Many times. Is Duvan really dead? Oscar texted me about what they saw.

I lift my watery gaze to find her staring at me with such hope in her eyes. Hope that it was all a bad dream. Hope that I'll somehow save her from this motherfucking Esteban, too.

Clenching my jaw, I give her a slight shake of my head before storming off to comfort my daughter. Her broken wails behind me seep their way into my soul and crack it wide open.

Esteban is going to fucking die.

The asshole won't die easily.

I'm going to peel his skin from his sorry body and feed it to him until he chokes to death.

And I'm going to make sure he feels every second of excruciating pain.

Nobody touches my daughter.

Fucking nobody.

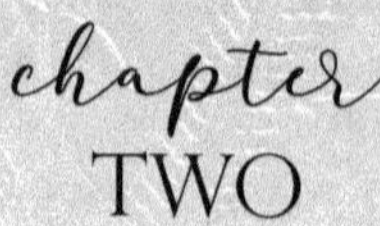

TWO

War

Several days later…

"Your move, Daddy."

Hannah's blue eyes glitter with clarity. The meds seem to be working. I don't notice the darkness overtaking her when she looks at her mother or when Toto acts out. She seems…normal.

Of course, with Hannah, there is no normal.

She can never be normal.

My daughter will always teeter on a delicate line between here and…*there*.

We absolutely can't have her go *there* again.

Out of all my children, Hannah's always been my most worthy opponent on the chess board. She's calculating and smart as a whip. That's what makes her so dangerous. The girl isn't just rash and impetuous. A lot of the time, she plans out her moves. Always thinking about the end game. She contemplates the other moves. The outcomes. The consequences.

"You're stuck," she tells me smugly as she sits back in her chair, rubbing her swollen belly. In another few months, I'll have a grandson.

I arch an eyebrow at her and am met with a satisfied grin. She's given me that smile ninety-seven times since she's been here. I count them because I need to figure her out. It benefits my family if I can think several moves ahead of our most unpredictable piece. For her safety…and ours.

"I'm not stuck," I say with a grunt. I have three options to take out her queen within just a couple of moves. But something tells me she knows this and is setting me up so she can obliterate me when I go for the most obvious moves.

She starts humming something sweet, but coming from my daughter, it sounds haunted and borderline fucking scary. Her blue eyes darken several shades as she looks past me out the window at the beach, the moonlight casting an eerie glow on her face. Baylee used to get the same look in her eye when she thought about Gabe. There's no doubt in my mind, Hannah is thinking about him too. And whatever it is, I certainly don't want to think about it.

"When did you know you were different, Daddy? When did you realize you were sick?" she asks and reaches for her mug of tea on the end table. She sips it and looks at me over the steam.

I scrub at my face and shrug. "I don't know."

But that's a lie. I remember the exact second I realized something was completely wrong with me. It wasn't long after my high school girlfriend moved on because I was going insane. Dad was at his wits' end with me. I'd become antisocial and refused to leave my room. But that isn't when the realization occurred.

It happened almost like a crack in a glacier.

Small at first.

Then it seemed to run from me. Zigzagging back and forth away from me at light speed.

I'd desperately tried to hold the fissure together. Dug my fingernails into the black ice of my mind. Watched them rip from my fingers as the divide spread open. The crack became a valley, and I fell. So far, I fell. Into the nothingness. Alone.

That day, I attempted to calculate how many seconds I'd known my mother before she passed away. I'd obsessed over those last moments of her life. Grew confused on the calculations because I wasn't exactly sure of the exact moment she'd left this world. I replayed the horrific scene of her blood and brain matter all over my parents' bathroom over and over again. Sometimes the calculation would vary by a few hundred seconds. Other times just a few seconds.

It maddened me.

I needed to know.

I'd had a burning desire to cut open my head and demand the memories to become clearer for me. To pull out the part of me that actually paid attention in that exact moment. It was then that I went into the bathroom and buzzed all of the hair off my head. Each strand fluttered into the bathroom sink until my flesh-covered skull was on display. The answers were all inside. I just needed to cut them out.

I'd held a kitchen knife out before me and glared at it for hours. Actually, it was fourteen hundred and fourteen seconds to be exact. But who's counting?

I imagined seeing the blood run down my forehead. To see it dripping down over my eyelids, blinding me with red. The very idea of the horror show replaying again was enough to make me drop the knife with a clatter. I'd gagged and gagged and gagged until I expelled my lunch into the toilet. Then, I'd become fixated on the hair discarded in the sink.

How many were there?

Hundreds?

Thousands?

I found a pair of tweezers and a Ziplock bag. That afternoon, I stood in front of the sink counting my hairs. Each and every one of them. Dad worked late that night. When he'd come home, I was still counting. He'd taken one look at me and broken down. Sobbed and sobbed in the doorway as he regarded my crazed self.

And I *was* crazed.

It was the beginning of my confusion. My mental hurricane. My self-hate.

I'd cracked. That afternoon, I cracked and it wasn't until I met Baylee that I was able to bridge the divide. She healed me. Not only did she place bandages on the splits in my mind but she also showed me how to bring the two torn parts of me back together. With steady, sure hands, she stitched me until I was no longer ripped in two. One day at a time, she healed me.

"Your move," I tell Hannah as I slide my rook into place.

She groans. "Ugh! Dad! How do you always know what I'm going to do?"

I'm still smirking at her when the front door swings open and Ren stalks in. He slams the door, and I cringe hoping he didn't wake the babies or Bay. Calder is out with friends. Not that the kid ever sleeps, anyway.

Hannah frowns at me. "He's still mad at me?" Her expression is crestfallen.

I close my eyes and expel a deep breath. Being mad is the biggest understatement of the year. Ren hates Hannah for the path of destruction she left in her wake. I know this because he's screamed it at me on more than one occasion since Gabe dropped her off on our doorstep to go find Heath.

"He's not mad," I lie.

She makes a humming sound but then leans forward to focus on her move.

"I'll be right back, Han. I'm going to go talk to your brother." I stand and press a kiss to the top of her head before striding down the hallway after my boy.

I hate that they once had such a close relationship, yet now he won't even speak to her. Not that I can blame him. Hannah's ruined so many lives with her choices. But what Ren and Bay don't get is that Hannah can't help it. She doesn't operate like they do. Her mind doesn't know the lines of right and wrong. Hell, even Gabe has some sense of right and wrong—otherwise he wouldn't be so damn protective over Toto.

But Hannah?

She's like me.

Darker, though. Unpredictable. Certainly not reachable.

Her mind isn't a crevice that can be pushed back together.

No…

Her mind is a black hole.

Empty. Crushing. Never ending madness.

Anything that gets sucked up into her twisted vortex gets decimated. She ruins people. Lives. Hearts.

Which is why I watch her every move. Just like in our chess games. It is absolutely imperative I learn everything I can about her darkness. Because if I understand it, then I can keep her away from it. Keep my once sweet baby girl in the light. Gabe, surprisingly, keeps her fairly level-headed. But he doesn't understand her. He feeds her inner monster when she's ravenous. He protects her from herself. And protects those he loves from her. But he simply doesn't get her. Not like I do.

One day, I'll learn about her black hole.

I will figure out her inner algorithms. Crack the code of her head. Cross all the *T*s and dot all the *I*s. I'll turn her black hole inside out. I'm so sure of it.

By the time I push into Ren's bedroom, he's standing with his back to me, his shoulders tense. When I reach out and pat his back, he flinches. It's then that I see the bandages sticking out of the neck of his shirt.

"Did you add more to it?" I question.

He turns to regard me. My sweet son—always the boy who did what he could to please Bay and I—is gone. After witnessing the bloodshed online recently, he's been a little fucked up. His steely blue eyes are hardened. All the softness of my son is hidden from me. He clenches his jaw and glares. "I got it filled in."

I'm not one hundred percent on board with my oldest son getting a full back tattoo, but it seems to be therapeutic for him. It started not long after Brie officially moved on from him. Every couple of weeks, he'd get more added on. But after the massacre, he's seemed almost obsessed with finishing it.

"Can I see?" I question.

He shakes his head. "Later. Why is she still here?"

Ren. Straight to the point. Just like his mother.

I let out a sigh of frustration. "We're the only ones who can look after her properly until Gabe gets back. It's not safe for her to be alone…" I trail off. We both know why.

His eyes narrow and his nostrils flare. "I want access to my trust fund."

I gape at his sudden change of discussion. "Why?"

"I'm moving the fuck out of here. The dorms are just temporary, and when I'm not there, I have to come back here. And I can't stay here any longer. This isn't home," he seethes. "Not when that monster prances around as if nothing happened." He rips at his hair and lets out a guttural growl. "Everything happened."

My heart races in my chest. *Thump. Thump. Thump.* I try to focus on my boy rather than the urge to count the loud beats. He needs me. He needs my focus.

"I can give you your money," I tell him, my voice hoarse. "But, Ren, I really wish you would reconsider—"

"THERE IS NOTHING TO RECONSIDER!"

His entire body quakes with rage. Both of his hands are fisted. My son is no longer a boy. He stands taller than me. Nineteen looks good on him. The past couple of months, he's spent more time in our home gym than anywhere else, and his muscles have really filled out. He avoids Hannah at all costs. Lives in his headphones with his music blasting continuously to block out his family.

It's cutting my chest wide open.

I want to fix my boy.

But right now, I have to fix my daughter.

Ren is smart. He'll figure it out. The kid just needs his space.

"I'll write you a check in the morning. Whatever you need," I assure him. My tone sounds resigned to the fact that Ren will only heal if he gets away from his sister, who was instrumental in his life being torn apart.

"Thank you," he manages. Barely. He turns and starts yanking clothes from his dresser and shoving them into a bag. I'm leaned against the wall watching him when the door squeaks open. When Hannah's blonde head comes into view, I open my mouth to ask her to leave us be.

But Ren sees her before I get a chance to.

"Get out," he snarls, his muscled arm quivering with rage as he points at the door behind her. "Get the fuck out of my room and out of my goddamned life!"

She tenses at his words and shoots me a sad look. "Ren—"

He stalks over to her with lightning speed. I tense, preparing myself to yank him away if his temper flares any more. His finger points at her chest as he glares down at her. Their bodies are nearly touching. "I hate you, Han. Do you understand that in your fucked-up little head? Hate."

Tears well in her eyes. "You don't mean that."

He scoffs, narrowing his gaze. "Every word. You ruined my life. You ruined Brie's life."

She tenses at the mention of Brie. I know this look too. The look she regards Bay with on occasion. The one she flashes to Toto at times. I'm not at all comfortable with this look. It's one that screams: *I could make you disappear with a snap of my fingers.*

I fucking hate the look.

"Okay, you two," I grumble and grab Ren's elbow. I drag him away from her and stand between them. "Han, go to bed. Ren, pack your stuff. We'll talk about this later when tempers aren't hot."

Tears roll down my daughter's cheeks and she launches herself into my arms for a hug. I know those tears, though. They aren't real. They aren't genuine. They're the ones she uses to get what she wants. Right now, she wants Ren to forgive her.

Unfortunately, I don't think Ren will ever forgive her.

"We'll talk soon, son," I say to him, giving him a nod of my head.

"Yep," he grunts out before he goes back to packing.

I usher Hannah out of his room and into hers. We don't speak as I give her the pills that seem to be helping. Once she's settled into bed, I kiss her goodnight and shut the door. Now that she's not acting so crazy, I don't have to lock her in the room at night.

But Baylee and I lock ourselves in our room.

With both Mason and Toto.

You can never be too sure with Hannah.

By the time I make it back to my bedroom, Ren's already gone. I hear the thump of his bass as he peels away.

Poor kid.

My bedroom is dark, aside from the glow from the closet. Toto sometimes gets scared, so we leave it on for her. She's passed out in her pack-n-play. Her blonde curls glow in the light from the closet. God, I love that little girl. Next, I peek in on Mason. He's in a basinet beside Baylee. She swaddled him up, and he looks serene sucking on his pacifier. The boy looks just like Ren did at that age. My heart swells at how beautiful our children are.

"Come to bed," Bay murmurs in her thick, sleepy voice.

I peel off my T-shirt and shove down my lounge pants. As I crawl into our bed, I'm assaulted with her scent. It's a permanent happy place in my mind. So feminine and clean and just Baylee.

"What was all the yelling about?" she asks in a whisper.

I haul her to me and press a kiss to her forehead. "Hannah and Ren." Our eyes meet, both of us wearing matching frowns. "He wants access to his trust fund. He's moving out, baby."

A storm brews in her eyes, and she chews on her bottom lip for a moment while she contemplates my words. After a moment, she darts her eyes to mine. "I don't want him to go, but maybe he'll be happier."

I nod and slide my palm to her hip before slipping it under her shirt to stroke the delicate flesh on her back. "He needs his space. It's better to let him have his money than for him to quit college or something."

Her fingers skim over my chest and she sniffles. "Everything is a mess right now, War."

I lean forward and capture her lips. So soft. So fucking supple. "This mess is ours. We're the only ones who can clean it up. This mess is our responsibility." I kiss her deep enough to draw out a needy moan from her. "But we *will* get it cleaned up. Then we can be happy again."

Pushing her onto her back, I lick away her tears as I strip her out of her clothes. We've only been able to go back to having sex in the last couple of weeks. Thankfully, though, we don't have to worry about birth control because she got her tubes tied after Mason.

"War…" My name on her lips is a prayer. She needs me to fix it all for her. Of course I will. I'll always owe her for fixing me.

"Shhh," I murmur against her mouth as I part her legs and settle myself between them. I tug my hardened cock from my boxers and tease her wet opening. Then, with a low growl, I push into my perfect wife.

Once I'm seated deep inside her heat, I lift up to look at her. "I love you, Bay."

Her fingernails dig into me and her heels press into my ass as she urges me to fuck her. I suck on her sweet tongue as I deliver the thrusts she wants. Exactly the way she likes them. Exactly the right pace.

With every pound into her tight body, I feel my own climax taunting me. It's so close, but I don't want to lose control unless she's unraveling with me. Now that we have two small kiddos to deal with, our sexual times have been limited. I want her to orgasm and give me all of her, even if only briefly.

"Come all over my cock, baby," I urge. My fingers slip between us and I massage her swollen clit. Having been married for nearly two decades, I know exactly where to touch her. I know how many seconds it will take her to explode with pleasure the moment I find her sweet spot.

"Oh," she moans in the softest of whispers.

Her body clenches around mine. It drives me mad with need. My nuts tighten for a brief moment before I'm draining my desire into her.

"God," I say with a grunt and nip at her bottom lip. "You make the hottest sounds when I fuck the pleasure out of you."

She lets out a quiet laugh and grins up at me. Her blue eyes sparkle. "War?"

"Yeah, Bay?"

"I *am* happy." She palms my cheek. "Everything is a mess, no doubt about it. But I'm happy. As long as you're here taking care of me and the kids, my life is complete. You're a good man."

I flash her a lopsided grin. My cock, which had been softening, hardens up rather quickly. "I'm about to make you happy again. Then, we're going to shower." I buck into her hard enough to make her yelp. The time for sweetness is over. It's now time to bring out her claws. I fucking love it when she digs them into me. "And after we shower, you'll make me happy too when you let me suck on that sensitive clit of yours. It's been far too long, baby."

My hips buck powerfully into her. The pain of her fingernails has me groaning with pleasure.

"Don't stop," she begs against the shell of my ear.

I'll never stop.

chapter
THREE

Brie

I'm broken.

Used up.

Empty.

Fucking lost.

The pillow beneath me is soaked from my tears. Days and days. They all bleed together. I'm lost inside this vortex of pain. Unsure where it all starts and where it ends. One thing's for sure, though.

Duvan's not here with me.

Heath ripped him away from me. He came into my life, one last time, and took what never belonged to him. The ache in my chest intensifies. A pain unlike one I've ever known claws from within me. It's like a caged beast desperate to escape. But God has punished me—again—for some reason. Because, this time, I'm to manage this beast all on my own. This beast of despair devoured the old one within me. Before that, I only thought it was bad after my mother was taken from me. Now, I realize it wasn't a beast at all. Just some sad little animal.

But the feral animal in me now is not small at all. It's devastated and crushed and growing by the second. The animal is also very angry. She has a thirst for blood. The one she wanted to devour is already gone. That only leaves the thirst for one man.

Esteban.

The cravings that used to surge through me were because of what he could give me. The heroin. Heated bliss that stole all the pain away. I know that if I wanted it again, I could figure it out myself this time. I could drive into the city, purchase the product, and get high.

If I wanted to.

If I didn't have Duvan's baby growing inside of me.

But I don't want to.

The craving when I think about Esteban now isn't about the drugs. It's about making him bleed. It's about punishing him because he deserves it after all he's done. It's about vengeance. I want him to be the recipient of the pain I can't dole out to Heath because he's dead.

Esteban will be the one to pay for the sins of Heath.

I want his blood to coat my fingers as I cut his heart from his chest.

Swiping a tear from my cheek, I sit up and look over at Duvan's empty spot. The first night we'd arrived back home, Daddy tried to comfort me. As soon as the bed dipped with his weight, I screamed at him to leave. I was so afraid he'd steal away the lingering scent Duvan left. That he'd take away the memories of my husband.

Plus, I didn't want Daddy's comfort.

My heart still bleeds from when he left me. When he took off with my mother's murderer. As grateful as I was that he saved me from Heath, I still can't help but be angry with him.

The tears constantly roll down my cheeks. But it isn't sadness that is threatening to eat me alive. It's fury and hate and anger. I've welcomed them wholeheartedly. Those fiery emotions don't hurt. They crave to do the hurting.

I want to make someone pay for all the wrongs that were done to me.

My eyes settle on a frame on Duvan's bedside table. It's a selfie of the two of us. One of those times when we were curled up watching movies together. Back when we were happy—just like he always wished for me to be.

I'll never be happy again.

Not ever.

Bile rises in my throat, and it once again reminds me that I'll be forced to be happy at some point. I scramble out of the bed and make it to the toilet in time to vomit. This little gift from Duvan has made me so sick.

I close my eyes and wallow in the misery of losing him. Had Daddy arrived ten minutes sooner, he could have saved Duvan too. Life is just unfuckingfair.

My hands shake as I clutch the toilet seat. I glance down at my wedding ring. Yesterday, I found the strength to go through the bag my dad had packed for me. Inside, I'd found my laptop, some pictures of Duvan and I, my clothes, a T-shirt of Duvan's, and his wedding ring.

Now that, I will be thankful for.

My father may have abandoned me but he always understood love. And in a tense, hasty moment, he had the foresight to grab something that was important to me. Now, Duvan's giant ring hangs on the chain around my neck, which Ren gave me. Safe, just above my heart, where he'll always be.

Just the thought of Duvan's body decomposing in the same room as Heath's corpse has me throwing up again. Tears roll out and my throat stings. If I were to call out, Luciana or Daddy would be here in an instant to take care of me.

But I don't want them.

I want to deal with this alone.

It's mine.

The hurt. The pain. The loss. It's all I have left of him.

Finally, I manage to feel okay and stand on shaky legs. The shower is hot and does something to soothe my soul into a numb state. If I think too hard about it all, I feel overwhelmed. The crushing weight of reality is too much. I crave to cut my wrists open and find my husband out there in the afterlife.

But each time those dark thoughts enter my mind, I think about our baby. It's enough to snuff out those dark ideations.

I tie a towel around my still wet body and shakily make my way into my bedroom. I've been going through every nook of the house finding items that remind me of Duvan. Collecting them. Sorting through his paperwork. Looking through old pictures. Anything to feel closer to him.

I wish I had someone I could talk to. Sure, Luciana has tried via text. Daddy has held me through a couple of soul-crushing cries. But it's not enough. Climbing onto the bed, I grab my laptop and open it up. The Skype app tells me that one of my friends is on. When I open it, I'm oddly satisfied to notice that it's Ren who's on.

Is he waiting for me to log on?

Does he want to talk to me?

I know from overhearing my dad that his family knows what happened. Ren was a witness to the horror. It makes me wonder if he was secretly happy to watch my husband die. The thought makes me sick and rage has me dialing him.

The program makes a chiming sound as it rings and then Ren's face is on my screen. I didn't think through my actions. I'm now sitting here, gaping at his haggard face like I'm a deer caught in a pair of headlights. His once navy blue eyes are hardened into a darker color. Almost black.

The hair on his face has grown into a stubble. Dark circles ring his eyes from what looks like stress or lack of sleep. If I thought he'd be happy for my loss, I was mistaken.

Ren's my friend.

At one time he was my lover.

He doesn't want my pain.

"Brie," he murmurs. "Jesus Christ."

Emotion chokes my throat but I swallow it down and blink away the tears forming in my eyes. He doesn't ask me how I am. He doesn't blurt out how horrific it was watching two men die just a few days ago. He does nothing but stare at me with his jaw clenching and unclenching.

I don't reply to him. My heart aches too fucking badly to find words. Instead, I let out a ragged breath and stare back. Eventually, I grab Duvan's ring hanging from my necklace and grip it in my fist. Hot tears streak down my face, but again, no words come out.

We remain silent for quite sometime. Me crying quietly and him sending me a thousand words with just one simple expression.

The two of us are different.

Two new people.

Two people scarred and ruined by our pasts.

I don't even know who he is anymore.

And I certainly don't know myself.

After what feels like hours, but based on the clock on my screen, has only been a minute or two, I let out a ragged sigh.

"Have you heard from Ozzy?" My question is a tiny whisper—one I barely push out of my throat.

His eyes close and he nods. When they reopen, his gaze pins me. "He left that day. Said he had to go see his dad." His gaze lowers until it's no longer locked with mine. "He said they had to dispose of the bodies."

Guilt surges through me. I left my dead husband's body in that beach rental and hopped in a ride with my dad. We drove thirty-one hours to my home in Colombia without a backward glance.

Had I been a better wife and not so shaken to my core, I'd have begged my father to call the police. For us to give Duvan a proper burial. But I didn't. I wallowed in my despair. Until I snapped out of it today. Until anger took over. Until clarity began to set in.

Unfortunately, it's too late.

"If you speak to him, will you tell him to call me?" I ask. Just the thought of seeing Oscar broken over the loss of his brother has me nearly in tears again.

"I will," he vows, his voice raw. "Promise me you'll call me if things get too rough. I'll be out there in a second. Just say the words, Brie."

I force a smile but I don't think it even reaches my lips. It feels as though my lips simply twitch instead. "I'm fine."

"Brie…" His brows furl together. "Be careful."

The tone of his warning has a chill shivering through me. "Take care of yourself, Ren."

As soon as I end our call, despair crashes back down around me. I clutch Duvan's T-shirt to my heart and curl up on the bed. My stomach growls after having emptied it, but I don't move to get up.

I never want to get up.

One week is all it took to dry up. I went from crying at every turn to walking around like a zombie. Luciana is barely able to get me to eat when she tries. Which is often. My dad tries to get me to speak. But I have nothing to say. I'm a shell. Simply going through the motions.

That is…

Until Ren calls me.

Our Skype conversations aren't really conversations at all.

They're more like staring contests. I listen to him bounce a tennis ball off the wall while Nine Inch Nails blares in the background. He watches me as I thumb through photo albums of when Duvan was a kid. Ren occasionally barks out at Calder. I, at times, yell at my dad to leave me alone. We're both sort of existing on the same plane but never intersecting.

I don't understand what's going on inside his head. But I sense the fury just below the surface. I like that he's angry for me. The heat from his wrath warms me like rays from the sun on a warm California summer day. I'm curious about the anger rolling from him. Ren was always so gentle and sweet. I've never really seen him get mad about anything.

I crave to scratch my fingernails along his flesh until the irritation seeps out. To see exactly why it exists. To prod until it becomes infected and spreads. I want to see more of it.

His anger feeds mine.

My inner animal craves to devour it.

"Where do you want them to put the couches?" I hear Calder question him.

My brows furrow together and I sit up to listen better.

"Don't know. Don't care. You're a big boy," Ren grunts. "Figure it out."

When Calder leaves, Ren goes back to bouncing his ball off the wall.

"Couches?"

His head snaps over to the screen and he frowns. "Moved out."

"Of the dorms?"

"And house," he grumbles.

He's angry and this time it doesn't seem to be about me. I'm dying to know what's upsetting him. I feel like he's holding back from me.

"Why?" I murmur.

He yanks off his baseball cap and tosses it away. His dark brown hair is messy. Longer than I remember. A lock of it falls into his eye for a brief moment before he rakes his fingers through his hair, pushing it back. Dark eyebrows furl together and his blue eyes darken. "Hannah. I can't stay there while…" he trails off. His eyes flicker with rage and it ignites something within me.

He can't stay there because of what she did to my family.

I'm not sure why that makes me happy, but it does.

I feel as though I won some battle I didn't know I was fighting.

"How can you afford it?"

He shrugs. "Dad let me into my trust fund. Calder's rooming with me because he doesn't like our fuckwit sister either. Plus, I don't think he's keen on being the backup babysitter at every turn."

I fight a smile imagining big 'ol Calder with a baby in his lap watching *Terminator* and eating greasy pizza. He'd be a terrible babysitter. Calder would probably give the baby Mountain Dew in its bottle or something.

My hand automatically splays out over my own belly. Would Duvan have been like that? Would he have been a laid back father or would he have been overprotective?

I guess I'll never know.

"You going to stay there forever?" he questions. "I mean, it's your house now, right?"

I swallow before dragging my gaze over to a pile on the bed. I've gone through all of his paperwork. When I'd been here before, Duvan would bring things for me to sign. I didn't pay much attention because I didn't care. Only cared about being with him—not his assets. But now…

I realize I have a lot to deal with.

For one, I have to figure out what to do with this house. I'm not sure I'll stay here but if I don't, I'll need to sell it. And his building where he manufactured his coke, I'll need to figure out what to do with that. If I could get a hold of Ozzy, he could help me. But according to Ren, he's gone AWOL.

So has Vee.

I haven't tried to call her, but Ren said he's called many times and even went by her apartment a few times. She's just gone. I know my best friend. Despite Heath being a lunatic, she loved her father. Watching him die had to have been hard on her. She's probably holed up at her parents' house in mourning.

I miss her.

"Brie…"

I blink away my thoughts and look at Ren. His face is scruffy from not having shaved for several days. That, coupled with the fierce gleam in his eyes, makes him look rougher. So different than the boy I remember.

"I guess one day I'll come back. There's just so much to deal with here first. Have you been able to get ahold of Oscar?"

He shakes his head. "Nope."

I'm about to say something else when my door cracks open. Daddy's watchful eyes find me. I wonder if he ever regrets leaving me. We haven't even spoken about it. Simply gone through the motions.

"I need to go," I tell Ren.

"I guess I need to as well. Calder isn't the brightest crayon in the box. Those couches will probably end up in his room," he complains and stretches his arm forward to end the call. His shirt slides up his arm and reveals some black from a new tattoo hiding beneath.

"New tat?"

"Yeah. It's still in progress."

"Can I see?"

He gives me a half smile that warms me and nods. Then, he grabs the bottom of his black T-shirt, peeling it off his body and up over his head. The first thing I notice on the gritty Skype image is how big he's gotten. When we were lovers for that brief stint, he was built but lean. Now, he's massive. Every surface of his chest is hardened and defined. His tribal wave tattoo has been added to and covers the entire upper half of his chest, whereas before it was small and only covered his pectoral muscle.

But what has me curious are what appears to be black tendrils or something creeping around his rib cage and collar bone. Like some creature is behind him and is about to drag him away. It's spooky but looks good on him.

"It's a back tattoo. I'm still having it worked on," he tells me as he turns.

When his back comes into view, I lean forward to get a better look. Even with the pixilation from our spotty connection, I can tell it's really well done. From the base of his skull to nearly his ass is a giant tree. No leaves. Just gnarly branches and roots that seem to reach around the sides of his body toward the front.

"Wow…"

He lets me stare at it for a few minutes. From behind, he hardly looks like Ren anymore. His shoulders are broader, his neck a little thicker, and his back is rippled with newly defined muscles.

"Do you just work out all the time? To hell with school," I tease. Or at least it's meant to come out in a teasing way. But lately, I'm not me and as soon as the words leave my mouth I realize they seem more condescending and borderline rude.

He turns back around and glares. I'm not used to his hardened gazes. A shiver ripples through me.

"I'm only taking a couple of classes this semester. I needed a break. Both are online courses. So, yeah," he grunts. "I've been using my extra time to lift."

I chew on my bottom lip as I stare at him. "Will you be on later?"

He grabs his T-shirt and starts to put it back on. "I'll find you, Brie." His head pops back through the shirt and his steely blue eyes are on mine. They make promises I don't understand. Promises I don't want to understand. His words, although simple, are thick with double meaning.

"Right," I say with a slight shake of my head. "Talk later."

Quickly, I mash the button to end our call. When I look back up, Daddy is still in the cracked doorway.

"Come in," I groan. I'm not in the mood for him to try and talk to me. I'm not in the mood to eat. I'm not in the mood for anything.

He pushes through the door and strolls in as if this is his house. Walking past the bed, he makes his way over to the window. With his back to me, he speaks in a gruff tone. "Are we going to talk about what happened?"

A shiver trembles through me. "You saw what happened. You were there," I bite out.

He looks at me over his shoulder, his brown eyes narrowed. "Not that, Brie baby. Us. How I left you."

Pain stabs at me from the inside out and I have to break our gaze. I look down at my hands to keep from crying. "I didn't understand why you left me. I still don't understand. It hurt so bad, Daddy."

His footsteps near, but I still don't look back at him. He moves the laptop and then sits beside me. I don't fight him when he takes my hand. Truth be told, I miss my dad's comfort. I miss how close we were. Mom was always working so it was me and him. Always.

"I thought I was doing the right thing. When I left you, I never meant for anything to happen to your mother. And then…" he trails off, his voice hoarse.

"Hannah cut open Mom's throat," I remind him, my tone bitter.

He squeezes my hand. "I didn't know she'd done that. I swear I would never have left you to find such a terrible scene. But then, it wasn't safe to come back home. I was a wanted man. I mean, I've always been a wanted man, but the spotlight was back on me. They'd have taken me to prison the moment I came for you."

The thought of Daddy in prison saddens me. I remember being a little girl and him warning me. How he said that if he ever got taken away, that he'd always loved me. That it was never a lie. Our love was real. I'd never understood it at the time. But after Mom died, his real story was all over the news. The terrible things he'd done in the past. The people he'd killed.

It should have made me afraid of him but it never did. The dad I knew wasn't like that. At least not with me. And when he'd eliminated Heath, all I wished for was that he'd done it sooner.

"Heath Berkley imprisoned me. I was his little pawn," I choke out.

I can sense his rage from beside me. It's like a wave of hate clouding the air around us. It doesn't suffocate and destroy me. Instead, it warms me. I breathe it in and hold on to it.

"War was supposed to make sure you were safe. I swear, baby, I kept tabs on you. A few times, I even snuck into that fucker's parties just to get a glimpse of you. Each time, you looked so…"

He must have seen me hanging out with Oscar and Vee. When I was with them, I was happy.

"Ren looked after me," I tell him and finally meet his gaze.

Daddy's eyes are bloodshot and his brows are furled together. His beard has thickened since we've been here. "He didn't do a very good job," he utters under his breath.

I feel oddly defensive over Ren. Sure, he wasn't protective like Daddy or even Duvan. And when his secret came out, I was crushed. But Ren was always there for me. He loved me when not many people did. He made me laugh. He made me feel. He gave me hope in an otherwise hopeless environment.

"You don't know anything about him," I tell him firmly. "How did you know to come find me, anyway? Why didn't you come sooner?" I want to scream at him and say, "Had you been there five minutes earlier, I would still have my husband." But I don't. I bite back the nasty words.

"Ren," he admits with a huff. "He spilled the beans about Heath and that he'd forced you to marry. That he was involved with the Colombian cartel. That he was a motherfucking dragon, and I'd willing left you there. He told me the ways he would touch you. How he'd hit you. All I saw was red. I'd sat by thinking you were happy. That you would go off to school and get a degree, like your mom. That you'd do great things in your life without my toxic decisions affecting you any longer. But it wasn't that way. You were nothing but a goddamned prisoner primed to marry into another bad family."

I shake my head. "Duvan was a good husband. Don't speak badly of him. And Oscar is my friend. The only bad person in this family is Esteban."

He scratches his beard before pinning me with a heartbroken look. "Luciana told me what that scum did to you." His palm finds my cheek and he strokes it. Fire blazes in his eyes as he spits out the words. "I promise you, Brie baby. I will find him and I will make him pay. It won't be a simple shot to the head either. I will torture him. Drain him of all his blood—one drop at a time. He'll suffer because he made you suffer. He'll hurt because he made you hurt. He'll die and you will live. Even if it's the last thing I do, I'll make sure he dies under my watch."

My heart flutters at his words. Esteban may not have killed my husband, but at one time, he killed my spirit. He'd made me hate myself. I want him dead. "Thank you."

Surprise flickers in his eyes but he schools the look away. "Baby, I need you to know that I'm never leaving you again. I know we'll never have a traditional family—and quite frankly, Hannah is difficult—but I'm going to find a way to make it work. We'll find a way to live together. Toto will love you. She's so beautiful and funny. You'll really like your sister."

An ache presents itself in my chest. I shake my head at him. "I'm not going to live with you. I am eighteen now and a widow. I've been imprisoned for far too long. I won't be locked away again."

Hurt flashes in his eyes. "But how will you live? Where will you live? Here?"

Reaching over to the stack of papers, I hand them to him. "All of this is mine. And this," I point at the address of the manufacturing plant, "is my business. At least my part of it."

His eyes widen. "You can't be serious. You're not going to be some cartel queen, Brie. I won't fucking allow it."

Gritting my teeth, I snatch the papers from him. "You don't have a say in the matter. Besides, I'm not going to run it. I'm going to sell it. That's where I'll need your help. I'm afraid these people are dangerous."

His gaze softens and a smile plays at his lips. "You look just like your momma. Alejandra had the same fire in her eyes when she was passionate about something. Beautiful. You've blossomed into an amazing woman. She would have been so proud of you. I certainly as fuck am. You've been dealt some bullshit and yet here you are. Alive. Fire blazing in your eyes. Fierce." He drags my wrist over to him and his thumb swipes over the heart with Duvan's name in it. "The tiger stripes are fitting. Anyone who fucks with you will meet the claws."

My heart patters and a genuine smile tugs at my lips. It's been so long since I actually laughed or truly grinned. Daddy always had that way of being able to cheer me up no matter what.

"I missed you," I admit, my throat tight with emotion.

He tugs my wrist until I'm flush against him. My dad always smelled so good. Safe and loving. A scent I couldn't seem to recall when I was living with the Berkleys but I missed it so badly. Now, I inhale it and hope to never lose it again.

"Brie baby," he whispers against my hair before kissing my head. "I'm not ever going anywhere again. I'll always be there for you if you need me. All you have to do is say the words. I'll slaughter anyone in my path to make sure I get to you."

I hug his middle. Tears roll out, but this time they are ones of relief. I don't feel so alone with my dad here to help me fight my war. His vow can be felt all the way into my soul. He won't leave me again. We're in this together.

"These Colombians won't know what hit 'em," he says with a chuckle. "Mickey and Sylvia are on the warpath."

I crack a smile. "Nobody puts Baby in the corner."

He pats my back. "Damn straight."

"Daddy," I murmur and look up at him. "I'm pregnant."

His smile falls from his face, and for the first time ever, a look of distress passes over my father's fearsome features.

chapter
FOUR

Gabe

The sensation of being watched has really been fucking with my head. Of course I don't mention it to Brie or Luciana, but someone is out there in those woods. I can feel it with every fiber of my being.

And tonight, I'm going to find out whom.

I located Duvan's weapon stash. Found me a big fucking knife and a Glock. Tonight, after the girls go to bed, I'm going hunting. If it's that Esteban asshole, I'm going to enjoy the hell out of skinning him alive.

"Still no word from Oscar?" Brie's voice carries out into the hallway from her room. She doesn't talk much, but each day is getting better. Ever since we had our heart to heart a few days ago, her spirits have lifted. She's still gutted over the loss of her husband, but I see signs of my child hiding behind the sadness. My baby girl lurks inside, just waiting to come out when it's safe.

I'll make her world safe for her if it's the last thing I do.

I'm sitting in her yellow office with the lights out and my eyes trained on the tree line past the barn. I know whoever is out there can't see me from this vantage point so it gives me the advantage. Eventually, I'll find this motherfucker.

"Where do you think he is?" she asks, her voice somewhat muffled.

I can't hear what Ren is saying but I know it's him. He's the only person she truly talks to. Sometimes, they do this weird-ass thing where they don't talk at all. As much as I want to ask why they do this, I don't. Whatever sort of comfort he provides her seems to improve her moods. Ren, despite being War's kid, is actually okay in my book. I'd much rather have her talking to the likes of him than that Oscar kid she keeps fretting about. I don't trust these Colombians as far as I can throw them.

I still can't believe she's pregnant. With Duvan's child, she later told me. I'm too young to be a grandfather. Hell, I have a baby of my own on the way. She stunned me speechless. I'm still trying to process her words. Not only do I have to protect my baby…but I also have to protect my baby's baby. I think I'm going to develop a fucking ulcer from all this stress.

Something glows for a brief moment beyond the trees, jerking me away from thoughts of my little girl's stomach swelling with child, and my suspicions are confirmed. Someone is out there. Their cell phone just gave them away.

I slip out of the room and creep down the hall past Brie's room. Luciana has already retired to her room above the garage for the evening, so I'll be able to sneak out undetected. The last thing I need is one of those girls following me out there and getting themselves hurt. I make my way out the front door and then creep around the massive house until I reach the backyard. Darting through the shadows, I make a wide arc to the woods. I move like the night. The fucker won't see me coming. Once I get into the thick vegetation of the forest, I have to slow down and be mindful of my steps as not to alert the prick to my presence. As I near, I can hear his breathing. He's crunching on some leaves. When his phone lights up again, he lets out a groan of frustration as he quickly answers it.

"Yes," he hisses. "I'm here. Where are you?"

He nods his head as he listens and his eyes remain fixed on the house. I inch forward and draw my knife, ready to exact damage on the lurker.

"She's here. Some man is with her." A pause. "Could be. They don't come out much." A pause. "Haven't seen Esteban." A pause. "Trust me, I will, *hermano*."

I'm much closer now and can hear the voice speaking rapidly on the other end, although I can't make out the words. The fucker is bigger than me. Broad shoulders. Looks meaner than hell. But I'm the one with the element of surprise here. I'm the one with my weapon drawn and ready.

"You think he'll come for her?" he asks, his voice weary. "Has Camilo even spoken to Esteban since Duvan ran him off?"

I don't make out what the other person says but I'll find out soon enough.

"Right. I'll keep watch. Call me when you need me to do it."

It takes everything in me to wait until he ends his call before I pounce. He's not going to touch one hair on my daughter's head. Grabbing the back of his jacket, I yank him backward and push the knife against his throat. It isn't hard enough to puncture the flesh but if he moves, he might cut himself wide open.

"Who the fuck are you?" I seethe. "And why are you stalking my daughter?"

He raises both hands in surrender. "Chill out, hombre. I'm here to protect her," he says through clenched teeth. "Not hurt her."

"Name," I bark.

"Rafe."

"Do you know my daughter?" I demand.

He groans. "I've met her once but I'm not even sure she remembers me. Although, I'm sure Duvan probably spoke of me to her. I'm his right-hand man. His protection." He lets out a hiss of frustration. "Was. I was those things. Now, I'm hers."

He is nothing to her.

I'm her motherfucking protection detail.

"Who were you talking to?"

"Oscar."

The name has me calming a bit. I draw my gun and step away. "Turn around."

He slowly turns around and regards me with narrowed eyes. "Listen, old man," he grunts, "you're in the lion's den out here. Word has gotten out that Duvan was murdered. I have some trusted men protecting his factory and I'm looking after his wife and the house. But it won't take long for the enemies of the Rojas family to pounce on this weakness. Esteban is missing. Duvan is dead. And that just leaves Camilo and Oscar to pick up the pieces. Camilo is at the shipyard eight hours away, and Oscar is with him until he can come out this way. We need to get the little princess out of here before she's in the middle of a drug war. Diego Gomez is just waiting to make his move and steal the Bogotá territory. It's only a matter of days before he can assemble a big enough army for what will be a hostile takeover."

Once again, I'm furious at myself for having let my daughter go. She was sucked up into something a thousand times more dangerous than Hannah. At least with my wife, when she gets crazy, I can manhandle her and tie her ass up. This whole Colombian army shit is way out of my league.

Fuck!

"Walk," I bark out. "We're going to talk to Brie and Luciana about this. If they even look at you wrong, I'm putting a bullet in your skull and letting the fucking forest animals snack on you. No funny moves. You do not know who the fuck you're messing with."

He sighs and nods. "Oscar told me you eliminated that sick fuck, Heath. There's been a hit out on him for years. Gomez just couldn't ever get to him. The Rojas family never got rid of him because he was an asset. I know Duvan hated him, though. You just carried out your son-in-law's wishes."

I motion with my gun toward the house. He trots through the brush and across the grass. Once we're on the porch, he turns to regard me.

"You may not trust me, but Duvan did. We were thick as thieves. He always took care of my mother and sisters when money was tight. I want to return the favor and make sure his woman isn't harmed. It would appear you and I share the same interests, *hermano.*"

The man smirks and it boils my blood. "I don't fucking share," I growl out before I pistol-whip him upside the head. "And I'm not your brother."

Brie sits perched on the arm of the couch with her dark eyebrows furrowed together. She glares at Rafe tied to a kitchen chair I dragged in here. Blood drips from his brow, where I've hit him. He still hasn't come to. The fierceness rippling from her is so thick in the air, you could cut it.

"Did you have to knock him out, Daddy?" Her brown eyes cut to mine and irritation flickers in them. She may have her mother's features, but the look in her eyes is all mine. I've seen it a thousand times in the mirror.

"I don't trust him," I grumble. Walking over to him, I grab a handful of his black hair and yank his head back. "Wake up, asshole."

His eyes slowly blink open, confusion twisting his features. When his eyes lock onto my daughter's, he smiles. If I didn't think she'd beat my ass, I'd knock him out again. "Hey, Brie. Remember me?"

She stiffens and tears her gaze from his. Her fingers twist together. I can tell he makes her anxious and that makes me really fucking anxious.

"You have exactly three minutes to make that look on her face disappear, punk," I snap. "Get to talking real fast." I release his hair and sit down in the chair beside him, my gun casually pointed at his head.

He side-eyes the gun before looking at her with a less confident expression. "Brie. You may not remember me, but I came here once when you two were first married. Remember, you went and fetched us the blow?"

She squints her eyes at him. "I remember there being several men there but I'm not sure."

He frowns. "Do you remember getting high out of your mind on Ex at the restaurant? I drove you two home that night."

My blood boils that her asshole husband gave her drugs. I'm glad the prick is dead.

"I thought you looked familiar. The name is familiar, though. Duvan did speak highly of you," she murmurs. "My dad says Oscar sent you? Why isn't he answering my calls?"

Rafe lets out a sigh. "Duvan and Heath left a mess for little Ozzy and Camilo. With Esteban hiding who the fuck knows where, they've got their hands full trying to keep control of their operation. Oscar has made it known, though, that I am to protect you and to get you out of Bogotá as soon as possible."

Brie's eyes flit over to mine, questions dancing in her eyes. She's eighteen goddamned years old, for crying out loud. This isn't something a woman her age should be dealing with. I'm keen on the idea of getting her the hell out of this country. I can protect her better on my own soil.

"My dad," she tells him, "and you, for that matter, can keep me safe from Esteban. I'm not leaving until I've settled my husband's assets. I owe it to him." She bites down on her bottom lip and her eyes become watery. "Did Oscar mention anything about Duvan's body? Did they bury him or cremate him?" Her shaking hand finds her necklace and she fingers his ring that sits on it.

He shrugs. "He just said that he had his men take care of things in Venezuela. I didn't ask much else. But, Brie, I was serious. We need to get you out of here. You're a target now that Duvan's gone. Diego wants that factory and—"

Holding her hand up, she nods her head. "Good. Set up a meeting with him."

Both Rafe and I growl at the same time. "What?"

Her eyes dart between us. She straightens her back and presses her lips together in a firm line. Then, she speaks in a calm tone. "If he wants it, I'll sell it to him. All the product, the building, the territory."

"He wants to take it," Rafe snarls. "Not buy it."

She stands and crosses her arms over her chest before leveling him with a glare. "You worked for Duvan, did you not?"

He nods.

"So now you work for *me*. Set it up. He'll buy it or he won't get it all. I'll sell it to Camilo if he's not interested."

Rafe shakes his head in vehemence. "Little girl, you don't understand. That operation *is* Camilo's. Duvan just ran things. You can't fucking sell a territory out from under a cartel king pin. You just don't understand!"

His tone is pissing me right the fuck off. I'm about to shut his ass up when Brie snaps.

"I understand things clearly. That building," she bites out, "legally belongs to my husband. I have the paperwork to prove it. I also have the paperwork he had me sign that puts me as a co-owner. Same goes for his house. His land. His money. It's mine. And, as a result, so is this territory. Duvan and I spent many late nights discussing his business. He always wanted me to rule with him. I wasn't just some trophy wife. Camilo receives a cut. That's it. When I sell it, Camilo will get his cut as pre-negotiated. Now, you can either help me, and honor your friend and employer's wishes or you can disobey a direct order." She stands directly in front of him with her hands on her hips. The anger emanating from her is hot like a flash fire. If he's not careful, he's going to get burned. "I have no qualms about having my father take you out back and punish you for insubordination. Do you remember how Duvan dealt with those who were against him?"

Rafe's shoulders hunch in defeat. "You don't have to kill me, little princess. But just remember this discussion when Diego has his knife at your throat. When he steals everything you once owned. Including your life."

Brie doesn't flinch. I'm about three seconds from disemboweling him in her living room but I hold back, just barely.

"My life was stolen last week when I tried to hold my dying husband's throat closed. It drained away along with his blood. Diego can't take anything from me that hasn't already been taken." She darts her gaze over to the clock. "Set up a meeting for tomorrow. Tell him I'm not here to play games. I'm here to do business."

Brie

Of course the first time I see Duvan's building would be after he's dead. He won't be there to show me around. It'll just be the three of us. Me, Daddy, and Rafe. Once we realized Rafe wasn't there to hurt me, we untied him. He's much like Duvan was in the fact that he worries over everything. These guys are full of heart. They may be hardened coke kings but they're soft inside.

Diego actually agreed to meet with me. Rafe suspects a trap. Daddy wants to murder everyone. And I just want to do what Duvan would have wanted. He would have wanted me to sell his assets and get the hell back to California. My safety was always his primary concern.

We pull up to a gigantic metal building, probably forty thousand square feet in size, located on the outskirts of town not far from the house. Several employees' cars are lined up in the grass outside. Rafe assured me business continued on as usual in Duvan's absence despite him being in Venezuela with me. They will have learned of his death by now but won't try anything stupid. The punishment for stealing or trying to con your boss is death. End of story. Most of the people working in the coke warehouse are fathers and mothers. People simply doing their job to provide for their family. At first, I'd wanted to judge them. Being a spoiled girl from the US, I secretly scoffed and thought they were terrible people.

Until I realized it was how Duvan provided for his family. With Duvan, it didn't seem as bad. Just like the many times I'd partaken in his drugs. It simply didn't seem like the dirty drug world I'd learned about. It was different.

"Who's the guy with the assault rifle strapped to his chest?" my dad questions from the back seat.

"There are seven more guys like him surrounding the property. Duvan always had proper security, but after what happened with Esteban, he upped it. They're here for our safety," Rafe assures me before climbing out of the car.

Dad and I follow after him. I'd not bothered to dress fancy for this guy. I'm wearing a black pair of yoga pants and a fitted white tank with a pair of tennis shoes. My hair, which has gotten a little longer, is pulled into a messy bun. I've gone without makeup too. This Diego character will have to get over it.

Rafe speaks in Spanish to the scary looking guy with the big gun. But after a long gaze at my father and I, the man motions for us to go inside. Once in the door, we pass by a room lined with glass windows. Inside, more men with guns stand guard as people undress until they're naked. They hand them uniforms to wear. After they're dressed, they disappear through a door which must lead somewhere else in the factory.

I pick up my pace to keep up with Rafe. He strides along the hallway at a breakneck speed. Dad takes up the rear. When we come to an office door at the end of the hallway, Rafe uses a key to unlock it. He ushers us inside.

As soon as I enter, my heart drops to the floor. The room smells of Duvan's lingering cologne which causes a pang in my chest. I inhale his familiar scent with deep gulps of air. I'm desperate to lock his scent up inside of me and never exhale.

"Have a seat," Rafe says and motions to Duvan's chair.

I walk over to the expensive leather desk chair and plop down. There aren't any pictures, which I'm sure is for my protection, but when I wiggle his mouse, there is a picture of us saved to his desktop.

It was from one of the times when we first got together and I was high as a kite on blow. His tatted up arm is draped across my tits. I can almost recall exactly how he felt at that moment. Soft yet so strong. In the picture, his lips are to my ears, telling me naughty secrets. My eyes are almost black with dilation and my lips are parted with desire.

"How much time do we have?" I question, swallowing down my emotion.

Rafe flicks his gaze to his watch. "Forty-five minutes or so. Knowing Diego, he'll show up late to make a statement."

I give him a clipped nod. "Can you show my dad the place? I'm going to look through Duvan's computer a bit. I want to make sure I'm ready for Diego."

Rafe lets out an annoyed sigh but nods. "Sure. But here," he says and pulls out a handgun, slapping it on the desk in front of me. "It's loaded and ready to go. Just point and pull the trigger if anyone so much as looks at you wrong."

My eyes dart over to Daddy's. He merely nods in agreement. I'm still staring at the gun long after they've gone. If Duvan were here, he'd probably take me out back and show me how to shoot it.

Thinking about the *could have beens* is depressing. Focusing on the task at hand, I type in Duvan's password and begin rummaging through his files. I make sure to email myself any and all pictures of the two of us he has saved before I do anything else.

Soon, I become engrossed in his notes, his documents, and his calendar. I send myself anything of importance and delete everything. Before I leave, I'll have Rafe destroy the hard drive, though, just to be safe.

A rap on the door startles me from my thoughts.

"Come in," I chirp, a little too cheerful for a cartel queen. I do manage to pull the gun into my lap to hide it away in case it is anyone besides Rafe or Dad.

The door swings open and in strides a man. A scary yet handsome man. Black suit. Near black hair slicked back. Silvery scars crisscrossing all over his cheeks and forehead. His cheeks are smooth shaven and he wears a distinguished goatee that's been groomed neatly. When his pale brown eyes meet mine, a black eyebrow arches up in surprise.

"You must be Duvan's little play thing," he says smoothly.

I don't see any weapons in his possession, but I'm not stupid. I clutch the gun under my desk and expel a ragged breath. Three men file into the room behind him. All intimidating. Dangerous looking. All scowling.

"He preferred the term wife. You must be Dora's cousin," I grit out.

He regards me in confusion. "Who the hell is Dora?"

"Forget it," I utter. "Diego Gomez?"

He straightens his tie and saunters over to the desk. I motion for him to sit. His eyes are all over my body, sizing me up. Once he decides I'm not a threat, he waves at his men. "Outside."

They don't argue. They step out and leave me alone with this slimeball.

"I must say, *cariño*," he utters as he drops down into the chair across from me, "you're not at all what I expected. You're nothing but a little girl."

My hackles rise and I straighten my back. "I'm little, I'll give you that." My voice drops to a whisper. "But you have no idea who I am or what I'm made of."

The threat hangs in the air as Diego scrutinizes me. After a long moment, he lets out a boisterous laugh that echoes off the walls. "Fucking adorable is what you are." He stands and begins nosily walking around the office. Touching artwork on the wall. Running his fingertip along the mahogany of the desk. Tipping over a binder on the back credenza behind me. I remain frozen in my spot. My hand sweats from holding the gun and I fear I'm going to have to use it. When he swivels the chair around, I let out a squeak of surprise. His strong hand finds my throat and he lifts me easily to my feet.

"You don't threaten me, bitch," he spits out, his eyes flickering with rage. "I'll fuck you over this desk like the useless whore you are. I take what I want, cariño."

With a growl, I shove the loaded gun against his hard dick. "Back it up before I make you *my* bitch."

His eyes widen in shock and he releases me. Slowly, he steps backward. As soon as he's stepped out of my reach, I glare at him. "I'm here to do business, asshole. Not let you take what belongs to me. Are you interested or am I selling to Camilo?"

He swallows and his body ripples with anger. "You're fucking feisty, bitch."

"Call me bitch again and I'm going to unload every bullet I've got into your cock and sorry ass balls," I snap. "Are we doing business or what?"

"I came here expecting to slap a whore around and instead, I meet you. No wonder Duvan gave his nuts to you. You probably fuck like a wild beast." His light brown eyes fall to my chest and he smirks. "I'd certainly like to have a go to see if I'm right." Despite having a loaded gun pointed at his junk, he's sporting a very large hard-on.

"Dream on, dick," I mutter. "How much are you offering?"

He rolls his eyes, as if I'm the annoying one here. He's the one who thinks he can stroll in, slap me around, fuck me, and then take what he wants. Over my dead body. "Three million pesos."

I almost laugh at him. I may be young and way out of my league and totally American, but I am not fucking stupid. "Nice try. We're talking good 'ol US dollars here. Not pesos. You and I both know this is worth a helluva lot more than a measly hundred grand."

His eyes widen in surprise once again. For a drug king, he sure does a piss poor job of hiding his thoughts. "I see. What did you have in mind?"

I know he wants me to throw out some over-the-top number as if I have no idea what I'm talking about. But I do. I've spent days learning of his properties, the value of the coke based on the amount we have in production, and all of his other assets.

"Twelve million."

His laugh is so loud that one of his men peeks in briefly to check on us. Once he closes the door and Diego sees I'm not kidding, his laughter dies. "No fucking lie. You are as smart as you are sexy. You sure you don't want to let Daddy Diego fuck your tight cunt. I'll put a ring on your finger if that makes you happy. What's one more wife?"

Bile rises in my throat, and I wish I'd have eaten more this morning than the two pieces of buttered toast. As soon as I get to California, I'm going to need to see a doctor to make sure I'm taking care of this baby properly.

"I don't want your dick," I tell him softly. "I just want your money."

He smirks. "You sure you don't want to be one of my wives? You sure as hell act like them."

I cringe wondering what it must be like married to this man. At least Duvan was good to me. He loved me and tried desperately to keep the dark parts of his business out of my sight.

"Twelve million. I want it wired to this account." I slide a handwritten piece of paper toward him. When he grabs my wrist, I have the urge to shoot him in the head, but I don't have to. He's simply inspecting my tattoo.

"Ten," he counters and lets go of my hand. Respect flickers in his eyes. I'm not some whore. I loved Duvan. He was my husband, and I won't let his hard work be stolen from us.

"Twelve, Diego."

His eyes flit to my chest. "Twelve and a blow job."

I roll my eyes. "No."

"Eleven and I see your tits."

"Jesus, you're a pig."

"You make me hard as fuck, cariño. I'm not leaving without seeing those pretty nipples."

I cross my arms over my chest. "You can forget it. Do we have a deal?"

He stands and reaches his hand across the desk. "Let me smell your cunt and the money is yours."

I gape at him for one long moment of hesitation, and it's a terrible mistake. He grabs me by the elbow in a brutal grip. His other hand is fast as he wrenches the weapon from my hand. With a growl, he drags me over the desk and papers hit the floor. I attempt to claw at him but before I know it, he has me twisted and pushed over the desk with both wrists in his grip. The mahogany is cold against my cheek.

"Help!" I cry out.

His laughter is cold. "My men have your men. Cariño, it's just us now."

Tears roll out when he presses his hardened cock against my ass. My wrists are locked in his strong hand and he uses the other one to stroke my hair. He fucking pets me like I'm a cat.

"So soft," he says with a growl.

"Please don't rape me," I beg. "I'm pregnant."

His grip on my hands loosens. "With Duvan's child?"

"Of course," I snarl.

He fingers a strand of my hair and gives it a gentle tug. "You'd be such a pleasure to tame."

"Please don't."

I'm so sure he's going to rape me that I start to mentally check out. I remain completely still for what feels like forever, praying to God he doesn't fuck me. But he doesn't fuck me. He just keeps me trapped as if I'm the pet he never was allowed to have as a child. I shiver when he presses a kiss to the back of my skull.

"I'm not a villain, cariño," he says in a firm tone as he releases my hands. He then gives me a playful slap to my ass before pulling away. "I'm a businessman. Now that I've gotten what I want, I'll give you what you want."

He helps pull me upright and steadies me on my feet. I'm in too much shock to do anything but gape at him. I'm disgusted by the sleaze but I don't dare do or say anything to set him off. He didn't rape me but it doesn't mean he won't. My hands tremble as he sifts through some papers on the floor. Eventually, he pulls up the wiring instructions and winks at me. Then, he stands before offering me back my gun.

"Luis!" he barks toward the door.

One of the scary men storms inside. His eyes never even glance over at me. Diego hands him the slip of paper.

"Make it happen."

Luis nods and pulls out his phone. A few moments later, the transaction is done. Once he proves it to me on the phone, he dismisses Luis.

"This office and everything in it, now belongs to me, cariño," he says with a growl. "Are you sure you want to stand there looking so fucking fine? Don't you have a flight to catch back to your pussy country? If you wait around any longer, I'll claim you too."

I start past him toward the door, but before I get to it, he once again grabs on to me. He takes the gun from me and shoves it into the back of his slacks. His light brown eyes are narrowed and he seems to inhale me. My heart rate is thundering right out of my chest.

"I'm leaving," I assure him.

His grip on my bicep tightens as he walks me toward the wall. Once my ass hits the drywall, I let out a yelp. He travels his gaze over my forehead, then my eyes, along my nose, lingers on my lips, before landing on my throat.

"This," he hisses as he clutches the necklace Ren gave me with Duvan's ring on it. "Is mine. As collateral."

I cry out when he yanks the chain, breaking it. A tear races down my cheek and I shake my head. "N-No. Please don't take that."

His black eyebrow lifts up in surprise. "Not so fearless, are you?"

"Why do you need collateral? I'm giving it to you. I'll sign over the deed. Just please don't take my necklace."

He pockets my jewelry and his lips lift up on one side. "You will sign over the deed. But I need to own something that you cherish, so that if Camilo loses his mind over our deal, I'll know how to get back in touch with you and that you'll listen. Once this all blows over, you can have it back. I promise, cariño."

I shake my head. "I can't let you take my jewelry. Anything else. Please."

His hand palms my stomach. "Anything?"

I'm seconds away from vomiting at his insinuation. He'll never get my child.

"I'm a very patient man. I could keep you until you give birth to this child and then keep the baby as collateral if you'd rather," he tells me, his voice low and threatening.

Another tear strolls down my cheek. He leans forward and kisses the wetness. "I didn't think so. I'll keep it safe. I promise." His suffocating presence pulls away from me. "Now you better go, little lady, before I change my mind. Letting you go is taking all of my self-control. I've been tempted by how sweet you are and I'm starved for a tiny little taste. My cock is dying to have the whole fucking buffet."

I shudder and stumble over to the door.

"Wait," he barks out. "Danilo!"

Another man walks into the office, this one dressed as nice as Diego, and carries a briefcase.

"We still have to sign a few things, cariño," he tells me. "My attorney will get them ready for us. Then you're free to go."

The next twenty minutes are torture. He won't quit staring at me as if he's going to eat me. And my heart aches knowing my husband's wedding ring sits in his pocket. I scribble my signature on the necessary documents all the while counting down the seconds until I can leave.

Once we're finished and his attorney stacks the papers in the briefcase, Diego regards me with a wolfish grin.

"Nice doing business with you, Gabriella Rojas. I never expected things to go so…" His words trail off as his gaze drops between my legs. "Beautifully."

I storm away from him toward the door. Once I wrench it open, I glare at him over my shoulder. "I want my ring back. I suggest you find a way to make that happen sooner rather than later."

"Ahh," he chuckles. "Another threat by the feisty little fox."

"It's tigress to you, asshole."

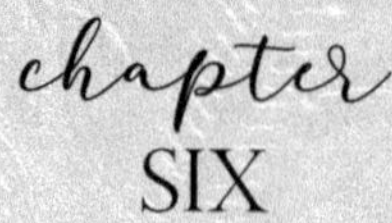

SIX

Brie

It's been a month since I sold my soul to the devil at the tune of twelve million dollars. He hasn't messed with me anymore but he also still hasn't returned my ring. I've managed to finally sell the house and have liquidated the last of Duvan's assets.

Everything has gone well.

Too well, in fact.

And that keeps me on alert.

Camilo and Esteban are still nowhere to be found. Vee is still in hiding. I've been waiting for something bad to happen but each day is just another day. One more day further away from the last time I saw Duvan.

My belly is still small. I've finally started to get over my morning sickness. At least a little bit. Luciana gets me to eat and Daddy gets me to talk. After that day at the warehouse, I'd found my dad's beaten body lying beside our vehicle. Rafe was bleeding from his nose but wasn't in as bad of shape. I learned from Rafe that my father went crazy when he found out I was alone with Diego. They had to beat the hell out of him to keep him from interrupting our business.

I still never told him exactly what happened.

And I never will.

If he knew that Diego had been all over me and throwing out threats left and right, he'd have murdered that creep and brought the entire cartel's wrath down upon us. A shudder ripples through me. That will be a secret I keep to myself for as long as I live.

I walk through the now fairly empty house. Ren told me to ship the important stuff to his townhouse and that he'd keep up with it until I was ready to come for it. Everything else, we sold with the house.

Speaking of Ren, I haven't been able to get ahold of him for a few days. It is weird not to talk to him. After a month of Skyping every day, I feel isolated and all alone by not getting to hear his voice. Even if we don't really talk that much.

Tomorrow morning, Daddy, Luciana, and I have planned to fly out of Colombia. I'm equal parts sad and happy. On one hand, I'll be happy to leave the nightmare behind. But by leaving the nightmare, I'll also be abandoning my memories with Duvan. As much as I would rather stay and raise my baby in this house where we can feed the chickens every day, I know it isn't safe for my child. Not with people like Esteban and Diego lurking about.

In America, we can be free from all of this.

I push down my yoga pants and kick out of them. It's late and even though I'm not tired, I know I'll be exhausted on the trip tomorrow. I need to try and sleep at least. Duvan's old T-shirt swallows my small frame and my swollen bare breasts hang heavy beneath the fabric. I've outgrown all of my bras lately. I'll definitely have to do some shopping in California. I switch off the overhead light and am just crawling into our bed for the last time when I hear a crash downstairs.

I scramble across the bed to the table where I keep a gun. I'll never feel one hundred percent safe, especially here, but the gun sure helps. Men are shouting downstairs. More crashing. On shaky legs, I slide off the bed and frantically look for a place to hide. I'm just darting toward the bathroom when I hear footsteps thundering up the stairs. My heart lurches in my throat. I freeze and instantly hate myself for not running. It's almost as if I'm waiting for…

The door swings open and a madman enters. Blood trickles from his bottom lip. The muscles in his neck are taut with tension. His brown hair is messy and overgrown. It hangs into his eyes, making him appear as though he's some untamed animal. His cheeks are scruffy and his jaw is sharp. The black Soundgarden T-shirt molds to his sculpted body. I'm frozen in shock, no longer in fear.

"Ren?"

"Your dad's an asshole," he utters, his hands fisted. He seems to snap out of his rage and his eyes skim over my clothing while his gaze softens. He wipes the blood away from his bottom lip with the back of his hand before he flashes me a grin I remember from when times were simpler. "Do I get a hug?" When our eyes meet again, a familiar glimmer flickers in his.

I jolt out of my shocked stance, set the gun down on the end table, and run over to him. He doesn't wait, stalking toward me to meet halfway. The moment he gathers me in his arms, I relax. I relax for the first time in over a month. All of my friends, aside from Luciana, have gone radio silent. All but *this* friend.

This friend is here.

Hugging me so tight, I think I might break.

Inhaling my hair as if I'm a delicate and rare rose.

Muttering out words of relief.

"Jesus," he utters, embracing me tighter. "It's been forever since I've hugged you."

I let out a laugh but it soon turns into tears. The relief is overwhelming, and I lose myself to it. Within seconds, I'm sobbing so hard, I think I might collapse. When my knees buckle, Ren slides his strong arm under my legs and lifts me. I cry against his chest, soaking his shirt as he carries me over to my bed. At first, I stiffen because if he crawls into this bed with me, it'll be his scent that replaces Duvan's. The thought terrifies me. But tomorrow it won't matter, anyway. I'll be gone. The idea of Ren holding me like old times seems to soothe my battered heart.

His scent is comforting too.

The springs groan in protest when Ren sets me down on the bed. He kicks off his shoes and scoots in beside me. As soon as he drags the covers over us, I clutch his T-shirt and bury my face against him. His fingers stroke through my hair. I cry for my loss. For the unfairness of this life. For the assaults I've suffered. The men who have abused me. I cry for my child who will never know its father. I cry for…me.

Ren, just like on our Skype sessions, doesn't speak. His strength speaks volumes. It steadies me. Roots me into the ground so I don't blow away in the wind. Like the gnarly branches of his tree tattoo, he holds me against his solid frame, keeping me safe from the awful world I know.

When my tears finally dry up and all that can be heard is Ren's soft breathing, I look up at him. The lamp light casts dark shadows on his face. It's so different than I remember. Where is the smile that used to light up his whole face? Where are his blue eyes that would twinkle with delight when he saw me?

Ren is different, just like me.

He's seen unspeakable horrors. I've lived them.

He's teetered an impossible line with his sister. She stole from me.

He's lost his love. I've lost my love.

Our hearts have been slayed and left for dead.

The innocence we once knew has been obliterated. There's no collecting those pieces and putting them back together again.

"Did you and Daddy get in a fight?" I murmur in question.

His eyes that had been staring off toward the window find mine. A storm brews in his dark gaze. It makes me shiver. Thinking I'm cold, he pulls me tighter. Absently, he presses a kiss to my forehead and it stills my racing heart. "Your dad thought I was someone else. Three months ago, he'd have probably been able to gut my ass. Unfortunately for him, I've been spending a lot more time lifting than he has. We scuffled until he realized it was me, and that I wasn't coming here to kill you. Now he's downstairs on the phone with my dad, bitching."

A chuckle rumbles in my chest. Poor Daddy has done nothing but either kick ass or get his ass kicked since he came for me. He always looks so tired. I know he just wants to get back to California so he can have his life back again.

My smile falls.

Does that life involve me?

How can he have Hannah and I both?

The answer is…he can't.

I won't be able to see that woman without wanting to claw her eyeballs out.

"I wasn't expecting you to show up," I tell him after a few moments.

His fingers find my overgrown bangs and he tucks them behind my ear. "I could've waited a couple more days to see you, but I didn't want to. I also didn't think you travelling with a wanted felon was a good idea. The last thing you need is to get dragged to prison because you were in the wrong place at the right time."

My eyes find his—his gaze boring a hole through me. When did Ren become so intense? I reflect back on all the things I've dealt with in the past month. When did I become so intense? We're both strung so tight, we're sure to snap at any moment.

"Thank you for coming," I murmur. "I've been so lost and lonely. With Vee and Oscar gone too, I've been drifting. If it weren't for you, I'd have already lost my mind."

His brows furl together. He grits his teeth together as if he's holding in a mouthful of words. I want to pry his lips apart and pull them from him.

"What?" I ask.

He swallows. "I'm so fucking sorry, Brie."

Tears sting my eyes, but I quickly blink them away. "My life is a mess."

"I'm here now. I'll help you clean it all up. Your mess is mine." He leans forward and kisses the corner of my mouth. It stirs old feelings in my belly. "Go to sleep, Juliet. You've got a big day tomorrow."

I drift off, losing myself to nostalgic memories of when life was easy and fun. Before the cartel, before my dad came back, before Heath tried to ruin my life. Back when I was just a girl looking out a window, wishing for a boy to climb the tower and save me.

"Tigress…"

I groan in protest. I'm too sleepy to get up.

"Tigress…"

"Mmmm," I grumble.

"Tigress…"

My dreams tease me and bleed into reality. I hate that I can have him there and not in real life. Sometimes, when I wake up, his scent lingers. I can almost still hear his whispers against the shell of my ear. I'm oftentimes still wet from remembering the way he would touch me.

And now, in the pitch black of my bedroom, I'm once again taunted by his memory. He seems so real. I dance my fingertips along his bare chest. Solid muscle. Smooth contours and lines. So perfect.

My breasts ache to have him gripping them to the point of pain. I'd do anything to have his teeth on my nipples one last time. Greedy not to lose him in this moment, I regain full clarity and I straddle him. His cock is erect and at full attention.

God he feels so real.

"I missed you so much," I murmur in the dark, my fingernails raking along his chest.

His body tenses as if I've just woken him. Strong hands slide up my bare thighs and grip my hips just under my shirt. I want to glue them to me so he'll never let me go. Between the thin fabric of his boxers and my barely-there panties, I'm sure he can feel how wet I am as I rub against his throbbing cock. It's been so long.

"Brie…" His voice is all wrong but it's real. So fucking real.

"Shhh," I tell him, needing the fantasy to remain. Reality is a goddamned bitch.

He lets out a low growl and his thumbs dig into my flesh. I rock against him almost painfully. My body needs this release. I grab on to his muscular shoulders so I can stabilize myself. Grinding against him feels so good. So perfect.

Tendrils of pleasure begin lazily making their way through my veins as if they've suddenly awoken from a long slumber. Much like the bliss of the heroin I once loved, I quiver with anticipation as it snakes its way through me, leaving a delicious sting in its wake. My pussy throbs with need. It won't be long before I come.

And like so many nights before, I'll reawaken with a pillow between my legs. My fantasy nothing more than a sad dream. But it never stops me from giving in to these dreams. I greedily steal them each time.

His hands grip the bottom of my T-shirt and he starts to drag it up my body. Reality is hiding just beyond the door of my mind. Reminding me this isn't real. That he's not real. That my fantasy is an imposter.

I turn my back on that door.

Lifting my arms, I let him tug the shirt from me. His palms slide to my swollen breasts and he squeezes them. Admires them. Gets used to the new size of them. He sits up on the bed until our stomachs press together. His hot mouth finds my nipple. So tentative at first but then he suckles on it. Bites it. Draws pleasure from such a small area just with his mouth. My panties are drenched.

This isn't enough.

I need more.

So much more from him.

Raking my fingers through his hair, I blatantly ignore the fact that his hair is different. I don't get caught up in reality. This fantasy is mine. I'll live in it forever.

He grips my ass to the point I know I'll be bruised. His need to consume me—to tear me apart—has me flying higher and higher toward ecstasy.

"I need you," I whisper so quietly I don't think he hears.

But then his hot breath is between my breasts, sending chills down my spine. "I'm not him."

I'm not him.

A tear streaks down my cheek and I shake my head. "Shhh."

When I grind into him hard, he lets out a sound of pure bliss. But then his hands are in my hair almost painfully. He jerks my head back so that my breasts jut right into his face. His teeth drag along my flesh before he sinks them into my skin. I cry out in pain—but it's pain mixed with pleasure, and I need it. "I'm not him, baby."

I slap my hand over his mouth so he'll shut up. This seems to spark a reaction from him because he flips us around and presses me into the bed. His strong hands grab my wrists as he jerks them above my head. My legs are still spread apart. He never loses our stride and continues rubbing against me in a way that has me so close to climaxing.

I just need to hold on to the fantasy a moment longer.

Then I can hate myself all I want.

Then I can force myself to face the truth.

Then I can apologize.

"I'm not him," he growls in a no-nonsense way. He grips my chin almost brutally before crashing his lips to mine. This kiss tastes familiar, but the harsh way he delivers it isn't familiar. Despite not recognizing it, I crave it.

"I need you inside me," I plead, hot tears rolling from my eyes. I'm fully aware of my betrayal but I won't let it win. Not now.

"Jesus fucking Christ!" he hisses.

At one time, he'd have been the gentleman. Made me come to terms with reality. Held me through what I'd almost done.

But this isn't the boy I remember. I don't know this man at all. I let out a sigh of relief when he lifts up long enough to pull his cock from his boxers. My panties are hastily pushed to the side. There isn't any time to change my mind. To focus on the wrongness. To erase this mistake.

With one painful thrust, he's deep inside me, drawing out a crushing wail. His cock splits me wide open all the way down to my soul. Flashes of a simple past flit through my mind like blinding white zaps. Each one electrocuting me with realization. This isn't my fantasy at all, and yet I'm soaking it all in. Drawing comfort from the sound of the waves. The warm sunshine. The way he used to kiss me until my mouth was raw on the beach. How we'd dry hump long before he took my virginity.

His fingers are back to biting into my jaw as he kisses me. There's nothing soft about the way he mauls me. He thrusts into me so hard, I imagine I'll be bruised. My clit throbs out of control each time his body hits mine.

So close…

Don't think about it, just do it, I tell myself.

I make the mistake of opening my eyes. Moonlight peeks in through the window, casting a sliver of light across his face. One steely blue eye is illuminated and it bores into me. His one eye flashes with anger and love and need. And it's too much.

I want to run away from it all.

Pretend this never happened.

"Goddammit, Brie," he growls. "Look at me."

His fierce command has my eyes popping back open and my pussy clenching in response. His gaze softens before he kisses me in a gentler way. A way I remember. A way I used to dream about late at night before my world turned upside down.

"Relax, baby," he murmurs against my lips. "Just let it go."

I shut off my mind and allow my orgasm to overtake me. My nerve endings take on life as they all seem to explode at once. The shudder that wracks through me is so strong, I actually jerk from beneath him. When my body clamps down around his, he lets out a guttural groan. A gush of his hot seed fills me. Throb after exhilarating throb.

"What have I done?" I whisper mostly to myself.

He releases his grip on my wrists and slides a palm over my heart. "You were letting go of some of the pain."

I blink in the darkness, stunned by his words. My body is relaxed. My mind is calm. It's just my heart that is destroyed. I feel like a whore who can't keep her legs closed.

"My heart still belongs to him," I blurt out.

He flinches at my words. But then he takes my tattooed wrist and draws it to his lips. The way he kisses it reminds me of how Duvan would. It makes my chest ache painfully. "I know, Brie. Nobody's asking you to forget about him. But having that orgasm was probably the best thing you could do for yourself right now. You were so fucking tense."

He slips his softened cock out of me and then climbs off the bed. Soon, the bathroom light blinds me. It sheds light on the horror of what I've just done. When he returns, carrying a wet cloth, I can't bear to look at him.

"Brie."

I clench my eyes closed, hoping he'll get a clue.

"Open your eyes, dammit." His words are harsh and it makes me open them so I can see his expression. He's never been the angry type. I don't understand who he is anymore.

"I'm sorry," I whisper.

He grabs my panties and tugs them down my thighs. They're soaked with his cum and need to go. He clutches my knees and pulls me open once he's removed the last of my clothing. I start to drag my knees back together, but he's stronger and he wins. The warm cloth travels over my still pulsating clit as he cleanses me between my thighs. He does it in such a gentle, protective way, I think I might burst into tears. My emotions are all over the place. When he's finished, he stalks back over to the bathroom. I get a better peek at his back tattoo, which seems to have a lot more going on with it since my last perusal. Thankfully, he's pulled his boxers back into place.

"You didn't do anything wrong," he tells me as soon as the room goes dark again. I should probably make moves to find my shirt or a new pair of panties or a wall to put between us. Instead, I remain frozen.

He slips into the bed and hauls me to him. His sculpted chest presses firmly against my back while his arm wraps possessively around me. Now that I'm fully aware of my situation, it's more brutal to my psyche admitting that I need him comforting me right now. If I could fall asleep forever like this and never wake up, I would.

His lips kiss my shoulder, and I shiver. I don't know what to do. I should push him away and yet I don't. I should ask him to sleep elsewhere and yet I don't. I should warn him I'll only fuck up his heart because I'm a mess and yet I don't.

I let him hold me.

I let him kiss my neck.

I let him snuggle his flaccid cock against my ass.

I'll allow myself this one night. Then, tomorrow, with reality, I can deal with the consequences of my actions. Right now, though, I refuse to let them win.

For the first time in over a month, I fall asleep with a blank mind.

My heart aches but not as much as usual.

Tonight, for a short while, I am free.

chapter
SEVEN

Ren

I've slept like shit for months. My mind has been plagued by all the wrongs and I can't focus on anything right. Everything seemed to be spiraling out of control.

Until now.

Sleeping with Brie tucked in against my chest was calming. The anger that had been simmering below my surface seemed to cool. For once in what seems like forever, I slept easily.

But last night?

Last night was probably a big fucking mistake. As much as I wanted to be inside of her, it was wrong. She was lying to herself and wanted me to play along with her little charade.

I fucking did.

Fucked her right into a sleepy stupor.

Her scent still clings to me and my dick twitches to ram into her again. Her body simply responded so differently than the other two times we'd had sex. It wasn't lovemaking, like before. It was carnal, animalistic, unapologetic fucking. And, my God, it was amazing.

But now she's locked herself in the bathroom. As soon as her alarm went off, she bolted from the bed, and out of my arms, to lock herself away from the reality of what we'd done.

I need to make her understand it wasn't a mistake.

It was simply…a release.

A release she needed more than I did.

With a sigh, I climb out of bed and walk over to the window. The sky is overcast and ominous as a storm looms. I catch sight of my reflection in the glass. My eyebrows are furled together in a contemplative manner. The stubble on my cheeks has grown in recently. I'm normally one to keep my face clean-shaven, but lately, I like the way it scratches my palm when I'm in one of my moods. Tiny bites of pain keep me alive.

I wonder if they could keep her alive too.

Would the hair scratch her inner thighs in a way that hurts so good?

Finding my jeans, I pull them up quickly and forgo a shirt. When I make it over to the bathroom door, I raise my hand to knock but pause when I hear her sniffling inside.

"Brie," I murmur, "open up."

The sink turns on and then, after a moment, she opens the door. Her face is splotchy and red from crying. But it's the hollow look in her brown eyes that's haunting.

"What I did…what we did…" Her bottom lip wobbles as tears well in her pretty eyes.

Stalking over to her, I grip her chin and tilt her head up so I can look at her. The tears break free from her eyelids and race each other down her cheeks. Her two eyebrows are pinched together as if she's in pain.

I caused this pain.

But I can take it away too.

"Nobody is judging," I tell her firmly. "Nobody." When I hug her to me, she doesn't resist. Instead, she clings to my bare chest and cries. Brie has always been so strong. It's a hidden strength that not many see. I've always seen it, though. Seen the fierce glint in her eyes when she'd talk about her future. And when she was with Duvan, her strength seemed to intensify. He was good for her. I'll always be grateful for the love he gave her when not many people would. It was a love she needed—something I couldn't quite give to her at the time.

One day, I will find exactly what she needs and I will give it to her.

My heart. My soul. My devotion.

Of course, now's not the time. What she needs from me now is my strength. This poor woman is broken and slayed. She's bleeding uncontrollably from a wound in her heart.

I'm going to help her soothe the pain.

I'll wrap her up tight in my safe, loving heart and keep her protected from the hurt that plagues her.

"I'm going to be sick," she hisses a second before jerking from my embrace.

She clambers over to the toilet and barely pushes the lid open before she's puking inside. I storm over to her and grab a handful of her hair to keep it from her face. Between her heaves, she sobs so loudly, I'm sure God can hear. I hope he hears her pain and fucking does something about it. I hope he gives her some peace.

Once she's done throwing up, I release her to get a cold, wet cloth. She still hugs the toilet bowl but has shifted to sit on her ass.

"I'm going to get you something to drink," I tell her.

I stalk out of the bathroom and through her bedroom on a mission to the kitchen. The rest of the house is dark and quiet. But when I reach the kitchen, Gabe sits perched on a bistro chair. His hair is disheveled. A dark, black circle rings his eye where I managed to get a swing in on him last night.

While I can respect his need to protect Brie, I wasn't going to be deterred.

When he notices me, his tired brown eyes meet mine. The usual anger doesn't flicker in them. Sadness does.

"How's Brie?" he mumbles before sipping from his mug of black coffee. His gaze rakes over my bare chest. I'm sure he knows we've been intimate but I don't give a rat's ass what he thinks about it.

"She'll be fine. A little sick this morning," I grunt back as I rummage in some cabinets on a hunt for crackers. The house is all packed up, but I do find a basket of snacks on the counter.

"How am I going to fix this, Ren?" His voice is choked. Broken. Vulnerable even.

I pluck a sleeve of peanut butter crackers from the basket before regarding him. "Fix what?"

He runs his fingers through his messy hair. "Your sister. My daughter. How do I get to have this family? My family? Together. Under one roof."

Just the mention of my sister has my blood boiling. "You chose Hannah over Brie. I don't understand how. She certainly doesn't."

He flinches at my words. With a scowl, he twists his wedding ring on his finger. "Love is fucking messy."

Tell me about it.

"You can't have the best of both worlds," I finally utter out. "You want true love and children with Hannah but then you have this amazing daughter too. Unlike most normal blended families, they can't be around each other, because Hannah is a fucking murderer. She killed your daughter's mother. So, Gabe, I'm sorry, man, but you're just going to have to accept that you can't have both. You can't fix it."

He clenches his eyes shut and lets out a ragged sigh. "Toto would love Brie. You know she would."

Toto's pretty brown eyes are at the forefront of my mind. I love that kid like you would not believe. "Brie will love her too. With time. You can't rush into it, though. Maybe one day I can bring Toto with me to visit her. Brie is a good person," I tell him vehemently. "She has so much love in her heart. It's just been crushed in the past few years. Once she begins to heal again, I think she'll be ready to show some of that love."

He stares at me for a long moment. "You're okay, kid."

I let out a humorless chuckle as I snag one of the last cans of Sprite from the refrigerator. "I'm not a kid anymore, man. I kicked your old ass last night."

His lips tug into a smile. "You caught me at a weak moment. Next time, your ass is mine."

I smirk and flip him off before trotting back to Brie's room. She's still in the bathroom on the floor where I left her. Kneeling beside her, I pop open the Sprite and help her take a sip. When she notices the crackers, her nose scrunches up.

"I don't think I can eat anything," she murmurs.

I stroke her hair and set the drink on the counter. "You need to if you want to feel any better. When my mom was pregnant with Mason, she did okay as long as we kept food in her. It was when her stomach was empty that she would get sick."

She turns and regards me with sad brown eyes. If I could cut open my own chest and give her my beating heart, I would. If only somehow that would fill her empty one up. I sit beside her so that I'm facing her.

"Tell me about…" I trail off as I clutch her shaking hand. I draw it toward me so I can look at her tattoo. "Him."

Her eyes snap to mine and she frowns. "You want to know about him? I thought you hated him."

Bringing her wrist to my mouth, I kiss the flesh there, my eyes never leaving hers. "He made you happy. How could I hate him for that?"

Tears pool in her eyes and she breaks our gaze. For a moment, I don't think she'll speak, but then she does.

"He was good to me. Found ways to make me laugh. Wanted me to make my own decisions. He paid attention to the small details, and sometimes I thought maybe he knew me better than I knew myself. Duvan filled parts of me I didn't know were empty." Her lips curve up on one side, and I see a small flash of a smile. "He encouraged me to be a better person. Loved me without rules or conditions. He was so excited to be a father." Her voice cracks and her tears fall freely down her cheeks. "We were going to have such a good life together."

I squeeze her hand. "But it was stolen from you."

That day online, when I watched as Heath appeared behind the finally-happy woman and her husband, will forever be etched into my brain. I've never been so fucking terrified in my life. The scene unfolded like that of a horror movie, but it was real. Every single awful second was real. Their love, so visible on the screen was literally cut open and drained before my very eyes. I was disgusted to see something so beautiful ruined because of the greed of another. Heath had vacant eyes as he slit open Duvan's throat. Her screams had been otherworldly as her love died in her arms. I still remember how Oscar tried desperately to shield Vee from the gruesome scene—a scene her father played a leading role in, and his brother the victim. And just when I thought I'd lose Brie next to a brutal rape and murder, Gabe showed up. Too little, too late, though. It'll be a guilt he'll have to bear on his shoulders until the day he dies. How he wasn't quick enough to get to them. To save Duvan. Watching Gabe stab Heath to death was oddly satisfying. If I were there, I'd have wanted to do it myself. Duvan was always the better man when it came to the two of us in Brie's eyes, but I never once wished him dead.

Because his death meant the death of her heart.

And her heart has always been my focus.

"Your mother would have liked Duvan, huh?" I ask as I pull some tissue off the roll to dab her cheeks with.

She nods and gives me a brief wobbly smile. "Daddy would have hated him but Mom would have thought he was perfect." Her eyes flit to mine and an apology flickers in them. She has nothing to be sorry for.

"Why would your dad have hated him? Besides the fact that he hates everyone, of course," I say in a light tone.

She laughs through her tears. "He does hate everyone." Her finger brushes against the scab on my lip from where he split it with his fist. "Including you."

"After the black eye I gave him, I can agree with that." I wink at her.

Her smile falls and she regards me with a serious expression. "Actually, Daddy would have hated the life I was exposed to with Duvan. We'd made a plan to get away from it all but for a while there…" she trails off and nervously starts to open the crackers.

I know she's thinking of what Esteban did to her. The drugs. The rape. The terror.

"Duvan may have led a dangerous life," I admit, "but your safety was his main priority. You were loved, Brie."

You're still loved.

She starts to cry, so I wrap my arms around her and haul her to me. For what seems like forever, we sit on the bathroom floor in an emotional embrace. When I hold her like this, I feel like I can keep the broken parts of her held together. That maybe, even if only for a moment, she'll feel whole again.

"I'm so lost," she murmurs against my chest. "I'm drifting. No home. No future. No anything. I don't even know who I am anymore. I'm sinking, Ren, and it feels like I'll never hit the bottom."

I kiss the top of her head. "I've got you. You may feel lost or alone, but you're not. I'm right behind you. When you feel like falling, I will catch you."

She lifts her chin and peers up at me. Her swollen lips are so goddamned kissable, but I refrain. "I'm so scared."

Using my thumb, I swipe away a drying tear. "Even the bravest, toughest of people have moments of weakness. You're going to lick these wounds and then you're going to come out swinging." I smile at her. "You have his child inside of you. And that baby is going to need its mother to be strong."

Hope, such a rarity in her world, flickers in her eyes as if she believes every single word coming out of my mouth. My chest swells with happiness. I hope she hears them. Draws them inside her tattered heart and puts them on a shelf so she can stare at them. I mean every single word.

"You're going to cry it out," I tell her firmly. "And then you're going to sharpen those claws. The world is about to hear you roar, baby."

"Where do you want to go?" I ask as I toss the last of her and Luciana's bags into the back of my truck.

Brie glances over at Gabe, who is pacing beside my truck in the parking lot. When her eyes find mine again, she seems stressed. Probably wondering where the fuck she will go. Her dad seems confused on what to do as well. Talk about a clusterfuck.

"I'm taking her with me," Gabe says finally, his menacing gaze boring into me. "The girls are coming with me. I'll make it work."

Brie tenses and it's all I need. "Nope, old man. Remember, you have Hannah Bananas. They can stay at my place for the time being."

Gabe growls like a big grizzly bear but it doesn't faze me.

"Brie," he utters and stalks over to her. "I'll find a way for this to work. Just give me some time." He pulls her into a tight embrace, but she doesn't hug him back.

"Goodbye, Daddy."

He reluctantly lets her pull away from his hug. I give him a shrug of my shoulders as both women climb into the truck. Once they close the door, he storms toward me. His eyes are manic. I can tell he's losing his mind over the whole ordeal. I'd almost feel sorry for him, but I don't.

I feel sorry for Brie.

He had a hand in doing this to her.

My sister did this to her.

If anyone fixes things for her, it'll be me. I'm probably one of the few people she will let help her.

"Make sure she stays safe, Ren," he grumbles. "My baby girl needs protection. If she won't let me, then it has to be you."

"I'll never let anyone hurt her," I vow. My eyes narrow and my jaw clenches. The air seems to crackle with my heartfelt promise. "Now go see your *other* daughter. She needs you too."

Without waiting for a response, I stride over to the driver's side of the truck and hop in. Both women are somber. The entire ride to the townhouse is silent. Brie sits in the back seat. Occasionally our gazes meet in the mirror. When I finally pull into my neighborhood, Brie perks up and stares at all the modest townhomes. I liked this neighborhood because the homes were newer, but not gigantic, and fairly affordable compared to others in the area. And the best part is that it's within walking distance of the ocean.

I pull into the driveway next to Calder's black Tahoe and shut off the truck. "You both are welcome to stay for as long as it takes for you to get back on your feet," I say, making sure to look at both of them. "We have an extra bedroom. If you can deal with Calder eating all the food and leaving the toilet seat up, I think you'll be okay."

We all get out of the truck. Brie shields her eyes against the sun as she looks down the street. Between the townhouses, you can see the ocean. A salty breeze whips around us. Brie's T-shirt flaps in the wind, and it almost seems as if a gust will catch her just right and blow her away from me.

I would find her again.

I always do.

When she turns to look at me, she's wearing a small smile. Small smiles eventually lead to breathtaking ones. I'll take them all. "I like it here."

"Good." I flash her and Luciana a grin. "Let's get your stuff inside. Calder may eat a lot but he's actually a pretty decent cook. I texted him from the airport to tell him we'd be hungry."

They both trail inside behind me. The house is a little messy, because two bachelors aren't exactly good housekeepers, but it's still a nice place. I'm only renting for now. I'd wanted to buy, but Dad asked me to wait. Said it had nothing to do with the money I would spend from my trust fund but everything to do with the fact that I should wait before I plant my roots. Something about his words had halted me from making such a huge decision, like buying a house.

The place smells good. Calder's obsessed with Italian food and cooks it a lot. With Dad being vegan, we ate some pretty bland stuff growing up. It would seem my brother is as far from vegan as one could get.

"We're here," I holler as I waltz into the kitchen. My brother stands at the stove in nothing but a pair of jeans that barely stay on his ass and a blue beanie on his head. He's not wearing a shirt because, let's face it, he's Calder and he never wears a shirt. I smirk when I notice he's gotten yet another tattoo. Unlike my tats that make sense to me and are large pieces, he has a bunch of random shit all over his chest and arms. Mom knows about my tattoos but she would kill his ass if she saw his. Calder is still her baby boy despite being eighteen now and also having Mason on the scene.

"You kids hungry?" he questions, turning his gaze our way.

I roll my eyes when I see he's wearing a fucking *Blue's Clues* beanie. Where does he find this shit to taunt me with? He's beaming at me like the cat that ate the goddamned canary. That is, until his gaze falls behind me. When his smile falters, I assume it's because he sees how broken my Brie is. But when I turn, I realize his focus has landed somewhere else.

"Remember Luciana from when we visited? I know we weren't there very long, and she didn't come out much..." I glance up at my brother. A storm brews in his eyes before he seems to shake it away, replacing the odd look with one of smug assholeness, which he wears so well.

"Hey, Luci." He winks at her before going back to stir his sauce.

Luciana's face grows bright red. Her eyes remain on my brother's muscled body as he cooks. Maybe he'll stop obsessing so much over Vee and give some other chicks a chance. One can only hope.

"While he finishes up, I'll show you to your room," I tell the girls. Brie's face is impassive. I've seen the look on her face a thousand times over the past three years.

Block out the pain.

Focus on what's right in front of her.

Force a smile when necessary.

Deny tears from falling.

She's so fucking strong all the time. In those rare moments when she breaks, I get to see down to her fragile core. I don't *want* her to have to be strong all the time. I want to be strong for her, so for once, Brie can relax.

"This is the guest room." I motion toward the neutrally decorated room. "The bed is big enough for the both of you, but if you don't want to sleep together, I can always take the couch and one of you can take my bed."

Brie sets her bags down and walks over to me. "Can I talk to you for a second?"

My hand finds the small of her back. She lets me guide her down to the master bedroom. Once we push inside the door and close it behind us, she turns her sad gaze to mine. Confusion and heartache storm behind her eyes. I can tell she wants to say something but simply doesn't have the words yet.

"Brie—"

"Can I sleep here tonight?" she blurts out.

Our eyes meet and shame washes over her features. Her bottom lip quivers and she bites it to keep it from moving. I want to bite it too. Like last night when I marked her perfect tit with my teeth.

"Of course you can," I tell her with a smile. "Like I said, I can take the couch and—"

"No," she interrupts. "*With* you." Her eyes close and her nose turns pink as she desperately fights her tears. "I just want to be held again."

I stalk over to her and pull her against my chest. Her rigid frame relaxes in my grip. "Brie, I will hold you until you don't want me to hold you anymore. Don't ever feel bad for wanting that."

Her head tilts up and she swallows. Pain hides in her eyes. I wish I could reach inside of her and patch it all up. I'm dying to heal every infliction she's ever suffered. "Hug buddies," she says softly, a false chuckle following.

Sliding my palms to her cheeks, I hold her face so I can stare deeply into her chocolate eyes. "And other kind of buddies too. Like last night. If that's what you need."

Her cheeks blaze red. "T-That was a mistake," she stammers out.

I run my thumb across her bottom lip, staring for just a moment at how her flesh resists and pulls with it. "Taking away some of your pain, if only for one night, was not a mistake. It was necessary."

Brie

The semi cold shower did nothing to cool the flames of embarrassment that had painted my skin earlier. I'd basically, in a moment of desperation, begged Ren to let me sleep in his bed. My emotions have been chaotic for the past month. The only time I've felt even remotely okay was last night with his heavy arm wrapped across my middle.

I'm selfish because I want it again.

I want to close my eyes and feel safe.

Running a brush through my wet hair, I wonder how to navigate my messy world. I'd told Ren I was lost…and I am. The feeling isn't far off from when I was holed up in the basement with Esteban. I was drifting and alone. I never thought I'd be found again.

Thank God for Ren showing up when he did. He grounded me. I had begun to spin slightly out of control and he slowed the dizzying movement. Brought it to a screeching halt.

"Beh."

Luciana's brown eyes meet mine in the foggy mirror. She looks pretty with her hair hanging down in long waves in front of her face. She usually has it pulled back into a bun. It's weird seeing her look so casual.

"Everything okay?" I question.

She looks over her shoulder to the doorway and then back at me. Quickly, she nods her head but her cheeks light up in a pink hue.

"What's going on?"

With a frustrated huff, she pulls her phone from her pocket. Her long fingers fly across the keys. Seconds later, she hands me the phone that's pulled up to the Notes app.

He looks like Justin Bieber!

Frowning, I lift my gaze to meet hers. "Who?"

She grunts and steals the phone back. Then hands it back to me.

Calder. OMG, did you see his chest? His muscles are huge. I want to lick them!

At this, I burst out laughing. That girl has Bieber Fever bad. The fact that she thinks Calder looks like him has me quite amused. I personally don't see it, but Luciana seems convinced.

"Have you ever actually licked anyone's muscles before?" I ask with a lifted eyebrow.

Her gaze falls to the floor and she shakes her head. She taps away on the phone until she has a new message for me.

I was a virgin until two summers ago. :(

Her expression has lost the joviality from moments ago.

"Esteban?" I can hardly say his name without wanting to throw up.

Luciana nods and taps away some more.

Yes. Esteban. He is the only one. He let his friends touch me sometimes but never let them do more.

Memories of him assault me. The spaghetti we ate earlier is threatening to make a reappearance.

"I'm sorry," I mutter. "Getting fucked against your will doesn't count. One day, I hope you get to learn the difference with someone you care about."

She stares at me for a long moment before her fingers type away at another message.

Don't be sad, Brie.

I close my eyes. Flashes of the way the heroin numbed me taunt me. Truth be told, I loved the feeling. How it made my pain disappear. How I faded into oblivion. Not a day goes by where, at some point, I don't physically crave it.

"I'm not feeling so hot," I lie when I reopen my eyes. "I'll see you tomorrow."

She gives me a quick hug and pecks my cheek before leaving. I shakily make my way over to the bed and sit. After dinner, Ren went to the basement to work out. He's been gone a couple of hours, and I wish he'd come back. At least when he's here, my mind clears some. I'm not trapped in a drug-induced haze in that basement or holding together my dead husband's neck.

I'm in the present.

The door clicks closed and I snap my attention over to it. Ren stands in the doorway looking too good for the way I feel. My hormones are all over the place. And right now, seeing him all sweaty in nothing but a pair of low-slung basketball shorts and tennis shoes, enables my mind to lose focus on all my stress, and instead, hone in on him.

At one time, I used to sit in my window and stare at him for hours. I loved how he'd drip with sweat, all of his muscles glistening. Now, he's larger and his skin is more colorful. He's the same boy and yet he's also this man.

A distracting man.

"You okay?" he asks as he kicks off his shoes. His eyebrows are pinched together in concern.

I nod and scoot further up the bed toward the headboard. His bed smells just like he always does. Leather and soap and safety. An odd yet extremely satisfying combination. His eyes travel along my bare legs before he clears his throat and turns his back to me as he heads toward the shower.

Once I hear the water turn on, I slip under the covers. My entire body is on edge. The dead organ that once beat in my chest has turned to stone. Each time I think of Duvan, another piece of it chips away. The only solution I have to keep it from whittling down to nothing is to completely shut out those parts. When Ren held me early this morning in my bathroom, I'd wanted to lock my mind down. Instead, he started asking questions. Drew out answers from me about my love for Duvan. It was therapeutic, in a way, but now that it's just me again, I don't want to be alone with my devastation.

My nerve endings seem to pulsate with energy. Each time I close my eyes, Duvan's purple-black irises shine back at me. It hurts so fucking badly to think about him. I dig my fingernails into my palms and attempt to drive away the pain.

I'm not sure how long I remain in this position, but it isn't until the overhead light above me is shut off that I finally drag myself from my inner torture chamber. A warm body slides into the bed beside me. I let out a relieved groan when he hauls me into his arms.

He smells so good.

Clean and strong.

Ren.

"You're crying," he says softly. "What can I do to help?"

I didn't even realize I was crying. When my fingertips touch my cheek, I feel the wetness there. "I don't know."

"Were you thinking about him?" he murmurs, his fingers stroking the flesh on my upper arm.

"Always."

"I'm sorry this happened to you. It's not fair. You of all people deserved better."

I choke out my words. "I don't want to talk right now," I whisper. "I just need..." My fingertips lightly skate down his sculpted chest toward his stomach. In the dark, his physique reminds me of Duvan's.

The smells are all wrong.

The voice is all wrong.

But the heat rippling from him is all right.

By the time my palm reaches his shorts, his cock is erect and straining against the fabric. Last night, he split me apart with pleasure. With every stroke and thrust, he drove away my sadness. It was fleeting but for a while, I was high.

Just like the heroin once did for me.

I was able to blur out all the heartache and focus on something nice for just a moment. Something that didn't destroy me, but instead, fulfilled me.

"I need you," I utter. "You're my distraction."

I hate myself for using Ren. For literally turning out the lights on our friendship to gain a high from his body. His warmth. His companionship. His pleasure. When daylight returns, I'll once again regret my actions. I'll detest my decision-making skills. Hate how weak I am.

Yet, right now, I don't care about any of that.

In the darkness, I crave the real life ecstasy that surges through my veins when I'm touched in just the right way. When his hot breath tickles the tender flesh along my throat. When his teeth bite me in a way that hurts so good.

"You're going to just keep pretending?" he asks, his lips pressing soft kisses below my ear.

My fingers find his still wet hair. "It's easier that way."

In the dark, I'm free to say whatever I want.

"Do you imagine it's him here instead of me?" He's not angry. At least I can't tell if he is. He sounds curious. As though he's trying to figure me out.

"Sometimes."

An animalistic sound rumbles from him tickling my throat as he trails south toward my chest. His palm cups my breast in an almost reverent way. But then his teeth are on my still tender nipple. He's not gentle as he sucks and nips at it. The contrast between his rough handling of one breast and his worshipping way of the other has me squirming beneath him. When he bites me once more, I dig my fingernails into his shoulder. A hiss escapes him. I expect him to move along but he bites me over and over, causing me to cry out and claw him again.

"I can see why he called you tigress," he murmurs against my sore nipple before kissing my skin softly. He suckles the flesh until he gets to my stomach. My pussy is throbbing with anticipation. The idea of having his lips on me between my thighs has my entire body thrumming with excitement.

In the dark, I'm transfixed in this moment.

Sadness and despair and regret aren't haunting me.

I'm lost in the best possible way.

My attention is torn away from my inner thoughts and is honing in on his lips. So soft. So tender. So loving. He kisses me just below my belly button. His palm splays across my midsection, which is beginning to soften and expand. He whispers something against my belly that I can't hear, but I feel. *So hot.*

"What did you say?" I question, my body practically twitching with the need to have him tear me apart.

His tongue flicks out and he drags it down my skin—lower and lower until he reaches my panty line just above my pubic bone. I'm so wet for him. If he were to touch my panties, he'd feel just how wet. His teeth find the fabric and he playfully tugs at it. I let out a mewl of pleasure when his thumb rubs along my clit through my panties to the part of me that practically drips with need.

"So wet," he says with a smug tone.

"What did you say before?" I ask again.

"I said, 'You're going to love your mom. Everyone does.'"

I'm stunned stupid, realizing he just spoke to my unborn baby. My entire body shivers from head to toe. His strong hands find my panties and he jerks them from my body. I am still thinking of his words until his nose rubs against my clit, sending fire shooting through me.

He's going to burn me alive from the inside out.

"Oh, God!" I cry out, my hips lifting to seek his mouth.

I'm not forced to wait much longer because a second later, his lips and tongue are all over my pussy. Tasting and sucking and licking and biting. So much sensation. Too much. But I need it all. I'm greedy, and it's addicting. The pleasure surging through me is better than any drug. His breath scorches my sensitive skin as he whispers sweet things against my flesh. I hear those words and lock them up inside of me for safe keeping. Tuck them away in a memory box of my mind to open up and look at later when it's no longer dark.

"You're dripping for me, baby," he growls against my pussy. "I want to devour you all night long. Feast on this perfect part of you."

His hungry words only serve to drive me crazier than I already feel. I grip his hair when he starts to make good on his promise to consume me. My entire body—which had felt like an empty shell not even twenty minutes ago—comes alive. I jolt and squirm and cry out with every flick of his tongue. I beg and plead for I don't know what until he gives it to me. His teeth find my clit and he tugs. It hurts for just a moment until he sucks away the pain. I'm dizzy with the assault of sensations blasting through me from where his mouth is connected to me.

An orgasm with the ferocity and sudden onset like that of an unexpected tornado rips through me and decimates everything in its path.

"Ren!"

He jerks away from my throbbing sex and pushes my thighs apart. I let out a needy whine when I feel the head of his cock rubbing against my slick opening. Thankfully, he doesn't tease me, and instead drives into me with one hard thrust. My fingernails dig into his arms as he bucks into me like a savage beast. I like him like this.

Uncontrolled.

Hungry.

An animal who's starved only for me.

Possessive.

"Say it again," he orders, his voice deep and authoritative. The echoes of it rumble their way straight to my core. "Nobody has to hear it but us."

"Ren," I murmur so softly, I wonder if he even hears it.

His mouth crashes against mine and we kiss unlike any time before. This kiss is greedy. Soul consuming. Two people with needs only the other can fulfil.

I want to touch every part of him as he fills me. To dance my fingers over his flesh and memorize each contour. Deep in my heart, I want to imagine it's Duvan taking me. But even as I think those words, I know they aren't one hundred percent true.

Ren isn't one I can simply block out.

He loves too hard. With such loyalty. It never waivers. A love that one can lean upon during life's biggest storm and not get blown away.

Here in the dark, I don't have to hide *from* Ren and pretend. It's now that I actually feel alive. It's everyone else I'm hiding from…*with* him. He's once again there for me. I'm not sure I'll ever be able to convey to him how much that means to me.

"Our little secret," he whispers against my lips, like he has direct access to my thoughts.

A secret with Ren.

Wouldn't be the first time.

"Okay, Romeo," I agree, my voice ragged as another orgasm clutches greedily at my body.

My response spurs him on and he fucks me so hard I know I'll be sore tomorrow. I dig my nails into his flesh and hold on for the duration of the ride.

Together we peak with hissed breaths. Wet lips. Tangled souls.

And then together we come back down. Fast and hard. Hurtling toward gravity at breakneck speed.

Reality trickles its way into my brain as his seed trickles its way out of my body. His massive arms slide between my back and the mattress. He then rolls us over onto our sides. I nearly whimper when his fingers brush my hair out of my face. My skin is hot and sticky.

I wish I could see him.

Give a face to the secret.

For now, the dark keeps us hidden.

"What did Duvan want from you?" he questions, his tone sad.

My heart aches in my chest. "For me to be happy. No agendas. No ulterior motives. Nothing in exchange for it. Just to see me smile." Emotion chokes me. "It was that simple."

Ren leans forward and kisses my forehead. "It seems he and I have that in common then," he breathes against me. "I *will* fulfil his wish. We *will* see you smile. You *will* be happy, Juliet."

A smile tugs at my lips from hearing the nickname.

In his pitch-black bedroom, he may not see it, but I sure hope he can feel it.

chapter

NINE

Ren

Sunlight pours in through my window and blankets Brie in its warmth. Even the sun wants her. She's the gravity. We all simply orbit around her.

Lifting up on my elbow, I watch her as she sleeps. Her brows aren't pinched together in pain. Her lips aren't drawn into a sad frown. Her brown eyes don't pool with unshed tears.

She's at peace.

Asleep in my bed.

Pride fills my chest. She hasn't run from me. If anything, she's run straight for me. It's where she belongs now that her world has been blown to bits. I won't let anything or anyone touch her again. Her tattered heart belongs to me. I'll mend it until the day I die. I'm still watching her when my phone buzzes from the table. With a groan, I roll over to see who's texting. I see I've missed a few.

Calder: You do realize there are other people in this house?

Calder: I thought you'd be a one-minute man or some shit but that crap went on for hours. WTF dude?

Calder: Would have been cooler if she would have accidentally called you Steve…

Calder: Oh, Teev! Give it to me! I've got a clue for you right here…

I roll my eyes at his stupid texts from early this morning.

Me: You're a dick.

His response is immediate.

Calder: A dick that didn't get any sleep because your girl's moans kept me up all night. Oh, Romeo! Oh, Juliet! What is that anyway? Some sort of Shakespearean kink? Must be a thing. I'm googling it.

I steal a glance at Brie. Last night had been fucking fabulous. And afterward, I held her while she slept. She was more relaxed than the night before. It felt good to give her some relief.

Calder: Fucking forget it. I can't believe I just googled that shit. Luciana won't stop laughing now.

He then sends me some Shakespeare porn that has me choking back laughter, so I don't wake up Brie.

Me: You're a sick fuck.

I slide out of bed and throw on a pair of jeans before slipping out of the bedroom. Calder and Luciana are nowhere to be found. After I start some coffee, I text him back.

Me: Where are you?

Calder: Denny's. Thought Luci might want to get out of the house.

Luci?

Me: Thanks for the invite, asshole.

Calder: According to my eavesdropping, you ate your fill last night.

Me: I hate you.

While I wait for him to respond, I stir some sugar into my coffee. Eventually, my punk-ass brother replies.

Calder: You're going to hate me even more. Mom's on her way. I was supposed to warn you but then I thought it would be funny if she saw you butt-ass naked with Gabe's daughter. Bye, Teev.

A growl rumbles from me just as the doorbell rings.

Fucking hell.

I don't even make it to the door before it swings open. Mom beams at me. Toto sits on her hip and she has Mason in his carrier in her other hand.

"Teev!" Toto screeches and wiggles herself out of Mom's grip.

I can't help but grin at my little buddy and scoop her up as soon as she makes it over to me. "Hey, Toto. Miss me?"

She hugs my neck and lets out another squeal. "Teev!"

Patting her blonde curls, I arch an eyebrow up at Mom. "You can't just blast in through the door, Mom. I have company."

Mom's mouth drops open and her gaze takes in my appearance. I'm sure my hair has that just-fucked look and I'm not even wearing a shirt, for crying out loud. Her cheeks turn bright red as she wrestles Mason's tiny body out of the car seat. "Well, I didn't know!" she exclaims. "I told your brother I was coming. He said you'd be here."

Toto, now curious about my home, wiggles out of my grip. I set her back on her feet to go on a hunt for my coffee. It's too early to deal with this crap without my liquid caffeine. "Want any coffee?" I call out.

Mom follows me into the kitchen. "Wow…"

Looking over my shoulder, I frown at her. "What?"

"That tattoo. It's…"

"Big?" I quip with a smirk.

She laughs. "That too. It's beautiful, Ren."

I'm just taking my first sip of much needed coffee when I hear Brie screech my name from the other room. I slam down my mug and trot toward the bedroom. When I burst through the door, I'm frozen at what I see.

Toto, a big toothy grin on her face, sitting on Brie's chest and petting her dark brown hair. Brie's eyes are wide and horrified but she makes no move to push Toto away.

"Ahhh, fuck," I hiss.

Mom swats at my back. "Don't cuss around her. She learned the word *shit* the other day from your father and has said it probably a thousand times since." When she pushes past me, she too, pauses. "Oh, dear. You do have company."

Fucking Calder.

"Uh, Jesus," I groan and run my fingers through my hair before I stalk over to the bed. "I'm sorry." I scoop Toto's nosy ass up and storm back toward the door. "Mom, take Toto and wait in the living room. Please. Brie and I'll be out in a sec."

Mom's eyes are wide with understanding. She steals another glance at Brie before she ushers Toto out of my room. When I turn to look at Brie, she's chewing on her bottom lip. God, she looks so fuckable this morning with her messy bed hair. She's every man's wet dream with the sheet barely tugged over her generous breasts. If my mother weren't waiting for an explanation in the other room, I'd rip the sheet from Brie's grip and give her something to smile about this morning.

"I'm sorry it had to happen this way," I groan. "If you want, I can make them leave. You don't have to meet…" I close my eyes and let out a huff. "Your sister."

When I risk a glance at her, she's still frowning. "Technically, I just met her." Her tone is cold but then she seems to soften. "I can do this."

Her simple words mean so much. I love Toto. Who wouldn't love Toto? I want Brie to love her too. Both Toto and Brie could use a sister. Their dad is a little on the special side.

"You're so fucking brave, Brie," I tell her as I stride over to her. I grip her tousled hair and tilt her head back. She lets out a soft moan when I give her a hard kiss. When I finally pull away from her, her eyes flash with anger.

"I haven't brushed my teeth!"

I smirk and shrug my shoulders. "Tasted pretty sweet to me. You don't hear me complaining."

"Who said it was *my* breath I was disgusted about?" she retorts back, her brow lifted up in challenge.

Laughing, I shake my head. "Keep looking at me that way, woman, and I'll give my mother something to be disgusted about when I fuck you so hard you scream loud enough to scare the babies."

She gapes at me. "You wouldn't…"

I slide my leg between her thighs. "Want to test me?" My knee slides up and I nudge her right where I'll put my dirty little mouth if she keeps up the sassy talk.

She's about to respond when Toto starts banging her tiny fists on my door. "Teev! Teev!"

I snap my gaze to Brie and give her a wolfish grin. "We'll continue this discussion later."

The flicker in her previously dull eyes tells me she's looking forward to it.

Awkward doesn't even begin to describe this moment. Brie sits beside me on the couch. Toto is in my lap and keeps petting Brie like she's some sort of exotic animal. And Mom stares at Brie in wonder with Mason suckling on her tit.

Where is Dad or Calder or fucking Gabe?

"Toni is your sister," I tell Brie, my voice soft.

Toto turns and grins at me. "Sissy?" She points at Brie in question.

Brie's hard gaze softens a bit. I know she's uncomfortable around my sister's toddler but these people are her family whether she likes it or not. Toto didn't do anything wrong. If anything, she's the only thing that Hannah and Gabe ever did right.

"Yep," I tell her and tug at a curl. "That's your sissy."

"Why do you call her Toto?" Brie questions.

I can tell Toto wants to crawl into Brie's lap but she hesitates, probably sensing the stress that seems to be rippling from her.

"Your dad calls her that so it kind of stuck."

Toto lets out a needy little whine and regards Brie with the saddest puppy dog eyes I've ever seen. That's a look she learned from her momma. Brie bites on her lip as if she's mentally battling with herself. Finally, though, she reaches for her sister. Toto crawls into her lap and lays her head on her shoulder. Her tiny hands begin playing with Brie's hair.

"Sissy pwetty."

Brie, who was stiff, relaxes and she pats Toto on her back. "You're pretty too."

I flash Brie a supportive smile before turning to look over at Mom. Tears roll silently down her cheeks. After a moment, she finds her voice. "You look just like your dad," Mom says, her voice quivering.

Brie regards her with a frown. "I look like my mother too. But she was killed."

Mom flinches as if Brie's words were an actual slap to her face. "I'm so sorry, sweetheart. I am so, so sorry."

Brie, who seemed poised for a fight, deflates just as quickly as she'd puffed out. "That was rude. I didn't mean to…" she trails off and jerks her teary gaze to mine.

"Some bad shit happened," I assure her, "and you're not wrong to feel angry or to lash out. If anyone knows how it feels, it's Mom." I smile at Mom and hope she can see how broken Brie is. That she's not being a bitch…she's just hurt.

"My mother died too. And then my father was killed by my high school boyfriend." Mom lowers her gaze. "People hurt me. They stole from me. They took away everything I loved." She sniffles as she burps Mason. "Your father was one of those people."

Brie snaps her gaze to my mother. "What?"

"They told me what that man did to you in Colombia. And then what happened to your husband," Mom says. "I'm so sorry, honey. I just want you to know that if you ever need someone to talk to, I'm here. I know how it feels to be raped and held against your will. I know how it feels to be a captive. I know how it feels to watch the ones you love bleed out in front of you." She dabs at her cheek with Mason's bib. "And I also know how awful it feels to have to have contact with those who hurt you. The hardest thing I ever had to do was accept your sister. My rapist's child."

Brie starts to cry. "But he's my daddy." Even though she argues with my mom, I can sense she believes every word. "He wouldn't do that, right?"

Mom swallows and her lips purse into a firm line. "He did. It was a long time ago but he did."

I attempt to comfort Brie by pulling her closer but she's still on her quest to understand and shakes me away.

"I don't know if I can accept this—what you're saying," she chokes out, her voice breathless. Her eyes flit over to her little sister and she frowns. "Any of this."

"I can't imagine how it would feel to have to accept your mother's murderer's child," Mom murmurs. "I know that it hurts. That it is confusing. That it makes you angry."

"Mom-mom," Toto says sadly as she climbs off Brie's lap and runs over to Mom. "Don't cwy."

Mom pulls her into her side and kisses her blonde head. "But some of us just have to be stronger because the rest of the world simply is not."

Brie buries her face into my side as a loud sob escapes her. I hold her to me as she cries. My poor, broken, beautiful girl.

"Daddy always told me that people would say he did bad things. I just never understood what those things were. He certainly never explained them." Brie lets out a painful cry but sits up to look at my mother. "He might have hurt you, and for that I'm sorry, but he was the best father anyone could have asked for."

Mom nods and smiles at her. "I don't doubt that for a minute, sweetheart. I've seen how he behaves around Toto. Gabe isn't all bad. For ten years of my life, he was my entire world. I'm not trying to turn you against him. I'm simply telling you I understand how you feel."

Brie's hand finds mine and she squeezes it as if she requires my strength. "I still love him."

"I know." Mom winks at her.

Something passes between them. Something powerful. Something solid.

"Umm, Mrs. McPherson…"

"Baylee," Mom corrects.

Brie swipes away her tears with the back of her hand and begins resurrecting the wall that protects her. "Can I get the name of your obstetrician? I'm not sure who to go to and I'm going to need to get some prenatal tests done soon."

Mom's eyes drop to Brie's stomach and then flicker to mine. I give her a slight shake of my head. *I'm not the father.* Understanding flashes in them. Not relief, though. Sadness. "Of course, Brie. I've got a card in my bag. In another month or two, Mason will be too big for his bassinet. I could loan it to you if you'd like."

"I would like that," Brie assures her. "And, Baylee?"

"Yes, honey?"

"I'm sorry he hurt you. I wouldn't wish that on anyone."

Mom smiles at her. "What doesn't kill us makes us stronger. They may try to tear our hearts apart…" She strokes at Toto's hair and looks fondly at her. "But they don't understand, our hearts are made of steel. Women like us are unbreakable. Even when we're shattered into a thousand bits. We just find a way to gather up what's left, walk into the fire otherwise known as life, and weld our most precious piece back together again." Mom kisses Mason's forehead before leveling her gaze at Brie. "This is life, baby. And you're going to conquer it."

chapter
TEN

Brie

I fidget on the exam table as I wait for the doctor to see me. The nurse had me pee in a cup and drew some blood after having me fill out a mountain of paperwork. Baylee had offered to come with me, but I'm glad that it's Ren who's here with me.

His shoulders are tense as he stares out the window. It's been a week since I met my sister and his mother. A whole week of us being intimate at night but friends during the day. Something about the daylight makes me feel exposed. Like I've done something wrong. Like I've betrayed Duvan by letting Ren put me back together again.

The daylight instills guilt.

Which is why I keep him at arm's length.

Until his bedroom door closes at night.

When he draws me into his arms and kisses away all the pain. I count down the minutes until we're alone in the dark. It's the only time I feel somewhat normal. I'd thought he'd be upset with me. That my standoffishness during the day would hurt his feelings.

But Ren is strong.

It's as if he has direct access into my head. I don't have to tell him because he gets it. Ren respects my boundaries and doesn't breach them.

I hate what I'm doing to him but it helps me. I'm selfish because I need him to be two different people for me at two different times.

"Are you nervous?" he questions, his steely blues darting to mine.

I stop chewing on my fingernail and nod. "I am. What if I'm not really pregnant? What if I don't have his baby inside me? It's all I have left of him…" The stupid emotions overwhelm me once again. Tears streak down my cheeks. But before they can even drip from my jaw, Ren is out of his seat and standing beside the exam table pulling me into his arms.

"You're sick every morning, Brie. Your tits are huge. And you haven't had a period in a while, right? You're pregnant. Stop worrying. His baby is safe," he assures me.

I let my best friend hug me tight. We may not carry on a sexual relationship when the sun can stare at me with disdain in its eyes, but we still touch. His hugs are soothing to me. They're needed and always come at the right time.

Luciana and I are tight, but she can't give this to me.

Vee, at one time could have, but she's nowhere to be found.

The thought of Vee has my heart aching. I don't know where she went. Ren's father is looking into tracking her whereabouts. According to his records, her apartment and parents' house are still being paid for. It's as if she and her mom left on a vacation or something. Knowing her stupid mom, she probably took Vee to some resort so they could deal with the stress of losing Heath by getting pedicures and massages and sipping mimosas.

I'd ask Oscar but he's unreachable. He won't answer his phone or his emails. The last I'd heard about him was from Rafe. But I can't get in touch with Rafe now either. Everything is all so weird.

The door clicks open and someone walks in. Ren kisses the top of my head before releasing me to go sit back down. An Asian woman with black hair and a pretty smile walks in wearing a lab coat.

"Hello, Mrs. Rojas. I'm Dr. Ling," the woman greets and extends her small hand.

I shake it and force a smile. "Hi."

She sits down on a stool and opens the laptop on the counter. Quickly, she scans through the information. "Well, you're definitely pregnant according to your bloodwork and urine sample. Congratulations," she says with a grin. "And based on when you said your last period was, that puts you at twelve weeks."

My heart races in my chest.

This is real.

I'm pregnant with Duvan's baby.

I will carry on a piece of him.

"Would you like to see your baby?" she questions. "At this stage, we should be able to get a pretty good picture for you."

My gaze jerks over to Ren and he's beaming. He nods his head before rising and striding back over to me. He takes my hand. "Brie, this is exciting."

Tears well in my eyes, and I nod at the doctor. "Yes. Please."

She calls in a nurse and they begin prepping me for a vaginal ultrasound. My hand squeezes Ren's strong one as anxiety spikes through me. The only thing keeping me sane through this entire ordeal is the breathtaking smile on his handsome face.

He's happy for me.

That thought elates me.

"This will feel a little uncomfortable, but just try to relax," Dr. Ling says in a calm voice. I feel pressure as she pushes the lubricated wand into me. The nurse turns some dials on the screen beside the bed.

"You're doing a great job," Ren whispers before kissing me on the forehead.

I smile back at him.

"You two are a cute couple," the young nurse says with a grin. "How long have you been married?"

My heart stops beating in my chest. Her simple question reminds me of the fact that my child will never have a father. That we'll have to deal with these questions until the day we die.

"What's that?" Ren interjects, pointing at the screen. I'm thankful for the distraction and the fact that he reads me so well.

The nurse turns her attention to the screen. Her smile falls immediately. "Umm, Dr. Ling?"

Dr. Ling's eyebrows furrow together as she concentrates. "Yes," she murmurs. "I see that. Let me make sure first."

Ren's gaze snaps to mine and terror flickers in his eyes. I don't like the look because it scares me. Everything about the way they're acting is scaring me.

"Volume, Nurse Ellie," Dr. Ling instructs.

A moment later, a loud thumping fills the room. All fear drains away from me as I focus on the beautiful sound.

"That is your baby's heartbeat," Dr. Ling says. She moves the wand around inside of me. A moment later, I hear another sound. The cadence slightly different. "And this is your other baby's heartbeat."

Time stands still as I process her words. Nurse Ellie is beaming at me pointing to two different grainy blobs on the screen.

"T-Two?" I stutter out.

Ren bends over and boldly kisses me on the mouth. "Two babies," he breathes against my lips. "Congratulations, Momma."

Tears roll out of my eyes and Ren swipes them away with his thumbs. His eyes twinkle with delight and it fills me with warmth. Two babies. This is better than good. This is perfect. Of course Duvan would knock me up with a litter of little tiger cubs. Of course he would.

"I'm speechless," I manage to choke out.

Dr. Ling chuckles. "Most parents are when they find out they're having twins. Come back in another month for your sixteen-week checkup and we may be able to determine the sex of the babies."

Ren gives me a lopsided grin that makes my heart flop in my chest. Nurse Ellie pulls some photographs from the printer and then hands a stack to me. When she hands Ren a picture, she beams at him. "Congratulations to you too, Daddy. You did good work." She gives him a wink.

I don't have the heart to tell her he isn't the father. Thankfully, Ren doesn't confirm nor deny her words. He simply takes the picture and stares proudly at it. My heart is too small and shredded to handle all of this happiness at once. I'm overwhelmed.

"I'm going to set you up with some prenatal vitamins, but other than that, keep doing what you're doing. Your weight is a healthy amount and the babies look great," Dr. Ling tells me as she stands.

Babies.

I'm having two.

The moment we exit the building and the late October breeze whips around us, Ren scoops me into his arms. I let out a laugh when he spins me in a circle before putting me back on my feet.

His hair is styled in a messy way that looks good on him. The stubble on his cheeks has gotten thicker and I love the way it feels when his mouth kisses me in the dark all over my most sensitive places. Steely blue eyes shine with pride and love and excitement. I don't think he's ever looked as sexy as he does now.

"Brie," he says, his tone low. His smile falls and he regards me with a severe look. "You keep looking at me that way, and I won't be able to control what happens next." His head lifts up to the sky, making his Adam's apple bulge from his throat. "In case you didn't notice, it's broad daylight." He draws his chin back down and glares at me with a wicked gleam in his eyes. "The things I want to do to you are too sinful for this time of day."

His words cause my panties to dampen. The rules and boundaries I have in place with Ren are slightly skewed and greyed out right now. For once I'd like to watch the way his full lips suck on my inner thigh until it leaves a mark. For once, I'd like to see the way his cock stretches me open as he slowly slides into me. For once I'd like to stare into his blues as he drives into me. Thoughts of sex with Ren aren't helping my situation. Like always, he reads me so well. Hunger flashes in his gaze.

"God," he growls. "You're so fucking sexy. I know it isn't what you want to hear right now but I can't not say it." His fingers spear into my hair and he tugs until I'm looking up at him. The parking lot is full of people but he doesn't care. His mouth once again descends upon mine like when he so boldly kissed me in the exam room. This time, though, his intent is darker—like our nights. I let out a moan the second his lips press against mine. A starved growl rumbles from him as he deepens our kiss.

I clutch his shirt to hold him in place. Truth is, I don't want the kiss to ever end. In the daylight, the kiss warms me. It's freeing. People can see. We can see. Our teeth clash together as we kiss, as though there might not be another chance. Having lost Duvan has shown me that you never know what the future holds so you have to take those chances when they're presented to you.

He finally breaks our kiss when we're both panting for air and slides his palms to the sides of my neck. His forehead leans against mine as he grins at me.

"Oh, Romeo," I say with a chuckle. I can't help but think that several months ago, when I was still locked away in my tower, I'd have gone wild over a kiss like that. Very romantic. Very Romeo. Very Ren.

"Speaking of, Juliet, do you want to go to the costume store? Calder's having a Halloween party tomorrow night. He's been inviting a shit-ton of people. It could be fun," he says, waggling his eyebrows at me.

My heart sinks.

Ren probably wants us to dress up as Romeo and Juliet.

"I want to be a tigress," I blurt out.

His dark brown eyebrow lifts up in amusement, not disappointment like I would have thought. "I wouldn't expect anything less." He gives my ass a squeeze. "Now get in the truck before I turn into a beast and maul you."

The visual has me stalling for just a moment.

I like it when Ren goes into beast mode.

"There," I tell him, pointing at a townhouse at the end of his street. "Let's go look."

He pulls his truck into the driveway. This townhouse is two-story and stucco and has a direct view of the ocean. I like that it's close to Ren. As much as I've enjoyed sleeping in his bed each night, I need to think of giving my babies a real home.

A multicolored strand of flags flaps in the wind. A sign boasting Open House hangs above the garage. I've not even been inside yet and I already feel drawn to this place. We climb out and Ren takes my hand. His grip makes me feel secure. Together, we enter the place. Before we even make it through the front door, a man in a black suit with a blinding white smile greets us. As soon as he quickly assesses us, his smile falters. I'm sure he was hoping for someone older.

"What can I help you kids with?" he questions, irritation bubbling in his voice.

Ren bristles at his tone. "Well," Ren bites out, dropping his gaze to the realtor's nametag, "Conrad, you can start by giving us a tour. Unless you're too busy for that. We can certainly show ourselves around."

Conrad opens his mouth to reply when another couple walks in the front door. He sizes the older couple up and makes a quick decision. "Please," he says, "feel free to show yourselves around."

Ren tenses but I tug him away from the asshole. "I'd rather take the tour with you instead. He's a douchebag," I mutter.

He chuckles and lets me guide him down the hallway. Everything is perfect. Brand new hardwood floors. Granite countertops in the kitchen. Fancy stainless steel appliances and fixtures. Once I'm satisfied I've properly looked at everything downstairs, I let Ren guide me up the stairs of the fully furnished home.

"Do you think they'll sell the furniture too?" I ponder aloud.

He stops at the top of the steps and frowns at me. "You really want to buy it?"

I swallow and nod. "I want to give my babies a home."

His gaze bores into mine for a long moment. "Okay, then. Let's check out the rest, Momma." That's twice now he's called me Momma and both times, it's filled me with warmth.

We carefully inspect each bedroom. There are two smaller bedrooms and a larger master. So Luciana will have a place to stay too. I'll probably put the twins together. This house is perfect.

Ren drags me into the master bathroom. He grins when I shriek over the size of the jet bathtub and walk-in shower.

"I'm going to buy it," I tell him proudly.

He walks over to the bathroom door and locks it. Then, he saunters over to me. "It's perfect. Just like you." I let out a whimper when he grabs my hips and turns me to face the mirror.

Compared to Ren, I look like a shrimp. My dark brown hair is messy and windblown, but the look on my face isn't one I've seen in a while. Happiness. Hope. Pride. I'm smiling, and it looks good on me. He, of course, looks like perfection in a tight white T-shirt that showcases every single one of his muscles. His large hands seem to swallow my waist as he rests them on my hips.

The lines have become blurry with him.

I want him in this moment.

Not tonight after the lights have gone out.

Now.

As if back inside my head, he reaches for the light switch. I shake my head at our reflection. "Leave them on."

He gives me a clipped nod before he sweeps my hair away from my neck. His lips are soft on my flesh as he places hot kisses there. One of his massive hands slides to my front and grips my breast through a Nirvana shirt of his I stole.

"Are you sure you want to see this?" he murmurs and then his teeth tug at my flesh near my ear. "I'm going to fuck you right now against this counter. In this house. For those assholes downstairs to hear. Can you handle seeing it happen? Last chance for me to turn off the lights, baby."

My eyes flutter closed at his bold words. I'm wet and needy for him. Screw my boundaries. I want to see this. Grabbing on to his hand, I guide him lower until his fingers graze against my clit through my yoga pants. Pleasure jolts through me at the simple touch.

"I want to see," I whisper, my unsure eyes meeting his. "I need to see."

He grabs the bottom of my shirt and pulls it hastily from my body. The bra I'm wearing is way too small now and my tits are spilling out of the top of it. His hands cup them in a reverent way for a moment before he dances his fingers along to my back to unlatch my bra. When it falls to the floor and my heavy breasts are freed, our eyes once again meet in the mirror.

"You're so goddamned beautiful, Brie. I'll never get tired of looking at you," he growls. His tongue finds my neck and he laps at me. "I'll never get tired of tasting you." Then, he sinks his teeth into my skin in a playful way. "I'll never get tired of biting you." He roughly hooks his thumbs into the top of my pants and shoves them down. With one of his large hands, he pushes the middle of my back until my palms are on the countertop and my face is inches from the glass. His hands grope my ass cheeks for a second before he runs a long fingertip between my thighs. He finds my wet opening and breaches it with his finger. I let out a needy moan and wiggle my hips at him.

"Ren…"

He does that sexy man thing where he reaches behind his neck and yanks his shirt up over his head in a way that looks sinful. I watch him jerk at his belt and then his jeans slide to the floor. His impressive cock is freed and slides along the crack of my ass, causing me to shiver with anticipation. He fists his erection and guides it into my wet opening, drawing a whine from me. When he's pushed in to the hilt, he flashes me a wicked grin that has me clenching around him.

Seeing this makes it better.

Reality isn't always a bitch.

The darkness isn't always preferable to the light.

"I'll never get tired of fucking you, baby."

He slides all the way out before slamming into me again. I cry out and grip the countertop. When my eyes close as I give in to the pleasure, pain at my skull forces them back open. Ren's blue eyes glimmer wildly and he has my hair tangled in his grip.

"Eyes open," he growls as his hips piston into me.

My mouth is parted open and my eyes are hooded. Swollen breasts bounce in front of me with every thrust he delivers.

This is hot.

We're hot.

"Oh, God…" I whimper, my legs beginning to shake with impending pleasure.

His rough palm slides around my hip to my front where he captures my clit between his thumb and finger. The hand that's gripping my hair pulls me toward him so his chest is up against my back. He can't thrust with me standing upright so he focuses on massaging my clit. My eyes start to close again, so he tugs my hair hard enough to remind me of his command. I bite down on my lip and meet his gaze head on. The fire that blazes in his blues consumes me. I give in to the expert way he touches me and cry out as my entire body convulses. The moment my legs begin to wobble, he pushes me back down onto the counter. Slam after beautiful slam, he thunders into me until he grunts signifying his own release. His heat gushes into me without warning. He slows, and when his cock stops throbbing, he flashes me a crooked, mischievous grin.

"You."

I raise an eyebrow. "Me?"

"Yep. You." Chuckling, he pulls out of me and his seed runs down my inner thigh. Uncaring that we're in a house that doesn't belong to us, he yanks a hand towel off the rack and sets to cleaning me up. We're just pulling on the last of our clothes when someone beats on the door.

Ren smirks at me before sauntering over to the door, his T-shirt still in hand. When he slings it open, Conrad glares at us.

"You need to leave," he snaps.

The couple behind him gapes at us. The woman's neck turns bright red when she sees Ren with no shirt on. It's obvious what we've been up to.

"No," I tell him. "How much?"

Conrad frowns. "I'm sorry but Mr. and Mrs. Sanchez here are putting in an offer. We're about to work up the paperwork as soon as you leave."

Ren lets out a menacing growl, and I flash him a smile letting him know I've got this.

"Conrad. How much are they offering?" I ask again, my voice calm.

He lifts his chin in a snotty way. "Six hundred."

Turning to the couple, I smile. "Is that as high as you can go?"

Mr. Sanchez puffs out his chest. "We have room to negotiate if you're insinuating a bidding war. I assure you, we'll outbid you. We want this townhouse."

I laugh and shake my head. "You may want this townhouse, but I *need* this townhouse. I have two little cubs on the way, am obsessed with the beach, and my best friend lives on this street. I also have more money than I know what to do with. So, make your best offer so I can outbid you and we can all move along with our day." Turning toward Conrad, I give him a shrug of my shoulders. "Did I mention I can pay cash?"

Four hours later and a seven hundred grand wire transfer, I'm the proud owner of my first home.

chapter
ELEVEN

"I can't believe I bought a house," Brie murmurs to herself in the dark.

I'm glad she wanted to spend one more night at my house before moving in to hers. I am selfish and like her in my bed. Having her down the street will be nice, but I don't know where that leaves us.

"Conrad sure changed his tune. Ran that poor couple right out of the house once he realized you were serious." I chuckle just thinking about the greedy sleezeball. My palm finds her bare breast under the sheet and I give her nipple a little pinch. "It was nice getting to see you while we fucked."

She stiffens, but I don't regret my words. It *was* nice. I won't forget the look on her face when I made her come. All stress and worry and sadness was gone as she succumbed to the bliss. *I* made her feel good.

"Ren." A pause. "I'm sorry."

I chuckle and playfully bite her tit. "You weren't sorry when you were coming all over my dick."

She pulls away and then light from the bedside lamp floods the room. When she looks at me, her gaze is sad. "I don't want to use you. I just…" she trails off. "I don't understand how to feel or what to do right now. I'm doing it all wrong, I know. But…"

"It feels so fucking right?"

Her eyes snap to mine and she nods. I grin at her and press soft kisses to her breast that's closest to me. My palm splays out over her stomach that's not as tight as I remember. I'm looking forward to watching it swell. When I look back up at her, a storm brews in her eyes.

"What?" My palm stills on her stomach. "Am I hurting you?"

Her nostrils flare and she shakes her head. "No. You're just…"

"Perfect? Sexy? Amazing?" I tease and nip at her flesh.

She lets out a gasp. "You're just…"

"I could go all night. Funny? Have a beautiful cock? Smart? Hot as fuck?"

A giggle escapes her and it makes my heart rate speed up. "Thank you."

"For being all of the above?" I quirk up a playful eyebrow.

She nods. "Thanks for always being here for me. Through all of my storms, you've been there. Steadying me. Holding me. Assuring me everything would be okay. I feel thankful is all."

I slide back up the bed so I can kiss her. She lets me pull her into my arms and seems just as eager for my mouth. Her fingers thread into my hair as I kiss her deep enough to steal her breath. After a hot, wet kiss, I pull away to look at her. Her plump lips are swollen and red from my facial hair. I love making her flesh turn crimson.

"Am I a bad person?" she questions, tears welling in her chocolate eyes.

I shake my head as I push her onto her back. She parts her legs willingly and lets me slide inside of her. Her breath hitches. I cup her cheek and stare into her glimmering orbs. Neither of us moves, we just remain connected—both physically and emotionally.

"You're one of the best people I know," I tell her firmly. "You've always been strong and resilient. Like a dandelion in a hurricane. The wind rips away parts of you, but you're still left standing after the storm. Sure, you're weathered and changed, but you're still there."

She laughs. "This is me, baby. A hairless dandelion."

I smirk at her and then steal her smile with a kiss. "You're a smartass too."

"Are you going to just sit there with your dick inside me or are you going to fuck me?" she sasses.

I let a growl escape as I snatch both her wrists and press them into the bed. She squirms as she waits for me to fuck her. I'll tease her a bit first. Locking eyes with her, I slowly thrust into her in a teasing manner. Then, I drag my gaze down to watch how my thick cock stretches her with each slide inside her body. My dick is coated with her wetness, which is a total turn on. Lately, in the dark, we've missed some of the small details that mean so much.

Seeing her arousal on my cock is most definitely a detail I never want to miss again.

"Faster, Ren," she grumbles. Very much a growly tigress.

I shake my head and continue teasing her in a torturous way. She resists at first but then begins to learn this rhythm. Her body quakes and trembles as it anticipates each of my movements.

"You're so fucking wet, baby," I murmur.

She bites on her bottom lip and desire flickers in her eyes.

"I want you to come just like this. Think you can orgasm without me touching your needy clit?" I question, my voice husky.

Panic flashes in her eyes. "I don't know. I want to come so badly."

"You're going to come that way," I tell her in a matter-of-fact tone. "In fact, I have an idea to help make that happen."

She lets out a squeal when I roll us over to where I'm on my back. I release her wrists while she settles herself over my hips. A gasp rushes from her when my cock hits her in the right spot.

"Do more of that," I instruct as I slide my finger along the place where my cock is pushed into her opening, now dripping with arousal. She gasps when I slip it inside along with my dick. I make sure to coat it well before pulling it back out. "Twist around so I can see your sexy ass."

Her eyes widen with fear, but when I grin at her she obeys. Once she's settled with her round ass facing me, I grab her hip to urge her to move. She begins rocking her body and rolling her hips. It feels so fucking good but this is about her. I want her to come without any clitoral stimulation.

"Relax a minute, Brie," I murmur as I tease the tight hole of her ass with my wet finger.

"Ren…"

"Shhh," I urge.

Her dark hair hangs down her back as she looks up at the ceiling. I notice the moment her rigid body seems to relax. Slowly, I push my thick finger into her tight ass.

"Ohhhh…." she moans.

God, she's so fucking tight.

"That's it, beautiful. Now ride that cock. Make it feel good. I want your hands all over those perfect fucking tits. That clit is off limits, understand? If you're a good girl and come like this, I'll suck on it until you see stars."

She lets out another sound of bliss and begins riding both my dick and my finger. Her ass clenches with each movement. I want to come so fucking badly but I don't dare do it until she's screaming my name.

"You're doing such a good job," I praise. "I love seeing your body. Fuck this bullshit darkness. I only ever want to see you in the light from here on out. Got it, baby?"

She nods and quickens her pace. Her breaths come out quick and ragged with each passing second. "Oh God!" Her body clenches around me for a second before she lets out a roar. A motherfucking roar. Like a woman possessed, she shudders wildly as pleasure takes over. It steals her away from me for a moment, and I allow her the brief, torrid affair with bliss because I know she'll be back with me soon. As she crashes back to reality, I release my own climax into her. I'll never grow tired of fucking this beautiful, broken woman.

When we both still, I slip my finger slowly out of her body. Then, she eases herself off my cock. Before she gets too far away, I give her sexy ass a *thwap*.

"Hey!" she screeches and scrambles away from me. Her smile is so fucking pretty.

"You liked it," I tell her smugly as I sit up on my elbows. "Seems like you're into a lot of kinky shit these days. I'd be an asshole if I didn't deliver what you secretly want."

She arches a brow at me. "Who says it's a secret?"

"So it's public knowledge that you want my cock in your ass?" I retort back.

"Ren!" she scoffs. Heat colors her chest and throat.

"I guess you *do* still have some secrets," I tell her with a big-ass grin. "I won't tell anyone. But you'll have to be quiet when I'm fucking that pretty little ass because they're going to hear you otherwise. You're the loud one, not me."

"Oh my God," she grumbles. Despite her tone, her smile gives her away. "You're impossible." She bounces off toward the bathroom, her butt jiggling at me as if to fucking tease me.

I scramble off the bed, trailing after her. "Don't deny it, baby. The heart wants what the heart wants."

My words—meant to tease—seem to strike a chord with her because her smile falls in the bathroom mirror. Her eyes well with tears and she drops her gaze to the sink. Coming up behind her, I wrap my arms around her and bury my nose in her hair.

"Don't feel guilty for being happy, Gabriella Rojas," I murmur to her. "He would have hated that."

Her eyes snap back up to mine, understanding flashing in them. She doesn't have to say a word. I've always been able to read my girl.

And she's always been my girl…even when she wasn't.

I slide both palms to her stomach and smile at her. "Are you happy?"

Her smile is shy and she nods. "I am."

"Good," I tell her firmly. "Harness that feeling and don't ever fucking let it go. You deserve it, baby. You've always deserved it."

"You're seriously not wearing that," Calder says, barely holding in a chuckle.

I look down at my carefully put together costume and shrug before I start bouncing my tennis ball at the wall again. "What's wrong with it?"

"You look like a douchebag. An 80s one at that." He shakes his head as if he's embarrassed of me.

"And your costume is any better? What the hell are you supposed to be, anyway?" I question as I toss the tennis ball at him.

He catches it and flashes me a wicked Calder grin. "A puppeteer."

"Like Geppetto?"

The ball gets launched back at me. "You'll see." He whistles and soon my bedroom door opens. Luciana waltzes in wearing a grin that matches his. Those two are up to something. Two partners in a crime I haven't figured out just yet. If Brie were here, she'd be calling her friend out right about now, demanding to know what's going on. But she wanted to get ready at her house. I'm supposed to pick her up in half an hour.

"Luci," Calder says, and beckons for her to come to him. Her makeup has been done up artfully so that she looks kind of like a doll. Dark hair pulled into pigtails. Rosy red cheeks. Two black lines drawn down her chin from each corner of her mouth to her jaw. I put it together and I'm already shaking my head.

"Don't you think this is a little insensitive," I mutter through clenched teeth.

Calder stiffens as if the thought just now occurred to him. He snaps his wide-eyed gaze to

Luciana. "I thought it would be funny—" He runs his fingers through his hair in frustration. "Not insulting. Jesus! Am I insulting you, Luci?"

She shakes her head in vehemence and steps closer to him. Her brown eyes sparkle with delight. He raises his palm to her cheek for a brief moment as if he's caught up in her gaze. But then, as if cold water has been splashed on him, he jerks his hand away. Disappointment mars her pretty features for just a moment before she forces it away with a smile.

Calder clears his throat before sliding his hand up under the back of her shirt. Her white T-shirt tightens around her breasts and her midriff shows.

"Hey Teev," Calder chirps in a cheesy girl voice through clenched teeth. "The 80s called, they want that abomination you call an outfit back." As he speaks, Luciana animatedly moves her mouth as if the words are coming from her.

"A ventriloquist and a dummy," I grumble. "Unbelievable."

Calder once again talks in his stupid voice as Luciana acts out, as if she's speaking. "I only see one dummy here and I'm staring right at him." Luciana leans forward and waggles her eyebrows at me. I can't help but laugh because they are so damn stupid.

"Go away," I groan. "Don't you have some Martha Stewart shit in the oven for your lame Halloween party?"

"Fuuuuck," Calder grumbles and runs out of the room.

Luciana starts giggling, and I flip her off. "Laugh it up." But then I grow serious and sit up on my bed. "You two seem fast friends," I probe.

The blush that creeps up her neck immediately gives her away. She pulls her phone out of her pocket and starts tapping away like mad before handing it to me.

He's not into me or anything. Not like you're thinking. He just likes me as friend.

I lift an eyebrow up. "I've known Calder for nearly two decades. That's more than just friendship."

Hope flashes in her eyes as she steals her phone back. She taps out a response.

The Beebs is not into me. He can't even kiss me. I have no tongue, remember?

Tears well in her eyes and she looks down at her feet. I grab her wrist and pull her to sit down beside me. Wrapping an arm around her, I hug her to me.

"Luciana," I tell her firmly, "you can kiss without tongue."

She types on her phone and holds it up for me.

I've never been kissed at all. I'm afraid I'll disgust anyone who tries...

At this I laugh. "Calder is pretty fucking disgusting. He'd be lucky to get to kiss you."

She giggles and it's like little bells ringing on Christmas day.

"Now tell me about this Beebs nickname," I urge and flash her a grin.

She bites on her bottom lip and her neck turns bright red again. Finally, she lets out a resigned sigh and taps out a message.

He looks like Justin Bieber. Soooo hot. Don't tell him I said that!

I start laughing so hard tears roll down my cheeks. She slaps me and then flips me off. I'm still rolling when Calder comes sauntering back in. His gaze snaps between Luciana and me sitting next to each other on the bed. Then, he stalks over to her. "Is he making fun of you?" he demands as he hauls her to her feet and into his protective arms.

"N-No," I laugh. "I'm making fun of *you*, dumbass."

She shoots me a warning glare, and I wink at her. "Don't worry," I assure her, "your secret is safe with me."

Calder growls at me before escorting her out of my room. My stomach hurts from laughing so hard. The Beebs. I guess he sort of looks like him. They both have stupid tattoos. But does Justin Bieber know how to make pigs-in-a-blanket and put on a party that Martha Stewart would be proud of? I think not.

I'm just getting ready to go pick up Brie when my phone rings.

Without looking at the caller ID, I answer it.

"Yeah?"

"Let me talk to my daughter."

Gabe.

Rolling my eyes, I start gathering what I need before I leave the house. "She's not here. What do you want?"

He lets out a frustrated sigh. "Rafe called me. He's a friend of Duvan's. Was there with us when she made that deal with Diego." He growls and anger ripples from him. "I'm going to fuck him up one day."

I scowl. "Who the hell is Diego?"

"An asshole who's going to get what's coming to him. I still don't know what he said or did to Brie, but she was pretty shaken up after we left. If I find out he touched her—"

Red blurs my vision and my hand fists. I'm seconds from sending it through the sheetrock. "She didn't say anything about this Diego shit. What would she make a deal with him about?"

He grumbles. "Sold the crack factory."

I don't correct him even though it was coke.

"Made a cool twelve mil for it too," he continues, pride in his voice. "My baby is a master negotiator."

And rich, I think.

I'd assumed Gabe gave her money or that she'd had some leftover from when she'd sold the house. I didn't know she sold the coke plant too. And to a cartel king, no less.

"Why did Rafe call?"

"He said trouble is on the horizon. He thinks Diego might be in cahoots with that Esteban fuck. Another bastard I'm going to murder. I wanted her to be on the lookout. The last thing we need is some drug trafficker hurting my daughter. It happened once before but it won't happen again," he snarls.

"Right. I'll keep a close watch on her." I'm already gathering my shit and walking out the door after her.

"Ren," he grunts. "I'm coming to your party tonight. Your dad told me about it. If I were some criminal cocksucker, a costume party would be the perfect place to find someone. I'll stay out of sight but I'm going to be there in case any shady shit goes down."

I roll my eyes. Ever since Toto came onto the scene, Dad and Gabe act like they're best fucking pals. I don't even know how Mom puts up with that crap.

"Whatever," I mutter. "Just don't upset her. She's happy, man. Let's keep her that way."

He lets out a resigned sigh. "She'll be happier when I serve her Esteban's dead cock on a platter."

Brie

I stare into the same bathroom mirror Ren fucked me in front of and frown. The outfit I'd bought at the Halloween store yesterday doesn't look as cute on today. Perhaps spandex was not a good idea for a pregnant-with-twins woman to be wearing. At least if I'd gone with Juliet, I'd be wearing a big, flowy dress.

Grumbling, I paint on whiskers and a black nose. My hair has been pulled back into a sleek ponytail and I've put on a headband with tiger ears on it. The tiger striped cat suit I'm wearing fits like a glove. But when I turn to the side, I can see my belly protrude. It doesn't look like a pregnancy swell…it just looks like I ate too many tacos at lunch.

I did eat too many tacos at lunch thanks to Calder. Between him and Luciana in the kitchen, they cooked us up one helluva lunch.

I let out a huff of frustration. Too late to change my outfit now. I'm just attaching my tail and slipping into some black flats when I hear music. I step out of my bathroom and walk over to my bedroom window, which overlooks the driveway. As I near it, I recognize the music.

"In Your Eyes" by Peter Gabriel blasts from outside.

A smile tugs at my lips.

Ren gets me.

He always has.

With a cheesy grin on my face, I run over to the window and draw back the curtains. Sure enough, Ren stands in my driveway in front of his black truck. The music booms from his truck but he's holding up a handmade cardboard boom box. His dark hair has been styled into a geeky 80s style to match that of John Cusack's from the *Say Anything* movie. He's nailed the costume. But unlike nerdy John, Ren looks hotter than hell in his 80s movie getup. The white Clash T-shirt fits him like it was painted on. He wears a tan trench coat over it with the sleeves pushed up to his elbows. But the pants and shoes are what have me giggling. His grey pants have red stripes going down the sides and are tapered at the bottom. The white high-top sneakers have to have been stolen from an old man's closet somewhere because I know they don't make shoes like that anymore.

Lifting the window, I lean out and laugh. "Lloyd!"

He fist pumps the air because he knows I get his silly costume. "Get your sexy ass down here, little tigress. I've been dying to see your tight body in spandex ever since you bought that damn outfit."

Not exactly what Lloyd said in the movie…but it's definitely better.

I've long forgotten about my insecurities as I close the window to head downstairs. By the time I sling open the front door, he's abandoned his cardboard box and is waiting on the porch with his hands shoved in his pockets. Even though he tried to dork himself out, he's still so good looking.

Strong, chiseled jaw.

Piercing steel blue eyes.

Sexy stubble sprinkled on his handsome face.

Rushing over to him, I throw my arms around his neck and hug him. "You're such a nerd," I say with a chuckle.

His powerful arms squeeze me to him and he inhales my hair. "Good thing you're a nerd too. A sexy nerd but still a total nerd. You're the one who likes these goofy movies, not me."

I pull away and regard him with a lifted brow. "Is that right? How many times did you watch *Say Anything* to get this costume perfect?"

He grins at me sheepishly. "Yeah, yeah. Get your pretty butt in the car."

When I pull away, he gives my ass a slap. I narrow my eyes at him and make a growling sound. He grabs me by the tail and pulls me back into his arms. His hot mouth breathes against my neck near my ear as his palms roam my spandexed front, settling on my tits.

"You're hot as fuck, kitty."

I laugh. "Kitty? Have you seen the claw marks I left on you last night? I am tigress. Hear me roar."

He pinches my nipple through the spandex. "Okay, tigress," he concedes. "And for the record, I like your claw marks on me. Gotta love a woman who marks her territory."

Territory. Is he mine?

My heart rate quickens in my chest.

He is.

I don't let guilt steal away our moment. Instead, I close my eyes and relax in his arms. He peppers kisses along the outside of my neck. Then, he twists me back around so we're facing one another. His strong fingers grip my jaw in a gentle way.

"You're so beautiful, Brie." His brows are furrowed as he makes this proclamation.

I stare deep into his intense blue eyes. "So are you, Ren."

We hold each other's stares for a long moment. Then, he dips down and brushes a soft kiss on my lips. It's only a tease and I crave more. A car door slams loudly from nearby and it makes him tense. He starts to tug me to the truck.

"We're too exposed out here," he mutters, a slight bite to his voice.

I jolt at the sudden change in his demeanor. "No more darkness," I remind him.

He shuts me in the truck and then soon joins me. The keys sit in the ignition but he makes no move to turn the engine over. When he turns his head toward mine, worry is etched in his features.

"What?" I demand.

He swallows and reaches for my hand. "What happened with Diego?"

I frantically pull open the glove box, where I'd shoved some crackers for emergencies, and attempt to stall by eating. When I don't answer him and instead munch on the snack, he lets out a sigh and reverses the truck. By the time we reach his townhouse at the end of the street, I've nearly downed the entire sleeve of crackers to avoid spilling the icky details of "Daddy" Diego. As soon as he puts the car in park, I launch out and hightail it up to the house. Cars are parked everywhere and people in costumes are heading to the front door. I'm almost to the porch when someone grabs my arm.

I yelp out in surprise.

"It's me," Ren assures me. He comes to stand in front of me and scowls. "Tell me. Something bad happened. Something you didn't even tell your dad. You need to tell me."

I purse my lips together. "Why?" A shudder passes through me.

"Because something happened to you, goddammit. I need to know…" he trails off and runs his fingers through his hair, messing up his 80s hair style. "I need to know what happened and who I need to kill." His glare is severe. If this were old Ren, I would have laughed after such a proclamation. New Ren is serious.

"I had it handled," I lie. I was scared shitless when I thought he was going to rape me. I'd gotten myself into something that was way over my head.

"Did he touch you?" he demands, his jaw ticking with fury.

I swallow down my emotion and shake my head. "No."

His eyes narrow as he studies me. "I don't believe you."

Tearing my gaze from his, I shrug my shoulders. "I'm sorry." I run past a group of people and push through the front door. Luciana and Calder really went all out decorating the place. There's food too. My stomach grumbles with delight but I charge past the kitchen toward the bedrooms. Once I make my way into Ren's, I make a run for the bathroom. I've barely shut the door when it's being pushed back open.

My eyes flip up to the mirror. Ren stands behind me looking more like the bad guy in the 80s movies than the good guy. And I look absolutely ridiculous in a tiger outfit that's two sizes too small. He places his large hands on my hips and twists me to face him.

"Tell me."

I purse my lips together and pout. "You're being a bully."

He winces and I instantly feel bad. Then, his fingers are under my chin, lifting it up so he can look into my eyes.

"I'm not sorry for worrying about you. You may be all fierce and tough and have claws, but people can still hurt you. For that reason alone, I'll always fucking stress out about you." He leans forward and drops a soft kiss on my lips. "Have you told anyone?"

Emotion clogs my throat and I fight tears. "N-No."

"No secrets, Brie. Bring it into the light. We'll face it together."

My chest aches but I know he's right. I don't want to carry that burden alone. He's always been the one I can confide in. "He was just going to take what he wanted…"

He stiffens, and I can sense the rage bubbling from him, yet he somehow manages to remain quiet.

I continue, my voice slightly wobbling. "We made a deal. But then…" I choke out. "I thought he was going to rape me. He overpowered me and he…and he…"

"So help me, Brie, I'm going to cut out his fucking throat," he growls in a low, threatening tone.

"But he didn't." I drop my voice to a whisper. A tear sneaks out and I worry if it'll smear my cat whiskers. "He just exerted his power over me is all. I felt helpless and alone. I was in over my head with him. He could have…if he wanted…" Thank God he didn't.

A roar, louder than any sound my tiger of a husband ever made, rips from Ren. His entire body ripples with fury. I hug his middle so he doesn't do anything stupid, like destroy his bathroom. "You're not alone. Not anymore."

"Then he took the necklace you gave me and Duvan's wedding ring." At this statement, I burst into tears.

His strong arms hug me tight. For the longest time, he doesn't speak a word. "Gabe doesn't know those details, I'm guessing?"

"Daddy had already gotten his ass beat all to hell that day. If he'd known Diego was anything other than pure business with me, he'd have gotten himself killed," I say softly.

He grips my sleek ponytail and tugs until I'm looking up at him. "I'll keep you safe from those motherfuckers," he vows. "You're going to get away from that crooked life. Here, you're going to have a normal one. You're going to take care of those babies without having to look over your shoulder. Brie," he murmurs and dips his head down, "you're safe here."

His lips crash against mine.

When we finally pull away from our soul consuming kiss, he regards me with a fierce look on his face. "Be careful tonight."

I nod and give him a smile. He grabs my hand and we leave his room to go back into the fray of people dancing and drinking in his house. I see lots of cool costumes but Ren's is the best hands down. Only he could make looking like an 80s nerd seem so hot. I'm smiling as we enter the kitchen where Calder and Luciana are putting on a show. A puppet show that is. The sight is hysterical— her looking like a dummy with his hand up under the back of her shirt. Both of them are all smiles as they perform their little show.

"Oh my God," I shout over the music to Ren. "What is even happening there right now?"

He chuckles and pulls me to his side. "Whatever it is, they're both happy to do it. Did you know Luciana thinks my brother looks like Justin Bieber?"

I snort and nod. "I don't see it."

Ren smirks at me. "He does kinds look like a douchebag, so maybe she's on to something."

He pulls away from me to pour me some Pepsi into a red Solo cup. I notice he abstains from the alcohol too. Not sure if it's in solidarity with me because of the pregnancy or if it's because he wants to remain alert. By the way his eyes skim the crowd every so often and he keeps me within touching distance lets me know it's the latter. As much as Diego terrifies me and as much as Esteban haunts my every thought, I doubt either one of them would be so bold as to come to this party. Hell, for all I know, they're probably still in Colombia. I don't feel threatened right now. For once, I feel kind of normal. A young adult at a party full of college-aged people who are dressed up and drinking and laughing. Ren has always wanted a simple, happy life for me. One where I was free to make my own choices and do my own thing. I've been here a week and he's already done so much to help make that happen.

"I'm going to run to the restroom," I tell him.

His features harden, but the last thing I want is for him to follow me to pee. "I can stand outside the door."

Shaking my head, I put my palm on his firm chest and stand on my toes. Our lips brush against each other briefly. I did it. I kissed him in front of others for the first time. His big hands slide to my ass and he pulls me flush against him.

"That was only a tease," he murmurs, his hot breath tickling my lips. "That will never be enough."

He kisses me hard enough to steal my breath and pull a moan from me. When I finally manage to free myself from his magnetic touch, he flashes me a knowing smirk. I laugh and stick my tongue out before heading to the bathroom. I'm just about to twist the knob to the front bathroom when the door flies open. The bathroom is dark from the lights being cut off, so all I get is a flash of blonde pigtails before she brushes up against me. I notice her belly is huge with pregnancy. When I lift my gaze, I meet curious blue eyes.

Familiar.

I open my mouth to speak but she grips my elbows and drags me into the bathroom. She shuts the door behind her and blocks my path to it. The lock clicks as the light turns back on.

I'm staring at Harley Quinn. Well, not the *real* Harley Quinn—The Joker's insane girlfriend—from the *Suicide Squad* movie. But someone who's nailed her costume with precision. The real-live version might be a little more frightening than the character from the movie though.

Blonde pigtails with streaks of pink and blue. Bright red lipstick on a devious grin. She wears a white T-shirt that says "Daddy's Lil Monster" that has been shredded, revealing her very pregnant belly. Tiny red and blue sequined shorts sparkle in the light.

But what's alarming is the baseball bat she's holding.

"Gabriella," she says, a small bite to her voice that has my hackles rising. She smacks on her gum as she takes her time sizing me up.

I'm too frozen in fear to move.

"Hannah," I choke out. My voice is barely a whisper. When she lifts the baseball bat and runs her hand over it, I flinch and protectively clutch at my stomach.

Calculating eyes dart to my midsection and her hard gaze softens. "You pregnant?" she questions as she lets the bat swing lazily beside her like a pendulum. Then, she blows a bubble with her pink gum.

A cold sweat breaks out over my flesh. The terror has swallowed me whole. This woman cut open my mother's throat and ran off with my father. For years, I imagined how this conversation would go. How I would scream at her and rip her hair out. How I would make her pay for what she did to Mom. I never imagined I'd be so scared of her.

"P-Please don't hurt me," I utter. "Or my babies."

At this, her eyes widen with glee and that sends my heart thumping right out of my chest.

"Twins?" She beams at me as if this is the coolest thing she's ever heard.

Swallowing, I nod. My eyes quickly dart around the room in search of a weapon. Calder and Ren don't keep weapons in their bathroom. I decide right then and there that if I make it out of this bathroom alive, my house will have hidden weapons in all the rooms.

"I'm pregnant." She rubs her belly and smacks her gum. "Second baby. Your brother."

I inch away from her because I don't like how she keeps swinging the bat, the arc growing wider and wider. "That's nice," I blurt out.

She flashes me another grin. "Do you ever get cravings?"

I blink at her in confusion. "Uh, not really. Mostly I try not to be sick. I eat a lot of peanut butter crackers."

Her head bobs up and down knowingly. "Morning sickness is the worst. Try keeping some saltines by your bed and eat a couple before you even get up. That way, you have something on your stomach when you go to eat something a little more substantial."

Pregnancy advice from my…psycho, murdering stepmother.

"Thanks." I chew on my bottom lip and look past her to the door. Surely any minute Ren will come looking for me. "I really need to pee. Do you think you could—"

She charges for me and all I can do is squeak. My palms go in the air in a defensive move. I expect the baseball bat to crack me over the head but it doesn't. Her belly presses against mine wedging me between her and the wall. All humor and sweetness is gone as she glares down at me.

"He told me what happened," she snaps, fury flickering in her steely blue eyes that look more fierce than her brother's ever could be.

"W-Who? What?" I stammer, my heart thundering to the point of pain.

She reaches her hand up and I flinch. Her red lips purse into a line as she pets me—fucking pets me like I'm a little kitten. "Gabe. He told me about him."

"Who?"

"Estebaaaaaaan," she hisses through clenched teeth.

I'm thoroughly confused at this point. I don't understand her misplaced rage.

"He," she snarls as her mouth gets close to my ear, "raped you."

Shuddering, I let out a sob. I'm confused when this psychopath hugs me rather than hurts me. I stand still, afraid to move or speak. She releases me and glares at me.

"He'll pay for what he did. That's what happens to rapists." Her eyes narrow. "They pay with their life."

Anger, my most recent familiar emotion, finally claws up inside of me from whatever depths it was hiding in. "And what do murderers pay with?" I don't remind her that my father and Hannah's husband, according to Baylee, is also a rapist. She's proven once that she will kill the ones I love. The last thing I want is for her to snap and kill Daddy too.

Her blue eyes soften and she gives me a shy grin that makes my insides quake with more fear. "Oh, baby girl, I was just curious."

I scoff and fist my hands. "Curious?" My tone is shrill. "Your fucking curiosity killed my mother?!"

She shrugs her shoulders but then levels me with another one of her scary stares. "And the fact that she was in my way. Are you in my way?"

A threat.

"Unbelievable," I hiss. "How are you even cut from the same cloth as Ren?"

At the mention of his name, she smiles sweetly at me. "Take care of my brother and I'll take care of your father." Then the smile melts away. "Hurt my brother and I'll hurt you."

"Fuck you, crazy!" I screech. "You killed my mother!"

She points the bat at me. "In the past, baby girl."

Shaking my head, I start for her but she pokes the bat in the center of my chest stopping me. "I'm sorry," she hisses. "Okay? I didn't know it would hurt so many people. It was an accident, kinda. Just know if I could go back, I wouldn't do it again."

A flicker of deception in her gaze tells me that's a lie.

"Just go. I don't ever want to see you again," I tell her, my voice ragged. I'm exhausted from this little run in.

She drops the bat back down to her side and once again sizes me up, her gaze lingering on my rounded stomach. "Fine. I'll stay away. But remember what I said."

My brows drag together in confusion.

"Rapists pay with their life," she spits out. "That's a motherfucking promise, baby girl." She blows another bubble and then waves. When she opens the bathroom door, Ren stands on the other side with his hand poised to knock. It takes him three seconds to take in the scene before him before he's charging inside and has his sister by the throat. I've never seen him so furious.

The bat clangs to the floor as she grabs at his wrist. He walks her to the wall beside me and gets right in her face.

"You're not welcome here," he snaps, his entire body quaking with rage.

"Let her go." Daddy's voice from the bathroom doorway is strained. Tired even.

My gaze flits over to him. He's dressed in dark jeans and a black leather jacket with a dark red colored scarf around his neck that's tucked into his jacket. His chocolate-colored hair has been tousled and styled differently than usual. It's his weapon that scares the shit out me. Who twists barbed wire around a wooden baseball bat?

"Hey puddin'," Hannah chokes out. All psychopathic looks are gone. She regards my father as if he's the sun and she wants to bask in his warmth.

Ren releases Hannah and points at the door. "Brie, go to my room and lock the door. I'll be there in a minute."

I give him a nod and start past Daddy. Before I pass him, though, I point at his costume. "Who are you supposed to be, anyway?"

He smirks. "I am Negan."

"Who?"

"The Walking Dea—"

"Brie. Now," Ren interrupts with a barely contained growl.

I push past Daddy and leave Ren to deal with them. Once I slip into Ren's room and lock the door behind me, I kick off my flats and head toward the bathroom. I finish my business, which I never even got to start because I ran into that crazy woman, and then quickly wash away my smeared makeup.

Another shudder ripples through me as realization sets in. I was alone in the bathroom with my mother's killer. And she was fucking terrifying. I don't understand, after knowing Ren and Calder and then later meeting their mother, how Hannah is even a part of their family. They're all so normal and she's so…scary.

I peel off the stupid cat suit until I'm in nothing but my panties. Walking over to the closet, I catch my reflection in the mirror. My hands are trembling and I'm wearing a grim expression. This whole run in with her has wiped me out. I locate a T-shirt of Ren's from his closet—which swallows me up—before turning off the lights and crawling into his bed. Light from the cracked bathroom door streams in and doesn't leave me totally in the dark.

I'm distracted by my thoughts when I think I see the closet door move. Terror skitters over me like a thousand bugs on the move.

"Who's there?" I demand, sitting up.

The door swings open and a blur charges toward me. I've barely opened my mouth to scream when a large hand clamps over it. His other hand manages to collect both my wrists and pin them to the bed. The giant man's heavy body presses against me and his hot breaths warm my face. I start to fight my attacker, whose face is hidden by shadows until he speaks.

"Stop freaking out," he growls. "It's me."

The familiar voice slices right through me. His voice confuses me. It's deeper and lower than I remember. Harsher. I squint in the darkness to try and take in his features. All I can see is the outline of his head. His hair is longer than before.

"Miss me?" The normally playful tone in his voice is gone. It feels forced.

Swallowing, I give a clipped nod and when he lets go of my mouth, I speak. "Ozzy, where have you been?"

He relaxes but doesn't release me. I squirm but he ignores the movement. "I've been putting out fires," he snips out. "Fires *you* started."

I once again wriggle in his grasp. "You're hurting me," I lie. "Why are you holding me down?"

He huffs. "I'm holding you down because I want to talk to you and I don't need you running off to your little boyfriend."

I chew on my bottom lip. Ren will be in here at any moment. Things could get ugly quick. "He's not my boyfriend." Another lie. But is it? My mind squashes the thought because now is not the time to analyze me and Ren's relationship status.

"Sure looked like your boyfriend when you were sucking face in the kitchen earlier," he bites out. "How long did you wait before you moved on? Was my brother's body even cold yet, Brie?"

I choke at his words and if my hands were free, I'd slap him.

"Fuck you!" I screech. "Let go of me!"

At one time, I used to enjoy Ozzy's playfulness. How we'd cuddle up in bed and laugh. How he'd touch me as close friends often do. Nothing about the way he's touching me now is playful.

"Just tell me why it is you couldn't even make sure my brother was dead first before you moved on to Ren. I thought you were my friend. Hell, I even thought he was my friend. Were you two fucking behind Duvan's back the whole time?" he demands.

This time, I do manage to free my hand. And as I wanted to do the first time, I smack the shit out of him. He lets out a snarl as he pins it back to the mattress.

"Just answer the goddamned question," he snaps.

I spit at him. "You know that's not the truth. I loved your brother."

His grip loosens and he sags against me. My angry friend chokes on his emotion. "I had to watch. Jesus Christ, I can't get that image of Heath cutting him open out of my head." He burrows his face against my hair and inhales me. "I missed you, Brie. Everything has gone to shit."

Guilt crawls its way up my spine. Oscar lost Duvan too. He's hurting just as much as I am. This time, when my hands are released, I slide them around his back to hug him.

"You've started a war," he murmurs. "I don't know how to fix any of it. I'm supposed to be here… I'm supposed to…" he trails off. "My father wants me to…but I just can't. God, I've missed you."

Fear clutches at my throat. "W-What did Camilo want you to do?"

"To come get you. So he could *discuss* what you did with Duvan's territory." He starts sniffling but true to Oscar, his hands start roaming and his mouth is on the flesh below my ear. "You're not safe. He'll hurt you."

I freeze at his words just as his hand slips under my shirt. He starts kissing my neck and when he presses his hardness against my thigh, I'm jolted to reality.

"Oscar," I groan, trying to push his heavy body away. "Get off me. We need to talk about this."

His palm grips my sore breast and I let out a yelp of surprise. I'm still ordering him to get off me when I hear a noise and then Oscar's weight is ripped off my body. Ren's face is positively murderous as he rears back his fist. Then, I hear a crunch. Ozzy crumples to the floor with a groan. Ren's furious glare meets mine, assessing me for damage for a quick moment before he lunges at Oscar.

Crunch.

Crunch.

Crunch.

He gets three solid punches in on Ozzy before I snap out of my daze and scramble after him. I manage to slide my arms around Ren's middle to pull him away.

"I'm okay," I tell him. "Please stop hitting him."

Ren is tense as hell but he allows me to pull him away from a now bloodied Oscar. We both sit on our asses on the carpet. Ren's shoulders hunch forward as I hug him from behind.

"He…he was…" he trails off.

"It looked worse than it was," I assure him. "I promise."

When Oscar manages to get up on his hands and knees, Ren tenses again.

"Remember what I said," Ozzy murmurs as he wipes his nose with the back of his hand. "You're not safe. I just wanted to talk to you about that and about Vee—"

"You're never talking to her again," Ren roars and rises to his feet, despite my clutching for him. I'm left on the floor as he towers over Ozzy who clumsily gets back on his feet.

Ozzy shoots me a desperate look with one eye. The other one is already swelling shut. "Please…"

"Where's Vee?" I demand, a quiver of worry shuddering through me.

Oscar hunches as he lets out a howl of frustration. "I don't know for sure but…"

Ren pulls me against his side and I'm assuming it's because if he's not holding me then he'll have the urge to beat Oscar's face in some more.

"I think she might be with Esteban," Oscar growls. Then his voice cracks. "Unwillingly."

Ren

"Stop pacing." Brie's voice cuts through my mental anguish, and I give her a sharp look.

"I can't help it," I snap. "These people just won't leave you the fuck alone."

She tugs her towel from her body and starts drying her wet hair with it. After Oscar stumbled from my room, I gathered her up and took her back to her house. Where there weren't a million people. Where I could turn on the alarm and keep her safe.

"He didn't hurt me," she tells me. Her tits bounce as she towel dries her mane. I become momentarily distracted and find myself staring at them.

She lets out a small chuckle and approaches me where I'm pacing manically at the end of her bed. Her towel drops to the floor and then she grabs for mine that's tied around my waist. I let out a groan when she pulls it away. Then it's just us. Naked and together.

"Ren," she coos. "Stop stressing out. I'm okay."

I frown down at her. "Camilo is out there. Diego is out there. Fucking Esteban is out there. They all want something from you. You are *not* okay."

A dark look swims across her features. "So we'll figure it out. But I won't live my life in fear," she tells me with a huff.

I slide my fingers into her wet hair and tilt her head up so I can inspect her perfect features. "You were alone in that bathroom with my whack job baseball bat wielding sister. I'm fucking afraid for you. Don't be naïve, Brie. There are monsters everywhere."

Her nostrils flare and she pushes against my chest but I still have a grip on her hair. "Thinking about them twenty-four-seven solves nothing!"

I slide one hand to the front of her throat and capture her jaw in my fingertips. My lips ghost over hers. "But burying your head in the sand won't make it go away either," I growl. I nip at her bottom lip.

"You're bossy and rude. Where's my sweet Ren?" she huffs but then lets out a moan when I suckle on the lip I was just abusing. Her palms, which were pushing on my chest, have started to slide south where my cock is hard and at attention.

"He died."

She freezes at my words, and I instantly feel like a dick.

"I'm sorry—"

A fierce roar escapes her as she shoves me, breaking our connection. I expect to have to chase after her. Not for her to start attacking me. Her tiny fists beat against my chest as she lets out her emotions.

"Don't even say shit like that to me! You're the only person I have left who I can truly count on! I'm scared too but I'll go mental if I stress about it all damn day!" With each hit to my chest, she pushes me farther back until my ass is against the wall. She delivers a particularly powerful blow to my stomach that has my breath hissing out. I slide my palms to her ass and lift her up before pushing my body between her thighs. I twist us around until it's her back pressed against the wall. Another shift and my cock slides easily into her tight cunt. We both freeze for a moment.

"I said I'm sorry," I utter and thrust into her hard enough for her head to bounce against the wall.

She grips at my wet hair and lets out a hiss. "Apology accepted. Now harder."

Our lips bump against each other as I drive into her pussy with powerful thrusts. Her angry yet needy mewls urge me on. I fuck her against the wall so fast and so hard that a picture falls off and crashes to the floor. All that can be heard is the slapping of skin, desperate sounds we're both making, and the occasional bump of her head against the wall. When she lets out a scream that sounds like my name and rips at my hair, I lose it. Her pussy clutches my dick so hard I see stars. With a groan, I release my seed into her. My mouth seals against hers so I can breathe in her sounds of pleasure. The moment we both come down from our high, I walk her over to the bed. I lie her flat on her back and begin trailing soft kisses all over her full tits. Then, I make my way south.

She lets out a hiss when my mouth covers her mound. I lap at our juices running out of her and taste what only our lovemaking creates. Salty and musky and us.

"I can't believe you're doing that," she murmurs, her body jolting on the bed.

I nip at her clit and then run my tongue back down her seam to her opening. "We taste good, baby. I could spend all night licking every part of you."

She moans and spreads her legs further apart. "I want you to. I like your tongue on me. In me."

With a growl, because her sexy as hell words turn me on, I push her thighs until they're pressed against her belly. I drag my tongue lower teasing another delicious part of her.

"Ren…I don't know…" she utters but doesn't try to stop me.

Undeterred, I spread her ass cheeks apart and run the tip of my tongue along the puckered hole. She gasps and wriggles but doesn't tell me no. My tongue meets resistance, but I manage to breach the tight hole. I hear my name on her lips that quickly turns into a chant as I fuck her this way. While I taste her in such a foreign place, I pinch and rub her clit. It doesn't take long for her to cry out as she comes again. Gently, I tug my tongue free from her bottom and breathe against the tender flesh.

"I'm going to put my cock there next. Tell me no, Brie." I bite the inside of her ass cheek and she gasps. "You're fragile and broken and your heart is in shreds. Yet…" I groan and then press a soft kiss to her pussy. "I want to fuck and defile you. I want to see you forget it all as you lose yourself to unknown pleasure. I know it's too much for you. You deserve gentle. You deserve love and respect. And all I want to do is fuck you raw while you chant my motherfucking name. You asked where your sweet Ren is," I groan as I grab her hips. "Truth is, I don't know. I don't care either. All I care about is you. Being inside you. Taking care of you. Fucking and claiming and loving you." Our eyes meet and her hooded eyes glimmer with emotion. My fingers dig into her hips as I roll her over onto her stomach. "I'm not the man you deserve." I suck on my finger before teasing her asshole with it. "But I'm the man you're going to get." She lets out a low moan into the pillow when I push my longest digit into her ass. "Tell me no, baby. Tell me you need me to take you in there and bathe you and whisper sweet nothings in your ear." I drive my finger in and out of her tightness.

She reaches for her night table and yanks open the drawer. When she grabs the bottle of lube we've been using on occasion, my rock hard cock bounces in excitement. I let out a growl as I slip my finger from her and take the bottle. Pouring a healthy amount on my dick, I rub it in to thoroughly lubricate it before using the excess to prime her opening.

"Last chance. Tell me you need it sweet," I murmur.

On shaky arms and legs, she rises to her knees and elbows. "I need you to fuck me. Hard."

An animalistic sound rasps from me as I grab on to her sexy hip with one hand and use the other hand to help push the tip of my dick inside her tightest hole. She fists the blankets while simultaneously letting out a groan when I begin easing into her.

"Say no," I beg, my voice shaking. The pleasure is too much.

"Claim me, Ren McPherson. Fucking claim me."

Her scream isn't one of pain or horror or fear. It's raw, carnal pleasure as I do exactly as she wishes. I drive into her without apology. My death grip on her hips will leave bruises. Her ass will be sore for days. But right now, none of that matters as I stake claim on this woman.

"You're mine," I snarl, my hips bucking hard against her.

"Yours," she moans in agreement against the blanket. "Yours."

I brush my fingertips over her clit and it's enough to send her over the edge. Her ass contracts around my cock, causing me to go blind with bliss that is only associated with Brie.

Gabriella Rojas is mine.

Fucking finally.

I'm awoken in the middle of the night when I hear Brie whimper in her sleep. She calls out Duvan's name, which makes my stomach twist into a knot. I hate that she's having a nightmare. The way she says his name is the exact same way she called out for him when he bled out right before her eyes on that fateful day.

"Shhh," I murmur against her hair. "I'm here."

My words don't wake her but she does calm. Her fingernails dig into my pectoral as she seems to hang on for dear life. When her breathing evens out again, I drift off thinking about one of our first dates.

"He likes her," I tell her and point off in the distance where Calder chases Vee down the beach.

Brie looks up at me with a sweet smile. "She likes him." Even though her reply is about my brother and her friend, I can't help but wonder if there is a double meaning.

"He thinks she's beautiful. So fucking beautiful," I murmur as I take both her hands.

Her black eyelashes flutter and her cheeks turn rosy. "She thinks he's pretty good looking as well."

I release one hand and gently grip her jaw. I tilt her head up so I can look into her deep chocolate eyes, that hide a past that hurts. I'm dying to learn every part of her and take away some of that hurt. "He wants to kiss her."

Her lips part and her eyes close. "She wants him to kiss her."

I smile and then drop my lips to hers. Her soft mouth is like a shot of vodka on a cold day. It sends surges of warmth shooting through me. With a groan, I deepen our innocent kiss. The taste of her tongue is sweet and so damn delicious. Her fingers grip my T-shirt as she pulls me closer. What started out as gentle, quickly becomes ravenous. She clutches on to me as if she never wants to let go. I don't want that to ever happen. This girl…she's mine. No way around it.

When I finally release her lips, she's breathless. Her arms wrap around my middle and I hug her against my chest. I like her right here. I'm never going to get enough of her.

One day she'll find out your secret.

The thought hits me like a Mack truck. All hope for a normal relationship with this girl flies out the window. Truth is, if she ever finds out who I am…exactly what role I play in her world, she'll hate me. God, I don't want her to hate me.

She'll never know if I have anything to do with it.

I'm brooding over the stupid predicament my selfish sister put me in when Brie looks up at me. All inner fury at my sister melts away as this girl beams at me. Her smile is enough to chase away all dark thoughts. Her smile is perfect.

"She wants him to kiss her again," she tells me with a shy grin.

I smirk at her. "He's going to do whatever it takes to make her happy."

I'm jolted from the past when Brie once again murmurs a name. This time it's mine and she doesn't sound pained. Fierce male pride fills my chest as I hold her tight against me and kiss her hair. I know I will spend my life doing whatever it takes to dissolve her stress and worries.

He's going to do whatever it takes to make her happy.

chapter
FOURTEEN

Brie

I wake up in the wee hours of the morning to Ren's finger lazily tracing lines on my bare stomach. The intimate way in which he does it has my heart flopping wildly in my chest. For the first time since I lost Duvan, I feel a sense of peace. Like maybe, just maybe, I can one day be happy. And with Ren, it certainly feels possible.

His dark hair is messy from sleep and his eyes are still closed, but the small smile on his face tells me he's awake. I try not to let on that I'm awake so I can watch him. My world has been nothing but chaos for months. Even with Duvan, I always had a sense of worry surrounding me.

Right now, though…

In this exact moment…

I am relaxed.

My world is quiet and I want to savor it.

I find myself staring at Ren's full lips. Dark hair is growing on his face—hair that never existed when we dated what seems like eons ago. His new look makes him seem edgier. Slightly rugged. All man. I like that he seems a little unkempt and no longer guided by rules and order. He left his home because of me. Because his twisted sister staying there was an insult to me. It may seem like something small but it means a lot to me. More than he'll ever know.

His palm splays out over my belly and my breath hitches. I like that he's curious about my stomach and how he sometimes talks to the babies. If Duvan were here, I know it would be what he'd do. In a selfish way, I'm glad these little ones have someone who cares, besides me. And Ren does care. He does more than care.

He loves me.

The thought makes my heart clench. Ren has loved me for a long time. That never went away. Even when I was off loving someone else, Ren was here, his entire heart beating for me. The thought of him longing for me while I was gone causes my eyes to burn with tears. Nothing about how our relationship ended before was fair.

"Why are you crying?"

I blink away the blur and find steely blue eyes boring into me. Those eyes. So loving and fierce and undeterred. I get lost in them a lot lately. Those eyes make me feel safe.

"No reason," I lie as I run my fingers through his unruly hair.

His eyebrows furl together and he leans forward to brush a kiss against my cheek. "You're lying. Tell me what has you upset this morning. I want to fix it."

Those words only make the tears fall more freely. I let out a ragged breath of emotion as I try desperately not to cry. Being pregnant has my normally tough exterior reduced to flimsy shreds. He kisses my wet cheek as if to encourage me.

"I can't ever love you like I loved him," I blurt out, my voice hard despite the tears. There. I said it.

His body tenses and his fingertips that had been tracing lines on my belly stop. As soon as the words pierce the quiet air, I want to reel them back in and tuck them back in the dark parts of my head where they belong. Those words cut. And the last thing I want to do is cut Ren. But not being honest will only build what we have on lies and untruths.

I expect him to get upset. To yell or accuse me of leading him on. Something. Instead, he simply resumes tracing his finger on my stomach again. I bite on my bottom lip as I wait for him to say something. His brows are still pinched together and his gaze is somewhere else in the room as if he's lost in thought. After what feels like forever, he sits up on one elbow and reaches for my tattooed wrist.

Our eyes meet and he gives me such a sweet smile, it makes my chest ache. His thumb swipes over my wrist before he pulls it to his lips. Hot breath tickles my flesh and then he kisses the heart tattoo with another man's name on it.

"Your heart…"

"Is torn and useless and not much of it is left."

His lips press to my flesh again as his blue eyes dart to mine, locking on me. "It's still your heart. It still deserves love."

A tear streaks down my cheek and my bottom lip wobbles. "What if I don't have any love left to give? What if it's always just partial and clouded and obstructed? How can you love someone who will never be able to reciprocate fully?" I slide my palm to his cheek and he leans into my touch as if I'm the magnet he can't help but be attracted to.

"That's simple, baby," he says with an easy grin. "I'll love enough for the both of us. My heart is big enough to hold yours." His hand rubs my stomach again. "My heart is big enough to love all of you."

At this, I begin to full on sob. He pulls me to his chest and I mold myself against his strong body. I'm warmed when he kisses my forehead.

"Brie," he tells me, his voice low and gravelly. "You're it for me. You always have been. I lost you once and I won't lose you again. If all you can give me are broken parts, I'll fucking take them because they're still you. Broken or not, the girl I remember from that window all those years ago still exists. I'll weather whatever storms that hit *for you*. I want to keep you safe and see you smile again. Let me love you. I'm not asking for anything in return."

I hug his middle but don't speak right away. I don't trust myself not to break down into a million pieces.

"If it were possible to love again," I finally say, my voice ragged and but a whisper. "It would be with you. I'll always try for you. I just hope that it will be enough."

He chuckles and his long fingers stroke the outside of my arm, making me shiver. "Having you right here, right now, is enough. You'll always be more than I ever expected."

I slide my hand lower down his ridiculously toned stomach until my fingertip traces his dark trail of hair that disappears under the sheet. His cock jolts under the covers and it makes me smile. "Make love to me," I murmur and slip my hand under the fabric to grip his nice cock. "I want to feel the love you insist on giving me."

A growl rumbles from him as he rolls over on top of me. His lips begin peppering kisses all over my face. He does it in such a playful way, I find myself giggling and running off the last of my tears. Our eyes meet and his blaze intensely with his dedication to me. My laughter dies the moment he pushes his cock into me.

He rests on one elbow as he slowly rocks into me. The other hand whispers touches all over my breast, throat, face, and hair. His worshipping touch repairs parts of my broken soul. The way he stares at me as if I'm the only thing in this world has me praying to God that I can one day be the woman he deserves. I'll try. For Ren, I'll try. Because if anyone deserves all-encompassing selfless love, it's Ren McPherson.

"You're beautiful," he murmurs.

I smile at him. "So are you."

He smirks and thrusts a little harder into me. "Guys prefer the term 'sexy as fuck' but beautiful will do. Just remember for next time." He winks at me before diving in to nip at my throat.

"Definitely sexy as fuck," I agree but trail off with a moan. The way he grinds against me delivers pleasure to my clit. It's exhilarating and I want all that he has to give me.

Our love making quickly becomes ravenous. What started off as gentle soon becomes grunts and groans and growls. Fingernails and teeth scraping flesh. Begging and pleading for release.

"I love you, Brie," he murmurs against the shell of my ear. The words, even though I'm not sure I'll ever be able to say them back, send me over the edge. My eyes close as an intense soul healing orgasm sears through me. His heat pours into me, chasing my release. A few more thrusts and he nuzzles against me, reminding me of an animal caring for his mate.

The tigress may have lost her tiger.

But this tigress is *not* alone.

After a moment, he sits up so he can look down at me. A panty-melting grin spreads across his most definitely *sexy-as-fuck* face.

"I'm going to wash your pretty ass in the shower and then…" he trails off as he looks down between us. "I'm going to feed you and the babies. Waffles covered in whipped butter and warm syrup. Maybe a side of strawberries. What do you think?" He waggles his brows at me.

I laugh and lock away the perfect moment with him in my memory for whenever I have a sad day. This memory will most definitely make me happy.

"I think you're going to make me orgasm again," I tease.

His cock twitches inside me. "Oh," he says with a wolfish smile. "I can make that happen before we even leave this bed."

A growl on his part is my only warning before he makes good on his promise.

"The question is," I say as calmly as I can. "Will you be able to find her?"

Ren's father, War, looks up from his laptop and frowns. "I'm sure as hell going to try." War has a gentleness about him that had me relaxing almost as soon as I met him. Maybe it's that he looks so much like Ren, and Ren equals safety in my mind. Either way, I just like him.

An entire week has passed since Oscar came to see me and it's eating me alive. Vee's missing. She's not at a spa like I'd hoped. She's gone. Oscar still won't take my calls, but I did receive some texts from him over the week to which he never replied when I answered back.

Ozzy: Her car is at her parents' house, but I broke in. She's not there.

Ozzy: The apartment was empty too.

Ozzy: Nothing seems out of sorts except that she's just gone. My father claims innocence but I'm not sure.

Ozzy: My father wants me to meet with Diego. I'm supposed to take our territory back. How the fuck am I supposed to do that?

Ozzy: If Diego has her, I'll gut him.

Ozzy: My father got a call from Esteban but won't tell me what he said. I think it may involve you.

None of his texts made much sense, but they have my anxiety on high. Ren seems to notice my rigid shoulders because he walks up behind the chair at my kitchen table and rubs on my neck.

"Did Oscar mention anymore about Esteban?" Daddy questions from across the table. Toto has fallen asleep in his arms and he absently strokes at her blonde curls. She clutches onto her favored Veggie Tales stuffed animal, Larry the Cucumber. My sister is so sweet and innocent. If she didn't represent the psycho who killed my mother, I'd be warmed by the sight of her looking so serene in our daddy's arms. But the chill always remains.

"No," I say with a sigh. "His texts are sporadic at best. That's why we need to find Vee. Ozzy is too distracted by what his father is making him do. I'm afraid she might be hurt somewhere."

War taps away at his computer but speaks. "I've looked up all of her credit cards. All activity ceases the day after..." His blue eyes dart to mine, and I see pity in them. "Anyway, all activity stops. Same with her mother. Neither of them has purchased a thing since then. I've hacked into their bank accounts. All the money they had is still there. Everything is just sitting."

"What about Esteban?" Daddy demands. "Can you find where the hell he's been holed up? He and I need to have some words." Rage ripples from him. The crazed look on his face reminds me of a demon. And the fact that he's holding a little blonde cherub in his arms only makes the whole thing seem a little more comical.

"Maybe I could ask Diego and—"

"Fuck no!" Both Daddy and Ren growl at the same time.

War gives me a supportive smile and a wink—one that says he'll research Diego and follow any leads. I give him a slight nod before grabbing Ren's hand. When I look up at him, he's gazing at me with such love and fierce protection, I almost waver under it.

"Can you get me something to drink?" I ask. "I'm not feeling so well."

He gives me a nod and then presses a kiss to my head. Once he leaves, I find Daddy and War watching me. I'm still not used to me and Ren's relationship being public, but it is. Nobody, except for Oscar, has criticized us for it either. As much as Ozzy's words had broken my heart, I refuse to feel guilty for letting Ren into my heart. Truth is, he never left. Ren is my best friend and my protector. My lover and a million other things all rolled up into one person. When I vowed a week ago that I belonged to him, I meant it. He may only get a broken sliver of who I used to be, but that's all I have to give.

Daddy and War get into a heated discussion about the "Colombian cunts" as my dad calls them. My phone buzzes in my lap and I quickly lift it up to see if it's Ozzy with any news.

Unknown Number: We need to talk, cariño. Privately. I have something you want, remember? And I need something from you.

Ice slides through my veins, freezing me in my seat. With shaky hands, I quickly type out a response.

Me: Talk with you ends up with you trying to either fuck me or fuck me over.

He buzzes back immediately.

Unknown Number: Camilo is on my ass. Tell me where you live and I'll come see you.

Me: Absolutely fucking not. We meet in public or we don't meet at all.

Unknown Number: I'm here in San Diego. There's a restaurant at one of the piers. Come alone and I'll give you your precious jewelry back. I'm not going to hurt you. Daddy Diego swears on his big dick.

I suppress a shiver at the thought of him here in my city.

"Does Oscar have any news?" Daddy questions, jerking me away from my inner shuddering over the thought of Diego's dick. His eyes dart to my phone. I hold it to my chest.

"Uh," I murmur. "Nope."

His eyes narrow and he gives War a pointed look that I'm not meant to interpret. It annoys me. When they go back to discussing how Daddy plans on murdering the whole lot of them, I look back down at my phone and tap away my response.

Me: Fine. Get me the address. I'll shoot you if you try anything funny.

Unknown Number: I have no doubts, cariño. We both know you've got bigger balls than most men. Meet me in an hour. Wear something sexy. I want to see your nipples through your clothes.

I quickly delete the horndog's texts and then bite on my bottom lip. I'm about to have to lie to these guys.

"Everything okay?" Ren questions from behind me causing me to jump. I nod quickly—too quickly—and take the glass of Sprite from him. In several gulps, I down half the glass.

"I'm fine but I was going to go over to your house for a bit and see Luciana," I lie. "May I borrow your truck?"

He frowns. "Let me get the keys and I'll drive you."

I'm already shaking my head and attempting to give him a bright smile. "Stay here with them and sort out our next plan of action."

Ren stares at me for a long moment before he nods. "Fine." I thank God that Ren's not the smothering type. "I'll walk you out and make sure you get there okay."

My outfit is far from sexy. Too damn bad, Diego. I'm wearing something similar to the last time he saw me. Black yoga pants and this time a hoodie because it's chilly outside. Ren walks me out to his truck and gives me a chaste kiss. I drive slowly over to his house down the street and make a great show of climbing out and waving. He remains from his watch until I disappear onto the porch. I wait a few minutes before peeking around the house. He's gone back in side. With shaky legs, I hurry back to the truck and haul ass out of the neighborhood. It isn't until I'm several miles away with nobody following me that I relax.

I spend the entire half-hour drive to the restaurant worrying. I didn't bring a weapon. I don't have my wallet. I didn't tell anyone where I was going. All I have is my phone shoved into the pocket of my hoodie. When I pull up to the restaurant, I'm happy to see it's bustling with people. Busy is good. Busy means he can't do anything stupid like accost me.

I wait several minutes before climbing out of the truck. My feet carry me inside to the hostess stand. I'm queasy, and the scent of seafood mixed with my nerves makes my stomach roil. I am just about to ask the server for a table when an arm slips around my waist. Before I can let out a scream, warm breath tickles my ear.

"Looking sexy as ever, cariño," Diego murmurs and bites my lobe. "Table for two." The hostess's eyes linger on us for a moment before she waves for us to follow her. I attempt to jerk out of his grip, but he holds me like we're lovers. The moment we reach the booth, he guides me into the seat and slides in beside me. I glare at him and he simply chuckles.

"My wife will have water," he tells the woman. "She's expecting. I'll have a glass of your house wine."

When she leaves, I punch him in his side. "You're such a fucking dick."

"You're the only person I have ever known who is brave enough to not only hit me but also to call me such names." He leans in and kisses my cheek. "I've killed men for much less. But you, my dear sweet kitten, I'm amused by you. If we're being honest, it gets me really fucking hard." His hand grips mine. "Would you like to feel just how hard?"

"I'm going to be sick," I groan, shaking my head.

He laughs and releases me. "Don't be so dramatic, Mrs. Rojas. Where I'm from, most women are actually quite attracted to me."

"I'm not most women."

He reaches across the table and snags a package of crackers from the basket. After he opens them up, he hands me a cracker.

"So I can see," he says with a chuckle.

With a huff, I accept the cracker and begrudgingly munch on it. He leans on his elbow on the table so he can watch me eat. His lips curve into a pleased smile. Once I've downed the cracker, I meet his stare.

"Why are we here?" I demand.

He hands me another cracker, which I take. "Camilo. The old fuck is really losing his poor mind. Seems that you, cariño, really stirred some shit up."

I suppress a shudder at the very thought of Camilo being angry with me. The man is scary. All the tales of him torturing the people who wronged him replay in my head.

"You need protection, no?"

I snap out of my daze and frown at him. "From you?" I scoff. "I don't think so. I have protection."

He narrows his eyes at me and strokes his goatee with his finger and thumb in a contemplative manner. "Who exactly is your protection detail? Rafe Gonzalez? Your daddy? Because if you recall, they didn't protect you so well the last time we met."

"It doesn't matter," I spit out. "I'm protected."

The asshole leans in and sniffs me like I'm some piece of meat he wants to cook up and eat later. "My men took down your men easily once before. I'm sure it won't be hard for Camilo to do the same. But Camilo Rojas doesn't incapacitate, he kills."

He unwraps another cracker and hands it to me. We're momentarily interrupted when the server comes to our table. Diego blurts out an order and sends her back on her way. Then, his predatory gaze is back on me.

"What do you want from me?" I ask. "Beside something sexual."

He laughs and stretches his arm across the booth behind me and leans closer. "I want all the information you have in that pretty little head of yours on the Rojas operations. I know you were friends with the little red headed girl. I know you saw how things worked with her father and the shipyard. Then, you were a witness to everything Duvan did. I want the details because I'm going to be running the show very soon."

"You're just going to take it all away from Oscar?" I question with a glare.

He lifts a black eyebrow and smirks. "The boy?"

I almost laugh at him. "When exactly was the last time you saw Oscar? He's far from a boy."

Shrugging, he runs his finger along the outside of my arm. "No matter. I want their territory. You're going to help give it to me. And in exchange, I keep you safe from retaliation."

The very idea of betraying Oscar sickens me. I don't trust Diego one single bit.

"No."

He slaps the table hard enough to make our glasses slosh and me yelp out in surprise. "No is not the answer I was looking for. So far, I have been generous with you, cariño. But you're pushing me right now. You're pissing me off and I'm three seconds from dragging you out of here by your hair and taking you back home with me so I can teach your smart mouth what I do to little girls who misbehave." I let out a whimper when he clutches my thigh to the point of pain.

The woman arrives with the food and Diego flirts with her while I consider his words. Carefully, I unwrap my cloth napkin and set it in my lap. When he's distracted, I slip the knife inside the sleeve of my hoodie. She leaves and he picks up a crab leg. I remain silent as he cracks it open with a crab cracker. Then, he dips a big chunk of meat in some butter sauce before holding it to my lips.

I shake my head and his face darkens.

"Don't make me pry your mouth open in front of all these people because I will. Do as you're told," he hisses.

Suppressing a grumble, I open my mouth and accept the food. He smirks and then pulls off a piece of meat for himself. The entire meal goes on this way. Even though the food is surprisingly good, I'm disgusted by this man. Once he finishes, he wraps his arm around me and hugs me to him. I remain frozen as he pets me as though I'm a small animal. What is it with this guy and petting? He should get a dog.

"I want the information," he says softly, his touch gentle.

"I'll only help you under one condition."

He tenses but releases me. "Go on."

"If I tell you, you can't hurt Oscar."

"Done."

"And I want that protection extended to my friends and family."

He reaches into his pocket and retrieves something. "Of course, cariño. Text me a list. It'll be done."

"Once I tell you what I know, Camilo and Esteban and their people will come after me. I'm pregnant and somewhat happy. I don't want this disrupting my life." Our eyes meet and he nods.

"Anything else?"

"Please don't tell them where you got this information. I know you're an asshole of epic proportions but I'd like to think of you as a business acquaintance. I'll tell you what I know but I'm counting on you to uphold your end of all parts of our deal."

He strokes my cheek with his thumb. "So beautiful. I do a lot of business with men in South America but you've been my most worthy opponent. It would seem I have a soft spot for you." He smirks and slides his thumb over my bottom lip. "I often think of your big round ass when I'm balls deep in one of my wives. Perhaps one day the fantasy will come true."

I start to tell him off but then he dangles something shiny in front of me. My necklace and Duvan's ring.

"You fixed it," I choke out.

He smirks. "Well, I did break it."

At seeing my jewelry, I can't help but burst into tears. He fastens it around my neck and hugs me to him. I don't want to be in his embrace but I feel like I've just made a necessary deal with this devil.

His hand that strokes me in a comforting move slides under my hoodie and up my front. I let out a yelp when his finger strokes my bare belly.

"It would be so easy just to take you home with me," he murmurs against my hair.

The knife hidden in my sleeve slides into my hand and I press the sharp tip against his hard cock that strains against his slacks. He lets out a hiss of shock.

"It would be so easy just to take this," I poke hard enough to make him grunt, "home with me."

His hand retreats from under my shirt and he chuckles. I reluctantly pull the knife away from his junk and glare at him.

"Cariño," he says with a wolfish grin. "Did I ever tell you I like you?"

I roll my eyes and point at his phone. "Too many times. Now take some notes. I have a lot to say."

chapter
FIFTEEN

Ren

Calder: Luci and I are going to see that new Ryan Reynolds movie. You guys want to come?

Me: Sounds cool. Just ask Brie if she's feeling up to it.

Calder: Ummm. She's probably on YOUR lap. You ask her.

Me: Ha. Seriously, just ask her.

Calder: Duuuude. Do you want me to text her? Wtf.

Me: Stop being a dumbass. She's over there so just ask her.

Calder: Ren, she's not here.

Panic slices through me, and I nearly knock back the kitchen chair I was sitting in to bolt to the front door. As soon as I open the door and look down at my house, my heart nearly explodes.

"She's gone!" I holler over my shoulder to Dad and Gabe.

I've already taken off running down the road to my house. I'm barefoot and not nearly dressed warm enough for the chilly November air but I don't want to lose any time. While on my run, I dial Brie's number. It goes straight to voicemail.

"Fuuuuck!" I yell as I pound up my driveway.

When I sling open the front door, Luciana and Calder look over their shoulders from the couch in confusion.

"She's gone," I breathe out as I hurry to my room to grab a pair of shoes. Snagging a hoodie on the way back out, I bark at Calder. "I need your keys, man. She's gone."

My brother jolts to his feet. "I'm coming with you. Luci, go over to Brie's until I get back."

We both trot back out to his Tahoe and, by this point, Dad and Gabe are in the driveway both looking as panicked as I feel.

"She's not answering. Dad, pull up the location on her phone and text me the address. Gabe, keep trying to call her. I knew something wasn't right when she left in such a hurry," I growl as I climb into the driver's seat.

Gabe hands off a sleeping Toto to Luciana before he and my father take off running back to her house. I don't look back as I peel out of the neighborhood.

"So she's just gone?" Calder questions in confusion.

"Yep," I huff as I gas it down the road.

"Where the fuck are we going?"

"I don't know," I roar and beat my fist on the steering wheel. "Keep calling her but keep an eye out for Dad's call."

I've just merged onto the highway when Dad calls. Calder puts him on speaker.

"Phone records show some texts from an unknown number. Looks like some guy named

Diego Gomez." He rattles off the address to a seaside restaurant. Thank fuck I'm already headed in the right direction. "Gabe and I are ten minutes behind you. Don't do anything stupid." I can hear Gabe snarling in the back ground. "Hold on," Dad grunts in annoyance.

"THAT'S THE CRAZY COLOMBIAN CUNT!" Gabe bellows. "She's not fucking safe with him. I'm going to cut his eyeballs out if he so much as looks at her."

I run my fingers through my hair and hit the accelerator. Calder's knuckles turn white as he holds on to the dash. I'm easily going ninety—it'll be a miracle if I don't get pulled over. We weave in and out of traffic as Gabe tells me how dangerous Diego is. And he doesn't even know the half of it. The asshole terrified the hell out of Brie and made promises of brutality. She can't handle someone so ruthless and powerful by herself.

The ride should take at least thirty minutes but Calder and I fly into the parking lot in just under twenty-three. I don't even shut off the ignition before I'm clambering out of the Tahoe and hauling ass into the restaurant.

"Hispanic male. Scary looking. Younger Hispanic woman wearing a grey hoodie," I huff out. "Have you seen them?"

The hostess nods. "Yeah, they just left, actually. Maybe five minutes ago."

I nearly knock Calder over in the doorway but then shove past him back into the parking lot. I see my truck but it's empty. I'm about to go fucking nuts when a black Town Car slowly rolls past. Charging for it, I launch myself on the hood of it to stop it. An old man with a grey beard and an equally old woman stare back at me in horror. The man slams on the brakes and I slide back off the car.

"Over here, crazy!" Calder hollers. "Jesus! You trying to get killed?"

My gaze snaps over to his. Beside him stands my favorite person. And she looks unharmed.

"Fuck, Brie!" I trot over to her and nearly tackle her. With a groan of relief, I wrap my arms around her and crush her against my chest. "What the fuck? You scared the shit out of me!"

She stiffens in my arms. "I had to go."

My palms find her cheeks and I glare at her. "The fuck you did! You just snuck off and met with a man who's known for being a psychopath. Alone! What were you thinking, goddammit?!"

She huffs and tries to push away from me, but I refuse to let her go. "I had to!" Her lips tremble as the fear from meeting with him becomes present. That prick scares her. Hell, he scares me.

"Come here," I growl and smash my lips to hers. She kisses me frantically as if I have the power to erase whatever stressful situation she just encountered. When our lips break apart, she starts to sob.

"I-I didn't think about it. I j-j-just wanted to get my jewelry back," she cries against my chest.

I squeeze her tight and kiss the top of her head. "We do this shit together, Brie. Please. You've got two babies you need to protect. You can't do that alone. You've got to stop trying to fix all these problems by yourself. I'm here. Let me be here for you."

She nods. "I'm sorry, Ren. I'm so sorry."

I'm stroking her hair and assuring her everything will be okay when another car flies into the lot. Seconds later, Gabe jerks her from my grip.

"What the fuck, Brie baby?" he snaps but squeezes her tight enough that I'm afraid he'll crush her. "I'm going to kill that motherfucker! Where the hell is he?"

She pushes away from her father and launches herself back into my arms. "He's gone. I made a deal with him."

Dad gives me a wide-eyed stare while Gabe kicks the gravel under his feet.

"We don't make deals with that fucker," Gabe snaps.

I squeeze her to me and level him with a *calm-the-fuck-down* stare. "Let her talk."

She sniffles and lets out a sigh. "He wanted to know every detail of the Rojas operations. I told him because he promised me protection. He promised protection to all of you."

Gabe grips at his hair and shakes his head. "Oh, sweet girl," he growls. "And you believed him?"

Her chin tilts up and she looks at me. Uncertainty flickers in her brown eyes. "I trusted him to do the right thing. I honestly don't have a choice. Camilo is pissed. He wants to get me back for selling off Duvan's assets. That old man is scary. The things he's done to people for far less…" She shudders and buries her face against my chest.

"This was stupid—" Gabe starts but I cut him off.

"Enough," I snap. "She did what she thought she needed to do. You and Dad keep digging into the cartels. I don't trust them at all. Not even Oscar. So find out what they're up to. Let's stay ahead of this." Looking down at Brie, I kiss her nose. "And you," I murmur. "Please don't do that ever again. You scared the shit out of all of us. Promise me, baby."

She nods. "He scares me so bad." Her body trembles again as if the thought of him simply terrifies her.

"I want a gun," I bite out to Gabe. If anyone can get me illegal and untraceable shit, it would be him. "For all of us. Luciana. Calder. Me and Brie. I'm not going to feel settled until we all have a way to protect ourselves."

Gabe is already storming back to Dad's vehicle but he's nodding. Dad grips my shoulder and gives me a firm stare. "I'm going to find out where they're holing up. If I must leak the info to the Feds, I will. We're going to get rid of this threat," he assures me before stalking off after Gabe.

Calder holds his hand out for his keys. "Drive the speed limit on the way home, you crazy freak. I'd really like to go to that movie later and I can't do that if you and Brie are splattered all over the highway."

I chuckle and toss his keys at him. Once he's gone, I guide Brie over to my truck. I open her door for her. She shakily sits down inside. By the time I'm inside with her, she's somber and quiet but much calmer than before.

"Are you okay?" I question.

She swallows and nods. "I just hate when he touches me." Then a beat of silence. "It reminds me of him. Esteban." Her body shudders. "I can't ever go through something like that again."

Rage blooms in my chest, and I fist my hands. If that prick were here, I'd bash his head in. "He better not ever touch you. If I have anything to do with it, he won't."

Her lips tug into a half smile as she relinquishes my keys. "You're cute when you're protective."

Smirking, I shrug my shoulders and start the truck. "Must mean I'm cute all the time."

It's been nearly a month since Brie gave us the disappearing act scare. We've all been on high alert, but I have to say, sleeping with a gun under my pillow each night certainly helps. Brie is always on edge, and I hate that she must live her life that way.

"I can't deal if she's going to be there," Brie murmurs as we walk hand in hand to my house. I can see Mom and Dad's car in the driveway next to Calder's. No trace of Gabe and Hannah, thank God.

"Dad already asked them not to come. I think Toto will be there, though," I tell her.

She doesn't pull a face at the mention of her sister. "I thought your dad was a vegan."

"He is. Calder told him he could eat vegetables but we were having turkey on Thanksgiving for once," I say with a chuckle.

Brie laughs. "I actually like your parents. Do you think this is hard on them? Especially your mom?"

I let out a breath of air. "Yeah. Gabe is the villain in her eyes. He's the villain in mine too. But he's also your dad and the father of my adorable niece. It's complicated, but I think we're doing better than most families with this much baggage."

She stops when we get to the front porch. I can hear voices inside and can smell food already.

"I can't imagine my daddy doing those terrible things to Baylee. My heart begs me not to believe her, but I saw the look in her eyes. I've seen that same terrified look in my own eyes in the mirror whenever I think about Esteban and what he did to me. Why would he hurt her?" she questions, her chin quivering.

I stroke her bangs from her face and kiss her forehead. "I don't know, babe. I don't know. But Mom has always kind of been a badass. And I can kick your dad's ass if I need to. He's not hurting anyone else in this family ever again."

"Do you think he's hurt other women?"

I think about all the stories Dad told me recently about their past. Gabe was more than a villain. He was psychopathic and predatory. Dad told me about the other women he "trained." Something tells me that Brie doesn't need the image of her dad tarnished further. She has enough going on in her head right now.

"I'm not sure," I lie. "But all that matters now is that he's trying to be a better person. He's good to my sister, even though she doesn't deserve it. And he loves you and Toto with everything he has. I'm not saying he's a good man," I tell her with a sigh. "But I'm not saying he's completely bad either. He's still your dad no matter what he's done or no matter what he will do."

She nods and lifts her chin. "Thank you."

Smirking, I nuzzle her nose with mine. "For what? For this morning? I can still taste your sweet cunt on my lips."

A squeal erupts from her and she shoves me, but a grin turns her full lips up. "No, punk. Thank you for being my friend. I mean, you're more than a friend because we practically live together, but you know what I mean. Thank you for being a friend *and* a lover. Thank you for being you."

I snag her wrist and haul her into my arms. Twisting her so her back is flush against my chest, I splay both palms on her much fuller stomach. Next week, we get to find out the sex. "One day I'm going to be more than just a friendly lover," I murmur against her hair. "One day I'm going to be so much more, Momma."

She relaxes against me, and I kiss her neck. The front door opens and Calder steps out with his hands on his hips. He's not wearing a shirt, no surprise there, but he's wearing a stupid apron that says "Kiss the Cook" on it.

"Everyone's waiting to eat while you guys practically fuck on the front porch," he chides. "Seriously. If my mashed potatoes get cold, so help me, I'm going to kick your ass."

Brie laughs and pulls away from my grip. She gives Calder a kiss on the cheek before going inside.

"You're more of a woman than Martha Stewart is," I tell him with a smirk.

"Laugh it up now, fucker," he grumbles. "You won't be laughing when you come in your pants after you taste those mashed potatoes."

"Make your own gravy?" I taunt to get a reaction out of him.

When he gags, I snort with laughter.

The punch to my gut was worth the look of pure horror on his face.

chapter
SIXTEEN

Brie

A boy and a girl.

I'm still in shock. Two healthy little babies according to the sonogram. The moment was bittersweet. Duvan wasn't there to share it with me but Ren was. And despite not being the father, he was thrilled.

"Any word from Oscar?" Ren questions from the doorway of what will be the nursery. We've still yet to decorate it. The only thing I've bought so far is a glider. Sometimes, I sit in here for hours. Especially when Ren is distracted with his online courses. It relaxes me. In a way, I feel closer to Duvan in these quiet moments while I absently stroke his ring, which hangs at the base of my throat. Just his memory, our babies, and the quietness. During those times, we're the family that we'll never truly get to be.

"Not in a month," I tell him with a sigh before turning my attention to him. Big mistake. He's just gotten out of the shower after a workout over at his house. The white towel hangs dangerously low on his tapered hips revealing a delicious V and a happy trail of hair that leads right to his impressive cock. Said cock, although flaccid now, can be seen bulging from behind the towel. The doctor warned me my hormones would be off the charts. And lately, now that my morning sickness has gone away for the most part, I find myself physically craving Ren's cock inside of me. A lot.

He saunters into the room past me and looks out the window. The window in the babies' room faces the ocean. When it's warmer, I'll be able to open it and hear the waves crashing.

"Do you think Vee is okay?" he questions. His shoulders are tense and it squashes all of my sexual thoughts as reality rushes back in.

"I don't know. I'm worried about her. She's just gone. Oscar filed a police report ages ago. Of course the cops have no leads. Has your dad found out anything else?" I ask as I stand and make my way over to him. His back tattoo is finished now. Every time I see it, I want to cry. The tree is big and strong and takes up most of his back. But it's what's under the tree that steals my heart. A fierce tigress with a no-nonsense gleam in her eyes. Curled up in front of her are two baby cubs. I don't have to ask him to know that he's the tree. And truth be told, I see him as the tree in my life. Steady. Unyielding. Protective from the harsh storms that always seem to whip my way from every direction. The fact that he cares for all of me, including my little cubs, has my heart stammering in my chest. His love is too much sometimes. I feel undeserving of it.

"Dad will find something. I'm sure of it," he says softly.

He relaxes once I wrap my arms around his solid middle. My cheek presses against his colorful back and I let out a sigh. His palms cover mine on his lower stomach and we remain silent for a bit.

"What if she's dead?" A choked sob escapes me.

Ren turns in my arms and hugs me to him. "Shhh," he murmurs. "Don't talk like that."

Tears roll out, and I once again curse myself for all these stupid emotions swirling around me twenty-four-seven. Vee is tough but she's also sheltered. I'm afraid if something bad happened to her, she wouldn't be able to cope.

"Calder was making lasagna when I left. Wanted to know if we were coming for dinner. Luciana misses you," he tells me, changing the subject.

I yawn and shrug my shoulders. "We can go but I'm so tired. I hate that I'm sleepy all the time."

He chuckles and kisses my forehead. "How about you just relax? I'll go grab us a plate in a bit and bring it back. Luciana can come visit tomorrow."

I give him a wicked grin as I tug at his towel. "Maybe you should tuck me into bed first."

Before the towel even hits the floor, he scoops me into his arms and charges back to my room—I say it's *my* room, but he's practically moved all his clothes into the closet and drawers. I'd be lying if I said I didn't like his crap all over the place, mingled with mine. It feels homey and comfortable having him here all the time.

He strides into the room and sets me on the bed. All I have on is one of his T-shirts and a pair of panties. Both get torn from me in a matter of seconds. Before I can utter another word, he climbs on top of me and is inside of me before my next breath.

Sex with Ren is fulfilling and exciting.

But the part I crave the most from it is that I can feel his love pouring from him like a never ending fountain. I drink greedily from it. I try to reciprocate the best I can but I'm not as good at it. He makes it seem like loving me is as easy as breathing.

"We won't get as many of these moments when our babies get here," he murmurs against my throat as he thrusts into me. "Gotta steal them while we can."

I freeze at his words.

Our babies.

I'm hit by a thousand emotions at once. Joy. Fury. Happiness. Anger. Despair and sadness. Excitement. Dread.

"Oh, fuck," he grunts and slows to a stop. He lifts to give me a pained expression. Dark hair that's growing longer hangs down past his eyebrows into his eyes. His full lips are parted as he attempts to find the right words to say.

He becomes a blur as emotion overcomes me. I want to tell him I'm glad he wants to take care of the three of us. I want to explain to him that despite this being a sad time for me, he makes me happy. But none of those things come out. Instead, words I don't mean trickle out. They taste dirty and wrong on my tongue.

"They're *my* babies," I choke out. "Me and Duvan's babies."

The look of heartbreak on his face makes it feel as though someone is cracking open my chest. He's inside of me with a look of frustration and horror painted on his face. Neither of us move. Both of us are confused about how we're supposed to feel.

"Brie," he murmurs and buries his face against my neck. His thick cock pushes deeper inside of me at the action causing me to gasp. "I'm sorry. I just can't help but feel possessive over every part of you. You know I love you. I love them too."

I sob as I clutch his hair. Rocking against him, I urge him to continue fucking me despite the raging storm of emotions whipping around inside me.

"I won't feel guilty for loving you or them," he bites out, the fierceness something I can feel cutting permanent grooves in my heart. "Not ever."

His words are like an accelerant on my impending orgasm. My body shudders as I lose myself to the pleasure. All conflicting emotions fly out of me as I allow myself one moment of undiluted bliss. He bucks into me a few more times before his own heat surges into me. When he finishes, we remain tangled up in silence. After some time, he kisses my throat and pulls out of me.

"I'm going to go get us some food," he says in a husky voice, his gaze not meeting mine. "Try and get some rest." His back muscles ripple as he yanks clothes on—the inked tree moving but still unbreakable. He's angry at me. Deservedly so. Hell, I'm angry at me. Sometimes my emotions are confusing but how I feel about Ren is unwavering. So why did I say something to hurt him? Truth is…I don't know. I wish I were brave enough to climb out of the bed after him and beg him to understand the conflicting slew of emotions wreaking havoc inside of me. The way he's tearing my heart right from my chest and keeping it as his own. He casts one more troubled look at me that makes my heart rate quicken. The flash of anger in his eyes unsettles me.

I want to be yours, Ren.

I want them to be yours.

But the words don't fall from my mouth like I want them to and my bottom lip does nothing but tremble as I watch him walk right out the door.

I clench my eyes closed and will the ache in my chest to subside. When he gets back, I'll explain to him. I'll let him know that he's everything to me. That sometimes I say things I don't mean because the guilt inside of me is a curse I can't escape.

I wasn't supposed to be happy.

But I am.

Because of Ren.

So why is it so hard admitting that out loud?

I wake to my phone buzzing on the nightstand. One look at the clock tells me I've only just fallen asleep. That Ren hasn't been gone more than five minutes.

Ozzy: I found her. She's in bad shape. I need your help.

I blink away my sleep as I sit up.

Me: Where? What happened?

Ozzy: I'm at your front door. Come now. We don't have time to waste.

I jolt into action and throw on some yoga pants. Then, I find one of Ren's hoodies that smells like him to throw on over my T-shirt. I stuff my feet into a pair of Ugg's and grab my phone before hurrying downstairs. When I sling the door open, Ozzy stands there looking horrible.

His eyes have dark circles under them and his hair is even longer than the last time I saw him. He's an utter wreck. As soon as he sees me, he grabs my elbow.

"Hurry," he snaps.

I put on the brakes and shake my head. "I need to call Ren."

He rolls his eyes and releases me. "Fine. Do it in the car. Tell him to meet us at her parents' house."

We both climb into Oscar's car and I dial Ren. He doesn't answer, so I leave him a voicemail telling him Ozzy found Vee and that we're headed to her parents' now. I shove the phone back into the pocket of my hoodie and regard my friend. He looks nothing like the boy I remember.

He's a lost, broken man.

"Are you okay?" I question and reach for his hand.

"Peachy," he snaps and jerks his hand away. "Really. What do *you* think, Brie?"

Tears prickle at my eyes, but I refuse to cry in front of him. He's upset so I'll allow him to be an ass. Under normal circumstances, I'd be telling him where to stick his attitude. But he managed to find Vee and it sounds bad. If there was ever a time for allowances, the time is now.

Oscar easily drives fifteen miles over the speed limit the entire way there. I'm so lost in thought that I don't even realize we're heading in the opposite direction of her parents' house, until we're pulling into Heath's shipyard.

"Wait," I say, sitting up and pointing through the glass. "I thought you said we were going to their house."

He gives me a noncommittal shrug as he parks the car and climbs out. I scramble out after him, suddenly wishing I would have spoken to Ren before I left in such a hurry.

"This way," he tells me over his shoulder as he stalks toward the gate that leads to all the shipping containers.

"Hold on," I blurt as I dial Ren again. It rings and rings until it goes to voicemail again. I'm about to leave a message when my phone gets torn from my hand. Oscar's face is positively murderous as he heaves it as far as he can throw it. I gape at him in shock for a long second before I begin to process what just happened.

This was a trick.

Vee isn't here.

But I can bet my entire bank account that his crazy father is.

"Shit," I hiss as I back away from him.

He lets out a growl as he charges after me. Oscar is bigger and stronger than me. So when he grabs my elbow, he's easily able to drag me behind him despite my fighting him off. Someone opens the gates, and I yell out to them. The howl of the biting wind seems to carry my voice away, right along with the sunlight. It's dark and grey and dreary…much like what awaits me.

"Help!" I swat at Ozzy. "Let me go!"

He ignores me as he storms along at a breakneck speed. My tears fall freely now. I don't know what's about to happen but every nerve ending in my body promises that it won't be good. I'm dragged through a maze of containers that are stacked on top of each other until he stops in front of one. The door is ajar. Panic immobilizes me as I imagine what sort of horrors wait for me on the other side. When he has trouble getting me to follow, he hooks his arm just under my breasts and lifts me. I kick and scream to no avail.

The moment we enter the container, a foul stench wafts around me and makes me gag. Oscar hands me off to two larger men who easily wrangle me into a chair. I scream at them to let me go but, within minutes, they have me tied to the chair. Oscar delivers the blow of betrayal when he slaps a strip of duct tape over my mouth.

It's dark inside the container aside from the grey light streaming in from the doorway. I frantically look around to see what I'm up against. There's movement and sound coming from the dark part of the metal cage but I can't see what it is.

Realization hits me like a cold splash of water.

I'm going to die in here.

Both my babies and I are never leaving this box.

As hot tears race down my cheeks, the only thing I can think of is Ren. How as soon as he realizes I'm gone, he'll go mad trying to find me. A sob fights for escape in my throat but the tape keeps it locked away.

"If it isn't the little *puta* who keeps screwing over my sons," a familiar, heavily accented voice snarls. Camilo. All three of Camilo's sons look a lot like him, but not one, not even Esteban, have that sick gleam in their eyes. Eyes that point to an evil past. And an empty soul. A shudder wracks through me the moment he comes into view. Blood soaks the front of his white dress shirt and a look of rage is painted on his normally cool features. I tremble and shake my head at him pleading for him to not do whatever it is he has planned.

"First, you get my middle son killed because of your precious little *bollo*," he bites out, gesturing between my legs. "My own business partner betrayed me because he wanted it so bad." He comes to stand right in front of me. "*Débiles*. Weak." With the toe of his dress shoe, he pokes at me between my spread legs and regards me as if I'm vermin. "What exactly is so special about it? Is it lined with *cocaína*? What makes grown men *estúpido* over your whore snatch?"

I shake and attempt to free myself from the restraints.

"*¿Dónde está mi cuchillo?*" he snaps over his shoulder.

My cries become too much with the tape over my mouth and I start to hyperventilate. I frantically look for Oscar in the shadows, but he's nowhere to be found. When Camilo kneels in front of me, I meet his hate-filled gaze. I close my eyes, though, the moment I see the knife in his grip.

God, please no.

A ripping of fabric has my heart beating right out of my chest. Thankfully, aside from a quick bite or two from the knife against my flesh, he leaves me otherwise unharmed. Naked from the waist down but alive.

"*Mírame,*" he growls. "Look at me."

I'm shaking badly but I open my eyes to meet his gaze. With the tip of the knife, he pokes at the lips of my pussy. Not hard enough to break the skin, but hard enough to scare the crap out of me.

"My wife's snatch was better looking," he observes. "What makes yours so special? I mean, my eldest son broke the rules of our family to fuck it. Went against our code to put his dick inside of you. And we all know how goddamned distraught Oscar was when he found out he wasn't winning *this* prize." He pokes me again. "*Me das asco.*"

I shake my head and plead with him. He wants answers but he won't let me even speak. A scream resounds from behind the tape the moment he touches me with his pudgy fingers. They prod at me. Tug at my pubic hair. And then, to my horror, enter me. Bile threatens to rise up my throat but being that I have tape over my mouth, I decide I'll do whatever it takes to keep it down.

Closing my eyes, I think of Ren. I think of the way he proudly called these precious babies ours. I'd give anything to rewind a couple of hours and agree that we're his family now. That I want him to take care of us.

That I love him too.

The realization of that fact has me sobbing harder than before. Camilo fingers me almost painfully, but it's better if I disconnect my mind from the physical act.

Ren. Ren. Ren.

God, I miss him.

If he were here, he'd protect me.

"That's enough, Papá," Oscar snarls from the shadows.

I pop my eyes open to see Camilo glaring in the direction he's in. "Son, I must be honest," Camilo says with a cold laugh as he pulls his fingers from within me. "I don't see what's so fucking special about her cunt. But clearly, you see it. It's a goddamned cunt *del otro mundo.*" He sniffs his fingers and I gag. This seems to anger him though because with a quick, hard swing, he cracks his knuckles across my cheek.

Stars blind my vision for a moment.

"You like that, *puta?*" He raises his hand like he's going to hit me again but he never strikes.

Oscar emerges from the darkness and glowers at his father. "She's pregnant. That's enough."

Camilo stands, no longer interested in hitting me, and faces off with his son. "*Hijo,* we talked about this. She's going to pay for what she's done to our family."

Oscar's gaze meets mine, and I see a flash of regret in his eyes. I plead with mine for him to help me. With reluctance, he drags them away to glare back at his father.

"If you have such a problem with my methods, then *you* exact our revenge," Camilo barks. "Did you want to fuck her magical pussy once more? By all means, get your rocks off, *hijo.* The boys and I will leave if that will make you feel better. Rafe, though, stays."

My eyes dart into the darkness. If Rafe is here, maybe he'll help me.

"Fine," Oscar bites out. "Just go."

"If I don't hear the puta screaming in fifteen minutes, I'm coming back to finish the job," Camilo warns. "*Esto es tu deber.*"

His son gives him a clipped nod. Camilo and several other men file out. They shut the doors, leaving us in pitch-black darkness. All that can be heard are my whimpers.

"Why?" Oscar chokes out after several moments. "Why did you fuck everything up?"

When I don't answer, he walks closer to me. I can sense his presence within touching distance. His breath is ragged, and for the first time, I smell liquor on it. Warm hands clutch my thighs, and I hear his knees bang on the metal as he falls in front of me. I wriggle in my bindings, praying I can get loose.

"If things went differently, you'd be pregnant with *my* baby," he utters, his words nostalgic almost.

I whimper when his thumbs rub circles on my inner thighs.

"I lost my chance with you. A chance to make my father proud. Then, I lost her. A chance at something else…something good. But both chances were stolen from me. I can't fucking win," he snips out in a disgusted tone.

His head falls against my breasts, and I can really smell the alcohol on him.

"I don't know how to fix this," he admits, his voice ragged with emotion. "I don't want you to die."

When he reaches up and tears the tape from my mouth, I let out the long sob I'd been holding in.

"P-P-Please, Ozzy. Don't let him hurt me. I'm pregnant with twins. Your brother's babies. Don't let them die. Please. You c-can help me. We can get out of this. P-Please," I plead through my tears.

"Shhh," he groans before his mouth presses against mine in a sloppy drunk kiss. "Shhh." His hands roam my body clumsily. "This is all so fucked up."

"Just untie me," I plead. "We c-can fix it." My teeth chatter as the terror of my situation completely consumes me.

"My father is right," he says in a husky tone. "There's something about you that we can't ignore." His fingers, much gentler than his father's, prod at my opening. "For so long I wanted to fuck you, Brie."

"Well, you can't," I bite out, squirming against his unwanted touch. "I'm not yours. But you can do right by your brother and get me out of here. I'm pregnant with two babies. Your brother's babies. Snap the hell out of whatever it is you're going through, Ozzy. You're no better than Esteban."

My words have him jerking away from me. I can't see him in the dark but I can hear him pacing on the metal floor.

"I'm not like him," he snaps.

"No and you're not like your father either," I try, my tone gentler. "You're like Duvan. You're good. Please come back to me. I need my friend right now…not this…not this monster your father wants you to be."

Someone beats on the doors and yells, "Ten more minutes."

This seems to jolt Oscar into action. A flashlight comes on and he points it in my face. I squint against it as he starts untying me. Relief floods through me until he jerks me to my feet. He drops the flashlight with a clang and it points into the darkened part of the container from earlier. I let out a scream when I see Rafe tied to a chair in the corner. His eyes have been cut from their sockets and his intestines hang out of his stomach.

"Noooooo," I shriek as I fight against Oscar.

He grunts as he drags me over to a dirty mattress in the corner. I'm tossed on my ass. Before I can even move, he's pinning me to the filthy makeshift bed.

"This will only take ten minutes," he assures me loud enough to make the container echo with his words. "Now hold fucking still. It's my turn."

chapter
SEVENTEEN

Ren

I drop the keys on the island in the kitchen and put the lasagna in the refrigerator. Chances are, she's passed out so I won't wake her to eat. While over at my house, I tried not to obsess over her crushing words.

They're my babies. Me and Duvan's babies.

Those words, spoken so vehemently, rocked me to my core. It reminded me that no matter how much time passes, no matter how many times I love her with my body, that we're never really any further than we were when we started. I ache knowing she'll never love me like she loved him.

And yet…

I don't give up. She's mine. Even though she said she couldn't love me, she did promise me that. That she belonged to me. In my head, they're one in the same. One day she'll let down her guard just a little and I'll be there to swoop her into my arms. I won't ever give up on her. If we go round and round until our deaths, so be it. At least I'll have her. At least I can love her with everything I have. I don't need it back. I just need her.

I tiptoe up the stairs, careful not to wake her. Before heading into her bedroom, I stop off in the nursery. We still have so much to do before the babies get here. I'm scratching my jaw, figuring out if two cribs will fit along one wall when I remember I bought an app the other day for this purpose. It allows you to measure walls. When I reach into my pocket, I remember I left my phone charging on my nightstand in Brie's room.

I'm still mulling over our conversation from earlier when I walk into our room. The first thing I notice is the utter silence. She's not in bed.

"Babe?" I call out and storm into the bathroom. When I find it empty too, my heart rate starts thundering. "Babe!" I stomp into the bedroom and yank my phone from the charger.

Two missed calls from Brie.

Fuck!

I start listening as I clomp down the stairs two at a time. In the first message, she tells me Oscar showed up and they found Vee. That they're going to Vee's parents' house. I snag my keys from the island and break into a sprint out to my truck as I listen to the next message. She curses. Then I hear a crunching sound. And finally…shrieks to let her go that sound far off.

I'm stunned frozen until reality hits me. He fucking took her. Oscar fucking took my girlfriend and is taking her straight to Camilo. Turning on my heel, I run back in the house to collect the gun Gabe gave me and call Dad along the way.

When he answers, I bark out orders. "Find the location of Brie's phone and then send Gabe. They fucking took her!"

It took Dad fifteen minutes to hack in and find the last ping of her cell phone. As soon as he gave me the location of the shipyard, I hauled ass there. I should wait for Gabe who I know will come ready to slaughter the entire lot of them, but I don't. All I can think about is the fact that they have my pregnant girlfriend. Crazy, evil, psychotic men have my Brie.

Fuck!

As soon as the shipyard comes into view, I pull off alongside the dirt road. I launch out of the truck with my gun locked and loaded. I'm ready to blow the head off any motherfucker who stands in my way. I should sneak up on them or something, but it's hard to do when time is of the essence. Quickly, I prowl down the road hunched over until I reach an open gate. Once inside, I see several vehicles parked in front of what looks like an office. Another gate stands open that leads straight to where the shipping containers are stacked at least ten high. I'm slinking along the outside, hoping to sneak in when I hear a blood-curdling scream from somewhere inside one of the containers. The scream came from Brie—I would recognize the sound of her voice anywhere.

"Brie!!" I yell, no longer worried about my cover. I charge forward but before I make it very far, something cracks me over the head. Stumbling, I attempt to blink away the blurriness in my vision when another blow hits my skull from behind.

Blackness steals away my sight and consciousness. And the last thing I hear until I completely fade away are her screams.

"Wake up, asshole."

Pain slices through my head as I attempt to shake away the buzzing in my skull. I'm in a dark room of sorts. The only light that shines through is from a door. Once I blink a few times, I realize I'm in a shipping container.

"You must be the little boyfriend." An old man laughs. It's cold and harsh. "The lawn boy, I presume. You're the little cunt who was fucking my boy's wife on the side?"

I shake my head in a daze. "I don't know what you're talking about."

He swings his fist and it connects with my jaw. My teeth bite down on my bottom lip from the impact and metallic blood gushes into my mouth.

"Don't lie to me. Are you or aren't you the cunt who the little girl was in love with before my son married her?" he snarls.

I go to rub at my jaw but realize through my haze that I'm bound to a chair I'm sitting on. "I never touched her while they were married," I grit out as I spit some blood from my mouth.

The old man comes into the light and squats in front of me. "She's not talking. My youngest boy has been in there with her trying to extract information from her. You see," he says and scratches at his white beard. "Your puta girlfriend sold my son's territory to our motherfucking enemy. Territory that's been in our family for decades. It wasn't hers to give away. Now she not only pays with her magical cunt but also with her life."

"WHERE THE FUCK IS SHE?" I roar and struggle against the ropes.

He smirks and pats my knee. "My boy Oscar is getting his fill of her pussy before I get her back. I promise you, I'm going to extract the debt from her one square inch of her flesh at a time."

"She's pregnant," I snap. "With your son's babies."

He's silent for a moment.

"Twins, huh?" The old fuck simply shrugs his shoulders. "Presumed. But as far as I know, they're yours."

I spit at him. "What if they're Esteban's?" It's a lie but I don't want him thinking the babies are mine because then he'll have no reason to keep her alive.

Camilo puffs out his chest and fists his hand. "Esteban is disowned. He abandoned our family in our time of need."

"The doctor said they were Duvan's," I try again. "You'd kill your own grandchildren?"

He stands and paces. I hope my words get to him. "I suppose I could keep her around. As a fuck toy for my youngest son until the babies are born. Then, I'll kill her. Smart thinking, lawn boy."

I'm about to go off on him when we hear a struggle outside the container. Then four loud pops of a gun. Camilo runs out the door. A few minutes later, he returns dragging Gabe in by his hair.

Fuck!

"And who the fuck are you?" Camilo demands as he shoves Gabe to the floor. Gabe scrambles back up to his feet and wipes blood off his chin. Camilo aims a hand gun at his face. "I asked who the fuck you are."

Gabe growls. "Your worst motherfuckin' nightmare."

At this, Camilo laughs. "Bind him," he orders to two of his men, who are in the container with us. "This day just keeps getting better and better."

Gabe puts up one helluva fight and ends up head-butting one of the men. But between Camilo and the still-standing man, they wrestle him into submission.

"Where the fuck is Pedro?" Camilo demands, his chest heaving. "This is his shit to deal with."

The man who's not sprawled out unconscious on the floor shakes his head. "This fucker took out four of ours before I tackled him."

Camilo glares at Gabe before turning back to the man. "As in incapacitated or—"

"He blew their heads off."

With a rage-filled roar, Camilo punches Gabe in the stomach hard enough to have him gasping for air.

"Where's Brie?" I demand, hoping to distract them.

"I already told you. Getting her brains fucked out by my son. While he gets what he so desperately wants, I'm going to enjoy myself." He unsheathes a knife from his belt. "Starting with you."

Gabe grunts and struggles from the chair beside me as Camilo slowly prowls toward me. The blade of his knife points right at me as a taunt.

"People who fuck with the Rojas family eventually meet my blade," he seethes. He punches me hard in the gut. Searing pain explodes from the impact. It takes only a second to realize he didn't punch me. He fucking stabbed me.

"J-Just let her go," I choke out. The pain in my stomach steals my breath.

He laughs again. It's cold and ugly. Slowly, he pulls his blade from my middle. I hiss when blood rushes from the gaping hole.

"If you want to fucking slaughter someone, I'm right here," Gabe bellows and struggles against his restraints. "Right the fuck here. Man to old fucking man. Cut me loose and see just how many jabs you can get on *this* man."

Pain throbs from my stomach, and I struggle for air. Camilo looks over at Gabe and smirks. "I would gut you in a heartbeat."

"Wanna fucking bet?" Gabe snarls.

Camilo shakes his head and storms back over to me. He grabs a handful of my hair and jerks my head up. "You don't want this boy to die. Is he yours? Better yet is *she* yours?"

Gabe utters out a *fuck you*.

My eyes keep rolling back in my head, but I fight desperately to keep them open.

"You must be the evil fuck who sent her off to live with Heath. Did you know he was a twisted man? Did you know he wanted to fuck your sweet little girl even back when she was just fifteen years old? She resembles you now that I'm really looking at you." Camilo shrugs and slashes his arm out in front of me. Fire skates across my chest, and I gape down at the slice across my pectoral muscles.

"JUST FUCKING STOP!" Gabe roars.

Camilo wipes his blade against the thigh of his slacks. "I won't stop until I drain the life out of both of you."

"Ren," Gabe snaps, making me jolt with sudden awareness. "Fucking stay with me."

I blink again and attempt to struggle against the ropes. But I'm weak. So damn weak.

"Where was I?" Camilo questions as if we were discussing a football game or some shit. "Oh," he says with a wicked grin that reveals his teeth. "I remember. I was gutting this little piggy."

Pain explodes in my thigh this time as he plunges the knife deep into the muscle. My dizziness evaporates as I scream. Fire lashes at the entry point. I'm feeling overwhelming pain from so many places that I'm starting to lose touch with reality.

Brie.

I close my eyes and envision her sad eyes. Eyes that on occasion twinkle with happiness. I live for those small moments with her. Moments that are worth all the other hard times. Her smiles are like heaven. She's my angel.

"REN!"

I blink my eyes open to Gabe's voice. Turning my head, I manage to see him going fucking crazy in his chair. The man behind him simply laughs. My gaze fixates on the way Gabe loosens his binds around one wrist without our captors even noticing.

"I-I-I love her," I tell my beautiful girl's father. Not that he cares. Not that it matters. I just want it to be heard. The darkness keeps creeping up on me and if it steals me away, I want those words to be the last ones on my lips. "I l-love Brie. I l-l-love the b-babies."

Camilo kneels in front of me. "Cue the fucking tears. We have us a modern day Romeo here." He hollers as if she can hear him wherever she is. "Juliet! Juliet! Your Romeo's heart is bleeding for you."

"J-Just let her go," I murmur. I'm not even sure if the words make it outside my mouth.

My eyes fall closed and my head flops forward. The only pain I feel right now is in my heart. Sadness and loss. I don't want to lose her. I finally fucking got her back. Duvan died and it was up to me to be there for her. To see it to the end with her. We were going to be a family. As fucked up as it was, a family.

I think about the first time I made love to her. What feels like eons ago when we were so innocent. Just the two of us under the moonlight by the ocean. Our bodies meeting for the first time in an intimate way.

God, I fucking love her.

Gabe shouts over and over again. I can feel bites and licks of pain but they don't matter anymore. All that matters are her pretty browns staring at me. The way her lips press against mine in the middle of the night. At one time I'd craved having her in the light. But now I want her to find me in this dark.

Find me, Brie.

Fucking find me.

Black swarms in like a cloud of a million bees.

It shadows my world.

Blinds me.

I can't see her anymore.

Fucking find me, Brie.

chapter
EIGHTEEN

I brace for Ozzy to enter me against my will. My friend. Someone who I thought I loved is about to betray me in the worst possible way. In some ways, this will be worse than it was with Esteban. With Ozzy, I care.

But he doesn't.

I'm jolted to reality when he whispers against the shell of my ear. "They think I'm raping you. We don't have much time. Just scream and make it sound like you're struggling while I figure out what the hell we're going to do."

I gape up at him in the darkness. The small beam of light from the flashlight isn't enough for me to see his face. I'd like to imagine that if I could see him, he'd have the same mischievous expression I remember from before.

He climbs off me and rises to his feet. Then, he grabs hold of my shoulders and helps me to my feet as well. I'm still wearing Ren's hoodie, so it thankfully covers my ass as it hits about mid thigh and I still have my Ugg's on.

"Scream," he hisses as I hear the click of his weapon.

I let out an ear-piercing scream that muffles our footsteps toward the door. With his gun poised and ready to shoot, he slowly drags open the door a crack and peeks outside.

"There's no one out here," he mutters, his voice sounding confused. He drags the door the rest of the way open and we both wince at the screeching sound it makes. Then, he motions for me to follow him. Sunlight is still not visible as a winter storm begins to roll in. The wind is cold and powerful.

"This way," he tells me and motions for me to follow.

I run after him but then stumble to a halt when we come across a dead body. A man who has a bullet through his skull. I can't help but have a surge of hope welling inside me. Maybe Ren was able to find me.

We're headed toward the gate when I hear a familiar voice.

"Daddy?" I murmur.

"We need to go," Oscar hisses and jerks at my arm.

I wriggle from his grasp. "No! My dad is here! I hear him over there!" Pointing, I begin running toward the sound. Oscar curses behind me but quickly passes me with his gun raised. We pass three more unmoving bodies, and I can't help but pray they're all dead. Grunts and cursing and shouting can be heard from a shipping container fifty feet or so ahead that has its door open. When I hear Daddy's horrified voice shouting Ren's name, all thought vanishes from my brain—except for reaching them—as I bolt ahead of Oscar.

As soon as I burst through the door, my entire world tilts on its axis. Blood. So much blood. Like Mom. Like Duvan. It causes me to stumble over my feet and gag from the sight of it. My eyes fixate on my dad for one second. He's bloody and furious, but alive. Ren on the other hand...

"What have you done?" I hiss at Camilo, no longer concerned about my own safety. "WHAT HAVE YOU DONE?"

One of his men appears from the shadows and grabs me from behind. I go crazy trying to escape. He's stronger and slaps a hand over my mouth to keep me quiet. My eyes land on Ren. Sweet, sexy, beautiful, perfect Ren. Completely drenched in blood. His head hangs in front of him and his hair hides his eyes from me. I can't tell if he's still alive or not. A sob catches in my throat as hot tears streak down my cheeks.

"I should have known my son wouldn't have been able to manage you. You probably sweet talked him right out of that container," Camilo says in disgust as he stalks over to Ren. His bloody knife is the only thing I see, though. It's a threat to my Ren.

A man groans from the floor and stands on wobbly feet. When he regains focus, he roars at my father and pistol whips him. Everything blurs in front of me as the tears become too plentiful. We will all die here. All three of us. Two of the people I love most in the world sit in those chairs, bloody and weak. Camilo is going to end them all because of me.

I squirm against the man holding me and when his hand slips off my mouth, I manage to cry out, "Oscar! Help us!"

He charges into the container, but Camilo stops him with his harsh words. "That's enough, *hijo!*"

Camilo goes to stand behind Ren and grabs a handful of his hair. He yanks his head back so I can see Ren's face. His eyes slowly blink open. When they fixate on me, he utters something unintelligible before attempting to smile at me. It breaks my heart into a thousand pieces.

"Say goodbye to your lawn boy," Camilo hisses. His blade comes into view and it takes me a half a second to realize what he's about to do. He's about to deliver the same fate to Ren that Heath did to Duvan. I should close my eyes. Not witness another horrifying act, but I refuse to abandon Ren in his last moments.

The storm must be picking up because I swear I hear chaos ensuing outside of the metal containers. I wish the storm would pick us all up and carry us out to the sea. Drowning would be quick and painless. I wouldn't have to watch those I love bleed out.

"B-Brie." Ren's reverent way of saying my name has me sobbing so hard, I can't breathe. I lock eyes with his half-lidded ones and convey every ounce of love I have for him with just one look.

Camilo's movement is quick as he slashes his knife across the front of Ren's throat. I'm frozen even as a million things happen at once. Daddy freeing a hand and throwing a punch that lands in Camilo's stomach, which jolts him. The man holding my mouth releases me as he's tackled by Oscar.

And then I'm running.

Running. Running. Running.

I must get to him.

Movement and shadows race around me but I ignore them as I all but tackle Ren in the chair. Blood runs from a slice in his throat and it's Duvan all over again as I desperately hold my palm over the wound. I sob and kiss his bloody face.

"D-Don't leave me," I beg through my tears. "Please don't you dare leave me. I love you!"

I slide out of his lap and hit the floor. I'm on a mission to free him from this chair. Shouts and thumping of metal resound behind me, but I don't care. All that matters is untying Ren and getting him to a hospital.

He. Will. Live.

I will not go through this. Not again.

Daddy's voice shouts at me through my haze, but I attempt to ignore it. That is until he jerks me to my feet. I scream and fight him.

"Shhhh, *cariño*," Diego says and flashes me a bright smile in the darkness. "I must deal with Camilo and I can't do that if you're screaming."

I'm still gaping in shock at his surprise appearance when he quickly sheds his jacket and then rips at his dress shirt. The buttons go flying everywhere and echo in the container. A quick sweep of the room shows Oscar in one of Diego's men's grip and the other of Camilo's men sprawled out on the floor. Daddy attempts to hold me back from the knife fight that is about to go down. Camilo appears enraged as he glares at Diego, his own knife out in front of him.

"Long time, *viejo*," Diego says as he tosses his knife back and forth between his hands.

"I spared your life last time because you were a boy," Camilo hisses. "I won't make that mistake this time."

Diego laughs, a laugh that at one time scared me. But this time, I'm thankful for it. "I bear those scars all over my face and abdomen. Scars you decorated me with. A man doesn't wear such scars without making a promise to himself to return them to the man who originally gave them to him." Lightning quick, he slashes Camilo across the belly. It's shallow but Camilo grunts in pain.

"Why are you here?" Camilo hisses as he attempts to stab at Diego. Diego is fast, though, and he gashes Camilo's forearm. The old man howls and stumbles back.

"A deal is a deal," Diego remarks and then flashes me another one of his flirty grins. "I promised the girl protection. So protection is what she shall get."

Camilo's screams of rage echo through the container. "The bitch got you too?!"

Diego does a series of quick arm movements that I soon realize are brutal stabs to Camilo's stomach. Camilo grunts and falls to his knees.

"Am I to make him suffer or am I to make him die, cariño?" Diego questions as he tosses his bloody knife back and forth between his hands again. Camilo has dropped his own knife with a clatter as he desperately attempts to block the holes in his abdomen that are gushing with blood.

Oscar fights against the man holding him. His eyes are on his father, heartbreak shining in them. If I didn't hate Camilo so much, I'd feel bad for him. Oscar jerks his gaze to me and pleads with his eyes, since his mouth is covered by his assailant.

"Make him die," I spit out, my entire body trembling with anger.

Oscar's eyes harden at my words and then he hangs his head, surely to avoid watching what's about to happen. I, however, drag my gaze over to Diego who grins at me like he's just won the biggest prize at a carnival game. I give him a nod. He lets out a hiss as he delivers a series of fatal stabs to Camilo's heart. When the old man falls forward with a *thunk*, Diego starts toward me.

Daddy growls. "Stay the fuck away from my daughter."

Diego narrows his eyes at him. "Want me to kill him too, *cariño*?"

I shake my head. "H-He's under my protection. As is Oscar and…" I trail off as a sob escapes me. Ren remains unmoving in his chair. "We need to get him to a hospital. Help me," I plead.

Diego motions at one of his men. "Leave the Rojas boy. Gather this other one and put him in a vehicle." He snatches me out of my dad's grip and hauls me to him for a hug. "Thank you, *cariño*. You've just made me a very rich man. You're untouchable, little princess. If you need anything, even some cock every now and again, you call Daddy Diego."

"Touch her again and you'll be Daisy Diego when I cut your dick off," Daddy barks.

Diego laughs and releases me. He struts out of the container and out of my life.

Two men pull Ren from the chair and work together to carry him from the container. Another man hits Oscar in the head with the butt of his gun. Ozzy crumples to the floor beside his father's corpse. I know he'll get out of here. Alive. And that's all that matters. But right now, I can't worry about Oscar's well-being. The most important person is Ren.

Please God, don't let him die. I can't do this again.

"Sweetheart, you should eat something," Baylee says, concern lacing her voice. "You're pale."

I wave away the package of crackers she attempts to hand me and swallow down the urge to puke. When I lift my gaze, her eyes are bloodshot from crying. Her bottom lip trembles.

"I love him," I admit to her. "I always have. It's just different but it's love."

She pulls me into her arms, and I break down into gut-wrenching sobs for the tenth time today. Baylee strokes my hair in a way that reminds me of how Mom would when I was upset or sick. This only saddens me more. I desperately hug her, afraid she'll suddenly leave me too.

I'm the worst kind of luck.

People who love me end up hurt. Or worse.

"Brie baby," Daddy murmurs from the chair on the other side of me. "I should take you home. You need rest."

Baylee hisses at him over my head. "Go check on my grandbaby. I can stay with her. You know it's never a good idea for Hannah to be alone."

He grunts but there is resignation in his voice. I feel him kiss the top of my head. "Call me when you hear something."

Once he's gone, I pull away from her embrace to look at her. "It's been hours. This is bad, right?"

Baylee darts her gaze to someone behind me. Then, I hear War's voice. "The probability of him living is high. If they're still in surgery, hopefully that means they've been able to repair the damage. Worse news would have been if they came out right away. At least we know they're doing something back there."

"But his throat," I murmur. "I watched Camilo slash it."

Baylee shudders and lets out a choked sob but it's War who speaks again. "Gabe described the wound to me. It doesn't sound as if it was as deep as you are thinking. You said yourself, he cut across the front. Had it been situated to one side, his carotid could have been severed but it doesn't sound like it was."

Carotid.

The same artery that was cut on my mother.

I shiver and swipe away my tears so I can look at him. Right now, with worry etched on his face, he looks so much like Ren that it makes me start crying again. He sits down beside me and pulls me against his side.

"He's going to be okay," he promises. I don't know how he can promise such things but he says it with such conviction that I believe him.

"This is all my fault," I tell him through my tears. "If I'd have just come here and abandoned Duvan's whole life, I could have avoided all this. I'm so sorry."

Baylee pats my knee. "This is not your fault, sweetheart. You were dragged into that life. And we're the ones sorry for that. Hannah started this course. She's sick and unstable. We failed her but we won't fail you and Ren."

You and Ren.

As if we're a team and they're our support network.

I don't know why this fills me with such joy, but it does.

Mason stirs in his baby seat and Baylee absently rocks him. "We're here for you, Brie," she assures me and squeezes my hand. "The world has played some pretty cruel jokes on me by sending your father back into my life, only for him to fall in love with my mentally unstable child, but the joke was on me. I was given Toto." She smiles at me. "And I was given you. We're here for you."

Mom is gone. Duvan is gone. Ren is barely hanging on by a thread. But these two people are here. They provide the strength that two parents who love their children with everything they have. Ren is lucky to have them as parents.

"McPherson family?" a deep voice calls out.

All three of us jolt and War stalks over to the doctor. They speak in hushed tones, which makes my anxiety spike. But when War turns around to beam at me and give me a thumbs up, I break down in hysterical sobs.

He's okay.

He's going to be okay.

chapter
NINETEEN

Ren

An annoying beeping wakes me from my slumber, and I suppress a groan. My dreams were filled with brown eyes and sweet smiles. I dreamed of Brie. A heaviness seems to hold me to my bed. I attempt to blink my eyes open to figure out what's come over me. The beeping gets more annoying but then something warm grips my hand.

"Shhhh," the sweet voice murmurs. "I'm here. Calm down."

I relax because I like the sound of her voice. Like an angel. Am I in heaven?

"My baby boy," another female voice utters.

My eyelids feel as though they have heavy lead weights attached to them, but I slowly manage to blink them open. The room is bright white and I squint against it. I hear some shuffling and the room dims. I'm able to open my eyes a little more. Dad stands at the end of my bed with Mom on his left. The angel with the pretty brown eyes sits to my left, clutching my hand.

I try to tell her she's beautiful, but my mouth doesn't seem to work. So I settle for squeezing her hand. Tears streak down her cheeks and she leans forward bringing her beautiful face near mine.

"You made it," she assures me with a tearful grin. "You didn't die on me."

I try to smile but it's too difficult.

"You're still intubated," Dad explains. "Try not to move or talk. Give it some time."

My eyes never stray from hers, though. I could stare at her for eternity.

"We're going to go grab some coffee," Mom tells the angel. "We'll give you two some time alone." Mom kisses my forehead while Dad pats my foot. Once they're gone, the beautiful one grins.

"You scared me to death," she murmurs.

Brie.

Her name is Brie.

I could never forget such a pretty name.

Sweet Gabriella. An angel in more ways than one.

"And I thought I wouldn't ever be able to tell you the words I so desperately need you to hear," she chokes out. Her lips press kisses all over my face. I close my eyes because I want to relish in the way it feels.

"I love you." She pulls away to stare down at me. "Did you hear that? I love you, Ren McPherson. I have pretty much since the first moment you looked up at me in that window. Something snapped into place then. A missing piece. A part of my heart that wasn't fully formed. You slotted yourself right in and, truth be told, never left. My heart was dragged through the mud, stomped on, shredded, and abused. And yet, at the end of it, you were still there. Still hanging on for dear life. Embedded deep inside. There wasn't much left of my heart at the end, but what was left was the part you still held on to. Here I was worried I wouldn't have room for you in my tiny sliver of a heart," she murmurs, tears freely falling down her face. "And yet the only room left was for you." She draws my hand to her chest and presses it against her, so I can feel the thundering just beneath her flesh. "My heart is yours, Ren."

I reach for her with my other hand, despite the sharp pains that pull across my torso. With shaky movements, I swipe away her tears. Then, I tug her hand to my chest, mimicking her action. My heart pounds just as hard for her. I can't say the words, but I hope she feels them. They're thick as they cloud the air around us.

I love you too.

With every part of my being and then some.

You're mine, Gabriella Rojas, and I am yours.

Fatigue threatens to steal me from Brie. I desperately attempt to burn her face into my mind, so that when I'm sleeping, I'll think only of her.

"I love you," she reminds me as my eyes blink closed.

I love you too.

"She had the baby," Brie tells me as she folds a small onesie and tucks it into a drawer.

"Hannah?" I question as I sit up in the rocker that's in the nursery. Pain ripples through my entire body, but I try not to let Brie know I'm hurting. She'll try and shove more pain pills down my throat. It's been three weeks since I left the hospital, but she still treats me as if I've just left surgery.

"Daddy called," she says. "It's a boy. They're calling him Land."

"After my grandpa?" I'm mildly irritated that Hannah has successfully stolen all our grandparent's names for her babies. She always was selfish. One day I'd hoped to pass on one of their names to one of my own children.

"He wants us to come see the baby, but I told him you weren't up to it," she says softly, her back to me.

"We can go if you wan—"

She cuts me off with a wave of a hand. "I'll see him when Daddy brings him by one day. I'd rather not spend one second with your sister."

The feeling is mutual.

"How are Duvan and Alejandra today?" I question.

She turns and beams at me. Then, she rubs her stomach before dropping to the floor in front of me. Her head rests on my uninjured thigh. I stroke her hair as she lets out a contented sigh. "They're good. I think I'm finally getting cravings."

I chuckle but it makes my abdomen ache. Despite the many stab wounds Camilo inflicted, most were superficial. The one that tore a hole in my spleen was the worrisome one, which took hours to repair. Thankfully, the surgeons were excellent ones. "What sort of cravings?"

She groans and looks up at me, embarrassment tinting her cheeks. "Gross things. Like crab from that seaside restaurant I met up with Diego at." I grit my teeth but swallow back a growl. Despite my hating that prick, in the end, he did save our lives. If he protects my woman and our babies, I'll tolerate him.

"Crab is good," I say with a smile.

She shrugs. "And tacos but with ranch dressing instead of sour cream."

At this, I shake my head. "Okay, that is gross. Anything else?"

"Cherry pie filling. Like the kind out of the can." She makes a grumble of annoyance. "It sounds so good right now. Who eats that stuff straight out of the can? It's all I can think about."

I run my fingers through her silky hair and wink. "Help me out of this chair and I'll go with you right now. We'll buy twenty cans if that makes you happy."

She stands and shakes her head. "I don't think so, buddy. You're not fit to grocery shop. I'll call Calder. He'll go with me."

"And leave me here all alone with Luciana? Why do you insist upon her babysitting me, anyway? Our conversations are always one-sided." When she scoffs, I continue. "Because all she does is drone on and on about how much Calder looks like "The Beebs." I throw up in my mouth at least ten times during every conversation we have." And it's true. Luciana's fingers fly across her phone as she writes out twenty different ways to tell me how hot she thinks my brother is.

Brie laughs and clutches my hands. I wince but we finally get me to my feet. I take her cheeks, which have finally started to round out now that she's able to keep food down, and grin at her.

"When did the doctor say I could have sex again?" I tease and steal a kiss.

She rolls her eyes. "Six weeks. You're not even close, buddy. No funny business."

I draw her closer to me, careful not to press her against my sore flesh. My cock, though, has a different plan and pokes at her belly. "You're going to deny an injured man?"

Her palm rubs against my erection and she looks up at me with a salacious stare. "I said we weren't going to have sex." Then she smirks and it's devious and goddamned beautiful. "I never said anything about blow jobs."

Before I can process her words, she's on her knees and gently tugging down my shorts and boxers.

"Did I ever tell you how much I love y—" My words die in my throat the moment her mouth wraps around my neglected cock. "Jesus Christ, woman, you're so fucking good at that." I grip her hair as she takes me deep, careful not to gag.

The woman pulls out every trick in the book until I'm murmuring her beautiful name repeatedly in a chant.

She sucks me dry, and I hiss in pain the moment my stomach clenches with my release. The moment she pops off my cock and looks up at me with my seed running down her chin and a happy smile on her face, I know right then…

No matter what storms come our way, we'll endure them.

Together.

Because our love is strong and unflappable.

Love destroys demons and obliterates broken pasts.

Love is ours—finally—and we fucking earned it.

TWENTY

Brie

Two months later…

His mouth is on my swollen tit and he's driving me crazy by sucking on the flesh everywhere except my needy nipple. My state of duress has the babies rolling around like wild in my stomach.

"Staaaahp," I complain in the darkness.

He pulls away and soon the light from the lamp floods the room. His dark brows are pulled together in concern. "Is everything okay? Are my little cubs okay in there?" His large hands splay over my big round belly. The babies respond to his touch and roll around some more. A look of pure joy passes over his features.

"They're fine," I assure him with a smile.

My hands cover his and I stare at him as he watches my stomach.

"I still can't get over how weird this feels. To touch them. I mean, I felt Mason in my mom's stomach, but this is different. They're…" he trails off as if he doesn't want to say anything to hurt me.

"They're yours?" I finish.

His steely blue eyes dart to mine, and the heat in them nearly scorches me. "Ours."

I nod and clutch his hand. He starts talking to the babies, but I'm distracted by his bare torso. Three months ago, he was toned and flawless. Since he can't work out much yet, his defined lines aren't as prominent. It's his scars that haunt me, though. One day they'll fade to silvery white but right now they're still puffy and dark pink. A daily reminder that he almost died. When I sniffle, he curls up beside me and pulls me into his strong arms.

"What's wrong, beautiful?"

I swallow down my emotion. "Nothing. I just think about how I almost lost you from time to time, and it upsets me."

He sits up on one elbow and frowns at me. My gaze falls to the red scar across his neck. That one affects me the most. That one I see whether he's dressed or not. That one reminds me that he was lucky when Mom and Duvan were not. I reach up and tenderly stroke the pink flesh.

Understanding washes over him and he gently plucks my hand away. He pins it on the bed and a low growl rumbles from him.

"I'm not going to wither away," he tells me, his gaze fierce. If I had any doubts that he isn't as strong as he once was, they get squashed under that tough look he's giving me. His grip is firm and unmovable as he holds my wrist against the bed. "Now tell me how you want to be fucked, little momma."

I laugh and spread my legs. "Just like this. So I can see you."

His brow arches as he makes a point to stare at my big belly. "And how exactly do you think we'll manage?"

Sticking out my tongue, I grab my pillow and swat it at him. "Put this under my ass," I instruct in a bossy tone. "Then fuck me from your knees where I can watch."

An evil smirk quirks up his features. "My bossy girl is so dirty. I love it." He folds the pillow in half and slips it beneath me. Then, he slides a leg over each of his broad shoulders. His cock is thick and heavy as it rests against my bare pussy. From this vantage point, I can see all his scars. It sickens me yet it reminds me that he's made it through alive.

"Fuck me, Daddy," I tease.

He laughs and gives my clit a tiny pinch that has me shuddering with need. "You're a bad girl."

I bite on my bottom lip and that steals his smile. Pure, starved need paints his handsome features as he grabs my hips and then slides into my very wet opening. I let out a ragged sound of bliss as he bucks into me slowly.

"Camilo said I had a magical cunt. Does it feel different to you?" I question, suddenly overwhelmed with need to know what makes me so special.

Ren rolls his eyes at me. "Are you seriously wanting to discuss this with my cock nine inches deep inside you?"

I let out a gasp when he gives my clit a little slap. It sends ripples of pleasure surging through me. "Just tell me."

He shakes his head as he thrusts into me hard. "It's not your pussy that makes you so special. I mean"—he flashes me a wolfish grin—"I love it. Don't get me wrong. But to me, it's your…"

His cock slides out of me and then he rolls me over onto my side. "On your knees, beautiful," he barks out. I get on my elbows and knees and wriggle my ass at him. He enters me hard enough to make me cry out. Then he slaps my ass.

"Oh, God," I moan and push back against him, meeting him thrust for thrust.

"Baby, this ass is what grown men turn fucking stupid over. It's perfect." Thrust. Slap. Another moan from me. "And it's mine."

"I'll be back in a bit," he murmurs, kissing my cheek before turning out the light. "Rest and then I'll feed you and those babies some ranch tacos."

I'm smiling even as I hear the front door slam shut and his truck drive away. Ren is the only man I know that doesn't even seem bothered to have to go hunt his woman some tacos down at midnight. My tummy grumbles. God, I really do love him.

After our wild fuck session, I'm tired despite my hunger. I find myself drifting in and out. When I hear the bedroom door creak open, I smile. Rolling over, I seek out my man.

"Were you able to get any?" I question.

But when he emerges from the shadows, and a sliver of moonlight from the window reveals his face, I'm frozen. A million emotions filter through me all at once.

"Looking stunning all naked, mi amor," he murmurs.

I blink in confusion. This is real. This isn't a dream.

"W-What are you doing here?" I stammer.

A low growl rumbles from him as he takes another step toward the bed. In an effort to hide, I drag the sheet up my naked flesh.

"Are you pregnant with my child?"

Emotion clogs my throat and no words come out. I don't understand.

"Duvan?"

Brie

"Oh, sourpuss," he utters softly. "Don't I wish I could give my brother back to you, but he's gone. Oscar gave me an urn with his ashes. Duvan is dead."

Bile rises in my throat as I fretfully look around for a weapon, shaking off the vision of my dead husband. Esteban isn't the cocky manipulator he once was. In fact, he appears ragged and not at all put together. His hair is messy and he's sporting some scruff. It's as though he's been hiding under some rock until now. "You need to leave, Esteban." No longer do I get a surge of need whenever I see him. Terror and helplessness and despair are what consume me. My hand clutches my belly in a subconscious desire to protect my children.

He stalks forward and then pounces. Like the black panther I always equated him to. This tigress isn't and never was a worthy adversary. I cry out as he pushes my wrists together and pins them above my head. His heavy body straddles my waist. A sob escapes me when he runs his large palm over my breast to my stomach. The babies roll in response.

His lips curl into a proud grin but I don't miss the possessive gleam in his eyes. "Is. This. Baby. Mine?" Then, his voice drops as he reaches for my face. "We fucked countless times, sourpuss." As if I need the reminder.

I spit at him. "Fuck you! Get out of my house!"

His brows crash together as hurt flashes in his eyes. "Is this baby mine?" he demands, irritation lacing his tone. "Your stomach is so big. You're further along, which means it's mine."

"Babies. They're your brother's *babies*. The doctor confirmed when I conceived."

Dark eyes widen in surprise. Then, a fleeting look of anger. "I've come for you."

I'm already shaking my head. "I'm not going anywhere with you! Leave, Esteban!"

He growls before reaching back and slapping my face. Not hard, but enough to have me dazed. "She's so lonely. I'm bringing you so she has someone to entertain her."

Her?

"I don't know what you're talking about," I argue, my voice becoming weaker by the second. But I do. Deep down, I do. And it sickens me.

"That would hurt little Red's feelings," he chides. "It's a shame how easily she was forgotten by her best friend."

Ice runs cold through my veins. I gave up months ago assuming one of Camilo or Diego's men or even Esteban had killed Vee.

"Y-You have Vee?" I stammer out in surprise.

His smile is tender and it confuses me. "I do. She is mine now."

I buck underneath him, but he's too strong. "Let me go! Tell me where she is, you fucking asshole!" I rage at him.

"I'll do better. I'll take you to her, sourpuss," he assures me with a cold grin.

I hear a sound behind him and then see the gleam of the baseball bat I keep behind the bedroom door.

"The hell you will," Ren roars a second before I hear the crack of the bat.

Esteban howls and rolls away from me. Ren pounces without hesitation, swinging that bat like he's trying to nail a homerun right out of the park. The cracking of Esteban's ribs is loud, and it makes me gag.

"Ren! Stop!" I screech and scramble to put myself between him and Esteban. But I'm too late. Ren swings another hard blow that hits Esteban right in the back of the head. The sickening pop actually does make me ill. I burst off the bed and rush into the bathroom, barely making it to the toilet in time to expel my guts. The bat clatters to the tile floor as Ren drops behind me, his hands flitting all over me checking for injuries.

"Is he dead?" I question through my tears.

He shakes his head. "I don't think so."

"Good!" I shriek. When he glowers at me, I quickly continue. "He knows where Vee is!"

Understanding washes over him. And then relief. "Call 911."

As soon as the call is made and help is on the way, I make my way back into the bedroom. Seeing Esteban bloody and helpless and unconscious causes my chest to tighten. It feels right. Like he deserves it and so much more. Full fucking circle. Not long ago, it was him staring over me, wielding all the power. I was his victim.

Not anymore.

Three days later...

"Sit down, woman," Ren orders and points his paintbrush at me.

I pout but do as I'm told. He looks hot as ever in a pair of holey jeans that hang low on his hips, revealing just a tiny view of his ass crack. Since he's painting, he's not wearing a shirt, and his entire tattooed back is on display for my visual pleasure. The entire thing is covered in his intricate tree. His tiger and cubs have long been filled in. It's beautiful and I love it.

With a smile, I rub my belly. "Are you sure you can paint those stripes? I think this looks harder than the YouTube video tutorial."

He looks over his shoulder and gives me a smoldering look. "Keep mouthing off and I'll have to keep that pretty mouth busy so I can paint in peace."

Laughing, I shoot him the bird. "Real funny."

We're quiet again as he paints. Ren truly is beautiful both inside and out. Sometimes I worry I don't tell him that enough.

"I love you," I blurt out.

He gives me a lopsided grin over his shoulder that has my heart thumping in my chest. "I love you too."

When he goes back to painting, I have the urge to say more. "I know I don't tell you enough but you mean the world to me. You were always there for me. Nobody has been there every step of the way like you have." My chin wobbles.

He sets his brush down and struts over to me. I find myself ogling this sexy-ass man who I can proudly call mine. His fingers grip my jaw, and he tilts my head up so he can kiss me. It's brief and sweet, but it knocks me over with his love. With Ren, I feel it always rippling from him. With Ren, I never feel his love waver.

"Thank you," I murmur against his warm lips.

He pulls away and something like pride shines in his eyes as he regards me. "Loving you is easy, Brie. Nothing about it ever feels like a chore. It's a gift. So thank you for my gift." He winks at me before making his way over to his project.

My mind is on thoughts of our future. One where Ren is my husband and these kids call him

Daddy. Thoughts of us going to T-ball games together, dinners and holidays with his wonderful family, late nights where he and I worship each other's bodies, family pictures and school plays. Normalcy. The American dream.

Love.

Ours.

My phone starts to ring and I see it's Daddy calling. He probably wants to drop by and visit. I refuse to admit it to anyone but I'm in love with my new little brother. It gives me a sneak peek of what it will be like to have my own babies. Sometimes, I hold baby Land for hours and inhale his sweet scent. Daddy is smart enough to leave the psycho with her parents when he brings my siblings by.

"Hey," I answer as my eyes drag back over to Ren. He's been able to work out a little more here and there. Painting will probably leave him tired, but he's insistent. I admire his back muscles while Daddy hisses on the other line. It takes me a second to pull my attention back to my phone call. "Wait? What? Say that again," I demand.

"Esteban escaped from the hospital," he snarls. "Tell Ren to put a bullet through anyone's skull who tries to come into your house."

Ren, sensing my distress, is already stalking over to me, wearing an alarmed expression.

"But he hasn't told them where Vee is yet," I mutter. "He can't escape. We have to find her."

Daddy grumbles on the line. "I'm sorry about your friend, but that's the least of my worries right now. My worry is your safety. I'll be over in fifteen minutes. Call your fuckface *friend*, who still has a death sentence."

When he hangs up, I stare up at Ren.

"What is it?" he demands and falls to his knees in front of me. He takes my hand and kisses the top of it. Fierce love and protectiveness shine in his gaze.

"Esteban escaped." I blink in shock. Then, I dial my "fuckface friend who still has a death sentence." I will *not* let my dreams and future with Ren be compromised by a madman.

"Ahhh, cariño. Ready for the big D?" his deep voice purrs as he answers.

I swallow and choke out my words. "It…It's Esteban. He escaped."

His breath rushes out in a hiss. "Ever since he got to you a few days ago, I've had men parked on your street watching. He won't get to you," he assures me.

"I'm not worried about me." And I'm not. At least not one hundred percent. This is bigger. "We have to find him. When we find him, we find her."

Diego chuckles on the other end. "Are you asking me for a favor, cariño?"

"Por favor."

EPILOGUE

Vee

He left me.

Promised to bring me something that would make me happy. What a ridiculous concept. *Happy.* I don't even understand what that means anymore. How can one be happy in a metal box with no light, no entertainment, no one to talk to? Nothing.

My stomach growls and the pains are too much to bear. I've slowly been starving to death. At first, I picked through the rations and attempted to share them with my mother. But she was too far gone on the heroin to care. She screamed and clawed, and at one point, tried to attack me as if I held her precious drug prisoner.

Newsflash, we were the prisoners.

But then the strangest thing happened. She stopped screaming and hissing and fighting. She stopped breathing altogether. And the moment it all became quiet, I let out a sigh of relief. My mother died from withdrawals. From a drug she'd never touched until Esteban forced it into her vein. And I was glad.

Not that I didn't love her.

I did.

Truly.

But she became some savage beast the moment he put us in this cage. He took joy in making her dependent on him for a simple high. But I depended on him for something altogether different.

A sob escapes me but no tears roll out. Sometimes I wish he had forced the heroin on me. Mom was blissed out of her mind for most of the months we've been here. I've been clear headed. I have been awake and coherent every time he's come for me.

I imagine his large body curled around mine. At one time it made me shudder. At one time I hated him. Hated that he stole so much from me. But now, I miss him. I miss his warmth. I miss his words in my lonely world. I miss the food he would feed me.

Why did he leave me?

I know I won't survive much longer without him. Mom's body has begun to decompose over in the corner. She didn't last a full day without the constant stream of drugs in her system. Since she didn't have medicine to help her withdrawal, she simply shut down. Her moans and screams are no more, but now I'm completely alone.

My mind begs to think about my past. Dad and Brie. Oscar. Even Ren and Calder. The funny thing is, though, I can't remember any of them. Oscar's face, because it's so similar to Esteban's, is the only one I can clutch onto through the haze.

Each time I attempt to remember my friends and family, only one frighteningly handsome face comes to mind. And I miss it. I would give myself willingly to him if he would just come back and save me from this slow, painful death.

Diabla Roja.

I smile in the darkness and touch the thin mattress where he used to sleep with me sometimes. If I close my eyes, I can almost smell him. Spicy and manly. In the early days, he would take my orgasms. I'd fought him tooth and nail, but in the end, I always gave in. Gave him what he wanted—what we both wanted.

"Diabla Roja."

I start crying because now I'm delirious. I can almost hear him. Am I dying?

"Shhhhh."

It's as though his palms are whispering touches along my outer arm. As if his fingers are running through my ratty red hair.

"You're alive." His phantom voice sounds real. Pained and desperate and relieved. "Can you stand, Roja?"

I blink slowly and roll toward the sounds that tease me. It's dark but I see his shadow looming above me. "Esteban?" I croak.

His palm strokes my cheek. "I went to fetch her for you. So you wouldn't cry so much," he tells me, his voice sad. "But then that motherfucker put me in the hospital. All I could think about was how you were starving here."

A tear slides down my temple. This is real. He came back for me. "I don't want her," I rasp out. "I need you."

He grunts as if he's in pain but he manages to scoop my weak frame from the mattress on the floor. With labored breaths, he carries me right past my mother's rancid body and out of the metal box. It's the first time in months I've left this prison. I let out a relieved sob and cling to his shirt.

"Shhh," he murmurs as he carries me through the darkness. Gently, he loads me into the car. As he drives, I simply stare at him. Such a simple gift, the gift of sight, I'm able to use on him. Drinking in his every feature. His longish black hair normally remains slicked back but today hangs in his eyes. Those calculating, nearly black eyes that dart over to me every so often. The scruff on his cheeks that my fingers crave to touch. We drive for what seems like forever until he pulls up to a secluded house on the beach.

"Where are we?" I'm shivering despite his hand constantly rubbing on my thigh in an oddly comforting manner.

"One of my father's safe houses. I sometimes stay here when I need to keep a low profile," he tells me before climbing out of the car. I don't have the energy to move. When he opens my car door, I drag my gaze to look at him in the moonlight. He reminds me of a hungry wolf. Starved for me.

Well, I'm starved too.

"I'm hungry," I tell him.

He nods and scoops me up. "I know, Roja. I'm going to fix you right up."

My heart thunders at his words. I believe them. I want him to fix me.

I'm in a daze for the next few hours. He feeds me broth and holds me. Eventually, he gets me under the hot spray of the shower. After not having properly bathed in months, it feels like heaven. I bawl until the water runs cold and I'm hiccupping and he has to carry my shivering body out. When he sets me on the bed, panic races up my spine. I clutch onto the front of his shirt and whine.

"Don't leave me."

His brows furrow and he strokes my wet hair. "Never again."

I wake for the first time in what feels like forever, comfortable and warm. A big hot body is draped over me. I'm not sure if he's trying to keep me from running or to keep me warm. I burrow further beneath him to seek out his protection. My movement wakes him as well.

"Let me see you," he murmurs, his voice gruff with sleep.

I tilt my head up and stare into his nearly black eyes. At one time, they terrified me. Months ago, when he'd take what he wanted whenever he wanted, I feared him with every fiber of my being. I prayed for someone to come save me.

Nobody came.

And then the strangest thing happened. I became reliant on him. He was the only person who wanted me. Everyone else forgot about me. So, soon, despite my outward denial, I came to look forward to his late night visits. I would bask in his expert touches and come from his fingers on my own accord. I'd never admitted I wanted him until now.

"I was so lonely," I choke out, my eyes welling with hot tears. "I thought I was going to die."

He lets out a fierce growl before his mouth finds mine. In the past, whenever he'd kiss me, I never participated. I'd lain there like a dead doll. Now, I crave his mouth more than the broth I desperately downed last night. My mouth parts and I shove my tongue into his. Every nerve ending in my body fires to life. I squirm with the need for him to touch me everywhere.

"What's come over you?" he murmurs against my lips as his palm roams over my round breast. He tweaks the nipple, which makes me cry out. Then, his hand trails down south toward my pussy.

"I...I...I just need..."

His finger grazes my clit and I jolt with a moan. A growl of approval resounds from him and it seems to stroke my poor, fragile heart. I want him to be happy with me. I want to be enough.

"Open your legs, Roja. Let me see you," he murmurs, his lips trailing down to my throat.

Like a whore, I jerk my knees apart to give him what he wants. His finger dips inside me dragging a mewl from me. "Oh, please...I need more."

He nips at my neck just as he inches another finger inside me. Before Esteban, I was a virgin. That first time had been painful, but every other time was surprisingly pleasure filled.

"Always so wet for me, Roja," he praises, his fingers working magic on my insides. "I see you've finally come to learn who owns this perfect cunt."

I nod and bite my lip. His mouth kisses along my chest until he has my pebbled nipple between his teeth. I grab my knee and pull it toward me. His two fingers aren't enough. I crave him. Deeper. Harder. His cock stretching me wide.

"What do you want?" he questions as his thumb begins working lazy circles on my clit while he fucks me with two fingers.

"I need you," I moan. "Please."

His fingers slip out of me, and I yelp at the loss. I'm squirming and helpless as he grabs a condom from the end table. It takes all of ten seconds to sheath his cock, but it's ten seconds too long. Thankfully, he climbs on top of me and suffocates me with his addicting presence. Our eyes lock when the tip of his cock teases my opening in a delightful way.

"You want this?" he demands, his free hand delicately stroking my throat.

I grab his wrist and nod.

With a powerful thrust, he drives into me. Hard. I scream in pleasure as I desperately claw his shoulders. He winces in pain but then quickly finds his stride. Esteban drives into me as if this single act will mold my soul to his.

I close my eyes and give myself to him.

The dead heart in my chest belongs to this man. It may not beat, but it's his.

"You belong to me, Roja," he growls, his grip on my throat tightening.

I let out a hissed "yessss" as my body ripples with desire. His mouth hovers over mine as he fucks me senseless. I become an animal the moment my orgasm explodes through me and I claw his flesh, needing to crawl inside him. His grunts and then the swelling of his cock tells me he finds his release too.

Esteban relaxes on me and nuzzles his nose against my ear. It's perfection, and I don't want to leave this moment. But then the phone on the bedside table is ringing and he's leaving me to answer it. I lick my lips as I watch him pull the wet condom off his large cock. He smirks as he answers. The voice on the other line is familiar. It jolts me out of my sex-induced fog and sends a shiver of memories down my spine. I can't make out all the words but I do hear some.

Thump.

Thump.

Why does my chest hurt?

"This is war, brother. We're going to slaughter every single one of Diego's men. Then…" The line goes quiet for a moment. "Then we take back our empire."

Thump.

Oscar.

Thump.

My simple world consisting of me and Esteban fucking all day suddenly dissipates as clarity sets in.

Thump.

I'm going to see Oscar.

Thump.

The dead heart in my chest thuds back to life.

Thump.

Because it's only ever truly beat for one man.

This Isn't Fair, Baby is up next…

THIS ISN'T FAIR,

baby

The king in my world fell and a new one slid into place.
He wasn't just.
He wasn't FAIR.

He was cruel and hateful and twisted.
But I had this black king figured out.
Or so I thought.

The game became complicated because my black king had some new moves and one of those involved my heart. Hope trickled in for the briefest of moments.

That is, until my black king and my heart sided against me. Those two didn't play FAIR. They used me as their pawn in a bigger game—a game I didn't know how to play.

The laws changed. I didn't play by their rules anymore, for the queen makes up her own.

I am not a pawn.
I am not theirs to use and abuse.
I belong to nobody.

There are new players on the board and they don't play FAIR either. But the white king does know how to treat his queen. And together, they will make them pay.

All's FAIR in love and war, right?

PROLOGUE

Vee

Five years old…

This house is pretty. Like the castle in my *Beauty and the Beast* movie. There are so many rooms to play hide-and-seek in. I wish Mommy would play with me. She never does, though.

Once I've looked inside every room in the castle, I run down the long hallway toward Mommy's and Daddy's room. We're on a vacation, Daddy told me. A work vacation. All I know is we're not in California anymore. We got on an airplane and flew far, far away to this castle.

"Mommy!" I call out. "Where are you?"

Maybe she is playing a game with me. The thought makes my heart thump in my chest. When I get close to her room, I can hear the music playing inside. And as I round the corner, I see her dancing.

Mommy is so pretty with her shiny red hair, which looks like it has gold strands in it sometimes. Like the mermaid in my favorite Disney movie. Her eyes even sparkle every now and again. I love when they sparkle because that means she's in a good mood. When she's in a bad mood, she makes me go play by myself.

I let out a squeal and drop my backpack full of toys and coloring books. I start dancing in circles and love the way my dress flares out around me. I'm a princess like Mommy.

"Dancing! Dancing!" I cheer out in delight.

As if my words make her angry, she stops dancing and turns to stare at me. Some white powder is on her nose and her green eyes look almost black. Her smile is gone. She bares her teeth at me and her lip curls up as if she's grossed out by me.

"I thought I told you to go play," she snaps and then sniffs, like she has a cold.

"But I thought we were dancing, Mom—"

"For crying out loud, Vienna! Mommy has to test Daddy's merchandise. I can't do that with you bothering me. Go play," she spits out and rubs at her nose.

"But Daddy said to stay inside and—"

"Now!"

Her harsh words used to make me cry, but I'm used to them now. Nothing makes me cry. Daddy says I'm fierce…like a dragon. I always smile when he says that, yet deep down I wish I were fierce, but also a princess. Why can't I be pretty and breathe fire at the same time?

Mommy's hand swats at me, and I scamper away from her. I scoop up my backpack along the way out the door. Eager to explore, I run along the narrow hallways until I find one that leads outside. As soon as I push through the door, the summer heat cloaks me like my warm blanket back home.

Even though Daddy told me to stay inside, I listen to Mommy's instructions and start exploring the outside of the castle. Daddy has taken us on lots of vacations to Colombia, but this is the first time we've visited this castle.

I'm humming a song when I hear voices. Shouting. Curiosity gets the best of me, and I sneak around the side of the stone wall to see what all the commotion is about. A man with big muscles and a scary smile is holding a huge knife. He's teasing someone, but I can't see who. I sneak over to a rose bush and crouch behind it. The roses are big and red, kind of like the ones in my *Beauty and the Beast* movie. I want to pick one but I know roses have thorns. Instead, I lean in and inhale the sweet scent.

"You'll pay for this," the scary man growls, stealing my attention away from the roses. His big knife gleams in the bright sunlight.

I peek around the bush to get a better look. Finally, I see who the scary man is yelling at. A skinny boy is sprawled out on the grass with his hands up, like he's afraid the man will hurt him. Sometimes I hold my hands up like that when Mommy is mad. She doesn't hit me often, but her eyes can be mean. I always worry she will.

"*No me robé ningúna cocaína,*" the boy says, his voice shaking. I don't know what he's saying, but it sounds like he's trying to make the scary man understand.

"*Te cojì con el producto en tu bolsa. Ahora vas a pagar con tu vida. Nadie le falta el respeto a mi familia,*" the scary man hisses. I half expect him to change into a monster right under the hot, sunny rays. Kind of like when Beast turns into a human. But backward and scarier.

"*Por favor, señor.*" The boy seems sad and afraid. I wish I could yell at the scary man to stop waving his knife at him.

While they continue to argue, I slide my backpack off and dig around. I don't have a real knife but I have a yellow plastic one I use to cut my Play-Doh. Once I have it in my tiny grip, I rise from behind the bush. I watch in awe for a moment as the scary man moves his arm fast and fancy, like he's a dancer but with just one arm. It's almost magical. Until I see the blood covering his white button-down shirt, like the ones Daddy wears.

"No!" I cry out from my hiding spot.

The scary man freezes and turns, his eyes locking onto mine. "Run along, child." His accent is thick, but I understand his words this time. "Run to your father." He breaks our stare to glare down at the bloody boy, who doesn't move. When he holds the knife up like he might stab him, I charge for the scary man.

"Noooooo!" I screech and hold my yellow knife up as I run.

The scary man laughs—loud and too cold for this hot day—as I try to stab him with my weapon. He snorts before easily pushing me to the grass beside the boy.

"*Hijos de puta,*" he grumbles and shakes his head before stalking off.

I turn to regard the boy. His face is covered in blood. The dirty white T-shirt he's wearing is now torn and bright red, like the roses on the bush. He's bleeding everywhere. When he lifts a shaking hand that drips with blood, I let out a small shriek. But he smiles through his pain.

"*Un ángel. Me estoy muriendo y tu eres mi ángel.*" His voice is deep like Daddy's. I can tell he's older like my cousin Seth who can drive.

"Shh," I coo to the boy. His lip wobbles and he looks lost. I can't see his eyes because they're squinted shut against the bright sunshine. "I have Band-Aids," I assure him. "They're *Toy Story,* so boys can like them too."

Tears streak down his cheeks and gurgling sounds escape him. The sounds scare me, but I can fix him. With newfound determination, I run back to the bush to grab my backpack. Once I snag it up, I rush back to my patient. He's quiet as I pull out my box of Band-Aids and carefully peel apart each one. The box was nearly full—Daddy bought it for me at the airport when we arrived in Colombia after I fell and skinned my knee—so I'm able to put them all over his bloody face. With Buzz Lightyear and Woody staring back at me with big smiles on their faces, I believe this boy will get better.

"*¡Llama ayuda, hermano!*" a boy shouts from somewhere behind us.

I turn to see an older boy with messy black hair running toward me. He doesn't seem scary like the man from before. In fact, he looks like he might cry.

"I fixed him," I assure the boy when he kneels beside me. "He's going to get all better now." I go to pat him, but he stares at my bloody hand as though he's afraid it will bite him. *Hands don't bite, silly.*

His eyes that are almost purple in the sunlight shimmer with tears. "Please go inside, little girl." He points at the house. "My little brother is in the kitchen. Have him help you clean up." I like this boy's accent.

I reach into my bag and tug out Mr. Snuffles, my new stuffed cat, which Daddy bought me in a gift shop before we came to the castle. Mr. Snuffles won't miss me. Besides, this bloody boy needs him more than I do. I'll just ask Daddy to buy me a new one.

"Here you go," I tell the bloody boy, who seems to have fallen asleep. "Mr. Snuffles wants to stay with you." I lift his messy arm and stuff the cat in the crook of it.

The purple-eyed boy beside me starts to cry. "I think he's dead."

I ignore the sad boy and give the bloody boy a hug goodbye. Then, I scoop up my backpack and walk slowly back to the castle. When I reach the doorway, I turn and look at the bloody boy and the sad boy. One sobs loudly. The other doesn't make a peep.

He's going to be okay.

I fixed him.

With a smile, I turn and run right into another boy. This boy looks to be my same age. This boy has the prettiest dark brown eyes I've ever seen.

"Hi," I wave a bloody hand at him and grin. "I'm Vee. Can we be friends?"

His eyes widen but he nods slowly. A small smile creeps on his face. "We can be friends if you can catch me." He gives me a tiny shove before turning and running away. Fast. My new friend is super fast.

But I'll catch him.

Tossing my backpack to the floor, I chase after him.

chapter ONE

Vee

Present

"Wake up, *diabla roja*," a deep voice rumbles as it parts its way through the fog clouding my mind.

I blink away the confusion and take in the eyes before me. Dark brown. Piercing. Calculating. Esteban.

"Morning."

He's not smiling, though. And while that's not uncommon for Esteban, I sense something is wrong.

"We need to discuss a few things," he bites out. When I stare at him with a frown for a second too long, his palm cracks across my thigh. "¡*Levantate!*"

My flesh stings, but I jolt into action. The last thing I want is Esteban angry with me. I don't want to see that fury flickering in his eyes, like the night he took my mother and I from her house after I witnessed the death of my father. That night he was furious and roaring about revenge and what was owed to him.

He stole me.

And my mother.

Our families were joined by business, and I'd always hoped they'd be by matrimony one day as well.

But nothing went as planned. Everything was destroyed.

"Whatever it is that's going on in your head, I want it gone," Esteban snaps as he snags my wrist in his brutal grip.

My heart rate skitters in my chest, and I clumsily follow him. He's fully dressed in a pair of slacks and a white button-down shirt that fits his muscled body like a glove. I, on the other hand, am dressed exactly how he likes me. Which is not dressed at all.

"Sit," he commands and points to the floor in front of a chair in the small living room.

I nod and fall to my knees. My head starts to throb much like it always does these days. I'm sure it's because I always feel so hungry. Maybe today he'll feed me more than just a sandwich. He takes a seat in the chair and gently grabs my throat to pull me between his thighs. I look up at him with wide eyes as my palms caress his knees through his slacks.

"What did I do wrong?" My voice is but a whisper, but I know he hears me. Esteban never misses a thing. Not when it comes to me. That's one thing I can say about him. I'm his entire focus. I've never been anyone's entire focus before.

His hard gaze softens as he leans forward. A large palm strokes the side of my head, and I lean against it. My eyes flutter closed as I relish his gentle touch.

"Look at me," he murmurs, his fingers twisting into my hair.

I pop my eyes back open and fixate on his mouth. Just thinking about where his mouth was last night sends a ripple of need coursing through me. He may not drug me like he did my mother, but I'm completely addicted to him. It's his touch I need. His dark eyes roaming over my body. The deep rumble of his voice quaking down to my very soul.

I've never felt so consumed before. Not even by Oscar.

My heart rate quickens at the thought of his name. Thinking about Ozzy confuses me. Several days ago, Esteban spoke to him over the phone. He said he'd be coming out to meet with us. I wonder if all connection with Oscar has been severed. If I'll ever feel about him the way I seem to feel about Esteban. My mind can't comprehend turning off all these feelings for Esteban in the blink of an eye and switching back on how I felt for Oscar. Everything is hazy and all messed up. If I could just get rid of this headache, maybe I could think clearly.

A sharp slap to my face stuns me, and I clutch my stinging flesh. The throb in my head intensifies. I dart my eyes up to Esteban's which are blazing with fury.

"We spent so many months teaching you how to behave. Who you belong to. And for what? For you to forget it the moment I take you out of your metal prison? Do we need to go back and start over?" he hisses, the brutal grip on my hair tightening.

I start to shake my head but I can't move it. Swallowing, I force out my words. "N-No. I'm just tired, I think. Hungry." While it's technically a lie about where my thoughts have been, I am tired and hungry. Ever since leaving the container, I can't help but feel starved all the time. Esteban brings me my meals. Esteban feeds me. But it never feels like enough. And everything seems foggy—as if Esteban is the lighthouse beaconing for me. Everything around me feels like a blur.

"You can eat later," he hisses. "We need to talk about tonight."

I try not to fixate on the way his nostrils flare with anger. Sometimes they flare when his face is between my thighs as he inhales me. Sometimes they flare when he grabs me by the throat and pins me to the bed.

Focus, Vee.

"You belong to me," he bites out, and his grip in my hair loosens. He goes back to petting the side of my head, like I'm his dog. "Whatever childhood fantasies you had of growing up to marry my little brother are over. At one time, our families would have supported that. Now that it's just the three of us left, everything will play out differently."

My gaze falls to his lips. I wonder if he's eaten anything today.

"Do you understand, Roja?"

Upon hearing the pet name he coined for me, my mind flashes to several days ago when I was his prisoner, trapped in a metal container he'd kept me in for months. When he'd left to try and steal Brie, so I'd have a friend. It ended up nearly getting him killed in the process. As a result, my mother died from heroin withdrawals, and I was on the brink of starvation. But he came back. He came back and plucked me from that nightmare. This safe house in San Diego feels like a dream in comparison.

"Roja!" he snaps, jerking me from my thoughts.

I nod rapidly and slide my palms higher along his thighs. Anything to coax him out of this tense mood he's in. "I'm yours."

His features relax, and I feel proud that I've pleased him. Maybe he'll fix me a giant sandwich with extra turkey and—

"He must not find out about…" he trails off and scratches his jaw as if to search for the correct word. "He must not find out about how you and I came to be a couple."

I may not be drugged up on heroin like my mother, but Esteban is definitely running through my veins. I don't understand how he burrowed his way under my skin. Months ago, I hated him. Now, my skin tingles at the mention of the word couple.

Deep down inside, a part of me screams. It's a silent scream, but I feel it in my bones.

He stole you. He raped you. He killed your mother. Fuck Esteban.

But since he's bubbling in my veins like the hot liquid drug that makes strong people weak, thoughts of him silence the part of me that screams in protest.

Esteban saved you from the metal box.

Esteban saved you from the stench of your mother's rotting corpse.

Esteban brought you to this home to feed and care for you.

"I love when you look at me that way, Roja," he murmurs, lust thick in his voice. "I want to see those adoring eyes on me while you worship my cock."

A smile touches my lips as my fingers skate along the hard outline of his erection in his slacks to his belt. He usually feeds me after sex, but especially if I blow him. Eager to not only please him but also to eat, I yank at the leather and work frantically to free his dick. I'm overwhelmed with the need to please him. The past few days have been heaven with him trapping me beneath him while he fucks me wildly. After all those months in the metal box, this life with him is manageable. I'm safe and cared for under his watch. Today, though, he's regarded me differently, and I hate it. I want the look of desire back in his eyes. The pure, unfiltered look of possession. And I want a damn sandwich.

His cock is hot in my hand the second I grip my fingers around it. My mouth waters to lick his tip and show him how good I can be for him. He lets out a slight hiss of air when my thumb runs along the side of his shaft, which is all I need to dive in. I slide my parted lips over the head of his length and let my tongue taste the underside of him. A grunt rumbles from him as he takes handfuls of my hair on each side of my head. His grip isn't harsh, like it sometimes can be. It's just firm enough to guide me the way he likes.

I work him up and down with my fist while dancing circles with my tongue. His girth is wide enough to make my jaw ache, but not bad enough that I can't push him deep into my throat. The moment I relax my muscles and swallow him, he lets out a string of curse words in Spanish. I smile against his cock but don't slow my movements. I'm about to pop off him for a moment to catch my breath, but his grip on my hair stops me. His hips thrust up as he shoves my face against him. His sudden deep intrusion causes me to gag. Drool runs out of my mouth and along his cock while I wriggle to get away.

"That's it," he hisses. "Take every inch."

Tears from not being able to breathe stream down my cheeks. I dig my fingernails into his thighs to let him know I can't take any more. This only seems to turn him on more because with a long grunt and an extra brutal thrust of his hips, he comes down the back of my throat.

I gag and gag but thankfully don't throw up—not that there's anything in my belly to expel, anyway. Finally, when I feel as though I might black out, he releases me. I jerk off his cock and gasp for air. Snot runs from my nose and down over my lips.

His face is impassive as he sets to putting his cock back inside his boxers and slacks. I stare at his features while they're distracted.

He will always be like this. Remember what he did to your best friend?

I silence my inner screamer with a flash of inner rage. My best friend abandoned me. Married into the family I was supposed to marry into, dragging grown men on their knees behind her in her wake. Oscar had been drawn to her. Duvan had fallen for her. And Esteban had fucked her.

Thoughts go to my father…

Daddy was obsessed with her and now he's gone.

While Brie was off living the good life, I'd been stolen by the man who hurt her. I was starved and beaten and fucked right out of my sanity. I was forced to listen to my mother die in a metal cage. All because Brie made smart men stupid. All because Brie was too selfish to come for me.

If the situation were reversed, I would have gone for her.

Tears don't fall, though. Instead, anger bubbles in my chest. This is my world now. Esteban may not be perfect, but at least he wants me. Unlike Oscar. Unlike Brie. Unlike anyone else.

"You're to do exactly as I say," Esteban growls as he tugs me into his lap.

My eyes find his and I straddle his muscular thighs. I can't help but touch him with greedy fingers. I'm sure I look a mess with my drool and snot and watery eyes, but he looks at me as though I'm perfect.

"Of course," I tell him with a smile. "Can you feed me now?"

He smirks before pulling me against him. "Oh, Roja," he says with a chuckle. "I just fed you." His fingertips stroke me until I'm dozing off. I inhale his scent and it reminds me of the first time I smelled him up close. It helps the pain in my belly disappear.

"Ozzy?" I question as I peek inside another door. My parents and I just arrived at the Rojas's for the summer. I'm dying to find him and hope he notices I'm wearing makeup. Daddy made me wait until I turned fourteen to start wearing it. Well, I'm fourteen now, so Oscar will have to notice me.

I adjust my push-up bra and wander along the hallway until I get a whiff of weed. My nose scrunches at the smell, but I follow it in hopes it'll lead to Ozzy. When I push through the door, I enter a darkened room. Dark curtains cover the window, and the only light comes from a black light on the wall.

"Oscar?"

A female giggles, and I jerk my head over to see a woman straddling Duvan's lap. She's blowing smoke into his mouth. My gaze lingers on them. Duvan is several years older than Ozzy and I. Where my best friend is lanky and boyish, Duvan is all man. He's in college now and has muscles.

I'm still staring at them when Duvan seems to notice me. "Vienna. Did you lose your way from your mommy?"

The dark-haired woman in his lap jerks her head to glare at me and then laughs upon seeing me. Her boobs are giant and bounce with her giggles. I suddenly feel like a kid in comparison. I mean…I am only fourteen but most days I feel grown up. Not today, though. Today I'm staring at her chest, wishing for humongous breasts like hers.

"I was looking for Oscar," I tell him, dragging my gaze from the woman's chest.

Duvan smirks and accepts more smoke from the woman who's no longer interested in me. His hands lazily roam her butt while I stare in wonder. Maybe one day, Oscar will touch me like that. I'll have boobs, and he'll want to squeeze them with his hands.

"I should go," I murmur and start to back out.

"You should stay." The deep voice behind me causes me to jump.

Esteban.

He's the scary brother.

When I turn around, he's staring at me like I'm a little mouse with its leg caught in a trap. Like he's a big cat with sharp teeth and he wants to shred my flesh straight from my body. I shiver but attempt to calm myself. Esteban won't do anything to me—not with Daddy downstairs. My dad would kill him.

"Sit, Roja," Esteban commands, his eyes unnaturally white and evil looking in the black light. "Hang out with the adults for awhile."

When I don't move, he grabs my elbow and ushers me into Duvan's room and over to the sofa. I'm forced to sit. Esteban sits down beside me and stretches out his long legs. He's a giant compared to Ozzy. When I look at Esteban, I see someone who's no longer the young teen from my youth. He's this grown man—a man who's done terrible things, based on what Oscar has told me. I don't like him one bit.

"You smoke?" he questions as he leans across me to access the side table.

His masculine scent envelops me, and I shiver.

"I haven't tried it, no."

Duvan is too busy playing with his girlfriend to notice that his brother is attempting to get me high. My daddy will be so angry if he finds out I've been up here with these men.

"Nice bra," Esteban says with a wolfish grin.

I snap my gaze down and gape in horror. My tight light-orange T-shirt is practically transparent in the weird lighting. The white push up bra underneath glows!

"Oh my God," I shriek and cross my arms over my chest.

He laughs at me as he lights a joint. I watch the way his stubbly cheeks suck in as he inhales. The way his full lips part and the smoke billows from his mouth. Then, he smirks and hands it to me.

"Your turn."

When I don't reach for it, he shrugs. "Didn't take you for a pussy, niñita. Guess I was wrong."

Fire flashes inside me, and I snap the joint out of his hand. I bring it to my lips and attempt to mimic his actions. As soon as the strange smoke fills my lungs, I start coughing. Esteban's booming laughter upsets me as I choke. When I can finally breathe normally again, I glare at him.

"Rude."

He shrugs and slings an arm over my shoulders, hugging me to him. "Tell me something I don't know."

I relax against his hold and attempt to remain calm. I've been following these boys around alongside Oscar for as long as I can remember. The fact that they're finally letting me hang out with them makes me happy—even if they are having fun at my expense.

"I used to think this house was a castle," I tell him. My body is starting to feel loose. Free even. "Your dad is the beast of the castle." I start to giggle, imaging Mr. Rojas big and furry like Beast from my favorite childhood movie.

Esteban chuckles as he takes another hit of the joint. His fingers are dragging up and down along my arm, making me feel tingly. "What am I then, princess?"

Moans start coming from the other side of the room, and I drift my gaze over to where Duvan has his hand under the woman's skirt. She rocks against him as if she's enjoying it. It makes me wonder exactly what he's doing under there.

I look up at Esteban. His eyes have turned nearly black and he looks completely chill. Nice even. I start to giggle again, which makes him grin. "You're the snake in the garden."

"Like from the Bible?" He smirks, and it reminds me of Oscar.

Where is that boy, anyway?

"Yep. And I'm not a princess, I'm the—"

"Angel?"

I snort and shake my head. "No, the queen."

His brows scrunch together. "Queen, huh?"

"Queen of everything."

"Is that right, Roja?"

"And I'm going to rule the world one day."

He inspects me with a narrowed gaze and passes me the joint. This time, I don't choke. It sucks that Oscar isn't around. It'd be even more fun with him here.

"I'm sleepy."

"Sleep then."

I drag my eyelids open but they feel heavy. I'm not sure why I'm so out of it. My thoughts linger in the past. I can almost smell the weed. Curling against Esteban, I close my eyes again. That day when I'd smoked pot with him, I'd woken up on the couch alone. When I sat up to try and figure out where I was, I realized that although I was fully dressed, my bra was gone.

"You took my bra off that day while I slept, didn't you?" I question softly.

He chuckles, and it reminds me so much of that day. "I wanted it. And I take what I want."

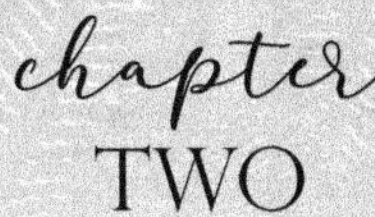

TWO

Oscar

I stare at my brother from across the table at the safe house and truly inspect him. It's been months since I last saw him. When he all but vanished after fucking up one of my best friends. My own brother fucked and drugged his brother's wife. Duvan had wanted to kill him but never got the chance.

An ache forms in my chest for the loss of my brother. And that ache only grows when I think about my father on his knees in the shipping container, desperately trying to hold the wounds in his stomach closed. I watched my father die that day. Watched him bleed out and collapse to the floor. It was as though Brie held his fate in her hands because she asked Diego to kill him. To my surprise, the motherfucker obeyed her. That's something I'll never be able to forgive her for. Colluding with a Rojas enemy is unforgivable.

I close my eyes for a moment but that only makes the memory more vivid. Quickly, I stare back at the man who is the only family I have left. My brother's dark eyes are narrowed and his jaw is clenched. The silvery scar that runs down the side of his face glistens under the light of the dining room table. I'd been eleven years old the day he got it. I watched my badass brother get his ass kicked by someone somehow scarier than him. All over a girl.

He reaches up and scratches at the dark hair that speckles his jaw as he scrutinizes me with a guarded expression. His hair once used to be closely shaved to his head, but it's long since grown out. Esteban looks more like Duvan and I when he has the unruliness about him. More passionate than calculating.

"Where is she?" My tone is calm even though my hands clench into fists.

"I've been taking care of her. She's sleeping right now."

The anxiety that's been swarming in my stomach like a storm of pissed-off bees lessens. "You didn't hurt her? Where's she been since her dad was killed? Where's her mother?"

He crosses his arms over his chest and leans back. Esteban is always dressed nicely. Duvan took a page from his book and dressed the same. Our father instilled that in us. *Dress like kings because you are all my little princes.* Now that Papá is gone, I dress how I want. Compared to my older brother, I'm nothing but a boy dressed sloppily in jeans and a T-shirt.

"Vee is not hurt," he tells me, his voice carrying a slight edge to it. "Her mother is off somewhere being the whore she always was. I've helped Vee manage the properties by paying the bills for her."

I let out a sigh of relief. "Can you wake her? I miss her."

Vee has been one of my closest friends since the day she showed up in our kitchen, covered in blood at the age of five. I remember thinking she was sort of scary, but when she smiled all fear evaporated. We'd been connected at the hip ever since. For the longest time, we'd even thought our fathers would arrange for us to marry. It seemed logical, but we both knew our hearts weren't in it. A marriage between the Berkleys and the Rojas' would have been on paper only. At least for our parents, anyway. But she was my best friend, and I'd always imagined I'd fall deeply in love with her the way she seemed to love me. *One day.*

"Let her sleep," Esteban says and pushes a bottle of tequila my way. "Tonight, we drink. I've missed you, *hermanito*."

I take a swig from the bottle and enjoy the way it burns my throat. It seems to sharpen my senses, something I am thankful for. Ever since Papá was brutally murdered by Diego Gomez, my mind has been muddled with confusion, heartache, and an all-consuming thirst for vengeance. The only thing that takes the edge off are the pills I take from time to time—something has to calm me the fuck down. Now that I'm here with Esteban, though, we can begin to formulate a plan and deal with this shit, so I don't have to obsess over it all the damn time.

"I want to kill him," I tell him in a blunt tone and swallow down more of the fiery tequila.

Esteban snags the bottle from me and takes a swallow. "Who are we killing?"

I growl and slam my fist on the table. "Diego!"

He narrows his gaze at me. "Diego is the most powerful man in Colombia right now. You think you're going to stomp right in there and kill him without any sort of resistance?"

My chest deflates as his words sink in. Anger consumes me but I have no outlet for it. "So we make a plan."

"We have no men," Esteban reminds me. "It will take some time to talk to Papá's and Duvan's men so that we can begin to gather our army. These things don't happen overnight, Oz."

I run my fingers through my wild hair. It now hangs in my eyes, but I can't be bothered to cut it. I'm sure to my put-together brother, I look like a bratty kid. That's how he's always seen me. But inside…inside I am raging like a beast. Duvan always favored our mother. And I thought perhaps I was like her too. At one time, maybe I was. Now, though, I am different. Anger throbs within me, like some uncaged beast waiting to be set free. Sometimes, when I look in the mirror, I don't see myself. I see the cold eyes of my father.

"He took our home."

Esteban is mid swallow when his eyes meet mine. "W-What?"

"After Diego killed Papá, he went back to Colombia and he took our childhood home," I hiss. "The same home Mami died in. He just moved the fuck in there like he's the goddamned king of our castle."

Esteban's eyes blaze with rage. He's normally calm and collected, but I know I struck a nerve. When our mother died, I think all the humanity in Esteban died with her. He'd taken it the hardest. It was at that point, I didn't know my brother anymore. All memories of us playing in the woods by our house and Esteban saving me from drowning in a nearby river when I was a toddler were wiped clean.

"We have to get it back," he growls and chugs more of the tequila before passing it back to me. "We will."

His black eyebrows pinch together, and I can see the wheels turning in his head. My brother is smart. Together we'll devise a plan.

Over the next two hours, we become more and more drunk. Our plans to take over the world are interrupted when a flash of red darts into the kitchen. Esteban is leaned back in his chair with his feet on the table, looking relaxed as fuck.

But as soon as she comes into view, we both sober up quickly.

"Ozzy?"

Vee's bright green eyes are wide and innocent looking. Her pink lips are parted in surprise at seeing me. Her trademark wild red mane is in messy tangles all over her head as if she hasn't brushed it in quite some time. Of course she's cute as ever—always has been—but what has my attention are her tits.

"Why are you naked?" I choke out, my dick hardening in my jeans. Once, at her apartment, she'd begged through her tears for me to take her virginity. Back then, I was a different man. I had morals and valued our friendship. Sure, I couldn't help but kiss her but I did refrain from popping her cherry. But now? Fuck…I'd hit that for damn sure.

Esteban growls and reaches for her. Her eyes tear away from mine to find his. The small moment of clarity seems to dissipate as she gets a glassy-eyed look. A small smile forms on her pouty lips. She all but runs to him. I gape in confusion as she sits in his lap and curls against him.

What the fuck is happening?

"Vee?" I snap, and ask again, through gritted teeth, "Why are you naked?"

Esteban strokes her messy hair and levels me with a hard gaze. "We're together, and she wasn't expecting company."

My gaze is fixated on her perfectly rounded tits. I have no words. I have no idea what the hell is going on. This is far from what I expected to find here. If she's "together" with Esteban, there's no doubt in my mind they're fucking. The thought that she isn't a virgin anymore saddens me. I guess I always thought she'd be there when I was ready.

"Can you put some clothes on?" I hiss through clenched teeth. There's no way I can carry on this conversation with her succulent tits on full display. She looks up at Esteban in question. As if she needs permission from him to dress. A flash of fire blazes inside me. This isn't the Vee I know. The Vee I know isn't controlled by anyone.

"Take my shirt," he tells her and strokes her cheek.

She leans in to his touch and smiles. It's creepy as fuck.

"Thank you," she murmurs as she starts delicately plucking through his buttons. Once she unfastens them all, he slips out of his dress shirt and helps her into it. He fastens one button in front of her tits before pulling her against his chest.

"How long you two been together?" I question, my voice coming out with a slight bite.

Vee stiffens for a moment but won't meet my gaze. "Months now, right Esteban?"

He continues to pet her and nods. "Yep. Might even be love." His gaze darts to mine and he smirks. The look says, *I won the fucking prize.* It makes my blood boil. Vee is *my* age. She was *my* friend growing up. She was *mine.*

Was.

She looks up at him in confusion. "Love?"

Esteban shrugs and runs his thumb across her bottom lip. "Could be. You hungry, Roja?"

Vee has pretty smiles. But the one she's giving him right now is unlike any other I've seen before. Brilliant like a thousand rays of sunlight.

"Please," she begs. "I'm so hungry."

He pushes her off his lap and gives her ass a little pinch. "Go take a quick shower, and I'll have it ready for you."

She lets out a squeal before throwing her arms around his neck. "Thank you!" Her lips find his and they kiss as if they're in a goddamned porno. It fucking nauseates me.

When she's gone, he rises and begins making a sandwich. He pours her a giant glass of milk. Then, he reaches into his pocket, retrieves a pill, crushes it with a knife, and drops the dust crumbles into the milk.

I scowl. "What the fuck did you just put in her drink?"

His eyes pierce mine. "She likes it. Mind your own fucking business."

Those words cut through me, and I'm transported to the past.

"Mind your own fucking business," Esteban growls.

I ignore the sounds of Duvan banging Luz in the corner. Her little sister and I go to school together. Both Luz and Ana are skanks. I don't know why Duvan sleeps with her. Everyone has slept with Luz and Ana. I know for a fact Esteban has been with Luz, too. And just yesterday, Ana sucked my dick between classes.

"Why do you have her bra?" I demand through clenched teeth. I may only be halfway through fourteen years of age, but I would try to kick his ass if I had to. Of course Esteban would pummel me, but I bet I'd get a hit or two in on him.

"She gave it to me," he says simply and brings one of the white padded cups to his nose to inhale. "So sweet."

I glare at him and then dart my gaze down to Vee. Her shirt is still on, but now I can see her small nipples through the fabric. She's sleeping peacefully. Did she really give it to him?

"Leave her alone," I mutter in defeat. "She deserves someone better than you fucking with her."

He smirks. "Like you? Have you stolen her V-card yet, Oz?"

"No," I snap.

"Why not? You've racked up quite the collection of V-cards lately, haven't you? Duvan tells me you've fucked your way through most of the girls at your school."

Irritation bubbles through me. "Vee's my friend. It's not like that."

"Ahhh," he says with a malicious grin. "So I'm free to take it."

"Fuck you!"

I hear a zipper behind me, and then Duvan saunters up next to me wearing nothing but a pair of jeans and stinking like sex. He slings an arm over my shoulder. I can tell he's high as fuck.

"Why are you two assholes fighting in my room?" Duvan questions, a lazy smile on his face.

I ignore him and squat down in front of the sofa. Vee looks so innocent with her head in Esteban's lap as she sleeps. Doesn't she know my brother is evil? I slide my arms beneath her to lift her up, but Esteban's giant hand pushes down on her breast through her shirt to keep me from lifting her.

"She stays," he taunts, a challenge gleaming in his eyes.

"Take your hand off of her before I break it," I snarl and meet his glare. "She goes with me."

Both him and Duvan start laughing at my valiant effort to protect my friend. I'm able to snag her and escape without any more crap from the two assholes. Once she's settled in my dark room under the blankets, I crawl in behind her to spoon her.

She's my best friend, and I'll be damned if I let them fuck with her.

"I missed you, Ozzy," she murmurs, half asleep.

"Missed you too, Vee. Now sleep this shit off so your dad doesn't kill us."

She squirms a little, which makes my cock harden against her ass. I'll have to go visit Ana later to get laid or I'll end up doing something stupid like fucking my best friend. The image of her naked and beneath me only makes my cock harder, so I try to envision other things that don't turn me on. Like Esteban, the fucker. But then my active imagination goes to him with Vee underneath him. His teeth on her tiny tits, marking her up like some kind of savage beast. My erection is gone but now I'm just raging with fury. With Vee turning into a woman, she'll start to be a problem when she visits. Esteban likes to conquer and Duvan likes to fuck. Between the two of them, one of them will corrupt her if I don't protect her.

"I'll keep you safe," I assure her in the faintest of whispers.

I'm snapped from my inner thoughts when a fresh-faced Vee bounces into the kitchen. Her eyes glitter with excitement, which makes my chest ache. At one time, she wanted me. Not him. Me. And now, one of the few people I have left in this world doesn't want me anymore.

"I'm so hungry," she tells Esteban as she eyeballs the sandwich he's set out for her on the table.

"I know. Sit." He motions for the chair that he's dragged right beside him. "Eat."

Her red hair looks darker now that it's wet. It hasn't been combed through and she isn't wearing any makeup whatsoever. It makes her seem younger, like that night I rescued her from Esteban's predator ass when she was just fourteen.

I guess it's too late to rescue her now. She's clearly head over fucking heels for him. Every look she flashes him is filled with adoration and love. I'm completely ignored. As she starts to eat, Esteban leans forward to watch her. She devours the sandwich in record speed. Then, she chugs the milk. It isn't until she finishes that I remember him putting something in it.

Fuck.

I'm the worst goddamned friend ever.

"Can I have more?" she pleads with him, sadness pulling on her cute features. "Please."

He pats her while he shakes his head. "No. Not right now. I don't want you to get sick."

She frowns but obeys. "Okay."

"Let's go outside on the porch and talk," Esteban says as he stands. She takes his hand as if it's normal and lets him guide her outside. I stare after them. The shirt he made her wear swallows her, but it's white and completely see-through. It's like she's fucked in the head or something.

I snag the tequila bottle and make my way outside. It's dark and the ocean is volatile as a storm starts to roll in. The wind is brusque and way too cold for her to be out here with no clothes on. Esteban is just wearing his wife beater, so I'm sure he's cold too. But neither of them seem bothered as they sit down in the wicker love seat. I sit across from them in a single chair.

Esteban and I discuss Diego Gomez. We each state what we know of his territory and inner workings. And as the night progresses, the liquor begins to numb me to my core. Esteban becomes more handsy, while Vee seems to squirm with need. Whatever he gave her appears to be working because she is practically humping his leg.

We've all gone quiet. The two of them are wrapped up in each other while I stare like some perverted voyeur. I guess I don't get how she's suddenly so into my brother. Everyone always knew Vee wanted me. I knew this. Vee knew this. Our friends and family. But I cared for her as a friend, which always had me keeping my dick in my pants. There were so many times when I could have fucked her, and she would have let me. I didn't, though.

And now, apparently, the time has passed.

My best friend has moved on to my fucking brother instead.

Vee wasn't ever supposed to be his.

I'm still lost in thought when I hear the pop of a button and then see a flash of white as the shirt falls to the floor. Her back is to me and she's straddling my brother's lap. I've seen both my brothers fucking before. Plenty of times. But seeing my best friend all but beg for my brother's cock pisses me off. What pisses me off more is that the curve of her ass has my cock harder than fucking stone.

Vee wasn't ever supposed to be his.

My gaze stays on her ass as she rubs herself against him through his slacks. Her fingers are locked in his hair and she keeps begging.

"Please, Esteban."

Her breathy tone is too much. I've never craved Vee sexually. Sure, I'd thought about boning her a time or two, because I was a horny little shit, but never once did I just crave her. Yet now, I can't stop thinking about her full tits and round ass. About the fact that my brother will soon be inside her.

I rub at my cock through my jeans, seeking relief. When I lift my gaze, I see that my brother caught the movement. He smirks, like all those times he'd fucked a woman in front of me before. A smirk that says, *it's okay, you can watch and maybe learn a thing or two.*

My jaw clenches when I hear the buckle of his belt jangle. Soon, he's got his pants pushed down his thighs. Then, I hear the tear of a condom packet. He's about to fuck her right in front of me. I should just get up and let them do their shit. I don't want to fucking see this.

But I don't move.

I do want to see.

"Oz is turned on, Roja," he growls. "Let my baby brother see what's mine." He grabs her hips and twists her so that she's facing me. My gaze falls to her large tits, which bounce with her movement, and then roam over her flat stomach to the thin tuft of red hair between her thighs. I can see my brother's dick sliding in and out of her. Her juices soaking his cock. I let out a groan as my eyes travel back up her creamy curves to her face.

"Mmm," she murmurs as she rubs at her nipples.

My brother grips her hair and yanks her back. Her tits stick out even farther. I'm aching to fist my cock right now. Vee looks so fucking hot, and I'm a damn idiot for not ever hitting that before. Her full lips are swollen and parted as she moans. Those green eyes—eyes that always light up with the fire typical of redheads—have been dulled. She's high as fuck on whatever he gave her.

"Whom do you belong to?" Esteban murmurs as he thrusts his hips up.

She shudders. "You."

Vee wasn't ever supposed to be his.

My cock is seriously straining in my jeans now. I can't fucking deal with how painful it is so I unzip my jeans and free it. When I start stroking myself, I pretend that it's me she's riding. I bet her pussy is so goddamned tight.

"Ahh," Esteban taunts. "Baby brother can't control himself around you."

I don't look at him but instead meet her gaze. The adoration she used to look at me with is vacant from her eyes. Instead, all I find there is desperation. Desperation to reach that high she's chasing.

Vee wasn't ever supposed to be his.

Her eyes lock on my cock and she bites her lip. It's when she lets out a moan as an orgasm overtakes her that I lose it. Hot semen shoots up my chest, wetting my T-shirt. My cock throbs as I drain the rest of my release. The moment I come down from my climax, reality sets in.

I just got off watching my rapist brother fuck my high-off-her-ass best friend.

I'm a fucking asshole.

chapter
THREE

Vee

The room spins around me as Esteban carries me inside. Everything is so foggy lately. Like I'm in a dream. And all I want to do is eat and fuck. As if I'm some animal.

"I'm hungry," I whine when Esteban lays me on the mattress.

"Tomorrow," he tells me and stumbles into the bathroom. When he emerges some time later, he's clean from a shower but still looks drunk. He falls into the bed face first.

Even through my haze, I realize this is the first time he's dropped his guard since he's had me here at this San Diego safe house. My brain is garbled and confused. A part of me feels like this is important. That I should do something about it. But a bigger part of me wonders if he'll notice if I sneak out to make a sandwich. My stomach growls as if to answer me.

Eventually, after what feels like hours, I decide to sneak out. The only goal in my head is food. I stumble through the darkness, now that all the lights have been shut off, in a journey to the kitchen. I'm careful as I tiptoe into the kitchen. I'll just sneak a banana or something and slip back into bed. Esteban will never know. As quietly as I can, I open the cupboards on a hunt for something quick and edible. I find the jar of peanut butter, which makes my stomach growl again. Quickly, I twist off the top and stick my finger inside to scoop out some. It tastes so good that I let out an embarrassing moan. I'm scooping out another heap with my fingers when I sense someone else's presence.

Jerking my head toward the doorway, I'm shocked to see Ozzy standing there in nothing but his boxers. His hair is messy like he's been sleeping. Now that I'm getting some food in my belly, I'm able to wade through some of the fog.

"I was hungry," I murmur as I suck on my finger.

His eyes darken and he prowls forward. Old familiar feelings stir in my belly. So many times I imagined scenes where he'd find me naked and then claim me. Lust swims in his gaze. Desire for me.

Esteban would kill him for looking at me like that.

"He doesn't let you wear clothes?" he questions, his voice husky as he steps closer.

I shake my head. "No."

He sways on his feet and I remember how much tequila he drank earlier. When he grips my wrist, I let out a whimper. I watch with sadness as he draws my peanut-butter-covered fingers to his mouth. My stomach continues to growl, and yet, here he is sucking the precious food off my hand.

"You're a natural seductress," he tells me as he licks his lips. Then, his mouth sucks on two of my fingers at a time. My nipples harden and I hate that my body responds to him. Esteban made it very clear that my feelings for Oscar were over.

"I just want to eat," I tell him.

He pushes my hand between my thighs and smears the creamy goodness still left on my fingers along the lips of my pussy. "So do I."

I start to argue but then he's on his knees. His mouth is on me, sucking off the peanut butter with vigor. I nearly drop the vat of peanut butter on his head. Stars glitter in my vision. My mind is still foggy, but I feel a niggling sensation creeping over me. Telling me this is wrong. That this will get me in a lot of trouble.

What if Esteban makes me go back to the metal box?

What if I starve again?

A tear snakes its way down my cheek, and I desperately shovel more peanut butter into my mouth. His tongue is on my clit, lapping at me as he licks away the food he smeared there. Small jolts of pleasure prickle through me here and there, but I mostly wish he would stop before everything blows up in our faces. I let out a groan when he urges my leg over his shoulder. His mouth cleans every single smudge of peanut butter off my pussy.

"You're so hot," he breathes against me.

I frown as I suck more peanut butter off my fingers. "Please stop."

He presses a kiss to my clit before standing. His lips are quirked up into the mischievous smile I remember so well. It makes my heart squeeze from the memory of how I used to feel about him.

"Did you come?" he questions as he steals my jar from me.

I growl. "Give it back."

"There she is. Guess the mollies or whatever the fuck he gave to you are fading. The bitch is waking up," he says with relief.

My eyes are fixated on the jar of peanut butter. I can't believe he stole it from me. I'm so damn hungry. Anger surges through me, and I attempt to take it back, but he holds it high over his head.

"While my tongue was between your legs, I came up with a plan. Tomorrow, we're going to Colombia."

I freeze and stare at him. "I'm staying with Esteban."

He gives me back my peanut butter and then sets to wetting a cloth. I'm too focused on my only source of food to even notice that he cleans me up between my legs.

"Vee," he tells me with a smile. "I have a plan to take back what belongs to our families. You'll be a Rojas one day, so this should be important to you."

A Rojas?

For so many years I wanted that…but with Oscar.

Now, I try to imagine being married to his brother.

My fantasies are jumbled and messy. Right now I don't think I like them either way. A thundering in my head starts to form again as I try to work out my future.

I don't want to believe it but I know, deep down, Esteban is drugging me and probably has been for some time.

That must be why I'm so out of it. So animalistic.

The only thing that explains the headaches and confusion.

"Go to sleep. Tomorrow, we're going to war. And you, Vee," he says with a smile as he strokes my cheek, "are going to help us."

"What is this place?" I question as I peer out a window that faces a pond. The dress that sticks to my body feels heavy and strange after months of not wearing anything. When I don't get a response, I turn to regard Esteban.

His arms are crossed over his chest while he glares at me as if the dress disgusts him as well. But we traveled to Colombia, and I couldn't exactly do it naked. I shiver under his gaze.

"Where are we?" I ask again, my voice softer this time. Now that the fog no longer confuses me and the headaches aren't crushing me, I've had a lot of time to think. I've had a lot of time to remember.

He took me and my mother. Seeing the gun pressed against my mother's temple was all the incentive I needed to willingly follow Esteban. Had I known I was subjecting myself to dark isolation for months in a metal box, I'd have run for the hills. Had I known he'd force his cock into me while I screamed in pain, I'd have put up a bigger fight. Had I known he'd make me watch my mother become addicted to heroin only to have to watch her die later, I'd have tried to kill him.

But I didn't know. Deep down, I trusted him not to hurt me. I thought we had history. I'd assumed that because our fathers had been business partners and I visited the Rojas's every summer, that Esteban would have a soft spot for me.

And yet he hurt me.

So many times.

He was the deliverer of pain, but then he'd follow it up with pleasure. All those nights in that dark box, he'd turned me into some sexually hungry animal that fed off him. Now that my mind has cleared, I know he drugged me then too. I'd been too out of my head to understand it for what it was.

He. Drugged. Me.

Just like my mother.

Just like Brie.

My heart squeezes at the thought of my adopted sister and best friend, other than Oscar. When Daddy told me he was adopting her, I'd been elated. I thought he wanted me to have a friend being that I was home schooled and lonely. Later, I learned he adopted her to take my place as the betrothed to the Rojas family. At the time, I was embarrassed but having her in my life has outweighed all of that.

If she were here, my feisty friend would tell me what to do. She'd tell me to get away from Esteban—that he's a monster. I bet she would even help me, too.

I swallow down the emotion in my throat. The last thing I need is for these two men to see me weak. I'll have to figure out what to do on my own.

I'm a Berkley.

A badass bitch.

I just need to be a calculating bitch.

It takes everything inside of me to remain calm and not fly off the handle. I need to be smart. Going off on Esteban for everything he's done seems like a dangerous move. And I still can't argue the way he makes me feel when it's just the two of us. That's the most frustrating part of it all. Despite my eagerness to make him pay, I still can't deny the way my pussy seems to flare to life around him. He truly did train my body. But he'll never own my mind if I have anything to say about it.

"Papá's safe house," Ozzy answers as he strolls into the room. My nostrils flare when I see him. Of course he looks sexy as ever in his playboy Ozzy way, but it doesn't excite me like it used to. Instead, irritation bubbles up inside me.

"So what's the plan?" I question as I let my gaze dart back and forth between the two men who each have their own special grip on my heart.

"It's better if you don't know the plan," Oscar says plainly.

I scowl at him and give Esteban a pleading look that sometimes works on him when he's being soft. His gaze loses some of its hardness as he holds a hand out to me. My gut instinct tells me to demand they tell me what's going on. To stomp my feet and scream at them both until I get my way. But the brain that had been locked away while Esteban kept me has begun to work full throttle again. And because of that, I go willingly to Esteban.

His arm snakes around my waist and he pulls me possessively against him. "I don't like the plan."

"Don't tell her," Ozzy warns.

The fire explodes inside of me, and I twist to glare at him. "Tell me the damn plan, asshole!"

Hurt flashes in his eyes, but I don't care. Oscar has given me the puppy dog eyes one too many times, and right now, I'm immune. Who knows? Maybe they'll never work on me again.

"Roja," Esteban murmurs as his lips find my neck. "The plan is fucking stupid."

"So what's plan B then?" I question as my eyes flutter closed. When he's touching me, I lose all sense of reality. That smart little brain shuts off and lets my pussy call the shots.

"There is no plan B. It's plan V," Oscar grunts. "You're the plan."

I tug away to unlatch myself from Esteban's dizzying kisses on my throat. "Care to explain?"

Esteban twists me in his arms so that we're facing each other. His hand slides to my throat and he holds me gently. "Women are his weakness. We'll use you to infiltrate his operation from the inside out. He has too many men to just attack. You'll kill him and then, by the time his men are in chaos over what to do after that happens, we'll have amassed our own men to take over." He growls and anger gleams in his dark eyes. "He stole our childhood home. We want it back."

I blink at him in confusion. "You want to send me straight to him? To flirt with him until his back is turned, and then what? Stab him in the back? I've never killed anyone before!" My chest heaves as I freak out. Are these two knuckleheads insane? They want me to invade this guy's life and kill him just because they want their stupid house back? This is the worst idea ever.

"Not flirt," Esteban snaps. "Fuck."

White heat colors my vision as fury seeps its way into my bones. Anger is a safer emotion than the terror that barely hides behind it. "What?" My voice is shrill. "But I thought I was yours!"

The monster that sometimes presents itself in his eyes rages forward. "You. *Are*. Mine. And the moment we have our shit back, I'm going to marry you and put fucking babies inside of you. But first," he snarls, his grip on my throat tightening. "First we fight. First we take."

My hands fist at my sides, but I refuse to lose control right now. I'm not one hundred percent myself so I need to chill the hell out before I make the wrong move. If Daddy ever taught me anything, it was to always know my enemy. It was to outsmart them all. He was so smart and successful. I can do this.

"He'll be suspicious. Won't he figure out who my father is? Won't he know I'm connected to you guys?" I hiss out my questions until Esteban releases my throat. I rub at my flesh and pin him with a fiery glare. "What if I don't *want* to have sex with him? What if he hurts me?" My voice cracks. "I'm scared." I will not cry. I will not whine. But a part of me is upset and furious. This thing with Esteban is wrong and fucked up, but it's the only evil I know right now. He even said babies and marriage. So why do I once again just feel like a pawn in their game? A little girl in a room full of big bad wolves.

Oscar lets out a snide laugh. "You're pretty good at shaking your tits when you want something. So shake your tits for Diego and kill him. Then you get what you so desperately want." He motions for Esteban, but I don't miss the flicker of jealousy in his eyes. At one time, I wanted to see that look so badly. Today it's infuriating me.

"You want to be a Rojas? Well, then there are just certain things you must do," Esteban snaps with a shrug. "This is one of them."

I'm stung by his words. "But—"

His fingers crush into my jaw as he draws me closer. "No buts. You do this and we move on. You don't fuck any other men ever again."

Rage is blooming up inside of me. My head is clear—so fucking crystal clear—and I can see the big picture. How could I let myself get caught up in this man? He's been toying with me since I was a child.

Emotion chokes me, but I refuse to cry. I wish Brie were here. The thought once again hits me like a sucker punch to my gut. She was a victim. *I* am a victim. Pain slices through my chest as realization sets in. She was never the villain.

The villain is right in front of me.

He presses a soft kiss to my lips, and I fight the urge to bite him.

"So tonight," Oscar says with a growl, "we implement part one of the plan. Then, we deliver you right to his den."

Terror fights its way up inside of me. What if this Diego is like their father? Camilo always scared me half to death. I'm headed for some crazy old man's house to let him fuck me so I can kill him in his sleep. Fucking wonderful.

"But—" I start, but Esteban crams something into my mouth.

An acrid taste makes me gag, but he pushes the pill toward the back of my throat until I'm forced to swallow.

"This should make you more compliant," Esteban says before he shoves me away from him.

I blink after him in confusion as he storms away, leaving me with Oscar. Jerking my head over my shoulder, I see him prowling forward. I'm about to lay into him when he rears his fist back and socks me in the eye.

I gape at him in horror and implore him with my stare as my trembling fingers touch my face that now screams in pain. Our eyes meet for a moment, and I search his gaze for guilt or sorrow or anything to indicate what just happened was an accident.

He clenches his jaw and his dark eyes are wild but regret swims just beneath the surface of his glare. I'm about to tearfully throw myself into his arms when he pulls his fist back again. The pain this time, as my best friend cracks me in the face, is overwhelming.

Make that my *ex* best friend.

The innocent boy I once knew has been slaughtered by this animal.

I crumple to the floor like a sack of potatoes and my world immediately fades to black.

I want to open my eyes but they feel too heavy. My mind is a cloud of darkness as I try and make sense of my surroundings. I can hear water running.

God, my face hurts. I groan and try to reach out for something to ground me. Whatever I'm touching is soft.

A bed.

I'm on a bed.

I crack an eye open and light streams in from the bathroom door that adjoins to the bedroom I'm in. Pipes squeak when someone turns off the shower. My limbs are heavy. Whatever they gave me is different than what I've had in the past.

I feel as though I'm paralyzed.

Panic skitters through me when a dark shadow fills the doorway.

Esteban.

He drops the towel that's wrapped around his waist and saunters toward the bed. I attempt to roll away from him but my body refuses to move. Hell, I can barely keep my eyes open.

"You must not forget who you belong to," he bites out as he fumbles around in the bedside drawer. He pulls out a condom and leaves the drawer sitting wide open. I can't look away as he rips open the foil and rolls the rubber down his cock.

The bed dips as he joins me. I can't move, so he manhandles my body so that my legs are spread wide open. My heart races so fast I think it'll explode at any minute.

Please don't.

My thoughts don't leave my mouth. They stay locked up inside my head. I beg him with my eyes, but I'm ignored.

"Don't worry," he assures me. "I'll lube you up so it doesn't hurt." He spits into his hand and then rubs his cock with it.

I want to close my eyes, but since they're the only things apparently working right now, I simply stare at him. He grips his cock as he pushes into me. I can feel the pressure but that's it. I've had sex with Esteban enough times to know that by the look of bliss on his face, he's deep inside me.

Anger surges within me and I glare at him. He doesn't notice.

Thrust after thrust, he takes what he wants, but I don't enjoy it this time.

If I was confused before, I certainly am not now.

Esteban is evil. Always has been. To think I thought he loved me in some fucked up way. Stupid girl. Hate for this man claws at me from the inside out. I'm nothing but an object to shove his dick into.

One day, when I'm not immobile, I will figure out a way to make him pay for this.

"You're mine," he hisses. "Mine."

Repeatedly he reminds me of this as he fucks me.

I am nobody's.

The closer he gets to orgasm, the angrier he seems to get. His palm finds my throat and he grips it so tight that the corners of my vision begin to darken. Nothing can be heard aside from his furious grunts and my ragged hisses of breath.

I black out completely.

When I come to, it's because I hear Oscar shouting at Esteban in the other room.

"Where are you going?" Oscar demands.

"I need to take a fucking walk to clear my head," Esteban snarls back.

The windows in the house rattle when he slams the door behind him. My heart is thundering in my chest and seems loud compared to the sudden silence. But then footsteps creak down the hallway. I can't see him but I feel his presence.

Help me, Oscar.

He hit me. Right in the face. Twice. But I could almost forgive him for that if he'd get me out of this mess.

Why did you hit me, Oscar?

That question plays over and over again in my head.

"Oh, Vee," he murmurs as he grabs something from the drawer. "We'll have to make this quick."

I want to ask him what he means, but then I hear his zipper go down and the familiar tear of a foil packet. I'm screaming inside for him to snap out of whatever shit he's going through. This is not Oscar. This is not the boy I've chased after since I was five years old. He rounds the side of the bed and climbs on to join me. His brows are furled together in concentration as he pushes my knees apart.

I try to meet his gaze, but he won't look at me. Instead, his focus is on his cock. More pressure within me. Some feeling is coming back. I know I'll be sore after this.

Please stop.

Nobody hears me.

Nobody fucking hears me.

He grabs the front of my dress and yanks it down to free one of my breasts. His mouth latches on to it. I can't feel it but I can hear the slurping sounds as he sucks on my flesh. A hard thrust slides me farther up the bed and a loud bang resounds.

Bang! Bang! Bang!

With each brutal thrust, my head slams against the headboard. Since some of my feeling is coming back, a thundering inside my skull begins to take hold. My vision blurs from being jarred by the repeated hits.

"Fuck," he murmurs, his eyes are wide, black, and unfamiliar as an animal takes over. "I knew you'd feel fucking amazing."

I check out.

I can't stare at someone who I thought I loved while they rape me as if I'm nothing more than a toy to be used and abused. Our history. Our friendship. Our bond. Gone in an instant.

Despite my numb state, the fire within me is beginning to roar. It intensifies with each breath I take.

I'm going to kill them.

Both of them.

"Yes," he grunts, his movement jerky and out of control. "Fuck yes!"

I glare at him. Our eyes eventually meet. Guilt flashes in his dark brown orbs.

"Vee…" he trails off and clenches his jaw.

"Y-You—" My voice is but a whisper but at least it's working. I start to try to scream but his palm slaps over my mouth.

"Shhh," he hisses, his thrusting harder than before. Conflict is written all over his face but the animal bucking into me seems to win. "Shhhh."

I send him the nastiest hate-filled stare I can muster, but he's once again not making eye contact. Beads of sweat form on his forehead as he concentrates on his brutality. I guess keeping the Oscar I thought I knew so well buried while this thing takes over is hard work. He lets out a grunt and his body stiffens. Then, as if his pants are on fire, he yanks out of me and lets go of my mouth. He all but runs to the bathroom, and soon the toilet flushes. When he remerges, his clothes have been righted and he's running a nervous hand through his hair.

"Y-You…" I whisper out, the accusation thick in the one word.

He shoves his hand into his pocket and quickly retrieves a pill. Then, he's striding over to me. The pill is pushed past my tongue and he forces it down my throat.

"Sleep now, Vee." His eyes darken as he leans forward and kisses my forehead. "This was all a dream."

I close my eyes because I can't look at him any longer. He's killed something that could have been beautiful. With this one single act, he's poured a lifetime of love down the drain.

This wasn't a dream.

It was a nightmare.

And when I wake up from it, I will make him pay.

Everything is blurry and confusing.

I can tell I'm in a car by the way it bounces along gravel and the sound of the engine loud in my ears. When I go to move my hands, I attempt to cry out upon noticing they're bound behind me. Tape covers my mouth, preventing me from making much noise. I'm hurting badly. Every muscle in my body aches. Bruises. Cuts. Hell, I may even have a broken rib judging from the way one side of me feels as though I'm on fire.

The plan.

Diego wouldn't be suspicious because they had *this* plan. Drop me off on the enemy's doorstep bloodied, raped, and beaten. Deliver me as a broken pawn that the cartel king can use to his advantage.

I've never hurt so much in my life. What concerns me most is the ache between my legs. Did they fuck me more while I was unconscious?

Tears should be falling yet they don't.

I'm fucking pissed.

My thoughts dissipate when the vehicle stops. Soon, the trunk opens, and Esteban appears in front of me. He grabs my elbow and hefts me out. His eyes are positively manic. There's no reaching the man who sometimes showed me some degree of humanity. The monster has been unleashed.

"Kill him and then you can come back home to me," he snarls against my ear as he roughly cups me between my legs. "Don't worry, I fucked you one last time so you'd stink of me when you meet that motherfucker."

I jerk my head to meet his gaze. The movement causes the dark night to spin around me due to whatever drugs he forced upon me. But when it slows back down and I lock onto his monstrous eyes, I send him a message of my own.

I'll kill him and then I'll come back to kill you too.

He must receive my message loud and clear because he fucking head butts me.

Can this night get any worse?

I'm thinking about how the night has only just begun when my world once again fades to black…

chapter
FOUR

Diego

"Claudia and Carmen are destroying the library," Jorge, one of my best men, announces. He's dressed neatly in a suit, but I know he's packing at least seven weapons under the fabric. Weapons meant to protect me. Not that I necessarily need protection, but when you have an entire country under your thumb, you tend to develop enemies along the way and unfortunately it becomes a necessity. I might be able to take them on one by one, but in the event they all come at me at once, I'd be fucked. So I suppose I do need Jorge and my men.

I exhale a puff of cigar smoke and arch an eyebrow at him. "Thank you for the warning, chico. I won't go into the library."

His jaw clenches in annoyance. "No, sir," he groans. "What do you want me to do about your wives?"

Only two out of my five women at war seems like a good day. About a year ago, my dick said, *let's have five wives*, against my brain's wishes. Now my dick takes back his goddamned words. They're all pissing me the fuck off. Pussy on demand had seemed like a grand idea back then, but of course it has supremely backfired on me. I should bring both Claudia and Carmen, wives number three and four, in here to fight over my cock since they're both in a bitchy mood. But then I'd have to look at them. Both are similar in appearance with their thick dark manes and olive-colored skin. Both bitches have the biggest fucking mouths in this country. I thought those mouths would be good for sucking cock. The problem is the other twenty-three hours of the day when they don't have a dick stuffed in their mouths.

"Get rid of them," I grumble and take another puff of my cigar.

He pulls a knife from his belt, and I shake my head.

"I didn't mean fucking off them, Jorge. I meant make them go away."

I pinch the bridge of my nose and will the tension to leave my shoulders. Everything is so goddamned complicated lately.

"You're not technically married to any of them. You don't owe them anything," he mumbles as he sheaths his knife.

"Fine. Send them away." Send them away forever.

"Even Olga?" he questions, a brief flash of hurt in his normally hard gaze. It's then I realize he's been fucking wife number two.

I meet his eyes with a glare. "Make her go away too. Even if it is to your bungalow. I don't give a fuck anymore. This was supposed to be for my benefit. They're worse than goddamned children."

"Martha and Rosa?" he questions.

Even though wives numbered in my head as five and six are the least problematic, they're both on the fucking needy side. If Rosa begs for a baby one more time, I'm going to force Jorge to knock her up.

"Gone. Give them money. Lots of it. Just make them leave," I snap and then crack my neck. "I have enough shit to worry about right now. In case you didn't notice, our territory has quadrupled since Camilo is no longer a factor."

He gives me a clipped nod. "Are they to leave indefinitely, sir?"

"Until the next time I need my goddamned dick sucked," I seethe. "Do I need to make you a fucking spreadsheet? Get them out of my damn presence before I send you packing along with them!"

My chest heaves with exertion. I bring a hand shaking with anger back to my mouth and suck more of the sweet cigar smoke into my lungs. Closing my eyes, I lean back in the leather chair in my office and tilt my head up to the ceiling. This new place doesn't feel like a home at all. It's massive and cold. Fitting for that bastard Camilo. I'd only wanted to live in it to prove who the winner truly was. He may have won a few battles along the way, but I'm the motherfucker sitting in his chair now. This is my kingdom. Camilo is nothing but a corpse rotting away in a metal container back in the States.

The smile on my face falls as thoughts of my mother filter into my head. She'd always been religious and spoke of angels and demons often. Especially near the end when she teetered the line between life and death. Back when I'd desperately tried to scrounge together money for medicines to help her. I was sure I could cure her ailments. It wasn't until I'd had a near death experience myself on one of my missions for her that I believed in her words. That day, as my life drained from me, I met both an angel and a demon.

I spent my entire life prowling the shadows just waiting for that demon. To eradicate him from this earth. If it weren't for him cutting me to within inches of my own life, I'd have been able to kiss my mother as she passed on from this world to the next. Instead, I was laid up in a hospital bed and kept breathing by machines. When I was finally released, she was gone. I missed her death, her funeral, everything. That demon had to pay. And he did.

Now, to find that angel…

"Diego!" Jorge bellows as he stalks back into my office. "We have a problem—"

"JUST MAKE THE CUNTS LEAVE BEFORE I LOSE MY TEMPER!" I roar back at him and slam my fist on the mahogany desk.

He doesn't flinch and switches to English. "The women are packing. Not a problem. This problem is that there is a vehicle on the perimeter."

I stiffen. "Do we know who it is?"

"No. Luis and Manuel have ridden ahead to check it out. I'm going to meet them out there."

I rise and snag my Glock from the desk. "I'm coming with you."

"Sir, you shouldn't come out there in case it is a threat."

I tuck the gun into the back of my pants beneath my suit jacket and toss the cigar into the ashtray. "I dare them to threaten me. I need to release some steam. What better way than to slice up a few motherfuckers." I pat the knife that's sheathed at my belt. "Let's go."

He grumbles but doesn't argue the fact any further. I stalk ahead of him down through the long hallways. Until I'm intercepted by Claudia.

"You can't make us leave!" she screeches and bares her teeth at me. "You promised to take care of us!" She starts screaming at me in Spanish and throws a vase my way. I duck and growl at her.

"I did take care of you until you got on my last fucking nerve. Now you'll leave in one piece or I'll slice you up and feed you to the pigs out back. Your decision, *Three*," I snarl. Her eyes narrow at my calling her by her number. They all fucking hate that, but I don't give a rat's ass. How else am I supposed to tell them apart? "Take the money and leave or try my patience. My blade is thirsty." I give her a wink.

"You prick!"

Ignoring her, I storm away to let someone else deal with her shit. Jorge gets held up for a minute but soon joins me outside. He wears claw marks down the side of his face. Better him than me.

We climb into his vehicle and haul ass along the gravel drive. Soon, the headlights reveal two men standing over a crumpled form. Looks like my men already eradicated the threat. As soon as the car stops, I climb out and stalk over to them.

"What is this?" I snap as I push past them.

"This was delivered a few minutes ago," Luis says, his tone gruff.

"With this note," Manual finishes and hands me a letter.

The cunt was a traitor. Thought she'd fit in quite well here. You're welcome.

The letter isn't signed. Fucking pussies. I dare them to speak these things to my face. With a growl, I squat beside the woman. Her hair is matted with blood. A once yellow dress is torn and dirty. Creamy white flesh is slightly blue from the cool temps and mottled with bruises all over. Small cuts dot her skin, making me cringe. I absently stroke the scars on my face.

"Bring her inside," I bark out.

"What? What if it's a trick?" Jorge questions.

"I don't give a goddamn!" I snarl as I rise to my feet. "She's a woman, and we're not leaving her here to fucking rot. Bring her inside and call for the doctor. We'll sort out the rest in the morning."

Jorge gives me a clipped nod before he scoops her into his arms. Her dress is torn down the front and her breast is bared to me and my men. Fury surges through my veins. I shrug out of my jacket and cover her before drawing her into my own arms. Jorge shoots me a questioning look, but I don't answer him as I stride back to the vehicle. I sit inside with her nestled against me in my lap. Dark red hair is covering her face. She can't be more than eighteen or nineteen years old as far as I can tell. When her head lolls back, I notice tape covering her mouth.

"Who is she?" Jorge questions as he starts the car.

"I don't know." *Sorry, ángel, but this is going to hurt.* I rip the duct tape away from her mouth. A small moan escapes her, and her lashes flutter from behind her hair but she doesn't reopen them. "But whoever pulled this shit is going to meet my goddamned blade."

Jorge wisely doesn't say a word in protest at my harsh declaration. Women seem to claw their way inside my heart and latch on to any sliver of vulnerability I possess. They get under my skin with their softness and sweet voices. And so help me when one is in distress, I want to be the mother-fucking knight to swoop in and save her. Like little Gabriella Rojas. That girl was sweet yet feisty. In way the fuck over her head and in dire need of protection. Those boys in her life can't look after her. She's lucky I'm weak for the female sex. Any other cartel fuck would have put a bullet in her skull the day she tried to make professional business deals with monsters. But the girl had amused me.

Fucking women.

That's my problem.

It's why I have five wives. Of course they're not legitimate wives. I'd die before I so carelessly married a woman in God's eyes and tied myself to her in every way. My mother married my father. He was the love of her life until he was shot in an alley one day when I was three. I'd never disrespect her, dead or not, by marrying without love. My "wives" are more like steady girlfriends. Permanent pains in my ass.

I smirk as we pull into the drive. Not so permanent. By morning, my home will be quiet. Free from catty-ass cunts. I look down at the girl in my arms. Except for this one. This one is going to get better and then she and I are going to have a long talk. I need to know how a young woman like her ends up beaten and abandoned in a cartel king's driveway. There's a story. Daddy Diego loves a good bedtime story.

I'm sitting in the leather chair in my office when Dr. Tatiana Morales walks in. She'd been the surgeon when I'd nearly lost my life. It wasn't until I made something of myself that I was able to hire her to be my full-time doctor, earning double what she did at the hospital. Tatiana held me when I sobbed in my bed upon learning of my mother's death. She's seen me at my weakest and she's the closest thing I have to family.

"You're looking tired, *hijo mío*," she says as she sits across from me. She waves away the cigar smoke. "Bad habit," she chides and leans forward to snuff out my cigar that's sitting in the ashtray.

I smirk and shrug my shoulders. "I'm sure I have much worse habits."

She purses her lips, and it reminds me of my mother so much it hurts. "Speaking of your ruthless ways, I want to talk about the girl."

Jolting upright, I lean forward and frown. "What are her injuries?"

Sadness washes over her features. "Her wounds aren't consistent with a struggle, but I think it's because she was drugged. I'm not sure what was given to her, but she's still quite out of it. There was some vaginal irritation. My gut tells me she was raped."

Rage burns through my veins, and I fist my hands. "Anything else?"

She sighs and switches to English. "Most of the wounds are superficial. The one on her eyebrow required a couple of stitches, though." Her gaze falls to her lap. "Diego, she was severely malnourished. Her weight is at least fifteen pounds below what someone her age and height should be. The bones of her ribs protrude. She reminds me of an anorexic patient I had once."

Starvation. I know plenty about this. My mother often struggled to feed us when I was a young child. It wasn't until I hit my early teenage years that I had the wit about me to steal food for us. Hunger is a pain much worse than that of a knife. It's deep and consumes you to your soul.

"I'll make sure she's fed," I bite out. "Is that all?"

"I've tested for STDs and pregnancy. She's clear."

"How long until she's able to talk?" I ask, suddenly feeling sick to my stomach.

"I went ahead and started an IV with fluids. I'll watch her overnight. By morning, most of that should be cleared from her system. She'll need to be fed and taken care of," she tells me. Her brown eyes meet mine and her gaze hardens. "If you want me to take her to a woman's shelter in the morning, I will." I understand the look in her eyes. A look that says, *don't take advantage of her.* A look that tells me the girl has been through enough already.

"She stays here. She won't be harmed," I vow. And that's the goddamned truth. But the assholes who brought her here, I will gut without a second thought.

"Get some rest, Diego. You're exhausted."

I give her a nod and watch her leave my office.

Tomorrow, I will get some answers.

chapter
FIVE

Vee

I wake with a start, a gnawing hunger pain clutching at my belly from the inside out. Bright sunshine pours in from a window, and I squint against it as I sit up.

"Good morning, little one," a woman says.

I find an older Hispanic woman smiling at me. Kindness shines in her eyes. Am I in a hospital? My brows scrunch up in confusion.

"You're safe now," she assures me as she reaches for my hand.

I look down to see that I'm attached to an IV. She sets to removing the needle and then bandages me up.

"W-Where am I?" I croak out. Pain assaults me from every direction, but I power through it to find out where I am.

"You're under Diego Gomez's protection now." The way she says his name is one of fondness. I can't help but shudder, though. I'm in the beast's lair. When my eyes focus on the room around me, I recognize it as the very one I used to stay in whenever we'd come to visit the Rojas family all those years ago.

"I, uh, I…" Panic shoots through me. I'm here. I'm supposed to kill this scary dude and then I can escape.

Back to Esteban?

I choke back bile. He fucking head butted me. And worse yet, he and his brother sent me here as a pawn. They drugged and raped me. Disgust is quickly squashed by anger. How dare they use me!

"Are you hungry, sweetheart?"

And just like that, my anger is snuffed out.

"I'm starving," I whisper.

"Let's get you dressed and then we'll go down to breakfast. Ingrid is making homemade waffles this morning," she tells me with a gentle smile.

I'm confused. I'd expected monsters and mayhem. Not motherly smiles and hospitality.

After a slew of embarrassing moments during which I needed this stranger to help me pee and then dress, I eventually make my way down the familiar hallways on shaky legs.

"I'm Tatiana," she tells me as we shuffle along the corridor.

"Vee."

We settle at a table—the same table I used to eat at every summer with three Colombian boys. Now, I sit with Tatiana. She watches me carefully as the old lady who must be pushing eighty waddles in, plopping plates down in front of us. I feel like an animal as I dive into the food. I've eaten nothing but sandwiches and soup for months. One bite of the waffles, and I feel like perhaps I died in that car last night. This must be heaven.

I stuff myself to the point of pain at breakfast. And yet, I still have the desire to push more food into the pockets of the lounge pants I'm wearing. Just in case.

"You're welcome to come eat whenever you're hungry," Tatiana tells me with a smile. "I'll also make sure we put some snacks in your room."

My shoulders relax. I keep waiting for something horrible to happen. When we finish, she guides me back to my room. I stand awkwardly as I wait to be told what to do next.

"Books are over there. Television. Bathroom is in there if you'd like to bathe. I'll go into town later and pick you up more clothes. Would you like a swimsuit? It's hot out there, so maybe you'd like to swim. Swimming is a great strength builder." She babbles her words as though she's nervous.

I jerk my head over to her. "Thank you. Umm…sure. A swimsuit would be nice." I force a smile but can't help thinking about all the times Oscar and I would swim together. Back when we were friends. Back when he wasn't a vengeful prick. I mean, the rape and beatings make sense for their plan. Send me here as a victim. What they didn't realize, though, is that they created another enemy in the process.

Nobody fucks with the queen.

I'll get rid of this Diego asshole and then figure out a way to make the Rojas brothers pay for what they did to me.

"Don't be afraid of him," she mutters from behind me.

I freeze at her words. "I'm not afraid of him. I'm not afraid of anyone." My gaze drifts to hers, and I pin her with a glare. "I'm not."

She blinks at me in shock. "Good. That's good."

Tatiana slips out of my room. I walk over to the bookshelf. It takes everything in me to pull down the book I know holds pictures inside. All the décor is the same as it was when I was here all those summers. Pulling *The Count of Monte Cristo* from the shelf, I settle into a chair by the window and open it. In the middle are a stack of Polaroids. Each picture is either of me or Oscar. We're making silly faces in each pose. In the last pic, we smartened up and stood in front of a mirror to get us both in the picture. In the photo, I'm fourteen and looking up at his lanky self. Love shines from my eyes and smile. He smirks at the mirror with one of his looks that got him more girlfriends than he knew what to do with. The only girlfriend it didn't get him was me. And it wasn't for lack of trying. That summer, I tried everything to get him to fall for me. I even swam nude in the pool for him. Nothing ever worked.

I grit my teeth and tear each photo of him in half. The pieces of the pictures flutter to my lap. With a sound of disgust, I swipe them all onto the floor along with the book. Then, I limp over to the bathroom. It's stocked with girly stuff. Hairbrushes, perfume, makeup. I can't help but become giddy over seeing such silly items. But these are simple items I've been denied for months.

A burst of fury explodes inside of me. Part of me wants to rage and push all the pretty things to the floor with a clatter.

But then I remember *my* plan.

My plan is to destroy them all.

I stare in the mirror and hardly recognize myself. My hair has been blown into soft red waves, and I'm wearing clothes. The dress is loose, but I love how the green is almost the exact shade of my eyes. I look like Poison Ivy from the *Batman* movies. Except I'm not trying to kill any good guys. I prefer the bad ones.

There is a basket full of unopened makeup, but most of it was meant for darker skin tones. I open a tube of mascara and brush some on my lashes and then opt for some lip gloss. Other than that, my bruises and cuts are on full display. I can even see the small dusting of freckles on my cheeks. At one time, I did everything in my power to hide them.

Now, I don't care.

The woman staring back at me is poisonous and vicious. She's not a victim or a delicate flower. This woman has thorns and deadly venom. This woman has a plan to hurt them all.

I smack my lips together before spritzing on some perfume and exiting the bathroom. I'm stopped dead in my tracks by the sight of a man wearing a suit on the other side of my bed, his back turned to me. He's staring at one of the halves of the pictures I'd torn up and holds the book in his other hand. In my moment of fury, I'd torn them all up and hadn't bothered to clean up the mess. Of course now, this implicates me as being somehow tied to the Rojas family.

"Jorge warned me this was a trick," the deep voice rumbles.

I'm stunned frozen. The man is much bigger than me. Broad shouldered with messily styled black hair on top of his head. He exudes strength and power.

"Diego Gomez?"

He turns to the side, and I get a brief look at his profile before he turns to shove the book into the empty spot it came from. I'd expected an old man like Camilo. Not someone closer to Esteban's age.

"I am," he states in a cold tone. "What's your name, *ángel*?"

He turns around fully to face me. The bed is between us and it seems like such a small obstacle between a cartel king and his captive. But I'm nobody's victim. Not anymore. Bravely, I tilt my chin and let my gaze bore into the lightest brown eyes I have ever seen. His eyes, not him, are the ones holding me captive as I momentarily get lost in them.

"Name," he grits out through clenched teeth.

I tear my gaze from its locked position on his eyes and study his face. Tiny silvery white scars crisscross all over his flesh. His cheeks are dusted with dark hair, thicker around his mouth and chin in a half-grown goatee. It's as if at one time, he kept it neat, but then one day simply forgot to care anymore, giving him the appearance of a wild man barely contained in a neat suit. My eyes land on his lips. Pink and full. So soft for a villain.

"Vienna Berkley," I tell him boldly and meet his light brown-eyed stare. "Vee."

His gaze softens as a half-smile tugs at his lips. The bad guys aren't supposed to be so damn handsome. They're supposed to be scarred and ugly. Yet here this one is—scarred up something terrible—yet he is anything but ugly. "I've been looking for you, *ángel*."

I tilt my chin up and bite out my words. "Here I am. And I am not an angel."

This earns me a wide smile which reveals every pearly white tooth in his mouth. The smile makes his light brown eyes twinkle with delight. "I can see I'm going to have fun with you, *mi diablita*. So much fun."

"Touch me and you die," I bite out, my voice slightly wobbling.

He chuckles. "You Americans are so feisty. It makes Daddy Diego so fucking hard."

I snort and lift an eyebrow at him. "We Americans also make fun of assholes who talk about themselves in third person."

He shoves his hands into the pockets of his grey pants, part of a crisp three-piece suit and a perfectly tied, navy-blue tie. He prowls around the edge of the bed. My hackles rise but I refuse to take a step back. His voice rumbles right through me when he says, "Americans are so quick to judge. I'm a friend, not a foe."

I tense when he rounds my corner of the bed. His movements are quick and stealthy. Like a jungle cat. In a matter of seconds, he's looming over me and toying with a lock of my hair. He brings it to his nose and he inhales me.

"Why are you here, Vienna?"

I turn to face him, refusing to cower under his intimidation. I've spent months cowering. This Diego prick is nothing in comparison to motherfucking Esteban. "Because they decided to hurt and betray me. Because they don't care about me. I'm here because they think I'm a pawn. I'm here because they don't know me at all."

"Fearless," he murmurs, his face inches from mine. I can smell the lingering scent of cigar smoke from this proximity.

"And angry," I admit, a slight crack to my voice.

His fingertip strokes my cheek. The movement is gentle and far from sexual, despite his earlier threatening words. "You want vengeance."

I swallow when his finger slides down the side of my throat. "That's part of the plan."

Our eyes lock and a storm brews in his eyes. "What's the other part of the plan?"

"I like to call it plan D."

His loud, abrupt laughter startles me. "Ahhh, you are too fucking adorable. I like you."

I growl after him as he strides to the door, his long legs eating up the distance in no time. "Well I don't like you!"

He twists the knob and looks over his shoulder at me. "Not yet, *mi diablita*, but you will. All women like me eventually." With a wink, he's gone. And I refuse to admit that his stupid wink made my stomach do a little twist.

I manage to hide out in my room for the next few days. Ingrid brings me food fit for a queen—actual feasts, God bless her—and Tatiana takes care of me in other ways. She fusses over my well-being and brings me gifts. Once she took out my stiches, she brought me some makeup that matched my skin tone and some clothes that were my size. The swimsuit she purchased is a sparkly green two-piece that I absolutely love. I'm not sure what I'm doing here in Diego's house or exactly what my plan is—despite my lie, telling him I had one—but one thing's for sure, I'm going to swim in that pool. I may as well enjoy myself before I go on a bad-guy killing spree.

I haven't seen Diego since he came into my room that day, thank God. I never dreamed he'd be as hot as he is. Not that it matters. But it does make the plan easier. Whatever the plan is. As I put on the new swimsuit, I ponder what the plan really could be. I could always manipulate Diego into liking me. If I earned his trust, then he could send his men after Esteban and Oscar. He could do the dirty work. Then, I could take him out while he sleeps one night.

That plan seems feasible.

But getting men to like me has always backfired on me. The one man I'd always wanted never once touched me until he decided to use me in a ploy for revenge. Punched me in the damn face as if our friendship meant nothing and then raped me, knowing I couldn't stop him. A normal woman would be reduced to tears. Not me, though. I'm positively fucking furious. The Rojas brothers once again used me for their own personal gain. This is no different than all those summers when Oscar would toy with my emotions and Esteban would laugh at my expense. Their family has always been number one, and I was never a part of it. I was nothing but a silly girl to them.

They are going to regret this.

I'm going to need to make this plan work.

It's time to show them they fucked with the wrong chick. I'm not playing their games anymore. This time, I'm running the show. This time, I'll be the one laughing as I make them pay.

I twist my wild red locks into a messy bun. I've spent some time on my makeup today and given myself a darker look than I normally wear. I decide I resemble a seductress like Oscar claimed. Good. The cover up Tatiana brought me is cream-colored and sheer. I slip it on over the swimsuit before leaving the safety of my room. I'm heading toward the back staircase that leads to the pool when I hear a voice. Curiosity gets the better of me, and I sneak down the hallway to Camilo's old office. When I peek around the doorway, I see Diego pacing the office with a phone pressed to his ear.

"She's fine, cariño. I promise on my big dick. Now take care of those babies. When have I ever not kept a promise to you?" He smiles. "That's what I thought." Then his voice grows serious. "Remember…you owe me big for this. And one day soon, I will call on you for repayment."

I'm dying to know who he is talking to. A wife? For some reason, that thought annoys me. A wife means more baggage. My plan to kill him will grow complicated with more people involved.

He hangs up the phone and his eyes dart over to where I'm standing. His shit-eating grin falls away as anger contorts his features.

"Why in the fuck are you walking around the house in your bra and panties?" he snarls, the muscle in his neck twitching.

I curl my lip at him. "Good afternoon to you too, asshole."

His fury melts away and he grins. "That mouth will get you in trouble one day, *mi diablita*."

"I'm going swimming. Want to come?" I grit out. He's making my plans of seduction very difficult.

Shock flashes in his eyes and his mouth parts. I've only encountered him a couple of times and each time, I could easily read his emotions. I'd love to play poker with this guy. I would take him for every penny he's worth with that expressive face.

"You want me to come swim with you? With you…" he utters and waves at me. "Looking like that?"

I'm stung by his words. "Jesus! Be a prick, why don't you? I thought I looked nice." My mouth forms a pout.

He stalks my way and looms over me without touching me. "You do not look nice."

I jerk away from him and storm toward the door. I've barely made it to the threshold when a strong hand grips my elbow. I'm forced up against the door jam, and Diego presses his entire hard body against me. His impressive erection stabs at me from behind. When he brings his mouth to my ear, his breath tickles me.

"*Nice* is a word for grandmas and fucking sunrises. You…" he murmurs as his palm roams around my front to touch my breast through my swimsuit. "You are like a thousand sunrises. Too bright and too goddamned beautiful for human eyes. I'm blind just looking at you, *mi diablita*."

His thumb rubs across my hardened nipple, and I gasp. So much for me being the seductress. The man pins me up against a doorframe and whispers a few sweet nothings into my ear and I'm seconds from begging him to strip me out of this *nice* swimsuit.

"I have too much work to do," he murmurs before nibbling at my earlobe. "But I can assure you, I'll be watching. I'll always be watching."

I shudder and it's not from disgust. I'm shocked that my body seems to respond to him whenever he's near. No fucking surprise there, though. My pussy seems to start flashing like a disco ball whenever a bad guy is in the vicinity.

Diego stalks off to somewhere in the house, and I stand there stunned for a moment. I'm really going to have to get my act together. Falling for the villain is not part of the plan. I've done enough of that to last a lifetime.

SIX

Diego

The sun today is killer and hot as hell. I could be inside in the air conditioning, working on shit, but instead, I'm standing on the deck staring at the redheaded vixen lying on a chaise lounge beside the pool. Her eyes are closed while one toe lazily swirls around in the sparkling pool water. Everything about her screams innocent and pure and fucking perfect. The best part about her is her rack. I swear those tits were hand sculpted by angels.

Speaking of angels…

I was given very direct orders by Gabriella Rojas not to touch her friend. When she found out Vienna was in my possession, she cried over the phone. It broke my heart a little to see the tough little thing reduced by her emotions. But when she asked to speak to her friend, I refused. I'm still certain the woman by my pool has an ulterior motive.

Until I figure out what that is, I'll play the girl's games. Clearly she's trying to get into my pants as part of her agenda. And I'd not be a gentleman if I didn't oblige.

I prowl silently over to where she bakes in the sun. The bruises still dot her flesh and small cuts remain. Despite her injuries, she's beautiful under the sun's rays. My hands crave to run my fingertips along her milky flesh, just to watch goose bumps form in their wake. She must have dozed off because she's fucking serene as she lies there without a care in the world. Her skin is slightly pink, and I know I'll need to make sure she stays covered so she won't burn.

"*Mi diablita.*"

She cracks an eye at me and peers at me with her piercing green orb. "Mi motherfucker."

I snort and shadow her from the sun as I loom over her. "Where were you all those months?"

She bites on her pink bottom lip and the action makes my cock jolt in my slacks. "How do you know I was missing?"

"I know things."

A flash of sadness flickers in her eyes, followed by fear. She quickly chases it away with the fiery look she does so well. "Esteban Rojas took me. Held me captive."

I glare at her. Those hadn't been the words I'd expected to hear. Sure, they dumped her on my property, but I'd figured it was a one-time thing. "Did he hurt you often?"

Her nostrils flare. "When *didn't* he hurt me?"

"So you're here seeking asylum?" I don't understand her game.

Her eyes drift off behind me. She appears to be lost. "I don't really know what I'm doing." The honesty in her words is raw.

"I can keep you safe here," I assure her as I squat down beside her and twist a stray strand of red hair in my fingertips.

Her lips pull into a frown. "I've been told that a time or two. You men are liars."

I give her hair a tug. "I'm not."

"Mmmm-hmmm."

"If I vow to keep you safe, I will keep you fucking safe. End of story," I growl.

She simply nods, but I can tell she doesn't believe me.

"After you dress, I want to have a little chat with you," I tell her as I release her hair and stand.

"What's there to talk about?" Her breasts jiggle as she heaves out a sigh. Those tits are too damn tempting.

"Everything," I murmur, dragging my gaze from her gorgeous rack. "Dinner. Seven. My office. Wear something sexy."

She hisses from her lounge chair, and I chuckle as I stride back toward the house.

"I'm not wearing anything sexy," she calls out after me.

"So don't wear anything at all," I say with a devilish grin and wink at her. "Such a naughty girl."

"You're disgusting."

I give her one last look and shrug before walking inside. I'll show her disgusting.

She walks through the darkness cloaked all in black. Her face is hidden from me. My fingertips twitch to pull the hood from her head, so I can see her. To see the angel who hides in shadows. But I'm bound. Bound and bleeding from a chair. Pain sears inside of me like never before and burns through my chest. She's somehow ripping me apart from the inside out. Maybe she's no angel at all.

A pale arm emerges from the dark clothing and points straight at me. The throbbing inside my chest intensifies. I feel as though the witch is trying to tear my heart right from my chest. She makes a motion with her finger. Down, starting from her left, and then up again to her right. It's a threat. I don't understand what she means but I know it's meant to hurt me.

I can't speak to her. My lips are sealed shut. I'm dying to plead with her to make the pain stop but I can't ask her anything. I am completely at her mercy.

"I could have killed you like five times," a sweet voice says, cutting through my nightmare.

I blink away the remnants of the dream and sit up in my chair abruptly. Apparently I passed the fuck out face first on my desk. Tatiana is right—I'm not sleeping well. These random catnaps throughout the day aren't cutting it.

"What time is it?" I grumble and swipe my fingers through my wrecked hair. My eyes finally dart over to find Vienna perched in a chair. She's wearing a dress that Claudia must have left behind. It's black and fitted. The low scoop neck reveals the full tops of her succulent tits while the short hem of the dress showcases her creamy thighs that now have a pink tinge to them.

"It's after eight," she murmurs. She fingers her messily styled red waves and arches an eyebrow at me. "I really could have killed you. But I didn't." Her lips quirk up into an amused grin.

I narrow my eyes at her and try to read the woman. A few days ago, she showed up on my property raped and beaten to a bloody pulp. I discovered she has a past with the Rojas family but no longer seems tied to them. She's the same girl Gabriella had me locate. I'd expected a victimized woman who I'd need to nurse back to health. What I have sitting before me is no victim. I can practically see the wheels turning inside her head. Vengeance is in every smile and calculation in each glance. She all but admitted to using me for some personal gain. So fearless and bold.

"Come sit in Daddy Diego's lap," I utter in a low tone, my gaze once again traveling her milky thighs. "We need to discuss this little plan of yours."

A flash of annoyance flickers in her shimmering green eyes but she slowly rises. The dress fits her well, even if it is a little on the short side. She's artfully done her makeup in such a way that she looks much older than her young age. My cock thickens against my thigh as she saunters over to me, swaying her hips. Despite the makeup and the clothes, I sense her nervousness. It doesn't change the fact, though, that she's a natural seductress without even trying. The woman is an expert at drawing a man's eye and getting his dick to do all the thinking. Right now, as she sashays over to me, my head is clouded with thoughts of her and I tangled up under the sheets. It's been days now since the last time I got laid, something my cock reminds me of as it tries to escape my slacks.

When she rounds the desk, I roll the chair away and lean back in it. I point in front of me. "Sit there, *mi diablita*."

Her palms find the mahogany surface and she hoists herself on top of it. I smirk when she primly crosses her ankles. Rolling back toward her, I keep my legs spread apart and pin her shins with the front of my chair. With my eyes on hers, I take my time pulling a cigar from the drawer. She watches me as I take my father's old metal lighter and flick the lid open to produce a flame. I burn the end of the cigar until it's lit and then suck in the rich smoke. Camilo left these Cohiba Esplendido cigars for me as a parting gift. Unlike Tatiana, Vienna doesn't flinch when I blow the smoke up at her pretty face.

"Esteban kidnapped and raped you. And then you escaped?" I question as I take another puff.

Her brows crash together and she shakes her head. "Not exactly. He kept me for months. I thought I…" A frown tugs at her perfect lips. "I thought maybe he cared about me, but I later realized he'd been drugging me. I'd only recently come out of my stupor when he and his brother came up with the plan to send me here."

I stiffen at her words. "To kill me?"

A blush creeps up her slender neck and she nods. "But I told them I'd never killed anyone before. I didn't want to do it."

Anger bubbles up inside of me. "So you agreed to—"

"I agreed to nothing," she hisses, her gaze fiery enough to melt glaciers.

"So they kicked your ass, raped you, and dumped you on my lawn?" This makes no fucking sense.

The hardness leaves her expression, and she once again appears to be lost. This is the side of her that plucks at my heartstrings. I cannot deal with a vulnerable woman without wanting to tear the heads off everyone who harmed her in her past.

"You forgot he also drugged me," she says with a dark laugh. "But what I told you was true. They betrayed me."

I inhale another long drag of my cigar and scrutinize her. Hurt flashes in her eyes but she won't let it surface. She is fierce, this one.

"Why do they think you are so loyal to them? That you'll actually follow through with their plan after what they did to you?" I demand, taking another puff from my cigar. "Did they really assume you'd do their bidding and kill me? That you are even capable of killing me? Assuming you could, *why* would you?"

She uncrosses her ankles, and I can't help but drop my gaze to her thighs. The dress hides what lies beneath but it doesn't keep my stare from lingering there in hopes of catching a peek.

"I'm a good actress," she tells me, her voice but a whisper. "When I finally snapped out of my haze, I continued to play the part of broken, submissive woman. Esteban assumes I'll behave and follow his orders." She shudders. "I'm done being told what to do. I'm not ever going back to him."

We hold each other's gaze for a long while until her stomach grumbles. I tug the cigar away and lift an eyebrow at her. "You waited to eat dinner with me?"

Her nostrils flare. "You told me to."

"I thought you were done being told what to do," I challenge and run my knuckle along the inside of her knee.

Her body shivers at my touch, but she doesn't move away from me. "I need your help," she murmurs.

"You want them killed. And then what? I am to set you free?"

When her stomach growls before she can answer, I yank my phone from my breast pocket. I call down to the kitchen and bark out an order for them to deliver our food. Once I hang up, I lean back in my chair once again. The need to touch her is strong, but my cock muddies my brain. I need to think clearly for a moment.

"*Mi diablita…*"

"Yes." Her voice catches and for a split second she seems conflicted by her answer. Sadness flickers in her eyes. But then, her nostrils flare and she lifts her chin bravely. "I am no one to you, I know this. But I have money. I can pay you for your services."

What is it with these fucking adorable American beauties trying to make deals with me? I'm a bad man. A conqueror. Not some fair and just douchebag who is swayed by a pair of pretty tits and a shy smile. Oh…oh, wait. Perhaps I am that douchebag.

"I'm sure we can work something out," I grumble as I take a drag from my cigar. "But I don't want your money."

She narrows her glittering green eyes at me. "Well, I don't care. You're not doing it for free."

With my cigar between my teeth, I laugh and wink at her. "Oh, I want something in exchange." My gaze travels to her perfect rack. "I want something so very badly." When I finally look back up at her, she's not wearing a look of fear like her cute friend Gabriella did when we were making deals not so long ago. This girl is all fire and fury. The fucking devil in female form. Her red eyebrow that's recently been plucked to perfection is arched in a challenge. I'm pretty sure the look she's giving me is going to bring me to my knees one day. That look will be my demise.

"You want sex?" Her voice is hard, but it quivers ever so slightly. I notice it and latch on to her sliver of fear.

"I want sex," I agree as my knuckle teases her inner thigh again. "I want other things, too."

"Like what?" she murmurs, her bottom lip looking quite bitable right now.

"I'm not sure yet but I'll let you know."

She reaches forward, lowering her cleavage closer to my face and plucks my cigar from my teeth. I let out a groan when she slides into my lap and straddles my thighs. This girl is playing a dangerous game—a game she won't win. Not with me.

"You need me for more than sex," she tells me, her tone confident as she takes the most erotic drag from my cigar. The way her plump lips wrap around the tip has my cock aching for relief. Then, her fingertips are ghosting over the scars on my face. Her thumb slips into my mouth and she pulls it open.

I've pursued lots of women.

Women may be my weakness, but I'm really fucking good at showing them my strength.

I know what they want and I give it to them.

Seduction is my game.

Yet right now, this red-haired devil is playing my game better than I do. She exhales the cigar smoke into my mouth and brushes her lips against mine. I let out a hungry growl as I dig my fingertips into her hips.

"Be careful how you tread, *mi diablita*," I hiss, my hands barely staying under control.

"Or what?"

I snag her wrist and bring the cigar to my lips. "You might get in too deep. Don't forget that you're playing with fire here."

She grinds against my lap, causing me to hiss in pleasure. When her eyes meet mine, they're downright fucking evil. "I know all about fire, so trust me, I won't be the one who gets burned."

This bitch delivers threat after threat, and yet I'm gritting my teeth to keep from blowing my load in my pants. She's got my head all twisted up. This girl, who days ago, I fucking nursed to health, has morphed into this sultry demon hell-bent on bringing me down. Sure, she wants vengeance on the Rojas brothers. That much is clear.

But she also wants me.

Dead.

I can see it in her eyes.

Feel it in her murderous glares.

Hear it in her softly spoken threats.

And yet, here I am, indulging the succubus of a woman. I'm wondering how many times I'll get to fuck her before she delivers that fatal blow when I least expect it. Leaning forward, I drag my nose along the bare part of her tit, peeking over the top of her dress. She lets out a gasp that has me grinning wolfishly.

"Well, Vienna," I murmur against her flesh. "Looks like you've made yourself a deal. I'll bring down the bastards who hurt you and then I'll bring you down to your knees where you'll suck my fat cock until you're blue in the face."

She sucks in a deep breath and leans away from me. Her lips are parted while her eyes are lit up like green flames. Hot with desire. On fire with lust.

"We have ourselves a deal, *mi diablita*?" I question as I take the cigar from her fingertips. "You for them?"

"Deal."

Vee

Plan D is in full effect. I hide my smirk as I slide off the desk the moment a young man rolls in a cart of food. He wants to have sex with me in exchange for killing Esteban and Oscar. It's almost too easy. Sex with a man like him would be kind of like a bonus, certainly not a chore. So I'll bang Diego and then bolt. Win, win. At one point, I thought I wanted him dead too, but things change. He'll make a better partner alive.

"Where are you going?" he questions, his voice low yet amused.

"I thought we were going to eat." My tone is pouty, and I instantly hate how transparent I am when it comes to food.

"We are," he growls. "But sit here."

He pats his thigh beside the hard length that is every bit visible through his slacks. Whatever he's packing in there looks dangerous. A big fat snake ready to strike. The cock he's hiding is what male porn stars only wish they had.

Knowing I need Diego to carry out my plan, I obey. I kick off my heels and pad back over to him. The guy who brought our food is busy setting out the dishes on the desk without saying a word. I sit on Diego's powerful thigh and can't help but shiver. Do these Colombian men live on the regiment of sleep, fuck, and work out twenty-four hours a day?

I'm distracted by the man setting out the food. He places many different styles of dishes all over the surface that smell heavenly. I remember many of them from when I used to come visit. Dishes that are native to the country. My mouth waters for a taste.

"I'm not sleeping with you until you carry out your end of the bargain," I tell him as I snag a hot seasoned piece of meat from a bowl. Flavor explodes on my tongue when I pop the sliver of steak into my mouth. A groan of pleasure rumbles from me. "Oh, God, that's so good."

Diego chuckles and his fingers run circles along my back through the fabric of the dress. "Carne Guisada con zanahoria," he tells me, his voice friendly. "My mother's recipe. It tastes better with the carrot sauce."

He leans past me and spoons some of the orange-colored sauce onto the meat that's been cut thinly. With a fork, he scoops up a mound of it and brings it to my face. My eyes dart over to his, searching for malice, but I only find eagerness in his expression. He wants me to like this dish.

I part my lips and accept the bite he feeds me. Esteban fed me sandwiches and soup. At one time, I'd thought it was borderline romantic.

Then I woke up.

Then I realized he was fucking with my head.

"Oh," I murmur between chews. "That's really good. Did your mother make it?"

His black eyebrows crash together and he scowls. "No. She's dead."

I swallow the morsels before regarding him sadly. "Mine's dead too. Esteban drugged her with heroin like he drugged my friend Brie. When Esteban finally came back for us in the shipping container, it was too late. I was half starved to death and my mother had died from withdrawals."

His eyes dart all over me. He clenches his teeth and scoops up another bite. I expect him to feed himself, but he once again gives me the bite. It should annoy me or remind me of Esteban. But it actually doesn't bother me at all. The food is good and he's not as evil as I originally thought.

At least I hope not.

I tend to see the best in the bad guys. They dazzle me with their evil grins and their bad boy muscles, and I fall hopelessly at their feet where they tend to kick me while I'm down.

"My mother died of pancreatic cancer. One day she was fine and strong. The next day, she was weak and dying." His jaw clenches as he looks past me toward the wall. I follow his gaze to a painting. The woman in the picture is young and beautiful. Her dark hair is curled and pulled to one side. She smiles but her features are sad. I don't have to be told it's his mother because I know. They look just alike.

"I'm sorry," I murmur, my eyebrows pinching together in pain. My mother was difficult and bitchy and unkind. It's my father who I loved unconditionally, despite his flaws and mistakes. I understand how it feels.

He grunts and stabs at more meat. Once again, he feeds me rather than himself. I can tell the talk about deceased mothers has soured his mood. A bad mood doesn't fare well with my need to keep him on my side. In order to keep the conversation light again, I pick up a different fork and poke at what looks like some shredded beef over rice. When I turn to look at him, he's still staring at the portrait.

"Open up." I flash him a smile before bringing the fork to his lips. "Partner."

He smirks but obeys. "Carne Desmechada o Ropa Vieja," he tells me after he swallows.

The rest of the meal carries on like this. I try many new dishes that I decide I very much love. After months and months of hardly any food at all with shit selection, dining with Diego feels like a royal feast.

"So you're the king of Colombia now?" I question.

He chuckles, the sound boyish in quality. My stupid heart stutters at the sound of it. "I suppose so," he agrees. "But if we're partners and I'm the king…" His light brown eyes flicker up to mine and he grins wide. A shiver races down my spine. "Then you're my queen."

I hold his stare despite my desire to look away. I think he's trying to intimidate me.

"I'm going to fuck you until those assholes are dead. That's my deal, *mi diablita*."

Mentally, I had hoped our deal just meant the one time. But deep down in my heart, I knew it would never be just once. "Whatever…" I trail off and reach forward to grab the knot of his tie. "Now?"

Surprise washes over his features, but then he hardens his expression. "When I want it, you will know. And when I come for it, you will give it to me."

I unknot his tie despite his words. "Are you going to force me?"

He grips my wrist in a painful way. "I've never had to force a woman." His eyes darken a shade. "They all beg for Daddy Diego's cock."

The moment of seriousness is swiped away when I snort with laughter. And as soon as one giggle escapes, an eruption of them soon follow. I laugh until tears stream out. When I sneak a glance at *Daddy* Diego, he's glaring at me, which only serves to make me giggle harder.

Striking with the quickness of a snake, he jolts to his feet and twists me toward the desk. I cry out when he shoves me down on the hard surface. My hand smashes into a half eaten dish while my cheek gets pressed against what feels like dinner rolls. I cry out when he rubs against me through our clothes. His erection is giant and rock hard as it slides along the crack of my ass.

"You will beg for it," he snarls, his fingers tangling up in my hair.

He's furious, but I can't help but start to giggle again. My villain sensor is broken and I can't seem to turn off the part of me that provokes them. His grip on my hair becomes almost painful, and yet I continue to snort with laughter. I'm completely flattened against the food when he covers my body with his.

"Oh, Daddy Diego," I choke out through amused tears, "please give me your cock."

The man freezes behind me and then his chest starts to rumble. "What is wrong with you?" he grumbles against my hair near my ear. "I have you bent over my desk, with food staining your dress, with my angry anaconda pressed against your ass, and you're still laughing. Have you no fear, woman?"

"Angry anaconda?" I snort again but then I relax despite the precarious position I'm in. "I haven't laughed in so long. I forgot what it truly felt like."

"I'm glad you're so amused," he bites out as he stands up, relieving me of his weight.

Carefully, I pull myself away from the desk. Plates clatter as I peel myself from them. When I look down, food is smeared all across the front of me.

"You're fucking filthy."

I stick my tongue out at him. "You made me this way."

His jaw clenches as he points toward the door. "Go get cleaned up and then meet me upstairs."

"What's upstairs?" I scrunch my nose up as I try to recall what's on the third floor. Last I remember, it was full of junk.

"You'll find out when you get there." His gaze falls to my breasts. "Dress comfortably."

Forty-five minutes later, my hair is clean and dried. The heavy makeup I had on before has been wiped away. He said to dress comfortably, so I'm standing in the bathroom staring at the white camisole and short silk shorts in the mirror, wondering if this is too comfortable.

The plan is to make him want me.

The plan is to make him kill them for me.

And per our agreement, I'm going to have to have sex with him. Lots of times, I'm sure. I meet my own green-eyed stare in the mirror. Dressed like this with no makeup, I look younger than my almost nineteen years of age. But the coy smile on my lips and the way my pink nipples show through my white shirt are far from innocent.

Esteban taught me that sex is animalistic and raw. Your mind shuts down as the nerves in your body take over. Pleasure exists where sanity cannot. It'll be just like it was with Esteban. I will turn off my mind and take pleasure in the deed.

Before I chicken out, I creep out of the bathroom and start for my bedroom door. The house is quiet. I know there are staff members and his men in different areas of the house, but right now they're being silent. I make my way down the dark hallways until I find the stairwell in the back. Hastily, I pound up the steps and push through the doorway at the top.

When I make my way through the door, I freeze.

Diego is no longer wearing a suit, looking dapper and distinguished as he usually does. No, right now he's looking kind of thuggish, dressed in a loose pair of holey jeans and a tight white wife beater. He's lean but muscular, like a fighter. Where Esteban is all bulk and strength, Diego seems more lithe and possesses a powerful grace.

I stare at him for longer than I should while his attention is on a gigantic television as he mashes buttons on the remote. Tattoos color his arms, and I can see more on his back through his shirt. Who knew all this was hiding under those suits.

"What are we doing?" I murmur, my gaze stalling at his beautifully curved shoulders. "I thought we were having sex."

He looks over his shoulder and his messy, now wet hair hangs in his eyes. I don't miss the smug grin on his face, though. "Patience, *mi diablita*. I'll sex you up when I am good and ready. It's all about the buildup." When he turns back to the television, I let out a growl of annoyance.

"Patience isn't a quality I possess, mi motherfucker." I huff and storm over to him. "I'm not doing whatever this is." I motion around the media room. "Dates aren't part of the deal."

He slams the remote onto the entertainment table and snaps his gaze to me. It's in this moment, as his eyes flicker with fury, I remember I'm in the lion's den. I've negotiated with a monster to do monstrous deeds all in exchange for my monstrous goddamned pussy. A vein in his neck pulsates and his jaw ticks as he regards me. And then, much like the snake he can be, he strikes.

His palm curls around my throat and he pushes me until my back hits the wall. He doesn't squeeze my neck, but his eyes convey to me that he could choke me dead in a matter of seconds if he wanted to. I need to make sure he doesn't want to.

I press a palm to his solid chest over his heart and clutch his wrist with the other. He loosens his grip, letting me peel him away from me. But he doesn't back off. His body crowds mine until I'm sandwiched uncomfortably between him and the wall.

"This is why I don't have wives anymore," he grumbles, his hot breath inches from my face.

I stiffen, no longer concerned about being trapped by a cartel bad boy. "Wives? As in plural?"

"Yes, wives," he says simply. "Plural. Past tense."

Tilting my head up at him, I frown. "Pig."

His lips curl into a grin. "So you think I'm disgusting and gross. I'm still waiting to show you how nasty I can be, *mi diablita*."

My nostrils flare and I open my mouth to tell him where he can stick that statement when he leans forward. His scent envelops me just a moment before his lips press against mine. The kiss is so sudden. So surprising. So…sweet. I'm stunned frozen. That is, until his palm curls around the side of my neck and he coaxes my mouth open with his tongue.

We both taste of toothpaste. I'm consumed by the way his tongue expertly dances with mine. Unrushed but deliberate. Soft but experienced. His thumb caresses my jaw and a whimper escapes me. I hate the vulnerable whine it carries. A sound that says I need his gentle touch more than I need air.

My fingers begin tugging at the bottom of his shirt, but he stops me with a growl. His hands find my wrists and he presses them against the wall above my head. This action makes my tits squeeze together.

"Sex," I whisper. "You…naked…"

He nips at my lip. "Not yet."

I want to argue, but his tongue is back in my mouth, owning me. He dizzies me with his kiss to the point that my knees buckle. My hands are released, and the next thing I know, I'm scooped into his arms. His lips are on mine again as he walks across the room. I'm tossed onto a comfy sectional sofa, but he doesn't join me.

"Want something to drink?" he questions as he saunters back over to the television.

"Are you kidding me right now?" I grumble. My body is trembling with desire over here, and I'm practically dripping with need. And he's playing hospitable host?

"I'll take that as a yes," he says with a chuckle.

I cross my arms over my chest and watch with irritation as he starts a movie and then begins digging around in a mini fridge. He grabs a couple of beers and pops the tabs. I accept one and down half of it as he flips off all the lights. Once it's dark, besides the glow from the television, he sits down beside me.

"What are you doing?" I question, annoyance in my tone.

He stretches his arm across the back of the sofa behind me and takes a pull from his beer. "I'm chilling the fuck out. What are you doing?"

I blink at him several times. "I don't know what to make of you."

He chuckles, and his gaze darkens. "Likewise. You're a pretty little puzzle I don't quite understand."

"But you're a big, badass cartel king who likes to fuck and kill," I snap.

He seems to consider this. "And you're a little girl with a big mouth who needs protection," he growls back.

I glare at him and grit my teeth. "So we're just going to pretend we aren't those people and have a sleepover?"

Amusement glitters in his eyes. "When was the last time you weren't stressed out about shit? When was the last time you just sat down, enjoyed a beer, and watched a movie?"

Forever. It's been forever. I think the last movie I watched was with Ren and Oscar at my apartment. That seems like ages ago. Back when life was simple and fun and hopeful.

Now life is dark and ugly.

"I'm not old enough to drink," I pout as I drain the rest of my bottle.

He regards me with a devilish grin. "And you're not in Kansas anymore, Dorothy. Here, under my roof, you can do whatever the fuck you want. Here, we live like kings." He winks. "*Mi reina.*"

I set the bottle down and let his words simmer. I'm so wound up, violence and vengeance running through my veins, that I don't know if I can fully relax. But soon, we're both chuckling at the stupid movie with Channing Tatum and Jonah Hill who are cops and go undercover at a high school.

When the air conditioner kicks on, I shiver and burrow against Diego's warm body. He smells good. Clean and manly. Maybe for a night, I can pretend I'm just me. Vee.

His fingertips stroke the outside of my arm, and I am comforted by his soothing touches. It makes no sense. According to Esteban and Oscar, he's a violent man who killed Camilo.

Maybe he's a hero.

Camilo was certainly the bigger villain of the two.

I'm sure Mr. Rojas deserved it.

Soon, I fully relax and fall asleep in the arms of a supposed monster. I've slept in the arms of a real life monster. This supposed one doesn't feel so scary at all.

chapter
EIGHT

Diego

"Please, sit."

Jorge's features are hard as he folds his bulky frame into the chair across from my desk. Despite his impassive features, I can tell he's nervous. A slight dart of his nearly black eyes. A tick of his jaw. An impatient glance at his watch.

"I've made a deal," I tell him, my voice low. "With the devil it would seem."

Jorge relaxes his shoulders. "You make deals with devils all the time."

But this devil is far more dangerous than anyone I've encountered before.

"How is Olga?"

Once again, he stiffens. "I'm sure Olga is fine."

I lift an eyebrow at him. "Did you sleep with her while she lived under my roof?"

He grits his teeth and nods. "I did."

Most men would lie to a cartel king to spare their life. Jorge is not a liar. He's extremely loyal—even if he did fuck one of my wives. She was weak—a habitual crier—and didn't even like anal. My loss is his gain. Good luck with that one, man.

"I should slit your throat for that," I growl. "Blatant disrespect."

His eyes narrow. "I would deserve it. Love makes you do unimaginable things, though. Stupid things."

"I wouldn't know," I bite out. "I'm not going to kill you, but we do need to get men out there hunting the remaining Rojas brothers. I want them brought to me alive."

"Do I need to know with whom you made this deal?" he questions.

I let out a sigh. "The girl. She's connected with the family. They wronged her, and she wants vengeance. And I…" I trail off and scrub at the scruff that's trying to grow in on my cheeks. "I want her."

"Another wife perhaps?"

I shrug and pick up a cigar. "I believe I'm done with wives for now."

He cracks a rare smile. "I'll believe that when pigs fly."

"Men. Rojas brothers. This week. Those are my orders," I grit out, ignoring his jab. "I also want Ricardo on the shipments going through Panama to get to Mexico. Tell him we—"

"I want to sit in on this meeting," Vienna interrupts from my office doorway. My gaze darts over to her like a heat-seeking missile. Last night, when she'd fallen asleep, I'd left her there despite my desire to strip and then fuck her. This morning, she's already showered and dressed. She's a picture of innocence in a knee-length white summer dress. Her silky red hair has been loosely braided to one side and her makeup is minimal. To an outsider, she resembles an angel.

I'm no outsider.

"Good morning, *mi diabliata*," I greet with a wolfish grin as I visually feast on her cleavage.

"Morning, mi motherfucker," she chirps back. "What's on the villain agenda for the day? Are we skinning anyone alive?"

Jorge raises his eyebrows in surprise at how she speaks to me so disrespectfully. I smirk at him before gesturing for Vienna to come closer. She shows no hesitation, despite whom she's approaching, and bounces over to me.

"Sit," I instruct.

She eyes Jorge with apprehension but eventually sits on the edge of my desk, facing me. Our eyes meet and her green eyes flicker with curiosity when I pat the side of her leg. When she lifts it, I grab her ankle and place her bare foot on top of my thigh. Once she has both feet on my thighs, I lean back in my chair and admire her beauty. Unlike the Colombian women I'm used to, this one stands out with her pale, slightly freckled flesh, brilliant red hair, and the plumpest dick sucking lips I have ever seen. Her glittering green eyes dance between good and evil, just barely hugging the line.

"Now what? When do we kill them?"

Jorge snorts, and I can't help but smile at her. "So eager. And we haven't even had breakfast yet."

She shrugs and picks up my steaming mug of coffee. I regard her with lifted eyebrows as she drinks from my cup as though it's hers. I'm not sure why that gets my dick hard, but it does. Goddamn this vixen.

I grip the inside of her thigh just above her knee and caress the flesh. She sets the coffee down and attempts to draw her knees together. I grip her by the ankles and spread my thighs apart, which in turn spreads her open to me. With my eyes back on hers, I lift the hem of her dress and peek underneath.

"Red. I like it." My voice has dropped several octaves.

"Should I go?" Jorge asks.

"Stay. We have business to conduct. My *partner* here wants in on the details. So, Jorge, fill her in on your plans," I instruct as I let my palm roam up her thigh again. When my longest finger brushes against her panties, she lets out a sharp gasp.

"Jorge…"

"Uh, right. So, ma'am, we—"

"Call me Vee," she interrupts.

My hands rub against her in a teasing manner. I'm dying to take a look at her cunt. This little girl wants to play big games with big bad men. I'll let her play. I wonder how long it'll be until she throws in the towel.

While Jorge drones on about shipments and territory changes, I attempt to distract her. I can tell she's trying to listen, but it must be difficult for her when I keep rubbing my thumbs along the sensitive flesh of her thighs near her panties. She doesn't protest when I kiss the inside of her thigh near her knee. A soft little peck is all she gets at first. But then I catch whiff of her arousal. And now I'm hungry. I nip at her pale flesh and grin when it starts turning pink immediately.

"Why not go through Buenaventura?" she questions, looking over her shoulder at Jorge.

I perk up. "What about Buenaventura?"

"It was where Camilo sent shipments to my father's shipyard," she says, turning back to look at me. Her red brows are crushed together as she thinks. "If you took over his territories, why aren't you utilizing his shipyard? Are the U.S. monies not that much?"

I narrow my eyes at her. Brie had detailed out everything she knew, but she played dumb when it came to the specifics about where the Berkleys were concerned. I'd assumed we were at their shipyard when I gutted Camilo like a fucking fish, but I had to get my ass back to Colombia. I knew shipping product to the U.S. was a huge part of Camilo's profits, but I simply didn't have the connections he had. Berkley was dead and his daughter was missing. But now?

"How much do you know about your father's business?" I question.

Her green eyes sparkle. "I've followed him around since I was little girl. I used to sit in his office and play with my toys or color while he discussed business and made deals. For as long as I can remember, I tagged along with my dad. When I got older, he tried to keep me out of the limelight because he considered me to be a vulnerability that someone could use against him, but I was still curious. I knew how things worked. And I know that when I turned eighteen, Daddy made sure to add me to his accounts and properties. He didn't fully trust my mother and he wanted me to hurt for nothing if anything ever happened to him." Her eyes become glassy with unshed tears but she quickly blinks them away. "Something did happen to him. He was murdered. While I was locked away in that metal container at my father's shipyard, Esteban brought me paperwork. He wanted everything to run as seamless as before." She bites on her bottom lip for a moment to keep it from quivering. "I signed checks in exchange for food. I paid bills for water. I did whatever Esteban asked of me so that I could survive."

I've hated Esteban Rojas since I was a teenager. We'd been two fucked-up kids on opposite sides of the line that had been drawn in the sand. He was a cartel prince. I was a thief who was slowly stealing bits and pieces that would build my empire. The privileged son against the son born of poverty. Two sides of a coin. A lifetime of war.

Nothing compares to the hate I have festering for him inside my chest. The fact that he could hurt women disgusts me. Esteban acquired quite the reputation for being a monster. He'd cut out the tongue of a friend of his younger brother's. I'd seen him nearly get killed by a small-time cartel leader when he'd fucked around with his sister. The only reason Bolo spared Esteban's life was because everyone in Colombia answered to Camilo.

But Camilo is dead.

Nobody can protect Esteban anymore.

The sins of his past are going to hang him in the end.

And I'll be holding the motherfucking noose.

"You're willing to give it all to me?" I ask, my brow lifted in question.

This gorgeous little devil before me grins. "Oh, mi motherfucker, of course not. I'm simply telling you that you *have* to partner with me if you want your shit in the U.S. Exporting to Mexico isn't nearly as profitable of a way to get the cocaine over the border because you have to pay a middle man. You need to go straight to the source if you want to keep most of your profit." Her fingers toy with the hem of her dress and she slides it farther up her thighs distracting me for a moment. I flash her a warning glare until she stops fucking with her dress and continues talking. "Killing Esteban and Oscar is what we've made a deal for. Them for sex. Easy peasy. But Buenaventura to San Diego is a *new* deal. You need *me* to push the coke into the U.S. My father had contacts within the feds and local authorities. At one time, they'd been on to my father and Camilo, but then they married my adopted sister Brie off to Duvan. It was a legitimate marriage that bound our two countries in a way that had them off their backs."

"So what are you saying?" I demand, irritation bubbling inside me. I knew this bitch had ulterior motives.

"I'm saying," she purrs as her foot slides to where my cock is still hard in my slacks. She rubs against it with the bottom of her foot. "You need me. This partnership, if you will, can be bigger than just one transaction. It can be a union. A deal bound by law—"

"And God," I finish with a growl. "A wife."

Jorge snorts. "Would you look at that? I think there's a pig outside flying."

I clench my jaw and glare at her, but it's hard to stay pissed when she rubs at my cock with her foot.

"It's just business, *Daddy* Diego," she says in her most seductive voice.

The bitch is playing me. I'm staring right into her calculating green eyes and I can see right through her bullshit. Yet…I am weak.

Goddamn women.

"Why would you subject yourself to this world? Drugs. Mayhem. Murder. A little girl like you belongs on the other side of a white picket fence in suburbia. Not in the middle of Colombia making deals with evil men. Why, Vienna?"

She leans forward and clutches my tie, pulling me closer to her. "Because I have nothing left. My legacy is all I have. It was my father's business and now it belongs to me. I won't hand it over to Esteban Rojas. And I certainly won't hand it off to you." Her voice becomes a whisper. "This is what I want, and you're going to give it to me."

I grab her hips and drag her into my lap. She lets out a yelp but settles herself against my throbbing cock. My palms slide under her dress so I can grab her ass that's covered by the silky panties I saw earlier.

"What if I just want to take it instead?" I demand as I yank the front of her dress down far enough to expose her nipple. "What if I just want to use you until I get what I want?" My mouth covers her pale pink nipple. I suck on the soft flesh until her nipple peaks and hardens. Then, I nibble on it. Her fingers thread into my hair and she whimpers.

Goddamn those whimpers.

"I'm going to go," Jorge states.

"No!" Vee and I both shout at the same time.

I jerk my gaze up to stare at her in confusion. "You like an audience?"

She rolls her eyes. "No, but I do like the idea of having a witness."

"Jorge is loyal to me. What makes you think he's a neutral factor here?" I'm amused by her implication.

Her green eyes darken as she eyes me cautiously. "You said you always make good on your promises. I'm simply making sure you'll remember we made such promises."

I narrow my eyes as I palm her tit through her dress. I'm looking for any weakness. Any sign that she can't handle what she's proposing. Her gorgeous face remains impassive. The girl is fire, and I want to get burned by her.

"You'd marry someone like me? For business?" I smirk and squeeze her tit through her dress.

"I'd wear your ring and all," she drawls with a fake southern U.S. accent as she bats her eyelashes.

I lean forward and inhale her sweet scent before eyeing her with a wicked stare. "If you married me, it would have to be binding and under the eyes of God for it to be legal. And if I take a *real* wife, under God, there is never any getting out of it. Ever."

"I understand," she says softly, a tiny twinge of fear in her voice.

"'Til death, *mi diablita*. The only way out is through the backdoor to hell. Do you understand?"

She swallows and levels me with a brave glint in her eyes. "I understand. The ultimate business partnership. What is mine becomes yours. And…" She clutches my tie at the knot and tugs me forward again. Her breath tickles my lips and my cock grows impossibly harder. "What's yours becomes *mine*. What was once theirs becomes *mine*. I'll be the queen of—"

"Everything."

I grip her neck and pull her to my mouth. Her kiss is hesitant at first but then she gives in to the slow tango of my tongue. I need the U.S. exports. It was such a huge facet of Camilo's territory. This partnership with little Vienna Berkley is a brilliant move. It further cuts the Rojas family. Esteban and Oscar may think they can regain what was theirs, but they are sadly mistaken. They are dead to this country. If they knew what was best for them, they'd leave while they still can. I may have promised Brie I wouldn't hurt Oscar back when I made my deal to protect her in exchange for information, but I didn't promise her that nobody else would. Colombia is mine. I am the king.

And Vienna wants to be my queen.

"Trust is a big thing for me," I growl. "I need to know you're not going to fuck me over the moment you get what you want."

"Sir—" Jorge starts, but I silence him with a wave of my hand.

"We'll sign a contract," she tells me as if that's the simplest idea in the world.

My wheels begin to turn. A contract is an excellent idea. But I want one written in blood. A constant fucking reminder.

"You're ready to be mine for life?" I question as I squeeze her thighs. I slip my palms under her dress and run my thumbs along the sides of her panties. She gasps and squirms. So responsive. I wonder what sort of sounds she makes when she comes.

"I'm ready to take what's mine. I'm tired of being kicked around and used. And if that means partnering with Diego Gomez to fuck over those who stole from me, then so be it."

"Sir—"

"It's done," I hiss to Jorge. "I've made my decision. Call Tatiana. I'll want her available tonight for what I have in mind. Get me a priest. This partnership begins tonight."

When he hesitates, I roar. "Go!"

Vienna doesn't flinch at my raised voice, but Jorge hustles from the room. Her eyes are on my face as she brushes her fingertips along my scars. "How'd you get these?"

"It doesn't matter," I snarl as I stand abruptly with her in my arms. Her eyes widen when I lie her back on my desk. "I want to celebrate our engagement."

She cracks a genuine smile that makes my heart thump. "I don't have a ring yet."

I push her dress up to her hips and begin sliding her red panties down her thighs. "I'll give you something better."

I sit back down in my chair as I toss her panties to the floor. Her cunt glistens with arousal. The tiny strip of red hair makes my mouth water for her.

What's one more wife?

But this one will be permanent…

The wife.

Wife number one. I never numbered any of my previous wives with that slot because I knew one day someone would fill it. Someone different and worthy.

I hope my mother isn't rolling over in her grave.

"Tell me no, *mi diablita*," I growl as I roll my chair forward so I can inhale her scent.

She sits up on her elbows and lifts a sculpted brow at me. "Why on earth would I ever do such a thing?" Her knees fall apart, inviting me. She bites on her bottom lip, her eyes heated with lust. "I want my gift, Daddy Diego."

My cock aches to slam into her. "You're a succubus aren't you? You were sent straight from hell to tempt me into giving up everything. So help me, if you fuck me over…" I trail off with a hiss.

"We both have a lot at stake here," she says softly. "I have nothing left except for my father's business. You're the only person who can help me hold on to that. Plus…"

I press a kiss to her sweet pussy. "You need protection."

Her breath hitches when I run my tongue along her seam. Sweet. This girl is so sweet and innocent despite her hard words.

"I can't be a prisoner again," she whispers.

I run my thumb along her opening as I tease her pink clit with my tongue. "Isn't that what marriage is? You'll be bound to me."

She reaches forward and grips my hair. Our eyes meet. Fire and determination and barely contained lust blaze in her glittery green orbs. "As equals."

I'm amused that she thinks she could ever be equal to a man such as myself who exudes power and strength. But something tells me she believes it with every shred of her being. I'll indulge the girl.

"If you fuck me over," I threaten and take her clit between my teeth. "I will kill you. Make no bones about it."

She whimpers when I bite hard enough to make my threat understood. Then, I suckle away the sting until she's squirming and begging me for more. I ease a finger into her and am satisfied when her tight cunt grips it. She'll feel amazing wrapped around my fat cock. My past wives were all used up whores. Their cunts had been nothing more than a wet hole to fuck. This cunt, though…it's a wet dream. A motherfucking fantasy come true.

"I won't fuck you over," she vows. "Please…I need…"

I take my time fingering her, making sure to locate her G-spot within. A tiny nub inside her that seems to beg to be touched. As I massage the pleasure spot, I tease her throbbing clit with the tip of my tongue. She squirms and wiggles and at times yanks on my hair. But it isn't until I suck hard on it that she comes with a scream. Her pussy clamps down around my finger as she shudders in ecstasy. I fuck her with my finger until she's ridden the orgasm into a relaxed state.

"Tonight, we seal the deal. All of it. You'll become Mrs. Diego Gomez. We'll get Buenaventura moving product again with your help. Together, we'll nail down the uncertain territories and make sure it is understood that we are bound. Everyone will know. Even Esteban and Oscar Rojas. There won't be a goddamned thing they can do about it." I grin at her as I make a dirty show of sucking her juices off my finger. "And I want you to wear this pretty white dress."

She sits up and attempts to right her dress. "I still want them dead. Knowing I've betrayed them won't be good enough. *I* want to kill them."

Sweet girl doesn't have it in her to kill anyone, but she has herself convinced. Who am I to crush her dark dreams?

"You'll get your chance," I vow. I give her a wolfish grin. "Aren't you afraid of marrying me? You have no idea what kind of man I am." When she narrows her eyes at me in annoyance rather than acting fearful, I stifle a laugh. "I hope you like anal."

"Ugh," she groans. "Don't be gross."

Finally, a motherfucking normal reaction.

"*Mi diablita*," I growl as I stand between her still slightly spread legs that are hanging off the desk. "There is nothing gross about my ten-inch cock buried deep inside your sweet ass. I bet you'll love it. You seem like the type of girl who has all sorts of sexual secrets. I'll discover them all."

She sobers up and presses her lips into a firm line. "I don't have secrets. What you see is what you get."

I grab her ass and pull her against my hard cock. I'm dying to unzip my pants and shove my cock into her. But now that we'll be married soon, I'll wait for the sole act of consummating our marriage later.

"I know you're a very sexual person, Vienna," I murmur as I brush a soft kiss to her lips. "Every time I'm near you, your body responds. You want to be touched and pleased. You, my dear girl, have secrets you don't even know you have. You're about to hand over the key, and I will unlock every single one of them."

"Don't fuck me over, Diego," she threatens, her eyes hard.

I grip her jaw and kiss her brutally.

"You'll be mine soon. And nobody fucks over my wife," I growl as I nip at her lip. "Not even me."

chapter
NINE

Vee

It isn't until I'm back in my room that my mind begins to clear. What have I just done? I sold my soul to the devil, that's what. But what choice do I have? If I leave Diego, even if he does manage to rid this world of Esteban and Oscar, I can't possibly keep up my father's business without him. My only option would be to seek out other cartels. And I'd much rather deal with the evils I know, thank you very much.

I pace around the room as my blood pressure rises. What if this is an awful mistake? The man is smooth. What if he's simply biding his time until he gets what he wants? Will he kill me at that point? I'd gotten lost in his promises and expert touches. Let him seduce me so easily. *You'll be mine soon.* So possessive. His true feelings are every bit the same as Esteban's. I'm a thing to him—a power play. There never will be a legitimate partnership. As I left his office without my panties and my dignity dripping from me quicker than my arousal, I was reminded that it will always be me against them. I refuse to be owned by anyone ever again.

With a roar of frustration, I yank off the dress and toss it to the floor. I'm about to storm into the bathroom to take a cold shower when the door flings open. I sense his presence before I even see him. And I hate that a little piece of my heart patters that he came after me.

Sick girl.

Sick, sick girl.

Villain bait is what I am.

"Leave!" I snap and turn to point a finger at him.

His black hair is messy and it gives him a boyish quality. But the way he prowls toward me is far from boyish. I yelp when he grabs my hips and walks me back toward the bed. My fists beat on his solid chest through his vest.

"We're not done talking," he growls as he shoves me to the bed. "You were making deals one minute while letting me eat that perfect pussy. The next minute you're stalking off and slamming doors."

Before I can roll away from him, he smashes me with his muscular body. He snatches my wrists and holds them above my head with one hand. His mouth presses sweet kisses on my face, which only pisses me off. The motherfucker knows how to seduce me. Well, unlucky for him, my brain has overruled my pussy and—*oh God!*

He's managed to wiggle his way between my thighs and grinds his erection against me. His clothes are a thin barrier between us, so I feel every ridge of his cock against my body.

"You're mine," he starts again, his mouth stealing another kiss.

I turn my head to the side and scream. "I am nobody's!"

My rage rushes from me the moment he tickles me. I'm pinned beneath him and have nowhere to go this time. Loud bellowing laughter escapes me as tears stream down my face. His fingers stop tickling me and he cups my bare tit. So many emotions are flooding through me that I'm getting dazed.

"Fine," he teases against my neck, the hot breath tickling me. "I'm *yours* then, fiancée."

He's clearly amused by my outburst because he chuckles. My hands are released as he starts kissing his way down between my breasts toward my stomach. I let out a gasp when he bites me near my belly button.

"I'm going to marry you in a few hours and then I'm going to fuck you so hard you won't be able to walk normally for days. Tell me no, *mi diablita.*" His light brown eyes glimmer with feral hunger. I don't tell him no because villains are my kryptonite.

After having sex all the time with Esteban, my body seems to be going through withdrawals. All I can think about is how much I want this man's cock inside of me.

"Tell me you want to play big games with a big boy," he breathes as he trails kisses back up to my bare breast, making my nipple harden. His hand cups me between my thighs as he sucks on my nipple. And just like earlier, my body is eager for his touch. He massages me in that expert way that leaves me writhing in need for him. Diego turns my world upside down.

Another all-consuming orgasm is on the horizon. I need it because I want to feel alive and free again. To get lost in pure bliss even if only for a moment or two. The orgasm he gave me earlier was intense. With my mind crystal clear, as opposed to the months with Esteban that seem like a confusing fog, I'm able to feel every nerve ending as they all explode to life and sing at once.

"Say it, *mi diablita,*" he growls, his fingers moving faster. "I'll do this all night until you say yes if I have to."

His words tip me over the edge and my orgasm tears through me with the force of a vicious tornado. I shudder from the sheer strength of it. Are all orgasms with him this intense?

He pinches my clit and I yelp. "Say it."

"I don't play games unless I know I can win."

His black eyebrow quirks up in amusement. "It's a good thing we're about to be on the same team then, huh? Because I *always* win."

I should feel threatened by this man but I'm not. Instead, I'm calculating a future. A future where I continue with my father's legacy and nobody fucks with me ever again. With Diego, I can make this happen. He's a necessary move on the game board.

And if he tries to fuck with me?

I'll end him.

I don't know how, but I will end him.

"Say yes," he implores. His mouth finds mine and he kisses me, like a lover would. When he's touching and kissing me, it's easy to forget who we are and simply give in to the sensations. I could almost close my eyes and pretend we're something we aren't. That this is more than a business transaction. "Say it." He sucks on my bottom lip before popping off and staring at me with those beautiful pale brown eyes of his.

"Yes." I grit out the word and attempt to glare at him. My anger melts away when his mouth presses back against mine. The woman inside of me who is desperate for love and touch and intimacy falls victim to this expert-level game he's playing. She's down to spread her legs and hopes for the best.

The wounded soul within, though, is weary and suspicious.

"Vienna," he utters and gives me a serious stare. "I can kill a man without breaking a sweat. But women…"

I bite on my lip waiting for him to continue. His gaze falls to my mouth and he gives a slight shake to his head.

"That," he says as he runs his thumb along my lip and tugs it loose. "That is what has me making stupid decisions. *You* make me weak. You think I'm going to pull some bullshit to trick you, but you have no idea how vulnerable you make me."

My suspicion fades some and I give him a genuine smile. "I guess we're even then. Villains are *my* weakness."

Marriage.

A business arrangement.

A new last name and the key to a fortune.

My future.

"Dinner is ready. Diego is waiting," Tatiana says from my doorway.

"I'll be right down," I assure her with a smile. She gives me a lingering, sad look before leaving.

I smooth out my long red locks with a shaky hand. Ever since he left me needy and wanting earlier today, I've had a hard time getting a handle on my emotions. At some points, I feel confident in my choice to marry a cartel king. It was always my plan for as long as I can remember. Just with a different cartel king.

Thoughts of Oscar fill my head. My heart still aches. Over and over throughout my life, he broke my heart. But most times, it was unintentional. Other times…. This last time, he did it on purpose.

I want to cry. My heart is tight in my chest, and I have to swallow down my emotion. But I don't cry. I've cried more times than I can count over Oscar since I was five. That day when I met him, he told me to chase him. I've been chasing him ever since.

This is the last chase.

The one where I make him pay for what he did to me. He's a monster—not the man I always thought he was.

And Esteban?

My core clenches but it's purely a physical response. For so many months, he made me rely on him for everything. He conditioned me to grow addicted to him. But now that I've been weaned off, I know he's a monster too.

This marriage will help me eradicate those monsters. I'm not the adoring and loving little girl who follows around assholes like a lost little puppy anymore. I am worthy and capable. I am powerful. I am Vienna soon-to-be Gomez. Queen of the Cartel.

"That's an evil-villain smile if I ever saw one. Sure you aren't a villain yourself, *mi diablita?*" The deep voice from the doorway steals my attention.

"I'm certainly no angel," I bite back.

He smirks and holds a hand out to me. "Come. We have important things to take care of."

I swallow and make my way over to him on shaky legs. My nerves are going crazy. When I'm near, he takes my hand and tugs me close. He's recently showered, and I inhale his masculine scent.

"You shaved," I observe, ignoring the way my heart beats wildly whenever he touches me. His goatee has been trimmed neatly. With his black hair styled messily and him looking dapper as hell in his three-piece black suit, I can't help but have a swell of pride. I know it's silly and girly and completely misplaced. But I allow the sensation to flood through me.

He'll soon be my husband.

I hope he doesn't kill me.

"You," he says, his voice low and gravelly. "You are a goddamned vision."

I laugh and shake my head. "No wonder you had so many wives. You're really good at this wooing stuff."

He smirks as he strokes my hair. I like that he pets me like I'm a kitten he's always wanted but nobody ever gave him, until now. The way he touches me makes me feel wanted and revered.

Please don't fuck with me, Diego.

"When you're my wife, I will cut out the eyes of all those who even look at you," he hisses as his mouth drops to mine. His hot breath tickles me. "And I will cut off the fingers of anyone who dares put his hands on you."

I shiver. My psycho villain siren should be wailing, but instead it is silent. The only sound is my heart thumping loudly in my chest. His violent words turn me on. I rub my thighs together and dart my gaze to his hooded one. "You're so romantic," I tease, my voice breathless.

His fingers slide into my silky hair, and he grips it. He tilts my head back so he can stare down at me. Light brown eyes flicker all over my face as he inspects me. Then, he leans forward and kisses my forehead.

"Let's go eat, Vienna."

My God, this man is a tease. I swear he gets off on bringing me to the brink of insanity just to back off and leave me hanging.

"Come," he growls when I don't immediately follow him.

"I'd like to, but someone is too busy playing the gentleman," I grumble back.

He smirks at me as his palm finds the small of my back so he can guide me out of my room. His hand slides to my ass where he grips it to the point of pain. "A gentleman doesn't grope his future wife on the way to their wedding."

I cut my eyes to his and grin at him. "I'm swooning, mi motherfucker."

He snorts and swats my ass. "I forgot you're a smartass."

"That's something you can't ever forget around me," I chide.

When we enter the dining room, I gasp. A feast has been laid out on the long rectangular table. Fancy silver and china decorate the space and several candles light up the room.

"It's beautiful," I breathe.

I'm not sure how this marriage thing will go, but it's already surpassed my expectations. Diego pulls out a chair beside the head of the table and gestures for me to sit. I take my place, folding my hands in my lap. He disappears and then reappears with Tatiana and Jorge. Once they're seated, he takes his place at the head of the table. A young male server comes out to fill our glasses with red wine and then he exits without a word.

"Tonight, we celebrate the union of two families," Diego says as he lifts his glass, his light brown eyes flickering with something that I hope is excitement. He certainly doesn't seem as apprehensive as I do. "Vienna and I will wed this evening under the eyes of God. If my mother, God rest her soul, were here, I know she would approve of my decision." His handsome smile warms me. The devil was an angel once. "Not only will this marriage be binding in the eyes of God, but it will be binding by our country's laws as well. And mostly," he says, his voice dropping to a low growl, "it will be binding to me."

I dart my gaze over to Jorge and Tatiana. Neither one of them speaks, but Tatiana flashes me a supportive smile.

"I keep my promises, Vienna," Diego murmurs. "I hope you keep yours as well."

I swallow and nod. The fierceness he's displaying would indicate that he believes what he says to be true.

I just wish I could believe it as easily as he seems to.

"So a toast to my future wife, a partnership that will strengthen my newly acquired empire, and for a play that will deliver ultimate revenge to our mutual enemies." He winks at me and holds his glass to mine. I clink it before quickly chugging down the bitter red wine.

"To Mr. and Mrs. Gomez," I agree, my voice shaking. "A power couple."

He reaches over and takes my clammy hand. "*Mi reina.*"

"You may kiss your bride."

I imagined this moment a thousand times, especially in my early teen years, but with a certain dark-eyed boy. A fancy beach wedding in California with my father walking me down the aisle. A big, frilly dress. A giant fancy cake. The whole nine yards. With Oscar. And for awhile there, while high off my ass in Esteban's bed, he'd taken place as the groom in my fantasies.

But reality is oh-so different.

Diego Renaldo Gomez and Vienna Martina Berkley are the star of this show.

I'm still so dazed and in shock over what just happened that *my husband's* kiss takes me completely by surprise. His kisses are always soft but demanding. This kiss, though, feels like a promise. I don't get to enjoy his tongue that still tastes of wine because he ends our kiss as quickly as it began.

"Come now, *mujer*."

He guides me out of the old church toward where his fancy black car awaits. I am still trying to make sense of what's happening and staring at the gold band that sits on my ring finger when I hear what sounds like a pop.

"JORGE!" Diego roars a moment before he shoves me face first into the dirt.

A shriek escapes me. My palms sting, and I'm sure my knees are now scraped all to shit. I start to rise but then I'm tackled.

Pop! Pop! Pop!

"Stay down," Diego hisses against my ear. His body heat is no longer enveloping me as he starts shooting at someone on the other side of the car. Everything is so loud. Even though it's night time, the moonlight is bright. Diego crouches at the back of the car near the trunk. I dart my eyes under the vehicle to see where the shots are coming from. When someone starts charging for us, I yell, "Two 'o clock!"

Pop! Pop!

The figure crumples into the dirt before they reach the vehicle. Shooting ensues from someplace else. I army crawl under the car until I'm close enough to take the gun from the dead man's grip. The shooting stops but my ears are still ringing. Two men are grunting, and I recognize one of them as Diego. Another figure emerges from the tree line on the other side of the road and starts charging for us. I squint my eyes to focus before squeezing the trigger.

Pop!

The bullet tears through his knee and he crashes to the dirt. When he looks up, he makes eye contact with me under the car. His weapon aims for me but then his head explodes. I'm gaping in horror when someone grabs my ankle.

"Diego!" I scream at the top of my lungs.

My attacker yanks me roughly out from under the car. As soon as I'm out, I aim the gun at his head.

"Whoa," Jorge says. "Whoa, *niña*."

He reaches for me, but I scramble to my feet without his help.

"Get in the car," he hisses. "Tatiana!"

She runs from the church and throws her arms around me. Her words are shaking and in Spanish. I yank the car door open before urging the frantic woman inside.

"Where's Diego?" I demand.

Two strong arms envelop me from behind, causing me to scream. Out of instinct, I drive the barrel of my gun behind me into what I hope is at my attacker's face. Before thinking twice, I squeeze the trigger.

Click.

"Fuck," Diego hisses into my ear. "Fuck, *mi diablita*."

Once I realize it isn't one of the bad guys, I collapse in his arms. He all but drags me to the car and shoves me inside. Tatiana sobs loudly as the men climb into the front seat. I pull her to me so I can stroke her hair.

"Shhhh," I coo. "We made it. We're safe."

She clutches my dirty dress, her tears soaking through my front. I hold her in a state of shock as Jorge hauls ass through the streets. He and Diego snarl in hissed tones the entire way home.

Her head tilts up and she palms my cheek. "I am so sorry, Vee. I worried this would happen. A marriage to a cartel leader is a lifetime of death and destruction."

I glance up to find Diego watching me, his jaw clenched. He's brutal and handsome and fierce in this moment. My words answer her question but I want him to hear.

"I know exactly what I signed up for and I am not afraid."

chapter
TEN

Diego

"I'm fine, Tatiana," I snap and swat her hand away. Her brown eyes are filled with tears. We've barely been safely home for five minutes and she's mothering the fuck out of me. "It's a scratch. Tend to Vienna."

Vienna's brilliant green eyes dart to mine and she shakes her head. "I'm fine too."

I glower at her. She's far from fine. Blood drips down her shins from her knees. Her once pretty white dress is dirty as fuck. The red mane she'd worked so hard to smooth out is messy and tangled. Compared to Tatiana, who is shaking like a leaf, Vienna stands there like a horror from a nightmare. Hate-filled eyes. Calm demeanor. Full, pouty lips pressed into a firm, pissed off line.

"Get cleaned up and rest," I tell my doctor and close friend. "You're shaken up. I'll take care of Vienna."

Tatiana nods before hugging us both. Then, she disappears from my office leaving me alone with my *wife*. Jorge is already rounding up my men and heavily securing the compound. Those motherfuckers attacked me on my wedding day. I'd hoped it was some other cartel wanting to take me out. But deep down I knew. These were Camilo's men. Esteban and Oscar have already begun their war.

They don't care about Vienna.

Those assholes shot at her.

She's a tool to get to me, nothing more.

Rage bubbles up inside of me at the thought of losing her. Our business union is of utmost importance, of course, but I *married* her, goddammit. She's mine to protect. They almost took her from me.

"Were they with the Rojas's?" she questions, her voice level and even. Christ, she scares me with how calm she is.

I give her a clipped nod before snagging my cutter from the drawer. I prep the cigar from the ashtray and then light it. When we got back, I gave Jorge explicit instructions of what I needed him to do. Now, it's a waiting game. We'll be protected here, but I want those motherfuckers hunted down and brought to me.

"Now we wait," I tell her as I exhale a plume of smoke.

She walks over to me and plucks the cigar from my fingers. This wife is unlike my other pretend ones. Despite their constant bitching and nagging, they still feared me. Vienna takes this partnership seriously, apparently, because now we share *everything*. Even my fucking cigars and coffee. Her swollen lips wrap around the fat cigar and she inhales the smoke, her wild green eyes on mine. Fire and vengeance storm within them. My sweet girl wants to make them pay. I yank the cigar from her fingers and snub it out in the ashtray.

With a growl, I grip her jaw and tilt her dirty face up so I can regard her. This woman would have shot me in the goddamned face today had she had any bullets left. She's not a princess at all. Hell, she even warned me.

Vienna is the motherfucking queen.

I kiss her pouty lips hard, my fingers never leaving her jaw. Her mouth opens to kiss me back.

Sweet. So fucking sweet. She grabs the front of my jacket to hold on as she jumps into my arms, her legs wrapping around my waist. I hold her perfect ass as we kiss. With her pressed against my eager cock, I'm dying to officially make her mine.

"We still have business, *mi diablita*," I growl between kisses.

She bites my lip and hisses. "Later, mi motherfucker."

We kiss hard with her grinding against my cock, but I can't proceed without knowing she's mine in every sense of the word. Her fingers start plucking at the buttons under my tie. Our kiss is messy and dirty.

"The contract," I snarl against her lips.

"Not now," she bites back.

I storm over to my desk and jerk her away from me to deposit her on the surface. The little minx tears her soiled dress from her body before tossing it at me. She's a goddamned dream sitting on my desk, looking hot as fuck in nothing but a simple matching nude-colored bra and panty set.

She's distracting me. For the future of our relationship, both personal and business, the contract needs to be carried out.

With my heated gaze on hers, I slip out of my jacket and pull off my tie. The vest hits the floor next and then I finish unbuttoning my shirt. Once I'm naked from the waist up, I grab one of my sharpest blades from my desk drawer. I flick it open, my eyes on hers to gauge her reaction. The little devil licks her dirty lips. My cock jolts, and I almost declare we fuck instead.

Almost.

"I want this gone," I tell her, pointing the tip of my blade at her bra.

"So do I," she says with a wicked smile.

I hook my finger under the bottom of her bra between her ample tits and pull it from her body. She remains still as I saw through the fabric with my knife. The material gives and frees her gorgeous tits. She tosses it away before leaning back on her elbows and putting her feet on my desk. Her knees fall apart as she offers her barely covered cunt to me. My dick is about to rip through my slacks to get to her.

"Danger makes your pussy wet. You really are a villain," I muse as I run my finger along the wet spot on her panties. "Such a naughty girl."

She bites her fat bottom lip and nods. I hook my finger into the side of her panties just below her clit to pull the material toward me. This too, I saw through eagerly. Once she's fully naked, I take a moment to appreciate her body. Young. Tight. Supple. She'd probably still be a virgin if Esteban hadn't have taken that away from her. Despite her past with him, she's still inexperienced. I love that she trusts me to take her to new places sexually. Whatever he did with her won't compare to what I'm going to do. I'm going to awaken her beast. I'm going to feed it and fuck it. There won't be any taming her beast. If anything, I'm about to free it.

"The contract is of utmost importance," I growl. "Then we can get back to what we both want and need." I tap my blade on the flesh over her heart. "I need *you* to remember every day that we have a promise to each other. Fuck witnesses."

"Just tell me where to sign," she grumbles, her voice breathless with need. "I need you."

I grab her left hand and pull it until she's sitting up. My mouth presses a kiss to the pale, perfect flesh on the back of her hand. The wedding ring that belonged to my mother sits proudly on her ring finger. Possessiveness thunders through me at seeing it there. I've held on to that one important item, the one materialistic thing my mother owned, for so long. Nobody was ever worthy of wearing it. But Vienna is the new owner, and I swear to God, it looks perfect on her.

"Do you need alcohol?" I question. "I might hurt you."

Her green eyes narrow. "I existed in a fog for too long. I want to feel everything."

I challenge her with my gaze as I tease her smooth flesh on the back of her hand with the tip of my blade. "A contract forged in blood. Still want to feel that?"

She snorts. "I'm not afraid."

I poke her flesh with my knife and become fixated on the crimson that wells around the hole before it spills down the side of her hand. She remains still as if to wait out my next move before breathing.

"Relax," I murmur. "It will be over soon."

A choked sound escapes her as I begin carving her flesh. I'm careful not to go too deep, but I brand my wife with a large *D* on the back of her hand. I don't want her to forget who she made this deal with. Ever.

When I finish, I meet her fiery gaze. Something that looks like a mix between hate and lust swims in her teary eyes. The tears don't fall, but I brought them to the brink.

"Fuck," I growl, my knife clattering to the desk. "You're so beautiful."

I grip her jaw and kiss her hard. Her fingers work at my belt and then zipper. Soon, she has my aching cock in her grip.

"Diego," she hisses as she fists my length. "I need you."

A groan rumbles from me as I rid myself of the rest of my clothes. I grip her hips and yank her to the edge of the desk. My cock is long and fat. She's so small. I should use lube to fit inside her without pain on her part.

But I can't wait.

I need her now.

"This is going to hurt," I warn through clenched teeth.

She claws at my biceps with blood running down her arm and draws me closer. "So hurt me."

The tip of my cock pokes at her slippery opening. She's practically dripping for me. Quick and fast. Like pulling off a bandage.

I slide an arm around her middle and meet her heat-filled gaze. My mouth crushes against hers a second before I drive powerfully into her. Her scream is snuffed out by my kiss, but I know I've probably hurt her. I'm about to black out from pleasure. She's the tightest fucking woman I've ever been with, and I'm inside her without a condom. I've been fucking women since I was fourteen. Not once did I ever do it without protection.

But this woman is mine.

"Jesus, you're perfect," I hiss out as my hips thrust into her again. Her fingernails continue to claw at my biceps, but she kisses me frantically. We're dirty and messy and so fucking needy for each other. Husband and wife. King and queen. Two avenging angels turned devils escaped from hell.

She wraps her arms around my neck and leans against me, her mouth still fused to mine. I lose my footing and fall on my ass with her in my arms and my cock still buried deep inside her. Those manic green eyes meet mine as she reaches behind her to the desk. My knife that still drips with her blood comes into view. She pushes her palm against my chest, urging me to lie back on the floor.

"We weren't finished with our contract," she hisses, her body slowly rocking against me. I reach forward and pinch her clit, which makes her already tight cunt strangle my cock.

"So finish it," I challenge as I offer her my hand.

She laughs. The sound of it is downright terrifying. "I have something better."

She wraps one hand around the hilt of the knife and she covers it with her other bloody one. She meets my nervous stare with a confident one of her own. "You don't have tattoos on your chest. How come? The rest of you is covered in tattoos."

Are we really fucking talking about this in the middle of the hottest, messiest, most psychotic sex I've ever had?

"I want those scars to remind me of my past," I grit out, my dick throbbing with the need to come.

Her green eyes gleam with decisiveness. Then, she starts at my right shoulder with the tip of the blade. The pain is sharp and intense. She slices slowly, almost as if to punish me, along my chest before stopping just below my naval. Blood runs down my ribs in its wake.

"Vienna," I warn when she lifts the blade again and pokes deep into the flesh opposite of where she started. "Not so deep."

She loosens her grip and drags the sharp tip down to meet the ending point of her last cut below my naval. *V is for vengeance.* The pain is intense, but the throbbing of my cock is worse. I swat the knife out of her hand and grab her throat. Her eyes are shining with pleasure when I pull her close to my mouth. She places her palms right over the cuts on my chest for leverage and begins riding my dick like it's her sole purpose in life. I squeeze her throat until her pale face turns a gorgeous shade of purple.

Our mouths meet for another needy kiss. My grip on her throat loosens the moment her full tits start sliding against my bloody chest. Fuck, this is intense.

"Partners," I growl as I lift my hips to thrust into her. "Lovers." Thrust. "Mine."

She cries out and her body seizes, like the other couple of times I've gotten her off. The moment her pussy clenches around me, I lose it. My cock explodes its release deep within her. It isn't until I've drained the last of it and her shaking has subsided, that I let go of her neck. She collapses against my stinging and bloody chest. I hug her to me and kiss her dirty hair. Not even an hour ago, we were in the middle of a gun battle. Now, we're in a whole new type of battle. This battle takes more skill and so much more is on the line.

"I'm not on birth control," she whispers.

I stroke her tangled hair. "I know."

"But…"

"In my country, family is everything."

She relaxes. "That was…"

"Intense? Hot? Sexy as hell?" I quip.

Her chest trembles as she laughs. "I was going to say fucked up."

My fingers thread into her hair, and I tilt her head up so I can see her pretty face. Those fiery green orbs have lulled into a sleepy state. I love the look on her. "*Mi diablita,* you haven't seen fucked up yet."

She smirks, which makes my softening cock jolt inside her. "Bring it on, big daddy."

The black coat she always wears is gone. This time, she wears all white. The one who haunts me isn't a demon. She's an angel. I'm stunned as she walks over to me. Her pale arm is outstretched. Blood drips from it. I want to fix her. To make it stop. She brushes her bloody fingertips along my chest and draws a letter against my flesh.

V is for vengeance.

The angel straddles my hips and cradles my face. Her scent—so sweet—envelops me. The hood of her white cloak keeps her hidden from me. But deep down, I know she's the one I am looking for.

"Diego…"

"Diego."

My dream mixes with reality, and I have a hard time shaking away the recurring dream. Lately, because I don't sleep as much, the dream comes more often. I'm always awoken with a sense of loss. In the darkness, though, I am anything but alone. Curled up beside me is my wife.

"Diego," she murmurs. "It was just a dream."

She slides out of bed and soon the bathroom light comes on. When she returns, she has a wet cloth. The bed dips as she climbs back in. At least I can see her now. She wipes away the sweat on my brow with a serene smile on her lips.

Is this what my mother would have wanted for me?

All those months I had one "wife" after another in my bed. I was looking for them to fill up a part of me that was empty. But the void always remained. Yet now…now I feel better than I ever have. Vienna in my bed feels right.

"Do you have nightmares often?" she questions as she runs the cloth along my neck. My chest feels tight with every deep breath I take. Last night, after we showered together, I took her down to where Tatiana keeps the medical supplies and I used the medical super glue to fuse our wounds shut.

"Fairly so. Mostly a recurring one. Tonight it was different," I tell her with a sigh.

"Better or worse?"

"Definitely better. I just wish I could see her."

Her brows scrunch together. "You can't see her?"

I frown. "My mother believed dreams were prophetic in a sense. If she were still alive, I'd ask her about them. They started when I was a teenager after…"

Her fingertips brush against the scars on my face. "After this?"

"I almost died. I think hovering between life and death opened my mind a little."

She discards the rag on the end table and then curls up against me. It feels too nice to have her here. "What happened?"

"Camilo."

She stiffens. "He hurts lots of people."

"Not anymore," I growl.

Her palm rubs along my uninjured flesh on my chest. "Not anymore."

"My mother was sick. I stole from him. All I wanted was to make enough money for her to get the medical treatment she needed," I whisper, my voice distant. "He tried to kill me."

"But you fought him off? You ran away?" she questions.

I shake my head and hug her to me. With her supple naked body pressed against mine, I am calm and relaxed. "Someone saved me."

"Big bad Daddy Diego needed saving," she says with a laugh. "Hard to believe."

I chuckle with her. "An angel saved me."

"You must not be all bad then, villain, if an angel saved you."

Sitting up, I give her a grin before sliding out of the bed. I make my way over to the closet to dig around in my chest that holds a few of my mother's things. It's all I have left of my past. I lift the lid and root around until I find what I'm looking for. When I approach the bed, she's lying with her bare back to me. The contrast of her crimson hair against my white pillows is a sight I'll never get tired of seeing.

"They say when I showed up at the hospital, I was clutching this," I tell her as I toss my only memory of my angel onto the bed in front of her. I climb in behind her and pull her back against my sore chest. Her fingers grip the stuffed cat and she draws it to her.

"The bloody boy."

I frown at the smiling cat who has dried blood still on his fur. "I suppose he is a little bloody."

"No, not Mr. Snuffles," she whispers. "*You're* the bloody boy."

She rolls onto her back, her green eyes the softest I've ever seen them. Her beauty temporarily distracts me from her words which don't make much sense. I've seen many expressions on Vienna's face but never one so tender and sweet. It's then that I hope I knock her up right away because I know she'll give our future children the same look my mother always gave me. My heart nearly explodes with the prospect of such an idea.

"I couldn't see my angel," I continue, my mind lost to that day. "I just heard her sweet little voice. A child. A child saved me, Vienna." I press a kiss to her forehead. "If it weren't for her stopping him, I'd be dead."

A tear streaks down her temple. "It was never supposed to be *them*."

I frown as I brush a red strand of hair away from her face. "Who, *mi diablita*?"

"You," she murmurs, awe in her voice. "It was *always* supposed to be you." Her fingertips dance across my scarred face. "I fixed you."

I fixed you.

It reminds me of all those years ago.

"I fixed him. He's going to get all better now."

My entire body stills as I stare down at her in confusion. A small, fearless girl. I'd never been able to recall what she looked like but I always remembered the sweet voice.

"*You* saved me," I murmur.

My palm reverently strokes her cheek. So often I thought about my angel. So many times I looked for her to thank her. The bold little girl who tried to scare off Camilo Rojas when he was dead set on slicing me to fucking bits for stealing from him.

I slide my palm to her breast and she lets out a gasp. I take advantage of her parted lips and kiss her. I'm dying to convey my thanks to her. Her voice and her gentle touches kept me hanging on as I bled out on the grass. My lips brush against hers softly at first, but then I lose control. She's sweet—unlike any other woman I've tasted—and I'm convinced it's because she's truly an angel. Her tongue is tentative, but I don't care. My tongue shows her the way. I kiss her in a way that tells a story. The kiss is reminiscent of a time when she, although small, held my delicate life in her hands. I was enraptured by my little angel and latched on to her voice that seemed to keep me away from the darkness pulling at me.

I nip at her bottom lip and suck it into my mouth before diving in for another deep kiss. We're both breathless and panting by the time I reluctantly pull away. But only because I want to look at her.

Her long fingers reach for my face again. With whispering touches that remind me of that fateful day, she brushes her fingertips along my scars. Her eyebrows scrunch together and the tip of her nose wrinkles. She's so fucking adorable I could scream. I'm flying high on this new revelation. An unknown sensation stirs in my chest, and I like it. I really fucking like it.

Her green eyes darken with emotion. Tears shimmer in her normally fierce eyes as she regards me. "I thought you died."

"You saved me."

Her eyes are darting all over me. "Those bandages…they couldn't have…"

"You ran off Camilo before he could deliver his death blow. Then, you stayed with me while I hovered between life and death. I knew I would find you again," I murmur before devouring her mouth once more.

I climb on top of her and ease my cock into her perfect cunt. In and out, I drive into her slowly. My eyes take in every little freckle that I took for granted until now. We fuck at an unrushed pace. She can't seem to stop touching my face, and I can't stop staring at her gorgeous features.

She is my angel. My fucking destiny.

She's mine.

And there's no way around it.

chapter
ELEVEN

Vee

I'm in a dream.

A dream that consists of lying in bed all day every day where my romantic villain ravishes me until I'm spent and exhausted. For two straight weeks, he's had his men doing the dirty work while he does me.

It's heaven.

But when we fuck, it's something straight out of a porn mag from hell. Diego is a freak. Apparently, so am I. I have the bruises to prove it.

"I have a gift for you," Diego murmurs, his face buried against my bare chest.

I smile as I run my fingers through his black hair. "I thought what you gave me after breakfast was my gift."

He chuckles. "Nah, I was just hungry for your cunt. This gift is different."

"Should I be afraid?" I question, a flutter of butterflies dancing in my stomach.

He lifts on an elbow and regards me with a sexy grin. His hair is wild and his facial hair has grown out some. I think he looks the hottest when he's messy and disheveled.

"You never have to be afraid with me." He leans forward and kisses my lips. "But get dressed. I can't put this off any longer or I'll have a five foot nothing tigress flying all the way out here to maul me."

I frown in confusion. What the hell is he talking about?

"Get dressed, *mi diablita*."

Fifteen minutes later, I'm dressed in a jade-colored sun dress and have my hair pulled into a sleek ponytail. I'm sitting on Diego's lap in front of a laptop staring at the open Skype app.

"What are we doing?" I demand as I absently rub my finger over the big D on my hand. I'm still attempting to pick glue scabs off it. His chest looks worse, though. Tatiana had a fit when she found out what we did and dosed us both up with antibiotics.

"We're making good on a promise."

"Okaaaaay," I huff. "I thought we were partners."

He bites the back of my bicep. "Remember that when she's yelling at me."

"Who—"

A beeping sound resounds from the computer. Diego leans forward to accept the call. Then, I'm staring straight into the big brown eyes of Brie. The sight of her has my chest squeezing and tears welling in my eyes. Last time I saw her, she was desperately trying to hold her husband's neck together.

"Vee!" she shrieks and leans forward to touch the screen. "Has he hurt you? He promised not to!"

I look over my shoulder at Diego and he gives me a smug grin.

"Wait? Are you sitting in his lap? Oh my God," she growls. "Is he forcing you? I'm sending Daddy and—"

I snap my gaze to hers and snarl my words. "Do not send that man anywhere near me."

Confusion mars her features but then it sinks in. Her father killed my father. My father killed her husband.

"I'm sorry!" We both blurt out at the same time. Brie blubbers about how it isn't my fault. None of it is either of our faults. I'm barely keeping it together because she's bawling her eyes out. Diego hugs my middle and kisses my back, which calms me considerably.

A rogue tear slips out and I lift my hand to swipe it away.

"What is that?" Brie chokes out. "YOU BRANDED MY FRIEND?!" That comment was for Diego.

"What I did to him is far worse," I assure her with a teary laugh. "How are you? How's the baby?"

She stands and shows me her gigantic stomach. My friend is an adorable pregnant woman. "Two babies."

"Oh my God!" I squeal and touch the screen. God, I miss her so much.

"We're naming them Alejandra and Duvan," she tells me with pride. Sadness flickers in her eyes but mostly she's happy. Actually, I haven't seen Brie this happy in a long time.

"We're?"

She gives me a shy smile but doesn't get to answer me because some muscular guy walks in to the room where she's at and stands behind her. He's tatted up and wears tons of scars.

"Hey, Little Mermaid," a familiar male voice rumbles. The man leans forward, and I realize it's Ren.

"Ren!" I cry out and laugh. "Oh, wow, you've been working out. You two are together now?"

He nods and presses a kiss to the top of her head. They're both so happy, which makes me thrilled for them.

Brie grows serious and guilt crumples her features. "I tried so hard to find you. You vanished. I had everyone exhausting their resources to find you. Even Diego," she says, motioning to him behind me.

His palm splays over my thigh and he slides it up under my dress, causing me to shiver.

"Esteban had me holed away in a shipping container," I tell her so softly it comes out as a whisper. "He hurt me."

Brie starts to cry and Ren comforts her. My man's way of comforting me is slipping his finger inside my panties to tease my clit. I bite on my bottom lip to stifle a moan. With a shaky voice, I recant my entire tale up until the part where they left me on Diego's lawn.

"Ozzie?" Brie asks in disbelief. "But he…how could he…"

I shrug. "And then Diego took me in. We made a pact."

At this, Brie winces. "You made a deal with him? Oh, honey, his deals suck."

I take offense to her words. Diego has been nothing but good to me for the past few weeks. "We're business partners," I grit out.

His palm creeps around to my grip my breast through the front of my dress. "And…"

I cover his hand with mine before meeting her gaze. "And he's my husband."

Brie's eyes widen and her mouth hangs open. "Oh, Vee…" Then she hisses at Diego. "What have you done? I trusted you! You promised to take care of her!"

With a growl of fury, I snap the laptop closed, ending her tirade against the only man who has my back.

"Calm down, *mi diablita*," he grumbles as he slips his entire hand into my panties. He pushes a finger inside me, causing me to groan in pleasure.

"She has no idea what we have," I snap, anger simmering in my veins. "What we have is strong. I don't feel as though I was victimized!"

He chuckles as he slowly finger-fucks me. "Gabriella worries about you."

I stand up abruptly and hate that it forces his hand out of me. With my hands on my hips, I turn around to glare at him. "How do you two know each other, anyway?"

He shrugs. "I bought Duvan's territory and factory from her. I've looked after her ever since."

Jealousy surges through me. "One of your *weaknesses*?"

All humor is wiped from his face as he also rises. Today he's dressed fairly casual in a pair of black slacks and white-button down shirt. He's rolled up the sleeves, revealing his toned, veiny, and tattooed forearms. Quite frankly, he looks good enough to eat. My pussy clenches with need, but I'm upset with him. So help me, if they had sex…

"Get that look off your face right now," he warns, taking a step toward me.

"Did you fuck her?" I hiss, my voice quivering. "Did she get to you like she gets to every other male on this planet?"

He launches himself at me, twisting me around with lightning speed before bending me over his desk. I scream and wriggle as he shoves my dress up. My panties are all but torn from me. And then he drives into me hard from behind. His fingers grip my ponytail and he yanks my head around, so I can see him as he fucks me.

"You're my wife," he snarls, his hips thrusting brutally against me. "She's a friend."

His thick cock stretches and fills me to the brink. With every pound into me, he brings me closer to orgasm. Our bodies were made for one another. A perfect fit.

"I'm inside *you*," he tells me, his voice soft. "I'm with *you*."

A jolting orgasm rips through me, and I shudder hard against the desk. He manages to thrust a couple more times before he comes with a roar. His hot seed spurts deep inside me. I love the way his body possesses mine.

Brie was wrong.

Diego is the best thing that's ever happened to me.

"Feel better?" he teases as he releases my hair before pressing a kiss to the back of my head.

"Much," I admit with a sigh.

He chuckles and slips out of me. His hot cum runs down my thighs. "Now put your panties back on. I'm hungry."

It came to me.

A sinister thought.

When Diego started pulling out fixings for sandwiches, my mind seemed to crack wide open. I fucking hate sandwiches.

"No," I grit out as I snag the loaf of bread. I storm over to the trash can and toss it inside. "No sandwiches ever."

His eyes widen in surprise, but then he does that thing he does where he reads me with one simple stare. I always feel exposed and transparent around him. But never vulnerable.

"Can we get something hot and filling?"

Understanding dawns in his light brown eyes. "I'll have Ingrid prepare one of my mother's dishes."

I beam at him and launch myself into his arms. "Thank you."

He palms my ass and bites my neck. "So easy to please."

"Speaking of," I tell him as I lean back to look at him. "I need some things from you."

"Like my ten-inch cock in your ass? All you have to do is ask, *mi diablita*."

I snort. "Ten inches. Kind of bragging there a little bit, huh?"

His grin is wolfish. "It'll feel like ten inches buried in your tight ass."

I press a kiss to his handsome mouth. "You make me happy."

He searches my eyes but then strokes my cheek with his thumb. "You make me happy, too. My mother would have loved you."

"And my father would have liked you, too."

"Where are we taking this discussion?" he questions.

I bite on my bottom lip as anxiety spikes through me. The things I need from him aren't going to be easy to acquire. "In your office. I think we need Jorge and Tatiana, too."

"Witnesses?" he muses with an arched eyebrow. Sometimes it's easy to get lost staring at his handsome face. When he sleeps, I often watch him for hours in the early morning light.

"More like helpers."

His eyes narrow, and I can practically see the wheels turning in his head. "I'm probably not going to like this."

I kiss him again. "You're going to hate it."

He closes his eyes and shakes his head. "Why do I sense a 'but' somewhere in there?"

"But," I say with a smile, "I know you'll give it to me."

A growl rumbles from his chest. "So confident, I see."

I reach down and stroke his dick through his slacks. "The king gives his queen what she wants."

"And if I don't?" he challenges, his cock hardening in my grip.

"You will."

"Humor me, Vienna."

I tug at his belt and then unfasten his pants. His pale brown eyes darken a few shades. The way to Diego's heart is through his dick. His very thick, very scary, very long dick. I drop to my knees in front of him and fist his length. He lets out a hiss when I lick the tip of him. I can taste myself from earlier, and I like it.

"Say yes, Daddy D," I beg, giving him the most seductive look I can muster.

He groans as he wraps his hand around my ponytail. "You can't strong arm me into getting what you want by sucking my cock—fuuuuuck!"

I take him deep in my mouth. His giant cock doesn't get far inside before he's hitting the back of my throat. I grip the base of him and relax my muscles. Slowly, I ease him into my throat. Esteban face fucked me so many times that I learned to relax my throat in order not to choke to death. With Diego, I want to pleasure him. I want him to see how good we can be together. He lets me set the pace, and I'm thankful. Diego is a generous lover. While at times he's rough in a delicious way, he's never cruel.

I start to gag and pull off him for a moment to catch my breath. When I look up at him, he's regarding me with a hungry emotion-filled gaze. I love how he stares as though I'm some god giving him a special gift. I lick my lips before sliding back down his length. The grunts and groans coming from him are making my panties grow wet. Him being so turned on is a complete turn on for me.

"*Mi reina*," he murmurs. *My queen.*

I hasten my efforts and pull out every pleasurable trick I can come up with. It's when I give his heavy balls a massage as I deep throat him that he lets out a familiar tell that he's about to come. His heat rushes down my throat, but I don't gag. I suck and swallow until he's gripping the sides of my head and pulling me from him.

"Come here, *mi ángel hermosa*," he growls.

I stand and he attacks me. His cock is still hanging out and his pants are around his thighs but it doesn't stop him from mauling me with a passionate kiss. He darts his tongue into my mouth and fucks it like he does my pussy at times. Hard and unrelenting. I'm so caught up in the kiss that I don't realize that his hand is under my dress and in my panties until his finger is rubbing my clit.

"Oh, God," I moan against his lips. His fingers are magical. He knows exactly how to touch me so that I'm practically humming with pleasure within seconds. And he does this little thing—"Diego!" I cry out and claw at his shoulders when he pinches my clit with his thumb and finger. Every time he does that, I swear I nearly explode. His cock, despite just coming, is pressing hard against me. "I need you."

He lifts me by my ass, and I help him out by wrapping my legs around his waist. His finger hooks into my soaked panties and he yanks them to the side. I whimper when he starts pushing the swollen head of his cock into me. Each time he stretches me to the brink of pain, but it feels so good, too. I feel complete. Like he's the missing part of me. Once he's seated inside of me, his free hand is back in my panties searching out my clit. He always assaults my nerve-endings from every direction so that I'm on fire with pleasure.

"Bounce on my cock, *mi diablita*. Own what belongs to you," he hisses against my mouth. He pinches my clit again, and it makes me clench around him. I'm being impaled by a cartel king and I've never been happier in my life.

I grip his neck and use my feet, digging into his ass as leverage to work myself up and down over his length. All it takes is another pinch before I'm seeing stars. I shudder so hard, he nearly drops me. Then, my ass hits the cold counter top when he sits me on the edge. He's tall enough that he never has to break stride and thrusts hard into me from our new position. I rip at his hair as I seek his mouth. The moment our lips touch and tongues collide, he lets out a groan that's so animalistic, it speaks to my own inner beast. I want him to mark me from the inside out. And he does. Hot delicious come spills deep inside of me.

"Mine," he hisses against my mouth. "Vienna Gomez."

I tremble at hearing my name. I love it. The name sounds powerful. The name is powerful. But mostly, I love it because it's his name too.

"What were we talking about again?" he jokes as he slides his thick cock from my throbbing body.

"How you love me and are going to give me what I want," I tease back, a smile spreading across my face.

His eyes regard me, mixed with awe and some other strong emotion. I'd said he loved me in jest, but one look in his expressive eyes and I know. This is more than a business deal for him. Diego's feelings for me are real.

And this is exactly why he's going to give me what I want.

chapter
TWELVE

Diego

Tonight, on our one-month wedding anniversary, we are celebrating with an enormous party. The wealthiest people from all over Colombia have been invited. Security has been tripled, but I still don't feel safe.

Give me what I want, Diego.

I grit my teeth. You'd think with five wives prior, I'd have plenty of practice telling a woman no. Instead, I fall into my wife's dick-sucking traps and hand her the keys to my kingdom without hesitation. She asks and I give. Every single time. I even had to call in the favor Gabriella owed me. Boy, was she upset, but she delivered.

I hold up the jewelry box—which arrived today, just in time—and lift the lid. Gabriella had to scramble to get me these earrings, but I wanted them for tonight's celebration. Perfect timing. Everything is going too smoothly, which has my chest tight with nerves.

"I don't like this," Tatiana tells me with a huff. Her gaze is on my bare chest and she fixates on one spot.

"I promised her," I snap as I start buttoning my shirt back up. "Vienna gets what she wants."

She frowns and crosses her arms over her chest. Tonight she's donning a black sequined gown for the fancy affair. "I don't like when her wants affect you."

I shrug as I knot my tie. "It doesn't matter what you like. This is bigger than how you feel, Tatiana."

"I just…" she trails off with tears in her eyes. "Would your mother want you risking it all on some woman?"

I pin her with a serious stare. "My mother would have wanted me to risk everything for love."

She swallows and her bottom lip trembles. "So this is love?"

"It is for me."

"And for her?"

"Only time will tell." I shrug on my black vest before pulling on my black suit coat. "Everything will be okay."

Her head bows but she gives me a small nod. "I hope so, Diego. You're like a son to me. I can't lose you over some girl. You fell too hard and too fast for her. It scares me."

I scrub my scruffy cheek with my palm before giving her a tender smile. "Vienna and I have a past that has led us to this moment. Fate was always playing an intricate game with our lives. We've finally gotten here. I'm not going to disregard what was designed for us. It's been a long road getting here and the road still has some twists and turns. We'll get to the end, though, together. I trust her and she trusts me."

Tatiana rushes over to me and hugs me. "You always were weak for women."

I pat my close friend's back and kiss her on the top of her head. "This woman makes me stronger. She's tough and resilient. Exactly what someone of my position and caliber needs. An equal, Tatiana. I don't have to take care of Vienna because she takes care of us both."

"I hope you know what you're doing," she says finally.

I wink at her when she pulls away. "I don't and that's half the fun."

"That's him," Vienna says, her long manicured nail pointing at the security monitor. "He'll come for me."

"He won't leave with you," Jorge assures her. "We'll have eyes on him at all times."

She turns to regard me, and I study her face for insecurity, fear, any-fucking-thing, but I find nothing. Her chin is lifted and her green eyes are sharp. My sweet wife isn't afraid. If anything, she's thirsty.

"Are you sure you want to do this?" I question, my brows pinched together. "Do you still have the knife?"

She slides up her silky brilliant green evening gown, past her knee to reveal a garter belt with a knife tucked inside. It's hot as fuck and if I didn't have one of my enemies in my home at this very moment, I'd screw her against the closest wall.

"I can do this, Diego," she assures me with a bright grin, releasing her dress as she walks toward me. "*We* can do this."

Her gorgeous red hair has been twisted and pinned into a fancy style behind her head. A tendril has escaped on the side of her pretty face, and I can't help but tuck it behind her ear. She's beaming at me. Confident. Fierce. Strong as hell. Mine.

"You look beautiful, *mi diablita*," I tell her and press a soft kiss to her glossy lips.

She slides her palms up over my chest to my neck. "You look handsome, mi motherfucker."

Everything inside of me screams to pull her into my arms and never let go. She'd be safer that way. In the short run. But what about the long run? What about for the rest of our lives? I have to let her fly away from me for a bit because that's the only way to keep her.

"I have something for you," I tell her with a wolfish grin as I pull out the jewelry box from my pocket.

Her lips quirk up on one side. "You're such a romantic."

"These," I say as I open the box to show her the two shiny diamonds, "came all the way from America. Your friend Ren's dad acquired them for me. They're special. Like you."

She stands on her toes and gives me a chaste kiss. "Thank you, Diego. Thank you for this." Her past hurts and injustices are written all over her face. I can give her security. I can give her safety. I can give her me.

She puts both earrings in and grins at me. "How do I look?"

I grab her hips and tug her to me. "Good enough to eat."

"He's headed toward the stairwell, Mrs. Gomez," Jorge says from his chair in front of the monitors. "You should go."

My hands are locked on her waist. It takes every ounce of self-control to remove my hands and not crush her to me. "Be safe, Vienna."

Her palms find my cheeks, and she tugs me down for a kiss. "I'll be okay as long as you have my back."

Our kiss turns frantic, but then she's pulling away.

"I have to go," she whispers.

I grip her jaw and glare down at her. "I love you, *mi diablita*."

Tears glisten in her gorgeous green eyes. "I love you too."

The moment she's gone, I prowl over to the wall of monitors. Jorge has her in view because as soon as she leaves the room, she's on the screen. When we'd discussed this party a couple of weeks ago, I spared no expense outfitting one of the spare rooms with wall-to-wall monitors of every part of the house, both inside and out. The equipment picks up sound as well because I needed to be able to have eyes and ears on her.

We watch my enemy slip into her old bedroom. She's long since moved into my room. I love that she's begun to add touches to the home to make it hers. Despite her and Gabriella's conversation ending with Vienna hanging up on her best friend a couple of weeks ago, she's still stayed in touch with her friend Ren. He even went by her parent's house and had some of her belongings shipped here. This is her home now. With me.

"What's he doing?" Jorge asks.

"He's looking for the book with their pictures in it."

Sure enough, he walks over to the bookcase and pulls *The Count of Monte Cristo* from the shelf. He's thumbing through it when Vienna walks into the room.

"Turn up the sound," I bark out.

Jorge turns the knob just as Vienna says in a choked voice, "Oscar?"

Over the past month, my wife has shared with me more and more stories of her past. A lot of them revolved around this man. Someone she trusted. Even loved. A man who should have protected her. Instead, he took from her and used her.

"Vee," Oscar replies as he shoves the book back into place and then turns to regard her. From my vantage point, I don't see any weapons. "You look well." His tone is flat and cold. It makes my hackles rise.

"I'm a good actress. I'm doing what I can to survive," she tells him, her voice shaky.

He takes a step forward, but my brave woman doesn't retreat. She lifts her chin to meet his gaze dead on.

"You were supposed to kill him," he bites out.

She stiffens. "And I told you, I'm not a killer. I'm scared."

His answering scoff is brief, but I catch it. "Kill him. Tonight. We'll be waiting for you to carry it out." He approaches her, and I hate how close he is to her. "Where'd we go wrong?" His hand lifts and he runs his finger along her jaw. She shivers as if she's waited for that touch her entire life. But I know my girl and I know when *I* touch her like that, it's different. Her reaction to me is so much better because it's real.

"You hurt me," she accuses, her bottom lip wobbling. "You *both* hurt me."

He runs his fingers through his long hair that touches his shoulders. "It was just because it was a part of the plan. None of it meant anything. You know that. A big game of fucking pretend, Vee."

I keep waiting for her to lash out, but she remains calm. She sniffles and he reaches to swipe away the tear. Instead of flinching, she leans into his touch.

Good girl.

"I'm sorry," he says, his voice raw. And I hear it. Remorse. Regret. But it doesn't forgive what he did to her. She'll never get over that.

"Oscar…"

"Does he hurt you?"

She looks away, as if to not meet his gaze, but her eye is on the hidden camera. "Yes." Her green eyes flicker with deception before she darts them back to him. "Every night in this bed. He takes and takes and takes. I was forced to become his wife." Her shoulders hunch as she starts to cry.

Fake. Fake. Fake.

My queen doesn't cry.

"Oh, Vee," Oscar croaks as he hugs her to him. "It was supposed to be us. How'd we get so lost along the way?"

I slam my fist on the table and hiss at Jorge. "Lost? He fucking ignored her their entire lives. Dragged her around like she was his fucking puppy. And then he raped her for authenticity?! This kid is fucking quacked out."

Jorge grunts in agreement.

"Can you get me out of here?" she pleads. "We can run away. Esteban doesn't have to know." Exactly what he wants. His sweet, adoring girl worshipping him at his feet.

He squares his shoulders and cups her cheeks so he can look at her. "We still need you to kill Diego. He'll always be a threat to us. Once he's gone, we can move on together."

"Esteban…" she murmurs.

He lets out a possessive growl. "We'll deal with Esteban later. He's unhinged, Vee. Together we'll take care of him. Then it will just be us." His mouth drops to hers where he places a soft kiss on her lips. Rage threatens to consume me, but Jorge is gripping my shoulder tight.

"Relax."

I crack my neck and clench my jaw. "I'll relax when that fucker is dead."

Vee pulls away from their kiss and darts her gaze to the camera again. She's playing the part of fearful girl, but I see the fire in her eyes. With one simple look, she assures me she knows exactly what she's doing. I have to trust her.

"How?"

He walks over to the bed, pulls a knife from his belt, and lies down. Then, he motions for her. "I'll show you."

She takes his hand as she climbs onto the bed with him. He urges her to straddle his waist. It takes some maneuvering in her fancy dress but she sits on him, her garter belt barely covered by the fabric. If he finds her knife, that could be a problem. I rise from my chair to ready myself to intervene if necessary.

"Use this knife," he instructs. "Put it under your pillow like this." He shoves his knife under the pillow. "Now, when you're fucking, lean in to kiss him but pull the knife out. Then, stab him. So easy, Vee. You can do this." His palm slides up her thigh.

"Wait," she blurts out and threads his fingers with hers before he notices her knife. "He's usually the one on top. What then?"

He smiles and flips her onto her back. His mouth finds hers as he kisses her hard. The motherfucker's hips are moving as he grinds against my wife's cunt.

Trust in Vienna.

Don't fuck this up by being a hothead.

"Mmm," she moans out in pleasure. But it's fake. When my sweet woman moans, it doesn't sound like that. Her moans are more ragged, more breathy, less controlled.

"If I had more time, I'd make love to you right here in this bed, Vee," he coos. "Just like I should have done all those years ago. It was supposed to be us. I've made so many mistakes."

"Rape is more than just a mistake, fucker," I snarl at the screen.

"But," he continues, "we can get past those. I wasn't in my right mind then. From here on out, I'll show you how good we can be together."

"Okay," she agrees. "Just us. Now show me how to kill Diego."

He holds her wrist with the knife in it and brings it to his chest. It would be so easy for her to kill him but that isn't part of the plan. At least not yet.

"You can do this, baby," he tells her and kisses her sweet mouth. He grinds against her again. "God, I wish we had more time."

"Soon," she promises.

When he pulls away, her dress reveals her hidden knife. She discreetly covers herself when he gets distracted by cupping her tit.

"Tonight," he reminds her in a gruff voice. "End this tonight and you can come home. We'll finish it together. Just you and me, baby."

She sits up and smiles at him. False and transparent. But only to someone who sees her genuine smiles each day. "You'll be waiting for me?"

"Just outside of the compound. If you're not out by morning, we'll know something went wrong. I'll come back for you if that's the case," he assures her.

Such a fucking hero.

She slides off the bed and launches herself into his arms. "I've missed you."

"I know you have," he agrees as he strokes her hair. "I have to go."

Her hand slides to his front and she gives him one of those sexy as fuck pleading looks she gives me sometimes. I'm unable to tell her no. The girl always gets what she wants. And this chump isn't immune.

"This isn't fair, baby," he groans. "You know we can't fuck right now and yet you're going to send me out of here with blue balls."

She pouts but releases his cock. "Fine."

He laughs and gives her a smug grin. "Soon, baby. I promise." He shoves a small piece of paper into her palm. "If shit gets too hard, this is how you can reach me."

Their mouths meet in a heated kiss and then he tears himself from her. He slips out of the room and down the hallway.

"Keep an eye on him," I growl at Jorge as I watch Vienna.

She walks into the bathroom and proceeds to immediately brush her teeth. I wish there were time to haul her into the shower with me to wash that man's stink off her, but there's not. We have a party to attend.

"He's at the tree line," Jorge tells me. "A car is waiting."

"Are there any others here? Any of his men?"

"Not as far as I can tell."

"Good."

I stalk from the room on a mission to find my wife. Once I'm in her old room, she throws herself into my arms.

"Oh, Diego," she murmurs, her voice quaking. "Why is this so hard?"

I kiss her neck. "It'll get harder before it gets easier. You did great, *mi diablita*."

She pulls away to regard me with guilt in her eyes. I hate that she feels guilty for what we both know had to be done. "It's hard to turn off love for someone. Even when you move on. Even when you hate that person."

I kiss her soft lips. "I know. It will all be over soon."

"Come here," I growl as I tug her to me in the hallway. I sway on my feet because my sweet wife has taken it upon herself to get me plastered at our celebration. She, on the other hand, is quiet and contemplative. She'd nursed the same glass of wine all night.

"No," she teases.

This girl loves it when I chase her down and fuck her into the next day.

"Now," I order.

"No!" she screeches as she bolts down the hallway.

I'm uncoordinated as I run after her, shedding my coat along the way. I see a flash of red hair dart into her old bedroom, so I charge after her. Once inside the room, I rip off my vest and begin working on my tie.

"Get naked," I bark, meeting her gaze with a heated one of my own.

"No," she challenges. "Leave me alone."

I smirk as I jerk the tie away from me. "I'll never leave you alone. In case you've forgotten, you bear my mark. Now take off your goddamned dress before I cut it off you."

She screams and backs herself into a wall. I stalk for her as I tear through the buttons on my shirt. When I'm near, she goes to dart past me, but I'm able to easily snag her into my arms. She wiggles in my grip, but I manage to rip the zipper down her back. My wife fights the entire time as I pull off her dress. The garter belt remains but the knife has long since been put someplace else.

"Get away from me," she hisses, her green eyes flaring with fury.

"Fucking never," I snarl back at her. "Take off your panties."

"No."

"Goddammit, woman!"

It takes some wrestling, but I manage to pull off her undergarments as well. I toss her onto the bed and drop my pants in the next instant. She starts to crawl away, but I snag her thigh in my brutal grip.

"Ahhh!" she cries out when I drag her back to me.

I pin her wrists at her hips. She wriggles but doesn't fight me when I start kissing the inside of her thigh toward her pussy.

"Stop," she breathes. "Don't do this."

Her cunt begs me to, though. It drips with her arousal. I run my tongue along her seam and lap up her sweet taste. She shudders in my grip.

"You're mine," I growl and tug at one of her pussy lips with my teeth.

"Never," she lies.

I suck on her clit until she starts convulsing with pleasure. Before she can recover, I climb over her body and press the tip of my cock against her wet opening. Her body accepts me despite her clawing on my shoulder and screams. Our eyes meet and an emotion I love dances in her eyes.

"I love you," I murmur softly against her lips.

She starts to cry, and I fucking hate it because it sounds so real. My fierce Vienna doesn't cry. "Please," she sobs. "I can't do this."

I nip at her lip. "Yes you can. *We're* doing this."

As I thrust into her, I lift up so I can watch my dick slide into her wet cunt. Her fingertip runs along my chest and she makes a cross motion.

"X marks the spot," she says sadly. Then, her hand disappears under the pillow. Everything happens so quickly. One minute I'm fucking my wife and the next, she's plunging a shiny knife into my chest.

"*Mi diablita*," I hiss in shock.

"I am not yours," she chokes out as she shoves me off her.

I roll onto my back and stare down at the knife that sticks out of my chest. Her green eyes are fixated on the wound that now gushes with blood. She's frozen in horror, and I'm in too much pain to move.

"Diego—"

I hiss the nastiest words I can muster. "So help me, cunt, you're going to die for this."

She snaps out of her daze and throws on a T-shirt and a pair of jeans. I clutch my chest but don't dare remove the knife.

"Vienna," I croak out. My eyelids grow heavy. Last time I got stabbed this deep, I nearly died on the lawn on the side of this very house. Back then, it was a demon who tried to kill me. This time, it's *mi ángel*.

The door clicks shut and I know she's gone.

The pain in my chest is from something altogether different than the knife stuck in my flesh.

Loss.

Heartache.

A crack in my soul.

Blackness floods in around me. I hear voices, two in particular, but I tune them out so I can chase the vision in my nightmares. She'd abandoned me when I'd married Vienna. But now she's back. My *ángel* wears all white, but her gown drips with blood as she beckons for me to follow her.

I know wherever she wants me to go is going to hurt.

But I'd follow her anywhere.

"Diego!"

The voices call to me, but I don't like them. The soft whisper of my angel is sweeter. It's more alluring. It drags me away from all of this.

I'm coming, *ángel* …

Black.

Black.

Black.

<p style="text-align:center">chapter
THIRTEEN

Vee

Run.

Run.

Run.

Tears stream down my face as I bolt out the front door barefoot and down the gravel drive. Rocks bite into my flesh as I run as fast as my legs can carry me.

They wanted me to kill him.

And they got what they wanted.

What about what I want?

I sob and swipe at my tears to clear my vision. It doesn't matter what I want. If I got what I wanted, I wouldn't be soaked in my husband's blood and running without a backward glance. My ankle rolls, and I nearly stumble face first into the rocks but I quickly recover.

Don't look back.

Don't look back.

I do look back, though. The house, giant and imposing—a castle to a fire-breathing dragon queen—mocks me. It practically hisses its hate at me. I'm a traitor.

Pop!

The sound of a gun behind me scares the shit out of me. It wouldn't be the first gunfight I've been in, but I don't have Diego and Jorge trying to protect me this time. This fight has Jorge firing *at* me rather than *with* me.

Pop! Pop!

The gravel near my feet kicks up as a bullet ricochets. I scream and run harder. The property is huge and it feels like the run down the driveway is the longest mile I've ever run. My lungs are seized up in pain and my calves scream from exertion.

Don't stop.

If you stop, you'll lose.

If you stop, everything you worked so hard for will be gone in a poof of smoke.

"Get back here, you bitch!" Jorge bellows from behind me. He's getting closer because now I can hear his grunts as he runs. With him wearing shoes, he'll catch up to me soon.

The sound of a car engine blares to life and then a car squeals from its spot on the road ahead, heading right for me. I wave my hand, hoping it's Oscar. The last thing I need is to run right into the arms of yet another monster. The monsters I know are the ones I'll keep.

"Stop!" Jorge roars from behind me as he gains speed.

The car slows to a stop at the end of the driveway and the passenger door gets flung open. Just like he promised, Oscar waits behind the wheel. A bullet whizzes past me and pings the metal of the car.

So close.

A few more feet.

I dive into the seat and Oscar wastes no time peeling away even before I manage to close the door. When I turn to look at him, he's grinning. His palm slides over my shirt and he cups my breast. Diego's blood has soaked through my clothes.

"You did it, baby," he says, pride in his voice. "We're getting you the fuck out of here."

I start to cry and he pulls me as close as he can to him with the console between us. My heart is hammering in my chest and the sense of loss is crushing.

I can't do this.

But I already am.

Of all the villains in my life, Oscar is the easiest to handle. I've known him since I was five. I can interpret his every expression. Every lie he tells, I can sense. For these reasons, he'll be both the hardest and the easiest man to beat. I'll know how to hurt him but in turn it'll hurt me because of the past we shared.

"Where are we going?" I question as the trees whiz by in the darkness.

His hand settles on my thigh and he squeezes. "Buenaventura."

"I thought Diego took over there."

He grins at me. "Diego has been distracted. I think he took on more than he can handle. Esteban and I rounded up some men. We were easily able to take it back over. Some of the men turned on him to spare their lives and fed Diego false information. Others, we've needed to torture to get what we want. But it's ours and it's only the beginning."

I frown as I frantically try to figure out what this means for me. I'd expected to encounter Oscar and Esteban. Not an entire branch of the cartel. I'm about to ask more questions when Oscar's phone rings.

"Yeah?"

I can't hear what he's saying but I recognize Esteban's deep voice on the other end.

"I have her. It's done." Oscar pauses to give me a chaste kiss. "We should be there by breakfast."

They hang up and he lets out a sigh. "We can't let him know about us at first."

I refrain from rolling my eyes. There will never be an "us," buddy. "Okay," I breathe and then let fear filter into my voice. The fear is real. With Esteban, there's no faking the emotion. "I'm scared he's going to hurt me. I don't want him to drug me again."

Oscar lets out a growl. "I'll do my best to not let that happen."

We drive several hours through the night without stopping. Eventually, Oscar pulls off onto a side road. Dawn has breached the horizon, but it's still fairly dark out due to a storm that's rolling in.

"I have to take a piss," he tells me as he climbs out.

I get out as well. My fingers go to my earrings and I rub them. They're so beautiful and important. The ring Diego gave me no longer resides on my finger, which makes my chest ache. It is sitting on the end table in the room he and I shared. Safe. Unlike me.

Breathe.

You've got this.

You knew it would be hard.

I'm jolted from my thoughts when Oscar hugs me from behind. A chill races down my spine as he gropes my breasts.

"All these years and we're just now getting together," he murmurs as he kisses my shoulder. "How stupid were we to wait this whole time?"

I let out a gasp when one of his palms slides to cup me between my legs. I know what needs to happen. What *will* happen. It just doesn't make it any easier.

"We better fuck now before we get there. Esteban is going to make things difficult for us until we carry out our plan," he tells me as he starts working to unfasten my jeans.

I grip his wrist to stop him. Distract him. Delay the inevitable. "What is our plan?"

He works my jeans down over my hips and rubs at my pussy. "We kill him."

"I know, but how," I demand, a little too harshly and out of character. I soften my words and lean against him as he massages me. "I want us to think of something before we get there."

His finger pushes into my dry opening, drawing a whimper from me. "I'll stab him in the back."

How appropriate…

"When?"

He works his finger in and out of me as if he's actually bringing me pleasure and not discomfort. "Next time he's balls deep inside you. That'll be when he least expects it."

"Maybe we should go then," I suggest, my teeth gritted in pain every time the edge of his fingernail scratches inside of me. "Get it out of the way."

"Soon," he assures me. "Your pussy is dry, baby."

I shudder. "It's been a long night."

He eases his finger out of me, and I let out a sigh of relief until he pushes me down over the hot hood of the car.

"Oscar," I start, disgust overwhelming me to the point I might throw up. "Maybe we should do this later." His belt jangles behind me, and I hear the tear of a foil. "Ozzy," I whimper. "Ozzy, why don't we—" Pain burns through me as he enters me dry from behind. Hot tears leak from the corners of my eyes as I clutch the hood. "Ahhh!"

"I know, baby," he coos as he thrusts into me hard and pets my hair. "Feels so good for me, too."

A sob catches in my throat, but I refuse to let it escape. My mind drifts to Diego.

"Mi diablita, these are bad men. They'll rape you," he hisses. Despite his horror-filled words, he's cupping my face in a gentle way that makes my heart flutter.

"It wouldn't be the first time," I clip out.

His expressive light brown eyes seem to flicker with his pain. "I don't know if I can allow this."

I lean forward and kiss his soft mouth. "It's the only way."

He rolls me over to my back on the bed and he starts pressing kisses all over my face. "I can't part with you."

I swallow, fighting stupid tears. "You can."

"What if they hurt you?"

"I'm stronger than you think."

He pushes his thick cock into my body, that is always wet for him, and makes love to me slow and sweet. Once he's come deep inside of me, his mouth finds my ear. "I want to trust in you, mi reina."

"You must," I whisper. "You absolutely must."

"Fuuuuck," Oscar groans, dragging me to the present. He pulls out and gives my ass a squeeze. I remain bent over the car as he ties off the condom and tosses it in the woods. "Plenty more of that in our future."

I pull myself up into a standing position and jerk my jeans back into place before hopping back in the front seat. He doesn't seem bothered at all by the fact that I was an unwilling participant. As he starts up the car, he fishes a couple of pills from his pocket. "Need something to take the edge off?"

"I told you, I don't want any drugs," I hiss.

He frowns and takes one. "I'm not going to hurt you. Not like him. I love you, Vee."

Too late, asshole.

All I want to do is curl up in a ball. But I need this guy with me…not against me. I lean against him and let my fatigue take over. He wraps an arm around me and strokes my hair as we drive. I want to stay awake but I'm too overcome with emotion.

I gladly run to Diego in my dreams.

"Like this," Diego tells me as he grips my wrist and guides the knife to his chest. "Plunge hard so it doesn't fall out. If it comes out, I'll bleed out."

I wince at his words. Hard. Got it. "Is this necessary?"

"You know how those motherfuckers are about their authenticity. They want authenticity, we'll give it to them."

"But…" I trail off, my throat squeezing with emotion. "What if it slips? What if Tatiana isn't right? What if we mess up?" I toss the knife onto the desk with a grumble.

His thumb drags along my jawline and he grins at me. Stupid fucker isn't scared of anything. Not even death. "If we mess up, I'll see you in hell, mi diablita."

I huff and roll my eyes before wriggling away from him. He grabs my hips and pushes me against the edge of his desk. His strong hands spread my knees apart, and he slides my dress up my thighs. A moan escapes me when he rubs my clit through my panties. He glares at me while he brings me pleasure. "I'm more worried about what happens to you afterward. What happens to me is nothing. What happens to you is everything."

I soften at his words and clutch his face. He kisses me hard as his finger rubs me between my legs. My panties are soaked with his assault, but I don't stop him. Pleasure with Diego comes so often that I've become greedy for it. Downright addicted.

"Just tell me no at any time and we'll find another way," he murmurs against my mouth. "I know this was your idea, but it's okay to change your mind."

An orgasm seizes me, and I shudder until my muscles feel as though they are jelly. When I come down from my high, I regard him sadly. "V is for vengeance. I want to make them pay and this way gets me right where I need to be."

He nips at my lip and grins. "So we give the girl what she wants. Anyone ever tell you you're spoiled?"

I laugh and tug his tie so he remains close. "You're the one who spoils me."

"And I'm about to spoil you with my mouth," he growls.

"Wake up," Oscar bellows.

I jolt upright and squint against the bright morning sun. We're parked in front of the shipyard. Shipping containers are stacked at least ten high for as far left and far right as the eye can see. Beyond the long strip of metal containers are the barges that ship cocaine, among other products, from Buenaventura to San Diego via the Pacific.

As a girl, we visited their shipyard often. But after my stay in one of the metal tombs for months back home in the States, I can't help but feel overly apprehensive about being near them again.

"Let's go," Oscar says as he climbs out.

I follow after him and squint against the sun. "I'm scared."

He gently grabs my elbow and leans into me. "There are eyes everywhere, baby. Just play it cool. I'm scared too, but we'll get through this."

I let him guide me across the gravel parking lot to the gate in the chain-link fence that stands wide open. A man with an assault rifle stands at the gate but nods at us to go on through. I shiver and try to stick close to Oscar.

"Where are we going?" I squeak out.

He points to the shipyard office. "Esteban wants to ask you some questions."

Terror climbs its way up through my throat at having to see him once again. Not that long ago, he had such a strong hold on my life. That won't happen again. I'm not his for the taking. At least not permanently.

I belong to someone else.

My heart skitters in my chest. So many what-ifs scream at me from the back of my mind but I refuse to give thought to any of them. Those what-ifs will knock me off my game. I can't afford that distraction.

I'm still trying to push those thoughts away when the cold air from the office billows out around me as Oscar opens the door. It's dark inside. I'm shivering but it has nothing to do with the temperature. It has everything to do with the beast that lives and breathes inside. The snarling beast who I will soon make my prey.

"Roja."

Vee

One word.

One simple nickname.

Spoken with such promise.

I'm scared shitless.

"Esteban," I choke out.

Unlike Oscar would, he doesn't run up to me for an embrace. Instead, he emerges from the shadows like the Boogeyman. Tall. Imposing. Powerful. I suppress a whimper of fear. Everything about him seems bigger and fiercer. His neck is most definitely thicker and his dress shirt is stretched to the limits across his bulky chest. Esteban has turned into the Colombian Hulk.

He narrows his eyes at me before flicking his gaze over to his brother. The way he watches us worries me. Esteban is like some feral animal who can probably smell the stink of his brother on me from halfway across the room. His nostrils flare in an angry way. I don't dare move a muscle.

"Diego is dead?"

I nod emphatically and motion for my bloody front. "This is his blood. I stabbed him. H-He bled out all over me."

Esteban prowls closer until he's towering over me. Oscar tenses from beside me but makes no move to come between my monster and me. He leans forward and inhales me. Then, he pokes me hard in the chest.

"Ow!" I cry out and rub the spot.

He seizes my wrist, gripping it painfully. And still, Oscar doesn't intervene. Fucking pussy. "How are you certain he's dead?"

I swallow down my unease and focus on everything I practiced. Breaking down in front of the enemy wasn't part of the plan. I lift my chin and meet his dark brown glare. "I stabbed him in the heart. He bled out. I ran. There's no way he survived."

He twists my wrist until I yelp. When he sees the scar on the back of my hand, he roars. "He fucking scarred you?!"

Terror sends tears skating down my cheeks. Diego thinks I'm brave. It's an act. It's *all* an act. With him, I *am* brave because he's the hero in my story. But I'm terrified of the monster in this tale called *Life*.

"He made me his wife," I whisper, my bottom lip wobbling wildly. "Did you really think he would be good to me?"

Esteban runs his fingers through his slick black hair and snarls. "I don't know what I fucking thought." He turns to Oscar and slaps him on the side of the head. "This is all your fault."

Oscar rubs at his temple and glares at his brother. Esteban seems to shift his weight back and forth on his two feet, like a fighter who's about to go in for the kill. It makes me want to provoke him. Tell him exactly what his little brother did to me on the way here.

Not now.

"We got what we want and—" Oscar starts but Esteban silences him by punching him in the gut.

Oscar grunts but recovers quickly to scowl at his brother.

"Diego fucked me bare," I rattle out, my tone accusatory. "So many times. I'm probably riddled with diseases now." I don't meet Oscar's gaze. "I suffered. So much." A choked sob escapes me.

Esteban grabs my bicep and yanks me to him. I'm tugged into his powerful embrace. I feel as though I'm trapped in the arms of a bear. His touch is gentle as he strokes my hair.

"He better be dead, Roja," he murmurs against my hair.

Oscar's phone buzzes and soon he's whistling with excitement. "She did it. She really fucking did it!" He hands over his phone. I peer at the screen with Esteban. An unknown number texted him.

Unknown: That bitch killed him. We're coming for all of you.

Unknown: VIDEO ATTACHED.

Unknown: Watch this video because that is how we are going to kill every one of you.

I shudder in Esteban's grip and he hugs me tighter. His scent suffocates me. At one time, I'd grown to anticipate it. I loved inhaling him. Now, I swear it makes me queasy. Just the thought of him on me and in me has me wanting to throw up all over this office.

Esteban presses play and the night before plays out exactly as rehearsed. The footage is from my old bedroom at me and Diego's home. To an outsider, it appears as though he chases me into the room and forces himself upon me. Tears spill down my cheeks. He'd whispered that he loved me against my mouth just seconds before I had to hurt him. In the video, though, you don't hear those whispered words. You do see me slide my hand under the pillow to retrieve the short blade Diego gave to me to use.

"You really fucking did it," Oscar says, pride in his voice.

I stare in horror as I plunge the knife right into his chest. Tatiana had drawn an *X* with a Sharpie on Diego's chest—*and thank God the video is too grainy to see it*—so I wouldn't miss my intended target. I made sure it went exactly in the right way. She'd located a spot that she could easily fix and no vital organs or arteries would be harmed.

But it was still a gamble.

He could bleed to death.

I tremble as I wait for their sign. The video shows me throwing on clothes and bolting. Moments later, Jorge and Tatiana rush in. I can't look at Diego's unmoving form. My heart is seized up in my chest as I keep my gaze on Tatiana's hands.

"We've lost him!" she cries out.

But then it's there. A subtle motion of her thumb pointing up. That was the signal—the signal that meant he was going to be okay.

I let out a sigh and quickly follow it with, "I'm glad he's dead."

"How do they have this number?" Esteban demands waving the phone at me once the video is over. "They can track us."

"I-I must have left the number Oscar gave me there," I choke out. "I'm sorry."

He slams the phone to the tile floor and then stomps on it until it's ruined. I wince because nobody will be tracking me that way now. Esteban shoos Oscar away. "Get lost. Me and Vee have some catching up to do."

Oscar clenches his jaw, shoots me a sad look, and turns to leave. To fucking leave. So much for stabbing Esteban in the back when he fucks me. I needed Oscar to kill Esteban for me. I know I can't take down Esteban, but I can sure as hell take down Oscar.

"Oscar," I murmur. He turns and gives me a slight shake of his head. Not now. Not fucking now. Pussy. I stand on my toes and whisper to Esteban. "Oscar forced himself on me this morning."

Esteban tenses and Oscar's mouth pops open in surprise.

"H-He has b-bad plans to kill you and take me for his own," I rattle out. "I d-don't want him. I w-want you." I'm shaking so bad I'm afraid I'll collapse.

Oscar's glare becomes murderous. "You traitorous bitch!"

He charges but doesn't get far before Esteban has him by the throat and against the wall. Esteban transforms into the beast he can be. Right now, he's a psychopathic one. His fist rears back and he slams it into his brother's face.

Crunch.

Crunch.

Crunch.

Over and over again.

So much blood.

I collapse to my knees, unable to take my eyes from the scene. If I don't stop him, Esteban will kill him. This is what I *want*. Right?

No. Not really. Not ever.

But this is what they made me *need*.

So with bile in my throat, I watch as one monster beats the other. Eventually, Esteban releases Oscar and he crumples to the floor. A part of me is disappointed to discover he's still alive. His sounds are gurgles and rasps. His teeth are broken and his nose is smashed. I'm sure more bones are broken, but I can't bear to look at his face anymore. It's too grotesque. He reaches for me, his hand touching my ankle, but I kick it away with a screech.

When Esteban yanks me up from the floor, I claw at him. Watching him hurt his own flesh and blood is a reminder that he's nothing but a horrific monster who will eventually kill me too.

"Stop!" he roars as he wrangles me into submission. His voice is softer. "We need to wash the blood off of both of us."

I'm helpless in his brutal grip as he drags me into the office bathroom. He locks the bathroom door behind us and stands between me and the door.

"Undress," he growls.

I shake my head at him. "No."

"I don't like that fire in your eyes," he hisses. "Undress."

Funny, because Diego loves my fire. "No."

His jaw clenches and his eyes turn nearly black with rage. This wasn't part of the plan. Oscar was supposed to kill him or at least give me the opportunity to do so. I wasn't supposed to provoke the beast.

Yet…here I am, telling him no.

I scream when he lunges for me. He tears my T-shirt straight from my body but my jeans take a little more work with me squirming. Eventually, after I'm naked, he rips away his own clothes and stalks me into the corner of the shower. I cower away from him, sobbing.

You endured months with this man.

You can endure a few more hours…

His hand grips my throat and he lifts me off my feet. I claw at his wrist, but he doesn't let me go. Ice-cold water suddenly showers down on me, causing me to shudder. He eases me back to my feet as the water warms but doesn't fully release my neck.

"Was it true? Diego fucked you bare? You could have fucking HIV or some shit?" he demands, spittle flying from his lips.

"Y-Yes," I hiss out.

He releases my throat some more. "And you could be pregnant with his child?"

My heart jackknifes in my chest. "N-No. They gave me birth control," I lie.

"Good," he snarls. "I'm not in the mood for a coat-hanger abortion today."

I shudder at his words but don't dare respond to that comment.

He grabs a bar of soap and begins aggressively scrubbing my body with it. I know he'll leave bruises by how forcefully he's pushing the bar against me. When he reaches my pussy with it, he stops to glare at me.

"My brother really fucked you?"

"Yes," I hiss.

"You didn't want it?" His tone is menacing.

"I didn't want it the last time either."

"What last time?" he demands through clenched teeth.

He starts scrubbing between my legs, and it hurts. The soap stings, and I squirm against it. I'm so focused on what he's doing that I barely realize he's asked me another question.

"I asked 'what last time,' goddammit!"

Pain slices through me when he rams the bar of soap inside of me. I choke and scream, but his grip on my throat tightens. His feral, evil face is inches from mine as he brutally fucks me with a bar of soap. It doesn't go deep, thank God, because he has it in his grip, but it goes deep enough to hurt really fucking bad.

I start to black out, my knees collapsing beneath me. The soap slips from his grip and hits the bottom of the shower with a thud. He pulls me into his arms to keep me from hitting the floor.

"What last time?" he asks, his tone much softer as he strokes my wet hair.

I'm shuddering in in his arms. "T-The n-night you t-t-took me to D-Diego's."

"That was me, Roja," he says with a chuckle.

I shake my head. "You stormed out and he…he…"

"He fucked you behind my back?" All humor is gone as the familiar possessiveness takes hold of his deep voice.

"Yes," I choke out. I'm overwhelmed and sick and hurting.

"Shhhh," he coos as he starts gently rinsing away all the soap. His hand cups my tender pussy as he rubs away the suds. Then, his fingers are inside of me, cleaning the soap out.

I'm in and out of a daze as he rinses me off. I barely register when he exits the shower to dress. I simply hug myself and sob as the water turns to ice. The water is turned off and Esteban stands before me, fully dressed.

"Time to go," he snaps.

I shiver uncontrollably and I can't tell if it's from the chill of the air or my nerves. "Where?"

I'm a stupid girl because I expect him to say "home."

"Time to break your fierce little spirit again. I was a fucking fool to let you go. You're mine, and they had no right touching you," he says in a low voice that makes my hair stand on end.

"Is he dead?"

He smirks. "He will be by the time I finish with him. He's not going anywhere, though. Little Oz won't be able to see after those hits to his face."

"Esteban," I start and hold a shaking hand up to him. "Please—"

He backhands me across the cheek, and I stumble into the wall. "At one time you worshipped the very ground I walked on."

I chance a look at him. He's rage personified. Nearly black eyes that glitter with evil. A clenched jaw that seems only seconds away from opening to devour me. "I'm sorry," I blurt out.

He shakes his head and his nostrils flare with fury. "We have a long road ahead of us, Roja. What was it last time? Four months?"

I fall to my knees and reach for him. "P-Please! No! I can't go in there again. I'll do whatever you want. Please, Esteban." My face throbs from where he hit me, but I keep my eyes on his. I try my hardest to summon the submissive look he's after.

He unbuckles his belt. If he wants to fuck me, so be it. Anything not to go back. But he whips off the belt instead with an elaborate swoosh. I can handle a spanking or a whipping or whatever else he has in mind with that thing. I can handle anything but being inside that container.

His entire body trembles with anger as he approaches. I close my eyes and await my punishment. The moment the leather tightens around my throat, I pop open my eyes in shock.

"W-What are you doing?"

"I'm reminding you who you belong to," he snaps and yanks the belt.

I fall forward and go to hold my hands out to stop me from crashing on my face, but then he yanks the belt high. I'm dragged to my feet while the belt cuts off my air supply. I grip the leather to try and free my throat so I can breathe to no avail. He drags me out of the bathroom, like I'm a fucking dog, and I'm powerless to fight against him.

He stalks past his abused and noisily breathing brother on the floor and out of the office. I'm naked and hurting and scared out of my mind. But there's no time to process any of it. All I can do is practically run after him to keep from getting choked to death. Several men with assault rifles glare at me with hunger in their eyes. When I get out of here, I'll kill them all.

Esteban *will* suffer.

Esteban *will* feel the pain he's caused me.

And I *will* get out of here.

Diego

My eyes are closed but the small girl hums a sweet song from a Disney movie as she unpeels her Band-Aids and places them on my face. One by one. The birds chirp and a small breeze blows, but I'm too weak to open my eyes. Her hair must be long because it brushes against my arm. I'm numb. So numb. My mother is going to be so upset with me. That is, if I make it out of here alive. I'd gone into this dumb mission of mine a few months before my eighteenth birthday, thinking I'd steal the coke and make a quick sale to get her some medications she could take to make her feel better.

And now…

Now I'm screwed.

Camilo, our country's biggest cartel leader, has all but gutted me. And if it weren't for this little girl, he would have succeeded.

With each passing second, I grow weaker. I never had any siblings, but I know that I would feel protective over them. Especially a little sister. This little girl—who can't be very old, based on the sound of her voice—is someone I will protect.

She continues humming, and I latch on to the sound of it.

Maybe I'm already dead. Maybe this is heaven. Maybe she's an angel.

The warm breath has her hair tickling my arm again. I suppose there are worse ways to die and worse places to end up. If I had to spend the rest of eternity in this moment, I could.

I'm at peace.

"Fuuuuck," I wake with a hiss and squint against a bright light. "What the fuck?" Pain throbs from my chest, and I'm disoriented. Am I almost eighteen again? Am I bleeding out on the grass?

"Diego," a familiar voice chokes out.

Is that my mother?

"I was so worried you wouldn't come to!"

I blink my eyes open, and Tatiana comes into focus. The fog dissipates and everything comes back to me like a ton of crushing bricks.

"Vienna," I snarl, ignoring the biting pain in my chest. "Where is Vienna?"

Jorge stalks over to the bedside. "She's with them. I watched her climb into the car with the youngest Rojas brother."

I scrub at my face but it pulls at my chest. When I look down, I can see I'm sporting fresh new stiches from where Vienna stabbed me. "What did you give me?" I demand.

Tatiana holds up her hand in protest. "Nothing, just like you requested. However, you drank too much alcohol before this, which was not what I requested. It made your blood thinner, so you bled more. You're lightheaded from the blood loss but you'll be okay with rest."

"Rest?!" I hiss as I sit up. A blanket has been thrown over my waist but my cock is still sticky from being inside my wife recently. "How much time has passed?"

Jorge holds up his phone to show a tracker. "Almost two hours."

"Why didn't you fucking wake me up sooner?" I snarl and sling the sheet away, uncaring if they see my fucking cock. Tatiana reaches for me when I stumble, but I swat her away. "I'm fine. I need clothes and some goddamned coffee. And I need us to leave in the next five minutes."

I walk past Jorge and head toward my bedroom. Blindly, I grab a pair of holey jeans and a white T-shirt. Then, I throw on some socks and a pair of boots. Once I'm dressed, I storm into my office, feeling much clearer in the head. My chest hurts like a motherfucker, but I've received and lived through worse stab wounds.

"Where are they headed?"

"West. They haven't stopped," Jorge tells me. He begins checking his weapons.

I locate my Glock and holster. The movement is painful, but I finally get it strapped to my back under my shirt. My favorite knife gets hooked to my belt, and I snag my cigar from the ashtray. Once it's ready and lit, I inhale a plume of smoke and motion for the door.

"Let's go," I order, the cigar wiggling between my teeth.

He follows me out and Tatiana meets me in the hall. Her medical bag is on one shoulder and she holds a thermos in her hand.

"You shouldn't be smoking, Diego." When I glower at her, she quickly continues. "Coffee. And I have food in my bag for you to eat along the way." She lifts her chin bravely. "I'm coming with you."

I shake my head as I storm past her. "Fuck no."

"Diego! Yes!" she hollers after me. "You're not well, and I need to make sure you remain okay. And what if…" she trails off. "I need to be there for Vee."

I freeze at her words. She's right. Vienna and I discussed this at great lengths. I was sickened as she detailed out every single thing Esteban and Oscar had ever done to her. There was more of the same where they were concerned. We both knew this going into our plan. If she hadn't been so goddamned adamant, I'd have told her the fuck with her plan.

But my scarlet-headed vixen?

Nobody tells *mi diablita* no.

Not even me.

You let her wreak her havoc.

She's a storm and a hell-raiser.

And I have her back, which is why we need to get the hell on the road.

"Let's go," I bark out. "I want more men on this with us."

Jorge nods and pulls out his cell to make his orders. As we climb into Jorge's SUV, I notice several of my men emerge from the tree line, assault rifles in hand.

"They're right behind us," he assures me as we tear off down the driveway.

I set my cigar down in the ashtray and regard my right-hand man. "Where do you think they're going?" I ask and twist my wedding ring around my finger.

Jorge scrubs his face. "I don't fucking know."

I pull out my phone and call my little American friend. She answers on the first ring.

"Is Vee okay?" she blurts out in greeting.

"She will be if you continue to uphold your end of the deal, cariño," I grumble. Getting her to help me was like pulling fucking teeth. Eventually, she pulled the strings I needed her to because a deal is a deal and, like me, she's not one to break her word. "Is your boyfriend's dad still tracking the earrings?"

She swallows loudly into the phone. "He is. We're watching it on the monitor now. It's moving in the same direction as the phone. Oscar and Vee are together." She lets out a teary sob. "How could he do this to her?"

I don't remind her that he's a fucking Rojas. He's not my friend. Oscar is the scum on the bottom of my shoe. "It doesn't matter," I snap. "He did it. He's probably still fucking doing it. I want you to call me if anything changes on the GPS location of either trace."

"Of course," she breathes. "Diego…bring my friend back home. I can tell you care about her. It surprises me that you care about anyone but yourself, but apparently you do. You looked after and protected me. I know you'll do the same for her. Thank you."

My chest tightens. A year ago, I'd have laughed if someone would have told me I'd befriend a little feisty American and marry her even feistier best friend. "I love her, Gabriella."

She sniffles. "I know you do."

We hang up and Tatiana shoves a sandwich in my face. "Eat. You need the protein."

Jorge snorts, and I roll my eyes as I take the sandwich. I chomp on it but it only reminds me of my wife. That fucker never fed her. Fucking sandwiches like once a day. Bile rises in my throat at the thought of him torturing her further. I swallow down my bite and then toss the sandwich out the window. Tatiana grumbles, but I ignore her as I chug down the hot coffee instead. Once I'm feeling better, I prepare my cigar and relight it, sticking it between my teeth. Nothing will bring me comfort right now, but this is a start.

Be brave, mi amor.

Be fucking brave.

I jolt awake at the sound of my phone ringing. "Yes?"

"The cell phone is gone. They must have destroyed it," Gabriella tells me, her voice urgent. "The earrings are still picking up a signal. But Diego?"

"What?" I demand.

"They've been stopped at the same location for the past fifteen minutes. It's a location we know…"

"And?"

"Buenaventura. Camilo's old shipyard."

I seethe into the phone. "You mean my new shipyard."

"They're there. If it's yours, why haven't your men called to tell you?" she questions.

Because I've been fucking betrayed. I should have known Esteban and Oscar would have been able to sway some of their old men. "Call me if anything changes," I bark at her before hanging up.

"What is it?" Jorge demands.

"Buenaventura. They've taken over. Alert our men," I growl. "We're about to fucking go to war."

We're still two hours behind when Vienna left with Oscar. It pains me knowing she'll be in their custody for two minutes, much less two hours. My wife is strong and brilliant and tougher than nails but…

Esteban is fucking crazy.

Fury bubbles up inside of me. The men who betrayed me will all die. One by one, I will end them all. I'll save Esteban for last. I'll slice him up, like I sliced up his father. The Rojas fucks will be nothing but shit on the sole of my shoes when I'm finished with them.

I unsheathe my blade and it glints in the morning light. I'm going to fuck them all up. Nobody hurts my wife and lives to tell about it. Fucking nobody.

"This is such a bad idea," Tatiana complains from the backseat. "Ever since you met this girl, your life has been topsy turvy."

I inhale a sharp breath. "Ever since I met her, my life has come into focus. I love her and I'd take a million stabs to the chest if it means I'll get to have her in the end. Vienna is a flame I want to get burned by, don't you see? I don't want to feel safe and secure if I can't have her. I'd much rather live and die fighting as long as I can do it with her."

Tatiana reaches forward and clutches my shoulder. "I just worry about you."

I turn and give her a wicked grin. "You should worry about them. They're all about to be slaughtered."

She frowns and nods. "I knew that day you showed up on my operating table that you'd be trouble. And yet…" she trails off and flashes me a proud smile. "You're always worth it because you're the boy I could never have."

Warmth floods my chest, and I close my eyes as we continue our drive. My mother would be proud of me. Not for the cartel shit and all that comes with it. She'd be proud of me for loving Vienna and finding a motherly friend in Tatiana. Integrity was always a big deal for my mother, which is why I've always kept my word in every situation. "A man's word is his honor," she'd said. I'm sure she'd be proud of the man I've become.

Now I need to continue to live up to her expectations.

I'll fulfil them all.

And that starts with rescuing my queen.

I'm coming, mi diablita. *Just hold on for me, beautiful.*

chapter
SIXTEEN

Vee

As soon as the rusty old container comes into view, I know that's where we're going. Intuition, if you will. Esteban had put me in one like it once before. Hidden away in the back of the lot where nobody would hear my screams.

"No!"

He yanks on the belt, and I stumble forward. I tug at the leather but it's so tight, I can't even get my finger between it and my throat. I'm hissing for air when I'm dragged into the dark unit. Panic washes over me. My heart races so fast in my chest, I'm afraid I'll black out. Memories of so many months locked away threaten to consume me. I can't do this again.

Diego.

Diego will find you.

Breathe.

The door is left open behind us and Esteban shoves me toward the back. I fall to my knees but I take the moment to yank the belt from my throat and toss it away. The morning sunlight shines in and illuminates the space. But not for long. Never for long. Soon it will be nothing but me and the darkness. His heavy footsteps thunder behind me. He wants to corner me, and like the scared little animal I am right now, I run straight for the corner as if it will offer me an escape.

My knees land on a dilapidated mattress. It's then when I realize he was going to put me in here whether or not I behaved. A sick game to him. Breaking me is his brand of fun. Fire blazes inside my chest, and I turn to face my attacker. When he nears, I kick him and the bottom of my heel slams onto his jaw. Pain rips up my foot, but it knocks him off his game for a second. I scramble past him, but he hooks me around my waist.

"Not so fast," he snarls against my hair. "You need to calm the fuck down, Roja."

He tries to pry open my mouth, and instead of fighting him, I open and then bite down hard.

"FUCKING CUNT!" he roars as he rips at my hair.

I release him and cry out. I'm tossed down onto the mattress. Before I can move, he tackles me. I squirm, but he wrangles me onto my back. He pins my body with his massive weight and binds my wrists together with one hand.

"Open," he orders.

I shake my head.

"So help me," he snarls, his spit showering down on me, "if you don't open your goddamned mouth, I'll cut your tongue out and shove it up your ass."

A shudder ripples through me.

But I open my goddamned mouth.

He shoves a pill deep into my mouth until I'm forced to swallow it. I know what it is. Same hazy drug from last time. With the sun shining in from the doorway, it casts a shadow on his face, but illuminates him from behind.

A demon.

Esteban was sent straight from where nightmares are made to torment me in this life.

One day, I'll send him back to hell.

He holds me in his tight grip until my eyelids grow heavy and I give in to exhaustion. Fifteen minutes pass, maybe longer, but the drug is taking effect. When he realizes I've relaxed, he releases my hands. They're throbbing but a buzzing has already begun to course through me.

I hate this feeling.

"I missed you," he tells me, his voice a low growl that echoes through every nerve ending in my body.

I shiver and squirm. My body is pulsating, especially between my legs. "Fuck you," I murmur.

He slaps me hard across the face. The sting of it zings through my body and feels as though it ricochets off every inch of my flesh. I'm still reeling when he stands up. I hear the jangle of his belt even before I see it. With a quickness I can barely register, he binds my wrists with the leather.

The only thing he can do that he hasn't done already is kill me.

And as psycho as Esteban is, I don't think he has it in him. He'd much rather keep me as his toy to torment.

"Your pussy still belongs to me," he tells me as he clutches my knees and pries them apart.

I don't have the strength to fight against him. The more I fight, the more he hurts me. I knew this was what would happen. I ensured Diego I could handle it.

I *can* handle it.

But after today, I won't have to handle it ever again.

"Did Oscar make you come?" he asks, his long finger dragging a trail from my belly button down south. He stops right before he reaches my clit. "Hmm?"

"N-No," I rasp out. My duplicitous body shudders with need. Those fucking pills are the devil.

"Good. That kid got more pussy than anyone I know, but can you imagine how many unsatisfied girls are out there?" he questions. His finger circles my clit, and I jolt in response. "Now me…" he trails off, his dark eyes finding mine. "Every girl I touch comes without fail. Your mother came many times for me."

He's fucking with me.

I hope.

"I hate you," I tell him but my hips are lifting as if they're drawn like a magnet to him.

"Hate is just as intense as love." He rubs my clit with his one finger. My entire body thrums with pleasure. If I could escape my body, I'd find a way to choke him with his belt. "You like this, don't you? When I touch you this way?"

Tears roll out and I shake my head. But my quivering body says otherwise.

"Lies, Roja. Your cunt is dripping."

My body is sore from his brutalization in the shower, but it doesn't stop the need from coursing through me. He slides his finger down my seam and he barely pushes the tip of it inside me.

"Wet," he tells me. "Don't worry. You don't have to be ashamed. What we have is beautiful."

His finger inches in slowly, stretching my bruised flesh. I groan when he easily pushes another finger inside me.

"I'm going to make you come," he tells me in a smug tone. "And then I'm going to wrap my cock up so you don't give me any goddamned diseases so I can fuck that needy pussy until you scream. You want that, Roja?"

"Fuck you," I whisper. "Oh God…"

Pleasure zings through me and I'm confused. The haze he likes to cloud me with is intense. As much as I hate him, I feel like my body needs the pleasure. I close my eyes when he starts kissing his way down my stomach.

Diego.

Lightest brown eyes I've ever seen.

Charming and sexy to a fault.

Mine. Mine. Mine.

Esteban's mouth latches on to my clit and he begins sucking as he finger-fucks me slowly. I hate that he steals me away from thoughts of my husband. Every part of my body is on fire. It feels good. So wrong but good.

One day I'll make him pay for all of this.

Even in my haze, I realize these sensations coursing through me are induced by the drugs. With Diego, they're real. He doesn't have to drug me to get me to come. I want every part of him.

Esteban has dedicated his life to being nothing but a low-life cheater.

He steals what he wants but doesn't deserve a thing.

Someone screams, jerking me from my thoughts. I realize this person is me as an unwanted orgasm cuts through me. At one time, emotion had been attached to them but now it's nothing more than physiological.

Find me, Diego.

I close my eyes when Esteban slips his fingers out of me and unzips his pants. The tear of the condom wrapper makes me shudder, but I don't dare watch him. He spreads my knees apart so that he can worm his hulk-like body between them.

And then he's hammering one more nail into his coffin. By taking me again, he's sentencing himself to a painful death. This foolish man fell for the bait. I walked right into his trap so that I could annihilate him from the inside out.

"Look at me," he hisses as he thrusts painfully into me.

I pop my eyes open, ignoring the bruises inside of me, and glare at him. "You're going to die."

He fucks me so hard I scream, but I stare him down with the promise of a long, torturous death glimmering in my eyes. The sick fucker must like it because he comes with a grunt.

Pop! Pop! Pop!

"What the fuck?" he snarls as he stiffens. He yanks out of me and shoves his still sheathed dick inside his pants. "What did you do?"

His accusation makes me start laughing.

"I fucked *you*!" I screech. My body is numb and tingling but fire blazes within me. "You're going to die."

He grabs my jaw and then turns my head forcefully to the right. A scream rips through me when he snatches the diamond stud out of my earlobe. "You set me up!" he roars. "You fucking set me and my brother up!"

Pain radiates from my torn ear, but I find the energy to spit in his face. "Damn right I did."

He stands and yanks me to my feet by my hair. I'm dragged beside him toward the door when a shadow steps in front of the doorway. My heart leaps at the sight of him.

Lean and fierce.

Terrifyingly beautiful.

My partner and lover.

My husband.

"Diego," I moan.

I can't make out his facial features because the sun streaming in is too bright, but by the way his shoulders heave, I can tell he's infuriated.

"Don't move or I'll cut her throat wide open," Esteban threatens. A blade pokes my flesh, hard enough that he breaks the skin.

"Always such a pussy," Diego growls. "Just like your father. Always picking on those smaller than you."

Esteban drags the knife along my flesh, tearing the skin along the way. It isn't deep but it hurts, even through my drugged state. "You're going to kill me anyway, so I may as well take her with me."

Diego remains calm and still. His blade glints in the sunlight. "She's not yours to take. Never was. Vienna has always been mine. Since before she ever laid eyes on you. Fate, they call it. And you're about to meet yours."

"She belongs to me, but you tried to take that, too," Esteban snarls. "Just like you took my father's life."

Diego takes a step into the container. "Let her go and fight like a fucking man. At least your father had the balls to do that much."

Esteban growls and he hugs me possessively. The knife digs a little deeper into my flesh.

"Do you want to go to your grave like a pussy or do you want to go with some dignity?" Diego taunts.

Esteban stiffens. "I've killed many men. I'll kill you too."

Diego laughs and it warms me to my soul. "You can fucking try."

To my surprise, Esteban shoves me to the floor. I go down hard on my knees, and the container echoes with the sound. Diego's eyes never fall to me. His eyes are locked on his target. Esteban practically huffs like a bull trapped in a cage. Ready to charge at any second.

"Did you fuck my wife?" Diego questions as he quickly tears off his T-shirt and tosses it my way.

Esteban laughs like a madman. "I fucked her good. She'll be feeling me inside her cunt for days."

Diego's frame is thinner—solid lean muscle compared to Esteban's hulkish build. He bounces from foot to foot, like a graceful dancer, while Esteban throbs with barely contained rage. With shaking hands, I pull the shirt on over me and inhale the scent of my man.

"You won't touch her ever again," Diego hisses and waves his knife in front of him in a fluid motion.

Esteban hisses and jumps back. "Motherfucker!"

Blood soaks the front of his shirt, and I smile. I hope he makes him fill up this entire container with his blood.

"Pussy," Diego hisses and bounces forward on his toes. Slash. And then he bounces back. Esteban groans but waves his knife out in front of him in defense. Diego has already moved out of reach. His eyes stay on his target but his presence is like a warm hug.

"Your family name is a disgrace," Diego tells him.

Esteban lunges for him with his knife raised. Diego does some fancy arm movements before ducking around him. Now he stands between me and the monster. My hero.

"You run out that door and they'll mow you down with every bullet in their arsenal," Diego warns with a laugh.

I want to wrap my arms around my husband, but he needs to stay focused. Esteban charges again, but Diego slashes him across his face with the knife. A groan rips from Esteban and he drops to his knees. His knife clatters to the metal floor, and he clutches the wound that is gushing blood.

Diego pounces like a stealthy cat and grabs a handful of Esteban's hair while pressing his blade to his carotid artery.

"*Mi diablita,*" he hisses my way. "What do you want me to do? I can end this now…"

I stand on shaky legs and wobble toward them. "Or I can."

His beautiful eyes meet mine, and I almost collapse under the weight of the love shining in them. I bend over and retrieve Esteban's abandoned knife. His enraged glare meets mine from his kneeling position.

"Just kill me," he snarls. "Fucking kill me, Roja."

Diego rips harder at his hair. "Don't talk to your queen like that, motherfucker."

I narrow my eyes at Esteban but speak to my husband. "Are his wounds lethal?"

"All superficial at this point," he growls.

I smile. "Good."

Esteban's evil face scrunches into one of confusion. "You're going to let me live?"

I bend over and glower at him. "I'm going to break you."

"What the fuck, Vee?" Esteban demands. For the first time in my entire life, I see fear in the monster's eyes. Fear of me.

"What do you think, baby?" I ask Diego. "Four months? Is that long enough?"

"FUCKING KILL ME NOW!" Esteban screams. "NOW!"

I kick him hard in the balls, and with the drugs still buzzing in my body, I nearly come from the way he screeches in pain. The sound of his pain is beautiful. Four months isn't nearly long enough.

"I want to keep him right here. I want him to relive every single second of what I went through. Put his piece of shit brother in here after you make sure he's dead so he can be forced to live with that rotting scent every hour of every day." My eyes dart to Diego's. "I want him to pay. Dying is too easy."

Diego slashes his knife along the back of Esteban's calves through his slacks. Esteban's screams are otherworldly. When Diego releases him, Esteban falls to his side as he clutches his calves.

"He's not leaving this container on his two feet," Diego assures me with a wicked gleam in his eyes. "I'll station a trusted man at the door. Whatever you want, *mi diablita*, we'll make it happen."

While Esteban writhes in pain, I wobble over to Diego. He's shaking, and I wonder if it's from anger or from the wound that's seeping blood on his chest. I wince upon realizing he's torn some stiches.

"A hero would carry his queen right out of here," he says with a grunt, his fingers brushing through my tangled hair.

I grip his hand with mine and tug him toward the door. "Good thing we're villains because we're going to walk out of here together. Equals. King and queen. Heroes are for fairytales." I rest my head on his shoulder. "Our story is one from the horror section."

He kisses the top of my head. "With a little erotica thrown in?"

I laugh as we slowly make our way into the bright sunlight. "With a lot of erotica thrown in."

His palm finds my face and he kisses me hard. "I love you."

"I love you more."

Diego

"I'm so exhausted," Vienna murmurs as she shakily makes her way to our bed. We've been home for only a few hours. Long enough to feed our starving bodies and for me to wash every inch of the scum from her. My sweet wife cried for a short while in the shower but her quiet strength didn't allow the tears to fall for long. I can't begin to imagine what she's going through right now.

"Let's sleep." I turn off the lights and join my naked woman in the bed. She feels warm and soft in my grip. I'm thankful I can't see her bruises and lacerations in the dark. "I'm so sorry."

She stiffens in my arms. "For what?"

"For today. I know we talked about everything that would happen. But planning it and going through with it are two different things. I should never have agreed," I grit out.

Her palm slides up my bare chest but avoids the stitched flesh. "I didn't give you a choice."

I lean forward and kiss her somewhere on her face. "I should have told you no."

She scoffs. "As if I would have listened."

"I could have made you see a different way," I growl. "It didn't have to end with two men—your two enemies—raping and beating you, goddammit."

"It was the only way," she murmurs. "I was the bait."

I'm still unsettled but I know she won't back down on this. We spoke for hours while setting up this plan. She told me in detail what they would do to her based on what they'd done before. My fiery Vienna wanted this. Her claws were bared and ready to exact damage. She just needed to get inside their den first.

It still pisses me off that their "den" was my goddamned port. Several of the men turned against me for the Rojas brothers. Those men are dead now. But Ricardo and many others refused to sell out. They'd been tortured. Some killed. When Jorge discovered them in another shipping container, it took three men to hold Ricardo back from trying to kill Esteban. But once Vienna explicitly asked him what she needed him to do for her, Ricardo wholeheartedly agreed.

Ricardo is Esteban's warden now.

Except when Vienna comes to visit.

Until then, Ricardo will feed him sandwiches once a day. He'll change out his piss bucket once a week if he's lucky. And he's not, under any circumstances, allowed to talk to Esteban. But he is allowed to fuck him. Ricardo's exact words were, "His ass is mine."

Esteban is getting to see exactly what he put Vienna through.

A severe and fitting punishment.

One of the men was instructed to finish off Oscar, if he was still alive, and put his body in with Esteban. Esteban could smell his brother as he decayed just as Vienna was forced to smell her mother.

An eye for a motherfucking eye.

"How long do you think he'll live?" she whispers, hate giving her voice a slight edge.

"Tatiana cleaned his wounds and stitched him up. Ricardo has been instructed not to hurt him more than necessary. I suppose he'll live as long as you want him to," I tell her and brush my fingers through her hair.

"I don't want him to die easy. This punishment will satisfy me until I can come up with some-thing better." She cuddles against me and presses her lips to my jaw. "Thank you for trusting me. Together we did this." Her palm cups my face and the metal from her wedding ring, which she put back on, cools my face.

"We're going to do so much more together," I assure her. "Together we're going to rule our little corner of the fucking world."

She lets out a contented sigh. "Nobody will mess with us. And if they try, we'll make them pay."

I chuckle and twist my finger in her hair before tugging it in a playful way. "So you're into tor-turing now? You're barely a cartel queen, yet here you are so goddamned serious about your job. I love your drive, *mi diablita*."

She laughs too and then we're both quiet.

The exhaustion of the day steals us from our moment, but at least we enter the dream world in each other arms. Just like everything else we do. Together. Side by side.

Three months later…

"How's our little captive?" I ask Ricardo on speakerphone.

He laughs and it's evil as hell. "His ass is a little sore and the big fucker has lost some major weight, but he's hanging in there."

I smirk. "I thought you were into the ladies."

Ricardo grunts. "The ladies get plenty of Ricardo. But Ricardo puts his dick wherever he wants."

"Don't tell me every Colombian asshole around here speaks of himself in third person," Vienna groans from my office doorway.

I motion for her to come sit in my lap. My stunning bride wears a short tank top dress that barely hits the top of her thighs. Too short. She likes to torment me while I work.

"My little Vienna," Ricardo greets, a smile in his voice. "How is my little hellraiser? Already time for another visit?"

She chuckles as she straddles my lap. "You just want to show off again. We all know you're amazing at butt sex," she teases.

They chat a bit while I grab her hips and make her rub her pussy against my cock through our clothes. Vienna gets a little too eager when they talk torture. One day, once the pain of what Esteban did to her settles, she'll probably ease off a bit. But as it stands, at least once a week, we drive out to Buenaventura for a visit. She makes Ricardo bind Esteban and then fuck him in front of her. And whenever she's in charge, Ricardo makes it real nice for Esteban. Just like Esteban used to do for her. He pleasures the straight man until Esteban is coming with a big Colombian meat-head deep in his ass. Every visit ends with a kiss to the top of Esteban's head before she kicks him in the balls. It's funny as fuck.

"Is our first shipment to San Diego ready to go?" I question.

He grunts. "Will be in the next day or so. You'll have plenty of time to get to the States and sort out your business before the shipment arrives."

We talk a little while longer before we hang up. The moment he's off the phone, my gorgeous wife mauls me. Her mouth attacks mine and she starts tugging at my tie.

"This. Off. Now," she orders between kisses.

Ignoring her request, I lift her dress up off her body and then discard it. My naughty little thing isn't wearing anything under her dress. This makes my cock really fucking hard.

"You're so bad," I growl.

She laughs and leans back so I can regard her swollen tits. They're tender these days and my fucking God are they huge. I lean forward and tongue one of her nipples.

"These are so goddamned beautiful," I praise.

Her fingers undo my tie and she tosses it away. Then, she is on a quick mission to unbutton my vest. "Why do you wear so many clothes?" she complains.

I chuckle and reach between us to rub on her clit. "I like to tease you, *mi diablita*. I like to watch you go hungry for my cock."

She licks her plump bottom lip and it makes my dick thump against her. "I'm always hungry for your cock. Especially when you're naked. You should be naked more often."

I lift an eyebrow at her. "This is just the hormones talking."

A few weeks after we came back, Vienna learned she was pregnant. Tatiana said we probably conceived during the week after our wedding. I've been walking around with my chest filled with pride since the moment two little blue lines showed up on that stick. It's been surreal thus far but lately, her flat stomach has begun to protrude with our child. She's hot as fuck carrying my baby.

"Shut up and take your clothes off already," she orders with a wicked smile. "Momma needs Daddy's fat cock inside her."

I growl because I love when she talks dirty to me. My little wife knows this and uses it like a weapon. Together we're all but ripping my clothes off me.

"Beg Daddy Diego for his anaconda."

She snorts. "Put that big snake in me, Daddy."

I lift her by her hips and plop her on the edge of my desk while I push down the rest of my clothes. She's fucking glorious to look at with her brilliant red hair and blazing green eyes. Her tits are carved from God's finest materials. And she's mine. All mine.

"Show me your needy cunt. I want to see how it weeps for me," I mumble as I stroke my dick.

Her eyes fall to my cock and she grins before leaning back on my desk. She puts her feet on the edge of the desk so that her pussy is on full display. Then, she slides her fingers down her cute belly and touches her clit. Our eyes find each other as we pleasure ourselves. My cock aches to get the fuck out of my hand and into this gorgeous woman.

"Is it wet for me?"

She nods and pushes a finger inside her body. When she removes it, it glistens with her arousal. I lean forward so she can slip it into my mouth. I suck off her sweet taste. My God, this woman makes me horny as fuck. I can be having a shit day, yet one look at her supple body and all is forgotten.

"Beg for it."

"Please," she whines, "give me your cock. Fuck me good and hard."

I groan in pleasure. Her words are like fucking fire. They burn me in the best possible way. Everything in me buzzes to slam into her, but I like making her wait. I like seeing her arousal leak from her body.

I reach forward and swat her hand away so I can take over touching her clit. She can come at her own touch, but she goes fucking crazy when I do it for her. I thought that after all that happened with Esteban and Oscar a few months ago, she'd be gun shy. But my woman is tough as shit because as soon as her body healed, she was all over me, begging for my cock. Each time I'm inside her, it's just one more time they won't ever be.

"Diego," she murmurs. "Oh, God…"

Her body writhes as I bring her pleasure. I rub her faster and smile when the opening of her pussy shimmers in the light. Like a fucking magical unicorn, this cunt of hers. I'll ride it all the way to hell.

"You ready for Daddy D's big cock?"

"Yessss," she moans.

"When you come, I'll put my dick inside you. Come, beautiful."

It takes her another few moments, but soon she's crying out my name. I make good on my promise the moment she stops jolting in pleasure and tease her wet entrance with the tip of my cock. Vienna doesn't like it slow often. Usually, at night, she'll let me make love to her. But during the day, in my office, is the time reserved for hard fucking.

With a growl, I slam into my wife so hard, the desk scrapes against the wood floors. She cries out and fondles her tender breasts. I almost come, imagining my son or daughter latched onto one in the near future.

Fucking Vienna is the best reward this life has given me. Nothing else in this world matters. Not this giant house. Not my empire. Not this country. Just her. We could be poor and living in a shack on the other side of the world and I'd be happy as a fucking lark to have her in my bed and in my heart.

"Come here, mi amor," I growl as I pull her into my arms. Her legs wrap around my waist when I lift her. I prefer having her big tits pressed against me when my dick is inside her. But mostly, I want her mouth on mine.

She kisses me hard as I sit back in my chair. We settle into a position where she can ride me. I tangle my fingers in her hair and give her love bites all over her throat until her telling whimpers warn me of an upcoming orgasm.

"I love you," I murmur against her flesh.

Her fingers run through my hair and she moans. "I love you too."

Her cunt clenches hard around me a second before she screams out my name. I let out a guttural groan as I blow my load deep inside of her. We're both breathing raggedly as we come down from our high.

"So this is the life, huh?" she asks, burying her face against the side of my neck. "It doesn't get any better than this."

I grin and hug her tight. It jostles her enough that I feel my cum run back down the side of my cock to the chair below me. "This is everything, baby."

Vee

I chew on my bottom lip as I stare up at the nice home through the windshield. We've been in San Diego for three weeks now, and I still haven't found the nerve to see Brie. I'm not sure why, but I feel like our friendship is broken. How do two wronged teenage girls who were forced to grow up way too fast find their way back together?

She knows everything.

I know she knows.

I've heard Diego talking to her on the phone. It's definitely me, not her. She wants to repair our friendship. And if it weren't for Diego forcing me to see her, I'd have chickened out.

I don't think twice about barking out orders to men three times my size who carry assault weapons, but when it comes to facing my best friend, I am weak.

"Are we going to sit in her driveway all day?" Diego asks, his palm resting on my thigh.

I turn to regard him and shrug. "Maybe."

He smirks and relaxes in his seat. "Take all the time you need. I'm on vacation."

I roll my eyes, but it's true. Diego has let me handle all of my father's affairs and has only stepped in when I've needed him. Together we made sure we fortified our shipyard here in California, but he let me be the one to boss everyone around. Most of the men have known me since I was a kid, so they weren't opposed to being under my leadership. The Gomez empire has come together over the past few months because we've done it together as partners.

And just like usual, he's waiting until I'm ready.

We go in together.

I'm still deep in thought when someone beats on my window with their fist. I shriek in surprise, and Diego already has a gun drawn from his belt aimed across me at our attacker. When I meet the familiar face of my ex-boyfriend, I swat Diego's arm away.

"Calder," I cry out, surprisingly happy to see him.

He pulls open the car door and tugs me into his arms. His hug is strong. Much different than I remember.

"When did you get so big?" I tease.

He chuckles and shrugs when we pull apart. "Probably about the same time you did."

We both look down at my growing belly and smile.

Calder's grin falls when a dark shadow comes up behind me. His eyes lift and worry flickers in them.

"Calder, this is my husband, Diego."

He nods and holds his hand out to shake Diego's. Diego shakes his hand but then points near the garage door. "Who's she?"

"Luciana," Calder says, pride in his voice. "My fiancée."

Her cheeks turn pink as she hesitantly makes her way over to him. He wraps a possessive arm around her before hugging her to him.

"Fiancée, huh?" I say with a grin. "Wow. Congrats."

"Nice to meet you," Diego says.

She gives him a shy wave.

"You can't speak?" He snorts. "What's the matter? Cat got your tongue?"

"A cat named Esteban," Calder growls.

A silent understanding blankets the air around us.

Luciana begins using her hands to speak in sign language. Calder translates for us.

"He cut out my tongue. I thought he ruined my life. But then I met a stunning sex god named Calder the Great." As soon as he says the last line, she swats at him and grumbles. Her sign language goes faster but he translates quickly to keep up. *"I didn't say that. Calder is just being Calder. We recently took a sign language course together so we could communicate but he gets lost in translation sometimes. I'm so happy you came to see Brie. She talks about you all the time."* Her nose crinkles and she points at Diego. *"You too."*

"How do you two kiss?" Diego questions point blank.

I elbow him in the side, but he simply winks at me.

Luciana raises her hands to answer, but Calder decides to show us instead. His fingers slide into her hair and he tilts her head up. Her black lashes bat shyly at him but she parts her mouth open in anticipation. Their lips press together softly at first but then he kisses her hard. Nothing about their kiss from the outside appears abnormal. Just possessive and consuming and filled with love. It makes my heart threaten to burst. Calder was always a good guy, but he was meant for a good girl.

I was a villain.

And I finally found my match.

When they finish their public display of affection, Calder motions us inside. "The food will be shit. Just warning you right now. Brie can cook macaroni and that's it. Ren knows how to heat up the leftovers we bring over. If we didn't live at the end of the street, these two knuckleheads would starve. Let's just pray they ordered pizza. So help me if Brie tries to make enchiladas again…"

Luciana groans and holds her stomach. "Ew."

Calder reaches for the door when it swings open. Ren, a giant version of the guy I remember, stands in the doorway with a baby swaddled in a pink blanket in his arms. All apprehension fades away the moment I see the baby.

"Oh my God!" I screech as I run straight to him and give him a quick hug. "Is this Alejandra?"

He chuckles. "We call her Ally for short but yes. Fussy as fuck."

I playfully swat his stomach and steal the sweet infant from him. Her big nearly black eyes stare up at me. I love her and she isn't even mine. "You're so beautiful. You and your brother are going to be best friends with our little baby."

Ally lets out a big sigh, and I laugh.

"Come inside," Ren says with a chuckle. "Brie's feeding little D right now."

I peer over my shoulder and Diego stands in the threshold with stiff shoulders. Ren's gaze drifts to his and his jaw clenches.

"Bygones, man," Ren says, if anything a little begrudgingly. "You're married to one of my good friends and she's happy. Let's move forward."

Diego told me of his previous flirtations and advances with Brie. He said he was like that with all women until I put his balls in my purse forever. Such a romantic, that guy.

"Come on, babe," I tell him and walk inside.

The house smells good. Like something has been cooking all day. Calder saunters past me tugging Luciana behind him and hollers. "What is this sorcery?"

Brie rounds the corner with another brown-haired baby, but this one is latched to her breast. She sees Calder first and sticks her tongue out at him. "I can read directions, asshole. Luci gave me a crockpot recipe to try. Shut your pie hole and eat my food or I'll make you change the twins next time they have a monster diaper blowout."

He gags which makes Ren snort with laughter. These people, my friends from ages ago, are happy. Happy looks good on them. Diego wraps an arm around me and kisses the top of my head. It's then that Brie sees us. Her smile falls as tears well in her eyes.

"Vee."

She walks over to me and we stare at each other, both of us with babies in our arms. Silly tears sneak out of my eyes as I regard my friend. I thought it would be weird, but mostly I'm just happy to see her.

"You look well," she tells me with a huge grin. "Is this punk still being good to you?"

Diego chuckles and the deep rumble warms me to my soul. "I'm good to her every single night, cariño. So good. I think even the people three towns over can vouch for how good I am to her."

Brie snorts and shakes her head. "I forgot how perverted you are."

"I highly doubt that," he retorts.

Ally starts fussing and Ren comes to the rescue. He's big and bulky now but the way he looks at the babies melts my heart. I wonder if Diego will regard our future children with such a brilliant look of raw love.

I know so.

As soon as he walks away with the baby, Brie's eyes bug out. "YOU'RE PREGNANT?!" she screeches which makes baby Duvan jump in surprise.

Diego hugs me from behind and palms my belly. "*Mi familia.*"

She shakes her head but beams at us. "Would you look at us? We're all grown up now."

"But Vienna still likes to call me daddy," Diego says as his teeth nip at my ear.

Brie laughs. "Oh my God. I don't even know how you put up with him, but I'm glad you're happy, Vee."

She reaches her hand for mine and I take it. Of course I take it. Brie is my best friend. Some shit happened, some time happened, and some distance happened. But our friendship still exists. A sturdy tree that still stands after one helluva hurricane.

As she pulls me toward the living room, I can't help but make sure my other half is coming with me. Where I go, he goes. We're two halves of a very perfect whole. His lips are quirked up into an amused smile. I love how his light brown eyes seem to twinkle with mischief.

With my best friend tugging me along and my husband having my back, I can't help but think life doesn't get any better.

I feel a tiny nudge in my stomach and it reminds me.

The best is yet to come.

"I can have Dan update me by phone. We don't have to go," Diego says, his black brows furled together in concern.

I reach over and brush his black hair out of his eye. "We need to go. The new shipment arrived late last night, and we need to make sure everything goes smoothly. These first few shipments are important."

He frowns. "But you're sick, Vienna."

Bile rises in my throat, and I wince. The morning sickness, I thought, was supposed to end after my first trimester. But Tatiana tells me some women are lucky to have bouts of it throughout their entire pregnancy. Today I'm having a damn bout of it.

"I'll drink some ginger ale and it'll pass," I assure him. My stomach gurgles, and I groan. "Actually, just go. If I need you, I'll call. The shipyard isn't but ten minutes from here."

He sighs and leans forward to kiss my swollen belly. "I'll be back in an hour. I will make it quick, and Dan will take care of what needs to be done." His hot breath tickles my stomach. "Daddy will be back soon," he tells our baby. Tatiana had asked if we wanted a scan to discover the sex, but we both decided we wanted it to be surprise.

"Be careful," I tell him, my voice cracking with emotion. Lately, I have all these fears that my husband will die. At the hands of others, a horrific accident, dropping dead of a heart attack. Every terrible way to die, I've thought it. Some nights I can't sleep after having a panic attack over losing him.

He leans forward and kisses my lips. His lips pull up on one side. My body burns with desire every time he looks at me with that sexy smirk of his. "Feed my baby and then I'll come home and feed you."

I laugh and watch him as he crawls out of bed to start dressing. We've been staying at my parent's old house, which now belongs to me, while we stay in the States. Ever since I saw Brie for the first time a couple of weeks ago, we've visited just about each day. I didn't realize how much I missed her. Ren and Calder and Luci are a packaged deal. It's nice having them in my life. And I even got to meet War and Baylee. War was the favor Diego called in several months ago. He acquired some earrings that were fit with a tracking device. It was how they found me in that shipping container.

"Bring back those yummy buffalo wings from that pizza place down the street," I order. When he lifts a brow, I flash him a sweet smile. "Please, Daddy."

He shakes his head. "So demanding, *mi diablita*."

I shrug and stare at his ass as he bends over to grab some socks from a drawer. "I thought you like it when I get all feisty."

"Feisty for my cock," he corrects and then looks over his shoulder to give me a smoldering grin.

If he weren't about to leave, I'd beg him to stay. I'll show him feisty…

But then another wave of nausea ripples through me. I don't even realize I've closed my eyes until I reopen them and see Diego squatted in front of me beside the bed. Concern has chased away all playfulness in his features.

"I should stay," he murmurs, his thumb dragging along my jaw.

I reach forward and touch his lips. "Go. I'll sleep. When you get back, you can take care of me for the rest of the day."

He stares for a long moment but then gives me a clipped nod. His lips press to mine before he stands upright. "Thirty minutes tops. Sleep."

When the bedroom door clicks shut, I drift off to sleep with my husband as the star of my dirty dreams.

Glass.

I jolt awake and find that I'm drenched in sweat. I'm about to sit up and yank off the T-shirt I'm wearing when I hear heavy footsteps pounding down the hallway. Something about the urgency in the steps tells me my visitor is not Diego.

Shit.

He warned me months ago. The cartel is a dangerous business. Just because we're in love and happy doesn't mean that we aren't still in the thick of the most dangerous criminals in the world. We must always be vigilant and aware. And despite always having men on guard, things can still happen. People can still slip through.

The door flings open and crashes into the wall behind it. I'm stunned frozen when the figure enters the room. The monster before me is horrific. Straight from a nightmare. I am wondering how he came back from the dead just as he speaks.

"Hello, Vee," he snarls, a shiny metal gun in his grip.

I can't help but gape at his disfigured face. Oscar was once so handsome. The sexiest man I knew. But then he lost himself. He turned into this thing. And that was all before his brother bashed his face in. His nose is severely crooked. One of his eyes doesn't open all the way and the eyeball seems to drift. He's baring his teeth at me. Most are broken. The dark hair that he used to wear in a stylish way is bushy and hangs in his face.

"Oscar," I murmur. "What are you doing here? I thought…Esteban… You were so close to death…"

He growls, and the sound sends a shiver up my spine. "After he left with you, I got the hell out of there."

What?

It makes me wonder whose body they threw in with Esteban. Diego told his men to obtain Oscar from the office. Apparently they grabbed the wrong dead guy along the way.

"Why are you here?" I try again. I'm attempting to distract him with words while I work out a plan to defend my baby and myself from this monster.

"You know why I'm here," he hisses. "I'm here to fuck you up like you made my own goddamned brother fuck me up. Then, I'm going to tear your ass up before I put a bullet in your skull."

He yanks the blanket off me, and I scream. His eyes peruse my bare legs but when his gaze finds my rounded belly, he glares.

"I'm pregnant, Oscar," I tell him softly. "Just go. Nobody has to know you were here."

Our eyes meet. His are hate-filled and lost and full of vengeance. Mine are fierce and violent and full of the need to save my child. One of us won't leave this room today.

"Take off your shirt," he demands. "I want to see what you're hiding under there."

I shake my head. "Please leave." *I'm warning you.*

"Vee," he barks. "Take off your goddamned shirt and let me see your stomach."

Time seems to stand still as I'm reminded of when I was seventeen.

"Show me," Oscar begs, his dark eyebrows scrunched together as he gives me a sad face.

I want to show him more than my fake belly button ring but everything is a mess right now. Daddy says I need to squash my feelings for Oscar because he may end up being the one who is to be married to Brie.

But I don't want to squash anything.

I want him.

Brie left earlier, complaining of a headache, so Oscar and I drank by ourselves. Normally, he's wedged between us on the bed as we flirt and cut up. Now, it's just the two of us. I've been friend-zoned hard with him. But sometimes I wonder, if I wasn't too shy to make the first move, could things change between us?

"Show me," he pleads again. His palm rests on my bare thigh. Despite it being an innocent touch, I can't help but tremble from the sensation. His fingers inch up under my cocktail dress, sending ripples of excitement coursing through me.

"I don't think your girlfriend would like me showing you," I snip. I've been trying to play hard to get, a new tactic, but I'll be damned if that isn't hard as hell.

"You know I don't have any girlfriends. There are only two girl friends I love." He gives me a lopsided sexy grin that turns my insides to mush.

"Okay," I breathe.

His eyes darken as he grips the bottom of my dress. He drags the silky material up my thighs over my panties. Our gaze is broken when he darts his eyes to look at my panties. When his palm brushes over my pubic bone, I shiver. He palms my stomach and then runs his thumb over the piece of metal that just pinches my skin versus piercing it. I bravely reach forward and pull my dress up to just under my breasts to expose my entire stomach to him. The liquor we'd downed earlier does nothing to calm my nerves.

"Vee," he murmurs as he leans forward. "I like it."

I exhale a sharp breath when he kisses my stomach. So innocent yet so full of intent. This could happen. I could finally have Oscar. My panties are wet with excitement. I squirm in need for his touch, but he seems unaware.

"Any other fake piercings I should know about?" he questions, his finger brushing over my clit through my panties.

I jolt and let out a whimper. Say, yes, Vee. "No."

He frowns. "Too bad."

I'm mentally berating myself for being a wussy when his mouth finds my belly button. His teeth latch on to the metal and he tugs on it. It pulls my skin but breaks loose. Our eyes meet for a heated moment, and I know that if we keep flirting at the rate we're going, we're going to have sex. The thought thrills me.

His hand grips the top of my panties just as someone knocks on the door. I shove my dress down quickly and he sits up. "Who is it?"

"You're being summoned," Esteban grumbles from the other side of the door.

Oscar groans and climbs off the bed, a giant boner in his slacks. So close. So damn close. He flashes me a guilty smile before answering the door.

Esteban glances over Oscar's shoulder at me on the bed and smirks. "Two naughty kids up to naughty deeds. Need someone to show you how things work?" He makes a vulgar motion of his finger going in a hole. "I could perform an example, little Oz."

Oscar punches him in the arm. "Shut up. We were just talking. Like always. Friends, fucker."

Esteban snorts and winks at me. "Tell her that."

"Vee." The voice is cold and it drags me out of my warm memory. This man—this monster—is not the boy from my past. That boy died a long time ago. Probably not long after his brother Duvan.

"I always loved you," I murmur, my voice tight with emotion. "I loved you from the moment I walked into your kitchen and you told me to chase after you. I've chased you ever since."

He growls. "I was always here."

"And so was I until…" *You raped me.* I sniffle and shake my head. "Doesn't matter. We weren't meant to be."

His hand shakes but he keeps his weapon pointed at me. "I miss those days."

A tear leaks out, and I slide my hand under the pillow to grip the cold metal Diego gave me for emergencies. This constitutes as an emergency. "So do I."

"We can't ever get them back, can we?" His voice cracks. The sadness nearly splits me in two.

"No," I whisper. "We can't. Not ever."

A harsh sob catches in his throat. "But I want them. I want them back."

"Oscar, you should leave." *Don't make me do this…*

His lip trembles. "I don't want to be this person."

"So don't be," I whisper.

He falls to his knees as a gut-wrenching sob escapes him. My heart shatters and breaks. The person who raped me and abused me is long gone. The boy from my past is hurting and lost. I wish I could fix him. I honestly wish I knew how.

"I'm sorry, Vee. I'm so sorry for everything."

He lifts the gun and I panic. I'd been focused on his words, not readying the weapon under my pillow. I stare in horror as the gun slides into his mouth, rather than to point at me. Tears stream down his cheeks.

"Oscar!"

Pop!

So many times I visualized his death after he hurt me. So many times I planned on making him pay. But then…then he broke down in front of me. I didn't see the monster, I saw him. Oscar. Playful, funny, flirtatious Oscar.

A loud sob pierces the air, and I realize it's me. When I scramble to the floor, I know he's gone. Half of his skull is blown out on the wall in front of me. Blood pools on the carpet beneath his head.

I know he's dead.

Yet, I pull him into my arms and hug him anyway.

I tell him everything's going to be okay. That I forgive him. That I love him.

"R-Remember that time we found that p-puppy one summer and we hid him in the woods b-behind your house?" I question through my tears as I hold him to me. "Savvy was her name. She was so cute. How old were we? Eight and Nine?"

He doesn't answer.

He'll never answer again.

"She'd gotten loose from the rope one day and had run away. We both cried so much our dads thought something bad had happened." I laugh and stroke the side of his face. "Your dad kept asking us to give him a name. All we could get out was Savvy. How long did he search for 'the motherfucker who hurt his kid named Savvy' anyway?"

I lie him back and take his hand in mine. I try not to look at his mangled face or messed up head. Instead, I kiss his knuckles and pretend we're kids again. I'm not sure how long I clutch him, but I'm brought out of my daze when two strong arms lift me. I'm carried like a child into the giant bathroom that used to be my parents. My hero sets me down on the counter before starting the bath. Then, he peels the bloodstained shirt from my body and undresses himself. Carefully, he helps me into the tub and settles behind me.

"What happened, mi amor?" Diego murmurs, his mouth pressing kisses against the back of my head.

I sob and shudder in his arms. "He said he was sorry."

He hugs me tight and doesn't let go.

I hope he never lets go.

NINETEEN

Diego

Several months later...

"I'm a fool," I growl as I spear my fingers through my hair and pace my office.

Jorge laughs—fucking laughs—that asshole. "Never said you weren't."

"How could I do this? How could I let this happen?" I snag my still lit cigar—pink of all fucking colors and straight-up shitty quality—from the ashtray and inhale a big puff.

"Well, everyone knows you think with your cock, man," he snorts.

I glare at him and snub out the abomination in the ashtray. "This is fucked up. I'm a fucked-up person. Karma, _hermano_. Karma. I have a shitload coming my way."

He smirks. "Why? Because you had five wives at once?" Fucking prick knows how to goad me.

"YES!" I roar.

He stands and dusts off his jacket even though it's in pristine condition. Then he reaches inside to pull out his Glock. "See this?"

I arch a brow at him. "Fuck yeah."

"There are hundreds more where this came from. And just as many badass motherfuckers who will be holding them."

"Your point," I grumble.

"They touch her, they die. Simple."

Some tension eases from my chest. "Simple."

"Now, can we stop celebrating with these lame-ass cigars Tatiana bought and go see this princess I'm going to have to help guard until the day I die?" He grins at me.

I smirk and shake my head. "Let's go see the princess."

She's gorgeous. I'm blown away by how she can look like two people at once. Mine.

"I love that look," Vienna murmurs from our bed, a soft smile on her face. Not four hours ago, she gave birth in her old room to our daughter, Valentina Martina Gomez.

"What look?"

"That one right there. The way you look at her. As if she's your entire world."

I kiss the sweet baby's forehead. "She's not my entire world."

Vienna frowns. "Oh."

I smirk. "You're right there with her."

"There's my romantic," she says with a grin. "You should let her sleep and come lie down with me." Her hand pats the bed beside her.

I stand from the glider we put in our room and gently place our sleeping child into the bassinet. Once I'm sure she's settled, I crawl in beside my wife. I'm afraid to touch her. I watched Tatiana deliver our daughter and some things can't be unseen. The blood. The stitches. I'd been so disturbed once Tatiana placed a bloody Valentina in Vienna's arms that she asked me to leave until she got them all cleaned up. I close my eyes and gently run my hand along her arm. I hope I never have to see that again.

"You're tense, Diego. What's wrong?"

"I don't like seeing you in pain," I admit and kiss her temple.

"It was worth it," she tells me in a fierce tone.

It's then I know that my brave wife could handle anything, especially childbirth. She's hell on heels with her flaming red hair and fiery spirit. The bastards who wrong her suffer under her iron fist. Just ask Esteban…he knows first hand.

"It was worth it," I agree.

"Everything…"

"Completely."

She turns her head to gaze up at me. I drop a kiss on her forehead and then her nose. And then her sweet, pouty mouth.

"I love you, *mi diablita*," I murmur.

"I love you too, mi motherfucker."

We both grin.

And then I kiss her again.

And again.

And again.

And again.

And again.

And again until the end.

EPILOGUE

Gabe

I wake with a start. Something heavy sits on my chest in the darkness. My arms are pinned beneath the weight, and for a split second, I almost toss it off me. But then I feel her palms on my chest. Exploring. Soft and gentle.

"Why are you awake in the middle of the night, baby?" I murmur as I slide my arms out to grip her hips.

"I've been thinking." Her voice is a whisper. A scary-as-fuck whisper. I hate those goddamned whispers.

"Toto and Land?"

"Sleeping," she assures me. Her fingers brush along my beard in the darkness. "Can we talk?"

I swallow down the tension building inside me. "Of course, angel."

Angel, my ass.

Hannah eats angels for dinner.

But when she's in a mood, I placate her at any cost. I know this. Her parents and brothers know this. Our kids even know this.

She slides off my lap and turns on the bedside lamp. Her blonde hair is messy and wild, but it's her eyes that are distant. So dark. Fuck.

"Talk, beautiful."

The darkness flickers in her eyes as she beams at me. My sweet girl never lets a compliment go. She fucking loves them.

"The medicine doesn't work anymore," she tells me, a slight wobble to her bottom lip. "I think those…things. The bad things."

I jolt upright and reach for her wrist. When I pull her into my arms, she sags against me.

"We'll find something different. Your dad is always researching meds for you." I kiss her tit through her thin nightshirt and then bite it. Sometimes I can distract her from her dark thoughts with sex.

"But what if nothing works. We need a plan."

I stiffen at her words. "A plan for what?"

"Sometimes I stare at them at night. I don't feel like they belong to me. I think terrible things, but then I leave. I'm strong enough to leave." Her voice cracks. "But what happens when one day I'm not?"

Fuck. Fuck. Fuck.

"You're the strongest girl I know," I tell her, squeezing her tight. "Maybe you just need a vacation, baby. You're a good mom. You keep the house in perfect shape and you're a great cook. But you might be working too hard. Why don't we go on a vacation? We'll ask War and Baylee to watch the kids."

She seems to mull over my answer, and I pounce. I peel off her tank top and squeeze her tit before sucking on the soft flesh. Her breath catches when I nibble on her.

"Gabe…"

"Shhh," I murmur. "We'll figure it out in the morning. Until then, let me love you."

My words work because her fingers thread into my hair as she straddles me on the edge of the bed. I flip her onto her back and flash her a wolfish grin before I peel her panties and shorts down her thighs. Once my stunning-but-crazy-as-all-fucking-hell wife is naked, I climb off the bed for a necessity on nights like this.

Rope.

She bites on her bottom lip when I come sauntering back to the bed with the nylon rope. Her eyes are hooded as I tie intricate knots around her wrists so that they don't come loose. Then, I tie the end of the rope to the bed frame.

"Spread 'em," I growl.

My good little girl obeys and shows me her pink pussy. I'm going to punish her cunt for what I can't punish her mind for. I slap it hard enough to make her cry out.

"You want my dick stretching out your ass, don't you, sweet girl?"

She nods. "I want you to hurt me."

I slap her cunt again. "Don't worry. I'm going to hurt you real bad tonight."

Her body shudders in response. Distraction is the best thing I can do for her right now.

"Tell me who owns you," I murmur as I lean forward and suck on her clit.

She jolts against her bindings and releases a long moan.

"Tell me," I order.

When she doesn't answer, I bite her clit hard enough to make her scream out a string of cuss words at me.

"Tell me, goddammit," I snarl against her wet cunt.

"Y-You. You always have."

"Good girl." I kiss her pussy softly. As I take my time teasing her, my brain is elsewhere. This shit gets worse every day. The meds don't work. Nothing fucking works. It scares the hell out of me the way she looks at our children.

Fuck. Fuck. Fuck.

"Mmmmm," she moans.

"That's it, sweet girl. Come for me and then I'll put my dick inside you. If you're a real good girl, I might put it in your ass later, too."

My words turn her on because she whimpers as her orgasm nears. I suck on her swollen clit until she cries out in pleasure. Her entire body trembles, but I don't give her time to recover. I shove my boxers down and flop my hard cock out. I'm always hard for my sweet girl.

"Oh, Hannah," I growl as I thrust hard inside her tight cunt. I lean over her and find her perfect mouth. Our kiss is needy and hungry and unhinged—like our entire relationship. Fucking hell, it's perfect.

But it's *not* perfect because when she's not tied to my bed, letting me fuck her, she's on a train by herself riding full speed ahead to crazy town. And she's going to mow down my family in the process.

"God, I fucking love you," I tell her with a grunt.

She whimpers and sucks on my tongue. "I fucking love you, too."

I pound into her until we're both moaning with our release. I come deep inside her cunt because my shit is fixed. No more babies with my hot ass wife. I can barely protect the two we've got.

I grin as I look deep into her blue eyes that have found clarity again. Love shines in them. It's real and genuine.

For now.

With a stifled sigh, I stroke her hair and memorize her face.

One day, I won't see this look in her eyes anymore.

One day, I'm going to have to kill my wife.

This is the End, Baby is up next…

THIS IS THE END,
baby

This queen knows all the rules. She plays the game better than the king.
In my game, the queen will knock the king right off the board if she must.

Game over.
The END.

But, I love him.

The darkness threatens to make me lose sight of my strategy from time to time, but in the
END, love always prevails.
Problem is, my black king is playing by a different set of rules. His END game is one he
shields from me.

It's a game he plays closely with the white king, the most brilliant player of all. Together,
they want to END my game.

They want to END me.

This queen doesn't go down without a fight.
This queen makes her own rules.
This queen will outsmart those who play against her.

This is the END, baby.
In the END, I am going to win it all.

PROLOGUE

Hannah

His dark hair is soft. So soft. I could stare at him for hours while he sleeps. Sometimes I do. He's beautiful and mine. Every night, when I look at him, I am reminded that I am happy. *He* makes me happy.

Other times, he maddens me.

I can't pinpoint it exactly. It isn't any one thing. Just that his presence rubs me the wrong way. Every day, it worsens. I don't like that feeling at all.

I stroke his hair again and murmur, "I love you."

It's times like these I must remind myself that I *do* love him. That he *is* mine. I have to remind myself that I am in charge of my thoughts…the darkness is *not* in charge of me.

I close my eyes and start to hum a song I remember Mom humming when I was a child. It would always calm me when I was in the middle of a tantrum. For as long as I can remember, my mother and I have always butted heads. It's only recently that we've talked a little more. We mostly tolerate each other. You'd think Gabe would be a deal breaker for her, but she puts up with him. Despite everything that went on between them in the past, she welcomes him into her home.

It makes me wonder if she still has feelings for him.

I often wonder if Dad were to suddenly die, would she go after my husband?

Would she remember what a good lover he was and want that back?

Anger bubbles up inside my chest. Mom is beautiful and looks younger than her actual age. She runs most days and eats well. If she wanted to seduce him, she probably could.

I try to imagine her as a teen having sex with my husband. Thoughts of my mother beneath him moaning his name have me fisting my hand and gritting my teeth. I can almost hear her moans.

Gabe…

Gabe…

More…

"Sweet girl?"

I snap my eyes open and cast an irritated glare at him. That perfect mouth has been on my mother's pussy. He's been inside her.

"Hannah," he utters as he strides into Land's nursery. "Let me put him back in his crib and then we can go back to bed."

I stop gliding in the rocker but don't release my baby to him. His eyes narrow but he doesn't challenge me. Instead, my sleepy husband drops to his knees and hugs us both. Some of the tension releases from my chest. While Land sleeps in one of my arms, I can't help but reach over with my free hand and stroke Gabe's hair.

"How are you feeling?" he asks, his voice muffled against my breast.

"Just thinking about things."

He tilts his head up. "What things?"

I frown and dart my eyes over to the window. "Things that make me angry."

His fingers grip my jaw and he turns my head to look down at him. "What things, baby?"

"You and Mom," I seethe, the accusation heavy in my voice.

"She and I were over before you were even conceived." His brows furl together and an annoyed sigh escapes him. "We've been through this a thousand times."

My tone is bitter. "I'm your second choice."

"Hannah," he warns. "How many times—"

"Daddy?"

He and I both jerk our heads around to see our sleepy toddler standing in the doorway, rubbing her eyes. My heart warms to see her in her cute pink polka-dot zip-up pajamas. Her blond curls are fuzzy from sleep. She's been wandering a lot more in the middle of the night and early mornings since we recently switched her from her crib to a toddler bed.

"Come here, Toto," I coo and motion for her.

Gabe twists to sit on his butt with his back against my shins. Toto walks over and climbs into his lap. He holds her against his chest and strokes her soft hair. A smile plays at my lips. She reaches a small hand up, and I grab it. Land stirs but doesn't wake.

"*We* are a family, Hannah," Gabe murmurs, but his tone is fierce. "You and I and these babies."

My eyes sting but tears don't form. Sometimes I hate that I'm broken. The emotions that normal people have aren't in my hollow chest anymore. They've dried up and crumbled away. Anger is my most prevalent emotion. It feels like it takes over more often than not.

"I hate being sick," I hiss as though the words themselves are tainted.

A growl rumbles from my husband. "You're not sick…you're just in desperate need of a vacation."

Toto peers over her father's shoulder at me with her big brown eyes and smiles. It reminds me of Gabe. The love in that smile nearly knocks the breath out of me.

"Are you going to take me on vacation so you can off me and dump me somewhere in the Pacific Ocean?" I question, my voice only half teasing in nature. "Then find a new wife? Someone normal?"

Toto smiles shyly at me again. Those smiles are distracting. A trick she most definitely learned from her daddy.

"I'm not even entertaining those questions with an answer. I love you more than anything in this world," he grumbles. "You know this."

"I love you, Mommy," Toto agrees.

My heart expands, and I grin at her. "I love you too, baby."

She starts whining to climb into my lap, so Gabe sets her on her feet so he can relieve me of the baby. As soon as Land is in his daddy's arms, Toto crawls into my lap. Her small hands touch my face as she beams at me. I run my fingers through her messy hair and study her features.

Her light blonde hair is soft. So soft. I could stare at her for hours while she watches me with her cute grins and adoring eyes. Sometimes I do. She's beautiful and mine. Every day, when I look at her, I am reminded that I am happy. *She* makes me happy.

Other times, she maddens me.

I can't pinpoint it exactly. It isn't any one thing. Just that her presence rubs me the wrong way. Every day, it worsens. I don't like that feeling at all.

I stroke her hair again and murmur, "I love you."

After Land is back in his crib, Gabe stares out the window for a long time with his strong arms crossed over his chest and his back to me. After some time, Toto falls asleep. I stand and carry her back to her bedroom. Once I've kissed her and shut the door behind me, I start down the hallway.

I sense his heat before he even touches me. A moment later, a hand covers my mouth from behind, and I'm captured in his powerful arms.

His mouth finds my ear, and I shiver when he nips at my lobe with his teeth. "You have to stay out of that head of yours and with me, sweet girl. It's the only way for us to be happy."

I whimper when his free hand slides to my breast through my silky gown. He trails kisses down the side of my neck before releasing me to twist me around. His dark eyes are narrowed as his palm grips my throat. My head thumps the wall when he pushes me against it. I love when he possesses me. He keeps me focused on what matters. Us.

"God, sweet girl," he mutters as he nips at my bottom lip and chin and jaw. "You have to get your shit together. You *have* to."

"I'm trying," I promise as I grip his hair to guide him down to my aching breasts. He bites my nipple through the fabric and regards me with a wicked glare that makes my panties wet. I tug his hair to the left so he'll bite my other nipple too.

His chocolate brown hair is soft. So soft. I could stare at him for hours while he devours me, his touches demanding and consuming. Sometimes I do. He's beautiful and mine. Every day, when I look at him, I am reminded that I am happy. *He* makes me happy.

Other times, he maddens me.

I can't pinpoint it exactly. It isn't any one thing. Just that his presence rubs me the wrong way. Every day, it worsens. I don't like that feeling at all.

I stroke his hair again and murmur, "I love you."

Gabe

As much as I love the beach, I know we can't live here forever. This home doesn't meet our needs anymore. We're too close to people. Hannah doesn't do well around people.

"We've tried everything on the market," War complains on the other end of the line.

I run my fingers through my hair and huff in frustration. "So we try everything *not* on the market. Come on, man, you have access to this shit. Find something. Anything. It's absolutely necessary we find a solution."

He's quiet for a moment, and I listen for Land. Thankfully he's still napping, so I can keep my focus on Hannah and Toto playing in the sand not two hundred feet from where I stand inside the house.

"Is it getting worse?"

Worse? Hannah is always worse than the day before. But this is different. This is darker and more unpredictable.

"I can't read her anymore," I hiss. "She's a fucking live wire, and I am scared as hell it'll be one of the kids that gets hurt."

I hear him tapping away on his keyboard but he remains silent. Then he sighs. "Have you thought about putting her back in an institution?" Even though he says the words, which sound like scripted shit straight from Baylee's mouth, I know that isn't what he wants.

"Fuck the institutions," I snap. "I told you how she was when I took her from the one Baylee sent her to. My sweet girl was so fucked in the head. They were supposed to make her better, not pump her full of bullshit that makes her talk to goddamned walls. She will not ever go to an institution in my lifetime."

His tapping stops. "I don't know that I like where this conversation is going."

"Fuck you, War. You know that if you don't get your shit together and find something that works, my hands will be tied. I'll be forced to do something neither of us wants. She's the fucking mother of my children. You think I want to hurt her?"

"Touch her and I'll—"

"You'll what, man? Turn me in?" I rub the tension from the back of my neck. "This isn't just about her. It's about my fucking kids."

"Bay and I can keep them. Send them to us, and we'll raise them. Take her somewhere safe. Just don't hurt her," he pleads.

I swallow and dart my gaze out to see Toto running circles around her mother, squealing with laughter as Hannah tries to tickle her. "I can't do that. I can't not see my kids. I already made that fucking mistake once with Brie. I won't do it again."

Land fusses in the other room but doesn't cry yet.

"I'll intensify my searches. I can go on the deep web and hunt for something on the black market. I'll keep digging." His chair creaks and he grumbles. "But this shit isn't tested, Gabe. I have no idea what the side effects will be. We're playing with fire, and it involves my daughter—"

"She's my fucking wife! You think I don't know this already?" I snarl. My outburst makes Land start to cry. I stalk into his bedroom. "Time is running out. You should have seen her last night. It's getting fucking creepy. One of these days, I feel like she's going to snap."

Land squirms in his crib but his cries lessen when he sees me.

"Hey there, baby boy," I coo as I scoop him into my arms and pull him against my chest. I redirect my attention to War on the phone as I walk back over to the window to watch my girls who are outside. "Just keep looking."

He sighs. "I will. Also, I was going to tell you when I had more information but I think I found what you were looking for. It's a hunch, based on some cryptic texts, but I believe it's what you're searching for."

My chest tightens. "You have a location?"

"I do. Like I said, it hasn't been one hundred percent verified, but all signs point to it. Are you really going to do it?" he questions.

I kiss Land's soft forehead while he gnaws on his fist. He's hungry, and I'll need to have Hannah come back in to feed him soon. "Of course I am."

"What about Hannah?"

"I'm going to take her with me this time. She needs to get away," I tell him. "I think it will be good for her for it to be just her and I for a few days. Plus, it's a helluva lot easier keeping her in line when it's just the two of us."

"Bring my grandbabies over, and we'll keep them. It needs to be done, and she certainly needs a break," he agrees. "Do I need to procure new fake IDs or are the last ones still okay?"

Translation: *Did my innocent little girl murder anyone while using her last ID?*

"They're fine. Book us a flight and find us a hotel. We'll leave as soon as we can. I'm not sitting on this," I order. Land grins up at me, slobber running down his chin. I grin back at him. Cute as fuck little boy.

"On it," War assures me.

I smirk and give him some shit because, why the hell not? "Most fathers would not approve of this."

He grunts. "Spare me the lesson on morality, Gabe. You and I both know the rules are different with Hannah. Not to mention, if it weren't you going to deal with this, my son would be on the first plane out of here."

A smile tugs at my lips. That Ren kid is all right in my book. "Maybe we could invite him along—"

"Don't start," he snaps. "I'll text you with the details."

He hangs up and I chuckle. That is, until I don't see my girls. A quick scan of the beach tells me they aren't there anymore. Panic rises in my chest, and I dart for the sliding glass door. Just as I pull it open, Toto and Hannah bounce over from the side of the house, screaming "Gotcha!"

Land lets out a peal of laughter, and Toto runs to hug me around my knees. Hannah's blue eyes are glittering with light and love. God, I wish I could keep her like this. These moments are rare. Fucking beautiful, but rare.

"You scared me," I tell them both as I tug at one of Toto's pigtails.

Hannah laughs. "That was the point." She holds her hands out for Land. As soon as he sees her, his legs start kicking. Kid loves his momma.

I usher them inside, and while Hannah feeds Land, I let Toto help me pull out everything we'll need to make lunch.

I love my family.

I love moments like these.

I love my broken wife.

Which is exactly why I need take care of this shit.

"Where are we going?" Hannah questions for the millionth time since I told her about our romantic getaway. "I mean, I know *where* we're going but *what* are we going to do there?"

I palm her thigh just below the hem of her dress and grin at her. "It's a surprise, sweet girl. We haven't done anything like this in awhile, just the two of us. I want you all to myself."

My answer pleases her because she clasps her hand over mine and teases me by pulling my hand further up her thigh. The young guy who's been eyeballing her thighs the entire flight discreetly watches our little display. I'd offered her the seat by the window, but she wanted the middle. My wife likes the attention.

The cabin lights have been dimmed, and many people are sleeping. But not this guy in our row. It's as if he's been waiting for me to fall asleep so he can chat my wife up. I'll give him something to talk about.

My eyes meet Hannah's as I slip my palm under her dress. She spreads her knees to grant me access, bumping the other guy's knee in the process. He lets out a choked sound and shifts uncomfortably in his chair.

I smirk as I run my finger along the outside of her panties where her clit is. A gasp of pleasure escapes her. When I glance over at the guy, who's closer to her age than I am, he's staring shamelessly at the way my hand moves under her dress.

My Hannah is naughty because she likes putting on a little show.

I lean forward and bite her tit through her dress, my eyes finding the horny guy's beside her. He gives me a deer-in-the-headlights stare as I nip at my woman. The glare I give him back says, *You can watch as long as you don't fucking touch.*

He hisses out a breath of air and slouches in his seat, his palm covering his crotch. Fucking pervert.

"Your panties are wet, sweet girl," I murmur, my breath hot against her dress.

She smiles at me. "They are."

"Does it turn you on that some guy is watching your husband touch you?" I question, my eyebrow lifting.

Her blue eyes flicker with darkness, and she nods. The guy beside her groans.

"Do you want my finger inside your slippery cunt?"

I lift up and scan the cabin for anyone noticing our little party, but nobody is. Nobody but Horny Fuck next to her. I grab hold of her panties and start inching them down. She lifts her ass to help, and together we slide them down her thighs.

When I pull them off her ankles, I hold them out to Horny Fuck. "Can you hold these a second?"

He stares at me with flames of desire flickering in his eyes and he takes the panties. Who wouldn't? This girl is a fucking knockout. Tall. Blonde. Legs for days. And a rack that most men would only dream of getting to come all over. Once he has her panties in his fist with his other hand resting on his crotch, I slide my palm back under her dress.

"Spread them further," I whisper and lean in to bite her ear lobe.

She does but the space doesn't allow for much room. Her leg lifts and she hooks it over Horny Fuck's thigh. "I hope you don't mind," she purrs at him.

He grips her panties so tight his knuckles turn white. I almost start laughing. He's probably imagining all the ways he'd fuck her. I smirk, knowing she'd fuck *him* up before he even got the chance. She hooks her other leg over my knee and now she's spread wide open for me.

"That's better," I murmur, my tone low and deadly, as I slide my finger along her wetness. When I push a finger inside her, she moans softly. I can tell the guy beside me would like to help. I'll rip his entire arm off if he touches her, though.

"You're such a naughty girl," I chide as I slowly fuck her with one finger. "I forgot how naughty you can be."

She whimpers and squirms in the seat. "I need more," she pleads under her breath.

I smirk at Horny Fuck, who is staring at us with his mouth hanging wide open. "How many fingers?"

"All of them," she breathes.

"Jesus Christ," Horny Fuck hisses.

I wink at her as I ease two more fingers into her. My cock is much bigger than three of my fingers. But this girl, with the right amount of lube, has been able to take my entire fist before. She's fucking magical.

"Your body is making so much noise," I observe. Each time I push inside her, her juices make a loud sound. "Maybe we should do something to cover up that sound." When I rub my thumb over her clit, she moans loudly. An old sleeping woman across the aisle stirs but doesn't wake. When I glance back at Horny Fuck, he's discretely rubbing the palm of his hand against his cock, which is hard and noticeable through his sweatpants.

I focus on fingerfucking my wife. She's attempting to be quiet but is having trouble. With my fingers buried in her pussy, she is on the verge of a scream.

"When we get to the hotel," I whisper against her throat, "I'm going to put my dick in your ass. You want that sweet girl?"

"Mmm-hhhmmmm," she moans.

Horny Fuck curses again.

Her legs are beginning to quiver and she has no control over her body. When she runs her heel farther up his thigh, I know it isn't a loss of control. My sweet girl is dirty and likes to make people suffer. The moment her foot touches his cock, I know he's really fucking suffering.

"You're not innocent," I snarl as I nip at her ear. "You're going to fucking pay for that little move."

Her fingers find my hair and she kisses me hard. I know it's to distract me because five bucks says she's trying to get Horny Fuck off with her foot. My girl is dangerous like that. Always playing with fire. She doesn't want that dork. She wants me to punish her for touching him.

"You can't distract me," I hiss as I pull away from our kiss. Sure enough, her foot is rubbing against him, and he's groaning in pleasure. I yank my fingers from her body, causing her to whimper from the loss before I snag the panties from Horny Fuck's fist. "These are mine." Her juices get smeared across the back of his hand in the *exchange*. He gapes at me in horror but then his eyes roll back in his head when she rubs against him again.

I snap my gaze to hers, and she challenges me with her dark stare. I glare at her as I stuff her panties into her mouth. "I need to stifle your scream," I hiss.

My hand goes back under her dress. I get two of my fingers good and wet in her pussy before sliding them to the puckered hole of her ass. She cries out when I push them fully into her. My thumb slips inside her wet cunt and I fuck both holes ruthlessly.

The noises coming from our row are straight up from a porno, and this almost makes me laugh. My own cock is desperate to be inside her, but that'll have to wait until we arrive at the hotel. Horny Fuck just sits back and enjoys a foot rub against his cock.

An old guy in front of us turns to give us a dirty look, but when he sees what we're doing—and most likely gets a firsthand view of what's going on under her dress—he gasps before turning around. Hannah whimpers again and her body begins to tremble. I suck on her earlobe until she's convulsing hard. Her pussy and ass both clench simultaneously around my fingers as she finds her release. Horny Fuck groans too.

They fucking came together.

This makes me snort.

I pull my hand out from under her dress and then yank her knee back to where it belongs—in front of her and away from him. Then, I pull the panties from her mouth and put them in my pocket. Horny Fuck is tense as hell as he stares down at the wet spot soaking through his sweatpants.

"You made a mess there," Hannah says with a loud giggle.

He turns to look at her, his throat turning bright red. If we weren't on an airplane, I'd make his throat *red* all right but with his own blood—brilliant crimson and gushing. Horny Fuck is lucky I'm not free to do what I please. Because it would please me to slaughter him for his part in our little sex show.

"Oh," she says when she notices her wetness smeared on his hand. "That's mine. Sorry about that." She grabs his wrist and brings it to her mouth. Her eyes dart to mine as she licks off the remnants of her arousal from Horny Fuck's hand. When she releases him, he bolts from his chair and all but runs to the bathroom closest to us.

"You're so getting punished for that."

She curls her body to face mine and runs her palm over my cock through my jeans. "Good. I deserve it."

I'm not about to come in my pants like Horny Fuck. So I unzip my jeans and pull my cock out. "Suck it, bad girl. Hurry."

She leans forward and licks my tip. I grab a handful of her hair as she starts bobbing up and down my length. Her teeth are sharp as she lets them graze along my sensitive flesh. Always reminding me what a fucking monster she can be.

Well, I'm a monster too.

I grip her hair and twist it until I know it hurts. Then, I push her farther down my cock until I feel the head of my dick sliding into her throat. Her throat tenses as she gags but then she relaxes, so I can use her. I make her facefuck me for several long moments until I come with a grunt. My cum rushes down her throat. She doesn't gag but stays relaxed so she can swallow it all down like a good girl.

The old fucker in front of us turns on the light, alerting the stewardess that he needs something. I know the prick just wants to tattle on us. My dick still throbs with its release when I make eye contact with the stewardess who is now making her way toward us.

I release Hannah and she quickly puts my wet cock away. She's just sitting up and righting her dress when the woman asks the old fucker what he needs.

"I need a stiff drink, ma'am," he drawls out.

I smirk and wave at the lady. "Bring one for this row too."

She hustles away, and Horny Fuck shows back up. I can tell he tried to clean up his cum, but it didn't work. He avoids making eye contact with us as he sits back down.

This vacation is already off to one helluva start.

This is exactly what we needed.

chapter
TWO

Hannah

I'm not sure why he brought us to this seemingly run down city, but at least the hotel is nice, and we have a view of the beach. The pool is killer. While Gabe sleeps, I stare out the window and watch a barge move slowly across the water.

It's peaceful here.

I like it.

My chest aches and I miss my kids. I've been slowly weaning Land off the breast because I haven't been producing as much milk as my hungry boy needs. This trip was the little push he and I both needed to quit for good. But now my breasts are sore. It just reminds me how much I miss having him nurse from me, even if he could only do it once or twice a day.

A buzz comes from Gabe's phone plugged in on the table. Curiosity gets the better of me, and I walk over to see who's texting him.

Brie.

Irritation claws its way up inside of me, but I swallow it down. I vowed I would do my best when it came to Brie. That I'd be nice to her. She has my brother, and they seem happy with the babies. It makes me angry, though, that she now hogs my brother *and* my husband. Stingy bitch.

I read her text to my husband.

Brie Baby: The photographer can do that date. Ren and I have been tasting cakes this week. One more month, Daddy. :)

A huff of breath escapes me, and I roll my eyes. Another little annoyance in my life. Brie and her wedding to my brother. I'm surprised he's so eager to take on some other man's kids. But sweet, stupid Ren dove in without hesitation to play daddy to her twins. Ren was always soft when it came to girls. Always wanted to be the hero.

It was Calder who surprised me. My younger brother fell hard for that chick with no tongue. They actually come over to the house, from time to time, to see Toto and Land. It's Ren and Brie who refuse to see us.

Well, me, actually.

Neither of them want to see me.

I'm not even allowed at their wedding.

Fury surges through me, and I decide I need to let off some steam. I throw on a tank top and some mid-shin-length black workout pants. Once I've laced up my tennis shoes and pulled my long blonde hair into a ponytail, I grab my key from the desk in the room and head out. Despite this hotel being nice enough, it's still old school with real keys. I'd balked at that, but my old man husband didn't even notice until I pointed it out. They were all like this back in the day, he'd said. *The olden days…*

I smirk as I walk down the long hallways on a search for the fitness room we'd passed. When I reach the door, I'm irritated to find it's locked. With a huff, I travel downstairs and through the lobby to go outside.

Today, it's warm out. It'll be dark soon, so I don't want to stay out too late considering I don't know this country very well. We've barely been here a day, and my poor husband is wiped out. After a day of fucking and eating room service, he spent the rest of the afternoon sleeping.

I start jogging down the narrow road. My ponytail swings back and forth along the back of my shoulders as I run. This country isn't one I've been to before. Gabe told me I had to be careful. Freaks are everywhere, he'd said. Don't I know it.

As I jog, I pass several stray animals, but they scamper off when they see me. A couple of cars pass by and one honks. I run until I find access to the public beach. The chain-link fence I come to is beat up, but once I walk through the gate, I find a nice beach. Not as nice as the ones back home, but it'll do. I run past an old fat man with a hairy white chest lying in the sand and dart along the shore. It feels good to run. I fill my lungs with the warm air and grin.

Gabe was right.

I did need a vacation.

I love my kids so much, and I can keep my darkness at bay. But sometimes…it's like I'm not me. I'm this other person. I stare at them with a stranger's eyes. Sometimes, I wish it were just me and Gabe. And those thoughts scare me. I wonder if the stranger within me will make that happen one day.

With a frown, I trot to a stop and bend over to catch my breath. Someone catcalls me. I jerk my head over to see that I'm standing in front of a dilapidated beach house. A man stands in the shadows under the porch.

"*Oye mamita linda!*" he hollers in a thick Spanish accent and follows it with a whistle. He emerges from the shadows, puffing on a cigarette, and crudely grabs his crotch.

My chest aches from exertion and my calves are on fire. I look over my shoulder to see how far I've run. At least a mile…maybe two. I can't even see the hotel from this distance. Unease creeps up my spine.

"I don't speak Spanish," I yell back as I start hobbling away. My throat is on fire from thirst. I wish I'd have thought this out before I just ran off without my phone or telling my husband where I was going while in a foreign country.

"I speak English, pretty lady. Come a little closer. Are you thirsty? You look like you need a rest."

I turn to regard him. I *am* thirsty.

His eyes widen in shock when I start walking in his direction. When I'm close, he blatantly eye-fucks me. The guy is sort of cute, I guess. Probably late twenties. He needs a shower, but I don't think he has problems getting women.

"I'm Hannah," I tell him and give him a shy smile. "Staying over there with my husband."

He frowns and scratches his scruffy jaw with a finger while somehow managing to hold on to his cigarette. "Husband, eh?"

"Yep." I smile primly at him.

His gaze falls to my chest. I look down and frown to see two wet spots from where my nipples have leaked.

"Oh no," I groan. "Babies."

He takes a long drag of his cigarette while his eyes linger on my tits. "You look good, Mama."

I bask in his praise and bat my eyelashes at him. "Thanks. I thought you had something for me to drink."

He nods and licks his lips before tossing the cigarette into the sand. "I'm Pico." With a wave of his hand, he motions for me to follow him.

I wobble after him, wishing my calves didn't hurt so badly. I'll drink some water and then head back to the hotel. He slides open a dirty glass door at the back of the house. I follow him inside. One quick glance tells me this is an abandoned home. Trash litters the space and it reeks of feces.

"Where's the water?" I croak out.

The glass door slides shut behind me, and he stands between it and me. "There is no water."

I turn to him and frown. "Then why'd you invite me in?"

His brown eyes seem to darken and he lifts his T-shirt to reveal a gun tucked into his waistband. "You know why, white girl."

I curl up my lip. "Let me out of here, asshole."

A dark laugh rumbles from him. "No, cunt."

"My husband—"

He snorts and pulls the gun from his belt. "Your husband can't do shit."

I narrow my eyes at him and crack my neck. "I was going to say," I hiss, "that my husband will be angry if I kill you."

This sets him off because he attacks me. I'm tackled backward, and we land on a dirty mattress in the middle of the floor. He shoves the barrel of the gun under my chin as he uses his other hand to yank my pants down.

I don't fight or wiggle or anything.

I wait.

When he senses I'm not putting up a struggle, he glares at me. "What's wrong with you, puta? Are you fucking crazy?"

"You have no idea."

He snarls and roughly grabs me between my legs. His dirty finger pushes past my panties, seeking entrance. It burns when he gets it inside me. The gun feels cold against my jaw, but I'm not afraid. His zipper goes down, and he manages to take his cock out once he yanks his finger back out.

The wait is over.

He still holds the gun loosely in his one hand while the other is trying to help his cock thrust past my panties. I grip the key in my hand to form a weapon and I stab at his eyes.

Poke. Poke. Poke.

"Fuuuuck," he roars, abandoning his gun and me to cover his now bleeding face.

I grin as I shimmy my panties and pants back up my thighs. Sitting up on my knees, I grab his gun and point it at him. "You're going to regret ever waking up this morning."

He whimpers like a pussy. "Y-You fucking stabbed me in the eye!"

"Y-You tried to rape me," I mock and then cackle. "You messed up, buddy. You messed up real bad."

His cock is out and I laugh. Thin and the big bush of black hair surrounding it makes it seems shorter, too. No wonder he must resort to rape. Nobody wants his tiny pecker. Poor fucker.

"Get naked."

He hisses. "What?"

"You wanna fuck? Let's fuck," I taunt.

"Fuck you, bitch."

I stand over him and kick his shoulder until he's on his back. With my gun pointed at his face, I snap at him, "I said get naked, asshole."

Terror flickers in his uninjured eye. With a shaking hand, he shoves his dirty underwear down and kicks away his jeans. Then, he pulls away his T-shirt. His chest is littered with poorly done tattoos, and it makes me giggle.

What a fucking loser.

"That's better," I coo. "Now, tell me how many girls you've raped."

He doesn't answer, so I fire a shot into his shoulder. The scream he lets out belongs to a teenaged girl, not a man.

"You psycho cunt!"

"How many girls have you raped?"

Snot dribbles down his lip and he shudders. "I don't know."

"Guess, asshole!"

He trembles. "Uh, six maybe?"

Six maybe?

Somehow I doubt that's true.

"Don't lie to me."

"Fuck, uh, fine. Maybe twenty or thirty."

I snort and straddle his waist. His one eye widens as he gapes at me in horror. But his stupid dick hardens beneath me. This asshole will always fuck with girls because he can't even manage to keep his cock soft when his eyeball is about to fall out and he has a bullet in his shoulder.

"Oh," I chide. "You're very bad, Pico."

He starts to cry, but I'll be damned if his cock doesn't throb beneath me.

"You need some relief, baby," I purr as I grip his jaw. "Need me to take care of that dick of yours?"

"Get away from me, puta!"

I laugh and obey the prick. For a moment. I find a discarded cola can and shove the barrel of the gun into the opening. The metal of the gun widens the opening. When I fire off another round, Pico screams. With the bottom of the can now bearing a hole, I push the gun through that hole too. Then, I regard him with an evil grin.

"Ready, Pico?"

"Get the fuck away from me," he hisses as he holds up his free hand, as if that'll protect him.

I pounce on him. When he tries to escape, I push the gun into his belly and fire off a shot that makes him scream louder than before. Both of his hands cover the hole that now spills with blood. While he's distracted, I grab his mediocre dick in my hand and shove the can down over his erection. And then I crush the aluminum can around him with my fist.

Screams.

One long continuous one followed by another garbled one.

I sit on my butt and admire my handiwork. The head of his penis pokes out of the top of the can. Blood is everywhere.

"God, Pico, you're messy," I chide.

His hands try to pull the can away, but the sharp pieces of aluminum are digging into his sensitive flesh and preventing him from pulling it off. This makes me giggle.

"Y-You c-crazy f-f-fucking c-cunt," he chatters through his tears.

I stand and glower at him. "You should have just given me the water."

"Bitch!"

I smirk. "This bitch just fucked you up. By the way you're bleeding, I suspect you'll be dead before I even make it halfway back to the hotel. Goodbye, Pico."

He moans and groans, but I can tell he's weak. Blood spills from the hole in his stomach with every movement he makes. There's no way he'll live.

With a little wave at him, I tuck the gun into the back of my workout pants and tug the tank top over it to hide the bulge. As soon as I close the sliding glass door, I can no longer hear his cries over the waves. In the distance, the clouds are dark as a storm rolls in, making the water choppier.

I sprint the entire way back to the hotel with a giant smile on my face.

Pico, that sick rapist, really knew how to cheer a girl up.

chapter

THREE

Gabe

I wake to the sound of a shower running. It's dark out now and thunder rumbles nearby. I can't believe I slept for half the day. Now that we're here, away from my family, I can relax a bit. I don't have to watch Hannah's every move. We both needed the breather.

I slip out of bed and push my boxers down to join her in the shower. After a quick brush of my teeth, I find her under the spray, washing her hair.

"Hey, beautiful," I murmur as I draw her soapy body to me.

Her sudsy fingers find my shoulders and she beams at me. Clarity makes her eyes shimmer with light. She's fucking stunning. "Hey, handsome."

I tug her hair, so she looks up, and help her rinse the soap from it. Once she's clean, I grip her jaw and kiss her plump lips.

"What'd you do while I slept?"

My little liar bites on her lip. "Nothing much."

I snort. "Try again."

"Went for a run." Deception still flickers in her pretty eyes.

"Hannah," I warn, my fingers biting into her flesh. "Don't fucking lie to me."

Her fingers wrap around my cock, and she grips it hard. "I met a rapist."

I stiffen and glare at her. "Did he hurt you?"

A sexy smile plays on those dick sucking lips. "He tried."

I pull her to me and kiss the top of her head. She wraps her arms around my body. Her tits seem fuller than normal, smashed between us.

"What did you do?"

She looks up at me and wickedness gleams in her eyes. "I made sure he won't rape any more girls ever again."

My heart is hammering in my chest. I should yell at her for so many things. But all I can do is kiss her supple lips.

"My good girl," I praise. "God, I love you."

I grip her ass and lift her. She wraps her legs around my backside just as I push my cock into her wet cunt. I fuck her hard against the wall until she's screaming my name and clawing her nails down my shoulder. After I come deep inside her, I pull out of her and continue cleaning her perfect body. Small silvery stretch marks color the pale flesh near her hips, but I love the physical reminder of the children she grew inside her. _Our_ children.

"What are we doing tonight?"

I cradle her face in my palm and grin at her. "I'm taking you to dinner. And then…"

"Dancing?"

I snort. "Better than that. We're going to do something fun after a little shopping."

"Oooh," she says, her eyes glimmering with mischief. "I'm excited."

"Wear black."

She arches a blonde brow at me. "This gets better and better."

"And maybe real shoes. Don't wear any fucking flip-flops."

"Yes, sir," she sasses and gives me a faux salute. "Anything else?"

I cup her pussy. "I'd like if this was easily accessible. Can you do that, sweet girl?"

She beams at me and nods.

"Good girl. Now get your ass ready so we can have some fun."

While Hannah blow dries her hair, I call Ren.

"How's my girl?" I ask in greeting when he answers.

"Good. What's up?"

I launch into what I need from him. It's asking a lot, I know. But, unlike his father, he doesn't argue. He simply takes note of my instructions and vows to fulfill my requests. Lastly, I give him the address before hanging up.

Just in time too.

Hannah shuts off the hairdryer and saunters into the room, with just a towel wrapped around her. I want to yank it off and nibble on her tits but I'm fucking starving for real food.

"Hurry and get dressed," I tell her as I pinch her ass through the towel. "We have reservations in twenty minutes."

She throws on a halter top black dress with a lovely open back and a plunging neckline. And like the obedient girl she is, she leaves off her panties and bra. I love that she's a stunner even without any makeup on. Then, she pulls on a tiny pair of white socks before slipping into a pink pair of Chucks. The shoes don't go with the dress, but she still looks fuck hot.

"Keep looking at me like you want to eat me and we may never leave this place," she says with a smirk.

I laugh and grab her hand. "Come on. We have shit to do."

Dinner was at the hotel and it was fucking delicious. They reserved a romantic table near the windows for us where we could watch the lightning. The storm seems to have stalled off in the distance and hasn't come ashore yet, but it won't be long before it reaches us. Once we've eaten, I pull up the address War found me, and we take a cab to the location, which is in a seedy part of town. The building is a pile of crap but it holds what we need.

"Let's do this, sweet girl," I instruct as I toss a wad of bills at the driver.

She climbs out, and the wind whips her dress up. My sexy girl doesn't even bother with fighting to push it back down. With the moon shining on her blonde head and her round ass on full display, she's like some bad angel cast from heaven, luring men straight to hell. She simply struts up to the dilapidated building with her fine ass on display for me and the cabbie. And sure enough, when I glance at him, he's checking her out.

"Beat it," I snarl before trotting after her.

I tug the dress back down over her ass and guide her inside the building. It's dark and run-down inside, but a friendly guy greets us.

"Can I help you? Americans?" he chirps, his eyes nearly bugging out with dollar signs, like in the cartoons. He's a slimy bastard and greedy as hell. I can practically see him trying to calculate how much money he can make off us.

"Knives. I was told you had knives." I smile at him. "And other things."

His gaze flickers over to Hannah before he meets my stare. A question dances in his eyes. *Are you going to kill her?*

I smirk. *Eventually, I'm sure. But not today.* "My girl needs one too."

At this, he laughs. It's boisterous and over the top. "Oh, I have something to suit both your needs."

We follow him down the dark hallway toward the back. Hannah squeezes my hand. Not because she's nervous but because she's excited. My wife loves an adventure.

The room is brightly lit up with weapons lining the walls. Guns and knives and shit I wouldn't even know what to do with hang from hooks all over the place. I point at a backpack. "I want that."

The man pulls it down and sets it on a table. "You going to fill it up?"

Hannah glances over at me. "Please, Daddy?"

I snort and nod. "Fill it up, sweet girl."

The man, upon realizing that Hannah might be my daughter, takes a moment to check out her tits. So I walk up behind her and give them a squeeze. I meet his shocked stare and shrug. "She's got nice tits," I tell him and give one of her nipples a pinch. "Am I right?"

He nods and quickly picks up sharp long blade with an ivory handle. "This one is good for skinning."

She takes it from him and holds it up. "Too big."

I snag it from her and run my thumb along the blade. "Skinning you say?"

He nods again.

"I want it."

Hannah laughs and gives me a quick smile before picking up a smaller knife. "I like this one."

"Bag it, baby."

The man seems pleased with our splurge. I toss in some handcuffs and a bundle of rope. He has everything we could possibly need—even a battery-operated light and a fifth of the country's best rum.

"Is that all?" the man questions, a weasel smile on his face.

I point behind him at a black-handled machete. "I want that too."

He obliges and then starts calculating my total. It's astronomical and obnoxious but I pull out a wad of bills and pay the man. After he counts it three times, he waves us toward the door.

"Thank you for doing business with us. Colombia welcomes you."

With the heavy-ass backpack slung over my shoulder, I take Hannah's hand and start walking toward our destination. I had War book us our hotel for a reason. It was close to where I wanted to go.

"A storm is coming," she says and points to the ocean where lightning illuminates the sky.

I squeeze her hand. "You have no idea, baby."

Under the moonlight with the wind kicking up her hair, I'm reminded of how much I love her. Hannah is my soulmate. My dark, dirty, hellion of a woman. It's been quite the ride to get us to this point. I don't want to lose her. Not now, not ever.

As we walk, I think about that emptiness I see in her eyes sometimes. I hate when that look presents itself in front of the children. They don't understand that their mother is sick. Toto takes it the hardest because she's older. She cries when Mommy is being cold toward her. I wish I could reach into Hannah's sick mind and patch up the hole that sometimes sucks all humanity from her.

And God how I've tried.

War and I have made her take every medicine we could get our hands on. Baylee has spent countless hours researching her daughter's mental illnesses. I've tried to preempt her moods and intervene. I'm good at distracting my wife but I never know how long it will work. And what happens when I'm *not* there to distract her? All it takes is one moment.

Guilt surges through me. I can't do that to my kids. I can't risk their lives. Their mother is unhinged and unstable. She's a vase full of cracks, and one day, water will gush out, drowning those she loves in the process. I've plugged those cracks, but I'm afraid I can't do that any longer.

There is only one way to save them.

"You're quiet," she murmurs.

I pull her into my arms and kiss her forehead. "I love you, baby. No matter what. Always and forever. And when this life is no longer ours, we'll rejoin in hell where nothing can stop us."

She tilts her chin up and beams at me. "My Hades."

I cup her jaw with my palm and run my thumb along her pink bottom lip. "My Persephone."

Her fingers grip the front of my shirt as she pulls me to her. Our mouths meet in a needy kiss. I'll never get enough of kissing her. If I had it my way, I'd keep kissing her until I'm old and on my deathbed. Then, I'd just kiss her until I take my last breath.

Something tells me it won't be so easy.

I slide my palm to her throat and run my fingertips along her vein. Her pulse is steady. Always so steady.

A crack of thunder makes us both jump. We pull away from our kiss, both of us panting for more.

"Come on," I bark. "We're almost there."

We pick up the pace down a desolate road that seems like it hardly ever sees any travelers. This is good because I don't need anyone seeing my ugly mug and screwing up my plans. The first raindrop that hits the back of my neck is cold. The second and third seem colder. When the heavens open up and rain down on us, I start running toward a chain-link fence. It's not electric, thank God, so I easily snap through the metal with the wire cutters I bought from the weasel guy earlier. I make a hole big enough for us to crawl through and send her through it first.

I should worry about dogs or some shit, but War has already given me the layout of the premises, and they don't have any vicious animals protecting the property. What they have is worse. They have big-ass Colombians with AK-47s strapped to their chests surrounding the perimeter. But, according to War, they don't have as many at night, and they mostly protect the front gate. Hannah and I should be good.

"What are we doing here?" she hisses. Her eyes flicker with excitement. My sweet girl is always down to be bad.

"You'll see," I tell her.

According to War's intel, one particular shipping container sees a lot of action. It isn't guarded at night, but during the day, people come and go. Even Brie's friend Vee and that fuckface Diego. War sent me some footage from when he hacked into their security system. What I've been looking for was last seen dragging a naked girl into the container months and months ago. He never came out, but she did. If he were dead, I doubt they would visit all the time, nor would it be so well guarded. And with what Brie told me about what happened to Vee when she went missing, I know it has to be *him*.

"This way," I bark out above the howling wind and pouring rain.

She runs behind me, along the outer perimeter. The shipping containers are stacked high and go on for as far as the eye can see. I finally find the one I'm looking for. It's older than the rest and hidden in the very back.

"What's inside?" she demands.

I smirk and use yet another tool I bought from that weasel. The fucker didn't even blink twice when I filled my bag with all this bizarre shit. But, he had all of said bizarre shit up for sale, so I guess it isn't that strange to a guy like him.

A bolt lock sits on the door handle. I unzip my backpack and pull out a crowbar. Once I wedge the metal in the lock, I throw all my weight down over and over again until the lock snaps. Hannah reaches forward and pulls the broken lock away.

I grab the machete and ready my weapon as I tug open the door with a noisy creak that is drowned out by the storm. My wife stands behind me, and together we walk inside. She manages to turn the light on, and soon the long narrow container is lit up. It reeks of feces and body odor and death. The emaciated form on the mattress rolls over and squints against the light.

"Is this…" Hannah trails off and takes a step forward, her wet shoes squeaking on the metal.

"Yep."

Her voice becomes a hiss. "Estebaaaaaaaaaaan."

chapter
FOUR

Hannah

He promised me. Not long ago, after we found out what happened to Brie, I'd been enraged on her behalf. Having been a rape victim myself, it made me crazy furious that this Esteban dude fucked my husband's daughter. What's his is mine. Esteban raped what's mine. I told her I would kill him one day. Gabe promised me our chance would come. I never doubted my man for a second.

Esteban is naked and shivering. His black hair is long and hangs in his face. A black, coarse beard covers his cheeks and mouth.

"Help," he croaks out.

Gabe stays back, but I approach and set the lamp on the floor once I'm close. "Help with what, honey?" I coo in a sugary sweet voice.

"Help me, please."

I look over my shoulder and Gabe stands with his back to the open container. His shoulders are broad and his chest heaves. My man is a barely contained storm. He wants to rage and make this man suffer for what he did to Brie. And what kind of wife would I be if I didn't help him?

"Can you move?" I question, my voice soft and concerned.

He tries to sit up but he's too weak. "I can't," he grunts. "You have to get me out of here."

I stroke his hair out of his face so I can look into the eyes of a sicko. "Who's done this to you?"

"Vienna, that fucking cunt. And her husband Diego Gomez. They're vicious. If they find you here, they'll have you killed," he hisses. "We have to go."

Gabe snorts and I suppress a grin.

"Shhh," I coo as I roll him to his back and straddle his stomach. My wet hair drips on his chest and he licks his lips. "Are you thirsty?"

He nods and stares up at me as if I'm an angel who's come to rescue him. *Hell's angel.* I grab a handful of my drenched hair and wring the water out over his mouth. A groan rumbles from him as he catches the wetness.

"Thank you," he murmurs.

I sit up on my knees and hold my dress out. "More? I can wring it out from my dress."

His gaze falls between my legs and his eyes widen. My pussy is naked and on full display. Since he doesn't answer, I wring my dress out into his open mouth. Then, I sit back down on his bare chest. My wet-from-the-rain pussy slides against his skin.

"W-Who are you people?" he demands, suspicion dancing in his eyes.

I rest my palms on his shoulders and rub against him. "I'm Hannah."

"Why are you here?" His jaw clenches as he glares at me. His fingers dig into my thighs over my dress. "Why the fuck are you here?"

Gabe grunts and stalks over to us, his heavy footsteps thundering in the metal tomb. He drops the bag beside Esteban and yanks his wrists above his head. "Don't talk to my fucking wife like that."

"D-Did Ricardo send you? Are you here to rape me too?" Esteban snarls up at my husband.

I laugh because it's fucking funny. This big, scary man is weak and helpless as Gabe cuffs him and then pins the cuffs with his knee. Esteban tears his gaze from Gabe to glower at me. Pleasure courses through me as I rub my pussy against his flesh. I scoot down until I meet the trail of hair below his belly button. His cock jolts and bounces against my ass crack through my dress.

"You like this," I accuse, a wicked smile on my face. Then, I flick my eyes up to Gabe. He watches me with narrowed eyes and a clenched jaw as I grind against this rapist's happy trail. With my thumb between my teeth, I lift my dress so my husband can see what I'm doing.

"Don't fuck him," Gabe orders.

I smirk. "I only fuck you."

"Damn right."

"You two are fucked up!" Esteban roars, his entire body coming alive with adrenaline. He must sense his fate. "Those cunts sent you, huh?"

"Shhh," I hiss as I rake my fingernails down his chest, breaking the skin as I go. "I want my knife, baby."

Gabe grunts and digs around in the bag. Once he hands me the small knife, he grips my wrist and yanks me until I fall into him. I kiss him hard with my thighs smashing Esteban's head. I'm getting into our kiss when Esteban bites the inside of my thigh. I screech and lift off from him. The knife clatters to the metal floor loudly.

"He bit me!"

Gabe snarls and grabs a handful of Esteban's hair. His wild eyes are on mine. "You okay, baby?"

I lift my dress and frown at the teeth marks. He didn't draw blood, but it still hurts. "Tape his mouth," I snap.

Gabe lets him go and finds the duct tape we bought earlier at the ghetto store. He rips off a giant strip and slaps it over Esteban's mouth. I stick my tongue out at the little biter and then straddle his face again so I can continue kissing my man. Esteban's hot breath comes out hard through his nose and it tickles my sensitive flesh. A tiny moan escapes me.

"You're such a dirty girl," Gabe mutters against my mouth as he grabs my ass through my wet dress. "What are you doing under there?"

I rub myself against Esteban's nose and jolt when the tip of it touches my clit. "Nothing."

"Little liar," Gabe says with a grin. "Show me. Take this shit off."

I match his wicked smile and peel off my soaked dress. It hits the metal floor with a slap. Gabe and I look between us. Esteban's wild eyes are staring up at us as if we're crazy, his chest heaving.

Maybe we are.

Gabe's eyes find mine as he grabs my hips. He urges me closer to him. Esteban's nose pokes inside me and it feels good. My eyes roll back when his hot breath rushes inside me.

"Oh!" I cry out.

Esteban jolts from beneath me as he struggles to breathe. Gabe pins my hips so that I can't move anywhere.

"Touch your clit, baby," Gabe instructs.

I reach down and rub at my sensitive bundle of nerves. With Esteban fighting for breath inside me and his face moving back and forth, I'm overcome with a delicious sensation. Gabe's mouth finds mine and he kisses me hard. I close my eyes and give into the wonderful feelings surging through me. Esteban stills just as I climax. I shudder wildly. The moment Gabe lets me go, I lift up to let my little biter friend have some air.

He inhales a deep breath and then breathes so heavily, I wonder if he'll hyperventilate.

"Hold his hands." Gabe's eyes are nearly black with fury and madness. I fucking love that look in his eyes.

I take Esteban's wrists and hold them down. Not that he's going anywhere anyway. His body is weak and his eyes are barely open. Gabe stands and walks off. I stroke Esteban's hair from his eyes.

"Awww," I coo. "You okay, sweetie?"

Esteban's eyes widen for a minute and then he shakes his head.

I tug at his facial hair. "You survived. Just like Gabe's daughter did when you drugged and raped her multiple times."

He closes his eyes as realization sets in.

I give his cheek a slap. "Open up, honey. The sins of your past have come back to haunt you."

His dark eyes are wild as they glare up at me. Despite his weak body, fire still burns inside him. Some monsters don't die easily.

"What are we doing?" I question as I look over my shoulder at Gabe.

He runs his fingers through his dripping hair and levels me with a hard gaze. "I want to punish him for everything he did to her but I'm so pissed I can't think straight."

I beam at my husband. "That's why you have me." I pick up the knife and turn back to Esteban. He brings his cuffed hands in front of him and attempts to push me away but he's weak. I use my knee to pin his cuffed arms against his lower belly. Then, I wiggle the knife at him.

"Ready, Esteban? Ready to tell Gabriella you're sorry?" I scream, my spittle spraying him.

He starts shaking his head, but I ignore him as I begin carving his apology into his flesh. The garbled and choked sounds he makes fuel my adrenaline. When I finish, I shake away my daze and find Gabe kneeling beside me, his attention fully on me. A beautiful smile adorns his handsome face.

"I'm sorry for raping you, Gabriella," Gabe says as he reads my bloody artwork.

Esteban is breathing heavily, his eyes dilated. Sweat pours from his face. But it's the blood rushing down the sides of his abdomen that is so pretty. Red against his pale flesh. I drop my knife to the side and rub my palms through the blood. It smears, and new blood rushes out in its wake.

Turning my head to regard Gabe, I catch his gaze before rubbing the blood all over my breasts and belly. Gabe growls and licks his lips.

"You're so fucking hot, baby," he utters in a soft, deadly voice. "I want to fuck your pretty little ass."

I rub my bare bottom against Esteban's sweaty lower stomach. "So do it."

"That dickhead will probably like it," he snarls.

My gaze drifts back to Esteban's. "We'll punish him if he does."

Gabe stands and kicks off his shoes. He tugs his shirt off and his pants drop to the floor. My man is gorgeous in all his naked, masculine glory. And, dear God, his cock is amazing.

"Give me your ass, Hannah," he orders as he kneels behind me.

I rest my forearms on Esteban's chest as I straddle his hips. My ass pokes in the air, ready for my man. When I feel his cold palm on my lower back, I let out a breath of anticipation. Esteban is staring at me with hate in his eyes. I expect him to try to shove me away, but he's too weak and his hands remain cuffed, resting on his lower belly.

"Is your pussy wet, baby?" Gabe questions as the tip of his cock rubs against my clit.

"Mmm-hmmm."

"It better be," he bellows. "If you want lube for your ass, your cunt better provide it."

His words turn me on, and a shiver ripples through me. "I'm so wet."

As if to test me, he pushes his cock inside of me. My body is soaked and easily accepts his thickness. He drives into me with a few thunderous thrusts. When he pulls all the way out, I know where he'll go next. The moment he pushes against the tight hole of my ass, I cry out. He's so big, but I love when he stretches me wide open and threatens to tear me apart. Inch by inch, he drives into me until he's completely buried.

"Touch yourself," Gabe orders, his cock throbbing but unmoving inside me.

I reach between my legs and brush against Esteban's bound hands before I find my clit. The moment I find the sweet spot, I let out a whimper of pleasure. Gabe takes this as his moment to start pounding into me. The faster he goes, the faster I move my fingers. My eyes lock on Esteban's. His dark eyes are positively manic. And when I tear my gaze from his to look between us, I can see how turned on he is, despite his helpless state. His cock jolts and his bound hands reach for it.

"He likes this," I breathe.

Gabe groans and thrusts almost painfully into my ass. I'm turned on as I touch myself and watch this sick fuck attempt to fondle himself. A scream escapes me when Gabe grabs a handful of my hair and yanks me all the way upright. He glares over my shoulder to see what Esteban is up to. Then, his mouth attacks mine. The pleasure of having him buried deep in my ass, coupled with how I'm rubbing my clit, has me crashing into oblivion. A long moan erupts into Gabe's mouth as I lose myself to ecstasy. The moment I begin to shudder, Gabe explodes with his orgasm inside my ass. Esteban groans loudly enough to steal me from my husband's kiss. I look down in time to see his semen spurt up his belly.

"Oh, no," I chide. "Bad boy wasn't supposed to do that."

Gabe snarls when he slides out of my ass. He storms over to his clothes and throws his jeans back on. Then, he grabs me by the elbow and jerks me up to my feet. My legs still quiver from my orgasm, and I nearly collapse.

"I want to hear his screams. Rip the tape off his mouth, baby," he orders as he releases me. "But I want to see your sexy naked body, so don't dress yet. I want to watch you while my cum leaks out of your ass."

I grin at him as I bend over to remove the tape. His cum does run out of me and down my thighs. My husband is so dirty. I fucking love it.

Esteban doesn't make a sound when I rip off the tape but the moment he realizes it's gone, he starts babbling.

"M-Money. Whatever you want. I'll give it to you," he murmurs, his voice weak and breathless. His eyes are on mine, as if I have the ability to sway Gabe's mind on what he plans to do.

"We don't want money. We want your life," I tell him simply.

"P-Please…"

I kneel beside him and swipe his sweaty hair from his eyes. "Stop begging. Bad guys don't beg. They take their punishment and they die like the motherfucking villains they are. Got it, Esteban? Stop acting like a pussy and take it like a man."

His eyes turn hard. "Just cut my throat."

I pick up my knife and tease his neck with it. "That would be too easy, baby doll. I think my husband wants your dick—and not in a sexual way."

Esteban groans as a tear leaks from the corner of his eye.

"And I think you owe us a tongue. Gabe is quite disturbed about the fact that you took that sweet little girl's tongue," I tell him as I run my bloody finger over his bottom lip. "It takes a lot to disturb my husband. But late at night, he asks me about it. We discuss how painful that must have been for that little girl. She's big now, though. And even without a tongue, she somehow still found love with my brother. They kiss. I've seen pictures on his Facebook. You could probably kiss without your tongue too." I drag my knife along his torn chest to his belly button. I skim over his handcuffed hands, letting the blade hit the metal with a clink before I poke his flaccid dripping cock. "But can you fuck without your cock?" He attempts to steal the knife, but I hold it away, laughing. "Not so fast, bud."

Gabe drops to his knees on the other side of Esteban and cups my cheek with his hand. "You're so beautiful when you're free. I wish I could free you forever."

I frown and regard his sad eyes for a moment. "I'm free when I'm with you."

His gaze darkens as his palm slides to my throat. "You think so?"

My fingers grip his wrist and I smile at him. "I know so."

The sadness seems to dissipate and determination sets in. I love how fierce my man is. "I'm going to pry his mouth open and you take his tongue. For Luci," Gabe snarls, his glare firm.

"My pleasure, baby," I tell him.

It's a struggle, but my husband is much stronger than the weak man in captivity. He manages to pry his mouth open. And with glee, I saw right through the muscle until I free Esteban of his tongue. He gurgles and blood spurts from his mouth.

I grip Gabe's bearded face with my bloody fingers and motion my head toward Esteban's lower region. "Now, for Brie."

He nods and scoots farther down. I straddle Esteban's chest and hold his face in my palms. The life is draining from his eyes as the blood gushes from his mouth. He chokes and spits. His tongue sits discarded beside his head, and the sight of it makes me wonder what happened to Luci's. Did he just throw it somewhere?

"You're dying, pig," I whisper and kiss his nose that smells like me. "Accept it, baby."

Tears stream down his cheeks, and then an unholy scream makes it past the blood in his throat as Gabe delivers his final vengeance. The sound of his flesh tearing is sickening and unlike anything I've ever heard before. Something hot sprays against my bare back and I shiver. It's done. Esteban's been robbed just like he robbed so many before him. Gabe is the dark avenging angel straight from the catacombs of hell tasked with sending the demon to meet his maker. An eternity of suffering for his sins. I hug the bloody dying man as he quickly slips from our world into the next. His entire body spasms until it doesn't move anymore. The rise and fall of his chest stops. The gurgling and choking is silenced.

"Good boy," I say with a grin and kiss his cheek before I stand. My gaze skims to where Esteban's cock once was. Blood is everywhere. What a mess.

Gabe glares down at him, but the rage is calming. I wrap my arms around him and rest my cheek to his bare chest.

"We should get back soon. It's late," I tell him with a yawn. "If we want to make the buffet breakfast in the morning, I need sleep."

His strong hand finds my throat and he glares down at me. The wild look in his eyes is one I don't recognize. Monstrous. Cold. Not my husband. "Who said we were leaving?" He squeezes hard enough to cut off my air supply. I start to black out.

This is it. He's made his decision to end me once and for all.

Black.

Black.

Silence.

When I reopen my eyes, I realize the cold rain hitting my naked flesh is what woke me. Gabe carries me through the storm past the rows of containers and back toward the fence. I wrap my arm around his neck and bury my face into his flesh.

"I love you," I croak, my voice hoarse from his choking.

He kisses the top of my head as a low growl escapes him. "I love you too, baby."

Maybe he doesn't have it in his heart to kill me.

At least for now…

chapter
FIVE

Gabe

One month later…

I'm staring up at the ceiling with my entire life in my arms. Hannah is on one side of me with our son sleeping between us. Toto is curled up against my side with her small arm slung across my middle. Everyone is asleep. It's been a few weeks since we came back from our "vacation" where we ended that sicko. And it's as if my entire little family knows our world is about to dramatically shift. We all cling together in these moments.

It fucking kills me.

My heart breaks for them.

Their mother is dangerous. I'd hoped the trip would sort her out. If anything, it only made her more blood thirsty. The feral look in her eyes—that same manic one from the shipping container—hasn't dissipated. I can't leave her alone with the children. I'm scared to fucking death I'm going to wake up to another bloodbath, but this one will steal my soul.

I reach over and stroke her hair. So soft and silky. How can I ever let her go? Truth is, I can't. But I have to fix this. Everyone in my family is relying on me.

Thank God I have Ren on my side.

He's been helping me plan.

Tomorrow night, on the eve of his wedding to my daughter, is when we will carry it out. Hannah can't go to the wedding anyway because my Brie loathes her. It has to be done then.

Land stirs, so I scoop him up and lay him across my chest. I stroke his dark hair before kissing the top of his head. Babies have made me soft. Ever since Brie came into my life, I've become weaker. My children have made me this way. Love makes you weak. So fucking weak. But, fuck, if I don't like being weak from it.

Hannah lifts her hand and strokes our son's back before whispering. "He's so cute."

I smile and turn to see her eyes softer than usual. The darkness is gone as love shines through. I wish to hell I knew how to keep that look in her eyes.

"Because he looks like me," I tell her in a smug tone.

She laughs, which makes Land jump but not wake up. "Sometimes I wish you wouldn't have gotten fixed. We could have more."

My chest aches. I'd love to have more children. But the fact is, we can't. Not with her mental health situation. We've tried every drug imaginable. There is no bringing light to her darkness. It's just who she is. War is still in denial, but I've come to peace with it. There's no fixing her, unfortunately.

Death is the only way out of her darkness.

"Come on," I tell her, changing the subject. "Let's take the kids to the beach today. One last family day."

She tenses. "One *last* family day?"

"Before all this wedding stuff takes over our lives starting this evening. Toto has to try on her flower girl dress. I have to pick up my tux. Brie wants me to come see the babies and have dinner with them before the rehearsal. Just a lot going on," I tell her softly.

"I wish Ren would just get over it and let me come," she huffs.

"It's not Ren who has the problem, baby."

"It was an accident." Her response to killing Alejandra is always the same. But since it isn't true, nobody believes her. Especially not Brie.

"I know," I lie, indulging her. "They'll come around eventually and I'll make sure to get pictures for you."

Satisfied, she curls against me and kisses my cheek. "Let's sleep for a little while longer. The beach will wait for us."

Toto squeals as Hannah chases her along the shore. Land sleeps sprawled next to me on our blanket under the umbrella. My attention never leaves my girls. All it would take is one second. My phone buzzes, and I quickly read the message.

Ren: Done. All ready. All you have to do is get her here. Then this nightmare will be over.

I bristle at his abrupt tone. His sister, my wife, is not a nightmare. She's troubled. I hate that I must do this to her. I scrub my face and scan the beach for her. Her eyes are on mine as she walks hand in hand with Toto. I grin and wave at her. She smiles back. Today she wears a skimpy black bikini that makes my cock hard. I'm going to miss moments like these after tomorrow.

Me: I'll take the kids to your parents tonight. Give me more time with her. Then, I'll bring her.

He responds right back.

Ren: Fine, but I want it done before the wedding. Consider it your gift to your daughter.

I grumble but type out my reply.

Me: Done.

After I delete all the messages, I tuck my phone away in the beach bag. Land wakes and starts squirming.

"Hey, baby boy," I coo and kiss his belly through his onesie. "Let's go play with Mommy and your sister. Looks like our time is limited."

He grunts and waves his fist at me as if he's trying to argue. If there were any other way, I'd be arguing too. But there's not. This is it. This is the end, baby.

I scoop him into my arms and stand. When Toto sees me, she squeals and runs for me. Hannah's smile is brighter than the sun beaming down on us.

Why can't all days be like this one?

"A date the night before the wedding?" Baylee grumbles as she rocks Land in her arms. "I still have to cut up all that fruit and a mountain of vegetables for the reception. How am I supposed to do that if I have to babysit?"

Calder saunters in with his no-tongue girlfriend on his heels. That kid and I don't like each other, but at least he loves my children. He takes Land from his mother while Luciana signs to her.

"We can babysit," Calder translates. "Or we can cut vegetables. It's fine."

Hannah remains silent as she refuses to speak to her mother. They talk sometimes about the kids, but the conversation is usually strained. Sometimes, like tonight, they don't speak at all. I pull her to my side and thank Calder. "We *need* this."

Our eyes meet, and he gives me a clipped nod. It makes me wonder if Ren's confided in him about what we have planned. Wouldn't surprise me. I am shocked, though, that he doesn't try to stop me. The only one who would try would probably be Baylee. For Hannah's biggest thorn, she's always been the fiercest about protecting her.

Not this time, Baylee.

The plan is in motion, and your fucking boys are going to help me.

"Let me tell Toto bye and then we'll leave," I grit out as I release Hannah to go hunt for my daughter. I find her in War's office, sitting in his lap. He's turned on a computer game for her and only winces a little bit when she beats on his keyboard.

"We're about to head out," I tell him as I enter the office.

Toto ignores me, so I ruffle her hair and kiss the top of her head. "Bye, baby girl."

"Bye, Daddy," she chirps and bangs her fist again.

"How are the new meds?" War questions.

I meet his steely gaze and shrug. "Same as the others. Fucking worthless."

His lips press into a firm line. "I'll keep trying."

"Soon it won't matter."

Hard blue eyes dart to mine and his jaw clenches. "I told you I didn't want the specifics."

I snort. "Well, neither do I but here we fucking are."

Toto is oblivious as she plays her game. Meanwhile, War pinches the bridge of his nose, and I pace his office.

"It's our only option," I mutter. "If there were any other way, you know I'd be up for it." I swallow and pat Toto's head. "I can't lose these kids."

Understanding washes over him and he nods. "I know. I just…" His jaw clenches again. "I just don't want to know about it. It hurts too fucking much. Because in order to protect *your* kids, we have to hurt *mine.*"

I place my hands on my hips and give him a hard stare. "This protects your other children as well, you know. You and Baylee too."

He closes his eyes, and a ragged breath escapes him. "I know, but I don't like it."

"Neither will she."

"Where are we going?" Hannah asks from the passenger seat.

Tonight, she looks killer in a pale blue summer dress that shows off her toned thighs. I'm dying to mark them up with my teeth. I reach over to squeeze her leg and then run my pinky under her dress and along the seam of her panties.

"Somewhere special."

She smiles, and it's so beautiful I almost change my mind. For a split second, I almost turn the car the fuck around. But when her blue eyes flicker with that ever-present darkness, I'm reminded that this ends tonight.

"Would you ever kill me?" I ask as I tease her flesh while I drive.

She's quiet but manages to give me a shrug.

I give her skin a little pop. "I asked you a yes or no question, baby."

Her glare snaps to mine. "If I had to, then yes."

"The things we do for love," I say softly.

The two-hour drive is intense. With every passing mile, I feel a part of my soul chipping away. And she must sense the foreboding because she's tense. I glance over and catch her chewing on her fingernail.

I need to calm her down.

To ease her nerves.

I drive until I find a road that's lined with thick trees on either side. When I shut off the car, she stiffens.

"Is this the part where you kill your wife?" she demands, her small hands fisted.

"Don't be fucking ridiculous," I snap.

"Then what?"

I reach up and pinch her tit through her dress. "Get your skinny ass over here."

Her shoulders relax. "You just want to fuck?"

"I always want to fuck you."

A small laugh escapes her as she climbs over the center console into my lap. Our mouths connect in a needy kiss as she scrambles to pull my hard cock from my jeans. I barely mange to pull her panties to the side before she's guiding me inside her. Her body slides down my length and she pulls away to stare at me. I grip her hip with one hand to urge her body to move but use my other hand to stroke her soft blonde hair.

She's mine.

Ever since the day I knew she existed in her mother's belly.

"I love you," I tell her, my tone fierce. "No matter what."

She chews on her bottom lip and nods. Fat, genuine-as-fuck tears well in her pretty blue eyes. My girl is intuitive. Always has been. She knows that life as we've known it ends tonight.

"I'm sorry," she chokes out as her lips attack mine. "I'm sorry I can't be better for you."

I drown out her stupid words by kissing her deeply. Her seated on my cock with her tongue in my mouth is where she belongs. I slip my thumb to her front and rub it against her clit through her panties.

"Gabe," she moans as her head tilts back in pleasure.

"That's it, sweet girl," I growl. "Come all over my big dick. Get me messy, baby."

I lean forward and bite her tit through her dress. She trembles as her fingers clutch my hair. All it takes is a moment more of me rubbing her needy pussy before she's climaxing with my name on her lips as though it's a curse.

I've always been her curse.

The black fucking plague.

Hannah's own little nightmare.

I bury my face against her tits as my orgasm explodes from me. I'm in heaven when her body is wrapped around my cock. All the bad in our life feels good for just one moment. I can forget it all and pretend we're okay. But as soon as my seed trickles back out of her body, awareness settles over me.

No more putting this off.

I have to drive her to the place that she'll never leave.

chapter
SIX

Hannah

The end is near. I can feel it. Despite his denial, a sense of foreboding has washed over me. Finality. I'm perceptive enough to know when my husband's behavior changes. He's not the loving, doting husband he usually is.

He's hard.

His jaw is clenched and he's white-knuckling the steering wheel.

Poised and ready to kill.

I should be worried or panicking but I'm not. I know something is wrong with me. We both know this. If I keep barreling down this path called Life, I'm going to eventually crush the ones I love. The thought of hurting my children sickens me. I love them as much as I love Gabe. And if I were to hurt them, he'd never forgive me.

It's better this way.

Tears swim in my vision, and I quickly blink them away.

I'm a strong woman. I can handle this.

My mind begins to wander. How will he kill me? With a rope around my throat? I'd rather it be his strong hand. With a knife tearing open my flesh like we cut up Esteban? I hope he does it slow so I can savor his beauty while my life bleeds out. Shot to the head? As long as he's holding me when I go, I'm okay with that.

A quiver shakes through me.

I don't want to die.

I'm too young and I have too much love to give. Fighting my demons is a daily battle, but it's always worth it because my prize is my family. Gabe and Toto and Land need me. Only I know how to cut up Toto's apples the way she likes them. It's only me who knows that when you brush your thumb along Land's brow after he eats, he falls asleep quicker. And nobody but me knows that when you cradle Gabe against your breast, his breathing evens out and all the stress leaves his body—that he snores ever so softly, and that's how you know he's fully at peace.

It's the little things.

They're mine to love and take care of.

I shouldn't be taken away from them.

"Almost there," Gabe says in a husky tone. He won't look at me, which crushes a deep piece of my soul.

I squint in the darkness as we drive slowly down a winding road lined with trees. The speed limit said forty miles per hour, and yet he's dipping way below. He doesn't want to do this. I don't want him to either.

"Gabe," I choke out, my tears falling freely now.

"Shhh," he murmurs and takes my hand. "It'll all be over soon."

I start to sob. My chest feels as though it's going to explode. The love is all inside. It's locked up but it seeps out through my cracks. This love belongs to him and our babies. One drip at a time might be all they get, but it's theirs. And there is so much more where that love came from. I just don't know how to make the holes bigger.

He turns down a gravel driveway that leads to a pretty house with many windows. On the side of the yard is a newly built swing set. It appears to be a perfect home for a family. The thought makes me cry harder. But when I see my brother Ren's truck, my blood runs cold.

That fucking traitor.

Of course, Ren would want to help kill me. He'd do it himself if he had his way. Hell, that may be why he's here. Maybe Gabe knew he wouldn't be able to do it by himself.

"Hannah," Gabe mutters before turning his head to frown at me. "I love you."

I swallow. "I love you too."

"If there were any other way…" he trails off. His brows pinch together as pain flickers in his eyes. He tugs my hand to pull me closer. Then, his other hand is in my hair. I let out a sad moan when his lips press to mine. Soft and sweet. He deepens the kiss, and I try to memorize the taste of his tongue. His manly scent that comforts me. The way his love follows him around like a warm fog always blanketing me.

"Promise me something," I whisper against his lips. "Promise me *you'll* do it. Don't let Ren be the one to kill me. I want it to be you."

A growl rumbles from him. "Hannah…"

"But first"—I whimper as I pull away to regard his handsome face. I free my hand from his and touch his wiry beard—"First, you have to catch me."

His brown eyes flare to life with need and desire and love and animalistic fury all swirled into one storm. A storm only I can create. I don't give him time to react before I yank on the handle and throw myself out of the car. I abandon my flip-flops in the car as I take off running through the soft grass toward the tree line.

"HANNAH!" he roars from behind me as he climbs out of the car.

I don't look back.

I just run.

He's going to catch me.

He always does.

My hair flies out behind me as I bolt. The air is fairly warm tonight. It's a beautiful night to die. His heavy footsteps thud behind me, so I pick up my pace. The moment I enter the woods, I know it by the bite of the underbrush on my bare feet. Twigs and pinecones and thorny plants tear at my soles, but they don't stop me.

I run and run and run.

His heavy breathing grows closer. I bet if I were to turn around, he'd be just a few feet away. So I don't turn around. I can't afford one small mistake. My tears seem like a permanent fixation on my cheeks. I know that I'll die with those tearstains on my cheeks. I just hope I also die with his face being the last thing I see. Fingers brush against the back of my dress, and I screech. I run faster.

Just not fast enough.

With a grunt from him, he tackles me to the forest floor. The crash and fall is brutal. Sticks poke at me and thorns seem to stab at me from every direction. His weight crushes me to the earth. My husband easily wrangles my wrists behind my back as he presses his hard body against me. We're both breathing heavily, so neither of us speaks at first.

This is it.

All over now.

"Why'd you run, sweet girl?"

I swallow down my emotion. "So you'd catch me one last time."

His lips press to my cheek as he seeks my mouth from behind. I turn my head to steal one last kiss. But the kiss isn't enough for either of us. He rips my dress up over my ass and yanks my panties down my thighs. Then, he struggles with his pants until his hot cock is freed and pressing against me. He works his knee between mine. When I try to move my wrists, he tightens the grip.

"I'll never get tired of fucking you, wild woman," he says as he guides his cock to my opening. I'm slick and hot for him. When he pushes into my pussy, I cry out in need. With one hard thrust, he drives all the way into me.

Pain assaults me from every direction, but the pleasure always supersedes the pain. I'd take all the pain as long as Gabe was the one doling it out. He fucks me hard against the brush. He utters beautiful words about love and family and destiny the whole time. I get lost in them—in him—and unravel with a scream. A grunt and then a growl escape him before he's gushing inside of me. When we're no longer moving, but he's still buried deep inside me, I let out the breath I'd been holding.

"I'm ready," I tell him, my voice quivering slightly.

"Ready for what?"

"This is the end, baby. Kill me, so I don't kill them." My voice cracks. "Or you."

He slides out of me and his cum leaks out. I'm then released as he pulls his pants back up. "Come here."

I'm unable to move, so he tugs my panties into place before hooking his arm around my waist to haul me to my feet. I lean my back against his chest in an effort to steal another moment with him. His palm slides up to grip my tit through my dress as his mouth finds my ear. A shiver ripples through me at having his hot breath there.

Soon, I'll never feel his hot breath again.

It'll be so cold without him.

"I love you," he assures me again.

A crunch in the woods jerks my attention toward the direction we came from. Not even thirty feet away, a giant shadowy figure stalks toward us. Fear races down my spine until I catch a glimpse of the familiar face. More of my love seeps out through my stupid cracks.

"Did you really have to do that when I'm within shouting distance?" Ren asks.

My eyes fall to the hammer in his grip. I freeze in Gabe's arms. A hammer? Fucking really?

"J-Just shoot me," I beg, tears once again hot in my eyes. "Don't bludgeon me to death!"

Ren snorts and shakes his head. "If it were my way, big sis, I'd have shot your ass a long time ago." The hate in his eyes doesn't mask the love he still harbors, though. I see it. A slight flicker of light amidst his dark rage.

"I'm sorry," I choke out. I truly am sorry for what became of my relationship with my brother.

"Not sorry enough," he snarls as he storms toward us. He has something in his other hand, but I'm not able to make out what it is because in the next second, everything turns black.

Black.

Black.

Cold.

"I love you, sweet girl."

And then nothing.

chapter
SEVEN

Gabe

My daughter is getting married. Again. The girl is barely twenty years old and she's on her second marriage. I never knew the first guy, but this guy is okay. He's a product of Baylee, so how could he not be?

I let my gaze drift over to where Baylee is fussing over the dark purple bow on Toto's white dress. The woman I once loved is still just as beautiful as she was when I had her for the very first time. Fuck, she might even be more beautiful. Age has done her well. A spitting fucking image of her mother, Lynn. The teal-colored dress she's wearing hugs her body in all the right ways, accentuating the globes of her breasts. Hannah would have been so jealous of her mother had she been able to be here today for this wedding.

Guilt and heartache have my jaw clenching.

Last night was the worst night of my life.

I'm hollow now.

"He'll take care of her," War assures me as he clutches my shoulder in a supportive way. Twenty years ago I'd have murdered him for merely looking at me. And yet, here we are. Friends of sorts. I'm sure Baylee is proud.

I smirk and shrug. "Brie is a tough cookie. If he does her wrong, she has enough of her daddy in her to make sure it doesn't happen again."

War chuckles and shifts their baby Mason to his other hip. "You're right about that."

Toto squeals and runs over to me. I scoop her into my arms and plant a kiss on her soft cheek. "You'll always stay my baby girl, huh? You're never going to get married."

"Daddy's baby," she agrees, her brown eyes wide and happy.

My heart swells when she nuzzles against me and hugs me with her small arms. I'm grinning like a fool when my gaze meets Baylee's. Normally, she glares at me. Cold stares filled with hate.

But not today.

Today, Baylee regards me like she did long ago, back when I was someone in her life who she cared for. Her eyes shine with love for my daughter, and a smile plays at her lips. It hurts me how fucking much she and Hannah resemble each other.

"How much longer?" I question.

She reaches forward and adjusts the boutonniere on my lapel, which Toto jostled. "Ren and Calder are finishing up. Luci's in with Brie, making sure her makeup is just right. I think we're ready to begin."

"Where are the twins?" I question.

She pulls a baby monitor from her clutch and waves it at me. "Same place as Land. Napping in the church nursery. Brie wanted them in the wedding, but they've been extra fussy lately so she decided to let them sleep."

"Is the devil even allowed in church?" Calder questions with a laugh from behind me. "Shouldn't your skin be sizzling or some shit?"

"Calder!" Baylee chides. "Don't say 'shit' in church. I can't take you anywhere."

I snort and eyeball the Justin Bieber looking kid with a raised eyebrow. "The devil was an angel once." That comment earns me an eye roll from both him and Baylee, which has me chuckling.

I sober up, though, when Ren walks out and stands beside his brother. Had I not had his help last night, I'm not sure where my life would have ended up. I'll owe him that debt until the day I can repay him. But now he's about to vow to take care of my Brie baby for the rest of his life. For that, I'll never be able to repay him.

"I'm counting on you," I tell him as I reach out to shake his hand.

He gives me a firm shake. The kid is a man now. He'll fuck up anyone who even looks at my daughter wrong. I'm thankful she has a built-in bodyguard for her and the twins.

"So is she," he replies. "I love her and I'm going to spend the rest of my life showing her that."

"You better," I say with a grin. "I know where you live. And you know what I can do if you slack off. Don't fucking slack off."

"Gabriel Sharpe!" Baylee hisses. "Church. Stop trying to get us kicked out."

Calder starts laughing, but Ren starts shoving him down the aisle in a playful brotherly way. My heart rate picks up. I can't wait to see my daughter all dressed up and ready to marry a McPherson.

"You asleep, sweet girl?" I coo to Toto.

She lifts her head and beams at me. "I big girl. No nap."

War ruffles her hair before taking Baylee's hand. Together, the two of them along with their small son, walk down the aisle and find a seat.

I kneel and set Toto to her feet. "Where's your basket?"

She points over to the table but then regards me with a frown. "Mommy?"

A pang of guilt slices through me. "Mommy's sleeping," I lie.

"Nap like baby?"

I hug her to me and kiss her soft blonde hair. "Yep. Now go get your basket."

She runs off just as the music starts playing. By the time she returns, the door down the hallway opens. Luci steps out wearing a knee-length dark purple, almost black, dress. Her long black hair has been pulled up in a fancy style on top of her head. The engagement ring Calder gave her glimmers in the light. She smiles broadly when she sees me. Luci and I hit it off pretty easily. For being a mute, the girl has a lot to say. But if she texts me one more Justin Bieber meme… Sometimes I regret bringing her that bastard's tongue as a vacation souvenir because apparently that means we're best goddamned friends now.

"Luci!" Toto shrieks and runs over to her, losing half her flower petals along the way.

The pretty Colombian woman squats to hug my daughter. It warms my once-cold heart. She signs to Toto. Toto sets her basket down and signs *I love you,* which is something Calder has been teaching her. Luci grins and signs it back before kissing her on the forehead. She stands and looks back in the room. Her hands do some fancy motions. Then I hear my other daughter.

"I'm too big for this dress," Brie pouts.

As I stalk toward the room where I can hear her mumbling to herself, I can't help but smile. Inside, I find an angel. *My* angel. A lump forms in my throat upon seeing my beautiful girl. She looks so much like Alejandra, it's dizzying. Her mother would be so proud of the woman she's grown into.

"Daddy," she chokes out.

"You look gorgeous, Brie baby. Fucking gorgeous."

A laugh escapes her. "I've gained weight since I bought the dress. I look terrible."

At this, I raise an eyebrow. "You could never look terrible. Even if you tried."

Her smile is radiant. "Ren says the same thing. You both are strange."

"*Love* is strange."

When I start humming her favorite *Dirty Dancing* song, she giggles just like she used to when she was a kid.

"Sylvia?" I ask with a grin and hold out my hand.

"Yes, Mickey?"

I tug her to me, and she steps on my fancy shoes. While I hum the song "Love is Strange," we dance around the small dressing room, until she begins humming the melody along with me. She rests her head against my chest. I dance with my daughter, enjoying the moment, until Luci knocks on the door, motioning to us that it is time for us to go with her.

Leaning forward, I press a kiss to Brie's forehead and then I offer her my arm. She hooks her arm in mine, and I walk my daughter out to marry her off to her husband. I may be giving her away, but she'll always be my baby.

❧

The ceremony is a blur.

Two kids who have been through so fucking much vowing to love each other till the end. It's beautiful, and I wish Hannah could have seen it. My heart is heavy but it was the right thing to do. The only way.

The vows. The rings. The kiss.

It's all a haze.

Regret and sadness try to steal me from the moment. It almost does. But then these two strong kids raise their conjoined hands as if to say, *We did it*, and I'm grinning with pride. An old familiar 80s song plays on the speakers. "Don't You (Forget About Me)" by Simple Minds. Everyone claps and Calder whistles. Toto runs into the aisle and spins around in circles with excitement.

Jesus, I wish I could have shared this moment with my wife.

I'm in a daze through pictures, and it isn't until a new song is playing in the reception hall that I snap out of it. The reception is small, just family, but it feels right. My oldest daughter beams happily at me.

I reach for her and touch a sparkly diamond stud in her ear.

"Something borrowed," she whispers sadly. "Vienna sent them."

Guilt settles in the pit of my belly. I don't regret killing Heath Berkley—not after what he did to Brie and Duvan. I do, however, regret that it put a wedge between Brie and her best friend. Brie confided in me that as much as Vee wanted to come to the wedding, she wouldn't be able to be around me without "accidentally" stabbing me while I wasn't looking. Not to mention, she's still pissed as hell that we "stole" her kill. Apparently she was saving Esteban for a rainy day. Well it rained that day and my wife and I seized the opportunity. Carpe fucking diem.

Another song comes on, dragging me from my dark thoughts.

"Father-daughter dance," she says with a smile as she takes my hand.

I chuckle and bring her hand to my lips before kissing it. "May I have this dance, princess?"

She nods and she reminds me of the little girl from years ago who'd dress up and make me play the prince from her storybooks. I never had the heart to tell her I was the villain. Today, she doesn't look at me any differently. As if I've always been her hero.

"Which song, Daddy?"

Ren stands beside the speakers grinning. "I have just the one for you two."

When Bill Medley's "(I've Had) the Time of My Life" comes on, I choke up. Her brown eyes shimmer with tears as I hug her to me. The song is perfect, and dancing with her is even better.

"Daddy," she whispers. "I'm pregnant again. We just found out."

I snap my stare to hers. "Again?"

She laughs. "Again. Ren promises me we can do this. I'm not so sure. The twins are hard."

"Brie baby, you can do whatever you set your heart to. You've always been strong like your mother. She'd be so fucking proud of you. I know I sure as hell am."

A tear races down her cheek. "Thank you, Daddy."

"Now let's hope this baby looks like you and not like Ren," I tease with a grin.

We both chuckle and the rest of the dance is free of conversation. Just enjoying the moment. I don't ever want to let go, but much too soon, the song ends, and Ren whisks her away to dance. Their eyes are glued to one another, and the love radiating from them is overwhelming. I hope it never wavers for a second. My daughter deserves all the love in the world.

"Daddy," Toto chirps as she tugs on my pant leg. "Dance."

I tug her into my arms and dance much faster to the beat with my baby girl in my arms. She almost falls asleep, until Calder's big mouth takes over the microphone.

"I'd like to dedicate this song to Teev," he says with a shit-eating grin before the *Blue's Clues* theme song starts playing. This perks Toto back up as she starts singing loudly.

"Teev! Teev!" she screeches happily and then squirms out of my arms to go chase after her favorite uncle. Or is it brother-in-law now? Fuck, I really messed up the family tree.

"You're getting soft in your old age," Baylee says. "I think I even saw you crying."

I smirk and regard the angel in the teal dress. "I don't cry," I snap.

She laughs. "Don't try that villainous shit on me. You don't intimidate me anymore."

"You said 'shit' in church," I grumble, but a smile sneaks its way out.

I snag her wrist and she lifts a brow at me.

"Dance?"

My hand gets forcibly removed from hers and War flashes me an annoyed glare. "Nope. This one's mine." He pulls her away to dance closely with her, their sleeping baby sandwiched between them. The sight of them makes me happy. I'm glad that fucker lived after me shooting him in one of my crazed moments. I'm glad he stole my girl from me. So fucking glad.

I scan the room and can't help but think of who we're missing. The girl who I made mine. The girl who rocked my world to its core. The girl who stole my heart and my soul.

My Hannah Bananas.

My goddamned wife.

My everything.

But it's better this way.

Right?

EPILOGUE

Gabe

Five years later…

"Time to come inside," I holler out the back door. "Dinner's ready."

When I walk back to the kitchen to start dishing out the kids' plates, I groan to find Land still swinging despite Toto's obvious attempts to boss him around. Her blonde hair is in uneven pigtails because I kind of suck at doing little girl hair. They bounce each time she yells at him and points at the house. He sticks his tongue out at her but refuses to get off the swing. *Little shit.*

I put their plates in the refrigerator to cool off while I go round up my kids. As soon as I step out onto the back porch, Land flies off the swing set Ren put together for us several years back. He regards me with an innocent stare. Problem is, that little boy is just like his momma. The innocent looks don't work on me. Especially when I know he's been bad.

"In the house, Toto," I tell my daughter.

She huffs. "Daddy, you promised you'd start calling me Toni Lynn. Jackie at school says I'm the dog from *The Wizard of Oz.*"

That little Jackie is a fucking bully, and if I knew where she lived, I'd scare the living daylights out of the mini bitch so she'd leave my Toto alone.

"Okay, sweet girl. Go get the plates out of the refrigerator please," I instruct.

She hugs me before running inside. When I turn my attention to Land, he manages to produce tears for theatrics. I hate seeing my kids cry, and this kid fucking knows it.

"Come here."

He runs over to me and hugs my legs. "I'm sorry, Daddy."

I scoop the tiny thing into my arms and kiss his messy dark hair. "Don't rile your sister up, okay?"

He nods and rests his head on my shoulder as we go back inside. Once they've both washed up and are at the table, Toto takes it upon herself to say grace.

"Dear Jesus. Thank you for this yummy food Daddy made. I love you and Daddy and Mommy and all the squirrels that eat the bird seed out of the feeders. Amen." She beams sweetly at me.

Land huffs. "What about me?"

"What about you?"

"Daddy," Land cries out and glares at his sister. "She said she doesn't love me."

I groan. "Your sister loves you—"

"No I don't," Toto argues.

"Daddy!"

"Toto," I grumble. "Tell your brother you love him."

"No," she says before bursting into tears. "H-He's mean and he doesn't listen. I hate him."

They start yelling at each other, both of them crying now, and I rub my palm across my face. This parenting thing is hard to do alone.

"I miss Mommy," Land wails.

I manage to calm them both down and urge them to eat a little more. They both end up passing out the moment I put a movie on after dinner. I tuck them both into bed and take my time picking up the house. Tomorrow, they'll just ransack it again. If I don't clean every night before bed, it's fucking atrocious by the end of the week. Once the alarm is set, so I'll know if they escape the house, I go to my room and grab my lanyard from the top of my closet and slip it over my head. I make a pass through the kitchen, snagging a few things, before I head down to the basement for some me time. Daddies need me time.

The door is triple locked and tricky to unlock with all the shit in my hands, which is why I put the key on a lanyard, but I eventually get it open. It's quiet, but I'm not alarmed. My footsteps are heavy as I thud down the stairs. When I reach the bottom, my head darts to the left. Always to the left.

God, what a beautiful sight.

"Hey, babe," Hannah chirps, her eyes never leaving the screen in front of her.

"Who's winning?" I ask as I set down her plate of leftovers on the table just outside her door.

"Daddy," she groans.

I smirk to see War wearing the same intense expression as her on the screen. Those two spend countless hours playing chess online together. I'm pretty sure he kicks her ass every time, but it doesn't stop her from trying to win.

"Where are the kids?"

"Asleep. They were both tired as fuck. If I would have brought them down, they'd have begged to spend the night with you and that would have just led to more temper tantrums," I grunt.

I grab on to one of the bars outside her cell and stare in at her. Five years ago, I discovered a way to keep my wife without having her be a danger to herself or others. I didn't have to kill her. And while we were in Buenaventura, Ren did me a solid and finished out this basement for me so I could keep her safe. And everyone else safe *from her*.

My gaze skims over her makeshift prison. There's plenty of space for my girl to roam. She has a comfortable bed that we can both sleep in easily, a bathroom complete with a tub, and a table. Her space is painted in bright colors and the kids' drawings decorate the walls. It looks like any other room in our home—except this room has bars and a locked door. My little inmate has been sentenced for life. And, thank fuck, she's happy.

Getting her inside it proved to be tricky, though, but once she realized I had no intention of killing her, she settled into her new home easily. It gives her peace of mind, knowing she can still have her family but that when the dark thoughts consume her, she can't hurt them.

At one time, I didn't have an answer when it came to Hannah. I thought I would have to kill her. Hell, that's the reason I brought her to Colombia with me. Despite my conversations with Ren about making her a cell, I'd had my doubts it could work. After she and I had eliminated Esteban, I had my hand around her throat. I almost murdered my wife in the pouring rain. It would have been easy to dump her beside Esteban's body. But goddamn was she beautiful. Mine. I was too fucking selfish to let her go. Ren and I would have to make it work. We *did* make it work.

"Checkmate," War says smugly.

I laugh and Hannah shoots me the bird. "Goodnight, Daddy. Same time tomorrow?"

"Of course, sweetheart."

They end the call and she sits up in the bed on her knees. My little hellion is the picture of innocence in her pink T-shirt and jean shorts. But the moment she starts stripping off her shirt, I'm reminded of how not-so-innocent she is.

"You coming in here, babe?" she purrs.

I laugh as I rip off my own T-shirt. "Fuck yeah I am. I've been dealing with bad ass kids all day. I need some mommy and daddy alone time."

She giggles and tugs away her bra, freeing her luscious tits. We both pull off the rest of our clothes pretty much at the same time. Now that my dick is heavy but free, I unlock the door to her cell.

"I'm hungry for you right now," she says, her voice husky. "Dinner can wait."

I chuckle as I saunter in and lock the door behind me. "Didn't I already feed you my cock today while the kids were at school?"

She lies back on the soft bed, her blonde hair spilling on the pillow around her, and bites her lip as she caresses her tits. "You know you have to feed your little animal often."

I growl as I pounce. Her squeals are music to my ears when my mouth finds her neck. I may be old as fuck but this girl keeps me young and on my toes. Never a dull moment with this one. She wraps her long legs around my waist and urges me closer. My fingers tangle in her pretty hair as she grips my cock to guide me inside her. Once I push into her, we both groan in unison.

This is exactly where I'm supposed to be.

"I love you," I breathe against her perfect plump lips. "I love you so goddamned much. All of this is for you." I thrust into her hard enough to make her cry out. "You know this, right? It's always been for you."

She nods and kisses me hard. Our bodies are one as I fuck my wife right into an explosive orgasm. I'll eventually get mine but until then, I plan on pleasuring her with my tongue and fingers.

For most of my life, I screwed shit up and took the wrong paths. It was engrained in me. But with Hannah, I did something right. With my kids, I did something right. Even the bad guys can be good every once in a while. I try not to make it a habit. Don't want to get soft, like War.

"Oh, God!" my wife cries out in ecstasy, her body clenching hard around mine.

"That's it, sweet girl. Give it all to me. It's mine," I growl. "*You're* mine."

She unravels with my name on her lips, and it makes me so goddamned happy. This life—our life—is perfect. Undeserving but ours. Nobody will ever take this away from us. Not now. Not ever.

Happy endings aren't for villains…

But we fucking take them anyway.

I hope you enjoyed the War and Peace series in Love and War.
To read a free novella about Gabe and Hannah's son, Land, you can check it out here.
https://dl.bookfunnel.com/3gr0sjwze7

Looking for your next heart-stopping dark romance read?
Start Sweet Jayne next!

about
THE AUTHOR

K Webster is a USA Today Bestselling author. Her titles have claimed many bestseller tags in numerous categories, are translated in multiple languages, and have been adapted into audiobooks. She lives in "Tornado Alley" with her husband, two children, and her baby dog named Blue. When she's not writing, she's reading, drinking copious amounts of coffee, and researching aliens.

To see the full list of K Webster's books, visit authorkwebster.com/all-books.

Download at authorkwebster.com/free-books

Join my Newslettter
at authorkwebster.com/newsletter

Join my Private Group

at www.facebook.com/groups/krazyforkwebstersbooks

Follow K Webster here!

Website: authorkwebster.com

Email: kristi@authorkwebster.com

Facebook: www.facebook.com/authorkwebster

Twitter: twitter.com/KristiWebster

Goodreads: www.goodreads.com/user/show/10439773-k-webster

Instagram: www.instagram.com/authorkwebster

BookBub: www.bookbub.com/authors/k-webster

EXCERPT FROM
SWEET JAYNE

prologue

Nadia

I fucking hate Donovan Jayne.

A furious scream is lodged in my throat, but one desperate, pleading look from my mother, and I'm trotting away from the asshole in our expensive kitchen toward the front door with my lips firmly pressed together.

Words like, *Fuck you*, or *Eat shit and die*, or *Stop checking out your seventeen-year-old stepdaughter, you prick*, all remain unsaid and poised on the tip of my tongue that craves to lash out at him. If it weren't for my mother actually loving the asshole, I'd have already given him a piece of my mind.

But she does love him—or so she says. And Mamá deserves any morsel of happiness she can get. She's been unhappy for so long. Ever since Papá died in an accident at the mill he worked at, just outside of Buenos Aires six years ago, she's been lost. The pretty smile that used to light up her face had darkened. It was by chance that she ran into the cocky hotel and resort magnate, Donovan Jayne. She'd been working as a housekeeper at one of the biggest hotels in Argentina. During her rounds, she pushed through his door, ready to collect the dirty towels thinking no one was in at the time. He was just coming out of the bathroom after a shower as she was entering. She apologized profusely and went to leave, but he wouldn't let her go. Love at first sight, they both claim.

Gag.

How anyone could love that self-centered asshole is beyond me. He not only uprooted us and moved us to Colorado to marry her, but I also had to leave all of my friends behind during my last year of high school. We'd gone from our simple two-bedroom apartment which Mamá was able to afford in the city on her meager housekeeping salary to a breathtaking mansion on a fucking mountain. But, her smile is back again. Mamá smiles like she did when Papá was still alive and that's the only reason I put up with Donovan's shit.

And by shit, I mean his possessiveness over his "family." The way he struts around this town showing us off like we're a couple of prized horses. But when someone so much as looks at us remotely wrong, he turns into a narcissistic idiot who reminds them who owns this town. *We do*, he says. Quite frankly, I'm embarrassed to be a part of the "we."

Ten more months. I can suck it up, bite my tongue, and let him pull my strings for ten more months. And then I'm off to college. I'm not sure where I'll go yet but it will most definitely be far, far away from Donovan and his superiority complex.

"Nadia Jayne!"

I cringe on the bottom step of the front porch and consider running the rest of the way to the bus stop to avoid having to talk to him. But Donovan doesn't give up so easily. He's shrewd and determined. It's best to let him spout his bullshit and then move on. So, instead, I lift my chin and turn to regard him with a raised eyebrow, no doubt revealing my disdain for him.

"What?" I hiss out my question, hoping the venom in my voice stings.

A small flinch at my tone is the only indication I've hurt him before he quickly masks it away with a look of indifference. He must've gotten ready for work early this morning, as he's already donning a pristine dark grey suit. I've never, not once, seen him *not* in a suit. For thirty-six, he's well-built and handsome. His dark hair is styled in a way that's meant to look messy and his grey-blue eyes are piercing. Always calculating and determining his next move. I'm not blind to the fact that his physical traits are attractive. But it's what's on the inside that makes him a creep. And he's the biggest damn creep around. I've seen the way he looks at me as if he wants to fuck me.

His eyes linger on my bare legs, unhidden by my ridiculously short school uniform because I've purposefully rolled it up as not to appear to look like an old maid on my first day, before he drags them up to meet my simmering gaze. "You forgot your lunch money," he says, waving a crisp hundred-dollar bill at me, "and you forgot to give your old man a hug goodbye."

Anger causes my chest to heat up. I can feel it clawing up my neck, revealing itself to him. His smirk tells me he knows he's struck a chord with me. I fist my hands at my sides to keep from doing something stupid like flipping him off. I'm already grounded from the car he bought me after we officially moved here this summer. I hadn't even gotten to drive it once. *You talk back around here and your privileges get taken away. My house, my rules.* Fuck him and his house rules.

"You're not my dad," I snap. Visions of my own loving father flit through my head and I feel the familiar ache in my chest at losing him.

He takes a few steps toward me and flashes me a wide grin, revealing perfect, white teeth. "Technically I *am* your daddy. If you forgot, maybe you should check your ID again."

Tears well in my eyes but I clench my jaw. I won't let them spill over and give him the satisfaction of knowing that he can so easily rile me up. But he's right. Donovan's good at what he does. He swoops in, buys property—in this case, my mother and me—and stamps his name all over it. The asshole made sure he legally adopted me so I would bear the Jayne name too.

I'm no longer Nadia Blanco.

As of two months ago, I'm officially Nadia Jayne.

With a huff, I stomp up the steps and make my way up to where he's standing. His eyes glimmer with excitement as I approach. Five bucks says he's sporting a hard-on, too. More heat floods through me, this time making its way to my cheeks, and I shiver at that idea. God, my poor mother.

He holds out the money but when I reach for it, he clutches onto my wrist. His gaze darkens and he affixes me with a firm glare. "Don't embarrass me. The principal at your school sits on the board of my company. I won't have you tarnishing the Jayne name," he says coolly. "I wouldn't want to have to spank you over my knee for being a bad girl."

My jaw drops and I gape at him. I knew the bastard was a pervert but he's crossed over onto a whole new plane of twistedness.

"Oh, don't act so shocked, Nadia. You know I'm not opposed to disciplining you. If I remember correctly, you're still grounded from your car because of your attitude. I'd be more than happy to try other methods of punishment. Clearly, your attitude still fucking sucks. Maybe a little ass whipping will be good for you."

When I try to wriggle my hand out of his grasp, he grips it tighter and pulls me closer. His cologne invades my lungs and I nearly choke from the potent smell.

"¡Te odio!" I hiss. *I hate you.* Jerking my hand away, I take several steps back.

The corner of his mouth lifts up in a devilishly handsome grin. "Tell me you'll be a good girl."

I glare at him and nod my head, not giving him the satisfaction of my words. His eyes lazily skim over my face and stop at my lips.

"Good," he says, his smile faltering and his eyes finding mine again. "Have a great first day of school, sunshine." His gaze softens for a brief moment. For one tiny second I think Donovan Jayne may even be human. Not some asshole I've been forced to obey until the day I turn eighteen and can bolt. "Come here." His voice is hoarse this time.

With his arrogance taking a surprising backseat for once, I find myself going to him willingly. Almost seeking his comfort for some odd reason. When I'm close enough, he eats up the rest of the distance with his long legs and then his powerful arms are around me, pulling me against his solid chest. The stiffness I always carry when I'm around him melts away as he hugs me. Our hug is different this time. It's not forced for once. His scent, like always, cloaks me and I know from experience

I'll smell him all day long. A constant reminder of his iron grip on my life. Today, though, I'm hoping it will give me even an ounce of his confidence as I attempt to make new friends in my new school.

"The boys are all beneath you here," he says with a playful growl. "I know this because I grew up here. Stay away from them. They don't deserve you."

A small smile tugs at my lips. That's probably the sweetest thing he's ever said to me. I lift my head up and look into his eyes that sparkle with an emotion I can never quite put my finger on. "Maybe I'm not into boys." I quirk up an eyebrow in a challenging way.

His soft features pinch into a hard scowl, momentarily stunning me. "You shouldn't be into anyone. School should be your primary focus. I'll forbid you from dating—boys or girls—if your grades start to suffer."

God, I hate him. How could I have so easily forgotten?

Before releasing me, he pats my ass with one hand and kisses the top of my head. As soon as he pulls away, I snatch the money from his hold and storm away from him. It isn't until I'm halfway down the long gravel driveway that I realize tears are streaking down my cheeks.

"Nadia," he calls out to me, a hint of remorse in his voice.

Swiping away a tear, I turn to regard him. His face has an apology written all over it but his stubborn mouth refuses to let it out.

"What?" I prod.

He scrubs at his cheeks with his palms, an almost angry scowl forming after. His steps are rushed as he strides back over to the front door and swings it open, calling out to me over his shoulder. "Have a good day at school."

I don't respond as the door slams behind him but instead wave him off. If it weren't for him and his "undying" bullshit love for my mother, I'd be texting with my friend Julienne as we speak, trying to figure out a way to skip out on our last class of the day. Instead, I'm in another country, going to a brand new school, and completely friendless with nobody to talk to aside from my mother and annoyingly good-looking stepfather. *Thanks, Daddy.*

Once I reach the road beside the mailbox, I sit down in the grass and ignore the cold morning dew soaking my bottom through my skirt. I swipe the tears away with the back of my hand and try to overlook the fact that my stepfather is a prick. It was stupid to think there was an actual likable person behind the suit and hard eyes. Doubt I'll ever make the mistake of letting my guard down again.

"Please don't tell me you live *there*," a voice calls out from the road.

I look up to the sound of the young voice and see a girl who looks to be around my age walking toward me. Her hair is dyed black on top and pale blonde underneath. She's got it pulled up in a messy bun that reveals multiple piercings in her ears. The school uniform she's wearing looks just like mine, but wrinkly and slightly baggy.

"Please tell me you're here to help me run away," I joke back.

Her eyebrows furrow together as she approaches and inspects me. "Why are you crying?"

I drop my gaze to my lap and tug at a loose thread on my skirt. "I hate my stepdad."

She plops down beside me and mimics my cross-legged position. I watch with fascination as she pulls out a pack of cigarettes and lights one. "Funny. I hate my stepdad, too."

A puff of smoke surrounds us as she exhales. We sit in silence for a moment while she smokes and I plan ways to kill Donovan.

Finally, she says, "I'm Kasey."

She hands me her cigarette and I gingerly take it from her. I'm not a smoker but I don't want to scare away my first potential friend with being snooty.

"Nadia."

I take a puff and then cough before handing her back the cigarette.

"You new to Aspen High?" she questions.

Glancing up at her, I take in her features. Despite the dark eyeliner and heavy purple lipstick, a pretty face hides beneath. Her hazel eyes look sad, as if she has a whole lifetime of stories to tell.

"Yep. I moved here from Argentina this summer."

Her eyebrows furrow together in confusion. "You don't sound foreign."

I laugh and roll my eyes. "What exactly does foreign sound like?"

Her cheeks turn slightly pink but she tries to hide her embarrassment with another puff of her cigarette. "I don't know. Like, you don't speak another language or have an accent or whatever."

"Los Americanos pueden ser tan ignorantes," I tell her with a smile. *Americans can be so ignorant.* "Is that better?"

She scrunches her nose up at me. "What did you say?"

"I insulted you," I say shrugging my shoulders. "It takes out all the fun if I tell you."

"Bitch," she says with a grin and flips me off.

I run my fingers through my long, dark locks that are still smooth from straightening them this morning. "In my old school, we had to learn both English and Spanish. Everyone there could speak both languages fluently. My mother always drilled into me that knowing multiple languages would help me be successful one day, especially if I went to college in another country like the U.S. Her dream, not mine. I guess her dream came true."

She laughs. "College. Must be nice to have that option."

"Everyone has that option," I say with a frown, furrowing my brows together.

She stands quickly and flicks the half-smoked cigarette into the street. "Not when you're trailer trash," she says and points at a mobile home through the tree line across the road. "When you're poor, your only option is to find a job in this shitty-ass town and pop out a couple of babies. Your destiny, when you're like me, is being some asshole's punching bag. A wife to a drunk who beats you. You have no future. No love. Happily fucking ever after. Just ask my mom."

I lift my chin to see her visibly shaking. Not really knowing anything about this girl and also not wanting to upset her, I rush to blurt out the first thing that comes to mind. "Cheers," I say with a sneer, "to moms everywhere who married fucking assholes."

She snaps her gaze to mine and a small smile plays at her lips. With a few rapid blinks, she chases away the despondency in her eyes and is once again composed. "Cheers."

"You know," I tell her as I pick a blade of wet grass and try to tie it in a knot, "you could go to college. You don't have to be like your mom."

A sardonic chuckle is tossed back at me. "God, you sound like Taylor," she says wistfully but then her bottom lip trembles.

"Who's Taylor?" I question, wondering about her sudden mood change.

She gapes at me as if I've lost my mind but then waves off the question. "He's just someone I used to know." I sense the lie in her words. He was more than that. Much more than that. "Besides," she says, changing the subject, "with what money would I go to college with, anyway?"

This time it's me who looks at her like she just crawled out from under a rock. "Um, grants? Scholarships? Duh."

She shrugs her shoulders. "Maybe. But college isn't what I want to do."

I wait for her to elaborate but she doesn't. Finally, after a few minutes, I ask. "Well, what do you want to do then?"

She turns to regard me with a look of embarrassment, her teeth tugging at her bottom lip. The expression makes her seem younger, a stark contrast to her harsh makeup. Kasey hides behind the emo look for some reason. I wonder what she'd look like with her natural hair color, whatever that may be.

"You'll just laugh at me."

I roll my eyes. "Fine, I'll go first. Mine is laughable too. We can laugh together."

The corners of her lips draw up into a small smile. "Okay then."

"I always wanted to be a cook. Maybe a sous chef or a pastry chef. I'm not one hundred percent sure, but I love food. Clearly," I mutter and motion at my curvy body.

She places her hands on her hips and arches a brow at me. "Are you kidding me right now? I'd kill to have your body. I'm still waiting for the boob fairy to show up and sprinkle me with some titty dust. But obviously she accidentally spilled the whole jar on you."

We both burst out into a fit of giggles and I swipe at tears—this time from laughter.

"Be careful what you wish for," I tease. "Now tell me already."

She lights up another cigarette as if she's working up the courage to start talking. After a couple of drags, she meets my gaze. "I want to work at a day care."

"That seems completely doable. Is this like a gothic day care?" I question with a grin. "Would all the babies wear Metallica T-shirts and cuss? Would they take smoke breaks instead of recess?"

"Bite me." She laughs and kicks some rocks from my driveway toward me.

I'm still smiling when a squeal of tires draws my attention down the road. Kasey flicks her still burning cigarette into the street and we both watch as a black SUV comes barreling down the street, headed our way.

"Slow down, asshole!" she yells and flips off the vehicle as it nears.

A screeching of the tires deafens me as it comes to a complete stop right in front of where I'm sitting beside the mailbox. The door is wrenched open, and I see black combat boots first before seeing who they belong to.

Flickering my gaze over to Kasey, I notice the nervousness on her face as she starts to take a step back. When I jerk my head back over to the car, I see why.

A big man, dressed entirely in black with a ski mask covering his face, is charging for her. It happens so quickly that I'm frozen with my ass planted on the earth and I can only watch what's unfolding right in front of me. She lets out an ear-piercing screech as he runs for her. Kasey doesn't make it far before he's got his massive arms wrapped around her middle. Her long legs kick wildly around her as he drags her back toward the car. The moment her terrified gaze meets mine, I jolt into action.

"No! Stop!" I scream as I scramble to my knees when he passes by me. "Let her go."

He grunts in exertion at her struggling but has the ability to meet my stare. The eyes behind the mask are wild and crazed. I'm trying to get a better look at the man when he raises his knee in the air. The bottom of his gigantic boot slams into my cheek with the force of a hurricane. Blackness explodes in front of me, blinding me from the man who is forcefully kidnapping my friend, and I fall back into the grass, slamming my head against the ground.

As I try to regain my wits, I hear a car door slam once as he shoves her into the vehicle. Another slam sounds after he climbs back in. The SUV screeches into drive and hauls ass down the road. A wave of dizziness washes over me but I quickly roll to my side to try and read the license plate.

Too blurry.

Too far away.

Another blanket of darkness clouds my vision and I black out.

I'm not sure if it's minutes or hours later when I hear Donovan's concerned voice and I slowly regain consciousness.

"Nadia, baby," he murmurs as he cradles my head in his hand. "What happened?"

My eyes are fixated on the road where Kasey's half-smoked cigarette rolls around in the wind, the cherry still red on the end. When I don't respond, he slides his arms beneath me and pulls me into them against his chest. Normally, I hate Donovan but right now, I need him.

I need him to hold me like Papá would have.

To tell me everything's going to be okay.

For him to assure me that Kasey and the man who took her were all just a silly figment of my teenage imagination.

"Selene!" Donovan hollers to Mamá. "Call 911! I think Nadia was assaulted. Her nose is bleeding and she's disoriented."

His dark eyebrows are pinched together in genuine concern and it comforts me.

"Kasey," I murmur and blink slowly. A massive migraine is wrapping its evil claws around my skull and crushing in on me. "He took Kasey."

His eyes widen and he darts his gaze back down the street as if to see the vehicle that's now long gone. When he turns to look back down at me, he presses a chaste kiss to my forehead and then pins me with a searing stare. "Shhh. We'll tell the police. But you're safe now, Nadia. I'll make sure nothing happens to you." He then curses, "Jesus Christ, it could have been you instead."

I want to feel comforted that it wasn't me but I don't. All I can think about is her terrified expression. The fact that someone took her. How, if the police aren't able to find her and soon, she'll never get to hold the babies at the day care like she dreamed about.

Someone could abuse her. Rape her even.

And what's worse, they may kill her.

Kasey was right.

She has no future.

Donovan carries me up the steps of our house where moments earlier he was acting like a pervert and fondling my ass. It seems so miniscule in comparison to what Kasey is now facing—being taken by some twisted predator. While I was annoyed and creeped out over my stepdad, she's probably scared out of her fucking mind in the clutches of a lunatic. I really am just a spoiled brat. A girl who doesn't know how good she really has it.

"Please help me find her," I beg him with tears in my eyes.

He stares at me for a long minute, a frown tarnishing his otherwise handsome face. When he eventually snaps out of whatever thought held him, he nods. "I'll do what I can, baby. I swear to fucking God, I will do everything in my power to find her." The intensity in his vow to find a random girl who is a stranger to him shocks me. A newfound respect for him begins taking root deep inside me.

In this moment, I realize Donovan might not be so bad. The glimmer of the man he'd shown me earlier is making a reappearance. I see the promise in his penetrating gaze—a promise to make me happy. To indulge his little girl.

And if sucking up to Donovan is what it takes to find Kasey, then that's what I'll do.

I have to save her.

I swear to God, I'll find and save her somehow.

She'll have her future.

Her happy ending.

I'll make sure of it.